Also by David Foster Wallace

The Broom of the System

Girl with Curious Hair

Infinite Jest

A Supposedly Fun Thing I'll
Never Do Again

Brief Interviews with Hideous
Men

Everything and More

Oblivion

Consider the Lobster

McCain's Promise

This Is Water

THE PALE KING

An Unfinished Novel

DAVID FOSTER WALLACE

LITTLE, BROWN AND COMPANY

LARGE PRINT EDITION

Little, Brown and Company
Hachette Book Group
237 Park Avenue, New York, NY 10017
www.hachettebookgroup.com

First Large Print Edition: April 2011

Little, Brown and Company is a division of Hachette Book Group, Inc. The Little, Brown name and logo are trademarks of Hachette Book Group, Inc.

The following chapters have appeared previously, in slightly different form, in the following publications:

Chapter 6, published as "Good People" in *The New Yorker*.
Chapter 16, published as "A New Examiner" in *The Lifted Brow* and *Harper's*.
Chapter 33, published as "Wiggle Room" in *The New Yorker*.
Chapter 35, published as "The Compliance Branch" in *Harper's*.

ISBN: 978-0-316-17793-1
LCCN 2011921952

10 9 8 7 6 5 4 3 2 1

RRD-IN

Jacket design by Mario J. Pulice
Jacket art by Karen Green

Printed in the United States of America

Editor's Note

In 2006, ten years after the publication of David Foster Wallace's *Infinite Jest,* Little, Brown made plans to release an anniversary edition of that glorious novel. Celebrations were set up at bookstores in New York and Los Angeles, but as the events neared, David demurred about attending. I telephoned to try to persuade him. "You know I'll come if you insist," he said. "But please don't. I'm deep into something long, and it's hard for me to get back into it when I'm pulled away."

"Something long" and "a long thing" were the terms David used to talk about the novel he'd been writing in the years since *Infinite Jest.* He published many books in those years—story collections in 1999 and 2004 and gatherings of essays in 1997 and

2005. But the question of a new novel loomed, and David was uncomfortable speaking about it. Once when I pressed him, he described working on the new novel as like wrestling sheets of balsa wood in a high wind. From his literary agent, Bonnie Nadell, I heard occasional reports: David was taking accounting classes as research for the novel. It was set at an IRS tax return processing center. I had had the enormous honor of working with David as his editor on *Infinite Jest*, and had seen the worlds he'd conjured out of a tennis academy and a rehab center. If anyone could make taxes interesting, I figured, it was him.

At the time of David's death, in September 2008, I had not seen a word of this novel except for a couple stories he had published in magazines, stories with no apparent connection to accountancy or taxation. In November, Bonnie Nadell joined Karen Green, David's widow, to go through his office, a garage with one small window at their home in Claremont, California. On David's desk Bonnie found a neat stack of manuscript, twelve chapters totaling nearly 250 pages. On the label of a disk containing those chapters he had written "For LB advance?" Bonnie had talked with David about pulling together a few chapters of his novel to send to Little, Brown in order to commence negotiations for a new contract and advance against royalties. Here was that partial manuscript, unsent.

Exploring David's office, Bonnie and Karen found hundreds and hundreds of pages of his novel in progress, designated with the title "The Pale King." Hard drives, file folders, three-ring binders, spiral-bound notebooks, and floppy disks contained printed chapters, sheaves of handwritten pages, notes, and more. I flew to California at their invitation and two days later returned home with a green duffel bag and two Trader Joe's sacks heavy with manuscripts. A box full of books that David had used in his research followed by mail.

Reading this material in the months after returning, I found an astonishingly full novel, created with the superabundant originality and humor that were uniquely David's. As I read these chapters I felt unexpected joy, because while inside this world that David had made I felt as if I were in his presence, and was able to forget awhile the awful fact of his death. Some pieces were neatly typed and revised through numerous versions. Others were drafts in David's minuscule handwriting. Some—those chapters from the desk among them—had been recently polished. Others were much older and contained abandoned or superseded plotlines. There were notes and false starts, lists of names, plot ideas, instructions to himself. All these materials were gorgeously alive and charged with observations; reading them was the closest thing to seeing his amazing mind at play upon the world. One leather-bound work-book was still closed around a green felt marker with which David had recently written.

Nowhere in all these pages was there an outline or other indication of what order David intended for these chapters. There were a few broad notes about the novel's trajectory, and draft chapters were often preceded or followed by David's directions to himself about where a character came from or where he or she might be headed. But there was no list of scenes, no designated opening or closing point, nothing that could be called a set of directions or instructions for *The Pale King.* As I read and reread this mass of material, it nevertheless became clear that David had written deep into the novel, creating a vividly complex place—the IRS Regional Examination Center in Peoria, Illinois, in 1985—and a remarkable set of characters doing battle there against the hulking, terrorizing demons of ordinary life.

Karen Green and Bonnie Nadell asked me to assemble from these pages the best version of *The*

Pale King that I could find. Doing so has been a challenge like none I've ever encountered. But having read these draft pages and notes, I wanted those who appreciate David's work to be able to see what he had created — to be allowed to look once more inside that extraordinary mind. Although not by any measure a finished work, *The Pale King* seemed to me as deep and brave as anything David had written. Working on it was the best act of loving remembrance I was capable of.

In putting this book together I have followed internal clues from the chapters themselves and from David's notes. It was not an easy task: even a chapter that appeared to be the novel's obvious starting point is revealed in a footnote, and even more directly in an earlier version of that chapter, to be intended to arrive well after the novel begins. Another note in the same chapter refers to the novel as being full of "shifting POVs, structural fragmentation, willed incongruities." But many of the chapters revealed a central narrative that follows a fairly clear chronology. In this story line, several characters arrive at the Peoria Regional Examination Center on the same day in 1985. They go through orientation and begin working in and learning about the vast world of IRS tax returns processing. These chapters and these recurring characters have an evident sequence that forms the novel's spine.

Other chapters are self-contained and not part of any chronology. Arranging these freestanding sections has been the most difficult part of editing *The Pale King*. It became apparent as I read that David planned for the novel to have a structure akin to that of *Infinite Jest,* with large portions of apparently unconnected information presented to the reader before a main story line begins to make sense. In several notes to himself, David referred to the novel as "tornadic" or having a "tornado feeling"—suggesting pieces of story coming at the reader in a high-speed swirl. Most of the non-chronological chapters have to do with daily life at the Regional Examination Center, with IRS practice and lore, and with ideas about boredom, repetition, and familiarity. Some are stories from various unusual and difficult childhoods, whose significance gradually becomes clear. My aim in sequencing these sections was to place them so that the information they contain arrives in time to support the chronological story line. In some cases placement is essential to the unfolding story; in others it is a matter of pace and mood, as in siting short comic chapters between long serious ones.

The novel's central story does not have a clear ending, and the question inevitably arises: How unfinished is this novel? How much more might there have been? This is unknowable in the absence of a detailed outline projecting scenes and stories yet to be written. Some notes among David's manuscript pages suggest that he did not intend for the novel to have a plot substantially beyond the chapters here. One note says the novel is "a series of set-ups for things to happen but nothing ever happens." Another points out that there are three "high-end players...but we never see them, only their aides and advance men." Still another suggests that throughout the novel "something big *threatens* to happen but doesn't actually happen." These lines could support a contention that the novel's apparent incompleteness is in fact intentional. David ended his first novel in the middle of a line of dialogue and his second with large plot questions addressed only glancingly. One character in *The Pale King* describes a play he's written in which a man sits at a desk, working silently, until the audience leaves, at which point the play's action begins. But, he continues, "I could never decide on the action, if there was any." In the section titled "Notes and Asides" at the end of the book I have extracted some of David's notes about characters and story. These notes and lines from the text suggest ideas about the novel's direction and shape, but none strikes me as definitive. I believe that David was still exploring the world he had made and had not yet given it a final form.

The pages of the manuscript were edited only lightly. One goal was to make characters' names consistent (David invented new names constantly) and to make place names, job titles, and other factual matters match up throughout the book. Another was to correct obvious grammatical errors and word repetitions. Some chapters of the manuscript were designated "Zero drafts" or "freewriting," David's terms for first tries, and included notes such as "Cut by 50% in next draft." I made occasional cuts for sense or pace, or to find an end point for a chapter that trailed off unfinished. My overall intent in sequencing and editing was to eliminate unintentional distractions and confusions so as to allow readers to focus on the enormous issues David intended to raise, and to make the story and characters as comprehensible as possible. The complete original drafts of these chapters, and the entire mass of material from which this novel was culled, will ultimately be made available to the public at the University of Texas's

Harry Ransom Center, which houses all of David Foster Wallace's papers.

David was a perfectionist of the highest order, and there is no question that *The Pale King* would be vastly different had he survived to finish it. Words and images recur throughout these chapters that I am sure he would have revised: the terms "titty-pinching" and "squeezing his shoes," for example, would probably not be repeated as often as they are. At least two characters have Doberman hand puppets. These and dozens of other repetitions and draft sloppinesses would have been corrected and honed had David continued writing *The Pale King*. But he did not. Given the choice between working to make this less-than-final text available as a book and placing it in a library where only scholars would read and comment on it, I didn't have a second's hesitation. Even unfinished, it is a brilliant work, an exploration of some of life's deepest challenges, and an enterprise of extraordinary artistic daring. David set out to write a novel about some of the hardest subjects in the world—sadness and boredom—and to make that exploration nothing less than dramatic, funny, and deeply moving. Everyone who worked with David knows well how he resisted letting the world see work that was not refined to his exacting standard. But an unfinished novel is what we have, and how can we not look? David, alas, isn't here to stop us from reading, or to forgive us for wanting to.

—Michael Pietsch

THE PALE KING

We fill pre-existing forms and
when we fill them we change them
and are changed.

—Frank Bidart, "Borges and I"

§1

Past the flannel plains and blacktop graphs and skylines of canted rust, and past the tobacco-brown river overhung with weeping trees and coins of sunlight through them on the water downriver, to the place beyond the windbreak, where untilled fields simmer shrilly in the A.M. heat: shattercane, lamb's-quarter, cutgrass, sawbrier, nutgrass, jimsonweed, wild mint, dandelion, foxtail, muscadine, spinecabbage, goldenrod, creeping charlie, butterprint, nightshade, ragweed, wild oat, vetch, butcher grass, invaginate volunteer beans, all heads gently nodding in a morning breeze like a mother's soft hand on your cheek. An arrow of starlings fired from the windbreak's thatch. The glitter of dew that stays where it is and steams all day. A sunflower,

3

four more, one bowed, and horses in the distance standing rigid and still as toys. All nodding. Electric sounds of insects at their business. Ale-colored sunshine and pale sky and whorls of cirrus so high they cast no shadow. Insects all business all the time. Quartz and chert and schist and chondrite iron scabs in granite. Very old land. Look around you. The horizon trembling, shapeless. We are all of us brothers.

Some crows come overhead then, three or four, not a murder, on the wing, silent with intent, corn-bound for the pasture's wire beyond which one horse smells at the other's behind, the lead horse's tail obligingly lifted. Your shoes' brand incised in the dew. An alfalfa breeze. Socks' burrs. Dry scratching inside a culvert. Rusted wire and tilted posts more a symbol of restraint than a fence per se. NO HUNTING. The shush of the interstate off past the windbreak. The pasture's crows standing at angles, turning up patties to get at the worms underneath, the shapes of the worms incised in the overturned dung and baked by the sun all day until hardened, there to stay, tiny vacant lines in rows and inset curls that do not close because head never quite touches tail. Read these.

§2

From Midway Claude Sylvanshine then flew on something called Consolidated Thrust Regional Lines down to Peoria, a terrifying thirty-seater whose pilot had pimples at the back of his neck and reached back to pull a dingy fabric curtain over the cockpit and the beverage service consisted of a staggering girl underhanding you nuts while you chugged a Pepsi. Sylvanshine's window seat was in 8-something, an emergency row, beside an older lady with a sacklike chin who could not seem despite strenuous efforts to open her nuts. The core accounting equation $A = L + E$ can be dissolved and reshuffled into everything from $E = A - L$ to beyond. The craft rode the updrafts and downdrafts like a dinghy in a gale. The only service into Peoria was regional out of either St. Louis or the two Chicagos. Sylvanshine had an inner ear thing and couldn't read on planes but did read the emergency laminated card, twice. It was mostly illustrations; for legal reasons, the airline had to presume illiteracy. Without being aware that he was doing so, Sylvanshine mentally repeated the word *illiterate* several dozen times until the word ceased to mean anything and became just a rhythmic sound, not unlovely but out of sync with the propellers' flux's pulse. It was something he did when he was under stress and did not want an incursion. His point of departure was Dulles after a Service shuttle from Shepherdstown/Martinsburg. The three major codifications of US tax law being of course '16, '39, and '54, with '81 and '82's indexing and anti-abuse provisions also relevant. The fact that another major recodification was on the horizon would not, obviously, be on the CPA exam. Sylvanshine's private goal was to pass the CPA exam, thereby immediately advancing two paygrades. The extent of the recodification would, of course, depend in part on the Service's success in carrying out the Initiative's directives. The job and the exam had to occupy two separate parts of his mind; it was crucial that he maintain separation of powers. Separation of the two areas. Calculating depreciation recapture for §1231 assets is a five-step process. The flight took fifty minutes and seemed much longer. There was nothing to do and nothing would hold still in his head in all the confined noise and after the nuts were gone there was nothing else for Sylvanshine to do to occupy his mind but try to look at the ground which appeared close enough that he could make out house colors and the types of different vehicles on the pale interstate the plane seemed to tack back and forth across. The card's figures opening emergency doors and pulling cords and crossing their arms funereally with their seat cushions on their chests seemed amateurishly drawn and their features little more than bumps; you couldn't see fear or relief or really anything on their faces as they slid down the emergency chutes in the drawing. Emergency doors' handles opened in one way and emergency hatches over the wings opened in a totally different way. Components of equity include common stock, retained earnings, and how many different types of SE transaction. Distinguish between perpetual and periodic inventory and explain the relation(s) between a physical inventory and the cost of goods sold. The darkly gray head ahead of him gave off a scent of Brylcreem that was even now surely soaking and staining the little paper towel on the seat top. Sylvanshine wished again that Reynolds was with him on the flight. Sylvanshine and Reynolds were both aides to Systems icon Merrill Errol ('Mel') Lehrl although Reynolds was a GS-11 and Sylvanshine only a miserable and pathetic GS-9. Sylvanshine and Reynolds had lived together and gone everywhere together since the Rome REC debacle in '82. They weren't homosexual; they just lived together and both worked closely with Dr. Lehrl at Systems. Reynolds had both his CPA and a degree in Information Systems Management although he was only slightly more than two years Claude Sylvanshine's senior. This asymmetry was just one more thing that compromised Sylvanshine's self-regard since Rome and made him doubly loyal and grateful to Systems Director Lehrl for having salvaged him from the debris of the catastrophe in Rome and believing in his potential once his niche as a cog in the system was found. The double-entry method invented by Italian Pacioli during the same period as C. Columbus et alia. The card indicated that this was the type of aircraft whose emergency oxygen was a fire-extinguisherish thing beneath the seats rather than dropping from overhead. The primitive opacity of the figures' faces was actually scarier than fear or some kind of visible expression would have been. It was unclear whether the card's primary function was legal or PR or both. He briefly tried to remember the definition of *yaw*. Every so often while studying for the exam this winter Sylvanshine would burp and it would seem like more than a burp; it would taste like he'd almost thrown up a little. A light rain made a moving lace on the window and distended the cross-hatched land they went over. At root, Sylvanshine saw himself as a dithering ninny with at most one marginal talent whose connection to him was itself marginal.

Here is what occurred at the Service's Rome NY Northeast Regional Examination Center on or about the date in question: Two departments had fallen behind and reacted in a regrettably unprofessional fashion, an atmosphere of extreme stress was allowed to cloud judgment and overrule set procedures, the department attempting to hide the growing pile of returns and cross-audit receipts and W-2/1099 copies rather than duly reporting the backlog and requesting that some of the excess be rerouted to other centers. There failed to be full disclosure and prompt remedial action. Just where the failure and breakdown had occurred was still a matter of controversy despite blamestorming sessions at the very highest levels of Compliance, though ultimately the responsibility lay with the Rome REC

Director despite the fact that it was never quite established whether the department heads had made her fully aware of the extent of the backlog. The dark Service joke about this Director now had been that her desk had had a Trumanesque wooden plaque on it which read: WHAT BUCK? It had taken three weeks for District Audit sections to start howling over the shortfall of examined returns for audit and/or Automated Collections Systems and the complaints had slowly worked their way up and over into Inspections as anyone should have been able to figure was only a matter of time. The Rome Director had taken early retirement and one Group Manager had been fired outright, which was exceedingly rare for GS-13s. It was obviously important that remedial action be quiet and that undue publicity not compromise the public's full faith and confidence in the Service. No one threw forms away. Hid, yes, but not destroyed or discarded. Even in the midst of disastrous departmental psychosis no one could bring himself to burn, shred, or pack in Hefties and discard. That would have been a real disaster—that would have become public. The emergency hatch's window was nothing more than several layers of plastic, it appeared, the inside of which gave ominously under digital pressure. Over the window was a stern injunction against opening the emergency hatch accompanied by an iconic triptych explaining how to open just this hatch. As a system, in other words, it was poorly thought through. What was now called *stress* used to be called *tension* or *pressure*. Pressure was now more like something you put on someone else, as in high-pressure salesmen. Reynolds said one of Dr. Lehrl's interbranch liaisons had described the Peoria REC as a 'real pressure cooker,' although that was in terms of Exams, not Personnel, to which latter Sylvanshine was posted as advance and ground-laying for *a possible Systems full-out.* The truth, which Reynolds had stopped just short of expressing as such, was that the assignment couldn't be that sensitive if they trusted it to Sylvanshine. There were, according to his researches, registration slots for the CPA examination at Peoria College of Business on November 7 and 8, and at Joliet Community College November 14–15. Duration of this posting unknown. One of the most effective isometric exercises for the deskbound is to sit up quite straight and tighten the large muscles of the buttocks, holding for a count of eight, then release. It tones, aids blood flow and alertness, and can, unlike other isometric exercises, be performed even in public, being largely obscured by the desk's material mass. Avoid grimacing or loud exhalations upon release.

Preferential transfers, liquidation provisions, unsecured creditors, claims against bankruptcy estate as per Ch. 7. He had his hat in his lap, over the belt. Systems Director Lehrl had started as a GS-9 auditor in Danville VA before the éclat and rapid rise. He had the strength of ten men. When Sylvanshine studied for the exam now the worst thing was that studying any one thing would set off a storm in his head about all the other things he hadn't studied and felt he was still weak on, making it almost impossible to concentrate, causing him to fall ever further behind. He'd been studying for the CPA exam for three and a half years. It was like trying to build a model in a high wind. 'The most important component in organizing a structure for effective study is:' something. What killed him were the story problems. Reynolds had passed the exam on his first sit. Yaw was rotating slightly from side to side. The word for pitching forward and back was something else. Axes were involved. There was something called gimble or 'gimbal' that came into his mind whenever he saw the Donagan kid at Lombard High who then later ended up at Mission Control for the last two *Apollos* and had his picture in a glass case by the Office at Lombard. The worst then was that he knew what teachers were the last people suited for their jobs, and they then smelled some part of this knowledge on him and were at their worst when he was watching. It was a loop. Sylvanshine's senior yearbook in his trunk in storage in Philly was almost wholly unsigned. The older party next door was still trying to open her package of nuts with her teeth but had been clear on not wanting help or needing help. The projected benefit obligation (PBO) equals the present value of all benefits attributed by the pension benefit formula to employee services rendered prior to that date. If you spell it fast with stress on the *h* and the *a* and then the second *a* and the *h* again then *headache* becomes a lilting children's rhymed refrain, something to jump rope to. Look down your shirt and spell *attic*. One of the teenagers outside the video arcade next to the facilities at Midway had worn a black tee shirt with the words SYMPATHY FOR NIXON TOUR and then a long list of cities in tiny appliqué letters. The teen, who was not on the flight, had then sat briefly across from Sylvanshine in the gate area and had picked at his face with a concentration that wasn't at all like the absent face-picking and feeling at parts of the face that accompanied concentrated work in the Service. Sylvanshine still dreamed of desk drawers and air ducts stuffed with forms and forms' edges protruding from grilles over the ducts and the utility closet stacked to the top with Hollerith cards and the Inspections Division lady forcing the door and the cards all falling out on her like McGee's closet as the whole debacle caught up to them after they fell behind on cross-audit receipts at the Rome REC. He dreamed still of Grecula and Harris disabling the Fornix mainframe with something poured from a thermos into the rear vent as hisses and bits of blue-tinged smoke issued. The teen had had no vocational aura at all; this happened with some people. Ethical standards comprising the exam's whole first unit, about which there were also many Service jokes. A violation of the profession's ethical standards most likely would have occurred when: Such was the propellers' otherworldly sound that Sylvanshine now could hear nothing more than drifting syllables of the exchanges around him. The woman's claw on the steel armrest between them was a horrible sight that he declined to attend to. Old people's hands frightened and repelled him. He'd had grandparents whose hands he could remember in their laps looking alien and clawlike. Upon incorporation, Jones, Inc. issues common stock at a price in excess of its par value. It was difficult not to imagine the faces of those whose jobs were writing these questions. What they thought about, what their professional hopes and dreams were. Many of the questions were like little stories with all the human meat left out. On December 1, 1982, Clark Co. leases office space for three years at a monthly rental of $20,000. For a count of one hundred, Sylvanshine tried flexing first one buttock and then the other instead of both buttocks at once, which required concentration and a strange type of noncontrol, like trying to wiggle your ears in the mirror. He tried the inclined-to-the-side thing of stretching out his neck's muscles on each side very gently and gradually but still got a look from the older lady, who with her dark dress and staved-in face appeared more and more skull-like and frightening and like some type of omen of death or crushing failure on the CPA exam, which two things had collapsed in Sylvanshine's psyche to a single image of his silently, expressionlessly pushing a wide industrial mop down a corridor lined with frosted-glass doors bearing other men's names. Even the sight of a mop, rollable bucket, or custodian with his name woven in red Palmer script on the breast pocket of his gray jumpsuit (as at Midway, outside the men's room whose little yellow sign warned bilingually of wet floors, the cursive name something beginning with *M*, Morris or Maurice, the man fitted to his job like a man to the exact pocket of space he displaces) now rattled Sylvanshine to the point where precious time was lost before he could even think about how to set up a workable schedule for maximally efficient reviewing for the exam, even mentally, which he did every day. His great weakness was strategic organization and apportionment of time, as Reynolds pointed out at every opportunity, enjoining Claude to for Christ's sake just take a book off the stack and study instead of sitting there noodling impotently about how best to study. Stuffing returns behind cabinets and into air ducts. Locking desk drawers so filled with cross-reference forms that they could not open anyhow. Hiding things beneath other things in Tingles' baskets. Reynolds had simply appeared at the Director's office before the hearing and the whole personal disaster seemingly vanished in some bureaucratic puff of violet smoke and a week later Sylvanshine was unpacking his boxes at Systems in Martinsburg under Dr. Lehrl. The whole thing felt like being in a near traffic fatality avoided by inches and later not being able even to think of the whole thing lest you begin shaking and be unable to function, it had been such a near-disaster. The entire Fats Pod had melted down. The small sound of a simulated bell accompanied the overhead glyph of seat belts and cigarettes lighting up or disappearing; Sylvanshine looked up every time without con-

sciously intending to. In obtaining evidential matter in support of financial statement assertions, the
auditor develops specific audit objectives in light of
those assertions. An infant keened in some aisle
behind him; Sylvanshine imagined the mother simply unbuckling and withdrawing to some other
aisle and leaving it there. In Philly, after the frenzy
surrounding the introduction of inflation indexes
that new templates had to be configured for in '81,
he had been diagnosed with a stress-related pinched
nerve in his neck and upper back which the enforced
unnatural posture of the tiny narrow 8-B and the
deathlike claw on the armrest beside him aggra-
vated if he gave it his attention. It was true: The
entire ball game, in terms of both the exam and life,
was what you gave attention to vs. what you willed
yourself to not. Sylvanshine viewed himself as weak
or defective in the area of will. Most of what others
esteemed or valued in him was unwilled, simply
given, like a person's height or facial symmetry.
Reynolds called him weak-minded and it was true.
He had a serial memory of their neighbor Mr. Satterthwaite filling in scuffs on his postal uniform's
shoes with a black pen which then before he was
aware of it expanded into a whole narrative memory
of Mr. and Mrs. Satterthwaite, who were childless

and did not if you first met them appear all that friendly or interested in children, nevertheless allowing their backyard to become the de facto HQ for all the children in the neighborhood and even the slapdash and unsound tree house they had allowed Sylvanshine and the Roman Catholic boy with the tic like a chronic wince to try to construct in one of their trees, and Sylvanshine could not recall whether it was because the boy's family had moved away that the tree house was not completed or whether the move had taken place later and the tree house had simply been too slapdash and sap-soaked to continue with. Mrs. Satterthwaite had had lupus and was often indisposed. Deviation rates, precision limits, stratified sampling. As Dr. Lehrl had explained it, entropy was a measure of a certain type of information that there was no point in knowing. Lehrl's axiom was that the definitive test of the efficiency of any organization structure was information and the filtering and dissemination of information. Real entropy had zippo to do with temperature. Another effective concentration device was to summon into one's mind a soothing and low-pressure outdoor scene, either imagined or from memory, which was even more effective if the scene comprised or included a pond lake brook or stream, as water had been proven to have a calming and centering effect on the involuntary nervous system, but try as he might after the buttock exercises Sylvanshine could summon only a jagged primary-color array that looked like a psychedelic poster or something resembling what you see if you're poked in the eye and then close your eye in pain. The oddness of the word *indisposed.* Prove that the relation of long-term bond prices to long-term capital gains tax rates is not inverse. He knew who on the plane was in love, who would say they were in love because it was what you were supposed to say, and who would say they were not in love. Reynolds's own professed take on marriage/family was that from boyhood on he had never liked fathers and had no wish to be one. In three separate venues in today's various airports Sylvanshine had found himself locking eyes with thirty-year-old men who had infants in high-tech papooselike packs on their backs, their wives with quilted infant-supply bags at their sides, the wives in charge, the men appearing essentially soft or softened in some way, desperate in a resigned way, their stride not quite a trudge, their eyes empty and overmild with the weary stoicism of young fathers. Reynolds would call it not stoicism but acquiescence to some large and terrible truth.

The term *dependent* includes any person who qualifies as a dependency exemption, or would otherwise qualify as a dependency exemption except that the gross income and joint return tests are not met. Name two standard devices by which fiduciaries may legally shift tax liability to beneficiaries. The term *passive losses* was not even on the CPA exam. It was vital to divide Service priorities and Exam priorities into two exclusive modules or networks. One of four stated projects was to enhance Peoria 047's ability to distinguish legitimate investment partnerships from tax shelters whose entire purpose was to avoid taxes. The key was identifying passive vs. active losses. The actual project was to create both a case and a control structure for the automation of crucial Examination functions at the Peoria Center. The goal was to have automation in place by the time Revenue Rulings against certain passive-loss provisions were codified in next year's tax law. The older lady's rouge very red and a paperback with a bookmark's tongue unopened in her lap; the veinous and piebald claw. Sylvanshine's seat number was right there stamped onto the brushed steel of the armrest, next to the claw. Its nails were deeply, perfectly red. The smell of his mother's polish remover, of her makeup compact, the way wisps of her hair escaped the bun and curled down the back of her neck in the steam of the kitchen when he and O'Dowd had returned from the Satterthwaites' backyard with hammered thumbs and sap in their lashes. Wisps and flashes of uncolored cloud flashed past the window. Above and below were a different story, but there was always something disappointing about clouds when you were inside them; they ceased to be clouds at all. It just got really foggy. *Yaw* was *way* in a mirror, it occurred for no reason. Sylvanshine then spent some time trying to feel the fact that his personal body was traveling at the same speed as the craft he was inside. On a large jet it felt like merely sitting in a loud narrow room; here at least the changes in the seat's and belt's pressures against him allowed him to be aware of movement, and there seemed to be some security in the physical candor of this, which partly offset the fragility and spatter-potential of the sound of the propellers, which Sylvanshine tried to think of what the props sounded like but could not except as a gnawingly hypnotic rotary hum so total that it might have been silence itself. A lobotomy involved some kind of rod or probe inserted through the eyesocket, the term was always 'frontal' lobotomy; but was there any other kind? Knowing that internal stress could cause failure on the exam merely set up internal stress about the prospect of internal stress. There must be some other way to deal with the knowledge of the disastrous consequences fear and stress could bring about. Some answer or trick of the will: the ability not to think about it. What if everyone knew this trick but Claude Sylvanshine? He tended to conceptualize some ultimate, platonic-level Terror as a bird of prey in whose mere aloft shadow the prey was stricken and paralyzed, trembling as the shadow enlarged and became inevitability. He frequently had this feeling: What if there was something essentially wrong with Claude Sylvanshine that wasn't wrong with other people? What if he was simply ill-suited, the way some people are born without limbs or certain organs? The neurology of failure. What if he was simply born and destined to live in the shadow of Total Fear and Despair, and all his so-called activities were pathetic attempts to distract him from the inevitable? Discuss important differences between reserve accounting and charge-off accounting in the tax treatment of bad debts. Surely fear is a type of stress. Tedium is like stress but its own Category of Woe. Sylvanshine's father, whenever something professionally bad happened—which was a lot—had a habit of saying 'Woe to Sylvanshine.' There is an anti-stress technique called Thought Stopping. The excess present value index is the ratio of the present value of future cash inflows to the initial investment. Segment, significant segment, combined segment revenue, absolute combined segment revenue, operating profit. Material price variance. Direct material price variance. He thought of the removable grate over the air duct above his and Ray Harris's desk in the Rome REC and the sound of the grate being removed and then jammed back into place and driven home with the heel of Harris's hand, and then recoiled from the thought in a way that made it feel as if the craft were accelerating. The interstate highway below disappeared and then sometimes reappeared at a spot Sylvanshine had to squash his cheek right up against the plastic inner window to see, then as the rain recommenced and he could tell they were beginning descent it reappeared in the window's center, light traffic crawling with a futile pointless pathos you could never sense on the ground. What if it felt as slow to actually drive as it looked from this perspective? It would be like trying to run under water. The whole ball game was perspective, filtering, the choice of perception's objects. Sylvanshine tried to envision the small plane as seen from the ground, a cruciform shape against the old-bathwater color of the cloud cover, its lights blinking complexly in the rain. He imagined rain on his face. It was light, a West Virginia rain; he hadn't heard one unit of thunder. Sylvanshine had once been on a first date with a Xerox rep who had complex and slightly repulsive patterns of callus on her fingers from playing the banjo semiprofessionally as her off-time passion; and he remembered, as the overhead bell again rang and the sign lit, the no-cigarette glyph legally redundant, the pads' calluses deep yellow in the low dinnerlight as he'd spoken to the musician about forensic accounting's intricacies and the hivelike organization of the Northeast REC, which was only one small part of the Service, and the Service's history and little-understood ideals and sense of mission and the old joke (to him) about how Service employees in social situations would go to such absurd lengths to avoid telling people that they worked for the IRS because it often cast such a social pall because of popular perceptions of the Service and its employees, all the while watching the calluses as the woman worked her knife and fork, and that he'd been so nervous and tense that he'd yammered on and on about himself and never asked her sufficiently about herself, her history with the banjo and what it meant to her, which was why she hadn't liked him enough and they hadn't connected. He'd never given the woman with the banjo a chance, he saw now. That what appears to be egoism so often isn't. In some ways, Sylvanshine was a whole different person now in Systems. Their descent was mainly a heightening of the specificity of what lay below—fields revealed as plowed and perpendicularly furrowed and silos as adjoined by canted chutes and belts and an industrial park as individual buildings with reflective windows and complicated clumps of cars in the parking lots. Each car not only parked by a different human individual but conceived, designed, assembled from parts each one of which was designed and made, transported, sold, financed, purchased, and insured by human individuals, each with life stories and self-concepts that all fit together into a larger pattern of facts. Reynolds's dictum was that reality was a fact-pattern the bulk of which was entropic and random. The trick was homing in on which facts were important—Reynolds was a rifle to Sylvanshine's shotgun. The feeling of a slight trickle of blood from his right nostril was a hallucination and to be ignored absolutely; the feeling simply did not exist. Sinus trouble ran in Sylvanshine's family in the worst way. Aurelius of ancient Rome. First principles. Exemptions vs. deductions, for AGI vs. from AGI. A loss sustained from a nonbusiness bad debt is always classified as a short-term capital loss and may therefore be deducted on Schedule D as per the following IRC §: One building's roof had what was either a marked helipad or a complicated visual signal to the planes descending overhead, and the pitch of the propellers' doubled hum was different and his right sinus was even now ballooning redly in his skull and they really were descending, the term was controlled descent, the interstate now rococo with exits and half-cloverleafs and the traffic denser and with something insistent about it, and the claw rose from the steel armrest as there appeared a body of water below, a lake or delta, and Sylvanshine felt one of his feet was asleep as he tried to recall the peculiar crossed-arm configuration with which the figures on the card held their seat cushions to their chests in the unlikely event of a water landing, and now they did really and truly yaw and their speed became more evident in the rate of passage of things below in what had to be an older district of Peoria *qua* human city, close-packed blocks of sooty brick and angled roofs and a television antenna with a flag attached, and a flash of a bourbon-colored river that was not the previous body of water but might have been connected to it, nothing like the stately and befrothed stretch of Potomac that obtruded through Systems' windows on Antietam's hallowed site, noting that the stewardess in her fold-down seat had her head down and arms about her own legs where at year's end the aggregate fair value of Brown's salable securities exceeds the aggregate carrying amount at the beginning of the year as out of nowhere appeared an expanse of pale cement rising to meet them with no warning bell or announcement and his soda can wedged in the seat pocket as the gray death's-head beside whipped right and left and the propellers' shimmering sound shifted either pitch or timbre, and the older lady stiffening in her seat and raising her pleated chin in fear and repeating what sounded to Sylvanshine like the word *chump* as veins stood bluely in the fist before her, in which was enclosed the crushed and bulbous but still unopened foil pack of off-brand nuts.

'The fifth effect has more to do with you, how you're perceived. It's powerful although its use is more restricted. Pay attention, boy. The next suitable person you're in light conversation with, you stop suddenly in the middle of the conversation and look at the person closely and say, "What's wrong?" You say it in a concerned way. He'll say, "What do you mean?" You say, "Something's wrong. I can tell. What is it?" And he'll look stunned and say, "How did you know?" He doesn't realize something's *always* wrong, with everybody. Often more than one thing. He doesn't know everybody's always going around all the time with something wrong and believing they're exerting great willpower and control to keep other people, for whom they think nothing's ever wrong, from seeing it. This is the way of people. Suddenly ask what's wrong, and whether they open up and spill their guts or deny it and pretend you're off, they'll think you're perceptive and understanding. They'll either be grateful, or they'll be frightened and avoid you from then on. Both reactions have their uses, as we'll get to. You can play it either way. This works over 90 percent of the time.'

And stood—having squeezed by the powdery older lady, she being the type that waits in her seat until all others have deplaned and then exits alone, with a counterfeit dignity—holding his effects in an aisle whose crammed front portion was all regional business travelers, men of business, willfully homely midwestern men on downstate sales calls or returning from the Chicago HQs of companies whose names end with '-co,' men for whom landings like this yaw-wobbled horror just past are business as usual. Paunched and blotchy men in double-knit brown suits and tan suits with attaché cases ordered from in-flight catalogues. Men whose soft faces fit their jobs like sausage in its meaty casing. Men who instruct pocket recorders to take a memo, men who look at their watches out of reflex, men with red foreheads all mashed standing in a metal chute as the props' hum descends the tonal scale and ventilation ceases, this the type of commuter airplane whose stairs must be rolled up alongside before the door opens, for legal reasons. The glazed impatience of businessmen standing closer to strangers than they would ever choose to, chests and backs nearly touching, suit bags slung over shoulders, briefcases knocking together, more scalp than hair, breathing one another's smells. Men who cannot bear to wait or stand still forced to stand still all together and wait, men with calfskin Day-Timers and Franklin Quest Time Management certificates and the classic look of unwilled tight confinement, the look of a local merchant on the verge of an SSI-withholding lapse, undercapitalized, illiquid, trying to cover the monthly nut, fish thrashing in the nets of their own obligations. Two eventual suicides on this plane, one forever classed as an accident. In Philly there had been a whole subgroup of implacable metal-minded GS-9s tasked to nothing but going after small businesses who'd fallen behind on

SSI withholding, although in Rome for almost a year the only Compliance staff taking SSI alerts from Martinsburg had been Eloise Prout, a.k.a. Dr. Yes, a fortyish GS-9 in a macramé hat who ate lunch at her desk out of a complex system of Tupperware containers and was a dinner whore of the most pathetic sort, the boys in Examinations christening her Dr. Yes after she'd reportedly slept with Sherman Garnett on nothing but the promise—not honored—of a walk around the town commons with the snow stopped and everything crisp and white. The Eloise Prout who came in so low every month on referral and recovery quotas that any other GS-9 would have worn the brown helmet but dim kindly REC Mr. Orkney had kept her on, Prout apparently a car-crash widow with a GS-9 salary that barely bought cat food, Sylvanshine was well aware, his foot pulsing with new blood and excusing himself each time someone bumped his carry-on, his third post in four years and still a GS-9 with a promise of 11 if he passed the CPA exam this spring and acquitted himself well in this post as Systems' eyes on the ground through the March 15 corporate and then April 15 storms of 1040s and ESTs for Peoria 047 to examine, having sat for the exam twice so far and so far passing only Managerial with a Low Pass, Sylvanshine's rep in Philly following him to Rome and locking him firmly into Level 1 Returns, not even Fats or Review, which had made him little more than a professional letter-opener, which Soane, Madrid, et al. had not been shy about observing.

Sylvanshine tended to do his deskwork in a kind of frenzy as opposed to the slow, austere, methodical disposition of truly great accountants, his first group supervisor in Rome had told him, a lifetime third-shifter who wore an eccentric coat and always left the REC carrying a little rhomboid carton of delivered Chinese for his wife, who was said to be some kind of shut-in. This GS-11 had early in his career been posted at the St. Louis Service Center, literally in the shadow of the strange scary giant metal arch thing, to which mail came daily in great wheezing eighteen-wheel trailer rigs backing up to the dock's long conveyor, and on breaks in the break room the group leader had liked to lean back holding his umbrella and blow silvery clouds of cigar smoke up at the fluorescent lights and reminisce about summer in the Midwest, of which region Sylvanshine and the other young eastern GS-9s were ignorant and in whom the group leader somehow planted visions of fishing barefoot on the banks of motionless rivers and a moon you could read the paper by and everyone always saying Hi to everyone else every time they saw them and moving in a kind of cheery slo-mo. Named Bussy, Mr. Vince or Vincent Bussy, who wore a Kmart parka with a hood with a fake fur fringe, and could walk chopsticks over his knuckles like a magician with a shiny coin, and disappeared following Sylvanshine's second REC Christmas party, when his wife (i.e., Mrs. Bussy) had suddenly appeared in the midst of the revel in an off-white nightie and identical unzipped Kmart parka and approached the Assistant Regional Commissioner for Examinations and, speaking slowly and atonally and with total conviction, told him that her husband Mr. Bussy had said that he (the ARCE) had the potential to be a really truly evil person if he grew a somewhat larger set of balls, Bussy one week thereafter gone so abruptly that his umbrella remained hanging from the Pod's communal coatrack for almost a quarter until someone finally took it down.

They deplaned and descended and collected the carry-on bags that had been confiscated and tagged at Midway and now rested in a motley row on the wet tarmac beside the airplane, and stood then briefly en masse on a complexly painted cement expanse while someone with orange earmuffs and clipboard counted them and then crosschecked the count with a previous count undertaken at Midway. The whole operation seemed somewhat ad hoc and slapdash. On the steep and portable staircase, Sylvanshine had derived the usual satisfaction from putting his hat on his head and adjusting its angle all with one hand. His right ear popped and crackled slightly with each swallow. The wind was warm and steamy. A large hose extended from a small truck to the commuter plane's stomach and appeared to be refueling the craft for its turnaround to Chicago. Up and back again and again all day. There was a strong scent of fuel and wet cement. The older lady, evidently uncounted, now descended the frightening stairs and went to some type of long automobile that Sylvanshine had not noticed parked off the airplane's starboard side. A wing obtruded, but Sylvanshine could see that she did not open her own door. A distant tree line's tops bent left in the wind and came straight again. Because of previous problems with accidents traceable to poor snap decisions in Philly, Sylvanshine no longer drove. He was over 75 percent certain that the packet of nuts was now inside the older lady's handbag. There was some type of consultation between the employee with the clipboard and another person with orange earmuffs. Several of the other passengers were making pointed gestures of looking at their watches. The air was warm and close and well beyond humid or muggy. They were all becoming damp on the sides of themselves that faced the wind. Sylvanshine now noticed that the dark topcoats many of the businessmen wore were quite similar, as were the flares of the upturned collars. No one else wore any type of hat. He was trying to pay close attention to his surroundings as a way to avert thought and anxiety. The administrative or logistical delay was occurring under a baggy sky and a rain so fine it seemed to come sideways with the wind instead of fall. There was no sound of rain on Sylvanshine's hat. The fur of Mr. Bussy's hood's fringe had been dirty in a sort of queasy way that got worse over the two years he served as Sylvanshine's group supervisor in Returns Processing. Some of the more assertive passengers were walking unguided down the red-lined path that led through the fence's gate and toward the terminal. Sylvanshine, who had checked bags, was concerned about sanctions for unauthorized departure from the tarmac. On the other hand, he had an assigned schedule to keep. Part of what kept him standing in the restive group of men awaiting authorization to enter the airport was a kind of paralysis that resulted from Sylvanshine's reflecting on the logistics of getting to the Peoria 047 REC—the issue of whether the REC sent a van for transfers or whether Sylvanshine would have to take a cab from the little airport had not been conclusively resolved—and then how to arrive and check in and where to store his three bags while he checked in and filled out his arrival and Post-code payroll and withholding forms and orientational materials then somehow get directions and proceed to the apartment that Systems had rented for him at government rates and get there in time to find someplace to eat that was either in walking distance or would require getting another cab—except the telephone in the alleged apartment wasn't connected yet and he considered the prospects of being able to hail a cab from outside an apartment complex were at best iffy, and if he told the original cab he'd taken to the apartment to wait for him, there would be difficulties because how exactly would he reassure the cabbie that he really was coming right back out after dropping his bags and doing a quick spot check of the apartment's condition and suitability instead of it being a ruse designed to defraud the driver of his fare, Sylvanshine ducking out the back of the Angler's Cove apartment complex or even conceivably barricading himself in the apartment and not responding to the driver's knock, or his ring if the apartment had a doorbell, which his and Reynolds's current apartment in Martinsburg most assuredly did not, or the driver's queries/threats through the apartment door, a scam that resided in Claude Sylvanshine's awareness only because a number of independent Philadelphia commercial carriage operators had proposed heavy Schedule C losses under the proviso 'Losses Through Theft of Service' and detailed this type of scam as prevalent on the poorly typed or sometimes even handwritten attachments required to explain unusual or specific C-deductions like this, whereas were Sylvanshine to pay the fare and the tip and perhaps even a certain amount in advance on account so as to help assure the driver of his honorable intentions re the second leg of the sojourn there was no tangible guarantee that the average taxi driver—a cynical and ethically marginal species, hustlers, as even their smudged returns' very low tip-income-vs.-number-of-fares-in-an-average-shift ratios in Philly had indicated—wouldn't simply speed away with Sylvanshine's money, creating enormous hassles in terms of filling out the internal forms for getting a percentage of his travel per diem reimbursed and also leaving Sylvanshine alone, famished (he was unable to eat before travel), phoneless, devoid of Reynolds's counsel and logistical savvy in the sterile new unfurnished apartment, his stomach roiling in on itself in such a way that it would be all Sylvanshine could do to unpack in any kind of half-organized fashion and get to sleep on the nylon travel pallet on the unfinished floor in the possible presence of exotic Midwest bugs, to say nothing of putting in the hour of CPA exam review he'd promised himself this morning when he'd overslept slightly and then encountered last-minute packing problems that had canceled out the firmly scheduled hour of morning CPA review before one of the unmarked Systems vans arrived to take him and his bags out through Harpers Ferry and Ball's Bluff to the airport, to say even less about any kind of systematic organization and mastery of the voluminous Post, Duty, Personnel, and Systems Protocols materials he should be receiving promptly after check-in and forms processing at the Post, which any reasonable Personnel Director would expect a new examiner to have thoroughly internalized before reporting for the first actual day interacting with REC examiners, and which there was no way in any real world that Sylvanshine could expect himself to try to review and internalize on either a sixteen-hour fast or after a night on the pallet with his damp raincoat as a pillow—he had been unable to pack the special contoured orthotic pillow for his neck's chronic pinched or inflamed nerve; it would have required its own suitcase and thereby exceeded the baggage limit and incurred an exorbitant surcharge which Reynolds refused to let Sylvanshine pay out of simple principle—with the additional problem of securing any sort of substantive breakfast or return ride to the REC in the morning without a phone, or how without a phone one was supposed even to verify whether and when the apartment phone was going to be activated, plus of course the ominous probability of oversleeping the next morning due to both travel fatigue and his not having packed his traveler's alarm clock—or at any rate not having been certain that he'd packed it instead of allowing it to go into one of the three large cartons that he had packed and labeled but done a hasty, slipshod job of writing out Contents Lists for the boxes to refer to when unpacking them in Peoria, and which Reynolds had pledged to insert into the Service's Support Branch shipping mechanism at roughly the same time Sylvanshine's flight was scheduled to depart from Dulles, which meant two or possibly even three days before the cartons with all the essentials Sylvanshine had not been able to fit in his bags arrived, and even then they would arrive at the REC and it was as yet unclear how Claude would then get them home to the apartment—the realization about the traveler's alarm having been the chief cause of Sylvanshine's having to unlock and open all the carefully packed luggage that morning on arising already half an hour late, to try to locate or verify the inclusion of the portable alarm, which he had failed to do—the whole thing presenting such a cyclone of logistical problems and complexities that Sylvanshine was forced to do some Thought Stopping right there on the wet tarmac surrounded by restive breathers, turning 360° several times and trying to merge his own awareness with the panoramic vista, which except for airport-related items was uniformly featureless and old-coin gray and so remarkably flat that it was as if the earth here had been stamped on with some cosmic boot, visibility in all directions limited only by the horizon, which was the same general color and texture as the sky and created the specular impression of being in the center of some huge and stagnant body of water, an oceanic impression so literally obliterating that Sylvanshine was cast or propelled back in on himself and felt again the edge of the shadow of the wing of Total Terror and Disqualification pass over him, the knowledge of his being surely and direly ill-suited for whatever lay ahead, and of its being only a matter of time before this fact emerged and was made manifest to all those present in the moment that Sylvanshine finally, and forever, lost it.

§3

'Speaking of which, what do you think of when you masturbate?'

'...'

'...'

'What?'

Neither had said a word for the first half hour. They were doing the mindless monochrome drive up to Region HQ in Joliet again. In one of the fleet's Gremlins, seized as part of a jeopardy assessment against an AMC dealership five quarters past.

'Look, I think we can presume you masturbate. Something like 98 percent of all men masturbate. It's documented. Most of the other 2 percent are impaired in some way. We can forgo the denials. I masturbate; you masturbate. It happens. We all do

41

it and we all know we all do it and yet no one ever discusses it. It's an incredibly boring drive, there's nothing to do, we're stuck in this embarrassing car—let's push the envelope. Let's discuss it.'

'What envelope?'

'Just what do you think of? Think about it. It's a very interior time. It's one of life's only occasions of real self-sufficiency. It requires nothing outside you. It's bringing yourself pleasure with nothing but your own mind's thoughts. Those thoughts reveal a lot about you: what you dream of when you yourself choose and control what you dream.'

'...'

'...'

'Tits.'

'Tits?'

'You asked me. I'm telling you.'

'That's it? Tits?'

'What do you want me to say?'

'Just tits? In isolation from anybody? Just abstract tits?'

'All right. Fuck off.'

'You mean just floating there, two tits, in empty space? Or nestled in your hands, or what? Is it always the same tits?'

'This is me learning a lesson. You ask a question like that and I go what the hell and I answer it and you run a DIF-3 on the answer.'

'Tits.'

'. . .'

'. . .'

'So what do *you* think about, then, Mr. Envelope Guy?'

§4

From the *Peoria Journal Star,*
Monday, November 17, 1980, p. C-2:

IRS WORKER DEAD FOR FOUR DAYS
Supervisors at the IRS's regional complex
in Lake James township are trying to determine why no one noticed that one of their
employees had been sitting dead at his desk
for four days before anyone asked if he was
feeling all right.

Frederick Blumquist, 53, who had been
employed as a tax return examiner with the
agency for over thirty years, suffered a heart
attack in the open-plan office he shared
with twenty-five coworkers at the agency's

Regional Examination Center on Self-Storage Parkway. He quietly passed away last Tuesday at his desk, but nobody noticed until late Saturday evening when an office cleaner asked how the examiner could still be working in an office with all the lights off.

Mr. Blumquist's supervisor, Scott Thomas, said, 'Frederick was always the first guy in each morning and the last to leave at night. He was very focused and diligent, so no one found it unusual that he was in the same position all that time and didn't say anything. He was always absorbed in his work, and kept to himself.'

A postmortem examination by the Tazewell County Coroner's Office yesterday revealed that Blumquist had been dead for four days after suffering from a coronary. Ironically, according to Thomas, Blumquist was part of a special task force of IRS agents examining the tax affairs of medical partnerships in the area when he died.

§5

It is this boy who dons the bright-orange bando-
lier and shepherds the lower grades' kids through
the crosswalk outside school. This is after finishing
his Meals on Wheels breakfast tour of the charity
home for the aged downtown, whose administrator
lunges to bolt her office door when she hears his
cart's wheels in the hall. He has paid out of pocket
for the steel whistle and the white gloves held palm-
out at cars while children who did not dress themselves cross behind him, some trying to run despite
WALK, DON'T RUN!!, the happy-face sandwich board
he also made himself. The autos whose drivers he
knows he waves at and gives an extra-big smile and
tosses some words of good cheer as the crosswalk
clears and the cars peel out and barrel through,

46

some joshing around a little by swerving to miss him only by inches as he laughs and dances aside and makes faces of pretended terror at the flanks and rear bumpers. (The time that one station wagon didn't miss him really *was* an accident, and he sent the lady several notes to make absolutely sure she knew he understood that, and asked a whole lot of people he hadn't yet gotten the opportunity to make friends with to sign his cast, and decorated the crutches very carefully with bits of colored ribbon and tinsel and adhesive sparkles, and even before the minimum six weeks the doctor sternly prescribed he'd donated the crutches to Calvin Memorial's pediatrics wing in order to brighten up some other less lucky and happy kid's convalescence, and by the end of the whole thing he'd been inspired to write a very long theme to enter in the annual Social Studies Theme Competition about how even a painful and debilitating accidental injury can yield new opportunities for making friends and reaching out to others, and while the theme didn't win or even get honorable mention he honestly didn't care, because he felt like writing the theme had been its own reward and that he'd gotten a lot out of the whole nine-draft process, and was honestly happy for the kids whose themes did win prizes, and told them he was 100-plus percent sure they deserved it and that if they wanted to preserve their prize themes and maybe even make display items out of them for their parents he'd be happy to type them up and laminate them and even fix any spelling errors he found if they'd like him to, and at home his father puts his hand on little Leonard's shoulder and says he's proud that his son's such a good sport, and offers to take him to Dairy Queen as a kind of reward, and Leonard tells his father he's grateful and that the gesture means a lot to him but that in all honesty he'd like it even more if they took the money his father would have spent on the ice cream and instead donated it either to Easter Seals or, better yet, to UNICEF, to go toward the needs of famine-ravaged Biafran kids who he knows for a fact have probably never even *heard* of ice cream, and says that he bets it'll end up giving both of them a better feeling even than the DQ would, and as the father slips the coins in the coin slot of the special bright-orange UNICEF volunteer cardboard pumpkin-bank, Leonard takes a moment to express concern about the father's facial tic again and to gently rib him about his reluctance to go in and have the family's MD look at it, noting again that according to the chart on the back of his bedroom door the father is three months overdue for his annual physical and that it's almost eight months past the date of his recommended tetanus booster.)

He serves as hall monitor for Periods 1 and 2 (he's half a grade ahead on credits) but gives far more official warnings than actual citations — he's there to serve, he feels, not run people down. Usually with the warnings he dispenses a smile and tells them you're young exactly once so enjoy it, and to go get out of here and make this day count why don't they. He does UNICEF and Easter Seals and starts a recycling program in three straight grades. He is healthy and scrubbed and always groomed just well enough to project basic courtesy and respect for the community of which he is a part, and he politely raises his hand in class for every question, but only if he's sure he knows not only the correct answer but the formulation of that answer that the teacher's looking for that will help advance the discussion of the overall topic they're covering that day, often staying after class to double-check with the teacher that his take on her general objectives is sound and to ask whether there was any way his in-class answers could have been better or more helpful.

The boy's mom has a terrible accident while cleaning the oven and is rushed to the hospital, and even though he's beside himself with concern and says constant prayers for her stabilization and recovery he volunteers to stay home and field calls and relay information to an alphabetized list of relatives and concerned family friends, and to make sure the mail and newspaper are brought in, and to keep the home's lights turned on and off in a random sequence at night as Officer Chuck of the Michigan State Police's Crime Stoppers public-school outreach program sensibly advises when grown-ups are suddenly called away from home, and also to call the gas company's emergency number (which he has memorized) to have them come check on what may well be a defective valve or circuit in the oven before anyone else in the family is exposed to risk of accidental harm, and also (secretly) to work on an immense display of bunting and pennants and WELCOME HOME and WORLD'S GREATEST MOM signs which he plans to use the garage's extendable ladder (with a responsible neighborhood adult holding it and supervising) to very carefully affix to the front of the home with water-soluble glue so that it'll be there to greet and cheer the mom when she's released from Critical Care with a totally clean bill of health, which Leonard calls his father repeatedly at the Critical Care ward pay phone to assure him that he has absolutely no doubt of, the totally clean bill of health, calling hourly right on the dot until there's some kind of mechanical problem with the pay phone and when he dials it he just gets a high tone, which he duly reports to the telephone company's special 1-616-TROUBLE line, remembering to include the specific pay phone's eight-digit Field Product Code (which he'd written down all of just in case) as the small-print technical material on the 1-616-TROUBLE line at the very back of the phone book recommends for most rapid and efficient service.

He can produce several different kinds of calligraphy and has been to origami camp (twice) and can do extraordinary freehand sketches of local flora and can whistle all six of Telemann's *Nouveaux Quatuors* as well as imitate just about any birdcall that Audubon could ever have thought of. He sometimes writes academic publishers about possible errors of category and/or syntax in their textbooks. Let's not even mention spelling bees. He can make over twenty different kinds of admiral, cowboy, clerical, and multiethnic hats out of ordinary newspaper, and he volunteers to visit the school's K–2 classrooms teaching the little kids how, an offer the Carl P. Robinson Elementary principal says he appreciates and has considered very carefully before declining. The principal loathes the mere sight of the boy but does not quite know why. He sees the boy in his sleep, at nightmares' ragged edges — the pressed checked shirt and hair's hard little part, the freckles and ready generous smile: anything he can do. The principal fantasizes about sinking a meat hook into Leonard Stecyk's bright-eyed little face and dragging the boy facedown behind his Volkswagen Beetle over the rough new streets of suburban Grand Rapids. The fantasies come out of nowhere and horrify the principal, who is a devout Mennonite.

Everyone hates the boy. It is a complex hatred, one that often causes the haters to feel mean and guilty and to hate themselves for feeling this way about such an accomplished and well-meaning boy, which then tends to make them involuntarily hate the boy even more for arousing such self-hatred. The whole thing is totally confusing and upsetting. People take a lot of aspirin when he's around. The boy's only real friends among kids are the damaged, the handicapped, the fat, the last-picked, the *non grata* — he seeks them out. All 316 invitations to his eleventh-birthday *BLOWOUT BASH* — 322 invitations if you count the ones made on audiotape for the blind — are offset-printed on quality vellum with matching high-rag

envelopes addressed in ornate Phillippian II calligraphy he's spent three weekends on, and each invitation details in Roman-numeraled outline form
the itinerary's half-day at Six Flags, private PhD-
guided tour of the Blanford Nature Center, and
Reserved Banquet Area w/ Free Play at Shakee's
Pizza and Indoor Arcade on Remembrance Drive
(the whole day gratis and paid for out of the Paper
and Aluminum Drives the boy got up at 4:00 A.M.
all summer to organize and spearhead, the balance
of the Drives' receipts going to the Red Cross and
the parents of a Kentwood third-grader with terminal spina bifida who dreams above all else of seeing the Lions' Night Train Lane play live from his
motorized wheelchair), and the invitations explicitly call the party this—a *BLOWOUT BASH*—
in balloon-shaped font as the caption to an
illustrated explosion of good cheer and -will and
no-holds-barred-let-out-all-the-stops *FUN,* with the
bold-faced proviso **PLEASE—NO PRESENTS
REQUIRED** in each of each card's four corners;
and the 316 invitations, sent via First-Class Mail to
every student, instructor, substitute instructor,
aide, administrator, and custodian at C. P. Robinson Elementary, yield a total attendance of nine
celebrants (not counting parents or LPNs of the
incapacitated), and yet an undauntedly fine time is

had by all, and such is the consensus on the Honest Appraisal and Suggestion Cards (also vellum) circulated at party's end, the massive remainders of chocolate cake, Neapolitan ice cream, pizza, chips, caramel corn, Hershey's Kisses, Red Cross and Officer Chuck pamphlets on organ/tissue donation and the correct procedures to follow if approached by a stranger respectively, kosher pizza for the Orthodox, designer napkins, and dietetic soda in souvenir *I Survived Leonard Stecyk's 11th Birthday Blowout Bash 1964* plastic glasses w/ built-in lemniscate Krazy Straws the guests were to keep as mementos all donated to the Kent County Children's Home via procedures and transport that the birthday boy has initiated even while the big Twister free-for-all is under way, out of concerns about melted ice cream and staleness and flatness and the waste of a chance to help the less fortunate; and his father, driving the wood-panel station wagon and steadying his cheek with one hand, avows again that the boy beside him has a large, good heart, and that he is proud, and that if the boy's mother ever regains consciousness as they so very much hope, he knows she'll be just awful proud as well.

The boy makes As and enough occasional Bs to keep himself from getting a swelled head about marks, and his teachers shudder at the sound of even just his name. In the fifth grade he undertakes a district collection to provide a Special Fund of nickels for anyone at lunch who's already spent their milk money but still might for whatever reason want or feel they need more milk. The Jolly Holly Milk Company gets wind of it and puts a squib about the Fund and an automated line drawing of the boy on the side of some of their half-pint cartons. Two-thirds of the school ceases to drink milk, while the Special Fund itself grows so large that the principal has to requisition a small safe for his office. The principal is now taking Seconal to sleep and experiencing fine tremors, and on two separate occasions is cited for Failure to Yield at marked crosswalks.

A teacher in whose homeroom the boy suggests a charted reorganization of the coat hooks and boot boxes lining one wall so that the coat and galoshes of the student whose desk is nearest the door would themselves be nearest the door, and the second-nearest's second-nearest, and so on, speeding the pupils' egress to recess and reducing delays and possible quarrels and clots of half-bundled kids at the classroom door (which delays and clots the boy had taken the trouble this quarter to chart by statistical incidence, with relevant graphics and arrows but all names withheld), this tenured and highly respected veteran teacher ends up brandishing blunt scissors and threatening to kill first the boy and then herself, and is put on Medical Leave, during which she receives thrice-weekly Get Well cards, with neatly typed summaries of the class's activities and progress in her absence sprinkled with glitter and folded in perfect diamond shapes that open with just a squeeze of the two long facets inside (i.e., inside the cards), until the teacher's doctors order her mail to be withheld until improvement or at least stabilization in her condition warrants.

Right before 1965's big Halloween UNICEF collection three sixth-graders accost the boy in the southeast restroom after fourth period and do unspeakable things to him, leaving him hanging from a stall's hook by his underpants' elastic; and after being treated and released from the hospital (a different one than his mother is a patient in the long-term convalescent ward of), the boy refuses to identify his assailants and later circumspectly delivers to them individualized notes detailing his renunciation of any and all hard feelings about the incident, apologizing for whatever unwitting offense he might have given to provoke it, exhorting his attackers to please put the whole thing behind them and not in any way self-recriminate over it—especially down the line, because the boy's understanding was that these were the sorts of things that could sometimes really haunt you later on down the line in adulthood, citing one or two journal articles the attackers might have a look at if they wanted documentation on the long-term psychological effects of self-recrimination—and, in the notes, professing his personal hope that an actual friendship might conceivably result from the whole regrettable incident, along which lines he was also enclosing an invitation to attend a short no-questions-asked Conflict Resolution Round-table the boy has persuaded a local community services outreach organization to sponsor after school the following Tuesday *'(Light Refreshments Served!),'* after which the boy's PE locker along with the four on either side are destroyed in an act of pyrotechnic vandalism that everyone on both sides in the subsequent court trial agrees got totally out of hand and was not a premeditated attempt to injure the night custodian or to do anything like the amount of structural damage to the Boys' locker room it ended up doing, and at which trial Leonard Stecyk appeals repeatedly to both sides' counsel for the opportunity to testify for the defense, if only as a character witness. A large percentage of the boy's classmates hide—take actual evasive action—when they see him coming. Eventually even the marginal and infirm stop returning his calls. His mother has to be turned and her limbs manipulated twice a day.

§6

They were up on a picnic table at that one park by the lake, by the edge of the lake with part of a downed tree in the shallows half hidden by the bank. Lane A. Dean Jr. and his girlfriend, both in blue jeans and button-up shirts. They sat up on the table's top portion and had their shoes on the bench part that people sat on and picnicked in carefree times. They had gone to different high schools but the same junior college, where they had met in campus ministries. It was springtime, the park's grass was very green and the air suffused with honeysuckle and lilacs both, which was almost too much. There were bees, and the angle of the sun made the water of the shallows look dark. There had been more storms that week, with some downed trees and the sound of chainsaws all up and down his parents' street. Their postures on the picnic table were both the same forward kind with their shoulders rounded and elbows on their knees. In this position the girl rocked slightly and once put her face in her hands but she was not crying. Lane was very still and immobile and looking past the bank at the downed tree in the shallows and its ball of exposed roots going all directions and the tree's cloud of branches all half in the water. The only other individual nearby was a dozen spaced tables away by himself, standing upright. Looking at the torn-up hole in the ground there where the tree had gone over. It was still early yet and all the shadows wheeling right and shortening. The girl wore a thin old checked cotton shirt with pearl-colored snaps with the long sleeves down and she always smelled very good and clean, like someone you could trust and deeply care about even if you weren't in love. Lane Dean had liked the smell of her right away. His mother called her *down to earth* and liked her, thought she was good people, you could tell—she made this evident in little ways. The shallows lapped from different directions at the tree as if almost teething on it. Sometimes when alone and thinking or struggling to turn a matter over to Jesus Christ in prayer, he would find himself putting his fist in his palm and turning it slightly as if still playing and pounding his glove to stay sharp and alert in center. He did not do this now, it would be cruel and indecent to do this now. The older individual stood beside his picnic table, he was at it but not sitting, and looked also out of place in a suit coat or jacket and the kind of older men's hat Lane's grandfather wore in photos as a young insurance man. He appeared to be looking across the lake. If he moved, Lane didn't see it. He looked more like a picture than a man. There were not any ducks in view.

One thing Lane Dean did was reassure her again that he'd go with her and be there with her. It was one of the few safe or decent things he could really say. The second time he said it again now she shook her head and laughed in an unhappy way that was more just air out her nose. Her real laugh was different. Where he'd be was the waiting room, she said. That he'd be thinking about her and feeling bad for her, she knew, but he couldn't be in there with her. This was so obviously true that he felt like a ninny that he'd kept on about it and now knew what she had thought every time he went and said it; it hadn't brought her comfort or eased the burden at all. The worse he felt, the stiller he sat. The whole thing felt balanced on a knife or wire; if he moved to put his arm up or touch her the whole thing could tip over. He hated himself for sitting so frozen. He could almost visualize himself tiptoeing through something explosive. A big stupid-looking tiptoe like in a cartoon. The whole last black week had been this way and it was wrong. He knew it was wrong, he knew something was required of him and knew it was not this terrible frozen care and caution, but he pretended to himself he did not know what it was that was required. He pretended it had no name. He pretended that not saying aloud what he knew to be right and true was for her sake, was for the sake of her needs and feelings. He also worked dock and routing at UPS, besides school, but traded to get the day off after they'd decided together. Two days before, he had awakened very early and tried to pray but could not. He was freezing more and more solid, he felt like, but he hadn't thought of his father or the blank frozenness of his father, even in church, that once had filled him with such pity. This was the truth. Lane Dean Jr. felt sun on one arm as he pictured in his mind an image of himself on a train, waving mechanically to something that got smaller and smaller as the train pulled away. His father and his mother's father had the same birthday, a Cancer. Sheri's hair was colored an almost corn blond, very clean, the skin through the central part pink in the light. They'd sat up here long enough that only their right side was shaded now. He could look at her head, but not at her. Different parts of him felt unconnected to each other. She was smarter than him and they both knew it. It wasn't just school — Lane Dean was in accounting and business and did all right, he was hanging in there. She was a year older, she was twenty, but it was also more — she had always seemed to Lane to be on good terms with her life in a way age could not account for. His mother had put it that she *knew what it was she wanted,* which was nursing and not an easy program at Peoria Junior College, and plus she worked hostessing at the Embers and had bought her own car. She was serious in a way Lane liked. She had a cousin that died when she was thirteen, fourteen, that she'd loved and been close with. She only talked about it that once. He liked her smell and the downy hair on her arms and the way she exclaimed when something made her laugh. He had liked just being with her and talking to her. She was serious in her faith and values in a way that Lane had liked and now, sitting here with her on the table, found himself afraid of. This was an awful thing. He was starting to believe he might not be serious in his faith. He might be somewhat of a hypocrite, like the Assyrians in Isaiah, which would be a far graver sin than the appointment—he had decided he believed this. He was desperate to be good people, to still be able to feel he was good. He rarely before had thought of damnation and hell, that part of it didn't speak to his spirit, and in worship services he more just tuned himself out and tolerated hell when it came up, the same way you tolerate the job you have got to have to save up for what it is you want. Her tennis shoes had little things and items doodled on them from sitting in her class lectures. She stayed looking down like that. Little notes or reading assignments in Bic in her neat round hand on the rubber elements around the sneaker's rim. Lane A. Dean looking at her inclined head's side's barrettes in the shape of blue ladybugs. The appointment was for afternoon, but when the doorbell rang so early and his mother'd called to him up the stairs, he had known, and a terrible kind of blankness had commenced falling through him.

He told her that he did not know what to do. That he knew if he was the salesman of it and forced it upon her that was awful and wrong. But he was trying to understand, they'd prayed on it and talked it through from every different angle. Lane said how sorry she knew he was, and that if he was wrong in believing they'd truly decided together when they decided to make the appointment she should please tell him, because he thought he knew how she must have felt as it got closer and closer and how she must be so scared, but that what he couldn't tell was if it was more than that. He was totally still except for moving his mouth, it felt like. She did not reply. That if they needed to pray on it more and talk it through, why then he was here, he was ready, he said. He said the appointment could get moved back; if she just said the word they could call and push it back to take more time to be sure in the decision. It was still so early in it, they both knew that, he said. This was true, he felt this way, and yet he also knew he was also trying to say things that would get her to open up and say enough back that he could see her and read her heart and know what to say to get her to go through with it. He knew this without admitting to himself that this is what he wanted, for it would make him a hypocrite and a liar. He knew, in some locked-up little part of him,

why it was that he'd gone to no one to open up
and seek their life counsel, not Pastor Steve or the
prayer partners at campus ministries, not his UPS
friends or the spiritual counseling available
through his parents' old church. But he did not
know why Sheri herself had not gone to Pastor
Steve—he could not read her heart. She was blank
and hidden. He so fervently wished it never happened. He felt like he knew now why it was a true
sin and not just a leftover rule from past society.
He felt like he had been brought low by it and
humbled and now did understand and believe that
the rules were there for a reason. That the rules
were concerned with him personally, as an individual. He'd promised God he had learned his lesson. But what if that, too, was a hollow promise,
from a hypocrite who repented only after, who
promised submission but really only wanted a
reprieve? He might not even know his own heart
or be able to read and know himself. He kept
thinking also of 1 Timothy 6 and the hypocrite
therein who *disputeth over words*. He felt a terrible
inner resistance but could not feel what it was it so
resisted. This was the truth. All the different
angles and ways they had come at the decision
together did not ever include it, the word—for
had he once said it, avowed that he did love her,

loved Sheri Fisher, then it would have all been transformed, it would be a different stance or angle but a difference in the very thing they were praying and deciding on together. Sometimes they had prayed together over the phone in a kind of half code in case anybody accidentally picked up another extension. She continued to sit as if thinking, in the pose of thinking like almost that one statue. They were on that one table. He was the one looking past her at the tree in the water. But he could not say he did, it was not true.

But nor did he ever open up and tell her straight out he did not love her. This may be his *lie by omission*. This may be the frozen resistance — were he to look straight at her and tell her he didn't, she would keep the appointment and go. He knew this. Something in him, though, some terrible weakness or lack of values, would not tell her. It felt like a muscle he just did not have. He didn't know why, he could not do it or even pray to do it. She believed he was good, serious in his values. Part of him seemed willing to more or less just about lie to someone with that kind of faith and trust and what did that make him? How could such a type of individual even pray? What it really felt like was a taste of the reality of what might be meant by hell. Lane Dean had never believed in hell as a lake of fire or a loving God consigning folks to a burning lake of fire—he knew in his heart this was not true. What he believed in was a living God of compassion and love and the possibility of a personal relationship with Jesus Christ through whom this love was enacted in human time. But sitting here beside this girl as unknown to him now as outer space, waiting for whatever she might say to unfreeze him, now he felt like he could see the edge or outline of what a real vision of hell might be. It was of two great and terrible armies within himself, opposed and facing each other, silent. There would be battle but no victor. Or never a battle—the armies would stay like that, motionless, looking across at each other and seeing therein something so different and alien from themselves that they could not understand, they could not hear each other's speech as even words or read anything from what their faces looked like, frozen like that, opposed and uncomprehending, for all human time. Two hearted, a hypocrite to yourself either way.

When he moved his head, the part of the lake farther out flashed with sun; the water up close wasn't black now and you could see into the shallows and see that all the water was moving but gently, this way and that, and in this same way he

besought to return to himself as Sheri moved her
leg and started to turn beside him. He could see
the man in the suit and gray hat standing motionless now at the lake's rim, holding something
under one arm and looking across at the opposite
side where little forms on camp chairs sat there in
a row in a way that meant they had lines in the
water for crappie, which mostly only your blacks
from the East Side ever did, and the little white
shape at the row's end a Styrofoam creel. In his
moment or time at the lake now just to come, Lane
Dean first felt he could take this all in whole;
everything seemed distinctly lit, for the circle of
the pin oak's shade had rotated off all the way and
they sat now in sun with their shadow a two-
headed thing in the grass to the left before them.
He was looking or gazing again at where the
downed tree's branches seemed to bend so sharply
just under the shallows' surface when he was given
then to know that through all this frozen silence
he'd despised he had, in truth, been praying all the
while, or some little part of his heart he could not
know or hear had, for he was answered now with a
type of vision, what he later would call within his
own mind a vision or *moment of grace*. He was not
a hypocrite, just broken and split off like all men.
Later on, he believed that what happened was he

had a moment of almost seeing them both as Jesus might see them — as blind but groping, wanting to please God despite their inborn fallen nature. For in that same given moment he saw, quick as light, into Sheri's heart, and was made therein to know what would occur here as she finished turning to him and the man in the hat watched the fishing and the downed elm shed cells in the water. This down-to-earth girl who smelled good and wanted to be a nurse would take and hold one of his hands in both of hers to unfreeze him and make him look at her, and she would say that she cannot do it. That she is sorry she did not know this sooner, she hadn't meant to lie, she'd agreed because she wanted to believe she could, but she cannot. That she will carry this and have it, she has to. With her gaze clear and steady. That all night last night she prayed and searched herself and decided this is what love commands of her. That Lane should please please sweetie let her finish. That listen — this is her own decision and obliges him to nothing. That she knows he does not love her, not that way, has known it all this time, and that it's all right. That it is as it is and it's all right. She will carry this, and have it, and love it and make no claim on Lane except his good wishes and respecting what she has to do. That she releases him, all claim, and hopes he finishes up PJC and does so good in his life and has all joy and good things. Her voice will be clear and steady, and she will be lying, for Lane has been given to read her heart. To see her. One of the opposite side's blacks raises his arm in what might be greeting, or waving off a bee. There is a mower cutting grass someplace off behind them. It will be a terrible, make-or-break gamble born out of the desperation in Sheri Fisher's soul, the knowledge that she can neither do this thing today nor carry a child alone and shame her family. Her values block the way either way, Lane can see, and she has no other options or choice, this lie is not a sin. Galatians 4:16, *Have I then become your enemy?* She is gambling that he is good. There on the table, neither frozen nor yet moving, Lane Dean Jr. sees all this, and is moved with pity and with also something more, something without any name he knows, that is given to him to feel in the form of a question that never once in all the long week's thinking and division had even so much as occurred — why is he so sure he doesn't love her? Why is one kind of love any different? What if he has no earthly idea what love is? What would even

Jesus do? For it was just now he felt her two small strong soft hands on his, to turn him. What if he is just afraid, if the truth is no more than this, and if what to pray for is not even love but simple courage, to meet both her eyes as she says it and trust his heart?

§7

'New?' There were agents on each side of him and Sylvanshine thought it a bit odd that it was the one with the pink little timorous face of a hamster who turned as if to address him but the one on the other side looking away who had said it. 'New?' They were four rows back from the driver, about whose posture in his seat there was something odd.

'As opposed to what?' Sylvanshine's neck down through his shoulder blade was on fire, and he could feel the start of a jumping muscle in one of his eyelids. Explain the tax treatment of somebody giving appreciated stock to a charity vs. that same person selling the stock and giving the proceeds to the charity. The sides of the rural road looked chewed. The light outside was the sort of light that makes you turn on your headlights but then keeps them from doing any good because technically it's still light out. It was unclear if this was a van or a max. capacity 24 bus. The one who'd asked had a sideburn and the invulnerable smile of someone who's had two airport cocktails and nothing but nuts. The driver of the last van, to which Sylvanshine as a GS-9 had been assigned, rode the wheel as if his shoulders were too heavy for his back. As if clinging to the wheel to support himself. What kind of driver wore a white paper cap? A strap was all that held the vertiginous pile of bags in place. 'I'm the Special Assistant to the new Human Resources Systems Deputy, whose name is Merrill Lehrl, who is coming soon.'

'New to the Post. Freshly assigned I meant.' The man's voice was clear even though he seemed to address the window, which was unclean. Sylvanshine felt hemmed in; the seats were more a cushioned bench and there were no armrests to provide even the illusion or impression of personal space. Plus the van swayed alarmingly on the road, which was either a road or a sort of rural highway, and you could hear the chassis's springs. The rodential man, whose aura was timid but kind, a sad kind man who lived in a cube of fear, had his hat in his lap. Capacity 24 and full. There was the yeasty smell of wet men. The energy level was low; they were all coming back from something that had consumed a lot of energy. Sylvanshine could almost literally see the small pink man drinking Pepto-Bismol straight out of the bottle and going home to a woman who treated him like an uninteresting stranger. The two men either worked together or knew each other very well; they were talking in tandem without even being quite aware of it. An alpha-beta tandem, which meant either Audit or CID. It occurred to Sylvanshine that the window held a faint oblique reflection of him and that the alpha of the two men was amusing himself slightly by addressing Sylvanshine's reflection as if it were him, while the hamster affected the facial expression of address but said nothing. Stock donations are disguised capital-gains treatments— there was also a sound, gassy and tinkly like half a bar of calliope, when the driver downshifted or the boxy van swayed hard on a reverse-S next to a billboard that read DOWNSIZE THIS and then a picture Sylvanshine didn't catch, and while the urbane man was offhandedly introducing them (Sylvanshine didn't catch the names, which he knew would cause trouble because it was insulting to have forgotten people's names, especially if you were attached to an alleged wunderkind in

Personnel and Personnel was your business, and he would have to go through all sorts of conversational gymnastics in the future to avoid using their names, and God help him if they were climbers and expected one day to come up and have him make introductions to Merrill, although if they were CID this would be less likely because Investigations and Fraud usually had their own infrastructure and office space, often in a separate building, at least in Rome and Philly, because forensic accountants like to think of themselves more as law enforcement than Service, and didn't as a rule much mix, and in fact the taller man, Bondurant, did identify both himself and Britton as CID GS-9s, which Sylvanshine was too occupied with mortification at missing their names to internalize until much later that evening, when he would recollect the substance of the conversation and experience a moment of relief). The timorous man rarely lied; the more urbane CID agent lied rather a lot, Sylvanshine could feel. The window clicked with a fine rain, the sort of rain that stabs you but doesn't get you wet. Little drops—tiny drops—peened on the glass, in which the less strictly dependable of the two cupped his chin and let out a sigh that was at least partly for effect. Somewhere behind was the sound of a handheld video game, and the small sounds of other agents watching the game's progress over the shoulder of the man who was playing the game, who was silent. The van or bus's wipers made a small shrieking sound on every second pass—it occurred to Sylvanshine that the driver looked as if he was almost resting his chin on top of the wheel because he was leaning way forward to try to get closer to the windshield the way anxious people or people with poor eyesight will do when they're having trouble seeing. The slicker of the two CIDs in the window had an almost kite-shaped face, both square and pointy at the cheekbones and chin; Bondurant could feel the sharp pressure of his chin in his palm and the way the edge of the window's casement dug in a straight line between the bones of his elbow. Everyone but Sylvanshine knew where they'd all been and what they'd been doing in Joliet, but none of them were thinking about it in any kind of informative way because that's not how people think about what they've just done. From outside the vehicle it was clear what it was—both the shape and the sway of it, as well as the fact that the top layer of tan paint had been shoddily applied and in places the headlights of the cars behind it picked up flashes of the bright colors beneath, the ballooned letters and icons on sticks at angles that suggested yumminess in some mysterious way only children get. Inside was the sound of the engine and the fluctuant murmur of small conversations melted by anticipation of the end of something—a conference or retreat, perhaps, or maybe an in-service training; Rome personnel had always been going to Buffalo or Manhattan for In-Service Trainings—and the handheld game, and a slight rustle or twitter in the breathing of the pale pink fellow, who Sylvanshine could feel was looking at the right side of his face, and the sound of Bondurant asking Sylvanshine about the Rome post's CID division, and from one spot ahead and one behind and to the right the tinny whisper of people listening to things on possible headphones—a sure sign of a younger agent, and it occurred to Sylvanshine that the last time he'd seen any sort of black or Latin person had been at the Chicago airport that wasn't O'Hare but he couldn't quite seem to lasso the name and felt odd getting his ticket receipt out of his case— while the smaller appeared to be watching him, waiting for him to do something that would betray some sort of inadequacy or deficit in retention. Describe the advantages of Octal Machine Language over Binary Machine Language in designing a Level-2 program for tracking regularities in the cash-flow sheets of related corporations, name two essential advantages for a franchise to filing Schedule 20-50 returns as a subsidiary of its parent company rather than filing as an autonomous corporate entity—and there it was again, the snatch of forced-air music that Sylvanshine couldn't place but made him want to leave his seat and go chase something on foot in the company of all the children in the neighborhood, all of whom come boiling out of their respective front doors and hotfooting it up the street holding currency aloft, and before he could think, Sylvanshine said, 'Bizarre as this sounds, can either of you every so often hear—?'

'Mister Squishee,' now said the agent to his right in a baritone that didn't go with his body at all. 'Fourteen Mister Squishee iterant-route frozen-confection S corp out of East Peoria trucks seized together with office facilities, receivables, and equity holdings of four out of the seven members of the family who owned what the Region's counsel convinced the Seventh Circuit was de facto a privately held S corp,' Bondurant said. 'Disgruntled employee, falsified depreciation schedules for everything from freezers to trucks like this here—'

'Jeopardy assessment,' Sylvanshine said, mostly to show he knew the lingo. The seat directly ahead of Sylvanshine was unoccupied, yielding a view of the crossed and meaty neck of whoever sat ahead of that, his head covered by a Busch hat pushed back to communicate relaxation and informality.

'This is an ice-cream truck?'

'Wonderful for morale, isn't it? Like the paint job fools anybody that you've got the Post's cream riding back in something that used to sell Nutty Buddies and was driven by a guy in a big lumpy white outfit and rubber face so he looked like a blancmange.'

'Driver used to drive this for Mister Squishee.'

'That's why we're going so slowly.'

'Limit's fifty-five; take a look at what-all's stacked up behind us flashing their brights if you want.'

The smaller, pinker man, Britton, had a round, downy face. He was in his thirties and it wasn't clear if he shaved. The odd thing was that Sylvanshine's neighborhood in King of Prussia had been a planned community, with speed bumps, whose neighborhood association had prohibited solicitation of any kind, especially with a calliope—Sylvanshine had never in his life chased an ice-cream truck.

'Driver still bonded—the seizure just went through last quarter, the DD decides that the margin on keeping the trucks and drivers in service through the length of the bond so outweighs what's realized auctioning them that everybody below G-11 now rides in Mister Squishee trucks,' Bondurant said. His hand moved with his chin when he spoke, which struck Sylvanshine as awkward-looking and false.

'Mrs. Short-Run Thinking.'

'Terrible for morale. Not to mention the PR debacle of kids and their parents seeing trucks they associate with innocence and delicious Caramel Crunch Pushups now seized and as it were shanghaied by the Service. Including surveillance.'

'We conduct surveillance in these trucks, if you can believe it.'

'They practically throw stones.'

'Mister Squishee.'

'Some of the music's worse; some of the trucks there's a snatch of it every time they shift.'

They passed another sign, this out the right side but Sylvanshine could see it: IT'S SPRING, THINK FARM SAFETY.

Bondurant, ass tired from two days in a folding chair, was looking without really looking at a twelve-acre expanse of cornfield—they plowed the cornstalks under just as they were harrowing the fields for seed in April instead of plowing them under in the fall so they'd have all winter to rot and fertilize the ground, which with organophosphate fertilizers and such Bondurant supposed it wasn't worth the two days in the fall to plow them under, plus for some reason Higgs's daddy had told him but he'd forgot they liked to have the ground all clodded up in the winter, it protected something about the ground—and without being aware of it found himself thinking about the nubbly field reminiscent of the armpit of a girl who didn't shave her armpits very often, and without being conscious of any of the connections between the field that now passed and was replaced in the window by a stand of wild oak and the armpit and the girl was thinking in a misdirected way of Cheryl Ann Higgs, now Cheryl Ann Standish and now a data-entry girl at American Twine and a divorced mother of two in a double-wide trailer her ex had apparently been arrested for trying to burn up shortly after Bondurant got GS-9'd over to CID, who'd been his date at Peoria Central Catholic prom in '71 when they'd both made Prom Court and Bondurant was second-runner-up to king and wore a powder-blue tux and rented shoes too skinny for his feet and she didn't fuck him that night even at post-Prom when all the other fellows took turns getting fucked by their dates in the black and gold Chrysler New Yorker they'd gone in and rented for the night from the shortstop's daddy at Hertz and got stains in so the shortstop had to spend the summer out at the airport at the Hertz desk working off the detailing of the New Yorker. Danny something, his daddy died not much later, but he couldn't play Legion ball that summer because of it and couldn't stay sharp and barely made the team in college ball at NIU and lost his scholarship and God knows what-all became of him but none of the stains were Bondurant and Cheryl Ann Higgs's despite all his entreaties. He hadn't used the bottle of schnapps because if he'd brought her home drunk her daddy'd have either killed him or grounded her. Bondurant's life's greatest moment so far was on 5-18-73 as a sophomore and the pinch-hit triple in the last home game at Bradley that drove in Oznowiez the future triple-A catcher to beat SIU-Edwardsville and get Bradley into the Missouri Valley playoffs, which they lost but still hardly a day at the desk with his feet up and clipboards stacked in his lap goes by that he doesn't see the balloon of the SIU slider hanging and feel the vibrationless thip of the meat of the bat connecting and hear the two-bell clatter of the aluminum bat fall as he sees the ball kind of pinball off the l.f. fence post by the foul line and twang off the other fence of the foul line and see and he could swear hear both fences jingle from the force of the ball, which he'd hit so hard he'll feel it forever but can't summon anywhere near that kind of recall of what Cheryl Ann Higgs felt like when he slipped inside her on a blanket by the pond out back past the stand past the edge of the pasture of the small dairy spread Mr. Higgs and one of his uncountable brothers operated, though he does well remember what each of them had been wearing and the smell of the pond's new algae near the runoff pipe whose gurgle was nearly brooklike, and the look on Cheryl Ann Higgs's face as her posture and supine position became acquiescent and Bondurant had known he was home free as they say but had avoided her eyes because the expression in Cheryl Ann's eyes, which without ever once again thinking about it Tom Bondurant has never forgotten, was one of blank terminal sadness, not so much that of a pheasant in a dog's jaws as of a person who's about to transfer something he knows in advance he can never get sufficient return on. The next year had seen them drop into the crazy-obsessive love spiral in which they'd break up and then not be able to stay away from each other, until one time she was able to stay away, and that was all she wrote.

The small light-pink CID agent Britton had, without any sort of throat-clearing or segue, asked Sylvanshine what he was thinking, which seemed to Sylvanshine grotesquely and almost obscenely inappropriate and invasive, rather like asking what your wife looked like naked or what your private restroom functions smelled like, but of course it would be impossible to say any of this aloud, particularly for someone whose job here involved cultivating good relations and uncluttered lines of communication for Merrill Lehrl to exploit when he arrived—to mediate for Merrill Lehrl and to at once gather information on as many aspects and issues involved in the examination of returns as possible, since there were some difficult, delicate decisions to make, decisions whose import extended far beyond this provincial post and any way it went it was going to be painful. Sylvanshine, turning slightly but not all the way (a flare of orange in his left shoulder blade) to meet at least Gary Britton's left eye, realized that he had very little emotional or ethical 'read' on Britton or anyone on the bus but Bondurant, who was having some kind of wistful memory and was cultivating the wistfulness, reclining a bit in it as one would in a warm bath. When something large and oncoming passed, the windshield's big rectangle was for a moment incandesced and opaque with water, which the wipers heaved mightily to displace. Britton's gaze—seemed to Sylvanshine more like looking *at* his right eye than *into* it. (At this time it moved through Thomas Bondurant's mind, which lended to be tornadic, as he looked out the window but more back and in at his own memory, that one could look out a window, look in a window as there was the gold ponytail and a flash of creamy shoulder *in* the window, through a window [close to 'out'], or even *at* a window, as in examining the pane's clarity and whether it was clean.) The gaze nevertheless seemed to be one of expectancy, and Sylvanshine felt again past the emptiness of his stomach and the pinched nerve in his clavicle how opaque the bus's overall mood was and different from the horror-fraught tension of the Philadelphia 0104's hundred and seventy agents or the manic torpor of tiny 408's dozen in Rome. His own mood, the complex hybrid of destination-fatigue and anticipatory fear one feels at the end not of a journey but a move, did not in any way complement the mood of the former Squishee truck nor of the urbane wistful older agent to his left nor of the human blank-spot who'd asked an invasive question whose honest answer would entail acknowledging the invasion, putting Sylvanshine in a personnel-relations bind before he'd even arrived at the Post, which seemed for a moment terribly unfair and flushed Sylvanshine with self-pity, a feeling not as dark as the wing of despair but tinged carmine with a resentment that was both better and worse than ordinary anger because it had no specific object. There seemed no one in particular to blame; something in Gary or Gerry Britton's aspect made it obvious that his question was some inevitable extension of his character and that he was no more to be blamed for it than an ant was to be blamed for crawling on your potato salad at a picnic — creatures just did what they did.

§8

Under the sign erected every May above the outer highway reading IT'S SPRING, THINK FARM SAFETY and through the north ingress with its own defaced name and signs addressed to soliciting and speed and universal glyph for children at play and down the blacktop's gauntlet of double-wide show-pieces past the rottweiler humping nothing in crazed spasms at chain's end and the sound of frying through the kitchenette window of the trailer at the hairpin right and then hard left along the length of a speed bump into the dense copse as yet uncleared for new single-wides and the sound of dry things snapping and stridulation of bugs in the duff of the copse and the two bottles and bright plastic packet impaled on the mulberry twig, seeing through shifting parallax of saplings' branches sections then of trailers along the north park's anfractuous roads and lanes skirting the corrugate trailer where it was said the man left his family and returned sometime later with a gun and killed them all as they watched *Dragnet* and the torn abandoned sixteen-wide half overgrown by the edge of the copse where boys and their girls made strange agnate forms on pallets and left bright torn packs until a mishap with a stove blew the gas lead and ruptured the trailer's south wall in a great labial tear that exposes the trailer's gutted insides to view from the edge of the copse and the plurality of eyes as the needles and stems of a long winter noisomely crunch beneath a plurality of shoes where the copse leaves off at a tangent past the end of the undeveloped cul-de-sac where they come now at dusk to watch the parked car heave on its springs. The windows steamed nearly opaque and so alive in the chassis that it seems to move without running, the boat-sized car, squeak of struts and absorbers and a jiggle just short of true rhythm. The birds at dusk and the smell of snapped pine and a younger one's cinnamon gum. The shimmying motions resemble those of a car traveling at high speeds along a bad road, making the Buick's static aspect dreamy and freighted with something like romance or death in the gaze of the girls who squat at the copse's risen edge, appearing dyadic and eyes half again as wide and solemn, watching for the sometime passage of a limb's pale shape past a window (once a bare foot flat against it and itself atremble), moving incrementally forward and down each night in the week before true spring, soundlessly daring one another to go get up close to the heaving car and see in, which the only one who finally does so then sees naught but her own wide eyes reflected as from inside the glass comes a cry she knows too well, which wakes her again each time across the trailer's cardboard wall.

There were fires in the gypsum hills to the north, the smoke of which hung and stank of salt; then the pewter earrings vanished without complaint or even mention. Then a whole night's absence, two. The child as mother to the woman. These were auguries and signs: Toni Ware and her mother abroad again in endless night. Routes on maps that yield no sensible shape or figure when traced.

At night from the trailer's park the hills possessed of a dirty orange glow and the sounds of living trees exploding in the fires' heat did carry, and the noise of planes plowing the undulant air above and dropping thick tongues of talc. Some nights it rained fine ash which upon contacting turned to soot and kept all souls indoors such that throughout the park every trailer's window possessed of the underwater glow of televisions and when many were identically tuned the sounds of the programs came clear to the girl through the ash as if their own television were still with them. It had vanished without comment prior to their last move. That last time's sign.

The park's boys wore wide rumpled hats and cravats of thong and some displayed turquoise about their person, and of these one helped her empty the trailer's sanitary tank and then pressed her to fellate him in recompense, whereupon she promised that anything emerging from his trousers would not return there. No boy near her size had successfully pressed her since Houston and the two who put something in her pop that made them turn sideways in the air and she could not then fight and lay watching the sky while they did their distant business.

At sunset then the north and west were the same color. On clear nights she could read by the night sky's emberlight seated on the plastic box that served as stoop. The screen door had no screen but was still a screen door, which fact she thought upon. She could fingerpaint in the soot on the kitchenette's rangetop. In incendiary orange to the deepening twilight in the smell of creosote burning in the sharp hills upwind.

Her inner life rich and multivalent. In fantasies of romance it was she who fought and overcame thereon to rescue some object or figure that never in the reverie resolved or took to itself any shape or name.

After Houston her favorite doll had been the mere head of a doll, its hair prolixly done and the head's hole threaded to meet a neck's own thread; she had been eight when the body was lost and it lay now forever supine and unknowing in weeds while its head lived on.

The mother's relational skills were indifferent and did not include truthful or consistent speech. The daughter had learned to trust actions and to read sign in details of which the run of children are innocent. The battered road atlas had then appeared and lay athwart the counter's medial crack opened to the mother's home state over whose representation of her place of origin lay a spore of dried mucus spindled through with a red thread of blood. The atlas stayed open that way nigh on one week unreferred to; they ate around it. It gathered wind-drift ash through the torn screen. Ants vexed all the park's trailers, there being something in the fire's ash they craved. Their point of formication the high place where the kitchenette's woodgrain paneling had detached in prior heat and bowed outward and from which two vascular parallel columns of black ants descended. Standing eating out of cans at the anodized sink. Two flashlights and a drawer with different bits of candles which the mother eschewed for her cigarettes were her light unto the world. A little box of borax in each of the kitchenette's corners. The water in buckets from the coinwash tap, the trailer a standalone with sides' wires hanging and its owner's whereabouts unreckoned by the park's elders, whose lawn chairs sat unmolested by ash in the smoke tree's central shade. One of these, Mother Tia, told fortunes, leathery and tremorous and her face like a shucked pecan fully cowled in black and two isolate teeth like a spare at the Show Me Lanes, and owned her own cards and tray on which what ash collected showed white, calling her *chulla* and charging her no tariff on terms of the Evil Eye she claimed to fear when the girl looked at her through the screen's hole with the telescope of a rolled magazine. Two ribby and yelloweyed dogs lay throbbing in the smoke tree's shade and rose only sometimes to bay at the planes as they harried the fires.

The sun overhead like a peephole into hell's own self-consuming heart.

Yet one more sign being when Mother Tia refused then to augur and doing so in terms of pleading for clemency instead of bare refusal to the reedy laughter of the shade's other elders and widows; no one understood why she feared the girl and she would not say, lower lip caught behind one tooth as she traced the special letter over and over on nothing in the air before her. Whom she would miss, and whose memory in trust therefore the doll's head also would carry.

The mother's relational skills being indifferent to this degree since the period of clinical confinement in University City MO wherein the mother had been denied visits for eighteen business days and the girl had evaded Family Services during this period and slept in an abandoned Dodge vehicle whose doors could be secured with coat hangers twisted just so.

The girl looked often at the open atlas and the city thereon marked with a sneeze. She had herself been born there, just outside, in the town that bore her own name. Her second experience of the kind her books made seem sweet through indifferent speech had occurred in the abandoned car in University City MO at the hands of a man who knew how to dislodge one coat hanger with the straightened hook of another and told her face beneath his fingerless mitten there were two different ways this right here could go.

The longest time she had ever subsisted wholly on shoplifted food was eight days. Not more than a competent shoplifter. Their time at Moab UT an associate once said that her pockets had no imagination and was soon thereafter pinched and made to spear litter by the highway as she and the mother had passed in the converted camper driven by 'Kick,' the seller of pyrite and self-made arrowheads around whom the mother said not ever one word but sat before the radio painting each nail a different color and who had once punched her stomach so hard she saw colors and smelled up close the carpet's grit base and could hear what her mother then did to distract 'Kick' from further attentions to this girl with the mouth on her. This being also how she learned to cut a brake line so the failure would be delayed until such time as the depth of the cut determined.

At night on the pallet in the ruddled glow she dreamt also of a bench by a pond and the somnolent mutter of ducks while the girl held the string of something that floated above with a painted face, a kite or balloon. Of another girl she would never see or know of.

Once on the nation's interstate highway system the mother had spoken of a headless doll she herself had kept and clung to through the hell on earth years of her Peoria girlhood and her own mother's *nervous illness* (her profile bunched up as she pronounced it) during which the mother's mother had refused to let her outside the house over which she had engaged itinerant men to nail found and abandoned hubcaps to every inch of the exterior in order to deflect the transmissions of one Jack Benny, a rich man whom the grandmother had come to believe was insane and sought *global thought control* by radio wave of a special pitch and hue. (' "Nobody that mean's going to let the world go" ' was an indirect quotation or hearsay when driving, which the mother could do while simultaneously smoking and using an emery board.) The girl made it her business to read signs and know the facts of her own history past and present. To beat broken glass into powder requires an hour with a portion of brick on a durable surface. She had shoplifted ground chuck and buns and kneaded powdered glass into the meat and cooked it on a windowscreen brazier at the rear of the abandoned Dodge and had left such painstaking meals of sandwich on the front seat for days running before the man who had pressed her used his coat hanger tool to jimmy the vehicle and steal them whereupon he returned no more; the mother then released into the girl's care soon. Imbrication by disk is impossible, but the grandmother's specifications were that each hubcap touch those on every possible side. Thus the electrification of one became the charge of all, to counter the waves' bombardment. The creation of a lethal field which jammed radios all down the block. Twice cited for diverting the home's amperage, the old woman had found a generator someplace that would run if noisily on kerosene and bounced and shook beside the bomb-shaped propane tank outside the kitchen. The young mother was sometimes permitted outside to bury the sparrows that alit on the home and sent up their souls in a single flash and bird-shaped ball of smoke.

The girl read stories about horses, bios, science, psychiatry, and *Popular Mechanics* when obtainable. She read history in a determined way. She read *My Struggle* and could not understand all the fuss. She read Wells, Steinbeck, Keene, Laura Wilder (twice), and Lovecraft. She read halves of many torn and castoff things. She read a coverless *Red Badge* and knew by sheer feel that its author had never seen war nor knew that past some extremity one floated just above the fear and could blinklessly watch it while doing what had to be done or allowed to stay alive.

The trailer park's boy who had pressed her there in the hanging smell of their own sewage now assembled his friends outside the trailer at night there to lurk and make inhuman sounds in the ashfall as the daughter's daughter drew circles within circles about her own given name on the map and the arteries leading thereto. The gypsum fires and the park's lit sign were the poles of the desert night. The boys burped and howled at the moon and the howls were nothing like the real thing and their laughter was strained and words indifferent to the love they said swelled them and would visit upon her past counting.

In these the mother's absences with men the girl sent for catalogues and Free Offers which daily did arrive by mail with samples of products that people with homes would buy to enjoy at their leisure like the girl, who considered herself home tutored and did not ride the bus with the park's children. These all possessed the stunned smeared look of those who are poor in one place; the trailers, sign, and passing trucks were the furniture of their world, which orbited but did not turn. The girl often imagined them in a rearview, receding, both arms raised in farewell.

Asbestos cloth cut carefully into strips one of which placed in the pay dryer when the mother of the would-be assailant had deposited her load and returned to the Circle K for more beer caused neither the boy nor mother to be seen anymore outside their double-wide, which rested on blocks. The boys' serenades ceased as well.

A soup can of sewage or roadkill carcass when placed beneath the blocks or plasticized lattice of a store-bought porch attachment would fill and afflict that trailer with a plague's worth of soft-bodied flies. A shade tree could be killed by driving a short length of copper tubing into its base a handsbreadth from ground; the leaves would commence to embrown straightaway. The trick with a brake or fuel line was to use strippers to whet it to almost nothing instead of cutting it clean through. It took a certain feel. Half an ounce of packets' aggregate sugar in the gas tank disabled all vehicles but required no art. Likewise a penny in the fuse box or red dye in a trailer's water tank accessible through the sanitation panel on all but late-year models of which the Vista Verde park had none.

Begat in one car and born in another. Creeping up in dreams to see her own conceiving.

The desert possessed of no echo and in this was like the sea from which it came. Sometimes at night the sounds of the fire carried, or the circling planes, or those of long-haul trucks on 54 for Santa Fe whose tires' plaint had the quality of distant surf's lalation; she lay listening on the pallet and imagined not the sea or the moving trucks themselves but whatever she right then chose. Unlike the mother or bodiless doll, she was free inside her head. An unbound genius, larger than any sun.

The girl read a biography of Hetty Green, the matricide and accused forger who had dominated the Stock Market while saving scraps of soap in a dented tin box she carried on her person, and who feared no living soul. She read *Macbeth* as a color comic with dialogue in boxes.

The performer Jack Benny had cupped his own face with a hand in a manner the mother, when lucid, had told her she'd seen as tender and pined for, dreamt of, inside the home and its carapace of electric shields while her own mother wrote letters to the FBI in code.

Near sunrise the red plains to the east undimmed and the terrible imperious heat of the day bestirred in its underground den; the girl placed the doll's head on the sill to watch the red eye open and small rocks and bits of litter cast shadows as long as a man.

Never once in five states worn a dress or leather shoes.

At dawn of the fires' eighth day her mother appeared in a vehicle made large by its corrugated shell behind whose wheel sat an unknown male. The side of the shell said LEER.

Thought blocking, overinclusion. Vagueness, overspeculation, woolly thinking, confabulation, word salad, stonewalling, aphasia. Delusions of persecution. Catatonic immobility, automatic obedience, affective flattening, dilute I/Thou, disordered cognition, loosened or obscure associations. Depersonalization. Delusions of centrality or grandeur. Compulsivity, ritualism. Hysterical blindness. Promiscuity. Solipsismus or ecstatic states (rare).

This Girl's D./P.O.B.: 11-4-60, Anthony IL.
Girl's Mother's D./P.O.B.: 4-8-43, Peoria IL.
Most Recent Address: 17 Dosewallips Unit E, Vista Verde Estates Mobile Home Park, Organ NM 88052.
Girl's H.W.E./H.: 5' 3", 95 lbs., Brown/Brown.
Mother's Stated Occupations, 1966–1972 (from IRS Form 669-D [Certificate of Subordination of Federal Tax Lien, District

063(a)], 1972): Cafeteria Dish and Food Area Cleaning Assistant, Rayburn-Thrapp Agronomics, Anthony IL; Skilled Operator of Silkscreen Press Until Injury to Wrist, All City Uniform Company, Alton IL; Cashier, Convenient Food Mart Corporation, Norman OK and Jacinto City TX; Server, Stuckey's Restaurants Corp., Limon CO; Assistant Adhesive Product Mixing Scheduling Clerk, National Starch and Chemical Company, University City MO; Hostess and Beverage Server, Double Deuce Live Stage Night Club, Lordsburg NM; Contract Vendor, Cavalry Temporary Services, Moab UT; Canine Confinement Area Organization and Cleaning, Best Friends Kennel and Groom, Green Valley AZ; Ticket Agent and Substitute Night Manager, Riské's Live XX Adult Entertainment, Las Cruces NM.

They drove then once more at night. Below a moon that rose round before them. What was termed the truck's backseat was a narrow shelf on which the girl could sleep if she arranged her legs in the gap behind the real seats whose headrests possessed the dull shine of unwashed hair. The clutter and yeast smell bespoke a truck that was or had been lived in; the truck and its man smelled the same. The girl in cotton bodice and her jeans gone fugitive at the knees. The mother's conception of men was that she used them as a sorceress will dumb animals, as sign and object of her unnatural powers. Her spoken word aloud for these at which the girl gave no reproof, *familiar*. Swart and sideburned men who sucked wooden matches and crushed cans with their hands. Whose hats' brims had sweatlines like the rings of trees. Whose eyes crawled over you in the rearview. Men inconceivable as ever themselves being children or looking up naked at someone they trust, with a toy. To whom the mother talked like babies and let them treat her like a headless doll, *manhandle*.

At an Amarillo motel the girl had her own locked room out of earshot. The hangers were affixed to the closet's rod. The doll's head wore lipstick of pink crayon and looked at TV. The girl often wished she had a cat or some small pet to feed and reassure as she stroked its head. The mother feared winged insects and carried cans of spray. Mace on a chain and melted cosmetics and her faux-leather snap case for cigarettes and lighter at once in a handbag of imbricate red sequins the girl had produced for Christmas in Green Valley with only a very small tear near the base where the electronic tag had been forced with a file and then used to carry out the same bodice the girl now wore, on which stitched pink hearts formed a fenceline at breast level.

The truck smelled also of spoilt provision and had a window with vanished crank he rolled up and down with pliers. A card taped to one visor proclaimed that hairdressers teased it till it did stand up. His teeth were missing at one side; the glovebox was locked. The mother at thirty with face commencing to display the faint seams of the plan for the second face life had in store for her and which she feared would be her own mother's and in University City's confined time sat with knees bunched up rocking and scratched at herself essaying to ruin the face's plan. The sepia photo of the mother's mother at the girl's own age in a pinafore on horsehair seat rolled into the doll's head and carried with soapscraps and three library cards in her given name. Her diary in the round case's second lining. And the lone photo of her mother as a child outdoors in winter dazzle in so many coats and hats that she and the propane tank might be kin. The electrified house out of view and the circle of snowmelt around its base and the mother behind the little mother holding her upright; the child had had croup and such a fever she was feared not to live and her mother had realized she had no pictures of her baby to keep if she died and had bundled her up and sent her out into the snow to wait while she begged a snapshot with a neighbor's Land Camera so her baby might not be forgotten when she died. The photo distorted from long folding and no footprints in view anywhere in the picture's snow that the girl could see, the child's mouth wide open and eyes looking up at the man with the camera in trust that this made sense, this was how right life occurred. The girl's plans for the grandmother, much refined with age and accrued art, occupied much of the latest diary's first third.

Her mother and not the male was at the wheel when she woke to the clatter of gravel in Kansas. A truck stop receded as something upright ran in the road behind them and waved its hat. She asked where they were but did not ask after the man who through three states had driven with the same offending hand on the mother's thigh that had touched her, a hand studied through the seats' gap by the doll's head held just so and its detachment and airborne flight seen in the same dream the lurch and sounds first seemed part of. The daughter thirteen now and starting to look it. Her mother's eyes were distant and low-lidded in the company of men; now in Kansas she made faces at the rearview and chewed gum. 'Ride up front up out of there up here why don't you.' The gum smelt cinnamon and its folded foil could make a glovebox pick by wrapping round to smooth a file's emery at the point.

Outside a Portales rest stop, under a sun of beaten gold, the girl supine and half asleep in a porous nap on the little back shelf had suffered the man to hoist himself about behind the truck's wheel and form his hand into an unsensual claw and send it out over the seatback to squeeze her personal titty, to throttle the titty, eyes pale and unprurient, she playing dead and staring unblinking past him, the man's breathing audible and khaki cap pungent, manhandling the titty with what seemed an absent dispassion, leaving off only at the high heels' sound in the lot outside. Still a stark advance over the previous year's Cesar, who worked at painting highway signs and had green grains forever in the pores of his face and hands and required both mother and girl to keep the washroom door open no matter what their business inside, himself then in turn improved over Houston's district of warehouses and gutted lofts whereat had fallen in with them for two months 'Murray Blade,' the semiprofessional welder whose knife in its forearm's spring clip covered a tattoo of just that knife between two ownerless blue breasts the squeeze of a fist made swell at the sides which amused him. Men with leather vests and tempers who were tender when drunk in ways that made your back's skin pebble up.

The 54 highway east was not federal and the winds of oncoming rigs struck the truck and its shell and caused yaw the mother steered against. All windows down against the man's stored smell. An unmentionable thing in the glovebox the mother said to shut she couldn't look. The card with its entendre made French curls in their backwash and disappeared against the past road's shimmer.

West of Pratt KS they purchased and ate Convenient Mart burritos heated in the device provided for that purpose. A great huge unfinishable Slushee.

Behind her carapace of disks and foil the mother's mother held when madman Jack Benny or his spiral-eyed slaves came for them the best defense at hand was to play dead, to lie with blank eyes open and not blink or breathe while the men holstered their ray guns and walked about the house and looked at them, shrugging and telling one another they were too late because look here the woman and her nubile daughter were already deceased and best left be. Forced to practice together in the twin beds with open bottles of pills on the table betwixt and hands composed on their chests and eyes wide and breathing in such a slight way that the chest never rose. The older woman could hold her open eyes unblinking a very long time; the mother as child could not and they soon enough closed of their own, for a living child is no doll and does need to blink and breathe. The older woman said one could self-lubricate at will with the proper application of discipline and time. She said her decade on a carnival necklace and had a small nickel lock on the mailbox. Windows covered with foil in the crescents between the caps' black circles. The mother carried drops and always claimed her eyes were dry.

Riding up front was good. She did not ask about the truck's man. It was his truck they were in but he was not in the truck; it was hard to locate something to complain about in this. The mother's relatings were least indifferent when the two faced the same; she made small jokes and sang and sent small looks the daughter's way. All the world beyond the reach of the headlamps' beams was much obscured. Hers was her grandmother's maiden name, Ware. She could put her soles against the truck's black dash and look out between her knees, the whole of the headlights' tongue of road between them. The broken centerline shot Morse at them and the bone-white moon was round and clouds moved across it and took shape as they did so. First fingers then whole hands and trees of lightning fluttered on the west horizon; nothing came behind them. She kept looking for following lights or signs. The mother's lipstick was too bright for the shape of her mouth. The girl did not ask. The odds were high. The man was either the species of man who would file a report or else would essay to follow like a second 'Kick' and find them for leaving him waving his hat in the road. If she asked, the mother's face would go saggy as she thought of what to say when the truth was she hadn't thought at all. The girl's blessing and lot to know their two minds both as one, to hold the wheel as Murine was again applied.

They had a sit-down breakfast in Plepler MO in a rain that foamed the gutters and beat against the café's glass. The waitress in nurse-white had a

craggy face and called them both honey and wore
a button which said I have got but one nerve left
and you are upon that nerve and flirted with the
workingmen whose names she knew while steam
came out of the kitchen over the counter above
which she clipped sheets from her pad, and the girl
used their toothbrush in a restroom whose lock
had no hasp. The front door's hung bell sounded
on use to signal custom. The mother wanted bis-
cuits and hashbrowns and mush with syrup and
they ordered and the mother sought a dry match
and soon the girl heard her laughing at something
the men at the counter said. Rain rolled through
the street and cars passed slowly and their truck
with its shell faced the table and still had its parking lights on, which she saw, and saw also within
her mind the truck's legal owner still there in the
road outside Kismet holding his hands extended
into claws at the space where the truck had receded
from view while the mother beat the wheel and
blew hair from her eyes. The girl dragged toast
through her yolk. Of the two men who entered
and filled the next booth one had similar whiskers
and eyes beneath a red cap gone black with rain.
The waitress with her little stub pencil and pad
said unto these:

'What are you settin' in a dirty booth for?'
'So as I can be closer to you, darling.'
'Why you could have set over right there and been closer yet.'
'Shoot.'

§9

AUTHOR'S FOREWORD

Author here. Meaning the real author, the living human holding the pencil, not some abstract narrative persona. Granted, there sometimes is such a persona in *The Pale King,* but that's mainly a pro forma statutory construct, an entity that exists just for legal and commercial purposes, rather like a corporation; it has no direct, provable connection to me as a person. But this right here is me as a real person, David Wallace, age forty, SS no. 975-04-2012,[1] addressing you from

---

1 Little-known fact: The only US citizens anywhere whose Social Security numbers start with the numeral 9 are those who are, or at some time were, contract employees of the Internal Revenue Service. Through its special relationship with the Social Security Administration, the IRS issues you a new

my Form 8829–deductible home office at 725 Indian Hill Blvd., Claremont 91711 CA, on this fifth day of spring, 2005, to inform you of the following:

All of this is true. This book is really true.

I obviously need to explain. First, please flip back and look at the book's legal disclaimer, which is on the copyright page, verso side, four leaves in from the rather unfortunate and misleading front cover. The disclaimer is the unindented chunk that starts: 'The characters and events in this book are fictitious.' I'm aware that ordinary citizens almost never read disclaimers like this, the same way we don't bother to look at copyright claims or Library of Congress specs or any of the dull pro forma boilerplate on sales contracts and ads that everyone knows is there just for legal reasons. But now I need you to read it, the

---

SS number on the day your contract starts. It's like you're born again, ID-wise, when you enter the Service. Very few ordinary citizens know about this. There's no reason they should. But consider your own Social Security number, or those of the people close enough to you that you're entrusted with their SS. There's only one digit that these SS numbers never start with. That number is 9. 9's reserved for the Service. And if you're issued one, it stays with you for the rest of your life, even if you happen to have left the IRS long ago. It sort of marks you, numerically. Every April — and quarterly, of course, for those who are self-employed and pay quarterly ESTs — those tax returns and ESTs whose filers' SS numbers start with 9 are automatically pulled and routed through a special processing and exam program in the Martinsburg Computer Center. Your status in the system is forever altered. The Service knows its own, always.

disclaimer, and to understand that its initial 'The characters and events in this book…' includes this very Author's Foreword. In other words, this Foreword is defined by the disclaimer as itself fictional, meaning that it lies within the area of special legal protection established by that disclaimer. I need this legal protection in order to inform you that what follows[2] is, in reality, not fiction at all, but substantially true and accurate. That *The Pale King* is, in point of fact, more like a memoir than any kind of made-up story.

This might appear to set up an irksome paradox. The book's legal disclaimer defines everything that follows it as fiction, including this Foreword, but now here in this Foreword I'm saying that the whole thing is really nonfiction; so if you believe one you can't believe the other, & c., & c. Please know that I find these sorts of cute, self-referential paradoxes irksome, too—at least now that I'm over thirty I do—and that the very last thing this book is is some kind of clever metafictional titty-pincher. That's why I'm making it a point to violate protocol and address you here directly, as my real self; that's why all the specific

---

2 This is a term of art; what I really mean is that everything that surrounds this Foreword is essentially true. The Foreword's having now been moved 130 pages into the text is due to yet another spasm of last-minute caution on the part of the publisher, re which please see just below.

identifying data about me as a real person got laid out at the start of this Foreword. So that I could inform you of the truth: The only bona fide 'fiction' here is the copyright page's disclaimer—which, again, is a legal device: The disclaimer's whole and only purpose is to protect me, the book's publisher, and the publisher's assigned distributors from legal liability. The reason why such protections are especially required here—why, in fact, the publisher[3] has

---

3 At the advice of its corporate counsel, the publishing company has declined to be identified by name in this Author's Foreword, despite the fact that anyone who looks at the book's spine or title page will know immediately who the company is. Meaning it's an irrational constraint; but so be it. As my own counsel has observed, corporate attorneys are not paid to be totally rational, but they are paid to be totally cautious. And it is not hard to see why a registered US corporation like this book's publisher is going to be cautious about even the possibility of appearing to thumb its nose at the Internal Revenue Service or (this from some of the corporate counsel's hysterical early memos) to be 'abetting' an author's violation of the Nondisclosure Covenant that all Treasury employees are required to sign. Nevertheless—as my lawyer and I had to point out to them about 105 times before the company's counsel seemed to get it—the version of the Nondisclosure Covenant that's binding on *all* Treasury employees, not just on agents of the Bureau of Alcohol, Tobacco and Firearms and of the Secret Service, as formerly, was instituted in 1987, which happens to be the year that computers and a high-powered statistical formula known as the ANADA (for 'Audit–No Audit Discriminant Algorithm') were first used in the examination of nearly all individual US tax returns. I know that's a pretty involved and confusing data-dump to inflict on you in a mere Foreword, but the crux here is that it is the ANADA,[a] and the constituents of its formula for determining which tax returns are most apt to yield additional revenue under audit, that the Service is concerned to protect, and that that was why the Nondisclosure

insisted upon them as a precondition for acceptance of the manuscript and payment of the advance—is

---

Covenant was suddenly extended to IRS employees in 1987. But I had already left the Service in 1987. The worst of a certain personal unpleasantness had blown over, and I'd been accepted for transfer at another college, and by autumn of 1986 I was back on the East Coast and again up and running in the private sector, albeit of course still with my new SS number. My entire IRS career lasted from May 1985 through June 1986. Hence my exemption from the Covenant. Not to mention that I was hardly in a position to know anything compromising or specific about the ANADA. My Service post was totally low-level and regional. For the bulk of my time, I was a rote examiner, a.k.a. a 'wiggler' in the Service nomenclature. My contracted civil service rank was a GS-9, which at that time was the lowest full-time grade; there were secretaries and custodians who outranked me. And I was posted to Peoria IL, which is about as far from Triple-Six and the Martinsburg Center as anyone could imagine. Admittedly, at the same time—and this is what especially concerned the publishing company's counsel—Peoria was a REC, one of seven hubs of the IRS's Examination Division, which was precisely the division that got eliminated or, more accurately (though this is arguable), transferred from the Compliance Branch to the newly expanded Technical Branch, by the advent of the ANADA and a digital Fornix network. This is

> (a) By the way, no kidding about the formula's name. Were the Technical Branch statisticians aware that they were giving the algorithm such a heavy, almost thanatoid-sounding acronym? It's actually doubtful. As all too many Americans now know, computerized programs are totally, maddeningly literal and nonconnotative; and so were the people in Technical Branch.

rather more esoteric, contextless Service information than I'd anticipated having to ask you to swallow right at the beginning, and I can assure you that all this gets explained and/or unfolded in much more graceful, dramatically apposite terms in the memoir itself, once it gets under way. For now, just so you're not totally flummoxed and bored, suffice it to say that Examinations is the IRS division tasked with combing and culling various kinds of tax returns and classifying some as '20s,' which is Service shorthand for tax returns that the same reason the disclaimer is, when you come right down to it, a lie.[4]

---

are to be forwarded to the relevant District office for audit. Audits themselves are conducted by revenue agents, who are usually GS-9s or -11s, and employed by the Audit Division. It's hard to put all this very smoothly or gracefully—and please know that none of this abstract information is all that vital to the mission of this Foreword. So feel free to skip or skim the following if you wish. And don't think the whole book will be like this, because it won't be. If you're burningly interested, though, each tax return pulled, for whatever reason(s) (some of which were smart and discerning and others, frankly, wacko and occult, depending on the wiggler), by a line examiner and forwarded for audit is supposed to be accompanied by an IRS Series 20 Internal Memo, which is where the term '20' comes from. Like most insular and (let's be frank) despised government agencies, the Service is rife with special jargon and code that seems overwhelming at first but then gets internalized so quickly and used so often that it becomes almost habitual. I still, sometimes, dream in Servicespeak. To return to the point, though, Examinations and Audits were two of the main divisions of the IRS's Compliance Branch, and the publishing company's house counsel's concern was that the IRS's own counsel could, if they were sufficiently aggrieved and wanted to make trouble over the Nondisclosure Covenant thing, argue that I and several of the Post 047 REC coworkers and administrators who feature in this story should be grandfathered in under the constraints of the Nondisclosure Covenant, because we were not only employed by the Compliance Branch but posted at the REC that ended up figuring so prominently in the run-up to what came to be known variously as 'the New IRS,' 'the Spackman Initiative,' or just 'the Initiative,' which was ostensibly created by the Tax Reform Act of 1986 but was actually the result of a long, very complicated bureaucratic catfight between the Compliance Branch and the Technical Branch over Examinations and the Exam function in IRS operations. End of data-dump. If you're still reading, I hope enough of all that made sense for you to at least understand why the issue of whether or not I explicitly say the name of the publishing company was not one that I chose to spend a lot of time and editorial goodwill arguing about. You sort of have to pick your battles, as far as nonfiction goes.
4 (excepting the 'All rights reserved' part, of course)

Here is the real truth: What follows is substantially true and accurate. At least, it's a mainly true and accurate partial record of what I saw and heard and did, of whom I knew and worked alongside and under, and of what-all eventuated at IRS Post 047, the Midwest Regional Examination Center, Peoria IL, in 1985–86. Much of the book is actually based on several different notebooks and journals I kept during my thirteen months as a rote examiner at the Midwest REC. ('Based' means more or less lifted right out of, for reasons that will doubtless become clear.) *The Pale King* is, in other words, a kind of vocational memoir. It is also supposed to function as a portrait of a bureaucracy—arguably the most important federal bureaucracy in American life—at a time of enormous internal struggle and soul-searching, the birth pains of what's come to be known among tax professionals as the New IRS.

In the interests of full disclosure, though, I should be explicit and say that the modifier in 'substantially true and accurate' refers not just to the inevitable subjectivity and bias of any memoir. The truth is that there are, in this nonfiction account, some slight changes and strategic rearrangements, most of these evolving through successive drafts in response to feedback from the book's editor, who was sometimes put in a very delicate position with respect to balancing literary and journalistic priorities, on the one hand, against legal and corporate concerns on the other. That's probably all I should say on that score. There is, of course, a whole tortuous backstory here involving the legal vetting of the manuscript's final three drafts. But you will be spared having to hear much about all this, if for no other reason than that relating that inside story would defeat the very purpose of the repetitive, microscopically cautious vetting process and of all the myriad little changes and rearrangements to accommodate those changes that became necessary when, e.g., certain people declined to sign legal releases, or when one mid-sized company threatened legal action if its real name or identifying details of its actual past tax situation were used, disclaimer or no.[5]

---

5 This latter is a good example of the sort of thing that threw the publisher's legal people into a swivet of anality and caution. People often don't understand how seriously large US corporations take even a threat of litigation. As I eventually realized, it's not even so much a question of whether or not the publisher would lose a lawsuit; what really concerns them is the cost of defending against it, and the effect of those costs on the company's liability insurance premiums, which are already a major operating expense. Legal trouble is, in other words, a bottom-line issue; and the editor or in-house counsel who exposes a publishing company to possible legal liability had better be able to demonstrate to his CFO that every last reasonable bit of caution and due diligence was exercised on the manuscript, lest he wear what we in Exams

In the final analysis, though, there are a lot fewer of these small, identity-obscuring changes and temporal rearrangements than one might have expected. For there are advantages to limiting a memoir's range to one single interval (plus relevant backstories) in what seems to us all now like the distant past. People don't much care anymore, for one thing. By which I mean people in this book. The publishing company's paralegals had far less trouble getting signed legal releases than counsel had predicted. The reasons for this are varied but (as my own lawyer and I had argued ahead of time) obvious. Of the persons named, described, and even sometimes projected into the consciousness of as so-called 'characters' in *The Pale King*, a majority have now left the Service. Of those remaining,

---

used to call 'the brown helmet.' At the same time, it isn't fair to attribute every last tactical change and deviation here to the publisher. I (meaning, again, the actual human David Wallace) also fear litigation. Like many Americans, I've been sued—twice, in fact, though both suits were meritless, and one was dismissed as frivolous before I was even deposed—and I know what so many of us know: Litigation is no fun, and it's worth one's time and trouble to try to head it off in advance whenever possible. Plus, of course, looming over the whole vetting-and-due-diligence process on *The Pale King* was the shadow of the Service, which no one in his right mind would ever even dream of wanting to piss off unnecessarily, or actually even to come to the full institutional attention of, since the Service, like civil litigation, can make your life miserable without ever getting one extra dime from you.

several have reached levels of GS rank where they are more or less invulnerable.[6] Also, because of the time of year when drafts of the book were presented for their perusal, I am confident that certain other Service personnel were so busy and distracted that they did not really even read the manuscript and, after waiting a decent interval to give the impression of close study and deliberation, signed the legal release so that they could feel they had one less thing they were supposed to do. A few also seemed flattered at the prospect of someone's having paid them enough notice to be able, years later, to remember their contributions. A handful signed because they have remained, through the years, my personal friends; one of these is probably the most valuable, profound friend I've ever made. Some are dead. Two turned out to be incarcerated, of which one of these was someone you never would have thought or suspected.

Not everyone signed legal releases; I don't mean to suggest that. Only that most did. Several also consented to be interviewed on-record. Where appropriate, parts of their tape-recorded responses have been transcribed directly into the text. Others

6 E.g., one is now an Assistant Regional Commissioner for Taxpayer Assistance in the Western Regional Commissioner's Office at Oxnard CA.

have graciously signed additional releases authorizing the use of certain audio-visual recordings of them that were made in 1984 as part of an abortive IRS Personnel Division motivational and recruitment effort.[7] As an aggregate, they have provided reminiscences and concrete details that, when combined with the techniques of reconstructive journalism,[8] have yielded scenes of immense authority and realism, regardless of whether this author was actually corporeally right there on the scene at the time or not.

The point I'm trying to drive home here is that it's still all substantially true—i.e., the book this Foreword is part of—regardless of the various ways some of the forthcoming §s have had to be distorted,

---

7 A signed, notarized 2002 FOIA request for copies of these videotapes is on file at the Internal Revenue Service's Office of Public Information, 666 Independence Avenue, Washington DC.... And yes: The Service's national HQ's street number really is '666.' So far as I know, it's nothing more than an unfortunate accident in the Treasury Department's assignment of office space after the Sixteenth Amendment was ratified in 1913. On the Regional levels, Service personnel tend to refer to the national office as 'Triple-Six'—the meaning of the term is obvious, though no one I was able to talk to seemed to know just when it came into use.

8 This loose term is meant to connote the dramatized reconstruction of an empirically real occurrence. It is a common and wholly respectable modern device used in both film (q.v. *The Thin Blue Line, Forrest Gump, JFK*) and literature (q.v. Capote's *In Cold Blood*, Wouk's *The Caine Mutiny*, Oates's *Zombie*, Crane's *The Red Badge of Courage*, Wolfe's *The Right Stuff*, & c., & c.).

depersonalized, polyphonized, or otherwise jazzed up in order to conform to the specs of the legal disclaimer. This is not to say that this jazzing up is all just gratuitous titty-pinching; given the aforementioned legal-slash-commercial constraints, it's ended up being integral to the book's whole project. The idea, as both sides' counsel worked it out, is that you will regard features like shifting p.o.v.s, structural fragmentation, willed incongruities, & c. as simply the modern literary analogs of 'Once upon a time...' or 'Far, far away, there once dwelt...' or any of the other traditional devices that signaled the reader that what was under way was fiction and should be processed accordingly. For as everyone knows, whether consciously or not, there's always a kind of unspoken contract between a book's author and its reader; and the terms of this contract always depend on certain codes and gestures that the author deploys in order to signal the reader what kind of book it is, i.e., whether it's made up vs. true. And these codes are important, because the subliminal contract for nonfiction is very different from the one for fiction.[9]

9 The main way you can tell that the contracts are different is from our reactions to their breach. The feeling of betrayal or infidelity that the reader suffers if it turns out that a piece of ostensible nonfiction has made-up stuff in it (as has been revealed in some recent literary scandals, e.g. Kosinski's *Painted Bird* or that infamous Carcaterra book) is because the terms of the nonfiction

What I'm trying to do right here, within the protective range of the copyright page's disclaimer, is to override the unspoken codes and to be 100 percent overt and forthright about the present contract's terms. *The Pale King* is basically a nonfiction memoir, with additional elements of reconstructive journalism, organizational psychology, elementary civics and tax theory, & c. Our mutual contract here is based on the presumptions of (a) my veracity, and (b) your understanding that any features or semions that might appear to undercut that veracity are in fact protective legal devices, not unlike the boilerplate that accompanies sweepstakes and civil contracts, and thus are not meant to be decoded or 'read' so much as merely acquiesced to as part of the cost of our doing business together, so to speak, in today's commercial climate.[10]

Plus there's the autobiographical fact that, like

---

contract have been violated. There are, of course, ways to quote-unquote cheat the reader in fiction, too, but these tend to be more technical, meaning internal to the story's own formal rules (see, e.g., the mystery novel's first-person narrator who doesn't reveal that he's actually the murderer until the last page, even though he obviously knew it all along and suppressed it just to jerk us around), and the reader tends to feel more aesthetically disappointed than personally dicked over.

10 Apologies for the preceding sentence, which is the product of much haggling and compromise with the publisher's legal team.

so many other nerdy, disaffected young people of that time, I dreamed of becoming an 'artist,' i.e., somebody whose adult job was original and creative instead of tedious and dronelike. My specific dream was of becoming an immortally great fiction writer à la Gaddis or Anderson, Balzac or Perec, &c.; and many of the notebook entries on which parts of this memoir are based were themselves literarily jazzed up and fractured; it's just the way I saw myself at the time. In some ways, you could say that my literary ambitions were the chief reason I was on hiatus from college and working at the Midwest REC at all, though most of that whole backstory is tangential and will be addressed only here in the Foreword, and very briefly, to wit:

In a nutshell, the truth is that the first pieces of fiction I was ever actually paid for involved certain other students at the initial college I went to, which was extremely expensive and highbrow and attended mainly by graduates of elite private schools in New York and New England. Without going into a whole lot of detail, let's just say that there were certain pieces of prose I produced for certain students on certain academic subjects, and that these pieces were fictional in the sense of having styles, theses, scholarly personas, and authorial names that were not my own. I think you get the idea. The chief motivation behind this little enterprise was, as it so often is in the real world, financial. It's not like I was desperately poor in college, but my family was far from wealthy, and part of my financial aid package involved taking out large student loans; and I was aware that student-loan debt tended to be very bad news for someone who wanted to pursue any sort of artistic career after college, since it's well known that most artists toil in ascetic obscurity for years before making any real money at their profession.

On the other hand, there were many students at that college whose families were in a position not only to pay their whole tuition but apparently also to give their kids money for whatever personal expenses came up, with no questions asked. 'Personal expenses' here refers to things like weekend ski trips, ridiculously expensive stereo systems, fraternity parties with fully stocked wet bars, & c. Not to mention that the entire campus was less than two acres, and yet most of the students had their own cars, which it also cost $400 per semester to park in one of the college lots. It was all pretty incredible. In many respects, this college was my introduction to the stark realities of class, economic stratification, and the very different financial realities that different sorts of Americans inhabited.

Some of these upper-class students were indeed

spoiled, cretinous, and/or untroubled by questions of ethics. Others were under great family pressure and failing, for whatever reasons, to work up to what their parents considered their true grade potential. Some just didn't manage their time and responsibilities well, and found themselves up against the wall on an assignment. I'm sure you get the basic picture. Let's just say that, as a way of positioning myself to pay off some of my loans at an accelerated rate, I provided a certain service. This service was not cheap, but I was quite good at it, and careful. E.g., I always demanded a large enough sample of a client's prior writing to determine how he tended to think and sound, and I never made the mistake of delivering something that was unrealistically superior to someone's own previous work. You can probably also see why these sorts of exercises would be good apprentice training for someone interested in so-called 'creative writing.'[11] The enterprise's proceeds were invested in a high-yield money market account; and interest rates at that time were high, whereas student loans don't even start accruing interest until one leaves school. The overall strategy was conservative, both financially and academically.

---

11 (which, FYI, there were few or no formal classes in at that time)

It's not as if I was doing several of these commissioned fictional pieces a week or anything. I had plenty of my own work to do too, after all.

To anticipate a likely question, let me concede that the ethics here were gray at best. This is why I chose to be honest, just above, about not being impoverished or needing the extra income in order to eat or anything. I was not desperate. I was, though, trying to accumulate some savings against what I anticipated[12] to be debilitating post-grad debt. I am aware that this is not an excuse in the strict sense, but I do believe it serves as at least an explanation; and there were also other, more general factors and contexts that might be seen as mitigating. For one, the college itself turned out to have a lot of moral hypocrisy about it, e.g., congratulating itself on its diversity and the leftist piety of its politics while in reality going about the business of preparing elite kids to enter elite professions and make a great deal of money, thus increasing the pool of prosperous alumni donors. Without anyone ever discussing it or even allowing themselves to be aware of it, the college was a veritable temple of Mammon. I'm not kidding. For instance, the most popular major was economics, and the best

12 (correctly, it turned out)

and brightest of my class all seemed obsessed with a career on Wall Street, whose own public ethos at the time was 'Greed is good.' Not to mention that there were retail cocaine dealers on campus who made a lot more than I ever did. Those were just a few of what I might, if I chose, offer as extenuating factors. My own attitude about it was detached and professional, not unlike a lawyer's. The basic view I held was that, whereas there may have been elements of my enterprise that might technically qualify as aiding or abetting a client's decision to violate the college's Code of Academic Honesty, that decision, as well as the practical and moral responsibility for it, rested with the client. I was undertaking certain freelance writing assignments for pay; why certain students wanted certain papers of a certain length on certain topics, and what they chose to do with them after delivery, were not my business.

Suffice it to say that this view was not shared by the college's Judicial Board in late 1984. Here the story gets complex and a bit lurid, and an SOP memoir would probably linger on the details and the rank unfairnesses and hypocrisies involved. I'm not going to do that. I am, after all, mentioning all this only to provide some context for the ostensibly 'fictional'-looking formal elements of the non-SOP memoir that you have (I hope) bought and are now enjoying. Plus, of course, also to help explain what I was even doing in one of the most tedious and dronelike white-collar jobs in America during what should have been my junior year at an elite college,[13] so that this obvious question isn't left to hang distractingly all through the book (a type of distraction I personally despise, as a reader). Given these limited objectives, then, the whole Code-of-AH debacle is probably best sketched in broad schematic strokes, to wit:

(1a) Naive people are, more or less by definition, unaware that they're naive. (1b) I was, in retrospect, naive. (2) For various personal reasons, I was not a member of any campus fraternity, and so was ignorant of many of the bizarre tribal customs and practices in the college's so-called 'Greek' community. (3a) One of the college's fraternities had instituted the phenomenally stupid and shortsighted practice of placing behind their billiard

---

13 Junior year, by the way, was when many of the college's other, more privileged students, including several who'd been my freelance clients, were enjoying their traditional 'semester abroad' at places like Cambridge and the Sorbonne. I'm just mentioning this. There's no expectation that you're going to wring your hands over whatever hypocrisy and unfairness you may discern in this state of affairs. In no sense is this Foreword a bid for sympathy. Plus it's all water long under the bridge now, obviously.

room's wet bar a two-drawer file cabinet containing copies of certain recent exams, problem sets, lab reports, and term papers that had earned high grades, which were available for plagiarism. (3b) Speaking of phenomenally stupid, it turned out that not just one but *three* different members of this fraternity had, without bothering to consult the party from whom they'd commissioned and received them, tossed papers that were not technically their own into this communal file cabinet. (4) The paradox of plagiarism is that it actually requires a lot of care and hard work to pull off successfully, since the original text's style, substance, and logical sequences have to be modified enough so that the plagiarism isn't totally, insultingly obvious to the professor who's grading it. (5a) The type of spoiled, cretinous frat boy who goes into a communal file cabinet for a term paper on the use of implicit GNP price deflators in macroeconomic theory is also the type who will not know or care about the paradoxical extra work that good plagiarism requires. He will, however incredible it sounds, just plunk down and retype the thing, word for word. (5b) Nor, even more incredibly, will he take the trouble to verify that none of his fraternity brothers is planning to plagiarize the same term paper for the same course. (6) The moral system of a college fraternity turns out to be classically tribal, i.e., characterized by a deeply felt sense of honor, discretion, and loyalty to one's so-called 'brothers,' coupled with a complete, sociopathic lack of regard for the interests or even humanity of anyone outside that fraternal set.

Let's just end the sketch there. I doubt you need a whole diagram to anticipate what came down, nor much of a primer in US class dynamics to understand, of the eventual five students placed on academic probation or forced to retake certain courses vs. the one student formally suspended pending consideration of expulsion and possible[14] referral of the case to the Hampshire County District Attorney, which one of these was yours truly, the living author, Mr. David Wallace of Philo IL, to which tiny lifeless nothing town neither I nor my family were at all psyched about the prospect of having me return and sit around watching TV for the at least one and possibly two semesters that the college's administration was going to take its sweet time considering my fate.[15] Meanwhile, by

14 (but highly unlikely, given the college's concern with its reputation and PR)
15 Sorry about that text sentence. The truth is that the whole frat-cabinet-and-cascading-scandal's-need-for-a-scapegoat situation still sometimes gets me jacked up, emotionally speaking. Two facts might make the durability of these emotions easier to understand: (a) of the five other students found by the

the terms of the 1966 Federal Claims Collection Act's §106(c-d), the repayment clock on my Guaranteed Student Loans started running, as of 1 January 1985, at 6¼ percent interest.

Again, if any of that seems vague or ablated, it's because I am giving you a very stripped down, mission-specific version of just who and where I was, life-situation-wise, for the thirteen months I spent as an IRS examiner. Moreover, I'm afraid that just how I landed in this government post at all is a background item that I can explain only obliquely, i.e., by ostensibly explaining why I can't discuss it.[16] First, I'd ask you to bear in mind the above-cited disinclination to have me return and serve out my limbo at home in Philo, which mutual reluctance in turn involves a whole lot of issues and history between my family and me that I couldn't get into

---

J-Board to have either bought term papers or plagiarized from those who had, two ended up graduating *magna cum laude,* and (b) a third now serves on the college's Board of Trustees. I'll just leave those as stark facts and let you draw your own conclusions about the whole shabby affair. *Mendacem memorem esse oportet.*

16 And please forgive the contrivance here. Given the familio-legal strictures detailed just below, this kind of anti-explanation is the only permissible way for me to avoid having my whole presence at IRS Post 047 be some enormous, unexplained, and unmotivated blank, which in certain types of fiction might be (technically) OK, but in a memoir would constitute a deep and essential breach of contract.

even if I wanted to (see below). Second, I would inform you that the city of Peoria IL is roughly ninety miles from Philo, which is a distance that permits general familial monitoring without any of the sort of detailed, close-quarters knowledge that might confer feelings of concern or responsibility. Third, I could direct your attention to Congress's 1977 Fair Debt Collection Practices Act §1101, which turns out to override the Federal Claims Collection Act's §106(c-d) and to authorize deferment of Guaranteed Student Loan repayments for documented employees of certain government agencies, including guess which one. Fourth, I am allowed, after exhaustive negotiations with the publisher's counsel, to say that my thirteen-month contract, posting, and GS-9 civil service paygrade were the result of certain *sub-rosa* actions on the part of a certain unnamed relative[17] with unspecified connections to the Midwest Regional Commissioner's Office of a certain unnamed government agency. Last and most important, I am also permitted to say, albeit in language not wholly my own, that members of my family were almost unanimous in declining to sign the legal releases required for any further or more specific use, mention, or representa-

17 (*not* a parent)

tion of the aforesaid relatives or any likeness thereof in any capacity, setting, form, or guise, inclusive of references *sine damno,* within the written work heretofore entitled *The Pale King,* and that this is why I can't get into anything more specific about the overall hows and whys. End of explanation of absence of real explanation, which, however irksome or opaque it may come off, is (again) still preferable to having the question of why/how I was working at the Midwest Regional Examination Center just hang there huge and unaddressed through the whole text to follow,[18] like the proverbial elephant in the room.

Here I should also probably address one other core-motivation-type question that bears on the matter of veracity and trust raised several ¶s above, viz., why a nonfiction memoir at all, since I'm primarily a fiction writer? Not to mention the question of why a memoir restricted to a single, long-past year I spent in exile from anything I even remotely cared about or was interested in, serving out time as little more than one tiny ephemeral dronelike cog in an immense federal bureaucracy?[19] There are

18 Q.v. FN 2, *supra.*

19 The word *bureaucracy* is notwithstanding that part of the run-up to the whole 'New IRS' thing was an increasing anti- or post-bureaucratic mentality on the part of both Triple-Six and Region. See, for one quick example, this

two different kinds of valid answer here, one being personal and the other more literary/humanistic.

---

snippet from an interview with Mr. Donald Jones, a GS-13 Team Leader in the Midwest REC's Fats group from 1984 through 1990:

> Perhaps it would help to define *bureaucracy*. The term. What we're talking about. All they said you had to do was refer to the dictionary. Administration characterized by diffusion of authority and adherence to inflexible rules of operation, unquote. Inflexible rules of operation. An administrative system in which the need or desire to follow complex procedures impedes effective action, unquote. They had transparencies of the definition projected up on the wall during meetings. They said he had them all recite them as nearly some type of catechism.

Meaning, in discursive terms, that the couple of years in question here saw one of the largest bureaucracies anywhere undergo a convulsion in which it tried to reconceive itself as a non- or even anti-bureaucracy, which at first might sound like nothing more than an amusing bit of bureaucratic folly. In fact, it was frightening; it was a little like watching an enormous machine come to consciousness and start trying to think and feel like a real human. The terror of concurrent films like *Terminator* and *Blade Runner* was based around just this premise... but of course in the case of the Service the convulsions, and fallout, although more diffuse and undramatic, had an actual impact on Americans' lives.

N.B. Mr. Jones's 'they' is referring to certain high-level figures who were exponents of the so-called 'Initiative,' which it is totally impractical here to try to explain abstractly (although q.v. Item 951458221 of §14, Interview Documentary, which consists of a long and probably not ideally focused version of such an explanation from Mr. Kenneth ['Type of Thing Ken'] Hindle, one of the oldest wigglers in the Rotes group to which I ended up [after a great deal of initial confusion and misassignment] being tasked), except to say that the only such figure anyone at our low level ever even laid eyes on was the Technical Branch's M. E. Lehrl and his strange team of

The personal stuff it's initially tempting to say is just none of your business...except that one disadvantage of addressing you here directly and in person in the cultural present of 2005 is the fact that, as both you and I know, there is no longer any kind of clear line between personal and public, or rather between private vs. performative. Among obvious examples are web logs, reality television, cell-phone cameras, chat rooms...not to mention the dramatically increased popularity of the memoir as a literary genre. Of course *popularity* is, in this context, a synonym for profitability; and actually that fact alone should suffice, personal-motivation-wise. Consider that in 2003, the average author's advance[20] for a memoir was

---

intuitives and occult ephebes, who were (it emerged) tasked to help implement the Initiative as it pertained to Examinations. If that doesn't make any sense at this point, please don't worry about it. I went back and forth on the issue of what to explain here vs. what to let unfold in a more natural, dramatic way in the memoir itself. I finally decided to offer certain quick, potentially confusing explanations, betting that if they're too obscure or baroque right now you just won't pay much attention to them, which, again, I hasten to assure you is totally OK.

20 If you're interested, this term is shorthand for an unrefundable advance payment against the author's projected royalties (through a 7½%–15% set of progressive margins) on sales of a book. Since actual sales are difficult to predict, it is in the writer's financial interest to receive the largest possible advance, even though the lump-sum payment can create tax problems for the year of receipt (thanks largely to the 1986 Tax Reform Act's elimination of

almost 2.5 times that paid for a work of fiction. The simple truth is that I, like so many other Americans, have suffered reverses in the volatile economy of the last few years, and these reverses have occurred at the same time that my financial obligations have increased along with my age and responsibilities[21]; and meanwhile all sorts of US writers—some of whom I know personally, including one I actually had to lend money to for basic living expenses as late as spring 2001—have

---

income averaging). And given, again, that predicting actual sales is an inexact science, the size of the up-front author advance that a publishing company is willing to pay for the rights to a book is the best tangible indication of the publisher's willingness to 'support' that book, w/ the latter term meaning everything from the number of copies printed to the size of the marketing budget. And this support is practically the only way for a book to gain the attention of a mass audience and to garner significant sales—like it or not, that's just the commercial reality today.

21 By age forty, artist or no, the reality is that only an imprudent chump would neglect to start saving and investing for eventual retirement, especially in this era of tax-deferred IRA and SEP-IRA plans with such generous annual tax-exempt caps—and extra-especially if you can S-corp yourself and let the corporation make an additional annual pension contribution, over and above your IRA, as a contractual 'employee benefit,' thereby exempting that extra amount from your taxable income, too. The tax laws right now are practically down on one knee, begging upper-income Americans to take advantage of this provision. The trick, of course, is earning enough to qualify as an upper-income American—*Deos fortioribus adesse.*

recently hit it big with memoirs,[22] and I would be a rank hypocrite if I pretended that I was less attuned and receptive to market forces than anyone else.

As all mature people know, though, it's possible for very different kinds of motives and emotions to coexist in the human soul. There is no way that a memoir like *The Pale King* could be written solely for financial gain. One paradox of professional writing is that books written solely for money and/or acclaim will almost never be good enough to garner either. The truth is that the larger narrative encompassing this Foreword has significant social and artistic value. That might sound conceited, but rest assured that I wouldn't and couldn't have put three years' hard labor (plus an additional fifteen months of legal and editorial futzing) into *The Pale King* if I were not convinced it was true. Have, e.g., a look at the following, which was transcribed verbatim from remarks by Mr. DeWitt Glendenning Jr., the Director of the Midwest Regional Examination Center during most of my tenure there:

---

22 (Despite his sudden celebrity and windfall I am still, almost four years later, awaiting repayment of the loan's principal from this unnamed writer, which I mention not to whinge or be vindictive, but merely as one more small part of my financial condition *qua* motivation.)

> If you know the position a person takes on
> taxes, you can determine [his] whole phi-
> losophy. The tax code, once you get to
> know it, embodies all the essence of
> [human] life: greed, politics, power, good-
> ness, charity.

To these qualities that Mr. Glendenning ascribed
to the code I would respectfully add one more:
boredom. Opacity. User-unfriendliness.

This all can be put another way. It might sound
a bit dry and wonkish, but that's because I'm boiling it down to the abstract skeleton:

1985 was a critical year for American taxation
and for the Internal Revenue Service's enforcement
of the US tax code. In brief, that year saw not only
fundamental changes in the Service's operational
mandate, but also the climax of an involved intra-
Service battle between advocates and opponents of
an increasingly automated, computerized tax system. For complex administrative reasons, the
Midwest Regional Examination Center became
one of the venues in which this battle's crucial
phase played out.

But that's only part of it. As alluded to in an
FN way above, subtending this operational battle
over human vs. digital enforcement of the tax code

was a deeper conflict over the very mission and *rai-son* of the Service, a conflict whose fallout extended from the corridors of power at Treasury and Triple-Six all the way down to the most staid and back-water District office. At the highest levels, the struggle here was between traditional or 'conserva-tive'[23] officials who saw tax and its administration as an arena of social justice and civic virtue, on the one hand, and those more progressive, 'pragmatic' policymakers who prized the market model, effi-ciency, and a maximum return on the investment of the Service's annual budget. Distilled to its essence, the question was whether and to what extent the IRS should be operated like a for-profit business.

Probably that's all I should say right here in terms of summary. If you know how to search and parse government archives, you can find volumi-nous history and theory on just about every side of the debate. It's all in the public record.

But here's the thing. Both then and now, very few ordinary Americans know anything about all this. Nor much about the deep changes the Service underwent in the mid-1980s, changes that today directly affect the way citizens' tax

23 (meaning, somewhat confusingly, classically liberal)

obligations are determined and enforced. And the reason for this public ignorance is not secrecy. Despite the IRS's well-documented paranoia and aversion to publicity,[24] secrecy here had nothing to do with it. The real reason why US citizens were/are not aware of these conflicts, changes, and stakes is that the whole subject of tax policy and administration is dull. Massively, spectacularly dull.

It is impossible to overstate the importance of this feature. Consider, from the Service's perspective, the advantages of the dull, the arcane, the mind-numbingly complex. The IRS was one of the very first government agencies to learn that such qualities help insulate them against public protest and political opposition, and that abstruse dullness is actually a much more effective shield than is secrecy. For the great disadvantage of secrecy is that it's interesting. People are drawn to secrets; they can't help it. Keep in mind that the period we're talking was only a decade after Watergate. Had the Service tried to hide or cover up its conflicts and convulsions, some enterprising journalist(s) could have done an exposé that drew a lot of attention and interest and scandalous fuss.

24 (attitudes that are not wholly unjustified, given TPs' hostility to the Service, politicians' habit of bashing the agency to score populist points, & c.)

But this is not at all what happened. What happened was that much of the high-level policy debate played out for two years in full public view, e.g., in open hearings of the Joint Committee on Taxation, the Senate Treasury Procedures and Statutes Subcommittee, and the IRS's Deputy and Assistant Commissioners' Council. These hearings were collections of anaerobic men in drab suits who spoke a verbless bureaucratese — terms like 'strategic utilization template' and 'revenue vector' in place of 'plan' and 'tax' — and took days just to reach consensus on the order of items for discussion. Even in the financial press, there was hardly any coverage; can you guess why? If not, consider the fact that just about every last transcript, record, study, white paper, code amendment, revenue-ruling, and procedural memo has been available for public perusal since date of issue. No FOIA filing even required. But not one journalist seems ever to have checked them out, and with good reason: This stuff is solid rock. The eyes roll up white by the third or fourth ¶. You just have no idea.[25]

---

25 I'm reasonably sure that I am the only living American who's actually read all these archives all the way through. I'm not sure I can explain how I did it. Mr. Chris Acquistipace, one of the GS-11 Chalk Leaders in our Rote Exams

Fact: The birth agonies of the New IRS led to one of the great and terrible PR discoveries in modern democracy, which is that if sensitive issues of governance can be made sufficiently dull and arcane, there will be no need for officials to hide or dissemble, because no one not directly involved will pay enough attention to cause trouble. No one will pay attention because no one will be interested, because, more or less *a priori*, of these issues' monumental dullness. Whether this PR discovery is to be regretted for its corrosive effect on the democratic ideal or celebrated for its enhancement of government efficiency depends, it seems, on which side one takes in the deeper debate over ideals vs. efficacy referenced on p. 141, resulting in yet another involuted loop that I won't tax your patience by trying to trace out or make hay of.

To me, at least in retrospect,[26] the really interesting question is why dullness proves to be such a powerful impediment to attention. Why we recoil

---

group, and a man of no small intuition and sensitivity, proposed an analogy between the public records surrounding the Initiative and the giant solid-gold Buddhas that flanked certain temples in ancient Khmer. These priceless statues, never guarded or secured, were safe from theft not despite but because of their value—they were too huge and heavy to move. Something about this sustained me.

26 (which is, after all, memoirs' specialty)

from the dull. Maybe it's because dullness is intrinsically painful; maybe that's where phrases like 'deadly dull' or 'excruciatingly dull' come from. But there might be more to it. Maybe dullness is associated with psychic pain because something that's dull or opaque fails to provide enough stimulation to distract people from some other, deeper type of pain that is always there, if only in an ambient low-level way, and which most of us[27] spend nearly all our time and energy trying to distract ourselves from feeling, or at least from feeling directly or with our full attention. Admittedly, the whole thing's pretty confusing, and hard to talk about abstractly ... but surely something must lie behind not just Muzak in dull or tedious places anymore but now also actual TV in waiting rooms, supermarkets' checkouts, airports' gates, SUVs' backseats. Walkmen, iPods, BlackBerries, cell phones that attach to your head. This terror of silence with nothing diverting to do. I can't think anyone really believes that today's so-called 'information society' is just about information. Everyone knows[28] it's about something else, way down.

The memoir-relevant point here is that I

27 (whether or not we're consciously aware of it)
28 (again, whether consciously or not)

learned, in my time with the Service, something about dullness, information, and irrelevant complexity. About negotiating boredom as one would a terrain, its levels and forests and endless wastes. Learned about it extensively, exquisitely, in my interrupted year. And now ever since that time have noticed, at work and in recreation and time with friends and even the intimacies of family life, that living people do not speak much of the dull. Of those parts of life that are and must be dull. Why this silence? Maybe it's because the subject is, in and of itself, dull... only then we're again right back where we started, which is tedious and irksome. There may, though, I opine, be more to it... as in vastly more, right here before us all, hidden by virtue of its size.

§10

Notwithstanding Justice H. Harold Mealer's famous characterization, included in the Fourth Appellate Circuit's majority opinion on *Atkinson et al. v. The United States,* of a government bureaucracy as 'the only known parasite larger than the organism on which it subsists,' the truth is that such a bureaucracy is really much more a parallel world, both connected to and independent of this one, operating under its own physics and imperatives of cause. One might envision a large and intricately branching system of jointed rods, pulleys, gears, and levers radiating out from a central operator such that tiny movements of that operator's finger are transmitted through that system to become the gross kinetic changes in the rods at the periphery. It is at this periphery that the bureaucracy's world acts upon this one.

The crucial part of the analogy is that the elaborate system's operator is not himself uncaused. The bureaucracy is not a closed system; it is this that makes it a world instead of a thing.

§11

From Assistant Commissioner of Internal Revenue for Human Resources, Management & Support's Office of Employee Assistance & Personnel Overview Internal Memorandum 4123-78(b)

Conclusion of ACIRHRMSOEAPO Survey/Study 1-76—11-77: AMA/DSM(II)-authorized syndromes/ symptoms associated with Examinations postings in excess of 36 months (average term of posting on report: 41.4 months), in reverse order of incidence (per medical/EAP service claim per IRSM §743/12.2(f-r)):

Chronic paraplegia
Temporary paraplegia
Temporary paralysis agitans
Paracatatonic fugues
Formication
Intracranial edema
Spasmodic dyskinesia
Paramnesia
Paresis
Phobic anxiety (numerical)
Lordosis
Renal neuralgia
Tinnitus
Peripheral hallucinations
Torticollis
Cantor's sign (dextral)
Lumbago
Dihedral lordosis
Dissociative fugues
Kern-Børglundt syndrome (radial)
Hypomania
Sciatica
Spasmodic torticollis
Low startle threshold
Krendler's syndrome
Hemorrhoids

Ruminative fugues
Ulcerative colitis
Hypertension
Hypotension
Cantor's sign (sinistral)
Diplopia
Hemeralopia
Vascular headache
Cyclothymia
Blurred vision
Fine tremors
Facial/digital ticcing
Localized anxiety
Generalized anxiety
Kinesthetic deficits
Unexplained bleeding

§12

Stecyk started at the end of the block and came up the first flagstone walkway with his briefcase and rang the bell. 'Good morning,' he said to the older lady who answered the door in what was either a robe or very casual housedress (it was 7:20, so bathrobes were not only probable but downright appropriate) whose collar she was holding tightly closed with one hand and was looking through the door's crack at different points over Stecyk's shoulders as if certain there must be someone else behind him. Stecyk said, 'My name is Leonard Stecyk, I go by Leonard but Len is also perfectly fine as far as I'm concerned, and I've recently had the opportunity to move in and set up housekeeping in 6F in the Angler's Cove complex just up the street there, I'm

152

sure you've seen it either leaving home or returning, it's just right up the street there at 121, and I'd
like to say Hello and introduce myself and say I'm
pleased to be part of the neighborhood and to offer
you as a token of greetings and thanks this free
copy of the US Post Office's 1979 National Zip
Code Directory, listing the zip codes for every
community and postal zone in each state of the
United States in alphabetical order, and also' —
shifting the briefcase under his arm to open the
directory and hold it out open to the woman's
view — something seemed wrong with one of the
lady's eyes, as if she were having trouble with a contact lens or perhaps had some foreign matter under
the upper lid, which could be uncomfortable — 'additionally listing here on the back of the last page and
inside the rear cover, the cover's the continuation,
the addresses and toll-free numbers of over forty-
five government agencies and and services from
which you can receive free informational material,
some of which is almost shockingly valuable, see
I've put small asterisks next to those, which I know
for a fact are helpful and an extraordinary bargain,
and which are of course after all when you come
right down to it paid for with your tax dollars, so
why not extract value from the contributions if you
know what I mean, though of course the choice is

entirely up to you'—the lady was also turning her head slightly in the way of someone whose hearing wasn't quite what it used to be, noting which Stecyk put the briefcase down to ink one or two extra asterisks by numbers that in this case might be of special help. Then making a large motion of handing it over and letting the postal directory hang there in midair just outside the door while the lady had her face screwed up and seemed to be deciding whether to disengage the door's chain in order to accept it. 'Maybe I'll just be leaning it up here against the milkbox'—pointing down at the milkbox—'and you can peruse it at leisure at your own convenience later in the day or really whatever you might choose to do,' Stecyk said. He liked to make a small jest or sally of employing a motion as if he were tipping his hat even though his hand never made contact with the hat; he felt it was both courtly and amusing. 'Hidey ho, then,' he said. He proceeded back down the walkway, missing all the cracks and hearing the door behind him close only as he reached the sidewalk and made a sharp right and took eighteen strides to the next walkway and a sharp right to the door, which had a wrought-iron security door installed before it and at which there was no answer after three rings and shave-and-haircut knock. He left his card with his new address and the gist of his greeting and offer and another 1979 zip code directory (the 1980 directory would not be out until August; he had an order in) and proceeded down the walkway, a spring to his step, his smile so wide it almost looked like it hurt.

§13

It was in public high school that this boy learned the terrible power of attention and what you pay attention to. He learned it in a way whose very ridiculousness was part of what made it so terrible. And terrible it was.

At age sixteen and a half, he started to have attacks of shattering public sweats.

As a child, he'd always been a heavy sweater. He had sweated a lot when playing sports or when it was hot, but it didn't especially bother him. He just wiped himself off more often. He couldn't remember anyone ever saying anything about it. Also, it didn't seem to smell bad; it's not like he stank. The sweating was just something particular about him. Some kids were fat, some were unusually short or tall or had crazy teeth, or stuttered, or smelled like mildew no matter what clothes they wore—he just happened to be someone who sweated heavily, especially in the humidity of summertime, when just riding his bike in dungarees around Beloit made him sweat like crazy. It all barely even registered on him, so far as he could remember.

In his seventeenth year, though, it started to bother him; he became self-conscious about the sweating thing. This was surely related to puberty, the stage where you suddenly get much more concerned about how you appear to other people. About whether there might be something visibly creepy or gross about you. Within weeks of the start of the school year, he became both more and differently aware that he seemed to sweat more than the other kids did. The first couple months of school were always hot, and many of the old high school's classrooms didn't even have fans. Without trying to or wanting to, he started to imagine what his sweating might look like in class: his face gleaming with a mixture of sebum and sweat, his shirt sodden at the collar and pits, his hair separated into wet little creepy spikes from his head's running sweat. It was the worst if he was in a position where he thought girls could maybe see it. The classrooms' desks were all crammed together. Just the presence of a pretty or popular girl in his sight line would make his internal temperature rise—he could feel it happening unwilled, even against his will—and start the heavy sweating.[1]

Except at first, as autumn of that seventeenth year deepened and the weather cooled and dried and the leaves turned and fell and could be raked for pay, he had reason to feel that the sweating problem was receding, that the real problem had been the heat, or that without the muggy summer heat there would now no longer be as much occasion for the problem. (He thought of it in the most general and abstract terms possible. He tried never to let himself think of the actual word *sweat*. The idea, after all, was to try and be as unself-conscious about it as possible.) Mornings now were chilly, and the high school's classrooms weren't hot any-

1 Psychodynamically, he was, as a subject, coming to a late and therefore traumatic understanding of himself as also an object, a body among other bodies, something that could see and yet also be seen. It was the sort of binary self-concept that many children attain as early as age five, often thanks to some chance encounter with a mirror, puddle, window, or photograph seen in just the right way. Despite the boy's having the average ration of reflectors available to him in childhood, though, this developmental stage was retarded in his case somehow. The understanding of himself as also an object-for-others was in his case deferred to the very cusp of adulthood—and, like most repressed truths, when it finally burst through, it came as something overwhelming and terrible, a winged thing breathing fire.

more, except near the rears' clanking radiators. Without letting himself be wholly aware of it, he had started hurrying a little bit between periods to get to the next class early enough that he wouldn't get stuck in a desk by a radiator, which was hot enough to jump-start a sweat. But it involved a delicate balance, because if he hurried too fast through the halls between periods, this exertion could also cause him to break a light sweat, which increased his preoccupation and made it easier for the sweating to get more severe in the event that he thought people might be noticing it. Certain other examples of balancing and preoccupation like this existed, most of which he tried to keep from conscious thought as much as possible without being wholly aware of why he was doing this.[2]

For there were, by this time, degrees and gradations of public sweating, from a light varnish all the way up to a shattering, uncontrollable, and totally visible and creepy sweat. The worst thing was that one degree could lead to the next if he worried about it too much, if he was too afraid that

---

2 In clinical terms, he was fighting to re-repress a truth that had been too long repressed in the first place, a confinement from which it had taken on far too much psychic energy ever, once it had burst through the mirror (so to speak), to be willed back out of conscious awareness. Consciousness just doesn't work this way.

a slight sweat would get worse and tried too hard to control or avoid it. The fear of it could bring it on. He did not truly begin to suffer until he understood this fact, an understanding he came to slowly at first and then all of an awful sudden.

What he thought of as easily the worst day of his life so far followed an unseasonably cold week in early November where the problem had started to seem so manageable and under control that he felt he might actually be starting to almost forget about it altogether. Wearing dungarees and a rust-colored velour shirt, he sat far from the radiator in the middle of a middle row of student desks in World Cultures and was listening and taking notes on whatever module of the textbook they were covering, when a terrible thought rose as if from nowhere inside him: *What if I all of a sudden start sweating?* And on that one day this thought, which presented mostly as a terrible sudden fear that washed through him like a hot tide, made him break instantly into a heavy, unstoppable sweat, which the secondary thought that it must look even creepier to be sweating when it wasn't even hot in here to anyone else made worse and worse as he sat very still with his head down and face soon running with palpable rivulets of sweat, not moving at all, torn between the desire to wipe the sweat from his face before it actually began to drip and someone saw it dripping and the fear that any kind of wiping movement would draw people's attention and cause those in the desks on either side of him to see what was happening, that he was sweating like crazy for no reason. It was by far the worst feeling he had ever had in his life, and the whole attack lasted almost forty minutes, and for the rest of the day he went around in a kind of trance of shock and spent adrenaline, and that day was the actual start of the syndrome in which he understood that the worse his fear of breaking into a shattering public sweat was, the better the chances that he'd have something like what happened in World Cultures happen again, maybe every day, maybe more than once a day—and this understanding caused him more terror and frustration and inner suffering than he had ever before even dreamed that somebody could ever experience, and the total stupidity and weirdness of the whole problem just made it that much worse.

Dating from that day in World Cultures, his dread of it happening again, and his attempts to avert or avoid or control this fear, began to inform almost every moment of his day. The fear and preoccupation only happened in class or lunch at school — not in last-period PE, since sweating in PE wouldn't be seen as all that weird and so didn't inspire the special kind of fear that primed him for an attack. Or it also happened at any crowded function like Scout meetings or Christmas dinner in the stuffy, overheated dining room of his grand-parents' home in Rockton, where he could literally feel the table's candles' extra little dots of heat and the body heat of all the relatives crowded around the table, with his head down trying to look like he was studying his plate's china pattern as the heat of the fear of the heat spread through him like adrenaline or brandy, that physical spread of internal heat that he tried so hard not to dread. It didn't happen in private, at home in his room, reading — in his room with the door closed it often didn't even occur to him — or in the library in one of the little private carrels like an open cube, where no one could see him or it would be easy to just get up anytime and leave.[3] It happened only

3 It especially didn't happen when he was alone in the upstairs bathroom in front of the mirror, trying to make an attack happen so he could study it in the mirror and see for himself, objectively, how bad and obvious it looked from various angles and how far away it was visible from. He hoped, and on some level believed, that it maybe wasn't as obvious or bizarre-looking as he was always afraid it was during an actual attack, but he could never verify this

in public with people around him and crowded in rows or around a well-lit table where you had to wear your new red Christmas sweater and your shoulders and elbows were almost actually touching the cousins crammed in on both sides and everyone all trying to talk at the same time over the steaming food and all looking at each other so there was every chance that people could see even the first flushed little pinpricks of it on his forehead and upper face that then, if the fear of it getting out of control grew too great, would swell to shining beads and soon start to visibly run, and it was impossible to wipe his face off with a napkin because he feared that the weird sight of wiping his face in wintertime would draw all his relatives' attention to what was going on, which is what he would have traded his very soul not to have happen. It could basically happen anyplace where it was hard to leave without drawing attention to himself. To raise your hand in class and ask for a bathroom pass as heads turned to look—just the thought of it filled him with total dread.

He could not understand why he was so afraid of people possibly seeing him sweat or thinking it

---

because he could never get a real attack to happen when he wanted it to, only when he totally, totally did not.

was weird or gross. Who cared what people thought? He said this over and over to himself; he knew it was true. He also repeated—often in a stall in one of the boys' restrooms at school between periods after a medium or severe attack, sitting on the toilet with his pants up and trying to use the stall's toilet paper to dry himself without the toilet paper disintegrating into little greebles and blobs all over his forehead, squeezing thick pads of toilet paper onto the front of his hair to help dry it— Franklin Roosevelt's speech from US History II in sophomore year: *The only thing we have to fear is fear itself.* He would mentally repeat this to himself over and over. Franklin Roosevelt was right, but it didn't help—knowing it was the fear that was the problem was just a fact; it didn't make the fear go away. In fact, he started to think that thinking of the speech's line so much just made him all the more afraid of the fear itself. That what he really had to fear was fear of the fear, like an endless fun-house hall of mirrors of fear, all of which were ridiculous and weird. He started to sometimes catch himself talking to himself about the sweating thing and fear in a kind of very fast faint whisper that he'd been doing without being aware of it, and now he began to really consider that he might be going crazy. Most of the craziness he'd seen on TV involved people laughing maniacally, which now seemed totally bizarre to him, like a joke that wasn't only not funny but made no sense at all. Imagining laughing about the attacks or the fear was like imagining trying to come up to somebody and start trying to explain what was going on, like his Scoutmaster or the guidance counselor—it was unimaginable; there was no way.

High school became a daily torment, even as his grades improved even more, due to the increased reading and studying he did because it was only when he was in private and totally absorbed and concentrating on something else that he was OK. He also got into word search and number puzzles, which he found absorbing. In class or the lunchroom, it was a constant preoccupation to not think about it and not let the fear reach the point where his temperature went up and his attention telescoped to where all he could feel was the uncontrolled heat and sweat starting to pop out on his face and back, which, the minute he felt the sweat popping out and beading, his fear went through the roof and all he could think of was how he could get out of there to the restroom without drawing attention. It only happened sometimes, but he dreaded it all the time, even though he knew all too well that the constant dread and preoccupation were what primed him to have these attacks. He thought of them as *attacks,* though not from anything outside him but rather from some inner part of himself that was hurting or almost betraying him, as in *heart attack.* Similarly, *primed* became his inner code word for the state of hair-trigger fear and dread that could cause him to have an attack at almost any time in public.

His main way of dealing with being constantly primed and preoccupied with the fear of it all the time at school was that he developed various tricks and tactics for what to do if an attack of public sweating started and threatened to go totally out of control. Knowing where all the exits were to any room he entered wasn't a trick, it became just something he now automatically did, like knowing just how far the nearest exit was and if it could be got to without drawing much attention. The school's lunchroom was an example of someplace that was easy to get out of with no one really noticing, for instance. Leaving the classroom during an attack in a class was out of the question, however. If he just got up and ran out of the room, as he always yearned to do during an attack, there would be all kinds of disciplinary problems, and everyone would want an explanation, including his parents—plus when he came back to that class the next day, everyone would know he'd run out and would want to know what had made him freak out, and the net result would be a lot of attention on him in the class, and the fear that everyone would be noticing him and looking at him, which would prime him all over again. Or if he ever actually raised his hand and asked the teacher for a restroom pass, it would draw all the bored students in the rows' attention to who'd spoken up, and their heads would all turn to look and there he would be, sweating and dripping and looking bizarre. His only hope then would be that he'd look sick, people would think he was sick or about to maybe throw up. This was one of the tricks—to cough or sniff and feel uncomfortably at his glands if he feared an attack, so if it got out of control he could hope people would maybe just think he was sick and shouldn't have come to school that day. That he wasn't weird, he was just sick. It was the same with pretending he didn't feel well enough to eat his lunch at lunch period—sometimes he wouldn't eat and would bus the full tray and then leave and go eat a sandwich he brought from home in a baggie in a restroom stall. That way, people might be more apt to think he was sick.

Other tactics included sitting in a row as far back in the classroom as he could, so most people would be in front of him and he didn't have to worry about them seeing him if he had an attack, which only worked in classes without a seating chart,[4] and could also backfire in the nightmare scenario he tried so hard not to think about. And also avoiding the hot radiators, naturally, and desks between girls, or trying to secure the desk at the very end of a row so that in case of emergency he could avert his head from the rest of the row, but in a subtle way that didn't look weird—he'd just swing his legs out from the row into the aisle and cross his ankles and lean out that way. He stopped riding his bike to the high school because the exercise of riding could warm him up and prime him with anxiety before first period had even started. Another trick, by the start of third quarter, was walking to school without a winter coat in order to get cold and sort of freeze his nervous system, which he could only do when he was the last one to leave the house, because his mother would have a spasm if he tried to leave

4 This boy's surname, which was *Cusk,* placed him near the front of those classes with assigned seating.

without a coat. There was also wearing multiple layers that he could remove if he felt it coming on in a class, although removing layers could look weird if he was also coughing and feeling his glands—in his experience, sick people didn't normally remove layers. He was somewhat aware he was losing weight but didn't know how much. He also began to cultivate a habitual gesture of brushing his hair back from his forehead, which he practiced in the bathroom mirror in order to make it look like just an unconscious habit but was really all designed to help brush sweat from his forehead out of sight into his hair in the event of an attack—but this too was a delicate balance, because past a certain point the gesture was no longer helpful, since if the front part of his hair got wet enough to separate into those creepy little wet spikes and strands, then the fact that he was sweating became even more obvious, if people were to look over. And the nightmare scenario that he dreaded more than anything was for him to be in the back and to start having such a shattering, uncontrollable attack that the teacher, all the way up at the front of the room, noticed he was soaked and running with visible sweat and interrupted class to ask if he was all right, causing everyone to turn way around in their chairs to look. In the nightmares there was a literal spotlight on him as they all turned in their seats to see who the teacher was so worried and/or grossed out by.[5]

In February his mother made a breezy, half-joking comment about his love life and if there were any girls he especially liked this year, and he almost had to leave the room, he almost burst into tears. The idea now of ever asking a girl out, of taking a girl out and having her looking at him from right there close up, expecting him to be thinking about her instead of how primed he was and whether he was going to start sweating — this filled him with dread, but at the same time it made him sad. He was bright enough to know there was something sad about it. Even as he gladly quit Scouts just four badges short of Eagle, and turned down a shy, kind of socially anonymous girl from College Algebra and Trigonometry's invitation to the Sadie Hawkins dance, and faked being sick at

---

5 Under any reputable Depth-based interpretation, a search- or spotlight serves as a manifest dream-symbol of human attention. On the level of latent content, however, the recurring nightmare could be interpreted as signifying anything from, e.g., a repressed narcissistic desire for others' notice to an unconscious recognition of the boy's own excessive preoccupation with himself as the suffering's proximate cause. At clinical issue would be such questions as the dream-spotlight's source, the teacher-figure's status as either imago or archetype (or, perhaps, as projected self-image, since it is in this figure that distress is externalized as affect), and the subject's own associations concerning such terms as *gross, attack,* and *shattering.*

Easter so he could stay home by himself reading ahead in *Dorian Gray* and trying to jump-start an attack in the mirror of his parents' bathroom instead of driving down with them to Easter dinner at his grandparents', he felt a bit sad about it, as well as relieved, plus guilty about the various lies of the excuses he gave, and also lonely and a bit tragic, like someone in the rain outside a window looking in, but also creepy and disgusting, as though his secret inner self was creepy and the attacks were just a symptom, his true self trying to literally leak out — though none of all this was visible to him in the bathroom's glass, whose reflection seemed oblivious[6] to all that he felt as he searched it.

---

6 There are secrets within secrets, though — always.

§14

It's an IRS examiner in a chair, in a room. There is little else to see. Facing the tripod's camera, addressing the camera, one examiner after another. It's a cleared card-storage room off the radial hall of the Regional Examination Center's data processing pod, so the air-conditioning is good and there's none of summer's facial shine. Two at a time are brought in from the wiggle rooms; the examiner on deck is behind a vinyl partition, for prebriefing. The prebriefing is mostly just watching the intro. The documentary's intro is represented as coming from Triple-Six via the Regional Commissioner's HQ up in Joliet; the tape's case has the Service seal and a legal disclaimer. The putative working title is *Your IRS Today*. Possibly for public TV. Some of them are told it's for schools, civics classes. This is in the pre-briefing. The interviews are represented as PR, with a serious purpose. To humanize, demystify the Service, help citizens understand how hard and important their job is. How much at stake. That they're not hostile or machines. The prebriefer reads from a series of printed cards; there's a mirror in the near corner for the on-deck subject to straighten his tie, smooth out her skirt. There's a release to sign, specially crafted—each examiner reads it closely, a reflex; they're still on the clock. Some are psyched. Excited. There's something about the prospect of attention, the project's real purpose. It's DP Tate's baby, conceptually, though Stecyk did all the work.

There's also the VCR monitor for letting them see the provisional intro, whose crudeness is acknowledged up front in the prebriefing, the need for tweaking. It's all set pieces and shots from photo archives whose stylized warmth does not fit the voiceover's tone. It's disorienting, and no one is sure what is up with the intro; the prebriefers stress it's just for orientation.

'The Internal Revenue Service is the branch of the United States Treasury Department charged with the timely collection of all federal taxes due under current statute. With over one hundred thousand employees in more than one thousand national, regional, district, and local offices, your IRS is the largest law enforcement agency in the nation. But it is more. In the body politic of the United States of America, many have likened your IRS to the nation's beating heart, receiving and distributing the resources which allow your federal government to operate effectively in the service and defense of all Americans.' Shots of highway crews, Congress as seen from the Capitol's gallery, a porch's mailman laughing about something with a homeowner, a contextless helicopter with the archive code still in the lower right corner, a Welfare clerk smiling as she hands a check to a black woman in a wheelchair, a highway crew with their hardhats raised in greeting, a VA rehab center, & c. 'The heart, too, of these United States as a team, each income earner chipping in to share resources and embody the principles that make our nation great.' One of the prebriefers' cards directs her here to lean in and insert that the voiceover script is a working draft and that the final product's voiceover will have real human inflections — to use their imagination. 'The lifeblood of this heart: the men and women of today's IRS.' Now a number of shots of what may be real but unusually attractive Service employees, mainly GS-9s and -11s in ties and shirtsleeves, shaking hands with taxpayers, bent smiling over the books of an auditee, beaming in front of a Honeywell 4C3000 that is in fact an empty chassis. 'Far from faceless bureaucrats, these [inaudible] men and women of today's IRS are citizens, taxpayers, parents, neighbors, and members of their community, all charged with a sacred task: to keep the lifeblood of government healthy and circulating.' A group still of what's either an Exams or Audit team arranged not by grade but by height, all waving. A shot of the same incised seal and motto that flank the REC's north facade. 'Just like the nation's *E pluribus unum,* our Service's founding motto, *Alicui tamen faciendum est,* says it all — this difficult, complex task must be performed, and it is your IRS who roll up their sleeves and do it.' It's laughably bad, hence its intrinsic plausibility to the wigglers, including of course the failure to translate the motto for an audience of TPs who all too often actually misspell their names on returns, which the Service Center systems catch and kick over to Exams, wasting everyone's time. But are presumed to know classical Latin, it seems. Perhaps really testing whether the prebriefed examiners catch this error — it's often hard to know what Tate's up to.

The chair is unpadded. It's all very spartan. The light is the REC's fluorescence; there are no lamps or bounces. No makeup, though in the prebriefing examiners' hair is carefully combed, sleeves rolled up exactly three flat turns, blouses opened at the top button, ID cards unclipped from the breast pocket. No director per se in the room; no one to say to act natural or tell them about the loopholes of editing. A technician at the tripod's camera, a boom man with headphones for levels, and the documentarian. The Celotex drop ceiling's been removed for acoustical reasons. Exposed piping and four-color bundles of wire running above the former ceiling's struts, out of the frame. The shot is just the examiner in the folding chair before a cream-colored screen that blocks off a wall of blank Hollerith cards in cardboard flats. The room could be anywhere, nowhere. Some of this is explained, theorized in advance; the prebriefing is precisely orchestrated. A tight shot, they explain, from the torso up, extraneous movements discouraged. Examiners are used to keeping still. There's a monitor room, a former closet, attached, with Toni Ware and an off-clock tech inside, watching. It's a video monitor. They are miked for the earplug that the documentarian/interlocutor stops wearing when it turns out to emit a piercing feedback sound whenever the Fornix card reader across the wall runs a particular subroutine. The monitor is video,

like the camera, with no lighting or makeup. Pale
and stunned, faces' planes queerly shadowed—
this is not a problem, though on video some of the
faces are a drained gray-white. Eyes are a problem.
If the examiner looks at the documentarian instead
of the camera, it can appear evasive or coerced. It's
not optimal, and the prebriefer's advice is to look
into the camera as one would a trusted friend's
eyes, or a mirror, depending.

The prebriefers, both GS-13s on loan from
some Post where Tate has unspecified suction,
were themselves prebriefed in Stecyk's office. Both
are credible, in coordinated navy and brown, the
woman with something hard beneath the charm
that suggests an ascent through Collections. The
man is a blank to Ware, though; he could be from
anywhere.

As is to be expected, some examiners are better
than others. At this. Some can actuate, forget the
setting, the stilted artifice, and speak as from the
heart. So that with these, briefly, the recording techs
can forget the job's sheer tedium, the contrivance,
the stiffness of standing still at machines that could
run on their own. The techs are, in other words,
engaged by the better ones; attention requires no
effort. But only some are better...and the question
at the monitor is why, and what it means, and

whether what it means will matter, in terms of results, when the whole thing is given to Stecyk to track down the line.

Videotape File 047804(r)
© 1984, Internal Revenue Service
Used by Permission
945645233

'It's a tough job. People think deskwork, pushing papers, how hard can it be. Government work, the job security, pushing papers along. They don't get it why it's hard. I've been here now three years. That's twelve quarters. All my reviews have been good. I won't be doing rotes forever, trust me. Some of the fellows in our group are fifty, sixty. They've been doing rote exams over thirty years. Thirty years of looking at forms, crosschecking forms, filling out the same memos on the same forms. There's something in some of their eyes. I don't know how to explain it. My grandparents' apartment building had a boiler man, a janitor. This was up near Milwaukee. Coal heat, this old fellow fed the coal furnace every couple hours. He'd been there forever; he was almost blind from looking into the mouth of that furnace. His eyes were... The older ones here are like that; their eyes are almost like that.'

968223861

'Three or four years ago, the new president, the current one, got elected into office on the promise of big defense spending and a massive tax cut. This is known. The idea was that the tax cut would stimulate economic growth. I'm not certain how this was supposed to work—a lot of the, like, upper policy ideas didn't reach us directly, they just trickled down to us through administrative changes in the Service. The way you know the sun's moved because now the shadows in your room are different. You know what I'm saying.'

Q.

'All of a sudden there were all these reorganizations, sometimes one right after the other, and repostings. Some of us stopped even unpacking. This is where I've been the longest now. I had no background in exams. I came out of Service Centers. I got reposted here from 029, the Northeast Service Center, Utica. New York, but upstate, in the third quarter, '82. Upstate New York is beautiful, but the Utica Center had a lot of problems. At Utica I was in general data processing; I was more like a troubleshooter. Before that I was at Service Center substation 0127, Hanover NH—I was in payment processing, then refund processing. The Northeast districts were all in octal code and the forms with sprocket holes that they hired Vietnamese girls to sit there and tear off. Hanover had a lot of refugees. It was eight, nine years ago, but a whole different era. This here is a much more complex organization.'

Q.

'I'm single, and single men are the ones in the Service that get reposted the most. Any repost is a hassle for Personnel; reposting a family is worse. Plus you have to offer incentives for people with families to move, it's a Treasury reg. Regulation. If you're single, though, you stop even unpacking.

'It's hard to meet women in the Service. It's not the most popular. There's a joke; can I tell it?'

Q.

'You meet a woman you like at, like, a party. She goes, what do you do. You go, I'm in finance. She goes, what kind. You go, sort of a type of accounting, it's a long story. She says, oh, who for. You go, the government. She goes, city, state? You go, federal. She goes, oh, what branch. You go, US Treasury. On it goes, narrowing down. At some point she figures it out, what you're dancing around, and she's gone.'

928874551

'Sugar in a cake has several different functions. One, for instance, is to absorb moisture from the butter, or perhaps shortening, and release it slowly over time, keeping the cake moist. Using less sugar than the recipe calls for produces what's known as a dry cake. Don't do that.'

973876118

'Suppose you think along the lines of power, authority. Inevitability. You've got your two kinds of people now, when you get down to it. On one hand you've got your rebel mentality whose whole bag or groove or what have you is going against power, rebelling. Your spit-in-the-wind type that feels powerful going against the power and the Establishment and what have you. Then, type two, you've got your other type, which is the soldier personality, the type that believes in order and power and respects authority and aligns themselves with power and authority and the side of order and the way the whole thing has got to work if the system's going to run smoothly. So imagine you're a type two type. There's more than they think. The age of the rebel is over. It's the eighties now. If You're a Type Two, We Want You — that should be their slogan. In the Service. Check out the blowing wind, man. Join up with the side that *always* gets paid. We shit you not. The side of the law and the force of the law, the side of the tide and gravity and that one law where everything always gradually gets a little hotter until the sun up and blows. Because you got your two unavoidables in life, just like they say. Unavoidability — now that's power, man. Either be a mortician or join the Service, if you want to line yourself up with the real power. Have the wind at your back. Tell them listen: Spit *with* the wind, it goes a whole lot further. You can trust me on that, my man.'

917229047

'I had an idea I'd try and write a play. Our stepmother always went to plays; she'd drag us all down to the civic center all the time on weekends for matinees. So I got to know all about the theater and plays. So this play, because they'd ask me — family, fellows at the driving range — to give an idea what it was like. It would be a totally real, true-to-life play. It would be unperformable, that was part of the point. This is to give you an idea. The idea's that a wiggler, a rote examiner, is sitting poring over 1040s and attachments and cross-filed W-2s and 1099s and like that. The setting is very bare and minimalistic — there's nothing to look at except this wiggler, who doesn't move except for every so often turning a page or making a note on his pad. It's not a Tingle — it's just a regular desk, so you can see him. But that's it. At first there was a clock behind him, but I cut the clock. He sits there longer and longer until the audience gets more and more bored and restless, and finally they start leaving, first just a few and then the whole audience, whispering to each other how boring and terrible the play is. Then, once the audience have all left, the real action of the play can start. This was the idea—I told my stepmom all about it, it was going to be a realistic play. Except I could never decide on the action, if there was any, if it's a realistic play. That's what I tell them. It's the only way to explain it.'

965882433

'There have been frequent studies. Two-thirds of taxpayers think an exemption and a deduction are the same thing. Don't know what a capital gain is. Four percent every year don't sign their returns. Shit, two-thirds of people don't know how many senators a state has. Something like three-quarters can't name the branches of government. This is not rocket science we're doing here. The truth is, most of our time is wasted. The system kicks us mostly shit. You spend ten minutes filling out a 20-C on an unsigned return, it goes back to the

SC, a bullshit letter audit requesting a signature, nothing at stake. And then now in Rotes we're reviewed on the basis of increased revenue from audits down the line. It's a joke. Most of the stuff we're looking at isn't auditable, it's just rank stupidity. Carelessness. You should see people's handwriting—average people, educated people. The truth is, they waste our time. They need a better system.'

981472509

'Tate is a moth at the arc lights of power. Pass it on.'

951458221

'It's a fascinating question. The background is interesting, if you delve into it. Type of thing. One of the tenets of the incoming administration was the belief that marginal tax rates could be lowered, especially in the top brackets, without causing a catastrophic loss of revenue. This had been an explicit part of the campaign. Platform type of thing. I'm no economist. I know the theory was that lower marginal rates would spur investment and increased productivity, type of thing, and there would be a rising tide that would cause an increase in the tax base that would more than off-

set the decrease in marginal rates. There is a whole
technical theory behind this, though some dismissed this as voodoo science. Type of thing. By
late in the first year, sure enough, the regs are different, the top brackets are lowered. It goes on that
way. By, say, two years in, though, it's fair to say
the results contradicted the theory. Revenues were
down, and these were hard numbers that could
not be fudged or massaged. There were also, I
believe, very large increases in defense spending,
and the federal budget deficit was the greatest in
history. In adjusted dollars type of thing. You have
to understand that this was all playing out at a far
higher level of government than the level we're
working at here. But anyone could understand the
budget problems were a real rock-and-hard-place
type of thing, since backpedaling and raising marginal rates again was politically unacceptable,
ideologically you could say, as was compromising
on the military, and gutting social spending any
further would make relations with Congress
unworkable. Type of thing. All of this one could
almost know just from reading the newspaper, if
you knew what to look for.'

Q.

'Yes, but in terms of what we knew here, at our
level here in the Service. Some of it was not in the

papers. I know the executive branch had several different plans and proposals they were considering, to address this problem. The deficits, the hard place. My sense is that most of these were not appealing. Type of thing. Understand, all this is filtering down from a great height, administratively. The version we got here on the regional level is that someone very high up in the Service's structure, someone close to what's known around here as the Three-Personed God, resurrected a policy paper originally written in either 1969 or 1970 by a macroeconomist or systems consultant on the staff of the former Assistant Commissioner for Planning and Research at Triple-Six. The one that resurrected it was, under this account, an Assistant Deputy Commissioner for Systems, which by that time had absorbed the Planning and Research Branch as now a division of Systems in a reorganization, Systems had, type of thing, although that previous Planning and Research AC was also now the DCS.'

Q.

'Now meaning in terms of when the Spackman Memo was resurrected, which was in or around the fourth quarter of 1981.'

Q.

'The DCS is part of what's known as the Three-

Personed God, the [inaudible] term for the top triad of Commissioner, Deputy Commissioner for Systems, and Chief Counsel. The three top spots in the Service organization. The national office of the Service is known as Triple-Six because of the address. Type of thing.'

Q.

'These types of high-level proposals and white papers are generated all the time. Planning and Research has what amounts to think tanks type of thing. This is common knowledge. Full-time teams exclusively tasked to generating long-range studies and proposals. There's a famous policy paper from a P&R group in the 1960s, type of thing, on the implementation of tax protocols following a nuclear exchange. Called "Fiscal Planning for Chaos," which became rather a famous term around here, a kind of joke when things became hectic, chaos type of thing. Overall, few of them are made public. From the mid-sixties. Your tax dollar at work type of thing. This one that was resurrected in this context, though, was far less grand or explosive. I don't know its precise title. Sometimes it's known as the Spackman Memo or the Spackman Initiative, but I know of no one that knows who the eponymous Spackman was, type of thing, whether he was the author of the policy paper or the P&R official for whom the thing was written. It was generated, after all, in 1969, which was lifetimes ago in the institutional life of the Service. Most of them get filed away, type of thing. Understand, this is a compartmented agency. Many of the procedures and priorities of Triple-Six are simply out of our area. Type of thing. The Initiative's reorganizations, though, affect us directly, as I'm sure someone has explained. The original paper was said to be several hundred pages in length and very technical, as economics tends to be. Type of thing. But on a general level, the effective principle of the part or parts that came to later light was said to be quite simple, and it—[inaudible]—through routes unknown, it came to the attention of parties at the very highest levels of either the Service or the Treasury Department, and created interest because, in the budgetary impasse of the current executive branch, it appeared to describe a politically more appealing way to ameliorate the rock-and-hard-place of unexpectedly low tax revenues, high defense outlays, and an uncuttable base floor in social spending. At root, type of thing, the paper's proposal was said to be very simple, and of course the current executive approves of simplicity, arguably because this administration is somewhat of a reaction type of thing, or backlash, against the complex social engineering of the Great Society, which was a very different era for tax policy and administration. But its preference for simple, instinctive arguments is common knowledge. Type of thing. By the way, I can't help noticing you're wincing.'

Q.

'By all means.'

Q.

'As we understood it, the Spackman paper's root observation was that increasing the efficiency with which the Service enforced the extant tax code could provably increase net revenues to the US Treasury without any corresponding change in the code or a raising in marginal rates. Type of thing. Meaning it directed attention to Compliance and the tax gap. Should I define the gap, type of thing? Is this already defined by someone else? Are you asking everyone the same type of thing for this? Would the Service prefer that I not go into this?'

Q.

'I suppose it's self-evident, type of thing. It's the difference between total tax revenues lawfully due the US Treasury in a given year and total taxes actually collected by the Service in that year. It is rarely spoken of openly, largely [inaudible]. It is now the *bête noir* type of thing of the Service's

focus. Though not at the time. It had been estimated, in the Spackman paper, that between six
and seven billion dollars lawfully due the US Treasury in 1968 had not been remitted. Spackman's
econometric projections placed the tax-gap figure
for 1980 at close to twenty-seven billion, which
appeared, by the time of the paper's resurrection,
to be overly optimistic. Excluding appeals and litigation, the measured tax gap for 1980 was actually
in excess of thirty-one and a half billion dollars.
What was remarkable was that the tax gap's size
had not been much remarked on or made the
object of serious attention. I believe this is why it's
rarely spoken of openly, the institutional stupidity
of this, type of thing. Or that this is why the
Spackman paper never received serious attention,
although as I said, policy papers like this are generated by Systems all the time. Institutions can be
much less intelligent than the individuals that
make them up. Type of thing. There's also the fact
that the Service is concerned to have the taxpaying
public see it as nothing but a completely efficient,
all-knowing instrument of tax collection—there
are complex psychodynamics involved in taxation
and the public's willingness to comply with tax
law. For one thing, too much efficiency can be
misconstrued as hostility, excessive aggression

type of thing, which increases TP hostility and can actually negatively affect the public's compliance and the Service's mandate and budget, type of thing. Meaning the whole matter is complex, type of thing, and the psychodynamics are outside our area, and my understanding of it all is quite vague and general, type of thing, though we know that it is a matter of considerable interest and study at Triple-Six. Spackman's report, the subsection of interest, was resurrected by some person or persons close to the Three-Personed God. There are conflicting versions as to just whom. Type of thing. I'm speaking of a period roughly two and a half years ago.'

Q.

'At root, according to the policy paper, the gap was a matter of compliance. Type of thing. Obviously — since the gap represented a given percentage of noncompliance. But the subsection of the memo of interest concerned the parts of the tax gap that could be profitably addressed by the Service. Reduced, ameliorated. Type of thing. Meaning heightened revenue. A certain portion of the annual tax gap was due to an underground cash economy, barter mechanisms and in-kind exchanges, illicit income, and certain very sophisticated tax-avoidance mechanisms for the wealthy that could not be addressed in the short term. But Spackman's paper's analysis argued that a significant portion of the gap was the result of remediable misreporting, including Individual Forms 1040, which he argued could be addressed and ameliorated in the short term. The short term, for understandable reasons, the current administration was particularly keen on. Hence the intersection of technical policy and politics, which is how change occurs at the national level, then trickles down to us in the trenches, type of thing, through reorganizations and changes in Performance Review criteria, since 1040s are the purview of Rote Exams. Should I explain the different areas and types of examinations done here?'

Q.

'Not at all. On a root level, Spackman's memo broke the remediable, 1040-related portions of the tax gap down into three broad areas, categories, type of thing—nonfiling, underreporting, and underpayment. Nonfiling, in most cases, is the purview of CID. Criminal Investigations. Underpayment is handled through the Collections Division, a very different outfit, both philosophically and operationally, from what we do here in Exams, type of thing, although our two divisions, Exams and Collections, along, of course, with Audits, form the brunt of the Initiative. Which is also, organizationally, the Compliance Branch. At root, as examiners, we here deal with underreporting. Type of thing. Understated income, invalid deductions, overstated expenses, improperly claimed credits. Discrepancies, type—'

Q.

'At the root level, the argument of the Spackman Initiative, as it's come to be called here, both philosophically and organizationally, was that these three elements of the tax gap could be ameliorated by increasing the efficiency of the IRS respecting compliance. It's not difficult to see why this notion caught the political administration's eye as a potential third option, a way to help address the increasingly untenable revenue shortfall without raising rates or cutting outlays. Type of thing. Needless to say, this is all very simplified. I am attempting to explain the extraordinary developments that have taken place in the structure and operations of the Service as we here at the regional level experience it. It has been, to say the least, an unusually exciting year. And the root cause of the excitement, and also a certain amount of controversy, is the Spackman Initiative. This is what it came to be called. A sweeping, far-reaching reorientation in the Service's institutional sense of

itself and its role in policy. Type of thing. Listen —
are you all right?'

Q. [Pause, interval of static.]

'— of thing, which Triple-Six also found advan-
tageous, argued that, under certain technical conditions, each dollar added to the Service's annual
budget could be made to yield over sixteen dollars
in additional revenue to Treasury. A good deal of
this argument's body was devoted to considering
the IRS's peculiar status and function as a federal
agency. A federal agency is, by definition, an institution. A bureaucracy. But the Service was also the
only agency in the federal apparatus whose function was revenue. Income. Meaning whose mandate was to maximize the legal return on each
dollar invested in its annual budget. Type of thing.
More than any other, then, according to the resurrected Spackman, there was compelling reason
to conceive, constitute, and operate the IRS as a
business — a going, for-profit concern type of
thing — rather than as an institutional bureaucracy.
At root, the Spackman report was intensely anti-
bureaucratic. Its model was more classically free-
market. The attractiveness of this to the free-market
conservatives of the current administration should
be understandable. This, after all, is an era of business deregulation. How best, and how much, to in

a sense deregulate the IRS—which, of course, as a federal agency, was set up and operates as a set of legal regulations and mechanisms for enforcement— this was a thorny and still-evolving type of question type of thing. Some saw Spackman as an ideologue. Not every proposal in the original paper was resurrected—not everything became part of the Initiative. But the time was right, politically speaking, type of thing, for at least the root essence of Spackman's proposal. It would be difficult to overemphasize the consequences of this shift in philosophy and mandate for those of us on the ground of the effort. The Initiative. For example, an intensive new recruitment and hiring effort and an almost 20 percent increase in Service personnel, the first such increase since TRA '78. I refer also to a massive and seemingly endless restructuring of the Service's Compliance Branch, the most relevant [inaudible] of which to us here was the fact that the seven Regional Commissioners have assumed more autonomy and authority under the more de-decentralized operational philosophy of the Spackman Initiative.'

Q.

'This is another complicated subject, one that involves an extensive knowledge of US tax law and the history of the Service as part of the executive branch and yet also overseen by Congress. A critical part of what's now known as the Spackman Initiative involved finding an efficient middle way between two opposing tendencies that had hampered the Service's operations for decades, one being the decentralization mandated by the 1952 King Commission in Congress, the other being the extreme bureaucratic and political centrism of the national administration at Triple-Six. One could say that the 1960s was an era, speaking within the institutional history of the Service, in which the District office predominated. The 1980s is shaping itself to be the era of the Region. Type of thing. As an organizational middle ground between the many Districts and unitary Triple-Six administration. Administrative, structural, logistical, and procedural decisions are now far more in the hands of the Regional Commissioner and his deputies, that, in turn, delegate responsibilities according to flexible but coherent operational guidelines, type of thing, which results in more root autonomy for the centers.'

Q.

'Each Region including one Service Center and, with one current exception, one Examination Center. Shall I explain the exception?'

Q.

'At root, under the Initiative, Regional Service and Examination Centers are allowed considerably more latitude in structure, personnel, systems, and operations protocols, resulting in increased authority and responsibility on the part of these facilities' Directors. The guiding idea is to free these large central processing facilities from oppressive or hidebound regulations which impede effective action. Type of thing. At the same time, extreme pressure is applied with respect to one and only one primary, overarching goal: results. Increased revenue. Reduced noncompliance. Reduction of the gap. Not quite quotas, of course—never that, of course, for reasons involving fairness and public perception—but close. We've all watched the news, you and I, and yes, more aggressive auditing is part of the picture. Type of thing. But the shifts and emphases in the Audits Divisions are largely changes of degree, a quantitative type of thing—including the advent of automated letter audits, which again is outside our area of working knowledge here. For us, however, in Examinations, there has been a dramatic, qualitative shift in operational philosophy and protocols. It can be felt by the lowliest GS-9 at her keypunch console. If Audits are the Initiative's

197

weapon, type of thing, we in Exams are the telemetrists, tasked with determining where best to point that weapon. As deregulated, there is now only one overriding operational question: Which returns are most profitable to audit, and how are those returns most efficiently to be found?'

947676541
'I have an unusually high tolerance for pain.'

928514387
'Well, my dad used to like to mow the lawn in little patches and strips. He'd do the east corner of the front yard, come in the house for a while, then do the southwest strip of the back lawn and a little square at the south fence, come back in, and like that. He had a lot of little rituals like that, it's how he was. You know? It took a while to realize he did this with the lawn because he liked the feeling of being done. Of having a job and feeling like he did it and it was done. It's a solid little feeling, it's like you're a machine that knows it's running well and doing what it was made to do. You know? By dividing the lawn into like seventeen small little sections, which our mom thought was nuts as usual, he could feel the feeling of finishing a job seventeen times instead of just once. Like, "I'm done. I'm done again. Again, hey look, I'm done."'

'Well, some of the same thing is at work here. In Rotes. I like it. An average 1040 takes around twenty-two minutes to go through and examine and fill out the memo on. Maybe a little longer depending on your criteria, some teams tweak the criteria. You know. But never more than half an hour. Each completed one gives you that solid little feeling.

'The thing here is that the returns never stop. There's always a next one to do. You never really finish. But on the other hand, it was the same with the lawn, you know? At least when it rained enough. By the time he got around to the last little section he'd marked off, the first patch would be ready to mow again. He liked a short, groomed-looking lawn. He spent a lot of time out there, come to think of it. A lot of his time.'

951876833

'It was on either *Twilight Zone* or *Outer Limits*—one of those. A claustrophobic guy who gets worse and worse until he's so claustrophobic that he starts screaming and carrying on, and they trundle him off to a mental asylum, and in the asylum they put him in isolation in a straitjacket in a tiny little room with a drain in the floor, a room the size of a closet, which you can see would be the worst thing possible for a claustrophobic, but they explain to him through a slit in the door that it's the rules and procedures, that if somebody's screaming they have to be put in isolation. Hence, the guy's damned, he's in there for life — because as long as he's screaming and trying to beat himself unconscious against the wall of the room, they're going to keep him in that little room, and as long as he's in that little room, he's going to be screaming, because the whole problem is that he's a claustrophobic. He's a living example of how there has to be some slack or play in the rules and procedures for certain cases, or else sometimes there's going to be some ridiculous foul-up and someone's going to be in a living hell. The episode was even called "Rules and Procedures," and none of us ever forgot it.'

987613397

'I don't believe I have anything to say that isn't in the code or Manual.'

943756788

'Mother called it being in a stare. She referred to my father in this, a habit he had in the midst of almost whatever. He was a kindly individual, a bookkeeper for the school district. Being in a stare referred to staring fixedly and without expression at something for extensive periods of time. It can happen when you haven't had enough sleep, or too much sleep, or if you've overeaten, or are distracted, or merely daydreaming. It is not daydreaming, however, because it involves gazing at something. Staring at it. Usually something straight ahead—a shelf on a bookcase, or the centerpiece on the dining room table, or your daughter or child. But in a stare, you are not really looking at this thing you are seeming to stare at, you are not even really noticing it—however, neither are you thinking of something else. You in truth are not doing anything, mentally, but you are doing it fixedly, with what appears to be intent concentration. It is as if one's concentration becomes stuck the way an auto's wheels can be stuck in the snow, turning rapidly without going forward, although it looks like intent concentration. And now I too do this. I find myself doing it. It's not unpleasant, but it is strange. Something goes out of you—you can feel your face merely hanging loose, with no muscles or expression. It frightens my children, I know. As if your face, like your attention, belongs to someone else. Sometimes now in the mirror, in the bathroom, I'll come to myself and catch myself in a stare, without any recognition. The man has been dead for twelve years now.

'This is the new challenge of it here. From out-side the examiner, there was no guarantee that anyone could distinguish the difference between doing the job well and being in what she called the stare, staring at the returns files but not engaged by them, not truly paying attention. So long as you processed your given number of returns each day for throughput, they could not be sure. Not that I did this, my being in stares occurs after the day here, or before, when preparing. But I know they would worry: Who is the good examiner, and who is fooling them, spending their day in a stare, or thinking of other things. This can happen. But now, this year, they can know, they know who is doing the job. It becomes true later, the difference. Because they now log your eventuated revenue instead of your throughput. This is the change for us. Now it is easier, we are looking for something, what will cause ER, not just how many returns can one put through. This helps us pay attention.'

984057863

'Our house was outside of the city, off one of the blacktop roads. We had us a big dog that my daddy would keep on a chain in the front yard. A big part German shepherd. I hated the chain but we didn't have a fence, we were right off the road there. The dog hated that chain. But he had dignity. What he'd do, he'd never go out to the length of the chain. He'd never even get out to where the chain got tight. Even if the mailman pulled up, or a salesman. Out of dignity, this dog pretended like he chose this one area to stay in that just happened to be inside the length of the chain. Nothing outside of that area right there interested him. He just had zero interest. So he never noticed the chain. He didn't hate it. The chain. He just up and made it not relevant. Maybe he wasn't pretending— maybe he really up and chose that little circle for his own world. He had a power to him. All of his life on that chain. I loved that damn dog.'

§15

An obscure but true piece of paranormal trivia: There is such a thing as a *fact psychic*. Sometimes in the literature also known as a *data mystic,* and the syndrome itself as *RFI* (= *Random-Fact Intuition*). These subjects' sudden flashes of insight or awareness are structurally similar to but usually far more tedious and quotidian than the dramatically relevant foreknowledge we normally conceive as ESP or precognition. This, in turn, is why the phenomenon is so little studied or publicized, and why those possessed of RFI almost universally refer to it as an affliction or disability. In what few reputable studies and monographs exist, examples nevertheless abound; indeed, abundance, together with irrelevance and the interruption of normal thought and attention, composes the essence of the RFI phenomenon. The middle name of the childhood friend of a stranger they pass in a hallway. The fact that someone they sit near in a movie was once sixteen cars behind them on I-5 near McKittrick CA on a warm, rainy October day in 1971. They come out of nowhere, are inconvenient and discomfiting like all psychic irruptions. It's just that they're ephemeral, useless, undramatic, distracting. What Cointreau tasted like to someone with a mild head cold on the esplanade of Vienna's state opera house on 2 October 1874. How many people faced southeast to witness Guy Fawkes's hanging in 1606. The number of frames in *Breathless*. That someone named Fangi or Fangio won the 1959 Grand Prix. The percentage of Egyptian deities that have animal faces instead of human faces. The length and average circumference of Defense Secretary Caspar Weinberger's small intestine. The exact (not estimated) height of Mount Erebus, though not what or where Mount Erebus is.

In the case of GS-9 fact psychic Claude Sylvanshine on, say, 12 July 1981, the precise metric weight and speed of a train moving southwest through Prešov, Czechoslovakia, at the precise moment he's supposed to be crosschecking 1099-INT receipts with the tax return of Edmund and

Willa Kosice, whose home's shutters were replaced in 1978 by someone whose wife once won three rounds of bingo in a row at St. Bridget's Church in Troy MI, even though the Kosices' residential address is Urbandale IA—reason for RFI incongruity unknown to Sylvanshine, for whom the factoids are just one more distraction he has to shake off in the noise and overall frenzied low morale of the Philadelphia REC. Then the Toltec god of corn, except in Toltec glyphs, so that to Sylvanshine it looks like an abstract drawing of origin unknown. The winner of the 1950 Nobel Prize in physiology slash medicine.

Datum: At least one-third of ancient rulers' seers and magicians were in fact fired or killed early in their tenure because it emerged that the bulk of what they foresaw or intuited was irrelevant. Not incorrect, just irrelevant, pointless. The human appendix's real reason. Norbert Wiener's name for the little leather ball that was his only friend as a sickly child. The number of blades of grass in the front lawn of one's mailman's home. They intrude, crash, rattle around. One reason Sylvanshine's gaze is always so intent and discomfiting is that he's trying to filter out all sorts of psychically intuited and intrusive facts. The amount of parenchyma in a certain fern in the waiting room of an orthodontist in Athens GA, though not and never what parenchyma might be. That the 1938 featherweight WBA champ had mild scoliosis in the region T10-12. Nor does he look it up — you don't chase these facts down; they're like lures that lead you nowhere. He's learned this from hard experience. The rate in astronomical units with which System ML435 is moving away from the Milky Way. He tells no one of the intrusions. Some are connected, but rarely in any way that yields what someone with true ESP would call meaning. The metric weight of all the lint in all the pockets of everyone at the observatory in Fort Davis TX on the 1974 day when a scheduled eclipse was obscured by clouds. Perhaps one in every four thousand such facts is relevant or help-ful. Most are like having someone sing 'The Star-Spangled Banner' in your ear while you're trying to recite a poem for a prize. Claude Sylvanshine can't help it. That someone he passes in the street's great-great-great-grandmother's baby sister who died of whooping cough in 1844's name was Hes-per. The cost, in adjusted dollars, of that obscured eclipse; the FCC broadcasting license of the Chris-tian station the observatory's director listened to as he drove home, where he'd find his wife frazzled and the milkman's hat on the kitchen counter.

The shape of the clouds on the afternoon two people he's never met conceived their child, who was miscarried six weeks in. That the pioneer of pullable consumer luggage was the ex-husband of a People Express stew who'd spent over eighteen months driving himself almost insane trying to research luggage manufacturing specs and pending patent applications because he couldn't believe no one had thought of mass-marketing this feature already. The USPTO registration number of the machine that attached the paper housing to the milkman's hat. The average molecular weight of peat. The affliction kept a secret from everyone everywhere since fourth grade when Sylvanshine knew the name of his homeroom teacher's husband's first love's childhood cat who'd lost one side's whiskers in a mishap near the coal stove in Ashtabula OH, verified only when he wrote a little illustrated booklet and the husband saw the name and whiskerless crayon drawing of Scrapper, turned ivory white, and dreamed intensely for three nights, unknown to anyone.

The fact psychic lives part-time in the world of fractious, boiling minutiae that no one knows or could be bothered to know even if they had the chance to know. The population of Brunei. The difference between mucus and sputum. How long

a piece of gum has resided on the underside of
the third-row fourth-from-left seat of the Virginia
Theater, Cranston RI, but not who put it there
or why. Impossible to predict what facts will
intrude. Constant headaches. The data sometimes
visual and queerly backlit, as by an infinitely bright
light an infinite distance away. The amount of
undigested red meat in the colon of the average
forty-three-year-old adult male resident of Ghent,
Belgium, in grams. The relation between the Turkish lira and the Yugoslavian dinar. The year of
death for undersea explorer William Beebe.

Tastes a Hostess cupcake. Knows where it was
made; knows who ran the machine that sprayed a
light coating of chocolate frosting on top; knows
that person's weight, shoe size, bowling average,
American Legion career batting average; he knows
the dimensions of the room that person is in right
now. Overwhelming.

§16

Lane Dean Jr. and two older examiners from a different Pod are outside one of the unalarmed door exits between Pods, on a hexagram of cement surrounded by maintained grass, watching the sun on the fallow fields just south of the REC. None of them are smoking; they're just being outside for a bit. Lane Dean hasn't come outside with the other two; he just happened to step out for air on the break at the same time. He's still looking for a really desirable, diverting place to go during breaks; they're too important. The other two guys know each other or work on the same team; they've come out together; one senses it's a routine of long standing.

One of the men gives a sort of artificial-looking gap

and stretch. 'Jeez,' he says. 'Well, Midge and I went over to the Bodnars' on Saturday. You know Hank Bodnar, from over in K-team at Capital Exams, with the glasses with the lenses that turn dark by themselves outside, what are they called.' The man has his hands behind his back and goes up and down on his toes rapidly, like someone waiting for a bus.

'Uh-huh.' The other man, who's perhaps five years younger than the man who went to the Bodnars', is contemplating some kind of benign cyst or growth on the inside of his wrist. The heat is accumulating at mid-morning, and the electric sound of the locusts in the wild grasses rises and falls in the parts of the fields the sun is striking. Neither man has introduced himself to Lane Dean, who's standing farther from them than they are from each other, though not so far away that he could be seen as wholly disconnected from the conversation. Maybe they're giving him privacy because they can see he's new and still adjusting to the unbelievable tedium of the exam job. Maybe they're shy and awkward and not sure how to introduce themselves. Lane Dean, whose slacks have ridden up so far he'd have to go into a stall in a men's room to extract them, feels like running out into the fields in the heat and running in circles and flapping his arms.

'We were supposed to go over the weekend before, the what, the seventh that would be,' the first man says, looking out at a vista with nothing really particular to hold the eye, 'but our youngest had a temperature and a little bit of a sore throat, and Midge didn't want to leave her with the sitter if she had a temperature. So she called to cancel, and Midge and Alice Bodnar worked it out so we all just moved it up a week, seven days to the day, that way it was easy to remember. You know how mama bears get when their little cubs run a temperature.'

'Don't have to tell me,' Lane Dean inserts from several feet away, laughing a little too heartily. One shoe is in the shadow of the pod's overhang and one is in the morning sun. Lane Dean is starting now to feel desperate about the fact that the break's fifteen minutes are ticking inexorably away and he is going to have to go back in and examine returns for another two hours before the next break. There's an empty Styrofoam cup on its side in the ashtray unit of a small waste can in the alcove. Being in a conversation makes the time pass differently; it's not clear whether it's better or worse. The other man is still examining his wrist's thing, holding the forearm up like a surgeon after scrubbing. If you think of the locusts as actually screaming, the whole thing becomes much more unsettling. The normal protocol is not to hear them; they cease to register on you after a while.

'So anyhow,' the first examiner says. 'We go over, have a drink. Midge and Alice Bodnar get to talking about some new drapes they're looking at for the living room, on and on. Pretty dry stuff, wife stuff. So Hank and me end up in the den, because Hank he collects coins — seriously, he's a serious coin collector from what I could see, not just those cardboard albums with circular holes, he really knows his business. And he wanted to show me a picture of a coin he was thinking about acquiring, for his collection.' The other man had looked up for the first real time when the guy telling the story mentioned coin collecting, which is a hobby that to Lane Dean, as a Christian, has always seemed debased and distorted in a number of ways.

'A nickel, I think,' the first fellow is saying. He keeps lapsing into what seems like almost talking to himself, while the second man starts and stops examining the growth thing. You get the idea that this is the sort of interchange the two men have had on breaks for many, many years — it's such a habit it's not even conscious anymore. 'Not a buffalo nickel, but some kind of five-cent piece with an alternate backing that's well-known; I don't know much about coins but even I'd heard of it, which means it must be pretty well-known. But I can't think of the correct term for it.' He laughs in a way that sounds almost pained. 'Right out of my head. I can't remember it now.'

'Alice Bodnar's a pretty good little cook,' the other fellow says. The plastic tabs of a light-brown clip-on tie show slightly around his shirt's collar. The knot of the tie itself is tight as a knuckle; there'd be no way to loosen it. From where he stands, Lane Dean has a better, more circumspect view of this second examiner. The growth on the inside of his wrist is the size of a child's nose and composed of what looks almost like horn or hard, outgrowthy material, and appears reddened and slightly inflamed, though this may be because the second fellow picks at it so much. How could one not? Lane Dean knows that he might well become sickeningly fixated on the man's wrist's thing if they worked at adjoining Tingles in the same Pod — trying to look at it without being observed, making resolutions not to look at it, etc. It slightly appalls him that he almost envies whoever is at that table, imagines the reddened cyst and its career as an object of distraction and attention, something to hoard the way a crow hoards shiny useless things it happens to find, even strips of aluminum foil or little bits of a locket's broken chain. He feels an odd desire to ask the man about the growth, what is its deal, how long, etc. It's happened, just as the man said: Lane Dean no longer needs to look at his watch on breaks. There are now six minutes left.

'Jeez, well, there was a whole plan to poach some salmon fillets and eat out on the porch with the salmon with this special little sage glaze Midge and Alice wanted to make up and scalloped potatoes — I think scalloped; maybe you call them au gratin. And a big salad, so big you couldn't pass the bowl around, even; it had to be on a little separate table.'

The second man is now carefully rolling his shirtsleeve down and buttoning it back over the wrist with the thing, though when he sits over returns and the sleeve pulls back slightly Dean bets that the rim of the cyst's red penumbra will still show slightly over the cuff, and that the cuff's movement back and forth over the growth throughout the examination day might be part of what makes it look red and sore — it might hurt in a tiny, sickening way each time the man's cuff pulls forward or back over the little growth of horn.

'But it was such a nice day. Hank and I were in the den, that has a set of those large types of windows that look out over part of the front lawn and the street; there were some neighborhood kids riding bicycles up and down the street and yelling and just having a hell of a time. We decided, Hank did, what the hell, it's such a hell of a nice day, let's see if the girls want to barbecue. So we got out Hank's grill, a big Weber model with wheels that you could roll it out if you leaned it backwards; there were three legs but only two with wheels — you know what I'm talking about.'

The second man leans out and spits neatly through his teeth into the grass at the edge of the hexagram. He's maybe forty, silver hairs in the hair on the side of his head in the sun, Lane Dean can see. Lane Dean imagines running out into the field in an enormous circle, flapping his arms like Roddy McDowall.

'So we did, wheeled it out,' the first man says. 'And barbecued the salmon instead of poaching it, though everything else was the same, and Midge and Alice talked about where they got the salad bowl, that had all these little carvings around up near the rim, the thing had to weigh five pounds. Hank grilled them on the patio, and we ate there on the porch because of the bugs.'

'What do you mean?' Lane Dean asks, aware of the slight edge of hysteria in his voice.

'Why,' says the first, heavier guy, 'the sun was going down. The skeeters come down off the golf course out by Fairhaven. No way we're going to sit out on the patio, get eaten alive. Nobody even had to say anything about it.' The man sees Lane Dean still looking at him, his head cocked exaggeratedly in a curiosity he didn't one bit feel.

'Well, it's a screen porch.' The second man is looking at Lane Dean like, who is this guy?

The man who'd eaten supper at the other people's house laughs. 'Best of both worlds. A screen porch.'

'Unless it rains,' the second man says. Both of them laugh ruefully.

§17

'I'd always from early on as a child I think somehow imagined Revenue men as like those certain kinds of other institutional heroes, bureaucratic, small-*h* heroes—like police, firemen, Social Service workers, Red Cross and VISTA people, the people who keep the records at SSI, even certain kinds of clergy and religious volunteers—trying to stitch or bandage the holes that all the more selfish, glitzy, uncaring, "Me-First" people are always making in the community. I mean more like police and fire department office and clerical personnel rather than the ones who everyone knows about and get in the newspaper for what they do. I don't mean the kind of heroes that "put their lives on the line." I suppose what I'm saying is that there are other kinds. I wanted to be one. The kind that seemed even more heroic because nobody applauded or even thought about them, or if they did it was usually as some enemy. The sort of person who's on the Clean Up Committee instead of playing in the band at the dance or being there with the prom queen, if you know what I mean. The quiet kind who cleans up and does the dirty job. You know.'

§18

'And Desk Names are back. This is another plus under Glendenning. Nothing against the Pale King, but the consensus is that Mr. Glendenning is more agent-morale-oriented, and Desk Names are one example.'

[Off-camera prompt.]

'Well, they're just what it says. Instead of your name. There's a plate on your desk with your Desk Name. Your Name de Gear as they say. No more worrying some burger whose shoes you maybe have to squeeze a little bit knows your name, maybe they find out where you and your family live—don't think this isn't on an agent's mind.'

[Off-camera prompt.]

'Though it's not exactly like before the Pale King.

It got out of hand, there's no denying. There's no obvious joke Desk Names now. Which to be honest got old fast and nobody misses; nobody wants a taxpayer thinking he's silly. We are far from silly around here. No more Phil Mypockets or Mike Hunt or Seymour Booty. Although nobody least of all Mr. Glendenning says you can't still use the Desk Name as a tool. In the great battle for the hearts and minds. If you're smart, you'll use it as a tool. We rotate; seniority chooses the plate. This quarter, my Desk Name is Eugene Fusz — you can see it right on the nameplate here. They look pretty good now. One type of tool is you use a Desk Name where the subject isn't sure how to pronounce it. Is it like *fuse,* is it like *fuss,* is it like *fuzz?* The burger sure doesn't want to offend you. Other good ones are Fuchs, Traut, Wiener, Ojerkis, Büger, Tünivich, Schoewder, Wënkopf. There's over forty-three plates extant. La Bialle, Bouhel. Umlauts are always good; umlauts seem to drive them especially nuts. It's just one more little off-balance tactic. Plus a small little smile on a gray day and so forth and so on. Hanratty applied for a Peanys plate for third quarter — it's under review, Mr. Rosebury said. There's a line, after all, under Glendenning. This is about revenue. It ain't exactly the Chuckle Hut we're running here.'

§19

'There's something very interesting about civics and selfishness, and we get to ride the crest of it. Here in the US, we expect government and law to be our conscience. Our superego, you could say. It has something to do with liberal individualism, and something to do with capitalism, but I don't understand much of the theoretical aspect—what I see is what I live in. Americans are in a way crazy. We infantilize ourselves. We don't think of ourselves as citizens—parts of something larger to which we have profound responsibilities. We think of ourselves as citizens when it comes to our rights and privileges, but not our responsibilities. We abdicate our civic responsibilities to the government and expect the government, in effect, to legislate morality. I'm talking mostly about economics and business, because that's my area.'

'What do we do to stop the decline?'

'I have no idea what we do. As citizens we cede more and more of our autonomy, but if we the government take away the citizens' freedom to cede their autonomy we're now taking away their autonomy. It's a paradox. Citizens are constitutionally empowered to choose to default and leave the decisions to corporations and to a government we expect to control them. Corporations are getting better and better at seducing us into thinking the way they think—of profits as the *telos* and responsibility as something to be enshrined in symbol and evaded in reality. Cleverness as opposed to wisdom. Wanting and having instead of thinking and making. We cannot stop it. I suspect what'll happen is that there will be some sort of disaster—depression, hyperinflation—and then it'll be showtime: We'll either wake up and retake our freedom or we'll fall apart utterly. Like Rome—conqueror of its own people.'

'I can see taxpayers not wanting to part with money. It's a natural human thing. I didn't like getting audited either. But shit, you've got basic facts to counterbalance that — we voted these guys in, we choose to live here, we want good roads and a good army to protect us. So you ante up.'

'That's a little simplistic.'

'It seems like, suppose you're in a lifeboat with other people and there's only so much food, and you have to share it. You've only got so much and it's got to go around, and everybody's really hungry. Of course you want all the food; you're starving. But so is everybody else. If you ate all the food you couldn't live with yourself afterward.'

'The others'd kill you, too.'

'But the point is psychological. Of course you want it all, of course you want to keep every dime you make. But you don't, you ante up, because it's how things have to be for the whole lifeboat. You sort of have a duty to the others in the boat. A duty to yourself not to be the sort of person who waits till everybody is asleep and then eats all the food.'

'You're talking like a civics class.'

'Which you never had, I'm betting. What are you, twenty-eight? Did your school have civics when you were a boy? Do you even know what civics is?'

'It was a cold war thing they started in the schools. The Bill of Rights, the Constitution, the Pledge of Alliance, the importance of voting.'

'Civics is the branch of political science that quote concerns itself with citizenship and the rights and duties of US citizens.'

'*Duty*'s kind of a harsh word. I'm not saying it's their duty to pay their taxes. I'm just saying it doesn't make any sense not to. Plus we catch you.'

'I don't think this will be the conversation you want to have, but if you really want my opinion I'll tell you.'

'Fire away.'

'I think it's no accident that civics isn't taught anymore or that a young man like yourself bridles at the word *duty*.'

'We've gotten soft, you're saying.'

'I'm saying that the sixties—which God love them did a lot for raising people's consciousness in a whole lot of areas, such as race and feminism—'

'Not to mention Vietnam.'

'No, mention it, because here was a whole generation where most of them now for the first time questioned authority and said that their individual moral beliefs about the war outweighed their duty to go fight if their duly elected representatives told them to.'

'In other words that their highest actual duty was to *themselves*.'

'Well, but to themselves as *what?*'

'This all seems pretty simplistic, you guys. It's not like everybody that was protesting was doing it out of duty. It became fashionable to protest the war.'

'Neither the ultimate-duty-is-to-self element nor the fashionable element is irrelevant.'

'You're saying that protesting Vietnam led to tax cheating?'

'No, he's saying it led to the sort of selfishness that has us all trying to eat all the boat's food.'

'No, but I think whatever led to it becoming actually fashionable to protest a war opened the door to what's going to bring us down as a country. The end of the democratic experiment.'

'Did I tell you he was a conservative?'

'But that's just a put-down. There are all kinds of conservatives depending on what it is they want to conserve.'

'The sixties were America's starting to decline into decadence and selfish individualism—the Me generation.'

'There was more decadence in the twenties than there was in the sixties, though.'

'You know what I think? I think the Constitution and *Federalist Papers* of this country were an incredible moral and imaginative achievement. For really the first time in a modern nation, those in power set up a system where the citizens' power over their own government was to be a matter of substance and not mere symbolism. It was utterly priceless, and it will go down in history with Athens and the Magna Carta. The fact that it was a utopia which for two hundred years actually *worked* makes it beyond priceless — it's literally a miracle. And — and now I'm speaking of Jefferson, Madison, Adams, Franklin, the real church Fathers — what raised the American experiment beyond great imagination and made it very nearly work was not just these men's intelligence but their profound moral enlightenment — their sense of civics. The fact is that they cared more about the nation and the citizens than about themselves. They could have just set America up as an oligarchy where powerful eastern industrialists and southern landowners controlled all the power and ruled with an iron hand in a glove of liberal rhetoric. Need I say Robespierre, or the Bolsheviks, or the Ayatollah? These Founding Fathers were geniuses of civic virtue. They were heroes. Most of their effort went into restraining the power of government.'

'Checks and balances.'

'Power to the People.'

'They knew the tendency of power to corrupt —'

'Jefferson supposedly boinking his own slaves and having whole litters of mulatto children.'

'They believed that centralizing power in its dispersal among a concerned, educated, civic-minded electorate would ensure against America devolving into one more instance of nobles and peasants, rulers and serfs.'

'An educated landowning *white male* electorate, we should keep in mind.'

'And this is one of the paradoxes of the twentieth century with its apex in the sixties. Is it good to make things fairer and to allow the whole citizenry to vote? Yes, plainly so, in theory. And yet it's very easy to judge ancestors through the lens of the present instead of trying to see the world as they might have seen it. The Founding Fathers' enfranchisement of only wealthy landed educated males was designed to place power in the hands of the people most like themselves—'

'Doesn't sound all that new or experimental to me, Mr. Glendenning.'

'They believed in rationality—they believed that persons of privilege, literacy, education, and moral sophistication would be able to emulate them, to make judicious and self-disciplined decisions for the good of the nation and not just to advance their own interests.'

'It's certainly an imaginative and ingenious rationalization of racism and male chauvinism, that's for sure.'

'They were heroes, and like all true heroes they were modest and didn't regard themselves as all that exceptional. They assumed their descendants would be like them — rational, honorable, civic-minded. Men with at least as much concern for the common good as for personal advantage.'

'How did we get from the sixties to this?'

'And instead we get the dickless or crooked leaders we've got today.'

'We elect what we deserve.'

'But it's something very odd. That they could have been so prescient and farsighted about erecting checks against the accumulation of power in any one branch of government, their healthy fear of government, and yet their naive belief in the civic virtue of the common people.'

'Our leaders, our government is us, all of us, so if they're venal and weak it's because we are.'

'I hate it when you synopsize what I'm trying to say and get it wrong, but I don't quite know what to say. Because it's stronger than that. I don't think the problem is our leaders. I voted for Ford and I'll likely vote for Bush or maybe Reagan and I'll feel solid about my vote. But we see it here, with TPs. We're the government, its worst face — the rapacious creditor, the stern parent.'

'They hate us.'

'They hate the government — we're just the most convenient incarnation of what they hate. There's something very curious, though, about the hatred. The government *is* the people, leaving aside various complications, but we split it off and pretend it's not us; we pretend it's some threatening Other bent on taking our freedoms, taking our money and redistributing it, legislating our morality in drugs, driving, abortion, the environment — Big Brother, the Establishment —'

'The Man.'

'With the curious thing being that we hate it for appearing to usurp the very civic functions we've ceded to it.'

'Inverting the Founding Fathers' device of ceding political power to the people instead of the government.'

'Consent of the governed.'

'But it's gone farther than that, and the sixties idea of personal freedom and appetite and moral license has something to do with it, though I'm damned if I can quite figure it out. Only that something queer is going on in terms of civics and selfishness in this country, and we here in the Service get to see it in some of its most extreme manifestations. We now, as citizens and businessmen and consumers and what-all, we expect government and law to function as our conscience.'

'Isn't that what laws are for?'

'You mean our superego? In loco parentis?'

'It has something to do with liberal individualism, and something to do with the Constitution's overestimate of individual character, and it has something to do with consumer capitalism —'

'That's pretty vague.'

'It is vague. I'm not a political scientist. But it's not vague in its consequences; the concrete reality of its consequences is what our jobs are about.'

'But the Service has been around since long before the decadent sixties.'

'Let him finish.'

'I think Americans in 1980 are crazy. Have gone crazy. Regressed somehow.'

'The quote lack of discipline and respect for authority of the decadent seventies.'

'If you don't shut up I'm going to put you up on the roof of the elevator and you can stay there.'

'It may sound reactionary, I know. But we can all feel it. We've changed the way we think of ourselves as citizens. We don't think of ourselves as citizens in the old sense of being small parts of something larger and infinitely more important to which we have serious responsibilities. We do still think of ourselves as citizens in the sense of being beneficiaries—we're actually conscious of our rights as American citizens and the nation's responsibilities to us and ensuring we get our share of the American pie. We think of ourselves now as eaters of the pie instead of makers of the pie. So who makes the pie?'

'Ask not what your country can do for you...'

'Corporations make the pie. They make it and we eat it.'

'It's probably part of my naïveté that I don't want to put the issue in political terms when it's probably irreducibly political. Something has happened where we've decided on a personal level that it's all right to abdicate our individual responsibility to the common good and let government worry about the common good while we all go about our individual self-interested business and struggle to gratify our various appetites.'

'You can blame some of it on corporations and advertising surely.'

'I don't think of corporations as citizens, though. Corporations are machines for producing profit; that's what they're ingeniously designed to do. It's ridiculous to ascribe civic obligations or moral responsibilities to corporations.'

'But the whole dark genius of corporations is that they allow for individual reward without individual obligation. The workers' obligations are to the executives, and the executives' obligations are to the CEO, and the CEO's obligation is to the Board of Directors, and the Board's obligation is to the stockholders, who are also the same customers the corporation will screw over at the very earliest opportunity in the name of profit, which profits are distributed as dividends to the very stockholders-slash-customers they've been fucking over in their own name. It's like a fugue of evaded responsibility.'

'You're leaving out Labor Unions advocating for labor and mutual funds and the SEC's effects on share-price over basis.'

'You are a complete genius of irrelevancy, X. This isn't a seminar. DeWitt's trying to get at the heart of something here.'

'Corporations aren't citizens or neighbors or parents. They can't vote or serve in combat. They don't learn the Pledge of Allegiance. They don't have souls. They're revenue machines. I don't have any problem with that. I think it's absurd to lay moral or civic obligations on them. Their only obligations are strategic, and while they can get very complex, at root they're not civic entities. With corporations, I have no problem with government enforcement of statutes and regulatory policy serving a conscience function. What my problem is is the way it seems that we as individual citizens have adopted a corporate attitude. That our ultimate obligation is to ourselves. That unless it's illegal or there are direct practical consequences for ourselves, any activity is OK.'

'I'm regretting this conversation more and more. It—you like movies?'

'You bet.'

'Are you kidding?'

'Nothing like cozying up on a rainy evening with a Betamax and a good film.'

'Suppose it was determined that the increasing violence of US films correlated with a rise in violent-crime statistics. I mean, suppose the statistics weren't merely *suggestive* but actually demonstrated *conclusively* that the increasing number of graphically violent films like *Clockwork Orange* or *The Godfather* or *The Exorcist* had a causal correlation with the real-world rates of mayhem.'

'Let's not forget *The Wild Bunch*. Plus *Clockwork Orange* is British.'

'Shut up.'

'Define *violent,* though. Can't it mean vastly different things to different people?'

'I'll throw you off this elevator, X, I swear to God I will.'

'What would we expect the Hollywood corporations that make the movies to do? Would we really expect them to care about their films' effect on violence in the culture? We might posture and send nasty letters. But the corporations, underneath all the PR bullshit, reply that they're in business to make money for their stockholders, and that they'd give one fart in a stiff wind about what some statistics say about their products only if the government forced them to regulate the violence.'

'Which would run into some First-Amendment trouble, big-time.'

'I don't think Hollywood studios are owned by stockholders; I think the vast bulk of them are owned by parent companies.'

'*Or* if what? If ordinary moviegoing people stopped going in droves to see ultraviolent movies. The movie people can say they're only doing what corporations were designed to do—meet a demand and make as much money as is legally possible.'

'This whole conversation is dull.'

'Sometimes what's important is dull. Sometimes

it's work. Sometimes the important things aren't works of art for your entertainment, X.'

'My point is this. And I'm sorry, X, because if I knew more about what I was talking about I could make the point faster, but I'm not used to talking about it and have never been much able even to put it into words in any sort of order—the whole thing is usually more a tornado in my head as I'm driving in in the morning thinking about what's on the docket for the day. My only point on the movies is this: Would these statistics cause much of a decline in the crowds that go to see these ultraviolent movies in such droves? They wouldn't. And that's the craziness; that's what I mean. What would we do? We'd bitch at the water cooler about these damn soulless corporations who don't give a shit about the state of the nation but only care about making a buck. A few of them might write the *Journal Star*'s op-ed page or even their Congressman. There ought to be a law. Regulate it, we'd say. But come Saturday night, they'd still go see whatever damn violent movie they and the Mrs. want to see.'

'It's like they expect the government to be the parent that takes away the dangerous toy, and until it does they'll go right on playing with it. A toy dangerous to *others*.'

'They don't think of themselves as responsible.'

'I think what's changed somehow is they don't think of themselves as *personally* responsible. They don't think of it like that their personal, individual going and buying a ticket for *The Exorcist* is what adds to the demand that keeps the corporate machines coming out with more and more violent movies to satisfy the demand.'

'They expect the government to do something about it.'

'Or corporations to grow souls.'

'That example makes it a lot easier to see your point, Mr. Glendenning,' I said.

'I'm not sure *The Exorcist* is the best example. *The Exorcist* isn't all that violent so much as sick. Now *The Godfather* — that's violent.'

'Never did see *The Exorcist,* because Mrs. G. said she'd rather have all her fingers and toes cut off with dull scissors than sit through a piece of trash like that. But from what I heard and read it was damn violent.'

'I think the syndrome is more the not-voting one, the I'm-so-small-and-the-mass-of-everyone-else-is-so-big-what-possible-difference-does-what-I-do-make, so they stay home and watch *Charlie's Angels* instead of going to vote.'

'And then they bitch and moan about their elected leaders.'

'So maybe it's not a sense of the individual citizen not being responsible so much as they're so tiny and the government and rest of the country is so big they've got no chance of having any kind of real impact, so they just have to look out for themselves as best they can.'

'Not to mention how big corporations are; like how is one guy not having a *Godfather* ticket going to influence Paramount Pictures one way or the other? Which is all still bullshit; it's a way to rationalize not being responsible for your tiny part of which way the country goes.'

'All this is part of it, I think. And it's hard to peg just what the difference is. And I'm wary about doing the old-fart move of saying people aren't civic-minded like they were in the good old days and the country's going to shit. But it seems like citizens—whether on taxes or littering, you name it—did feel like they were part of Everything, that the huge Everybody Else that determined policy and taste and the common good was in fact made up of a whole lot of individuals just like them, that they were in fact *part* of Everything, and that they had to hold up their end and pull their weight and assume what they did made some difference the same way Everybody Else did, if the country was going to stay a nice place to live.'

'Citizens feel alienated now. It's like me-against-everyone-else.'

'*Alienated*'s one of those big sixties words.'

'But how did this alienated small selfish make-no-difference thing result from the sixties, since if the sixties showed anything good it showed that like-minded citizens can think for themselves and not just swallow what the Establishment says and they can band together and march and agitate for change and there can be real change; we pull out of 'Nam, we get Welfare and the Civil Rights Act and women's lib.'

'Because corporations got in the game and turned all the genuine principles and aspirations and ideology into a set of fashions and attitudes—they made Rebellion a fashion pose instead of a real impetus.'

'It's awful easy to vilify corporations, X.'

'Doesn't the term *corporation* itself come from *body,* like "made into a body"? These were artificial people being created. What was it, the Fourteenth Amendment that gave corporations all the rights and responsibilities of citizens?'

'No, the Fourteenth Amendment was part of Reconstruction and was intended to give full citizenship to freed slaves, and it was some corporation's sharpy counsel that persuaded the Court that corporations fit the Fourteenth's criteria.'

'We're talking C corps here, right?'

'Because it's true — it's not even clear now when you say *corporation* whether we're talking about Cs or Ss, LLCs, corporate associations, plus you've got closely-helds and public, plus those sham corporations that are really just limited partnerships loaded up with non-recourse debt to generate paper losses, which are basically just parasites on the tax system.'

'Plus C corps contribute by double taxation, so it's hard to say they're nothing but a negative in the revenue sphere.'

'I'm giving you a look of complete scorn and derision, X; what do you imagine it is we *do* here?'

'Not to mention fiduciary instruments that function almost identically to corporations. Plus franchise-spreads, flowthrough trusts, NFP foundations established as corporate instruments.'

'None of this matters. And I'm not even really talking about what we do here except in the sense that it puts us in a position to see civic attitudes close up, since there's nothing more concrete than a tax payment, which after all is your money, whereas the obligations and projected returns on the payments are abstract, at the abstract level the whole nation and its government and the commonweal, so attitudes about paying taxes seem like one of the places where a man's civic sense gets revealed in the starkest sorts of terms.'

'Wasn't it the Thirteenth Amendment that blacks and corporations exploited?'

'Let me throw him off, Mr. G., I'm pleading with you.'

'Here's something worth throwing out there. It was in the 1830s and '40s that states started granting charters of incorporation to larger and regulated companies. And it was 1840 or '41 that de Tocqueville published his book about Americans, and he says somewhere that one thing about democracies and their individualism is that they by their very nature corrode the citizen's sense of true community, of having real true fellow citizens whose interests and concerns were the same as his. This is a kind of ghastly irony, if you think about it, since a form of government engineered to produce equality makes its citizens so individualistic and self-absorbed they end up as solipsists, navel-gazers.'

'De Tocqueville is also talking about capitalism and markets, which pretty much go hand in hand with democracy.'

'I just don't think this is what I was trying to talk about. It's easy to blame corporations. DeWitt's saying if you think the corporations are evil and it's the government's job to make them moral, you're deflecting your own responsibility to civics. You're making the government your big brother and the corporation the evil bully your big brother's supposed to keep off you at recess.'

'De Tocqueville's thrust is that it's in the democratic citizen's nature to be like a leaf that doesn't believe in the tree it's part of.'

'What's interesting in a depressing way is that tacit hypocrisy — I, the citizen, will keep buying big gas-guzzlers that kill trees and tickets for *The Exorcist* until the government passes a law, but then when the government *does* pass a law I'll bitch about Big Brother and getting the government off our back.'

'See for instance the cheat-rate and the appeals percentage after audit.'

'It's more like I want a law to keep *you* from gas-guzzling and seeing *The Wild Bunch,* but not me.'

'Not in my backyard is the hue and cry.'

'Lady gets stabbed over off the river, houses up and down the block hear her screaming, nobody even sets foot outside.'

'Not get involved.'

'Something's happened to people.'

'People saying those damned tobacco companies while they smoke.'

'It's not fair to put down any critique of the corporate role in this kind of civic decline as just a simple knee-jerk demonization of corporations, though. The corporate agenda of maximizing profit by creating demand and trying to make demand inelastic can play a catalyst role in this syndrome Mr. Glendenning's trying to limn without being the devil or bent on world domination or something.'

'I believe Nichols has another two cents here.'

'I think he's trying to say something.'

'Because I think it goes beyond politics, civics.'

'I'm listening at least, Stuart.'

'Not even on a tree but more like leaves on the ground in the wind, blown this way and that way by the wind, and each time a gust blows it the citizen says, "Now I choose to blow this way; this is my decision."'

'With the wind being Nichols's corporate menace.'

'It's almost more a matter of metaphysics.'

'Yee ha.'

'Hoo doggy.'

'Say what we're in now is some transition in the economy and society between the age of industrial democracy and the stage that comes after, where what industrial democracy was about was

production and the economy depended on constantly increasing production and the democracy's
big tension was between industry's needs for policies that abetted production and citizens' needs to
both benefit from all the production and still have
their basic rights and interests protected from
industry's simpleminded emphasis on production
and profits.'

'I'm not sure where the metaphysics comes in
here, Nichols.'

'Maybe it's not metaphysics. Maybe it's existential. I'm talking about the individual US citizen's
deep fear, the same basic fear that you and I have
and that everybody has except nobody ever talks
about it except existentialists in convoluted French
prose. Or Pascal. Our smallness, our insignificance
and mortality, yours and mine, the thing that we
all spend all our time not thinking about directly,
that we are tiny and at the mercy of large forces
and that time is always passing and that every day
we've lost one more day that will never come back
and our childhoods are over and our adolescence
and the vigor of youth and soon our adulthood,
that everything we see around us all the time is
decaying and passing, it's all passing away, and so
are we, so am I, and given how fast the first forty-
two years have shot by it's not going to be long

before I too pass away, whoever imagined that there was a more truthful way to put it than "die," "pass away," the very sound of it makes me feel the way I feel at dusk on a wintry Sunday—'

'Anybody got the time? How long we been in here, three hours?'

'And not only that, but everybody who knows me or even knows I exist will die, and then everybody who knows those people and might even conceivably have even heard of me will die, and so on, and the gravestones and monuments we spend money to have put in to make sure we're remembered, these'll last what—a hundred years? two hundred?—and they'll crumble, and the grass and insects my decomposition will go to feed will die, and their offspring, or if I'm cremated the trees that are nourished by my windblown ash will die or get cut down and decay, and my urn will decay, and before maybe three or four generations it will be like I never existed, not only will I have passed away but it will be like I was never here, and people in 2104 or whatever will no more think of Stuart A. Nichols Jr. than you or I think of John T. Smith, 1790 to 1864, of Livingston, Virginia, or some such. That everything is on fire, slow fire, and we're all less than a million breaths away from an oblivion more total than we can even bring ourselves to even try to imagine, in fact, probably that's why the manic US obsession with production, produce, produce, impact the world, contribute, shape things, to help distract us from how little and totally insignificant and temporary we are.'

'This is supposed to be news to us. News flash: We're going to die.'

'Why do you think people buy insurance?'

'Let him finish.'

'Now this is depressing instead of just boring.'

'The post-production capitalist has something to do with the death of civics. But so does fear of smallness and death and everything being on fire.'

'I smell Rousseau at the root here, the same way you were talking about de Tocqueville before.'

'As usual DeWitt's way ahead of me. It probably does start with Rousseau and the Magna Carta and the French Revolution. This emphasis on man as the individual and on the rights and entitlements of the individual instead of the responsibilities of the individual. But corporations and marketing and PR and the creation of desire and need to feed all the manic production, the way modern advertising and marketing seduce the individual by flattering all the little psychic delusions with which we deflect the horror of personal smallness and transience, enabling the delusion that the individual is the center of the universe, the most important thing — I mean the individual individual, the little guy watching TV or listening to the radio or leafing through a shiny magazine or looking at a billboard or any of the million different daily ways this guy comes into contact with Burson-Marsteller's or Saachi & Saachi's big lie, that *he* is the tree, that his first responsibility is to his own happiness, that everyone else is the great gray abstract mass which his life depends on standing apart from, being an individual, being *happy*.'

'Doing your own thing.'

'That's your bag.'

'Shaking off the shackles of authority and conformity, of authoritarian conformity.'

'I'm going to need to use the head very soon, I'm afraid.'

'That's more the sixties than the French Revolution, man, then.'

'But if I'm getting DeWitt's thrust, the fulcrum was the moment in the sixties when rebellion against conformity became fashionable, a pose, a way to look cool to the others in your generation you wanted to impress and get accepted by.'

'Not to mention laid.'

'Because the minute it became not just an

attitude but a fashionable one, that's when the corporations and their advertisers can step in and
start reinforcing it and seducing people with it into
buying the things the corporations are producing.'

'The first time was 7 Up with its *Sgt. Pepper*
psychedelia and kids in sideburns and saying "the
Uncola."'

'But wait. The sixties rebellion in lots of ways
opposed the corporation and the military-industrial
complex.'

'The man in the gray flannel.'

'What *is* gray flannel anyway? Has anybody
ever seen anybody ever in gray flannel?'

'The only flannel I've got is PJs, man.'

'Is Mr. Glendenning even awake?'

'He looks awful pale.'

'Everybody looks pale in the dark, man.'

'I mean is there any more total symbol of conformity and marching in lockstep than the corporation? Assembly lines and punching the clock
and climbing the ladder to the corner office?
You've done field audits at Rayburn-Thrapp,
Gaines. Those guys can't wipe their ass without
a policy memo.'

'But we're not talking about the interior reality
of the corporation. We're talking about the face
and voice the corporate advertisers start using in

the late sixties to talk the customer into thinking he needs all this stuff. It starts talking about the customer's psyche being in bondage to conformity and the way to break out of the conformity is not to *do* certain things but to *buy* certain things. You make *buying* a certain brand of clothes or pop or car or necktie into a gesture of the same level of ideological significance as wearing a beard or pro-testing the war.'

'Virginia Slims and women's libbers.'

'Alka-Seltzer.'

'I think the I'm-going-to-die connection slipped by me at some point here.'

'I think Stuart's tracing the move from the production-model of American democracy to some-thing more like a consumption-model, where cor-porate production depends on a team approach whereas being a customer is a solo venture. That we're turning into consuming citizens instead of producing citizens.'

'Just wait sixteen quarters till '84. Just wait for the tidal wave of ads and PR that promote this or that corporate product as the way to escape the gray 1984 totalitarianisms of the Orwellian present.'

'How does buying one kind of typewriter instead of another help subvert government control?'

'It won't be government in a couple years, don't you see?'

'There won't be typewriters, either. Everyone'll have keyboards cabled into some sort of central VAX, and things won't even have to be on paper anymore.'

'The paperless office.'

'Rendering Stu here obsolete.'

'No, you're missing the genius of it. It'll all be played out in the world of images. There'll be this incredible political consensus that we need to escape the confinement and rigidity of conforming, of the dead fluorescent world of the office and the balance sheet, of having to wear a tie and listen to Muzak, but the corporations will be able to represent consumption-patterns as the way to break out—use this type of calculator, listen to this type of music, wear this type of shoe because everyone else is wearing conformist shoes. It'll be this era of incredible prosperity and conformity and mass-demographics in which all the symbols and rhetoric will involve revolution and crisis and bold forward-looking individuals who dare to march to their own drummer by allying themselves with brands that invest heavily in the image of rebellion. This mass PR campaign extolling the individual will solidify enormous markets of people whose innate conviction that they are solitary, peerless, non-communal, will be massaged at every turn.'

'But what role will government play in this 1984 scenario?'

'Just as DeWitt said—the government will be the parent, with all the ambivalent love-hate-need-defy charges that surround the parent-figure in the mind of the adolescent, which in this case I'm respectfully disagreeing with DeWitt in the sense that I don't think the American nation today is infantile so much as adolescent—that is, ambivalent in its twin desire for both authoritarian structure and the end of parental hegemony.'

'We'll be the cops they call when the party gets out of hand.'

'You can see where it's going. The extraordinary political apathy that followed Watergate and Vietnam and the institutionalization of grass-roots rebellion among minorities will only deepen. Politics is about consensus, and the advertising legacy of the sixties is that consensus is repression. Voting'll be unhip: Americans now vote with their wallets. Government's only cultural role will be as the tyrannical parent we both hate and need. Look for us to elect someone who can cast himself as a Rebel, maybe even a cowboy, but who deep down we'll know is a bureaucratic creature who'll operate inside the government mechanism instead of naively bang his head against it the way we've watched poor Jimmy do for four years.'

'Carter represents the last gasp of true New Frontier sixties idealism, then. His obvious decency and his political impotence have been conjoined in the voter's psyche.'

'Look for a candidate who can do to the electorate what corporations are learning to do, so Government — or, better, Big Government, Big Brother, Intrusive Government — becomes the image against which this candidate defines himself. Though paradoxically for this persona, to have weight the candidate'll also have to be a creature of government, an Insider, with a flinty-eyed entourage of bureaucrats and implementers who we'll be able to see can actually run the machine. Plus of course a massive campaign budget courtesy of guess who.'

'We're now very very very far afield from what I started out trying to describe as my thinking about taxpayers' relation to government.'

'This describes Reagan even better than Bush.'

'The Reagan symbolism's just too bold. This is just my opinion. Of course the marvelous thing for the Service about a possible Reagan presidency is that he's already anti-tax on the record. Flat-out, no hedging. No rise in the tax rates—in fact in New Hampshire he went on record as wanting to lower marginal rates.'

'This is good for the Service? Another politician trying to score points by trashing the tax system?'

'My own view: I see a Bush-Reagan ticket. Reagan for symbolism, the Cowboy, Bush the quiet insider, doing the unsexy work of actual management.'

'Not to mention his hike-defense-spending rhetoric. How are you going to lower marginal rates and increase defense spending?'

'Even a child could see the contradiction in that.'

'Stuart's saying it's good for the Service because lowering marginal rates but increasing spending can happen only if collection of tax is made more efficient.'

'Meaning the reins are off. Meaning the Service's quotas go up.'

'But also meaning a quiet reduction in the constraints on our auditing and collection mechanisms. Reagan'll set us up as the black-hatted rapacious Big Brother he secretly needs. We—the stitch-mouthed accountants in dull suits and thick specs, punching the keys on our adding machines— *become* the Government: the authority everyone gets to hate. Meanwhile Reagan triples the Service budget and makes technology and efficiency serious objectives. It'll be the best era the Service has had since '45.'

'But meanwhile increasing taxpayers' hatred of the Service.'

'Which paradoxically, a Reagan would need. The Service's more aggressive treatment of TPs, especially if it's high-profile, would seem to keep in the electorate's mind a fresh and eminently disposable image of Big Government that the Rebel Outsider President could continue to define himself against and decry as just the sort of government intrusion into the private lives and wallets of hardworking Americans he ran for the office to fight against.'

'You're saying the next president will be able to *continue* to define himself as an Outsider and Renegade when he's actually *in* the White House?'

'You're still underestimating the taxpayers' need for the lie, for the surface rhetoric they can keep telling themselves while deep down they can rest assured that Daddy's in control and everyone's still safe. The way adolescents make a big deal of rebelling against parental authority while they borrow

the keys to Daddy's car and use Daddy's credit
card to fill it with gas. The new leader won't lie
to the people; he'll do what corporate pioneers
have discovered works far better: He'll adopt the
persona and rhetoric that let the people lie to
themselves.'

'Let's get back to how a Bush or Reagan would
triple the Service budget for a second? Is this good
for us on a District level? What are the implications for a Peoria or a Creve Coeur?'

'Of course the marvelous double irony of
the Reduce Government candidate is that he's
financed by the corporations that are the backs
government tends to be the most oppressively on
the back of. Corporations, as DeWitt pointed out,
whose beady little brains are lit by nothing but net
profit and expansion, and who we deep-down
expect government to keep in check because we're
not equipped to resist their consumerist seductions
by the strength of our own character, and whose
appeal to the faux rebel is the modern rhetoric
that's going to get Bush-Reagan elected in the first
place, and who are going to benefit enormously
from the laissez-faire deregulation Bush-Reagan
will enable the electorate to believe will be undertaken in their own populist interests—in other
words we'll have for a president a symbolic Rebel

against his own power whose election was under-written by inhuman soulless profit-machines whose takeover of American civic and spiritual life will convince Americans that rebellion against the soulless inhumanity of corporate life will consist in buying products from corporations that do the best job of representing corporate life as empty and soulless. We'll have a tyranny of conformist nonconformity presided over by a symbolic out-sider whose very *election* depended on our deep conviction that his persona is utter bullshit. A rule of image, which because it's so empty makes every-one terrified — they're small and going to die, after all —'

'Christ, the death thing again.'

'— and whose terror of not really ever even existing makes them that much more susceptible to the ontological siren song of the corporate buy-to-stand-out-and-so-exist gestalt.'

§20

The quiet, pleasant family two houses down
from Lotwis (who was retired after thirty years of
service in the County Recorder of Deeds) and his
wife were then replaced by a single female of
unknown background and occupation who had
two large dogs that tended to make a lot of noise.
That was all right. Lotwis had a dog of his own
that barked a lot sometimes, and so did some of the
other people in the neighborhood. The neighborhood was one where people's dogs were going to
bark behind their fences and people were sometimes going to burn their trash or keep junked cars
in their yards. The neighborhood was now classed
Semirural in the Recorder's office, but in the Eisenhower and Kennedy and Johnson years it had been

classed Subd. Class 2, a development class, in fact the city's first recorded subdivision. It hadn't taken off and gone upscale and spread like Hawthorne 1 and 2 or Yankee Ridge, built out in the seventies on repossessed farmland out east of town. It was twenty-eight houses on two perpendicular black-top roads and had stayed that way, and the part of the city that spread out south to approach it was not upscale, it was light industry and some ware-houses and seed concerns, and the only develop-ments in terms of your basic housing out anywhere near were one large trailer park and one smaller one that hemmed the old subdivision in on the north and west; to the south was the interstate and serious farmland all the way to the pleasant little grain-town of Funk's Grove thirteen miles south on 51. But so. Within sight if Lotwis was up on his roof tending to gutters or the screen on his chim-ney was an auto wrecker's yard and Southtown Wholesale and Custom Meats, which was, when you cut through all the fancy language, a butch-er's. But so the folks that lived out here that the Lotwises had watched slowly move in and settle the neighborhood were folks with an independent streak that were willing to live out near trailer parks and a slaughterhouse and have a rural mail-man who brought the mail in his own private car and leaned way over to get it in the boxes out by the street, all in return for the benefits of living in a Class 2 zone without hemmed-in houses and subheaded ordinances on burning your trash or having your washer's outflow pipe empty into the gulley by the road or dogs with some spirit that were protective and barked up a storm at night.

'I'm glad you said this,' she said. Her name was Toni; she'd introduced herself when he came to her door. 'Now I'll know. If anything happens to these dogs. If they run off, or limp, or anything—I'll kill you, your family, burn your house down, and sow salt. I have nothing to live for but these dogs. If they want to run they're going to run. If you don't like it you can take it up with me. But if anything gets done to these dogs I'll decide it was you and I'll sacrifice my life and freedom to destroy you and everyone you love.'

So Lotwis just let her alone.

§21

Rubbing his eyes wearily. 'So let me get this straight. On $218,000 of gross billing on your Schedule C you realize $37,000 net.'

'It's all documented. I've supplied all receipts and W-2s.'

'Yes, the W-2s. We've got $175,471 in W-2s on sixteen employees—investigators, support personnel, research aides.'

'It's all right there. You've got copies of their returns.'

'Except what I found striking is they're all in terribly low marginal brackets. Terribly low-paid. Why not four or five employees highly paid?'

'The logistics of my business are complex. Much of the work is low-paid but time-consuming.'

'Except I dropped in on one of your researchers—a Mrs. Thelma Purler.'

'Ulp.'

'At the Oakhaven Assisted Living Center, where she resides.'

'Ulp.'

'In a wheelchair, with one of those old-fashioned ear horns even to hear your questions, and to which she replied—let me see'—checking his notes—'Roodle, roodle roodle roodle.'

'I um er.'

Turning off his recorder, which has no tape in it.

'So we're looking at potential criminal fraud, which is CID and not my department. We could go talk to—or dig up—these other employees. You'll go to jail. So here's what we can do. You have a one-hour opportunity to fill out an amended 1040 for last year. On which you omit the employee salary deductions. You pay real tax due, plus penalties for underpayment and late filing. You proceed with an employee of this department to your bank, where you cut a cashier's check for the total. At which time I destroy your original return, and the CID receives no referral.'

§22

I'm not sure I even know what to say. To be honest, a good bit of it I don't remember. I don't think my memory works in quite the way it used to. It may be that this kind of work changes you. Even just rote exams. It might actually change your brain. For the most part, it's now almost as if I'm trapped in the present. If I drank, for instance, some Tang, it wouldn't remind me of anything— I'd just taste the Tang.

From what I understand, I'm supposed to explain how I arrived at this career. Where I came from, so to speak, and what the Service means to me.

I think the truth is that I was the worst kind of nihilist—the kind who isn't even aware he's a nihilist. I was like a piece of paper on the street in the wind, thinking, 'Now I think I'll blow this way, now I think I'll blow that way.' My essential response to everything was 'Whatever.'

This was especially after high school, when I drifted for several years, in and out of three different colleges, one of them two different times, and four or five different majors. One of these might have been a minor. I was pretty much of a wastoid. Essentially, I had no motivation, which my father referred to as 'initiative.' Also, I remember that everything at that time was very fuzzy and abstract. I took a lot of psychology and political science, literature. Classes where everything was fuzzy and abstract and open to interpretation and then those interpretations were open to still more interpretations. I used to write my class papers on the typewriter the day they were due, and usually I got some type of B with 'Interesting in places' or 'Not too bad!' written underneath the grade as an instructional comment. The whole thing was just going through the motions; it didn't mean anything—even the whole point of the classes themselves was that nothing meant anything, that everything was abstract and endlessly interpretable. Except, of course, there was no argument about the fact that you had to turn in the papers, you had to go through the motions themselves, although nobody ever explained just why, what your ultimate motivation was supposed to be. I'm 99 percent sure that I took just one Intro Accounting class during all this time, and did all right in it until we hit depreciation schedules, as in the straight-line method vs. accelerated depreciation, and the combination of difficulty and sheer boredom of the depreciation schedules broke my initiative, especially after I'd missed a couple of the classes and fallen behind, which with depreciation is fatal—and I ended up dropping that class and taking an incomplete. This was at Lindenhurst College—the later Intro class at DePaul had the same title but a somewhat different emphasis. I also remember that incompletes peeved my father quite a bit more than a low grade, understandably.

I know three separate times during this unmotivated period I withdrew from college and tried working so-called real jobs. One was that I was a security guard for a parking garage on North Michigan, or taking tickets for events at the Liberty Arena, or briefly on the production line at a Cheese Nabs plant working the cheese product injector, or working for a company which made and installed gymnasium floors. Then, after a while, I couldn't handle the boredom of the jobs, which were all unbelievably boring and meaning-less, and I'd quit and enroll someplace else and essentially try to start college over again. My transcript looked like collage art. Understandably, this routine wore thin with my father, who was a cost systems supervisor for the City of Chicago—although during this time he lived in Libertyville, which is describable as an upper-bourgeois northern suburb. He used to say, dryly and with a perfectly straight face, that I was shaping up to be an outstanding twenty-yard-dash man. This was his way of squeezing my shoes. He read a great deal and was into dry, sardonic expressions. Although on one other occasion, after taking an incomplete or withdrawing somewhere and coming back home, I remember I was in the kitchen getting something to eat and heard him arguing with my mother and Joyce, telling them I couldn't find my ass with both hands. That was the angriest I think I ever saw him get during this unfocused period. I don't remember the exact context, but knowing how dignified and essentially reserved my father usually was, I'm sure I must have just done something especially feckless or pathetic to provoke him. I don't remember my mother's response or exactly how I came to overhear the remark, as eavesdropping on your parents seems like something that only a much smaller child would do.

My mother was more sympathetic, and whenever my father started squeezing my shoes about the lack-of-direction thing, my mother would stick up for me to some extent and say I was trying to find my path in life, and that not every path is outlined in neon lights like an airport runway, and that I owed it to myself to find my path and let things unfold in their own way. From what I understand of basic psychology, this is a fairly typical dynamic—son is feckless and lacks direction, mother is sympathetic and believes in son's potential and sticks up for him, father is peeved and endlessly criticizes and squeezes son's shoes but still, when push comes to shove, always ponies up the check for the next college. I can remember my father referring to money as 'that universal solvent of ambivalence' in connection with these tuition checks. I should mention that my mother and father were amicably divorced by this time, which was also somewhat typical of that era, so there were all those typical divorce dynamics in play as well, psychologically. The same sort of dynamics were probably being played out in homes all over America—the child trying to sort of passively rebel while still financially tied to the parent,

266

and all the typical psychological business that goes along with that.

Anyhow, all this was in the Chicagoland area in the 1970s, a period that now seems as abstract and unfocused as I was myself. Maybe the Service and I have this in common — that the past decade seems much longer ago than it really was, because of what's happened in the intervening time. As for myself, I had trouble just paying attention, and the things I can remember now seem mostly pointless. I mean really remember, not just have a general impression of. I remember having fairly long hair, meaning long on all four sides, but nevertheless it was also always parted on the left side and held in place with spray from a dark red can. I remember the color of this can. I can't think of this period's hair without almost wincing. I can remember things I wore — a lot of burnt orange and brown, red-intensive paisley, bell-bottom cords, acetate and nylon, flared collars, dungaree vests. I had a metal peace-sign pendant that weighed half a pound. Docksiders and yellow Timberlands and a pair of shiny low brown leather dress boots which zipped up the sides and only the sharp toes showed under bell-bottoms. The little sensitive leather thong around the neck. The commercial psychedelia. The obligatory buckskin jacket. The dungarees whose cuffs dragged on the ground and dissolved into white thread. Wide belts, tube socks, track shoes from Japan. The standard getup. I remember the round, puffy winter coats of nylon and down that made us all look like parade balloons. The scratchy white painter's pants with loops for supposed tools down the side of the thigh. I remember everyone despising Gerald Ford, not so much for pardoning Nixon but for constantly falling down. Everyone had contempt for him. Very blue designer jeans. I remember the feminist tennis player Billie Jean King beating what seemed like an old and feeble man player on television and my mother and her friends all being very excited by this. 'Male chauvinist pig,' 'women's lib,' and 'stagflation' all seemed vague and indistinct to me during this time, like listening to background noise with half an ear. I don't remember what I did with all my real attention, what-all it was going towards. I never did anything, but at the same time I could normally never sit still and become aware of what was really going on. It's hard to explain. I somewhat remember a younger Cronkite, Barbara Walters, and Harry Reasoner — I don't think I watched much news. Again, I suspect this was more typical than I thought at the time. One thing you learn in Rote Exams is how disorganized and inattentive most people are and how little they pay attention to what's going on outside of their sphere. Somebody named Howard K. Smith was also big in news, I remember. You almost never hear the word *ghetto* anymore, now. I remember Acapulco Gold versus Colombia Gold, Ritalin versus Ritadex, Cylert and Obetrol, Laverne and Shirley, Carnation Instant Breakfast, John Travolta, disco fever, and children's tee shirts with the 'Fonz' on them. And 'Keep On Truckin'' shirts, which my mother loved, where walking people's shoes and soles looked abnormally large. Actually preferring, like most children my age, Tang to real orange juice. Mark Spitz and Johnny Carson, the celebration in 1976 with fleets of antique ships coming into a harbor on TV. Smoking pot after school in high school and then watching TV and eating Tang out of the jar with a finger, wetting my finger and sticking it in, over and over, until I'd look down and couldn't believe how much of the jar was gone. Sitting there with my wastoid friends, and so on and so forth — and none of it meant anything. It's like I was dead or asleep without even being aware of it, as in the Wisconsin expression 'didn't know enough to lay down.'

I remember in high school getting Dexedrine

from a kid whose mother had them prescribed for her for pep, and the weird way they tasted, and the remarkable way they made the thing of counting while reading or speaking disappear—they were called black beauties—but the way after a while they made your lower back ache and gave you terrible, terrible breath. Your mouth tasted like a long-dead frog in a cloudy jar in Biology when you first opened the jar. It's still sickening just to think about. There was also the period when my mother was so upset when Richard Nixon got reelected so easily, which I remember because it was around then that I tried Ritalin, which I bought from a guy in World Cultures class whose little brother in primary school was supposedly on Ritalin from a doctor who didn't keep track of his prescriptions very well, and which some people didn't think were anything special compared to black beauties, Ritalin, but I liked them very much, at first because it made sitting and studying for long periods of time possible and even interesting, and which I really, really liked, but it was hard to get much of—Ritalin was—especially after evidently the little brother wigged out one day at primary school from not taking his Ritalin and the parents and doctor discovered the irregularities with the prescriptions and suddenly there was no pimply guy in pink sunglasses selling four-dollar Ritalin pills out of his locker in junior hall.

I seem to remember in 1976 my father openly predicting a Ronald Reagan presidency and even sending their campaign a donation—although in retrospect I don't think Reagan even really ran in '76. This was my life before the sudden change in direction and eventually entering the Service. Girls wore caps or dungaree hats, but most guys were essentially uncool if they wore a hat. Hats were things to make fun of. Baseball caps were for the rednecks downstate. Older men of any seriousness still sometimes wore business-type hats outside, though. I can remember my father's hat now almost better than his face under it. I used to spend time imagining what my father's face looked like when he was alone—I mean his facial expression and eyes—when he was by himself in his office at work at the City Hall annex downtown and there was no one to shape a certain expression for. I remember my father wearing madras shorts on weekends, and black socks, and mowing the lawn like that, and sometimes looking out of the window at what he looked like in that getup and feeling actual pain at being related to him. I remember everyone pretending to be a samurai or saying, 'Excuse *me!*' in all sorts of different contexts—this was cool. To show approval or excitement, we said, 'Excellent.' In college, you could hear the word *excellent* five thousand times a day. I remember some of my attempts to grow sideburns at DePaul and always ending up shaving them off, because at a certain point they got to where they looked just like pubic hair. The smell of Brylcreem in my father's hatband, Deep Throat, Howard Cosell, my mother's throat showing ligaments on either side when she and Joyce laughed. Throwing her hands around or bending over. Mom was always a very physical laugher— her whole body gets involved.

There was also the word *mellow* that was used constantly, although even early on in its use this word bugged me; I just didn't like it. I still probably used it sometimes, though, without being aware I was doing it.

My mother's the sort of somewhat lanky type of older woman who seems to become almost skinny and tough with age instead of ballooning out, becoming ropy and sharp-jointed and her cheekbones even more pronounced. I remember sometimes thinking of beef jerky when I would first see her, and then feeling terrible that I had that association. She was quite good-looking in her day, though, and some of the later weight-loss was also nerve-related, because after the thing with my father her nerves got worse and worse. Admittedly, too, one other factor in her sticking up for me with my father as to drifting in and out of school was the past trouble I'd had with reading in primary school when we'd lived in Rockford and my father had worked for the City of Rockford. This was in the mid-1960s, at Machesney Elementary. I went through a sudden period where I couldn't read. I mean that I actually could read — my mother knew I could read from when we'd read children's books together. But for almost two years at Machesney, instead of reading something I'd count the words in it, as though reading was the same as just counting the words. For example, 'Here came Old Yeller, to save me from the hogs' would equate to ten words which I would count off from one to ten instead of its being a sentence that made you love Old Yeller in the book even more. It was a strange problem in my developmental wiring at the time which caused a lot of trouble and embarrassment and was one reason why we ended up moving to the Chicagoland area, because for a while it looked as though I would have to attend a special school in Lake Forest. I have very little memory of this time except for the feeling of not especially wanting to count words or intending to but just not being able to help it—it was frustrating and strange. It got worse under pressure or nervousness, which is typical of things like that. Anyhow, part of my mother's fierce defense of letting me experience and learn things in my own way dates from that time, when the Rockford School District reacted to the reading problem in all sorts of ways that she didn't think were helpful or fair. Some of her consciousness-raising and entry into the women's lib movement of the 1970s probably also dates from that time of fighting the bureaucracy of the school district. I still sometimes lapse into counting words, or rather usually the counting goes on when I'm reading or talking, as a sort of background noise or unconscious process, a little like breathing.

For instance, I've said 2,752 words right now since I started. Meaning 2,752 words as of just before I said, 'I've said,' versus 2,754 if you count 'I've said'—which I do, still. I count numbers as one word no matter how large a given number is. Not that it actually means anything—it's more like a mental tic. I don't remember exactly when it started. I know I had no trouble learning to read or reading the Sam and Ann books they teach you to read with, so it must have been after second grade. I know that my mother, as a child in Beloit

WI, where she grew up, had an aunt who had a thing of washing her hands over and over without being able to stop, which eventually got so bad she had to go to a rest home. I seem to remember thinking of my mother as in some way associating the counting thing more with that aunt at the sink and not seeing it as a form of retardation or inability to just sit there and read as instructed, which is how Rockford school authorities seemed to see it. Anyhow, hence her hatred of traditional institutions and authority, which was another thing that helped gradually alienate her from my father and imperil their marriage, and so on and so forth.

I remember once, in I think 1975 or '76, shaving off just one sideburn and going around like that for a period of time, believing the one sideburn made me a nonconformist—I'm not kidding—and getting into long, serious conversations with girls at parties who would ask me what the lone sideburn 'meant.' A lot of the things I remember saying and believing during this period make me literally wince now, to think of it. I remember KISS, REO Speedwagon, Cheap Trick, Styx, Jethro Tull, Rush, Deep Purple, and, of course, good old Pink Floyd. I remember BASIC and COBOL. COBOL was what my father's cost systems hardware ran at his office. He was

incredibly knowledgeable about the era's computers. I remember Sony's wide pocket transistors and
the way that many of the city's blacks held their
radios up to their ear whereas white kids from the
suburbs used the optional little earplug, like a CID
earbud, which had to be cleaned almost daily or
else it got really foul. There was the energy crisis
and recession and stagflation, though I cannot
remember the order in which these occurred—
although I do know the main energy crisis must
have happened when I was living back at home
after the Lindenhurst College thing, because I got
my mother's tank siphoned out while out partying
late at night with old high school friends, which
my father was not thrilled about, understandably.
I think New York City actually went bankrupt for
a while during this period. There was also the
1977 disaster of the State of Illinois's experiment
with making the state sales tax a progressive tax,
which I know upset my father a lot but which I
neither understood nor cared about at the time.
Later, of course, I would understand why making
a sales tax progressive is such a terrible idea, and
why the resulting chaos more or less cost the governor at the time his job. At the time, though, I
don't remember noticing anything except the
unusually terrible crowds and hassle of shopping

for the holidays in late '77. I don't know if that's relevant. I doubt anyone outside the state cares very much about this, though there are still some jokes about it among the older wigglers at the REC.

I remember feeling the actual physical feeling of hatred of most commercial rock—such as for disco, which if you were cool you pretty much had to hate, and all rock groups with one-word place names. Boston, Kansas, Chicago, America—I can still feel an almost bodily hatred. And believing that I and maybe one or two friends were among the very, very few people who truly understood what Pink Floyd was trying to say. It's embarrassing. Most of these almost feel like some other person's memories. I remember almost none of early childhood, mostly just weird little isolated strobes. The more fragmented the memory is, though, the more it seems to feel authentically mine, which is strange. I wonder if anyone feels as though they're the same person they seem to remember. It would probably make them have a nervous breakdown. It probably wouldn't even make any sense.

I don't know if this is enough. I don't know what anybody else has told you.

Our common word for this kind of nihilist at the time was *wastoid*.

I remember rooming in a high-rise UIC dorm with a very mod, with-it sophomore from Naperville who also wore sideburns and a leather thong and played the guitar. He saw himself as a nonconformist, and also very unfocused and nihilistic, and deeply into the school's wastoid drug scene, and drove what I have to admit was a very cool-looking 1972 Firebird that it eventually turned out his parents paid the insurance on. I cannot remember his name, try as I might. UIC stood for the University of Illinois, Chicago Campus, a gigantic urban university. The dorm we roomed in was right on Roosevelt, and our main windows faced a large downtown podiatric clinic—I can't remember its name, either—which had a huge raised electrified neon sign that rotated on its pole every weekday from 8:00 to 8:00 with the name and mnemonic phone number ending in 3668 on one side and on the other a huge colored outline of a human foot—our best guess was a female foot, from the proportions—and I remember that this roommate and I formulated a kind of ritual in which we'd make sure to try to be at the right spot at our windows at 8:00 each night to watch the foot sign go dark and stop rotating when the clinic closed. It always went dark at the same time the clinic's windows did and we theorized that everything was on one main breaker. The sign's rotation didn't stop all at once. It more like slowly wound down, with almost a wheel-of-fortune quality about where it would finally stop. The ritual was that if the sign stopped with the foot facing away, we would go to the UIC library and study, but if it stopped with the foot or any significant part of it facing our windows, we would take it as a 'sign' (with the incredibly obvious double entendre) and immediately blow off any homework or supposed responsibility we had and go instead to the Hat, which at that time was the currently hip UIC pub and place to hear bands, and would drink beers and play quarters and tell all the other kids whose parents were paying their tuition about the ritual of the rotating foot in a way that we all appeared nihilistically wastoid and hip. I'm seriously embarrassed to remember things like this. I can remember the podiatrist's sign and the Hat and what the Hat looked and even smelled like, but I cannot remember this roommate's name, even though we probably hung out together three or four nights a week that year. The Hat had no relation to Meibeyer's, which is the main sort of pub for rote examiners here at the REC, and also has a hat motif and an elaborate display-rack of hats, but these are meant to be historical IRS and CPA hats, the hats of serious adults. Meaning the similarity is just a coincidence. There were actually two Hats, as in a franchise—there was the UIC one on Cermak and Western, and another one down in Hyde Park for the more motivated, focused kids at U of Chicago. Everybody at our Hat called the Hyde Park Hat 'the Yarmulke.' This roommate was not a bad or evil guy, although he turned out to be able to play only three or four real songs on the guitar, which he played over and over and over, and blatantly rationalized his selling of drugs as a form of social rebellion instead of just pure capitalism, and even at the time I knew he was a total conformist to the late-seventies standards of so-called nonconformity, and sometimes I felt contemptuous of him. I might have despised him a little. As if I was exempt, of course—but this kind of blatant projection and displacement was part of the nihilist hypocrisy of the whole period.

I can remember the 'Uncola,' and the way Noxzema commercials always played a big bump-and-grind theme. I seem to remember a lot of wood-pattern designs on things that were not wood, and station wagons with side panels engineered to look like wood. I remember Jimmy Carter addressing the nation in a cardigan, and something about Carter's brother turning out to be a wastoid and public boob embarrassing the president just by being related to him.

I don't think I voted. The truth is that I don't remember if I voted or not. I probably planned to and said I was going to and then got distracted somehow and didn't get around to it. That would be about par for the period.

Obviously, it probably goes without saying that I partied heavily during this whole period. I don't know how much I should say about this. But I didn't party any more or less than everyone else I knew did—in fact, very precisely neither more nor less. Everyone I knew and hung out with was a wastoid, and we knew it. It was hip to be ashamed of it, in a strange way. A weird kind of narcissistic despair. Or just to feel directionless and lost—we romanticized it. I did like Ritalin and certain types of speed like Cylert, which was a little unusual, but everyone had their idiosyncratic favorites when it came to partying. I didn't do incredible amounts of speed, as the kinds I liked were hard to get— you more had to stumble across it. The roommate with the blue Firebird was obsessed with hashish, which he always described as *mellow*.

Looking back, I doubt if it ever occurred to me that the way I felt towards this roommate was probably the way my father felt about me — that I was just as much a conformist as he was, plus a hypocrite, a 'rebel' who really just sponged off of society in the form of his parents. I wish I could say I was aware enough for this contradiction to sink in at the time, although I probably would have just turned it into some kind of hip, nihilistic joke. At the same time, sometimes I know I worried about my directionlessness and lack of initiative, how abstract and open to different interpretations everything seemed at the time, even about how fuzzy and pointless my memories were starting to seem. My father, on the other hand, I know, remembered everything — in particular, physical details, the precise day and time of appointments, and past statements which were now inconsistent with present statements. But then, I would learn that this sort of close attention and total recall was part of his job.

What I really was was naive. For instance, I knew I lied, but I hardly ever assumed that anybody else around me might be lying. I realize now how conceited that is, and how unfocused that lets actual reality be. I was a child, really. The truth is that most of what I really know about myself I learned in the Service. That may sound too much like sucking up, but it's the truth. I've been here five years, and I've learned an incredible amount.

Anyhow, I can also recall smoking pot with my mother and her partner, Joyce. They grew their own, and it wasn't exactly potent, but that wasn't really the point, because with them it was more of a sort of liberated political statement than a matter of getting high, and my mother almost seemed to make it a point to smoke pot whenever I was over there visiting them, and while it made me a little uncomfortable, I don't ever remember refusing to 'fire up' with them, even though it embarrassed me somewhat when they used college terms like this. At that time, my mother and Joyce co-owned a small feminist bookstore, which I knew my father resented having helped finance through the divorce settlement. And I can remember once sitting around on their Wrigleyville apartment's beanbag chairs, passing around one of their large, amateurishly rolled doobersteins—which was the hip, wastoid term for a joint at that time, at least around the Chicagoland area—and listening to my mother and Joyce recount very vivid, detailed memories from their early childhoods, and both of them laughing and crying and stroking one another's hair in emotional support, which didn't really bother me—their touching or even kissing one another in front of me—or at least by then I'd had plenty of time to get used to it, but I can remember becoming more and more paranoid and nervous at the time, because, when I tried hard to think of some of my own childhood memories, the only really vivid memory I could remember involved me pounding Glovolium into my Rawlings catcher's mitt, which my father had gotten me, and that day of getting the Johnny Bench Autograph mitt I remembered very well, although Mom and Joyce's was not the place to wax all sentimental about my father getting me something, obviously. The worst part was then starting to hear my mother recount all these memories and anecdotes of my own childhood, and realizing that she actually remembered much more of my early childhood than I did, as though somehow she'd seized or confiscated memories and experiences that were technically mine. Obviously, I didn't think of the term *seize* at the time. That's more a Service term. But smoking pot with my mother and Joyce was usually just not a pleasant experience at all, and often totally weirded me out, now that I think about it—and yet I did it with them almost every time. I doubt my mother enjoyed it much, either. The whole thing had an air of pretense of fun and liberation about it. In retrospect,

I get the feeling that my mom was trying to get me to see her as changing and growing up right there with me, both on my side of the generation gap, as though we were still as close as we were when I was a child. As both being nonconformists and giving my father the finger, symbolically. Anyhow, smoking pot with her and Joyce always felt a bit hypocritical. My parents split up in February 1972, in the same week that Edmund Muskie cried in public on the campaign trail, and the TV had clips of him crying over and over. I can't remember what he was crying about, but it definitely sunk his chances in the campaign. It was the sixth week of theater class in high school where I first learned the term *nihilist*. I know I didn't feel any real hostility towards Joyce, by the way, although I do remember always feeling sort of edgy when it was just her and me, and being relieved when my mother got home and I could sort of relate to both of them as a couple instead of trying to make conversation with Joyce, which was always complicated because there always felt like a great deal more subjects and things to remember not to bring up than there were to actually talk about, so that trying to make chitchat with her was like trying to slalom at Devil's Head if the slalom's gates were only inches apart.

In hindsight, I realized later that my father was actually kind of witty and sophisticated. At the time, I think I thought of him as barely alive, as like a robot or slave to conformity. It's true that he was uptight, anal, and quick with the put-downs. He was a hundred percent conventional establishment, and totally on the other side of the generation gap—he was forty-nine when he died, which was in December 1977, which obviously means he grew up during the Depression. But I don't think I ever appreciated his sense of humor about all of it—there was a way he sort of wove his pro-establishment views into a dry, witty style that I don't remember ever getting or understanding his jokes in at the time. I didn't have much of a sense of humor then, it seems, or else I did the standard child's thing of taking everything he said as a personal comment or judgment. There was stuff I knew about him, which I'd picked up through the years of childhood, mostly from my mother. Like that he'd been really, really shy when they'd first met. How he had wanted to go to more than just technical college but he had bills to pay—he was in logistics and supply in Korea but had already gotten married to my mother before he was posted overseas, and so upon discharge he immediately had to find a job. This is what people her age did then, she explained — if you met the right person and were at least out of high school, you got married, without even ever really thinking about it or questioning yourself. The point is that he was very smart and somewhat unfulfilled, like many of his generation. He worked hard because he had to, and his own dreams were put on the back burner. This is all indirectly, from my mother, but it fit with certain bits and pieces that even I couldn't help being aware of. For instance, my father read all the time. He was constantly reading. It was his whole recreation, especially after the divorce — he was always coming home from the library with a stack of books with that clear library plastic wrap on the covers. I never paid any attention to what the books were or why he read so much — he never talked about what he was reading. I don't even know what his favorite kinds were, as in history, mysteries, or what. Looking back now, I think he was lonely, especially after the divorce, as the only people you could call his friends were colleagues from his job, and I think he essentially found his job boring — I don't think he felt much personal investment in the City of Chicago's budget and expenditure protocols, especially as it wasn't his idea to move here — and I think books and intellectual issues were one of his escapes from boredom.

He was actually a very smart person. I wish I could remember more examples of the sort of things he'd say—at the time, I think they seemed more hostile or judgmental than like he was making fun of both of us at the same time. I do remember he sometimes referred to the so-called younger generation (meaning mine) as 'This thing America hath wrought.' That's not a very good example. It's almost like he thought the blame went both ways, that there was something wrong with the whole country's adults if they could produce kids like this in the 1970s. I remember once in October or November 1976, at twenty-one, during another period of time off, after being enrolled at DePaul—which actually didn't go well at all, the first time I was at DePaul. It was basically a disaster. They kind of invited me to leave, actually, which was the only time that had happened. The other times, at Lindenhurst College and then later at UIC, I'd withdrawn on my own. Anyhow, during this time off, I was working the second shift at a Cheese Nabs factory in Buffalo Grove and living there at my father's house in Libertyville. There was no way I was crashing at my mother and Joyce's apartment in the Wrigleyville section of Chicago, where the rooms all had bead curtains instead of doors. But I didn't have to punch in at this mindless job until six, so I'd mostly just hang around the house all afternoon until it was time to leave. And sometimes during this period my father would be away for a couple of days—like the Service, the City of Chicago's financial departments were always sending their more technical people to conferences and in-services, which I would come to learn later here in the Service are not like the big drunken conventions of private industry but are usually highly intensive and work-centered. My father said the city in-services were mostly just tedious, which was a word he used a fair amount, *tedious*. And on these trips it was just me living in the house, and you can imagine what used to happen when I'd be there on my own, especially on weekends, even though I was supposed to be in charge of looking after the house while he was gone. But the memory is of him coming home early one afternoon in '76 from one of these work trips, like a day or two before I'd thought he told me he was going to be home, and coming in the front door and finding me and two of my old so-called friends from Libertyville South high school in the living room—which, due to the slightly raised design of the front porch and front door, was in effect a sunken living room that more or less started right inside the front door, with one small set of stairs leading down into the living room and another set leading up to the house's second floor. Architecturally, the house's style is known as a raised ranch, like most of the other older homes on the street, and it had another set of stairs leading from the second-floor hallway down into the garage, which actually supports part of the second story—that is, the garage is, structurally, a necessary part of the house, which is what's distinctive about a raised ranch. At the moment he entered, two of us were slumped on the davenport with our dirty feet up on his special coffee table, and the carpeting was all littered with beer cans and Taco Bell wrappers—the cans were my father's beer, which he bought in bulk twice a year and stored in the utility room closet and normally drank maybe a total of two per week of—with us sitting there totally wasted and watching *The Searchers* on WGN, and one of the guys listening to Deep Purple on my father's special stereo headphones for listening to classical music on, and the coffee table's special oak or maple top with big rings of condensation from the beer cans all over it because we'd turned the house's heat way up past where he normally allowed it to be, in terms of energy conservation and expense, and the other guy next to me on the davenport leaning over in the middle of taking a huge bong hit—this guy was famous for being able to take massive hits. Plus, the whole living room reeked. When then, suddenly, in the memory, I heard the distinctive sound of his footsteps on the broad wooden porch and the sound of his key in the front door, and only a second later my father suddenly comes in on a wave of very cold, clear air through the doorway with his hat and overnight bag—I was in the paralyzed shock of the totally busted kid, and I sat there paralyzed, unable to do anything and yet seeing each frame of him coming in with horrible focus and clarity— and him standing there at the edge of the few stairs down to the living room, taking his hat off with the trademark gesture that involved both his head and his hand as he stood there taking in the scene and the three of us—he'd made no secret of not much liking these old high school friends, who were the same guys I'd been out partying with when my mom's gas cap was stolen and the tank siphoned out, and none of us had any money left by the time we found the car, and I had to call my father and he had to take the train down after work to pay for gas so I could get the Le Car back to my mom and Joyce, who co-owned it and used it for bookstore business—with the three of us now slumped there all totally wasted and paralyzed, one of the guys wearing a ratty old tee shirt that actually said FUCK YOU across the chest, the other coughing out his mammoth hit in shock, so that a plume of pot smoke went rolling out across the living room towards my father—in short, my memory is of the scene being the worst confirmation of the worst kind of generation-gap stereotype and parental disgust for their decadent, wastoid kids, and of my father slowly putting down his bag and case and just standing there, with no expression and not saying anything for what felt like such a long time, and then he slowly made a gesture of putting one arm up in the air a little and looking up and said, *'Look on my works, ye mighty, and despair!,'* and then picked up his overnight bag again and without a word walked up the upstairs stairs and went into their old bedroom and closed the door. He didn't slam it, but you could hear the door close quite firmly. The memory, strangely, which is horribly sharp and detailed up to there, then totally stops, like a tape that's just run out, and I don't know what happened after that, like getting the guys out of there and hurriedly trying to clean everything up and turn the thermostat back down to sixty-eight, though I do remember feeling like complete shit, not so much like I'd been 'busted' or was in trouble as just childish, like a spoiled little selfish child, and imagining what I must have looked like to him, sitting there in litter in his house, wasted, with my dirty feet on the marked-up coffee table he and my mother had saved up for and gotten at an antique store in Rockford when they were still young and didn't have much money, and which he prized, and rubbed lemon oil in all the time, and said all he asked was that I should please keep my feet off of it and use a coaster—like, for a second or two seeing what I actually must have looked like to him as he stood there looking at us treating his living room like that. It wasn't a pretty picture, and it felt even worse as he hadn't yelled or squeezed my shoes about it—he just looked weary, and sort of embarrassed for both of us—and I remember for a second or two I could actually feel what he must have been feeling, and for an instant saw myself through his eyes, which made the whole thing much, much worse than if he'd been furious, or yelled, which he never did, not even the next time he and I were alone in the same room—which I don't remember when this was, like whether I skulked out of the house after cleaning everything up or whether I stayed there to face him. I don't know which one I did. I didn't even understand what he said, although obviously I understood he was being sarcastic, and in some way blaming himself or making fun of himself for having produced the 'work' that had just thrown the Taco Bell wrappers and bags on the floor instead of bothering to get up and take like eight steps to throw them away. Although later on, I just stumbled on the poem it turned out he was quoting from, in some kind of weird context at the Indianapolis TAC, and my eyes just about bulged out of my head, because I hadn't even known it was a poem—and a famous one, by the same British poet who evidently wrote the original *Frankenstein*. And I didn't even know my father read British poetry, much less that he could quote from it when he was upset. In short, there was probably much more to him than I was aware of, and I don't remember even realizing how little I knew about him, really, until after he was gone and it was too late. I expect that this sort of regret is typical, as well.

Anyhow, this one terrible memory of looking up from the davenport and seeing myself through his eyes, and of his sad, sophisticated way of expressing how sad and disgusted he was—this kind of sums up the whole period for me now, when I think of it. I also remember both of those former friends' names, too, from that fucked-up day, but obviously that's not relevant.

Things began to get much more vivid, focused, and concrete in 1978, and in retrospect I suppose I agree with Mom and Joyce that this was the year I 'found myself' or 'put away childish things' and began the process of developing some initiative and direction in my life, which obviously led to my joining the Service.

Though it's not directly connected to my choice of the IRS as a career, it's true that my father being killed in a public-transit accident in late 1977 was a sudden, horrible, and life-changing kind of event, which I obviously hope never to have to repeat in any way again. My mother took it especially hard, and had to go on tranquilizers, and she ended up being psychologically unable to sell my father's house, and left Joyce and the bookstore and moved back into the house in Libertyville, where she still lives today, with certain pictures of my father and of them as a young couple still in the house. It's a sad situation, and an armchair psychologist would probably say that she blamed herself somehow for the accident, even though I, more than anyone, would be in a position to know that that wasn't true, and that, in the final analysis, the accident was no one's fault. I was there when it happened — the accident — and there is no denying that it was one hundred percent terrible.

Even today, I can remember the whole thing in such vivid, concrete detail that it almost seems more like a recording than a memory, which I'm told is not unusual for traumatic events—and yet there was also no way to recount for my mother exactly what happened from start to finish without almost destroying her, as she was already so grief-stricken, although just about anyone could have seen that a lot of her grief was unresolved conflicts and hang-ups over their marriage and the identity crisis she'd had in 1972 at age forty or forty-one and the divorce, none of which she got to really deal with at the time because she'd thrown herself so deeply into the women's lib movement and consciousness-raising and her new circle of strange, mostly overweight women who were all in their forties, plus her new sexual identity with Joyce almost right away, which I know must have just about killed my father, given how straitlaced and conventional he tended to be, although he and I never talked about it directly, and he and my mother somehow managed to stay reasonably good friends, and I never heard him say anything about the matter except some occasional bitching about how much of his agreed-upon support payments to her were going into the bookstore, which he sometimes referred to as 'that financial vortex' or just 'the vortex'—all of which is a whole long story in itself. So we never really talked about it, which I doubt is all that unusual in these sorts of cases.

If I had to describe my father, I would first say that my mother and father's marriage was one of the only ones I've seen in which the wife was noticeably taller than the man. My father was 5' 6" or 5' 6½", and not fat but stocky, the way many shorter men in their late forties are stocky. He might have weighed 170. He looked good in a suit—like so many men of his generation, his body almost seemed designed to fill out and support a suit. And he owned some good ones, most single-button and single-vent, understated and conservative, in mainly three-season worsteds and one or two seersucker for hot weather, in which he also eschewed his usual business hat. To his credit—at least in retrospect—he rejected the so-called modern style's wide ties, brighter colors, and flared lapels, and found the phenomenon of leisure suits or corduroy sport coats nauseating. His suits were not tailored, but they were nearly all from Jack Fagman, a very old and respected men's store in Winnetka which he had patronized ever since our family relocated to the Chicagoland area in 1964, and some of them were really nice. At home, in what he called his 'mufti,' he wore more casual slacks and double-knit dress shirts, sometimes under a sweater vest—his favorite of these was argyle. Sometimes he wore a cardigan, though I think that he knew that cardigans made him look a little too broad across the beam. In the summer, there was sometimes the terrible thing of the Bermuda shorts with black dress socks, which it turned out were the only kind of socks my father even owned. One sport coat, a 36R in midnight-blue slubbed silk, had dated from his youth and early courtship of my mother, she had explained— it was hard for her to even hear about this jacket after the accident, much less help tell me what to do with it. The clothes closet contained his best and third-best topcoats, also from Jack Fagman, with the empty wooden hanger still between them. He used shoe trees for his dress and office footwear; some of these were inherited from his own father. ('These' obviously referring to the shoe trees, not the shoes.) There was also a pair of leather sandals which he'd received as a Christmas gift, and not only had never worn but hadn't even removed the catalogue tag from when it fell to me to go through his clothes closet and empty out the contents. The idea of lifts in his shoes would just never have occurred to my father. At that time, I had never to my knowledge seen a shoe tree, and didn't know what they were for, since I never took care of any of my shoes, or valued them.

My father's hair, which had evidently been almost light brown or blond when he was younger, had first darkened and then become suffused with gray, its texture stiffer than my own and tending to curl in the back during humid weather. The back of his neck was always red; his overall complexion was florid in the way that certain stocky older men's faces are florid or ruddy. Some of the redness was congenital, probably, and some psychological—like most men of his generation, he was both high-strung and tightly controlled, a type A personality but with a dominant superego, his inhibitions so extreme that it came out mainly as exaggerated dignity and precision in his movements. He almost never permitted himself any kind of open or prominent facial expression. But he was not a calm person. He did not speak or act in a nervous way, but there was a vibe of intense tension about him—I can remember him seeming to give off a slight hum when at rest. In hindsight, I suspect he was probably only a year or two from needing blood pressure medication when the accident occurred.

I remember being aware that my father's overall

posture or bearing seemed unusual for a shorter man—many short men tend to stand ramrod straight, for understandable reasons—in terms of his seeming not slumped but more like slightly bent forward at the waist, at a slight angle, which added to the sense of tension or always walking into some kind of wind. I know that I wouldn't understand this prior to entering the Service and seeing the bearing of some of the older examiners who spend all day for years at a desk or Tingle table, leaning forward to examine tax returns, primarily to identify those that should be audited. In other words, it's the posture of someone whose daily work means sitting very still at a desk and working on something in a concentrated way for years on end.

I really know very little about the reality of my father's job and what-all it entailed, though I certainly now know what cost systems are.

On the face of it, my entering a career in the IRS might appear connected to my father's accident—in more humanistic terms, connected to my 'loss' of a father who was himself an accountant. My father's technical area was accounting systems and processes, which is actually closer to data processing than real accountancy, as I would later understand. For myself, however, I am convinced that I would now be in the Service regardless, given the dramatic event that I remember totally changing my focus and attitude which occurred the following fall, during the third semester of my returning to DePaul and when I was retaking Intro Accounting, along with American Political Theory, which was another class I'd gotten an incomplete in at Lindenhurst through basically not knuckling down and putting in the work. It's true, though, that I may have done this—retaking Intro Accounting—at least partly to please or try to pay back my father, or to at least lessen the self-disgust I had felt after his walking into the nihilistic scene in the living room which I just mentioned. It was probably only a couple days after that scene and my father's reaction that I took the CTA commuter line down to Lincoln Park and started trying to reenroll for my last two years— in terms of credits, four terms—at DePaul, although due to certain technicalities I couldn't officially reenter until the fall of '77—another long story—and, thanks to knuckling down and also swallowing my pride and getting some extra help to deal with depreciation and amortization schedules, finally did pass, along with DePaul's version of American Political Theory—which they called American Political Thought, although it and the Lindenhurst version of the course were nearly identical—in the Fall 1978 semester, though not exactly with final grades to write home about, because I largely neglected serious studying for these two classes' final exams due to (somewhat ironically) the dramatic event, which occurred accidentally during an entirely different DePaul class, one I was not even really taking but sort of bumbled into through an inattentive screw-up during the final review period just before Christmas break, and was so dramatically moved and affected by that I barely even studied for my regular courses' final exams, though this time not out of carelessness or sloth but because I decided I had some very important, sustained, concentrated thinking to do after the dramatic encounter with the substitute Jesuit in Advanced Tax, which was the class I've mentioned sitting in on by mistake.

The fact is that there are probably just certain kinds of people who are drawn to a career in the IRS. People who are, as the substitute father said that final day in Advanced Tax, 'called to account.' Meaning we are talking about almost a special kind of psychological type, probably. It's not a very common type—perhaps one in 10,000—but the thing is that the sort of person of this type who decides that he wants to enter the Service really, really wants to, and becomes very determined, and will be hard to put off course once he's focused in on his real vocation and begun to be actively drawn to it. And even one in 10,000, in a country as large as America, will add up to a fair number of people—roughly 20,000—for whom the IRS fulfills all the professional and psychological criteria for a real vocation. These twenty or so thousand comprise the Service's core, or heart, and not all of them are high-ranked in the IRS administration, although some of them are. These are 20,000 out of the Service's total of over 105,000 employees. And there are no doubt core characteristics that these people have in common, predictive factors which at some point or other kick in and cause a genuine calling to pursue tax accounting and systems administration and organizational behavior and to devote themselves to helping administer and enforce the tax laws of this country as spelled out in Title 26 of the Code of Federal Regulations and the Revised Internal Revenue Code of 1954, plus all the statutes and regulations entailed by the Tax Reform Act of 1969, the Tax Reform Act of 1976, the Revenue Act of 1978, and so on and so forth. What these reasons and factors are, and to what extent they coexist with the particular talents and dispositions the Service is in need of — these are interesting questions, which today's IRS takes an active interest in understanding and quantifying. In terms of myself and how I got here, the important thing is that I discovered I had them — the factors and characteristics — and discovered this suddenly, by what seemed at the time like nothing more than a feckless mistake.

I've left out the matter of recreational drug abuse during this period, and the relation of certain drugs to how I got here, which in no way represents an endorsement of drug abuse but is just part of the story of the factors that eventually drew me to the Service. But it's complicated, and somewhat indirect. It's obvious that drugs were a big part of the whole scene in this era — this is well-known. I remember in the later seventies, the supposedly coolest recreational drug around Chicagoland college campuses was cocaine, and given how anxious I was at that time to conform, I'm sure I would have used more cocaine, or 'coke,' if I'd liked the effects. But I didn't — like it, I mean. It didn't cause euphoric excitement for me, it more just made me feel as though I'd had a dozen cups of coffee on an empty stomach. It was a terrible feeling, even though people around me like Steve Edwards talked about cocaine as if it was the greatest feeling of all time. I didn't get it. I also didn't like the way it made the people who had just done cocaine's eyes bulge out and their lips move around on their face in strange, uncontrollable ways, and the way even shallow or obvious ideas suddenly seemed incredibly profound to them. My overall memory of this cocaine period was of being at some kind of party with someone on cocaine who kept talking to me in this very rapid, intense way, and of me trying to subtly back away, and of every time I take a step backwards they take a step forwards, and so on and so forth, until they've backed me against a wall of the party and my back is literally up against the wall and they're talking very fast only inches from my face, which was something I didn't like at all. This actually happened at parties during this period. I think I have some of my father's inhibition. Close bodily proximity to someone who's very excited or upset is something I've always had a difficult time with, which is one reason why the Audits Division was out of the question for me during the selection and posting phase at the TAC—which I should explain stands for 'Training and Assessment Center,' which roughly one quarter of today's Service's contract personnel above the grade of GS-9 have started out by attending, especially those who—like me—entered through a recruitment program. As of now, there are two such centers, one in Indianapolis and a slightly larger one in Columbus OH. Both TACs are divisions of what is commonly known as Treasury School, as the Service is technically a branch of the US Treasury Department. But Treasury also includes everything from the Bureau of Alcohol, Tobacco, and Firearms to the US Secret Service, so 'Treasury School' now stands for over a dozen different training programs and facilities, including the Federal Law Enforcement Academy in Athens GA, to which those posted to Criminal Investigations from the TAC are sent for specialized training which they share with ATF agents, the DEA, federal marshals, and so on and so forth.

Anyhow, downers like Seconal and Valium simply made me go to sleep and sleep through whatever noise, including alarm clocks, happened to occur for the next fourteen hours, so these were not high on my list of favorites, either. You have to understand that most of these drugs were both plentiful and easy to get during this period. This was especially true at UIC, where the roommate I watched the foot and hung out so frequently at the Hat with was something of a human vending machine of recreational drugs, having established connections with mid-level dealers in the western suburbs, whom he always got extremely paranoid and suspicious if you asked him anything about, as if these were mafiosi instead of usually just young couples in apartment complexes. I know one thing he liked about me, though, as a roommate, was that there were so many different types of drugs that I didn't like or that didn't agree with me that he didn't have to be constantly worried about my discovering his stash—which he usually kept in two guitar cases in the back of his half of the closet, which any idiot could have figured out from his behavior with the closet or the number of cases he had back there versus the one guitar he actually brought out and played his two songs over and over with—or ripping him off. Like most student dealers, he did not deal cocaine, as there was too much money involved, not to mention coked-out people pounding on your door at 3:00 in the morning, so that cocaine was handled more by slightly older guys in leather hats and tiny little rat-like mustaches who operated out of bars like the Hat and King Philip's, which was another fashionable pub of the period, near the Mercantile Exchange on Monroe, where they also serviced younger commodity traders.

The UIC roommate was usually generously

stocked in psychedelics, which by that time had definitely passed into the mainstream, but personally psychedelics frightened me, mostly because of what I remembered happening to Art Linkletter's daughter—my parents had been very into watching Art Linkletter in my childhood.

Like any normal college student, I liked alcohol, especially beer in bars, though I didn't like drinking so much that I got sick—being nauseated is something I essentially can't stand. I'd much rather be in pain than sick to my stomach. But I also, like almost everyone else who wasn't an evangelical Christian or part of Campus Crusade, liked marijuana, which in the Chicagoland area during that period was called pot or 'blow.' (Cocaine was not called blow by anyone I ever knew, and only hippie posers ever called pot 'grass,' which had been the hip sixties term but was now out of fashion.) This pot usage had peaked during high school, but I still sometimes smoked pot in college, although I suspect this was largely a matter of just doing what everyone else did—at Lindenhurst, for instance, almost everyone smoked marijuana constantly, including openly on the south quad on Wednesdays, which everyone called 'hash Wednesday.' I should add that now that I am with the IRS, of course, my pot-smoking days are long

behind me. For one thing, the Service is technically a law enforcement agency, and it would be
hypocritical and wrong. Relatedly, the whole culture of the Examinations Division is inimical to
smoking pot, as even rote exams requires a very
sharp, organized, and methodical type of mental
state, with the ability to concentrate for long periods of time, and, even more important, the ability
to choose what one concentrates on versus ignoring, an ability which smoking marijuana would all
but destroy.

There was, however, sporadically throughout
this whole period, the matter of Obetrol, which is
chemically related to Dexedrine but did not have
the horrible breath and taste-in-the-mouth thing
of Dexedrine. It was also related to Ritalin, but
much easier to get, as Obetrol was the prescription
appetite suppressant of choice for overweight
women for several years in the mid-seventies, and
which I liked very much, somewhat for the same
reasons I'd liked Ritalin so much that one time,
though also partly—in this later period, with me
five years older than high school—for other reasons which are harder to explain. My affinity
for Obetrol had to do with self-awareness, which
I used to privately call 'doubling.' It's hard to
explain. Take pot, for instance—some people

report that smoking it makes them paranoid. For me, though, although I liked pot in some situations, the problem was more specific—smoking pot made me self-conscious, sometimes so much so that it made it difficult to be around people. This was another reason why smoking pot with my mother and Joyce was so awkward and tense— the truth is that I actually preferred to smoke pot by myself, and was much more comfortable with pot if I could be high by myself and just sort of space out. I'm mentioning this as a contrast with Obetrol, which you could either take as a regular capsule or untwist the halves of and crush the tiny little beads into powder and snort it up with a straw or rolled bill, rather like cocaine. Snorting Obetrols burns the inside of the nose something terrible, though, so I tended to prefer the old-fashioned way, when I took them, which I used to privately refer to as Obetrolling. It's not like I went around constantly Obetrolling, by the way—they were more recreational, and not always easy to get, depending on whether the overweight girls you knew at a given college or dorm were serious about dieting or not, which some were and some weren't, as with anything. One coed that I got them from for almost a whole year at DePaul wasn't even very overweight—her mother sent them to her, along

with cookies she'd baked, weirdly—evidently
the mother had some serious psychological conflicts about food and weight that she tried to project onto the daughter, who was not exactly a
fox but was definitely cool and blasé about her
mother's neurosis about her weight, and more or
less said, 'Whatever,' and was content to offload
the Obetrols for two dollars apiece and to share
the cookies with her roommate. There was also one
guy in the high-rise dorm on Roosevelt who took
them by prescription, for narcolepsy—sometimes
he would just fall asleep in the middle of whatever
he was doing, and he took Obetrol out of medical
necessity, since they were evidently very good for
narcolepsy—and he would every once in a while
give a couple away if he was in an expansive mood,
but he never actually sold or dealt them—he
believed it was bad karma. But for the most part,
they were not hard to get, although the roommate
from UIC never carried Obetrols for sale and
squeezed my shoes about liking them, referring to
the stimulants as 'Mother's little helper' and saying that anyone who wanted them could just ring
the doorbell of any overweight housewife in the
Chicagoland area, which was obviously an exag-
geration. But they were not all that popular. There
weren't even any street names or euphemisms for

them—if you were looking for them, you had to just say the brand name, which for some reason seemed terribly uncool, and not enough people I knew were into them to make *Obetrolling* any kind of candidate for a hip term.

The reason I bring up pot is for contrast. Obetrolling didn't make me self-conscious. But it did make me much more self-aware. If I was in a room, and had taken an Obetrol or two with a glass of water and they'd taken effect, I was now not only in the room, but I was aware that I was in the room. In fact, I remember I would often think, or say to myself, quietly but very clearly, *'I am in this room.'* It's difficult to explain this. At the time, I called it 'doubling,' but I'm still not entirely sure what I meant by this, nor why it seemed so profound and cool to not only be in a room but be totally aware that I was in the room, seated in a certain easy chair in a certain position listening to a certain specific track of an album whose cover was a certain specific combination of colors and designs—being in a state of heightened enough awareness to be able to consciously say to myself, *'I am in this room right now. The shadow of the foot is rotating on the east wall. The shadow is not recognizable as a foot because of the deformation of the angle of the light of the sun's position behind the sign.*

I am seated upright in a dark-green easy chair with a cigarette burn on the right armrest. The cigarette burn is black and imperfectly round. The track I am listening to is "The Big Ship" off of Brian Eno's Another Green World, *whose cover has colorful cut-out figures inside a white frame.'* Stated so openly, this amount of detail might seem tedious, but it wasn't. What it felt like was a sort of emergence, however briefly, from the fuzziness and drift of my life in that period. As though I was a machine that suddenly realized it was a human being and didn't have to just go through the motions it was pro-grammed to perform over and over. It also had to do with paying attention. It wasn't like the normal thing with recreational drugs which made colors brighter or music more intense. What became more intense was my awareness of my own part in it, that I could pay real attention to it. It was that I could look at, for instance, a dorm room's walls of institutional tan or beige and not only see them but be aware that I was seeing them — this was the dorm at UIC — and that I normally lived within these walls and was probably affected in all kinds of subtle ways by their institutional color but was usually unaware of how they made me feel, unaware of what it felt like to look at them, unaware usually of even their color and texture, because I never really looked at anything in a precise, attentive way. It was kind of striking. Their texture was mostly smooth, but if you really focused your attention there were also a lot of the little embedded strings and clots which painters tend to leave when they're paid by the job and not the hour and thus have motivation to hurry. If you really look at something, you can almost always tell what type of wage structure the person who made it was on. Or of the shadow of the sign and the way that the placement and height of the sun at the time affected the shape of the shadow, which mainly appeared to contract and expand as the real sign rotated across the street, or of the way that turning the little desk lamp next to the chair on and off changed the room's interplay of light and the different objects in the room's shadows and even the specific shade of the walls and ceiling and affected everything, and — through the 'doubling' — also being aware that I was turning the lamp off and on and noticing the changes and being affected by them, and by the fact that I knew I was noticing them. That I was aware of the awareness. It maybe sounds abstract or stoned, but it isn't. To me, it felt alive. There was something about it I preferred. I could listen to Floyd, say, or even one of the roommate's constant records from his bedroom like *Sgt. Pepper,* and not only hear the music and each note and bar and key change and resolution of each track, but know, with the same kind of awareness and discrimination, that I was doing this, meaning really listening—*Right now I am listening to the second chorus of the Beatles' "Fixing a Hole"'*—but also being aware of the exact feelings and sensations the music produced in me. That may sound all drippy-hippie, getting in touch with inner feelings and all that business. But based on my experience during that time, most people are always feeling something or adopting some attitude or choosing to pay attention to one thing or one part of something without even knowing we're doing it. We do it automatically, like a heartbeat. Sometimes I'd be sitting there in a room and become aware of how much effort it was to pay attention to just your own heartbeat for more than a minute or so—it's almost as though your heartbeat wants to stay out of awareness, like a rock star avoiding the limelight. But it's there if you can double up and make yourself pay attention. Same with music, too, the doubling was being able to both listen very closely and also to feel whatever emotions the music evoked—because obviously that's why we're into music, that it makes us feel certain things, otherwise it would just be noise—and not only have them, listening, but be aware of them, to be able to say to yourself, *'This song is making me feel both warm and safe, as though cocooned like a little boy that's just been taken out of the bath and wrapped in towels that have been washed so many times they're incredibly soft, and also at the same time feeling sad; there's an emptiness at the center of the warmth like the way an empty church or classroom with a lot of windows through which you can only see rain on the street is sad, as though right at the center of this safe, enclosed feeling is the seed of emptiness.'* Not that you'd necessarily say it that way, just that it was distinct and palpable enough to be said that specifically, if you wanted to. And being aware of that distinctness, as well. Anyhow, this was why I was into Obetrol. The point wasn't just to zone out on pretty music or back somebody up against a party wall.

And nor was it just good or pleasurable things you were aware of, on Obetrol or Cylert. Some of the stuff it brought into awareness wasn't pleasant, it was just reality. Like sitting in the UIC dorm room's little living room and listening to the roommate-slash-social-rebel from Naperville in his bedroom talking on his phone—this so-called nonconformist had his own phone line, paid for by guess who — talking to some coed, which if there was no music or TV on, you couldn't help overhearing through the walls, which were notoriously easy to put your fist through if you were the type that punched walls, and listening to his rap of ingratiating patter to this coed, and not only sort of disliking him and feeling embarrassed for him at the affected way he talked to girls — as if anybody who was paying any attention could miss seeing how hard he was trying to project this idea of himself as hip and radical without being the slightest bit aware of how it really looked, which was spoiled, insecure, and vain — and listening and feeling all this, but also being uncomfortably aware that I was, meaning having to consciously feel and be aware of these inner reactions instead of just having them operate in me without quite admitting them to myself. I don't think I'm explaining it very well. Like having to be able to say to yourself, *'I am pretending to sit here reading Albert Camus's* The Fall *for the Literature of Alienation midterm, but actually I'm really concentrating on listening to Steve try to impress this girl over the phone, and I am feeling embarrassment and contempt for him, and am thinking he's a poser, and at the same time I am also uncomfortably aware of times that I've also tried to project the idea of myself as hip and cynical so as to impress someone, meaning that not only do I sort of dislike Steve, which in all honesty I do, but part of the reason I dislike him is that when I listen to him on the phone it makes me see similarities and realize things about myself that embarrass me, but I don't know how to quit doing them—like, if I quit trying to seem nihilistic, even just to myself, then what would happen, what would I be like? And will I even remember this when I'm not Obetrolling, or will I just go back to being irritated by Steve Edwards without quite letting myself be aware of it, or why?'* Does this make sense? It could be frightening, because I would see all this with uncomfortable clarity, although I would not have used a word like *nihilism* during that period without trying to make it sound cool or like an allusion, which to myself, in the clarity of doubling, I wouldn't have been tempted to do, as I did things like this only when I wasn't really aware of what I was doing or what my real agenda was, but rather on some kind of strange, robotic autopilot. Which, when I did Obetrol—or once, at DePaul, a variant called Cylert, which only came in 10 mg. tablets, and was only available one time in a very special situation that never repeated—I tended to realize again that I wasn't even really aware of what was going on, most of the time. Like taking the train instead of actually driving yourself somewhere and having to know where you were and make decisions about where to turn. On the train, one can simply space out and ride along, which is what it felt as though I was doing most of the time. And I'd be aware of this too, on these stimulants, and aware of the fact that I was aware. The awarenesses were fleeting, though, and after I came off of the Obetrol—which usually involved a bad headache—afterward, it felt as though I barely remembered any of the things I'd become aware of. The memory of the feeling of suddenly coming awake and being aware felt vague and diffuse, like something you think you see at the outer periphery of your vision but then can't see when you try to look directly at it. Or like a fragment of memory which you're not sure whether it was real or part of a dream. Just as I'd predicted and been afraid of when I'd been doubled, of course. So it wasn't all fun and games, which was one reason why Obetrolling felt true and important instead of just goofy and pleasurable like pot. Some of it was uncomfortably vivid. As in not merely waking up to an awareness of my dislike of the roommate and his denim workshirts and guitar and all of the so-called friends who came around and had to pretend to like him and find him cool in order to get their gram of hash from him or whatever, and not just disliking the whole rooming situation and even the nihilistic ritual of the foot and the Hat, which we pretended was a lot cooler and funnier than it was—as it wasn't as though we did it just once or twice but basically all the time, it was really just an excuse not to study or do our work and instead be wastoids while our parents paid our tuition, room, and board—but also being aware, when I really looked at it, that part of me had chosen to room with Steve Edwards because part of me actually sort of enjoyed disliking him and cataloguing things about him that were hypocritical and made me feel a sort of embarrassed distaste, and that there must be certain psychological reasons why I lived, ate, partied, and hung around with a person I didn't even really like or respect very much...which probably meant that I didn't respect myself very much, either, and that was why I was such a conformist. And the point is that, sitting there overhearing Steve tell the girl on the phone that he'd always felt today's women had to be seen as more than just sex objects if there was going to be any hope for the human race, I would be articulating all this to myself, very clearly and consciously, instead of just drifting around having all these sensations and reactions about him without ever being quite aware of them. So it basically meant waking up to how unaware I normally was, and knowing that I'd be going back to sleep like that when the artificial effect of the speed wore off. Meaning it wasn't all fun and games. But it did feel *alive,* and that's probably why I liked it. It felt like I actually *owned* myself. Instead of renting or whatever—I don't know. But that analogy sounds too cheap, like a cheap witticism. It's hard to explain, and this is probably more time than I should take to explain it. Nor am I obviously trying to give any pro-drug-abuse message here. But it was important. I like now to think of the Obetrol and other subtypes of speed as more of a kind of signpost or directional sign, pointing to what might be possible if I could become more aware and alive in daily life. In this sense, I think that abusing these drugs was a valuable experience for me, as I was basically so feckless and unfocused during this period that I needed a very clear, blunt type of hint that there was much more to being an alive, responsible, autonomous adult than I had any idea of at the time.

On the other hand, it goes without saying the key is moderation. You couldn't spend all your time taking Obetrols and sitting there doubled and aware and still expect to take care of business effectively. I remember not getting Camus's *The Fall* read in time, for instance, and having to totally bullshit my way through the Literature of Alienation midterm — in other words, I was cheating, at least by implication — but not feeling much about it one way or the other, that I can recall, except a sort of cynical, disgusted relief when the prof's grader wrote something like 'Interesting in places!' under the B. Meaning a meaningless bullshit response to meaningless bullshit. But there was no denying it was powerful — the feeling that everything important was right there and I could sometimes wake up almost in mid-stride, in the middle of all the meaningless bullshit, and suddenly be aware of it. It's hard to explain. The truth is that I think the Obetrol and doubling was my first glimmer of the sort of impetus that I believe helped lead me into the Service and the special problems and priorities here at the Regional Examination Center. It had something to do with paying attention and the ability to choose what I paid attention to, and to be aware of that choice, the fact that it's a choice. I'm not the smartest person, but even during that whole pathetic, directionless period, I think that deep down I knew that there was more to my life and to myself than just the ordinary psychological impulses for pleasure and vanity that I let drive me. That there were depths to me that were not bullshit or childish but profound, and were not abstract but actually much realer than my clothes or self-image, and that blazed in an almost sacred way — I'm being serious; I'm not just trying to make it sound more dramatic than it was — and that these realest, most profound parts of me involved not drives or appetites but simple attention, awareness, if only I could stay awake off speed.

But I couldn't. As mentioned, usually afterwards I couldn't even recall what had seemed so clear and profound about what I'd come to be aware of in that cheap green previous tenant's easy chair, which somebody had just left there in the room when he'd moved out of the dorm, and which had something broken or bent in its frame under the cushions and kind of tilted to one side when you tried to lean back, so you had to sit up very straight and erect in it, which was an odd feeling. The whole doubling incident would be covered with a sort of mental fuzz the next morning, especially if I woke up late — which I usually did, given what was essentially a kind of amphetamine's effects on getting to sleep — and had to more or less hit the floor running and hurry to class without even noticing anyone or anything I was running past. In essence, I was one of those types that have a terror of being late but still always seem to be running late. If I came into something late I'd often be too tense and wound up at first even to be able to follow what was going on. I know I inherited the fear of lateness from my father. Plus, it's true that sometimes the heightened awareness and self-articulation of doubling on Obetrols could go too far— *'Now I am aware that I am aware that I'm sitting up oddly straight, now I'm aware that I feel an itch on the left side of my neck, now I'm aware that I'm deliberating whether to scratch or not, now I'm aware of paying attention to that deliberation and what the ambivalence about scratching feels like and what those feelings and my awareness of them do to my awareness of the intensity of the itch.'* Meaning that past a certain point, the element of choice of attention in doubling could get lost, and the awareness could sort of explode into a hall of mirrors of consciously felt sensations and thoughts and awareness of awareness of awareness of these. This was attention without choice, meaning the loss of the ability to focus in and concentrate on just one thing, and was another big incentive for moderation in the use of Obetrols, especially late at night—I have to admit that I know that once or twice I got so lost in the halls or stacked layers of awareness of awareness that I went to the bathroom right there on the sofa—this was up at Lindenhurst College, where there were three roommates per suite and a semi-furnished 'social room' in the suite's center, where the sofa was—which, even at the time, seemed like a clear sign of loss of basic priorities and failure to take care of business. For some reason now, I sometimes have a mental picture of me trying to explain to my father how I somehow became so totally focused and aware that I sat there and wet my pants, but the picture cuts off just as his mouth opens for a response, and I'm 99 percent sure this is not a real memory—how could he know anything about a davenport all the way up in Lindenhurst?

For the record, it is true that I miss my father and was very upset about what happened, and sometimes I feel quite sad at the thought that he is not here to see the career path I've chosen, and the changes in me as a person as a result, and some of my PP-47 performance evaluations, and to talk about cost systems and forensic accounting with from a vastly more adult perspective.

And yet these flickers of deeper awareness, whether drug-induced or not—for it is arguable how much that ultimately matters—probably had more of a direct effect on my life and direction's change and my entering the Service in 1979 than did my father's accident, or possibly even more than the dramatic experience I underwent in the Advanced Tax review class that I had sat in on by mistake during my second, ultimately much more focused and successful enrollment at DePaul. I've mentioned this mistaken final review already. In a nutshell, the story of this experience is that DePaul's Lincoln Park campus had two newer buildings that looked very alike, were literally almost mirror images of one another, by architectural design, and were connected at both the first floor and — by an overhead transom not unlike our own at the Midwest REC — at the third floor, and DePaul's accounting and political science departments were in the two different buildings of this identical set, whose names I don't recall at this moment. Meaning the buildings' names. It was the last regular class day for Tuesday-Thursday classes of the Fall '78 term, and we were to be reviewing for the final exam in American Political Thought, which was to be all essay questions, and on my way to the final review I know I was trying to mentally review the areas that I wanted to make sure at least someone in the class asked about — it didn't have to be me — in terms of how extensively they would be covered on the final. Except for Intro Accounting, I was still taking mostly psychology and political science classes—the latter ones mostly due to the requirements for declaring a major, which you had to satisfy in order to graduate—but now that I wasn't merely trying to squeak by on last-minute bullshit, these classes were obviously much harder and more time-consuming. I remember that most of DePaul's version of American Political Thought was on *The Federalist Papers,* by Madison et al., which I had had before at Lindenhurst but remembered almost none of. In essence, I was so intent on thinking about the review and the final exam that what happened is that I took the wrong building entrance without noticing it, and ended up in the correct third-floor room but the wrong building, with this room being such an identical mirror image of the adjoining building's correct room, directly across the transom, that I didn't immediately notice the error. And this classroom turned out to contain the final review day of Advanced Tax, a famously difficult course at DePaul that was known as the accounting department's equivalent of what organic chemistry was for science majors—the final hurdle, the weed-out class, requiring several prerequisites and open to senior

accounting majors and postgrads only, and said to
be taught by one of DePaul's few remaining Jesuit
professors, meaning with the official black-and-
white clothing ensemble and absolutely zero sense
of humor or desire to be liked or 'connecting' with
the students. At DePaul, the Jesuits were notoriously unmellow. My father, by the way, was raised
as a Roman Catholic but had little or nothing to
do with the church as an adult. My mom's family
was originally Lutheran. Like many of my generation, I wasn't raised as anything. But this day in
the identical classroom also turned out to be one
of the most unexpectedly powerful, galvanizing
events of my life at that time, and made such an
impression that I even remember what I was wearing as I sat there—a red-and-brown-striped acrylic
sweater, white painter's pants, and Timberland
boots whose color my roommate—who was a
serious chemistry major, no more Steve Edwardses
and rotating feet—called 'dogshit yellow,' with
the laces untied and dragging, which was the way
everyone I knew or hung out with wore their
Timberlands that year.

By the way, I do think that awareness is different from thinking. I am similar to most other people, I believe, in that I do not really do my most
important thinking in large, intentional blocks

where I sit down uninterrupted in a chair and know in advance what it is I'm going to think about—as in, for instance, *'I am going to think about life and my place in it and what's truly important to me, so that I can start forming concrete, focused goals and plans for my adult career'*—and then sit there and think about it until I reach a conclusion. It doesn't work like that. For myself, I tend to do my most important thinking in incidental, accidental, almost daydreamy ways. Making a sandwich, taking a shower, sitting in a wrought-iron chair in the Lakehurst mall food court waiting for someone who's late, riding the CTA train and staring at both the passing scene and my own faint reflection superimposed on it in the window—and suddenly you find you're thinking about things that end up being important. It's almost the opposite of awareness, if you think about it. I think this experience of accidental thinking is common, if perhaps not universal, although it's not something that you can ever really talk to anyone else about because it ends up being so abstract and hard to explain. Whereas in an intentional bout of concentrated major thinking, where you sit down with the conscious intention of confronting major questions like *'Am I currently happy?'* or *'What, ultimately, do I really care about and believe in?'* or — particularly if some kind of authority figure has just squeezed your shoes — *'Am I essentially a worthwhile, contributing type of person or a drifting, indifferent, nihilistic person?,'* then the questions often end up not answered but more like beaten to death, so attacked from every angle and each angle's different objections and complications that they end up even more abstract and ultimately meaningless than when you started. Nothing is achieved this way, at least that I've ever heard of. Certainly, from all evidence, St. Paul, or Martin Luther, or the authors of *The Federalist Papers,* or even President Reagan never changed the direction of their lives this way — it happened more by accident.

As for my father, I have to admit that I don't know how he did any of the major thinking that led him in the directions he followed all his life. I don't even know whether there *was* any major, conscious thinking in his case. Like many men of his generation, he may well have been one of those people who can just proceed on autopilot. His attitude towards life was that there are certain things that have to be done and you simply have to do them — such as, for instance, going to work every day. Again, it may be that this is another element of the generation gap. I don't think my father loved his job with the city, but on the other hand, I'm not sure he ever asked himself major questions like *'Do I like my job? Is this really what I want to spend my life doing? Is it as fulfilling as some of the dreams I had for myself when I was a young man serving in Korea and reading British poetry in my bunk in the barracks at night?'* He had a family to support, this was his job, he got up every day and did it, end of story, everything else is just self-indulgent nonsense. That may actually have been the lifetime sum-total of his thinking on the matter. He essentially said 'Whatever' to his lot in life, but obviously in a very different way from the way in which the directionless wastoids of my generation said 'Whatever.'

My mother, on the other hand, changed her life's direction very dramatically—but again, I don't know whether this was as a result of concentrated thinking. In fact, I doubt it. That is just not how things like this work. The truth is that most of my mother's choices were emotionally driven. This was another common dynamic for her generation. I think that she liked to believe that the feminist consciousness-raising and Joyce and the whole thing of her and Joyce and the divorce were the result of thinking, like a conscious change of life-philosophy. But it was really emotional. She had a sort of nervous breakdown in 1971, even though nobody ever used that term. And maybe she would eschew 'nervous breakdown' and say instead that it was a sudden, conscious change in beliefs and direction. And who can really argue with something like that? I wish I had understood this at the time, because there were ways in which I know I was kind of nasty and condescending to my mother about the whole Joyce and divorce thing. Almost as though I unconsciously sided with my father, and took it upon myself to say all the nasty, condescending things that he was too self-disciplined and dignified to allow himself to say. Even speculating about it is probably pointless — as my father said, people are going to do what they're going to do, and all you can really do is play the hand that life deals you to the best of your ability. I never knew with any certainty whether he even really missed her, or was sad. When I think of him now, I realize he was lonely, that it was very hard for him divorced and alone in that house in Libertyville. After the divorce, in some ways he probably felt free, which of course has its good sides — he could come and go as he pleased, and when he squeezed my shoes about something he didn't have to worry about choosing his words carefully or arguing with someone who was going to stick up for me no matter what. But freedom of this kind is also very close, on the psychological continuum, to loneliness. The only people you're really ultimately 'free' with in this way are strangers, and in this sense my father was right about money and capitalism being equal to freedom, as buying or selling something doesn't obligate you to anything except what's written in the contract—although there's also the social contract, which is where the obligation to pay one's fair share of taxes comes in, and I think my father would have agreed with Mr. Glendenning's statement that 'Real freedom is freedom to obey the law.' That all probably doesn't make much sense. Anyhow, it's all just abstract speculation at this point, because I never really talked to either of my parents about how they felt about their adult lives. It's just not the sort of thing that parents sit down and openly discuss with their children, at least not in that era.

Anyhow, it would probably help to provide some background info. The easiest way to define a tax is to say that the amount of the tax, symbolized as T, is equal to the product of the tax base and tax rate. This is usually symbolized as $T = B \times R$, so you can then get $R = T/B$, which is the formula for determining whether a tax rate is progressive, regressive, or proportional. This is very basic tax accounting. It is so familiar to most IRS personnel that we don't even have to think about it. But anyhow, the critical variable is T's relationship to B. If the ratio of T to B stays the same regardless of whether B, the tax base, goes up or down, then the tax is proportional. This is also known as a flat-rate tax. A progressive tax is where the ratio T/B increases as B increases and decreases as B decreases—which is essentially the way today's marginal income tax works, in which you pay 0 percent on your first 2,300 dollars, 14 percent on your next 1,100 dollars, 16 percent on your next 1,000, and so on and so forth, up to 70 percent of everything over $108,300, which is all part of the US Treasury's current policy that, in theory, the more annual income you have, the greater the proportion of your income your income tax obligation should represent—although obviously it does not always work this way in practice, given all of the various legal deductions and credits which are part of the modern tax code. Anyhow, progressive tax schedules can be symbolized by a simple ascending bar graph, each bar of which represents a given tax bracket. Sometimes a progressive tax is also called a graduated tax, but this is not the Service's term for it. A regressive tax, on

the other hand, is where the ratio T/B increases as B decreases, meaning you pay the highest tax rates on the smallest amounts, which arguably doesn't make much sense in terms of fairness and the social contract. However, regressive taxes can often appear in disguise—for instance, opponents of state lotteries and cigarette taxes often claim that what these things amount to is a disguised regressive tax. The Service has no opinion on this issue either way. Anyhow, income taxes are almost always progressive, given our country's democratic ideals. Here, on the other hand, are some of the types of taxes which are usually proportional or flat: real property, personal property, customs, excise, and especially sales tax.

As many people here remember, in 1977, during high inflation, high deficits, and my second enrollment at DePaul, there was a state fiscal experiment in Illinois in which the state sales tax was to be made progressive instead of proportional. This was probably my first experience of seeing how the implementation of tax policy can actually affect people's lives. As mentioned, sales taxes are normally almost universally proportional. As I now understand it, the idea behind trying a progressive sales tax was to raise state tax revenues while not inflicting hardship on the state's poor or discouraging investors, plus also to help combat inflation by taxing consumption. The idea was that the more you bought, the more tax you paid, which would help discourage demand and ease inflation. The progressive sales tax was the brainchild of someone high up in the State Treasurer's Office in 1977. Just who this person was, or whether he wore the brown helmet in some way after the resulting disaster, I do not know, but both the state treasurer and the governor of Illinois definitely lost their jobs over the fiasco. Whoever's fault it ultimately was, though, it was a major tax-policy boner, which actually could have been easily prevented if anyone in the State Treasurer's Office had bothered to consult with the Service about the advisability of the scheme. Despite the existence of both the Midwest Regional Commissioner's Office and a Regional Examination Center within Illinois's borders, however, it's an established fact that this never occurred. Despite state revenue agencies' reliance on federal tax returns and the Service's computer system's master files in the enforcement of state tax law, there is a tradition of autonomy and distrust among state revenue offices for federal agencies like the IRS, which sometimes results in key communication lapses, of which the 1977 Illinois sales tax disaster is, within the Service, a classic case, and the subject of numerous professional jokes and stories. As almost anyone here at Post 047 could have told them, a fundamental rule of effective tax enforcement is remembering that the average taxpayer is always going to act out of his own monetary self-interest. This is basic economic law. In taxation, the result is that the taxpayer will always do whatever the law allows him to do in order to minimize his taxes. This is simple human nature, which the Illinois officials either failed to understand or neglected to see the implications of for sales tax transactions. It may be a case of the State Treasurer's Office allowing the whole matter to get so complex and theoretical that they failed to see what was right in front of their nose — the base, B, of a progressive tax cannot be something which can be easily subdivided. If it can be easily subdivided, then the average taxpayer, acting out of his own economic interest, will do whatever he can legally do to subdivide the B into two or more smaller Bs in order to avoid the effective progression. And this, in late 1977, was precisely what happened. The result was retail chaos. At, for instance, the supermarket, shoppers would no longer purchase three large bags of groceries for $78 total and submit to paying 6, 6.8, and 8.5 percent on those parts of their purchases over $5.00, $20.00, and $42.01, respectively—they were now motivated to structure their grocery purchase as numerous separate small purchases of $4.99 or less in order to take advantage of the much more attractive 3.75 percent sales tax on purchases under $5.00. The difference between 8 percent and 3.75 percent is more than enough to establish incentive and make citizens' economic self-interest kick in. So, at the store, you suddenly had everyone buying under $5.00 worth of groceries and running out to their car and putting the little bag in the car and running back in and buying another amount under $5.00 and running out to their car, and so on and so forth. Supermarkets' checkout lines started going all the way to the back of the store. Department stores were just as bad, and I know gas stations were even worse—only a few months after the supply shock of OPEC and fights in gas lines over rationing, now, in Illinois that autumn, fights also broke out at gas stations from drivers being forced to wait as people ahead of them at the pump tried putting $4.99 worth in and running in and paying and running back out and resetting the pump and putting in another $4.99, and so on. It was the exact opposite of mellow, to say the least. And the administrative burden of calculating sales tax over four separate margins of purchases just about broke retail stores. Those with automated registers and bookkeeping systems saw the systems crash under the new load. From what I understand, the high administrative costs of the new bookkeeping burden got passed along and caused an inflationary spike in Illinois, which then further aggrieved consumers who were already peeved because the progressive sales tax was economically forcing them to go through checkout lines half a dozen times or more, in many cases. There were some riots, especially in the southern part of the state, which abuts Kentucky and tends not to be what you'd call understanding or sympathetic about government's need to collect revenue in the first place. The truth is that northern, central, and southern Illinois are practically different countries, culturally speaking. But the chaos was statewide. The state treasurer was burnt in effigy. Banks saw a run on ones and change. From the perspective of administrative costs, the worst part came when enterprising businesses saw a new opportunity and started using 'Subdividable!' as a sales inducement. Including, for instance, used-car dealers that were willing to sell you a car as an agglomeration of separate little transactions for front bumper, right rear wheel

well, alternator coil, spark plug, and so on, the purchase structured as thousands of different $4.99
transactions. It was technically legal, of course, and
other big-ticket retailers soon followed—but I
think it was when Realtors also got into the practice of subdividing that things really fell apart.
Banks, mortgage brokers, dealers in commodities
and bonds, and the Illinois Department of Revenue
all saw their data processing systems buckle—the
progressive sales tax produced a veritable tidal wave
of subdivided-sales information that drowned the
existing technology. The whole thing was repealed
after less than four months. Actually, the state legislators came back to Springfield from their Christmas recess in order to convene and repeal it, as
that period had been the most disastrous for retail
commerce—holiday-season shopping in 1977
was a nightmare that people still sometimes chat
ruefully about with strangers when they become
stuck in checkout lines here in the state even now,
years later. Rather the same way extreme heat or
mugginess will make people reminisce together
about other terrible summers they both remember.
Springfield is the state capital, by the way, as well
as the site of an incredible amount of Lincoln
memorabilia.

Anyhow, it was also at this time that my father

was killed unexpectedly in a CTA subway accident in Chicago, during the almost indescribably horrible and chaotic holiday shopping rush of December 1977, and the accident actually occurred while he was in the process of weekend Christmas shopping, which probably helped contribute to making the whole thing even more tragic. The accident was not on the famous 'El' part of the CTA—he and I were in the Washington Square station, to which we'd ridden in from Libertyville on the commuter line in order to transfer to a subway line going further downtown. I think we were ultimately headed to the Art Institute gift shop. I was back at my father's house for the weekend, I remember, at least partly because I had intensive studying to do for my first round of final exams since reenrolling at DePaul, where I was living in a dorm on the Loop campus. In retrospect, part of the reason for coming home to Libertyville to cram may also have been to give my father an opportunity to watch me apply myself to serious studying on a weekend, though I don't remember being aware of this motivation at the time. Also, for those who do not know, the Chicago Transit Authority's train system is a mishmash of elevated, conventional underground, and high-speed commuter rails. By prior agreement, I came into the city with him on Saturday in order to help him find some kind of Christmas gift for my mother and Joyce—a task I imagine he must have found difficult every year—and also, I think, for his sister, who lives with her husband and children in Fair Oaks OK.

Essentially, what happened in the Washington Square station, where we were transferring downtown, is that we descended the cement steps of the subway level into the dense crowds and heat of the platform—even in December, Chicago's subway tunnels tend to be hot, although not nearly as unbearable as during the summer months, but, on the other hand, the platforms' winter heat is undergone while wearing a winter coat and scarf, and it was also extremely crowded, it being the holiday shopping rush, with the additional frenzy and chaos of the progressive sales tax being under way this year as well. Anyhow, I remember that we reached the bottom of the stairs and the platform's crowds just as the train slid in—it was stainless steel and tan plastic, with both full and partially pulled-off holly decals around some of the cars' windows—and the automatic doors opened with a pneumatic sound, and the train stood idling for the moment as large masses of impatient, numerous-small-purchase-laden holiday shoppers pushed on and off. In terms of crowdedness, it was also the peak shopping hours of Saturday afternoon. My father had wanted to do the shopping in the morning before the downtown crowds got completely out of control, but I had overslept, and he had waited for me, although he was not pleased about it and did not disguise this. We finally left after lunch—meaning, in my case, breakfast—and even on the commuter line into the city, the crowds had been intense. Now we arrived on the even more crowded platform at a moment that most subway riders will acknowledge as awkward and somewhat stressful, with the train idling and the doors open but one never knowing for sure how much longer they'll stay that way as you move through the platform's crowds, trying to get to the train before the doors close. You don't quite want to break into a run or start shoving people out of the way, as the more rational part of you knows it's hardly a matter of life and death, that another train will be along soon, and that the worst that can happen is that you'll barely miss it, that the doors will slide shut just as you get to the train, and you will have barely missed getting on and will have to wait on the hot, crowded platform for a few minutes. And yet there's always another part of you—or of me, anyhow, and I'm quite sure, in hindsight, of my father—which almost panics. The idea of the doors closing and the train with its crowds of people who did make it inside pulling away just as you get up to the doors provokes some kind of strange, involuntary feeling of anxiety or urgency—I don't think there's even a specific word for it, psychologically, though possibly it's related to primal, prehistoric fears that you would somehow miss getting to eat your fair share of the tribe's kill or would be caught out alone in the veldt's tall grass as night falls—and, though he and I had certainly never talked about it, I now suspect that this deep, involuntary sense of anxiety about getting to idling trains just in time was especially bad for my father, who was a man of extreme organization and personal discipline and precise schedules who was always precisely on time for everything, and for whom the primal anxiety of just barely missing something was especially intense—although on the other hand he was also a man of enormous personal dignity and composure, and would normally never allow himself to be seen shouldering people aside or running on a public platform with his topcoat billowing and one hand holding his dark-gray hat down on his head and his keys and assorted pocket change audibly jingling, not unless he felt some kind of intense, irrational pressure to make the train, the way it is often the most disciplined, organized, dignified people who, it turns out, are under the most intense internal pressure from their repressions or superego, and can sometimes suddenly kind of snap in various small ways and, under enough pressure, behave in ways which might at first seem totally out of sync with your view of them. I was not able to see his eyes or facial expression; I was behind him on the platform, partly because he walked more quickly in general than I did—when I was a child, the term he used for this was 'dawdle'—although, on that day, it was partly also because he and I were in the midst of yet another petty psychological struggle over the fact that I had overslept and made him, according to his perspective, 'late,' there being therefore something pointedly impatient about his rapid stride and hurry through the CTA station, to which I was responding by deliberately not increasing my own normal pace very much or making much of an effort to keep up with him, staying just far enough behind him to annoy him but not far enough back quite to warrant his turning and actually squeezing my shoes over it, as well as assuming a kind of spacey, apathetic demeanor— much like a dawdling child, in fact, though of course I would never have acknowledged this at the time. In other words, the basic situation was that he was peeved and I was sulking, but neither of us was consciously aware of this, nor of how habitual, for us, this sort of petty psychological struggle was—in retrospect, it seems to me that we did this sort of thing to one another constantly, out of possibly nothing more than unconscious habit. It's a typical sort of dynamic between fathers and sons. It may even have been part of the unconscious motivation behind my indifferent drifting and lump-like sloth at all of the various colleges he had to get up on time every day and go to work to pay for. Of course, none of this entered into my awareness at the time, much less ever got acknowledged or discussed by either of us. In some sense, you could say that my father died before either of us could become aware of how invested we actually were in these petty little rituals of conflict, or of how much it had affected their marriage that my mother had so often been put in the role of mediator between us, all of us acting out typical roles which none of us were conscious of, like machines going through their programmed motions.

I remember, hurrying through the platform's crowds, that I saw him turn sideways to shoulder his way between two large, slow-moving Hispanic women who were heading towards the train's open doors with twine-handled shopping bags, one of which my father's leg jostled and caused to swing slightly back and forth. I don't know whether these women were actually together or were just forced by their size and the surrounding crowds' pressure to walk so closely side by side. They were not among those interviewed after the accident, which means they were probably on the train by the time it happened. I was only eight to ten feet behind him by this time, and openly hurrying to catch up, as there was the idling downtown train just ahead, and the idea of my father just making it onto the train but of me lagging too far behind him and getting to the doors just as they closed, and of watching his face's expression framed by holly decals as we looked at one another through the doors' glass portions as he pulled away in the train — I think anyone could imagine how peeved and disgusted he would be, and also vindicated and triumphant in our little psychological struggle over hurry and 'lateness,' and I could now feel my own rising anxiety at the thought of him making the train and me just barely missing it, so at this point I was trying to close the gap between us. I still, to this day, do not know whether my father was aware then that I was almost right behind him, or that I was nearly butting and shoving people out of the way myself in my hurry to catch up, because, as far as I know, he did not look back over his shoulder or signal to me in any way as he made for the train's doors. During all of the litigation that followed, none of the respondents or their counsel ever once disputed the fact that CTA trains are not supposed to be able to begin moving unless all of the doors are completely closed. Nor did anyone seek to challenge my account of the exact order of what happened, as at this point I was a few feet at most behind him, and witnessed the whole thing with what everyone conceded was terrible clarity. The two halves of the car's door had begun to slide shut with their familiar pneumatic sound just as my father reached the doors and shot out one arm in between the halves to keep them from closing so that he could squeeze his way in, and the doors closed on his arm — too firmly, evidently, to allow either the rest of my father to squeeze through the doors' gap or to allow the doors to be forced back open enough to let him withdraw his arm, which it turned out was caused by a possible malfunction involving the machinery that controlled the force with which the doors closed — by which time the subway train had begun moving, which was another blatant malfunction—special circuit breakers between the doors' sensors and the train operator's console are supposed to disengage the throttle if any of the doors on any car are open (as one can imagine, we all learned a great deal about CTA trains' design and safety specifications during the litigation following the accident)—and my father was being forced to trot with gradually increasing speed alongside it, the train, releasing his hold on his head's hat to pound with his fist against the doors as two or possibly three men inside the subway car were now at the slight gap in the doors, trying to pull or pry them open further enough to at least allow my father to extract his arm. My father's hat, which he prized and owned a special hat block for, flew off and was lost in the platform's dense crowds, in which a visibly widening gap or tear appeared—by which I mean it appeared in the crowd further down the platform, which I could see from my own place, trapped in the crowd at the platform's edge at a point further and further behind the widening gap or fissure that opened in the platform's crowds as my father was forced to run faster and faster at the accelerating train's side and people moved or leapt back to avoid being knocked onto the track. Given that many of these people were also holding numerous small, subdivided packages and individually purchased bags, many of these could be seen flying up in the air and rotating or spilling their contents in various ways above the widening gap as shoppers jettisoned their purchases in an attempt to leap clear of my father's path, so that part of the appearance of the gap was the illusion that it was somehow spurting or raining consumer goods. Also, the causal issues related to legal liability for the incident turned out to be incredibly complex. The manufacturer's specifications for the doors' pneumatic systems did not adequately explain how the doors could close with such force that a healthy adult male could not withdraw his arm, which meant that the manufacturer's claim that my father—perhaps out of panic, or because of injury to his arm—failed to take reasonable action to extricate his arm was difficult to refute. The male subway riders who appeared to be attempting so forcefully to pry the doors open from within subsequently vanished down the track with the departing train and were not successfully identified, this due partly to the fact that the subsequent transit and police investigators did not pursue these identifications very aggressively, possibly as it was clear, even at the scene, that the incident was a civil and not criminal matter. My mother's first lawyer did place personal ads in the *Tribune* and *Sun-Times* requesting that these two or three passengers come forward and be deposed for legal purposes, but for what they claimed were reasons of expense and practicability, these ads were quite small, and were buried in the Classified section towards the rear of the paper, and ran for what my mother would later claim was an unreasonably brief and unaggressive period of time during which all too many Chicagoland residents left the city for the holidays anyhow—so that this eventually became one more protracted, complex element of the litigation's second phase.

At the Washington Square station, the official 'scene of the accident'—which, in a fatality, is legally deemed to be '[the] location at which death or injuries causing death are sustained'—was listed at 65 yards off of the subway platform, in the southbound tunnel itself, at which point the CTA train was determined to have been traveling at between 51 and 54 miles per hour and portions of my father's upper body impacted the iron bars of a built-in ladder protruding from the tunnel's west wall—this ladder had been installed to allow CTA maintenance personnel to access a box of multi-bus circuitry in the tunnel's ceiling—and the trauma, confusion, shock, noise, screaming, rain of small individual purchases, and nearly stampede-like evacuation of the platform as my father cut an increasingly forceful and high-velocity swath through the dense crowds of shoppers all disqualified even those few people who still remained there on the scene—most of them injured, or claiming injury—as 'reliable' witnesses for authorities to interview. Shock is evidently common in situations of graphic death. Less than an hour after the accident, all that any bystanders could seem to remember were screams, loss of holiday purchases, concern for personal safety, and vivid but fragmentary details as to my father's affect and actions, various rippling things the onrushing air did to his topcoat and scarf, and the successive injuries he appeared to receive as he was borne at increasing speed towards the platform's end and fully or partly collided with a wire mesh trash receptacle, several airborne packages and shopping bags, a pillar's steel rivets, and an older male commuter's steel or aluminum luggage cart—this last item was somehow knocked by the impact across the tunnel and onto the northbound tracks, causing sparks from that track's third rail and adding to the stampeding crowds' chaos. I remember that a young Hispanic or Puerto Rican man wearing what looked to be a type of tight black hairnet was interviewed while holding my father's right shoe, a tasseled Florsheim loafer, of which the toe portion and welt were so abraded by the platform's cement that the sole's front portion had detached and was hanging loose, and that the man could not recall how he'd come to be holding it. He, too, was later determined to be in shock, and I can clearly remember seeing the Hispanic man afterward again in the triage area of the emergency room — which was at Loyola Marymount Hospital, only one or two blocks away from the Washington Square CTA station — seated in a plastic chair and trying to fill out forms on a clipboard with a ball-point pen attached by a piece of white string to the clipboard, still holding the shoe.

And the wrongful-death litigation was, as mentioned, incredibly complex, even though it all technically never even proceeded past the initial legal stages of determining whether the City of Chicago, the CTA, the CTA's Maintenance Division (the emergency brake's cord in the car to which my father was forcibly appended was discovered to have been vandalized and cut, although expert opinion was divided on whether the forensic evidence represented a very recent cut or one of weeks' duration. Evidently, the microscopic

evaluation of severed plastic fibers can be interpreted in just about any way one's interests lead
one to interpret it), the train's manufacturer of
record, the train's engineer, his immediate supervisor, AFSCME, and the over two dozen different
subcontractors and vendors of various components
of the various systems adjudged by the forensic
engineers retained by our legal team to have played
a part in the accident should, as respondents, be
classified in the action as strictly liable, liable, neg-
ligent, or FEDD, the latter abbreviation standing
for 'failure to exercise due diligence.' According to
my mother, our legal team's client liaison had con-
fided to her that the multiplicity of named respondents was just an initial strategic gambit, and that
we would ultimately be primarily suing the City
of Chicago—which was, of course, my father's
employer, in an ironic twist—citing 'common
carrier tort law' and a precedent case entitled
Ybarra v. Coca-Cola to justify collapsing liability
onto the shoulders of the respondent that could be
shown to have been most cheaply and efficiently
able to take reasonable steps to prevent the
accident—presumably by having required more
stringent quality-assurance of the doors' pneumat-
ics and sensors in the CTA's contract with the
train's manufacturer of record, a responsibility

which fell, in a further irony, at least partly to the City of Chicago's bursar's office's cost systems division, in which one of my father's own responsibilities had involved weighted evaluations of up-front cost versus liability exposure in certain classes of city agencies' contracts—although fortunately, it turned out that CTA capital equipment expenditures were vetted by a different detail or team in cost systems. Anyhow, to my mother's, Joyce's, and my dismay, it became evident to us that our legal team's major criterion for arguing for different companies', agencies', and municipal entities' different liability designations involved those different possible respondents' cash resources and their respective insurance carriers' record of settlement in similar cases—that is, that the entire process was about numbers and money rather than anything like justice, responsibility, and the prevention of further wrongful, public, and totally undignified and pointless deaths. To be honest, I'm not sure that I'm explaining all this very well. As mentioned, the whole legal process was so complicated as to almost defy description, and the junior associate that the legal team had assigned to keep us apprised of developments and evolving strategies for the first sixteen months was not exactly the clearest or most empathetic counsel one could have hoped for. Plus it goes without saying that we were also all really upset, understandably, and my mother—whose emotional health had always been pretty delicate since the breakdown or abrupt changes of 1971–72 and subsequent divorce—was going in and out of what could probably be classified as disassociative shock or conversion reaction, and had actually moved back into the house in Libertyville that she'd shared with my father prior to their separation, supposedly 'just temporarily' and for reasons that changed each time Joyce or I pressed her on whether this moving back there was a very good idea for her, and she was generally not in good shape at all, psychologically speaking. In fact, after only the first round of depositions in an ancillary lawsuit between one of the respondents and its insurance company over just what percentage of the legal costs for the respondent's defense against our ongoing suit were covered in the respondent's liability policy with the insurance company— plus, to further complicate matters, a former partner in the lead law firm that was representing my mother and Joyce was now representing the insurance company, whose national headquarters turned out to be in Glenview, and there was a subsidiary set of briefs and depositions in that case concerning whether this fact could in any way constitute a conflict of interest—and procedurally, this ancillary suit had to be resolved or settled before preliminary depositions in our own suit—which by that point had evolved into the twin classifications of civil liability and wrongful death, and was so complex that it took almost a year for the team's litigators even to agree on how to file it correctly—such that, by this point, my mother's emotional state reached the point where she elected to discontinue all litigation, a decision which privately upset Joyce very much but which she, Joyce, was legally powerless to enjoin or influence, and there was then a very complicated domestic struggle in which Joyce kept trying, without my mother's knowledge, to get me to reinitiate the suit with myself, who was over twenty-one and the decedent's dependent and son, as sole plaintiff. But for complicated reasons—chief among them that I had been listed as a dependent on both my parents' 1977 federal tax returns, which, in my mother's case, would have been promptly disallowed in even a routine office audit, but which escaped notice in the more primitive Examinations environment of the Service in that era—it emerged that in order to do this, I would have had to have my mother declared legally 'non compos mentis,' which would have required a mandatory two-week psychiatric hospitalization for observation before we could obtain a legal declaration from a court-authorized psychiatrist, which was something no one in the family was even close to having the stomach for. So after sixteen months, the whole litigation process ended, with the exception of our former legal team's subsequent suit against my mother for recovery of fees and expenses that, to all appearances, the contract that Joyce and my mother signed had explicitly waived in lieu of a 40 percent contingency fee. The recondite arguments by which our former team was attempting to have this contract declared null and void because of some ambiguity in the legal language of one of their own contract's subclauses were never explained or made clear enough to me to be able to tell if they were anything more than frivolous or not, as at this juncture I was in my final semester at DePaul and also in the process of recruitment by the Service, and my mother and Joyce had to hire yet another lawyer to defend my mother against the former lawyers' suit, which still, if you can believe it, still drags on to this day, and is one of the main reasons my mother will give as a rationale for having become a virtual shut-in in the Libertyville house, where she still now resides, and for letting the home's telephone service lapse, although evidence of some kind of major psychological deterioration had already appeared much earlier, actually probably even in the midst of the original litigation and her moving back home to my father's house following the accident, with the first psychological symptom I can remember involving her growing preoccupation with the welfare of the birds in a nest of finches or starlings that for years had been up over one of the joists on the large, open wooden porch, which had been one of the chief attractions of the Libertyville house when my parents had made the original decision to move there, the obsession then progressing from that one nest to the neighborhood's birds in general, and she began having more and more standing and tube-style feeders installed on the porch and the front lawn and buying and leaving out more and more seed and then eventually also all different kinds of human food and various 'bird supplies' for them on the steps of the porch, at one low point including tiny pieces of furniture from a dollhouse from her girlhood in Beloit, which I knew she had treasured as memorabilia as I'd heard her recount all sorts of childhood anecdotes to Joyce about how much she'd treasured the thing and had collected miniature furniture for it, and which she'd kept for many years in the storage room of the Libertyville house, along with a lot of memorabilia from my own early childhood in Rockford, and Joyce, who has remained my mother's loyal friend and sometimes virtual nurse — even though she did, in 1979, fall head over heels in love with the attorney who helped them close Speculum Books under Chapter 13 provisions, and is now married to him and lives with him and his two children in Wilmette — Joyce agrees that the tedious, complex, cynical endlessness of the accident's legal fallout was a large part of what kept my mother from processing the trauma of my father's passing and working through some of the prior, 1971-era unresolved emotions and conflicts which the accident had now brought rushing back up to the surface. Although at a certain point you have to just suck it up and play the hand you're dealt and get on with your life, in my own opinion.

But I remember once, during an afternoon on which he'd paid me to help him with some light yard work, asking my father why he never seemed to dispense direct advice about life the way my friends' fathers did. At the time, his failure to give advice seemed to me to be evidence that he was either unusually taciturn and repressed, or else that he just didn't care enough. In hindsight, I now realize that the reason was not the former and never the second, but rather that my father was, in his own particular way, somewhat wise, at least about certain things. In this instance, he was wise enough to be suspicious of his own desire to seem wise, and to refuse to indulge it—this could make him seem aloof and uncaring, but what he really was was disciplined. He was an adult; he had himself firmly in hand. This remains largely theory, but my best guess as to his never dispensing wisdom like other dads is that my father understood that advice—even wise advice—actually does nothing for the advisee, changes nothing inside, and can actually cause confusion when the advisee is made to feel the wide gap between the comparative simplicity of the advice and the totally muddled complication of his own situation and path. I'm not putting this very well. If you begin to get the idea that other people can actually *live* by the clear, simple principles of good advice, it can make you feel even worse about your own inabilities. It can cause self-pity, which I think my father recognized as the great enemy of life and contributor to nihilism. Although it's not as though he and I talked about it in any depth—that would have been too much like advice. I can't remember how he specifically answered that day's question. I remember asking it, including where we stood and how the rake felt in my hands as I asked it, but then there's a blank after that. My best guess, derived from my knowledge of our dynamics, would be that he would say trying to advise me about what to do or not do would be like the childhood fable's rabbit 'begging' not to be thrown in the briar patch. Whose name escapes me, though. But obviously meaning he felt it would have the reverse effect. He might have even laughed in a dry way, as though the question was comical in its lack of awareness of our dynamics and the obvious answer. It would probably be the same if I had asked him if he believed I didn't respect him or his advice. He might act as if he was amused that I was so unaware of myself, that I was incapable of respect but didn't even know it. It is, as mentioned, possible that he simply didn't like me very much, and that he used a dry, sophisticated wittiness to sort of try to deal with that fact within himself. It would, I imagine, be hard on someone not to be able to like your own offspring. There would obviously be some guilt involved. I know that even the slumped, boneless way I sat when watching TV or listening to music peeved him—not directly, but it was another thing I used to overhear him speaking about in arguments with my mother. For what it's worth, I accept the basic idea that parents instinctively do 'love' their off-spring no matter what — the evolutionary reasoning behind this premise is too obvious to ignore. But actually 'liking' them, or enjoying them as people, seems like a totally different thing. It may be that psychologists are off-base in their preoccupation with children's need to feel that their father or some other parent loves them. It also seems valid to consider the child's desire to feel that a parent actually likes them, as love itself is so automatic and preprogrammed in a parent that it isn't a very good test of whatever it is that the typical child feels so anxious to pass the test of. It's not unlike the religious confidence that one is 'loved unconditionally' by God — as the God in question is defined as something that loves this way automatically and universally, it doesn't seem to really have anything to do with you, so it's hard to see why religious people claim to feel such reassurance in being loved this way by God. The point here is not that every last feeling and emotion must be taken personally as about you, but only that, for basic psychological reasons, it's difficult not to feel this way when it comes to one's father — it's simply human nature.

Anyhow, all this is part of the question of how I came to be posted here in Examinations—the unexpected coincidences, changes in priorities and direction. Obviously, these sorts of unexpected things can happen in all sorts of different ways, and it's dangerous to make too much of them. I remember having one roommate—this was at Lindenhurst College—who was a self-professed Christian. I actually had two roommates in the Lindenhurst dorm suite, with a shared communal 'social room' in the center and three small single bedrooms leading off of it, which was an excellent rooming setup—but one of these roommates in particular was a Christian, as was his girlfriend. Lindenhurst, which was the first college I attended, was a peculiar place in that it was primarily a school full of Chicagoland-area hippies and wastoids, but also had a fervent Christian minority who were totally separate from the overall life of the school. *Christian* in this case meaning evangelical, just like Jimmy Carter's sister, who, if I remember it correctly, was reported as going around performing freelance exorcisms. The fact that members of this evangelical branch of Protestantism refer to themselves as just 'Christians,' as though there were only one real kind, is usually enough to characterize them, at least as far as I was concerned. This one had come in via the suite's third roommate, whom I knew and liked, and who arranged the whole three-way rooming situation without me or the Christian ever meeting one another until it was too late. The Christian was definitely not anyone I would have gone out and recruited to room with on my own, although in fairness, he didn't much care for my lifestyle or what rooming with me involved, either. The arrangement ended up being highly temporary, anyhow. I remember that he was from upstate Indiana, was fervently involved in a college organization called Campus Crusade, and had numerous pairs of dress chinos and blue blazers and Topsiders, and a smile that looked as though someone had plugged him in. He also had an equally evangelical Christian girlfriend or platonic female friend who would come over a great deal—she practically lived there, from what I could see— and I have a clear, detailed memory of one incident when the three of us were all in the communal area, which in these dormitories' nomenclature was called the 'social room,' but in which I often liked to sit on the third roommate's soft old vinyl sofa alone instead of in my tiny bedroom, to read, double on Obetrol, or sometimes smoke my little brass one-hitter and watch TV, prompting all sorts of predictable arguments with the Christian, who often liked to treat the social room as a Christian clubhouse and have his girlfriend and all his other high-wattage Christian friends in to drink Fresca and fellowship about Campus Crusade matters or the fulfillment of apocalyptic prophecy, and so on and so forth, and liked to squeeze my shoes and remind me that it was called 'the social room' when I asked them all whether they didn't have some frightening pamphlets to get out of there and go distribute somewhere or something. In hindsight, it seems obvious that I actually liked despising the Christian because I could pretend that the evangelicals' smugness and self-righteousness were the only real antithesis or alternative to the cynical, nihilistically wastoid attitude I was starting to cultivate in myself. As if there was nothing in between these two extremes—which, ironically, was exactly what the evangelical Christians also believed. Meaning I was much more like the Christian than either of us would ever be willing to admit. Of course, at barely nineteen, I was totally unaware of all this. At the time, all I knew is that I despised the Christian and enjoyed calling him 'Pepsodent Boy' and complaining about him to the third roommate, who was in a rock band besides his classes and was usually not around the suite very much, leaving the Christian and me to mock and bait and judge and use one another to confirm our respective smug prejudices.

Anyhow, at one juncture, I, the Christian roommate, and his girlfriend—who might technically have been his fiancée—were all sitting around in the suite's social room, and for some reason— quite possibly unprompted—the girlfriend was seeing fit to tell me the story of how she was 'saved' or 'born again' and became a Christian. I remember almost nothing about her except for the fact that she wore pointy-toed leather cowboy boots decorated with flowers—that is, not cartoons of flowers or isolated floral designs but a rich, detailed, photorealist scene of some kind of meadow or garden in full bloom, so that the boots looked more like a calendar or greeting card. Her testimony, as best as I can now recall, was set on a certain day an unspecified amount of time before, a day when she said she was feeling totally desolate and lost and nearly at the end of her rope, sort of wandering aimlessly in the psychological desert of our younger generation's decadence and materialism and so on and so forth. Fervent Christians are always remembering themselves as—and thus, by extension, judging everyone else outside their sect to be— lost and hopeless and just barely clinging to any kind of interior sense of value or reason to even go on living, before they were 'saved.' And that she happened, on this one day, to be driving along a county road outside her hometown, just wandering, driving aimlessly around in one of her parents' AMC Pacer, until, for no particular reason she was aware of inside herself, she turned suddenly into the parking lot of what turned out to be an evangelical Christian church, which by coincidence happened to be right in the middle of holding an evangelical service, and — for what she again claimed was no discernible reason or motive she could have named — she wandered aimlessly in and sat down in the rear of the church in one of the plushly cushioned theater-type seats their churches tend to use instead of wooden pews, and just as she sat down, the preacher or father or whatever they called them there evidently said, 'There is someone out there with us in the congregation today that is feeling lost and hopeless and at the end of their rope and needs to know that Jesus loves them very, very much,' and then — in the social room, recounting her story — the girlfriend testified as to how she had been stunned and deeply moved, and said she had instantly felt a huge, dramatic spiritual change deep inside of her in which she said she felt completely reassured and

unconditionally known and loved, and as though
now suddenly her life had meaning and direction
to it after all, and so on and so forth, and that
furthermore she had not had a down or empty
moment since, not since the pastor or father or
whatever picked just that moment to reach out
past all the other evangelical Christians sitting
there fanning themselves with complimentary
fans with slick full-color ads for the church on
them and to just kind of verbally nudge them aside
out of the way and somehow address himself
directly to the girlfriend and her circumstances at
just that moment of deep spiritual need. She talked
about herself as though she were a car whose pis-
tons had been pulled and valves ground. In hindsight, of course, there turned out to be certain
parallels with my own case, but the only real
response I had at the time was that I felt annoyed —
they both always annoyed the hell out of me, and I
can't remember what I could have been doing that
day sitting there in conversation with them, the
circumstances — and I can remember making a
show of having my tongue pressing against the
inside of my cheek in such a way as to produce a
visible bulge in my cheek and giving the girlfriend
in the boots a dry, sardonic look, and asking her just
what exactly had made her think the evangelical

pastor was talking to her directly, meaning her in particular, as probably everyone else sitting there in the church audience probably felt the same way she did, as pretty much every red-blooded American in today's (then) late-Vietnam and Watergate era felt desolate and disillusioned and unmotivated and directionless and lost, and that what if the preacher or father's saying 'Someone here's lost and hopeless' was tantamount to those *Sun-Times* horoscopes that are specially designed to be so universally obvious that they always give their horoscope readers (like Joyce every morning, over vegetable juice she made herself in a special machine) that special eerie feeling of particularity and insight, exploiting the psychological fact that most people are narcissistic and prone to the illusion that they and their problems are uniquely special and that if they're feeling a certain way then surely they're the only person who is feeling like that. In other words, I was only pretending to ask her a question — I was actually giving the girlfriend a condescending little lecture on people's narcissism and illusion of uniqueness, like the fat industrialist in Dickens or *Ragged Dick* who leans back from a giant dinner with his fingers laced over his huge stomach and cannot imagine how anyone in that moment could be hungry anywhere in the whole world. I also remember that the Christian's girlfriend was a large, copper-haired girl with something slightly wrong with one of the teeth on either side of her front teeth, which overlapped one of the front teeth in a distracting way, because during that day's conversation she gave me a big smug smile and said that, why, she didn't think that my cynical comparison was any kind of refutation or nullification of her vital Christ experience that day or its effect on her inner rebirth at all, not one little bit. She may have looked over at the Christian for reassurance or an 'Amen' or something at this juncture—I can't remember what the Christian was doing all through this exchange. I do, though, remember giving her a big, exaggerated smile right back and saying, 'Whatever,' and thinking inwardly she wasn't worth wasting time arguing with, and what was I even doing here talking to them, and that she and Pepsodent Boy deserved one another—and I know sometime soon after that I left them together in the social room and went off while thinking about the whole conversation and feeling somewhat lost and desolate inside, but also consoled that I was at least superior to narcissistic rubes like these two so-called Christians. And then I have a slightly later memory of me standing at a party with a red plastic cup of beer and telling somebody the story of the interchange in such a way that I appeared smart and funny and the girl-friend was a total fool. I know I was nearly always the hero of any story or incident I ever told people about during this period—which, like the thing with the lone sideburn, is a memory that makes me almost wince now.

Anyhow, it seems like a very long time ago. But the point of even remembering the conversation, I think, is that there was an important fact behind the Christian girl's 'salvation' story which I simply hadn't understood at the time—and, to be honest, I don't think she or the Christian did, either. It's true that her story was stupid and dishonest, but that doesn't mean the experience she had in the church that day didn't happen, or that its effects on her weren't real. I'm not putting it very well, but I was both right and wrong about her lit-tle story. I think the truth is probably that enor-mous, sudden, dramatic, unexpected, life-changing experiences are not translatable or explainable to anyone else, and this is because they really *are* unique and particular—though not unique in the way the Christian girl believed. This is because their power isn't just a result of the experience itself, but also of the circumstances in which it hits you, of everything in your previous life-experience which has led up to it and made you exactly who and what you are when the experience hits you. Does that make any sense? It's hard to explain. What the girl with the meadow on her boots had left out of the story was why she was feeling so especially desolate and lost right then, and thus why she was so psychologically 'primed' to hear the pastor's general, anonymous comment in that personal way. To be fair, maybe she couldn't remember why. But still, all she really told was her little story's dramatic climax, which was the preacher's comment and the sudden inward changes she felt as a result, which is a little like telling just the punch line of a joke and expecting the person to laugh. As Chris Acquistipace would put it, her story was just data; there was no fact-pattern. On the other hand, it's always possible that the 25,834 words so far of my own life-experience won't seem relevant or make sense to anyone but me—which would make this not unlike the Christian girl's own attempt to explain how she got to where she was, assuming she was even sincere about the dramatic changes inside. It's easy to delude yourself, obviously.

Anyhow, as mentioned, a crucial element in my entering the Service was ending up in the wrong but identical classroom at DePaul in December 1978, which I was so immersed in staying focused for the *Federalist Papers* review that I didn't even notice my error until the prof walked in. I couldn't tell whether he was the real fearful Jesuit or not. I only later found out that he wasn't the Advanced Tax instructor of record—there had evidently been some sort of personal emergency for the course's regular Jesuit prof, and this one had taken over as a sub for the last two weeks. Hence the initial confusion. I remember thinking that, for a Jesuit, the prof was in definite 'mufti.' He wore an archaically conservative dark-gray suit whose boxy look might have been actual flannel, and his dress shoes' shine was dazzling when the classroom's overhead fluorescents hit them at the proper angle. He seemed lithe and precise; his movements had the brisk economy of a man who knows time is a valuable asset. In terms of realizing my mistake, this was also when I stopped mentally reviewing the *Federalist* and became aware of a markedly different vibe among the students in this classroom. Several wore neckties under sweater vests, a couple of these vests being actual argyle. Every last shoe I could see was a black or brown leather business shoe, their laces neatly tied. To this day, I do not know precisely how I took the wrong building's door. I am not the sort of person who gets lost easily, and I knew Garnier Hall, as it's where the Intro Accounting class also met. Anyhow, to reiterate, on this day I had somehow gone to 311 Garnier Hall, instead of my own political science class's identical 311 Daniel Hall directly across the transom, and had sat down along the side wall near the room's extreme rear, a spot from which, once I came out of my preoccupation and realized my error, I would have had to cause a lot of disruption and moving of book bags and down jackets in order to get out — the room was completely filled by the time the substitute came in. Later, I learned that a few of the room's most obviously serious and adult-looking students, with actual briefcases and accordion files instead of backpacks, were graduate students in DePaul's advanced-degree business program — the Advanced Tax course was that advanced. Actually, DePaul's whole accounting department was very serious and strong — accounting and business administration were institutional strengths that DePaul was known for and spent a good deal of time extolling in its brochures and promotional materials. Obviously, this isn't why I had reenrolled at DePaul — I had next to no interest in accounting except, as mentioned, to prove something or compensate my father by finally passing Intro. The school's accounting program turned out to be so high-powered and respected, though, that nearly half of that classroom's Advanced Tax students were already signed up to take the February 1979 CPA exam, although at that time I barely knew what this licensing exam even was, or that it took several months of study and practice to prepare for. For instance, I learned later that the final exam in Advanced Tax was actually designed to be a microcosm of some of the taxation sections of the CPA exam. My father, by the way, also held a CPA license, though he rarely used it in his job with the city. In hindsight, though, and in the light of all that eventuated from that day, I'm not even sure I would have walked out even if the logistics of leaving hadn't been so awkward—not once the substitute came in. Even though I really did need that final-exam review in American Political Thought, I still may have stayed. I'm not sure I can explain it. I remember he came briskly in and hung his topcoat and hat on a hook on the corner's flag-stand. To this day, I can never be totally sure whether bumbling into the wrong building's 311 right before final exams might not just have been one more bit of unconscious irresponsibility on my part. You cannot analyze sudden, dramatic experiences like this

this way, though — especially in hindsight, which is notoriously tricky (though I obviously did not understand this during the exchange with the Christian girl in the boots).

At the time, I did not know how old the substitute was — as mentioned, I only learned later that he was filling in for the class's real Jesuit father, whose absence seemed unmourned — or even his name. My main experience with substitutes had been in high school. In terms of age, all I knew was that he was in that amorphous (to me) area between forty and sixty. I don't know how to describe him, though he made an immediate impression. He was slender, and in the room's bright lighting he looked pale in a way that seemed luminous instead of sickly, and had a steel-colored crew cut and a sort of pronounced facial bone structure. Overall, he looked to me like someone in an archaic photo or daguerreotype. His business suit's trousers were double pleated, which added to the impression of box-like solidity. Also, he had good posture, which my father always referred to as a person's 'carriage' — upright and square-shouldered without seeming stiff — and as he came briskly in with his accordion file filled with neatly organized and labeled course materials, all of the room's accounting students seemed unconsciously to shift and sit up a little straighter at their little desks. He pulled down the A/V screen before the board much as one would pull down a window's shade, using his pocket handkerchief to touch the screen's handle. To the best of my recollection, nearly everyone in the room was male. A handful were also oriental. He was getting his materials out and arranging them, looking down at his desktop with a little formal smile. What he was actually doing was the teacherly thing of acknowledging the roomful of students without looking at them. They in turn were totally focused, to a man. The whole room was different from political science or psychology classes, or even Intro Accounting, where there was always litter on the floor and people slouched back on their tailbones in their seats and looked openly up at the clock or yawned, and there was always a constant restless, whispery undertone which the Intro Accounting professor pretended wasn't there—maybe the normal profs no longer even heard the sound, or were immune to students' open displays of tedium and inattention. When the substitute accounting professor entered, however, this room's whole voltage changed. I don't know how to describe it. Nor can I totally rationally explain why I stayed—which, as mentioned, meant missing the final review in American Political Thought. At the time, continuing to sit there in the wrong class seemed like just one more feckless, undisciplined impulse. Maybe I was embarrassed to have the sub see me leave. Unlike the Christian girlfriend, I never seem to recognize important moments at the time they're going on — they always seem like distractions from what I'm really supposed to be doing. One way to explain it is that there was just something about him — the substitute. His expression had the same burnt, hollow concentration of photos of military veterans who'd been in some kind of real war, meaning combat. His eyes held us whole, as a group. I know I suddenly felt uncomfortable about my painter's pants and untied Timberlands, but if the substitute reacted to them one way or the other, he gave no sign. When he signified the official start of class by looking at his watch, it was with a crisp gesture of bringing his wrist sharply out and around, like a boxer's left cross, the force pulling up the sleeve of his suit jacket slightly to disclose a stainless steel Piaget, which I remember at the time struck me as a surprisingly racy watch for a Jesuit.

He used the white A/V screen for transparencies — unlike the Intro prof, he didn't write things in chalk on the blackboard — and when he put the first transparency on the overhead projector and the room's lights dimmed, his face was lit from below like a cabaret performer's, which made its hollow intensity and facial structure even more pronounced. I remember there was a sort of electric coolness in my head. The diagram projected behind him was an upward curve with bar graphs extending below its various sections, the curve steep near the origin and flattening somewhat at the apex. It looked a bit like a wave preparing to break. The diagram was unlabeled, and only later would I recognize it as representing the progressive marginal rate schedules for the 1976 federal income tax. I felt unusually aware and alert, but in a different way from doubling or Cylert. There were also several curves and equations and glossed citations from USTC §62, many of whose subsections had to do with complex regulations about the distinction between deductions 'for' adjusted gross income versus deductions 'from' AGI, which the substitute said formed the basis of practically every truly effective modern individual tax-planning strategy. Here—though I realized this only later, after recruitment—he was referring to structuring one's affairs so that as many deductions as possible were deductions 'for' adjusted gross income, as everything from the Standard Deduction to medical-expense deductions are designed with AGI-based floors (*floor* meaning, for example, that as only those medical expenses in excess of 3 percent of AGI were deductible, it was obviously to the advantage of the average taxpayer to render his AGI—known also sometimes as his '31,' as it was then on Line 31 of the Individual 1040 that one entered AGI—just as low as possible).

Admittedly, though, however alert and aware I felt, I was probably more aware of the effects the lecture seemed to be having on me than of the lecture itself, much of which was over my head—understandably, as I hadn't even finished Intro Accounting yet—and yet was almost impossible to look away from or not feel stirred by. This was partly due to the substitute's presentation, which was rapid, organized, undramatic, and dry in the way of people who know that what they are saying is too valuable in its own right to cheapen with concern about delivery or 'connecting' with the students. In other words, the presentation had a kind of zealous integrity that manifested not as style but as the lack of it. I felt that I suddenly, for the first time, understood the meaning of my father's term 'no-nonsense,' and why it was a term of approval.

I remember I did notice that the class's students

all took notes, which in accounting classes means that one has to internalize and write down one fact or point from the professor while at the same time still listening intently enough to the next point to be able to write it down next, as well, which requires a kind of intensively split concentration that I did not get the hang of until well into T&A in Indianapolis the following year. It was a totally different type of note-taking from the kind in humanities classes, which involved mainly doodles and broad, abstract themes and ideas. Also, the Advanced Tax students had multiple pencils lined up on their desks, all of which were extremely sharp. I realized that I almost never had a sharp pencil at hand when I really wanted one; I had never taken the trouble to keep them organized and sharpened. The only touch of what might have been dry wit in the lecture was occasional statements and quotes that the substitute interpolated into the graphs by sometimes writing them on the current transparency, projecting them onto the A/V screen without comment and then pausing while everyone copied them all down as quickly as possible before he changed to the next transparency. I still remember one such example — 'What we now need to discover in the social realm is the moral equivalent of war,' with the only written attribution at the end being 'James,' which, at the time, I believed referred to the biblical apostle James, for obvious reasons—although he said nothing to explain or reinforce the quote while the six straight rows of students—some of whose glasses reflected the projection's light in ways that gave them an openly robotic, conformist aspect, with twin squares of white light where their eyes should have been, I remember being struck by—dutifully transcribed it. Or one other example, which was preprinted on its own transparency and credited to Karl Marx, the well-known father of Marxism—

'In Communist society it will be possible for me to do one thing today and another tomorrow, to hunt in the morning, fish in the afternoon, rear cattle in the evening, criticize after dinner, just as I please'—

about which the substitute's only gloss was the dry statement 'Emphasis added.'

What I'm trying to say is that it was ultimately much more like the evangelist girlfriend with the boots' own experience than I could have ever admitted at the time. Obviously, through just the 2,235-word story of a memory, I could never convince anybody else that the innate, objective quality of the substitute's lecture would also have glued anybody else to their seat and made them forget about their final review in American Political Thought, or of the way that much of what the Catholic father (I thought) said or projected seemed somehow aimed directly at me. I can, though, at least help explain why I was so 'primed' for experiencing it this way, as I'd already had a kind of foretaste or temblor of just this experience shortly before the mistake in final-review classes' rooms occurred, though it was only later, in retrospect, that I understood it—meaning the experience—as such.

I can clearly remember that a few days earlier—meaning on the Monday of the last week of regular classes for the Fall '78 term—I was sitting there all slumped and unmotivated on the old yellow corduroy couch in our DePaul dorm room in the middle of the afternoon. I was by myself, wearing nylon warm-up pants and a black Pink Floyd tee shirt, trying to spin a soccer ball on my finger, and watching the CBS soap opera *As the World Turns* on the room's little black-and-white Zenith—not Obetrolling or blowing off anything in particular but essentially still just being an unmotivated lump. There was certainly always reading and studying for finals I could do, but I was being a wastoid. I was slouched way down on my tailbone on the couch, so that everything on the little TV was framed by my knees, and watching *As the World Turns* while spinning the soccer ball in an idle, undirected way. It was technically the roommate's television, but he was a serious pre-med student and always at the science library, though he had taken the trouble to rig a specially folded wire coat hanger to take the place of the Zenith's missing antenna, which was the only reason it got any reception at all. *As the World Turns* ran on CBS from 1:00 to 2:00 in the afternoon. This was something I still did too much during that final year, sitting there wasting time in front of the little Zenith, and several times I'd gotten passively sucked into CBS afternoon soap operas, where the shows' characters all spoke and emoted broadly and talked to one another without any hitch or pause in intensity whatsoever, it seemed, so that there was something almost hypnotic about the whole thing, especially as I had no classes on Monday or Friday and it was all too easy to sit there and get sucked in. I can remember that many of the other DePaul students that year were hooked on the ABC soap opera *General Hospital,* gathering in great avid, hooting packs to watch it — with their hip alibi being that they were actually making fun of the show—but, for reasons that probably had to do with the Zenith's spotty reception, I was more of a CBS habitué that year, particularly *As the World Turns* and *Guiding Light,* which followed *As the World Turns* at 2:00 P.M. on weekdays and was actually in some ways an even more hypnotic show.

Anyhow, I was sitting there trying to spin the ball on my finger and watching the soap opera, which was also heavily loaded with commercials—especially in the second half, which soap operas tend to load with more commercials, as they figure that you're already sucked in and mesmerized and will sit still for more ads—and at the end of every commercial break, the show's trademark shot of planet earth as seen from space, turning, would appear, and the CBS daytime network announcer's voice would say, '*You're watching* As the World Turns,' which he seemed, on this particular day, to say more and more pointedly each time—'*You're watching* As the World Turns,' until the tone began to seem almost incredulous—*You're watching* As the World Turns'—until I was suddenly struck by the bare reality of the statement. I don't mean any sort of humanities-type ironic metaphor, but the literal thing he was saying, the simple surface level.

I don't know how many times I'd heard this that year while sitting around watching *As the World Turns,* but I suddenly realized that the announcer was actually saying over and over what I was literally doing. Not only this, but I also realized that I had been told this fact countless times—as I said, the announcer's statement followed every commercial break after each segment of the show— without ever being even slightly aware of the literal reality of what I was doing. I was not Obetrolling at this moment of awareness, I should add. This was different. It was as if the CBS announcer were speaking directly to me, shaking my shoulder or leg as though trying to arouse someone from sleep—'*You're watching* As the World Turns.' It's hard to explain. It was not even the obvious double entendre that struck me. This was more literal, which somehow had made it harder to see. All of this hit me, sitting there. It could not have felt more concrete if the announcer had actually said, '*You are sitting on an old yellow dorm couch, spinning a black-and-white soccer ball, and watching* As the World Turns, *without ever even acknowledging to yourself this is what you are doing.*' This is what struck me. It was beyond being feckless or a wastoid—it's like I wasn't even there. The truth is I was not even aware of the obvious double entendre of *'You're watching* As the World Turns' until three days later—the show's almost terrifying pun about the passive waste of time of sitting there watching something whose reception through the hanger didn't even come in very well, while all the while real things in the world were going on and people with direction and initiative were taking care of business in a brisk, no-nonsense way— meaning not until Thursday morning, when this secondary meaning suddenly struck me in the middle of taking a shower before getting dressed and hurrying to what I intended—consciously, at any rate—to be the final-exam review in American Political Thought. Which may have been one reason why I was so preoccupied and took the wrong building's entrance, I suppose. At the time, though, on Monday afternoon, all that hit home with me was the reiteration of the simple fact of what I was doing, which was, of course, nothing, just slumped there like something without any bones, uninvolved even in the surface reality of watching Victor deny his paternity to Jeanette (even though Jeanette's son has the same extremely rare genetic blood disorder that's kept putting Victor in the hospital throughout much of the semester. Victor may in some sense have actually 'believed' his own denials, I remember thinking, as he essentially seemed like that kind of person) between my knees.

But nor is it as though I consciously reflected on all of this at the time. At the time, I was aware only of the concrete impact of the announcer's statement, and the dawning realization that all of the directionless drifting and laziness and being a 'wastoid' which so many of us in that era pretended to have raised to a nihilistic art form, and believed was cool and funny (I too had thought it was cool, or at least I believed I thought so — there had seemed to be something almost romantic about flagrant waste and drifting, which Jimmy Carter was ridiculed for calling 'malaise' and telling the nation to snap out of it) was, in reality, not funny, not one bit funny, but rather frightening, in fact, or sad, or something else — something I could not name because it has no name. I knew, sitting there, that I might be a real nihilist, that it wasn't always just a hip pose. That I drifted and quit because nothing meant anything, no one choice was really better. That I was, in a way, too free, or that this kind of freedom wasn't actually real — I was free to choose 'whatever' because it didn't really matter. But that this, too, was because of something I chose — I had somehow chosen to have nothing matter. It all felt much less abstract than it sounds to try to explain it. All this was happening while I was just sitting there, spinning the ball. The point was that, through making this choice, I didn't matter, either. I didn't stand for anything. If I wanted to matter—even just to myself—I would have to be less free, by deciding to choose in some kind of definite way. Even if it was nothing more than an act of will. All of these awarenesses were very rapid and indistinct, and the realizations about choosing and mattering were as far as I got—I was also still trying to watch *As the World Turns,* which tended to get steadily more dramatic and compelling as it progressed towards the hour's end, as they always wanted to make you remember to tune in again the next day. But the point was that I realized, on some level, that whatever a potentially 'lost soul' was, I was one—and it wasn't cool or funny. And, as mentioned, it was only a few days later that I mistakenly ended up across the transom in the final-class session of Advanced Tax—which was, I should stress, a subject which at that time I had zero interest in, I believed. Like most people outside the industry, I imagined tax accountancy to be the province of fussy little men with thick glasses and elaborate stamp collections, more or less the opposite of hip or cool—and the experience of hearing the CBS announcer spell out surface reality over and over, of suddenly really being aware of hearing him, and of seeing the little screen between my knees, beneath the spinning ball on my finger's point was part of what put me in a position, I think, whether mistakenly or not, to hear something that changed my direction.

I remember that the third-floor's hallway's bell had rung at the end of the scheduled time for Advanced Tax that day without any of the students doing that end-of-class thing in humanities classes of fidgeting around to gather their materials together or leaning over their desks to retrieve their bags and briefcases from the floor, even as the substitute turned off the overhead projector and raised the A/V screen with a smart snap of his left hand, replacing the handkerchief in his suit coat's pocket. They all remained quiet and attentive. As the room's overhead lights came back on, I remember glancing and seeing that the older, mustachioed student beside me's class notes were almost unbelievably neat and well-organized, with Roman numerals for the lecture's main points and lowercase letters, inset numbers, and double indents for subheadings and corollaries. His handwriting itself looked almost automated, it was that good. This was despite the fact that they were essentially written in the dark. Several digital watches beeped the hour in sync. Just like its mirror opposite across the transom, Garnier 311's floor was tiled in an institutional tan-and-brown pattern that was either checkerboard or interlocking diamonds, depending on one's angle or perspective. All of this I remember very clearly.

Though it would be over a year before I understood them, here are just a few of the substitute's review lecture's main areas, as denumerated in the older business student's notes:

Imputed Income → Haig-Simons Formula
Constructive Receipt
Limited Partnerships, Passive Losses
Amortization and Capitalization → 1976 TRA §266
Depreciation → Class Life System
Cash Method v. Accrual Method → Implications for AGI
Inter vivos Gifts and 76 TRA
Straddle Techniques
4 Criteria for Nontaxable Exchange
Client Tax Planning Strategy ('Tailoring the Transaction') v. IRS Exams Strategy ('Collapsing the Transaction')

It was, as mentioned, the final regular class day of the term. The end of the final regular class, in the humanities courses I was used to taking, was usually the moment for the younger professor to try to make some kind of hip, self-mocking summation—*Mr. Gorton, would you briefly summarize what we've learned over the past sixteen weeks, please?'*—as well as instructions about the logistics of the final exam or paper, and final grades, and perhaps wishes for a good holiday recess (it was two weeks before Christmas 1978). In Advanced Tax, though, when the substitute turned from raising the screen, he gave none of the bodily signals of completion or transition to final instructions or summary. He stood very still— noticeably stiller than most people stand when they stand still. Thus far, he had spoken 8,206 words, counting numeric terms and operators. The older males and Asians all still sat there, and it seemed that this instructor was able to make eye contact with all forty-eight of us at once. I was aware that part of this substitute's vibe of dry, aloof, effortless authority was due to the way the class's upperclassmen all paid such attention to his every word and gesture. It was obvious that they respected this substitute, and that it was a respect that he didn't have to return, or feign returning, in order to accept. He was not anxious to 'connect' or be liked. But nor was he hostile or patronizing. What he seemed to be was 'indifferent'—not in a meaningless, drifting, nihilistic way, but rather in a secure, self-confident way. It's hard to describe, although I remember the awareness of it very clearly. The word that kept arising in my mind as he looked at us and we all watched and waited—although all of this took place very quickly—was *credibility,* as in the phrase 'credibility gap' from the Watergate scandal, which had essentially been going on while I was at Lindenhurst. The sounds of other accounting, economics, and business administration classes emptying into the hallway were ignored. Instead of gathering together his materials, the substitute—who, as mentioned, I thought at the time was a Jesuit father in 'mufti'— had put his hands behind his back and paused, looking at us. The whites of his eyes were extremely white, the way usually only a dark complexion can make eyes' whites look. I've forgotten the irises' color. His complexion, though, was that of someone who had rarely been out in the sun. He seemed at home in thrifty, institutional fluorescent light. His bow tie was perfectly straight and flush even though it was the hand-tied kind, not a clip-on.

He said, 'You will want something of a

summation, then. An hortation.' (It is not impossible that I misheard him and what he actually said was 'exhortation.') He looked quickly at his watch, making the same right-angled movement. 'All right,' he said. A small smile played around his mouth as he said 'All right,' but it was clear that he wasn't joking or trying to slightly undercut what he was about to say, the way so many humanities profs of that era tended to mock themselves or their hortations in order to avoid seeming uncool. It only struck me later, after I'd entered the Service's TAC, that this substitute was actually the first instructor I'd seen at any of the schools I'd drifted in and out of who seemed a hundred percent indifferent about being liked or seen as cool or likable by the students, and realized—I did, once I'd entered the Service—what a powerful quality this sort of indifference could be in an authority figure. Actually, in hindsight, the substitute may have been the first genuine authority figure I ever met, meaning a figure with genuine 'authority' instead of just the power to judge you or squeeze your shoes from their side of the generation gap, and I became aware for the first time that 'authority' was actually something real and authentic, that a real authority was not the same as a friend or someone who cared about you, but nevertheless could be good for you, and that the authority relation was not a 'democratic' or equal one and yet could have value for both sides, both people in the relation. I don't think I'm explaining this very well—but it's true that I did feel singled out, spindled on those eyes in a way I neither liked nor didn't, but was certainly aware of. It was a certain kind of power that he exerted and that I was granting him, voluntarily. That respect was not the same as coercion, although it was a kind of power. It was all very strange. I also noticed that now he had his hands behind his back, in something like the 'parade rest' military position.

He said to the accounting students, 'All right, then. Before you leave here to resume that crude approximation of a human life you have heretofore called a life, I will undertake to inform you of certain truths. I will then offer an opinion as to how you might most profitably view and respond to those truths.' (I was immediately aware that he didn't seem to be talking about the Advanced Tax final exam.) He said, 'You will return to your homes and families for the holiday vacation and, in that festive interval before the last push of CPA examination study—trust me—you will hesitate, you will feel dread and doubt. This will be natural. You will, for what seems the first time, feel dread at your hometown chums' sallies about accountancy as the career before you, you will read the approval in your parents' smiles as an approval of your surrender—oh, I have been there, gentlemen; I know every cobble in the road you are walking. For the hour approaches. To begin, in that literally dreadful interval of looking down before the leap outward, to hear dolorous forecasts as to the sheer drudgery of the profession you are choosing, the lack of excitement or chance to shine on the athletic fields or ballroom floors of life heretofore.' True, some of it I didn't quite get—I don't think too many of us in the classroom had spent a lot of time 'shining on ballroom floors,' but that might have been just a generational thing—he obviously meant it as a metaphor. I certainly got what he meant about accounting not seeming like a very exciting profession.

The substitute continued, 'To experience commitment as the loss of options, a type of death, the death of childhood's limitless possibility, of the flattery of choice without duress—this will happen, mark me. Childhood's end. The first of many deaths. Hesitation is natural. Doubt is natural.' He smiled slightly. 'You might wish to recall, then, in three weeks' time, should you be so disposed, this room, this moment, and the information I

shall now relay to you.' He was obviously not a
very modest or diffident person. On the other
hand, his form of address didn't sound nearly as
formal or fussy at the time in Advanced Tax as it
now sounds when I repeat it — or rather his summation was formal and a bit poetic but not artificially so, like a natural extension of who and what
he was. It was not a pose. I remember thinking
that maybe the sub had mastered that trick in
Uncle Sam posters and certain paintings of seeming to look right at you no matter what angle you
faced him from. That perhaps all the hushed and
solemn older other students (you could hear a pin)
felt picked out and specifically addressed as well —
though, of course, that would make no difference
as to its special effect on me, which was the real
issue, just as the Christian girlfriend's story would
have already demonstrated if I'd been aware and
attentive enough to hear what the actual point she
was trying to make was. As mentioned, the version of me that listened to that story in 1973 or '74
was a nihilistic child.

After one or two other comments, with his
hands still clasped behind his back, the substitute
continued, 'I wish to inform you that the accounting profession to which you aspire is, in fact,
heroic. Please note that I have said "inform" and

not "opine" or "allege" or "posit." The truth is that what you soon go home to your carols and toddies and books and CPA examination preparation guides to stand on the cusp of is—heroism.' Obviously, this was dramatic and held everyone's attention. I remember thinking again, as he said this, of the A/V screen's quote I had thought was biblical: 'the moral equivalent of war.' It seemed strange, but not ridiculous. I realized that my thinking about this quote was probably the first time I'd ever considered the word *moral* in any context other than a term paper—this was part of what I had initially started to become aware of a few days prior, in the experience while watching *As the World Turns.* The substitute was only of about average height. His eyes did not cut or wander. Some of the students' glasses reflected light, still. One or two were still taking notes, but other than that, nobody except the substitute spoke or moved.

Continuing on without pause, he said, 'Exacting? Prosaic? Banausic to the point of drudgery? Sometimes. Often tedious? Perhaps. But brave? Worthy? Fitting, sweet? Romantic? Chivalric? Heroic?' When he paused, it wasn't just for effect—at least not totally. 'Gentlemen,' he said, '—by which I mean, of course, latter adolescents who aspire to manhood—gentlemen, here is a truth: Enduring tedium over real time in a confined space is what real courage is. Such endurance is, as it happens, the distillate of what is, today, in this world neither I nor you have made, heroism. Heroism.' He made a point of looking around, gauging people's reaction. Nobody laughed; a few looked puzzled. I remember I was starting to have to go to the bathroom. In the classroom's fluorescent lights, he cast no shadow on any side. 'By which,' he said, 'I mean true heroism, not heroism as you might know it from films or the tales of childhood. You are now nearly at childhood's end; you are ready for the truth's weight, to bear it. The truth is that the heroism of your childhood entertainments was not true valor. It was theater. The grand gesture, the moment of choice, the mortal danger, the external foe, the climactic battle whose outcome resolves all—all designed to appear heroic, to excite and gratify an audience. An audience.' He made a gesture I can't describe: 'Gentlemen, welcome to the world of reality—there is no audience. No one to applaud, to admire. No one to see you. Do you understand? Here is the truth— actual heroism receives no ovation, entertains no one. No one queues up to see it. No one is interested.'

He paused again and smiled in a way that was

not one bit self-mocking. 'True heroism is you, alone, in a designated work space. True heroism is minutes, hours, weeks, year upon year of the quiet, precise, judicious exercise of probity and care— with no one there to see or cheer. This is the world. Just you and the job, at your desk. You and the return, you and the cash-flow data, you and the inventory protocol, you and the depreciation schedules, you and the numbers.' His tone was wholly matter-of-fact. It suddenly occurred to me that I had no idea how many words he'd spoken since that 8,206th one at the conclusion of the review. I was aware of how every detail in the classroom appeared very vivid and distinct, as though painstakingly drawn and shaded, and yet also of being completely focused on the substitute Jesuit, who was saying all this very dramatic or even romantic stuff without any of the usual trappings or flourishes of drama, standing now quite still with his hands again behind his back (I knew the hands weren't clasped—I could somehow tell that he was more like holding the right wrist with the left hand) and his face's planes unshadowed in the white light. It felt as though he and I were at opposite ends of some kind of tube or pipe, and that he really was addressing me in particular—although obviously in reality he couldn't have been. The literal reality was that he was addressing me least of all, since obviously I wasn't enrolled in Advanced Tax or getting ready to take the final and then go home and sit at my childhood desk in my old bedroom in my parents' house cramming for the dreaded CPA exam the way it sounded as if many of these others in the room were. Nevertheless—as I wish I'd been able to understand earlier, since it would have saved me a lot of time and cynical drifting—a feeling is a feeling, nor can you argue with results.

Anyhow, meanwhile, in what essentially seemed to be a recapitulation of his main points so far, the substitute said, 'True heroism is *a priori* incompatible with audience or applause or even the bare notice of the common run of man. In fact,' he said, 'the less conventionally heroic or exciting or adverting or even interesting or engaging a labor appears to be, the greater its potential as an arena for actual heroism, and therefore as a denomination of joy unequaled by any you men can yet imagine.' It seemed then that a sudden kind of shudder went through the room, or maybe an ecstatic spasm, communicating itself from senior accounting major or graduate business student to senior accounting major or grad business student so rapidly that the whole collective seemed for an instant to heave—although, again, I am not a hundred percent sure this was real, that it took place outside of me, in the actual classroom, and the (possible) collective spasm's moment was too brief to be more than sort of fleetingly aware of it. I also remember having a strong urge to lean over and tie my boots' laces, which never translated itself into real action.

At the same time, it might be fair to say that I remembered the substitute Jesuit as using pauses and bits of silence rather the way more conventional inspirational speakers use physical gestures and expressions. He said, 'To retain care and scrupulosity about each detail from within the teeming wormball of data and rule and exception and contingency which constitutes real-world accounting—this is heroism. To attend fully to the interests of the client and to balance those interests against the high ethical standards of FASB and extant law—yea, to serve those who care not for service but only for results—this is heroism. This may be the first time you've heard the truth put plainly, starkly. Effacement. Sacrifice. Service. To give oneself to the care of others' money—this is effacement, perdurance, sacrifice, honor, doughtiness, valor. Hear this or not, as you will. Learn it now, or later—the world has time. Routine,

repetition, tedium, monotony, ephemeracy, incon-
sequence, abstraction, disorder, boredom, angst,
ennui—these are the true hero's enemies, and
make no mistake, they are fearsome indeed. For
they are real.'

One of the accounting students now raised his
hand, and the substitute paused to answer a question about adjusted cost basis in the tax classification of gifts. It was at some point in his answer to
this that I heard the substitute use the phrase 'IRS
wiggler.' Since that day, I have never once heard
the term anywhere outside of the Examination
Center at which I'm posted—it is a piece of
Service insider shorthand for a certain class of
examiner. In retrospect, then, this definitely
should have raised a red flag in terms of the substitute's experience and background. (By the way, the
term 'FASB' stood for Financial Accounting Standards Board, though obviously I would not learn
this until entering the Service the following year.)
Also, I should probably acknowledge an obvious
paradox in the memory—despite how attentive
and affected by his remarks about courage and the
real world I was, I was not aware that the drama
and scintillance I was investing the substitute's
words with actually ran counter to those words'
whole thrust. That is to say, I was deeply affected

and changed by the hortation without, as it now appears, really understanding what he was talking about. In retrospect, this seems like further evidence that I was even more 'lost' and unaware than I knew.

'Too much, you say?' he said. 'Cowboy, paladin, hero? Gentlemen, read your history. Yesterday's hero pushed back at bounds and frontiers—he penetrated, tamed, hewed, shaped, made, brought things into being. Yesterday's society's heroes generated facts. For this is what society is—an agglomeration of facts.' (Obviously, the more real Advanced Tax students who gingerly got up and left, the more my feelings of being particularly, uniquely addressed increased. The older business student with two lush, perfectly trimmed sideburns and incredible notes beside me was able to close his briefcase's metal clasps without any sound at all. On the wire rack beneath his desk was a *Wall Street Journal* that he'd either not read or had perhaps been able to read and refold so perfectly it looked untouched.) 'But it is now today's era, the modern era,' the substitute was saying (which was difficult to argue with, obviously). 'In today's world, boundaries are fixed, and most significant facts have been generated. Gentlemen, the heroic frontier now lies in the ordering and deployment of those facts. Classification, organization, presentation. To put it another way, the pie has been made—the contest is now in the slicing. Gentlemen, you aspire to hold the knife. Wield it. To admeasure. To shape each given slice, the knife's angle and depth of cut.' However transfixed I still was, I was also aware, by this point, that the substitute's metaphors seemed to be getting a bit jumbled—it was hard to imagine the remaining orientals making much sense of cowboys and pies, since they were such specifically American images. He went to the flag-stand in the corner of the room and retrieved his hat, a dark-gray business fedora, old but very well cared for. Instead of putting the hat on, he held it up aloft.

'A baker wears a hat,' he said, 'but it is not our hat. Gentlemen, prepare to wear the hat. You have wondered, perhaps, why all real accountants wear hats? They are today's cowboys. As will you be. Riding the American range. Riding herd on the unending torrent of financial data. The eddies, cataracts, arranged variations, fractious minutiae. You order the data, shepherd it, direct its flow, lead it where it's needed, in the codified form in which it's apposite. You deal in facts, gentlemen, for which there has been a market since man first crept from the primeval slurry. It is you—tell them that. Who ride, man the walls, define the pie, serve.' There was no way not to notice how different he looked now from the way he'd appeared at the beginning. Ultimately, it wasn't clear whether he'd planned or prepared his final hortation or exhortation or not, or whether he was just speaking passionately from the heart. His hat was noticeably more stylish and European-looking than my father's had been, its welt sharper and band's feather pegged—it had to be at least twenty years old. When he raised his arms in conclusion, one hand still held the hat—

'Gentlemen, you are called to account.'

One or two of the remaining students clapped, a somehow terrible sound when it's only a few scattered hands—like a spanking or series of ill-tempered slaps. I remember having a visual flash of something lying in its crib and waving its limbs uselessly in the air, its mouth open and wet. And then of walking back across the transom and down and out of Daniel and over to the library in a strange kind of hyperaware daze, both disoriented and very clear, and then the memory of that incident essentially ends.

After that, the first thing I can remember doing over the holiday recess in Libertyville was getting a haircut. I also then went to Carson Pirie Scott's in Mundelein and bought a dark-gray ventless wool suit with a tight vertical weave and double-pleat trousers, as well as a bulky box-plaid jacket with wide notched lapels, which I ended up almost never wearing, as it had a tendency to roll at the third button and produce what almost looked like a peplum when it was buttoned all the way. I also bought a pair of Nunn Bush leather wing tips and three dress shirts—two white oxfords and one light-blue sea island weave. All three collars were of the button-down type.

Except for practically dragging my mother to Wrigleyville for Christmas dinner at Joyce's, I spent nearly the whole holidays in the house, researching options and requirements. I remember I was also deliberately trying to do some sustained, concentrated thinking. My inner feelings about school and graduating had totally changed. I now felt suddenly and totally behind. It was a bit like the feeling of suddenly looking at your watch and realizing you're late for an appointment, but on a much larger scale. I had only one term left now before I was supposed to graduate, and I was exactly nine required courses short of a major in accounting, to say nothing of trying to sit for the CPA exam. I bought a Barron's guide to the CPA exam at a Waldenbooks in the Galaxy Mall off of

Milwaukee Road. It was given three times a year, and it lasted two days, and you were strongly advised to have had both intro and intermediate financial accounting, managerial accounting, two semesters of auditing, business statistics—which, at DePaul, was another famously brutal class—intro data processing, one or preferably two semesters of tax, plus either fiduciary accounting or accounting for nonprofits, and one or more semesters of economics. A fine-print insert also recommended proficiency in at least one 'high-level' computer language like COBOL. The only computer class I'd ever finished was Intro Computer World at UI-Chicago, where we'd mostly played homemade Pong and helped the prof try to recollate 51,000 Hollerith punch cards he'd stored data for a project on and then accidentally dropped on a slick stairway. And so on and so forth. Plus, I looked at a business-stats textbook and discovered that you needed calculus, and I hadn't even had trigonometry—in my senior year of high school, I'd taken Perspectives on Modern Theater instead of trig, which I well remembered my father squeezing my shoes about. Actually, my hatred of Algebra II and refusal to take any more math after that was the occasion for one of the really major arguments that I heard my parents have in the years before they separated, which is all kind of a long story, but I remember overhearing my father saying that there were only two kinds of people in the world—namely, people who actually understood the technical realities of how the real world worked (via, his obvious point was, math and science), and people who didn't—and overhearing my mother being very upset and depressed at what she saw as my father's rigidity and small-mindedness, and her responding that the two basic human types were actually the people so rigid and intolerant that they believed there were only two basic human types, on one side, versus people who believed that there were all different types and varieties of people with their own unique gifts and destinies and paths through life that they had to find, on the other, and so forth. Anyone eavesdropping on the argument, which had started as a typical exchange but escalated into an especially heated one, could quickly tell that the real conflict was between what my mother saw as two extremely different, incompatible ways of seeing the world and treating the people you were supposed to love and support. For instance, it was during this argument that I overheard my father say the thing about my being unable to find my ass even if it had a large bell attached to it, which my mother heard mainly as him passing cold, rigid judgment on somebody he was supposed to love and support, but which, in retrospect, I think might have been the only way my father could find to say that he was worried about me, that I had no initiative or direction, and that he didn't know what to do as a father. As is well-known, parents can have vastly different ways of expressing love and concern. Of course, much of my interpretation is just speculative—there's obviously no way to know what he really meant.

Anyhow, the upshot of all my concentrated thinking and research over the holiday recess was that it looked as though I would basically have to start college all over again, and I was then almost twenty-four. And the financial situation at home was in total flux due to the complex legalities of the wrongful death suit that was under way at the time.

As a side note, there was no amount of alteration that could have made my father's suits fit me. At that time, I was a 40L/30 with a 34 inseam, whereas the bulk of my father's suits were 36R/36/30. The suits and archaic silk blazer ended up being given to Goodwill after Joyce and I cleaned out most of his things from his closet and study and workshop, which was a very sad experience. My mother, as mentioned, was spending more and more time watching the neighborhood birds at the tube feeders which she'd hung around the front porch and the standing feeders in the yard—my father's house's living room had a large picture window with an excellent view of the porch, yard, and street—and often wearing a red chenille robe and large fuzzy slippers all day, and neglecting both her normal interests and personal grooming, which increasingly worried everyone.

After the holidays, just as it was beginning to snow, I made an appointment to speak with DePaul's Associate Dean for Academic Affairs (who was definitely a real Jesuit, and wore the official black-and-white uniform, and also had a yellow ribbon tied to the knob of his office door) about the experience in Advanced Tax and the turnaround in my direction and focus, and about now being so behind in terms of that focus, and to broach the possibility of maybe continuing my enrollment an extra year with deferred tuition in order to help make up some of my deficits in terms of an accounting major. But it was awkward, because I had actually been in this father's office before, two or three years prior, under, to put it mildly, very different circumstances—namely, getting my shoes squeezed and being threatened with academic probation, in response to which I think I may actually have said, aloud, 'Whatever,' which is the sort of thing that Jesuits do not take kindly to. Thus, in this appointment the Associate Dean's demeanor was patronizing and skeptical, and amused—he seemed to find the change in my appearance and stated attitude more comical than anything else, as if he regarded it as a prank or joke, or some kind of ploy to try to buy myself one more year before having to go out and fend for myself in what he termed 'the world of men,' and there was no way to adequately describe for him the awarenesses and conclusions I'd come to while watching daytime television and then later bumbling into the wrong final class without sounding childish or insane, and essentially I was shown the door.

This was in early January 1979, on the day it was just beginning to snow—I can remember watching large, tentative, individual flakes of snow falling and blowing around aimlessly in the wind generated by the train through the window of the CTA commuter line from Lincoln Park back up to Libertyville, and thinking, *This is my crude approximation of a human life.* As far as I recall, the yellow ribbons all over the city were because of the hostage trouble in the Mideast and the assault on US embassies. I knew very little about what was going on, partly because I had not watched any TV since that experience in mid-December with the soccer ball and *As the World Turns*. It is not as though I made any conscious decision to renounce television after that time. I just cannot remember watching any after that day. Also, after the pre-holiday experiences, I now felt far too far behind to be able to afford to waste time watching TV. Part of me was frightened that I'd actually become galvanized and motivated too late and was somehow going to just at the last minute 'miss' some crucial chance to renounce nihilism and make a meaningful, real-world choice. This was also all taking place during what emerged as the worst blizzard in the modern history of Chicago, and at the start of the Spring '79 term, everything was in chaos because DePaul's administration kept having to cancel classes because no one who lived off-campus could guarantee they could get in to school, and half of the dorms couldn't reopen yet because of frozen pipes, and part of my father's house's roof cracked because of the weight of accumulated snow and there was a big structural crisis that I got stuck dealing with because my mother was too obsessed with the logistical problems of keeping the snow from covering up all the birdseed she left out. Also, most of the CTA trains were out of service, and buses were abruptly canceled if it was determined that the plows couldn't keep certain roads clear, and every morning of that first week I had to get up very early and listen to the radio to see if DePaul was even having classes that day, and if they were, I'd have to try to slog in. I should mention that my father didn't drive — he'd been a devotee of public transportation — and my mother had given Joyce the Le Car as part of the arrangement they made regarding the dissolution of the bookstore, so there was no car, although occasionally I could get rides from Joyce, although I hated to impose — she was over there mostly to look in on my mother, who was obviously in a decline, and about whom we were all increasingly worried, and it later turned out Joyce had spent a great deal of time doing research into north-county psychological services and programs and trying to determine what kind of special care my mother might need and where it could be found. Despite the snow and temperatures, for instance, my mother now abandoned her practice of watching the birds from inside through the window and progressed to standing on or near the steps to the porch and holding up tube feeders herself in her upraised hands, and appeared prepared to stay in this position long enough to actually develop frost-bite if someone didn't intervene and remonstrate with her to come inside. The numbers and noise-level of birds involved were also problematic by this time, as some in the neighborhood had already pointed out even before the blizzard had struck.

On one level, I'm fairly sure that it was on WBBM-AM—a very dry, conservative, all-news station which my father had favored, but whose weather-related cancellations reports were the most comprehensive in the area—that I first heard mention of the Service's aggressive new recruiting-incentive program. 'The Service' obviously being shorthand for the Internal Revenue Service, better known to taxpayers as the IRS. But I also have a partial memory of actually first seeing an adver-tisement for this recruitment program in a sudden, dramatic way that now, in retrospect, seems so heavily fateful and dramatic that perhaps it is more the memory of a dream or fantasy I had at the time, which essentially consisted of me waiting in the Galaxy Mall food court area while Joyce was helping my mother negotiate another large deliv-ery order from Fish 'n Fowl Pet Plaza. Certain ele-ments of this memory are certainly credible. It is true that I had trouble seeing animals for sale in cages—I have always had difficulty with cages

and seeing things caged—and I often did wait for
my mother outside in the food court while they
were in Fish 'n Fowl. I was there to help carry
bags of seed in the event that delivery orders were
refused or delayed on account of the severe
weather, which, as many Chicagoans still recall,
remained intense for quite some time, all but para-
lyzing the whole area. Anyhow, according to this
memory, I was sitting at one of the many stylized
plastic tables in the Galaxy Mall's food court,
looking absently down at the table's pattern of
star- and moon-shaped perforations, and saw,
through one such perforation, a portion of the
Sun-Times that someone had evidently discarded
on the floor beneath the table, which was open
to the Business Classified section, and the memory involves seeing this from above the table
in such a way that a beam of light from the
food court's overhead lighting far above fell
through one of the star-shaped perforations in the
tabletop and illuminated—as if by a symbolically
star-shaped spotlight or ray of light—one particular advertisement among all the page's other ads
and notices of business and career opportunities,
this being a notice about the IRS's new recruitment-
incentive program under way in some sections of
the country, of which the Chicagoland area was

one. I'm simply mentioning this memory, whether it's actually as credible as the more pedestrian WBBM memory or not, as another illustration of how motivationally 'primed' I seemed to be, in retrospect, for a career in the Service.

The IRS recruiting station for the Chicagoland area was in a kind of temporary storefront-type office space on West Taylor Street, right near to the UIC campus where I'd spent a joyless and hypocritical 1975–76 school year, and almost across the street from the Chicago Fire Department Academy, whose apprentice firemen actually used to show up sometimes in full slicker-and-boot regalia at the Hat, where they were banned from drinks involving seltzer or carbonation of any kind—which involves a long explanation which I won't go into here. Nor, luckily, was the podiatrist's sign with the rotating foot visible from this side of the Kennedy Expressway. That huge, rotating foot represented one of the childish things I was anxious to put away.

I remember the sun had finally emerged— although this later turned out to be only a temporary break or 'eye' in the storm system, and there was more severe winter weather on the way two days hence. There were now four or more feet of new snow on the ground, and much more in places where high-speed plows had cleared the streets and formed mammoth drifts along the sides, and you had to pass through almost a kind of tunnel or nave to get to the sidewalk itself, where you then floundered whenever you passed a property whose owner wasn't civic-minded enough to shovel the sidewalk. I was wearing flared green corduroys whose cuffs were soon almost up around my knees, and my heavy Timberlands—which were not great on actual traction, I had discovered—were packed with snow. It was so bright that it was difficult to see. It felt almost like a polar expedition. When the sidewalks were simply too piled up, you had to try to clamber back over the drifts and walk in the street. Understandably, traffic was light. The streets were now more like canyons with sheer white sides, and the high drifts and business-district buildings beyond cast complex, flat-topped shadows that sometimes formed bar graphs you walked right across. I had been able to catch a bus transfer as far as Grant Park, but no closer. The river was frozen and piled high with snow which the plows had tried to dump there. By the way, I know that it's doubtful that anyone outside the Chicagoland area is very interested in the great 1979 winter storm anymore, but for me it was a vivid, critical time whose memory is unusually clear and focused. To me, this remembered clarity is a further sign of the clear demarcation in my own awareness and sense of direction before and after the substitute in Advanced Tax. It wasn't so much the rhetoric about heroism and wrangling, much of which seemed a bit over-the-top to me even then (there are limits). I think part of what was so galvanizing was the substitute's diagnosis of the world and reality as already essentially penetrated and formed, the real world's constituent info generated, and that now a meaningful choice lay in herding, corralling, and organizing that torrential flow of info. This rang true to me, though on a level that I don't think I even was fully aware existed within me.

Anyhow, it took a while even to find it. I can remember that a few corners' stop signs had only the polygonal sign portion visible above the drifts, and several storefronts' doors had their mail slots frozen open and long tongues of windblown snow on their carpet. Many of the city's maintenance and garbage trucks also had blades affixed to their grilles and were serving as extra plows as Chicago's mayor tried to respond to the public outcry over the inefficient disposal of snow. On Balbo, there were some remains of snowmen in front yards, whose heights indicated the ages of whoever had made them. The storm had blown some of their eyes and pipes away or rearranged their features—from a distance, they looked sinister or deranged. It was very quiet, and so bright that when you closed your eyes there was only a lit-up blood-red in there. There were a few harsh sounds of snow shovels, and a high distant snarling sound that I only later remembered as being one or more snowmobiles on Roosevelt Road. Some of the yards' snowmen wore a father's old or cast-off business hat. One very high, clotted drift had an open umbrella visible at its top, and I recall a frightening few minutes of digging and shouting downward into the hole, because it almost looked as if a person carrying an umbrella might have gotten abruptly buried in mid-stride. But it turned out to be just an umbrella which someone had abandoned by opening it and shoving it handle-down into the snowbank, perhaps as some kind of prank or gesture to play with people's minds.

Anyhow, it emerged that the Service had recently instituted a program of recruiting new contract employees in much the same way as the new volunteer armed forces—with heavy advertising and inducements. There turned out to be good institutional reasons for the aggressive recruiting, only some of which had to do with competition from the private accounting sector.

By the way, only lay and popular media refer to all IRS contract employees as 'agents.' Within the Service, where personnel are more often identified by the branch or division in which they're posted, 'agent' usually refers to those in the Criminal Investigation Division, which is comparatively small and handles cases of tax evasion so egregious that criminal penalties more or less have to be sought in order to make an example of the TP, which is essentially designed to motivate overall compliance. (By the way, given that the federal tax system still proceeds largely on voluntary compliance, the psychology of the Service's relation to taxpayers is complex, requiring a public impression of extreme efficiency and thoroughness, together with an aggressive system of penalties, interest, and, in extreme cases, criminal prosecution. In reality, though, Criminal Investigations is somewhat of a last resort, since criminal penalties rarely tend to yield additional revenue—a TP in prison has no income and is thus obviously not in a position to pay down his delinquency—whereas the credible threat of prosecution can function as a spur to repayment and future compliance, as well as having a motivating effect on other taxpayers considering criminal evasions. For the Service, in other words, 'public relations' is actually a vital, complex part of both mission and efficacy.) Similarly, while 'examiner' is often the popular term — even among some private tax professionals — for the IRS employee who conducts an audit, whether in the field or the appropriate District office, the Service's own internal term for such a post is 'auditor' — the term 'examiner' refers to an employee tasked with the actual selection of certain tax returns for audit, although he never deals with the TP directly. Examinations is, as mentioned, the responsibility of Regional Examination Centers such as Peoria's Midwest REC. Organizationally, Examinations, Audits, and Criminal Investigation are all divisions of the IRS's Compliance Branch. At the same time, though, it is true that certain mid-level auditors are known technically within the Service's personnel hierarchy as 'revenue agents.' It's also true that members of the Internal Inspections Division are sometimes classified as 'agents,' with the Inspections Division being rather like the Service's version of law enforcement agencies' Internal Affairs. In essence, they are tasked with investigating charges of malfeasance or criminal behavior on the part of Service employees or administration. Administratively, IID is part of the Internal Control Branch of the IRS, which also includes both the Personnel and Systems Divisions. The point, I suppose, is that, as with most large federal agencies, the structure and organization of the Service is highly complex — in fact, there are departments within the Internal Control branch tasked exclusively to studying the Service's own organizational structure and determining ways to help maximize efficiency in terms of the Service's mission.

Set amid the dazzling paralysis of the Chicago Loop, the IRS recruiting station was not, at first blush, a very dramatic or compelling-looking place. There was also a US Air Force recruiting office in the same storefront, separated from the IRS's space only by a large polyvinyl screen or shield, and the fact that the USAF office played an orchestral version of the familiar 'Off we go into the wild blue yonder' musical theme over and over again on a repeating track in its reception area may well have had something to do with the IRS recruiter's problem with his head and face, which were prone to small spastic jerks and grimaces at various times, and was, at first, difficult not to stare at and to act casual in the presence of. This Service recruiter, who appeared unshaven and had a cowlick that seemed to comprise almost the whole right side of his head, also wore his sunglasses indoors, and had an involved stain on one lapel of his suit jacket, and his necktie—unless my eyes had not yet adjusted from the brilliant dazzle of floundering southwest through fallen snow all the way from the Buckingham Fountain bus stop in Grant Park—might have been an actual clip-on. On the other hand, I had melted snow up to my groin, and frozen birdseed on my down coat, as well as two different winter-weight turtlenecks on beneath that, and probably did not look very promising either. (There was obviously no way that I was going to wear any of my new Carson's business apparel to clamber through chest-high snowdrifts.) Besides the distracting martial music from across the screen, the IRS recruiting station itself was overheated, and smelled of sour coffee and a brand of stick-style deodorant which I couldn't place. Several empty Nesbitt's soda cans were arranged atop an overfull wastebasket, around which a litter of balled-up papers suggested idle hours of trying to throw balled-up papers into it—a pastime I knew well from 'studying' at the UIC library on the evenings when the podiatrist's sign's foot had so ruled. I also remember an open box of doughnuts whose glaze had gone unappetizingly dull.

Nevertheless, I wasn't here to judge anything, nor to make hasty commitments. I was here to try to verify the seemingly almost incredible incentives for entering the Service that had been detailed by the advertisement I'd either heard or perhaps seen two days prior. It eventually emerged that the recruiter had been on duty without relief for several days because of the storm, which was probably the reason for his condition—the Service's standards for personal appearance on-post are normally fairly stringent. When one of the city's large, makeshift plows came by, the noise shook the storefront's window, which faced south and was untinted—forming another possible explanation for the recruiter's sunglasses, which I still found disconcerting. The recruiter's desk was flanked by flags and a large easel with institutional charts and advertisements on large pieces of posterboard, and hanging slightly askew on the wall above and behind the desk was a framed print of the Internal Revenue Service seal, which, the recruiter explained, depicted the mythic hero Bellerophon slaying the Chimera, as well as the Latin motto on a long furling banner along the bottom, *'Alicui tamen faciendum est,'* which essentially means *'He is the one doing a difficult, unpopular job.'* It turned out that, for reasons dating all the way back to the permanent institution of a federal income tax in 1913, Bellerophon was the Service's official symbol or figure, rather the way the bald eagle is the United States as a whole's.

In return for a commitment of two to four years, depending on the specific incentive scheme, the Internal Revenue Service was offering up to a total of $14,450 for college or continuing technical education. That was, of course, $14,450 before applicable taxes, I remember the IRS recruiter stipulating with a smile I did not, at that point, know how to interpret. Also, by an elaborate arrangement which the recruiter highlighted for me on a fold-out document that outlined all the Service's various incentive schedules in complex diagrams with dotted lines and extremely small type, if the continuing education led to either a CPA license or a master's degree in the accounting or tax fields from an accredited institution, there were several grades of further inducements to extend one's employee contract with the IRS, including an option to attend classes while posted at either a Regional Service Center or Regional Examination Center, to which the recruiter explained that newer Service personnel were commonly posted for their first several quarters after what the recruiter called 'T and A.' In order to qualify for the incentive package, one had to complete the twelve-week course at an IRS Training and Assessment Center, or TAC, which is what the recruiter's rather cynical 'T and A' also stood for. Also, employees nearly always refer to the IRS as 'the Service,' and the site at which one works as their IRS 'Post,' and they measure time of employment not in years or months but in terms of the Service calendar's four fiscal quarters, which correspond to the legal deadlines for mailing quarterly estimated tax, or 1040-EST, payments, the only unusual thing about which is that the second quarter runs from 15 April to 15 June, or only two months, and the fourth extends from 15 September to 15 January of the successive year — this is mainly so that the final quarter can comprise the entire taxable year through 31 December. The recruiter explained none of this in so many words at the time — much of it is just the sort of special institutional info one absorbs over time in an adult career.

Anyhow, by this time there were also two other would-be recruits in the office, one of whom I only remember as having a brightly colored one-piece snowsuit and a somewhat low, bulging forehead. The other, older man, though, had masking or duct tape holding his battered sneakers' soles on, and was shivering in a way that seemed to have nothing to do with temperature, and impressed me as quite probably an indigent or street person rather than a bona fide candidate for recruitment. I was trying to concentrate and study the incentive-schedule handout in my hand throughout the recruiter's more formal introductory presentation, and as a result, I know I failed to catch certain key details. Also, though, those details were sometimes actually drowned out by the cymbals and timpanis of the Air Force theme's crescendo portion on the screen's other side. We three, the recruiting presentation's audience, were in folding metal chairs arranged before his desk, which the recruiter initially stood to the side of, beside his display easel—I remember that the man with the low forehead had reversed his chair and was seated leaning forward with his hands on the chair's back and his chin atop his knuckles, whereas the third member of our audience was eating a doughnut after placing several others in side pockets of his khaki army coat. I remember the Service recruiter continually referred to an elaborate color chart or diagram that depicted the administrative structure and organization of the IRS. The depiction covered more than one chart, actually, and the recruiter—who sneezed several times without covering his nose or even averting his head, and also had more of the tiny neurological tic- or spasm-events at certain points in the unavoidably overheard 'Off we go...' — had to keep pulling different sections of posterboard to the front of the easel, and the whole thing was so complicated, and consisted of so many branches, sub-branches, divisions, and coordinating offices and sub-offices, as well as parallel or bilateral sub-offices and technology support divisions, that it appeared impossible to comprehend even the general sense of well enough to take a real interest in, though I obviously made it a conscious point to look as attentive and engaged as possible, if only to show that I was someone who could be trained to herd and process large amounts of info. At that juncture, I was obviously unaware that initial diagnostic screening of possible recruits was already under way, and that the excessive complexity and minutiae of the recruiter's presentation represented part of a psychological 'dispositional assessment' mechanism in use by the IRS's Personnel Division since 1967. Nor did I understand, when the other potential recruit (meaning the one who wasn't obviously just looking for a warm place off the street) began nodding off over his chair's back at the abstruseness of the presentation, that he had effectively eliminated himself as a candidate for all but the lowest-level IRS postings. Also, there were upwards of twenty different forms to fill out, many of which were redundant—it wasn't clear to me why one couldn't simply fill out one copy and then xerox a number of duplicates, but I again chose to keep my own counsel and simply fill out the same essential info over and over again.

Overall, despite comprising scarcely more than 5,750 total words, the initial recruiting presentation and processing lasted almost three hours, during which there were also several intervals when the recruiter trailed off and sat in a heavy, incongruous silence during which he may or may not have been asleep—the sunglasses made it impossible to verify. (I would later be informed that these unexplained pauses, too, were part of initial recruit screening and 'dispositional assessment,' that the shabby recruiting office was, in fact, under sophisticated videotape surveillance—one of the required forms had contained an 'Authorization to Record' buried in one of the subclause's boilerplate, which I obviously did not notice at the time—and that our fidget- and yawn-rates and certain characteristics of posture, position, and facial expression in certain contexts would be reviewed and compared to various psychological templates and predictive formulas which the Service's Internal Control Branch's Personnel Division's Recruitment and Training subdivision had developed several years prior, which is, in turn, a very long and complicated story involving the Service's emphasis, throughout the 1960s and '70s, on maximizing 'throughput,' meaning the highest possible efficiency in terms of the volume of tax returns and documents that could be processed, examined, audited, and adjusted in a given fiscal quarter. Though the Service's concept of efficiency would undergo changes in the 1980s, as new government priorities trickled down through the Treasury and Triple-Six, with an institutional emphasis on maximizing revenue rather than throughput of returns, the emphasis at the time — meaning January 1979 — required screening recruits for a set of characteristics that boiled down to an ability to maintain concentration under conditions of extreme tedium, complication, confusion, and absence of comprehensive info. The Service was, in the words of one of the Examinations instructors at the Indianapolis TAC, looking for 'cogs, not spark plugs.'

Eventually, it was beginning to get dark and to snow again by the time the recruiter announced that the process was over, and we — by this time there were perhaps five or six of us in the audience, some having drifted in during the formal presentation — were then each given a ream-sized stack of stapled packets of materials in a large blue IRS binder. The recruiter's final instructions were that those of us who felt we were still potentially interested should go home and read these materials closely, and return the next day — which would, if I remember right, have been a Friday — for the next stage of the recruitment process.

To be honest, I had expected to be interviewed and asked all sorts of questions about my background, experience, and direction in terms of career and commitment. I expected that they would want to verify I was serious and not just there to scam the IRS out of free tuition funding. Not surprisingly, I had expected that the Internal Revenue Service — which my father, whose job with the city had understandably involved dealings with the IRS on a variety of levels, feared and respected — would be acutely sensitive to the possibility of being scammed or conned in any way, and I remember, on the long trek in from the bus stop, that I had been apprehensive about what to say in response to tough questioning about the origin of my interest and goals. I'd been concerned about how to tell the truth without the Service's recruiters reacting the way the Associate Dean for Academic Affairs had just recently reacted, or thinking of me in anything like the way I had thought about the Christian girl with the multifloral boots in the Lindenhurst memory already mentioned. To the best of my recollection, though, I was required to say almost nothing that first day of recruiting after the initial hello and one or two innocuous questions—as well as my name, of course. Nearly all my input was, as I've mentioned, in the form of forms, many of which had bar codes in the lower left corners—this detail I remember because these were the first bar codes I can remember ever being aware of in my life up to then.

Anyhow, the recruiting office's binder full of homework was so unbelievably dry and obscure that you essentially had to read each line several times to derive any sense of what it was trying to say. I almost couldn't believe it. I had already gotten a taste of real accounting language from the assigned textbooks for Managerial Accounting and Auditing I, which were both just under way— when weather permitted—at DePaul, but the Service material made those textbooks look like child's play by comparison. The largest single packet in the binder was something on low-toner Xerox called *Statement of Procedural Rules,* which is actually from Title 26, §601 of the *Code of Federal Regulations*. A ninety-five-word section of a page that I remember that I flipped to at first at random and read, just to get an idea of what I would be having to try to read and process, was ¶1910, §601.201a(1)(g), subpart xi:

> For ruling requests concerning the classification of an organization as a limited partnership where a corporation is the sole general partner, see Rev. Proc. 72–13, 1972–1 CB 735. See also Rev. Proc. 74–17, 1974–1 CB 438, and Rev. Proc. 75–16, 1975–1 CB 676. Revenue Procedure 74–17 announces certain operating rules of the Service relating to the issuance of advance ruling letters concerning the classification of organizations formed as limited partnerships. Revenue Procedure 75–16 sets forth a checklist outlining required information frequently omitted from requests for rulings relating to classification of organizations for Federal tax purposes.

Essentially, the whole thing was like that. Nor, at the time, did I know we would have to try to practically memorize the entire 82,617-word *Procedural Rules* manual at the Training and Assessment Center, less for informational purposes — since every IRS examiner's Tingle table would have the *Procedural Rules* included in the *Internal Revenue Manual* right there in the bottom-right drawer, attached with a little chain so no one could take or borrow it, as we were all supposed to have it at our Tingle at all times — but more as a type of diagnostic tool for seeing who could sit there hour after hour and apply themselves to it versus who couldn't, which obviously bore on who could cut it at various levels of complexity and dryness (which, in turn, is why the Examinations component of the TAC's training course was known at the TAC as 'Camp Concentration'). My best guess at the time, sitting there in my childhood room in my father's house in Libertyville (the dorm at DePaul still wasn't open, as some frozen pipes had ruptured — the storm and its fallout still had much of the city paralyzed), was that requiring us to read this material was some kind of test or hurdle to help determine who was truly motivated and serious and who was just drifting around attempting to scam some easy tuition money from the government. I kept picturing the indigent character who ate all the doughnuts from that afternoon's presentation lying in a cardboard appliance box in an alley, reading a page of the packet and then setting it afire to provide light for reading the next page. In a certain way, I think that that was essentially what I was doing, too — I had to blow off nearly all my next day's accounting class assignments in order to stay up nearly all night getting through the Service material. It didn't feel feckless, though it also didn't feel especially romantic or heroic. It was more as if I simply had to make a choice of what was more important.

I read more or less the whole thing. I won't even say how many words in toto. It took until almost 5:00 A.M. At the very back — not all the way, but tucked between two pages of the transcript of a 1966 USTC case called *Uinta Livestock Corporation v. U.S.* near the back of the binder — were a couple of more forms to fill out, which reinforced my assumption that it really had been a kind of test to see if we were committed and interested enough to nut up and plow all the way through. I can't say I read everything carefully, of course. One of the few packets that wasn't totally eye-glazing was a rundown on the IRS Training and Assessment Centers and on the various types of entry-level posts available to recruits who came

out of the TAC course with various levels of education and incentive packages. There were two
IRS Training and Assessment Centers, in Indianapolis and Columbus OH, about which the
packet had photos and regulations but nothing
specific on what the training was actually like. As
usually happens with photocopied photos, the
images were mostly black masses with some indistinct white blobs; you couldn't really make out
what was going on. Unlike the present day, the
protocol in that era was that if you wanted a serious career in the Service, with a contract and civil
service rank above GS-9, you had to go through
a TAC course, which lasted twelve weeks. You
also had to join the Treasury Employees union,
although info on that criterion was not included
in the packet. Otherwise you were, in essence, a
temporary or seasonal worker, which the Service
uses a lot of, especially in the lower levels of
Returns Processing and Exams. I remember that
the Post List's representation of the Service's
structure was much simpler and less comprehensive than the recruiter's presentation's diagram,
although this one also had a lot of asterisks and
single and double lines connecting various parts of
the page's grid, and the legend for these marks had
been half cut off due to someone having xeroxed

the thing at an angle. In that era, the six main nodes or Service branches consisted of Administration, Returns Processing, Compliance, Collections, Internal Control, Support Services, and something called Technical Branch, which was the only branch with the actual word *Branch* in its name on the diagram, which at the time I found curious. Each branch then branched into several subordinate divisions—thirty-six divisions in all, though in today's Service there are now forty-eight separate divisions, some with cross-coordinated and overlapping functions which have to be streamlined and overseen by the Divisional Liaison Division, which is itself—somewhat confusingly—a division of both the Administration and Internal Control Branches. Each division then also comprised numerous subdivisions, some of whose typeface got extremely small and hard to read. The Compliance Branch's Examinations Division, for example, comprised positions—though only those postings marked in italic font (which was practically impossible to make out on the Xerox) required a federal contract or TAC course—in clerical, cart, data entry, data processing, classification, correspondence, district office interface, regional office interface, duplicating services, procurement, research audit interface, secretarial, personnel, service center interface, computer center interface, and so forth, as well as formal 'rote examiner' posts grouped (in that era, though here at the Midwest REC now the group characterizations are quite a bit different) by the types of returns one specialized in, encoded on the diagram as 1040, 1040A, 1041, EST, and 'Fats,' which refers to a complex 1040 with more than four schedules or attachments. Also, corporate 1120 and 1120S tax returns are examined by special examiners known in Exams as 'immersives,' which the recruiting page did not include information on, as immersive exams are conducted by special elite, highly trained examiners who have their own special section of the REC facility.

Anyhow, as I still can recall, the obvious idea was that anyone who was truly serious would make their best attempt to read the whole contents of the binder, would see and complete the relevant portions of the forms at the back, and then would make the effort to somehow commute back in, weather permitting, to the West Taylor recruiting station the next day by 9:00 A.M. for something which the final sheet termed 'advanced processing.' It also snowed all night again, though not as heavily, and by 4:00 A.M. you could hear the terrible sound of the City of Libertyville's plows scraping the street's concrete raw outside my childhood room's window—also, the bird-sounds at sunrise were incredible, causing lights in some of the other houses along our street to come on in irritation— and the CTA was still only running a staggered schedule. Still, even given the rush of commuters at that time of day and the rigors of the trek in from Grant Park, I arrived back at the storefront recruiting station no later than 9:20 A.M. (albeit covered with snow again), to find no one else there from the prior day except the same Service recruiter, looking even more exhausted and disheveled, who, when I came in and said I was ready for advanced processing, and gave him the forms from the homework I'd plowed through, looked from me to the forms and back again, giving me the exact kind of smile of someone who, on Christmas morning, has just unwrapped an expensive present he already owns.

§23

Dream: I saw rows of foreshortened faces over which faint emotions played like the light of distant fire. The placid hopelessness of adulthood. The complex regret. One or two, the most alive, looked better in an objectless way. Many others looked blank as the faces on coins. At the edges were office workers bustling at the endless small tasks involved in mailing, filing, sorting, their faces blankly avid, filled with the mindless energy you see in bugs, weeds, birds. The dream seemed to take hours, but when I'd come awake Superman's arms (the clock was a gift) would be in the same position as the last time I looked.

This dream was my psyche teaching me about boredom. I think I was very often bored as a child, but boredom is not what I knew it as—what I knew was that I *worried* a lot. I was a fretful, nervous, anxious, worried boy. These were my parents' words, and they became mine. Wet distended Sunday afternoons, while my mother and brother were at a recital and my father lay asleep on the couch in front of a Bengals game, with the libretto to *Norma* open on his chest, I felt the sort of soaring, ceilingless tedium that transcends tedium and becomes worry. I do not recall the things I worried about, but I remember the feeling, and it was an anxiety whose lack of a proper object is what made it horrible, free-floating. I'd look out the window and see the glass instead of anything past it. I'd think of the sorts of small games and toys and developmental projects my mother always suggested and within the boredom not only find them unappealing but be unable to imagine how anyone anywhere could possibly have the mindless energy to undertake any sort of child's amusements, or sit still in the silence long enough to read a picture book—the whole world was torpid, enervated, worry-logged. My parents' words and feelings became my own, as I took on the responsibilities of my role in the family drama, the nervous delicate son, object of my mother's concern, as my brother was the gifted, driven son whose piano filled the house after school and kept the twilight outside the windows where it belonged. In psychotherapy after the incident with my own son, I free-associated my way into recalling a Great Books presentation on Achilles and Hector in the eleventh grade, and I remembered realizing vividly that my family was Achilles, that my brother was Achilles' shield and I the family's heel, the part of the family my mother held tight to and made undivine, and that the recognition had come in the middle of my speech and left again so fast I'd not had time to grab it, though I did for much of my adolescence and early adulthood conceive of myself in terms of a heel or foot—my internal remonstrances often took the form of calling myself a 'heel,' for example, and it was true that people's feet, shoes, socks, and ankles were often the first things about them I noticed. Just as my father was the beaten but obdurate warrior— ground down every day in a campaign whose pointlessness was part of its corrosive power. My mother's role in the Achilles corpus remains unclear. I'm not sure, either, whether as a child my brother was conscious of the fact that his afternoon practice always coincided with my father's return home; in some respects I think my brother's whole piano career was designed around this requirement that there be light and music at 5:42 for my father's reentry, that in a way his life depended on it—every evening he made the opposite transition from that of the sun, death to life.

It is not surprising that I had trouble in grammar school, with its rows of empty faces and shadowless lights and wire mesh in the windows and a regimentation to primary education that still held on in the Midwest—memorization and regurgitation, tables, prescriptive grammar and diagrams of sentences, the only decorations the alphabet in construction paper on a cork guilloche that ran above the blackboard. Each classroom contained thirty student desks in five rows of six; each had flooring of white tile with insubstantial cloud-shapes of brown and gray that were discontinuous because whoever laid the tile didn't bother to match the patterns. Each room had a wall clock, manufactured by Benrus, with no second hand and a minute hand whose movements were discrete clicks instead of silent continuous clicks; the system of clocks was wired to the school's bell, which sounded at 55 past the hour, again at 00, and in a somehow more dire way at 02, signaling tardiness and interrupting each instructor's opening remarks. The school smelled of adhesive paste, rubber boots, sour cafeteria food, and a warm biotic odor of many bodies and the fixative of the tile floor as three hundred mammals slowly warmed the rooms throughout the day. Most of the teachers were sexless females, old (meaning older than my mother) and severe but not unkind, with a small dilution of younger males—one, in fourth-grade Mathematics, with the actual name Mr. Goodnature—drawn to teach children by the vague political idealism then just beginning to build (unknown to me) on college campuses far beyond my world. The young men were the worst, some actual martinets, depressed and bitter, because the idealism that had brought them to us was no match for the petrified bureaucracy of the Columbus School System or the listless passivity of children they'd dreamed of inspiring (read, indoctrinating) to a soft liberalism (*peace* was a big word with these men) that would replicate and flatter their own, children who were instead locked tight inside themselves and an institutional tedium they couldn't name but had already lost their hearts to.

§24

Author here.[1] I arrived for intake processing at Lake James IL's[2] IRS Post 047 sometime in mid-May

1 I won't keep saying this each time that I, the living author, am actively narrating. For now, I'm including it just as an innocuous cue to help you keep the book's various sections and agonists straight, since (as explained in the Author's Foreword) the legal situation here entails a certain degree of polyphony and flux.

2 At that time, Lake James was something between a suburb and an independent township of metropolitan Peoria. The same is true of other little outlying communities like Peoria Heights, Bartonville, Sicklied Ore, Eunice, & c., the latter two of which adjoined Lake James along certain unincorporated zones to the east and west. The whole separate-but-attached-district thing had to do with the city's inexorable expansion and encroachment into the rich agricultural land around it, which over time brought certain small, formerly isolated farming communities into Peoria's orbit. I know that these little satellite towns each had their own property-tax structure and zoning authority, but in many other respects (e.g., police protection) they functioned as outlying districts

447

of 1985. It was quite probably on or very near Wednesday, May 15.[3] In any event, the point is that

---

of Peoria proper. The whole thing could be extremely involved and confusing. For instance, the Regional Examination Center's street address was listed as 10047 Self-Storage Parkway, Lake James, IL, whereas the REC's official postal address was 'Internal Revenue Service Examination Center, Peoria IL 67452.' This may be because Peoria's USPS center on G Street downtown had a whole separate three-bin area for the REC, however, plus a pair of special tandem trucks that came out the restricted back road three times a day to the REC's loading docks behind the Annex. I.e., the mailing address may have been Peoria simply because that's where the REC's daily mountain of mail actually came to. That is, it may have been more a function of the relationship between the US Postal Service and the IRS than anything else. Like so many other features of the REC and Service, the answer to the physical-vs.-postal-location-incongruity question is doubtless incredibly complicated and idiosyncratic and would require far more time and energy to ferret out and truly understand than any sane person would want to expend. Another example: The really relevant, representative thing about Lake James as a township is that it has no lake. There is, in fact, a body of water called Lake James, but as a practical matter it's more of a large fetid pond, choked with algae from ag-runoff, a good dozen miles northwest of Lake James proper, closer to Anthony IL, which latter really is a separate township of Peoria and has its own zip code, & c., & c. . . . In other words, incongruities like these are complex and puzzling but not really all that important unless you're invested in the geographical minutiae of Peoria (the possibility of which I have decided I can safely presume is remote).
3 N.B.: I'm not going to be one of those memoirists who pretends to remember every last fact and thing in photorealist detail. The human mind doesn't work that way, and everyone knows it; it's an insulting bit of artifice in a genre that purports to be 100 percent 'realistic.' To be honest, I think you deserve better, and that you're intelligent enough to understand and maybe even applaud it when a memoirist has the integrity to admit that he's not some kind of eidetic freak. At the same time, I'm not going to waste time noodling about every last

I journeyed to Peoria on whatever particular day in May from my family's home in Philo, to which my brief return had been shall we say untriumphant, and where certain members of my family had more or less been looking at their watches impatiently the whole brief time I was home. Without mentioning or identifying anyone in particular, let's just say that the prevailing attitude in my family tended to be 'What have you done for me lately?' or, maybe better, 'What have you achieved/earned/attained lately that may in some way (imaginary or not) reflect well on us and let us bask in some kind of reflected (real or not) accomplishment?' It was a bit like a for-profit company, my family, in that you were pretty much

gap and imprecision in my own memory, a prime cautionary example of which is 'Irrelevant' Chris Fogle's vocational soliloquy (q.v. §22 above, which is actually heavily edited and excerpted) as part of the abortive 1984 Personnel Division motivational/recruitment faux documentary debacle, which ended up as a debacle in part because Fogle and two or three other maundering grandstanders took up so much film and time, and because Mr. Tate had failed to have his deputy, Mr. Stecyk, assign anyone on-site the responsibility of keeping someone's answer to the 'documentary question' under a certain sane ceiling, which meant that the supposed 'documentarian' and his crew had every incentive to let Fogle et al. go on and on while they stared into space and calculated the running amount of tiered overtime pay they were accruing. The whole thing, while obviously of archival value, was evidently an immense cluster-fuck, one of many that Tate authored when he indulged his administrative brainstorms instead of simply letting Stecyk do all the work of the Personnel office as usual.

only as good as your last sales quarter. Although, you know, whatever. I most definitely was not offered any kind of family ride to Peoria, though I may have gotten a quick lift to the bus station, which in Philo comprised one corner of the local IGA parking lot, which was not all that far but would have been ghastly to walk to wearing my three-piece corduroy suit in the gluey humidity of pre-dawn (which, in the lower Midwest, is also one of the two prime times of day for mosquito activity, the other being dusk, and mosquitoes there are not just a nuisance but serious business indeed) while carrying two heavy suitcases (this was a couple years before the sudden advance of someone in the luggage industry realizing that suitcases could be fitted with little wheels and telescoping handles so they could be pulled, which was just the sort of abrupt ingenious advance that makes entrepreneurial capitalism such an exciting system—it gives people incentive to make things more efficient). Plus I also had my beloved dispatch case, which was inherited from an older, non-immediate relative who'd been a staff officer in Hawaii during the latter part of World War II, and was a bit like a briefcase (i.e., the dispatch case was) except that it had no handle, and was therefore carried tucked under one's arm, and which contained the sorts of intimate or irreplaceable personal effects, toiletries, customized ear-plug case, dermatological salves and ointments, and important papers that any thinking person carries with him instead of trusting to the vagaries of baggage handling. These papers included my recent correspondence with both the Guaranteed Student Loan people and the IRS's Midwest Region's Office of the Deputy Regional Commissioner for Personnel, as well as my copy of the signed IRS contract and the Form 141-PO constituting my so-called 'Posting Orders' to the Midwest REC, both of which (i.e., both latter documents) I would evidently need in order to acquire my Service ID badge, which I'd been directed to do straightaway upon my arrival at the 'GS-9 Intake Station' at a certain particular time that was filled in by hand on a smeary, indifferently stamped line near the bottom of the Posting Orders.[4]

(Quick aside here. *Pace* his overall self-indulgence and penchant for hand-wringing, §22's 'Irrelevant' Chris Fogle was actually on the money about one thing. Given the way the human mind works, it does tend to be small, sensuously specific details

---

4 I no longer have this original two-page Form 141-PO, which vanished into the maw of the REC's Personnel and Internal Control Systems Problem Resolution filing systems during the whole eventual swivet and comedy of errors surrounding my initial misassignment to an Immersive Exams Pod, the story of which unfolds in full pathetic, ur-bureaucratic detail below.

that get remembered over time—and unlike some so-called memoirists, I refuse to pretend that the mind works any other way than it really does. At the same time, rest assured that I am not Chris Fogle, and that I have no intention of inflicting on you a regurgitation of every last sensation and passing thought I happen to recall. I am about art here, not simple reproduction. What logorrheic colleagues like Fogle failed to understand is that there are vastly different kinds of truth, some of which are incompatible with one another. Example: A 100 percent accurate, comprehensive list of the exact size and shape of every blade of grass in my front lawn is 'true,' but it is not a truth that anyone will have any interest in. What renders a truth meaningful, worthwhile, & c. is its relevance, which in turn requires extraordinary discernment and sensitivity to context, questions of value, and overall point— otherwise we might as well all just be computers downloading raw data to one another.)

There was also, in one of the leather dispatch case's myriad ingenious little inner sleeves and snap pockets, a certain piece of supporting documentation in the form of personal intrafamily correspondence from a certain unnamed and non-immediate relative who enjoyed what today would be called significant 'juice' with the IRS's Midwest

Regional Commissioner's Office in Joliet upstate,[5] which technically I was not supposed to even have (and which was somewhat rumpled after its retrieval from the wastebasket of an unnamed and more immediate relative), but which it seemed prudent to have with me in case of some kind of bureaucratic emergency or last-resort need.[6] In general, my

---

5 N.B.: With possible competition only from East St. Louis, Peoria and Joliet are well-known as the two grimmest, most blighted and depressed old factory cities in Illinois*, which fact turns out not to be a coincidence, since it affords statistically verifiable savings to the Service in terms of both facilities and labor. The location of most Regional HQs, RECs, and Service Centers in blighted and/or devitalized cities, which is traceable all the way back to the Service's big reorganization and decentralization after the King Commission's report to Congress in 1952, is just one sign of the deep pro-business and -bottom-line philosophies beginning to gather force in the Service as early as the Nixon administration.

  * As part of the overall relevant context, be advised that Illinois's five largest cities and metro areas by population (excluding Chicago, which is more like its own galaxy) c. 1985 were, in descending order, Rockford, Peoria, Springfield, Joliet, and Decatur.

6 I do, by the way, still possess this letter, which for legal reasons I am told I cannot reproduce more than one single fair-use sentence of, for 'general flavor,' the sentence I've chosen being from the second immaculately copperplate-handwritten paragraph; to wit: 'He will be given only a small job to begin with, and it will be his business to work his way up by diligence and attentiveness,' in the margin next to which the unnamed addressee of this letter had absently jotted either 'HA!' or 'HAH!,' depending on how one tried to parse the spiky and almost indecipherable hand of someone for whom a 'quick cocktail before supper' involved a sixteen-ounce tumbler and no ice.

attitude toward bureaucracies was the same as that of most ordinary Americans: I hated and feared them (i.e., bureaucracies) and basically regarded them as large, grinding, impersonal machines— that is, they seemed rigidly literal and rule-bound the same way machines are, and just about as dumb.[7] Dating at least from a 1979 tangle with the state's DMV and our insurance provider over the terms and coverage of my Learner's Permit after an incident so laughably minor it could barely even be called a collision, my primary association with the word *bureaucracy* was an image of someone expressionless behind a counter, not listening to any of my questions or explanations of circumstance or misunderstanding but merely referring to some manual of impersonal regulations as he stamped my form with a number that meant I was in for some further kind of tedious, frustrating hassle or expense. I doubt that you need much prompting to understand why my recent experience with the college's Judicial Board and Dean of Students's office (q.v. §9 above) had done nothing to mitigate this view. Shameful or not, I figured that any possible bit of

7 This was, keep in mind, the tail end of the era of mainframe computers, tape- and card-based data storage, & c., which now seems almost Flintstonianly remote.

evidence of extra connective juice might serve to lift
me out of some long gray line of faceless supplicants
in the event of trouble or confusion[8] at the Regional
Exam Center, which I had conceived ahead of time
as some kind of ur-bureaucratic version of Kafka's
castle, an enormous DMV or Judicial Board.

By way of foreshadowing and advance explana-

8 However puerile it seems now, I know that I sometimes felt an irrational
anxiety about the possibility that the recent unpleasantness at school might
have found its way into some shadowily comprehensive data retrieval system to
which the IRS was somehow linked, and that some kind of bell or siren would
suddenly sound when I presented at the counter for my ID and badge, and so
on... an irrational fear that I knew was irrational and so did not admit fully
into my consciousness, though at the same time I know that I spent at least
some of the interminable time aboard the bus to Peoria idly constructing
emergency plans and scenarios for how, if and when the bell or siren sounded,
I might avoid returning home to Philo the same day I'd left and facing
whoever it was who opened the door to my knock and saw me there on the
home's filthy screen porch with my bags and dispatch case — at some moments
I know that the unconscious anxiety consisted only of envisioning the
expression on the face of whatever immediate relative opened the door, saw me,
and opened his mouth to say something, at which time I became aware of the
fact that I was having anxious fantasies and waved them away on the bus ride,
returning to the unbelievably insipid book I'd been presented with as a 'gift' by
my family, their idea of useful wisdom and support, this 'gift' presented to me
at supper on the evening before my departure (which special farewell supper,
by the way, had consisted of [a] leftovers and [b] steamed ears of corn that I
had just had my braces tightened and couldn't even have hoped to try to eat),
after first being told to open the gift very carefully so that the wrapping paper
could be reused.

tion, I'll also admit up front here that there are portions of that arrival and intake day that I do not
remember very well, due at least in part to the tsu-
nami of sensuous input, technical data, and
bureaucratic complication that awaited me when I
arrived and was personally taken in hand and
escorted—with a degree of solicitude that, however unexpected and confusing, would have been
gratifying to just about anyone—to the REC's
Personnel office, bypassing the GS-9 Intake Station (whose location was anyone's guess) that I'd
been directed to find and stand in line at by the
smeared and typo-ridden Posting Orders inside my
dispatch case. As nearly always happens with
human minds inundated by excessive input, I've
retained only flashes and incomplete clips from
that day, which I'll now go ahead and recount some
specially selected relevant portions of, not only as a
way to introduce the atmospherics of the REC and
the Service, but also to help explain what might
initially look like my passivity (it was more simple
confusion[9]) in the face of what may seem, in the

---

9 (plus, I'll admit, a certain amount of slack relief at what seemed to be the
opposite of bells/sirens and possible rejection for ethical unfitness or whatever
my unconscious had conjured; I think I'd been more afraid than I'd
acknowledged to myself)

clarity of hindsight, like an obvious case of misassignment or mistaken identity. It was not obvious at the time, though; and expecting a person to have immediately seen it, understood it as an error, and taken immediate steps to correct it is a bit like expecting someone to have noticed and fixed some incongruity in his surroundings at the very moment that a hundred flashbulbs suddenly went off in his eyes. There's only so much complex input the human nervous system can take, in other words.

I do remember standing there at the edge of the IGA supermarket lot in my suit with my bags and case as dawn officially broke. For those who've never experienced a sunrise in the rural Midwest, it's roughly as soft and romantic as someone's abruptly hitting the lights in a dark room. This is because the land is so flat that there is nothing to impede or gradualize the sun's appearance. It's just all of a sudden there. The temperature immediately goes up ten degrees; the mosquitoes vanish to wherever exactly it is that mosquitoes go to regroup. Just to the west, the roofline of St. Dymphna's church sprayed complex shadows over half the downtown. I was drinking a can of Nesbitt's, which is sort of my version of morning coffee. The IGA's lot abuts the downtown's main drag, which is the in-town extension of SR 130 and ingeniously named. Directly across this Main

Street from the IGA were the bubbletop pumps and
saurian logo of Clete's Sinclair, outside of which the
best and brightest of Philo High used to gather on
Friday nights to drink Pabst Blue Ribbon and search
the adjacent lot's weeds for frogs and mice to throw
at Clete's bug zapper, which he'd modified to hold
225 volts of charge.

This was, so far as I know, the only time I'd ridden a commercial bus line, and it was not an experience I'm eager to repeat. The bus was unclean,
and some of the passengers appeared to have been
aboard for several days running, with all that that
entails in terms of hygiene and inhibition. I remember that the seatbacks seemed unnaturally high,
and there was some kind of aluminum-alloy bar
for your feet, and a button on the seat's arm for
causing the back to recline, which in the case of my
seat failed to work correctly. The arm's little flip-
top ashtray was a nightmare of gum-wads and
butts too numerous for the little lid even to close all
the way. I remember seeing two or more nuns in
full habit in one of the forward sections, and thinking that requiring nuns to travel by filthy commercial bus must have been in line with their sect's vow
of poverty; but it still seemed incongruous and
wrong. One of the nuns was doing a crossword
puzzle. The trip took over four hours in toto, since

the bus stopped at an endless number of sour little
towns just like my own. The sun began shortly to
broil the bus's rear and port side. The air-
conditioning was more like a vague gesture toward
the abstract idea of air-conditioning. There was a
horrific piece of graffiti incised with knife or leather
punch in the plastic of the seatback in front of me,
which I looked at twice and then made a point of
never looking directly at again. The bus had a lava-
tory in the wayback rear, which no one ever made
any attempt to use, and I remember consciously
deciding to trust that the passengers had good reason for not using it instead of venturing in and
discovering that reason for myself. Empiricism has
its limits. There is also, in memory, a contextless
flash of some female's feet in clear polyurethane
thongs, a tattoo of what was either ivy or barbed
wire around one of her ankles. And a round-faced
little boy[10] in shorts in the seat directly across the
aisle, with red sprays of impetigo on his knees and
a presumable guardian asleep in the adjoining seat
(her seatback did recline), watching me as I ate the

---

10 This boy had also spent the first several minutes after I'd boarded and
gotten settled staring wide-eyed at the condition of the side of my face, making
no effort to hide or disguise the clinical interest with which little children
stare, all of which I'd of course seen (and in some ways almost appreciated) out
of the corner of my eye.

small box of raisins from the bag lunch I'd had to pack myself in the dark kitchen, the boy moving his whole head to follow the path of each raisin I brought to my mouth, and I peripherally trying to decide whether to offer to share some of the raisins or not (ultimately not: I was reading and didn't want to converse, not to mention that God only knew what this child's situation or story was; plus impetigo is notoriously contagious).

I will spare all of us much sensuous reminiscence about Peoria's main bus terminal—which was ghastly in the special way of bus stations in depressed downtowns everywhere—or of my over-two-hour wait there, except to say that its air was not conditioned or even circulated, and it was extremely crowded, and that there were a certain number of lone men and groups of two or three men, nearly all wearing suit coats and hats, or else holding their hats or slowly fanning themselves with them as they sat (none of them ever seemed to think to remove their coats or even loosen their ties); and I remember remarking even then that it was strange to see men in their adult prime wearing the business-type hats that normally one saw only on much older men of a certain background and station. A few of the hats were eccentric or unusual.

I know that I saw, during my survey of the payphone and vending-machine area near the entrance to the restrooms, what may have been an actual prostitute.

I well remember the subsequent roil of these same hatted men in the humidity and diesel fumes outside the terminal; and I well remember the two baked-bean-brown IRS transport sedans' arriving, finally, and pulling up at the terminal curb, and there turning out to be far too many other newly arrived or transferred IRS personnel,[11] all with abundant luggage, to fit everyone in the sedans, and the order of departure being determined not by the mandatory reporting times stamped on people's respective Forms 141-PO (as would appear to have been fair and rational) but by GS grade as evidenced by Service ID—which I didn't have, and my argument that it was precisely in order to *acquire* Service ID that I had been specifically ordered to be at the GS-9 Intake Station by

11 I.e., all these men with hats, which hats I would soon suspect and then outright learn were an Exam Division trademark (just as flat square shoulder-holsters for one's pocket calculator were the signature accessory of Audits, earbuds and stylized tie clips were Systems, and so on) such that the REC's group rooms, whether for rotes or immersives, all featured at least one wall with a peg-board of hooks for examiners' hats, since individual hat racks or hooks screwed into the edge of one's Tingle table created impediments for cart boys' carts…

1340h. made no impression whatever, perhaps since several other, pushier personnel were also at that same time exclaiming to the driver while holding up their extant IRS IDs; and, slightly later, quite a few of us standing there watching the overfilled sedans recede from the curb into downtown traffic, and many of the other new personnel simply shrugging and going passively back inside the terminal, and my personal feeling that the whole thing was not only unfair and disorganized but a grim little foretaste indeed of what bureaucratic life was going to be like.

Here, by the way, as a brief interpolation, is some preliminary general background that I have opted not to massage or smuggle in through the sort of graceless dramatic contrivance[12] so many stock memoirs resort to; to wit:

The IRS's Midwest Regional Examination Center is a roughly L shaped physical structure located off Self-Storage Parkway in the Lake James district of Peoria IL. What makes the facility's L shape only rough is that the REC's two perpen-

---

12 (e.g., having one character inform another of stuff they both actually already know, in order to get this information across to the reader—which I've always found irksome in the extreme, not to mention highly suspicious in a 'nonfiction' memoir, although it is true [if mysterious] that mass-market readers seem not to mind being jerked around this way)

The Pale King

dicular buildings are closely proximate but not continuous; they are, however, connected at the second and third floors by elevated transoms that are enclosed in olive-green fiberglass carbonate as a shield against inclement weather, since important documents and data storage cards are often conveyed across them. Neither heating nor air-conditioning service was ever reliably achieved in these elevated tunnels, and in summer months the Post's personnel refer to them as bataans, an apparent reference to the Bataan Death March of World War II's Pacific theater.

The larger of the site's two buildings, originally constructed in 1962, basically comprises Post 047's administrative offices, data processing, document storage, and Support Service facilities. The other, which is where the bulk of actual examinations of US tax returns takes place, is not owned by the IRS but instead back-leased through a proprietary holding company established by the shareholder trustees of one Mid West Mirror Works (*sic*), a glass-and-amalgam manufacturer that vanished into the protections of UCC Ch. 7 in the mid-1970s.

Incorporated in 1845 and perhaps best known as the birthplace of barbed wire in 1873, Peoria plays a vital role in the IRS's Midwest Regional

463

structure. Located medially between East St. Louis, Illinois's Regional Service Center, and Joliet, Illinois's Regional Commissioner's Office, and serving the region's nine states and fourteen IRS districts, the Midwest REC's staff of more than 3,000 employees examines the math and veracity of some 4.5 million tax returns per year.[13] Though the Service's nationwide structure comprises seven regions in toto, there are (following the Rome NY REC's spectacular administrative meltdown in 1982)[14] only six currently operating Regional Examination Centers, these being located at Philadelphia PA, Peoria IL, Rotting Flesh LA, St. George UT, La Junta CA, and Federal Way WA, to which tax returns are forwarded by either the relevant region's Service Center or the IRS's central computer facility in Martinsburg WV.

13 N.B.: Some of this is more or less lifted from the packet of IRS orientation materials that new hires and transfers received at Intake & Processing; hence the somewhat dead, bureaucratic flavor, which I have elected not to jazz up or prettify.

14 I have, however, worked in relevant details that were obviously not in the official materials. The Rome debacle was not something the Service had any interest in publicizing, even internally; but it also figured prominently in the whole high-level struggle over the so-called 'Initiative' and its implementation. None of which I had any idea of or interest in on this first day, it goes without saying.

Among the notable businesses and industries
based in metropolitan Peoria as of 1985 are
included Rayburn-Thrapp Agronomics; American
Twine, the nation's second-largest manufacturer
of string, wire, and low-diameter rope; Consolidated Self Storage, one of the first corporations in
middle America to utilize the franchise financing
model; the Farm & Home Insurance Group; the
Japanese-owned remains of Nortex Heavy Equipment; and the national HQ of Fornix Industries, a
privately held maker of keypunch and card-
reading equipment, one of whose largest remaining customers of that time was the US Treasury.
Of Peoria's employers, however, the Internal Revenue Service has ranked first ever since American
Twine lost exclusive patent rights to Type 3 barbed
wire in 1971.

End of interpolation; return to mnemonic real
time.

After who knows how many attempts, back in
the fetid terminal, to find a working pay phone
and to prevail on someone at the Form 141-PO's
'employee assistance number' (which turned out
to be incorrect or out of order), it was eventually
in either the fourth or fifth Service vehicle to
appear at the terminal that I finally secured transport to the REC, now direly late for my appointed

check-in time, which tardiness I could imagine being blamed for by some expressionless person whose finger also controlled the Intake system's moral bell/siren.

The next salient fact of that day is that traffic along the city's circumambient Self-Storage Parkway was totally horrible. The section of SSP around Peoria's east side was lined with franchise restaurants and things like Kmarts, and auto dealerships with gaudy tethered parade balloons and blinking neon signs. There was an entire separate four-lane access road leading to something called Carousel Mall, which one shuddered even to think about.[15] Behind all this commerce (i.e., behind as seen from the east side, heading south around the city's perimeter, with the slow and silty Illinois River coming in and out of view on the Gremlin's left side) was the ruined-looking skyline of downtown Peoria, a bar graph

---

15 One of the pieces of freelance work I'd completed just before the fraternity-file idiocy blew up in everyone's face had been the first two chapters of a rather likable but disorganized sociology major's senior thesis on shopping malls as the modern functional analog of medieval cathedrals (with some of the parallels being downright striking), and I had no stomach left for shopping malls, even though they were often the only places anymore that had movie theaters, the grand old downtown palaces being now either shuttered or converted to Adult.

of sooty brick and missing windows and a sense of hard pollution even though no smoke issued from any of the smokestacks. (This was several years before attempted gentrification of the old downtown.)

The Service vehicle in question was a two-door orange or yellow AMC Gremlin, albeit fitted with a high-powered whip antenna and a Service-seal decal on the driver's-side door. Interior signs prohibited smoking and/or food. The vehicle's rigid plastic interior was clean, but it was also extremely hot and stuffy. I could feel myself beginning to perspire, which is obviously not a pleasant sensation at all inside a three-piece corduroy suit. No one spoke to me or even acknowledged my existence—although I had, as I may or may not have mentioned, a severe dermatological condition during this period, and was more or less used to not being looked at or acknowledged after an initial involuntary gasp and expression of sympathy or distaste (depending), which is to say that I no longer took it all that personally. There were no general offers to adjust the air-conditioning, or even standardly polite questions about whether any of the AC's trickle was reaching us in the cramped backseat, where between myself and an older GS-11 whose homburg was mashed down almost around his eyes by the roof's pressure on its crown sat a long-jawed younger man in a gray polyester sport coat and tie, maybe roughly my age, his feet on the medial hump and knees thus up almost to his chest, who was already sweating prodigiously, and who kept surreptitiously wiping rivulets of sweat off his forehead and then wiping his fingers off on his shirt with a motion that looked strangely as if he were pretending to scratch himself under his sport coat rather than wipe off his wet fingers. He did this over and over in my peripheral vision. The whole thing was very strange. His smile was an anxious and totally false rictus, his profile a branching mass of running droplets, some of which were actually falling onto his sport coat and dappling the lapels. He gave off a palpable aura of tension or fear, or perhaps claustrophobia—there was the unexplainable feeling that I'd hurt him terribly if I spoke to him or asked if he was feeling OK. Another older IRS employee sat up front beside the driver, both men also hatless (the driver with a monastic-looking *coupe de zéro* haircut) and staring straight ahead, neither of them speaking or moving, even when the vehicle was completely stopped in traffic. From the side, the skin of the older employee's chin's underside and upper throat had the scrotal or lizardy cast of some men's advanced middle age (not unlike the then-current US president's, whose face, on television, often looked as though it was melting down into his throat, which I remember making his jet-black pompadour and harlequin ovals of rouge look all the more incongruous). We alternated between sitting stopped in traffic and moving at roughly cortege speed. The sun beat palpably on the Gremlin's metal roof; a franchise bank's digital Time & Temp sign, which we sat idling in view of for several minutes, kept flashing first the time and then YOU DONT WANT TO KNOW, presumably for temperature, which seemed to me an ominous preview of Peorian wit and culture. You can imagine for yourself the air quality and overall smells involved.

I had never before been in a crowded vehicle for so long a time with no radio playing and no one in the car saying anything, even once, ever, feeling utterly isolated at the same time that I was crammed in so closely with other people that we were all breathing one another's air the whole time.[16] Every so often, the IRS driver would knead the back of his neck, which

---

16 True, there had been silent rides aplenty with my own family, though the AM radio then was always playing Easy Listening music at high volume, which helped explain-slash-cover the absence of conversation.

had obviously become stiff from the strange position he was forced to hold his head in in order to see through the dashboard's set of protrusive signs. The early part of the ride's chief excitement: A period of furious itching along the left side of my ribcage gave rise to fears (understandable, but luckily unfounded) that the former boy on the bus's impetigo had somehow been pneumatic or contagious without direct contact, which fears I had to quell because there was obviously no way to untuck my shirt and check the area's appearance. Meanwhile, the older Serviceman in the antiquated hat had opened an accordion file and spread two or three dark-brown manila folders in his lap and was perusing various forms and printouts, moving them from one folder to another according to some scheme or system I had no way of understanding, since I was watching the whole thing in my leftward peripheral vision past the steady cascade of droplets of sweat off the tip of the nose of the man on the hump, who was now sweating in a way I had previously seen only on the squash courts of college and in the case of a mild infarction suffered by an unnamed older relative on Thanksgiving Day 1978. I spent much of my own time drumming my fingers impatiently on the dispatch case—which was now especially soft and moist from the heat of the Gremlin's interior, and made a satisfying series of splattish noises when drummed on—which, though drumming absently on something in an otherwise silent space is usually one of the fastest ways to drive those around you crazy and get them to speak to you, if only to ask you to knock it off, no one in the Gremlin commented on or even seemed to notice.

Self-Storage Parkway more or less circles Peoria and composes the boundary between the city proper and its outlying suburbs. It is what now, in 2005, would be just a typical multilane exurban highway, complete with the paradoxical combination of high speed limit and traffic lights every quarter-mile, which lights were obviously placed to help give consumers and commuters access to all the retail commerce packed along SSP's length down at least the entire east side we were trying to traverse. As of the mid-1980s, Self-Storage Parkway was elevated over interstate junctions, and crossed the tobacco-colored Illinois River at two points via WPA-era iron bridges whose rivets wept orange rust and inspired, shall we say, less than total confidence.

Moreover, the closer we came to metro Peoria's southeast side and the special access road to the Examination Center, the worse the traffic became. The reason for this was apparent from that first day: It was institutional stupidity in all its manifold forms and names. Item one. The highway people were broadening this section of Self-Storage Parkway into three lanes, but the construction served to reduce the extant two lanes to just one; the right lane was closed off with orange cones, even in sections where no construction was ongoing and the lane looked clear and navigable. And, of course, single-lane traffic always moves exactly as fast as the very slowest vehicle in line. Item two. There were, as mentioned, traffic lights every eighth- to quarter-mile, and yet the single southbound lane's line of traffic was substantially longer than the distance between any two such traffic lights, so that our progress was dependent not just on the color of the next traffic light ahead but also on the colors of the two or three lights beyond that. It was the obverse of gridlock. It seemed like very bad urban planning or traffic-management or whatever exactly the discipline involved here was, and I could feel the corduroy of my suit getting sodden along the entire area of contact with the Gremlin's patterned plastic seat, as well as along the hip and upper thigh that were mashed up against the human sprinkler next to me, who was by now radiating both heat and an acrid, panicky smell that made me turn my head and pretend to be concentrating hard on something in view beyond the window (which rolled down only halfway, due to some design flaw or obscure safety feature). There is no point in describing the gauntlet of franchise retail and shopping centers and auto and tire and motorcycle/Jet Ski outlets and self-serve gas plazas with built-in convenience stores and national fast food brands we crawled through, since it's now the same basic gauntlet around every US city—I believe the economic term is 'monoculture.' Item three. It emerged, finally, that the turnoff from the parkway to the Examination Center was *not* serviced with a traffic light, even though it also became visually obvious, when we got within view, that a good percentage of the cars currently in the single lane ahead of us on SSP were also bound for and hence turning in to the REC and its blacktop access road. (Though it would be a maddeningly long time before even this simple fact was explained to me, the REC's two main eight-hour shifts in that period were 7:10 A.M. to 3:00 P.M. and 3:10 P.M. to 11:00 P.M., which meant that there was a tremendous amount of Service- and employee-owned vehicle traffic between the hours of 2:00 and 4:00.) Meaning that it was actually the Exam Center itself, together with the absence of a traffic

light and the abortive SSP construction,[17] that had
helped cause the hellacious backup, because there

17 GS-9 Chris Fogle would later explain (probably as I and whoever else was
around rotated our hand in the air in the please-get-on-with-it way that almost
everyone started involuntarily rotating their hand to convey whenever
'Irrelevant' Chris was on a roll) that the widening of Self-Storage Parkway had
been stalled for over a year, first because a supplementary bond issue was being
challenged in district court by a conservative Illinois citizens' taxation
watchdog group, and second because the extremely harsh regional winters and
abrupt spring thaws that then so often refroze again a day later (all of which is
true) caused whatever part of the new, freshly built SSP third lane that had not
been treated with a special type of industrial sealant to heave and crack, and
the courts had halted the previous year's construction at just the point when
this sealant was going to be applied with some kind of rare and very expensive
piece of heavy machinery that had to be rented far in advance from a single
specialty-distributor in either Wisconsin or Minnesota (I still have an actual
sense-memory of the way my hand would begin rotating in the air, almost
involuntarily, when Fogle started foundering in extraneous detail — he was
unpopular out of all proportion to his character, which was actually decent
and well-meaning to a fault; he was one of the low-level True Believers on
whom the Service depended so heavily for so much of the inglorious
gruntwork and heavy lifting of day-to-day operations, and what eventually
happened to him was a great injustice, I've always thought, since in his case he
really did need the drugs and took them entirely for professional reasons; it
wasn't recreational by any means), with, of course, the legal injunction and
failure to apply the sealant then causing heavy damage the following winter
and spring, and roughly doubling the cost of the construction over the civil
engineering firm's initial bid. Meaning that it was all a horrific mess of
litigation and engineering mishaps that, as usual, placed a chronic, annoying,
tedious burden on the ordinary commuters of the city. By the way, it emerged
that another reason traffic on the circumambient SSP was so chronically bad
even before the construction nightmare was that, understood not as an

were also a large number of vehicles in the oncoming, northeastbound lanes trying to turn left, i.e. across our single lane, to enter the REC's access road as well, which required that the vehicle at the front of our lane's line for the right turn wait and wave the oncoming car through its left turn, which only a very few did, since traffic jams often bring

---

agglomeration of human beings but as a going economic concern, Peoria had come in the 1980s to assume the same basic doughnut shape as so many other formerly industrial cities: The downtown center was empty and denuded, all but dead, while at the same time a robust collection of malls, plazas, franchises, business and light-industrial parks, town house developments, and apartment complexes had pulled most of the city's life out into an exurban ring. The mid-1990s would see a partial renaissance and gentrification of the riverside downtown—some of the factory and warehouse sites were converted to condos and high-concept restaurants; artists and younger professionals took some others for division into lofts, & c.—though much of this optimistic development was spurred by the establishment of riverboat casinos just off what had been the main industrial set of offload docks, casinos that were not locally owned and whose base revenues Peoria never even got a plausible cut of, the entire downtown rejuvenation spurred by incidental, small-potato tourist spending...viz., on the part of people who came for the casinos, which, since casinos are in the business of separating people from the cash they would otherwise use to shop and dine out, meant that the actual relationship between casino revenues and tourist spending was inverse, which, given casinos' deserved reputation for extreme profitability, meant that any levelheaded person could have predicted the steeply declining revenue curve that within just a few years caused most of the 'New Downtown' renaissance to sputter, especially when the casinos (after prudently waiting a decent interval) all opened their own restaurants and retail shops. And so on...the same basic thing played out in cities all over the Midwest.

out the most aggressive, me-first elements of the human makeup and cause behavior that itself, perversely, exacerbates the traffic jam — this right here perhaps being the place to mention a behavior that we began seeing more and more of as we inched closer to the REC turnoff. Certain private vehicles[18] in our lane veered rightward into the narrow gravel 'breakdown lane,' in which they sped up and were able to pass dozens of other vehicles, illegally, which in and of itself would not have been a big deal except for the fact that as the REC turnoff approached and the breakdown lane began to narrow and disappear they then sought to merge left back into the legal single lane, which required someone in that lane to stop to let them in again, which further clotted traffic in the regular lane... meaning that the selfish, me-first vehicles were significantly worsening the very jam that they'd sought to bypass; they gained an extra couple of minutes by making the jam and delay slightly worse for everyone else in the shimmering line of

18 (identifiable as such in memory because they were not Gremlins, Mercury Montegos, or Ford Econoline vans. It emerged that the REC's Support Service fleet of government vehicles were nearly all derived from a jeopardy-assessment seizure against a conjoint auto dealership in downstate Effingham, an explanation of which would be way too long and digressive to inflict on you here.)

cars in our lane. Within a couple weeks of daily commutes down SSP from the special low-cost Service housing[19] to the REC each day, this selfish, me-first behavior with the breakdown lane began to fill me with such disgust and malice that I can still, to this day, remember some of the vehicles that chronically did it, i.e., the same kind

---

19 Brief, unavoidable aside: For the first six quarters of a contracted posting, examiners without dependents could avail themselves of special Service housing in a set of apartment complexes and converted motels along the eastern edge of SSP's circumambient ring, government-owned through either seizures or tax sales during the recession of the early 1980s. There is, of course, a whole other long and tediously involved story here, including the fact that the housing situation had been vastly complicated by the large number of transfers and personnel reshufflings all RECs had undergone as (a) a result of the mid-Atlantic REC's foundering and dissolution in 1981 and (b) the early phases of the so-called 'Intiative' which it turned out bore directly on the Midwest REC. The point, though, was that this housing was offered both to facilitate ease of transfers and to offer a financial inducement, since the monthly rent at (for instance) the Angler's Cove complex was at least $150 a month less than the going rents for comparable housing in the private sector. My own motives for accepting this housing option should be clear...although it is also true that the IRS in 1986 began treating the difference between the subsidized and free-market rents as 'implied income' and taxing it, which as you can imagine caused no end of ill will among Service employees, who are also of course US citizens and taxpayers, and whose annual tax returns receive special scrutiny every year because of the distinctive '9's at the head of our ID/ SS numbers, & c., & c. In retrospect, the whole Service housing thing was probably not worth it, given all the bureaucratic hassles and idiocies involved (q.v. below), although the monthly savings in rent were substantial.

of idiotic, solipsistic behavior that causes stampedes in public places in the event of a fire and results in the authorities finding huge numbers of blackened, trampled bodies at the front doors of places after the fires or riots have been quelled, people prevented from getting out precisely by the panic and selfishness with which they all rushed and clotted the exit and got in each other's way, causing everyone to die horribly, which I have to admit is what I began wishing for the various Vegas, Chevettes, and a particular light-blue AMC Pacer with one of those fish-shaped Christian decals on the bubble of a back window[20] that made this maneuver almost every morning.

An additional bit of bureaucratic idiocy: As

---

20 We observed that it was almost always the private cars and pickups that clotted things by selfishly trying to shortcut through the breakdown lane and then merging back in. Service vehicles, including the Support Services vans that ran back and forth between the wiggler housing at north Peoria's Angler's Cove and the Oaks, never deviated from the legal lane, the Service drivers being non-contract hourly workers who had no incentive to hurry or try to cut corners, which presented a different set of problems for us who were required to be at our Tingle tables by a certain very definite time at the start of the shift; but from the point of view of orderly traffic it was still probably a good administrative move on Support Services' part, although it meant that the Support Services drivers, whose jobs were chiropractically sadistic as well as boring and repetitive beyond belief, couldn't join the Treasury union, didn't qualify for health insurance, & c.

mentioned, plastic signs within the car interdicted smoking, eating, & c., as turned out to be the case in all Service vehicles used for employee transport, by internal regs cited in the lower-right portion of the signs themselves[21]—except that AMC Gremlins' interiors were so cramped, and the plastic used therein so cheap and thin, that there was nowhere to mount the eight-inch signs except on the dashboard's top, where they blocked sections of the lower windshield and forced our driver to assume a contorted position with his tonsured head almost over on his right shoulder in order to see the road just ahead between the edges of the mandatory signs. This, so far as I could see, was beyond the pale in terms of both safety and anything like sense.

Set within a large expanse of very green close-clipped grass bordered on both sides by cornfields'

21 These cited regulations, when the Internal Revenue Manual's whole code of regulations was perused in a period of examination downtime with literally nothing else to do to occupy one's time, exposed a strange kind of error: The cars' and vans' interior signs' citations actually referred to the regulation that required the signs to be 'displayed in a prominent, unobscured location' within each vehicle; it was really a regulation two regs above that cited reg that interdicted eating, tobacco, & c. within Service-owned transport. That is, the signs' cited reg referred to the sign itself, not to the regulation the sign was supposed to signify.

windbreaks of trees and tangled shrubbery, the Midwest Regional Examination Center lay a good five hundred yards back from the parkway, these five hundred yards filled with nothing except verdant and weirdly dandelionless grass mowed to the consistency of baize. The contrast between the baronial splendor of the lawn and the squat, institutional ugliness of the REC itself was stark and incongruous, and there was plenty of time to ponder it as the Gremlin crawled along and the guy next to me dripped steadily onto both of us. The older man at the other end of the backseat had what looked at first to be a green thimble on one finger, which turned out to be the green traction-rubber that most wigglers wore and all called PCs for 'pinkie cheaters.' A large 4-H billboard some distance past the REC's one-way entrance read IT'S SPRING, THINK FARM SAFETY, which I knew to be a 4-H sign because every March–May there was an identical one just out past the instant-coffee factory on SR 130 west of Philo.[22] The state 4-H

22 At 158 employees, the vacuum-sublimation-and-caffeine-supplementation works for Bright Eyes Instant Coffee represented Philo's last remaining claim to industry. A subsidiary of Rayburn-Thrapp Agronomics, Bright Eyes was a regional high-caf brand, recognizable in Midwest stores by the jar's crude graphic of an electrified-looking squirrel with bulging blazing suns for eyes and what looked like tiny bolts of cartoon lightning shooting out from its

held bake sales and car washes all year to provide for these billboards (w/ comma splice *sic*), which by 1985 were so ubiquitous that no one paid any attention to them.[23]

I also remember that I had to move and twist my own neck awkwardly in order to make out the Exam Center's various features through the impediments of the car's required signs. From this distance and set of perspectives, the REC appeared at first to be a single huge right-angled structure, with its facing[24] tan or beige cement side mammoth and sheer, and just a bit of foreshortened

---

splayed extremities. When Archer Daniels Midland Co. absorbed Rayburn-Thrapp Agronomics in 1991, Bright Eyes was (mercifully*) discontinued. More than this I am legally enjoined from telling you by the refusal of certain members of my family to sign the appropriate legal releases. Suffice it to say that I know a lot more about the chemistry, manufacture, and ambient odors of instant coffee than anyone would voluntarily want to, and that the smells were not at all the cozy comforting breakfastish aromas that one might naively imagine (they were closer to burning hair, actually, when the wind was right).

* As early as the 1970s, there had been evidence linking artificially enhanced caffeine to everything from arrhythmias to Bell's palsy, though the first class-action suit was not filed until 1989.

23 A further irony: During an April 1987 tornado outside De Kalb, a detached portion of one of these FARM SAFETY billboards whirled in and for all practical purposes decapitated a soybean farmer—that was pretty much it for the 4-H sign.

24 (i.e., facing south and SSP, on which we were moving west at literally the rate of a toddler's crawl)

side-building's roof visible past the access road, which road extended in a broad one-way curve around the main building's rear, which rear itself turned out to actually be the REC's front, with its enormous self-regarding facade. In a similar distortion, what looked, from a distance, like a bona fide circumambient 'road' from the parkway in to and around the REC turned out to be more like a crude rural mew or driveway, narrow and high, banked with deep runoff ditches, and with freakish speed bumps set at such close intervals that travel over about five mph on the access road was impossible; one could see the occupants of any vehicle traveling faster than that being thrown about their cars' interior like rag dolls by the impact with the speed bumps, which were each over eight inches high. Beginning a couple hundred yards in from SSP, parking lots of various modest sizes extended outward from the access road, rather like square-cut jewels encrusting a bracelet or tiara.[25]

There was, from our vantage, no visible sign

25 Again, much of this is from the actual notebook in which these impressions were recorded. I'm aware that I'm describing the access road from a distance but attributing to it qualities that became evident only as we got very slowly closer and closer and then were actually on it. Part of this is artful compression; part is that it's next to impossible to take coherent notes in a moving auto.

identifying the site as an IRS or even government facility (which, again, was semi-explained by the fact that what appeared from Self-Storage to be the REC's front was in fact the rear, and of only one of the two distinct buildings). All there were were two small wooden directional signs — ENTRANCE ONLY; EXIT ONLY — at the semicircular access road's two junctions with SSP. The former sign also included what turned out to be the REC's street (though not postal) address. Given the access road's circular shape, the exit was some thousand or more yards farther west down the parkway, almost within the shadow of the FARM SAFETY billboard. I could hear the man up next to me breathing rapidly, as if almost beginning to hyperventilate; neither of us had even once looked directly at the other. I noticed that only the ENTRANCE side of the access road had parking lots appended; the distant EXIT side, which curved out from behind the rear (i.e., it later emerged, the two separate buildings' fronts) of the REC was a one-way vector back out to Self-Storage Parkway, with the exit's intersection also minus any kind of traffic light or directional signal, which absence caused further snarls and delays for commuters trying to reach the REC's entrance from the west.

As I may or may not have mentioned, it was

already well past the mandated 1340h. reporting time stamped on my 141-PO. Certain obvious and understandable emotions attended this fact, especially since (a) 0.0 percent of this lateness was my fault, and (b) the closer we got to the REC, the slower our progress in traffic became. In order to distract myself from these facts and emotions, I began to compile a list of the logistical absurdities that became evident once the Service vehicle got close enough to the entrance for the REC's access road to become visible through my unoccluded side window. The following are condensed from an unusually long, intense, unpunctuated notebook entry[26] composed at least in part within the Gremlin itself. To wit:

Besides the oncoming left turns and the loathsome me-firsters trying to remerge from the breakdown lane, the main cause of the excruciating slowness with which our line of cars on the westbound Self-Storage south of the city inched forward to make the right turn into the Examination Center's access road was what emerged as the even worse, more costive and paralyzed jam of vehicles on the access road itself. This was chiefly caused by

26 (inscribed with a pencil that had long since gone blunt and dull, which is something I detest; there would have had to be considerable psychic pressure/incentive for me to be willing to write with a dull pencil)

the fact that the access road's appended parking lots were already quite full, and that the farther along the access road the lots were, the fuller they were, and full also of IRS employee vehicles trolling for available parking places. Given the extreme heat and humidity, the most desirable parking lots were clearly the ones directly behind[27] the main building, less than a hundred yards from the central REC entrance. Employees in the more peripheral lots were required to walk along the narrow, ditch-flanked access road all the way around behind[28] to that central entrance, which resulted in a great deal of teetering along the access road's unpaved edge, plus some staggering and windmilling of arms; and we saw at least one employee slip and cartwheel into the drainage ditch by the road's side and have to be pulled manually back up by two or three others, all of whom held their hats to their heads with one hand, such that the rescued employee then had an enormous smeary grass stain all the way up one side of his slacks and sport coat, and dragged one seemingly injured leg behind him

27 Again, the 'behind' is from the perspective of the parkway. Given that what we were approaching was the main building's rear, the premium lots were actually 'in front' of the REC, though that front faced away from Self-Storage.
28 Ibid.

as he and his companions passed from view along the road's curve.[29] The whole problem was as obvious as it was stupid. Given the heat, hassle, and actual danger of pedestrian travel along the access road, it was totally understandable that most employee vehicles seemed to eschew the nearer (that is, nearer to us, hence farther from the REC itself) lots and to proceed to the far more desirable lots around back, lots that turned out to be closest to the main REC entrance and to be separated from it only by a wide, paved, and easily traversed plaza. But if those best, closest lots were full (as of course, given human nature and the above incentives, they were likely to be; the most desirable lots will obviously also be the most crowded lots), the incoming vehicles could not backtrack out the way they came in order to settle for spots in the progressively more distant and less desirable lots they had passed on their way in quest of the best lots—for,

29 Let's mainly skip the issue of the additional crowding and dysfunction caused by outer lots' pedestrians trying to negotiate the access road's narrow edge past the solid line of cars that filled that road, much of which problem could have been solved simply by installing a sidewalk across the immaculate lawn and some kind of entrance in the front (i.e., what appeared to be the front; it was actually the building's rear). In essence, the baronial splendor of the REC's grass was a testament to the idiocy and hassle of the whole thing's planning.

of course, the access road was one-way[30] all the way around its curve, so vehicles that couldn't find a spot in the best lots had now to proceed forward all the way back out away from the REC to the EXIT ONLY sign, turn left without any kind of light onto Self-Storage, drive the several hundred yards east back to the REC entrance with its ENTRANCE ONLY sign, and then try to turn left (against oncoming traffic, which obviously further slowed our own, westbound lane's tortured progress) into the access road again in order to park in some of the less desirable lots out nearer the parkway, from which they then had to join the line of pedestrians tightrope-walking along the road's edge back toward the main entrance around back.

In short, it all seemed like just phenomenally bad planning, resulting in gross inefficiency, waste, and frustration for everyone involved.[31]

---

30 It had to be: It wasn't nearly wide enough to sustain two-way traffic, not to mention the additional space taken up by pedestrians trying to walk to/from their vehicles along the road's edge.

31 What I did not at that time know was that, as the result of certain complex Compliance Branch reorganizations related to the implementation of the 'Initiative,' the Midwest REC had had a net gain of more than three hundred new employees over the previous two fiscal quarters. One theory among the rote examiners at Angler's Cove was that this had helped tip some delicate balance in the REC's parking situation, exacerbated by the construction on Self-Storage and the elimination, for what were represented as morale reasons,

Three obvious remedies presented themselves, which were sketched in outline form in my notebook, although whether I jotted them down right there *in situ* during the maddening Sisyphean so-near-and-yet-far stasis or entered them later that day—during which there were plenty of additional stretches of downtime with nothing to do except read the vapid book I'd already begun mordantly annotating on the bus ride—I will not pretend to recall. One remedy would be to institute some form of reserved parking, which would eliminate a good deal of the backup and clot resulting from people trolling for available spaces in the lots, as well as the 'incentive' problem of employee vehicles all beelining for the most desirable two or three lots near the REC's central entrance (which of course we hadn't yet seen from Self-Storage Parkway; the entrance's location was deduced from the apparent desirability of the parking lots behind [from our perspective] the building, given the number of cars heading for it, which was

---

of reserved parking for those with civil service grades above GS-11. The latter had been the idea of Mr. Tate, the REC's Director of Personnel, who'd regarded reserved parking as elitist and corrosive to REC morale. The syndrome of DP Richard Tate's instituting a policy that resulted in far more problems than it resolved was so familiar that wigglers referred to it as 'dicktation.'

clearly linked to some form of tangible incentive. The employee beside me now looked, peripherally, as though he'd been mechanically raised out of a body of water, which made the pretense of my not noticing the incredible sweating even more creepy and farcical). Another anodyne would obviously be to widen the access road and make it two-way. Admittedly, this could expose the REC to some additional short-term inconvenience and snarl along the same general lines as the widening of Self-Storage Parkway, although it was difficult to envision the widening of the access road taking anywhere near as long, since it wouldn't be subject to the delays and conflicting agendas of the democratic process. The third remedy would be to sacrifice, for the greater good and convenience of everyone except perhaps the REC's landscaping contractor, the virid expanse of the empty front (i.e., what turned out to be the rear) lawn, and to place on it not only a paved walkway but maybe an actual transverse spur that would allow vehicles on the EXIT portion of the road to cross back over to the ENTRANCE portion without having to make lightless left turns both onto and off the jammed parkway. Not to mention of course simply placing some goddamn traffic lights at the two intersections, which it was next to impossible to imagine the Internal Revenue Service not having enough suction with the municipal and state authorities to be able to demand just about any time it pleased.[32] Not to mention the sheer strangeness of having it be (it emerged) the REC's mammoth *rear* facing Peoria's main orbital road. It seemed, on slow approach, both craven and arrogant, like pre-modern priests who faced away from the communicants during Catholic mass. Everything from logistics to elementary civics would seem to dictate that a major government facility's front should face the public it serves. (Recall that I had not yet seen the REC's stylized front facade, which was identical to those of the nation's other six RECs, and had been installed after an uncaught typo in the enlarged construction and technology budget after the King Commission IRS reforms had been permitted to pass into law, that typo mandating that Regional Service and Examination Centers' facades' 'form specifications' rather

32 At the time, I knew nothing of the bureaucratic hostilities between the IRS and the state of Illinois, these dating all the way back to the state's brief introduction of a progressive sales tax, which top officials at Triple-Six under the Carter administration had joined others in the editorial pages of major financial dailies in ridiculing and in abusing the 'brain trust' behind the state's revenue scheme, causing bad blood which continued, in the form of many small types of petty hassles and inaccommodation, through the 1980s.

than 'form*al* specifications' be '…matched as closely as possible to the specific services the centers perform.'[33])

As to our actual physical arrival at the center's main entrance on that first day, all I can say by way of summary is that there is an indescribable thrill about seeing one's own printed name on a sign held up at a crowded place of disembarkation. I suppose part of it is that one feels especially picked out and — to use the bureaucratic term — validated. The special sign with my name on it held aloft by an attractive, official-looking woman in a bright-blue blazer was also, obviously, after all the ignominies and demeaning hassles, and consequent lateness, surprising, though not so surprising that any person could be reasonably expected to have seen it as immediate evidence of some error or confusion — there was, after all, the aforementioned matter of nepotistic juice and the letter in my dispatch case.

This was also when it emerged that the REC's ostensible rear was really the front, and that the two orthogonal parts of the center were not continuous, and that the main building's facade was stylized in a strange and kind of intimidating way

33 Factoid courtesy of GS-9 Robert Atkins (knows all, tells all).

that one would concede it was maybe prudent to keep from facing, or looming over, the crowded public road just south. Even without the crowding and chaos, the whole huge main-entrance area was complex and disorienting. There were flags, coded signs, directional arrows, and a kind of broad concrete plaza with what looked to have been a fountain but had no water spurting.[34] The main building's square shadow extended almost all the way across the plaza to the two highly desirable parking lots opposite, neither of which was all that large. And there was the REC's elaborate and obviously expensive facade, which extended from just above the main entrance to the middle of what appeared to be the fifth floor; it was some kind of tile or mosaic representation of a blank IRS 1978 Form 1040, both pages of it, complete in all detail down to verso Line 31's slot for the computation of **'Adjusted Gross Income'** and recto Line 66's terminal **'BALANCE DUE'** box, which box served, along with the form's myriad other slots and boxes and inset squares, as what looked to be windows. The detail was striking and the cream, salmon, and celadon of the offset colors realistic, if slightly

---

34 (It turned out that the fountain was broken and an obscure hydraulic part was on order.)

dated.[35] Also, to make the whole thing even more overwhelming/disorienting when seen all at once from the circular spur off the access road whence Service vehicles could pull right up and offload their passengers without having to park (which would have necessitated going all the way back out and around again, since the parking lots just opposite the entrance, across the plaza, were completely full and even had some extra vehicles parked in prohibited corner spaces that would keep other vehicles from being able to back out of their spaces and exit), the giant 1040, which was realistically proportioned to scale and so was slightly longer than it was wide, was flanked at either distant end by a large, round inset intaglio or glyph of some kind of chimerical combat and a Latin phrase, indecipherable in the right-hand side's deep shadow, which turned out to be the Service's official seal and motto (none of which I had been told in my contractual materials [which, as mentioned, tended to be both cryptic and tonally stern or urgent, really little more than engines of apprehension as far as I'd been concerned, sitting in my

35 There had been certain changes and modifications in the 1040 since 1978, the details of which I would come to know all too well over the coming months.

family's unused parlor and trying to parse them]). By way of one more detail, the whole elaborate facade assembly was reflected—though in an angled and laterally foreshortened way that made the edge's glyph and motto look closer together than they actually were—by the garishly mirrored exterior side of the REC's other structure, a.k.a. the 'REC Annex,' which lay at almost a perfect right angle to the main facade and was connected at two floors to the main building's west edge by what then appeared to be large green tubes supported by blinding (since not in the main building's shadow) forests of slender anodized or stainless steel poles, which metal supports looked strange and millipedic from this angle and were further reflected in blinding little angled slices by the edges of the Annex's mirrored exterior.

One or two of the mirrored panels were broken or cracked, however, I remember noting.[36]

(Also, please keep in mind that I knew none of the REC structures' actual history or logistics on that initial day; I'm trying to stay faithful to the memory

---

36 N.B. that a detailed illustrative photo of the REC's mirrored Annex's west side's junction with the main building's facade circa 1985, which I made a point of including as Plate 1 in the original memoir, has been here deleted by the publisher for 'legal' reasons that (I opine) make no sense whatsoever. *Hiatus valde deflendus.*

of that experience itself, although there is no avoiding a successive description of various elements that were, at the time, obviously simultaneous—certain distortions are just part and parcel of linear English.)

Re the human element: The broad cement area around the main entrance, as first seen by us from over the mass of other brown and orange/yellow Service vehicles disgorging passengers, was an enormous teeming roil of Service employees all milling around, holding 141-POs in their distinctive dark-yellow Service envelopes, with luggage and briefcases and accordion files, many of them hatted, and various REC or perhaps Regional HQ support personnel in gas-blue blazers with clipboards and sheaves of printout paper that they had rolled into ad hoc megaphones that they spoke through while they held their clipboards up in the air to get people's attention, evidently trying to collect those arrivals with similar 141-PO job designations and/ or GS-grades into cohesive groups for 'targeted check-in' at various 'Intake Stations' set up around the REC's main lobby, which lobby, as seen through the entrance's glass doors, was surprisingly small and cheesy-looking, and had various battered-looking folding tables set up with crude signs made of tented manila folders—the whole thing looked haphazardly jerry-rigged and chaotic, and one figured that there couldn't possibly be this many newly arrived and/or reassigned transfers to the REC as a typical daily thing, or else the disembarkation and check-in system would be much more permanent-looking and streamlined and less like some small-scale reenactment of the fall of Saigon. Again, though, all this was being perceived and processed in nothing more than a distracted flash—which occurred as the Gremlin finally broke out of the access road's snarl and pulled up in the almost chilly air of the building's shade to double-park in the semicircular spur just outside the entrance[37]— because, as mentioned, a person's attention is more or less automatically drawn to a sign with one's name on it, especially if it seems to be one of only two named signs being held up in the whole madding bureaucratic roil outside the main entrance, and so I had almost immediately seen the ethnic-looking woman in the loud blazer standing a few paces to the right of the rightmost group of new arrivals clumped around a man with a raised clip-

---

37 Which we had to do because several other vehicles had double- and even triple-parked just ahead, and it was impossible to go any farther, and the driver simply put the car in park and sat rotating his neck stiffly, with both hands still on the steering wheel, as the more experienced Service employees began piling out.

board and paper horn,[38] the female slightly off to the side and maybe ten feet directly beneath the facade's slot for reporting AGI on line 31, against the wall, holding either a piece of white cardboard or a small erasable whiteboard with the name DAVID WALLACE in neat block capitals. She was standing in a way that managed to connote weariness and boredom without any actual slumping, her legs well out and back supported by the wall, from bottom to crown, and staring straight ahead, holding the sign at chest level and staring into space with neither interest nor resignation. Of course I was now, as mentioned, through no fault of my own, terribly late, the anxiety of which mixed with the inevitable thrill of seeing one's name on a sign, not to mention a sign held by an exotic-looking female, plus a whole separate set of Ozymandian awe-and-folly reactions to the conjunction of the monumental 1040 mosaic combined with the self-appending chaos of the entrance area's crowds, to form a sort of sensory and emotional power-surge that I remember now much

38 Some of the entrance area's milling crowd's men were in shirtsleeves, and a swirling wind caused by the contrast in temperatures in and out of the building's shadow blew some of their neckties either back over their shoulders or (for a second or two) out straight from their chests in an arrowy way, as if they were impaled on their own neckties, which is what accounts for the strange memorability of this fragment as we pulled up.

more vividly than any of the myriad details and impressions (of which there were thousands or even millions, all obviously incoming at the same moment) of arrival. For she was visibly ethnic, even as seen in the deep pool of shade at the facade's base with various bits of blinding glare from the Annex's mirrored exterior, parts of which were catching bits of sun as it moved slightly west of due south. My initial guess was upper-caste Indian or Pakistani— one of my freshman roommates at college had been a wealthy Pakistani, with a marvelously burbly sing-song accent, though he'd revealed himself over the year to be an unbelievable narcissist and general prick.[39] She was, at the distance from which the Gremlin disgorged us, more striking than pretty, or maybe you might say that she was pretty in a some-what mannish, hard-faced way, with very dark hair and wide-set eyes in which was, as mentioned, the look of someone who was 'on duty' in the sort of way that involves having really nothing to do but stand there. It was the same expression one sees on security guards, college research-librarians on a Fri-day night, parking-lot attendants, grain silo opera-

---

39 The Personnel representative, Ms. Neti-Neti, turned out to be what she called Persian. It was she whom 2K Bob McKenzie and some of the others in Hindle's Rotes group had christened 'the Iranian Crisis.'

tors, & c.—she stood there gazing into the middle distance as though at the end of a pier.

It was only outside the cramped Gremlin, when the cool air of the facade-shadowed front area first hit and chilled it, that I became aware that the whole left side of my suit was now wet from the ambient perspiration of the young man I'd been mashed up next to through the whole ride, though when I looked around for him in order to make a gesture at the darkened corduroy and give him an appropriate look of distaste, he was now nowhere to be seen.

Ms. F. Chahla Neti-Neti (according to her ID badge)'s expression changed, actually several different times, as I approached her with bags and a degree of direct eye contact that would have been inappropriate if she hadn't been holding a sign with my name on it. Here, if I haven't already done so, I should explain that in this period of what was basically late adolescence I had very bad skin— very, very bad, as in the dermatological category 'severe/disfiguring.'[40] On meeting or encountering me for the first time, most people either (a) looked only briefly at my face and then looked away, or

---

40 It had been the Pakistani roommate, in fact, who as early as Freshman Orientation Week had christened me with the unkind name that followed me throughout the next three semesters, 'the young man carbuncular.'

(b) looked involuntarily stricken or pitying, or repelled, then could be seen struggling with themselves to superimpose on that expression another one that signified they either didn't see the bad skin or weren't especially bothered by it. The whole skin thing is a long story and for the most part not worth mentioning, except to emphasize again that by that time I was more or less reconciled to the skin thing and it didn't much bother me anymore, although it did make it difficult to shave with any precision, and I did tend to be very aware of whether I was standing in direct light and, if so, from just what angle that light originated— because in certain kinds of light the problem was very, very bad indeed, I knew. On this first encounter, I don't remember whether Ms. Neti-Neti was an (a) or a (b),[41] perhaps because my attention/

41 There is actually a third general class of reactive person, whose eyes would linger on my face in a kind of nakedly horrified fascination. These were usually people with a personal history of various kinds of moderate skin problems and a consequent interest in worst-case-type examples of bad skin that overrides (i.e., the interest does) their natural tact or inhibition. I had actually had strangers come up to me and start expounding on their own past or present skin problems, assuming that I couldn't fail to care or be interested, which I will admit I found irksome. Children, by the way, are not members of this (c) category—their interested stare is very different, and in general they (= children) are exempt from the whole taxonomy of reactors, since their social instincts and inhibitions are not yet fully evolved and it's impossible to take

memory was occupied by the way the Service ID badge clipped to her Personnel jacket's breast pocket had a head-shot photo that looked taken in very bright, almost magnesium-looking light, and I remember instantly calculating what this sort of photo's hideous light was going to do in terms of my face's blebular cysts and scabs, just as it had made this creamily dark Persian woman's complexion look dark gray, and had exaggerated the wide-setness of her eyes so that in the ID photo she looked almost like a puma or some other strange kind of feline predator, along with the badge's displaying her first initial and surname, GS grade, Personnel affiliation, and a series of nine digits that I would only later understand to be her internally generated SS, which also functions as one's Service ID number.

The reason for even taking the time to mention the (a) or (b) reaction thing is that it is the only way to make sense of the fact that Ms. Neti-Neti's greeting was so verbally effusive and deferential—'Your reputation precedes you'; 'On behalf of Mr. Glendenning and Mr. Tate, we're just so extremely pleased to have you on board'; 'We're extremely

---

their reactions or lack of tact personally—see e.g. the kid on the bus, although obviously he also had a repellent problem of his own.

pleased you were willing to take this posting'—
without her face and eyes registering any such enthusiasm or even displaying any affect or interest in me
or in why I was so late in arriving and had forced her
to stand there holding up a sign for God only knew
how long, which I personally would very much have
wanted some kind of explanation of. Not to mention that the whole left side of my suit was wet,
which I would have at least commented on in some
concerned way, e.g. had the person fallen into a puddle or what. In short, not only was it surprising to be
greeted in person with such enthusiastic words, but
it was doubly surprising when the person reciting
these words displayed the same kind of disengage-
ment as, say, the checkout clerk who utters the words
'Have a nice day' while her expression indicates that
it's really a matter of total indifference to her whether
you drop dead in the parking lot outside ten seconds
from now. And this whole doubly disorienting
affectless monologue occurred as the woman led me
away beneath the **'Paid Preparer's Information'**
slots at the base of the great 1040's recto side toward
a smaller, much less ostentatious set of doors some
hundred yards west along the REC's tile facade.[42] At

42 Nor did she offer to help me with any of my bags, despite the fact that the
one I held with the same arm with which I had to sort of clamp my dispatch

this close range, it was possible to see that some of the facade's tiles were chipped and/or stained. We could also see various distorted parts of our reflections in the facade of the Annex building directly ahead (i.e., east), though it was several hundred yards distant and the partial reflections were very tiny and indistinct.

Ms. Neti-Neti chattered along almost the whole length of the facade. It goes without saying that it was hard to comprehend all this personal attention and (verbal) deference being directed at a GS-9 who was probably going to get assigned to opening envelopes or carrying stacks of obscure files from one place to another or something. My initial theory was that the unnamed relative who'd helped get me in the door here as a way to defer the mechanisms of Guaranteed Student Loan collection had a lot more administrative juice than I'd originally thought. Although, of course, as I tried to clunk my way along behind the ethnic lady in the shadow of the building's rear/front, that business about my 'reputation preced[ing]' me was worrisome, given

---

case against my side clunked painfully against the same knee it had been clunking against all day whenever I had to carry my bags from one spot to another, while my left side's wet clothes caused the spot on my ribs to start itching like mad again.

some of the irrational anxieties I've already given more attention than they deserved just above.

Now it's becoming clear that I could spend an enormous amount of both our time just on describing this initial arrival and the compounding stack of confusions, miscommunications, and overall fuck-ups (at least one of which was mine—viz., leaving one of my suitcases in the outer waiting area of the REC's Personnel office, which I didn't even realize I'd done until I was on the shuttle back from the REC to the Angler's Cove apartment complex where my assigned IRS housing was located[43]) that attended that first day of posting, some of which took weeks to iron out. But only a few of these are relevant overall. One of the quirks of real human memory is that the most vivid, detailed recall doesn't usually concern the

43 Given the large number of both new employees and transfers who arrived with luggage that day (for reasons I wouldn't understand for some time), though, it's only fair to observe that the REC Personnel office might have done well to have set up some system whereby people got taken to housing first, dropped off their bags, and were only then conducted to the REC for intake and orientation. However difficult the logistics of that scheme might have been, the alternative was an enormous number of IRS employees having to carry their bags with them everywhere they went on that first day at the REC, including in cramped elevators and stairways, as well as piles of unattended bags in the corner of whatever rooms the various orientations and ID productions were going on in.

things that are most germane. The as it were forest. It's not just that real memory is fragmentary; I think it's also that overall relevance and meaning are conceptual, while the experiential bits that get locked down and are easiest, years later, to retrieve tend to be sensory. We live inside bodies, after all. Random examples of recalled snippets: Long and windowless interior halls, the burning in my forearms just before I had to set down the bags for a moment. The particular sound and cadence of Ms. Neti-Neti's heels on the hallways' flooring, which was of light-brown linoleum whose wax smelled strong in the unmoving air and reflected an endless series of shining parenthetical arcs where a custodian had swung his autowaxer from side to side in the empty hall at night. The place was a labyrinth of hallways, staircases, and fire doors with coded signs. Many of the halls seemed curved as opposed to straight, which I remember thinking was an illusion of perspective; the REC's exterior had nothing rounded or podular about it. In sum, the place was too overwhelmingly complex and repetitive to describe one's first experience of in any detail. Not to mention confusing: For instance, I know that our initial destination on arrival was one level below the main entrance and lobby. I know this in retrospect, because it's where the REC's Personnel office was, which I know was where Ms. Neti-Neti had been instructed to route me around the lobby check-ins and bring me directly... but I also have what feels like a clear sensuous memory of *climbing* at least one short set of stairs at some point, since it was climbing stairs with the luggage that caused the severest clunking of that one suitcase against the outside of my knee, which I could almost visualize the swelling and flamboyant bruising of. On the other hand, I don't suppose it's impossible that I'm confusing the order in which various parts of the REC were traversed.

I do know that at one point Ms. Neti-Neti herself apparently got confused or distracted, and opened the wrong door, and in the wedge of light before she could push the heavy door closed again I caught a glimpse of a long room filled with IRS examiners in long rows and columns of strange-looking tables or desks, each of which (desks) had a raised array of trays or baskets clamped to its top,[44] with flexible-necked desk lamps in turn clamped at angles to these fanned-out arrays, so that each of

---

44 These were Tingle tables, an Examinations convention with which I became all too familiar—although no one I ever talked to knew the origin of 'Tingle,' as in whether it was eponymous, or sardonic, or what.

the IRS examiners worked in a small tight circle of light at what appeared to be the bottom of a one-sided hole. Row after row, stretching to a kind of vanishing point near the room's rear wall, in which there was incised another door. This, although I didn't know it at the time, was my first glimpse of an Immersives Room, of which the main REC structure contained a handful. The most striking thing about it was the quiet. There were at least 150 men and/or women in that room, all intently occupied and busy, and yet the room was so silent that you could hear an imperfection in the door's hinge as Ms. Neti-Neti pushed it closed against the force of its pneumatic strut. This silence I remember best of all, because it was both sensuous and incongruous: For obvious reasons, we tend to associate total quiet with emptiness, not with large groups of people. The whole thing lasted only a moment, though, after which we continued on our complex way, with Ms. Neti-Neti occasionally greeting or nodding at other Personnel officers in distinctive bright-blue jackets conducting small groups the other way—which in hindsight should have been additionally confusing, though I have no memory of feeling one way or another about it; I was still as it were reverberating from the sight of all those intent, totally silent examiners.

Here is probably an apt place for some exposition on my background re: silence and concentrated deskwork. In hindsight, I know that there was something about the silent, motionless intensity with which everyone in that opened door's instant was studying the tax-related documents before them that frightened and thrilled me. The scene was such that you just knew that if you were to open the door for another brief instant ten, twenty, or forty minutes later, it would look and sound just the same. I had never seen anything like it. Or rather I had, in a way, for of course television and books often portray concentrated study or deskwork just this way, at least by implication. As in e.g. 'Irving knuckled down and spent the entire morning plowing through the paperwork on his desk'; 'Only when she had finished the report did the executive glance at her watch and see that it was nearly midnight. She had been completely absorbed in her task, and was only now aware that she had worked through supper, and was famished. Gracious, wherever did all the time go? she thought to herself.' Or even just as in 'He spent the day reading.' In real life, of course, concentrated deskwork doesn't go this way. I had spent massive amounts of time in libraries; I knew quite well how deskwork really was. Especially if the task at hand was dry or repetitive, or dense, or if it involved reading something that had no direct relevance to your own life and priorities, or was work that you were doing only because you had to—like for a grade, or part of a freelance assignment for pay from some lout who was off skiing. The way hard deskwork really goes is in jagged little fits and starts, brief intervals of concentration alternated with frequent trips to the men's room, the drinking fountain, the vending machine, constant visits to the pencil sharpener, phone calls you suddenly feel are imperative to make, rapt intervals of seeing what kinds of shapes you can bend a paperclip into, & c.[45] This is because sitting still and concentrating on just one task for an extended length of time is, as a practical matter, impossible. If you said, 'I spent the whole night in the library, working on some client's sociology paper,' you really meant that you'd spent between two and three hours working on it and the rest of the time fidgeting and sharpening and organizing

45 For me, the pencil sharpener is a big one. I like a very particular sort of very sharp pencil, and some pencil sharpeners are a great deal better than others for achieving this special shape, which then is blunted and ruined after only a sentence or two, requiring a large number of sharpened pencils all lined up in a special order of age, remaining height, & c. The upshot is that nearly everyone I knew had distracting little rituals like this, of which rituals the whole point, deep down, was that they were distracting.

pencils and doing skin-checks in the men's room mirror and wandering around the stacks opening volumes at random and reading about, say, Durkheim's theories of suicide.

There was none of this diffraction in that split-second view of the room, though. One sensed that these were people who did not fidget, who did not read a page of, say, dull taxpayer explanation about the deduction of some item and then realize that they'd actually been thinking about the apple in their lunchbag and whether or not to maybe eat the apple right here and now until they realized that their eyes had passed over all the words (or, given the venue here, perhaps columns of figures) on the page without actually having read them at all—with *read* here meaning internalized, comprehended, or whatever we mean by really reading vs. simply having one's eyes pass over symbols in a certain order. Seeing this was kind of traumatic. I'd always felt frustrated and embarrassed about how much reading and writing time I actually wasted, about how much I sort of blinked in and out while trying to absorb or convey large amounts of information. To put it bluntly, I had felt ashamed about how easily I got bored when trying to concentrate. As a child, I think I'd understood the word *concentrate* literally and viewed my prob-

lems with sustained concentration as evidence that
I was an unusually dilute or disorganized form of
human being,[46] and had laid much of the blame
for this on my family, who tended to need a lot of
loud noise and distraction going on at all times
and undertook almost every kind of activity with
every available radio, stereo, and television set on,
such that I'd taken to wearing special high-filter
customized earplugs at home from the age of fourteen on. It took me all the way up to the age of
finally getting away from Philo and entering a
highly selective college to understand that the
problem with stillness and concentration was more
or less universal and not some unique shortcom-
ing that was going to prevent me from ever really
rising above my preterite background and achieving something. Seeing the enormous lengths that
those elite, well-educated undergrads from all over
the nation went to to avoid, delay, or mitigate concentrated work was an eye-opening experience for
me. In fact, the school's social structure was set up

---

46 This sense of personal disorganization, which of course is very common,
was for me heightened by the fact that I had very little trouble analyzing other
people's basic character and motivations, strengths and weaknesses, & c., while
all attempts at self-analysis resulted in a tangle of contradictory and hopelessly
complex facts and tendencies, impossible to sort out or draw general
conclusions from.

to prize and esteem students who could pass their classes and assemble a good transcript without ever working hard. People who skated by, doing the absolute minimum required for institutional/ parental approval, were regarded as cool, while people who actually applied themselves to their assignments and to the work of their own education and achievement were relegated to the status of 'grinds' or 'tools,' the lowest caste in the college's merciless social hierarchy.[47]

47 I am reminded of an observation made during one of the wigglers' evening bull sessions in the room of Chris Acquistipace, who was a Chalk Leader and one of the only REC wigglers housed on the second floor of the Angler's Cove complex to display any friendliness or even an open mind toward me, despite the administrative foul-up that at first had me promoted even above the floor's other GS-9s. It was either Acquistipace or Ed Shackleford, whose ex-wife had taught high school, who observed that what was then starting to be codified as 'test anxiety' may well really have been an anxiety about *timed* tests, meaning exams or standardized tests, where there is no way to do the endless fidgeting and self-distraction that is part of 99.9 percent of real people's concentrated deskwork. I cannot honestly say that I remember whose observation it was; it was part of a larger discussion about younger examiners and television and the theory that America had some vested economic interest in keeping people over-stimulated and unused to silence and single-point concentration. For the sake of convenience, let's assume it was Shackleford. Shackleford's observation was that the real object of the crippling anxiety in 'test anxiety' might well be a fear of the tests' associated stillness, quiet, and lack of time for distraction. Without distraction, or even the possibility of distraction, certain types of people feel dread—and it's this dread, not so much the test itself, that people feel anxious about.

The upshot, though, was that up until entering college, where everyone often lived and did homework together in plain mutual view, I'd had no opportunity to realize that fidgeting, distraction, and frequent contrived breaks were more or less universal traits. In high school, for example, homework is literally that—it's done at home, in private, with earplugs and KEEP OUT signs and a chair jammed up underneath the knob. Same with reading, working on journal entries, tabulating one's accounts from a paper route, & c. You're with your peers only in social or recreational settings, including classes, which at my own public high school were academic jokes. In Philo, educating yourself was something you had to do in spite of school, not because of it—which is basically why so many of my high school peers are still there in Philo even now, selling one another insurance, drinking supermarket liquor, watching television, awaiting the formality of their first cardiac.

Ms. Neti-Neti of Personnel, by the way, continued talking during much of the circuitous trip to Personnel. The truth is that most of what she said is no longer available to memory. Her tone was pleasant, professional; but she chattered so nonstop that one more or less involuntarily stopped listening to her after a little while, rather as with a six-year-old. Some of what she was saying was probably helpful and apposite REC information, though, and it's a bit of a shame that I can't resummon it now, since it would probably be useful and concise, memoir-wise, in ways that my own impressions and memories were not. I know that I kept stopping and switching various suitcases from one hand to the other to attenuate the burning sensation that comes from carrying the heavier bag on just, say, the right side for any length of time, and that it took a few such moments for Ms. Neti-Neti to understand what was happening and pause instead of continuing and ending up twenty or more yards ahead of me, at which time the fact that she was still talking became absurd, since there was literally no one there to hear her. The complete absence of any offers to help with any of the luggage was OK; that was attributable to gender codes, which I knew were especially rigid in the Middle East. But nothing drives home the awareness that someone's volubility and chatter are her own trip and have nothing to do with you quite like your falling behind and being literally absent and the chatter still proceeding, reaching you only as an indistinct stream of echoes off the hallways' surfaces. It would be disingenuous to say much more about the Iranian Crisis in the context of the first day, since what more I learned about her off-duty eccentricities and their origins in the Iranian upheavals of the late 1970s came only later when she seemed to emerge from a different wiggler's housing unit almost every morning during the month of August 1985. Her accent was mild and sounded more British than Mideastern or foreign, and her hair was a very dark black, with an almost liquid aspect to the perfect straightness with which it hung—from the rear, its contrast with the ghastly bright blue of the Personnel office's jacket was the only interesting or comely thing about that jacket. Also, because I spent so much time in various parts of her wake, I remember that she smelled faintly—as if the scent belonged not to her but to the Personnel jacket— of a certain mall-bought perfume that some unnamed member of my own family used to practically drench herself with eye-watering quantities of every morning.

Unlike the upper floors, the REC building's lower level is sectioned into roughly hexagonal pods, with corridors radiating from a central hub like spokes in a misshapen wheel. As you can imagine, this radial floor plan, so popular in the 1970s, made no immediate sense, given that the REC building itself was starkly rectangular, which added to the overall disorientation of that first day's descent toward the Intake mechanism.[48] The array of directional signs at each hub was so

[48] Once again, I would only later learn that most wigglers and Support Services workers at the REC referred to the whole Intake/Orientation process as 'disorientation,' which was another bit of clumsy inside humor. On the other hand, no one in authority expected me to be as completely confused and overwhelmed as in fact I was on arrival, since it emerged that the Personnel office had mistaken me for a completely different David Wallace, viz. an elite and experienced Immersives examiner from Philadelphia's Northeast REC who had been lured to 047 through a complex system of shell-transfers and bureaucratic finagling. I.e., that there were not one but two David Wallaces whose contracted postings to 047 were to begin in this mid-May week. The computer-system problem behind this error is detailed in §38. It goes without saying that all these facts emerged only after a great deal of time, misunderstanding, and convoluted hassle. They were the real explanation for Ms. Neti-Neti's scripted effusion and deference: It was actually that other, GS-13's name, ontologically speaking, that had been on her special whiteboard sign, though it's not as if 'David Wallace' is so common a US name that anyone could have reasonably expected me to posit right away that there'd been some freakish confusion about names and identities, especially during all the other confusion and ineptitude of 'disorientation.'

(N.B. Purely as an autobiographical aside, I'll insert that my use of my full middle name in published writing has its origins in this early confusion and trauma, i.e., trauma at being threatened at first with blame for the whole snafu, which, though egregious bullshit, was still understandably traumatic for a twenty-year-old green recruit with a fear of bureaucracies and one so-called 'honor code' violation, however specious and hypocritical, in his background already. For years afterward, I had morbid anxieties about there being God only knew how many other David Wallaces running around out there, doing God knows what; and I never again wanted to be professionally mistaken for or conflated with some other David Wallace. And then once you've fixed on a detailed and complex that it seemed designed only to increase the confusion of anyone not already sure where they were going and why. This level had white flooring and walls with battleship-gray trim, and very bright inset fluorescents—it might as well have been a galaxy away from the main floor just above. At this point, it's probably best to keep the explanations as terse and compressed as possible, for realism's sake. The longer-term truth is that since I eventually came to be employed here—or, rather, it's better to say that I came to rest here, like a racquetball or caroming projectile, after the series of administrative mix-ups that almost resulted in disciplinary charges and/or Termination For Cause in the following weeks had been cleared up—it would be easy to impose on the Level 1 layout[49] and Personnel office a whole

---

certain *nom de plume,* you're more or less stuck with it, no matter how alien or pretentious it sounds to you in your everyday life.)

49 The subterranean level, which had been excavated and added (at staggering expense) to the main building in 1974–75, was designated Level 1, and the ground floor was therefore technically Level 2, which was additionally confusing because not all of the REC's older, pre-excavation-and-addition signs had been changed out, and these signs and directories still identified the main, ground level as 1, the level above that 2, and so on, so that one could get any orientational help from these older directories and 'You Are Here' maps only if one knew in advance to recalibrate every level number upward by one, which was another piece of easily correctable institutional idiocy that Mr.

welter of detail, explanation, and background that was actually gleaned only later and not part of my arrival and dazed scurrying around with the Iranian Crisis at all. Which is a quirk of temporal memory—one tends to fill in gaps with data acquired only later, sort of the same way the brain automatically works to fill in the visual gap caused by the optical cord's exit through the back of the retina. As in, for example, the fact that the madhouse at the Exam Center's main entrance and lobby area upstairs, and the extremely long line of travel-weary employees in hats with baggage and brown Service expandable files of documentation and posting orders that now extended (i.e., this line did) all the way out through one of the heavy

Stecyk was grateful to have brought to his attention but embarrassed that he hadn't seen and fixed before, and in essence took full responsibility for, even though technically it was the responsibility of Mr. Lynn Hornbaker and the Physical Plant office to have seen and amended the signs many years before, which is one reason why the process of getting the new design and makeup of the signs contracted and requisitioned then turned out to be so fraught and pointlessly complex—by making the sign thing as difficult and complex as possible, Hornbaker's staff helped allay and diffuse responsibility for the signs' not having been caught and amended years before, such that by the time the REC Director's office heard about the issue, it was through a cloud of internal memos and cc's so involved and opaque that no one not directly involved would have paid anything more than vague attention to the very general details of the snafu.

hermetic fire doors[50] out into the fluorescent rotary at what later turned out to be the center of the central pod of Level 1, which line consisted of newly posted and/or transferred personnel waiting to have their passport-sized photo taken and their new Post 047 ID printed and run through the laminator, after which it would be almost too hot to hold for several minutes, such that you could see personnel holding their new IDs by one corner and fanning them rapidly back and forth through the air in order to cool them before attaching the gator clips to their breast pockets (as was required at all times on-post)...that all this mid-May roil and crowding was in fact due to a major restructuring of the IRS's Compliance Branch that was ongoing at all six operational RECs and over half of all Districts' Audit facilities (whose sizes varied widely) nationwide, scheduled to begin (i.e., the restructuring had been) exactly one month after the national individual income tax filing deadline of April 15, in order to allow the annual massive inflow of returns to have gone through its initial sorting and processing at the Regional Service

---

50 These double doors were gray steel, and this was the overall color scheme of Level 1 — searing white and matte gray.

DAVID FOSTER WALLACE

Centers[51] and the attached checks to have been processed and deposited in the US Treasury via the six Regional Depository mechanisms...all of this uncovered later, informally, through confabs at Angler's Cove with Acquistipace, Atkins, Redgate, Shackleford, & c. Such that it would be misleading to go into any substantive detail or explanation at this point, since none of these truths yet existed, realistically speaking. Or the fact that it turned out one needed a valid IRS ID to access any of the shuttles from the complex to any of the special low-cost Post housing at two former commercial apartment complexes farther up Self-Storage Parkway, which was a Systems regulation nationwide and therefore the reason it was not Mr. Tate's or Stecyk's fault per se that new arrivals were required to schlep their luggage all over and stand in line with it as they waited to have their ID photo taken and fresh internal Social Security number generated, & c., though it was still irksome and idiotic not to have some mechanism in place for dealing with the luggage of new employees who didn't yet have an ID—all these facts are postdated, as it were.

51 (the Midwest of which RSCs was in that era located in East St. Louis, two hours southwest)

What can validly be included among the experiences of the first day is that I was naturally surprised—a little thrilled, even—when I was exempted from the long and excruciatingly slow line that stretched from the central Level 1 rotary in to the makeshift ID station and instead got taken up to the front of the ID line and posed and shot and given my hot and redolently laminated ID card and gator clip right there on the spot. (I didn't yet know what the nine-digit sequence of numbers below the bar code signified, or that my old Social Security number, which as an American over age eighteen I knew pretty much by heart, would never again be used by anyone; it simply disappeared, from an identification standpoint.) Like being met by someone in authority with your name on a sign, it's almost inevitably gratifying to be specially escorted to the front of a line, no matter what looks of resentment or (in my case[52]) revulsion you receive from the preterite people in line who watch you being conducted up front and exempted from all the ordinary hassle and crowded wait. Plus some of the new personnel in line were

[52] (FYI, late spring was always an exceptionally bad time, skin-wise, during this era; and the harsh fluorescents of Level 1 threw every blister, scab, and lesion into merciless relief.)

clearly high-ranking transfers, and I was again both gratified and curious or even apprehensive about what kind of suction the distant relative who'd helped me arrange for the posting might turn out to have, and about what-all personal or biographical information had been relayed about me ahead of time, and to just whom. This bit of special treatment is legitimately part of the real memory-chain only if it's made clear that it (i.e., my being specially conducted to the front of the line) happened somewhat later on arrival day, after Ms. Neti-Neti had already taken me on a slightly different route along this central pod's rotary to the REC Personnel office itself, which was in a large suite of connected offices and reception areas in Level 1's southwest corner or vertex.[53] It had been her impression that I was supposed to have some kind of personal introductory audience with the DDP,[54] but either the Iranian Crisis was wrong about this, or the travel and traffic delays had

53 The logistical information, too, is postdated, strictly speaking. On the day itself, I couldn't have told you where in the building we even were by this time; no one could have.

54 = Deputy Director of Personnel, which was Mr. Stecyk's official job title. My IRS contract, by the way, was signed not by Mr. Stecyk or by DP Richard Tate, but by Mr. DeWitt Glendenning Jr., whose bivalent titles were DREC (Director — Regional Examinations Center) and ARCE (Asst. Regional

caused me to forfeit the interview slot, or else some type of Personnel crisis had obtruded on the DDP's attention. For when we had descended to this level and negotiated the central rotary and skirted various parts of the line for ID, and had taken a number of labyrinthine turns and opened various fire doors, pausing ever more often so that I could redistribute the weight of my luggage, and had finally arrived at the Personnel office, we found the waiting area, outer offices, copier corridor, and special bisected room with a UNIVAC 1100 and remote terminal (connected, I learned later, by half-duplex Dataphone line to Region in upstate Joliet) across the hall already completely filled with IRS personnel sitting, standing, reading, staring into space, holding and twidgeling their various hats, and (I assumed—wrongly, as it turned out, although it's also true that Ms. Neti-Neti did nothing to disabuse me, instead disappearing into a side office and entering into a line of blue-jacketed people waiting to speak with a Personnel superior[55]

Commissioner for Examinations), but who was referred to by almost everyone as 'Dwitt.'

55 (This turned out to be Mrs. Marge van Hool, Mr. Stecyk's adjutant and right arm, who had the lashless, protuberant, unblinking eyes of a reptile or squid, something that could kill and eat you without its bulging alien stare ever changing, although Mrs. van Hool turned out to be the veritable salt of

in order to report my [i.e., the ostensible elite transfer's] arrival and to receive instructions about how
to proceed in the absence of the special interview.
It was this Assistant DDP who signed the internal
Form 706-IC authorizing my being taken right up
to the front of the line for Service ID processing,
although it took Ms. Neti-Neti over twenty minutes[56] to reach the front of Mrs. van Hool's office's
line and present with her questions) doing nothing
but sitting around on the taxpayer's dime in some
kind of classic 'hurry up and wait' scenario.

Meanwhile, I was understandably tired and
disoriented, and also frazzled (what today would
be called 'stressed'), and hungry, and more than a
little irritated, and was seated in a recently vacated[57]
vinyl chair in the main waiting area, with my suitcases at my feet and dispatch case held against me
in such a way as to hopefully obscure the damp-

---

the earth, a classic instance of the truth that what most people look like has
very little to do with their intrinsic human qualities…a truth I held quite dear
at this time of my life.)

56 (during which interval, through momentary sight lines, I witnessed the
Iranian Crisis first reading a paperback book and then at a later point
attending to one sleeve of her gas-blue jacket with some kind of small portable
sewing implement — she was clearly someone well-suited by temperament
and/or experience to standing in long lines)

57 (i.e., nauseously warmed by the heat of some stranger's back and bottom)

ness of my suit's left side, in direct view of the desk
of the DDP's horrific secretary/receptionist, Mrs.
Sloper, who on this first day gave me the exact
same look of incurious distaste I would receive
from her for the next thirteen months, and wore
(this I sure remember) a lavenderish pantsuit
against which the abundant rouge and kohl were
even more ghastly. She was maybe fifty, and very
thin and tendony, and had the same asymmetrical
beehive coiffure as two different older females in
my own family, and was made up like an
embalmed clown, the stuff of nightmares. (Her
face looked somehow held in place with pins.)
Several times, at moments when there was enough
of a gap in the mass of personnel to constitute a
real line of sight, this secretary and I glanced at
each other with mutual hatred and revulsion. She
might actually have bared her teeth at me for an
instant.[58] A few of the personnel seated or standing all around the room and connected hallways
were reading files or filling out forms that might
conceivably have had something to do with their

58 I would learn only much later that Mrs. Sloper's son had been badly burned
in some kind of vehicle accident while in the service, and that the state of my
skin hit her harder than the average mom. At the time, all I knew was that we
despised each other on sight, as of course can happen with some people.

assigned work, but most of them were staring vacantly into space or engaged together in wandering, desultory workplace conversations, the sort (as I learned) that neither start nor ever end. I could feel my pulse in two or three pemphigoid cysts along the line of my jaw, which meant that they were going to be really nasty ones. The nightmarish secretary had a small framed workplace cartoon on her desk's edge which featured a crude caricature of an angry face and below it the caption *'I have got one nerve left…AND YOU'RE GETTING ON IT!,'* which some of the administrative workers at Philo High had also displayed and expected people to applaud the wittiness of.

The fact that I was being paid for sitting here reading an insipid self-help book—my Service contract's period of employ had legally commenced at noon—while someone else who was being paid stood in a long line of similarly paid people simply in order to find out what to do with me: It all seemed massively wasteful and inept, a prime illustration of the view held among certain members of my family that government, government bureaucracy, and government regulation constituted the most wasteful, stupid, and un-American way to do anything, from regulating the instant-coffee industry to fluoridating the water.[59] At the same time, there were also flashes of anxiety that the delay and confusion might signify that the Service was considering whether to maybe disqualify and eject me based on some distorted record of allegedly unsavory behavior at the elite college I was on leave from, either with or without sirens. As every American knows, it is totally possible for contempt and anxiety to coexist in the human heart. The idea that people feel just one basic emotion at a time is a further contrivance of memoirs.

In short, I was there in the main waiting area for what felt like a very long time, and had all sorts of rapid, fragmentary impressions and reactions, of which I will include here only a few examples. I can remember hearing one middle-aged man who sat nearby saying 'Simmer down, boyo' to another older man seated kitty-corner to me across the doorway to one of the hallways extending out from the waiting area, except when I looked up from the book both these men were staring straight ahead,

59 In the usual way of twenty-year-olds, when home in Philo, I made a point of arguing with members of my family about their political attitudes, and yet then outside the home I often found myself reflexively holding, or at least sympathizing with, those same parental attitudes. I suppose all this meant was that I hadn't yet formed a stable identity of my own.

expressionless, with no sign of anyone needing to 'simmer down' in any conceivable way. Emerging from one radial hallway to traverse the edge of the waiting area and down another hallway was at least one good-looking girl, whose creamy pallor and cherrywood hair drawn to a knot with a store-bought bow I saw peripherally but then when I looked directly could see only the back of (i.e., the woman) as she went down the hall. I have to confess that I'm not sure just how much detail to actually indulge in, or how to keep myself from imposing on the waiting area and various personnel a familiarity earned only later. Telling the truth is, of course, a great deal trickier than most regular people understand. One of the waiting room's wastebaskets, I remember, contained an empty Nesbitt's can, which I interpreted as evidence that the REC's vending facilities might well include a Nesbitt's machine. Like all crowded rooms in summertime, the place was hot and stuffy. The smell of the sweat from my suit was not wholly my own; my flared collar was curling up slightly at the tips.

By this time, I had removed the mass-market paperback from my dispatch case and was reading it with partial attention—which was all that it deserved—while holding a ballpoint pen in my teeth. As I may have already mentioned in passing, the book had been given to me the day prior by an immediate relative (the same one whose wastebasket had contained the rumpled letter concerning my IRS posting from that other, less immediate relative) and was titled *How to Make People Like You: An Instant Recipe for Career Success,* and in essence I was 'reading' the book only to place certain tart, mordant margin-comments next to each bromide, cliché, or cloying bit of inauthentic pap, which meant just about every ¶. The idea was that I would mail the book back to this immediate relative a week or two hence, along with a voluble thank-you note filled with the gestures and tactics the book recommended — such as e.g. using the person's first name over and over again, emphasizing areas of agreement and shared enthusiasm, & c. — the overwhelming sarcasm of which this relative[60] would not detect until he then opened the book and saw the acerbic marginalia on every page. At school, I had once done certain freelance work for someone enrolled in an interdisciplinary course on Renaissance 'courtesy books' and the semiotics of etiquette, and the idea

---

60 (whose personal strengths did not include perceptiveness — and I am far from the only member of the family to observe this; trust me)

here was to allude to texts like *Peacham's Compleat Gentleman* and Chesterfield's *Letters to His Son* in the marginalia so as to make the implicit scorn all the more withering. It was just a fantasy, though. The truth was that I would never mail the book and note; it was a total waste of time.[61]

61 There was, though, an oral exchange that I overheard involving two or possibly three unseen voices in the narrow hallway my chair was near the ingress of, from two REC personnel presumably standing waiting in some sort of line in that hallway, which I remember (the exchange) in detail because the waiting area's fluorescent lighting was gray-white and blinding and shadowless, the kind of light that makes people want to kill themselves, and I couldn't imagine spending nine hours a day in light like this, and so I was emotionally primed to pick this exchange out of the overall ambient noise of the room's exchanges, even though I could see neither party who was speaking; and I actually transcribed parts of the conversation in real time in a kind of personal shorthand on the inside of the pop psychology book's front cover, in order to transfer it later to the notebook (which is why I am able now to recount it in such potentially suspicious-looking detail); to wit:

'That's the short version?'

'Well, the point is just that Systems is not uncreative. You can't paint them all with the same brush.'

'Not uncreative? What kind of word is that?'

'The up-front cost-savings of fluorescent lights were obvious. All you had to do was compare power bills. Fluorescent lighting in Exam Centers was doctrine. But Lehrl found, at least in La Junta, that replacing the inset fluorescents with banked incandescents and desk lamps increased efficiency.'

'No, all the Systems boys found is that throughput of returns increased after fluorescents were changed out for lamps.'

'Again, no. What Lehrl's team found was that the net audit receipts of the Western REC's monthly throughput increased, for each of the three quarters

Crowded offices' waiting areas have their own special choreography, and I do know that at a certain further point the configuration of personnel sitting and standing around altered enough that I enjoyed a sustained line of sight, over the book, into a select bit of the inner office of the Deputy Director of Personnel,[62] which office was basically a large wood-framed cubicle inset against the rear wall of the waiting area, the entrance to which was just behind and to the side of the nightmarish secretary/

---

following the installation of incandescents, by an amount next to which the combined installation cost and increased monthly power cost of incandescents was almost negligible, assuming you amortized the one-time expense of taking out all the fluorescents and fixing the ceiling.'

'But they never did prove that the incandescents had a direct causal link to the increased audit receipts.'

'But how do you prove that? A Region's balance sheet is thousands of separate pages. The increased receipts flowed from district offices spread all over the West. There's too many variables to account for—a single connection is unprovable. That's why it requires creativity. Lehrl's boys knew there was a correlation. They could just never get anyone at Triple-Six to accept it.'

'That's your interpretation.'

'They want everything quantified. But how do you quantify morale?'

...which transcription ended up making the book somewhat valuable, in terms of reproduction, decades later. So it was both a waste and not, depending on one's perspective and context.

62 The Personnel Director's own large office was down at the end of one of the waiting area's radial corridors. As I would learn later, Mr. Tate, like many senior administrators, preferred to work out of view; he rarely interacted with anyone below the rank of GS-15.

receptionist's desk, from which position she easily could and (one got the sense) often did shoot out a bony lavender arm into the space of the DDP's doorway to prevent someone from going in or even standing there knocking without her special *nihil obstat*. (Here being a veritable law of bureaucratic administration, it turned out: The more compassionate and effective the high-level official, the more unpleasant and Cerberusian the secretary who barred one's access to him.) Mrs. Sloper's desk's multiline telephone's handset had an attachment that let her rest it (i.e., the attachment) on her shoulder and be able still to use both hands for her secretarial tasks, without the violinish contortion of the neck required to hold a regular phone against one's shoulder. The little curved device or attachment, which was tan plastic, turned out to have been mandated by OSHA for certain classes of federal office workers. Personally, I'd never seen such a thing before. The office door behind her, which was partly ajar, featured frosted glass on which was inscribed the name and very long, complex title of the DDP (whom most of the Angler's Cove wigglers referred to by the facetious sobriquet of 'Sir John Feelgood,' which it took me several weeks to understand the Hollywood context and reference of [I detest commercial films, for the most part]). My sight line's particular angle was through the partly open door into a wedge-shaped section of the room inside. Within this section was a view of an empty desk with a name-and-title-plate so long that it actually extended beyond the width of the desk at both sides (i.e., of the desk), and a small bowler or rounded business hat hung at a slight angle from one of these protrusive sides, its brim occluding the last several letters on the plate so that what the desk's sign averred became:

L. M. STECYK DEPUTY ASSISTANT REGIONAL COMMISSIONER FOR EXAMINATIONS — PERSON which in a very different sort of mood might have been amusing.

To explain the context of this sight line into the office: Closest to me in terms of the personnel also sitting there waiting for something were two young unhatted males in two of a series of slightly different vinyl chairs at a slight angle to my left, both holding stacks of folders with color-coded tabs. Both seemed roughly college-age and wore short-sleeve shirts, poorly knotted ties, and tennis shoes, in contrast to the much more conventionally adult business-style dress of most of the rest of the room.[63] These boys,

63 These, I learned, were 'turdnagels,' which term referred to low-grade or seasonal IRS support staff tasked mainly to inputting or extracting data on the

too, were engaged in some kind of long, aimless exchange. Neither crossed his legs as he sat; both their breast pockets had arrays of identical pens. From my angle of sight, their badges reflected the overhead lights and were impossible to parse. Mine was the only luggage in our area, some of which luggage was technically encroaching on the nearer kid's part of the room's floor, near his off-brand sneaker; and yet neither of them seemed aware of or curious about the luggage, or me. One might normally expect a kind of instant unspoken camaraderie between younger people in a workplace crowded mostly with older adults—rather the way two unconnected black people will often go out of their way to nod at or otherwise specially acknowledge

---

REC's computer systems. Many of them were students at either the local junior college or Peoria College of Business, which was not an elite school. Like many low-caste or marginal groups, turdnagels turned out to be very tight-knit and exclusive, even when some of them were assigned to 'cart boy' duty and as a result tended to know and exchange pleasantries with many of the wigglers and higher-ranked immersives whose exam materials and supplies they (i.e., the turdnagels) had to courier back and forth in large carts filled with individual levels and boxes and trays that could be expanded like some enormous tackle box's tiers of compartments, so that the carts became enormous, complicated Rube Goldberg–like versions of a regular grocery or mail-room cart, and of which some (meaning the carts) clattered badly when they were pushed, because of all the moving parts and jerry-rigged tiers and compartments.

each other if everyone else around them is white —
but these two acted as if someone their approximate
age were not even there, even after I raised my head
from *How...Success* twice and looked pointedly
their way. It had nothing to do with the skin thing; I
had a good antenna for the various ways of and
motives for not being looked at. These two seemed
practiced at screening out input in general, rather
like commuters on subways in the larger cities of the
East Coast. Their tone was very earnest. E.g.:

'How can you constantly be this obtuse?'

'Me, obtuse?'

'Jesus.'

'I'm not aware of being the least bit obtuse.'

'   '[64]

'I don't even know what you're talking about.'

'Good God.'

...but I couldn't determine whether it was a serious argument or just cynical collegiate titty-pinching
to pass the time. At first, it seemed impossible to
believe that the second kid was unaware that his pro-
tests of being unaware that he was obtuse played right
into the hands of the colleague who was accusing him
of obtuseness, i.e., being unaware. I was unsure
whether or not to laugh, in other words. I had come

64 (signifying that the first kid said nothing)

to a ¶ in the book that explicitly recommended loud laughter at someone in a group's joke as being more or less an automatic way to signal or invite inclusion in that group, at least for purposes of conversation; the crude illustration was a line drawing of someone standing just outside a group of laughing people at a cocktail party or reception (they were all holding what were either shallow snifters or badly drawn martini glasses). The turdnagels, though, never turned their heads or even acknowledged my laughter, which was definitely loud enough to be audible even against the background noise. The point here being that it was at an extension of the angle over the shoulder of the 'nagel who denied having been obtuse, more or less pretending to be looking past them at something else in the way of someone whose attempt at eye contact or some moment of camaraderie has been rebuffed, that I enjoyed a momentary view into the actual office of the DDP, in which view the desk was empty but the office was not, for before the desk one man was squatting on his haunches before a chair in which another man[65] hunched forward with his[66]

65 More accurately, it was someone I presumed to be a man.... From my perspective, which was primarily behind the hunched person, he/she appeared to be wearing a suit jacket whose padded shoulders, in that era, were unisex.
66 (again, my assumption)

face in his hands. The posture, together with the movement of the suit coat's shoulders, made it pretty clear the second man was weeping. No one else among the crowds of personnel in the waiting area or standing in the lines that now extended out beyond the three narrow hallways[67] into the waiting room seemed

67 In effect, these people were standing in a kind of preliminary line just to enter the three hallways' lines in order to see various mid-level Personnel officers like Mrs. van Hool, who was just at that minute (extrapolating backward from Ms. Neti-Neti's imminent reappearance with the signed Form 706-IC) issuing her a crisp, decisive set of instructions as to what was to be done with and for the valued, veteran, high-ranking immersive exams specialist they believed me to be. (N.B. That examiner, transferred from Philadelphia's Northeast REC, being not only named David Wallace but having also been scheduled to arrive the following day, and whom the Iranian Crisis had actually been dispatched to wait for and personally escort, the Personnel computer systems having made a conflation error that will be explained in §38, and in effect collapsing that second, later-arriving David Wallace into me, explaining both the mistaken identity and the mistaken day...all of which it goes without saying is *post facto* knowledge that I had no way of either knowing or guessing at the time, since 'David Wallace,' though hardly the rarest name in the United States, is also not all that common. Nor did I or anyone else know, obviously, on May 15—on which date the other, older, more 'valuable' David Wallace was clearing out his Tingle table's trays and helping a senior cart boy collate and organize the files and supporting documents for distribution to other members of his Immersives Team in preparation for his transfer and flight the following day—that when, the following day, this senior transfer arrived at the appointed time and tried to check in at the GS-13 Intake Station in the Midwest REC lobby, he would be unable to do so—to check in and be permitted to proceed to the line for his new REC badge—because the GS-13 Intake Station would of course have

aware at that moment of this little tableau, or of the fact that the DDP's office door was partly open. The

---

him already listed as checked in and issued a new ID, that badge and GS-13 ID number (which was that other David Wallace's; he'd received it twelve years prior) having been already issued in Peoria to me, the author and 'real' (to me) David Wallace, who was obviously in no position to understand or explain (later) that the whole thing was an administrative fuck-up and not an intentional attempt to supplant or impersonate an IRS GS-13 with over twelve years of devoted service at a job whose difficulty and arcane complication I would shortly start discovering; but in any event, this snafu would end up explaining not just the effusive welcome and mistakenly high civil service grade and salary (which I won't pretend I wasn't pleasantly surprised by, albeit of course puzzled) but also, partly, the strange and — for me — pretty much unprecedented interlude in the dark electrical closet off one of the radial hallways extending from the Level 1 central corridor with Ms. Neti-Neti shortly after I was conducted to the head of the ID line and issued the new badge, in which (i.e., incident in the electrical closet) she backed me up against a warm series of inset circuit-boxes and administered what would, according to former president W. J. Clinton, not properly be considered 'sex,' but which to me was far and away the most sexual thing that had happened or would happen to me until almost 1989, all of which eventuated because of both the Personnel computer's failure to distinguish between two different internal David Wallaces and Mrs. van Hool's apparent instruction to Ms. Neti-Neti to extend to 'me' (i.e., to the GS-13 they'd so heavily recruited and gotten to transfer from the Northeast REC's elite Immersive Pod) 'every courtesy,' which it emerged was a very loaded and psychologically charged term for Chahla Neti-Neti, who'd come of economic age in the sybaritic but highly etiquette- and euphemism-intensive culture of pre-Revolutionary Iran (I learned this only later, obviously), and had, like many other nubile younger Iranian women with familial connections to the existing government, had to basically 'trade' or 'barter' sexual activities with high-level functionaries in weeper was facing away from me, for the most part,[68] but the man hunkered down before him with a hand on his padded shoulder and saying something in what you could tell was a not ungentle tone had a wide soft flushed or pinkish face with lush and (I thought) incongruous sideburns, a face slightly out of date, which, when his eye caught mine (I having forgotten, in my interest, that sight lines are by definition two-way) in the same moment when the loathsome secretary, still speaking on the phone, now saw me staring past her and reached out without even having to look at the door or its knob's position in order to pull it closed with an emphatic sound, spread (the administrator's face did, i.e., Mr. Stecyk's) in an involuntary

---

order to get herself and two or three other members of her family out of Iran during the tense period when the displacement of the shah's regime was becoming more and more certain, and to whom 'extend[ing] every courtesy' therefore translated into a rapid, almost woodpeckerishly intensive round of fellatio, this apparently being the preferred method of pleasuring government functionaries from whom one sought favor but upon whose face one did not wish or could not bear to look. But it was still really exciting, albeit — for obvious reasons — extremely brief, and also helps explain why it was such a long time before I even realized that I'd left one of my pieces of luggage on the floor of the Personnel office's waiting area....All of which background also would later explain the sobriquet 'Iranian Crisis' for Ms. Chahla Neti-Neti, whose breasts' shapes against the damp corduroy of my upper legs remain one of the most vivid sensuous memories of that whole cluster-fuck of my first several days as an IRS immersive.

68 (again helping to account for the gender confusion...)

expression of compassion and sympathy, an expression that seemed almost moving in its spontaneity and unself-conscious candor, which, as explained above, I was not at all used to, and which I have no idea how my own face registered my reaction to in that moment of what felt like highly charged eye contact before his stricken face was replaced with the door's frosted glass and my own eyes dropped quickly to the book once more. I had not had my facial skin provoke such an expression before, not ever once, and it was that soft, bureaucratically mod face's expression that kept obtruding on my mind's eye in the darkness of the electrical closet as the Iranian Crisis's forehead impacted my abdomen twelve times in rapid succession and then withdrew to a receptive distance that seemed, in that charged instant, much farther away than it really could have been, realistically speaking.

§25

'Irrelevant' Chris Fogle turns a page. Howard Cardwell turns a page. Ken Wax turns a page. Matt Redgate turns a page. 'Groovy' Bruce Channing attaches a form to a file. Ann Williams turns a page. Anand Singh turns two pages at once by mistake and turns one back which makes a slightly different sound. David Cusk turns a page. Sandra Pounder turns a page. Robert Atkins turns two separate pages of two separate files at the same time. Ken Wax turns a page. Lane Dean Jr. turns a page. Olive Borden turns a page. Chris Acquistipace turns a page. David Cusk turns a page. Rosellen Brown turns a page. Matt Redgate turns a page. R. Jarvis Brown turns a page. Ann

Williams sniffs slightly and turns a page. Meredith Rand does something to a cuticle. 'Irrelevant' Chris Fogle turns a page. Ken Wax turns a page. Howard Cardwell turns a page. Kenneth 'Type of Thing' Hindle detaches a Memo 402-C(1) from a file. 'Second-Knuckle' Bob McKenzie looks up briefly while turning a page. David Cusk turns a page. A yawn proceeds across one Chalk's row by unconscious influence. Ryne Hobratschk turns a page. Latrice Theakston turns a page. Rotes Group Room 2 hushed and brightly lit, half a football field in length. Howard Cardwell shifts slightly in his chair and turns a page. Lane Dean Jr. traces his jaw's outline with his ring finger. Ed Shackleford turns a page. Elpidia Carter turns a page. Ken Wax attaches a Memo 20 to a file. Anand Singh turns a page. Jay Landauer and Ann Williams turn a page almost precisely in sync although they are in different rows and cannot see each other. Boris Kratz bobs with a slight Hassidic motion as he cross-checks a page with a column of figures. Ken Wax turns a page. Harriet Candelaria turns a page. Matt Redgate turns a page. Ambient room temperature 80° F. Sandra Pounder makes a minute adjustment to a file so that the page she is looking at is at a slightly different angle to her. 'Irrelevant' Chris Fogle turns a page. David Cusk turns a page. Each Tingle's two-tiered hemisphere of boxes. 'Groovy' Bruce Channing turns a page. Ken Wax turns a page. Six wigglers per Chalk, four Chalks per Team, six Teams per group. Latrice Theakston turns a page. Olive Borden turns a page. Plus administration and support. Bob McKenzie turns a page. Anand Singh turns a page and then almost instantly turns another page. Ken Wax turns a page. Chris 'The Maestro' Acquistipace turns a page. David Cusk turns a page. Harriet Cande- laria turns a page. Boris Kratz turns a page. Robert Atkins turns two separate pages. Anand Singh turns a page. R. Jarvis Brown uncrosses his legs and turns a page. Latrice Theakston turns a page. The slow squeak of the cart boy's cart at the back of the room. Ken Wax places a file on top of the stack in the Cart-Out box to his upper right. Jay Landauer turns a page. Ryne Hobratschk turns a page and then folds over the page of a computer printout that's lined up next to the original file he just turned a page of. Ken Wax turns a page. Bob McKenzie turns a page. Ellis Ross turns a page. Joe 'The Bastard'

Biron-Maint turns a page. Ed Shackleford opens a drawer and takes a moment to select just the right paperclip. Olive Borden turns a page. Sandra Pounder turns a page. Matt Redgate turns a page and then almost instantly turns another page. Latrice Theakston turns a page. Paul Howe turns a page and then sniffs circumspectly at the green rubber sock on his pinkie's tip. Olive Borden turns a page. Rosellen Brown turns a page. Ken Wax turns a page. Devils are actually angels. Elpidia Carter and Harriet Candelaria reach up to their Cart-In boxes at exactly the same time. R. Jarvis Brown turns a page. Ryne Hobratschk turns a page. 'Type of Thing' Ken Hindle looks up a routing code. Some with their chin in their hand. Robert Atkins turns a page even as he's crosschecking something on that page. Ann Williams turns a page. Ed Shackleford searches a file for a supporting document. Joe Biron-Maint turns a page. Ken Wax turns a page. David Cusk turns a page. Lane Dean Jr. rounds his lips and breathes deeply in and out like that and bends to a new file. Ken Wax turns a page. Anand Singh closes and opens his dominant hand several times while studying a muscle in his wrist. Sandra Pounder straightens slightly and swings her head in a neck-stretching arc and leans forward again to examine a page. Howard Cardwell turns a page. Most sit up straight but lean forward at the waist, which reduces neck fatigue. Boris Kratz turns a page. Olive Borden raises the little hinged flag on her empty 402-C box. Ellis Ross starts to turn a page and then stops to recheck something higher up on the page. Bob McKenzie hawks mucus without looking up. 'Groovy' Bruce Channing worries his lower lip with a pen's pocket clip. Ann Williams sniffs and turns a page. Matt Redgate turns a page. Paul Howe opens a drawer and looks inside and closes the drawer without taking anything out. Howard Cardwell turns a page. Two walls' paneling painted over in Baker-Miller pink. R. Jarvis Brown turns a page. One Chalk per row, four rows per column, six columns. Elpidia Carter turns a page. Robert Atkins's lips are soundlessly moving. 'Groovy' Bruce Channing turns a page. Latrice Theakston turns a page with a long purple nail. Ken Wax turns a page. Chris Fogle turns a page. Rosellen Brown turns a page. Chris Acquistipace signs a Memo 20. Harriet Candelaria turns a page. Anand Singh turns a page. Ed Shackleford turns a page. Two clocks, two ghosts, one square acre of hidden mirror. Ken Wax turns a page. Jay Landauer feels absently at his face. Every love story is a ghost story. Ryne Hobratschk turns a page. Matt Redgate turns a page. Olive Borden stands and raises her hand with three fingers out for the cart boy. David Cusk turns a page. Elpidia Carter turns a page. Exterior temperature/humidity 96°/74%. Howard Cardwell turns a page. Bob McKenzie still hasn't spit. Lane Dean Jr. turns a page. Chris Acquistipace turns a page. Ryne Hobratschk turns a page. The cart comes up the group room's right side with its squeaky wheel. Two others in the third Chalk's row also stand. Harriet Candelaria turns a page. R. Jarvis Brown turns a page. Paul Howe turns a page. Ken Wax turns a page. Joe Biron-Maint turns a page. Ann Williams turns a page.

§26

A word or two on the 'phantom' phenomenon that's so much a part of Exams lore. Examiners' phantoms are not the same as real ghosts. *Phantom* refers to a particular kind of hallucination that can afflict rote examiners at a certain threshold of concentrated boredom. Or rather say the strain of trying to remain alert and punctilious in the face of extreme boredom can reach levels at which certain types of hallucination routinely occur.

One such hallucination is what's known in Exams as a visit from the phantom. Sometimes just as a visit, as in 'You'll have to forgive Blackwelder. He had a bit of a visit this afternoon, hence the tic.' Though most rote examiners suffer from hallucinations at one time or another, not every examiner gets visited. Only certain psychological types. One way you know they're not real ghosts: Every visitee's phantom is different, but their commonality is that the phantoms are always deeply, diametrically different from the examiners they visit. This is why they're so frightening. They tend to present as irruptions from a very rigid, disciplined type of personality's repressed side, what analysts would maybe call a person's shadow. Hypermasculine wigglers get visits from simpering queens in lingerie and clotted vaudevillian rouge and mascara, nancing about. Devout wigglers see demons; prudish ones see splayed harlots or priapistic gauchos. The immaculately hygienic get visits from filthy figures whose clothing jumps with fleas; the incredibly fussy and organized see whimpering wild-haired figures with strings around their fingers rummaging frantically through the Tingle's baskets for something crucial they've misplaced.

It's not like it happens every day. Phantoms afflict mainly certain sorts. Not so true ghosts.

Ghosts are different. Most examiners of any experience believe in the phantom; few know or believe in actual ghosts. This is understandable. Ghosts can be taken for phantoms, after all. In certain ways, phantoms serve as distracting background or camouflage from which it can be difficult to pick up the fact-pattern of actual ghosts. It's like the old cinematic gag of someone on Halloween being visited by a real ghost and complimenting what he thinks is a kid in a really great costume.

The truth is that there are two actual, non-hallucinatory ghosts haunting Post 047's wiggle room. No one knows whether there are any in the Immersive Pods; those Pods are worlds unto themselves.

The ghosts' names are Garrity and Blumquist. Much of the following info comes after the fact from Claude Sylvanshine. Blumquist is a very bland, dull, efficient rote examiner who died at his desk unnoticed in 1980. Some of the older examiners actually worked with him in rotes in the 1970s. The other ghost is older. Meaning dating from an earlier historical period. Garrity had evidently been a line inspector for Mid West Mirror Works in the mid-twentieth century. His job was to examine each one of a certain model of decorative mirror that came off the final production line, for flaws. A flaw was usually a bubble or unevenness in the mirror's aluminum backing that caused the reflected image to distend or distort in some way. Garrity had twenty seconds to check each mirror. Industrial psychology was a primitive discipline then, and there was little understanding of non-physical types of stress. In essence, Garrity sat on a stool next to a slow-moving belt and moved his upper body in a complex system of squares and butterfly shapes, examining his face's reflection at very close range. He did this three times a minute, 1,440 times per day, 356 days a year, for eighteen years. Toward the end he evidently moved his body in the complex inspectorial system of squares and butterfly shapes even when he was off-duty and there were no mirrors around. In 1964 or 1965 he had apparently hanged himself from a steam pipe in what is now the north hallway off the REC Annex's wiggle room. Among the staff at 047, only Claude Sylvanshine knows anything detailed about Garrity, whom he's never actually seen — and then most of what Sylvanshine gets is repetitive data on Garrity's weight, belt size, the topology of optical flaws, and the number of strokes it takes to shave with your eyes closed. Garrity is the easier of the wiggle room's two ghosts to mistake for a phantom because he's extremely chatty and distracting and thus is often taken by wigglers straining to maintain concentration as the yammering mind-monkey of their own personality's dark, self-destructive side.

Blumquist is different. When Blumquist manifests in the air near an examiner, he just basically sits with you. Silently, without moving. Only a slight translucence about Blumquist and his chair betrays anything untoward. He's no bother. It's not like he stares at you in an uncomfortable way. You get the sense that he just likes to be there. The sense is ever so slightly sad. He has a high forehead and mild eyes made large by his glasses. Sometimes he's hatted; sometimes he holds the hat by the brim as he sits. Except for those examiners who spasm out at any sort of visitation — and these are the rigid, fragile ones who are ripe for phantom-visits anyhow, so it's something of a vicious circle — except for these, most examiners accept or even like a visit from Blumquist. He has a few he seems to favor, but he is quite democratic. The wigglers find him companionable. But no one ever speaks of him.

§27

The Rotes orientation room was on the top floor of the REC building. You could hear the needly sounds of printers — next door was Systems. David Cusk had chosen a seat near the back below an air-conditioning vent that did not riffle the pages of his training packet and Internal Revenue Code. It was either a large room or a small auditorium. The room was brightly fluorescent-lit, and ominously warm. Industrial roller shade things were pulled over two broad sets of south windows, but you could feel the sun's heat radiating from the shades and from the Celotex ceiling. There were fourteen new examiners in a room that sat 108, not counting the raised stage thing with the podium and rotary slide projector, which Cusk's parents had one almost the like of.

The Compliance Training Officer was a woman with flat hair in a tan pantsuit and flats with two separate badges on either side of the jacket. She held a clipboard to her chest and had a pointer in one hand. The room had a whiteboard instead of a chalkboard. In the room's light her face was the color of suet. She was assisted by one of the Post's Personnel men whose bright-blue jacket was too short and showed the bones of his wrists. There was no one within six little bolted desks of Cusk on any side, and he'd also taken off his suit coat the way three other people in the desks had. The examiners who'd just come today had their luggage stacked neatly at the back on the opposite side of the room. Cusk had two pencils in his bag, both eraserless and so deeply chewed you couldn't tell what color they had been. He was teetering on the edge of an attack like the one in the car with the man with the horrible boiled-looking face watching him as his temperature spiked and it was all he could do not to clamber over the man and claw at the window for air. Like almost the other one only an hour later in the line for the badge, where once he had been in the line for a few minutes he was invested and couldn't leave the line without the man in the blue jacket asking a lot of questions that other people in the line would hear and look over, and by the time he got to stand there under the two hot lights he'd done the thing of pushing the hair back off his forehead so often that the hair stood up almost straight, which he didn't know until the ID came out all hot from the laminator and he saw the photo.

As Cusk discovered the year his grades had jumped in high school, his chances of an attack could be minimized if he paid very close and sustained attention to whatever was going on outside him. He had an associate's in Accounting from Elkhorn-Brodhead Community College. The problem was that at a certain level of arousal it was hard to pay attention to anything but the threat of an attack. Paying attention to anything but the fear was like hoisting something heavy with a pulley and rope—you could do it, but it took effort, and you got tired, and the minute you slipped you were back paying attention to the last thing you wanted to.

On the whiteboard was the acronym SHEAM, which had not yet been defined. Some examiners were transferring from other posts or had been through the twelve-week IRS training courses in Indianapolis or Rotting Flesh LA. Their orientation was somewhere else, and shorter.

The little desktops were bolted to the chairs' sides and forced people to sit in a very particular way. Little flexible lamps on stalks were bolted to the side of the desktop in the place where a right-handed person needed to place his elbow in order to take notes.

The whiteboard was rather small, and the new GS-9s had to refer to a small printed booklet for some of the diagrams that illustrated the procedures the Training Officer was explaining. Many of the diagrams were so complicated that they took more than one two-page spread and had to be continued on later pages.

First there were several forms to fill out. An oriental man collected them. The orientation people obviously believed that training sessions worked better and were easier to attend to if the presentation wasn't solo. This was not Cusk's experience. His experience was that the man with the prominent wrists and Adam's apple kept interrupting or providing unnecessary and distracting commentary. It was much easier and safer for David Cusk to pay attention to just one exterior thing at a time.

'One of the things you're going to hear a lot about is quotas. In the break rooms, the water cooler.'

'The Center has no illusions about gossip and scuttlebutt.'

'The older examiners like to tell tall tales about how things were in the bad old days.'

'On the public level, the Service has always denied quotas as gauges of work performance.'

'Because one of the things you'll be thinking, because it's natural, is: How will my work be evaluated? On what will my quarterly and annual performance reviews be based?'

The gangly man wrote a question mark on the whiteboard. Cusk's feet were hot in his dress chukkas, on one of which a scuff mark had been carefully colored in with a black pen.

The Training Officer said, 'Let's say, as a hypothetical, that at one point there were quotas.'

'But for what?'

'In 1984, the Service processed a total of over sixty million individual 1040s. There are six Regional Service Centers and six Regional Exam Centers. Do the math.'

'Well, in 1984, this Post had annual throughput of seven hundred sixty-eight thousand four hundred returns.'

'That math may not appear to add up.'

'That's because it's not sixty million divided by twelve.'

'It leaves out the factor of Martinsburg.'

Their employee handbooks contained a full-color photo of the Service's National Computer Center in Martinsburg WV, one of whose three layers of perimeter fencing was electrified and had to have its base swept up every morning during equinoctial bird migrations.

The problem was that the screen for the slide projector came down over the whiteboard, so that anything written on the whiteboard was obscured when a diagram or schema had to be projected. Also, the screen appeared to have something wrong with the lock on its roller mechanism and wouldn't stay down, so that the Personnel aide had to hunch down and grasp the pull ring to keep the screen in position while keeping his shadow off the screen, which required him to practically get on his knees. The image on the slide projector's screen was a crude map of the United States with six dots in various locales whose names were too blurred by the projector's diffracted beam to make out. Each dot had an arrowed line that terminated at a dot just slightly in and below the middle of the Atlantic Coast. Some of the room's new examiners were taking notes on the image, though Cusk couldn't have guessed what the notes contained.

'Let's say a 1040 return with a claim for a refund

comes into the Western Region Service Center in Ogden, Utah.' The lady pointed to the leftmost block. The man held up a Hollerith card, whose shadow on the screen was like the most complicated domino of all time.

One of the window shades was canted slightly in its own roller, and through the resultant gap a plane of light from the southern exposure empaled the screen's right side. A series of black-and-white photographs began to cycle through the automated slide projector, both too quickly and too irresolute in the sun to quite parse. There appeared to be two incongruous photos of some kind of beach or lake scene, but they went past too quickly to be seen.

'Of course, your own RSC is in East St. Louis,' the man said from his place hunched down at the screen's bottom. He had some kind of regional accent that Cusk did not recognize.

'During the intensive processing season—'

'Which this is the tail end of—'

'The procedure is basically this. Seasonal employees remove the pre-bundled bundles of envelopes from special trucks, remove the bundling restraints, and feed the envelopes into an automated mail processor, known also as AMP, which is one of the Systems Division's latest improve-

ments in the speed and efficiency of returns processing, with a peak of almost thirty thousand
envelopes an hour.' A Fornix Industries advertising photo of a room-sized machine with numerous belts, blades, and lamps had already cycled
past on the screen several images ago. 'Automated
AMP processes include sorting, opening with
ultra-fast milling knives, coding the edges of the
different returns, sorting them onto different belts
on which further temporary employees open them
by hand—'

'The empty envelopes are then run through a
special AMP candling scanner to ensure that
they're empty, a feature that has ameliorated a
great many administrative problems of the past.'

(Most of the shots just looked like a lot of people milling around a large room with a lot of bins
and tables. The slides were so out of sync with the
data being presented that it was impossible to pay
attention to both—most of the wigglers averted
their eyes from the screen.)

'When the envelopes are opened, the first task
is to remove all checks and money orders enclosed.
These are batched, recorded, and rushed by special courier to the nearest federal depository, which
in the Western Region is in Los Angeles. The
returns themselves are batched according to five

basic types and status.' The man let go of the screen, which ascended with a pop that made people in the first few rows jump. The projector was still on, and a photo of several black women in horn-rim glasses keypunching data was superimposed on the Training Officer as she pointed at the codes for corporate returns, 1120; trusts and estates, 1041; partnerships, 1065; and the well-known Individual 1040 and 1040A; plus S corporations, which also filed 1120s.

'Of these, you're going to be concerned only with individual returns.'

'Corporates and fiduciaries—fiduciaries are, as you know, estates and trusts—are done at the District level.'

The Personnel man, who was trying to turn the slide projector off, said, 'And 1040s divide into simples and Fats—Fats including schedules beyond A, B, and C, or an excess of supporting schedules or attachments or more than three total pages of Martinsburg printout.'

'We haven't yet covered the Martinsburg part of the process yet, though,' the TO said.

'The point for you is that 1040 exams are divided into rotes and Fats, and you're tasked to rotes, which are relatively simple 1040 and 1040As, hence Rote Exams. Fats are done in Immersive

Exams, which are staffed by more senior, umm, staff, which under some regional organizations also handle 1065s and 1120Ss for certain classes of S corporation.'

The lady extended her hand in a way that signified acquiescence.

Cusk noted that pretty much all the information the training team was offering was also in the orientation packet, although the team was presenting it in a different way. His seat was in the third row from the back and all the way to the right. His fear of an attack was considerably lessened by the fact that no one was around him or in a position to look at him closely. One or two of the new examiners toward the front were actually sitting in the planar column of sun from the damaged window shade. Cusk tried hard not to imagine how much warmer and more exposed these new hires or promotions must have felt, since he was aware that other people did not suffer from *phobic anxiety* about attacks, which combined with the other terms *ruminative obsession, hyperhydrosis,* and *parasympathetic nervous system arousal loop* in a self-diagnosis he had arrived at through scores of hours of covert research — he had even enrolled in psychology courses he had no interest in, in order to create a plausible cover for the research — in the

Elkhorn-Brodhead Community College library, and an awareness of his unique anxiety was one of twenty-two identified factors that could help prime him for an attack, though not one of the really super-drive factors. The sound of the door closing behind him was what first alerted David Cusk to the fact that a change in pressure he had felt was not due to the start of the pressurized room's AC, but to someone else having entered, though turning his head to see who had come in was a sure way to draw that person's attention to him, which was imprudent because there was a reasonable chance that a late-arriving person would sit behind him, near the door through which he had first entered, and Cusk did not relish the thought of a person he had made eye contact with sitting behind him and possibly looking at the back of his hair, which was still suspiciously damp. Just the thought of the prospect of being looked at was enough to send a small aftershock of heat through Cusk's body, and he could feel selected pinpricks of sweat breaking out along his hairline and just under his lower eyelid, which were the sites where sweat usually first appeared.

Cusk realized he had also missed a minute or more of the training presentation, to which he now returned his attention with an almost physical force. The CTO was referring to control cards and batches of returns being sent someplace that Cusk deduced might well still be in the Service Center.

'They're numbered by batch, then sent for key-punching.' She accentuated her stressed syllables with the pointer, which was approximately twice the length of a conductor's baton.

'Through both gang punching and specialized binary codes, GS-9 keypunch operators scan each return and generate a computer card with 512 key points of data on it, from the TP's Social Security number—'

'Which you might hear referred to as "tin." For TIN, for Taxpayer ID Number—' The man actually took time writing this on the whiteboard while the Compliance TO held up two computer cards that looked more or less identical from Cusk's vantage.

'Please note that both Service Centers and Martinsburg have gone to ninety-column cards,' the lady said, 'thereby increasing the computing power of the Service's IDS, or Integrated Data System.' The projector moved to an image of what looked more or less exactly like the cards the GS-11 was holding up, although the holes in the card of rectangle were round instead. The Fornix corporation logo on the side was almost as large as the image of the card. 'This can, in some cases, affect the lay-out of the printout you'll receive along with each return you'll be examining for audit.'

'For this is what you guys are doing,' the Personnel aide said, 'is examining returns for audit-potential.'

'Which we'll be getting to in exactly eight min-utes,' the CTO said, giving the Personnel aide something of a look.

Cusk was first aware of an unnaturally pleasant smell originating from somewhere behind him, more pleasant than the processed air of the room and considerably better than the faint sharp-cheddar smell he imagined came off his damp shirt.

'If the Powers card specs affect your IDS-360 in a significant way, you'll be given special supplementary training on this by your Group Manager.'

'Your Group Manager is your Team Leader's supervisor,' said the Personnel aide.

'Overall, the data include TIN, occupation code, dependents, classification of income and deductions, amounts on attached W-2s, 1099s, and similar information.'

'This is pure transcription,' the man said. 'There's no exams at this phase.'

'These are transported to Martinsburg, where

Card Readers transfer the information to the Central Computers, which check for arithmetic errors, crosscheck the W-2s and income statements—'

'And very basic discrepancies, which are recorded on the internal printout for each return.'

'The printouts are known as "Internal Memo 1040-M1s" or just "M1s."'

'Although appended to the 1 is the last two digits of the relevant year for the return; for instance, a 1040-M1-84 is a printout for a 1984 1040 Individual Tax Return.'

'Although these numbers refer to the return's classification in the Master Files, the printout itself has no real code designation.'

'In the Master Files, a specific return's location would be 1040-M1-79 plus the TP's TIN, so it's actually a seventeen-character designator.'

'They're not here for Systems orientation. The point is that all you'll see is a printout with the return, because the M1 printout and the return comprise the case file, and what rote examiners do is examine case files for audit potential.'

Cusk was starting to pick up on the rhythms of the dual presentation and the interrelational cues that came from the Training Officer when the presentation had veered into a digression or was covering something comparatively less important.

The main one was that she looked at her wrist-watch, which made the shadow of the pointer in her hand stick out to the side on the lit screen and point directly at the Personnel aide's shadow, even though the two were not equally close to the projector. Plus the relevant points were right there in the orientation packet. In the part of his mind that was aware of his own arousal-level, sweat-situation, the room's temperature, the location of all the exits, the locations and sight lines of all people in the room who might be able to see it if he had an attack—all of which, when he was in any kind of enclosed public situation, took up some part of his awareness no matter how intently he concentrated on whatever was going on in terms of the room's official business—Cusk was aware of the presence of someone behind and slightly above him, probably just inside the exit door, possibly standing there deciding where he or she would sit. And the possibility that it was a she—for the pleasant scent in the air was perfume, it was reasonable to assume, or else an unusually floral and effeminate kind of men's cologne—caused another wave of warmth to pass through Cusk's head and scalp, though not a really severe or attack-grade wave of heat.

'In essence,' the Compliance Training Officer said, 'the master files allow us to verify the arithmetic and check for discrepancies that would take several man-hours to do by hand.'

'Fact,' the Personnel aide said. 'Between six and eleven percent of average annual 1040s contain some basic arithmetical error.'

'But the Master Files also permit cross-year and cross-return checks,' the CTO said. 'Examples: 1040 Line 11 and Line 29—Alimony received and paid.'

'These are on your Rotes Protocol sheets,' the Personnel aide said. 'But they're essentially done by the time you get the file. Martinsburg's Master Files perform the crosschecks with the spouse's return. If there's a discrepancy, it's noted on the M1.... Your job will be to determine whether the amounts involved constitute an auditable item.'

'And, if so, whether it's a letter-audit through the REC's AC Pod—Automated Correspondence—or whether it's in the Service's interest to direct the entire return to its home District for an office audit.'

'In essence,' the Personnel aide said, 'this is your job. You are on the front lines of deciding which returns are audited and which are not. That's boiled down to the nutshell. And the criteria for auditability have changed substantially in the past two years, so...'

'One more example of how Martinsburg fits in the process,' the CTO said. 'Line 10.'

The Personnel aide slapped his forehead theatrically. 'This is one that drove them crazy in the seventies.'

'Line 10 in Income, on the 1040, requires you to declare state and local tax refunds *if* the refund is for a year in which you itemized deductions—'

'—meaning Line 34A, meaning Schedule A.'

'This was an open invitation to TPs to "misremember" whether they'd itemized the previous year. The incentive was to believe they had not itemized the previous year—'

'—because then the refunds were not income.'

'—and prior to the Master Files, it was reasonable of a clever TP to assume that this was not an item that would be checked in Exams. Because the previous year's return was something you had to fill out a Form 3IR plus 12(A) on.'

'Return Request Requisition,' the Personnel aide inserted.

'And the return had to be recovered from either the Service Center's archives or the National Records Center, and it was a pain, and took a week, and it was *expensive*, mainly in man-hours and transport and administration costs, costs which tended to far exceed the fairly small amounts of a state or local refund.'

'Line 10 was something we just could never afford to check,' the Personnel aide said. 'Not to mention the hassle of keeping a return in your Tingle's in-box for a week while you waited for the 3R to come through.'

'With the Master Files, the Line 34A option of the TP's previous return could be automatically checked—you now get alerts on the printout itself whether line 10 is tax-treatable or not, based on the previous returns and the state RE reports.'

'Although some states' computer systems aren't compatible with Martinsburg.'

The room's temperature, as experienced by David Cusk, was now 84 degrees. He heard the distinctive sound of a seat being pulled down into position directly behind him and someone sitting and placing what sounded like two or more cases or personal items in the seat next to her and unzipping what sounded like a portfolio—for it was definitely a female, there was a smell not only of floral perfume but of makeup, which has a distinct complex of scents in a warm room, as well as some type of floral shampoo, and Cusk could actually feel the twin disks of her eyes' pressure on the back of his head, since he could easily calculate that his head was at least partly within the girl's sight line of the podium. By watching the presentation, she would also be looking at at least part of the rear of Cusk's head, and also his neck's rear, which his short haircut left bare, meaning any droplets that might emerge from the rear of his hair might be clearly visible.

'That's not the point. The point is efficiency and economy, and the reason why we'll be going over the specs and layout of the Martinsburg M1 in detail in the next hour. We cannot overemphasize this. You are not inspectors — your job is not to catch every last little error and discrepancy and forward the 1040 for audit.'

'That would overwhelm District offices, whose audit resources are severely limited.'

'The truth — there is capacity in the present Audit Division to audit one-seventh of a percent of all 1040s and 1120s filed this year.'

'— although this year you'll be mostly occupied with 1984 returns, since there's an average ten-month lag between filing and exams, although in the Midwest Region they've got this down to closer to nine.'

'The *point*,' the CTO said with a bit of an edge to her voice, 'is that your job is to determine which returns give evidence of maximum auditability in terms of (a) profitability, and (b) expediency. Which are interlinked, since the more involved and time-consuming the audit, the more expensive it is for the Service, and the lower the net increase to the US Treasury at audit's end. At the same time, it is true that egregiousness of misreporting is tied to profitability, since negligence penalties kick in at certain pre-set levels of misreporting—'

'—as well as interest on all moneys due—'

'—which adds, sometimes significantly, to the audit's net proceeds.'

The worse it got, the colder the air from the overhead vent should have felt, by contrast. But perversely it didn't—the hotter Cusk's internal temperature got, the warmer the downdraft felt, until at a certain point it was like a scirocco or the air from an opened oven—positively hot. Cusk was not exactly having an attack, but he was in the fluttery initial stages of an attack, which in certain ways was worse because it could go either way. He had broken a light sweat, but this was not the problem—the nearby girl was behind him, and as long as the heat and sweat didn't escalate into a full-fledged attack, his haircut's rear would disguise any droplets of sweat. Only if it escalated into a real attack where the bits of sweat on his scalp beneath his hair grew and accreted into a density where they became actual droplets and followed gravity down over his exposed neck was there any real chance of the woman behind him noticing and seeing him as repulsive or weird. There was, by way of prophylaxis, the option of looking back and determining the age and attractiveness of the female examiner whose perfume and the faint leather scent of what was probably a purse enveloped Cusk. Since the room's clock was on the room's rear wall, there was an obvious excuse for turning quickly and looking backward.

At the podium, the Personnel aide was recounting the massive decentralization of the Service following the King Commission findings of 1952, which placed far greater authority and autonomy in the hands of the fifty-eight District offices, and the current partial re-centralization of processing and automated audit functions through Martinsburg and the Regional Centers, referring both to the 'era of Region' and something called 'the Initiative' of which Cusk had never heard. Cusk had not attended either of the twelve-week introductory sessions at the IRS's National Training Centers in Indianapolis and Rotting Flesh LA, both of which were filled through 1985. Instead, he had answered a recruiting advertisement in *Today's*

Accountant magazine, to which Elkhorn-Brodhead's library had subscribed. Cusk had had a part-time stacking job in this library as part of his financial aid package.

'There are two sets of Master Files, in essence one for business entities and one for individuals, in sets that are maintained for three-year periods—'

'Three years corresponding to the audit window for a given return, meaning we have until April 15 of next year to audit and recover taxes due on returns filed for 1982 taxes, some of which may cross your desk as parts of coordinated exam programs generated either through Compliance or Martinsburg.'

Cusk was now fighting desperately to attend to every last syllable enunciated at the podium. It was his one chance not to begin dwelling on his core temperature and perspiration, which were now severe enough that he felt a sort of yarmulke of heat at his head's crown, which was one of four main symptoms of a true attack. He knew his face was now starting to gleam with sweat, which was the main reason he had opted not to turn around and get a general attractiveness-level on the tardy female examiner behind him—which could either have possibly forestalled the attack or kick-started it into a full-out attack in which he would be unable to feel or pay attention to anything except his prodigious flow and feelings of uncontrollable heat and total panic at the idea of being seen sweating this way.

The Personnel aide was describing the 3,312 employees at IRS Post 047 in terms of both shift— 58 percent worked the 7:10 A.M.–3:00 P.M. (I) shift, 40 percent 3:10–11:00, plus some janitorial + physical plant activity overnight—as well as percentage breakdown of Exams, Clerical, Data Processing, and Administration, most of which Cusk missed because he had entered the incipient stages of an actual attack where his attention telescoped and the state of his own body and its emission of perspiration occupied almost 90 percent of his conscious awareness. He could hear the female behind him clicking her ballpoint pen in a nervous and arrhythmic way, and once a sound that had to be her uncrossing and recrossing her legs in what sounded like sheer hose, a sound that sent a terrible wave of internal heat through Cusk, and caused the first felt drops to go running from armpits down his torso's sides beneath the dress shirt. He automatically lowered his head during an attack, as well as slumping as far down in his plastic seat as would be inconspicuous, seeking to make himself as small as possible, visually, in terms of the woman behind him, whom he imagined by now to be a heart-stoppingly pretty girl of about Cusk's own age, with extraordinary posture and composure and a round porcelain face with intimidating blue eyes and overall an almost European hauteur about her. In short, she was Cusk's fantasy woman—which was as it were the price he paid for being too petrified with fear and self-consciousness to turn around and feign a look at the clock (which read 3:10 P.M.) in order to gauge the woman's threat in reality. The Compliance Training Officer, he could hear, was alluding to a page in the Exam Orientation Booklet that the current slide on the screen was a representation of that turned out to be exact, item for item, as Cusk lowered his running head further and pretended to study the relevant page of the booklet, circumspectly wiping away each fallen drop of perspiration before it could pucker its dime-sized section of the page, in case anyone would ever need to borrow his booklet and wonder what kind of grotesque, creepy thing had happened to p. B-3's diagram.

Cusk began gauging the exact distance to the exit in terms of both seconds and number of footsteps, another part of his brain calculating angles, sight lines, and intensities of light at various posts along the path of retreat—at as it were the periphery of his attention. Instinctively, he understood that not every item on the Rote Exams checklist was going to be equally important.

'What we have here are phases or the elements of triage,' the CTO said, then stopped briefly while the Personnel aide defined *triage* for those unfamiliar with the medical term. Claude Sylvanshine, three rows up and four seats to the left of Cusk, was battling between trying to resummon the distinctions between §162 and §212(2) deductions related to rental properties and data incursions of the annual rainfall in Zambia for even-numbered years since 1974, the latter appearing as highlighted columns on the page of a WHO atlas whose editor in chief had some form of psychomotor debility.

'If you think about it, you are not going to want to file a Memo 20 on a return just because, say, its Line 11 appears to understate alimony received by $200.'

'Since the additional tax due on $200 of income is less than 5 percent of the additional cost of conducting an audit.'

'You might, however, file a 20(a) and send the return to Automated Collections for a letter audit.'

'That will depend on your group protocols as stated by your Group Manager and group protocols packet in group orientation.'

'Which, in turn, will depend on your group assignment.' Someone whose pile of luggage was in the seat next to Sylvanshine several rows up raised his hand to ask what a group was in terms of Rote Exams assignments. What was odd was that there were no data incursions for Sylvanshine on the mysterious child that Dr. Lehrl traveled with and kept near him at all times but never seemed to talk to. Sylvanshine knew that it was not Dr. Lehrl's child, but that was only because Reynolds had told him so. It was as if the child were surrounded by a sort of impermeable factual membrane, or inhabited a fact vacuum. The big data Sylvanshine got for David Cusk, whose name he did not know, were the dimensions of his home's bathroom's medicine chest's mirror and certain temperature readouts in twin columns with the left column's numbers higher and illuminated in a kind of cheesy emergency red.

Page 16 had a diagram of the Compliance Branch's Rote Exams' Chalk—Team—Group—Pod organizational structure.

'The standard triage works like this. The M1 printout from Martinsburg will already note and

DAVID FOSTER WALLACE

list certain incongruities, either in arithmetic or a cross-reference of, say, an ex-spouse's return's Line 29 with your return's Line 11 —'

'That's one reason the returns are forwarded to Exams—Martinsburg catches something.'

'Others are forwarded because of criteria that may, as far as you're concerned, appear almost random.'

'Another advantage of the Master Files—now over 50 percent of the arithmetical and cross-file verification takes place automatically at Martinsburg, which vastly increases your efficiency and the number of returns this Post can process and reach audit determinations on.'

'Though volume and throughput are no longer the criteria by which a Post's performance is judged and evaluated.'

An involuntary grimace went over the Personnel aide's face as he spoke. Sylvanshine knew this aide's shoe size and total blood volume, but not his name.

'The evaluative criteria now concern return on audit,' the CTO said.

Without looking at it, the Personnel aide held aloft a Fornix twelve-column computer card and a sheet of printout.

The CTO said, 'These represent Memo PP-47

578

plus a subsection for one's Pod, Group, Team, Detail, and personnel margin.'

'Margin refers to the ratio of additional tax assessed through audit to costs.'

'—Including your own salary, benefits, housing allowance if any, etc.'

'—It's the new Bible,' said the Personnel aide.

Sylvanshine, his eyes rolling up slightly white, received a whole slew of facts about the CTO that he did not wish to know, including the specs of her mitochondrial DNA and the fact that it was ever so slightly nonstandard due to her mother's having taken thalidomide four days before it was abruptly yanked from the shelves. Training Officer Pam Jensen had a .22 revolver in her purse—she had promised herself a bullet in the roof of her mouth after her 1,500th training presentation, which at current rates would be July 1986.

'In the bad old days, it was throughput.'

'The average rote examiner could clear between twenty-seven and thirty files per day.'

'Now it could be four, five files a day—if your Audit-to-Cost ratios are good, you're in line for an outstanding six-month performance review.'

'Of course, the more files you throughput each day, the wider a field of possibilities for high-ratio files you're going to have, and the better your chances of filing 20s that realize substantial gains.'

'But you don't want to concentrate so hard on getting through as many files as possible that you fail to identify especially profitable returns.'

'We prefer not to use the term "profitable,"' the CTO said. 'We prefer the term "noncompliant."'

'But a flamboyantly noncompliant return could be operating off such a low Line 23 that it's actually more efficient to forbear on it but to 20 the return right next to it, which, while containing few errors or incongruities, actually realizes a far higher audit assessment.'

'These are matters best left to your group orientation.'

Now actual drops of sweat were falling off the ends of Cusk's hair, as an inaudible scream resounded inside him.

'Right,' the CTO said. 'Let's have a break and get you freshened up, and we'll proceed with general criteria for Audit / No Audit decisions.'

There was going to be a break. David Cusk had not allowed himself to consider this. The lights would come up. Everyone would get up and leave at the same time. If he stayed, the beautiful girl behind him would see his sopped collar and the

V-shaped darkening of sweat on his blue dress shirt, which it had been cocky and idiotic of him to wear instead of the more prudent and undarkenable white. He would sit there hunched over, pretending to study the M1 printout schema in his orientation packet, his core temperature well into three digits, drops of visible perspiration falling from the ends of his hair on all four sides to dot the packet, the arms of his shirt, the sizzling side of his nozzle lamp — there would be no way people could miss it. If he got up, though, and joined the crowds moving up the ramped aisles to the two exit doors, there would be no way people could fail to see what was happening with him, including the beautiful haughty French or maybe even Italian woman behind him. It was the nightmare scenario. Thinking this way was all but guaranteed to cause an attack, which was the absolute last thing in the world David Cusk wanted. He willed himself to raise his head. The hot spotlight he felt on him did not exist. The woman behind him was a person, had her own troubles, and wasn't paying close attention to him — that was an illusion. The only thing that mattered about his head was that it was in her way, that she had to cross her thighs tight and sit way over to the side to see the podium and screen, where a split-slide shot of two desks wavered while the CTO tried to focus the projector with a handheld appliance connected to the projector by a cord that had gotten tangled around one of her legs.

Sylvanshine, before the morning of travel, had forgotten to wash the shampoo from his hair. It was this that gave him the flame-shaped coiffure.

David Wallace, meanwhile, was not enjoying any general orientation with slick slide show. Instead, he had been conducted (by someone who was not Ms. Neti-Neti)—with no opportunity to eat anything—to the REC Annex and a small room in which he and four other men, all GS-13s, listened to a presentation of the Minimum Tax on Preferences, which evidently had its origin in the Democratic administration of Lyndon Johnson in the 1960s. The room was small, stuffy, and had no whiteboard or A/V facilities. It did, though, smell strongly of Dry Erase Marker. All the other men in the room were conservatively dressed and hatted and very serious, with Treasury notebooks that came in zip-up leatherette folders with the IRS seal and motto embossed on the cover, which David Wallace had not received, and was taking notes in his private notebook folded over so that the IGA price tag in the upper-right corner was not visible.

The presentation was dust-dry and appeared to be very high-level and was made by someone dressed in a black suit and black vest over what appeared to be either a white turtleneck—which would have been bizarre in such hot weather—or one of those detachable Victorian starched collars that men used to put on and fastened with studs as the very final part of the Victorian dressing process. He was very clipped and impersonal and all-business. He seemed very severe and austere, with great black hollows in his cheeks and under his eyes. He looked a little like a popular representation of death.

'We will note, however, that RA '78 revised the expansionist tendencies of the '76 provisions by removing both long-term capital gains deduction and excess itemized deductions from the index of relevant preferences.' The term *preferences* had been used several times already. It goes without saying that David Wallace didn't know what the term *preferences* meant, or that they were Congress's clever way of reducing a certain income group's tax burden without lowering its tax rate— one simply allowed special deductions or provisions that exempted certain portions of income from the taxable base, provisions collectively known in the Service as preferences. Later, thanks mainly to Chris Acquistipace, David Wallace would figure out that the MPT/AMT Group was tasked to enforce certain special provisions that the '76 and '80 acts had put in place to keep extremely wealthy individuals and S corps from paying, through the use of what are called 'tax shelters,' in effect, no tax at all. The Immersive Group to which David Wallace was assigned was part of the Immersive AT/S Pod (for Alternative Tax/Shelters). It would be embarrassing to state outright how long it took David Wallace to figure this out, even after several days of ostensibly examining files.

'We note, however, that the '78 act also added to the list of eligible preferences the excess of Intangible Drilling Cost deductions over any and all reported income from oil and gas production, effectively attacking the energy-based shelters of the mid-seventies oil shock, as in §312(n) of the revised code.' The way David Wallace was pretending to take notes was that he was simply copying down every last word or phrase the instructor uttered, much as he had for those college lecture classes in which he'd been hired to take notes for someone who was forced to miss class by a ski trip or extreme hangover. It was one reason why David Wallace's left hand was way more muscled and substantial—especially the muscle between his thumb and forefinger, which bulged when the pencil was pressed to the paper—than his right. He could transcribe like the wind.

'The provisions most relevant to your Memo 20 protocols are that '78 increased the ATP tax rate to 15 percent and established the standard ATP exemption to the larger of (a) $30,000 or (b) 50 percent of the requisite tax due for the *current year only*, a provision which the Master Files render otiose but which the '80 act's provisions failed to address.'

One of the GS-13s raised his pen—not his hand, but just his pen with a small cool move of his wrist—and asked some kind of absurdly recondite question that David Wallace didn't write down because he was flexing and unflexing his hand to ameliorate something that happened if he transcribed for more than a few minutes, which is that his left hand assumed a sort of automatic writerly claw shape and stayed that way after he finished transcribing, sometimes for more than an hour, forcing him to hide the hand in his pocket.

'As of March of 1981, and subject to refinement in the case of fiduciaries and certain specialized industries such as if memory serves timber, sugar, and select legumes, the relevant provisions this group is required to examine for ATP computation are, excluding code sections except where immediately relevant, which sections you'll find cross-indexed in your 1M specs 412, (1) Excess of accelerated depreciation on section 1250 property over straight-line depreciation. (2) Consequent to TRA '69, excess of sixty-month amortization of certain items associated with pollution-control, child-care facilities, mining safety, and national historic sites over straight-line depreciation. (3) Excess of percentage depletion over a property's adjusted basis at year's end. (4) Bargain elements in qualified stock options — TRA '76. (5) Excess IDC over fossil income as mentioned above.' (David Wallace had no time to look above in his notes. He was trying to circle words and terms he didn't know, figuring he could find a library. This list was not in his manual — they were given no manuals. It seemed expected that they'd already know this stuff. In order to deal with his feelings of confusion and fear, Wallace had opted to turn himself more or less into a transcription machine.) '(6) Being the excess of accelerated depreciation over straight-line depreciation on Section 1245 property leased to another.'

The man stood totally still as he spoke. David
Wallace didn't think he had ever before seen someone who didn't fidget in at least a few idle, unconscious ways when he spoke in public. The bodily
stillness would have been more thought-provoking
if David Wallace had felt less panicked and overwhelmed, and besides automatizing himself by
transcribing, David Wallace was doing the other
main compensatory thing he did when he was
in a room where everyone seemed to understand
exactly what was being talked about but him—
which had happened in certain social situations at
Philo High, at which David Wallace had not been
part of any one particular clique but had hung out
on the fringes of several different groups, from
second-tier athletes to student council and A/V
wonks, and was often privy to gossip or references
to group situations he had no direct knowledge of,
but had to stand there grinning and nodding like
he knew exactly what was being referred to. Not
to mention once when in a burst of absurd half-
drunken freshman hubris he'd accepted a massive
assignment that involved auditing a Russian Existential and Absurdist Literature class and writing
the papers for a wealthy and tormented son of a
Rhode Island State Supreme Court justice who
was actually enrolled in the class and discovering

that not only all the reading and critical background but the seminar itself was actually held in Russian, which David Wallace did not know or speak one garbled syllable of, and had to sit there with an enormous rigid grin, transcribing the phonetic versions of whatever unearthly and incredibly rapid sounds were being made by everyone else in the room every Tuesday and Thursday from 9:00 to 10:30 for three weeks before he was able to think of a plausible excuse and backed out of the arrangement. Leaving the client—who was still enrolled—with his own very special sort of existential dilemma. The point is that this is what David Wallace did in these situations, which was to assume and hold by main force an enormous grin that he imagined communicated ease and confident familiarity with whatever was going on but in fact, unbeknownst to him, in its rigid distension and lack of eye-involvement, together with the skin situation, actually looked like the agonized rictus of someone having the skin of his face slowly torn off, which luckily for him all the room's GS-13 Immersive Exam transfers and CTO shelter specialists were too serious and intent and engaged with the anti-shelter protocols—for that's what the Team to which David Wallace was mis-ID'd and erroneously assigned through no fault of his own (though this orientation might have been the place to put up his hand) turned out to be, the examination and evaluation of individual and limited-partnership shelters in realty, agriculture, and leveraged leasing, which was a small but serious component of the Spackman Initiative—to notice in anything more than a peripherally uncomfortable way, as well as David Wallace's youth, corduroy suit (which was the IRS equivalent of a Speedo and floppy clown shoes), and absence of hat.

A/NA, projected on its own b/w slide, was explained as the entire thrust and raison of Rote Exams.

'Are you cops?'

The Personnel aide raised his hands and shook them and shouted out 'Nooo.' This was the same fake evangelist bit Sylvanshine had seen at the Philadelphia REC when he was twenty-two years old. The Personnel aide's coin collection was kept in a portable safe in the rear of his mother or grandmother's closet, judging by the styles of dresses and coats on the rack overhead.

'Are you judges of civic virtue?'

'Nooo.'

'Are you sadistic bureaucrats arbitrarily deciding

which TPs' lives to make miserable by subjecting them to the anxiety and inconvenience of an audit, trying to squeeze every last drop of blood from the neck you've got your boot on?'

'No.'

'In essence, in today's IRS, you're businessmen.'

'And businesswomen. Businesspersons. Or rather in the employ of what you're urged to consider a business.'

'Which returns will be profitable to audit?'

'How do you determine this?'

'Different Exam groups do it different ways. Your group orientation will have the specifics.'

Aide: 'Or your Team, since some Group Managers here have different Teams tasked to different criteria.'

'You can almost think of them as filters — what gets through, what gets Memo 20'd and routed to District.'

'Or signs, flags — at least that some return deserves an exhaustive exam.'

'You won't be going over every last return with a microscope.'

'You want to work smart as well as fast.'

'And fast means some you'll know right away — this audit wouldn't produce anything.'

'That's the criterion — will an audit produce a

maximal increase when the cost of the audit is subtracted?'

'So that's one thing to discard—the idea that you're guardians of civic virtue.'

'There's another common misapprehension to disregard. Does anyone have any idea what it is?'

David Cusk had a terrible, totally ghastly impulse to raise his hand. Part of his strategy for surviving the close-order mingling of the break until he could make it to a restroom had been to think hard about the final projected image on the slide projector's screen, which the Training Officer never had gotten to quite resolve into focus but had been a split-screen view of two desks or tables, one strewn with papers and forms, plus a couple of items whose bright colors indicated they might have been food wrappers, the other clean and neat with items in piles and labeled baskets. Cusk was pretty sure the CTO wanted to stress order and organization and to banish the idea that a slovenly desk was the sign of a productive worker. Meanwhile, no one else had raised their hand. The idea came again of raising his hand and having the CTO point to him over all the turning heads, volunteering for the spotlight of all those people's attention, including the exotic Belgian transfer or émigré, whom Cusk had managed to avoid during the break, from which he had returned early, and did not know that the woman's glasses were so thick that if he'd ever seen her he'd have been able to tell that she was practically blind, at least in terms of objects more than three or four feet away, her eyes shriveled and oddly puckered in the irises, filled with cracks and fissures like a dry riverbed — she was about as exotic as a fire hydrant, and roughly the same shape — and he wouldn't have been as worried about being seen by her as wet or sweating. In any event, he was correct, it emerged:

'The common misapprehension is that a messy desk is a sign of a hard worker.'

'Get over the idea that your function here is to collect and process as much information as possible.'

'The whole mess and disorder of the desk on the left is, in fact, due to its excess information.'

'A mess is information without value.'

'The whole point of cleaning off a desk is to get rid of the information you don't want and keep the information you do want.'

'Who cares which candy wrapper is on top of which paper? Who cares which half-crumpled memo is trapped between two pages of a Revenue Ruling that pertained to a file three days back?'

'Forget the idea that information is good.'

'Only certain information is good.'

'*Certain* as in some, not as in a hundred percent confirmed.'

'Each file you examine in Rotes will constitute a plethora of information,' the Personnel aide said, stressing the second syllable of *plethora* in a way that made Sylvanshine's eyelids flutter.

'Your job, in a sense, with each file is to separate the valuable, pertinent information from the pointless information.'

'And that requires criteria.'

'A procedure.'

'It's a procedure for processing information.'

'You are all, if you think about it, data processors.'

The next slide on the screen was either a foreign word or a very complex acronym, each letter in bold and also underlined.

'Different groups and teams within groups are given slightly different criteria that help inform what to look for.'

The Personnel aide was thumbing through his laminated outline.

'Actually there's another example of the information thing.'

'I think they've got it.' The CTO had a way of

turning one foot out perpendicular to its normal direction and tapping it furiously to signal impatience.

'But it's right here under the desk thing.'

'You mean the deck of cards?'

'The checkout line.'

They seemed to believe their mikes were off.

'Christ.'

'Who'd like to hear another example illustrating the idea of collecting information versus *processing* data?'

Cusk was feeling solid and confident, as he often did after a series of attacks had passed and his nervous system felt depleted and difficult to arouse. He felt that if he'd raised his hand and given an answer that turned out not to be correct it wouldn't have been that big of a deal. 'Whatever,' he thought. The 'whatever' is what he often thought when he was feeling jaunty and immune from attack. He had twice actually asked women out when in this cocky, extroverted, hydrotically secure mood, then later failed to show up or call at the appointed time. He actually considered turning around and saying something jaunty and ever so slightly flirtatious to the noisome Belgian swimsuit model—on the upswing, he now *wanted* people's attention.

At age eight, Sylvanshine had data on his father's liver enzymes and rate of cortical atrophy, but he didn't know what these data meant.

'There you are at the market while your items are being tallied. There's an individual price for each item, obviously. It's often right there on the item, on an adhesive tag, sometimes with the wholesale price also coded in the corner—we can talk about that some other time. At checkout, the cashier enters the price of each grocery, adds them up, appends relevant sales taxes—not progressive, this is a current example—and arrives at a total, which you then pay. The point—which has more information, the total amount or the calculation of ten individual items, let's say you had ten items in your cart in the example. The obvious answer is that the set of all the individual prices has much more information than the single number that's the total. It's just that most of the information is irrelevant. If you paid for each item individually, that would be one thing. But you don't. The individual information of the individual price has value only in the context of the total; what the cashier is really doing is discarding information. What you arrive at the cash register with is a whole lot of information, which the cashier runs through a procedure in order to arrive at the one piece of information that's valuable — the total, plus tax.'

'Get rid of the layman's idea that information is good. That the more information the better. The phone book has lots of information, but if you're looking for a phone number, 99.9 percent of that information is just in the way.'

'Information per se is really just a measure of disorder.' Sylvanshine's head popped up at this.

'The point of a procedure is to process and reduce the information in your file to just the information that has value.'

'There's also the matter of using your time most efficiently. You're not going to spend equal time on each file. You want to spend the most time on the files that look most promising in terms of yielding the most net revenue.'

'Net revenue is our term for the amount of additional revenue generated by an audit less the cost of the audit.'

'Under the Initiative, examiners are evaluated according to both total net revenue produced and the ratio of total additional revenue produced over total cost of additional audits ordered. Whichever is the least favorable.'

'The ratio is to keep some rube from simply filling out a Memo 20 on every file that hits his Tingle in hopes of jacking up his net.' Cusk considered: An examiner who filed no Memo 20s ever would have a ratio of 0/0 which is infinity. But the net revenue total would, he reflected, also be 0.

'The point is to develop and implement procedures that let you determine as quickly as possible whether a given file merits closer examination—'

'—that closer examination itself involving some type or types of procedures blended with your own creativity and instinct for smelling a rat in the woodwork—'

'—although at the beginning of your service, as you're gaining experience and honing your skills, it will be natural to rely on certain tested procedures—'

'—a lot of these will vary by group or team.'

'Incongruities on the Master Files, for one thing. That's pretty obvious. Disagreement of W-2s plus 1099s with stated income. Disagreement of state return with 1040—'

'But by how much? Below what floor do you simply let an incongruity go?'

'These are the sorts of matters for your group orientation.'

Sylvanshine now knew that two separate pairs of new wigglers were actually, unbeknownst to them, related, one pair through a liaison five generations ago in Utrecht.

David Cusk was now feeling so relaxed and unafraid that he was almost getting drowsy. The two trainers sometimes established a rhythm and concert that was soothing and restful. Cusk's tailbone was a tiny bit numb from settling back and slumping slightly in his seat, resting his elbow casually on the foldout desk, the heat of the little lamp of no more direct concern than news of the weather somewhere else.

'Who has an unusually big dip in income or rise in deductions compared to previous years? These are just samples.'

'A major one—who has been fruitfully audited within the past five years? This appears on some, but not all, of the Martinsburg printouts.'

'—Sometimes you have to order additional specs from the Master Files.'

'But be disciplined about it. Avoid the temptation to think that you always need more information. You can drown in it.'

'Plus it's expensive.'

'Get to know your cart boy. Your cart boy is the GS-7 who liaisons with the examiners and the Technical Pod, where data processors can get you additional information from the Master Files if you fill out a DR-104 data requisition form.'

'Not all of them are boys. "Cart boy" is just a more historical term.'

'Plus cart boys are who keep the files circulating, particularly picking up files that you've cleared and keeping your Tingle's in-box filled.'

'They do not bring refreshments or do personal errands.'

Cusk was considering the possible advantages of being a cart boy if being an examiner turned out to be too dangerous in terms of subjecting him to attacks and making it difficult to leave the area. Cart boys sounded as if they were in more or less constant motion, and constant motion meant constant chances to nip into the restroom and check the sweat situation and wipe sweat off his forehead. On the other hand, it would probably mean a large pay cut. A small gurgling noise Cusk heard behind him at five-minute intervals was the sound of Toni Ware's glasses' auto-lubricant in her eyes.

'You'll meet your cart boy in your Group and Team orientations.'

'Other general examples: Who's in a largely cash business?'

'Who's got unusually high charitable deductions compared to the averages for his income level?'

'Who's getting divorced? For reasons they'll go into if relevant to your Group, divorces tend to generate unusually high net revenue from audits.'

'Partly because of liquidation of assets, partly because the proceedings often expose a great deal of the auditable situation without our having to incur the time and cost and uncovering things like hidden income.'

'Who's got unusually high depreciation write-offs that should be amortized over several years? Over 40 percent of accelerated depreciation on 1040s is illicit or at least challengeable in audit.'

'These are all just small, random examples of criteria.'

'You can't use them all—you won't be able to turn your files around fast enough.'

'Some teams examine each file in the context of the two prior years' returns. These are called interval terms. The point is to look for large dips in income or spikes in deductions.'

'Intuition plays a part. You can tell something's off. You can justify taking extra time on a file.'

'This is the great advantage of human examiners. Intuition, creativity.'

'Some people have a special talent for smelling a rat.'

'Guessing doesn't account for the nets of certain great examiners, some of whom are at this Post—'

'A rat that's worth pursuing.'

§28

10 Laws of IRS Personnel

All GS-9 Examiners want to be GS-11 Examiners. All GS-11 Examiners want to be Auditors. All Collections want to be CID. All Auditors want to be Appeals Officers or Supervisors. All Supervisors want to be Group Managers. All CIDs want to be almost anything that doesn't involve site surveillance. Some Appeals Officers want to be Group Managers. All Group Managers want to be Deputy District Directors, or else they dream of being Examiners again, alone at a desk with no one to bother you. All Deputy District Directors want to be District Directors — it's the ones who tell you they don't to watch out for. Some District Directors

want to be DRECs or DRSCs or Regional Commissioners, but all these are political appointments, and the best the District Director can do is
make their District's output look really good and
hope someone notices. Output is the ratio of collected tax to District expenses. It's the District's
net profit. The Service code is very simple as the
DDDs say as they circle the DD, plotting: Output
or Kaput; Supply or Die; Revenue or Au Revoir.
Au Revoir almost always means backwater
postings.

§29

'I only have one real story about shit. But it's a doozy.'

'Why shit?'

'What is it about shit? We're repelled but fascinated.'

'I'm not fascinated, I can tell you that.'

'It's like watching a car wreck, impossible to tear the eyes away.'

'My fourth-grade teacher had no eyelashes. Mrs. Something.'

'I mean I'm bored, too, but why shit?'

'My earliest memory of shit is dog shit. Remember as a kid how potent a presence and threat dog shit was? It seemed to be all over. Every time you played outside, somebody was stepping in it, and then everything stopped and it was like, "OK, who stepped in it?" Everybody has to check their shoes, and sure enough somebody had it on their shoe.'

'Embedded in the sole. In the pattern.'

'Impossible to scrape off.'

'New was always wet and yellow and horrible, the most horrible. But old got embedded more deeply in the sole. You had to set the shoes aside until it dried and then try to scrape out the sole's pattern with a stick or a rusty old knife out of the garage.'

'What time is it?'

'What are we supposed to see in all this? Somebody could go right by.'

'But it never got all the way out. Scrape and scrape. You'd have to try and run the sole under the faucet and wet it then and try to scrape out the rest.'

'The garage always had old butter knives, coffee cans full of screws and nails and little metal doodads that nobody ever even knew the function of.'

'And whoever had it on their shoe, it was discovered, then that person had some kind of terrible power.'

'Nobody'd have anything to do with him until he got it out.'

'Instant butt. Odd man out.'

'Like it was ever his fault if you were all playing football or at recess or whatever and somebody had the random misfortune to step in it. Suddenly it wasn't that he'd stepped in shit so much as *become* shit.'

'The way the cruelty in a group of kids swirls and shifts, at any moment you become the target, everybody constantly shifting for position all the time—now you're the one being cruel, now you're the target of someone else's cruelty.'

'And nothing like peeing or pooping your pants in a group playing baseball or kick the can or whatever out of excitement or a reluctance to leave the game even for a moment to turn you into the target of everyone's scorn and ridicule. Forever after you were the kid who shit his pants playing kick the can and it took only a few tackles for everyone to know it was you and it could be years later, it could be your junior prom, and everybody still knew you as the kid who shit his pants in 1961.'

No one said anything. The spools' turning was the only sound. The fog made the streetlights ghostly. This was the fourth hour of a third-shift CID Surveillance on Peoria Hobby 'n Coin. There was no wind; the fog just hung there.

'But a terrible power, too, as a kid, to have come into contact with shit—you were the butt, but you could repel people just by coming at them with the part that had contacted the shit; you could make them run screaming.'

The two agents who were younger had sunglasses folded and clipped to their shirts' necks by one arm.

'Kids' obsession with shit and dog shit and coming into contact with shit has to be connected to toilet training and their own infancy, which at this age isn't that far behind them.'

'It might have been third grade. We took a long time figuring it out, what made her eyes look piggy like that. No eyelashes. She had hair, head-hair, and eyebrows, but her eyes were piggy and lashless and blue.'

As much as two minutes elapsed between each remark, sometimes. It was 2:10 and even the agents' small personal movements were languid and underwater.

'Which if you think about it remember in high school when guys got together the whole thing was insulting each other's mom and saying you'd had sex with their mom and how she wasn't any good and couldn't get enough? What do you suppose that was all about? The sexuality of everyone's mom becoming an issue just as everybody hits puberty.'

'My shit story. Hide-and-seek, gang of neighborhood kids, twilight. I'm running for home base and trip over decorative logs somebody bordered his driveway with and went flying and put my hands out to like shield the impact and what do you suppose happens.'

'No.'

'Yes. Both hands first into a big new yellow steamer. Which I can still almost smell.'

'Jesus not even on the shoes but the hands. The personal skin.'

'You bet. I have maybe a dozen vivid, seared-in memories of early childhood, this is one of them. The feeling, the color, the dispersal, the rising smell. I howled, screamed, and everyone of course comes running, and as soon as they see it *they're* screaming and 180ing and running from me, and I'm both crying and roaring like some kind of horrible shit-monster and chasing after them, horrified and repulsed but also somehow underneath it all glorious in my role as monster, with the ability to make them all scream in terror and run for home where everybody's porch lights are just starting to come on and the little fake lamps by their driveways are on automatic timers; it's that time of day.'

'The hands being especially close to your idea of your identity of who you are, adding to the horror. Exceeded only by the face in terms of closeness, maybe.'

'There was no dog shit on my face. I held my arms out straight in front of me in order to like hold my hands as far out away from me as was humanly possible.'

'That only added to the monster-aspect. Monsters almost always hold their arms out straight in front of them as they chase you. I would have run like hell.'

'They did. I remember on one hand I was both screaming in horror just like they were and on the other I was roaring with monstrousness as I'd chase first one and then sort of peel off to chase somebody else. There were cicadas in the trees and they were all screaming in rhythm and somebody's radio was on through an open window. I remember the smell coming off my hands and how they didn't look like my hands anymore at all and feeling like how was I going to open the door without getting shit on it or even if I rang the bell. There'd be shit on my parents' doorbell.'

'What'd you do?'

'Jesus, what'd your *mom* do? Did she scream? Did you stand outside moaning and kicking the door and trying to ring the bell with your elbow?'

'Our house had a knocker. I would have been screwed.'

'I bet some of the other kids were in their houses cracking the curtains to look out the front window at you like staggering around moaning from house to house with your hands out straight like Frankenstein.'

'It's not like a shoe which you can just take off.'

'I've got a story about shit, but it's not pretty.'

'I don't remember. The memory ends with the shit and my hands and trying to chase everybody, which is odd, because up to then the memory is extraordinarily clear. Then it just stops and I don't know what happened.'

'I'm assuming I haven't talked before about running around with this odd gang of guys at Bradley and the strange thing we got into junior year of breaking into people's dorm rooms and holding them down while Fat Marcus the Money-lender sat on their face.'

'I think I would have remembered.'

'This was at Bradley; you know the weird shit you get into. There were five or six of us and this senseless thing got started where it was a tradition to cruise the freshman dorms at about four in the morning and find an unlocked door and all burst in and we'd all hold the guy in bed down and Fat Marcus the Moneylender would take his pants down and sit on his face.'

' . . '

'There was no reason to it. We just thought it was a gas.'

'Fat Marcus the Moneylender?'

'An enormous guy from the Chicago suburbs. Morbidly enormous. Always had cash and lent it out and kept his accounts in a small special ledger. Very careful bookkeeper, could compound daily without a calculator. Never even just Fat Marcus, it was always "the Moneylender." He was a Jew but I don't think that had anything to do with it. It was how he put himself through school after his parents had cut him off—this wasn't his first school but I don't remember his background too good.'

'Why the sitting on people's face?'

'The weirdness of it was the charm. That's all I can tell you. It was just something we started doing. I get a strange feeling even just thinking about how to describe it.'

'What did the guy in bed do?'

'The guy in the bed was not a happy camper, I can tell you that much. It would all happen real

fast where we'd all just burst in and be on the guy
before he was even awake. We'd each grasp
an extremity and quick as shit Fat Marcus the
Moneylender'd have his pants down and sit on
the guy's face and stay there just long enough
where the kid in the bed didn't smother. Then
we'd be out of there just as fast as we came in. That
was part of the whole point, so the guy in the bed
probably didn't even know if it was real or a nightmare or what the hell it was.'

They weren't far off the Sticky; the fog was a
storm coming in off the river. The very air was at
attention. Two ledge-chested older women were
peering in the window of the coin shop.

They all had unconscious habits of which
maybe only Hurd, as the new one, was fully aware.
Agent Lumm's habit on surveillance was in a blank
absent way to use his front teeth to peel a tiny fragment of dead skin from his lip and put it on the tip
of his tongue and gently blow it out his mouth to
land somewhere invisible. He was wholly unaware
that he did this, Hurd could tell. Gaines blinked
slowly in a stony mindless way that reminded
Hurd of a lizard whose rock wasn't hot enough.
Todd Miller wore a corduroy coat with a sheep-
skin collar and bunched and unbunched his left
sleeve; Bondurant stared at a point between his

shoes on the van's rug as if it were a chasm. It seemed staggering to Hurd that no one smoked. He himself was an endless catalogue of tics and fidgets.

One probationary agent whose sunglasses hung from his collar wore twelve-hole Doc Martens whose holes Hurd had counted several times.

'How does Marcus the Moneylender pull his pants back up while you all are running out?'

A long silence ensued while Bondurant gave Gaines a prison-yard stare. Gaines said, 'You ever try to get dressed while you're running? Can't be done.'

'The guy thinking it might have been a dream until that is he gets up to shave and sees his nose squished flat and a big ass-imprint on his face.'

'Did he scream?'

'In a muffled way they all screamed. Of course they screamed. But the thing that was making them scream was also the thing that muffled the scream.'

'Some fat man's ass coming down and covering their face.'

'Speed and quiet were the essence of the operation, and this was important because this was breaking in and assault of a sort, and Fat Marcus had already been expelled from at least one place, and none of us were what you might call on the Dean's List, and let's don't forget this was 1971 and the draft board was just about standing at the front gate waiting for you if you got kicked out.'

'This is why Bondurant was in the war. In The Nam.'

'I was a G-2 bookkeeper in Saigon, dickhead. That's not The Nam.'

'But you're saying this is what got you drafted? Assaulting freshmen with a big Jew's ass?'

'I'm saying it was just something that started happening and that we pulled off numerous operations all up and down the underclass dorms with a hundred percent operational success until the day the door we found open belongs to this kid, *Diablo,* that everybody called Diablo the Left-Handed Surrealist, this Puerto Rican mural-painter scholarship from Indianapolis that was crazy, that for example lost his student-aid job in the faculty dining hall because one day he came in on what we're pretty sure was acid and set all the place settings at everybody's place with all knives, and saw visions and painted these spiky fluorescent Catholic murals on walls on warehouses down by the river, and was crazy—Diablo the Left-Handed Surrealist.'

'Didn't anybody at your school ever have names like Joe or Bill?'

'That for the most part nobody ever messed with because he was crazy as a fucking mudbug, this little hundred-pound spic kid from some Indianapolis barrio, but by this time the operation was a finely honed mechanism built for speed, that plus nobody even placed who it was until we'd all bursted in and deployed around the bed. I had the left ankle I remember, and Fat Marcus was up on the bed undoing his belt and getting his feet distributed on either side of what was usually the guy's pillow except this kid didn't use a pillow or even sheets; it was just the bare dorm mattress with those stripes on them.'

The only truly fat person Gestine Hurd had ever known had been a Special Examination GS-9 in the Oneida Post who'd spent the entire two years Hurd knew of him back-auditing an Oneida firm so tiny and specialized that it made nothing but the corrugated dividers that went into the cardboard boxes used to ship a very particular kind of tiny lightbulb that went into tiny brass lamps that clicked onto the top of frames that display-quality paintings in historical homes and country restaurants often hang in.

'Which should have alerted us to trouble, plus

the fact that Diablo the Left-Handed Surrealist
seemed already awake when we boomed the door
and didn't sit up or yelp or rub his eyes or thrash
around or struggle when we all came booming in
and each grabbed us an extremity and Fat Marcus
the Moneylender got up on the bed and commenced to lowering his gargantuan white ass
down to his face; he just laid there very still with
his eyes glittering with Latin cunning and all-
around craziness. You didn't even want to know
the decor, what-all was on the walls; if the operation's total surreal speed had allowed it, if we'd
paid one bit of attention to the room or the expression on the kid's face on the mattress we could of
stopped and reconnoitered and saved us all a lot of
trouble and got to stay in school and not have to
spend a fucking year in Saigon learning requisition-
write-up accounting. Which I wouldn't wish on
a dog.'

The spools turned slowly with a slight triple
hiss. The IRS agents' expressions were those of
Cub Scouts around a Storytime fire. A quick bob
in the entry's mike's tape went unremarked.

'Waited until Fat Marcus the Moneylender's ass
was right down next to him, touching his face but
not with the full weight of the ass on him yet, and
jerked up and bit into Fat Marcus's ass. And I'm

not talking a lover-nip here, I'm talking a full front Doberman-type sinking of his whole frontal set of teeth into the buttock arc of Marcus's ass, so that even down by his ankle I could see blood going down the Surrealist's chin and see Fat Marcus the Moneylender's ass flexing as he reared back and let out a scream that made the windows shiver and knocked the two guys holding Diablo the Left-Handed Surrealist's shoulders back against the row of no-eye masks the spic's got on his wall that all fell and made a racket and could see the horrible thing of this unbelievably obese guy rearing back and up and trying with all his weight to get his ass out of the teeth of Diablo the Left-Handed Surrealist, who gentlemen just let me say wasn't letting go, the kid was a Gila monster, even as Fat Marcus had both hands hooked in the kid's nose's nostrils trying to peel him off his ass and Fat Marcus's main stooge Marvin "the Stooge" Flotkoetter actually bent in and was biting Diablo the Left-Handed Surrealist's ear and cheek, trying to make him let go, and both him and Diablo were growling and Diablo was shaking his head trying to tear the mouthful of ass clear out of Fat Marcus's ass and his nose and ear were bleeding and blood was just shooting I mean *arterially* shooting in all directions out of Marcus's ass and into the mattress

and his pants and Fat Marcus took a shit in fear
and pain and his screams brought everybody in
pajamas and underwear and pimple cream and
retainers to the still-open door, looking in at what
looked of course later though none of us realized it
at the time like a prison-type gang-type sexual
assault gone wrong.'

§30

'The Deputy DD's a man-of-the-people type. But very much Glendenning's boy. 907313433, a full CPA, Sheehan is, a GS-13, nine years in. He was auditing out of District 10 in Chicago before he got the degree. Came over with Glendenning. Kind of Glendenning's hatchet man, very hail-fellow, let's all be friends, all smiles but the eyes go right through you. Liaisons with Internal. Not well-liked. Plus a fashion-plate. Looks like the original seventies hipster almost. Very if you know what I mean mod.'

There were sounds of Reynolds doing something unrelated.

'Meaning you got the sideburns, the bell-bottoms, the pale blue workshirt. The little leather thong thing around the neck. The whole package.'

'Spare us the Mr. Blackwell, Claude.'

'Totally Glendenning's boy. But a serious 3-D in his own right. Performance Reviews all 8-plus. Nary a 7. Made GS-11 in '77 on an independent Promotion Board bid; Glendenning had nothing to do with it. But Glendenning's boy.'

'So he'll fight it?'

'He's an implementer. Admin was his choice; he applied. If things come down through channels he won't fight you. But he won't help you. He implements.'

'Glendenning's got a lot of boys in 047, from what you're saying.' The slight rise and rounding of Reynolds's voice indicated he was knotting his tie.

'Glendenning's got a high level of Group Manager support. Rosebury and Danmeyer in Exams and Quarterlies might have come with him, their periods in Syracuse overlapped, but the rest were here before Glendenning got the kick. Not yet clear how much of the support is political versus sincere, which would indicate how much of an operator Glendenning's been at 047. I haven't been able to squeeze even a private bad word on him out of anybody. Of course that could mean several things.'

'You don't have to tell us what things mean,' without heat. Reynolds's big gray Motorola had a violin's chin-cup welded on so he could hold it with his neck alone and free his hands, which whenever Sylvanshine tried this with his own he either forgot and moved his head wrong and the thing fell on the floor and broke and he had to spend time figuring out how to requisition his fourth field phone of the year or else it gave him a stabbing pain somewhere near his shoulder blade. He held a regular touch-tone phone with one hand and bit dead skin from the edge of his thumbnail while he turned sheets on the clipboard.

'Chaney has a picture of her and Glendenning up on her office wall if you can believe it.'

'Chaney.'

'Julia Drutt Chaney, forty-four, GS-10, 952678315, Administrative Supervisor for 047B across the complex. Big, big woman. Large. Stanton-sized in Philly if you recall her. As in muumuus. As in when you see her coming across the quad thing it looks like several women all cohabiting in just one garment. Big red cheeks. But nobody's fool, Performance—'

'We're only interested in 047B for Audits, and that's collateral.' Sylvanshine was trying to recall the name of his second-grade teacher, who stood at the terminus of a long chain of idle thought whose medial steps he'd already forgotten but which had started with the maneuvers by which Reynolds had arranged to stay in DC and Martinsburg for several weeks and to keep Mel Lehrl's ear by offering to analyze Sylvanshine's initial field reports and reduce them to relevant fact-patterns for Lehrl before eventually joining Claude in this horrible place after all his usual strategies were exhausted. 'Let's concentrate on the steak and not the peas here Claudie boy what do you say.' Jocularity was a tone Reynolds often used with subordinates or those of lower GS rank, and both he and Claude knew that Sylvanshine would be looking for a way to repay the insult. 'The steak is Examination.'

'ADD for Exams is Rosebury, Eugene E., forty, GS-13, 907313433, sandy hair, tall, a little stooped, glasses don't quite fit or else his ears aren't symmetrical, looks somehow scholarly but that might be the pipe, smokes a pipe, Glendenning's boy right down the spine. Don't like his hair, something about his hair. Implementer. Wind-sniffer. Neither help nor impede.'

'Second AD is Yeagle? Yagle?'

'Is Gary NMI Yeagle. Just-call-me-Gary type. Strange-looking specimen. Big heavy slabbish face, but a long jaw, but soft, the jaw, hanging with fat, which together with the lantern jaw makes you feel like somebody's hitting you with a melting fist when you look at him. Thirty-nine no, sorry, -eight, glad-hander but in a different way from Sheehan because Sheehan's glad-handing is professional and strategic whereas with Yeagle you feel it's that he's just insecure and needs everyone to like him or the world explodes or something.'

'Which'd make him a potential weak link.'

'The sort who's very shy and nervous around you but tries to be very bluff and hearty and outgoing but can't manage it and so it's excruciating for everyone. A jaw you could plow snow with.'

'So Yeagle might be one of our boys if we're going to fine-target Mel's efforts in the initial stages.'

'Plus eyebrows out to here. I kid you not. Tolkien-like eyebrows on a thirty-eight-year-old man. Very intense smile he feigns into trying to make it look like a wicked grin or grimace by drawing these incredible brows down. The sort that shakes your hand with both of his. A GS-13 but a Group Manager since second quarter '78, so he may have something on the ball but I haven't seen it. Not the sort of hard driver you'd expect from a Group Manager in an Exams Post.'

'Glendenning promoted him?'

'Yeagle's records are sketchy. You might have somebody there pull down Yeagle's whole file; his one here's sketchy that I could find.' Sylvanshine's thumb was bleeding slightly and he looked about him for something unimportant to blot it on. Both he and Reynolds knew how very very different the substance and form of Sylvanshine's report would be if he were speaking to Merrill Lehrl, and though there was no doubt that this irked Reynolds to some degree it in no way made up for the jocularity and its implication. They both knew accounts were not yet square. Sometimes Sylvanshine pictured himself and Reynolds as partners in a kind of courtly dance, very stately and prescribed, so that the tiniest variations were what communicated personality. 'He and Sheehan are mildly interesting counterpoints in glad-handing. Can't say I like either of them. Yeagle wore the same tie three days last week. Carries the pipe around with him even when it's not going. Something that might have been a condiment stain on the tie. Don't like him, that odd pendulous jaw. Saw him dab at a nostril with the back of his hand the other day.'

Throat-noise on the other end. Tiny bits of some conversation at the fringe of their bandwidth were audible in silences; they made Sylvanshine think of strands of hair in a dusty brush. The sink was piled with dishes and half-full cartons of Chinese take-out he'd sworn to himself he'd clean up two days ago; looking at the sink made it hard to inhale.

'Tell Mel the best I can do is indications. Yeagle not yet a known quantity. Seems ineffectual, but that may be part of some larger strategic presentation. Recommend an Informal soonest after Mel gets in — loosen him up, get him talking. Possible. That's as far out on the limb as I can go with Call Me Gary at this point.'

'Anything re Glendenning himself yet then?'

'Haven't gotten in to see him. Busy guy. Constant motion. Seems purposefully busy instead of ineffectually or flailingly busy, which if it's true it's worth noting for Mel.'

'Thanks.'

Not the thumb exactly, but it was true that Sylvanshine was now sucking the edge of his thumb. 'Seen him in the halls of what-was-it, whatever building his and Sheehan's offices are in. Disorienting place, the photos don't do it justice for sheer podular confusion. Looks more like a small college or community college campus than anything. You do know my father taught at a community college.'

'So when you saw Glendenning in these unre-called halls then...'

'Not much thus far. Tall silvery guy. Silver hair rigidly parted. The sort of older man you'd say "distinguished" or "formerly handsome." Medium-tallish I'd say. Nose looked a bit big but that was in moving profile.'

'Hey Claude, seriously, is there some process by which you decide I want to hear aesthetic apprais-als? Is there reasoning by which somewhere inside you decide this is useful data to have in Mel's head when he starts working with these people? Don't strain now, but think about it and sometime tell me the process by which you decide I have to wait through incidentals on dress and carriage before I hear material that's going to help me do my job here.'

'*Your* job, is the point. Boil it down. Reduce to fact-pattern, relevance. My job's the raw data. Do I recall right? Was I the one who asked for the field first? Am I confused?'

But the distressed sounds were only Reynolds trying to get under the knot with his fingers to do the top button, which he had always had trouble with. Sylvanshine waited the normal interval look-ing at his thumb and trying to see if he could taste any actual blood—which taste always made him think of touching a nine-volt to his tongue as a kid but the exact association evaded him—and listened to at least try to identify the gender of the ghostly conversation on the line, and finally said:

'Though his secretary—one of them, he seems to have two though one might be an Admin or liaison with the Group Managers—sent a memo, it's in Mel's in-box, Welcome and heard some fine things from Henzke re the skill of the turnaround at 0104—that's Philly Collections, the Auto—'

'You have to tell me that, I wasn't there?'

'—Henzke re the Collections turnaround at Philly, etc., please call Mrs. Oooley—that's the head secretary—Mrs. Oooley soonest on your arrival and processing—'

'What's that supposed to mean? He has to go through orientation like some turdnagel?'

'I don't have it, it's still in Mel's box, which by the way it's a good in-box, same size and same row as the ADDs' and over the GM's although it's got Mel's name on tape over some other fellow's name but that doesn't necessarily mean anything unless it's still like that when he comes. And I've got SS putting his name on his door in that one building; I gave them the stencil personally tell him, and told them about the elevator thing so it's on the ground floor. Tell him the door's locked and the window outside's locked and you can't see through but from the distance of the doors on either side tell him it seems spacious. Unfortunately nearest loo's third floor; have him advise if we want to risk making a fuss about that, but it's corner just as requested. No boiling down there, you know he'll want that. Tell him the doors on either side are 15 and 16.4 and change, respectively, which is almost Philly-sized.'

'You let them see you using a tape measure on the surrounding doors?'

'Don't be a maroon. I've got a front door key already and keys to two of the remaining four. At night before returning to field-quarters you and I need to have a good long talk about before you see it and get your shorts in a tangle. Angler's Cove apartment complex. Enough said? Makes the first Rome apartment look lavish, to give you an—'

'The memo was from the secretary or from Glendenning personally you're saying.'

'The bad news is it's not in the main building, where Glendenning and the DDs' officers are, whatever it's called. They've got an odd nomenclature for facilities here just like Chicago.'

'This is still Mel's office you're talking about.'

'I'm going right down my notes just as field protocol you might recall states and the way you did in Rome. I'm afraid it's in the outbuilding where they do the Corporates; it's also got the UNIVAC in there. The building's a bit of a madhouse I'm afraid. The first floor where all the offices for the keypunch people are. You just need to get Mel ready for this so he doesn't come and see where they put him and start shitting little green men about it.'

'And you may recall initial field-briefing calls are to be ten to twelve minutes, if you've memorized the protocol.' Sylvanshine knew just what Reynolds was doing physically at this minute but he couldn't think of what the right word for it was, even to himself. Nor was he talking about losing his license in the bank's drive-through yesterday, which really when you came down to it might be Merrill Errol Lehrl's concern but was not Reynolds's concern by any stretch of the imagination, though he knew what he'd say. Sometimes Sylvanshine's thumbnails had funny little white calciumoid lines in them, sometimes they didn't. He worried about it at odd moments, what the lines signified. Not adjusting, *smoothing, smoothing* his tie, which if it was Saturday would be either the light green or the light blue with the little red lozenge shapes in it, both of which were faux silk and butt-smooth at all times anyway. It was an unconscious gesture Reynolds had, and worked as a tell in cards, and Sylvanshine had sacrificed all sorts of opportunities to score off bringing it to Reynolds's attention because he didn't want Reynolds conscious of his unconscious gestures in any way, since reading them equaled power. In Martinsburg Sylvanshine had the bigger bedroom because the lease was in his name, but in field-quarters Reynolds always got the bigger room. This time, Angler's Cove's squalor aside, the bedrooms were exactly the same size, the door-distance wasn't the only thing Claude had measured, and he knew what Reynolds's face would do when he saw. Merrill Errol Lehrl always arranged his own quarters.

'Glendenning himself sent the memo, or the secretary?'

Sylvanshine held the thumb flat and got the overhead light on it and turned it this way and that. 'You would not believe how hot it is here. And muggy. The air's like somebody breathing right in your face. Philly on its worst summer day doesn't equal. 047's drinking fountains aren't refrigerated; they're low white toilet-porcelain fountains like some elementary school and the water's room temperature, which is to say hot.'

Reynolds exhaled so the phone transmitted the sound. 'I apologize for the tone, Claude.'

'What tone?'

'All right? Happy now?'

'You overestimate me, friend.'

'And yes, I am your friend. We're a team. I shouldn't have squeezed your shoes with the underling-tone like I did. It's high-pressure this week. I've had the same tension headache all week. I don't feel well at all. And none of that's an excuse, and I really am apologizing.'

If there were lines they weren't visible. 'Secretary or head secretary sent it I'm afraid. Oooley, Carolyn or Caroline maybe. File not located, it's not on the Support router. Crisp little woman, dry tight little face. Sweater over her shoulders like a cape. Main building's air-conditioned out the wazoo; that's where Exams is, so tell Mel the good news is the work environment itself is AC'd already although no halon, but the VAX room's haloned so we can assume SS has the wherewithal; if you want I'll call and—'

'So the memo was from the secretary, not Glendenning himself.'

'I'd urge Mel not to read anything into that. Glendenning's been gone two days out of three. He's been up to Region twice since last Wednesday.'

'He's running to Region a lot already? You wait

till now to include this and when you do it's an aside on the secretary's sweater?'

'From the way they approach her desk she's formidable, Oooley. You know how it is in the provinces. She may dominate Glendenning; she may be the real link. Small picture of a cat on her desk, but no visible cat hair on the sweater. Odd. And glasses on a little chain around her neck, those old-fashioned little silvery chains, what's the word. Potentially a formidable part of the equation. So far I've asked after the cat and given her a flower someone was selling on the median of the big road out here. To this comatose town. Tell Mel I'm working her already.' He didn't tell Reynolds there'd been no sign of the flower on her desk the next day.

Letting Sylvanshine hear him breathe again — 'And did the memo specifically say heard good things from Henzke, from Bill, or from Bill Henzke?'

'Just Henzke.'

'Damn.'

'Other secretary or liaison or whatever's been gone. Supposedly young and the District knock-out, two separate Collections fellows told me it's worth cooking up fallacious business and coming when Oooley's at lunch just for the full-frontal view.'

'I already apologized, Claude.'

'Rosebury's secretary's a big sheet-white woman named Bernays. Looks the ghost of a draft horse.'

Each Motorola mobile phone cost the Service $349 as opposed to the $380 retail and looked like an enormous walkie-talkie and weighed over two pounds and was something someone as dapper and diminutive as Reynolds Jensen Jr. looked a little silly holding.

'So. Let's sketch the week then.' Reynolds would be able to tell Dr. Lehrl they'd talked and he'd tried if what came next week wasn't what he wanted. Watching Reynolds try to maneuver politically was like watching a lumberjack dance, Harold Adny'd said. 'Need cogent relevant say again cogent relevant bios, Personnel data, evals, and impressions for Examinations by the seventeenth. This is the protocol I'm reading. The crew is what? There's Rosebury in Admin, there's this Yeagle as GM — group size is what, twenty? Exam budget's 2.4 times the size of Rome's, right, so what, twenty-two?'

'Twenty-four, maybe -five. There are some kind of unorthodox split-shift arrangements I haven't gotten a fact-pattern on yet, that Glendenning apparently vetted. Glendenning's done a lot of custom-tailoring of Exams which of course we can anticipate this will intensify. Say twenty-four to twenty-six, which doubles with then another whole twenty doing punch and sort work on cards during the Storm, though word is Glendenning's fought hard for Service personnel instead of Storm part-timers, which is understandable given the town; it's not like there's a sharp talent pool out there out here.'

'That's nice data. That's cogent.'

'Say twenty-six. Contact's been tough.'

'Guarded are they?'

'More like stupefied. They're full-timers. Glazed. What's the other word. Average burn here's three years. Obtundated is the word. Oh' — Sylvanshine winced at forgetting this before — 'and the big one's that Glendenning's first big move on arrival was the elimination of first-years on Exams.'

'You're kidding.' By Service custom, graduates of the three national IRS Training Centers spent their first years assigned to Examinations, which was the most brutal and unpopular assignment in the Service. A percentage then hurried to pass their certified exams, since a GS-11 revenue agent must have a CPA, and Audits was the natural promotion out of Exams. That Glendenning had eschewed first-years in his Exams branch indicated something important, though neither of them was sure quite what. It was so important Reynolds didn't even take time to squeeze Sylvanshine's shoes for waiting till now to tell him. 'Mel you know is going to want follow-up. Move that immediately to number one on next week's protocol.'

'I provisionally agree.'

'Glad you agree.'

'Glad you're glad.'

'Outstanding.'

'Though this is pending the rest of the report, as when I get to flows and outputs.'

'Outstanding. What's the flow look like then?'

'First individual Exams is one room, couple dozen desks plus Yeagle's little frosted cubicle thing. Either the room's symmetries are off or there are rough divisions—might be one section of 1040, one of 1040A, a smaller one for Fats the way Keene was. There's a Corporate branch that's a whole separate room.'

'If Corporate changes over it won't be till after, they've run the experiment with the DIF so—'

'Hence my not mentioning it.'

'If you're cozy with Glendenning's dry-skin lady then you must have a line on the specs.'

'The specs are a mess. They're not even on cards. They use old 904 forms I haven't seen since the Training Center.'

'Huge surprise.'

'They're all in horrible old dark-green cabinets in a basement complex even spiders would be hesitant to go into.'

'But you boldly went down there with a flashlight, you want Mel to know.'

'Today or tomorrow I have to get somebody in Martinsburg to input them and tabulate the mean values; the spec forms are a mess because the work's so periodic. Underline for Mel that they get returns from both Region *and* the St. Louis SC with no set procedures or even rhythms that I can see.'

'The trucks just back up and unload the returns you're saying.'

'So what I've got pending tabs—this is going to look very strange—is for the last six months a total 1,829 returns go through 047's Exams branch per month, but that figure includes everything from individual EZs to nightmare Fats with twenty schedules each to EST-reconciliations that Rosebury lets Danmeyer hit them with in nightmarish waves quarterly.'

'This is not broken down in a way that tells me anything, Claudie.'

'It's when you get here you're going to see why. It's Dickensian. There's one UNIVAC terminal in the room. The kicks from Martinsburg come round on big carts pushed by cart boys like they had, then the results get slid down slides two levels down where the keypunch girls prepare the kicks back for Region and Collections. And/or Collections. And the examiners are operating with pencils and NCR adding machines some of which still have I Like Ike and the ilk stickers on them. They've got those angled trays or drawer things coming in at their desks from all angles like those pictures of Philly Mel had in the nightmare days. Here they get standard kicks from Martinsburg, plus ESTs, plus exam requests from CID. They do Fats that St. Louis doesn't even bother to open they're so fat. They do contract work for Corporate Audits when a CA goes multiyear. The whole thing's almost Philly-grade, tell him. But this—'

'1,829 by 26 by 22 workdays is what, three a day?'

'3.198 a day by nine-hour shifts minus lunch minus Region average 45.6 minutes for breaks which I've got as seven hours 29.4 minutes so 3.2 over 7.5 is .4266 repeating 6 returns per man-hour, which for the Region is so totally average that—'

'So it's neither here nor there, as a productivity stat, which hurts our case with Glendenning maybe but also makes 047 Exams a fine test case.'

'No, Reynolds. I mean *totally* average. The

average for Region 4 for '82, '83, and the part of '84 Internal's got loads for—get this—is .42 repeating 6 returns per man-hour.'

'They're *exactly* average?'

'And anticipating just that reaction please tell Mel I checked this twice. All off cards, flowthrough totals, performance reviews, utilizations specs. .42 repeating 6. As if—'

'As if Glendenning and Rosebury and/or this Yeagle character were somehow cooking the Output books to produce an output so totally average that no one would ever suspect them of cooking the Output books.'

'I'll check it again if you like if you'll let me take just one moment here to discuss the apartment's water pressure and a commode with the single laziest flush I've seen in twelve US—'

The tone now was of Reynolds Jensen Jr. 100 percent focused, intent, which meant that whether sitting or standing he was bent slightly forward at the waist and not blinking at all. 'Do. Check. He'll want you to, you—or as if somehow Glendenning's been able to structure manpower and flow and morale in just such a way that he gets precisely the average out of Exams.'

'Meaning if and when he wants it to go up he just waves his wand and presto.'

'Could he be that good?'

'It would make him and/or the team of him and Rosebury a genius, a Mozart of production, whose management methods, if quantified and taught or if the other District Directors convinced DC it could be taught—'

'Could kill the project.'

'Especially if you could see these examiners. This is not an elite force, Reynolds. Not one over a GS-11 paygrade. Tics, spasms, eccentricities. Trembling hands. They're all in the men's room brushing their teeth after lunch. Whole lot of brushing going on. One has a violin on his desk. No reason. Just a violin. Another has a Doberman hand puppet on his hand without the rubber, which he talks to.'

'These should all be notated, Claudie.'

'These are shells of men I'm saying. If Glendenning can get any throughput he wants out of *this* crew...Some look catatonic. One might be an idiot savant. I haven't seen him yet.'

'None of which has to do with throughput.'

'And have I mentioned the wind out here? The sound it makes through cracks near the windows? Or the heat? Or the enormous mass of these tiny cruciform rural towns with exactly one intersection that appear to consist entirely of a grain silo and a gas station with names like Arrowsmith, Anthony, Shirley, Tolono, Stayne? There's a town called Big Thistle near here. Repeat: Big Thistle, Illinois. Hey, let's us go over to the Big Thistle Diner and snap Fanny's girdle. And the humidity. Towels don't dry; your windshield gets condensation like a glass of iced tea if you run the AC on the way in. The sky the color of motel ice—no color, no depth. It's like a bad dream. And the flatness. What's the horizon at sea level, eighteen miles?'

'Let's stay on task, Claudie.'

'He's posted me to the second dimension, R.J.'

'You were doing so well, Claudie.'

'And what if I said I miss you?'

'We're not going to get into this, not—'

'Because you know the way someone really old's eyes look, with cataracts? That milky spooky anybody-home quality? Imagine a whole face like that. Philly was frenzy. This is a kind of caul of boredom. Boredom past boredom. These examiners, most—'

'You realize this is good news in a way.'

'Well it's not good to look at, I can certainly—'

'Has any of the demo equipment arrived?'

'Glendenning's letting them personalize their desks. Listen to music if they—not smoke at their desks, but get this: A couple of them *chew tobacco* at their desks.'

'Where are we in terms of profiles of the actual hardware then?'

'Have you by chance ever actually *seen* an in-use spittoon, Reynolds, because I cer —'

'I miss you, too, Claude. Happy now?'

Once he'd chewed it so badly it got infected, which made it taste just awful. 'I haven't done a list per se as such yet.'

'What should I tell Mel?'

'That I've been here only a week and am under terrific duress from the primitiveness of the field-quarters, lack of contact vectors, and numbing heat. Tell Mel that.'

'Aren't we brave in absentia.'

'As you may recall the real hardware's over with Corporate in the out-site, and except for verifying Mel's facilities I've been lurking in Exams. Per specs I believe.'

'I wasn't squeezing, Claudie. Let's just get through this. I have a nasty commute ahead of me.'

'I have so far seen a Sperry UNIVAC 3- or 4000-series mainframe with terminals apparently all at Corporate. I've seen two IBM 5486 card sorters and have deduced the presence of related 5000-series keypunch and collating equipment.'

'And ninety-six-column cards for the IBMs.'

'Except UNIVACs still use the eighty-. They've apparently got something jerry-rigged to mix the two.'

'So the examiners are all hexadecimal-proficient, or is that the punch-girls? But the punch-girls are locals, no?'

'I don't have a training protocol yet. We can assume they're natural-language-translated for temps during March to May, yes?'

'Even Rome didn't mix ninety-six and eighties.'

'This is the provinces, I've been telling you. Mel's office is right down from the Central, which I deduce is a complete mutt of different systems. I've seen a Burroughs 1005 calculator-printer.'

'Does Burroughs even use cards anymore?'

'Burroughs work off tape since the 900 series. I've told you. The whole thing's a mutt. A garage sale. I've seen two IBM RPGs in a closet with an unbelievable tangle of co-ax leading up to a ragged and sub-code hole in the closet's ceiling, presumably meant to compatibilize the RPGs with the UNIVAC. It's all very ancient and scuzzy and I wouldn't be terribly surprised if there were monkeys with abacuses and string inside.'

'This is very good news. And their assembler's COBOL?'

'Unknown at this juncture.'

'We've got good news on the hardware front.'

'And if anything's arrived from DC then SS here isn't aware of it.'

'So it could just be sitting on the loading dock?'

'So I'm to be in Records with a flashlight in my teeth, on the horn to Martinsburg getting flowthrough analyses, probing Glendenning's No-First-Year implementation, inventorying the hardware, and cabbaging keys to get a firsthand at Mel's office all at once? Oh, and on the loading dock quizzing burly men on whether any of the boxes are from Martinsburg.'

'All I'm doing is lining up a protocol for next week's field-, Claudie.'

'What am I, a machine?'

§31

Shinn was long-bodied and had very light baby-fine blond hair that hung in bangs like an early Beatle's. The man seated next to him in the IRS van had exited Angler's Cove with several others as they all stood at the curb in the pastel dawn and waited for the van. The sweet wet heavy air of summer dawns. The men with Service nametags all knew each other and spoke among themselves. Some drank from mugs or smoked cigarettes they ground out against the curb as the van came into view. One had sideburns and a cowboy hat, which now in the van he'd removed two rows of bench seats up. Some read the paper. Some of the men in the van were as old as maybe fifty. The windows tilted out rather than rolling down; it was an odd vehicle, more like a small boxy truck that had bench seats welded in.

The van stopped at two other apartment complexes along Self-Storage Parkway; at one of these it idled for several minutes, apparently dilating time for a schedule. Shinn wore a powder-blue dress shirt. A conversation behind him featured someone telling someone else that if you cut a small notch in the center of your toenail's edge, it won't ingrow. Someone else yawned loudly and gave little shivers. The man next to Shinn, their hams touching with varied pressure as the van swung slightly side to side on a loose suspension, was reading an IRM supplemental pamphlet whose title Shinn could not see because the guy was one of those people who folded pamphlets back into a single square to read them. He had a small backpack in his lap. Shinn considered introducing himself; he wasn't sure what the etiquette called for.

Shinn had stood at the curb drinking his first Coke of his first day at the Post and felt his clothes unwrinkle and sag slightly in the humidity, smelling the same honeysuckle and cut grass as suburban Chicago, listening to the songs of dawn-stirred birds in the locust trees along Self-Storage, and his thoughts had drifted all over the place, and suddenly it occurred that the birds, whose twitters and repeated songs sounded so pretty and affirming of nature and the coming day, might actually, in a code known only to other birds, be the birds each saying 'Get away' or 'This branch is mine!' or 'This tree is mine! I'll kill you! Kill, kill!' Or any manner of dark, brutal, or self-protective stuff—they might be listening to war cries. The thought came from nowhere and made his spirits dip for some reason.

§32

'Don't ask me to do this.'

I switched my live-in sister Julie over to the speaker while she was still trying to get out of doing it. We were all in my part of the cubicle. I was sitting at my workstation and they were standing around it. 'I told them and they don't believe it. In the uncanny accuracy of it, that I keep trying to describe but I can't do it justice, especially this fellow here Jon whom I've been telling you about.' I was looking over at Soane as I persuaded her. Julie is my sister. Her voice sounded less like her own voice on the speaker — it had that tinny, desiccated quality. Steve Mead always wore a counter's rubber on his right pinkie. The constant ripping metallic dental sound of a printer came from

647

the Audit Room nearest the cubicle, a sound that set all our teeth on the edge when the printer ran. Steve Mead, Steve Dalhart, Jane Brown, and Likourgos Vassiliou were all standing around the speaker in my part of the cubicle, while Soane had rolled his chair back slightly from his own workstation to be included in the circle.

'I can't do it on demand. I feel stupid; don't make me,' Julie stated.

'Who this morning bought you three scrunchies when all you asked for was one?' I said, making a circle of affirmation with my thumb and finger and holding it up to the others.

There was silence from my younger sister's end of the phone.

'I already told them some of the effect will be lost on the phone. Without the eyes and face. Pressure's off, nobody's expecting perfection.'

'"What an excellent day for an exorcism, Father."'

Even on the speaker. Steve Mead visibly started. I had an urge to giggle and bite my knuckle in delight. Dalhart and Jane Brown were looking at each other and they let their bodies sag and lengthen a little to indicate how astounded they were.

'"Your mother sucks cocks in hell!"' Julie said, doing it.

'Astounding, Nugent.'

'My God' and 'It's uncanny,' Steve Mead said. He is always extremely pale and ill-looking. A Phillips screw was coming partway out of one of the supports at the back of Soane's chair's back support area. The ripping sound of the printer continued to set everyone's teeth on the edge.

Dale Gastine and Alice Pihl, who always conduct audits as a team, put their heads over the top of the cubicle to see what was going on.

'You should see the face if you could. She rolls her eyes all the way up and turns pale and puffs her cheeks out and it — she doesn't look like her at all until she does, then it's uncanny.' I said this. Soane, who is extremely cool and laid-back at all times, was doing something to his cuticle with a paperclip out of the dispenser.

Julie's regular voice came through the speaker. I consider Jane Brown attractive, but I can tell that Soane does not. 'Are we done?'

'You should see. They're all standing here agog. I really appreciate this,' I said. Jane Brown always wears the same orange blazer. 'Goggle-eyed. My credibility here has soared thanks to you.'

'We're going to talk about this when you get home, buckaroo, believe you me.'

'But can she lower the room down to freezing and write *Help* with her skin like when she —'

'One more,' whispered Mead, who does farm audits and goes out to the counter when a taxpayer rings the assistance bell (whole days go by without a taxpayer coming in for assistance, however) and has a soft square face and looks like he either never has to shave or uses moisturizer.

I told Julie on the phone, 'One more and then you'll have acquitted yourself in your usual out-standing way.'

'You promise.'

Likourgos Vassiliou, who is also unusually pale, especially for an ethnic Mediterranean, said to Dale Gastine and Alice Pihl, 'This new man Nugent does not exaggerate; make a note out of this.'

'"Can you spare a quotter fran old altaboy, Fadda. Dimmy. Why you do this to me, Dimmy? Let Jesus fuck you, fuck you!"'

'I'm practically getting the shivers,' Mead stated.

'This is positively the last time,' Julie emphasized on the speaker.

§33

Lane Dean Jr. with his green rubber pinkie finger sat at his Tingle table in his Chalk's row in the Rotes Group's wiggle room and did two more returns, then another one, then flexed his buttocks and held to a count of ten and imagined a warm pretty beach with mellow surf as instructed in orientation the previous month. Then he did two more returns, checked the clock real quick, then two more, then bore down and did three in a row, then flexed and visualized and bore way down and did four without looking up once except to put the completed files and memos in the two Out trays side by side up in the top tier of trays where the cart boys could get them when they came by. After just an hour the beach was a winter beach, cold and gray and the dead kelp like the hair of the drowned, and it stayed that way despite all attempts. Then three more, including one 1040A where the deductions for AGI were added wrong and the Martinsburg printout hadn't caught it and had to be amended on one of the Form 020-Cs in the lower left tray and then a lot of the same information filled out on the regular 20 you still had to do even if it was just a correspondence audit and the file going to Joliet instead of the District, each code for which had to be looked up on the pull-out thing he had to scoot the chair awkwardly over to pull out all the way. Then another one, then a plummeting inside of him as the wall clock showed that what he'd thought was another hour had not been. Not even close. 17 May 1985. Lord Jesus Christ have mercy on me a poor sinner. Cross-checking W-2s for the return's Line 7 off the place in the Martinsburg printout where the perforation if you wanted to separate the thing's sheets went right through the data and you had to hold it up against the light and almost sometimes guess, which his Chalk Leader said was a chronic bug with Systems but the wiggler was still accountable. The joke this week was how was an IRS rote examiner like a mushroom? Both kept in the dark and fed horseshit. He didn't know how mushrooms even worked, if it was true that you scooped waste on them. Sheri's cooking wasn't what you would call at the level of adding mushrooms. Then another return. The rule was, the more you looked at the clock the slower the time went. None of the wigglers wore a watch, except he saw that some kept them in their pockets for breaks. Clocks on Tingles were not allowed, nor coffee or pop. Try as he might he could not this last week help envisioning the inward lives of the older men to either side of him, doing this day after day. Getting up on a Monday and chewing their toast and putting their hats and coats on knowing what they were going out the door to come back to for eight hours. This was boredom beyond any boredom he'd ever felt. This made the routing desk at UPS look like a day at Six Flags. It was May 17, early morning, or early mid-morning you could maybe almost call it now. He could hear the squeak of the cart boys' carts someplace off at a distance where the vinyl panels between his Chalk's Tingles and the blond oriental fellow's Chalk one row up blocked the sight of them, the kids with the carts. One of the carts had a crazy wheel that chattered when the boy pushed it. Lane Dean always knew when that cart was coming down the rows. Chalk, Team, Group, Pod, Post, Division. He did another return, again the math squared and there were no itemizations on 34A and the printout's numbers for W-2 and 1099 and Forms 2440 and 2441 appeared to square and he filled out his codes for the middle tray's 402 and signed his name and ID number that some part of him still refused to quite get memorized so he had to unclip his badge and check it each time and then stapled the 402 to the return and put the file in the top tier's rightmost tray for 402s Out and refused to let himself count the number in the trays yet, and then unbidden came the thought that *boring* also meant something that drilled in and made a hole. His buttocks already ached from flexing, and the mere thought of envisioning the desolate beach unmanned him. He shut his eyes but instead of praying for inward strength now he found he was just looking at the strange reddish dark and the little flashes and floaters in there, that got almost hypnotic when you really looked at them. Then when he opened his eyes the In tray's stack of files looked to be still mainly the height it had been at 7:14 when he'd logged in in the Chalk Leader's notebook and started and there weren't enough files in his Out trays for Form 20s and 402s that he could see any over the side of the trays and he refused once more to stand up to check how many of them there were for he knew that would make it worse. He had the sensation of a great type of hole or emptiness falling through him and continuing to fall and never hitting the floor. Never before in his life up to now had he once thought of suicide. He was doing a return at the same time he fought with his mind, with the sin and affront of even the passing thought. The room was silent except for the adding machines and the chattering sound of that one kid's cart that had a crazy wheel as the cart boy brought it down a certain row with more files, but also he kept hearing in his head the sound a piece of paper makes when you tear it in half over and over. His six-man Chalk was a quarter of a row, separated off by the gray vinyl screens. A Team is four Chalks plus the Team Leader and a cart boy, some of these from Peoria College of Business. The screens could be moved around to reconfigure the room's layout. Similar rotes groups were in the rooms to either side. Far to the left past three other Chalks' rows was the Group Manager's office with the AGM's little cubicle of screens to the side of it. The pinkie rubbers were for traction on the forms for all deliberate speed. You were supposed to save the rubber at the end of the day. The overhead lights cast no shadow, even of your hand if you held it out like you were reaching at a tray.

Doug and Amber Bellman of 402 Elk Court, Edina MN, who itemized and then some, elected to have $1 go to the Presidential Election Campaign Fund. It took several minutes to crosscheck everything on Schedule A but nothing qualified for the specs of a promising audit, even though Mr. Bellman had the jaggedy handwriting of a crazy man. Lane Dean had filed far fewer 20s than protocol called for. On Friday he had the fewest 20s of anyone else in the Chalk. Nobody'd said anything. All the wastebaskets were full of the curled strips of paper from the adding machines. Everyone's faces were the color of wet lead in the fluorescent light. You could make a semiprivate cubicle out of the screens like the Team Leader had. Then he looked up despite all best prior intentions. In four minutes it would be another hour, a half hour after that was the fifteen-minute break. Lane Dean imagined himself running around on the break waving his arms and shouting gibberish and holding ten cigarettes at once in his mouth like a panpipe. Year after year, a face the same color as your desk. Lord Jesus. Coffee wasn't allowed because of spills on the files, but on the break he'd have a big cup of coffee in each hand while he imagined himself running around the outside grounds shouting. He knew what he'd really do on the break was sit facing the wall clock in the lounge and despite prayers and effort sit counting the seconds tick off until he had to come back and do this again. And again and again and again. The imagined sound made him remember different times he'd seen people rip paper in half. He thought of a circus strongman tearing a phone book; he was bald and had a handlebar mustache and wore a stripy all-body swimsuit like people wore in the distant past. Lane Dean summoned all his will and bore down and did three returns in a row, and began imagining different high places to jump off of. He felt in a position to say he knew now that hell had nothing to do with fires or frozen troops. Lock a fellow in a windowless room to perform rote tasks just tricky enough to make him have to think, but still rote, tasks involving numbers that connected to nothing he'd ever see or care about, a stack of tasks that never went down, and nail a clock to the wall where he can see it, and just leave the man there to his mind's own devices. Tell him to pucker his butt and think beach when he starts to get antsy, and that would be just the word they'd use, *antsy*, like his mother. Let him find out in time's fullness what a joke the word was, that it didn't come anyplace close. He'd already dusted the desk with his cuff, moved his infant son's photo in its rattly little frame where the front glass slid a bit if you shook it. He'd already tried switching the green rubber over and doing the adding machine with his left hand, pretending he'd had a stroke and was bravely soldiering on. The rubber made the pinkie's tip all damp and pale beneath it. Unable to sit still at home, unable to look at anything for more than a second or two. The beach now had solid cement instead of sand and the water was gray and barely moved, just quivered a little, like Jell-O that's almost set. Unbidden came ways to kill himself with Jell-O. Lane Dean tried to control the rate of his heartbeat. He wondered if with enough practice and concentration you could stop your heart at will the same way you hold your breath—like this right here. His heart rate felt dangerously slow and he became scared and tried to keep his head inclined by rolling his eyes way up and compared the rate to the clock's second hand but the second hand seemed impossibly slow. The sound of ripping paper again and again. Some cart boys brought you files with everything you needed, some did not. The buzzer to bring a cart boy was just under the iron desk's edge, with a wire trailing down one of the desk's sides and little welded-on leg, but it didn't work. Atkins said the wiggler who'd been at the station before him, who'd got transferred someplace, had pressed on it so much it burnt the circuit. Small strange indentations in rows on the blotter's front edge were, Lane Dean had realized, the prints of teeth that somebody'd bent down and pressed real carefully into the blotter's edge so that the indentations went way down and stayed there. He felt he could understand. It was hard to keep from smelling his finger; at home he'd find himself doing it, staring into space at the table. His little baby boy's face worked better than the beach; he imagined him doing all sorts of things that he and his wife could talk about later, like curling his fist around one of their fingers or smiling when Sheri made that amazed face at him. He liked to watch her with the baby; for half a file it helped to have them in mind because they were why, they were what made this worthwhile and the right thing and he had to remember it but it kept slipping away down the hole that fell through him. Neither man on either side of him seemed to ever fidget or move except to reach up and lift things onto the desk from their Tingles' trays, like machines, and they were never in the lounge at break. Atkins claimed that after a year he could examine and crosscheck two files at once, but you never saw him try and do it, though he could whistle one song and hum a different one. Nugent's sister did the exorcist on the phone. Lane Dean watched out of the corner of his eye as a parrot-faced man by the central aisle dividing Teams pulled a file out of his tray and removed the return and detached the printout and centered both documents on his blotter. With his little homemade seat cushion and gray hat on its hook screwed into the 402s tray. Lane Dean stared down without seeing his own open file and imagined being that guy with his sad little cushion and customized banker's lamp and wondered what he possibly had or did in his spare time to make up for these soul-murdering eight daily hours that weren't even a quarter through until he just couldn't stand it and did three returns in a row in a kind of frenzy where he might have missed things and so on the next file went very slowly and painstakingly and found a discrepancy between the 1040's Schedule E and the RRA annuity tables for poor old Clive R. Terry of Alton's pissant railroad pension, but a discrepancy so small that you couldn't tell if the Martinsburg printout had even made an error or had just accepted a wide roundoff for time's sake given the amount at stake, and he had to fill out both an 020-C and a Memo 402-C(1) kicking the return over to the Group Manager's office to decide how to classify the error. Both had to be filled out with duplicated data on both sides, and signed. The whole issue was almost unbelievably meaningless and small. He thought about the word *meaning* and tried to summon up his baby's face without looking at the photo but all he could get was the heft of a full diaper and the plastic mobile over his crib turning in the breeze the box fan in the doorway made. No one in either congregation ever saw *The Exorcist;* it was against Catholic dogma and an obscenity. It was not entertainment. He imagined that the clock's second hand possessed awareness and knew that it was a second hand and that its job was to go around and around inside a circle of numbers forever at the same slow unvarying machinelike rate, going no place it hadn't already been a million times before, and imagining the second hand was so awful it made his breath catch in his throat and he looked quickly around to see if any of the examiners around him had heard it or were looking at him. When he started to see the baby's photo's face melting and lengthening and growing a long cleft jaw and the face aging years in just seconds and finally caving in from old age and falling away from the grinning yellow skull underneath, he knew he was half asleep and dreaming but did not know his own face was in his hands until he heard a human voice and opened his eyes but couldn't see who it went with and then smelled the pinkie's rubber right under his nose. He might have drooled on the open file.

Getting a little taste, I see.

It was a big older fellow with a seamed face and picket teeth. He wasn't from any Tingle that Lane Dean had ever observed from his own. The man had on a headlamp with a tan cotton band like some dentists wore and a type of thick black marker in his breast pocket. He smelled of hair oil and some kind of food. He had part of his bottom on the edge of Lane's desk and was cleaning under his thumbnail with a straightened-out paperclip and speaking softly. You could see an undershirt under his shirt; he wore no tie. He kept moving his upper body around in a slight kind of shape or circle, and the movements left a little bit of a visual trail. None of the wigglers in either adjoining row was paying attention to him. Dean checked the face in the photo to make sure he wasn't still dreaming.

They don't ever say it, though. Have you noticed? They talk around it. It's too manifest. As if talking about the air you're breathing, yes? It would be as if saying, I see so-and-so *with my eye*. What would be the point?

There was something wrong with one of his eyes; the pupil of the eye was bigger and stayed that way, making the eye look fixed. His headlamp wasn't on. The slow upper-body motions brought him in closer and then back and away and around again. It was very slight and slow.

Yes but now that you're getting a taste, consider it, the word. You know the one. Dean had the uneasy sense that the fellow wasn't strictly speaking *to* him, which would mean that he was more like ranting. The one eye looked fixedly past him. Although hadn't he just been thinking about a word? Was that word *dilated?* Had he said the word out loud? Lane Dean looked circumspectly to either side. The Group Manager's frosted door was shut.

Word appears suddenly in 1766. No known etymology. The Earl of March uses it in a letter describing a French peer of the realm. He didn't cast a shadow, but that didn't mean anything. For no reason, Lane Dean flexed his buttocks. In fact the first three appearances of *bore* in English conjoin it with the adjective *French*, that French bore, that boring Frenchman, yes? The French of course had *malaise, ennui*. See Pascal's fourth *Pensée*, which Lane Dean heard as *pantsy*. He was checking for errant spit on the file before him. One ham in dark-blue work pants was inches from his elbow.

The man moved slightly back and forth like his waist was hinged. He appeared to be inspecting Lane Dean's upper body and face in a systematic gridlike fashion. His eyebrows were all over the place. The tan band was either soaked or stained. See La Rochefoucauld's or the Marquise du Deffand's well-known letters to Horace Walpole, specifically I believe Letter 96. But nothing in English prior to March, Earl of. This means a good five hundred years of no word for it you see, yes? He rotated slightly away. In no way was this a vision or moment. Lane Dean had heard of the phantom but never seen it. The phantom of the hallucination of repetitive concentration held for too long a time, like saying a word over and over until it kind of melted and got foreign. Mr. Wax's high hard gray hair was just visible four Tingles down. No word for the Latin *accidia* made so much of by monks under Benedict. For the Greek ακηδία. Also the hermits of third-century Egypt, the so-called *daemon meridianus,* when their prayers were stultified by pointlessness and tedium and a longing for violent death. Now Lane Dean was looking openly around as in like who is this fellow? The one eye was fixed at a point over past the row of vinyl screens. The tearing sound had gone, as had that one cart's squeaky wheel.

The fellow cleared his throat. Donne of course called it *lethargie,* and for a time it seems conjoined somewhat with melancholy, saturninia, *otiositas, tristitia*—that is, to be confused with sloth and torpor and lassitude and eremia and vexation and distemper and attributed to spleen, for example see Winchilsea's *black jaundice,* or of course Burton. The man was still on the same thumbnail. Quaker Green in I believe 1750 called it *spleen-fog.* Hair oil made Lane Dean think of the barber's, of the stripy pole that seemed to spiral eternally upward but you could see when the shop closed and it stopped really didn't. The hair oil had a name. No one under sixty used it. Mr. Wax used a men's spray. The fellow appeared unconscious of his upper body's underwater X-shaped rotations. Two of the wigglers in a Team near the door had long beards and black derbies and bobbed at their Tingles as they examined returns but their bobbing was rapid and back and forth only; this was different. The examiners on either side didn't look up or pay attention; their fingers on the adders never slowed. Lane Dean couldn't tell if this was a sign of their professional concentration or something else. Some wore the rubber on the left pinkie, most on the right. Robert Atkins was ambidextrous; he could fill out different forms with each hand. The fellow on his left hadn't blinked once all morning that Dean had been able to see. And then suddenly up it pops. *Bore.* As if from Athena's forehead. Noun and verb, participle as adjective, whole nine yards. Origin unknown, really. We do not know. Nothing on it in Johnson. Partridge's only entry is on *bored* as a subject complement and what preposition it takes, since *bored of* as opposed to *with* is a class marker which is all that ever really concerns Partridge. Class class class. The only Partridge Lane Dean knew was the same TV Partridge everybody else knew. He had no earthly idea what this guy was talking about but at the same time it unnerved him that he'd been thinking about *bore* as a word as well, the word, many returns ago. Philologists say it was a neologism—and just at the time of industry's rise, too, yes? of the mass man, the automated turbine and drill bit and bore, yes? Hollowed out? Forget Friedkin, have you seen *Metropolis*? All right, this really creeped Lane out. His inability to say anything to this guy or ask him what he even wanted felt a little like a bad dream as well. The night after his first day he'd dreamed of a stick that kept breaking over and over but never got smaller. The Frenchman pushing that uphill stone throughout eternity. Look for instance at L. P. Smith's *English Language,* '56 I believe, yes? It was the bad eye, the frozen eye, that seemed to inspect what he leaned toward. Posits certain neologisms as *arising from their own cultural necessity*—his words, I believe. Yes, he said. When the kind of experience that you're getting a man-sized taste of becomes possible, the word invents itself. The term. Now he switched nails. It was Vitalis that had soaked the headlamp's band, which looked more and more like a bandage. The Group Manager's door had his name on it painted on the same pebbled-glass window thing that older high schools have. Personnel's doors were the same. The wiggle rooms had windowless metal fire doors on struts up top, a newer model. Consider that the Oglok of Labrador have more than a hundred separate and distinct words for snow. Smith puts it as that when anything assumes sufficient relevance it finds its name. The name springs up under cultural pressure. Really quite interesting when you consider it. Now for the first time the fellow at the Tingle to the right turned briefly to give the man a look and turned just as fast back around when the man made his hands into claws and held them out at the other wiggler like a demon or someone possessed. The whole thing happened too fast to almost be real to Lane Dean. The wiggler turned a page in the file before him. Someone else had also called it that, *soul murdering.* Which now you will, too, yes? In the nineteenth century then suddenly the word's everywhere; see for example Kierkegaard's *Strange that boredom, in itself so staid and solid, should have such power to set in motion.* When he slid his big ham off the desktop the movement made the smell stronger; it was Vitalis and Chinese food, the food in the little white bucket with the wire handle, moo goo something. The room's light on the frosted glass was different because the door was slightly open, though Lane Dean hadn't seen the door open. It occurred to Lane Dean that he might pray.

It was the same gridlike swaying motion standing. The one eye was on the Group Manager's door, open a crack. Note too that *interesting* first appears just two years after *bore.* 1768. Mark this, two years *after.* Can this be so? He was halfway down the row; now the fellow with the cushion looked up and then back down right away. Invents itself, yes? Not all it invents. Then something Lane Dean heard as *bone after tea.* The man was gone when he reached the row's end. The file and its Schedules A/B and printout were right where they'd been, but Lane's son's picture was facedown. He let himself look up and saw that no time had passed at all, again.

§34

IRM §781(d) AMT Formula for Corporations: (1) Taxable income before NOL deduction, plus or minus (2) All AMT adjustments excepting ACE adjustment, plus (3) Tax preferences, yields (4) Alternative Minimum Taxable Income before NOL deduction and/or ACE adjustment, plus or minus (5) ACE adjustment, if any, yields (6) AMTI before NOL deduction, if any, minus (7) NOL deduction, if any (Ceiling at 90%), yields (8) AMTI, minus (9) Exemptions, yields (10) AMT base, multiplied by (11) 20% AMT rate, yields (12) AMT prior to AMT Foreign Tax Credit, minus (13) AMT Foreign Tax Credit, if any (Ceiling at 90% unless Exceptions 781(d) (13-16) apply, in which case attach Memo 781-2432 and forward to Group Manager), yields (14) Tentative Alternative Minimum Tax, minus (15) Standard tax liability before credit minus standard Foreign Tax Credit, yields (16) Alternative Minimum Tax.

§35

My Audit Group's Group Manager and his wife have an infant I can only describe as — fierce. Its expression is fierce, its demeanor is fierce, its gaze over bottle or pacifier — fierce, intimidating, aggressive. I have never heard it cry. When it feeds or sleeps, its pale face reddens, which makes it look all the fiercer. On those workdays when our Group Manager brought it in with him to the District office, hanging papoose-style in a nylon device on his back, the infant appeared to be riding him as a mahout does an elephant. It hung there, radiating authority. Its back lay directly against the Group Manager's, its large head resting in the hollow of its father's neck, forcing Mr. Manshardt's head out and down into a posture of classic oppression. They

671

made a beast with two faces, one of which was calm, bland, and adult, and the other unformed and yet emphatically fierce. The infant never wiggled or fussed in the device. Its gaze around the corridor at the rest of us gathered there waiting for the morning elevator was level and unblinking and, it seemed, somehow almost accusing.

The infant's face, as I experienced it, was mostly eyes and lower lip, its nose a mere pinch, its forehead milky and domed, its whorl of red hair wispy, no eyebrows or lashes or ever even eyelids that I could see. I never once saw it blink. Its features seemed suggestions only. It had roughly as much face as a whale does. I did not like it at all.

In the elevator, my customary spot is often in the middle, just behind Mr. Manshardt, and on the mornings when the child rides him and hangs there facing backward and I spend the time staring into the large, stern, lashless, fiery-blue eyes, I can only say that these rides are not pleasant at all, and often affect my mood and concentration for much of the subsequent work period.

On the third floor, in Mr. Manshardt's office, the infant had a crib and also a modern, ingenious, mobile supporting device which it spent much of its time in, a large ring-shaped contraption of heavy blue plastic and a type of cloth sling or saddle in the center's hole, in which the infant was placed in a position somewhere between sitting and standing—that is, the infant's legs were nearly straight, but the sling appeared to support its weight. The device or station had four short, squat supporting legs, which terminated in plastic wheels, and was designed to be movable under the infant's power, albeit slowly, rather the way our own workstations' wheeled chairs could be maneuvered this way and that by awkward motions of the auditor's legs. However, the infant declined to move the device, as far as I ever saw, or to play with any of the bright, primary-colored toys and small, amusing developmental tchotchkes built into sockets in the ring's blue surface. Nor did it ever seem to occupy itself with the books made of cloth, dump trucks and fire engines, teething rings of liquid-filled plastic, intricate mobiles, or pull-string music-and-animal-noise-emitting toys with which its play area was replete. It just sat there, motionless and mute, gazing fiercely at whichever GS-9 auditors happened to enter our Group Manager's small, frosted-glass office on the days when Mr. Manshardt—whose wife was liberated and had her own career—brought it in with him, for which he had reportedly received special permission from the District Director. At first, many a

GS-9 would enter the office on some thin pretext, trying to curry favor with the Group Manager by smiling and making soft, primal sounds at the infant, or by putting a finger or pencil in its field of vision, perhaps trying to stimulate its instinct for grasping. The infant, however, would just gaze at the auditor fiercely, with a combination of intensity and disdain, its expression rather as if it were hungry and the auditor were food but not quite the right kind. There are some small children who you can just tell are going to grow up to be frightening adults — this infant was frightening now. It was eerie and discomfiting to see something with hardly any bona fide human face yet to speak of nevertheless assume a fierce, intimidating, almost accusatory expression. For my own part, I had abandoned all ideas of ingratiating myself with Mr. Manshardt through his infant quite early on. To be honest, I was concerned that Gary Manshardt might be able to pick up my fear and dislike of the infant on some type of mysterious, occult parental radar.

His office's desk's personal-item area was lined with photos of Mr. Manshardt's infant — on a rug, newborn in an obstetrics ward, in boots and a tiny hooded coat, squatting nude with a red pail and shovel at the beach, and so on and so forth — and in all of the photos the infant looked fierce. Its presence seemed not to interfere with Manshardt's office duties, the bulk of which were administrative and required much less pure concentration than the Audit Group itself's. Once the working day began, however, the Group Manager appeared for the most part to ignore the infant, and to be ignored by it in return. Whenever I went in, try as I might, I could not interact with the infant. The nylon papoose appliance hung on a coat hook next to Mr. Manshardt's hat and jacket—he preferred to work in shirtsleeves, a further perquisite of Group Managers. Sometimes the office smelled slightly of powder or pee. I did not know when the GM changed the infant, or where, and avoided visualizing what-all might be involved or the infant's expression when this occurred. I myself could not imagine touching the infant or being touched by it in any way.

Due to our District 040(c)'s Audits Pod's administrative structure, Group Managers also did rotating duty as the District's Level 1 Appeals Officer, requiring Mr. Manshardt sometimes to put his suit jacket back on and proceed downstairs to one of the second floor's audit cubicles, where aggrieved TPs or their representatives would present their objections to a given audit's findings. And since, by the Service's Statement of Procedural Rules §601's specifications for Appeal of Findings, the GS-9 auditor himself was never present during a Level 1 Appeal, that auditor became the logical choice for Mr. Manshardt to approach at his or her desk and ask to move his or her work materials temporarily into the Group Manager's office, and to keep an eye on the infant while Mr. Manshardt handled the Level 1 Appeal.

In due course, the day eventually came when one of my audits' findings was appealed when Mr. Manshardt was 'up' as the Post's Appeals Officer. As luck would have it, the appeal was of a field audit that I had spent nearly eight full working days conducting at All Right Flowers, a small, family-owned S corporation specializing in the arrangement and delivery of bouquets for public functions, and whose Form 1120 Schedule A, E, and G deductions for everything from depreciation and spoilage to employee compensation were so grossly inflated that I'd been forced—despite terrible, long-standing hay fever—to back-audit them for the two previous years and to amend both their Schedule Js and 1120s' Line 33s heavily in the Treasury's favor. As the field audit came directly off a Form 20 directive from the Regional Examination Center, and as the combined adjustments, penalties, and interest assessed against All Right Flowers might well exceed the TP's ability to pay unless terms were made, the appeal was hardly a cause for surprise or alarm, Mr. Manshardt assured me in the bland, kindly tone that characterized his management style. But as the Level 1 would be conducted in the office of All Right Flowers' attorney on DeKalb Street downtown — as is the prerogative of certain categories of field auditees under SPR §601.105 — it would require that Mr. Manshardt be off-post for several hours, which in turn entailed that I was to have an extended period in the Group Manager's office in the company of his fierce and frightening infant, who could only be brought along on an L-1 in the field if Manshardt and the appellant's rep had a long-standing history of cordial relations, which he and All Right Flowers' attorney[1] unfortunately, he said, did not.

The Group Managers' offices were the only fully enclosed work spaces on the third-floor office's Audits Pod, and have doors, affording the luxury of privacy. But the offices are not large, Manshardt's own being perhaps at most eight feet by eight, with large frosted-glass windows on two sides — these being the sides

---

1 (a female Jew)

which did not abut the structural, load-bearing walls of the District building—and a double brass coat hook fixture, and a US flag and Service seal and motto flag on one corner's complex pole, as well as framed portraits of both Triple-Six's Commissioner of Internal Revenue and our own Regional Commissioner across town. In contrast to the cramped, impersonal metal desks of the Audit Group, Gary Manshardt's wood-grain desk, with its Tingle array of trays and hutches, took up nearly all of the space in the office not ceded to the infant, along with there being one of the large, multi-display easels on which all Group Managers charted both their auditors' present loads and, in a DD-mandated Charleston code that fooled no one,[2] each GS-9's total cases,

2 Production quotas are a reality in the Service. This is not difficult to understand. Given numerous and repeated public statements to the contrary by top officials at Triple-Six, however, all such internal quotas are required to be kept and recorded in code. At the same time, administrators view the knowledge of such quotas as valuable performance incentives, which is why the Compliance Branch mandates and authorizes internal codes that are laughably familiar to most auditors. The Charleston code, in which C stands for the number 0 and H stands for 1, dot, dot, dot, up to N's standing for 9, is today most commonly employed by retailers who use a perpetual inventory system which must include the nominal cost of goods sold in each transaction record. Thus, an item's retail price tag at, let us say, a rural IGA supermarket will include both the retail price in digits and the CGS or distributor's unit price in Charleston code, often at the tag's lower border. Thus, anyone familiar with the code can determine from, let us say, a $1.49 retail price and a tiny TE

adjustments, and assessed deficiencies so far in the present quarter. The air-conditioning was good.

And yet I'm now advised that none of this is directly to the point, the substance of which is: Imagine my surprise and discomfiture once I had moved my briefcase, Doberman hand puppet, desk nameplate, hat, personal items, Service notebook, expandable cardboard file of Hollerith cards, M1 printouts, Memo 20s, Form 520s and 1120s, blank forms, and at least two fat folders of crosschecks and receipt-request forms into the Group Manager's office, and—glancing as little as possible at Gary's forbidding infant, which was still wearing its lunch bib and standing-slash-sitting at its circular plastic play station gumming a liquid-filled ring

---

beneath it, that the unit markup here is nearly 100 percent, and that the IGA supermarket he is patronizing is either disposed to gouge or has extraordinary retail overhead, possibly involving poorly leveraged debt—a common problem with the management of Midwest supermarket chains. On the other hand, one advantage of the Charleston code is that inflating its Schedule A's Cost of Goods Sold is one of the most common and effective ways for a retail franchise to cook down its Line 33, especially if the retailer uses one type of code for CGS and its distributor another type of code for its receivables—and most distributors use a much more sophisticated octal PIS code. This is why so many large corporate audits are coordinated to review all different levels of the supply chain simultaneously. Such coordinated audits are handled out of Region, often also using specially selected GS-13 examiners from the Regional Exam Center; we do not conduct such audits at the District level.

in what I can describe only as a studious or contemplative way—was just managing to regather my concentration in order to organize a list of preliminary receipt and supporting-document requests from a vendor that made and affixed tempered handles on a line of galvanized pails for Danville's Midstate Galvanics Co. when I heard the unmistakable adult sound of a cleared throat, albeit at an extremely high pitch, as if from an adult who had recently inhaled helium out of a decorative balloon. The infant was, like Gary Manshardt's wife, a redhead, although in the infant's case its extreme pallor and the light-yellow pajamas or jumper—or whatever exactly one calls the small and fuzzy full-body snap-up chamois bodysuits which infants today tend to wear—made its fine wisps and spirals of hair appear, in the intensive light of the office, to be the color of old blood, and its fierce and concentrated blue eyes appeared now to be almost pupilless; and, to complete the incongruous horror, the infant had set aside its teething ring—rather carefully and deliberately, as a man might set aside a file on his desk once he has completed it and is ready to turn his professional attention to another—to lie moist and shiny next to an upright bottle of what appeared to be apple juice, and had placed its tiny hands folded adultly together before it on the vivid blue plastic of its play station,[3] exactly as Mr. Manshardt or Mr. Fardelle or any of the other Group Managers or District Director's senior staff would place their clasped hands before them on the desk to signal that you and the issue that had brought you into their office now occupied their full attention, and cleared its throat again—for it had indeed been it, he, the infant, who, like any other GM, had cleared its throat in an expectant way in order to get my attention and at the same time in some subtle way to upbraid me for requiring it to do something to get my attention, as if I had been daydreaming or digressing mentally from some issue at hand— and, gazing at me fiercely, said—yes, said, in a high and *l*-deficient but unmistakable voice—

'Well?'

It now seems probable that it was at first my shock, my as it were nonplussedness at being spoken that adultly to by an infant in diapers and jammies soaked with drool, that led me so automatically to answer, to respond as I would to any

3 (I observed that one of the elastic wristlets of its yellow chamois jumper was soaked through with saliva and appeared, for several inches up the infant's forearm, darker than the other wristlet, which the infant appeared to ignore and I certainly did not mention or foresee doing anything about)

expectant 'Well?' from a Service superior, functioning on, as it were, automatic pilot:

'Excuse me?' I said, as we stared at each other across our respectively wood-grain and lurid blue surfaces and the five or six fluorescent feet of air between us, both our hands now identically out and clasped, the infant's gaze fiercely expectant and a small, creamy gout of mucus appearing and receding in one nostril as it breathed, looking directly at me, the cowlick at its crown like a tag or receipt from a register's slit, its eyes lashless and without circumference or bottom, its lips pursed as if considering how to proceed, a bubble in its bottle of juice ascending slowly, leisurely towards the bottle's top, the salient nipple brown and shiny from recent use. And the moment hung there between us, borderless and distendant, my impulse to clear my own throat only blocked by a fear of appearing impertinent—and it was in that seemingly endless, expectant interval that I came to see that I deferred to the infant, respected it, granted it full authority, and therefore waited, abiding, both of us in that small and shadowless father's office, in the knowledge that I was, thenceforth, this tiny white frightening thing's to command, its instrument or tool.

§36

Every whole person has ambitions, objectives, initiatives, goals. This one particular boy's goal was to be able to press his lips to every square inch of his own body.

His arms to the shoulders and most of the legs beneath the knee were child's play. After these areas of his body, however, the difficulty increased with the abruptness of a coastal shelf. The boy came to understand that unimaginable challenges lay ahead of him. He was six.

There is little to say about the original animus or 'motive cause' of the boy's desire to press his lips to every square inch of his own body. He had been homebound one day with asthma, a rainy and distended morning, apparently looking through some of his father's promotional materials. Some of these survived the eventual fire. The boy's asthma was thought to be congenital.

The outside area of his foot beneath and around the lateral malleolus was the first to require any real contortion. (The young boy thought, at that point, of the lateral malleolus as the funny knob thing on his ankle.) The strategy, as he understood it, was to arrange himself on his bedroom's carpeted floor with the inside of his knee on the floor and his calf and foot at as close to a perfect 90-degree angle to his thigh as he could at that point manage. Then he had to lean as far over to the side as he could, bending out over the splayed ankle and the foot's outside, rotating his neck over and down and straining with his fully extended lips (the boy's idea of fully extended lips consisted at this point of the exaggerated pucker that signified kissing in children's cartoons) at a section of the foot's outside he had marked with a bull's-eye of soluble ink, struggling to breathe against the dextrorotated pressure of his ribs, stretching farther and farther to the side very early one morning until he felt a flat pop in the upper part of his back and then pain beyond naming somewhere between his shoulder blade and spine. The boy did not cry out or weep but merely sat silent in this tortured posture until his failure to appear for breakfast brought his father upstairs to the bedroom's door. The pain and resultant dyspnea kept the boy out of school for over a month. One can only wonder what a father might make of an injury like this in a six-year-old child.

The father's chiropractor, Doctor Kathy, was able to relieve the worst of the immediate symptoms. More important, it was Doctor Kathy who introduced the boy to the concepts of spine as microcosm and of spinal hygiene and postural echo and incrementalism in flexion. Doctor Kathy smelled faintly of fennel and seemed totally open and available and kind. The child lay prone on a tall padded table and placed his chin in a little cup. She manipulated his head, very gently but in a way that seemed to make things happen all the way down his back. Her hands were strong and soft and when she felt the boy's back he felt as if she were asking it questions and answering them all at the same time. She had charts on her wall with exploded views of the human spine and the muscles and fasciae and nerve bundles that surrounded the spine and were connected to it. No lollipops were anywhere in view. The specific stretching exercises Doctor Kathy gave the boy were for the splenius capitis and longissimus cervicis and the deep sheaths of nerve and muscle surrounding the boy's T2 and T3 vertebrae, which were what he had just injured. Doctor Kathy had reading glasses on a necklace and a green button-up sweater that looked as if it were made entirely of pollen. You could tell she talked to everybody the same way. She instructed the boy to perform the stretching exercises every single day and not to let boredom or a reduction in symptomology keep him from performing the rehabilitative exercises in a disciplined way. She said the long-term goal was not relief of present discomfort but neurological hygiene and health and a wholeness of body and mind he would someday appreciate very, very much. For the boy's father, Doctor Kathy prescribed an herbal relaxant.

Thus was Doctor Kathy the child's formal introduction both to incremental stretching and to the adult idea of quiet daily discipline and progress toward a long-term goal. This proved fortuitous. During his five weeks disabled with a subluxated T3 vertebra—often in such discomfort that not even his inhaler could help the asthma that struck whenever he experienced pain or distress—the heady enthusiasm of childhood had given way in the boy to a realization that the objective of pressing his lips to every square inch of himself was going to require maximum effort, discipline, and a commitment sustainable over periods of time he could not then (because of his age) imagine.

One thing Doctor Kathy had taken time out to show the boy was a freestanding 3-D model of a human spine that had not been taken proper care of in any real or significant way. It looked dark, stunted, necrotic, and sad. Its tubercles and soft tissues were inflamed, and the annulus fibrosus of its disks was the color of bad teeth. Up against the wall behind this model was a hand-lettered plaque or sign explaining about what Doctor Kathy liked to say were the two different types of payments for the spine and associated nervosa, which were *Now* and *Later*.

Most professional contortionists are, in fact, simply persons born with congenital atrophic/dystrophic conditions of major recti, or with acute lordotic flexion of the lumbar spine, or both. A majority display Chvostek's sign or other forms of ipsilateral spasticity. Very little effort or application is involved in their 'art,' therefore. In 1932, a preadolescent Ceylonese female was documented by British scholars of Tamil mysticism as capable of inserting into her mouth and down her esophagus both arms to the shoulder, one leg to the groin, and the other leg to just above the patella, and as thereupon able to spin unaided on the orally protrusive knee at rates in excess of 300 rpm. The phenomenon of suiphagia (i.e., 'self-swallowing') has subsequently been identified as a rare form of inanitive pica, in most cases caused by deficiencies in cadmium and/or zinc.

The insides of the small boy's thighs up to the medial fork of his groin took months even to prepare for, daily hours spent cross-legged and bowed, slowly and incrementally stretching the long vertical fasciae of his back and neck, the spinalis thoracis and levator scapulae, the iliocostalis lumborum all the way to the sacrum, and the interior thigh's dense and intransigent gracilis, pectineus, and adductor longus, which fuse below Scarpa's triangle and transmit sickening pain through the pubis whenever their range of flexibility is exceeded. Had anyone seen him during these two- and three-hour sessions, bringing his soles together and in to train the pectineus, bobbing slightly and then holding a deep cross-legged lean to work the great tight sheet of thoracolumbar fascia that connected his pelvis to his dorsal costae, the child would have

appeared to that person either prayerful or catatonic, or both.

Once the thighs' anterior targets were achieved
and touched with one or both lips, the upper portions of his genitals were simple, and were protru-
sively kissed and passed over even as plans for the
ilium and outer buttocks were in conception. After
these achievements would come the more difficult
and neck-intensive contortions required to access
the inner buttocks, perineum, and extreme upper
groin.

The boy had turned seven.

The special place where he pursued his strange
but newly mature objective was his room, which
had wallpaper with a repeating jungle motif. The
room's second-floor window yielded a view of the
backyard's tree. Light from the sun came through
the tree at different angles and intensities at different times of day and illuminated different parts of
the boy as he stood, sat, inclined, or lay on the
room's carpet, stretching and holding positions.
His bedroom's carpet was white shag with a furry,
polar aspect that the boy's father did not think
went well with the walls' repeating scheme of tiger,
zebra, lion, palm; but the father kept his feelings
to himself.

Radical increase of the lips' protrusive range

requires systematic exercise of maxillary fasciae such as the depressor septi, orbicularis oris, depressor anguli oris, depressor labii inferioris, and the buccinator, circumoral, and risorius groups. Zygomatic muscles are superficially involved. Praxis: Affix string to Wetherly button of at least 1.5" diameter borrowed from father's second-best raincoat; place button over upper and lower front teeth and enclose with lips; hold string fully extended at 90 degrees to face's plane and pull with gradually increasing tension on end, using lips to resist pull; hold for twenty seconds; repeat; repeat.

Sometimes his father sat on the floor outside the boy's bedroom with his back to the door. It's not clear whether the boy ever heard him listening for movement in the room, although the wood of the door sometimes made a creaky sound when the father sat against it or stood back up in the hallway or shifted his seated position against the door. The boy was in there stretching and holding contorted positions for extraordinary periods of time. The father was a somewhat nervous man, with a rushed, fidgety manner that always lent him an air of imminent departure. He had extensive entrepreneurial activities and was in motion much of the time. His place in most people's mental album was provisional, with something like a

dotted line around it—the image of someone saying something friendly over his shoulder as he
made for an exit. Most clients found the father
made them uneasy. He was at his most effective
on the phone.

By age eight, the child's long-term goal was
beginning to affect his physical development. His
teachers remarked changes in posture and gait. The
boy's smile, which appeared by now constant
because of the circumlabial hypertrophy's effects on
the circumoral musculature, looked unusual also,
rigid and overbroad and seeming, in one custodian's
evaluative phrase, 'like nothing in this round world.'

Facts: Italian stigmatist Padre Pio carried
wounds which penetrated the left hand and both
feet medially throughout his lifetime. The
Umbrian St. Veronica Giuliani presented with
wounds in one hand as well as in her side, which
wounds were observed to open and close on
command. The eighteenth-century holy woman
Giovanna Solimani permitted pilgrims to insert
special keys in her hands' wounds and to turn
them, reportedly facilitating those clients' own
recovery from rationalist despair.

According to both St. Bonaventura and Tomas
de Celano, St. Francis of Assisi's manual stigmata

included baculiform masses of what presented as hardened black flesh extrudent from both volar planes. If and when pressure was applied to a palm's so-called 'nail,' a hardened black rod of flesh would immediately protrude from the back of the hand, just exactly as if a real so-called 'nail' were passing through the hand.

And yet (fact): Hands lack the anatomical mass required to support the weight of an adult human. Both Roman legal texts and modern examinations of first-century skeletons confirm that classical crucifixion required nails to be driven through the subject's wrists, not his hands. Hence the, quote, 'necessarily simultaneous *truth* and *falsity* of the stigmata' that existential theologist E. M. Cioran explicates in his 1937 *Lacrimi si sfinti,* the same monograph in which he refers to the human heart as 'God's open wound.'

Areas of the boy's midsection from navel to xiphoid process at the cleft of his ribs alone comprised nineteen months of stretching and postural exercises, the more extreme of which must have been very painful indeed. At this stage, further advances in flexibility were now subtle to the point of being undetectable without extremely precise daily record-keeping. Certain tensile limits in the flava, capsule, and process ligaments of the neck and upper back were gently but persistently stretched, the boy's chin placed to his (solubly arrowed and dotted) chest at mid-sternum and then slid incrementally down — 1, sometimes 1.5 millimeters a day — and this catatonic and/or meditative posture held for an hour or more.

In the summer, during his early-morning routines, the tree outside the boy's window filled with grackles and became busy with grackles coming and going; and then, as the sun rose, the tree filled with the birds' harsh sounds, tearing sounds, which as the boy sat cross-legged with his chin to his chest sounded through the pane like rusty screws turning, some complexly stuck thing coming loose with a shriek. Past the southern exposure's tree were the foreshortened roofs of neighborhood homes and the fire hydrant and street sign of the cross-street and the forty-eight identical roofs of a low-income housing development beyond the cross-street, and, past the development, just at the horizon, the edges of the verdant cornfields that began at the city limits. In late summer the fields' green was more sallow, and later in the fall there was merely sad stubble, and in the winter the fields' bare earth looked like nothing so much as just what it was.

At his elementary school, where the boy's behavior was exemplary and his assignments completed and his progress charted at the medial apex of all relevant curves, he was, among his classmates, the sort of marginal social figure so marginal he was not even teased. As early as Grade 3, the boy had begun to develop along unusual physical lines as a result of his commitment to the objective; even so, something in his aspect or bearing served to place him outside the bounds of schoolyard cruelty. The boy followed classroom regulations and performed satisfactorily in group work. The written evaluations of his socialization described the boy not even as withdrawn or aloof but as 'calm,' 'unusually poised,' and 'self-containing [*sic*].' The boy gave neither trouble nor delight and was not much noticed. It is not known whether this bothered him. The vast majority of his time, energy, and attention belonged to the long-range objective and the daily disciplines thereby entailed.

Nor was it ever established precisely why this boy devoted himself to the goal of being able to press his lips to every square inch of his own body. It is not clear even that he conceived of the goal as an 'achievement' in any conventional sense. Unlike his father, he did not read Ripley and had never heard of the McWhirters—certainly it was no kind of stunt. Nor any sort of self-evection; this is verified; the boy had no conscious wish to 'transcend' anything. If someone had asked him, the boy would have said only that he'd decided he wanted to press his lips to every last micrometer of his own individual body. He would not have been able to say more than this. Insights or conceptions of his own physical 'inaccessibility' to himself (as we are all of us self-inaccessible and can, for example, touch parts of one another in ways that we could not even dream of with our own bodies) or of his complete determination, apparently, to pierce that veil of inaccessibility—to be, in some childish way, self-contained and -sufficient— these were beyond his conscious awareness. He was, after all, just a little boy.

His lips touched the upper aureoles of his left and right nipples in the autumn of his ninth year. The lips by this time were markedly large and protrusive; part of his daily disciplines were tedious button-and-string exercises designed to promote hypertrophy of the orbicularis muscles. The ability to extend his pursed lips as much as 10.4 centimeters had often been the difference between achieving part of his thorax and not. It had also been the orbicularis muscles, more than any outstanding advance in vertebral flexion, that had permitted him to access the rear areas of his scrotum and substantial portions of the papery skin around his anus before he turned nine. These areas had been touched, tagged on the four-sided chart inside his personal ledger, then washed clean of ink and forgotten. The boy's tendency was to forget each site once he had pressed his lips to it, as if the establishment of its accessibility made the site henceforth unreal for him and the site now in some sense 'existed' only on the four-faced chart.

Fully and exquisitely real for the boy in his eleventh year, however, remained those portions of his trunk he had not yet attempted: areas of his chest above the pectoralis minor and of his lower throat between clavicle and upper platysma, as well as the smooth and endless planes and tracts of his back (excluding lateral portions of the trapezius and rear deltoid, which he had achieved at eight and a half) extending upward from the buttocks.

Four separate licensed, bonded physicians apparently testified that the Bavarian mystic Therese Neumann's stigmata comprised corticate dermal structures that passed medially through both her hands. Therese Neumann's additional capacity for inedia was attested in writing by four Franciscan nuns who attended her in rotating shifts from 1927 to 1962 and confirmed that Therese lived for almost thirty-five years without food or liquid of any kind; her one recorded bowel movement (12 March 1928) was determined by laboratory analysis to comprise only mucus and empyreumatic bile.

A Bengali holy man known to followers as 'Prahansatha the Second' underwent periods of meditative chanting during which his eyes exited their sockets and ascended to float above his head, connected only by their dura mater cords, and thereupon underwent (i.e., the floating eyes did) rhythmically stylized rotary movements described by Western witnesses as evocative of dancing four-faced Shivas, of charmed snakes, of interwoven genetic helices, of the counterpointed figure-eight orbits of the Milky Way and Andromeda galaxies around each other at the perimeter of the Local Group, or of all four (supposedly) at once.

Studies of human algesia have established that the musculoskeletal structures most sensitive to painful stimulation are: the periosteum and joint capsules. Tendons, ligaments, and subchondral bone are classified as *significantly* pain-sensitive, while muscle and cortical bone's sensitivity has been established as *moderate,* and articular cartilage and fibrocartilage's as *mild.*

Pain is a wholly subjective experience and thus 'inaccessible' as a diagnostic object. Considerations of personality type also complicate the evaluation. As a general rule, however, the observed behavior of a patient in pain can provide a measure of (a) the pain's intensity and (b) the patient's ability to cope with it.

Common fallacies about pain include:

- People who are critically ill or gravely injured always experience intense pain.
- The greater the pain, the greater the extent and severity of damage.
- Severe chronic pain is symptomatic of incurable illness.

In fact, patients who are critically ill or gravely injured do not necessarily experience intense pain. Nor is the observed intensity of pain directly proportional to the extent or severity of damage; the correlation depends also on whether the 'pain pathways' of the anterolateral spinothalamic system are intact and functioning within established norms. In addition, the personality of a neurotic patient may accentuate felt pain, and a stoic or resilient personality may diminish its perceived intensity.

No one ever did ask him. His father believed only that he had an eccentric but very limber and flexible child, a child who'd taken Kathy Kessinger's homilies about spinal hygiene to heart the way some children will take things to heart and now spent a lot of time flexing and limbering his body, which as the queer heartcraft of children went was preferable to many other slack or damaging fixations the father could think of. The father, an entrepreneur who sold motivational tapes through the mail, worked out of a home office but was frequently away for seminars and mysterious evening sales calls. The family's home, which faced west, was tall and slender and contemporary; it resembled one half of a duplex town house from which the other half had been suddenly removed. It had olive-colored aluminum siding and was on a cul-de-sac at the northern end of which stood a side entrance to the county's third-largest cemetery, whose name was woven in iron above the main gate but not above that side entrance. The word that the father thought of when he thought of the boy was: *dutiful,* which surprised the man, for it was a rather old-fashioned word and he had no idea where it came from when he thought of him in there, from outside the door.

Doctor Kathy, who sometimes saw the boy for continuing prophylactic adjustments to his thoracic vertebrae, facets, and anterior rami, and was not a loon or a huckster in a shopping-center office but simply a DC who believed in the interpenetrating dance of spine, nervous system, spirit, and cosmos as totality—in the universe as an infinite system of neural connections that had evolved, at its highest point, an organism which could sustain consciousness of both itself and the universe at the same time, such that the human nervous system became the universe's way of being aware of and thus 'accessible [to]' itself—Doctor Kathy believed the patient to be a very quiet, inner-directed boy who had responded to a traumatic T3 subluxation with a commitment to spinal hygiene and neurospiritual integrity that might well signal a calling to chiropractic as an eventual career. It was she who had given the boy his first, comparatively simple stretching manuals, as well as the copies of B. R. Faucet's famous neuromuscular diagrams (©1961, Los Angeles College of Chiropractic) out of which the boy fashioned the freestanding four-sided cardboard chart that stood as if guarding his pillowless bed while he slept.

The father's belief in ATTITUDE as the overarching determinant of ALTITUDE had been unwavering since his own adolescence, during which awkward time he had discovered the works of Dale Carnegie and of the Willard and Marguerite Beecher Foundation, and had utilized these practical philosophies to bolster his own self-confidence and to improve his social standing—this standing, as well as all interpersonal exchanges and incidents which served as evidence thereof, was charted weekly and the charts and graphs displayed for ease of reference on the inside of his bedroom's closet door. Even as a provisional and secretly tortured adult, the father still worked tirelessly to maintain and improve his attitude and so influence his own altitude in personal achievement. To the medicine cabinet's mirror in the home's bathroom, for instance, where he could not help but reread and internalize them as he tended to personal grooming, were taped inspirational maxims such as:

'NO BIRD SOARS TOO HIGH, IF HE SOARS WITH HIS OWN WINGS— *BLAKE*'

'IF WE ABDICATE OUR INITIATIVE, WE
BECOME PASSIVE — RECEPTIVE VICTIMS OF
ON-COMING CIRCUMSTANCES — *BEECHER
FOUNDATION*'

'DARE TO ACHIEVE! — *NAPOLEON HILL*'

'THE COWARD FLEES EVEN WHEN NO
MAN PURSUETH — *BIBLE*'

'WHATEVER YOU CAN DO OR DREAM, YOU
CAN BEGIN IT. BOLDNESS HAS GENIUS, POWER
AND MAGIC IN IT. BEGIN IT NOW! — *GOETHE*'

and so forth, dozens or at times even scores
of inspirational quotes and reminders, carefully
printed in block capitals on small, fortune cookie–
sized slips of paper and taped to the mirror as written reminders of the father's personal responsibility
for whether he soared boldly, sometimes so many
slips and pieces of tape that only a few slots of
actual mirror were left above the bathroom's sink,
and the father had to almost contort himself even
to see to shave.

When the boy's father thought of himself, on
the other hand, the word that came unbidden first
to mind was always: *tortured*. Much of this secret
torture — whose causes he perceived as impossibly
complex and protean and involving both normal
male sexual drives and highly abnormal personal

weakness and lack of backbone—was actually quite simple to diagnose. Wedded at twenty to a woman about whom he'd known just one salient thing, this father-to-be had almost immediately found marriage's conjugal routines tedious and stifling; and the sense of monotony and sexual obligation (as opposed to sexual achievement) had caused in him a feeling that he felt must be almost like death. Even as a newlywed, he had begun to suffer from night terrors and to wake from nightmares of some terrible confinement feeling unable to move or breathe. These dreams did not exactly take any kind of psychiatric Einstein to interpret, the father knew, and after almost a year of inner struggle and complex self-analysis he had given in and begun seeing another woman, sexually. This woman, whom the father had met at a motivational seminar, was also married, and had a small child of her own, and they had agreed that this put some sensible limits and restrictions on the affair.

Within a short time, however, the father had begun to find this other woman kind of tedious and oppressive, as well. The fact that they lived separate lives and had little to talk about made the sex start to seem obligatory. It put too much weight on the physical sex, it seemed, and spoiled it. The father attempted to cool things off and to see the woman less, whereupon she in return also began to seem less interested and accessible than she had been. This was when the torture started. The father began to fear that the woman would break off the affair with him, either to resume monogamous sex with her husband or to take up with some other man. This fear, which was a completely secret and interior torture, caused him to pursue the woman all over again even as he came more and more to despise her. The father, in short, longed to detach from the woman, but he didn't want the woman to be able to detach. He began to feel numb and even nauseous when he was with the other woman, but when he was away from her he felt tortured by thoughts of her with someone else. It seemed like an impossible situation, and the dreams of contorted suffocation came back more and more often. The only possible remedy that the father (whose son had just turned four) could see was not to detach from the woman he was having an affair with but to hang dutifully in there with the affair, but also to find and begin seeing a third woman, in secret and as it were 'on the side,' in order to feel—if only for a short time—the relief and excitement of an attachment freely chosen.

Thus began the father's true cycle of torture, in

which the number of women with whom he was secretly involved and to whom he had sexual obligations steadily expanded, and in which not one of the women could be let go or given cause to detach and break it off, even as each became less and less a source of anything more than a sort of dutiful tedium of energy and time and the will to forge on in the face of despair.

The boy's mid- and upper back were the first areas of radical, perhaps even impossible unavailability to his own lips, presenting challenges to flexibility and discipline that occupied a vast percentage of his inner life in Grades 4 and 5. And beyond, of course, like the falls at a long river's end, lay the unimaginable prospects of achieving the back of his neck, the eight centimeters just below the chin's point, the galeae of his scalp's back and crown, the forehead and zygomatic ridge, the ears, nose, eyes—as well as the paradoxical *ding an sich* of his lips themselves, accessing which appeared to be like asking a blade to cut itself. These sites occupied a near-mythic place in the overall project: The boy revered them in such a way as to place them almost beyond the range of conscious intent. This boy was not by nature a 'worrier' (unlike himself, his father thought), but the inaccessibility of these last sites seemed so immense that it was as if their cast shadow fell across all the slow progress up toward his clavicle in the front and lumbar curvature in the rear that occupied his eleventh year, darkening the whole endeavor, a tenebrous shadow the boy chose to see as lending the enterprise a somber dignity rather than futility or pathos.

He did not yet know how, but he believed, as he approached pubescence, that his head would be his. He would find a way to access all of himself. He possessed nothing that anyone could ever call doubt, inside.

§37

'Certainly appears to be a nice restaurant.'

'Looks pretty nice.'

'I myself have never been here before. I'd heard good things about it, though, from some of the fellows in Administration. I've been anxious to try it.'

'...'

'And here we are.'

(Removing chewing gum and wrapping it in Kleenex removed from handbag.) 'Uh-huh.'

'...'

'...'

(Makes minute adjustments to placement of silverware.) '...'

'...'

'Do you suppose it's so much easier to make

conversation with someone you already know well than with someone you don't know at all primarily because of all the previously exchanged information and shared experiences between two people who know each other well, or because maybe it's only with people we already know well and know know us well that we don't go through the awkward mental process of subjecting everything we think of saying or bringing up as a topic of light conversation to a self-conscious critical analysis and evaluation that manages to make anything we think of proposing to say to the other person seem dull or stupid or banal or on the other hand maybe overly intimate or tension-producing?'

'. . .'

'. . .'

'What did you say your name was again?'

'Russell. Russell or sometimes "Russ," though to be honest I have a marked preference for Russell. Nothing against the name Russ; I just never quite cottoned to it.'

'Do you got any aspirin with you, Russell?'

§38

Until mid-1987, the IRS's attempts at achieving an integrated data system were plagued with systemic bugs and problems, many of them exacerbated by Technical Branch's attempts to economize by updating older Fornix keypunch and card-sorter equipment to handle ninety-six-column Powers cards instead of the original eighty-column Holleriths.[1]

---

1 Because of the heavy, more or less uninterrupted volume of data the IRS processes, its computer systems had been constructed on the fly and had to be maintained and upgraded the same way. The situation was analogous to maintaining a freeway whose high volume of traffic both necessitates and hinders serious maintenance (i.e., there is no way simply to close the road in order to fix the whole thing at one time; there's no way to divert all that traffic). In hindsight, it would ultimately have been cheaper and more efficient to shut the entire Service down for a brief period and transfer everything to a modern,

One particular bug is relevant here. The Personnel and Training Division's COBOL-based systems had long had special trouble with what were sometimes called 'ghost redundancies' in the processing of employee promotions. The problem was especially acute in Examinations staffing because of the unusually high rates of turnover and promotion among REC personnel. Suppose, for example, that Mr. John Q. Doe, a GS-9 rote examiner, was promoted in grade to GS-11. The system would then generate a whole new personnel file, and thereafter would recognize two separate files for what appeared to be two separate employees, John Q. Doe GS-9 and John Q. Doe GS-11, causing extraordinary hassle and confusion for both payroll and Systems planning protocols down the line.

As part of a multipronged debugging effort in 1984, a **GO TO** subroutine was inserted in all Per-

---

freshly installed disk-based system, nationwide. At the time, though, this seemed unimaginable, especially in light of the Rome NY REC's spectacular 1982 meltdown under the pressures of a cumulative backlog. So many of the fixes and upgrades were temporary and partial and, in retrospect, wildly inefficient, e.g. trying to increase processing power by altering antiquated equipment to accommodate slightly less antiquated computer cards (plus Powers cards had round holes instead of Holleriths' old square ones, requiring all kinds of violent alterations for Fornix equipment that was already old and fragile).

sonnel systems' **FILE** sections: In cases of what appeared to be two different employees with the same name and IRS Post code, the system was now directed to recognize only the 'John Q. Doe' of higher GS grade.[2] This led pretty much directly to the snafu at IRS Post 047 in May 1985. In effect, David F. Wallace, GS-9, age twenty, of Philo IL, did not exist; his file had been deleted, or absorbed into, that of David F. Wallace, GS-13, age thirty-nine, of Rome NY's Northeast REC. This absorption occurred at the instant that David F. Wallace (i.e., the GS-13)'s Regional Transfer Form 140(c)-RT and posting Form 141-PO were generated, which instant two different systems administrators in the Northeast and Midwest Regions would eventually have to go back through a combined 2,110,000 lines of recorded code in order to

2 What might appear to a layman as the obvious problem caused by this debugging—i.e., the loss of the system's ability to recognize and classify IRS demotions—was not in fact much of a problem, comparatively, for Personnel. The fact is that fewer than .002 percent of Internal Revenue Service employees are ever demoted in grade, thanks in large part to the collective-bargaining power of the National Association of Treasury Employees. In effect, the conditions and procedural hurdles required for demotion were gradually strengthened until in most cases they were no less stringent than those required for termination with cause...although this is all very much a side issue, mentioned only to head off certain possible confusions on the part of the reader.

find in order to override the **GO TO** absorption. None of this, of course, was explained in any detail to David F. Wallace (GS-9, formerly GS-13—meaning the David F. Wallace of Philo IL) until much later, after the whole administrative swivet was over and various outlandish charges had been retracted.

The problem was not, in other words, that no one in the Midwest Regional Examination Center's Personnel and Training office noticed that two separate David F. Wallaces were scheduled for intake and processing at the Midwest REC over two successive days. The problem was that the office's computer system recognized, and generated a Powers card and Intake Protocol Form for, only one such David F. Wallace, whom the system further conflated into both (a) the higher-ranked employee transferring from Philadelphia and (b) the employee whose physical arrival was scheduled first in the system, this latter viz. the twenty-year-old ephebe from Philo, whom the system also listed, in a further conflation, as arriving on CT Flight 4130 from Midway (due to the ticketing and travel information generated as part of the Form 140(c)-RT's arrival specs) rather than by Trailways bus, which was why no one was waiting to meet and transport the supposedly elite and valuable

David F. Wallace at the Peoria bus terminal on 15
May, and why the second (i.e., the 'real') David F.
Wallace, who arrived at the REC by ordinary commercial taxi the following day—which taxi this
other, older David Wallace was evidently so meek
and passive that it didn't even register on his consciousness that there'd been some foul-up in REC
transport, that his rank and value merited a special
pickup with his name on a cardboard sign, or even
that he should at least get a receipt from the taxi
driver so that he could apply for reimbursement,
and who furthermore arrived for permanent transfer and a complete change in residence with (rather
incredibly) his entire life contained in only one
carry-on bag—why that older, elite, highly valued
David F. Wallace spent almost two full working
days with his Xerox copies of the Forms 141 and
chintzy brown suitcase in first the lines for the
GS-13 Intake Station and then Problem Resolution desks in the REC's main building's lobby, then
sitting in a corner of the lobby itself, then in the
Security offices off Level 2's[3] southeast corridor,
sitting there with his neotenous face blank and his
hat in his lap, unable to proceed, since of course
the bureaucracy's computer system had him listed

3 (which, again, was actually the main building's ground floor)

as already having gone through Intake and received his Post 047 ID and badge—in which case where were his badge and ID, a Security part-timer kept asking him, over again each time he checked the system, and if he hadn't lost them then why couldn't he produce them? and so on and so forth.[4]

At the IRS's National Computer Center in Mar-

[4] It's probably worth noting two additional bugs or systemic weaknesses or whatever that contributed to the fuck-up and my initial misassignment at Post 047. The first problem was that, due to limitations imposed by the reconfiguration of certain core programs to accommodate round-holed ninety-column Powers cards, the Personnel computer system's file labels could accommodate only an employee's middle initial, which in the case of David Francis Wallace, incoming high-value transfer from Philadelphia, was not enough to distinguish him in the system from David Foster Wallace, incoming low-value contract hire. The second, much more serious problem was that IRS Personnel's original Social Security numbers (i.e., the civilian SSs issued to them in childhood) are always deleted and replaced systemwide by the new, IRS-issued SSs that serve also as Service IDs. An employee's original SS is 'stored' only on his original employment application—which applications are always copied to microfiche and stored in the National Records Center, which NRC by 1981 was dispersed throughout a dozen different regional annexes and warehouse complexes and was notoriously ill-managed and disorganized and difficult to extract specific records from in any kind of timely way. Plus the Personnel systems' file labels can accommodate only one SS # anyway, and that's obviously going to be the new '9'-based SS that functions as one's Service ID number. And since the 975-04-2012 that the new, low-value David F. Wallace was issued upon Expedited Intake was also the 975-04-2012 Service ID # of the older, high-value GS-13 David F. Wallace, the two employees became, so far as the Service's computer system was concerned, the same person.

tinsburg WV,[5] the 'ghost conflation' problem for
employees with identical names had been recognized

5 In retrospect, it's now clear that there was actually a third, even more severe
systemic problem, which was that, prior to 1987, the Service's computer
systems were organized around what's now known as a 'Bad Wheel' model of
network integration. Again, there's a great deal of arcana and explanation—
most of it involving not only the trying-to-maintain-a-freeway-while-still-
letting-people-use-it maintenance situation detailed above but also the
piecemeal and jerry-rigged quality of systems whose maintenance depended on
annual budget allocations to the Technical Branch, which for a variety of
bureaucratic/political reasons fluctuated wildly from year to year—but the
point of the Bad Wheel thing was that Technical Branch's networking setup
through the mid-1980s resembled a wheel with a hub but no rim. In terms of
computer interface, everything had to go through Martinsburg's NCC. A
transfer of data from Peoria's Midwest Regional Exam Center to Midwest
Region HQ up in Joliet, for example, actually entailed two separate data
transfers, the first from Peoria to Martinsburg and the second from
Martinsburg to Joliet. Martinsburg's modems and dedicated lines were (for
that era) high-baud and efficient, but there was still often a delay in 'routing
time,' which bland term actually referred to incoming data's sitting there in
Martinsburg's Fornix mainframes' magnetic cores until that data's turn came
up in the routing queue. Meaning there was always a lag. And, for
understandable reasons, the queue was always longest and the lag worst in the
weeks following April 15's tidal influx of individual tax returns. Had there
been anything like lateral networking in the IRS system—i.e., had the
Midwest REC's Systems/Personnel computers been able to interface directly with
their Systems/Personnel counterparts at the Northeast REC in Philadelphia, the
whole David F. Wallace swivet could have been resolved (and unjust blame
averted) much more quickly. (Not to mention that the whole rimless-wheel model
was at odds with the much-touted decentralization of the Service following the
1952 King Commission report, not much of which is relevant here except in that
it just adds to the overall Rube Goldberg idiocy of the whole setup.)

715

as early as December 1984—thanks mainly to a hideous mess involving two separate Mary A. Taylors at the Southeast Regional Service Center in Atlanta— and Technical Branch programmers were already in the process of inserting a **BLOCK** and **RESET** subsubroutine that overrode the **GO TO** subroutine for the thirty-two most common surnames in the United States: viz., Smith, Johnson, Williams, Brown, & c. But Wallace was, according to 1980 US Census figures,[6] only the 104th most common American surname, way down the list between Sullivan and Cole; and any override of **GO TO** that countenanced more than thirty-two surnames ran a statistically significant risk of reintroducing the original 'ghost redundancy' problem. In short, the name David F. Wallace fell in that statistical middle area where the original debugging's consequent 'ghost conflation' bug could still cause significant problems and woe, especially for any employee too new to understand why or whence these accusations of everything from contractual fraud to 'impersonation of an immersive' (that latter an unprecedented charge that may well

---

6 (This was the latest published data available, and the Service had to rely exclusively on published data because the US Dept. of Commerce's new UNIVAC system was incompatible with the more antiquated Fornix hardware that Martinsburg was still using.)

have been simply made up out of whole cloth by Dick Tate's hatchet men as a way of deflecting what at one point they feared might be construed as negligence or administrative error on the part of REC Personnel, a fear that even Mr. Stecyk, the DDP, conceded was simply bureaucratic paranoia, once the 'unreal' David Wallace [i.e., the author][7] had gotten in to see him and more or less thrown himself on his mercy).

7 (Now you can probably see why this occasional 'author' appositive thing is sometimes necessary; it turned out that there were two separate David Wallaces posted at the Midwest REC, of whom the one who ended up accused of impersonation was guess who.)

§39

GS-9 Claude Sylvanshine, back in the Martinsburg Systems compound as part of the April run-up to his advance work at the Midwest REC, went twice into the directed-input tank and tried, under Reynolds's audio supervision, running RFA[1] on Post 047's top brass, the first of which RFA sessions yielded some fruit. Sylvanshine got interpretable fact-sets on DeWitt Glendenning Jr.'s pathological hatred of mosquitoes born of his Tidewater childhood, his failed attempt to become a US Army Ranger in 1943, his violent allergy to shellfish, his evident belief that his genitals were somehow malformed, his run-in with the dreaded

1 Remote Fact Acquisition

Internal Inspections Division while a District Audit Director in Cabin John MD, parts of the home and/or office address of his psychiatrist in suburban Joliet, his memorization of the birthday of every last member of the Midwest Regional Commissioner's family, and a great deal of esoterica about home furniture-construction and -refinishing and power tools that led to an abrupt SDI[2] into certain specs surrounding a male adult's severed thumb. This leading some in Systems to conclude that current Midwest REC Director and Regional toady DeWitt 'Dwitt' Glendenning had lost or would shortly lose a thumb in some type of home woodworking accident, and to tailor certain plans and expectations around this fact.

The truth—which Claude Sylvanshine will and can never know despite the repeated column of figures on both the aerodynamics of arterial blood and the rates at which a 1420-rpm standing band-saw blade can cut through the various conic sections of a human hand of certain mass and angle—is that an adult severed thumb's factual relevance was actually to the life and psyche of Leonard Stecyk, Post 047's DDP, who as a practical matter undertook to do not only his own work

2 Spontaneous Data Intrusion

but much of his superior's. The severed-thumb incident figures in the psychic development that transformed L. M. Stecyk into one of the most brilliant and able Service administrators in the Region, though the thumb incident is by now buried deep in Mr. Stecyk's unconscious, his conscious life dominated by the REC's Personnel office and by issues surrounding the gathering storms in both Systems and Compliance.

The incident itself is not immediately relevant and so can be recounted quite fast. For reasons now lost in the administrative mists, Industrial Arts was then required of male tenth-graders across the upper Midwest, giving the Vocational Ed pupils a last chance to savage and torment the College Prep boys from whom they'd been (in Michigan) split off the previous year. And Leonard Stecyk had an especially hard time of it in Mr. Ingle's third-hour Industrial Arts class at Charles E. Potter High School in the autumn of 1969. It was not just that at almost sixteen Stecyk was 5' 1" and 105 pounds soaking wet, which he was (soaking wet) when the boys in his PE class's shower all urinated on him after knocking him to the tile floor, which ritual they called a Stecyk Special—he ending up the only boy in the history of Grand Rapids to carry an umbrella into a school's showers. Nor was it a matter just of the special OSHA-approved safety goggles and special homemade carpenter's apron inscribed in Palmer cursive with LEN'S THE NAME; WOOD'S THE GAME that he wore to class. Nor that third-hour IA featured two separate future convicted felons, one of whom had already served a week's suspension for heating an ingot of cast iron red-hot with an acetylene torch, waiting just until the last color had vanished from it, and then casually asking Stecyk to go bring him that one ingot over by the scroll saw real quick. The real problem was practical: Leonard turned out to have no talent or affinity whatsoever for Industrial Arts, whether it came to basic dynamics or welding, rudimentary construction or custom carpentry. True, the kid's drafting and measurement specs were, Mr. Ingle admitted, exceptionally (almost effeminately, he felt) neat and precise. It was with actual projects and operations of the machinery that Stecyk was terrible, whether it was cutting to an angle, following a pre-drawn jig, or even sanding smooth the base of the special pinewood cigar box that Mr. Ingle (who liked cigars) forced all the pupils to make for their fathers, but on which Stecyk's apparently loose or insufficiently masculine grip caused the belt-sander to shoot the box like a piece of ordnance across the

DAVID FOSTER WALLACE

Industrial Arts classroom, where it exploded against the cement wall not ten feet from the head of Mr. Ingle, who told Stecyk (whom he despised without guilt or reservation) that the only reason he didn't force him and his little apron over to Home Economics with the girls was that he'd probably burn the whole everloving school down! at which some of the larger and crueler tenth-grade boys (one of whom would be expelled the following autumn for not only bringing a USFWS bear trap onto school property but going so far as to open and set it—the dagger-sharp spring-loaded trap—outside the door to the vice principal's office, where it had to be deactivated with the pole of a custodian's push broom, which it snapped with a sound that caused students in classrooms all up and down the hall to duck and cover) actually pointed directly at Stecyk as they laughed.

On the other hand, it's possible that the severed-thumb incident did not so much actually change or shape Leonard Stecyk's character as alter his own perspectives on it (if any), as well as others' perceptions of him. As most adults know, the distinctions between one's essential character and value and people's perceptions of that character/value are fuzzy and hard to delineate, especially in adolescence. There is also the fact that a certain

722

amount of situational setup and context to the incident Leonard Stecyk no longer recalls, not even in dreams or peripheral flashes. It had to do with cutting a sheet of drywall into lathes or strips for some kind of reinforcement involving the framing and hanging of a door in an interior wall. The band saw was set in a broad metal table with gauges and calibrated clamps to hold what you were cutting just so while you pushed the piece carefully along the smooth surface so that the band saw's high-speed blade cut along the pencil line you'd drawn after measuring at least twice. There were, of course, detailed safety procedures as codified by Mr. Ingle in both the mimeographed Shop Rules and several stenciled all-cap signs on and around the band saw's rear housing, which procedures Leonard Stecyk had not only memorized but tried helpfully to point out some instances of typos or ambiguous phrasing in the terse imperatives of, which had caused one side of Mr. Ingle's big face to start jumping and crinkling involuntarily, a notorious sign that the man was just barely keeping his temper under control. The reality behind the surfeit of signs and yellow caution lines painted on the shop room floor was that Mr. Ingle operated under great felt pressure and constant borderline frustration and rage, since it

was his responsibility if anybody got hurt, and yet
at the same time many of the kids in the classes
were either inept effeminate 'mathlete' pansies like
Stecyk and Moss here or else long-haired delin-
quents in army coats that sometimes came to class
smelling of marijuana and peppermint schnapps,
and screwed around with rules and equipment
they didn't have the sense to respect the danger-
ousness of, including standing around watching
within the clearly marked yellow line to the side of
the band saw and its unshielded blade despite the
clearly painted instructions on both machine and
floor to STAY BEHIND LINE WHEN IN OPERATION,
where all it would then take is a careless shove or
even gesture where you waved one of your arms
around when standing in the unauthorized side
area; and in illustrating this at the top of his lungs
for maybe the fifth time this quarter as the sad
excuse for kids stood at the yellow line and watched
him exaggerate a childish gesture, his right hand
inadvertently made contact with the blade of the
band saw, which just as quickly as Mr. Ingle had
promised it could, took off his thumb and the surrounding material from the interdigital webbing
down to the abductor pollicis longus tendon, also
opening the radial artery, which caused a tremendous fan of blood-spatter as Mr. Ingle brought the

red thing to his chest and toppled sideways, gray
with shock and the paralytic reflexes of trauma.
As was more or less everyone else in the class —
gray-faced, openmouthed — watching from the
yellow line as blood from the radial and also first
volar metacarpal arteries shot rhythmically up and
out and spattered even some of the taller boys'
khaki coats and the control panel of the drill press
against which they bumped as they stepped reflexively back. This was not the slow welling of a
skinned knuckle or the trickle of a punched nose.
This was arterial blood under great systolic pressure, which shot up and fanned out from where
the teacher knelt cradling the hand against his
chest with the other hand and staring at the pha-
lanx of boys, mouthing something that could not
be heard over the band saw's A# scream, some of
the College Prep boys' faces also distended in
screams which could be seen but not heard, a few
others at the extreme back peeling off around the
drill press's clamps and running for the classroom
door with their arms up and hands waving in the
universal movement of blind panic, the rest splayed
against the nearest peer or machine with their eyes
wide and minds in deep neutral.

   . . . All but little Leonard Stecyk, who after only
the briefest neural pause moved forward, quickly

and decisively, came out around the group's flank, punching at the band saw's double-marked Power button with the heel of his bandaged hand as he swept around the back of the machine, looking neither right nor left in his apron and pressed white shirt, elbowing aside a large boy in a paisley headband who stood with his Keds' soles in human blood — a boy who only days before had menaced Stecyk with a pair of blacksmith's tongs behind the lathe's peg-board tool display — and seemed instantly to be at the side of Mr. Ingle, implementing the first rule of on-site treatment for hemorrhagic trauma, which was simultaneously to elevate the wound and to identify the severity of the trauma using the five-point Ames Scale from Cherry Ames RN's 1962 *First Aid for Industrial Injury,* which Stecyk had checked out of the public library as part of his standard preparation for the Autumn '69 class schedule. Stecyk simply lifted the hand as high as he could, to about eye level, while Mr. Ingle knelt hunched and slumped beneath it. It cannot be overstressed how fast this all was happening. The thumb and surrounding base tissues were not completely detached but hung by a flap of dermis such that Mr. Ingle's thumb itself pointed straight down in a parody of imperial judgment as Stecyk, ignoring both the blood and the high-pitched diminutives for 'Mother' that began to be audible as the band saw cycled down, removed with one hand first his slacks' belt and then the metric-conversion ruler he carried in a special narrow pocket of the carpenter's apron Mr. Ingle had ridiculed and—after running mentally through the protocols and determining à la Cherry Ames RN that digital pressure around the wrist did not alone control the bleeding—fashioned a deft two-knot tourniquet (w/ just a hint of Edwardian flourish to the top's four-loop bow, which was even more amazing given that Stecyk constructed the special knot with slippery scarlet hands that also supported a man's half-fainting weight) that stanched the flow with only one and a half turns of the ruler, such was the memorized precision with which Stecyk had placed the tourniquet just at the crucial branch between the forearm's ulnar and radial arteries. In the belling stillness after the saw's blade stopped you could now hear the sounds of the pneumatic jack from the Intro Auto Mechanics classroom next door. It was also now, with the spray's cessation, that Mr. Ingle lost consciousness, so that the last sight some of the taller boys at the flanks had was Stecyk cupping Mr. Ingle's skull at the back like a child's and gently lowering him—it, the big man's head—to the floor with one hand while the other held the tourniquet in place at the upraised wrist, there being something both dancerly and maternal and yet not one bit girlish about the sight that reverberated within the souls of a few in strange ways for days and even weeks after they were shouldered aside and told to break it up and give the man some air by the Auto Mechanics and Appliance Repair teachers, who also were brisk and adultly unfrozen but did not try to move Len aside or ask the Home Ec aide to shoo him outside with all the others and their red footprints but rather stood like subalterns at either side of the man's upraised arm with pendent thumb, awaiting instructions from the boy on whether they should wait for the ambulance or maybe try and put Mr. Ingle in one of their cheap but faultlessly tuned cars and rush him right to Calvin, speaking to Stecyk as more of a peer and being spoken to in return without deference or hesitation.

Voc Ed students tend not to be very sensitive or emotionally agile, and it would be too much to say that 'everything changed' after that day in Industrial Arts. It was not that Leonard Stecyk became popular, or that the hard boys started inviting him to come out with them on school nights to perpetrate vandalism or abuse gateway drugs. A few of them, though, were surprised—not ashamed so much as shaken—by their paralysis in the face of trauma and the noxious little faggot's actions. It was strange. These were tough boys: They fought freely, took beatings from stepdads and older brothers. For the brightest among them, their idea of what toughness was, of the relations between coolness and actual value, had now been somewhat fucked with. Their accounts of the incident were confused and varied from boy to boy. More than one alluded to *Lost in Space,* which was a popular show at the time. The main change in the quality of the future DDP's life was that most of the Stecyk Specials and sudden hallway punches in the upper arm's radial nerve and other daily bits of cruelty ceased, mostly because a strange unease came over the hard boys when they saw or even thought of Stecyk, and real cruelty—as every adolescent knows—requires a close attention to the object of that cruelty. Stecyk's actions that day did not make him more but less special; the hard boys ceased to see him or single him out. It was strange, and stranger still was how fast Stecyk himself forgot the whole thing, even after Mr. Ingle returned to C. E. Potter after Thanksgiving for his new duties as a Driver Ed instructor with his maimed right hand encased in some kind of protective black polyurethane glove or sheath, resulting in the student sobriquet 'Dr. No' throughout the early 1970s. Everyone seemed to have incentive to forget the whole thing. A Voc Ed hard boy who would serve in the Plaine des Joncs region of Indochina twenty months later was the only one with a clear conscious memory of Stecyk and Ingle's thumb that one day, and this when a fat-body draftee who'd almost flunked Basic and been the object of a savage blanket party had taken a squad that had lost its corporal and regrouped them and brought them around between two separate NVA platoons to reform with Able Company; he had just stood up and told them to strip ordnance off the dead and form a defilade against the opposite side of the creekbed, and everyone had obeyed— unthinkingly, for reasons they could not later explain or admit—and the hard boy had thought of Stecyk in his little apron and paisley bow tie (the latter a distortion of memory) and of the fact, again, that what they'd then thought was the wide round world was a little boy's preening dream.

§40

Cusk had been ushered into the psychiatrist's office and was counting the boxes of Kleenex in a little room lined with big books and diplomas. The sixth was on the little desk in the corner the psychiatrist used for filling out prescriptions. The office was minus the little sink some physicians had—he'd spent whole days girding himself for the sink. When his name had been called, Cusk had shaken the psychiatrist's hand and taken a padded chair the psychiatrist's other hand had indicated. The psychiatrist hitched her trousers up slightly at the knee and had sat down opposite Cusk across a glass coffee table on which were two boxes of Kleenex. Her hand had been large, warm, and soft. Her chair was the same model as Cusk's chair—one, maybe two levels of comfort below an easy chair—but seemed, unless it was his imagination, to be slightly taller than his chair.

... 'of spiders, of dogs, of mail,' Cusk was listing—the psychiatrist listened intently, nodding, but did not take notes, which relieved Cusk—'Fear of spiral notebooks, the kind with the spiral or wire down the spine; fear of fountain pens—though not felt-tip or ballpoint pens, unless the ballpoint is one of those expensive ones with an aspect of permanence—Cross, Montblanc, the kind that look gold—but not plastic or disposable ballpoints.' Having exhausted Kleenex boxes to count, Cusk was mentally repeating *large, soft, and warm, large, soft and warm,* over and over, a ruminative chant just below the level of thought.

'Fear of disks. Fear of drains. Fear of pretty much all spiral movements in liquid, across the board.'

The psychiatrist's eyebrows were extraordinarily thin and sparse, and when she raised them it meant she didn't quite follow—

'Whirlpools, maelstroms, bathtubs draining,' Cusk illustrated. He had a fine sheen of sweat on his upper lip, but could tell by feel that the forehead was staying dry, hanging in there. 'Briskly stirred beverages. Flushing toilets.'

§41

'You sent Cardwell to get him?'

'What's the problem?'

'He's demented, Charlie, that's what's the problem.'

'He's a good driver. He's dependable.'

'He'll rant at the guy the whole way here; the guy'll think it's a post of evangelist goons. This is Lehrl's aide, Charlie. Jesus.'

§42

There were long silences between periods of attention.

'Shit I got one for you. This was a while ago, though, when I was in school in St. Louis, when we were the Reserve Rangers.'

'I'll bite.'

'You won't get some of it. You had to be alive in the late sixties.'

'We weren't alive?'

'I don't mean playing-with-your-toes alive or squeezing-the-pores-of-your-nose alive. I mean of age, aware. I mean culturally.'

'Counterculturally you mean.'

'I could say to eat shit off a thick wooden stick, Gaines. But I don't. Instead I say if there's something cool with this unmistakable quality and I say the thing's quality is just so Beatles, you don't get it.'

'You had to be there.'

'It's not the same thing as just owning Beatles records, you're saying. You had to be *there*, in it.'

'Grooving. Being groovy.'

'That's just it. Nobody really said groovy. People that said groovy or called you man were just playing out some fantasy they'd seen on CBS reports. I'm saying if I say Baxter-Bathing or Owsley or mention Janis's one dress she wore you think in terms of data. There's none of the feeling attached to it—this was a feeling. It's impossible to describe.'

'Except as saying it's so very Beatles.'

'And some of it not even data. What if I say Lord Buckley? What if I say the Texas tower or Sin Killer Griffin on tape from jail or Jackson going on *Today* and sitting across from that J. Fred chimp in a shirt that's still got Martin's blood and brain matter on it and nobody says anything even though *Today's* in New York which means fucking Jackson flew all the way in from Memphis in that shirt so he could wear blood on TV—do you feel anything if I say that? Or *Bonanza* or *I Am Curious* parenthesis *Yellow*? J. Fred Muggs? Jesus, *The*

Fugitive—if I say the one-armed man, what interior state does it provoke?'

'You mean nostalgia.'

'I mean methamphetamine hydrochloride. Say *December's Children* or *Dharma Bums* or Big Daddy Cole at the House of Blues in Dearborn or crew cuts and horn-rims or even let me think of rolled-up Levi's showing three inches of white cotton over penny loafers and I taste the hydrochloride from the days at Wash U when we were the Reserve Rangers. How odd I can have all this inside me and to you it's just words.'

'We have our own little cultural signposts and cathexes and things that make us feel nostalgia.'

'It's not nostalgia. It's a whole set of references you don't even know you don't have. Suppose I say Sweater Puppies—you feel nothing. Christ, Sweater Puppies.'

'Not acid?'

'Pardon?'

'Why methamphetamine and not acid? LSD? Weren't grass and LSD the era's like defining drugs?'

'That's what I mean. None of the nuance or complexity introduces into your field. Acid was the West Coast and a small cell around Boston. Acid wasn't even in Greenwich Village until Kesey and Leary's thing upstate in '67. By '67 the sixties were over. The Midwest was meth and designer hallucinogens. We had a small sort of inner set at Wash U who were in with the Dogtown crowd; one reason I'm here instead of private is I don't think one of us cracked a book in two years, then I had to move because of the Rescue Rangers and this older guy named, perversely, McCool, who wanted in with us, hung around, but desperately uncool, from hunger we'd say but to you this means nothing. McCool was a district rep for Welch Lambeth. I presume Welch Lambeth is part of your cultural index.'

'Chemicals. Now part of Lilly. University City, Miz, heavily diversified, chemical and largely industrial solvents, medical supplies, adhesive, polymers, chassis molds.'

'Medical supplies at this time including for instance sometimes he'd bring stuff in, we'd be at the usual table at Jaegerschnitzel, a rathskeller for WU's most countercultural and antiestablishment but not mod or groovy crowd, and one night in the midst of some bull session in comes McCool, who had a larcenous heart, with a half-pound insulated box he'd got from some sample room and said, 'I know some of you fellows like this, so when I saw it I said, Holy Smokes I gotta liberate this for the fellows" and like that. From hunger, but plucky in that Eisenhower way. He's in his thirties and already bald with a blinky hunger for acceptance; you can only imagine what must have happened to him as a kid. The sort of guy who comes to your party and you get him drunk enough to pass out by nine and put him in the Rescue Rangers minibus and strip off everything but his shoes and socks and leave him propped up on a bus stop bench in East St. Louis and he'll not only survive somehow but the next night he'll be back at the Jaegerschnitzel punching you in the shoulder and saying Good One like you'd just given him a hotfoot, desperate to be one of the guys.'

'My brothers taught me that desperation is the chief, like, bar to being accepted as one of the guys. I learned this the hard way I can tell you. One time because as a kid I was scared of the water and they let me come with them on a camping trip and my oldest brother said this was my one big chance to be one of the guys and instead of camping it turned out it was a fishing trip and when I tried to climb in the boat it turned out they—'

'And we're like right, great, but then Eddie Boyce opens it up and inside are these long insulated corrugated-cardboard tubes, and inside each tube is a little three-inch double-stoppered test tube with...pharmaceutical-grade methamphetamine hydrochloride, three-point-something grams each. We're all sitting there looking at each other and Boyce's eyebrows are about on top of his head. McCool trying to play it casual but saying "See? What do you think?" Do you know what this means? There were 224 grams of pure pharmaceutical meth in that box. Do you know what even crummy adulterated garage-lab meth can do to a twenty-year-old nervous system?'

'I would have sold it off and used the net to establish a position in silver and then gone to my professors and pulled their beards, tell them I could buy and sell them now and they could put that in their pipes and smoke it.'

'We didn't sell enough of it, I'll tell you. But what we did wreaked havoc. Classes were a zoo. Carbuncular kids who'd sat in the back row and never made a peep were grabbing their profs by the lapels and citing the surplus theory of value in the voice of SS interrogators. Newman Club mainstays were copulating with abandon on the library steps. The infirmary was besieged by philosophy grad students begging someone to shut their heads off. Dining halls were empty. The entire Wash U defensive backfield was jailed for assault on the

Kansas State water boy. Coeds whose hymens could be used for a vault door were giving it up in the bushes outside Lambda Pi. Most of the next two months we spent as the Reserve Rangers, in the van, answering distress calls from boys who had gotten hold of a tenth of a gram of this stuff and now found their girlfriends hanging off the ceiling by their nails grinding their perfect little white teeth into nubbins. Reserve Rangers!

'Awake for a week at a time, all of us flying on meth and never coming down because coming down off meth is like having terrible flu while in hell, Boyce's palms with permanent indentations from gripping the bus's wheel so hard, and all our eyeballs looking like novelty-shop eyeballs. The closest we're coming to eating is shuddering in distaste when we see a restaurant sign on our way to the literally dozens of Rescue Ranger calls we're getting every night, booming the doors and scanning the elevators and taking stairs five at a time singing our Rescue Rangers on the Job fight song.'

'What's this Rescue Rangers angle, Todd, if—?'

'Because in very short order as the power and purity of this stuff starts to ramify throughout Dogtown we impress upon McCool the need for some kind of remedial help from the good offices of Welch Lambeth.'

'What possible medical use does methamphetamine have? Obesity? Sleep deprivation research? Controlled-psychosis experiments?'

'And two or three days later—just as all of us are reaching just about the limits of endurance and our ribs are showing and the skin around our eyes is starting to look like hamburger—there was one terrible accident where I was alone and I decided all right this time we take the emergency brake off and shoot almost an eighth of a gram uncut and was in a very very strange state of mind indeed one step short of clinical paranoia and the doorbell rings and I open it on the chain and all I see is a hat with plastic flowers on the brim and it's this tiny old little blameless Welcome Wagon lady, welcoming us in our caved-in rental house to the neighborhood with a little basket of cookies and hygienic products looking up at me but with those weird little hypnotic spirals of red in one eye and green in another and her little peanut of a face convexly bulging out horribly like a crocodile's face and then receding and then coming out up at me again, and I'll spare you the details of how I reacted except to tell you that this incident led directly to my having to drop out and move to Colorado less than two months later, which is how I got the Service Moniker Colorado Todd.'

§43

Tuesday morning I had an ENT appointment and clocked in at 10:05. The complex was even more subdued than usual. People spoke quietly and had a slight shoulder-first quality to their walk. A few of the women who were known to react to any sort of upset by becoming pale were pale. There was a quality of slow-motion milling to everybody's activities, as if they were all reacting to something but were aware of themselves reacting and that everybody else was reacting. I was out of aspirin. For some reason I was reluctant to ask anybody what had happened. I hate being the person who always doesn't know what's going on and has to ask somebody; it always seems like everybody else knows what's going on. This is a clear low-status marker, and I resisted it. It wasn't until after eleven that I overheard Trudi Keener, Jane-Ann Heape, and Homer Campbell in the UNIVAC room collating stacks of backdated EST vouchers.

There had been an explosion in another Region. In either Muskegon or Holland, both tenth annexes. Either a car or a light truck had parked directly in front of the District office and then at some later time blown up. Trudi Keener had quoted George Molesworthy as saying that the Posse Comitatus was known to be both extreme and active in Michigan. This meant that it was a terrorist attack on a Service Post, which in any depressed agricultural region is going to send chills. I stood in the room pretending to check something in the file catalogue for as long as I figured I could without Jane-Ann Heape being able to discern that I was eavesdropping and deduce that I was the sort of person who didn't know what was going on and recalibrate her idea of me accordingly. Her hair today was up and done in a complex set of curls and waves that appeared darker in the blue-end fluorescence of the UNIVAC room. She had on a pale blue acetate blouse and skirt whose plaid was so dark and low-contrast it was hard to identify it as true plaid. No casualty information emerged, but I did learn that two or three of 047's

Audit-Coordination Support Systems staff had been posted in Michigan early in their careers; I had no connection to Audit-Coordination Support Systems and didn't recognize the names.

When my break came the coffee room smelled sour, which meant that Mrs. Oooley hadn't cleaned out the pots and filters before clocking out last night. It was a personnel gold mine in there, however. Mr. Glendenning and Gene Rosebury were drinking coffee out of their complimentary Service mugs (for GS-13s and up) and Meredith Rand was eating a cup of yogurt out of the GS-9 refrigerator with a plastic fork (which meant Ellen Bactrim was hoarding spoons again). They were having the conversation, and Gary Yeagle and James Rumps and several others were standing just off to the side, listening. I came in in the middle and pretended to study the vending machines and then to count the coins in my hand.

'This isn't terrorism. This is people not wanting to pay their taxes,' Gene Rosebury said. There were faint remains of his customary Mylanta mustache. The 'this' indicated that there was a great deal of conversational context and information that had gone on heretofore.

'If I'm terrified, that doesn't make it terrorism?' Meredith Rand said. She removed a tiny bit of yogurt from the corner of her mouth with her little finger. It seemed significant that no one laughed, not even the GS-9s. Rand's was the sort of low-cal sally that was meant not so much to be funny as to give the room the opportunity to laugh and so dispel tension. No one took this opportunity. This seemed telling. Mr. Glendenning had on a tan suit and a string tie with a medallion of turquoise at the crux. The REC Director was a man who was accustomed to being the center of attention in any room he was in, although with him this manifested as an air of quiet self-possession instead of exhibitionism. I didn't know a person at the Post who didn't like and admire DeWitt Glendenning. I had been with the Service long enough by this time to understand that this was one quality of a successful administrator, to be liked. And not to *act* in such a way as to be liked, but to *be* that way. Nobody ever felt that Mr. Glendenning was putting on any kind of act, the way less gifted administrators do, even an act for themselves, for instance acting like a martinet because someplace inside they have a picture of a good administrator as a hard-ass and are trying to contort their own personalities to fit the picture. Or that glad-handing, my-door-is-always-open type who believes a good administrator needs to be everyone's friend and so acts very open and friendly even though the responsibilities of his office require him to discipline people or cut budgets and deny requests or reassign people to Examination or any number of things that aren't friendly at all. This type puts himself in a terrible position, because each time he has to do something for the good of the Service that is going to hurt some employee or piss her off, the action now carries the additional emotional freight of a friend dicking over a friend, and frequently the administrator feels so uncomfortable over this and his divided loyalties that he has to get personally angry — or act angry — at the employee to do it, which makes the thing personal in an inappropriate way and adds greatly to the dicked-over employee's hurt and resentment, and over time this totally undermines the administrator's authority, and in very short order everybody sees him as a fake and a backstabber, pretending to be your friend and colleague but ready to dick you over whenever he feels like it. It's interesting that these two false administrative styles — the tyrant and the fake friend — are also the two main stereotypes that books and television shows and comic strips present administrators as. One suspects, in fact, that the mental picture the insecure administrator erects inside himself is based partly on these pop-culture stereotypes.

Mr. Glendenning seemed not so much to subvert the stereotypes as to transcend them. His self-possession allowed him to be and act precisely as he was. What he was was a taciturn, slightly unapproachable man who took his job very seriously and required his subordinates to do the same, but he took them seriously as well, and listened to them, and thought about them both as human beings and as parts of a larger mechanism whose efficient function was his responsibility. That is, if you had a suggestion or a concern, and you decided that it merited his attention, his door *was* open (that is, you could make an appointment through Caroline Oooley), and he would pay attention to what you said, but whether and how he would *act* on what you said would depend on reflection, input from other sources, and larger considerations he was required to balance. In other words, Mr. Glendenning *could* listen to you because he did not suffer from the insecure belief that listening to you and taking you seriously obligated him to you in any way—whereas someone in thrall to the martinet-picture would have to treat you as unworthy of attention, and someone in thrall to the peer-picture would feel that he needed either to take your suggestion to avoid offending you, or give an exhausting explanation about why your suggestion wasn't implementable or maybe even enter into some kind of debate about it — to avoid offending you or violating his picture of himself as the sort of administrator who would never treat a subordinate's suggestion as unworthy of serious consideration — or get angry as a way of anesthetizing his discomfort at not welcoming the suggestion of someone he feels obligated to see as a friend and equal in every way.

Mr. Glendenning was also a man of style, the sort of man whose clothes hang on him just right even after he's ridden in cars and sat at desks in them. All his clothes had a sort of loose but symmetrical hang to them that I associated with European clothes. He always put one hand in his hip pocket and leaned back against the lip of the counter when he drank coffee. It was, in my opinion, his most approachable posture. His face was tan and ruddy even under the fluorescents. I knew one of his daughters was a gymnast of some national repute, and sometimes he wore a tiepin or brooch or something that seemed to consist of two horizontal bars and a platinum figure bent complexly over both. Sometimes I imagined coming into the coffee room and finding Mr. Glendenning alone, leaning back against the counter, staring down into the coffee in his mug and thinking deep administrative thoughts. In my fantasy he looks tired, not haggard but careworn, weighed down by the responsibilities of his position. I come in and get some coffee and approach him, he calling me Dave and I calling him DeWitt or even D.G., which was rumored to be his nickname around other District Directors and Assistant Regional Commissioners—Mr. G is up for Regional Commissioner, is the rumor—and I ask him what's up and he confides to me about some administrative dilemma he's on the horns of, like how the Systems guy Lehrl's constant reconfiguration of people's spaces and the passages between them was a ridiculous pain in the ass and waste of time and if it were up to him he'd personally pick the officious little prick up by the scruff of the neck and put him in a box with only one or two air-holes in it and FedEx him back to Martinsburg but that Merrill Lehrl was a protégé and favorite of the Assistant Commissioner for Taxpayer Service and Returns at Triple-Six, whose other big protégé was the Midwest Region's Regional Commissioner for Examination, who was essentially if not formally Mr. Glendenning's immediate superior in terms of Post 047's Corporate Examination Function and was the sort of disastrous administrator who believed in alliances and patrons and politics, and who could deny 047's application for an additional half-shift of GS-9 examiners on a number of pretexts that would appear reasonable on paper, and only D.G. and the RCE would know it was over Merrill Lehrl, and DeWitt felt beholden to the beleaguered examiners to get them some relief and to take some time off the Return Turnaround Schedule, which two different studies indicated could be accomplished better through relief and expansion than through motivation and reconfiguration (an analysis with which Merrill Lehrl disagreed, D.G. noted wearily). In the fantasy, D.G.'s head and mine are lowered somewhat, and we speak quietly, even though no one else is in the coffee room, which smells good and has cans of fine-ground Melitta instead of the Jewel-brand white cans with the khaki lettering, and it's then, perfectly in the context of the exact beleaguered-and-distracted-examiners problem he's confiding to me about, that I hit D.G. with the idea of these new Hewlett-Packard document scanners and the way the software could be reconfigured to scan both returns and schedules and to apply the TCMP code to red-flag selected items, so that examiners would have only to check and verify the important red-flag items instead of wading through line after line of unimportant OK stuff in order to reach the important items. D.G. listens to me intently, respectfully, and it's only his judiciousness and administrative professionalism that keep him from expressing on the spot the enormous acuity and potential of my suggestion, and his gratitude and care that here a GS-9 examiner has come out of nowhere and given a lateral, outside-the-box solution that will both relieve the examiners and free up D.G. to send the odious Merrill Lehrl packing.

§44

I learned it at just twenty-one or twenty-two, at the IRS's Regional Examination Center in Peoria, where I spent two summers as a cart boy. This, according to the fellows who saw me as fit for a Service career, put me ahead of the curve, to understand this truth at an age when most guys are starting only to suspect the basics of adulthood — that life owes you nothing; that suffering takes many forms; that no one will ever care for you as your mother did; that the human heart is a chump.

I learned that the world of men as it exists today is a bureaucracy. This is an obvious truth, of course, though it is also one the ignorance of which causes great suffering.

But moreover, I discovered, in the only way that

a man ever really learns anything important, the real skill that is required to succeed in a bureaucracy. I mean really succeed: do good, make a difference, serve. I discovered the key. This key is not efficiency, or probity, or insight, or wisdom. It is not political cunning, interpersonal skills, raw IQ, loyalty, vision, or any of the qualities that the bureaucratic world calls virtues, and tests for. The key is a certain capacity that underlies all these qualities, rather the way that an ability to breathe and pump blood underlies all thought and action.

The underlying bureaucratic key is the ability to deal with boredom. To function effectively in an environment that precludes everything vital and human. To breathe, so to speak, without air.

The key is the ability, whether innate or conditioned, to find the other side of the rote, the picayune, the meaningless, the repetitive, the pointlessly complex. To be, in a word, unborable. I met, in the years 1984 and '85, two such men.

It is the key to modern life. If you are immune to boredom, there is literally nothing you cannot accomplish.

§45

Toni's mom was a bit nuts, as was her own mom, who was a notorious recluse and eccentric who lived in the Hubcap House in Peoria. Toni's mom took up with a succession of bad-news men in the US Southwest. The last one was giving them a ride back to Peoria, where Toni's mom had decided to return after the relationship before that one had gone bad. Blah blah. On this ride, the mom had more or less gone crazy (stopped taking her meds) and stolen the guy's truck at a rest stop, leaving the guy behind.

Both the mom and the grandmother had been given to catatonic/cataleptic states, which as far as I can tell is a symptom of a certain kind of schizophrenia. The girl, ever since young, had amused herself by trying to imitate this state, which involved sitting or lying extremely still, slowing your pulse, breathing in such a way that your chest doesn't even rise, and holding your eyes open for long periods, such that you're blinking only every couple minutes. It's the last that's hardest — the eyes start to burn as they dry out. Very, very hard to push through this discomfort... but if you do, if you can resist the almost involuntary urge to blink that comes when the burning and drying is the very worst, then the eyes will start lubricating themselves without blinking. They will manufacture a kind of false or ersatz tears, just to save themselves. Almost no one knows this, because the incredible discomfort of having your eyes open without blinking stops most people before they hit that critical point. And there's usually damage, anyway. The girl had called it 'playing dead,' since that's the way her mother had tried to describe and discount the states to the girl when she was very tiny, saying that she was only playing and that the game was called 'play dead.'

The abandoned man had caught up with them somewhere in eastern Missouri. They'd been on a little blacktop highway, and the first sign that he was behind was a pair of headlights that showed just when they were on a downslope that extended

a mile or more—they'd see the headlights appear
when the trailing vehicle hit the crest, then they'd
lose them when they started to climb the slow
grade again.

As Toni Ware remembers it and recounted it
just one time to X on a night that turned out to be
the anniversary of the occurrence, the vehicle that
the man had commandeered or hired came up fast
behind them—it turned out to be going quite a
bit faster than the truck, which had a camper
shell—and the man was not driving the vehicle.
He was standing on the front hood of what
emerged to be the trailerless cab of an enormous
semi truck, swollen by rage and malice to at least
twice his normal size, holding his arms up and out
in a terrible gesture of almost Old Testament retri-
bution, and hollering (in the rural sense of 'holler,'
which is almost a special kind of art form; it used
to be the way that people who lived way out in hill
country out of sight of each other would
communicate—it was the way of letting other
people know that they were around, because otherwise it could seem, in the rural hills, like you
were the only person anywhere within thousands
of miles) with an ecstatic black evil rage and glee
that caused Toni's mother—who, let's recall, was
not a paragon of stability—to become hysterical

and floor the accelerator and try to outrun the vehicle while at the same time trying to extract from her purse a bottle of prescription pills and to open the childproof cap, which the mother was terrible at and usually needed Toni to open for her—causing the vehicle, which was top-heavy because of the LEER camper shell, to swerve off the road and go over on its side in some kind of field or area of weeds, injuring the mom terribly such that she was half-stunned and moaning and blood covering her face and Toni was lying against the passenger-side window, and in fact still has the window's crank imprinted into her side if you can get her to raise her top and show you the eerie reproduction. The vehicle came to rest on its right side, and the mom wasn't wearing a seat belt, which people like that never do, and she was lying partly on top of Toni Ware, pinning her against the window so that she couldn't move or even tell whether she was injured. There was nothing but that terrible silence and hissing and ticking of a vehicle that's just had an accident, plus the sound of spurs or maybe just a great deal of pocket change jingling as the man negotiated the downslope down to them. Her own window was driven into the ground and the driver's-side window was now pointing up at the sky, but the windshield, though buckled and hanging halfway off, had turned into a four-foot vertical slot through which Toni Ware got a full-length view of the man standing there, cracking his knuckles and looking at the occupants of the car. Toni lay there with her eyes opened and slowed her breathing and played dead. The mom's eyes were closed, but she was alive because you could hear her breathing and occasionally giving little unconscious exclamations in her coma or whatever it was. The man looked at Toni, locked eyes with her, for a long time—later, she understood that he was trying to ascertain if she was alive. It is unimaginably hard to be staring straight ahead and have someone lock eyes with you and yet to appear like you're not looking back at them. (This is what had started the story; David Wallace or someone else had remarked that Toni Ware was creepy because, even though she wasn't shy or evasive and would maintain eye contact, she seemed to be staring *at* your eyes rather than *into* them; it was a bit the way a fish in a tank swimming past as you watched through the glass and looked into its eyes looked back at you—you knew that it was aware of you in some way, but it was unsettling because it wasn't anything like the way a human being seems aware of you when he meets your gaze.)

Toni's eyes were open. It was too late to shut

them. If she suddenly did, the man would know she was alive. Her only chance was to appear so dead that the man didn't check her pulse or hold a piece of glass to her mouth to check. What would keep him from checking was if her eyes were open and stayed open — no living human being could hold its eyes open for long periods of time. There was no one around; the man had plenty of time to look through the windshield and see if they were alive. Her mother's face was right up against her face, but luckily the blood was dripping into some hollow of Toni's throat; if it had been dripping into her eyes it would have made her blink involuntarily. She stayed rigid like that with her eyes open. The man climbed up and tried the driver's-side door but it was locked from the inside. The man went back and got some kind of tool or crowbar and pried the windshield off, shaking the truck violently. He got on his side and edged through the slot of the windshield, looking first at the unconscious mom and then at the girl. The mom moaned and stirred slightly, and the man killed her by reaching in and pinching her nostrils shut with one hand and covering her mouth with a greasy rag with the other and pressing hard, so hard that the mom's head strained against the side of Toni's as she unconsciously resisted being suffocated. Toni stayed there, shell-breathing, with her eyes still open and only inches from the man's eyes as he suffocated her mother, which took over four minutes of pressure for the man to be totally sure. Toni staring sightlessly and not blinking even though the dryness and discomfort must have been terrific. And somehow succeeded in convincing the man she was dead, because he did not pinch her nostrils shut and use the greasy rag on her, even though it would only have taken an extra four or five minutes...but no regular living human can sit there with their eyes open that long without blinking, so he knew. And so he got one or two valuables out of the glove compartment and she heard him jingling his way back up the upslope and the tremendously powerful sound of the truck's motor starting up and the truck leaving, and then the girl lay there trapped between the door and her dead mom for what must have been several hours before someone happened by and saw the wreck and called the police, and then probably an additional long time for them to extract her from the truck, uninjured in any real physical sense, and put her in some kind of charity ambulance...

Sheesh.

So do not mess with this girl; this girl is damaged goods.

§46

What usually happens is that on Friday afternoons a percentage of Pod C's revenue officers meet for Happy Hour cocktails at Meibeyer's. As is the case with most of the north side's taverns that serve as Service hangouts, Happy Hour at Meibeyer's lasts exactly sixty minutes and features drink specials that are indexed to the approximate cost of gasoline and vehicle depreciation involved in the 2.3-mile drive from the REC to the Southport-474 interchange. Different levels and Pods tend to congregate at different places, some of which are downtown and ape in various ways the more stylized venues of Chicago and St. Louis. The Bell Shaped Men can be found nearly every evening at Father's, which is right there on Self-Storage Parkway and owned outright by the area's Budweiser distributor; its function is less social than intubatory. Many of the wigglers, on the other hand, frequent the steroidal college bars around PCB and Bradley. Homosexuals have the Wet Spot in the downtown arts district. Most of the examiners with children, of course, go home to spend time with their family, although Steve and Tina Geach are often at Meibeyer's together for Friday's 2-H. Nearly everyone finds it necessary to blow off some of the unvented steam that's accreted during a week of extreme tedium and concentration, or extreme volume and stress, or both.

Meibeyer's has ash-gray laminate paneling, electric tiki torches whose origins are unknown but may date from a past incarnation, a Wurlitzer 412-C jukebox, two pinball machines, a foosball table and an air hockey game, and a small darts area prudently set off apart near the little hallway for the pay phone and restrooms. Meibeyer's broad windows overlook Southport's highway-side franchises and the complicated exits of the I-474 overpass. There's been the same Friday bartender for at least the past three years, according to Chuck Ten Eyck. Drinks are somewhat expensive because Service employees do not, as a rule, drink very much or fast, even at Happy Hour, which affects what the tavern has to charge for drinks in order to stay solvent. In winter weather Meibeyer's plows its own lot with a bladed pickup. In the summer, the bar's neon sign, which features the semion of a disembodied trilby whose angle changes twice a second, is reflected off something unapparent before it and appears faintly, reflected at least twice, in the tavern's front windows. Meibeyer's brim goes up and down against the malarial light of a gathering dusk in which shelving clouds and a spike in humidity only sometimes mean real rain that hits the ground.

Being mainly single, heterosexual transfers and replacements fall right into this groove. Robby van Noght comes a lot, though not this Friday. Gerry Moeller has been here all five weeks he's been posted at the REC. Harriet Candelaria comes but nearly always leaves after one round whenever Beth Rath happens to bring Meredith Rand, with whom Candelaria has problems that none of the transfers has the slightest inkling of the origins of. Steve and Tina Geach, who work in different groups and have different break rotations, and who are very devoted to each other and by general consensus have the sort of marriage that increases the attraction and credibility of marriage a great deal for people who are wired to be in such a close, enduring relation, always arrive together in their rust-ruddled VW microbus, and sit close together, always consuming the very same type and brand of beverage, and usually leaving the moment the bell rings for Happy Hour's end, often showing an odd ability to embrace and walk at the same time without looking clumsy. Chris Acquistipace and Russell Nugent, Dave Witkiewicz, Joe Biron-Maint, Nancy Johnson, Chahla ('the Iranian Crisis') Neti-Neti, Howard Shearwater, Frank Brown, Frank Friedwald, and Frank De Chellis haven't missed a Meibeyer's Happy Hour night since their posting. Dale Gastine sometimes brings a date. Keith Sabusawa now always brings Shane ('Mr. X') Drinion, the UTEX transfer with whom Sabusawa now rooms at Angler's Cove in a suite with two other transfers who never seem to come to Meibeyer's. Schedule F specialists like Chris Fogle and Herb Dritz bat about .500 in terms of attendance. Chuck Ten Eyck and 'Second-Knuckle' Bob McKenzie (both at Peoria REC the longest) are reliable as iron and always seem to want to somehow preside. R. L. Keck and Thomas Bondurant usually come. Toni Ware and Beth Rath nearly always drop by, and, as mentioned, some of the time Beth Rath brings the legendarily attractive but not universally popular Meredith Rand. Rath and Rand work adjoining Tingle tables in Sabusawa's group, which is tasked to utility/overflow, and the two are confidantes. Drinion, who has no vehicle, must remain as long as Sabusawa stays and no longer. According to Sabusawa, the UTEX from La Junta CA has no problem with this, and his response to Sabusawa's invitations to come along to Meibeyer's after shift change is always either 'All right' or 'Why not.' Meredith Rand's deal is that she tends to come only if her husband is somehow stuck at work or out of town on business. Like Drinion, she doesn't seem to have her own vehicle or even a driver's license. Sometimes she catches a ride home from Meibeyer's with Beth Rath but more often gets picked up by her husband, whom she apparently calls from the Pod in advance to say where she'll be, and whom no one in Meibeyer's has ever met but always simply pulls up into the lot and toots the horn for Meredith Rand, who in turn often starts gathering her things a minute or two before the car horn sounds, rather (according to Nancy Johnson) like a dog that can hear the pitch of its master's approaching engine and assumes its position at the home's window long before the master's car heaves into view. She has been at Meibeyer's for the last five weeks running, which implies that her husband has been working late or on the road a great deal. According to Sabusawa, no one knows what he does.

It is not difficult to see the way the energy and dynamics of the Pod C table change when Meredith Rand is present for Happy Hour at Meibeyer's. In many respects, it's a phenomenon that happens at bars, taverns, and grills everywhere when a woman of sufficient prettiness appears. Meredith Rand is one of only a handful of females at the REC that every male with an opinion on such matters agrees is totally, wrist-bitingly attractive. Beth Rath is far from homely, but Meredith Rand is a whole different order. Meredith Rand has bottomless green eyes and exquisite facial bone structure and a creamy poreless complexion with almost no lines or signs of wear, and a great cataract of curly dark-blond hair that, according Sabusawa, when worn down and allowed to frame her face and shoulders has been known to produce facial tics even in gay or otherwise asexual men. She is a cut of pure choice prime, is the consensus, not always unspoken. Her entry into any sort of Service social setting produces palpable changes, especially in males. The specifics of these sorts of changes are familiar enough to everyone not to spend time enumerating. Suffice it that Meredith Rand makes the Pod's males self-conscious. They

thus tend to become either nervous and uncomfortably quiet, as though they were involved in a game
whose stakes have suddenly become terribly high,
or else they become more voluble and conversa-
tionally dominant and begin to tell a great many
jokes, and in general appear deliberately unself-
conscious, whereas before Meredith Rand had
arrived and pulled up a chair and joined the group
there was no real sense of deliberateness or even
self-consciousness among them. Female examiners, in turn, react to these changes in a variety of
ways, some receding and becoming visually smaller
(like Enid Welch and Rachel Robbie Towne), others regarding Meredith Rand's effect on men with
a sort of dark amusement, still others becoming
narrow-eyed and prone to hostile sighs or even
pointed departures (q.v. Harriet Candelaria).
Some of the male examiners are, by the second
round of pitchers, performing for Meredith Rand,
even if the performance's core consists of making a
complex show of the fact that they are not performing for Meredith Rand or even especially
aware that she's at the table. Bob McKenzie, in
particular, becomes almost manic, addressing
nearly every comment or quip to the person on
either the right or left side of Meredith Rand, but
never once addressing her or appearing even to

look at her. Since Beth Rath is usually one of the people on either the right or left side of Meredith Rand, McKenzie's habit of doing this tends visibly to either annoy or depress Rath, depending on her mood.

For the past four weeks, really only Shane Drinion has seemed unaffected by the presence of a terribly attractive woman. Granted, it's not clear to anyone just what Drinion is affected by. The other transfers from La Junta CA (Sandy Krody, Gil Haight) describe him as a very solid Fats and S corp examiner but a total lump in terms of personality, possibly the dullest human being currently alive. Drinion tends to sit very quiet and self-contained at his place with his hand around a glass of Michelob (which is what's on tap at Meibeyer's), his face expressionless unless someone tells a joke that's somehow directed at everyone around the table, at which time Drinion will smile briefly and then his face will go back to being expressionless. But not expressionless in a glazed or catatonic way. He watches whoever is speaking very intently. Actually, intently isn't even the right word. There is no particular kind of study in his gaze; he just gives whoever's speaking his complete attention. His bodily movements, which are minimal, give the suggestion of being clipped and precise without being fussy or prissy. He will respond to a question or comment directed explicity to him, but other than these rare times he is not one of the people who speaks. But he's not one of these people who shrinks or recedes in groups until he's barely there. There's no sense that he's shy or inhibited. He's there but in an unusual way; he becomes part of the table's environment, like the air or ambient light. It's 'Second-Knuckle' Bob McKenzie and Chuck Ten Eyck who've conferred on Drinion the name 'Mr. X,' short for 'Mr. Excitement.'

At one Happy Hour in June things eventuate such that Drinion and Meredith Rand are left alone together at the table, more or less right across from each other, at the part of the evening when a lot of the other examiners have left for home or other venues. But they're both still there. Meredith Rand is evidently waiting for a pickup from her husband, who is said to possibly be some kind of medical student. Keith Sabusawa and Herb Dritz are once again playing foosball while Beth Rath (who rather likes Sabusawa; they go all the way back to the IRS Training Center in Columbus) watches with her arms crossed and a More-brand cigarette going in one hand.

So they're sitting alone at the table. Shane

Drinion seems to be neither nervous nor not to be sitting alone opposite the galvanic Meredith Rand, with whom he's exchanged not one direct word since his posting in late April. Drinion looks directly at her, but not in the challenging or smoldering way of a Keck or Nugent. Meredith Rand has had two gin and tonics and is on her third, slightly more to drink than normal but has not yet smoked. Like most married examiners, she wears both an engagement ring and a wedding band. She looks back at him, though it's not as if they're staring into each other's eyes or anything. Drinion's expression could be called pleasant in the way that certain kinds of weather are called pleasant. He is on either his first or second glass of Michelob from one of the pitchers that's still on the table, some not wholly empty. Rand has asked Drinion one or two innocuous questions about his origins. The thing about the Kansas Youth Authority orphanage seems to interest her, or else it's just the flat candor with which Drinion says he spent much of his childhood in an orphanage. Rand tells Drinion a brief childhood vignette about her going to a girlfriend's house and their using their hands and feet to climb up inside doorjambs and remain there high up in the jambs splayed and as if framed, though later on she will not be able to remember the reason for telling this anecdote or any of the context behind it. She does notice, almost right away, the same thing that Sabusawa and many of the other examiners have noticed — which is that although Drinion seems only partly socially present in a large gathering, there is a very different quality to any kind of tête-à-tête with him; he has the quality of being easy or good to talk to, which is an attribute for which there is no good single word in English, which is slightly odd, although so is whatever is good about talking to Drinion, since he possesses nothing that could be called charm or social grace or even evident compassion. He is, as Rand will say later to Beth Rath (though not to her husband), a very odd bird indeed. There is a brief exchange that Meredith Rand won't remember so well, involving Drinion's being an itinerant examiner and the REC and Examinations and the Service in general, i.e., Rand: 'You like the work?' which it seems to take Drinion a moment or two to process. D: 'I think I don't like it or dislike it either.' R: 'Well, is there something else you'd rather be doing?' D: 'I don't know. I don't have any experience doing anything else. Wait. That's not true. I worked in a supermarket three evenings a week between the ages of sixteen and eighteen. I would not prefer working in a supermarket to what I'm doing now.' R: 'It sure doesn't pay as well.' D: 'I put things on shelves and affixed small adhesive price tags to them. There wasn't much to it.' R: 'Sounds boring.' D: '...'

'We look like we're having a tête-à-tête' is the first thing that Meredith Rand will later be able to remember clearly having said to Shane Drinion.

'That's a foreign term for a private conversation,' Drinion responds.

'Well, I don't know how private it is.'

Drinion looks at her, but not in the way of someone who's not sure what to say in reply. One thing about him is that he's completely the same, affectwise and demeanorwise, by himself as he is in a large group. If he gave off a sound it would be like a single long tone from a tuning fork or EKG flatline instead of anything that varies.

'You know,' Meredith Rand says, 'if you want to know the truth, you kind of interest me.'

Drinion looks at her.

'I'm guessing you don't hear that a lot,' Meredith Rand says. She gives a little bit of a dry smile.

'It's a compliment, that you find me of interest.'

'I guess it is, isn't it,' Rand says, smiling again. 'For one thing, it's that I could say something like that, that there's something sort of interesting about you, without you thinking I'm coming on to you.'

Drinion nods, one hand around the base of his glass. He is very still, Meredith Rand notices. He doesn't fidget or change positions in his chair. He's a bit of a mouth-breather; his mouth hangs slightly open. With some people the mouth hanging open thing makes them look not too bright.

'For instance,' she says, 'imagine if I said something like that to "2K" Bob, how he'd react.'

'All right.'

Something goes slightly opaque for a moment in Shane Drinion's eyes, and Meredith can tell he is literally doing it, imagining her saying 'I find you interesting' to Second-Knuckle Bob McKenzie. 'What would his reaction be, do you think?'

'Do you mean his outer, visible reaction or his inner reaction?'

'The visible one I kind of don't even want to imagine,' Meredith Rand says.

Drinion nods. He is, it is true, not all that interesting to look at, in terms of looks. His head is somewhat smaller than average, and very round. No one's seen him in any sort of hat or coat yet; it's always a white dress shirt and sweater vest. His hairline is receding in a way that makes his forehead seem elaborate. There are some pimple scars around his temple areas. His face isn't very defined or structured; his nostrils are two different sizes or shapes, she can see, which is usually bad news for how good-looking someone is. His mouth is slightly too small for the width of his face. His hair is that dull or waxy kind of dark blond that sometimes goes with a reddish complexion and not the greatest skin. He's the sort of person you'd have to look at very intently even to be able to describe. Meredith Rand has been looking expectantly at him.

'You're asking me to describe what I believe his inner reaction might be?' Drinion says. His face at least isn't quite the same abraded-looking red when they're not in the fluorescence of the Pod, a reddishness in people that for some reason always depresses Meredith Rand first thing in the morning.

'Let's say I'm curious.'

'Well, I don't know for certain. When I was imagining it, my impression was that he'd be frightened.'

There's a slight change in Meredith Rand's posture, but she keeps her facial expression very neutral. 'How come?'

'My impression is that he's frightened of you.

774

This is just my impression. It's hard to explain out loud.' He stops for a moment. 'Your attractiveness presents McKenzie with some kind of test that he is afraid he won't pass. He's anxious about this. When others are around and he can act out a role, he can go into an adrenalized state that makes him forget he's afraid. No, that's not right.' Drinion pauses again for a moment. He doesn't look frustrated, though. 'My sense is that the adrenaline of performing makes the fear feel like excitement. In this type of setting, he can feel as though you excite him. That's why he acts so excited and pays so much attention to you, but he knows that others are watching,' Drinion concludes and takes a sip of Michelob; the motion of his arm is very nearly right-angled without being stiff or robotic. There is a precision and economy of movement about him. Meredith Rand has noticed this also during work hours, when she stretches and looks around as a kind of break and looks over and sees Drinion sitting and removing staples and moving different forms into different piles at his Tingle table. His posture is very good without being stiff or rigid. He looks like a man whose back and neck never hurt. He appears confused, or speculative. 'Fear and excitement seem to be closely related.'

'Ten Eyck and Nugent do the same thing, though, when the whole table's going at it like that,' Rand says.

Drinion nods in a slightly off way that indicates that's not quite what she has asked to talk about. It's not the same as his registering impatience, though. 'In a private, tête-à-tête conversation with you, though, my impression is that he would feel the fear more as real fear. He wouldn't like being directly conscious of this. Of feeling it. He wouldn't be sure what it was even fear of. He would be on edge, confused, in a way that could not be made to feel like excitement. If you told him that you found him interesting, I believe he would not know what to say. He would not know how he was supposed to act. I think not knowing this would make Bob very uncomfortable.'

Drinion looks at her steadily for a moment. His face, which is a bit oily, tends to shine in the fluorescence of the Examination areas, though less so in the windows' indirect light, the shade of which indicates that clouds have piled up overhead, though this is just Meredith Rand's impression, and one not wholly conscious.

'You're pretty observant,' Meredith Rand says.

Drinion replies: 'I don't know that that's true. I don't think I have any direct observation or fact-pattern to base this on. It's a guess. But my guess, for some reason, is that he might actually burst into tears.'

Meredith Rand looks suddenly pleased, which almost literally lights up her face. She reaches out and pats the table smartly with the fingers of one hand. 'I think you're right.'

'Somehow it's awful to contemplate.'

'I think he might fall out of his chair and run away crying and flapping his hands hysterically in the air.'

Drinion says, 'That I couldn't guess at one way or the other. I do know that you dislike him. I know he makes you feel uncomfortable.'

Drinion is facing Meibeyer's front windows, Meredith Rand the tavern's rear section, where there is the hallway and darts area and a decorative display of different types of formal or business-type hats glued by the rims to a varnished board. Meredith Rand leans forward and makes as if to rest her chin on the knuckles of one hand, though it's easy to see that the actual weight of her chin and skull is not really resting on these knuckles; it's more a stance than a way of making herself comfortable. 'And then if I say you're interesting, though, what's your inward reaction?'

'That it's a compliment. It's a pleasantry, but

also an invitation to continue the tête-à-tête. To make it more personal or revealing.'

Rand waved that hand in a small gesture of impatience or acknowledgment. 'But how does it make you feel, as they say in Evaluation?'

'Well,' Shane Drinion says, 'I think an expression of interest like that makes a person feel good. Provided the person saying it isn't trying to propose a level of intimacy that makes you feel uncomfortable.'

'Did it make you uncomfortable?'

Drinion pauses for another brief moment, though he doesn't move and his expression does not change. There's again maybe the smallest instant of blankness or withdrawal. Rand has the sense of an optical reader scanning a stack of cards very fast and efficiently; there is a kind of ambient unsonic hum about him. 'No. I suppose if you meant it sarcastically it would be uncomfortable — I would think you were angry at me or found me unpleasant. But you gave no sign that you meant it sarcastically. So no, I'm not sure what you meant by interesting, but people naturally like to be found interesting to other people, so the curiosity about just what you mean is not uncomfortable. In fact, if I understand it, it is this curiosity that the remark "You know, if you want to know the truth, you kind of interest me" is meant to arouse. The conversation then becomes about just what the person who said it meant. Then the other person gets to find out just what about him interests another person, which is enjoyable.'

'Ex—'

'At the same time,' Drinion continues, showing no sign that he's noticed Rand starting to say something even though he's been looking right at her, 'someone who finds you interesting seems then suddenly, almost by virtue of their interest in you, more interesting to you. That is a very interesting dimension to it also.' He stops. Meredith Rand pauses a little extra bit of time to make sure he's now stopped for good. Like her own left pinkie, Drinion's left pinkie finger is noticeably puckered and pale from wearing the rubber all day in Exams. There's no way she even wants to notice Drinion's clothing enough to even catalogue or characterize it to herself. Just the sweater vest alone is a tremendous downer. She has her white vinyl cigarette case out and unsnaps it and withdraws a cigarette, since it's just the two of them at the table.

'So, and do you think you're interesting?' Meredith Rand asks him. 'Do you see how someone could think you're interesting?'

Drinion takes another sip from his glass and

DAVID FOSTER WALLACE

puts it back down. Meredith Rand notices that he places it perfectly centered on the napkin without trying to or without having to adjust the glass's base in small fussy ways to get it perfectly centered on the napkin. That Drinion in not graceful the way dancers or athletes are, but there is something graceful. His movements are very precise and economical without being prissy. The glasses on the table that are not on napkins have large and variously shaped pools of condensation around them. Someone has selected the same popular song to play twice in a row on Meibeyer's big jukebox, which has concentric rings of red and white lights on an integrated circuit that allows them to go on and off in such a way that they accompany the chosen song's bass line.

Shane Drinion says: 'I don't think I've ever really considered it.'

'Do you know why they call you Mr. X?'

'I think so.'

'Do you know why they call Chahla the Iranian Crisis?'

'I don't think so.'

'Do you know why they call McKenzie Second-Knuckle Bob?'

'No.'

Meredith Rand sees Drinion looking at the cig-

780

arette. Her lighter is in a special loop attached to the cigarette case, which is cheap pebbled vinyl—Meredith Rand ends up losing her cigarettes in different places so often that it makes no sense to have an expensive cigarette case. She knows, from the Pod's workday breaks, that it would be pointless to offer Drinion a cigarette.

'What about you? Do you think I'm interesting?' Rand asks Shane Drinion. 'I mean, apart from me saying you were interesting.'

Drinion's eyes are on hers—he makes a lot of eye contact without being in any way challenging or flirty—while he seems to do the same internal card-sorting thing he's done before. Drinion wears an argyle sweater vest, strange, pebbly-textured polyester slacks, and brown Wallabee knockoffs that might literally be from JC Penney. The cold stream from the vent overhead tears the smoke ring to shreds the minute she shapes and exhales it. Beth Rath is now playing foosball with Herb Dritz while Keith Sabusawa watches the pregame warmup to a Cardinals baseball game on the television above the bar. You can tell that Beth would rather be sitting with Sabusawa but isn't sure how forward to be about her feelings for Sabusawa, who has always struck Meredith Rand as awfully tall for an oriental. Drinion also has a way of nodding where the nod has nothing to do with etiquette or affirmation. He says: 'You're pleasant, and so far I'm enjoying the tête-à-tête. It's a chance to pay direct attention to you, which is otherwise hard to do, because it seems to make you uncomfortable.' He waits for a moment to see if she wants to say anything. Drinion's facial expression isn't blank, but it's bland and neutral in a way that might as well be blank for all it tells you. Meredith Rand has, without being quite aware of it, quit trying with the rings.

'Is liking paying attention the same thing as being interested in somebody?'

'Well, I would say almost anything you pay close, direct attention to becomes interesting.'

'Is that true?'

'I think so, yes.' Drinion says: 'Of course you're especially interesting to pay attention to because you're attractive. It's almost always pleasant to pay attention to beauty. It requires no effort.'

Rand's eyes have narrowed, though part of this may have been the bits of cigarette smoke being blown back into her face by the AC vent.

Shane Drinion says: 'Beauty is almost by definition interesting, if by interesting you mean something that compels attention and makes attention feel pleasant. Although the word you just used was *interested* rather than *interesting*.'

'You do know I'm married,' says Meredith Rand.

'Yes. Everyone knows you're married. You wear a wedding ring. Your spouse picks you up at the south entrance several days a week. His car has a small hole in the exhaust that gives the engine a powerful sound. A sound that makes the car sound more powerful than normal, I mean.'

Meredith Rand does not look pleased at all. 'Maybe I'm confused. If you just said that it makes me uncomfortable, why even bring up the attractiveness thing?'

'Well, you asked me a question,' Drinion says. 'I told you what I decided is the truth. It took a second to decide what the true answer is and what is and isn't part of it. Then I said it. It isn't intended to make you uncomfortable. But it isn't intended to keep you from being uncomfortable, either — you didn't ask about that.'

'Oh, and you're the authority on what the truth is because...?'

Drinion waits a moment. In just the same tiny interval as the pause, it occurs to Meredith Rand that Drinion's pausing to see whether there's more or whether the truncated question is meant to invite him to supply the answer. Meaning is it sarcastic. Meaning he has no natural sense of whether something was sarcastic or not. 'No. I'm not an authority on the truth. You asked me a question about me being interested, and I tried to determine the truth of what I felt, and to say that truth to you, because my assumption was that's what was wanted.'

'I notice you weren't nearly as, like, blunt and forthcoming about how me saying I found you interesting made you feel.'

Drinion's expression and tone haven't changed even a little bit. 'I'm sorry. I'm having a hard time understanding what you just said.'

'I'm saying when I asked you how me finding you interesting made you feel, you weren't as blunt about answering. You skittered and skipped all over. Now with me all of a sudden there's a sudden concern for the blunt truth.'

'Now I understand.' Again a slight pause. The light-brand's smoke does taste thin against the aftertaste of tonic and lime. 'I don't recall any part of me trying to be evasive or false in that answer. Maybe I'm able to express some things better than others. I think that's a common finding for people. Also, I don't usually speak very much. I'm hardly ever in a tête-à-tête, actually. It may be that I'm not as skilled as other people at speaking in a consistent way about how something makes me feel.'

'Can I ask you a question?'

'Yes.'

Rand is now having no problem looking directly at Drinion. 'It doesn't occur to you that all that might strike somebody as a little condescending?'

Drinion's brow moves ever so slightly upward as he thinks. The baseball game has now started on the television, which may explain why Keith Sabusawa, who's usually keen to leave after Happy Hour has ended, hasn't left yet, and so neither has Shane Drinion. Sabusawa is tall enough that he has his loafers partly on the floor instead of hooked into the little support near the barstool's base. Ron, the bartender, has a small towel and a glass in his hand and is making cleaning motions but is also looking up at the game, and he's saying something to Keith Sabusawa, who in fact sometimes keeps whole long lists of baseball statistics in his head, which according to Beth Rath he finds soothing and restful to think about. Two great flashing, twittering pinball machines stand against the wall just south of the air hockey game, which no Meibeyer's patron ever plays because there's some chronic malfunction that makes air blow too hard through the table's pinholes and the puck rides several inches off the surface and is next to impossible to keep from flying off the table altogether. On the nearer of the pinball machines, a beautiful Amazon in a Lycra bodysuit is lifting by the hair a man whose limbs appear to gyrate in time with the syncopated lights of the obstacles and gateways and flippers.

Drinion says: 'That doesn't occur to me. But I do notice that you've become angry or upset in response to something I've said. This I can tell,' he says. 'It occurs to me that you might want to end this tête-à-tête conversation even though your spouse hasn't arrived yet to pick you up, but that possibly you're not sure how to do it, and so you feel somewhat trapped, and this is part of what's angering you.'

'And you, you don't have to be someplace?'

'No.'

An interesting bit of trivia is that Meredith Rand actually outranks Drinion, technically, since she's a GS-10 and Drinion a GS-9. This even though Drinion is several orders of magnitude more effective than Rand as an examiner. Both his daily average of returns and his ratio of total returns examined to total additional revenue produced through audit are much higher than Meredith Rand's. The truth is that utility examiners have a harder time getting promoted, since promotions usually result from Group Managers' recommendations, and UTEXs are rarely at one Post or Pod long enough to develop the sort of rapport with superiors that makes the superior willing to go through the paperwork hassle of recommending someone for a promotion. Also, since utility examiners are often the best at what they do, there is a disincentive in the Service against promoting them, since at GS-15 a Service employee moves into administration and can no longer travel from Post to Post. One of the things that regular posted wigglers find mysterious about UTEXs is what motivations induce them to serve as UTEXs when the position is something of a career-killer in terms of advancement and pay raises. As of 1 July 1983, the difference between a GS-9's and a GS-10's annual salary is $3,220 gross, which is not pocket change. Like many wigglers, Meredith Rand assumes that there's a certain type of basic personality that's maybe drawn to the constant movement and lack of attachment of being a utility examiner, plus the variety of challenges, and that Personnel has ways to test for these personality traits and so to ID certain examiners as likely UTEX candidates. There is a certain prestige or romance to the UTEX lifestyle, but part of this is married or elsewise dug-in employees' romanticization of the unattached lifestyle of somebody who goes from Post to Post at the institutional whim of the Service, like a cowboy or mercenary. Lots of UTEXs have come to Peoria since late winter/spring '84—there are a variety of theories about why.

'Do you usually keep hanging out here after the hour and the whole Second-Knuckle crowd leaves?'

Drinion shakes his head. He doesn't mention the fact that he cannot leave Meibeyer's until Keith Sabusawa does. Meredith Rand doesn't know whether he fails to mention this obvious fact because he knows that Meredith already knows it, or whether this guy is so totally literal that what he does is just answer whatever question she asks, literally, like a machine, like with only a yes or a no if it's a yes-or-no question. She puts out her cigarette in the little yellow foil disposable-type ashtray that you have to request directly from Ron if you want to smoke, because Meibeyer's has had problems with ashtrays disappearing, hard as that is to really believe given their chintziness. She extinguishes the cigarette a bit more thoroughly and emphatically than she usually does, in order to reinforce a certain tonal impatience in what she says as she puts the cigarette out: 'All right then.'

Drinion rotates his upper body slightly in his chair to see just where Keith Sabusawa is at the bar. Rand is 90 percent sure that the movement isn't any sort of performance or anything that is meant to communicate something nonverbally to her. Outside in the sky to the northwest are great sheer walls of rim-lit sunset clouds in whose interior there is sometimes muttering and light. None of the people in Meibeyer's can see these clouds, although you can always tell physically that rain's on the way if you pay attention to certain subliminal physical signals like sinuses, bunions, a particular kind of incipient headache, a slight felt change in the quality of the cold of the air-conditioning.

'So tell me why you think the prettiness thing makes me uncomfortable.'

'I don't know for certain. All I could give you is a guess.'

'You know, you're not really quite as direct as you seem at first, it turns out.'

Drinion continues to look directly at Meredith Rand but without any sort of challenge or evident agenda. Rand, who is certainly in a position to know that guilelessness can be a form of guile, will tell Beth Rath that it was a little like having a cow or horse look at you: Not only did you not know what they were thinking as they looked at you, or if they were thinking at all—you had no sense of what they were even really seeing as they looked, and yet at the same time you felt yourself truly seen.

'All right, I'll play the little game here,' Meredith Rand says. 'Do you think I'm pretty?'

'Yes.'

'Do you find me attractive?'

'...'

'Well, do you?'

'I find that question confusing. I've heard it in movies and read it in books. It's strangely phrased. There's something confusing about it. It seems to ask for an objective opinion as to whether the person you're talking to would describe you as attractive. From the context it usually appears in, though, it seems almost always to be a way of asking whether the person you're talking to is sexually attracted to you.'

Meredith Rand says: 'Well, sometimes you have to let a roundabout way of saying things pass, don't you? Some things can't be said straight out or it's just too gross. Can you imagine somebody saying "Are you sexually attracted to me?"'

'Actually yes, I can.'

'But it'd be awfully uncomfortable to ask it that way, wouldn't it?'

'I can understand how it could be uncomfortable or even unpleasant, especially if the other person wasn't sexually attracted. I'm fairly sure that packed into the straightforward question is the suggestion that the asker is sexually attracted to the other person and wants to know whether the feeling is reciprocated. So—yes, this means I was wrong. There are questions or assumptions also packed into the underlying question, too. You're correct—the business of sexual attraction seems to be a subject that it's not possible to be wholly straightforward in talking about.'

Rand's expression is now patronizing enough to be irksome or annoying to the vast majority of people she might be speaking with. 'And why do you think that is?'

Drinion pauses a moment. 'I think it's probably because direct sexual rejection is intensely unpleasant for people, and the less directly you express information about your sexual attraction to someone, the less directly you feel rejected if there's no corresponding expression of attraction.'

'There's something kind of tiring about you,' Rand observes. 'Talking to you.'

Drinion nods.

'It's like you're both interesting and really boring at the same time.'

'I've certainly been told that people feel I'm boring.'

'The Mr. Excitement thing.'

'The nickname is obviously sarcastic.'

'Have you ever been on a date?'

'No.'

'Have you ever asked someone out, or expressed being attracted to somebody?'

'No.'

'Don't you get kind of lonely?'

A small pause for this. 'I don't think so.'

'Do you think you'd know if you did?'

'I think I would.'

'Do you know what's on the jukebox right now?'

'Yes.'

'Are you by any chance a homo?'

'I don't think so.'

'You don't think so?' Rand says.

'I don't think I'm really anything. I don't think I've ever had what you mean by sexual attraction.'

Rand is very good at reading affect on people's faces, and as far as she can tell there's nothing here on Drinion's face to read. 'Not even when you were a teenager?'

That little pause for scanning again. 'Not really.'

'Did you worry you might be a homo?'

'No.'

'Did you worry that something was maybe wrong with you?'

'No.'

'Did other people worry that something was wrong?'

Another pause, both blank and not. 'I don't think so.'

'Really?'

'You mean as an adolescent?'

'Yes.'

'I think the truth is that no one paid enough attention to me to even wonder what was going on inside me, much less to worry about it.' He hasn't moved a bit.

'Not even your family?'

'No.'

'Did that kind of bum you out?'

'No.'

'Were you lonely?'

'No.'

'Do you ever get lonely?'

Rand has come almost to be able to expect the pause after some questions, or to absorb it as a normal part of Drinion's conversational rhythm. Drinion doesn't acknowledge that she has already asked this before.

'I don't think so.'

'Not ever?'

'I don't think so.'

'Why not?'

Drinion takes another sip from his glass of warm beer. There is something about the economy of his movements that Rand enjoys watching without even being quite aware that she enjoys it. 'I don't think I know how to answer that,' the utility examiner says.

'Well, like when you notice other people having romances or sex lives, and you don't, or you can tell they feel lonely and you don't, what do you think about the difference between you and them?'

There is a pause. Drinion says: 'I think there's a doubleness about what it is you're asking. It's really about comparing. I think it's more like if I'm watching someone and paying attention to them and thinking about what they're like, I'm not paying so much attention to myself and what I'm like. So there's no way to compare.'

'You don't ever compare anything to anything?'

Drinion looks at his hand and the glass. 'I have a hard time paying attention to more than one thing at a time. I think it's one reason I don't drive, for instance.'

'But you know what's playing on the jukebox.'

'Yes.'

'But if you're paying attention to our little conversation here, how do you know what's on the jukebox?'

There is now a longer pause. Drinion's face looks slightly different when he comes to the end of his two-second-scan thing.

Drinion says: 'Well, it's very loud, and also I've heard this song several times on the radio, either four or five times, and when it plays on the radio when it's over they often give the song's title and artist. I believe this is how radio stations are able to play copyrighted songs without being required to pay any sort of per-use fee. The radio play is part of the advertising of the record album that the song is part of. It's a bit confusing, though. The idea that hearing the song several times for free on the radio makes the customer more likely to go to the store and buy the song seems somewhat confusing to me. Granted, often what is being sold is the entire record album that the song is only one part of, so it may be that the song on the radio functions a little bit like a preview of a movie that they show as an inducement to buy a ticket for that later movie, of which the preview is obviously only one small part. There's also the matter of how the record companies' accounting personnel treat the expenses involved in free radio play. It seems to be not a matter of corporate and ICE but rather *inter*-corporate, if you think about it. Surely there are significant shipping and distribution costs involved in placing the recording of the song in the hands of the radio stations that will play it. Can the record company or its parent write off these costs if the radio stations are not paying any fee for the rights to air the song and so there is no income against which to write off the expenses? Or can they be deducted as marketing and advertising expenses if in fact no moneys are being paid to the ostensible advertiser, here the radio stations or their parent companies, but rather only to the postal service or some private carrier? How would the Service examiner be able to distinguish such expenses from illicit or padded deductions if no larger compensation could be referenced against which to add or subtract these distribution costs?'

Meredith Rand says: 'Can I say that one of the reasons you come off as a little boring is that you don't seem like you have any sense of what the real topic of a conversation is? This stuff doesn't have anything to do with what we were just talking about, does it?'

Drinion looks slightly puzzled for a moment,

2736424851555861646770737679828588919497100

table, and the angle of incidence doesn't allow
Rand to see the design or motif of the machine.
The sun is not yet all the way down but the bar's
low lights in the artificial tiki torches on the wall
have come up, and the air-conditioner vents' rate
seems at least to have been cranked back a bit. As
baseball fans, real Peorians tend to be equally
divided between the Cubs and the Cardinals,
though in this era the Cubs fans tend to keep their
partisanship more to themselves. Baseball on television is just about the most tedious type of sport
there is, in Meredith Rand's husband's opinion. It
may or may not rain, as usual. There are different-
shaped puddles of condensation on all the places
that do or did have a glass, and none of these ever
evaporate. Drinion still hasn't spoken or fidgeted
or changed his facial expression much at all. This
now right here is cigarette number three since
5:10. There are no attempted rings.

Meredith Rand says: 'What are you thinking
now?'

'I'm thinking that you raise a number of points
that seem valid, and that I'm going to maybe have
to give the whole matter of what someone is thinking when I'm speaking to them about something
more thought.'

Rand does the thing she can do where she

smiles broadly with everything except the muscles around her eyes. 'Are you patronizing me?'

'No.'

'Are you being sarcastic?'

'No. I can tell you've become angry, though.'

She exhales two brief tusks of smoke. Because of less backdraft from the air-conditioner vent, some of the smoke is going into Shane Drinion's face. 'Did you know that my husband is dying?'

'No. I didn't,' Drinion says.

They both sit for a moment, doing the respective sorts of facial things they are inclined to do.

'Aren't you going to say you're sorry?'

'What?' Drinion says.

'It's what you say. It's the standard etiquette thing to say.'

'Well, I was considering this fact in the light of your asking me about sexual feelings and loneliness. Receipt of this fact changes the context for that conversation, it seems.'

'Should I ask how so?' Meredith Rand says.

Drinion inclines his head. 'I don't know that.'

'Did you think finding out he was dying might mean you've got some kind of sexual chance with me?'

'I had not thought that, no.'

'Good. That's good.'

Beth Rath has started back over to the table with her mouth partly open to maybe say something or try to join the conversation, but Meredith Rand gives her a look that makes Rath turn around and return to her place on the red leather stool at the bar, where Ron is changing out the club soda cartridge. Meredith Rand puts her purse on the table and rises to recharge her glass.

'Do you want another Heineken or whatever?'

'I still haven't finished this one.'

'You don't exactly party down, do you?'

'I get full quickly. My stomach doesn't seem to hold very much.'

'Lucky you.'

Rand, Rath, and Sabusawa have some kind of quick conversation while Ron is making Meredith Rand's gin and tonic, which Drinion doesn't hear, though he can see slight reflections of the people at the bar in Meibeyer's front window. Nobody knows what he looks like or what his face is doing as he sits at the table alone, or even what he's looking at.

'Do you know what cardiomyopathy is?' Rand asks when she sits back down. She looks at her purse, which is almost more of a bag in terms of shape. Half the gin and tonic is already gone.

'Yes.'

'Yes what?'

'I think it's a disease of the heart.'

Meredith Rand taps her cigarette lighter exper-
imentally against her front teeth. 'You seem like a
good listener. Are you? You want to hear a sad
story?'

After a moment, Drinion says: 'I'm not certain
how to answer that.'

'I mean my sad story. Part of mine. Everybody's
got their sad story. You want to hear part of mine?'

'...'

'It's actually a disease of the muscle of the heart.
Cardiomyopathy.'

'I thought that the heart was itself a muscle,'
Shane Drinion says.

'It means as opposed to the vasculature of the
heart. Trust me, I'm kind of an expert on this.
What they call heart disease is the major vessels.
As in a heart attack. Cardiomyopathy is the muscle of the heart, the stuff of it, the thing that
squeezes and relaxes. Especially when it's of
unknown cause. Which it is. They aren't sure what
caused it. The theory was that he'd had a terrible
flu or some virus when he was in college that
seemed to get better but nobody knew it had settled in his myocardium somehow, the muscle tissue of his heart, and gradually infected it and
compromised it.'

'I think I understand.'

'You're thinking how sad, maybe, to fall in love and get married and then have your husband get a fatal disease — because it is, it's fatal. Like the rich kid in that movie, what's it called, except there it's the wife, who's kind of a lump if you want my opinion, but the rich kid gets disinherited and everything and marries her and then she gets fatally ill. It's a tear-jerker.' Rand's eyes, too, change slightly when she's scanning some kind of memory. 'It's a little like congestive heart failure. Actually, in many cases of cardiomyopathy the actual cause of death when the person finally dies is listed as congestive heart failure.'

Shane Drinion has his hand around his glass with a little beer but does not raise the glass. 'Is this because the muscle of the heart becomes compromised and can't squeeze well enough to circulate the blood?'

'Yes, and he had it before we got married, he had it even before I met him, and I met him when I was super young, I wasn't even eighteen yet. And he was thirty-two, and a ward attendant in Zeller.' She is extracting a cigarette. 'Do you happen to know what Zeller is?'

'I think you mean the mental health center building near the Exposition Gardens on Northmoor.' Drinion's bottom is hovering very slightly—perhaps one or two millimeters at most—above the seat of his wooden chair.

'It's actually on University, the main entrance is.'

'...'

'It's a psych hospital. Do you know what a psych hospital is?'

'In a general sense, yes.'

'Are you just being polite?'

'No.'

'The bin. The mental Marriott. A nut ward. Do you want to know why I was there?'

'Were you visiting someone important to you?'

'Negative. I was a patient there for three and a half weeks. Do you want to know how come?'

'I can't tell whether you're really asking me, or whether this question is simply an overture to telling me.'

Meredith Rand makes her mouth into a sardonic sideways shape and clicks her tongue a couple times. 'All right. That's kind of annoying, but I can't say you don't have a point. I was a *cutter*. Do you know what a *cutter* is?'

There is no difference—Drinion's face remains composed and neutral without seeming in any way to be trying to stay neutral. Meredith Rand has a very good subliminal antenna for this sort of thing—she's allergic to performance. 'My assumption is that it's someone who cuts.'

'Was that like a witticism?'

'No.'

'I didn't know why I did it. I'm still not sure, except he taught me that trying to analyze it or understand all the whys was bullshit—the only important thing was knocking it off, because if I didn't it would land me right back in the psych ward, that the idea I could hide it with bandages or sleeves and keep it a totally private thing that didn't affect anybody else was arrogant bullshit. And he's right. No matter where you do it or how carefully you do it, there's always a time when somebody sees something and says something, or when somebody is funking around in the hall and pretending to beg you to cut algebra and go to the park and get stoned and climb on the statue of Lincoln and grabs your arm too hard and some of the cuts open up and you bleed through your long sleeves, even if you've got two shirts on, and somebody sends for the nurse even if you tell them to fuck off and it was an accident and you'll just go home and get it seen to at home. There always comes a day when somebody sees something in your face that tells them you're lying and then the next thing you know there you are, in a lit room with your arms and legs uncovered, trying to explain yourself to somebody with zero sense of humor, actually a little bit like talking to you right now.' With a quick tight smile.

Drinion nods slowly.

'That was kind of nasty. I need to apologize for that.'

'I don't have a very good sense of humor, it's true.'

'This is different. It's like they do this initial intake interview, with a legal form on a white clipboard they ask you questions from as required by law, and if they ask you if you ever hear voices and you say sure, I hear yours right now asking me a question, they don't think it's funny or even acknowledge you're even trying to be funny but just sit there looking at you. Like they're a computer and you can't proceed until you give the properly formatted answer.'

'The question itself seems ambiguous. For instance, what voices are they referring to?'

'So they have, like, three different kinds of wards at Zeller, and two of them are locked, and the one they put me on as a mental patient is the one that he also worked on, on the third floor, with mostly rich girls from the Heights who wouldn't eat or took a bottle of Tylenol when their boyfriend dumped them, et cetera, or stuck their finger down their throat every time they ate something. There were a lot of barfers there.'

Drinion keeps looking at her. Now no part of his bottom or back is touching the chair, although the separation is so slight that no one else could see this unless somehow a very bright light were shined from the side, illuminating the slight gap between Drinion and the chair.

'You might be asking how I got in there, since we definitely were not rich or from the Heights.'

'...'

'The answer is good insurance through my dad's union. He ran the baling wire line at American Twine and Wire from 1956 until it closed down. The only days of work he ever missed were some of the days I was in Zeller.' Rand makes a very brief distended horror-face whose exact meaning is unclear and lights the cigarette she has been holding and looking at. 'To give you an idea.'

Drinion finishes the last bit of the Michelob and wipes his mouth a little on the napkin the glass has rested on. He then replaces the napkin and the glass. His beer's been at room temperature for much too long to produce any new condensation.

'And it's true that he already looked sick when I met him. Not gross or anything, it's not like he oozed or went around coughing or anything, but pale, even for winter. He looked delicate, like somebody old. He was totally skinny, too, although compared to the anorexic girls it was hard to see right off how skinny he was — it was more like he was so pale and got tired easily; he couldn't move very fast. With the terrible dark circles under his eyes. Some of the time he looked tired or sleepy, although it was also late at night, because he was the second-shift ward attendant on the ward, from five to the middle of the night when the night guy came on, who we never even really saw except for breakfast or if somebody had a crisis in the middle of the night.'

'He wasn't a doctor, then,' Drinion says.

'The doctors were a joke. At Zeller. The psychiatrists. They came in in the afternoon for like an hour, in suits — they always wore nice suits; they were professionals — and talked more to the RNs and the parents when they came in, mostly. And then they'd finally come in and you'd have a weird, stiff conversation, like they were your dad or something. And they had zero sense of humor, and looked at their watch the whole time. Even the ones who you could halfway see might be human beings were more interested in your case, not in you. Like in what your case might mean, how it was like or different than other cases in the textbooks. Don't get me started on the medical establishment at psych wards. They were bizarre to deal with; it could really mess with your head. If you said you hated it there and it wasn't helping and you wanted to leave, they saw it as a symptom of your case, not as you wanting to leave. It was like you weren't a human being, you were a piece of machinery they could take apart and figure out how it worked.' She snaps and unsnaps her cigarette case. 'It was really scary, actually, because they could sign papers to keep you in there or move you to a worse ward, the other locked ward was a lot worse and people talked about it, you don't want to hear about it. Or they could decide to give you meds that turned some of the girls into zombies; it's like one day they were there and the next there was nobody home. Like zomboids in really nice bathrobes from home. It was just very creepy.'

   '   '

'They couldn't do horror-movie stuff, though, they couldn't give you electroshock treatments like in that one movie, because everybody's parents were right there practically every day and knew what was going on. If you were on that ward you weren't *committed* to Zeller, you were *admitted,* and after seven days they actually had to let you go if your parents said so. Which some of them did, of the zombie girls. But they could legally sign forms that changed you to *committed.* The doctors in the suits could, so they were the scariest ones.'

'. . .'

'Plus the food was beyond gross.'

'You had been giving yourself small, hidden cuts as some sort of psychological compensation,' Shane Drinion says.

Meredith Rand gives him a level look. She does notice that he seems to be sitting up slightly straighter or something, because the very lowest part of the display of different kinds of hats is obscured, and she knows she isn't slumped down. 'It felt good. It was creepy, and I knew it couldn't be good if I was so secret and creepy about it, but it felt good. I don't know that else to say.' Every time she taps ash, it's three taps of the same speed and angle with a red-nailed finger. 'But I had fantasies about cutting on my neck, my face, which was creepy, and I'd been moving further up my arms all year without being able to help it, which scared me in hindsight. It was good I was in there; it was crazy—so maybe they were right after all.'

Drinion simply watches her. There is no way to tell whether it is building up to really rain or if the mass will miss them. The light outside is the approximate color of a spent flashbulb. It's too loud in here to know if there is thunder. Sometimes the air-conditioning seems to get colder or more insistent when it is about to storm, but that is not what it feels like is happening now.

Meredith Rand says: 'You have to say little things occasionally, like it's a real conversation, to show you're at least interested. Otherwise the person just feels like they're yammering and the other person could be thinking about God only knows what.'

'But putting cuts on your face would have externalized the situation too much,' Drinion says.

'There you go. Plus I didn't want to cut my face. As he ended up showing me, my surface face was all I really thought I had. My face and my body, that I was supposedly a *fox*. I was one of the *foxes* at Central Catholic. That's a high school here. They called us that—the *foxes*. Most of them were cheerleaders, too.'

Drinion says: 'So you were raised in the Catholic faith.'

Rand shakes her head as she taps the cigarette. 'That's not relevant. That's not the kind of little occasional response I meant.'

'. . .'

'The connection is the stuff about prettiness and loneliness you were talking about. Or we were, which is hard to understand, probably, given how supposedly being considered as good-looking in high school is the female ticket to popularity and being accepted and all the things that are supposed to be the opposite of loneliness.' She sometimes uses direct questions as an excuse to meet his gaze directly: 'Were you lonely in high school?'

'Not really.'

'Right. Oh, right. Plus beauty is a form of power. People pay attention to you. It can be very seductive.'

'Yes.'

Only in close retrospect does Meredith Rand consider the strange intensity of talking to the utility examiner. Ordinarily very conscious of her surroundings and what other people around her were doing, Rand later realized that large blocks of the tête-à-tête at Meibeyer's seemed removed from any kind of environment at all. That within these blocks of intense engagement she had been unconscious of the jukebox's intrusive music or the thud of its excessive bass in her breastbone, the insistent burbles and dings of the pinball machines and video raceway game, the televised baseball above

811

the bar, the normally distracting roar of surrounding conversations in which different audible snatches sometimes rose out and commanded attention and then receded into the ambient distracting noise of mixed-together voices all raised to overcome the room's own noise. The only way she is able to explain it to Beth Rath is that it was as if a sort of insulated container had formed around their table and sometimes hardly anything else had penetrated through it. Even though it wasn't like she just sat there looking right at the utility man all the time; it wasn't like a hypnotic thing. She also hadn't been aware of how much time had passed or was passing, which for Meredith Rand was a very unusual thing.* The best theory Meredith Rand could come up with was that it was that 'Mr. X' paid such close, intense attention to what she was saying—an intensity that had nothing to do with flirting or anything roman-

* Meredith Rand becomes no less comely or beautiful when she speaks to someone else about ritualistically cutting herself and being pink-paper'd into the Zeller Center. But she does look abruptly older or more drawn. You can see, not just imagine but see the way her face will look at forty—which after all, as is well known, will be only a different form of beauty, a less received and more severe or 'earned' beauty, in which the emergent flaws and lines do not mar her beautiful features but rather frame them, show seams in a face that is made and not just stamped out at random. Meredith Rand's nose and chin's slight cleft shine slightly in the red light of the walls' fake flames.

tic; this was a whole different type of intensity—although it was also true to say that Meredith Rand had experienced absolutely zero romantic or sexual attraction to Shane Drinion at that table in Meibeyer's. It was something else entirely.

'It was him who told me this. Who laid it out that way. At night, after dinner, after all the groups and OT were over and the doctors in their nice suits went home and there was just one nurse on the meds desk and him. He had the white staff coat with a sweater and these plastic sneakers and a big ring of keys. You could hear him down the hall without looking, just from the ring of keys. We used to tell him it looked like the ring of keys weighed more than he did. Some of the girls gave him a lot of grief, because it wasn't like he could really do anything to them.'

'...'

'There wasn't anything to do after visits at night except watch TV in the community room, or play Ping-Pong on a table that had a really low net so even the girls on heavy meds could feel like they could play, too, and all he had to do was do med checks and give people passes for the phone, and at the end of his shift he had to fill out evals on everybody, which was totally routine unless there was some kind of psych crisis.'

'So you observed him closely, it seems,' Shane Drinion says.

'It wasn't like he was much to look at if you were going to call somebody good-looking or not. Some of the girls called him the corpse. They had to have their mean little names for everybody. Or they called him the grim reaper. It was all just physical. But it was like no part of him touched his clothes on the inside; they just hung on him. He moved like he was about sixty. But he was funny, and he really talked to you. If anybody wanted to talk about something, meaning really talk, he'd go in the conference room off the kitchen with them and talk.' Meredith Rand has a set of routines for putting the cigarette out, all of which, whether fast and stabbing or slow and more grinding from the side, are quite thorough. 'He didn't make anybody do it. It wasn't like he was tugging on your sleeve to go do tête-à-tête or let him practice on you. Most people just vegged out in front of the TV, or the ones in for drugs had to go to their drug meeting in the van. He had to put his feet up on the table, usually, when you had a one-on-one with him. The table in the conference room that the doctors spread out their files to talk to the parents at. He'd lean way back and put his sneakers up on the table, which he said it was because he had a bad back, but really it was because of the cardiomyopathy, which he'd gotten mysteriously in college and was why he didn't finish college, which was why he was working this shitty nut ward attendant job, even though he was about seven thousand times smarter and more perceptive about what was really going on with people than the doctors and so-called counselors were. They saw everybody through this professional lens that was about half an inch across—whatever didn't fit in the lens they either didn't see or twisted it or squished it in so it fit. And having his feet in those chintzy Kmart shoes up on the table like that made him seem more like at least a person, like somebody you were really talking to instead of somebody trying to just diagnose you or trace your etiology so they'd have something to say that fit their little lens. They were a total joke, those shoes.'

'May I ask a question?'

'Why not just ask the question instead of taking the time to make me say yes you can ask a question?'

'I see what you're saying.'

'So?'

'Elevating his feet was to help him circulate blood more efficiently?'

'That's what you wanted to ask?'

'Is that not the sort of small, reinforcing question you were talking about?'

'For Christ's sake,' Rand says. 'Yes, it's for circulation. Although at the time who knew why it was. It was believable he had a bad back. He sure didn't look comfortable. All you could really tell was that this was somebody who was not in great shape.'

'He appeared frail, especially for his age.'

Sometimes now Rand will every so often toss her head back and to the side a tiny bit, very rapidly, as if rearranging her hair's feathering without touching it, which certain types of adolescent girls do a great deal without necessarily being aware of it. 'By the way, he taught me the word *etiology*. And he explained why the doctors had to be so distant and stiff; it was just part of their job. He didn't force anybody, but at times it seemed like he picked certain people to talk to, and he made it hard to resist. The nights could be hard, and it wasn't like watching *Maude* with suicidal people or people on heavy meds was going to help very much.'

'   '

'Do you remember *Maude*?'

'No I don't.'

'My mom loved that show. It was about the last thing in the world I wanted to see in there. If her husband got mad and told her "Maude, *sit*," she'd sit, like a dog, and it got a big laugh on the canned laughter. Some feminism. Or *Charlie's Angels,* which was just totally insulting, if you were a feminist.'

'. . .'

'The way he started talking to me was in the pink room, which was the isolation room, which is where they put you if you were on suicide watch and the law said you had to be legally observed twenty-four hours a day, or if you acted out in a disciplinary way where they said you presented a danger or disruptive influence—they could put you in there.'

'Called the pink room because that was the room's color?' Drinion asks.

Meredith Rand smiles coolly. 'Baker-Miller pink, to be exact, because there had been experiments showing that seeing pink soothed mental agitation, and soon every nut ward everywhere started painting their isolation room pink. He told me that, too. He explained the color of the room they put me in; it had a sloped floor and a drain in

the middle like something out of the Middle Ages.
I was never on suicide watch, if you're wondering.
I have no idea how tripped out you are by any of
this, like uh-oh here's this crazy person, she was
in Zeller when she was seventeen.'

'I wasn't thinking that.'

'What I did was tell a doctor who wasn't even
my doctor, I mean the one my dad's insurance was
paying for, but this was a different doctor who'd
come in and *cover* for the doctor's cases when he
couldn't come in, they all covered for each other
all the time this way, so in like five days you'd talk
to three different doctors, and they had to spread
your file and case notes or whatever out on the
table to even remember who you were—and this
doctor, who never even blinked, kept trying to get
me to talk about being *abused and neglected* as a
child, which I never was, and I ended up telling
him he was a freaking idiot and that he could
either believe me when I told him the truth or just
stick it up his stupid fat butt. And then that night
I'm in the pink room, he'd ordered it, which was
bullshit. Not like they dragged me in there and
threw me in and slammed the door—everybody
was pretty nice about it. But you know, one of the
weird things about being in a psych hospital is you
gradually start to feel like you have permission to

say whatever you're thinking. You feel like it's OK or maybe even in some way expected to act crazy or uninhibited, which at first feels kind of liberating and good; there's this feeling like no more smiley masks, no more pretending, which feels good, except it gets kind of seductive and dangerous, and actually it can make people worse in there—some inhibitions are good, they're normal, he said, and part of the syndrome they call some people eventually getting *institutionalized* is that they get put in a nut ward at a young age or a fragile time when their sense of themselves is not really very fixed or resilient, and they start acting the way they think people in nut wards are expected to act, and after a while they really *are* that way, and they get caught in the system, the mental-health system, and they never really get out.'

'And he told you that. He warned you about using uninhibited insults with the psychiatrist.'

Her eyes have changed; she puts her chin in her hand, which makes her seem even younger. 'He told me a lot of things. A lot. We talked for like two hours the night I was in the pink room. We both laugh about it now—he talked way more than I did, which is not how it's supposed to be done. After a while every night we were in there like clockwork, ta—'

'You went to the isolation room?'

'No, I was just in there that one night, and the regular case doctor, I have to admit it, he got the substitute one in some kind of disciplinary trouble for signing me in there; he said it was reactive.' Rand stops and taps her fingers against the side of her cheek. 'Shit, I forget what I was saying.'

Drinion looks slightly upward for an instant. ' "Every night we were in there like clockwork." '

'In the conference room, after visits and whoever was freaking out because of something in visits got calmed down or medicated. We'd sit in there and talk, except he had to get up every so often to do checks on where everybody was and make sure nobody was in anybody else's room, and make whoever was due for meds go to the meds desk. Every night on weekday nights we'd go in, and he'd do this thing he always did of filling up a Coke can with water at the fountain, he'd use a Coke can instead of a cup, and we'd sit down at the table and he'd go, "So shall we go intense tonight, Meredith, or just do some laid-back chit-chat?" and I'd almost act like somebody looking at a menu and go, "Well, hmm, tonight I think I'd like to go intense, please." '

'Can I ask a question?'

'Grr. Go ahead.'

'Should I infer that *intense* refers to the cutting behavior and your reasons for doing it?' Drinion asks. His hands are now on the table with the fingers laced together, which for most people causes the back to bow and slump, but with Drinion does not—his posture stays the same.

'Negative. He was too smart for that. We didn't talk about cutting often. That wouldn't do any good. It wasn't the kind of thing you could come at directly that way. What he—it's more like he mostly just told me all these things about myself.'

One of Drinion's interlaced fingers moves very slightly. 'Not asked you things?'

'Negative.'

'And that didn't make you angry? Presuming to tell you about yourself?'

'The big difference is the way he was right. Just about everything he said was right.'

'In what he told you about yourself.'

'Look, and he did this mostly in the beginning, when he needed to establish credibility. That's what he told me later—he knew I wouldn't be there long, at Zeller, and he knew I needed to talk to somebody, and he needed to let me know very fast that he understood me, knew me, he wasn't just dealing with me as a case or a problem to be figured out for his own career, which he knew was how the doctors and counselors seemed to me, which he said it didn't matter if I was right about them or not, the point is that I believed it, it was part of my defenses. He said I was one of the most strongly defended people he'd ever seen come in there. In Zeller. Short of the outright psychotics, I mean, who were just about impregnable, but they got transferred out almost right away; he rarely had any one-on-ones with real psychotics. The psychotic thing is just defensive structures and beliefs so strong that the person can't get out, they become the real world, and then it's usually too late, because the structure of the brain gets changed. That person's only hope is medication and a whole lot of pink around him at all times.'

'He understood you as a person, you're saying.'

'What he did, right in the pink room, while I'm sitting there on the bunk and going oh my God there's a *drain* in the floor, he right away told me two separate things about myself that I knew but nobody else knew. Nobody. I'm serious,' Meredith Rand says. 'It's like, I couldn't believe it. He was dead-on.'

'...'

'Now you're wondering what the things are,' she says.

Drinion does that very small thing with the angle of his head. 'Are you saying you'd like me to ask you what they are?'

'No way.'

'Almost by definition, I doubt that you'd tell them to someone.'

'Bingo. Right. No way. Not that they're all that interesting,' she says. 'But he did. He knew them, and you can bet that got my attention. That made me sit up and take notice. How could it not?'

Drinion says: 'I can understand that.'

'Exactly. That he knew me, understood me, was interested in understanding. People always say that, *understand, I understand you, please help us understand you.*'

'I've said it several times, too, while we've been talking,' Drinion says.

'Do you know how many times?'

'Nine, though I believe only four in quite the sense that you appear to be referring to, if I understand what you mean.'

'Is that a joke?'

'My using the word *understand* again just now?'

Rand makes an exasperated expression and directs it off to one side and then the other as if there were still more people at the table with them.

Drinion says: 'Not if I follow the sense of

understand you mean, which doesn't refer to understanding a statement or somebody's implication but more a person, which seems to me less cognitive than a matter of empathy or I think even *compassion* would be the word you mean by this kind of understanding.'

'The thing,' she says, 'is he really did. Use whatever word you want. Nobody knew these things he told me—one of them I don't even think I knew, really, until he just put it out there in blunt words.'

'This made an impression,' Drinion says helpfully.

Rand ignores him. 'He was a natural therapist. He said it was his calling, his art. The way painting or being able to dance really well or to sit there reading the same thing for hours on end without moving or getting distracted is other people's calling.'

'. . .'

'Would you say you have a calling?' the POTEX asks Shane Drinion.

'I doubt it.'

'He wasn't a doctor, but when he saw somebody in there he thought he could maybe help, he'd try to help them. Otherwise he was more like a security guard, he said.'

'...'

'One time he said he was more just like a mirror. In the intense conversations. If he seemed mean or stupid, what it really meant was that you saw yourself as mean and stupid. If one time he struck you as smart and sensitive, it meant you were smart and sensitive that day—he just showed you what was there.

'He looked terrible, but that was also part of the power of sitting in there with him and doing these intense bits of work. He looked so sick and washed out and delicate that you never got the idea that here was this smug, normal, healthy, rich doctor judging you and being glad he wasn't you or just seeing you as a case to resolve. It was like really talking to somebody, with him.'

'Anyone could tell that he made a great impression on you in this difficult time, your future husband,' Shane Drinion says.

'Are you being ironic?'

'No.'

'Are you thinking, like, here's this messed-up seventeen-year-old falling in love with the therapist-type adult figure that she thinks is the only one that *understands?*'

Shane Drinion shakes his head exactly twice. 'That's not what I'm thinking.' It occurs to Rand that he could conceivably be bored out of his skull and she'd have no way of telling.

'Because that's pathetic,' Meredith Rand says. 'That's like the oldest story in the book, and however messed up you might think this is, it sure wasn't that.' She's sitting up very straight now for a moment. 'Do you know what monopsony is?'

'I think so.'

'What is it then?'

Shane Drinion clears his throat slightly. 'It's the reverse of monopoly. There's a single buyer and multiple sellers.'

'All right.'

'I think bids for government contracts, such as when the Service upgraded its card readers at the La Junta center last year, are an example of a monopsonistic market.'

'All right. Well, he taught me that one, too, although in a more of a personal context.'

'As in a metaphor,' Drinion says.

'Do you see what it could have to do with loneliness?'

Another very brief moment of inward scanning. 'I can see how it might lead to distrust, since contract-bidding situations are susceptible to rigging, dishonest cost-projections, and things like that.'

'You're a very literal person, did you know that?'

'...'

'Here's the literal thing, then,' Meredith Rand says. 'Say you're pretty, and there's things about being pretty that you like—you get treated special, and people pay attention to you and talk about you, and if you walk in someplace you can almost feel the room change, and you like it.'

'It's a form of power,' Drinion says.

'But at the same time you also have less power,' Meredith Rand says, 'because the power you have is all totally connected to prettiness, and at some point you realize that the prettiness is like a kind of box you're always in, or prison, that nobody's ever going to see you or think about you apart from the prettiness.'

'...'

'It's not like I even thought I was all that pretty,' Meredith Rand says. 'Especially in high school.' She's rolling a cigarette back and forth between her fingers but not lighting it. 'But I sure knew everybody else thought I was pretty. Ever since like twelve, people were saying how lovely and beautiful I was, and in high school I was one of the foxes, and everybody knew who they were, and it became sort of official, socially: I was pretty, I was desirable, I had the power. Do you get this?'

'I think so,' Shane Drinion says.

'Because this is what intense meant—he and I really talked about it, the prettiness. It was the first time I ever really talked about it with anybody. Especially a guy. I mean except for "You're so beautiful, I love you" and trying to put their tongue in your ear. Like that was all you needed to hear, that you were beautiful, and you were supposed to fall over and let them boff you.'

'. . .'

'If you're pretty,' Meredith Rand says, 'it can be hard to respect guys.'

'I can understand that,' Drinion says.

'Because you never even get to see what they might really be like. Because the minute you're around, they change; if they've decided you're beautiful, they change. It's like the thing in physics—if you're there to look at the experiment, it supposedly messes up the results.'

'There's a paradox involved in it,' Drinion says.

'And except for a while you like it. You like the attention. Even if they change, you know it's you making them change. You're attractive, they're attracted to you.'

'Hence the tongues in the ear.'

'Although with a lot of them it turns out it's got the opposite effect. They almost avoid you. They get scared or nervous — it makes them want something, and they're embarrassed or scared of wanting it — they can't talk to you or even look at you, or else they start putting on a little show like Second-Knuckle Bob, this flirty sexist thing where they think they're doing it to impress you but really it's to impress other boys, to show they're not afraid. And you haven't even done or said anything to start it; all you have to do is just be there, and everybody changes. Presto change-o.'

'It sounds taxing,' Drinion says.

Meredith Rand lights the cigarette she's been holding. 'Plus other girls hate you; they don't even know you or talk to you and they decide they hate you, just because of how the boys all react — like you're a threat to them, or they assume you're a stuck-up bitch without even trying to get to know you.' She has a definite style of averting her head to exhale and then bringing it back. Most people think she's very direct.

'I wasn't a ditz,' she says. 'I was good with figures. I won the algebra prize in tenth-grade algebra. But of course nobody cared about me being smart or good at math. Even the men teachers got all googly and nervous or pervy and flirty when I came up after or something to ask about something. Like I was a fox and there was no way anybody could ever even think to see anything more than that.

'Listen,' Meredith Rand says. 'Don't misunderstand me. It's not like I think I'm all that pretty. I'm not saying I'm beautiful. Actually I've never thought I was all that beautiful. My eyebrows are too heavy, for one thing. I'm not going to go around plucking them, but they're too heavy. And my neck is, like, twice as long as a normal person's, when I look in the mirror.'

'...'

'Not that it even matters.'

'No.'

'No what?'

'No, I understand it doesn't really matter,' Drinion says.

'Except it does. You don't get it. The prettiness thing—at least when you're that age, it's like a kind of trap. There's a greedy part of you that really likes the attention. You're special, you're desirable. It's easy to start thinking of the prettiness as you, like it's all you've got, it's what makes you special. In your designer jeans and little sweaters you can put in the dryer so they're even tighter. Walking around like that.' Although it's not as if what Meredith Rand wears at the Post is effacing or dowdy. They're professional ensembles, well within code, but many of the Post's examiners still bite their knuckles when she goes by, especially in cold months, when the extremely dry air produces static cling.

She says: 'The flip side being how you also start understanding that you're really just a piece of meat. Is what you are. Really desirable meat, but also that you'll never get taken seriously and never, like, be the president of a bank or something because no one will ever be able to see past the prettiness, the prettiness is what affects them and what makes them feel anything, and that's all that matters to them, and it's hard not to get sucked into that, to start, like, arranging yourself and seeing yourself the same way.'

'You mean seeing and reacting to people through whether or not they're attractive?'

'No, *no.*' You can see that Meredith Rand would have a hard time quitting cigarettes, since she uses the way she smokes and exhales and moves her head to convey a lot of affect. 'I mean starting to see yourself as a piece of meat, that the only thing you've got is your looks and the way you affect boys, guys. You start doing it without even knowing you're doing it. And it's scary, because at the same time it also feels like a box; you know there's more to you inside you because you can feel it, but nobody else will ever know—not even other girls, who either hate you or are scared of you, because you're a monopsony, or else if they're also the foxes or the cheerleaders they're competing with you and feel like they have to do this whole competitive catty thing that guys don't have any idea of, but trust me, it can be really cruel.'

The fact that one of Drinion's nostrils is slightly larger than the other sometimes makes it look as though he's cocking his head a little bit, even when he is not. It's somewhat parallel to the mouth-breathing thing. Meredith Rand usually interprets expressionlessness as inattention, the way someone's face blanks out when you're talking and they're pretending to listen but not really listening, but this is not the way Drinion's expressionlessness seems. Also, it's either her imagination or Drinion is sitting up steadily straighter and taller, because he seems to be slightly taller than when the tête-à-tête started. A collection of different kinds of old-fashioned fedoras and homburgs and various business hats glued or pinned somehow to a varnished rosewood board that had been visible on the opposite wall of Meibeyer's over Drinion's head is now partly obscured by the crown of his head and the slight cowlick that sticks up at his round head's apex. Drinion is actually levitating slightly, which is what happens when he is completely immersed; it's very slight, and no one can see that his bottom is floating slightly above the seat of the chair. One night someone comes into the office and sees Drinion floating upside down over his desk with his eyes glued to a complex return, Drinion himself unaware of the levitating thing by definition, since it is only when his attention is completely on something else that the levitation happens.

'Which is part of the feeling of the box,' Meredith Rand is continuing. 'There's the feeling, which in teenagers is really bad anyway, of feeling like nobody can really ever know you or love you for who you are because they can't really see you and for some reason you won't let them even though you feel like you want them to. But it's also at the same time a feeling that you know it's boring and immature and like a bad type of movie problem, "Boo hoo, no one can love me for who I am," so you're also aware that your loneliness is stupid and banal even while you're feeling it, the loneliness, so you don't even have any sympathy for yourself. And this is what we talked about, this is what he told me about, that he knew without me telling him: how lonely I was, and how the cutting had something to do with the prettiness and feeling like I had no right to complain but still being really unhappy at the same time believing that not being pretty seemed like it would be the end of the world, I'd just be a piece of meat nobody wanted instead of a piece of meat they did happen to want. Like I was trapped inside it, and I still really had no right to complain about it because look at all the girls who were jealous and thought no one who's pretty could be lonely or have any problems, and even if I did complain, then all the complaining was banal, he taught me *banal,* and *tête-à-tête,* and how this can become part of the whole loneliness—the truth of saying "I'm just meat, people only care about me as beautiful, no one cares what I really am inside, I'm lonely" is totally boring and banal, like something corny in *Redbook,* not beautiful or unique, or special. Which was the first time I thought of the scars and the cutting as letting the unbeautiful inside truth come out, be on the out-side, even if I was also hiding it under long sleeves—although your blood is really actually quite pretty if you really look at it, I mean when it first comes out, although the cut has to be very careful and fine and not too deep so the blood just more appears as a line that kind of slowly wells up, so it's thirty seconds or more before you have to wipe because it's starting to run.'

'Does it hurt?' Shane Drinion asks.

Meredith Rand exhales sharply and looks right at him. 'What do you mean does it? I don't do it anymore. I never have, since I met him. Because he more or less told me all this and told me the truth, that it doesn't ultimately matter why I do it or what it, like, represents or what it's about.' Her gaze is very level and matter-of-fact. 'All that matters is that I was doing it and to stop doing it. That was it. Unlike the doctors and small groups that were all about your feelings and why, as though if you knew why you did it you'd magically be able to stop. Which he said was the big lie they all bought that made doctors and standard therapy such a waste of time for people like us—they thought that diagnosis was the same as cure. That if you knew why, it would stop. Which is bullshit,' Meredith Rand says. 'You only stop if you stop. Not if you wait for somebody to explain it in some magic way that will presto change-o make you stop.' She makes a sardonic flourish with her cigarette hand as she says presto change-o.

Drinion: 'It sounds as though he really helped you.'

'He was very blunt,' she says. 'It turned out being blunt is something he's proud of—it's part of his act that there is no act. Only I only found that out later.'

'. . .'

'You can see, of course, how having somebody have this kind of compassion and understanding of what's really going on inside you, how this would affect somebody that thought her big problem was the impossibility of anybody seeing past the prettiness to what was inside. Would you like to know his name?'

Drinion blinks once. He doesn't blink very often. 'Yes.'

'Edward. "Ed Rand, partial BS," he'd say. So you can see why I was pretty much primed to fall in love with him.'

'I think so.'

'So I don't need to spell it out,' Meredith Rand says. 'In a way, if he was a perv or a creep that played things that way, it would be a perfect setup for getting pretty young girls to fall for him. Work in a place that everybody comes in all mucked up and lonely and in crisis, and find the young girls, whose basic problem is probably always going to be their looks. So all he had to do, if he was smart, and he'd seen hundreds of messed-up girls come through, who starved themselves, or stole clothes from shopping malls, or ate and couldn't stop eating, or cut on themselves, or got into drugs, or kept running away with older black guys and getting dragged back over and over again by the parents, whatever, you get the idea, but that all had the same really essential problem, each time one of them came in, no matter what they were officially in for, which was not feeling like they were really known and understood and that was the cause of their loneliness, of the constant pain they were in that made them cut, or eat, or not eat, or give blowjobs to the whole basketball team in a row out back behind the cafeteria dumpster, which is what one cheerleader I know for a total fact did all the time junior year, although she was never really quite one of the foxes because she was known as such a total slut; a lot of the foxes just hated her.' Rand looks briefly right at Drinion to see whether there is any visible reaction to the word *blowjob,* which he does not appear to provide. 'And it'd be easy to get them in the conference room, and to tell them some stuff about themselves that totally shocked and amazed them because they hadn't ever told *anybody* about it and yet it was totally easy to spot and know about because at the core it was all the same.'

Drinion asks: 'Did you tell him this, during the therapy sessions that were designated as intense?'

Rand shakes her head as she extinguishes the Benson & Hedges cigarette. 'They weren't therapy sessions. He hated that term, all that terminology. They were just tête-à-têtes, talking.' Again she uses the same number of stabs and partial rolls to extinguish it, although with less force than when she's appeared impatient or angry with Shane Drinion. She says: 'That was all he said it seemed like I needed, just to talk to somebody with no bullshit, which was what the Zeller Center doctors didn't realize, or like they couldn't realize it because then the whole structure would come down, that here the doctors had spent four million years in medical school and residency and the insurance companies were paying all this money for diagnosis and OT and therapy protocols, it was all an institutional structure, and once things became institutionalized then it all became this artificial, like, organism and started trying to survive and serve its own needs just like a person, only it wasn't a person, it was the opposite of a person, because there was nothing inside it except the will to survive and grow as an institution—he said just look at Christianity and the whole Christian Church.'

'But my question was whether you talked to him about your possible suspicion, the possibility that he didn't really understand you, and care, but was a creep?'

Sometimes throughout the conversation Meredith Rand looks down critically at her fingernails, which are almond-shaped and neither too short nor too long, and painted a lustrous red. Shane Drinion looks at her hands only when Rand does, as a rule.

'I didn't have to,' Rand says. 'He brought it up. Edward did. He said given my problem it was only a matter of time before it occurred to me that maybe he didn't understand and care but only understood me the way a mechanic understands a machine—this was a time in the second week in the nut ward that I was having all these dreams about different kinds of machinery, with gears and dials, which the doctors and so-called therapists wanted to talk about and get me to see the symbolism of, which he and I both laughed about because it was so obvious an idiot could have seen it, which he said wasn't the doctors' fault or that they were stupid, that was just the way the machine of the institution of in-patient therapy worked, and the doctors had no more choice about how much importance they put on the dreams than a little piece of machinery does about doing the little task or movement it's been put there to do over and over again as part of the larger operation of the larger machine.' Rand's rep at the REC is that she's sexy but crazy and a serious bore, just won't shut up if you get her started; they argue about whether they ultimately envy her husband or pity him. 'But he brought it up before I had a chance to even start thinking about it.' She unsnaps her white vinyl case but does not extract a cigarette from it. 'Which I have got to say was kind of surprising, because by this time I was eighteen, and I'd had such bad experiences with creeps and pervs and jocks and college boys' "I love you" on the first date that I was very suspicious and cynical about guys' double motives, and normally the minute this sickly little orderly started paying attention to me I'd have my defensive shields way up and be considering all kinds of creepy, depressing possibilities.'

Drinion's red forehead crinkles for just a moment. 'Were you eighteen, or seventeen?'

'Oh,' Meredith Rand says. 'Right.' As she acts younger, she begins to laugh sometimes in a fast and toneless way, like a reflex. 'I was just eighteen. I had my eighteenth birthday on my third day in Zeller. My dad and mother even came out and brought a cake and noisemakers during visiting hours and tried to have this celebration, like whoopee, which was so embarrassing and depressing I didn't know what to do, like, a week ago you're hysterical about some cuts and put me in the bin and now you want to pretend it's happy birthday, let's ignore the girl screaming in the pink room while I blow out the candles and you fix the elastic of the hat under your chin, so I just played along because I didn't know what to say about how totally weird it was for them to be acting like, happy birthday, Meredith, whoopee.' She is kneading the flesh of one arm with the other arm's hand as she recounts this. Sometimes, as Drinion sits with his hands laced on the tabletop before him, he changes having one thumb or the other be the thumb on top. His former glass of beer sits empty except for a semicircle of foamy material along the bottom's edge. Meredith Rand now has three different narrow straws she can choose to chew on; one of them is already quite thoroughly chewed and flattened at one end. She says:

'So he brought it up. He said it was probably going to occur to me on some level soon, so if I wanted it really intense we might as well talk about it. He'd always drop little bombs like this, and then while I sat there like':—she forms an exaggerated taken-aback expression—'he'd groan and swing his feet around off the table and go out with his clipboard to do checks—he had to officially check on everybody every quarter hour and note down where they were and make sure nobody was making themselves barf or looping pillowcases together to hang themselves with — and he'd go out and leave me there in the conference room with nothing to look at or do, waiting for him to come back, which tended to take him a long time because he never felt well, and if there was no nursing supervisor or anybody around to watch him he walked very slow and used to lean against the wall every so often to catch his breath. He was white as a ghost. Plus he took all these diuretics, which made him have to pee all the time. Except when I asked him about it all he'd say is that it was his own private business and we weren't in here talking about him, it didn't matter about him because all he really was was a kind of mirror for me.'

'So you didn't know that he had cardiomyopathy.'

'All he'd say was that his health was a mess but that the advantage of being a physical mess was that he looked like exactly as much of a mess as he really was, there was no way to hide it or pretend he was less of a mess than he felt like. Which was very different than people like me; he said the only way for most people to show the mess was to fall apart and get put someplace like this, like Zeller, where it was undeniably obvious to you and your family and everybody else that you were a mess, so there was at least a certain relief to being put in the nut ward, but he said given the realities here, meaning insurance and money and the way institutions like Zeller worked, given the realities it was almost sure that I wouldn't be in here that long, and what was I going to do when I got back out there in the real world where there were all these razor blades and X-Acto knives and long-slaved shirts. Long-sleeved shirts.'

'Can I ask a question?'

'You bet.'

'Did you react? When he brought up the idea that his helping you and intense conversations with you were connected to your attractiveness?'

Rand snaps and unsnaps her white cigarette case. 'I said something like, so you're saying you'd be in here with me all concerned and interested if I was fat with zits and a, like, big old jaw? And he said he couldn't say one way or the other, he'd worked with all kinds of people that came through, and some were plain girls and some were pretty, he said it had more to do with how defended people were. If they were too defended in terms of their real problems—or if they were just outright psycho, and when they looked at him they saw some shiny terrifying four-faced statue or something— then he couldn't do anything. It was only if he felt a kind of vibe off the person where he felt like he could maybe understand them and maybe offer real interpersonal talking and help with them instead of just the inevitable doctor-and-institution thing.'

'Did you accept that as an answer to your question?' Drinion says, without any kind of incredulous or judging expression that Meredith Rand can see.

'No, I said something sarcastic like blah blah blah whatever, but he said that wasn't his real answer, he wanted to answer the question because he knew how important it was, he could totally understand the anxiety and suspicion of would he really even care and pay attention if I wasn't pretty, because he said in actuality this was my whole core problem, the one that would follow me when I got out of Zeller, and that I had to find out how to deal with or I'd be back in here or worse. Then he said it was close to lights-out and we had to quit for today, and I was, like, you're telling me there's this major core problem I have to deal with or else and then that's it, time for noddy blinkums? I was so ticked off. And then the next two or three nights he wasn't even there, and I was totally spasming out, and there was only this other guy there from the weekends, and the day staff won't ever tell you *anything,* all they see is that you're agitated and they report that you're agitated but nobody actually cares about what you're agitated about, no one wants to even know what your question is, if you're an in-patient you're not a human being and they don't have to tell you anything.' Rand makes her face assume a look of frustrated distance. 'It turned out he'd been in the hospital — the real hospital; when the inflammation gets bad then the heart doesn't pump the blood out all the way, and it's a little like what they call congestive heart failure; they have to put you on oxygen and heavy-duty anti-inflammatories.'

'So you were concerned,' Drinion says.

'But at the time I didn't even know that, all I knew was he wasn't there, and then it was the weekend, so it was a long time before he got back, and at first when he did I was totally ticked and wouldn't even talk to him in the hall.'

'You'd been left hanging.'

'Well,' Rand says, 'I took it personally that he'd gotten me all involved and said all these heavy therapeutic things and then disappeared, like it was all just a sadistic game, and when he got back the next week and asked me in the TV room, I just pretended I was into the TV show and pretended he wasn't even there.'

'You didn't know that he'd been in the hospital,' Drinion says.

'After I found out how sick he was, I felt pretty bad about it; I felt like I acted like a spoiled child or some girl that was jilted for the prom. But I also realized I cared about him, I felt like I almost sort of needed him, and except for my dad and a couple friends when I was little I couldn't even remember how long it had been since I felt like I really cared and needed somebody. Because of the prettiness thing.'

Meredith Rand says: 'Have you ever only found out you cared about somebody when they're not around and you're like Oh my God, they're not around, now what am I going to do?'

'Not really.'

'Well anyway, but it made an impression. What came out when I finally said oh all right whatever and started talking to him in the conference room again is that maybe I'd felt like I'd ticked him off and sort of drove him away when I asked him if he'd be in here doing the intense tête-à-tête thing with me if I was fat and cross-eyed. Like that it ticked him off, or that he'd finally decided I was so cynical and suspicious of men only being interested in me because of the prettiness thing that he'd finally figured out that he wasn't going to be able to con me into thinking he actually cared enough that he'd get to boff me or even just feed his ego that here was this so-called beautiful girl that got into him and cared and wrote his name over and over in big loopy cursive in her diary or whatever his trip was. I think all this ugly stuff came out because I was mad because he'd disappeared like that, I thought, and just ditched me and left me here. But he was pretty good about it; he said he could see how I'd feel that way, considering what my real problem was, which then for a while after that I think he let me think he hadn't come in for work for those days just so I could start to see the problem for myself, to fig-ure out what it was and start to see it for what it was.'

'Did you demand any sort of explanation?' Drinion asks.

'A bunch of times. The weird thing is that now, so much later on, I can't remember for sure if he eventually spat it out or if he got me to figure it out for myself,' Meredith Rand says, now looking ever so slightly up in order to meet Drinion's eyes, which if she'd think about it is rather strange, given their respective heights and places at the table, 'the so-called core problem.' Drinion's fore-head crinkles slightly as he looks at her. She rotates

the fingers of one hand in a procedural or summa-
rizing way: 'Subject, who is seen as very pretty,
wants to be liked for more than her prettiness, and
is angry that she isn't liked or cared about for reasons that don't have anything to do with her prettiness. But in fact, everything about her is filtered
through her prettiness *for her*—she is so angry
and suspicious that she couldn't even accept real,
true, no-agenda caring even if it's offered to her,
because deep down inside *she,* the subject *herself,*
can't believe that anything except prettiness or sex
appeal is the motive for anybody's caring. Except
her parents,' she inserts, 'who are nice but not too
bright, and anyway they're her parents—we're
talking about people out in the world.' She makes
a summing-up gesture that may or may not be
ironic. 'Subject is really her own core problem, and
only she can solve it, and only if she quits wanting
to be lonely and feeling sorry for myself and going
"Poor me, I'm so lonely, nobody understands how
bad I hurt, boo hoo."'

'To be honest, I was asking about a different
explanation.' By now, Drinion appears considerably taller than he had when the tête-à-tête started.
The rows of hats on the wall behind him are
almost completely obscured. It is also odd to have
someone stare into your eyes this continuously

without feeling challenged or nervous, or even excited. It will occur to Rand later, as she's driven home, that during the tête-à-tête with Drinion she'd felt sensuously aroused in a way that had little to do with being excited or nervous, that she'd felt the surface of the chair against her bottom and back and the backs of her legs, and the material of her skirt, and the sides of her shoes against the sides of her feet in hose whose microtextured weave she could also feel, and the feel of her tongue against her teeth's rear and palate, the vent's air against her hairline and the room's other air against her face and arms and the taste of cigarette smoke's residue. At one or two points she'd even felt she could feel the exact shape of her eyeballs against her lids' insides when she blinked—she was aware when she blinked. The only kind of experience she could associate with it involved their cat that she'd had when she was a girl before it got hit by a car and the way she could sit with the cat in her lap and stroke the cat and feel the rumble of the cat's purring and feel every bit of the texture of the cat's warm fur and the muscle and bone beneath that, and that she could sit for long periods of time stroking the cat and feeling it with her eyes half-shut as if she was spaced out or stuporous-looking but had felt, in fact, like she was the opposite of stuporous — she felt totally aware and alive, and at the same time when she sat slowly stroking the cat with the same motion over and over it was like she forgot her name and address and almost everything else about her life for ten or twenty minutes, even though it wasn't like spacing out at all, and she loved that cat. She missed the feel of its weight, which was like nothing else, neither heavy nor light, and at times for almost the next two or three days she felt like she feels now, like the cat.

'You mean of the wanting to boff me thing?'

Drinion: 'I think so.'

Meredith Rand: 'He said he was basically a dead man, he used the words *dead man* and *walking dead,* so the point is he couldn't be into me in that way, he said. He wouldn't have the physical energy to try to get in my pants even if he'd wanted to.'

Shane Drinion: 'He told you about his condition, then.'

Meredith Rand: 'Not in so many words; he said it was really none of my business except in how it bore down on my problem. And I said my suspicion was starting to be that he was dropping all these hints about "my problem, my problem" but not just spitting out what it was supposed to be, to sort of string me along for some reason, and that I wasn't going to pretend I knew exactly what the reason was or what he wanted but it was hard not to think on some level it was creepy or pervy, which I simply flat-out told him. I'd quit being polite by then.'

'I'm a little confused,' Drinion says. 'This was all before he'd simply stated what he believed your main problem was?'

Meredith Rand shakes her head, though in response to what is now doubly unclear. One of the examiners' complaints is that she goes off on these long stories but at some point loses the thread and it's nearly impossible not to drift off or zone out when you can't understand what the hell she's getting at anymore. Several of the single posted examiners have decided she's simply crazy, great to look at from a distance but definitely a wide-berth-type girl, especially on breaks, when every moment of diversion is precious, and she can be worse than the work itself. She is saying: 'By this time I was either getting hit on or rapped to by every guy in Zeller, from the day attendant to the men on the second floor when we came down for OT, which was a major drag in all kinds of ways. Although he did point out that if it bummed me out so much, why did I put mascara on even if I was in a mental hospital. Which you have to admit was a valid thing to point out.'

'Yes.'

She is grinding the heel of her hand into one eye, to signify either fatigue or an attempt to stay on track in the story, although Drinion gives no sign of being bored or impatient. 'Plus also by around this time he said the Zeller doctors started saying that my so-called attachment to this one attendant—they also saw all the rapping and sniffing around everybody was doing—all the intense solo tête-à-têtes were starting to look dependent or unhealthy, and not saying anything to me about it but asking him all kinds of questions and basically starting to give him a really hard time, so we started having to wait for everybody to get all engrossed at TV time and then go talk in the stairwell just outside the ward, where it wasn't so public, where he'd usually lie down on the cement of the landing with his feet up on the second or third stair up, which by this time he admitted wasn't for his back but he needed the elevation to keep his circulation going. So we ended up spending a lot of the first couple days out in the stairwell talking about the whole business of my suspicions about what he wanted from me and why he was doing this, around and around, and he did tell me a little more about himself and getting cardiomyopathy in college, but he also kept saying

OK, he'd talk about all this as long as I wanted to, but that it was kind of a vicious circle because anything he said I could be suspicious of and attribute some kind of secondary agenda to if I wanted to, and I might think it was all honest and open but it wasn't really intense or efficacious, in his opinion, it was more like going around and around inside the problem instead of really looking at the problem, which he said because he was a walking dead man and not really part of the institution of the nut ward he felt like maybe he was the only person there who'd really tell me the truth about my problem, which he said was basically that I needed to grow up.'

Meredith Rand pauses here and looks at Shane Drinion in anticipation of his asking what that diagnosis was supposed to mean, exactly; but he does not ask. He appears to have become reconciled to something, or to have decided to accept the way Meredith Rand remembers the story on her own terms, or to have concluded that trying to impose a certain kind of order on her side of the tête-à-tête was going to have the opposite effect.

She is saying, 'And naturally the "grow up" thing ticked me off, and I told him to go sit on something sharp, but I didn't really mean it, because by around this time he'd said also that the word was

starting to come down that I was going to get discharged soon, the treatment team was starting to
talk about it, even though of course nobody ever
thought to tell me anything about what was going
on, and that my mother had been trying to set up
outpatient counseling and trying to get one of the
doctors to keep seeing me in his private practice,
which was very full and also not totally covered by
my dad's insurance, so the whole thing was a
bureaucratic nightmare, and it would take some
time, but it was starting to sink into me that this
wasn't forever, that by as early as maybe next week
or the week after I wouldn't be seeing him or having intense conversations with him anymore, or
even maybe ever see him again—I realized I
didn't know where he lived or even his last name,
for Christ's sake. This all sort of hit me, and I start
freaking out when I think about it, because I'd
already got a taste of what a couple days of suddenly not getting to talk to him or know where he
was was like, and I'm freaking out, and in my
mind I'm toying with the idea of sharpening something and doing some cutting that I didn't even
really feel like doing, just so I'd get kept in the nut
ward a little longer, which I knew was completely
nuts.' She looks up very quickly at Drinion to see
whether he's reacting to this information. 'Which

was crazy, and actually I think he knew this was going on, he knew how important he'd gotten to be to me by then, I think, so he had extra leverage or ammo to use to tell me to just cut the shit—I'd be sitting on the stairway up to Four and he'd be lying on his back at the bottom of the stairway with his feet up right below me, so I spent all this time looking at his shoe soles, which were like Kmart shoes and the soles were plastic—and that "grow up" meant *now*, right this second, and quit being childish, because it would kill me. He said the girls that came through Zeller were all the same, and none of us had any idea of what being a grown-up was. Which was totally condescending, and normally the totally wrong thing to say to an eighteen-year-old. So there was this little argument about that. His point was that being childish wasn't the same thing as being like a child, he said, because watch a real child play or stroke a cat or listen to a story and you'll see it's like the opposite of what we were all doing there in Zeller.' Shane Drinion is leaning slightly forward. His bottom is now almost 1.75 inches off the chair seat; his work shoes' gumlike soles, darkened at the perimeter by the same process that darkens pencils' erasers, swing slightly just above the tile floor. Were it not for the sport coat hanging off the back of his chair,

Beth Rath and others would be able to see light through the substantial gap between the seat of his chair and his slacks. 'It's more like he was explaining than arguing,' Rand says. 'He said there is a particular kind of stage of life where you get cut off from the, like, unself-conscious happiness and magic of childhood—he said only seriously disturbed or autistic children are without this childhood joy—but later in life and puberty it's possible to leave that childhood freedom and completeness behind but still remain totally immature. Immature in the sense of waiting or wanting some magical daddy or rescuer to see you and really know and understand you and care as much about you as a child's parents do, and save you. Save you from yourself. He also kept yawning a lot and hitting his shoes together, and I'd watch the soles go back and forth. He said this is how immaturity shows up in young women and girls; in men it's somewhat different in how it looks but really it's all the same, which is wanting to be distracted from what you've lost and fixed and saved by somebody. Which is pretty banal, it's like something out of a doctor's textbook, and I go so this is my core problem? This is what I've been stringing along waiting for? And he goes no, that's everybody's core problem, and it's why girls are so obsessed with prettiness and whether they can attract somebody and arouse enough love in that person to save them. *My* core problem, he said, and this connects to the core problem I told you about just now, was the neat little trap I'd made for myself to ensure that I never really had to grow up and so I could stay immature and waiting forever for somebody to save me because I'd never be able to find out that nobody else can save me because I'd made it impossible for me to get what I was so convinced I needed and deserved, so I could always be angry and I could always get to go around thinking that my real problem was that no one could see or love the real me the way I needed so I'd always have my problem to sit and hold and stroke on and make believe was the real problem.' Rand looks up sharply at Shane Drinion. 'Does that seem banal?'

'I don't know.'

'It kind of did to me,' Meredith Rand says. 'I told him that was incredibly helpful and now I knew just what to do when I got discharged from Zeller, which was click my heels together and transform diagnosis into cure, and how could I ever repay him.'

Drinion says, 'You were being deeply sarcastic.'

'I was pissed!' Meredith Rand says, a bit loudly.

'I told him lo and behold it looked like it turned out he was just like the diagnosis-is-cure doctors in their nice suits, except of course his diagnosis was also insulting, which he could call honesty and get extra jollies hurting people's feelings. I was just so pissed! And he laughed and said he wished I could see myself right now—he could see me because he was lying down and I was standing right over him, because every like fifteen minutes or so I had to help him up so he could sneak back in out of the hallway and go around with his clipboard and do checks. He said I looked like a little child that just had its toy taken away.'

'Which probably made you even angrier,' Drinion says.

'He said something like all right then, OK, he'd explain it like he was talking to a child, to somebody so locked into the problem that she can't even see that it's her problem and not just the way the world is. I wanted to be liked and known for more than just the prettiness. That I wanted people to look past the prettiness thing and the sexual thing and see who I was, like as a person, and I felt really mad and sorry for myself that people didn't.'

Meredith Rand, in the tavern, looks briefly up at Drinion. 'Didn't look past the surface,' he says, to signify that he understands what she's saying.

She cocks her head. 'But in reality everything was the surface.'

'Your surface?'

'Yes, because under the surface were just all these feelings and conflicts about the surface, and anger, about how I looked and the effect on people I had, and really all there was inside was this constant tantrum about how I wasn't getting saved and it was because of my prettiness, which he said if you think about it is really unattractive—nobody wants to get close to somebody who's in the middle of this constant tantrum. Who'd want that?' Rand makes a sort of ironic ta-da gesture in the air. 'So, he said, I'd actually set it up so that the only reason anybody *would* be attracted to me as a person was that I was pretty, which was exactly the thing that made me so angry and lonely and sad.'

'That sounds like a psychological trap.'

'His comparison was he compared it to making a kind of machine that gave you an electric shock every time you said "Ow!" Of course, he knew I'd been having the machine dreams. I know I kept just looking at him, giving him this death-ray look that all the foxes in school get good at giving people, like they're just supposed to melt away and die if you look at them like that. He was lying down with his feet up on the stairs as he's saying all this.

His lips were a little bit blue, the cardiomyopathy was getting worse all the time, and the Zeller stairways had those horrid fluorescent tube light things in the stairwell that made him look worse; he wasn't even pale as much as gray, with this kind of frothy paste on his lips, because he couldn't sip his little can of water when he was lying down on his back.' Her eyes look like she's really seeing him again *in situ* in the stairwell at Zeller. To tell the truth, he looked gross to me, scary, repulsive, like a corpse, or somebody in one of those pictures of people in stripes in concentration camps. The weird thing is that I cared about him at the same time I found him gross. He grossed me out,' she says. 'And that I was so deep in my problem that I couldn't accept real, genuine, nonsexual or non-romantic or non-prettiness-type interest in me even if it was offered to me — he was talking about himself, which I knew, even though he didn't spell it out; we'd gone over that ground for days and days before, and time was running out, we both knew. I'd be getting discharged and I'd never see him again. But I said some pretty horrible things.'

'You're referring to the stairwell,' Shane Drinion says.

'Because deep down inside, he said, I only saw myself in terms of the prettiness. I saw myself as so

860

mediocre and banal inside that I couldn't imagine anybody except my parents being interested in me for anything except what I looked like, as a fox. I was so angry, he said, that all anybody cared about or paid any attention to was the prettiness, but he said that was a smoke screen, theater of the human mind, that what really bothered me so much was I felt the same way, boys and men were treating me the same sort of way I really treated myself, and in reality it was really myself I was angry at except I couldn't see it — I projected it onto the pervs whistling on the street or the sweaty boys trying to boff me or the other girls deciding I'm a bitch because I'm stuck up about the prettiness.'

There is a brief moment of silence, meaning nothing but the noise of pinball and the baseball game and the sounds of people unwinding.

'Is this boring?' she asks Drinion abruptly. She's unaware of how she's looking at Drinion as she asks this. For just a moment she appears to be almost a different person. It has suddenly occurred to Meredith Rand that Shane Drinion might be one of those ingratiating but ultimately shallow people who could *seem* to be paying attention while in fact allowing their attention to wander hill and dale all over the place, including possibly to considering how he wouldn't be sitting here nodding politely and listening to this incredibly boring dribble, narcissistic dribble, if it didn't afford him a chance to look directly at Meredith's bottomless green eyes and exquisite bone structure, plus a bit of visible cleavage, since she'd taken off her flounce and unbuttoned her top button the minute the 5:00 buzzer had sounded.

'Is it? Is this boring?'

Drinion responds: 'The major part of it isn't, no.'

'What part of it is boring?'

'Boring isn't a very good term. Certain parts you tend to repeat, or say over again only in a slightly different way. These parts add no new information, so these parts require more work to pay attention to, alth—'

'Like what parts? What is it that you think I keep telling over and over?'

'I wouldn't call it boring, though. It's more that attending to these parts requires work, although it wouldn't be fair to call that effort unpleasant. It's that listening to the parts that do add new information or insights, these parts compel attention in a way that doesn't require effort.'

'What, is it that I keep going on and on about how supposedly beautiful I am?'

'No,' Drinion says. He cocks his head slightly. 'In fact, to be honest, in those parts where you do repeat the same essential point or information in a slightly different way, the underlying motive, which I get the feeling is a concern that what you're imparting might be unclear or uninteresting and must get recast and resaid in many different ways to assure yourself that the listener really understands you — this is interesting, and somewhat emotional, and it coheres in an interesting way with the surface subject of what Ed, in the story you're telling, is teaching you, and so in that respect even the repetitive or redundant elements compel interest and require little conscious effort to pay attention to, at least so far as I'm concerned.'

Meredith Rand extracts another cigarette. 'You sound like you're reading off a card or something.'

'I'm sorry it seems that way. I was trying to explain my answer to your question, because I got the sense you were hurt by my answer, and I felt that a fuller explanation would prevent the hurt. Or obviate it if you were angry. In my view, there was just a misunderstanding based on a miscommunication around the word *boring*.'

Her smile is both mocking and not. 'So I'm not the only one who's worried about misunderstanding and keeps trying to head off misunderstanding for emotional reasons.' But she can tell he is sincere; he is neither yanking her around nor kissing butt.

Meredith can feel it. There is a feeling that comes with sitting across from Shane Drinion and having his eyes and attention on you. It isn't excitement, but it is intense, a little bit like standing near the high-voltage transformer park south of Joliet Street.

'Can I ask,' Drinion says, 'is it projection when you project emotions about yourself onto other people? Or is that displacement?'

She makes another face. 'He hated those kinds of words, actually. He said they were part of the self-nourishing institution of the mental-health system. He said even the word was contradictory— mental-health *system*. This was the next night, in the service elevator now, because somebody on the stairs on some other floor heard our voices the night before because the stairwell was all cement and metal and echoey, and Ed got ragged on somehow by the nursing supervisor for encouraging my unhealthy attachment to him that they'd gotten the idea of from how upset I was the time when he was out for two days—it turned out he was right on the edge of getting fired, mainly because he'd started missing the fifteen-minute checks sometimes and one girl was putting her finger down her throat and throwing up dinner and somebody found some of the throw-up and Ed had missed it because he'd been lying in the stairwell and it was harder to get up from lying all the way down with his feet on the stairs, even if I helped him up, and he'd blown off getting up to do checks. Some of the girls had also gotten all bitchy about us having conversations, like I was the favorite or something, and started a whole rumor with the treatment teams that I was always pretending I had to talk secretly to him and dragging him off and trying to make out with him or whatever. A couple of those girls were just beyond horrible, they were such bitches I'd never seen anything like it.'

'. . .'

'And it was also the day I got discharged, or got told that I was getting discharged the next day; my parents had worked it out and there were about seven million papers to sign the next day and then I was going home. There'd been this whole thing with my mom getting some doctor to sign off on outpatient counseling, blah blah. Nobody used the service elevator at night after the supper trays, so he opened it up and we went in there and he sat on the floor, the floor had a metal pattern thing and you couldn't lie down. It stunk, it was worse than the stairwell.

'He said it was the last night, the last conversation, and when I said I wanted intense he said it was showtime, we probably wouldn't ever meet or see each other after this. I said what did he mean. I was totally freaking out, though. I was the one with double motives. It was showtime. I knew I couldn't pull some kind of scam so I could stay, I knew he'd see through that, he'd just laugh at me. But I was ready to say I had romantic feelings—that I was attracted to him, even though I felt like I really wasn't, sexually, even though later on it turned out I was. I just couldn't admit it to myself, how I felt about him, because of my problem. Although I have to say now I'm not so sure,' Meredith Rand says. 'Being married is totally different than being seventeen and in total identity crisis and idealizing somebody that seems to really see you and care.' She looks far more like herself now. 'But he was the first guy that it felt like told me the truth, that didn't just start having double motives and start performing or being all sweaty and intimidated and was willing to really see me and know me and just tell the truth about what he saw. And he really did know me—remember, he told me all those things about my mom and the neighbor that nobody knew.' Her face hardens again, somewhat, or tightens, as she looks directly at Drinion, holding the cigarette but not lighting it. 'Is this one of the parts that you said I repeat over and over?'

Drinion shakes his head a little bit and then waits for Meredith Rand to continue. The hyper-attractive POTEX continues looking at him.

Drinion says: 'No. I think the original subject of the story was you getting married. Getting married obviously assumes a mutual attraction and romantic emotions, so your first mention of a willingness to acknowledge romantic attraction is new information, and very relevant.' His expression hasn't changed at all.

'So it's not boring.'

'No.'

'And you've never had romantic attraction feelings yourself.'

'Not that I'm aware of, no.'

'And if you ever had them, wouldn't you be aware of them?'

Drinion: 'I think so, yes.'

'So your answer was a little bit slippery, wasn't it?'

'I suppose it was,' Drinion says. Later she'd consider that he didn't seem taken aback at all. It seemed like he was merely absorbing information and adding it to himself. And that (Rand wouldn't consider this so much as just remember it as part of the sensuous memory of her making a bit of fun of Drinion and the odd way he responded whenever she did this, which she could more or less at will, make fun of him, because in certain ways he was a total nerd and dweeb) the display of different kinds of hats on the rear wall was now completely obscured except for the very tip of the bill of a fisherman's cap in the upper row.

'Well, but anyway,' Meredith Rand says. She has had her chin in the same hand that holds the unlit Benson & Hedges, which looks like the opposite of comfortable. 'So I do know that that last night, in the elevator, I wasn't fully listening to him and, like, engaging with him on what he was telling me, because I was wrestling with all these inner feelings and conflicts about attraction to him and also totally freaking out about hearing that I'd never see him again, because the deal was that I was set up for outpatient counseling but that was on the second floor where all the doctors had their real offices, and he was only on on nights on the third floor, which was a locked ward. Just the idea that I didn't know where he lived freaked me out. Plus I knew he might get fired soon, because he could barely even do checks anymore, and there'd been trouble with one of the vomiters that had been vomiting and he hadn't checked her, plus I knew he hadn't told the Zeller people about his health thing, the cardiomyopathy, which had been more or less under control when they first hired him, it sounded like, but had gotten worse and worse—'

'He still hadn't told you about the cardiomyopathy, though.'

'Right, but whatever it was, the Zeller people didn't know about it, and they just thought that he didn't take care of himself very well, or he was hungover or lazy, something terrible. So I kept spacing out and thinking about what if I took my shirt off and, like, made out with him right here, would he let me or would he be grossed out or laugh at me, and how could I get him to see me again and still have intense conversations after I got out and had to go back to Mom and Central Catholic, and what if I told him I loved him, and what if he died after I got out and I didn't even know he died because I didn't know who he was or where he lived. It occurred to me I didn't even know how he really felt about me as me and not some girl he was helping, like did he think I was interesting, or smart, or pretty. It was so hard to think that somebody that seemed to understand me so well and tell me the truth didn't care for me in that special way.'

'You mean having romantic feelings.'

Rand shrugs a little with her eyebrows. 'He was a guy, after all. So...and then it occurred to me that I was sort of doing just what he said my core problem was — thinking about him and not losing him and that he could save me and that the way to keep him was through sexual feelings because that's all I had.

'So then I know at some point he gave me a quiz about the overall topics we'd covered. It was both a joke and not.' She lights the cigarette, finally. 'Later on, he confessed it was because he thought he was really dying from this spell of cardiomyopathy — it turned out there were whole days at a time that he couldn't catch his breath, like he was running even when he was just lying there; his lips were blue for a reason — and he said he'd been pretty sure he wouldn't ever see me again and be able to tell if he'd been any help, he wanted to reassure himself that he'd helped somebody a little before he died. And of course on my end I was freaking out, I couldn't figure out whether it would be better to ace the quiz or flunk it, in terms of getting to see him again. Even though he pretended the whole quiz was a joke, like I was a kindergartner getting quizzed by a kindergarten teacher. He was really good at being serious and making fun of himself at the same time — it's one reason I loved him.'

Drinion: 'Loved?'

'Like, question one: What have we learned about cutting ourself? And I said, like, we learned that it doesn't matter why I cut or what the psychological machinery is behind the cutting, like if it's projecting self-hatred or whatever. Exteriorizing the interior. We've learned all that matters is to not do it. To cut it out. Nobody else can make me cut it out; only I can decide to stop it. Because whatever the institutional reason, it's hurting myself, it's me being mean to myself, which was childish. It was not treating yourself with any respect. The only way you can be mean to yourself is if you deep down expect somebody else is going to gallop up and save you, which is a child's fantasy. Reality meant nobody else was for sure going to be nice to me or treat me with any respect—that was the point of his thing about growing up, realizing that—and nobody else was for sure going to see me or treat me the way I wanted to be seen, so it was my job to make sure to see myself and treat myself like I was really worthwhile. It's called being responsible instead of childish. The real responsibilities are to myself. And if liking my looks was part of that and part of what I thought was deep-down worthwhile, that was OK. I could like being pretty without making prettiness the only thing I had going for me, or feeling sorry for myself if people spazzed out about the prettiness. That was my answer to the quiz.'

Shane Drinion: 'As I understand it, though, your actual experience is that someone else *was* being nice to you and treating you as worthwhile.'

Rand smiles in a way that makes it seem as though she's smiling in spite of herself. She's also smoking her cigarette in a more thorough, sensuous way. 'Well, yes, that's what I was actually thinking about, standing there in the elevator and looking down at him and answering his quiz, which I did sincerely, but secretly I was totally freaking out. The truth is I felt like in reality he was just what he was saying was impossible and childish, he was exactly the other person he was saying I'd never really find. I felt like he loved me.'

'So there is a very intense emotional conflict going on,' Shane Drinion says.

Rand holds her hands to the sides of her head and makes a quick face that mimics someone having some kind of nervous breakdown. 'I was telling him about forgetting about other people and why they were or weren't attracted and if they really cared and just being decent to myself, treating myself like I was worthwhile, loving myself in a grown-up way—and it was all true, I really had learned it, but I was also saying it all for him, because it's what he wanted me to say, so he could feel like he'd really helped me. But if I said what he wanted me to say, would it mean he could leave and I'd never see him again, and he'd never miss me, because he'd think I was OK and going to be OK? But I still said it. I knew if I said I loved him or stripped down and kissed him right there, he'd think I was still in the childish problem, he'd think I still mixed up being treated like a valuable worthwhile person with sex and romantic feelings, and he'd think he wasted his time and it was hopeless, he'd think it was hopeless and he hadn't reached me, and I couldn't do that to him — if he was going to die or get fired then at least I could let him have this, the knowledge that he'd helped me, even though I really did feel like I was maybe in love with him, or needed him.' She puts out her cigarette without any of the previous stabbing aspect, almost sort of tenderly, as if thinking tenderly of something else. 'I all of a sudden felt like: Oh my God, this is what people mean when they go "I'll die without you, you're my whole life," you know, "Can't live, if living is without you," ' Meredith Rand accompanying this last bit to the tune of Harry Nilsson's 'Can't Live (If Living Is Without You).' 'All the terrible country songs my dad used to listen to in his shop in the garage, it seemed like every one of them was about somebody talking to some lover they'd lost and why and how they couldn't live without them, how terrible their life was now, and drinking all the time because it hurt so terribly to be without them, that I could never stand because I thought they were so banal and I never said anything but I couldn't believe he could listen to it all without almost barfing.... Actually he said if you listen to these songs and change the *you* to *me,* like, you understand that what they're really singing about is losing some part of themself or betraying themself over and over for what they think other people want until they're just dead inside and don't even know what *me* means, which is why the only way they can think of it and why they're feeling so dead and sad is to think of it as needing somebody else and not being able to live without them, this other person—which by some coincidence is the exact situation of a teeny baby, that without somebody to hold it and feed it and take care of it, it'll die, literally, which he said is not such a coincidence at all, really.'

Drinion's forehead is ever so slightly wrinkled with thought. 'I'm confused. Ed explained the true meaning of country-and-western songs in the elevator? So you told him about the lyrics and now understanding the lyrics' sentiments?'

Rand is looking around, possibly for Beth Rath. 'What? No, that was later on.'

'So you did see each other again, after the elevator.'

Rand raises the back of her hand to display the wedding ring. 'Oh, yes.'

Drinion says, 'Is there some extra information I need to understand this?'

Rand looks both distracted and annoyed. 'Well, he didn't die, obviously, Mr. Einstein.'

Drinion rotates his empty glass. His forehead has a definite wrinkle. 'But you've spent time describing the conflict between confessing love and your real motives, and how upset and uncomfortable you were at the prospect of not seeing him again.'

'I was seventeen, for Christ's sake. I was a drama queen. They take me home, I look in the phone book, and he's right there in the phone book. His apartment building was like ten minutes from my house.'

Drinion's mouth is in the distended position of someone who wants to ask something but isn't sure where to even start, and is signifying that facially instead of out loud.

Rand's arm is up in some kind of signal to Beth Rath.

'Anyway, that's how I met him.'

§47

Toni Ware stood at the pay phone on the lot's fringes. Instead of a booth it was just on a post. She leaned slightly against the front bumper of her car, which shone. One of the dogs' faces appeared over the backseat; when she looked hard at it a moment it dropped back out of sight. In the front passenger seat were a dozen standard six-pound bricks, each with a Return-Postage-Paid card from a different marketer. She was a standard-sized woman, just on the pale side of fair in slacks and a beige spring coat that flapped and popped in the wind. The man at the phone's other end was repeating her order, which was complex and involved several feet of #6 copper tubing angle-cut into four-inch lengths; the angle on the cuts was to be 60 degrees. This woman had twenty different voices; all but two were warm and pleasant. She didn't cup the phone's speaker to cut the wind but let it roar in the phone. Everyone has unconscious mannerisms they fall into on a telephone; hers was to look at the cuticles of the hand that didn't hold the phone and to use that hand's thumb to feel at each cuticle in turn. There were four women in the convenience store's lot, and a bust of the store's cashier through a gap between signs on the window for bulk-purchase beer. Two women were at the pumps; another was in a tan Gremlin waiting for a pump to free. They wore plastic wraps over their hair against the wind. There was a period when Toni had to wait for the hardware wholesaler to verify her credit card, which meant that the place was on a tight margin and couldn't afford even a four-hour float on the order, which meant they could be affected. Everyone conducts a rapid unconscious scan of each social sense object they encounter. Some scans' big concern involved fear and the threat-potential of each new datum; others' involved sexual potential, revenue potential, aesthetic grade, status indicators, power, and/or susceptibility to domination. Toni Ware's scans, which were detailed and thorough, were concerned entirely with whether the object could be affected. Her hair appeared grayish-blond, or the sort of dry blond that in certain kinds of light appears almost gray. The wind hit the door hard as people came out; she watched its force affect their faces and the small unconscious ingathering gestures they made as they attempted to huddle and walk quickly at the same time. It wasn't especially cold but the wind made it *seem* cold. The color of her eyes depended on what lenses she wore. The credit card number she gave the man was her own, but neither the name nor the federal ID# she gave belonged to her as such. Both dogs had the same name but knew without fail which one she was calling. Her love for the dogs transcended all other experience and informed her life. The voice she used with the Butts Hardware clerk was younger than she, conspicuously jejune, causing merchants whose emotional tastes were more refined than simple exploitation to feel paternal — superior and tender at the same time. What she said when he confirmed her order was: 'Great. Very great. Yay,' with 'Yay' stated instead of shouted. It was a voice that caused the listener to imagine someone with long blond hair and bell-bottoms who cocked her head and gave even statements an interrogative lilt. She played on this knife-edge most of the time—giving a false impression that was nevertheless concrete and tightly controlled. It felt like art. The issue was not destruction. Just as total order is dull, so is chaos dull: There's nothing informing about a mess. The store's cashier gave each customer a cool smile and engaged in a brief exchange. Toni Ware had twice in three years been part of an investigation of the store, whose name was QWIK 'N' EZ—its sign's icon was suspiciously like Bob's Big Boy—and was one of the first of the off-interstate stations to eliminate the full-serve pumps and attach a tiny grocery with cigarettes and soda pop and junk for Qwik Stop shopping. They did a phenomenal cash business and had been tagged by the local DIF function every year; but they were whistle-clean, field-audit was judged a waste of salary, their receipts jibed perfectly and their books were just messy enough to be uncooked, the owner a Pentecostal Christian who'd already started con- struction on another of what Bondurant called Ramp Tumors on the second 74 exit and had bids in for lots on two more.

She had two home lines and a bulky mobile phone and two office patch codes but used pay phones for personal business. She was neither attractive nor ugly. Except for a certain anemic intensity to her face there was nothing to attract or repel or cause any more notice than a thousand other Peoria women who'd been described as 'cute' in their bloom and were now invisible. She liked to come in under people's radar. The only person who might have noticed her hanging up the phone was someone who'd wanted to use it himself. Two women and a reddish man in flannel were filling their tanks. A child in one of the cars was crying, its face a knot. The cars' windows rendered its weeping a dumbshow. Its mother had a caved-in face and stared stolidly by the tank, smoothing her hair's plastic as the hose dispensed gas on auto. The station's flagpole's flag's rope's pulleys and joists clinked dully in the wind. Her own car's slight idled throb behind her, the two dogs hunkered down in identical postures. She slowed just enough to lock eyes with the child as she passed the rear right window, its face clenched and red, her own face empty of intent as for a moment the whole lot and street blazed with intensity, a non-connotative tone in her head like a rung bell. Interesting the way some people will stand still by the tank and let it fill and others like the pudgy woman up ahead cannot, must busy themselves with small tasks like squeegeeing the windshield or using blue towels to wipe at the brake lights, unable to stand still and wait. The man dispensed by hand, rounding off to an even sum. Half the child's face was cut off by the window's reflection of the sky and flag that popped high above her. And she liked the sound of her own footfalls, the solid sound and feeling the impact in her teeth. #6 tube was hard enough to go in all the way and soft enough that driving it made little sound; three at the base would do for any tree.

The Tumor's inside had a grocery's bleached light and was laid out with glass doors of pop at the back and two aisles of corporate gauge retail coffee and pet food and snacks E-W with your sundries and tobacco behind the orange counter where the young woman in denim workshirt and red bandanna done up slave-style with tiny rabbit ears at the back asked about fuel and totaled beer and snuff and sent change down an anodized chute into a steel cup. Behind the door at the rear of the second aisle was the stockroom and manager's office. The larger chain models had introduced video cameras, but these Ramp Tumors were blind. There were five other US citizens in the store and then a sixth when the woman sans child came in to pay, and while Toni selected enough items to fill a bag she observed them interact or not and felt again the acquaintance she always assumed all strangers in rooms she entered enjoyed, the conviction that everyone in the room all knew each other well and felt the connection and sameness they shared by virtue of what they had in common, the quality of not being her. None of them was affected by her in any way. One can of Mighty Dog Gourmet Beef was 69¢, which given wholesale and overhead was still a 20 percent margin of pure cream. The counter woman, who was in her early thirties and had incorporated her weight into a country mother presentation that involved pink cheeks and a laugh like a roar and a worldly good-humored sexuality, asked if she had any fuel today.

'Full up,' Toni said. 'Stopped to use the phone and come in to get out of the damn wind!'

'Still tootin' out there I see.' The counter woman smiled, totaling pet food Toni would throw away on a cut-rate NCR 1280 that totaled receipts on a one-day roll they stored in canisters and had to be taken out and unfurled to run a Field, the office filled with eighty-foot strips like a liner's bunting at sail.

'Like to blow me right off the road comin' in,' Toni said. The counter woman seemed unaware that Toni Ware was affecting the exact accent and cadence of her own speech. The assumption that everyone else is like you. That you are the world. The disease of consumer capitalism. The complacent solipsism.

'Got you some dogs that can do some eating.'

'Don't tell me. Don't I know.'

'That was $11.80.' The smile long-practiced to seem so sincere. As if Toni would be remembered one moment after she forced the door and staggered off under the flag like the rest of them. And why the conventional *was*? The stunted creature behind her smelled of hair oil and ambient breakfast; she imagined particles of meat and eggs in his facial hair and under his nails as she produced a Treasury note.

'The big Two-O,' the counter woman said, as if to herself, punching the keys with the slight extra force a 1280 takes.

A moment later Toni was out around the side of the store, sheltered from the lot's view by the Kluckman Ice dispenser, with the plastic bag's top whipping and popping between her shoes as she removed a traveler's Kleenex from her handbag, tore it in two and again, and wrapped a quarter of the tissue tightly around her little finger, whose nail was perfect and almond-shaped and done in arterial red. Up into the right nasal cavity and around in a comprehensive spiral, and what came out included a standard-colored clot, both viscous and hard, with even a tiny thread of capillary inside the right border. The only thing someone in a store or line might remark about her was a faint affective abstraction, a quality of detachment that was not the detachment of peace or a personal relation with Our Lord Jesus Christ. Which she carefully wiped onto the left lapel of her cream-colored coat, with enough pressure to give it some length but not enough to compromise its adhesion or distort the nougat at its heart. A plasticized flatness about her reminiscent of processed air, airline food, transistorized sound. This was merely to pass the time until her order at Butts Hardware was assembled. The stockroom as she entered it had only paper goods and large cardboard boxes and borax in the floor-wall seam for roaches, and the manager's little office door with its snap-on pinups and Peace with Honor poster of an eagle with a ski-jump nose and 5:00 shadow was ajar and emitted Dutch Masters and the mollified twang of country on a pocket radio. The day manager, who had no nametag (the counter woman was 'Cheryl') and had his feet up reading just what she'd have imagined, and who had a high convex forehead and one of those rapid and overhard blink rates like someone almost wincing when they blinked that signified something just a little neurally amiss, just a bit, swung his feet around and rose with complex squeaks of the chair as her timid knock and the force with which she all but staggered through the door spelled out all the innocent shock anyone'd need to read in her character. She'd drained her face of color and kept her eyes open in the wind on the way back from side to storefront, which wetted her eyes, and had her shoulders up and arms out in an attitude of speechless defilement. She appeared both smaller and larger than she really was, and the manager with the ticcy blink did not move or come around or find within himself the power to respond even during her setup, which was halting and hypoxic and sketched a scenario in which she was a frequent nay even habitual customer at this QWIK 'N' EZ Ramp Tumor and had always received not only good value for the hard-earned money she earned taking in mending at home which as the single mother of two was all she could do, even though she'd been trained as a legal secretary over five years of night school during the time she was nursing her blind mother through her lengthy terminal illness, not just value and gas but always cheerful and courteous service from the gals at the counter, until—here a shudder that brought the manager, still holding the remains of a Little Debbie product in his left hand, halfway around the desk to comfort her until he saw the two-inch mess on her left lapel, which was the result of several Q-Tipless days and near-sneeze feeling and was indeed a mucal clot of sheer clock-stopping horror—until today just now, just, she didn't know how to say this—her strongest impulse had just been to drive half-blind with tears home to throw the coat that had cost months of going without to buy so she could take her two babies to church in something they didn't have to feel ashamed to be with into the low-income housing development's dumpster and spend the rest of the day praying God to help her make some sense out of the senseless violation she'd just had happen and to avoid forever thereafter this QWIK 'N' EZ out of degradation and horror but no, she'd always had such good value and service at this establishment that she felt it almost her duty, however embarrassing and degrading to account, to tell him what the employee behind the cash register had done, even though it made no sense, to her least of all, who certainly looked normal and even friendly and to whom she'd tried to be pleasant and had done nothing more than try to pay for the items she'd elected to buy here, who had, while she'd reached for her change and while looking her steadily in the eye had, had, with the other hand put her finger up her nose and then reached out and...and...here giving way completely to sobs and a kind of high-pitched keening sound and looking down at the lapel of a coat she gave the impression of somehow trying to back away from in horror as if the only reason she hadn't already taken off the green-dolloped coat was that she couldn't bear to take it off, feeling the clonic blinks upon the wad to note even the thread of red blood that made it more ghastly, then turning to stagger out as if too upset to continue or press for redress, lurching out until the transistor's song of whiskey and loss had receded and she was back in the bleached light of the store itself, the sound of her heels in the aisle and lot rapid and satisfying as the counter woman's wave and farewell-till-next-time receded unacknowledged and the manager stood there working his way from the shock to outrage and the boys silent and docile as gar-goyles in the back even as she leapt into the car and all but peeled out, in case the manager had made it out front yet which she doubted, fishtail-ing onto the Frontage Road with such hysteric force that one dog was thrown into another, steadying herself with a right arm against the bag of bricks, half-humming the country tune's refrain, coat defiled and already half off one shoulder, mailbox-bound.

§48

'It's all a little hazy.'

'That's certainly understandable, Sir.'

'I think I should tell you I'm very upset.'

'We can certainly appreciate that.'

'No. No. I mean inside. Upset inside.'

'I think they've anticipated that, Sir, and that every possible—'

'Down low I mean.'

'Perhaps if you could just relay it to us as if you were relating data, Sir.'

'You know: *down low?* You take my meaning?'

'That's just the effects, Sir, lingering. Take your time.'

'It was the annual picnic. Is that what you want?'

'That we know already, Sir.'

'Every year, summer. In Coffield Park, bond-financed. Examinations annual picnic. Mummified fried chicken, potato salad. Deviled eggs I believe with flecked paprika like dots of dried blood—horrid. Great arrayed fans of luncheon meat. All this protein. Examiners eat like wild beasts, I'm sure you know. Audits more sparingly. You must know this. The variance in—'

'We've certainly had reports, Sir.'

'And grilled things. Those odd bolted park grills, also bond-financed to be sure. Wieners, patties in tiers on shiny white paper. Great swarms and shrouds of insects on the food on the table. Flies rubbing their little legs together. Do you know what that means when a fly does that? Hornets at the waste cans, hovering. Watermelon with ants on it. When it rubs its legs together like that?'

'…'

'A raw hamburger patty's like blood in the water to an insect, men.'

'You were just inventorying the picnic's provisions, Sir.'

'Iced tea, Kool-Aid. There was pop in a chest the GM brought. Some primary-colored Jell-O. Red or green or red-and-green. It's for morale, the annual picnic, change the interactive context.'

'Nothing wrong with a picnic, Sir.'

'See everyone's families, children. The children. One doesn't think of GS-9s having children, playing with children, little Line 40s. And yet every year there they are. The mothers arranged games. And bottles of beer in a chest Marge van Hool's husband brought.'

'We've spoken to Mr. van Hool, Sir.'

'And mosquitoes everywhere. The terrible kind, that cast a shadow and have hairy legs. You can hear them but you can't see them. Not until. Blood draws every—and Audits, Audits were playing some type of children's game with that flying disk from Hasbro. Aerodynamic disk, bright color, Hasbro, where did—?'

'A Frisbee, perhaps, Sir?'

'Hasbro now a division of I believe one United Amusements, supposedly based in St. Paul but with substantial offshore accounts.'

'...'

'And you know as well as I what that so often means.'

'And you noticed nothing out of the ordinary regarding the iced tea, the Jell-O.'

'They think it was the Jell-O then.'

'That wouldn't be our department, Sir.'

'The Jell-O had very small marshmallows in it

as I recall. One of those exceedingly bright primary colors, the Jell-O. The flies left it alone, although those bloody mosquitoes my God if you—'

'Yes, Sir.'

'I should tell you I'm extremely agitated and upset.'

'We're making a second note of that, Mr. Director, Sir, for emphasis.'

'I don't believe the effects have entirely worn off yet.'

'Just proceed on the assumption that we're the ones in the middle, please, Sir.'

'I spoke with law enforcement agents, I believe, unless that was the effects.'

'That was several hours ago, Sir. We're with the Service. I am Agent Clothier, this is Special Agent Aylortay.'

'Pleased to meet you, Sir, although it's damn unfortunate it has to be under these circumstances.'

'You're CID?'

'No, Sir, we're Inspections, out of Chicago, Post 1516.'

'They brought you down.'

'Everyone's very concerned, Sir, understandably.'

'Mosquitoes are just needles with wings.'

'Not entirely sure how to respond to that, Sir.'

'There were no CID at the picnic.'

'No, Sir, as you might recall CID had a forensic accounting in-service this weekend at Region, Sir.'

'They don't mix well, as a rule, CID.'

'No, Sir.'

'Hold themselves a bit aloof if you know what I mean. Vomiting.'

'Vomiting, Sir?'

'When they rub their legs together. It looks innocuous, but the flies are in fact vomiting digestive juices onto their legs and applying it to the food. They're one of the animals which pre-digest. Mosquitoes do the same thing.'

'Sir, I—'

'Vomit inside you. That's what raises the lump. They're pre-digesting the blood before they suck it out of you. Great hairy-legged things. They breed in the fields, you know. Needles with wings. Disease-vector. None finer. Whole civilizations down. Read your history.'

'We can appreciate the bug situation down here, Sir.'

'I was grilling. Brats and patties. At least for a time. They gave me an apron. Something witty on the front. A certain impertinence permissible at picnics, the Christmas party. Let everyone's hair down a bit if you get me.'

'You estimate you were grilling throughout the early intervals of the picnic, then, Sir, which would square with Mr. van Hool's account.'

'The iced tea was brewed, not that horrible mix iced tea with the slight scum on top.'

'The iced tea was consumed by you'd say how many at the picnic, Sir?'

'Copious. Terribly hot you understand. No one wants pop when it's hot, except of course children, which then they have sticky mouths, which then the sugar in the pop excites the bugs.'

'Jesus, Clothier, now with the bugs again.'

'Utitshay.'

'Nothing against CID, you understand. Indispensable part of the mechanism. Fine hardworking fellows. Notwithstanding all the junk cases, deplorable waste of resources, Region had figures on—'

'So if there was a common denominator, Sir, you might point at the iced tea, you're telling us.'

'We all drank it. Ungodly hot. Who wants beer under a sun like that? Do either of you hear a— a sound?'

'And yet you yourself you're saying did not see anyone bringing the iced tea into the picnic area or making the iced tea.'

'An urn. Dispenser. Orange pebbled plastic, nozzle like a barrel's bung, yes?'

'The iced tea, you're saying.'

'I don't know that I've ever felt this agitated. It's as if.'

'They tell us it will come and go for a time, Sir, as the blood level stabilizes.'

'You'll be up and around in no time they tell us, Sir.'

'Trying to be glad to be of help. Our boys in uniform.'

'Clothier, what say—'

'You were helping us identify the urn, Sir, with the iced tea.'

'Orange dispenser that said Gatorade on the side. Some of the older children were excited; they thought it was Gatorade.'

'No children drank the tea.'

'The examiners call their children their little Line 40s. That's of course where you enter your CCDC from Form 2441 on the 1040. Some of the children were playing Collections. Near the horseshoe courts. Some of the older children. Liens on the toys, a jeopardy assessment and seizure of some of the smaller childrens' plates; there was some of the usual crying.'

'And you'd say you might first have noticed any

unusual effects or anything out of the ordinary when, then, Sir, if you had to say?'

'Terrible activity to teach children. Collections is Ghent's problem. Was Ghent's. I avoid Collections.'

'Understandable from our vantage, Sir.'

'Are those sunglasses, then?'

'Sir, we're not wearing eye protection of any kind.'

'My nose itches something awful.'

'I'm afraid we aren't permitted to touch any part of your person, Sir.'

'My thoughts are normally so much more organized than this.'

'Please take all the time you need.'

'They seemed just awful. Whole clouds of them. Shrouds, clouds, crowds of them. They're a disease-vector you know. Read your history. Breed in the trees. When I looked in one of their shades two of the smaller children were covered. A shroud of them around both, in their eyes, nose, smothering them — I saw one of them fall; it couldn't cry out. Pendleton's little Line 40.'

'So then you'd say that was the first observable sign of any effect, then, Sir.'

'I had a very long fork, you know.'

'For the grilling you mean, Sir.'

DAVID FOSTER WALLACE

'Let's didi, Norm, man. This guy's still gone. Scratch his nose and let's go.'

'Aitway, Aylortay.'

'The *Culex* and malaria. The *Aedes aegypti* and dengue. Read it. It's written. Fork or no.'

'For your duties at the grill at the picnic area's southeast quadrant according to this schematic, Sir.'

'A *very* long fork. I don't think you can appreciate. Jagged tines. It cast a shadow.'

'And were—were you able to observe at this time any of the other agents or families behaving in any way out of the ordinary or engaged with the iced tea in any way, Sir?'

'Though I did notice the settings. At the tables. With checked cloths. The settings were all knives. No spoons, no forks. *I* had the fork. Knife, plate, knife, knife. Three wicked knives at each place. Some years the breeze blows the plates away. Not this year, I can tell you.'

'So this was an effect, or you were observing an effect, Sir, can you say which?

'Fechner has a glass eye.'

'That would be Revenue Agent Fechner, Sir. You observed him setting knives at the tables?'

'Lost an eye in the war. How he put it: "Lost an eye." The idea. Say there, fellows, anyone seen my *eye* by any chance?'

898

'So you hadn't observed any person or persons actually setting the table with all knives, then, Sir.'

'Norm, man, what knives? Let's didi.'

'That's a war term if I'm not mistaken. Agent Taylor. You think I don't know what this is?'

'It's Aylortay, Sir. Pleased to meet you, Sir, although it's damn unfortunate it has to be under these circumstances.'

'They were coming out of the *trees*.'

'They were rappelling, Sir. The incursion may or may not have been tactical, that much we know.'

'There was an egg-toss and gunny—the egg wouldn't move; it stayed there in midair. The three-legged race under way when they came from the trees and they were trying to run away, to get to their children but their legs were tied together. It was a feeding frenzy, the mosquitoes—I was waving the long fork around.'

'And you said you observed Revenue Agent Fechner suffering effects from the adulterated tea.'

'So it was the tea.'

'That's not our area, Sir, I'm afraid. We're collecting data.'

'On the knives.'

'A handsome set of knives indeed, Sir, would you care to see them?'

'Who is this really? Who are you men?'

'You were saying Revenue Agent Fechner and his glass eye.'

'That he was at van Hool's beer chest; he had his glass eye out so there was just the socket.'

'And did the knives oh by some chance look like . . . *this,* Sir?'

'Atiencepay, Aylortay. Onay uttingcay etyay.'

'You think I don't speak Latin?'

'Sir, I'm pleased you speak Latin.'

'Who is this man to your right and left?'

'Try to focus, Sir. I know it's difficult.'

'Fechner was at the chest, had the eye out and was . . . was opening bottles of beer with the socket. Socket as bottle opener. In goes the bottle, downward yank. The little Line 40s were watching — it was awful!'

'Revenue Agent Fechner's going to be fine, Sir. They found the eye and he's going to be right as rain.'

'Was it raining, Sir?'

'Placing the cap in the socket and then yanking down on the bottle, then the children would scream and clap because the cap was in the socket. A little gray sun in the eye. Eye eye!'

'I say we just cut it out of him right now. It's right there, Clothier, see it?'

'Scopolamine you say. Loco weed. Parentis. Mens

sano in corpus. And not plastic knives, either. And may I say what handsome skulls you have beneath that skin, boys.'

'And you last saw Revenue Agent Drinion before the tactical incursion, Sir, or after?'

'Drinion was at the table. Holding down the table as they say. Almost asleep he seemed. Drinion never takes part. They weren't touching him — the mosquitoes. His chin in his hand.'

'You don't mean that literally, Sir.'

'Note the honed edge. Note the seven-inch length, you old drone. Note the five stars on the blade and where it says No Stain and Ice Hardened and Zwilling and J.A. Henckels, Solingen FRG. You know what this is?'

'I just don't feel well at all, still. The examiners — a whole writhing boiling mass of them on the ground.'

'From the three-legged race you mean, Sir, you don't mean what Miriam calls your "third leg," back in the days when she wanted that leg, Sir, didn't she, Sir, before it repelled her.'

'They were rappelling. Ropes in the trees. Victor Charles. A writhing mass of GS-9 examiners — mass copulation among the examiners which I personally observed — it's all there in my report on a Form 923(a) for personal observations of impropriety; you Inspections men know all about 923(a)s, do you not.'

'You observed this from the grill, then, Sir.'

'I observed the effect of the tea in opened sockets and mass frenzied orgylike copulation and humping under the trees, on the table, under the tossed egg, on both ends of the horseshoe grotto. There were actual buttocks thrusting under my grill.'

'And I believe you said you were wearing an apron, Sir.'

'Cut him. Take it right off, Clothier.'

'So by this point in time everyone with the possible exception of the children was suffering definite effects, Sir, you're saying.'

'The wieners themselves were writhing, thrusting. Plump, thrusting, shiny, moist, there on the grill, on Mrs. Kagle's aluminum platter, in the air. I with the fork and observing it all until out of the *trees* where they breed! Breeding, ever breeding!'

'I think we've got a decent picture of the situation from your particular vantage, Sir.'

'You know it doesn't go, Sir. Not really. You'll stay like this. Look at me. You'll look like this, Sir. Always. We came to tell you. We'll cut it off right now if you like. Say the word.'

'Needles with wings. Knives with wings, all

dancing on their sharp tips, shrouds of mosquitoes making it dark. The sky is no longer the sky.'

'He doesn't want it, Clothier.'

'The air no longer white with it.'

'Get used to it, you impotent old fag. That's right: *fag.*'

'Ixnay, Taylor.'

'I have seen my wife take her skin off, you know. Since you came all the way down, eh? Peel the white skin of her arm clean off like an opera glove. Take off her face from the top down.'

'Like: *this,* Sir?'

'I think I'm going to be moving over to the next subject of the debriefing now, Sir. With much gratitude for taking the time.'

'As if it's even yours, eh, Dwitt? Eh?'

'I'm simply unprecedentedly upset. I don't think it's getting better.'

'You know what doctors do, don't you? When you're asleep. From the top down, like you're a soft old grape in the back of the fridge that someone's forgot to throw out. DeWitt, if I've told you once I've told you a thousand times.'

'I'm noting that, Sir, as well as Inspections' appreciation for your cooperation under the circumstances.'

'Well don't just lie there say something. Tell

them what they want or they'll cut it off. They've as much as said so. Are you a fool?'

'And I know they'll be back in, and doing everything possible for your comfort until it comes off, Sir. I mean wears off. The blood level.'

'I'm naked, you know. Under all this.'

'We may or may not be needing to interview you again, Sir. When the effects are less noticeable if you understand.'

'As a jaybird. Buck-naked. Birthday suit.'

'Tell them, hurry. It's *German.*'

'Yes and I do, I have a penis. Penis.'

'Hate that word, Clothier.'

'Dreadful word, eh? Penis? Like something you'd touch with a thick rubber glove if at all.'

'Why DeWitt you old scalawiggle! I'm still a woman, you know!'

'Say it with me, boys. Penis penis penis penis penis.'

'You didn't forget, oh DeWitt, *it's* lovely.'

'You just get some rest, Sir.'

'Its name is — I won't tell you. How do you like that? I won't!'

'I remember when you looked at *me* that way.'

'It's got a name. Its name is — I won't tell you. It's mine. It's my third leg, Miriam calls it. But never from the forehead. It's not a mask. They start with the chin. Upsy daisy. In comes the needle on wings!'

'Allweshay, Aylortay?'

'My proboscis itches so I sink it *deep* before vomiting.'

'Not in me, DeWitt. It's like you're vomiting inside me. Even your expression is as if you're taken ill. If you could ever see it you'd —'

'Miriam's frigid you know.'

'I'll be locking this behind me, Sir, but it's just procedural.'

'Since our third. A terrible labor. Stillborn. Blue and cold. You know what we named it?'

'Taylor?'

'That's right. Taylor. Fine little Clothier just like his gumpappy.'

'I just don't want it. Don't torture me for not, I beg you.'

'Shall we . . . there you are, Sir.'

'No interest since. Frigid. Dry as a fine martini, Bernie Cheadle'd say.'

'So then toodleoo, Sir.'

'Thank God we have our work, boys, eh? And our hobbies. Our home workshops, yes? Fashioning needles and wings for the commonweal? Yes, Aylor?'

'I'll be back with more of these if you don't lie

still like a good boy though, Sir, and wait for them to come for it, Sir, so you can look like: *THIS!* Just one firm tug and off she comes.'

'She'll say *Give it a tug yourself, you old degenerate.*'

'Barely feel a thing. This'll get 'em cracking at their desks, Sir, eh what?'

'I can inhale, but I can't seem to exhale.'

[Voices in hall.]

'My workshop *is* organized, it *is,* you should *see* it.'

[Voices in hall.]

'I can find anything in there.'

[Voices in hall.]

'You'll see.'

[Voices in hall.]

§49

Fogle sat waiting in the small reception area of the Director's office. No one knew what it meant that Merrill Errol Lehrl was using Mr. Glendenning's office. Mr. Glendenning and his senior staff were up at Region; it might just be a cordial professional-courtesy thing that Lehrl was using Mr. Glendenning's office. Mrs. Oooley wasn't at her desk in the reception area; instead at the desk was one of Lehrl's aides, whose either first or last name was Reynolds. He'd moved a certain amount of Caroline's stuff around, you could see. The area had a large rug whose geometric patterns, which were intricate, made the carpet look Turkish or Byzantine. The overheads were off; someone had placed several lamps around the little room, creating attractive oases in a general atmosphere of gloom. Fogle found low light gloomy. Dr. Lehrl's other aide, Sylvanshine, was in a chair just off to Fogle's right, so that the two aides were just outside the peripheries of Fogle's vision and could not both be seen at the same time, and he had to turn his head slightly to look at either directly. Which he was forced to do, rather a lot, because they appeared to be prebriefing him for some reason. Doing so in tandem. But also, in a way, to be talking across Fogle to each other. When they addressed Chris Fogle directly, they tended to wax a bit didactic, but at the same time it was not totally uninteresting. Both Reynolds and Sylvanshine were knowledge-able about various powerful administrators' career trajectories and résumés. It was the sort of thing that aides at National could be expected to know a lot about; they were a little like royal courtiers. Most of the names of the people they spoke of were people at Nation; only a few were known to Fogle. As was customary in the Service, the aides spoke in a rapid, excited way without either's face showing any excite-ment or even interest in the subject at hand, which started out with a small lecture on the two basic dif-ferent ways that a person could rise to prominence and large responsibility within the bureaucracy of the IRS. Bureaucratic aerodynamics and modes of advancement were very common topics of interest among examiners; it was unclear whether Reynolds and Sylvanshine didn't know that much of this was familiar ground to Fogle or didn't care. Fogle imagined that at whatever Post these two were normally at, they were legendary dickheads.

According to the two aides, one way to advance to managerial levels beyond GS-17 was through slow, steady demonstrations of competence, loyalty, reasonable initiative, interhuman skills with the people above and below you, etc., moving slowly up through the promotional ranks.

'The other, lesser known, is the éclat.'

'The éclat means the sudden, extraordinary idea or innovation that brings you to the notice of those at high levels. Even national levels.' One got the sense they were parroting others.

'Dr. Lehrl is the latter kind. The éclat kind.'

'Allow us to give you some background.'

'It's some time ago. Should I specify the year?'

The rhythms of Reynolds and Sylvanshine's back and forth were quite precise. There was no wasted time. Questions had a vaguely staged quality. If Dr. Lehrl himself was back behind that frosted door, it wasn't clear whether Reynolds and Sylvanshine thought that he could hear what they were saying.

'The details are unimportant. He was just one of a low-level audit group in a backwater district somewhere, and he got an idea.'

'He's not even on 1040s within the group, mind you. He's small business and S.'

'The idea, however, concerns 1040s.'

'Specifically exemptions.'

'An area not unfamiliar to you, I assume.' Neither had any accent at all.

'You may, for example, know or not know that up until 1979, filers could declare dependents just by name.'

'On the 1040 of the time.'

'Dependents. Children, elderly in the filer's care.'

'I think we can assume he knows what dependents are, Claude.'

'But do you know the 1040 of that period? What the filer had to do was put the dependent children's first names on Line 5c, others' names and relations on 5d.'

'Now, of course, it's all 6c and 6d. We're talking about 1977.'

'But the point is just the name and relation. Which you can see the problem.'

'There's no way to check,' Sylvanshine said.

'In retrospect, it appears absurd,' Reynolds said.

'But that's after the éclat that it looks so naive. Since there was no way to check.'

'Not really. Just a name and relation.'

'It was the honor system. There was no real way to ensure that dependents were real.'

'No efficient way, that is.'

'Oh sure, sure, they figured that the filer figured we *could* check, but as a practical matter we couldn't check. Not really. Not in any definitive way.'

'Especially since data processing was in such a primitive state. You could track consistency of dependents listed over successive years, but it was time-consuming and inconclusive.'

'A kid could have turned eighteen. An elderly dependent could have died. A new kid could have been born. Who was going to chase all this down? It wasn't worth the man-hours for anybody.'

'True, if there was an audit and some of the dependents were made up the filer was in huge trouble and there were criminal penalties plus interest and penalties. But that was just random chance. The dependents themselves couldn't trigger an audit.'

'Each dependent was I think two hundred dollars added to the standard deduction.'

'Which you guys now know as the zero bracket

amount.' Both aides were in their late twenties, but they spoke to Fogle as if they were much, much older than he. 'But before '78 everyone knew it as the standard deduction.'

'But this was '77.'

Sylvanshine gave Reynolds a look whose impatience was conveyed through duration instead of expression. Then he said: 'In case this sounds picayune or inconsequential, let's stress right here that we're talking $1.2 billion.'

'That's b-b-*billion,* from this one tiny change.'

Fogle wondered if he was supposed to ask what change, whether they were including him in the choreography here as a kind of prompter, whether the sophistication of their routine was that advanced.

Sylvanshine said: 'What Dr. Lehrl saw, as some no-account GS-9 auditor, was insufficient incentive for the filer to report dependents accurately. Institutional incentive. In retrospect, it seems obvious.'

'That's the way of genius, of éclat.'

'And his solution looks simple. He simply suggested requiring taxpayers to include the SS number of each dependent.'

'Requiring an SSN right next to each name.'

'Since everything in the Martinsburg database at the time was keyed to SSNs.'

'Which actually didn't make it all that much easier to really check.'

'But the filer didn't know that. The requirement would greatly increase the filer's fear of a phantom dependent being detected.'

'Such was the power of the SSN.'

'It created, in other words, an added incentive for compliance on dependents.'

'And it was very easy and inexpensive. Just add "and Social Security Number" in the directions for 5c and 5d.'

'His District Director had the sense to recognize an éclat and kicked the idea up to the Region, who routed it to the DC-Compliance's office at 666 Independence.'

'No one could believe it hadn't been thought of before.'

'The first tax year it's actually implemented is '78, as Section 151(e) of the Code. So '79 is the first year the new instructions are on 1040s. Six-point-nine million dependents disappear.'

'From the nation's 1040s.'

'Vanish, poof.'

'As compared to the '77 returns.'

'There are no sanctions. Everybody decides simply to pretend the fake dependents never happened.'

'Netting $1.2 billion the first year.'

'It's a textbook éclat.'

'It's also politically brilliant. There's more than one kind of éclat.'

'This was both.'

'Because although it costs next to nothing to implement, it requires a written change in Section 151 of the US Tax Code, which requires one of the Three-Personed God's senior staff to shepherd it through the Ways and Means process, to get codified as law.'

'Which means the idea gets bruited about at the very highest levels of Triple-Six.'

'And from out of nowhere Dr. Lehrl jumps four grades and even jumps Region after only two quarters and becomes in short order the DC-Systems' most valuable ——'

'Well, one of the most valuable, to be fair, since there's also —— in ——.'

'Who is a whole other story involving your more slow, conventional rise through the pipeline.'

'But certainly one of Systems' most valuable utility men.'

'Like an in-house consultant.'

'Especially since the Initiative.'

'Especially in Personnel Systems.'

'Which is where you come in, Mr. Fogle.'

'Essentially, he comes in and reconfigures Posts to maximize revenue.'

'Essentially, he's a reorganizer.'

'An idea man.'

'More bang for the buck.'

'True, largely at the District level.'

'But this is hardly his first Regional Center.'

'There's a certain amount of this we can't talk about.'

'We're enjoined.'

'You can think of him as a Personnel guy, or a Systems guy.'

'Personnel Systems, essentially.'

'But he answers to Systems. He serves at the pleasure of the Deputy Commissioner–Systems. He's the DCS's instrument, you could say.'

'But he's not a slave to any one system.'

'He's a reader of people.'

'He's an administrator, ultimately.'

'Or more like an administrator of administrators.'

'The Systems Division, you may or may not know, used to be called Administration.'

'It's a vague term, admittedly.'

'He'd describe himself more as a cyberneticist.'

'The Service is, after all, a system composed of many systems.'

'His job is to come in and redesign Posts to get the most out of them. To find ways to stream-line and enhance productivity, remove bottle-necks, debug. This blends an expertise in automation, personnel, support logistics, and over-all systems.'

'He goes where he's sent. His assignment is sim-ply a certain Post. The assignment memos are always about one line long.'

'Phase One is fact-finding. Feeling out the situation.'

'His real genius is incentive. Creating incentive. Finding out what makes people tick.'

'He'll take you apart like a little machine.'

'It's not as if Line 5 was his only éclat. We're just giving you an example. What he really is is a genius of human motivations and incentives and designing systems to achieve them.'

'He'll test you.'

'When you go in.'

'He reads people. It can be a little scary.'

'Be ready is all we mean.'

'But don't look nervous or like you're braced for some battery of tests.' Fogle knew of eastern cultures where any small piece of business had to be worked up to through involved systems of small talk and ritual indirection. Only an idiot would not have wondered whether this was what was going on, or whether Reynolds and Sylvanshine were just extremely boring and took a very long time to come to the point, assuming there was any point. Fogle had been away from his table for over half an hour already. Sylvanshine was continuing. 'Because it doesn't work like that. It's not that kind of testing.'

'Give him an example, maybe,' Reynolds said to Sylvanshine, indicating Fogle with a movement of his head as if there were anyone else he could possibly be referring to.

'OK.' Sylvanshine made a show of looking right at Chris Fogle. 'Where'd you go to school?'

'Umm, what kind of school?'

'Your college. Your alma mater.'

'I went to several, actually.'

If Sylvanshine was impatient, it was impossible to discern this. He had no poker tell whatsoever that Fogle could see. 'Pick one.'

'UIC. DuPage. DePaul.'

'Perfect. DePaul. So he'll ask, you'll say DePaul, he'll say "Ah, the Blue Demons." Well, it's not the Blue Demons, it's the Blue Devils. But do you correct him?'

'Actually, it is the Blue Demons. The Blue Devils is Duke.'

A one-beat pause. 'Whatever. Whatever the team

name is, he says the wrong team name. Now, though: Do you correct him?'

Fogle looked from Sylvanshine to Reynolds. Their suit coats were not identical, but their shirts and slacks were, he could see. Reynolds said, 'Do you?'

'Do I correct him?' Fogle said.

'That's the question.'

'I'm not sure exactly what you're asking.'

'You do. The correct answer is you do correct him,' Sylvanshine said. 'Because it's a test. He's testing as to are you a toady, are you intimidated, are you a yes-man.'

'A sycophant,' Reynolds said.

'It was a test?'

'If he says Blue Devils and you just nod and smile, he won't say anything, but you'll have failed a test.'

Fogle looked quickly up at the clock. 'Is there more than one?'

'Well, yes and no,' Sylvanshine said. 'It's extremely subtle. You'd have no idea anything was going on. But the whole time you're interfacing he'll be testing you, probing you. The whole time.'

'One other thing,' Reynolds said, forcing Fogle to turn his head again. 'There'll be a kid in there with him. A seven-, eight-year-old kid.'

There was a moment of silence. An unparsable look passed between Reynolds and Sylvanshine. Sylvanshine had a very small, thin, neatly groomed mustache.

'Is it Dr. Lehrl's kid?' Fogle asked finally.

'Don't ask him that. That's the thing. The kid will be in a corner, reading, playing with something. Don't acknowledge the kid. Nor do you ask him or refer to the kid. The kid won't acknowledge you, you don't acknowledge him.'

'There may also be a hand puppet. It's an old thing from Audits that he's hung on to. Call it an eccentricity. If I were you, I wouldn't mention the hand puppet, either.'

'For the record,' Sylvanshine said, 'it's not his kid.'

Fogle was looking straight ahead in a ruminative way.

'The kid's the kid of one of Dr. Lehrl's senior staff back at Danville,' Reynolds said. 'Dr. Lehrl just likes having the kid around.'

'Even if the dad isn't there.'

'It's all a long, tedious story. The point, as far as you're concerned, is don't acknowledge the kid, and it's up to you but our advice is don't acknowledge the Doberman hand puppet either.'

Fogle's eyelid was doing the maddening fluttery

thing again, which neither aide could see. He said: 'The thing is, can I ask a question?'

'Shoot.'

'The college sports team thing—how come you're telling me?'

Reynolds, at the desk, made a minute adjustment to one of his cuffs. 'What do you mean?'

'Well, if it's going to be a test when he asks me, why tell me in advance what I should say? Doesn't that defeat the purpose of the test?'

Sylvanshine opened the file on top of the stack beside him and made a small show of marking something inside. Reynolds leaned back in Caroline Oooley's chair and lifted his arms, smiling: 'Nice. You got us.'

'Pardon?'

'You got us. You passed. The test was: Are you just a toady, so anxious to please the hotshot from National that you'd suck up inside dope and go in there and say what we told you to?'

'Which you didn't,' Sylvanshine said.

'But I'm not even in there yet,' Fogle said.

'Instead, you challenged us on a point of logic.'

'Granted, a fairly obvious point.'

'But you'd be amazed how many don't. How many GS-9s will scuttle in there and correct

Dr. Lehrl's so-called mistake, trying to be a sycophant.'

'A brown-nose toaderooski.'

What his eyelid felt like was the eyelid equivalent of somebody shuddering. 'So then *this* was the test?'

'Consider yourself slapped five.'

Raising his arms in a gesture of surrender and congratulation had caused Reynolds's cuffs to protrude unevenly again from the sleeves of his jacket, and he was adjusting them again.

'So but can I ask another question?'

'The kid's on a roll,' Sylvanshine said.

'When I go in there, is Dr. Lehrl going to ask me about schools? Did you just make that up?'

'Let's turn that around,' Sylvanshine said.

So now he had to look back over at Sylvanshine again, who hadn't changed position in his chair over by the magazine and bulletin table even once the whole time, Fogle saw.

Sylvanshine said: 'Say you were to go in there and interface and at some point he misidentifies your football team—what do you do?'

'Because,' Reynolds said, 'if you don't correct his mistake, you're being a toady, and if you do correct him, you're maybe also being a toady in that you're acting on inside information we just gave you.'

'And he despises toadies,' Sylvanshine said, opening the file again.

'But is he even in there?' Fogle said. 'With some mysterious child I'm supposed to pretend isn't there? And is that another test—do I acknowledge the kid or not, given what you've said?'

'One item at a time,' Reynolds said. He and Sylvanshine were looking at Fogle very intently; Fogle thought, for the first time, that maybe they could see the eyelid thing. 'He calls it the Blue Devils—what do you do?'

§50

The office could be any office. Cove fluorescents on a dimmer, modular shelving, the desk practically an abstraction. The whisper of sourceless ventilation. You are a trained observer and there is nothing to observe. An open can of Tab whose color seems lurid against the beige and white. The stainless steel hook for your jacket. No photos or diplomas or personal touches—the facilitator is either newly posted or on outside contract. A woman with a pleasant, pop-eyed face, hair beginning to gray, in a padded chair identical to your own. Some protrusive eyes give the faces a creepy, staring aspect; the facilitator's do not. You have declined to remove your shoes. The knob beside the dimmer is your chair's control; it reclines and the feet go up. It is important that you be comfortable.

'You do have a body, you know.'

She has no notebook, it occurs. And given its position in the building's northwest leg, the office should by all rights have a window.

The setting at which you do not feel your own weight in the chair is two-thirds reclined. There is a disposable piece of paper attached to the headrest. Your sight line is the seam of the wall and drop ceiling; the toes of your shoes are visible at the lower periphery. The facilitator is not visible. The seam appears to thicken as the overheads are lowered to the level of a false dawn.

'The way we start is to relax and become aware of the body.

'It is at the level of body that we proceed.

'Do not try to relax.' Her voice is amused. It is gentle without being soft.

Since we all breathe, all the time, it is amazing what happens when someone else directs you how and when to breathe. And how vividly someone with no imagination whatsoever can see what he's told is right there, complete with banister and rubber runners, curving down and rightward into a darkness that recedes before you.

It is nothing like sleeping. Nor does her voice alter or seem to recede. She's right there, speaking calmly, and so are you.

Notes and Asides

Throughout the manuscript of *The Pale King,* David Foster Wallace wrote hundreds of notes, observations, and larger ideas. Some of these asides suggest where the plot of the novel might have headed. Others provide additional information about characters' backgrounds or their future development. Contradictions and complications abound among them. For instance, some notes say it's DeWitt Glendenning who is bringing examiners with unique abilities to Peoria; others that it's Merrill Errol Lehrl. A note from chapter 22 suggests that Chris Fogle knows a string of numbers that, when recited, give him the power of total concentration, but nowhere in the chapters we have does Fogle display this power. (Perhaps this ability is the reason Fogle has been summoned to meet Merrill Lehrl in chapter 49.) The hope in including this selection of notes is that they allow a fuller understanding of the ideas David was exploring in *The Pale King* and illuminate how much a work in progress the novel still was.

Notes that were attached to specific chapters in *The Pale King* appear first, followed by notes from other parts of the manuscript.

—Ed.

§7 Sylvanshine wants desperately to be CID— that's why he wants to pass the CPA exam. CID must be CPAs, just as FBI must be lawyers. Sylvanshine plays in front of mirror—"Freeze! Treasury!"

3 high end players—Glendenning, Special HR guy Glendenning needs to find gifted examiners, Lehrl. But we never see them, only their aides and advance men.

§12 Stecyk flown in via Lehrl's design to help drive examiners crazy.

§13 *Primed* is one of the IRS words for putting Examiners in a state where they pay maximum attention to returns.

footnote 34 The dragon-image always guards some priceless thing. This other boy never, in all his endless introspection and analysis, conceived the attacks as forms of all-body weeping or sadness itself—for childhood's end, for the split self required by society, for any number of possible traumas and estrangements. The disgust of others was a rank projection of his innermost secret, which the dragon both guarded and embodied—he was ignorant of mercy.

§15 It's Sylvanshine who's the fact psychic, and Lehrl, who believes in the occult, has sent him to find and place the very finest GS-7 wigglers he can in a given group, so that when the A/NADA outperforms them on revenue, it'll be convincing to Triple 6. This would require rewriting the Sylvanshine arrival sequence...S wants to become CPA because everyone else in Internal Control Systems is CPA? Or so that he can get out of the Service?

§19 It's the HR guys who ultimately get replaced by computers—they're too distractible, too into side-issues.

Glendenning's kid in navy on ship off Iranian coast? Terrified he's risking his life for an America that's no longer worth fighting for.

§22 'Irrelevant Chris' is irrelevant only on the subject of himself? On all other topics/subjects, he's focused & cogent and interesting? Dictum on him around REC is that he's OK as long as you keep him off the topic of himself—then you're in for it?

Fogle ends up in IRS as the insufferable do-gooder that Stecyk was, as child?

'Film interview' a sham? Point is to extract from Chris Fogle the formula of numbers that permits total concentration? Point is he can't remember—he wasn't paying attention when he happened to read the series of documents that added up to the string of numbers that, when held in serial in his head, allows him to maintain interest and concentration at will? Has to be sort of tricked into it? Numbers have downside of incredible headache.

§24 Richard 'Dick' Tate is Director of Personnel. Ned Stecyk is his Deputy Director. Tate opposes Lehrl and ICS because he wants power, control—no power if fewer living personnel.

Glendenning ineffectual—lost in a mist of civic idealism—the actual REC is run mostly by Tate and Stecyk, and by the Information Systems person.

When DW and Stecyk lock eyes as Stecyk is soothing guy in his inner office, a look of tremendous compassion and sympathy spreads over Stecyk's face, mainly because of DW's hideous skin. Stecyk thus searches out DW and tries to be nice to him, figuring that he's been shunned and traumatized his whole life. DW resents this—his position is that if people are shallow enough to regard someone's skin as the be-all and end-all of his value and character, then fuck them; he doesn't need them—but is ready to exploit Stecyk's kindness in order to win various advantages for himself.

David Wallace, once settled, has thing where he'll look out the window and see, in the other, more elite building, someone at a window in the computer center looking back. Wearing thick glasses. Their eyes meet but they never meet or say anything.

Light-blue Pacer with fish bumper sticker. This car is Lane Dean's—who has to hurry like crazy in the AM because he goes to church services (or Sheri, his wife, does) at dawn, and is always on the edge of being late (Dean has become less fervently Christian since starting at REC, while Sheri has gotten more so)—that made this maneuver almost every morning.

§26 Stecyk knows about Blumquist. He was at the REC when Blumquist died. He was just out of the IRS academy in Columbus and working as a chalk leader in rotes. He was the one who had to interview the wigglers (in 1978?) who had continued coming to work and working for something like three days while Blumquist sat rigidly at his desk, deceased. Some of them had felt bad about this. A few put in for transfers. Stecyk will discover that Examiners' total down-the-line audit revenue every month increases when Blumquist sits with them, not talking to them or distracting them but simply sitting there, being *with* them. Theorizes that double teams of Examiners might be worth the cost — the doubled salary might be exceeded by the overall realized audit-revenue. But how to get this idea sold? Region Personnel Director would want to know how this originally came to light...how can Stecyk refer to a ghost? Or perhaps this was the idea of a previous Personnel Deputy, who got in trouble, because Region figured that he'd tried the experiment with two actual examiners, meaning double salary. It this a plausible plotline?

What is Stecyk like now, as an adult? Still incredibly nice, but no longer a total dweeb? A bit sadder? A dispenser of pop-psych bromides? What happened to make him realize that the Niceness of his childhood was actually sadistic, pathological, selfish? That other people, too, want to feel nice and do favors, that he'd been massively selfish about generosity? In a college sport, did he keep letting other team score out of 'niceness,' and got a visit from a referee—someone dressed all in black and white, like Irrelevant Chris Fogle's Jesuit in college—who very bluntly told him he was full of shit and that true decency was very different from pathological generosity, because pathological generosity did not take into account the feelings of the people who were the object of the generosity? Stecyk had caused traffic jams at 4-way stops by always letting everyone else go first? Or referee magically gives Stecyk insight into how his mother had felt when Stecyk got up very early every morning to do her housekeeping for her—like she was useless, like the family felt she was incompetent, etc. Stecyk tells David Wallace the story of the butterfly—if you let it out of the cocoon when it seems to be struggling and dying, then its wings don't get strengthened and it can't survive.

The pathologically nice is one of the basic types who gravitate to the IRS, because it's such a grim, unpopular job—no gratitude, which only increases the sense of sacrifice.

Sylvanshine has a different take on Blumquist. Sylvanshine has educed that some of the very best Examiners—most attentive, most thorough—are those with some kind of trauma or abandonment in their past. He's there to intuit which are the best so that they can be auditioned for the test against A/NADA. Blumquist, it turns out, had had brutal Fundamentalist parents—the kind for whom fans and mattresses were luxuries. They had a special punishment: they made him face the wall in the parlor—blank wall—stand there facing it for hours at a time. This was the trauma. There had been a mirror on the other wall behind him; it showed only his back. This is the image Sylvanshine gets for Blumquist: a view of his childhood back, very still, with a scrolled wooden frame around it. Blumquist had had productivity numbers that were much, much higher than anyone else's, though he had declined offers to be promoted to higher civil service grade and managerial job. Sylvanshine looking for similarly great rote examiner, to do the series of tests against the A/NADA program and digital computer. Several of the recently transferred Examiners are among the very best tested rote examiners left at national RECs. Lehrl's Systems boys want a fair test, the computer and A/NADA against the very finest

rote examiners they can get . . . so that when the A/
NADA crushes them, the test'll be all that much
more definitive.

§30 LEHRL & PRO-TECH VS. GLENDEN-
NING & DISTRICT DIRECTORS: Project is
replacing human Examiners with computers
the way Lehrl invented Automated Collection Systems — the District Directors don't want it,
because they're Old School IRS-as-Civics believers, whereas the new school has a corporate philosophy: maximize revenue while minimizing
costs. Big Q is whether IRS is to be essentially a
corporate entity or a *moral* one.

Charles Lehrl preparing to computerize Exams
the way he computerized Automated Collection
System in Collections — the experiments there
were in Rome and Philadelphia. Invented the IRP
that compares W2s and 1099s to Returns — made
Examiners' jobs otiose.

Reynolds & Sylvanshine (lovers? roomies?) vie
for Lehrl's attention & favor like courtiers or children — it's how they pass the time in the dullness
of IRS intrigue.

Reynolds & Sylvanshine live together — sort of
like Rosencrantz & Guildenstern in *Hamlet*. They
have an incredibly nice reproduction of Gerard ter

Borch's *Parental Admonition* (28 x 29 in., Rijks-
museum, Amsterdam) that they hang wherever they
live—or else an incredibly good forgery, done by
one of the great painter-imitators of the modern US.

§38   DW, because of snafu, favors upgrading IRS
computer systems—Stecyk wants to preserve
human examiners?

§43   There is no bomb. It turned out that an
actual load of nitrate fertilizer had been blown up.
Again, something big *threatens* to happen but
doesn't actually happen.
    This becomes disaster—the scanners are
viewed as able to *replace* examiners—their jobs
are threatened: contest between Drinion + scanner set up.

§46   Rand works in Problem Resolution, not
Exams? Because her prettiness helps defuse appel-
lants and keep them from making as much trouble
as they would otherwise? Another Personnel coup
from X, the talent-arrangement genius?
    Drinion came home as child to find whole family
gone—at least that's the rumor. A lot of stuff about
Drinion, his manner of paying attention, should be
implicit, or should unfold over a much longer time.

IRS rap on Meredith Rand: She's pretty but a yammerer of the most dire kind, on and on, excruciating to be around—they speculate that her husband must have some kind of hearing aid that he can turn off at will.

At Rand and Drinion's last meeting, in book, Drinion asks: "Would you prefer it intense, or casual?" Rand breaks into tears.

Rand gets obsessed with Drinion (as type of "savior"?) in the same way she'd been obsessed with Ed Rand in hospital?

REC Center in outlying Peoria district called "Anthony, Illinois"? Who is Saint Anthony? The tornado continues . . .

End pt. 1. In pt. 2 (forthcoming?) Rand describes, quickly, how they got romantically involved (or Rath or someone else does, or it gets out through summary mediated by several different tellers): M.R. felt she needed Rand, or rather she felt sorry for him because he was sick and unattractive (additional repulsive symptoms in private) and going to die soon. Always expecting him to die in the near future. And she saw how lonely and sad his life was, his apartment was. So she married him, at just age 19 . . . But he didn't die, hasn't died; and now M.R. is trapped, miserable, especially because Ed isn't grateful to her, and would laugh spitefully at her if she ever tried to say to him that he should be grateful, that she'd taken pity — Rand would say that the real person she'd pitied was herself, and that marrying someone always on the edge of possible death was a great way to let herself feel both safe and heroic.

Every day at day's end they have the same exchange:

"How was your day?"

"I work in a mental hospital. How do you think my day was?"

It's not funny or intimate, no shared joke — they've been in the same basic relationship for 6 years, w/o growth or change, and Rand is looking for someone to save her, extract her from it.

* * *

Big issue is human examiners or machines. Sylvanshine is after the best human examiners he can find.

Embryonic outline:

2 Broad arcs:

1. Paying attention, boredom, ADD, Machines vs. people at performing mindless jobs.
2. Being individual vs. being part of larger things — paying taxes, being "lone gun" in IRS vs. team player.

David Wallace disappears 100 pp in.
Central Deal: Realism, monotony. Plot a series of set-ups for stuff happening, but nothing actually happens.

David Wallace disappears—becomes creature of the system.

Overall movement: Old IRS guard are driven by self-righteousness, tax cheats as deadbeats, tax payment as virtue, or to work out their own psych stuff like anger, resentment, subservience to authority, etc. Or else they're drab civil servants in it for security, standard government workers. New IRS guard are not only good accountants but good strategic and business planners: whole point is to maximize revenue—disregard civic virtue, disregard moral warrior aspect of being in tax collection. New Peoria REC Personnel guy is new guard: his whole deal is finding employees and organizing stuff so that examiners maximize the revenue that auditors/collections can yield. His willingness to experiment/think in fresh new ways leads, paradoxically, to deep mysticism: a certain set of numbers that lets examiners concentrate better, etc. The ultimate point is the question whether humans or machines can do exams better, can maximize efficiency in spotting which returns might need auditing and will produce revenue.

Drinion is *happy*. Ability to pay attention. It turns out that bliss — a second-by-second joy + gratitude at the guide of being alive, conscious — lies on the other side of crushing, crushing boredom. Pay close attention to the most tedious thing you can find (tax returns, televised golf), and, in waves a boredom like you've never known will wash over you and just about kill you. Ride these out, and it's like stepping from black and white into color. Like water after days in the desert. Constant bliss in every atom

STECYK?
There is a counterpart to Sylvanshine. This is a high-end Personnel person for the REC (for the side that advocates human examiners over computers and the DIF). He searches for immersives. Ringers who can be brought in and examine complex returns without the sort of boredom that numbs you. (Or it's Stecyk, an examiner totally devoted to his job — hated, an abstract application of probity and virtue — constantly on the lookout for ways to help. It's he who goes to Meckstroth's office with the idea of how to send receipts directly

to bank, save money and time.) Stecyk now in Personnel and Personnel Training?

They're rare, but they're among us. People able to achieve and sustain a certain steady state of concentration, attention, despite what they're doing. The first one Stecyk spotted was in the library of Peoria College of Business, in the reading room, an Asian kid in one of the reading chairs that looks a great deal more comfortable than it really is, slumped back and legs crossed ankle on knee, reading a statistics textbook. Stecyk goes by twenty minutes later, kid is still in exactly the same position, reading. Stecyk crosses the room just behind him to verify that the kid's several pages along. His notes are precise and flush-left in a tiny neat script. An hour later, the kid is <u>still</u> in same position, reading same book, now 14 pages later.

A guard working security outside a credit union. Standing at parade rest all day. Can't read or chat. Simply watching people come in and out, nodding when nodded at. In Midstate Security faux-police uniform. There in case of any trouble. Stecyk walks in and out several times, as occasion to watch guard. What's impressive is that the guard pays closer attention to him each time, meaning the guard registers the fact that Stecyk is coming in and out more than is normal. He's able to <u>pay attention</u> even in what has to be a staggeringly dull job.

Midwest meditation semifinals. Contestants hooked up to EEG — it's who can achieve and maintain theta waves for the longest period of time.

Woman on assembly line counting number of visible loops of twine on outside of bale of twine. Counting, over and over. When the whistle blows, every other worker practically runs for the door. She stays briefly, immersed in her work. It's the ability to be <u>immersed</u>.

About the Author

David Foster Wallace was born in Ithaca, New York, in 1962 and raised in Illinois, where he was a regionally ranked junior tennis player. He received bachelor of arts degrees in philosophy and English from Amherst College and wrote what would become his first novel, *The Broom of the System,* as his senior English thesis. He received a master of fine arts from the University of Arizona in 1987 and briefly pursued graduate work in philosophy at Harvard University. His second novel, *Infinite Jest,* was published in 1996. Wallace taught creative writing at Emerson College, Illinois State University, and Pomona College, and published the story collections *Girl with Curious Hair, Brief Interviews with Hideous Men,* and *Oblivion* and the essay collections *A Supposedly Fun Thing I'll Never Do Again* and *Consider the Lobster*. He was awarded a MacArthur Fellowship, a Lannan Literary Award, and a Whiting Writers' Award, and was appointed to the Usage Panel for *The American Heritage Dictionary of the English Language*. He died in 2008, leaving behind unpublished work of which *The Pale King* is a part.

Implementing Cisco IOS Network Security (IINS) Foundation Learning Guide

Second Edition

Catherine Paquet

Cisco Press

800 East 96th Street

Indianapolis, Indiana 46240 USA

Implementing Cisco IOS Network Security (IINS) Foundation Learning Guide
Second Edition

Catherine Paquet

Copyright© 2013 Cisco Systems, Inc.

Published by:

Cisco Press
800 East 96th Street
Indianapolis, IN 46240 USA

Printed in the United States of America

First Printing November 2012

Library of Congress Cataloging-in-Publication data is on file.

ISBN-13: 978-1-58714-272-7

ISBN-10: 1-58714-272-4

Warning and Disclaimer

This book is designed to provide information about implementing Cisco IOS network security with information necessary to prepare for Cisco exam 640-554, Implementing Cisco IOS Network Security. Every effort has been made to make this book as complete and as accurate as possible, but no warranty or fitness is implied.

The information is provided on an "as is" basis. The authors, Cisco Press, and Cisco Systems, Inc. shall have neither liability nor responsibility to any person or entity with respect to any loss or damages arising from the information contained in this book or from the use of the discs or programs that may accompany it.

The opinions expressed in this book belong to the author and are not necessarily those of Cisco Systems, Inc.

Trademark Acknowledgments

All terms mentioned in this book that are known to be trademarks or service marks have been appropriately capitalized. Cisco Press or Cisco Systems, Inc., cannot attest to the accuracy of this information. Use of a term in this book should not be regarded as affecting the validity of any trademark or service mark.

Corporate and Government Sales

The publisher offers excellent discounts on this book when ordered in quantity for bulk purchases or special sales, which may include electronic versions and/or custom covers and content particular to your business, training goals, marketing focus, and branding interests. For more information, please contact:

U.S. Corporate and Government Sales

1-800-382-3419

corpsales@pearsontechgroup.com

For sales outside the United States, please contact:

International Sales

international@pearsoned.com

Feedback Information

At Cisco Press, our goal is to create in-depth technical books of the highest quality and value. Each book is crafted with care and precision, undergoing rigorous development that involves the unique expertise of members from the professional technical community.

Readers' feedback is a natural continuation of this process. If you have any comments regarding how we could improve the quality of this book, or otherwise alter it to better suit your needs, you can contact us through email at feedback@ciscopress.com. Please make sure to include the book title and ISBN in your message.

We greatly appreciate your assistance.

Publisher: Paul Boger

Associate Publisher: Dave Dusthimer

Manager Global Certification: Erik Ullanderson

Business Operation Manager, Cisco Press: Anand Sundaram

Executive Editor: Brett Bartow

Managing Editor: Sandra Schroeder

Development Editor: Kimberley Debus

Senior Project Editor: Tonya Simpson

Copy Editor: Bill McManus

Technical Editor: Kevin Redmon

Editorial Assistant: Vanessa Evans

Book Designer: Louisa Adair

Cover Designer: Mark Shirar

Composition: Bronkella Publishing

Indexer: Tim Wright

Proofreader: Sheri Cain

Americas Headquarters
Cisco Systems, Inc.
San Jose, CA

Asia Pacific Headquarters
Cisco Systems (USA) Pte. Ltd.
Singapore

Europe Headquarters
Cisco Systems International BV
Amsterdam, The Netherlands

Cisco has more than 200 offices worldwide. Addresses, phone numbers, and fax numbers are listed on the Cisco Website at **www.cisco.com/go/offices**.

CCDE, CCENT, Cisco Eos, Cisco HealthPresence, the Cisco logo, Cisco Lumin, Cisco Nexus, Cisco StadiumVision, Cisco TelePresence, Cisco WebEx, DCE, and Welcome to the Human Network are trademarks; Changing the Way We Work, Live, Play, and Learn and Cisco Store are service marks; and Access Registrar, Aironet, AsyncOS, Bringing the Meeting To You, Catalyst, CCDA, CCDP, CCIE, CCIP, CCNA, CCNP, CCSP, CCVP, Cisco, the Cisco Certified Internetwork Expert logo, Cisco IOS, Cisco Press, Cisco Systems, Cisco Systems Capital, the Cisco Systems logo, Cisco Unity, Collaboration Without Limitation, EtherFast, EtherSwitch, Event Center, Fast Step, Follow Me Browsing, FormShare, GigaDrive, HomeLink, Internet Quotient, IOS, iPhone, iQuick Study, IronPort, the IronPort logo, LightStream, Linksys, MediaTone, MeetingPlace, MeetingPlace Chime Sound, MGX, Networkers, Networking Academy, Network Registrar, PCNow, PIX, PowerPanels, ProConnect, ScriptShare, SenderBase, SMARTnet, Spectrum Expert, StackWise, The Fastest Way to Increase Your Internet Quotient, TransPath, WebEx, and the WebEx logo are registered trademarks of Cisco Systems, Inc. and/or its affiliates in the United States and certain other countries.

All other trademarks mentioned in this document or website are the property of their respective owners. The use of the word partner does not imply a partnership relationship between Cisco and any other company. (0812R)

About the Author

Catherine Paquet is a practitioner in the field of internetworking, network security, and security financials. She has authored or contributed to ten books thus far with Cisco Press. Catherine has in-depth knowledge of security systems, remote access, and routing technology. She is a Cisco Certified Network Professional (CCNP) and a CCNP Security. Catherine is also a Cisco IronPort Certified Security Instructor (CICSI) and a Certified Cisco Systems Instructor (CCSI) with Cisco's largest training partner, Global Knowledge, Inc. She also works on IT security projects and implementations for different organizations on a part-time basis. Following her university graduation from the Collège Militaire Royal de St-Jean (Canada), Catherine worked as a system analyst, LAN manager, MAN manager, and eventually as a WAN manager. Later, she received a master's degree in business administration (MBA) with a specialty in management information systems (MIS) from York University.

Catherine has lectured for the Computer Security Institute and for Cisco Systems (Emerging Markets) on the topic of the business case for network security. In 2002 and 2003, she volunteered with the U.N. mission in Kabul, Afghanistan, to train Afghan public servants in the area of networking.

Catherine lives in Toronto with her husband. They have two children, who are both attending college.

About the Technical Reviewer

Kevin Redmon has been an employee of Cisco Systems, Inc. in Research Triangle Park, North Carolina since October 2000. He has a bachelor of science in computer engineering from Case Western Reserve University (Cleveland, Ohio) and a master of science in information security from East Carolina University (Greenville, North Carolina). Kevin was a customer support engineer with the Cisco TAC Firewall Team from September 2007 to March 2011 and now supports the TAC VPN team at Cisco. Kevin enjoys innovating new ideas to keep his mind fresh and currently has a patent listed with the United States Patent and Trade Office. Kevin spends his free time playing mandolin, writing software for home projects, hacking and modding home electronics, and relaxing with his wife and baby girl in Durham, North Carolina.

Dedication

This book is dedicated to my mother, Florence Jacques-Paquet, who became gravely ill during this project. She pulled through—all her life, my mother pulled through. She was ahead of her time, in her thoughts and in her actions, and she made it a priority that Hélène and I developed, like her, self-reliance. Mom, thanks for the gift of education, tenacity, and resiliency. I love you.

Acknowledgments

I'd like to give special recognition to Kevin Redmon for providing his expert technical knowledge in editing this book. Kevin's meticulous and holistic approach to security solutions is unsurpassed. He was not afraid to point out inaccuracies and make recommendations to improve the manuscript. Thank you, Kevin.

A big "thank you" goes out to the production team for this book: Brett Bartow, Drew Cupp, and especially Kimberley Debus, Tonya Simpson, and Bill McManus, who have been incredibly professional and a pleasure to work with. I couldn't have asked for a finer team.

Acknowledgements for this book wouldn't be complete without mentioning my husband of 25 years, Pierre Rivard. Another book, so another year where Pierre spent countless evenings and weekends alone while his wife was working on a manuscript. His understanding, patience, and personal delivery of splendid meals to my "eagle nest" were truly appreciated. Pierre is my rock, my shelter, my soulmate. Pierre, je t'aime.

Contents at a Glance

Contents

Icons Used in This Book

Router

Voice-Enabled
Router

Router with
Firewall

Wireless
Access Point

NAC
Appliance

Multilayer
Switch

Switch

ATM/Frame
Relay Switch

Secure Catalyst
Switch

Cisco ASA

IOS
Firewall

PIX Firewall

Firewall Services
Module

Firewall

VPN
Concentrator

Cisco Mars

Sensor/IDS

Access Server

Cisco Unity
Server

Cisco
CallManager

IP Phone

Analog Phone

PBX Switch

Phone

PC

Laptop

Security Management

Server

Web
Server

Wireless
Connection

Ethernet
Connection

Serial
Connection

Network Cloud

Command Syntax Conventions

The conventions used to present command syntax in this book are the same conventions used in the IOS Command Reference. The Command Reference describes these conventions as follows:

- **Boldface** indicates commands and keywords that are entered literally as shown. In actual configuration examples and output (not general command syntax), boldface indicates commands that are manually input by the user (such as a show command).

- *Italic* indicates arguments for which you supply actual values.

- Vertical bars (|) separate alternative, mutually exclusive elements.

- Square brackets ([ ]) indicate an optional element.

- Braces ({ }) indicate a required choice.

- Braces within brackets ([{ }]) indicate a required choice within an optional element.

Introduction

Network security is a complex and growing area of IT. As the premier provider of network security devices, Cisco Systems is committed to supporting this growing segment of the industry.

This book teaches you how to design, configure, maintain, and audit network security. It focuses on using Cisco IOS routers for protecting the network by capitalizing on their advanced features as a perimeter router, as a firewall, as an intrusion prevention system, and as a site-to-site VPN device. The book also covers the use of Cisco Catalyst switches for basic network security. While covering the topic of authentication, authorization, and accounting (AAA), this book also introduces Cisco Secure Access Control System (ACS). The final chapter also introduces how to use a Cisco Adaptive Security Appliance (ASA) for both clientless and full client remote-access VPNs. At the end of this book, you will be able to select and implement the appropriate Cisco appliances and services required to build flexible and secure networks.

This book provides you with the knowledge necessary to pass your CCNA Security certification (IINS v2.0) because it provides in-depth information to help you prepare for the IINS exam, which grants the CCNA Security certification. It also starts you on the path toward attaining your Cisco Certified Network Professional (CCNP) Security certification.

The commands and configuration examples presented in this book are based on Cisco IOS Releases 15, Cisco ASA 8.4, and Cisco ACS 5.2.

Goals and Methods

The most important and somewhat obvious goal of this book is to help you pass the IINS v2.0 exam (640-554). In fact, if the primary objective of this book were different, the book's title would be misleading; however, the methods used in this book to help you achieve the CCNA Security are designed to also make you much more knowledgeable about how to do your job.

Although this book has more than enough questions to help you prepare for the actual exam, the method in which they are used is not to simply make you memorize as many questions and answers as you possibly can. One key methodology used in this book is to help you discover the exam topics that you need to review in more depth, to help you fully understand and remember those details, and to help you prove to yourself that you have retained your knowledge of those topics. So, this book does not try to help you pass by memorization, but helps you truly learn and understand the topics. The IINS v2.0 exam, which grants the CCNA Security certification, is just one of the foundation topics in the CCNP Security certification, and mastering the knowledge covered by the exam is vitally important to consider yourself a truly skilled security specialist. This book would do you a disservice if it didn't attempt to help you learn the material. To that end, the book will help you pass the CCNA Security exam by using the following methods:

- Helping you discover which test topics you have not mastered

- Providing explanations and information to fill in your knowledge gaps

- Providing practice questions on the topics

Who Should Read This Book?

This book is not designed to be a general security topics book, although it can be used for that purpose. This book is intended to tremendously increase your chances of passing the CCNA Security exam. Although other objectives can be achieved from using this book, the book is written with three goals in mind: to improve your knowledge of Cisco IOS security, to introduce you to Cisco ASA, and to help you pass the CCNA Security exam.

So why should you want to pass the CCNA Security exam? Because it is one of the milestones toward getting the CCNP Security certification, no small feat in itself. What would getting the CCNP Security certification mean to you? A raise, a promotion, or other recognition? A way to enhance your résumé, and demonstrate that you are serious about continuing the learning process and that you are not content to rest on your laurels? A chance to work in one of the most thrilling and fastest growing sectors of IT, network security? An opportunity to please your reseller-employer, who needs more certified employees for a higher discount from Cisco? These are some of many reasons people pursue the CCNP Security certification.

Strategies for Exam Preparation

The strategy you use for CCNA Security might be slightly different from strategies used by other readers, mainly based on the skills, knowledge, and experience you already have obtained. For instance, if you have attended the IINS course, you might take a different approach than someone who learned firewalling via on-the-job training.

The best way to prepare for this exam is to focus on one chapter at a time and take notes. Some chapters are purely theoretical, such as Chapter 12, which introduces cryptography and VPN technologies. Other chapters are more hands-on where configuration of a Cisco router or a Cisco firewall is demonstrated. Ideally, you will practice the suggested configurations on Cisco equipment to sharpen your hands-on skills prior to attempting the IINS v2.0 exam, in order to achieve the CCNA Security certification.

How This Book Is Organized

Although this book could be read cover to cover, it is designed to be flexible and allow you to move between chapters. However, if you do intend to read every chapter, the order in the book is an excellent sequence to use. Chapters 1 to 15, separated in four parts, cover the following topics:

- **Chapter 1, "Network Security Concepts and Policies":** This chapter discusses how to develop a comprehensive network security policy to counter threats against information security. It also teaches you about possible threats and how to describe and implement the process of developing a security policy. It covers the identification of common vulnerabilities and threats, mitigation strategies, and the implementation of a security architecture using a lifecycle approach.

- **Chapter 2, "Security Strategy and Cisco Borderless Network":** This chapter discusses the concept of Borderless Networks. It discusses Cisco Borderless Network Architecture, including the components and underlying technologies. You will learn about the Cisco Security portfolio products that address specifically issues of Borderless Networks, and more precisely about Cisco SecureX. This chapter introduces Cisco threat control and containment products and VPN technologies that will be covered in greater detail in subsequent chapters.

- **Chapter 3, "Network Foundation Protection and Cisco Configuration Professional":** This chapter deals with Cisco IOS Network Foundation Protection (NFP) as a framework for infrastructure protection, all its components, and commonly used countermeasures as found in Cisco IOS devices. More precisely, this chapter differentiates the security measures to be implemented on the three conceptual planes of Cisco IOS devices: the control plane, the data plane, and the management plane. This chapter also discusses using Cisco Configuration Professional (CCP) to implement security controls on Cisco IOS routers.

- **Chapter 4, "Securing the Management Plane on Cisco IOS Devices and AAA":** This chapter describes how to securely implement the management and reporting features of Cisco IOS devices. It discusses technologies surrounding network management, such as syslog, Network Time Protocol, Secure Shell, and Simple Network Management Protocol. It discusses proper password management, the recovery procedure of the configuration file, and the safeguarding of the IOS. This chapter introduces the subject of authentication, authorization, and accounting (AAA) both locally and on an external database, including the Cisco Secure Access Control System (ACS).

- **Chapter 5, "Securing the Data Plane on Cisco Catalyst Switches":** This chapter explains how Cisco IOS routers and switches have their own set of network security requirements. It introduces fundamental switching concepts, such as VLANs, trunking, and Spanning Tree, and shows how attackers can exploit vulnerabilities in the switching infrastructure. It then describes a strategy for protecting the switch data plane using port security.

- **Chapter 6, "Securing the Data Plane in IPv6 Environments":** This chapter explains the need for IPv6 and presents its fundamental features, as well as enhancements when compared to IPv4. It covers IPv6 addressing scheme, components, and design principles and how routing functions. The chapter then presents potential threats and develops a strategy for IPv6 security.

■ **Chapter 7, "Planning a Threat Control Strategy":** This chapter suggests design principles to plan a threat control and containment strategy using firewalls and intrusion prevention systems in Cisco IOS environments. This chapter provides a general evaluation of the current state of enterprise security in the presence of evolving threats. It presents the design considerations for a threat protection strategy as part of a risk management strategy with Cisco threat control and containment solutions.

■ **Chapter 8, "Access Control Lists for Threat Mitigation":** Cisco provides basic traffic filtering capabilities with access control lists (ACL). This chapter covers the benefits of ACLs and describes their building blocks. The chapter describes summarizable address blocks in the context of CIDR and VLSM environments, demonstrating how ACL wildcard masks allow for threat mitigation in those environments. It also demonstrates how to configure ACLs using both CLI and CCP and how to use object groups. ACLs are examined in the context of IPv4 and IPv6.

■ **Chapter 9, "Firewall Fundamentals and Network Address Translation":** This chapter explains the operations of the different types of firewall technologies and the role they play in network access control and security architectures. It also describes guidelines for firewall rule set creation. The chapter then describes the function and building blocks of Network Address Translation.

■ **Chapter 10, "Cisco Firewalling Solutions: Cisco IOS Zone-Based Firewall and Cisco ASA":** This chapter explains the two Cisco Firewall solutions: Cisco IOS Zone-Based Policy Firewalls and Cisco Adaptive Security Appliance. It describes in detail Cisco IOS Zone-Based Policy Firewall, and how the solution uses the Cisco Common Classification Policy Language (C3PL) for creating firewall policies. The chapter then presents the Cisco ASA firewall, identifying key supported features and the building blocks of its configuration using ASDM. The chapter also briefly describes the deployment of policies using the Cisco Modular Policy Framework.

■ **Chapter 11, "Intrusion Prevention Systems":** This chapter describes the functions and operations of intrusion detection systems (IDS) and intrusion prevention systems (IPS). It explains the underlying IDS and IPS technology embedded in the Cisco IOS IPS solutions. It describe the use of signatures, the need for IPS alarm monitoring, and the design considerations in deploying IPS.

■ **Chapter 12, "Fundamentals of Cryptography and VPN Technologies":** This chapter introduces the concepts of cryptography and covers encryption, hashing, and digital signatures and how these techniques provide confidentiality, integrity, authenticity, and nonrepudiation. You will learn about algorithms, symmetric and asymmetric encryption, digital signatures, and Public Key Infrastructure (PKI).

■ **Chapter 13, "IPsec Fundamentals":** This chapter covers the role and operational impact of IPsec's main components and its modes of operation in various scenarios. It provides a detailed description of the phases of IPsec connectivity. It also provides an overview of IPv6 VPNs.

■ **Chapter 14, "Site-to-Site IPsec VPNs with Cisco IOS Routers":** This chapter explains how to configure site-to-site virtual private networks (VPN) using Cisco IOS routers. You will learn how to use both CLI commands and Cisco Configuration Professional to configure, validate, and monitor the VPN configuration. You will also learn site-to-site VPN troubleshooting techniques.

■ **Chapter 15, "SSL VPNs with Cisco ASA":** This chapter describes the use cases and operational requirements of SSL VPNs and offers a detailed presentation on the operations of SSL. The chapter explains configurations, deployment options, and design considerations. It describes the steps to configure both Cisco VPN clientless mode and Cisco full-tunnel mode on Cisco ASA using the Cisco AnyConnect client. The VPN configuration is demonstrated using Cisco ASDM.

Chapter 1

Network Security Concepts and Policies

In this chapter, you learn how to develop a comprehensive network security policy to counter threats against information security. You also learn about possible threats and how to describe and implement the process of developing a security policy. In this chapter, you learn about the following topics:

- Fundamental concepts in network security, including identification of common vulnerabilities and threats, and mitigation strategies

- Implementation of a security architecture using a lifecycle approach, including the phases of the process, their dependencies, and the importance of a sound security policy

The open nature of the Internet makes it vital for businesses to pay attention to the security of their networks. As companies move more of their business functions to the public network, they need to take precautions to ensure that the data cannot be compromised and that the data is not accessible to anyone who is not authorized to see it.

Unauthorized network access by an outside hacker or a disgruntled employee can cause damage or destruction to proprietary data, negatively affect company productivity, and impede the capability to compete. The Computer Security Institute reported in its *2010/2011 CSI Computer Crime and Security Survey* (available at http:// gocsi.com/survey) that on an average day, 41.1 percent of respondents dealt with at least one security incident (see page 11 of the survey). Unauthorized network access can also harm relationships with customers and business partners, who might question the capability of a company to protect its confidential information. The definition of "data location" is being blurred by cloud computing services and other service trends. Individuals and corporations benefit from the elastic deployment of services in the cloud, available at all times from any device, but these dramatic changes in the business services industry exacerbate the risks in protecting data and the entities using it (individuals, businesses, governments, and so on). Security policies and architectures require sound principles and a lifecycle approach, including whether the data is in the server farm, mobile on the employee's laptop, or stored in the cloud.

To start on our network security quest, this chapter examines the need for security, looks at what you are trying to protect, and examines the different trends for attacks and protection and the principles of secure network design. These concepts are important not only for succeeding with the IINS 640-554 exam, but they are fundamentals at all security endeavors on which you will be embarking.

Building Blocks of Information Security

Establishing and maintaining a secure computing environment is increasingly more difficult as networks become increasingly interconnected and data flows ever more freely. In the commercial world, connectivity is no longer optional, and the possible risks of connectivity do not outweigh the benefits. Therefore, it is very important to enable networks to support security services that provide adequate protection to companies that conduct business in a relatively open environment. This section explains the breadth of assumptions and challenges to establish and maintain a secure network environment.

Basic Security Assumptions

Several new assumptions have to be made about computer networks because of their evolution over the years:

- Modern networks are very large, very interconnected, and run both ubiquitous protocols (such as IP) and proprietary protocols. Therefore, they are often open to access, and a potential attacker can with relative ease attach to, or remotely access, such networks. Widespread IP internetworking increases the probability that more attacks will be carried out over large, heavily interconnected networks, such as the Internet.

- Computer systems and applications that are attached to these networks are becoming increasingly complex. In terms of security, it becomes more difficult to analyze, secure, and properly test the security of the computer systems and applications; it is even more so when virtualization is involved. When these systems and their applications are attached to large networks, the risk to computing dramatically increases.

Basic Security Requirements

To provide adequate protection of network resources, the procedures and technologies that you deploy need to guarantee three things, sometimes referred to as the CIA triad:

- **Confidentiality:** Providing confidentiality of data guarantees that only authorized users can view sensitive information.

- **Integrity:** Providing integrity of data guarantees that only authorized users can change sensitive information and provides a way to detect whether data has been tampered with during transmission; this might also guarantee the authenticity of data.

- **Availability of systems and data:** System and data availability provides uninterrupted access by authorized users to important computing resources and data.

When designing network security, a designer must be aware of the following:

- The threats (possible attacks) that could compromise security

- The associated risks of the threats (that is, how relevant those threats are for a particular system)

- The cost to implement the proper security countermeasures for a threat

- A cost versus benefit analysis to determine whether it is worthwhile to implement the security countermeasures

Data, Vulnerabilities, and Countermeasures

Although viruses, worms, and hackers monopolize the headlines about information security, risk management is the most important aspect of security architecture for administrators. A less exciting and glamorous area, risk management is based on specific principles and concepts that are related to asset protection and security management.

An *asset* is anything of value to an organization. By knowing which assets you are trying to protect, as well as their value, location, and exposure, you can more effectively determine the time, effort, and money to spend in securing those assets.

A *vulnerability* is a weakness in a system or its design that could be exploited by a threat. Vulnerabilities are sometimes found in the protocols themselves, as in the case of some security weaknesses in TCP/IP. Often, the vulnerabilities are in the operating systems and applications.

Written security policies might also be a source of vulnerabilities. This is the case when written policies are too lax or are not thorough enough in providing a specific approach or line of conduct to network administrators and users.

A *threat* is any potential danger to assets. A threat is realized when someone or something identifies a specific vulnerability and exploits it, creating exposure. If the vulnerability exists theoretically but has not yet been exploited, the threat is considered latent. The entity that takes advantage of the vulnerability is known as the threat agent or threat vector.

A *risk* is the likelihood that a particular threat using a specific attack will exploit a particular vulnerability of a system that results in an undesirable consequence. Although the roof of the data center might be vulnerable to being penetrated by a falling meteor, for example, the risk is minimal because the likelihood of that threat being realized is negligible.

Note   If you have a vulnerability but there is no threat toward that vulnerability, technically you have no risk.

An *exploit* happens when computer code is developed to take advantage of a vulnerability. For example, suppose that a vulnerability exists in a piece of software, but nobody knows about this vulnerability. Although the vulnerability exists theoretically, there is no exploit yet developed for it. Because there is no exploit, there really is no problem yet.

A *countermeasure* is a safeguard that mitigates a potential risk. A countermeasure mitigates risk either by eliminating or reducing the vulnerability or by reducing the likelihood that a threat agent will be able to exploit the risk.

Key Concepts:

An **asset** is anything of value to an organization.

A **vulnerability** is a weakness in a system or its design that could be exploited by a threat.

A **threat** is a potential danger to information or systems.

A **risk** is the likelihood that a particular vulnerability will be exploited.

An **exploit** is an attack performed against a vulnerability.

A **countermeasure** (safeguard) is the protection that mitigates the potential risk.

Data Classification

To optimally allocate resources and secure assets, it is essential that some form of data classification exists. By identifying which data has the most worth, administrators can put their greatest effort toward securing that data. Without classification, data custodians find it almost impossible to adequately secure the data, and IT management finds it equally difficult to optimally allocate resources.

Sometimes information classification is a regulatory requirement (required by law), in which case there might be liability issues that relate to the proper care of data. By classifying data correctly, data custodians can apply the appropriate confidentiality, integrity, and availability controls to adequately secure the data, based on regulatory, liability, and ethical requirements. When an organization takes classification seriously, it illustrates to everyone that the company is taking information security seriously.

The methods and labels applied to data differ all around the world, but some patterns do emerge. The following is a common way to classify data that many government organizations, including the military, use:

- **Unclassified:** Data that has little or no confidentiality, integrity, or availability requirements and therefore little effort is made to secure it.

- **Restricted:** Data that if leaked could have undesirable effects on the organization. This classification is common among NATO (North Atlantic Treaty Organization) countries but is not used by all nations.

- **Confidential:** Data that must comply with confidentiality requirements. This is the lowest level of classified data in this scheme.

- **Secret:** Data for which you take significant effort to keep secure because its disclosure could lead to serious damage. The number of individuals who have access to this data is usually considerably fewer than the number of people who are authorized to access confidential data.

- **Top secret:** Data for which you make great effort and sometimes incur considerable cost to guarantee its secrecy since its disclosure could lead to exceptionally grave damage. Usually a small number of individuals have access to top-secret data, on condition that there is a need to know.

- **Sensitive But Unclassified (SBU):** A popular classification by government that designates data that could prove embarrassing if revealed, but no great security breach would occur. SBU is a broad category that also includes the For Official Use Only designation.

It is important to point out that there is no actual standard for private-sector classification. Furthermore, different countries tend to have different approaches and labels. Nevertheless, it can be instructive to examine a common, private sector classification scheme:

- **Public:** Companies often display public data in marketing literature or on publicly accessible websites.

- **Sensitive:** Data in this classification is similar to the SBU classification in the government model. Some embarrassment might occur if this data is revealed, but no serious security breach is involved.

- **Private:** Private data is important to an organization. You make an effort to maintain the secrecy and accuracy of this data.

- **Confidential:** Companies make the greatest effort to secure confidential data. Trade secrets and employee personnel files are examples of what a company would commonly classify as confidential.

Regardless of the classification labeling used, what is certain is that as the security classification of a document increases, the number of staff that should have access to that document should decrease, as illustrated in Figure 1-1.

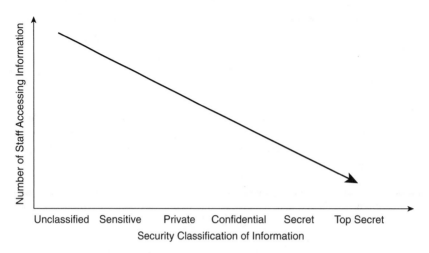

Figure 1-1 *Ratio: Staff Access to Information Security Classification*

Many factors go into the decision of how to classify certain data. These factors include the following:

- **Value:** Value is the number one criterion. Not all data has the same value. The home address and medical information of an employee is considerably more sensitive (valuable) than the name of the chief executive officer (CEO) and the main telephone number of the company.

- **Age:** For many types of data, its importance changes with time. For example, an army general will go to great lengths to restrict access to military secrets. But after the war is over, the information is gradually less and less useful and eventually is declassified.

- **Useful life:** Often data is valuable for only a set window of time, and after that window has expired, there is no need to keep it classified. An example of this type of data is confidential information about the products of a company. The useful life of the trade secrets of products typically expires when the company no longer sells the product.

- **Personal association:** Data of this type usually involves something of a personal nature. Much of the government data regarding employees is of this nature. Steps are usually taken to protect this data until the person is deceased.

Note   To further understand the value of information, think about the Federal Reserve Bank (commonly called the Fed) and the discount rate it sets. The discount rate is, in essence, the interest rate charged to commercial banks by the Fed.

Periodically, the Fed announces a new discount rate. Typically, if the rate is higher than the previous rate, the stock market reacts with sell-offs. If the discount rate is lower, the stock market rises.

Therefore, moments before the Fed announces the new discount rate, that information is worth gazillions of dollars. However, the value of this information drops to nothing when it hits the wire, because everyone then has free access to the information.

For a classification system to work, there must be different roles that are fulfilled. The most common of these roles are as follows:

- **Owner:** The owner is the person who is ultimately responsible for the information, usually a senior-level manager who is in charge of a business unit. The owner classifies the data and usually selects custodians of the data and directs their actions. It is important that the owner periodically review the classified data because the owner is ultimately responsible for the data.

- **Custodian:** The custodian is usually a member of the IT staff who has the day-to-day responsibility for data maintenance. Because the owner of the data is not required to have technical knowledge, the owner decides the security controls but the custodian marks the data to enforce these security controls. To maintain the availability of the data, the custodian regularly backs up the data and ensures that the backup media is secure. Custodians also periodically review the security settings of the data as part of their maintenance responsibilities.

- **User:** Users bear no responsibility for the classification of data or even the maintenance of the classified data. However, users do bear responsibility for using the data in accordance with established operational procedures so that they maintain the security of the data while it is in their possession.

Vulnerabilities Classifications

It is also important to understand the weaknesses in security countermeasures and operational procedures. This understanding results in more effective security architectures. When analyzing system vulnerabilities, it helps to categorize them in classes to better understand the reasons for their emergence. You can classify the main vulnerabilities of systems and assets using broad categories:

- Policy flaws
- Design errors
- Protocol weaknesses

- Software vulnerabilities

- Misconfiguration

- Hostile code

- Human factor

This list mentions just a few of the vulnerability categories. For each of these categories, multiple vulnerabilities could be listed.

There are several industry efforts that are aimed at categorizing threats for the public domain. These are some well-known, publicly available catalogs that may be used as templates for vulnerability analysis:

- **Common Vulnerabilities and Exposures (CVE):** A dictionary of publicly known information security vulnerabilities and exposures. It can be found at http://cve.mitre.org/. The database provides common identifiers that enable data exchange between security products, providing a baseline index point for evaluating coverage of tools and services.

- **National Vulnerability Database (NVD):** The U.S. government repository of standards-based vulnerability management data. This data enables automation of vulnerability management, security measurement, and compliance. NVD includes databases of security checklists, security-related software flaws, misconfigurations, product names, and impact metrics. The database can be found at http://nvd.nist.gov.

- **Common Vulnerability Scoring System (CVSS):** A standard within the computer and networking fields for assessing and classifying security vulnerabilities. This standard is focused on rating a vulnerability compared to others, thus helping the administrator to set priorities. This standard was adopted by significant players in the industry such as McAfee, Qualys, Tenable, and Cisco. More information can be found, including the database and calculator, at http://www.first.org/cvss.

Countermeasures Classification

After assets (data) and vulnerabilities, threats are the most important component to understand. Threat classification and analysis, as part of the risk management architecture, will be described later in this chapter.

Once threat vectors are considered, organizations rely on various controls to accomplish in-depth defense as part of their security architecture. There are several ways to classify these security controls; one of them is based on the nature of the control itself. These controls fall into one of three categories:

- **Administrative:** Controls that are largely policies and procedures

- **Technical:** Controls that involve electronics, hardware, software, and so on

- **Physical:** Controls that are mostly mechanical

Later in this chapter, we will discuss models and frameworks from different organizations that can be used to implement network security best practices.

Administrative Controls

Administrative controls are largely policy and procedure driven. You will find many of the administrative controls that help with an enterprise's information security in the human resources department. Some of these controls are as follows:

- Security-awareness training
- Security policies and standards
- Change controls and configuration controls
- Security audits and tests
- Good hiring practices
- Background checks of contractors and employees

For example, if an organization has strict hiring practices that require drug testing and background checks for all employees, the organization will likely hire fewer individuals of questionable character. With fewer people of questionable character working for the company, it is likely that there will be fewer problems with internal security issues. These controls do not single-handedly secure an enterprise, but they are an important part of an information security program.

Technical Controls

Technical controls are extremely important to a good information security program, and proper configuration and maintenance of these controls will significantly improve information security. The following are examples of technical controls:

- Firewalls
- Intrusion prevention systems (IPS)
- Virtual private network (VPN) concentrators and clients
- TACACS+ and RADIUS servers
- One-time password (OTP) solutions
- Smart cards
- Biometric authentication devices
- Network Admission Control (NAC) systems
- Routers with ACLs

Note   This book focuses on technical controls because implementing the Cisco family of security products is the primary topic. However, it is important to remember that a comprehensive security program requires much more than technology.

Physical Controls

While trying to secure an environment with good technical and administrative controls, it is also necessary that you lock the doors in the data center. This is an example of a physical control. Other examples of physical controls include the following:

- Intruder detection systems

- Security guards

- Locks

- Safes

- Racks

- Uninterruptible power supplies (UPS)

- Fire-suppression systems

- Positive air-flow systems

When security professionals examine physical security requirements, life safety (protecting human life) should be their number one concern. Good planning is needed to balance life safety concerns against security concerns. For example, permanently barring a door to prevent unauthorized physical access might prevent individuals from escaping in the event of a fire. By the way, physical security is a field that Cisco entered a few years ago. More information on those products can be found at http://www.cisco.com/go/physicalsecurity.

Convergence of Physical and Technical Security   One of the best examples of the convergence of physical and technical security I have witnessed was during a technical visit with a bank in Doha, Qatar, a few weeks before the grand opening of their new head office. They had extensive physical security, using a mix of contactless smart cards and biometrics.

They had cleverly linked the login system for traders to the physical security system. For instance, a trader coming to work in the morning had to use his smart card to enter the building, to activate the turnstile, to call the exact floor where the elevator was to stop, and to be granted access through the glass doors of the trading floors. The movements of the traders were recorded by the physical security systems. Minutes later, upon logging in to perform the first trade of the day, the trading authentication, authorization, and accounting (AAA) system queried the physical security system about the location of the trader. The trader was granted access to the trading system only when the physical security system confirmed to the trading AAA system that the trader was physically on the trading floor.

Controls are also categorized by the type of control they are:

- **Preventive:** The control prevents access.
- **Deterrent:** The control deters access.
- **Detective:** The control detects access.

All three categories of controls can be any one of the three types of controls; for example, a preventive control can be administrative, physical, or technical.

Note A security control is any mechanism that you put in place to reduce the risk of compromise of any of the three CIA objectives: confidentiality, integrity, and availability.

Preventive controls exist to prevent compromise. This statement is true whether the control is administrative, technical, or physical. The ultimate purpose for these controls is to stop security breaches before they happen.

However, a good security design also prepares for failure, recognizing that prevention will not always work. Therefore, detective controls are also part of a comprehensive security program because they enable you to detect a security breach and to determine how the network was breached. With this knowledge, you should be able to better secure the data the next time.

With effective detective controls in place, the incident response can use the detective controls to figure out what went wrong, allowing you to immediately make changes to policies to eliminate a repeat of that same breach. Without detective controls, it is extremely difficult to determine what you need to change.

Deterrent controls are designed to scare away a certain percentage of adversaries to reduce the number of incidents. Cameras in bank lobbies are a good example of a deterrent control. The cameras most likely deter at least some potential bank robbers. The cameras also act as a detective control.

Note To be more concrete, examples of types of physical controls include the following:
- **Preventive:** Locks on doors
- **Deterrent:** Video surveillance
- **Detective:** Motion sensor

Note It is not always possible to classify a control into only one category or type. Sometimes there is overlap in the definitions, as in the case of the previously mentioned bank lobby cameras. They serve as both deterrent and detective controls.

Need for Network Security

Business goals and risk analysis drive the need for network security. For a while, information security was influenced to some extent by fear, uncertainty, and doubt. Examples of these influences included the fear of a new worm outbreak, the uncertainty of providing web services, or doubts that a particular leading-edge security technology would fail. But we realized that regardless of the security implications, business needs had to come first.

If your business cannot function because of security concerns, you have a problem. The security system design must accommodate the goals of the business, not hinder them. Therefore, risk management involves answering two key questions:

- What does the cost-benefit analysis of your security system tell you?

- How will the latest attack techniques play out in your network environment?

Dealing with Risk   There are actually four ways to deal with risk:

Reduce: This is where we IT managers evolve and it is the main focus of this book. We are responsible for mitigating the risks. Four activities contribute to reducing risks:

- **Limitation/avoidance:** Creating a secure environment by not allowing actions that would cause risks to occur, such as installing a firewall, using encryption systems and strong authentication, and so on

- **Assurance:** Ensuring policies, standards, and practices are followed

- **Detection:** Detecting intrusion attempts and taking appropriate action to terminate the intrusion

- **Recovery:** Restoring the system to operational state

Ignore: This is not an option for an IT manager. The moment you become aware of a risk, you must acknowledge that risk and decide how to deal with it: accept this risk, transfer this risk, or reduce this risk.

Accept: This means that you document that there is a risk, but take no action to mitigate that risk because the risk is too far-fetched or the mitigation costs are too prohibitive.

Transfer: This is buying insurance against a risk that cannot be eliminated or reduced further.

Figure 1-2 illustrates the key factors you should consider when designing a secure network:

- **Business needs:** What does your organization want to do with the network?

- **Risk analysis:** What is the risk and cost balance?

- **Security policy:** What are the policies, standards, and guidelines that you need to address business needs and risks?

- **Industry best practices:** What are the reliable, well-understood, and recommended security best practices?

- **Security operations:** These operations include incident response, monitoring, maintenance, and auditing the system for compliance.

Risk management and security policies will be detailed later in this chapter.

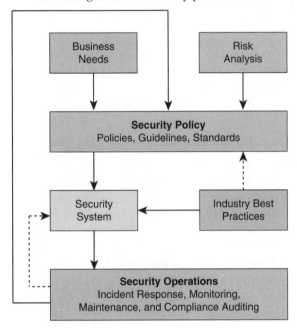

Figure 1-2   *Factors Affecting the Design of a Secure Network*

Intent Evolution

When viewed from the perspective of motivation intersecting with opportunity, risk management can be driven not only by the techniques or sophistication of the attackers and threat vectors, but also by their motives. Research reveals that hackers are increasingly motivated by profit, where in the past they were motivated by notoriety and fame. In instances of attacks carried out for financial gains, hackers are not looking for attention, which makes their exploits harder to detect. Few signatures exist or will ever be written to capture these "custom" threats. In order to be successful in defending your environments, you must employ a new model to catch threats across the infrastructure.

Attackers are also motivated by government or industrial espionage. The Stuxnet worm, whose earliest versions appear to date to 2009, is an example. This worm differs from its malware "cousins" in that it has a specific, damaging goal: to traverse industrial control systems, such as supervisory control and data acquisition (SCADA) systems, so that it can reprogram the programmable logic controllers, possibly disrupting industrial operations.

This worm was not created to gather credit card numbers to sell off to the highest bidder, or to sell fake pharmaceuticals. This worm appears to have been created solely to invade public or private infrastructure. The cleverness of Stuxnet lies in its ability to traverse non-networked systems, which means that even systems unconnected to networks or the Internet are at risk.

Security experts have called Stuxnet "the smartest malware ever." This worm breaks the malware mold because it is designed to disrupt industrial control systems in critical infrastructure. This ability should be a concern for every government.

Motivation can also so be political or in the form of vigilantism. Anonymous is currently the best known hacktivist group. As a recent example of its activities, in May 2012, Anonymous attacked the website of the Quebec government after its promulgation of a law imposing new requirements for the right to protest by college and university students.

Threat Evolution

The nature and sophistication of threats, as well as their pervasiveness and global nature, are trends to watch. Figure 1-3 shows how the threats that organizations face have evolved over the past few decades, and how the growth rate of vulnerabilities that are reported in operating systems and applications is rising. The number and variety of viruses and worms that have appeared over the past three years is daunting, and their rate of propagation is frightening. There have been unacceptable levels of business outages and expensive remediation projects that consume staff, time, and funds that were not originally budgeted for such tasks.

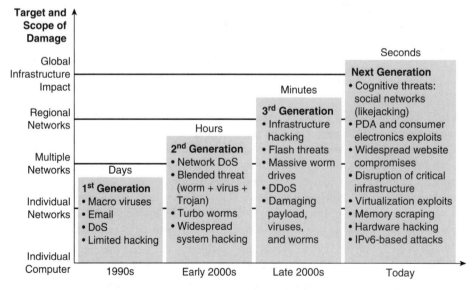

Figure 1-3 *Shrinking Time Frame from Knowledge of Vulnerability to Release of Exploits*

New exploits are designed to have global impact in minutes. Blended threats, which use multiple means of propagation, are more sophisticated than ever. The trends are becoming regional and global in nature. Early attacks affected single systems or one organization network, while attacks that are more recent are affecting entire regions. For example, attacks have expanded from individual denial of service (DoS) attacks from a single attacker against a single target, to large-scale distributed DoS (DDoS) attacks emanating from networks of compromised systems that are known as botnets.

Threats are also becoming persistent. After an attack starts, attacks may appear in waves as infected systems join the network. Because infections are so complex and have so many end users (employees, vendors, and contractors), multiple types of endpoints (company desktop, home, and server), and multiple types of access (wired, wireless, VPN, and dial-up), infections are difficult to eradicate.

More recent threat vectors are increasingly sophisticated, and the motivation of the attackers is reflected in their impact. Recent threat vectors include the following:

- **Cognitive threats via social networks (likejacking):** Social engineering takes a new meaning in the era of social networking. From phishing attacks that target social network accounts of high-profile individuals, to information exposure due to lack of policy, social networks have become a target of choice for malicious attackers.

- **PDA and consumer electronics exploits:** The operating systems on consumer devices (smartphones, PDAs, and so on) are an option of choice for high-volume attacks. The proliferation of applications for these operating systems, and the nature of the development and certification processes for those applications, augments the problem.

- **Widespread website compromises:** Malicious attackers compromise popular websites, making the sites download malware to connecting users. Attackers typically are not interested in the data on the website, but use it as a springboard to infect the users of the site.

- **Disruption of critical infrastructure:** The Stuxnet malware, which exploits holes in Windows systems and targets a specific Siemens supervisory control and data acquisition (SCADA) program with sabotage, confirmed concerns about an increase in targeted attacks aimed at the power grid, nuclear plants, and other critical infrastructure.

- **Virtualization exploits:** Device and service virtualization add more complexity to the network. Attackers know this and are increasingly targeting virtual servers, virtual switches, and trust relationships at the hypervisor level.

- **Memory scraping:** Increasingly popular, this technique is aimed at fetching information directly from volatile memory. The attack tries to exploit operating systems and applications that leave traces of data in memory. Attacks are particularly aimed at encrypted information that may be processed as unencrypted in volatile memory.

- **Hardware hacking:** These attacks are aimed at exploiting the hardware architecture of specific devices, with consumer devices being increasingly popular. Attack methods include bus sniffing, altering firmware, and memory dumping to find crypto keys.

- **IPv6-based attacks:** These attacks could become more pervasive as the migration to IPv6 becomes widespread. Attackers are focusing initially on covert channels through various tunneling techniques, and man-in-the middle attacks leverage IPv6 to exploit IPv4 in dual-stack deployments.

Trends Affecting Network Security

Other trends in business, technology, and innovation influence the need for new paradigms in information security. Mobility is one trend. Expect to see billions of new network mobile devices moving into the enterprise worldwide over the next few years. Taking into consideration constant reductions and streamlining in IT budgets, organizations face serious challenges in supporting a growing number of mobile devices at a time when their resources are being reduced.

The second market transition is cloud computing and cloud services. Organizations of all kinds are taking advantage of offerings such as Software as a Service (SaaS) and Infrastructure as a Service (IaaS) to reduce costs and simplify the deployment of new services and applications.

These cloud services add challenges in visibility (how do you identify and mitigate threats that come to and from a trusted network?), control (who controls the physical assets, encryption keys, and so on?), and trust (do you trust cloud partners to ensure that critical application data is still protected when it is off the enterprise network?).

The third market transition is about changes to the workplace experience. Borders are blurring in the organization between consumers and workers and between the various functions within the organization. The borders between the company and its partners, customers, and suppliers, are also fading. As a result, the network is experiencing increasing demand to connect anyone, any device, anywhere, at any time.

These changes represent a challenge to security teams within the organization. These teams now need to manage noncontrolled consumer devices, such as a personal tablet, coming into the network, and provide seamless and context-aware services to users all over the world. The location of the data and services accessed by the users is almost irrelevant. The data could be internal to the organization or it could be in the cloud. This situation makes protecting data and services a challenging proposition.

Note   Readers interested in staying current with Network Security trends and technologies could subscribe to some of the numerous podcasts available on iTunes, such as:

- Cisco Interactive Network TechWiseTV
- Security Now!
- Security Wire Weekly
- Silver Bullet Security
- Crypto-Gram Security

Attacks are increasingly politically and financially motivated, driven by botnets, and aimed at critical infrastructure; for example:

- Botnets are used for spam, data theft, mail relays, or simply for denial-of-service attacks (ref: http://en.wikipedia.org/wiki/Botnet).

- Zeus botnets reached an estimated 3.6 million *bots*, infected workstations, or "zombies" (ref: http://www.networkworld.com/news/2009/072209-botnets.html).

- Stuxnet was aimed at industrial systems.

- Malware is downloaded inadvertently from online marketplaces.

One of the trends in threats is the exploitation of trust. Whether they are creating malware that can subvert industrial processes or tricking social network users into handing over login and password information, cybercriminals have a powerful weapon at their disposal: the exploitation of trust. Cybercriminals have become skilled at convincing users that their infected links and URLs are safe to click, and that they are someone the user knows and trusts. Hackers exploit the trust we have in TinyURLs and in security warning banners. With stolen security credentials, cybercriminals can freely interact with legitimate software and systems.

Nowhere is this tactic more widespread than within social networking, where cybercriminals continue to attract victims who are willing to share information with people they believe are known to them, with malware such as Koobface. One noticeable shift in social engineering is that criminals are spending more time figuring out how to assume someone's identity, perhaps by generating emails from an individual's computer or social networking account. A malware-laden email or scam sent by a "trusted person" is more likely to elicit a click-through response than the same message sent by a stranger.

Threats originating from countries outside of the United States are rapidly increasing. Global annual spam volumes actually dropped in 2010, the first time this has happened in the history of the Internet. However, spammers are originating in increasingly varied locations and countries.

Money muling is the practice of hiring individuals as "mules," recruited by handlers or "wranglers" to set up bank accounts, or even use their own bank accounts, to assist in the transfer of money from the account of a fraud victim to another location, usually overseas, via a wire transfer or automated clearing house (ACH) transaction. Money mule operations often involve individuals in multiple countries.

Web malware is definitely on the rise. The number of distinct domains that are compromised to download malware to connecting users is increasing dramatically. The most dangerous aspect of this type of attack is the fact that users do not need to do much to get infected. Many times, the combination of malware on the website and vulnerabilities on web browsers is enough to provoke infection just by connecting to the website. The more popular the site, the higher the volume of potential infection.

Recently there have been major shifts in the compliance landscape. Although enforcement of existing regulations has been weak in many jurisdictions worldwide, regulators and standards bodies are now tightening enforcement through expanded powers, higher penalties, and harsh enforcement actions. In the future it will be more difficult to hide failures in information security wherever organizations do business. Legislators are forcing transparency through the introduction of breach notification laws in Europe, Asia, and North America as data breach disclosure becomes a global principle.

As more regulations are introduced, there is a trend toward increasingly prescriptive rules. For example, recent amendments introduced in the United Kingdom in 2011 bring arguably more prescriptive information protection regulations to the Privacy and Electronic Communications Directive. Such laws are discussed in more detailed later in this chapter. Any global enterprise that does business in the United Kingdom today will likely be covered by these regulations. Lately, regulators are also making it clear that enterprises are responsible for ensuring the protection of their data when it is being processed by a business partner, including cloud service providers. The new era of compliance creates formidable challenges for organizations worldwide.

For many organizations, stricter compliance could help focus management attention on security, but if managers take a "check-list approach" to compliance, it will detract from actually managing risk and may not improve security. The new compliance landscape will increase costs and risks. For example, it takes time and resources to substantiate compliance. Increased requirements for service providers give rise to more third-party risks.

With more transparency, there are now greater consequences for data breaches. For example, expect to see more litigation as customers and business partners seek compensation for compromised data. But the harshest judgments will likely come from the court of public opinion, with the potential to permanently damage an enterprise's reputation.

The following are some of the U.S. and international regulations that many companies are subject to:

- Sarbanes-Oxley (SOX)
- Federal Information Security Management Act (FISMA)

- Gramm-Leach-Bliley Act (GLBA)

- Payment Card Industry Data Security Standard (PCI DSS)

- Health Insurance Portability and Accountability Act (HIPAA)

- Digital Millennium Copyright Act (DMCA)

- Personal Information Protection and Electronic Documents Act (PIPEDA) in Canada

- European Union Data Protection Directive (EU 95/46/EC)

- Safe Harbor Act - European Union and United States

- International Convergence of Capital Measurement and Capital Standards (Basel II)

The challenge becomes to comply with these regulations and, at the same time, make that compliance translate into an effective security posture.

Adversaries, Methodologies, and Classes of Attack

Who are hackers? What motivates them? How do they conduct their attacks? How do they manage to breach the measures we have in place to ensure confidentiality, integrity, and availability? Which best practices can we adopt to defeat hackers? These are some of the questions we try to answer in this section.

People are social beings, and it is quite common for systems to be compromised through social engineering. Harm can be caused by people just trying to be "helpful." For example, in an attempt to be helpful, people have been known to give their passwords over the phone to attackers who have a convincing manner and say they are troubleshooting a problem and need to test access using a real user password. End users must be trained, and reminded, that the ultimate security of a system depends on their behavior.

Of course, people often cause harm within organizations intentionally: most security incidents are caused by insiders. Thus, strong internal controls on security are required, and special organizational practices might need to be implemented.

An example of a special organizational practice that helps to provide security is the separation of duty, where critical tasks require two or more persons to complete them, thereby reducing the risk of insider threat. People are less likely to attack or misbehave if they are required to cooperate with others.

Unfortunately, users frequently consider security too difficult to understand. Software often does not make security options or decisions easy for end users. Also, users typically prefer "whatever" functionality to no functionality. Implementation of security measures should not create an internally generated DoS, meaning, if security is too stringent or too cumbersome for users, either they will not have access to all the resources needed to perform their work or their performance will be hindered by the security operations.

Adversaries

To defend against attacks on information and information systems, organizations must begin to define the threat by identifying potential adversaries. These adversaries can include the following:

- Nations or states
- Terrorists
- Criminals
- Hackers
- Corporate competitors
- Disgruntled employees
- Government agencies, such as the National Security Agency (NSA) and the Federal Bureau of Investigations (FBI)

Hackers comprise the most well-known outside threat to information systems. They are not necessarily geniuses, but they are persistent people who have taken a lot of time to learn their craft.

Many titles are assigned to hackers:

- **Hackers:** Hackers are computer enthusiasts who break into networks and systems to learn more about them. Some hackers generally mean no harm and do not expect financial gain. Unfortunately, hackers may unintentionally pass valuable information on to people who do intend to harm the system. Hackers are subdivided into the following categories:
  - White hat (ethical hacker)
  - Blue hat (bug tester)
  - Gray hat (ethically questionable hacker)
  - Black hat (unethical hacker)
- **Crackers (criminal hackers):** Crackers are hackers with a criminal intent to harm information systems. Crackers are generally working for financial gain and are sometimes called black hat hackers.
- **Phreakers (phone breakers):** Phreakers pride themselves on compromising telephone systems. Phreakers reroute and disconnect telephone lines, sell wiretaps, and steal long-distance services.

Note   When describing individuals whose intent is to exploit a network maliciously, these individuals are often incorrectly referred to as hackers. In this section, the term hacker is used, but might refer to someone more correctly referred to as a cracker, or black hat hacker.

- **Script kiddies:** Script kiddies think of themselves as hackers, but have very low skill levels. They do not write their own code; instead, they run scripts written by other, more skilled attackers.

- **Hacktivists:** Hacktivists are individuals who have a political agenda in doing their work. When government websites are defaced, this is usually the work of a hacktivist.

Methodologies

The goal of any hacker is to compromise the intended target or application. Hackers begin with little or no information about the intended target, but by the end of their analysis, they have accessed the network and have begun to compromise their target. Their approach is usually careful and methodical, not rushed and reckless. The seven-step process that follows is a good representation of the methods that hackers use:

Step 1.   Perform footprint analysis (reconnaissance).

Step 2.   Enumerate applications and operating systems.

Step 3.   Manipulate users to gain access.

Step 4.   Escalate privileges.

Step 5.   Gather additional passwords and secrets.

Step 6.   Install back doors.

Step 7.   Leverage the compromised system.

> **Caution**   Hackers have become successful by thinking "outside the box." This methodology is meant to illustrate the steps that a structured attack might take. Not all hackers will follow these steps in this order.

To successfully hack into a system, hackers generally first want to know as much as they can about the system. Hackers can build a complete profile, or "footprint," of the company security posture. Using a range of tools and techniques, an attacker can discover the company domain names, network blocks, IP addresses of systems, ports and services that are used, and many other details that pertain to the company security posture as it relates to the Internet, an intranet, remote access, and an extranet. By following some simple advice, network administrators can make footprinting more difficult.

After hackers have completed a profile, or footprint, of your organization, they use tools such as those in the list that follows to enumerate additional information about your systems and networks. All these tools are readily available to download, and the security staff should know how these tools work. Additional tools (introduced later in the "Security Testing Techniques" section) can also be used to gather information and therefore hack.

- **Netcat:** Netcat is a featured networking utility that reads and writes data across network connections.

- **Microsoft EPDump and Microsoft Remote Procedure Call (RPC) Dump:** These tools provide information about Microsoft RPC services on a server.

- **GetMAC:** This application provides a quick way to find the MAC (Ethernet) layer address and binding order for a computer running Microsoft Windows locally or across a network.

- **Software development kits (SDK):** SDKs provide hackers with the basic tools that they need to learn more about systems.

Another common technique that hackers use is to manipulate users of an organization to gain access to that organization. There are countless cases of unsuspecting employees providing information to unauthorized people simply because the requesters appear innocent or to be in a position of authority. Hackers find names and telephone numbers on websites or domain registration records by footprinting. Hackers then directly contact these people by phone and convince them to reveal passwords. Hackers gather information without raising any concern or suspicion. This form of attack is called *social engineering*. One form of a social engineering attack is for the hacker to pose as a visitor to the company, a delivery person, a service technician, or some other person who might have a legitimate reason to be on the premises and, after gaining entrance, walk by cubicles and look under keyboards to see whether anyone has put a note there containing the current password.

The next thing the hacker typically does is review all the information that they have collected about the host, searching for usernames, passwords, and Registry keys that contain application or user passwords. This information can help hackers escalate their privileges on the host or network. If reviewing the information from the host does not reveal useful information, hackers may launch a Trojan horse attack in an attempt to escalate their privileges on the host. This type of attack usually means copying malicious code to the user system and giving it the same name as a frequently used piece of software.

After the hacker has obtained higher privileges, the next task is to gather additional passwords and other sensitive data. The targets now include such things as the local security accounts manager database or the Active Directory of a domain controller. Hackers use legitimate tools such as pwdump and lsadump applications to gather passwords from machines running Windows, which then can be cracked with the very popular Cain & Abel software tool. By cross-referencing username and password combinations, the hacker is able to obtain administrative access to all the computers in the network.

If hackers are detected trying to enter through the "front door," or if they want to enter the system without being detected, they try to use "back doors" into the system. A back door is a method of bypassing normal authentication to secure remote access to a computer while attempting to remain undetected. The most common backdoor point is a listening port that provides remote access to the system for users (hackers) who do not have, or do not want to use, access or administrative privileges.

After hackers gain administrative access, they enjoy hacking other systems on the network. As each new system is hacked, the attacker performs the steps that were outlined previously to gather additional system and password information. Hackers try to scan and exploit a single system or a whole set of networks and usually automate the whole process.

In addition, hackers will cover their tracks either by deleting log entries or falsifying them.

Thinking Outside the Box

In 2005, David Sternberg hacked the Postal Bank in Israel by physically breaking into one of the bank's branches in Haifa and connecting a wireless access point in the branch's IT infrastructure. Sternberg rented office space about 100 feet from the bank and proceeded to transfer funds to bank accounts in his name or in friends' names.

So instead of trying for months to break into the IT security of the bank, Sternberg thought outside of the box and broke through physical security to gain access to the IT system.

Sternberg was discovered when bank auditors noticed regular transfers from the main bank account to the same individual accounts.

I guess that Sternberg had not heard about the security axiom that says "predictability is the enemy of security."

A common thread in infosec forums is that information security specialists must patch all security holes in a network—a hacker only has to find the one that wasn't patched. Security is like a chain. It is only as strong as its weakest link.

Threats Classification

In classifying security threats, it is common to find general categories that resemble the perspective of the attacker and the approaches that are used to exploit software. Attack patterns are a powerful mechanism to capture and communicate the perspective of the attacker. These patterns are descriptions of common methods for exploiting vulnerabilities. The patterns derive from the concept of design patterns that are applied in a destructive rather than constructive context and are generated from in-depth analysis of specific, real-world exploit examples. The following list illustrates examples of threat categories that are based on this criterion. Notice that some threats are not malicious attacks. Examples of nonmalicious threats include forces of nature such as hurricanes and earthquakes.

Later in this chapter, you learn about some of the general categories under which threats can be regrouped, such as:

- Enumeration and fingerprinting

- Spoofing and impersonation

- Man-in-the-middle

- Overt and covert channels

- Blended threats and malware

- Exploitation of privilege and trust

- Confidentiality

- Password attacks

- Availability attacks

  - Denial of service (DoS)

  - Botnet

- Physical security attacks

- Forces of nature

To assist in enhancing security throughout the security lifecycle, there are many publicly available classification databases that provide a catalog of attack patterns and classification taxonomies. They are aimed at providing a consistent view and method for identifying, collecting, refining, and sharing attack patterns for specific communities of interest. The following are four of the most prominent databases:

- **Common Attack Pattern Enumeration and Classification (CAPEC):** Sponsored by the U.S. Department of Homeland Security as part of the software assurance strategic initiative of the National Cyber Security Division, the objective of this effort is to provide a publicly available catalog of attack patterns along with a comprehensive schema and classification taxonomy. More information can be found at http://capec.mitre.org.

- **Open Web Application Security Project (OWASP) Application Security Verification Standard (ASVS):** OWASP is a not-for-profit worldwide charitable organization focused on improving the security of application software. The primary objective of ASVS is to normalize the range in the coverage and level of rigor available in the market when it comes to performing web application security verification using a commercially workable open standard. More information can be found at https://www.owasp.org.

- **Web Application Security Consortium Threat Classification (WASC TC):** Sponsored by the WASC, this is a cooperative effort to clarify and organize the threats to the security of a website. The project is aimed at developing and promoting industry-standard terminology for describing these issues. Application developers, security professionals, software vendors, and compliance auditors have the ability to access a consistent language and definitions for web security-related issues. More information can be found at http://www.webappsec.org.

■ **Malware Attribute Enumeration and Characterization (MAEC):** Created by MITRE, this effort is international in scope and free for public use. MAEC is a standardized language for encoding and communicating high-fidelity information about malware based on attributes such as behaviors, artifacts, and attack patterns. More information can be found at http://maec.mitre.org.

Enumeration and Fingerprinting with Ping Sweeps and Port Scans

Enumeration and fingerprinting are types of attacks that use legitimate tools for illegitimate purposes. Some of the tools, such as port-scan and ping-sweep applications, run a series of tests against hosts and devices to identify vulnerable services that need attention. IP addresses and port or banner data from both TCP and UDP ports are examined to gather information.

In an illegitimate situation, a port scan is a series of messages sent by someone attempting to break into a computer to learn which computer network services (each service is associated with a well-known port number) the computer provides. Port scanning can be automated to scan a range of TCP or UDP port numbers on a host to detect listening services. Port scanning, a favorite computer hacker approach, provides information to the hacker about where to probe for weaknesses. Essentially, a port scan consists of sending a message to each port, one at a time. The kind of response received indicates whether the port is being used and needs further probing.

A ping sweep, also known as an Internet Control Message Protocol (ICMP) sweep, is a basic network-scanning technique that is used to determine which IP addresses map to live hosts (computers). A ping sweep consists of ICMP echo-requests (pings) sent to multiple hosts, whereas a single ping consists of ICMP echo-requests that are sent to one specific host computer. If a given address is live, that host returns an ICMP echo-reply. The goal of the ping sweep is to find hosts available on the network to probe for vulnerabilities. Ping sweeps are among the oldest and slowest methods that are used to scan a network.

IP Spoofing Attacks

The prime goal of an IP spoofing attack is to establish a connection that allows the attacker to gain root access to the host and to create a backdoor entry path into the target system.

IP spoofing is a technique used to gain unauthorized access to computers whereby the intruder sends messages to a computer with an IP address that indicates the message is coming from a trusted host. The attacker learns the IP address of a trusted host and modifies the packet headers so that it appears that the packets are coming from that trusted host.

At a high level, the concept of IP spoofing is easy to comprehend. Routers determine the best route between distant computers by examining the destination address, and ignore the source address. In a spoofing attack, an attacker outside your network pretends to be a trusted computer by using a trusted internal or external IP address.

If an attacker manages to change the routing tables to divert network packets to the spoofed IP address, the attacker can receive all the network packets addressed to the spoofed address and reply just as any trusted user can.

IP spoofing can also provide access to user accounts and passwords. For example, an attacker can emulate one of your internal users in ways that prove embarrassing for your organization. The attacker could send email messages to business partners that appear to have originated from someone within your organization. Such attacks are easier to perpetrate when an attacker has a user account and password, but they are also possible when attackers combine simple spoofing attacks with their knowledge of messaging protocols.

A rudimentary use of IP spoofing also involves bombarding a site with IP packets or ping requests, spoofing a source, a third-party registered public address. When the destination host receives the requests, it responds to what appears to be a legitimate request. If multiple hosts are attacked with spoofed requests, their collective replies to the third-party spoofed IP address create an unsupportable flood of packets, thus creating a DoS attack.

Technical Discussion of IP Spoofing

TCP/IP works at Layer 3 and Layer 4 of the Open Systems Interconnection (OSI) model, IP at Layer 3 and TCP at Layer 4. IP is a connectionless model, which means that packet headers do not contain information about the transaction state that is used to route packets on a network. There is no method in place to ensure proper delivery of a packet to the destination, since at Layer 3, there is no acknowledgement sent back to the source by the destination once it has received the packet.

The IP header contains the source and destination IP addresses. Using one of several tools, an attacker can easily modify the source address field. Note that in IP each datagram is independent of all others because of the stateless nature of IP. To engage in IP spoofing, hackers find the IP address of a trusted host and modify their own packet headers to appear as though packets are coming from that trusted host (source address).

TCP uses a connection-oriented design. This design means that the participants in a TCP session must first build a connection using the three-way handshake, as shown in Figure 1-4.

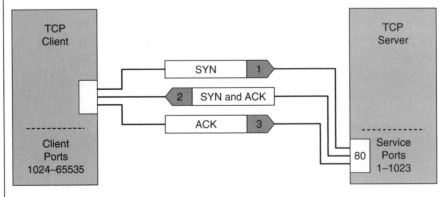

Figure 1-4 *TCP Three-Way Handshake*

After the connection is established, TCP ensures data reliability by applying the same process to every packet as the two machines update one another on progress. The sequence and acknowledgments take place as follows:

1. The client selects and transmits an initial sequence number.

2. The server acknowledges the initial sequence number and sends its own sequence number.

3. The client acknowledges the server sequence number, and the connection is open to data transmission.

Sequence Prediction

The basis of IP spoofing during a TCP communication lies in an inherent security weakness known as sequence prediction. Hackers can guess or predict the TCP sequence numbers that are used to construct a TCP packet without receiving any responses from the server. Their prediction allows them to spoof a trusted host on a local network. To mount an IP spoofing attack, the hacker listens to communications between two systems. The hacker sends packets to the target system with the source IP address of the trusted system, as shown in Figure 1-5.

Figure 1-5 *Sequence Number Prediction*

If the packets from the hacker have the sequence numbers that the target system is expecting, and if these packets arrive before the packets from the real, trusted system, the hacker becomes the trusted host.

To engage in IP spoofing, hackers must first use a variety of techniques to find an IP address of a trusted host and then modify their packet headers to appear as though packets are coming from that trusted host. Further, the attacker can engage other unsuspecting hosts to generate traffic that appears as though it too is coming from the trusted host, thus flooding the network.

Trust Exploitation

Trust exploitation refers to an individual taking advantage of a trust relationship within a network.

As an example of trust exploitation, consider the network shown in Figure 1-6, where system A is in the demilitarized zone (DMZ) of a firewall. System B, located in the inside of the firewall, trusts System A. When a hacker on the outside network compromises System A in the DMZ, the attacker can leverage the trust relationship it has to gain access to System A.

Figure 1-6 *Trust Exploitation*

A DMZ can be seen as a semi-secure segment of your network. A DMZ is typically used to provide to outside users access to corporate resources, because these users are not allowed to reach inside servers directly. However, a DMZ server might be allowed to reach inside resources directly. In a trust exploitation attack, a hacker could hack a DMZ server and use it as a springboard to reach the inside network.

Several trust models may exist in a network:

- Windows

  - Domains

  - Active Directory

- Linux and UNIX

  - Network File System (NFS)

  - Network Information Services Plus (NIS+)

Password Attacks

Password attacks can be implemented using several methods, including brute-force attacks, Trojan horse programs, IP spoofing, keyloggers, packet sniffers, and dictionary attacks. Although packet sniffers and IP spoofing can yield user accounts and passwords, password attacks usually refer to repeated attempts to identify a user account, password, or both. These repeated attempts are called *brute-force attacks*.

To execute a brute-force attack, an attacker can use a program that runs across the network and attempts to log in to a shared resource, such as a server. When an attacker gains access to a resource, the attacker has the same access rights as the rightful user. If this account has sufficient privileges, the attacker can create a back door for future access, without concern for any status and password changes to the compromised user account.

Just as with packet sniffers and IP spoofing attacks, a brute-force password attack can provide access to accounts that attackers then use to modify critical network files and services. For example, an attacker compromises your network integrity by modifying your network routing tables. This trick reroutes all network packets to the attacker before transmitting them to their final destination. In such a case, an attacker can monitor all network traffic, effectively becoming a man in the middle.

Passwords present a security risk if they are stored as plain text. Thus, passwords must be encrypted in order to avoid risks. On most systems, passwords are processed through an encryption algorithm that generates a one-way hash on passwords. You cannot reverse a one-way hash back to its original text. Most systems do not decrypt the stored password during authentication; they store the one-way hash. During the login process, you supply an account and password, and the password encryption algorithm generates a one-way hash. The algorithm compares this hash to the hash stored on the system. If the hashes are the same, the algorithm assumes that the user supplied the proper password.

Remember that passing the password through an algorithm results in a password hash. The hash is not the encrypted password, but rather a result of the algorithm. The strength of the hash is such that the hash value can be re-created only by using the original user and password information, and that it is impossible to retrieve the original information from the hash. This strength makes hashes perfect for encoding passwords for storage. In granting authorization, the hashes, rather than the plain-text password, are calculated and compared.

Hackers use many tools and techniques to crack passwords:

- **Word lists:** These programs use lists of words, phrases, or other combinations of letters, numbers, and symbols that computer users often use as passwords. Hackers enter word after word at high speed (called a *dictionary attack*) until they find a match.

- **Brute force:** This approach relies on power and repetition. It compares every possible combination and permutation of characters until it finds a match. Brute force eventually cracks any password, but it might take a long, long time. Brute force is an extremely slow process because it uses every conceivable character combination.

- **Hybrid crackers:** Some password crackers mix the two techniques. This combines the best of both methods and is highly effective against poorly constructed passwords.

Password cracking attacks any application or service that accepts user authentication, including the following:

- NetBIOS over TCP (TCP 139)

- Direct host (TCP 445)

- FTP (TCP 21)

- Telnet (TCP 23)

- Simple Network Management Protocol (SNMP) (UDP 161)

- Point-to-Point Tunneling Protocol (PPTP) (TCP 1723)

- Terminal services (TCP 3389)

Note   RainbowCrack is a compilation of hashes that provides crackers with a list that they can use to attempt to match hashes that they capture with sniffers.

Confidentiality and Integrity Attacks

Confidentiality breaches can occur when an attacker attempts to obtain access to read-sensitive data. These attacks can be extremely difficult to detect because the attacker can copy sensitive data without the knowledge of the owner and without leaving a trace.

A confidentiality breach can occur simply because of incorrect file protections. For instance, a sensitive file could mistakenly be given global read access. Unauthorized copying or examination of the file would probably be difficult to track without having some type of audit mechanism running that logs every file operation. If a user had no reason to suspect unwanted access, however, the audit file would probably never be examined.

In Figure 1-7, the attacker is able to compromise an exposed web server. Using this server as a beachhead, the attacker then gains full access to the database server from which customer data is downloaded. The attacker then uses information from the database, such as a username, password, and email address, to intercept and read sensitive email messages destined for a user in the branch office. This attack is difficult to detect because the attacker did not modify or delete any data. The data was only read and downloaded. Without some kind of auditing mechanism on the server, it is unlikely that this attack will be discovered.

Figure 1-7   *Breach of Confidentiality*

Attackers can use many methods to compromise confidentiality, the most common of which are as follows:

- **Ping sweeps and port scanning:** Searching a network host for open ports.

- **Packet sniffing:** Intercepting and logging traffic that passes over a digital network or part of a network.

- **Emanations capturing:** Capturing electrical transmissions from the equipment of an organization to deduce information regarding the organization.

- **Overt channels:** Listening on obvious and visible communications. Overt channels can be used for covert communication.

- **Covert channels:** Hiding information within a transmission channel that is based on encoding data using another set of events.

- **Wiretapping:** Monitoring the telephone or Internet conversations of a third party, often covertly.

- **Social engineering:** Using social skills or relationships to manipulate people inside the network to provide the information needed to access the network.

- **Dumpster diving:** Searching through company dumpsters or trash cans looking for information, such as phone books, organization charts, manuals, memos, charts, and other documentation that can provide a valuable source of information for hackers.

- **Phishing:** Attempting to criminally acquire sensitive information, such as usernames and passwords, by masquerading as trustworthy entities.

- **Pharming:** Redirecting the traffic of a website to another, rogue website.

Many of these methods are used to compromise more than confidentiality. They are often elements of attacks on integrity and availability.

Man-in-the-Middle Attacks

A complex form of IP spoofing is called man-in-the-middle attack, where the hacker monitors the traffic that comes across the network and introduces himself as a stealth intermediary between the sender and the receiver, as shown in Figure 1-8.

Figure 1-8   *IP Source Routing Attack*

Hackers use man-in-the-middle attacks to perform many security violations:

- Theft of information

- Hijacking of an ongoing session to gain access to your internal network resources

- Analysis of traffic to derive information about your network and its users

- DoS

- Corruption of transmitted data

- Introduction of new information into network sessions

Attacks are blind or nonblind. A blind attack interferes with a connection that takes place from outside, where sequence and acknowledgment numbers are unreachable. A nonblind attack interferes with connections that cross wiring used by the hacker. A good example of a blind attack can be found at http://wiki.cas.mcmaster.ca/index.php/The_Mitnick_attack.

TCP session hijacking is a common variant of the man-in-the-middle attack. The attacker sniffs to identify the client and server IP addresses and relative port numbers. The attacker modifies his or her packet headers to spoof TCP/IP packets from the client, and then waits to receive an ACK packet from the client communicating with the server. The ACK packet contains the sequence number of the next packet that the client is expecting. The attacker replies to the client using a modified packet with the source address of the server and the destination address of the client. This packet results in a reset that disconnects the legitimate client. The attacker takes over communications with the server by spoofing the expected sequence number from the ACK that was previously sent from the legitimate client to the server. (This could also be an attack against confidentiality.)

Another cleaver man-in-the-middle attack is for the hacker to successfully introduce himself as the DHCP server on the network, providing its own IP address as the default gateway during the DHCP offer.

Note   At this point, having read about many different attacks, you might be concerned that the security of your network is insufficient. Do not despair: many of the attacks described here are mitigated by techniques explained in this book or in other Cisco Press security books, such as *CCNP Security SECURE 642-637 Official Cert Guide*.

Overt and Covert Channels

Overt and covert channels refer to the capability to hide information within or using other information:

- **Overt channel:** A transmission channel that is based on tunneling one protocol inside of another. It could be a clear-text transmission inserted inside another clear-text protocol header.

- **Covert channel:** A transmission channel that is based on encoding data using another set of events. The data is concealed.

There are numerous ways that Internet protocols and the data that is transferred over them can provide overt and covert channels. The bad news is that firewalls generally cannot detect these channels; therefore, attackers can use them to receive confidential information in an unauthorized manner.

With an overt channel, one protocol is tunneled within another to bypass the security policy; for example, Telnet over FTP, instant messaging over HTTP, and IP over Post Office Protocol version 3 (POP3). Another example of an overt channel is using watermarks in JPEG images to leak confidential information.

One common use of overt channel is for instant messaging (IM). Most organization firewalls allow outbound HTTP but block IM. A user on the inside of the network can leak confidential information using IM over an HTTP session.

In Figure 1-9, the firewall allows outbound HTTP while a user on the inside of the network is leaking confidential information using instant messaging over HTTP.

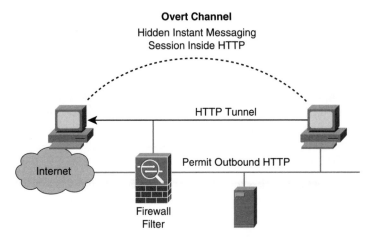

Figure 1-9 *Overt Channel*

Note You can use the advanced protocol inspection in the Cisco IPS products and Cisco ASA 5500 series appliances to counter attacks such as a hidden IM session being sent inside HTTP.

Steganography is another example of an overt channel. Steganography (from the Greek word *steganos*, meaning "covered" or "secret") literally means covered or secret writing. The combination of CPU power and interest in privacy has led to the development of techniques for hiding messages in digital pictures and digitized audio.

For example, certain bits of a digital graphic can be used to hide messages. The key to knowing which bits are special is shared between two parties that want to communicate privately. The private message typically has so few bits relative to the total number of bits in the image that changing them is not visually noticeable. Without a direct comparison of the original and the processed image, it is practically impossible to tell that anything has been changed. Still, it might be detected by statistical analysis that detects non-randomness. This non-randomness in a file indicates that information is being passed inside of the file.

Note Steganography is very difficult to detect or prevent.

With a covert channel, information is encoded as another set of events. For example, an attacker could install a Trojan horse on a target host. The Trojan horse could be written to send binary information back to the server of the attacker. The client, infected with the Trojan horse, could return to the hacker's server a ping status report in a binary format, where a 0 would represent a successful ping over a one-minute period, and a 1 would represent two successful pings over a one-minute period. The hacker could keep connectivity statistics for all the compromised clients he has around the world.

If ICMP is not permitted through a firewall, another tactic is to have the client visit the web page of the attacker. The Trojan horse software, now installed on the client, has a "call home" feature that automatically opens a connection to TCP port 80 at a specific IP address, the address of the hacker's web server. All of this work is done so that the hacker can keep precise statistics of how many compromised workstations he possesses around the world. One visit per day would be represented by a 1, and no visits would be represented by a 0. As you might imagine, this technique is usually quite limited in bandwidth.

Note   Covert channels are very difficult to detect or prevent.

Phishing, Pharming, and Identity Theft

Identity theft continues to be a problem. In computing, phishing is an attempt to criminally acquire sensitive information, such as usernames, passwords, and credit card details, by masquerading as a trustworthy entity. Phishing is typically carried out by email or instant message (IM), although sometimes phone contact is attempted; the phisher often directs users to enter details at a website, as shown on the left in Figure 1-10. Phishing is an example of social engineering.

Note   A variation on phishing is spear phishing. In this case, a hacker sends an email that appears genuine to all the employees of an organization and hopes that a few get hooked. As an example, the email could say: "This is Christina, your HR director. The Automatic Payment organization which processes your pay is unable to do so this week. Please email me directly your banking information, and I will ensure that your pay is directly deposited in your bank account for Thursday morning."

Figure 1-10   *Phishing and Pharming Attacks*

Pharming, also illustrated in Figure 1-10, is an attack aimed at redirecting the traffic of a website to another website. Pharming is conducted either by changing the hosts file on a victim computer or by exploiting a vulnerable Domain Name System (DNS) server. Pharming has become a major concern to businesses hosting e-commerce and online banking websites.

Note   Antivirus software and spyware-removal software cannot protect against pharming. Additional methods are needed such as server-side software, DNS protection, and web browser protection.

To protect against pharming, organizations implement "personalization" technologies, such as user-chosen images on the login page. Consider also supporting identified email initiatives such as DomainKeys Identified Mail (DKIM); these initiatives are beyond the scope of this book.

Availability Attacks

DoS attacks attempt to compromise the availability of a network, host, or application. They are considered a major risk because they can easily interrupt a business process and cause significant loss. These attacks are relatively simple to conduct, even by an unskilled attacker.

DoS attacks are usually the consequence of one of the following:

- The failure of a host or application to handle an unexpected condition, such as maliciously formatted input data or an unexpected interaction of system components.

- The inability of a network, host, or application to handle an enormous quantity of data, which crashes the system or brings it to a halt. Even if the firewall protects the corporate web server sitting on the DMZ from receiving a large amount of data and thus from crashing, the link connecting the corporation with its service provider will be totally clogged, and this bandwidth starvation will itself be a DoS.

Hackers can use many types of attacks to compromise availability:

- Botnets
- DoS
- DDoS
- SYN floods
- ICMP floods
- Electrical power
- Computer environment

Note   Many availability attacks can be used against confidentiality and integrity.

Botnets

Botnet is a term for a collection of software robots, or bots, that run autonomously and automatically. They run on groups of "zombie" computers controlled by crackers.

Although the term *botnet* can be used to refer to any group of bots, it is generally used to refer to a collection of compromised systems running worms, Trojan horses, or back doors, under a common command and control infrastructure. The originator of a botnet controls the group of computers remotely, usually through a means such as Internet Relay Chat (IRC).

Often, the command and control takes place via an IRC server or a specific channel on a public IRC network. A bot typically runs hidden. Generally, the attacker has compromised a large number of systems using various methods, such as exploits, buffer overflows, and so on. Newer bots automatically scan their environment and propagate using detected vulnerabilities and weak passwords. Sometimes a controller will hide an IRC server installation on an educational or corporate site, where high-speed connections can support a large number of other bots.

Several botnets have been found and removed from the Internet. The Dutch police found a 1.5-million node botnet (http://www.wisegeek.com/what-is-a-botnet.htm), and the Norwegian ISP Telenor disbanded a 10,000-node botnet. Large, coordinated international efforts to shut down botnets have also been initiated. Some estimates indicate that up to 25 percent of all personal computers are part of a botnet (http://everything.explained.at/Botnet/).

DoS and DDoS Attacks

DoS attacks are the most publicized form of attack. They are also among the most difficult to eliminate. A DoS attack on a server sends an extremely large volume of requests over a network or the Internet. These large volumes of requests cause the attacked server to slow down dramatically. Consequently, the attacked server becomes unavailable for legitimate access and use.

DoS attacks differ from most other attacks because DoS attacks do not try to gain access to your network or the information on your network. These attacks focus on making a service unavailable for normal use. Attackers typically accomplish this by exhausting some resource limitation on the network or within an operating system or application. These attacks typically require little effort to execute because they either take advantage of protocol weaknesses or use traffic normally allowed into a network. DoS attacks are among the most difficult to completely eliminate because of the way they use protocol weaknesses and accepted traffic to attack a network. Some hackers regard DoS attacks as trivial and in bad form because they require so little effort to execute. Still, because of their ease of implementation and potentially significant damage, DoS attacks deserve special attention from security administrators.

System administrators can install software fixes to limit the damage caused by all known DoS attacks. However, as with viruses, hackers constantly develop new DoS attacks.

A DDoS attack generates much higher levels of flooding traffic by using the combined bandwidth of multiple machines to target a single machine or network. The DDoS attack enlists a network of compromised machines that contain a remotely controlled agent, or zombie, attack program. A master control mechanism provides direction and control. When the zombies receive instructions from the master agent, they each begin generating malicious traffic aimed at the victim.

DDoS attacks are the "next generation" of DoS attacks on the Internet. This type of attack is not new. UDP and TCP SYN flooding, ICMP echo-request floods, and ICMP directed broadcasts (also known as Smurf attacks) are similar to DDoS attacks; however, the scope of the attack is new. Victims of DDoS attacks experience packet flooding from many different sources, possibly spoofed IP source addresses, which brings their network connectivity to a grinding halt. In the past, the typical DoS attack involved a single attempt to flood a target host with packets. With DDoS tools, an attacker can conduct the same attack using thousands of systems.

Figure 1-11 shows the process of a DDoS attack:

1. The hacker uses a host to scan for systems to hack.

2. After the hacker accesses handler systems, the hacker installs zombie software on them to scan, compromise, and infect agent systems.

3. Remote control attack software is loaded on agent systems.

4. When the hacker issues instructions to handlers on how to carry out the DDoS attack.

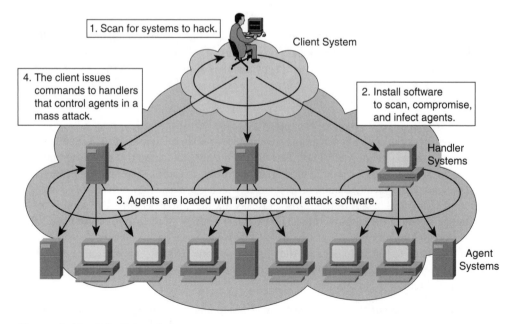

Figure 1-11 *DDoS Attack*

Note   *Stacheldracht*, which means "barbed-wire" in German, is a well-known tool used to conduct DDoS.

Blended Threats

The actual breach and vulnerability exploit is often accomplished using a combination of malware that infects, propagates, and delivers its payload following different techniques associated with traditional malware. Known as blended threats, these attack mechanisms combine the characteristics of viruses, worms, Trojan horses, spyware, and other malware.

A blended threat will exploit a vulnerability such as a buffer overflow or lack of HTTP input validation. Such attacks can spread without human intervention by scanning for other hosts to infect, embedding code in HTML, or by spamming, to name a few methods.

Blended threats plant Trojans and back doors. They are often part of botnet attacks, which try to raise privilege levels, create network shares, and steal data.

Most blended attacks are considered "zero day," meaning that they have not been previously identified. Blended attacks are ever-evolving and pretested by cybercriminals on common antivirus products before they are released. These threats easily breach firewalls and open channels, and they represent a challenge to detect and mitigate.

Offline Versus Online Password Cracking

Password cracking techniques can be classified as offline or online. Offline password cracking involves having the hashed result of the original password. At its own pace, the hacker could try hashing different combinations of characters until one of the hash results matches the hash of the original password. Online password cracking involves, as an example, different combinations of password on a live system. It is more difficult to achieve success with this method because most login pages lock after a certain number of unsuccessful login attempts.

Principles of Secure Network Design

In planning an overall strategy for security architecture design, sound principles are needed to accomplish an effective security posture. The selective combination of these principles provides the fundamentals for threat mitigation within the context of a security policy and risk management.

- **Defense in depth:** This is an umbrella term that encompasses many of the other guidelines in this list. It is defined by architectures based on end-to-end security, using a layered approach. The objective is to create security domains and separate them by different types of security controls. The concept also defines redundancy of controls, where the failure of one layer is mitigated by the existence of other layers of controls.

- **Compartmentalization:** Creating security domains is crucial. Different assets with different values should reside in different security domains, be it physically or logically. Granular trust relationships between compartments would mitigate attacks that try to gain a foothold in lower-security domains to exploit high-value assets in higher-security domains.

- **Least privilege:** This principle applies a need-to-know approach to trust relationships between security domains. The idea, which originated in military and intelligence operations, is that if fewer people know about certain information, the risk of unauthorized access is diminished. In network security, this results in restrictive policies, where access to and from a security domain is allowed only for the required users, application, or network traffic. Everything else is denied by default.

- **Weakest link:** This is a fundamental concept—a security system is as effective as its weakest link. A layered approach to security, with weaker or less protected assets residing in separated security domains, mitigates the necessary existence of these weakest links. Humans are often considered to be the weakest link in information security architectures.

- **Separation and rotation of duties:** This is the concept of developing systems where more than one individual is required to complete a certain task. The principle is that this requirement can mitigate fraud and error. This applies to information security controls, and it applies to both technical controls and human procedures to manage those controls.

- **Hierarchically trusted components and protection:** This principle applies a hierarchical approach to the compartmentalization and least privilege ideas, aiming at providing a more structured approach to data classification and security controls. The concept assumes that the hierarchy will be easier to implement and manage, resulting in similarly manageable and compartmentalized security controls.

- **Mediated access:** This principle is based on centralizing security controls to protect groups of assets or security domains. In that sense, firewalls, proxies, and other security controls act on behalf of the assets they are designed to protect, and mediate the trust relationships between security domains. Special considerations should be in place to prevent the mediation component from becoming a single point of failure.

- **Accountability and traceability:** This concept implies the existence of risk and the ability to manage and mitigate it, and not necessarily avoid or remove it. Information security architectures should provide mechanisms to track activity of users, attackers, and even security administrators. They should include provisions for accountability and nonrepudiation. This principle translates into specific functions, such as security audits, event management and monitoring, forensics, and others.

Cisco has always been a proponent of defense in depth. This was made clear in 2000 when it released its Cisco SAFE Blueprint for enterprise (SAFE is not an acronym), where it laid out its vision for defense in depth.

Defense in Depth

Addressing the fact that a security system is only as strong as its weakest link is often difficult when designing a system's security. The complexity of modern systems makes it hard to identify each individual weak link, let alone the weakest one. Thus, it is often most desirable to eliminate possible weaknesses by instituting several concurrent security methods.

Securing information and systems against all threats requires multiple, overlapping protection approaches that address the human, technological, and operational aspects of information technology. Using multiple, overlapping protection approaches ensures that the system is never unprotected from the failure or circumvention of any individual protection approach.

When a system is designed and implemented, its quality should always be questioned through design reviews and testing. Identification of various failure modes might help a designer evaluate the probability of element failure, and identify the links that are the most critical for the security of the whole system. Many systems have a security-based single point of failure, an element of functionality or protection that, if compromised, would cause the compromise of the whole system. It is desirable to eliminate or at least harden such single points of failure in a high-assurance system.

Defense in depth is a philosophy that provides layered security to a system by using multiple security mechanisms:

- Security mechanisms should back each other up and provide diversity and redundancy of protection.

- Security mechanisms should not depend on each other, so that their security does not depend on other factors outside their control.

- Using defense in depth, you can eliminate single points of failure and augment weak links in the system to provide stronger protection with multiple layers.

The defense-in-depth strategy recommends several principles:

- **Defend in multiple places:** Given that insiders or outsiders can attack a target from multiple points, an organization must deploy protection mechanisms at multiple locations to resist all classes of attacks. At a minimum, you should include three defensive focus areas:

  - **Defend the networks and infrastructure:** Protect the local- and wide-area communications networks from attacks, such as DoS attacks. Provide confidentiality and integrity protection for data that is transmitted over the networks; for example, use encryption and traffic flow security measures to resist passive monitoring.

- **Defend the enclave boundaries:** Deploy firewalls and intrusion detection systems (IDS) or intrusion prevention systems (IPS) or both to resist active network attacks.

- **Defend the computing environment:** Provide access controls and host intrusion prevention systems (HIPS) on hosts and servers to resist insider, close-in, and distribution attacks.

- **Build layered defenses:** Even the best available information assurance products have inherent weaknesses. Therefore, it is only a matter of time before an adversary finds an exploitable vulnerability. An effective countermeasure is to deploy multiple defense mechanisms between the adversary and the target. Each of these mechanisms must present unique obstacles to the adversary. Further, each mechanism should include both protection and detection measures. These measures increase the risk of detection for adversaries while reducing their chances of success, or make successful penetrations unaffordable. One example of a layered defense is to have nested firewalls (each coupled with IDS or IPS) that are deployed at outer and inner network boundaries. The inner firewalls may support more granular access control and data filtering.

- **Use robust components:** Specify the security robustness (that is, strength and assurance) of each information assurance component as a function of the value of what it is protecting and the threat at the point of application. For example, it is often more effective and operationally suitable to deploy stronger mechanisms at the network boundaries than at the user desktop.

- **Employ robust key management:** Deploy robust encryption key management and public key infrastructures that support all the incorporated information assurance technologies and that are highly resistant to attack.

- **Deploy an IDS or IPS:** Deploy infrastructures to detect and prevent intrusions and to analyze and correlate the results and react accordingly. These infrastructures should help the operations staff answer the following questions:

  - Am I under attack?

  - Who is the source?

  - What is the target?

  - Who else is under attack?

  - What are my options?

Evaluating and Managing the Risk

The security policy developed in your organization drives all the steps taken to secure network resources. The development of a comprehensive security policy prepares you for the rest of your security implementation. To create an effective security policy, it is necessary to do a risk analysis, which will be used to maximize the effectiveness of the policy and procedures that will be put in place. Also, it is essential that everyone be aware of the policy; otherwise, it is doomed to fail.

All design guidelines and principles, and the resulting security architecture, should be aimed at managing risk. Risk is, or should be, the building block of information security.

Levels of Risks

By its very nature, risk management is a tradeoff between the effort (cost) to protect organizational assets and the resulting level of exposure of those assets. This simple rule is a good starting point: the cost to protect an asset will likely not be greater than the value of the asset itself. There are obviously exceptions to the rule; for instance, cases that involve national security, or instances where the value of the asset is incalculable, such as cases where human life is involved.

The tradeoffs in risk management are based on its building blocks: assets and vulnerabilities, threats and countermeasures. Different values and scenarios for these components move the risk indicators up and down. Understanding these values and scenarios is critical in defining a risk management strategy.

For instance, would you use old, worn tires at high speed on a highway? The answer is obviously no. The asset that you are trying to protect (your life) is too valuable, and the countermeasure to mitigate the risk of navigating the highway, driving at a slow speed, is not good enough. It is inexpensive but not effective.

However, using a worn-down tire as a swing does not result in life-threatening risk in the majority of situations. The asset (your life) remains the same, but the threats that are able to exploit the vulnerabilities of the tire are mitigated or nonexistent. The premise changes again if you think that this worn-down tire will be used to swing your child. You may or may not risk using the old tire, but the value of the asset may prevent you from facing risk even if it is minimal.

The previous example is a simplistic view of information security risk. Imagine an organizational risk management effort, considering thousands of assets with different (and often subjective) valuation criteria, different (and often unknown) levels of vulnerability, and potentially exposed to an avalanche of threats that change by the minute. Risk management becomes a delicate balance and involves constant tuning of countermeasures in the face of sophisticated threat vectors, exploiting assets that are often located outside of corporate control.

Information security risk management is a comprehensive process that requires organizations to frame risk (in other words, establish the context for risk-based decisions), assess risk, respond to risk, and monitor risk on an ongoing basis. The result is a dynamic process in nature, evolving along with internal factors (assets, vulnerabilities, security policies, and architectures) and external factors (threats, and business, legal, and compliance forces).

Other sections in this chapter will expand on these concepts and present commonly used risk management strategies, within the context of a security policy and a security life-cycle process.

Risk Analysis and Management

Every process of security should first address the following questions:

- Which are the threats the system is facing?

- Which are the probable threats and what would be their consequence, if exploited?

The threat-identification process provides an organization with a list of threats to which a system is subject in a particular environment.

Note   An interesting method of modeling security threats is the attack trees method developed by Bruce Schneier. You can find more information about this method at http://en.wikipedia.org/wiki/Attack_tree.

Risk Analysis

Risk analysis is the systematic study of uncertainties and risks. Risk analysts seek to identify the risks that a company faces, understand how and when they arise, and estimate the impact (financial or otherwise) of adverse outcomes. Risk managers start with risk analysis, and then seek to take actions that will mitigate these risks. Risk analysis tries to estimate the probability and severity of threats faced by an organization's system that needs protection, and then provides to the organization a prioritized list of risks that the organization must mitigate. This allows the organization to focus on the most important threats first.

Two types of risk analysis are of interest in information security:

- **Quantitative:** Quantitative risk analysis uses a mathematical model that assigns monetary values to assets, the cost of threats being realized, and so on. Quantitative risk analysis provides an actual monetary figure of expected losses, which is typically based on an annual cost. You can then use this number to justify proposed countermeasures. For example, if you can establish that you will lose $1,000,000 by doing nothing, you can justify spending $300,000 to reduce that risk by 50 percent to 75 percent.

- **Qualitative:** Qualitative risk analysis uses a scenario model. This approach is best for large cities, states, and countries to use because it is impractical for such entities to try to list all their assets, which is the starting point for any quantitative risk analysis. By the time a typical national government could list all of its assets, the list would have hundreds or thousands of changes and would no longer be accurate.

Qualitative risk analysis is straightforward provided you have the resources to document all the assets. However, quantitative risk analysis is more tricky, so we will take a closer look at it.

Quantitative Risk Analysis Formula

Quantitative risk analysis relies on specific formulas to determine the value of the risk decision variables. These include formulas that calculate the asset value (AV), exposure factor (EF), single loss expectancy (SLE), annualized rate of occurrence (ARO), and annualized loss expectancy (ALE). The ALE formula is as follows: ALE = (AV * EF) *ARO.

The AV is the value of an asset. This would include the purchase price, the cost of deployment, and the cost of maintenance. In the case of a database or a web server, the AV should also include the cost of development. AV is not an easy number to calculate.

The EF is an estimate of the degree of destruction that will occur. For example, suppose that you consider flood a threat. Could it destroy your data center? Would the destruction be 60 percent, 80 percent, or 100 percent? The risk-assessment team would have to make a determination that evaluates everything possible, and then make a judgment call. For this example, assume that a flood will have a 60 percent destruction factor, because you store a backup copy of all media and data offsite. Your only losses would be the hardware and productivity.

As another example of EF, consider data entry errors, which are much less damaging than a flood. A single data entry error would hardly be more than a fraction of a percent in exposure. The exposure factor of a data entry error might be as small as .001 percent.

Caution   One of the ironies of risk analysis is how much estimating (guessing) is involved.

The SLE calculation is a number that represents the expected loss from a single occurrence of the threat. The SLE is defined as AV * EF.

To use our previous examples, you would come up with the following results for the SLE calculations:

- Flood threat
  - Exposure factor: 60 percent
  - AV of the enterprise: US$10,000,000
  - $10,000,000 * .60 = $6,000,000
- Data entry error
  - Exposure factor: .001 percent
  - AV of data and databases: $1,000,000
  - $1,000,000 * .000001 = $10 SLE

The ARO is a value that estimates the frequency of an event and is used to calculate the ALE.

Continuing the preceding example, the type of flood that you expect could reach your data center would be a "flood of the century" type of event. Therefore, you give it a 1/100 chance of occurring this year, making the ARO for the flood 1/100.

Furthermore, you expect the data entry error to occur 500 times a day. Because the organization is open for business 250 days per year, you estimate the ARO for the data entry error to be 500 * 250, or 125,000 times.

Risk analysts calculate the ALE in annualized terms to address the cost to the organization if the organization does nothing to counter existing threats. The ALE is derived from multiplying the SLE by the ARO. The following ALE calculations continue with the two previous examples:

- Flood threat
    - SLE: $6,000,000
    - ARO: .01
    - $6,000,000 * .01 = $60,000 ALE
- Data input error
    - SLE: $10
    - ARO: 125,000
    - $10 * 125,000 = $1,250,000 ALE

A decision to spend $50,000 to enhance the security of our database applications to reduce data entry errors by 90 percent is now an easy decision. It is equally easy to reject a proposal to enhance our defenses against floods that costs $3,000,000.

When you perform a quantitative risk analysis, you identify clear costs as long as the existing conditions remain the same. You compile a list of expected issues, the relative cost of those events, and the total cost if all expected threats are realized. These numbers are put into annual terms to coincide with the annual budgets of most organizations.

You then use these numbers in decision making. If an organization has a list of 10 expected threats, it can then prioritize the threats and address the most serious threats first. This prioritization enables management to focus their resources where it will do the most good.

For example, suppose an organization has the following list of threats and costs as the product of performing a quantitative risk analysis:

- **Insider network abuse:** $1,000,000 in lost productivity
- **Data input error:** $500,000
- **Worm outbreak:** $100,000

■ **Viruses:** $10,000

■ **Laptop theft:** $10,000

Decision makers could easily decide that it is of greatest benefit to address insider network abuse and leave the antivirus solution alone. They could also find it easy to support a $200,000 URL filtering solution to address insider network abuse and reject a $40,000 solution designed to enhance laptop safety. Without these numbers from a risk analysis, the decisions made would likely differ.

Building Blocks of Risk Analysis

Conducting a risk analysis starts with the gathering of pertinent information. The building blocks of the process follow the definition of risk used in this book: the organizational impact of threat vectors exploiting vulnerabilities of the assets you are trying to protect.

In that sense, the initial information gathering, in preparation for the risk calculations described in the previous example, should collect and define the following:

■ **Assets and their value:** This information, shown in Table 1-1, is typically obtained from data classification, inventories of assets, and other sources. A general principle is to use discrete numerical values for the exposure factor (EF) based on discrete values that reflect the impact of losing the asset. These values are generally based on data classification techniques (confidential, secret, top secret, and so on), and the impact is based on organizationally relevant criteria (replacement cost, liability, and so on).

Table 1-1 *List of Assets and Their Value*

	Confidentiality	Integrity	Availability
Low Value	Limited effect	Limited effect	Limited effect
Moderate Value	Serious effect	Serious effect	Serious effect
High Value	Severe effect	Severed effect	Severe effect

■ **Vulnerabilities:** This information is typically gathered from vulnerability assessments, which will be discussed further later in this chapter. Several tools are available, like Nessus and other commercial vulnerability assessment products. The use of public- or platform-specific vulnerability classification databases is commonplace. They include the Common Vulnerabilities and Exposures (CVE) effort by MITRE, http://cve.mitre.org, and the National Vulnerability Database (NVD) sponsored by the National Institute of Standards and Technology (NIST), http://nvd.nist.gov. An example of vulnerability categorization is shown in Table 1-2.

Table 1-2 *Example of Vulnerability Categorization Headings*

Categorization	Procedures	Processes	Systems	Network

- **Threats, their impact, and rate or probability of occurrence:** This information is commonly obtained from publicly available databases, such as the MITRE Common Attack Pattern Enumeration and Classification (CAPEC), http://capec.mitre.org. Calculating the rate of occurrence is a probabilistic exercise and is often considered subjective and specific for individual organizations or industries. Table 1-3 shows an example of this information gathering.

Table 1-3 *Example of Threats, Impact, and Probability of Occurrence*

Impact Category	Critical	Serious	Moderate	Minor	Negligible
Definition	Inability to achieve minimum requirements	Major cost and schedule increases	Moderate cost and schedule increases	Small cost and schedule increases	No effect

Risk Scores

With asset, vulnerability, and threat components defined, risk scores are obtained by applying formulas of quantitative risk analysis. Figure 1-12 illustrates the process.

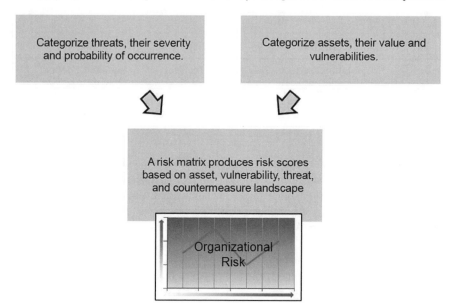

Figure 1-12 *Obtaining a Risk Score*

A risk matrix is then calculated, including risk scores for assets and groups of assets and, ideally, an organization risk score that can be used in security monitoring, incident response, and policy reviews. These risk scores provide an idea of the landscape of assets, threats, vulnerabilities, and countermeasures, the components of risk, at a given point in time.

A Lifecycle Approach to Risk Management

Managing risk is a complex, multifaceted activity that requires the involvement of the entire organization, including the following:

■ Senior leaders and executives who provide the strategic vision and top-level goals and objectives for the organization

■ Midlevel leaders who plan, execute, and manage projects

■ Individuals who operate the information systems supporting the organization's mission and business functions

Figure 1-13 shows that risk management is a comprehensive process that requires organizations to do the following:

■ Frame risk (that is, establish the context for risk-based decisions)

■ Assess risk

■ Respond to risk once determined

■ Monitor risk on an ongoing basis using effective organizational communications and a feedback loop for continuous improvement in the risk-related activities of organizations

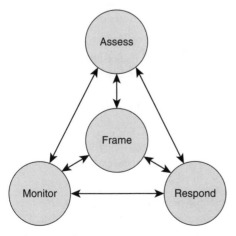

Source: NIST 800-39, 2011

Figure 1-13 *Lifecycle Approach to Risk Management According to NIST 800-39*

Risk management is carried out as a holistic, organization-wide activity that addresses risk from the strategic level to the tactical level. Approaching risk management in this way ensures that risk-based decision making is integrated into every aspect of the organization.

Regulatory Compliance

Compliance regulations have been a major driver for security in organizations of all kinds, and the following trends have emerged over the past decade:

- Strengthened enforcement
- Global spread of data breach notification laws
- More prescriptive regulations
- Growing requirements regarding third parties (business partners)
- Risk-based compliance on the rise
- Compliance process streamlined and automated

The compliance regulation defines not only the scope and parameters for the risk and security architectures of an organization, but also the liability for those who do not comply. Recently there have been major shifts in the compliance landscape:

- Although enforcement of existing regulations has been weak in many jurisdictions worldwide, regulators and standards bodies are now tightening enforcement through expanded powers, higher penalties, and harsh enforcement actions.

- In the future, it will be more difficult to hide information security failings wherever organizations do business. Legislators are forcing transparency through the introduction of breach notification laws in Europe, Asia, and North America as data breach disclosure becomes a global principle.

- As more regulations are introduced, there is a trend toward increasingly prescriptive rules. For example, laws in the states of Massachusetts and Nevada, which went into effect in 2010, apply not only to companies based in these states but also to all external organizations that manage the personal information of these states' residents.

- Regulators are also making it clear that enterprises are responsible for ensuring the protection of their data when it is being processed by a business partner, including cloud service providers.

- For many organizations, stricter compliance could help focus management attention on security; but if they take a "check-list approach" to compliance, it will detract from actually managing risk and may not improve security.

- The new compliance landscape will increase costs and risks. For example, it takes time and resources to substantiate compliance. Increased requirements for service providers give rise to more third-party risks.

- With more transparency, there are now greater consequences for data breaches. For example, expect to see more litigation as customers and business partners seek compensation for compromised data. But the harshest judgments will likely come from the court of public opinion—with the potential to permanently damage the reputation of an enterprise.

Table 1-4 illustrates some examples of relevant compliance regulations (most of which were introduced earlier in the chapter) that affect organizations all over the world. Geographic boundaries are blurring as globalization makes organizations subject to regulations in several countries. Industry scope boundaries are also blurring. For instance, many service organizations providing services to the U.S. government have to comply with U.S. federal regulations related to information security.

Table 1-4   *Examples of Compliance Regulations*

Regulation	Geographic Scope	Applies To
EU Data Protection Directive (EU 95/46/EC)	European Union	All organizations operating in the 27 EU member countries
Sarbanes-Oxley	United States	All publicly traded companies in the U.S. (exemption for smaller reporting companies)
PIPEDA	Canada	All organizations in Canada
PCI DSS	Global	All organizations processing credit card data
HIPAA	United States	All healthcare organizations in the U.S.
FISMA	United States	Federal agencies and service organizations
Basel II	Global	All internationally active banks with assets of $250 billion or more
DMCA	United States	Individuals and organizations in the U.S.
NERC	North America	North America users, owners, and operators of the bulk electric power system
GLBA	United States	All financial institutions in the U.S.
Safe Harbor Act	European Union	U.S. companies doing business in the EU

The following are descriptions of some of the regulations listed in Table 1-4:

■ The Gramm-Leach-Bliley Act (GLBA) of 1999 erased long-standing antitrust laws that prohibited banks, insurance companies, and securities firms from merging and sharing information with one another. The idea was that smaller firms would then be able to pursue acquisitions or alliances, or both, that would help encourage competition against many of the larger financial institutions. Included in the GLBA were several consumer privacy protections. Namely, companies must tell their customers what kinds of data they plan to share and with whom, and they must give their customers a chance to opt out of that data sharing.

■ On the healthcare side, the Health Insurance Portability and Accountability Act (HIPAA) of 2000 requires the U.S. Department of Health and Human Services to develop a set of national standards for healthcare transactions. These standards provide assurance that the electronic transfer of confidential patient information will be as safe as, or safer than, paper-based patient records.

■ The Sarbanes-Oxley (SOX) Act of 2002 is a U.S. law that was created in response to a number of major corporate and accounting scandals, including those affecting Enron, Tyco International, Peregrine Systems, and WorldCom. These scandals resulted in a decline of public trust in accounting and reporting practices.

■ The Federal Information Security Management Act (FISMA) of 2002 was intended to bolster computer and network security within the U.S. government and affiliated parties by requiring yearly audits. FISMA also brought attention within the U.S. government to cyber security, which the U.S. government had largely neglected previously.

Globalization, as with any other context, is changing the face of regulatory compliance. Regulators are not just looking at ways to strengthen existing laws. Regulators are also introducing new laws that are aimed at forcing more transparency, in a way that affects organizations on a global basis.

Data breach disclosure is becoming a global principle as jurisdictions worldwide adopt privacy and data protection laws that include a general obligation to notify government agencies, individuals, and other authorities such as law enforcement of unauthorized access or use of personal data. Requirements vary, including who must be notified, the type of data that triggers notification, and if there is a risk-of-harm threshold.

California's landmark legislation SB-1386 set off a wave of state breach notification laws that now cover almost the entire United States. Recently, this trend has spread to the European Union. The Privacy and Electronic Communications Directive (e-Privacy Directive) was amended in late 2009 to include data breach notification. It is now mandatory for telephone companies and ISPs in the EU to inform national regulatory authorities of any data security breach. Depending on the effects of the breach, they may also be required to inform subscribers. The upcoming overhaul of the EU Data Protection Directive is expected to include data breach notification requirements, which would broaden breach disclosure to cover all industries in all 27 member countries in the EU.

Table 1-5 shows how regulations are becoming the norm around the world.

Table 1-5   *Acceleration of Compliance Regulation Around the World*

Year	Country	Data Breach Notification Law
2003	U.S.	California's landmark SB-1386 starts wave of state laws.
2003–2010	U.S	46 states enact notification laws.
2008	U.K.	Information Commissioner's Office issues best practice guidance requiring notification.
2009	EU	e-Privacy Directive amended to include notification requirements for electronic communications sector.
	Germany	National privacy law amended to include notification.
2010	Austria	National privacy law amended to include notification.
	France	Draft legislation passed in senate would make notification mandatory.
	Canada	National privacy law amended to include notification.
	Mexico	New privacy law enacted that includes notification.
	Ireland	Code of Practice issued regarding notification.
	Hong Kong	Privacy Commissioner issues guidance note on breach notification.
	EU	Data Protection Directive under review for revision; proposed law expected by 2011 to include notification requirements for all industries; to be implemented in all 27 EU member countries.

Security Policies

Every organization has something that someone else wants. Someone might want that something for himself, or he might want the satisfaction of denying something to its rightful owner. Your assets are what need the protection of a security policy.

Determine what your assets are by asking (and answering) the following questions:

- What do you have that others want?

- What processes, data, or information systems are critical to you, your company, or your organization?

- What would stop your company or organization from doing business or fulfilling its mission?

The answers identify assets in a wide range, including critical databases, vital applications, vital company customer and employee information, classified commercial information, shared drives, email servers, and web servers.

A security policy comprises a set of objectives for the company, rules of behavior for users and administrators, and requirements for system and management that collectively ensure the security of network and computer systems in an organization. A security policy is a "living document," meaning that the document is never finished and is continuously updated as technology and employee requirements change.

The security policy translates, clarifies, and communicates the management position on security as defined in high-level security principles. The security policy acts as a bridge between these management objectives and specific security requirements. It informs users, staff, and managers of their obligatory requirements for protecting technology and information assets. It should specify the mechanisms that you need to meet these requirements. It also provides a baseline from which to acquire, configure, and audit computer systems and networks for compliance with the security policy. Therefore, an attempt to use a set of security tools in the absence of at least an implied security policy is meaningless.

The three reasons for having a security policy are as follows:

- To inform users, staff, and managers
- To specify mechanisms for security
- To provide a baseline

One of the most common security policy components is an acceptable use policy (AUP). This component defines what users are allowed and not allowed to do on the various components of the system, including the type of traffic that is allowed on the networks. The AUP should be as explicit as possible to avoid ambiguity or misunderstanding. For example, an AUP might list the prohibited website categories.

> **Note**   Some sites refer to an acceptable use policy as an *appropriate use policy*.

A properly defined security policy does the following:

- Protects people and information
- Sets the rules for expected behavior
- Authorizes staff to monitor, probe, and investigate
- Defines the consequences of violations

The audience for the security policy is anyone who might have access to your network, including employees, contractors, suppliers, and customers. However, the security policy should treat each of these groups differently.

The audience determines the content of the policy. For example, you probably do not need to include a description of *why* something is necessary in a policy that is intended for the technical staff. You can assume that the technical staff already knows why a particular requirement is included. Managers are also not likely to be interested in the technical aspects of why a particular requirement is needed. However, they might want the high-level overview or the principles supporting the requirement. When end users know why a particular security control has been included, they are more likely to comply with the policy.

In the policy, users can be organized into two audiences:

- Internal audience

  - Managers and executives

  - Departments and business units

  - Technical staff

  - End users

- External audience

  - Partners

  - Customers

  - Suppliers

  - Consultants and contractors

One document will not likely meet the needs of the entire audience of a large organization. The goal is to ensure that the information security policy documents are coherent with its audience needs.

Security Policy Components

Figure 1-14 shows the hierarchy of a corporate policy structure that is aimed at effectively meeting the needs of all audiences.

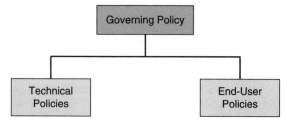

Figure 1-14 *Components of a Comprehensive Security Policy*

Most corporations should use a suite of policy documents to meet their wide and varied needs:

■ **Governing policy:** This policy is a high-level treatment of security concepts that are important to the company. Managers and technical custodians are the intended audience. The governing policy controls all security-related interaction among business units and supporting departments in the company. In terms of detail, the governing policy answers the "what" security policy questions.

■ **End-user policies:** This document covers all security topics important to end users. In terms of detail level, end-user policies answer the "what," "who," "when," and "where" security policy questions at an appropriate level of detail for an end user.

■ **Technical policies:** Security staff members use technical policies as they carry out their security responsibilities for the system. These policies are more detailed than the governing policy and are system or issue specific (for example, access control or physical security issues). In terms of detail, technical policies answer the "what," "who," "when," and "where" security policy questions. The "why" is left to the owner of the information.

Note   To assist you at drafting your security policies, consider the SANS security policies repository at http://www.sans.org/resources/policies.

For readers interested in security policies for academic institutions, visit the University of Toronto's Computer Security Administration website for a comprehensive example of a network security policy for a higher education institution:
http://www.cns.utoronto.ca/newsite/documentation/policies/policy_5.htm

Governing Policy

The governing policy outlines the security concepts that are important to the company for managers and technical custodians:

■ It controls all security-related interactions among business units and supporting departments in the company.

■ It aligns closely with not only existing company policies, especially human resource policies, but also any other policy that mentions security-related issues, such as issues concerning email, computer use, or related IT subjects.

■ It is placed at the same level as all companywide policies.

■ It supports the technical and end-user policies.

■ It includes the following key components:

   ■ A statement of the issue that the policy addresses

   ■ A statement about your position as IT manager on the policy

- How the policy applies in the environment

- The roles and responsibilities of those affected by the policy

- What level of compliance to the policy is necessary

- Which actions, activities, and processes are allowed and which are not

- What the consequences of noncompliance are

End-User Policies

End-user policies are compiled into a single policy document that covers all the topics pertaining to information security that end users should know about, comply with, and implement. This policy may overlap with the technical policies and is at the same level as a technical policy. Grouping all the end-user policies together means that users have to go to only one place and read one document to learn everything that they need to do to ensure compliance with the company security policy.

Technical Policies

Security staff members use the technical policies in the conduct of their daily security responsibilities. These policies are more detailed than the governing policy and are system or issue specific (for example, router security issues or physical security issues). These policies are essentially security handbooks that describe what the security staff does, but not how the security staff performs its functions.

The following are typical policy categories for technical policies:

- General policies

  - **Acceptable use policy (AUP):** Defines the acceptable use of equipment and computing services, and the appropriate security measures that employees should take to protect the corporate resources and proprietary information.

  - **Account access request policy:** Formalizes the account and access request process within the organization. Users and system administrators who bypass the standard processes for account and access requests may cause legal action against the organization.

  - **Acquisition assessment policy:** Defines the responsibilities regarding corporate acquisitions and defines the minimum requirements that the information security group must complete for an acquisition assessment.

  - **Audit policy:** Use to conduct audits and risk assessments to ensure integrity of information and resources, investigate incidents, ensure conformance to security policies, or monitor user and system activity where appropriate.

  - **Information sensitivity policy:** Defines the requirements for classifying and securing information in a manner appropriate to its sensitivity level.

- **Password policy:** Defines the standards for creating, protecting, and changing strong passwords.

- **Risk-assessment policy:** Defines the requirements and provides the authority for the information security team to identify, assess, and remediate risks to the information infrastructure that is associated with conducting business.

- **Global web server policy:** Defines the standards that are required by all web hosts.

- Email policies

  - **Automatically forwarded email policy:** Documents the policy restricting automatic email forwarding to an external destination without prior approval from the appropriate manager or director.

  - **Email policy:** Defines the standards to prevent tarnishing the public image of the organization.

  - **Spam policy:** The AUP covers spam.

- Remote-access policies

  - **Dial-in access policy:** Defines the appropriate dial-in access and its use by authorized personnel.

  - **Remote-access policy:** Defines the standards for connecting to the organization network from any host or network external to the organization.

  - **VPN security policy:** Defines the requirements for remote-access IP Security (IPsec) or Layer 2 Tunneling Protocol (L2TP) VPN connections to the organization network.

- Personal device and phone policies

  - **Analog and ISDN line policy:** Defines the standards to use analog and ISDN lines for sending and receiving faxes and for connection to computers.

  - **Personal communication device policy:** Defines the information security's requirements for personal communication devices, such as voicemail, smartphones, tablets, and so on.

- Application policies

  - **Acceptable encryption policy:** Defines the requirements for encryption algorithms that are used within the organization.

  - **Application service provider (ASP) policy:** Defines the minimum security criteria that an ASP must execute before the organization uses the ASP's services on a project.

  - **Database credentials coding policy:** Defines the requirements for securely storing and retrieving database usernames and passwords.

- **Interprocess communications policy:** Defines the security requirements that any two or more processes must meet when they communicate with each other using a network socket or operating system socket.

- **Project security policy:** Defines requirements for project managers to review all projects for possible security requirements.

- **Source code protection policy:** Establishes minimum information security requirements for managing product source code.

- Network policies

  - **Extranet policy:** Defines the requirement that third-party organizations that need access to the organization networks must sign a third-party connection agreement.

  - **Minimum requirements for network access policy:** Defines the standards and requirements for any device that requires connectivity to the internal network.

  - **Network access standards:** Defines the standards for secure physical port access for all wired and wireless network data ports.

  - **Router and switch security policy:** Defines the minimal security configuration standards for routers and switches inside a company production network or used in a production capacity.

  - **Server security policy:** Defines the minimal security configuration standards for servers inside a company production network or used in a production capacity.

- **Wireless communication policy:** Defines standards for wireless systems that are used to connect to the organization networks.

- **Document retention policy:** Defines the minimal systematic review, retention, and destruction of documents received or created during the course of business. The categories of retention policy are, among others:

  - **Electronic communication retention policy:** Defines standards for the retention of email and instant messaging.

  - **Financial retention policy:** Defines standards for the retention of bank statements, annual reports, pay records, accounts payable and receivable, and so on.

  - **Employee records retention policy:** Defines standards for the retention of employee personal records.

  - **Operation records retention policy:** Defines standards for the retention of past inventories information, training manuals, suppliers lists, and so forth.

Standards, Guidelines, and Procedures

Security policies establish a framework within which to work, but they are too general to be of much use to individuals responsible for implementing these policies. Because of this, other, more-detailed documents exist. Among the more important of these detailed documents are the standards, guidelines, and procedures documents.

Whereas policy documents are very much high-level overview documents, the standards, guidelines, and procedures documents are documents that the security staff will use regularly to implement the security policies.

Standards

Standards enable an IT staff to be consistent. They specify the use of specific technologies so that IT staff members can narrow the focus of their expertise to those technologies instead of trying to know everything about all sorts of technologies. Standards also try to provide consistency in the network, because supporting multiple versions of hardware and software is unreasonable unless it is necessary. The most successful IT organizations have standards to improve efficiency and to keep things as simple as possible.

Standardization also applies to security. One of the most important security principles is consistency. If you support 100 routers, it is important that you configure all 100 routers as similarly as possible. If you do not do this, it is difficult to maintain security. When you do not strive for the simplest of solutions, you usually fail in being secure.

Guidelines

Guidelines help provide a list of suggestions on how you can do things better. Guidelines are similar to standards, but are more flexible and are not usually mandatory. You will find some of the best guidelines available in repositories known as "best practices." The following is a list of widely available guidelines:

- National Institute of Standards and Technology (NIST) Computer Security Resource Center; http://csrc.nist.gov/

- National Security Agency (NSA) Security Configuration Guides; http://www.nsa.gov/ia/mitigation_guidance/security_configuration_guides/index.shtml

- The Common Criteria for Information Technology Security Evaluation; http://www.commoncriteriaportal.org/

- Defense Information Systems Agency (DISA) Field Security Operations Office – Security Technical Information Guides (STIG); http://iase.disa.mil/stigs/

Note   Note that the Rainbow Series from NIST was historically a reliable source for InfoSec guidelines but is now outdated.

Procedures

Procedure documents are longer and more detailed than the standards and guidelines documents. Procedure documents include the details of implementation, usually with step-by-step instructions and graphics. Procedure documents are extremely important for large organizations to enable them to have the consistency of deployment that is necessary to have a secure environment. Inconsistency is the enemy of security.

Table 1-6 provides a comparative chart for standards, guidelines, and procedures, which accompany security policies.

Table 1-6   *Comparison Between Standards, Guidelines, Procedures*

	Characteristics
Standards	Specify the use of specific technologies in a uniform way
	Improve efficiency
	Are usually mandatory
	Accomplish consistency and uniformity
Guidelines	Are similar to standards, but more flexible and not usually mandatory
	Can be used to define how standards should be developed or to guarantee adherence to general security policies
	Include NIST Computer Security Resource Center, NSA Security Configuration Guides, Common Criteria, and others
Procedures	Are usually required
	Are the lowest level of the policy chain
	Provide detailed steps used to perform specific tasks
	Provide the steps required to implement the policies, standards, and guidelines
	Are also known as practices

Security Policy Roles and Responsibilities

In any organization, it is senior management, such as the CEO, that is always ultimately responsible for everything. Typically, senior management only oversees the development of a security policy. The creation and maintenance of a security policy is usually delegated to the people in charge of IT or security operations.

Sometimes the senior security or IT management personnel, such as the chief security officer (CSO), the chief information officer (CIO), or the chief information security officer (CISO), will have the expertise to create the policy, sometimes they will delegate it, and sometimes it will be a bit of both strategies. But the senior security person is always intimately involved in the development and maintenance of security policy. Guidelines can provide a framework for policy decision making.

Senior security staff is often consulted for input on a proposed policy project. They might even be responsible for the development and maintenance of portions of the policy. It is more likely that senior staff will be responsible for the development of standards and procedures.

Everyone else who is involved in the security policy has the duty to abide by it. Many policy statements will include language that refers to a potential loss of employment for violation of the policy. IT staff and end users alike are responsible to know the policy and follow it.

Security Awareness

Technical, administrative, and physical controls can all be defeated without the participation of the end-user community. To get accountants, administrative assistants, and other end users to think about information security, you must regularly remind them about security. The technical staff also needs regular reminders because their jobs tend to emphasize performance, such as introducing new technologies, increasing throughput, and the like, rather than secure performance, such as how many attacks they repelled. Therefore, leadership must develop a nonintrusive program that keeps everyone aware of security and how to work together to maintain the security of their data. The three key components used to implement this type of program are awareness, training, and education.

An effective computer security-awareness and training program requires proper planning, implementation, maintenance, and periodic evaluation. In general, a computer security-awareness and training program should encompass the following seven steps:

Step 1. **Identify program scope, goals, and objectives.**

The scope of the program should provide training to all types of people who interact with IT systems. Because users need training that relates directly to their use of particular systems, you need to supplement a large, organization-wide program with more system-specific programs.

Step 2. **Identify training staff.**

It is important that trainers have sufficient knowledge of computer security issues, principles, and techniques. It is also vital that they know how to communicate information and ideas effectively.

Step 3. **Identify target audiences.**

Not everyone needs the same degree or type of computer security information to do his or her job. A computer security-awareness and training program that distinguishes between groups of people, presents only the information that is needed by the particular audience, and omits irrelevant information will have the best results.

Step 4.   **Motivate management and employees.**

To successfully implement an awareness and training program, it is important to gain the support of management and employees. Consider using motivational techniques to show management and employees how their participation in a computer security and awareness program will benefit the organization.

Step 5.   **Administer the program.**

Several important considerations for administering the program include visibility, selection of appropriate training methods, topics, and materials, and presentation techniques.

Step 6.   **Maintain the program.**

You should make an effort to keep abreast of changes in computer technology and security requirements. A training program that meets the needs of an organization today may become ineffective when the organization starts to use a new application or changes its environment, such as by connecting to the Internet.

Step 7.   **Evaluate the program.**

An evaluation should attempt to ascertain how much information is retained, to what extent computer security procedures are being followed, and the general attitudes toward computer security.

A successful IT security program consists of the following:

1. Developing IT security policy that reflects business needs tempered by known risks.

2. Informing users of their IT security responsibilities, as documented in agency security policy and procedures.

3. Establishing processes for monitoring and reviewing the program.

You should focus security awareness and training on the entire user population of the organization. Management should set the example for proper IT security behavior within an organization. An awareness program should begin with an effort that you can deploy and implement in various ways and be aimed at all levels of the organization, including senior and executive managers. The effectiveness of this effort usually determines the effectiveness of the awareness and training program and how successful the IT security program will be.

Secure Network Lifecycle Management

The lifecycle approach looks at the different phases of security, such as assessment, testing, implementation, monitoring and so forth, to provide methodology in securing our networks. The roles of risk, regulatory compliance, and security policies in designing and building effective security architectures have been described. How are these three components related?

IT Governance, Risk Management, and Compliance

Organizational efforts for IT governance, risk management, and compliance (sometimes known as IT GRC) are often separated by department or regulation type within organizations. This can create many problems, including unidentified risks, redundancies, and higher costs, requiring more resources, time, and effort to achieve a secure IT environment that meets regulatory compliance requirements. Moreover, while business processes and business process improvements are common practices in most organizations, this approach is often missing in the area of security.

Today, organizations of all kinds are making a conscious effort to simplify the process, given the multiple places in which these three areas operate concurrently. The result is a more effective process of defining risk within the context of existing organizational rules and business objectives, and within the framework of compliance regulations, as shown in Figure 1-15. The IT governance component creates stringent requirements for information security architectures, within the goal of adding business value, in addition to mitigating risk.

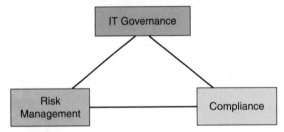

Figure 1-15   *Organization-wide Integration of IT Governance, Risk Management, Compliance*

This convergence results in an ideal framework and context to create a lifecycle approach to information security.

Secure Network Life Cycle

By framing security within the context of IT governance, compliance, and risk management, and by building it with a sound security architecture at its core, the result is usually a less expensive and more effective process. Including security early in the information process within the system design life cycle (SDLC) usually results in less-expensive and more-effective security when compared to adding it to an operational system.

A general SDLC includes five phases:

1. Initiation

2. Acquisition and development

3. Implementation

4. Operations and maintenance

5. Disposition

Each of these five phases includes a minimum set of security steps that you need to follow to effectively incorporate security into a system during its development. An organization either uses the general SDLC or develops a tailored SDLC that meets its specific needs. In either case, the National Institute of Standards and Technology (NIST) recommends that organizations incorporate the associated IT security steps of this general SDLC into their development process.

Initiation Phase

The initiation phase of the SDLC includes the following:

- **Security categorization:** This step defines three levels (low, moderate, and high) of potential impact on organizations or individuals should a breach of security occur (a loss of confidentiality, integrity, or availability). Security categorization standards help organizations make the appropriate selection of security controls for their information systems.

- **Preliminary risk assessment:** This step results in an initial description of the basic security needs of the system. A preliminary risk assessment should define the threat environment in which the system will operate.

Acquisition and Development Phase

The acquisition and development phase of the SDLC includes the following:

- **Risk assessment:** This step is an analysis that identifies the protection requirements for the system through a formal risk-assessment process. This analysis builds on the initial risk assessment that was performed during the initiation phase, but is more in depth and specific.

- **Security functional requirements analysis:** This step is an analysis of requirements and can include the following components: system security environment, such as the enterprise information security policy and enterprise security architecture, and security functional requirements.

- **Security assurance requirements analysis:** This step is an analysis of the requirements that address the developmental activities required and the assurance evidence needed to produce the desired level of confidence that the information security will work correctly and effectively. The analysis, based on legal and functional security requirements, is used as the basis for determining how much and what kinds of assurance are required.

- **Cost considerations and reporting:** This step determines how much of the development cost you can attribute to information security over the life cycle of the system. These costs include hardware, software, personnel, and training.

- **Security planning:** This step ensures that you fully document any agreed upon security controls, whether they are just planned or in place. The security plan also provides a complete characterization or description of the information system and attachments of or references to key documents that support the information security program of the agency. Examples of documents that support the information security program include a configuration management plan, a contingency plan, an incident response plan, a security awareness and training plan, rules of behavior, a risk assessment, a security test and evaluation results, system interconnection agreements, security authorizations and accreditations, and a plan of action and milestones.

- **Security control development:** This step ensures that the security controls that the respective security plans describe are designed, developed, and implemented. The security plans for information systems that are currently in operation may call for the development of additional security controls to supplement the controls that are already in place or the modification of selected controls that are deemed less than effective.

- **Developmental security test and evaluation:** This step ensures that security controls that you develop for a new information system are working properly and are effective. Some types of security controls, primarily those controls of a nontechnical nature, cannot be tested and evaluated until the information system is deployed. These controls are typically management and operational controls.

- **Other planning components:** This step ensures that you consider all the necessary components of the development process when you incorporate security into the network life cycle. These components include the selection of the appropriate contract type, the participation by all the necessary functional groups within an organization, the participation by the certifier and accreditor, and the development and execution of the necessary contracting plans and processes.

Implementation Phase

The implementation phase of the SDLC includes the following:

- **Inspection and acceptance:** This step ensures that the organization validates and verifies that the functionality that the specification describes is included in the deliverables.

- **System integration:** This step ensures that the system is integrated at the operational site where you will deploy the information system for operation. You enable the security control settings and switches in accordance with the vendor instructions and the available security implementation guidance.

- **Security certification:** This step ensures that you effectively implement the controls through established verification techniques and procedures. This step gives organization officials confidence that the appropriate safeguards and countermeasures are in place to protect the information system of the organization. Security certification also uncovers and describes the known vulnerabilities in the information system.

- **Security accreditation:** This step provides the necessary security authorization of an information system to process, store, or transmit information that is required. This authorization is granted by a senior organization official and is based on the verified effectiveness of security controls to some agreed upon level of assurance and an identified residual risk to agency assets or operations.

Operations and Maintenance Phase

The operations and maintenance phase of the SDLC includes the following:

- **Configuration management and control:** This step ensures that there is adequate consideration of the potential security impacts due to specific changes to an information system or its surrounding environment. Configuration management and configuration control procedures are critical to establishing an initial baseline of hardware, software, and firmware components for the information system and subsequently controlling and maintaining an accurate inventory of any changes to the system.

- **Continuous monitoring:** This step ensures that controls continue to be effective in their application through periodic testing and evaluation. Security control monitoring, such as verifying the continued effectiveness of those controls over time, and reporting the security status of the information system to appropriate agency officials are essential activities of a comprehensive information security program.

Disposition Phase

The disposition phase of the SDLC includes the following:

- **Information preservation:** This step ensures that you retain information, as necessary, to conform to current legal requirements and to accommodate future technology changes that can render the retrieval method of the information obsolete.

- **Media sanitization:** This step ensures that you delete, erase, and write over data as necessary.

- **Hardware and software disposal:** This step ensures that you dispose of hardware and software as directed by the information system security officer.

Models and Frameworks

The five-phase approach of the SDLC gives context to the process of designing, creating, and maintaining security architectures. It is based on NIST Publication 800-64 revision 2. Other frameworks and models exist, providing similar guidance to your security architecture:

- The ISO 27000 series is a comprehensive set of controls comprising best practices in information security. It is about information security, not IT security. It is also an internationally recognized information security standard, broad in scope and generic in applicability. It focuses on risk identification, assessment, and management. It is aligned with common business goals:

■ Ensure business continuity

■ Minimize business damage

■ Maximize return on investments

ISO 27000 standards are much more commonly applied in commercial organizations than in government. Originally created as BS17799, this framework was first submitted in 1995, and revised in 1998, but was not adopted by the ISO until 1999. Significantly revised in 2005, it was formally converted to two related ISO/ International Electrotechnical Commission (ISO/IEC) standards, 27001 and 27002.

■ Control Objectives for Information and Related Technology (COBIT) provides good practices across a domain and process framework and presents activities in a manageable and logical structure. The good practices provided by COBIT represent the consensus of experts. These good practices are strongly focused more on control and less on execution.

These practices will help optimize IT-enabled investments, ensure service delivery, and provide a measure against which to judge when things do go wrong. COBIT is generally considered complementary to ISO/IEC 27001 and 27002.

■ The Information Technology Infrastructure Library (ITIL) was developed under the supervision of the Central Computer and Telecommunications Agency in the UK. ITIL is a set of eight practice guidebooks covering most aspects of IT service management. The fourth service management set is Security Management. ITIL Security Management is based on the code of practice in ISO 27002.

Table 1-7 provides a summary of the different frameworks.

Table 1-7   *Comparison of Frameworks*

Framework	Strengths	Focus
COBIT	IT controls IT metrics	IT governance Audit
ISO 27000 series	Global acceptance Certification Security control	Information security Management system
ITIL	Processes Certification	IT service management
NIST 800 series	Detailed, granular Tiered controls Available for free	Information systems FISMA (federal government)

Network Security Posture

By assessing all aspects of the networked business environment, it is possible to determine the ability of the organization to detect, defend against, and respond to network attacks. The following are the key activities:

- **Security posture assessment (also known as vulnerability assessment):** The first step in planning network security requires an evaluation of the network security posture of the organization. The security posture assessment provides a snapshot of the security state of the network by conducting a thorough assessment of the network devices, servers, desktops, and databases. The effectiveness of the network security is analyzed against recognized industry best practices to identify the relative strengths and weaknesses of the environment and document specific vulnerabilities that could threaten the business. Because network security involves all aspects of the business, it is necessary to assess security from various perspectives, including the internal, external, dial-up, and wireless networks, and to provide recommendations on how to improve overall network security.

- **Internal assessment:** With so much attention devoted to threats and incidents by hackers, administrators may overlook the security of the internal, trusted network. The internal assessment is a controlled network attack simulation that is used to gauge the exposure present on internal systems, applications, and network devices. The assessment identifies the steps that are needed to thwart intentional attacks or unintentional mistakes from trusted insiders to effectively secure valuable information assets. To go beyond automated detection of vulnerabilities, you could simulate a real intruder in a controlled, safe manner to confirm vulnerabilities manually. The assessment provides a more structured approach to identifying vulnerabilities that may go undetected. This secondary exploitation may include attempting to exploit trusted relationships between hosts, exploiting password weakness, or gaining administrative access to systems.

- **External assessment:** The goal of an external assessment is to quantify the security risk that is associated with Internet-connected systems. After researching and confirming the registration of Internet devices, assessors scan the device for external visibility. Because most services have inherent and well-known vulnerabilities, it must be determined whether the services offered are potentially vulnerable.

- **Wireless assessment:** The wireless assessment provides an evaluation of the security posture of the wireless network within the organization and identifies risks and exposures that are associated with a wireless deployment. Assessors analyze the wireless technology architecture and configurations to identify authorized and unauthorized access points and to recommend solutions to strengthen the security of the wireless infrastructure. Assessors also check outside customer buildings to find wireless network traffic leaking from the buildings.

- **Security posture assessment analysis and documentation:** This assessment quantifies the security posture of the organization network by using metrics and graphs. The report should also provide technical details, including analysis of each IP address, an explanation of methods that are used to compromise network devices and systems, and a description of the likelihood that an attacker will use that same approach. The report then prioritizes the vulnerabilities, recommends actions to correct the security risks, and details remediation steps that will prevent future exploitation.

Network Security Testing

Security testing provides insight into the other SDLC activities, such as risk analysis and contingency planning. You should document security testing and make the documentation available for staff involved in other IT and security-related areas. Typically, you conduct network security testing during the implementation and operational stages, after the system has been developed, installed, and integrated.

During the implementation stage, you should conduct security testing and evaluation on specific parts of the system and on the entire system as a whole. Security test and evaluation (ST&E) is an examination or analysis of the protective measures that are placed on an information system after it is fully integrated and operational. The following are the objectives of the ST&E:

- Uncover design, implementation, and operational flaws that could allow the violation of the security policy

- Determine the adequacy of security mechanisms, assurances, and other properties to enforce the security policy

- Assess the degree of consistency between the system documentation and its implementation

Once a system is operational, it is important to ascertain its operational status. You can conduct many tests to assess the operational status of the system. The types of tests you use and the frequency in which you conduct them depend on the importance of the system and the resources available for testing. You should repeat these tests periodically and whenever you make a major change to the system. For systems that are exposed to constant threat, such as web servers, or systems that protect critical information, such as firewalls, you should conduct tests more frequently.

Security Testing Techniques

You can use security testing results in the following ways:

- As a reference point for corrective action

- To define mitigation activities to address identified vulnerabilities

- As a benchmark to trace the progress of an organization in meeting security requirements

- To assess the implementation status of system security requirements

- To conduct cost and benefit analysis for improvements to system security

- To enhance other lifecycle activities, such as risk assessments, certification and authorization (C&A), and performance-improvement efforts

There are several different types of security testing. Some testing techniques are predominantly manual, and other tests are highly automated. Regardless of the type of testing, the staff that sets up and conducts the security testing should have significant security and networking knowledge, including significant expertise in the following areas: network security, firewalls, IPSs, operating systems, programming, and networking protocols, such as TCP/IP.

Many testing techniques are available, including the following:

- Network scanning

- Vulnerability scanning

- Password cracking

- Log review

- Integrity checkers

- Virus detection

- War dialing

- War driving (802.11 or wireless LAN testing)

- Penetration testing

Common Testing Tools

Many testing tools are available in the modern marketplace that you can use to test the security of your systems and networks. The following list is a collection of tools that are quite popular; some of the tools are freeware, some are not:

- Nmap

- GFI LanGuard

- Tripwire

- Nessus

- Metasploit

- SuperScan by Foundstone, a division of McAfee

Many other excellent tools exist. This list is only a representative sampling.

Note   Visit http://www.backtrack-linux.org to download BackTrack 5, released in August 2011. BackTrack 5 is packed with hundreds of security tools to test and secure your network. Use BackTrack 5 responsibly and legally, which entails getting written permission from the organization where you would like to use BackTrack prior to using it.

Incident Response

Risk cannot be completely eliminated in some business environments.

Security Diminishing Returns and Residual Risk   Earlier I mentioned that a way to deal with risk is to reduce it by investing in security measures. The concept of diminishing returns applies to those security investments. Looking at Figure 1-16, you will notice that each additional security investment reduces risk (at least in theory). However, also notice that each additional security investment yields a lower additional risk reduction than the previous investment. In economics, this is what is called *diminishing returns*. Also, notice that regardless of how many resources you dedicate toward mitigating a risk, you can never reduce it to zero. There will always be residual risk. If that residual risk is unacceptable for your organization, you could consider buying insurance against it. Buying insurance against a risk would be considered *transferring the risk*.

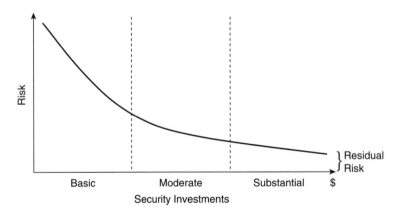

Figure 1-16   *Security Investment: Diminishing Returns and Residual Risk*

One way to eliminate risk is to simply withdraw from doing business at all, an unlikely scenario. For this reason, incident response has become an important component of the secure network life cycle. The breadth and sophistication of threat vectors in information security has increased exponentially. Every day new techniques emerge, and the motivation of the attackers becomes increasingly aggressive, driven by political reasons, industrial espionage, and terrorism. Preventative measures help, but not all incidents can be prevented. Risk avoidance is unlikely; risk mitigation is more realistic.

It is, then, almost required to implement an incident response capability to streamline the incident detection capabilities, contain the impact of those incidents to minimize loss and destruction, reduce the scope of weaknesses, and restore services within the parameters of the organization.

Implementing an incident response plan effectively can be challenging because of the amount and scope of the resources needed. The first critical step is to deploy an effective intrusion detection and prevention capability. Even if the incident response plan is not in place, incident detection and prevention can provide a first line of response. However, incident response is not completely effective without framing it within an incident response plan. Assessing the current and potential business impact of incidents is critical. Other crucial factors include the implementation of effective methods of collecting, analyzing, and reporting data. Also, it is important to define the framework of communication between the teams involved (for example, technical teams, human resources, legal) and between the organization and external entities (such as other incident response teams and law enforcement).

Incident Management

The incident response process has several phases:

- **Preparation:** As with any other activity, preparation is the building block of incident response methodologies. Preparation creates the foundation for a sound incident response plan and lays the groundwork for an incident prevention culture within the organization. These are some examples of the tasks typically implemented during the preparation phase:

  - Prepare the facilities (such as a central coordination room and storage facilities for collected evidence) and the communication mechanisms (cell phones, contact and on-call information, and others).

  - Define the incident analysis hardware and software tools, such as protocol analyzers and forensics software.

  - Define prevention procedures, such as patch management and user awareness and training methods.

- **Detection and analysis:** With any luck, this is where the incident response team will spend most of its time. This phase starts with the definition of a threat vector classification scheme, in order to define detection and analysis capabilities more effectively per type of threat. Clearly defining the difference between events and incidents is critical. The incident response team should analyze and implement tools for log and event correlation, in order to facilitate the navigation across eventually thousands of security-related events. Efficiently and effectively identifying the business- and risk-relevant incidents out of thousands of events is a key component of the detection strategy. The best way to start is to define a sound framework to prioritize, document, and provide notice about incidents.

- **Containment, eradication, and recovery:** When an incident has been detected and analyzed, it is important to contain it before the spread of the incident overwhelms resources or the damage increases. The containment strategy could start with a clear definition of tools to identify the attacker through IP addresses, usernames, and other means, followed by a clear definition of the context and time to perform this function (need for evidence preservation, time and resources to implement the strategy, sustainable service availability, and others). All containment strategies should also include steps to eradicate the threat and vulnerabilities, or at least mitigate them, and steps to recover operating systems, hardware components, and productive time. In light of this, ensure that the security policies are adapted to let remediation take place in a timely and effective manner if an attack is detected.

- **Post-incident activity:** This phase is crucial. The more the incident response team learns from past experience and (specially) mistakes, the more prepared it will be for future incidents. Focusing on how to collect and use data is a good first step. How to document what happened, especially the symptoms and fingerprint of the attack, should follow, leading to a full root-cause analysis. At this point, the incident response team should have a clear understanding of the options to go after the attacker (involve law enforcement, prosecution, and others).

Computer Crime Investigations

If you intend to successfully prosecute an individual who breaches your security, it is necessary to establish three things in most countries (in addition to evidence, the collection of which is covered next):

- **Motive:** Motive is concerned with why an individual performed the illegal act. As you investigate a computer crime, it is important to start with individuals who might have been motivated to commit the crime.

- **Opportunity:** Having identified a list of suspects, the next thing to consider is whether they had the opportunity to commit the crime. For example, if you can establish that three of the suspects were all participating in a wedding at the time of the security breach, they may have been motivated, but they did not have the opportunity. They were busy doing something else.

- **Means:** The means is an important thing to prove as well. Do not accuse someone who does not have the technical knowledge to accomplish the deed. Means is the ability to perform the crime. However, keep in mind that hacking tools have become easy for even a novice to use.

If you do not establish these three things, it is difficult to prove that the perpetrator is guilty of the offense should you decide to prosecute. When you can establish motive, opportunity, and means, and offer evidence, you are closer to a list of possible guilty parties.

Note   Different countries have different legal standards. Most countries and courts in the world accept this particular standard.

When working with computer data as part of a forensics case, you must maintain the integrity of the data if you will rely on the data in a court of law. It is difficult to maintain the integrity of the data in the virtual world of computers where it is trivial to change time stamps or any item of data. The flipping of a single bit can sometimes be all that is required to falsely establish an alibi.

Collection of Evidence and Forensics

Data collection is a volatile thing in the virtual world of computers. For this reason, a common procedure in response to security breaches is the immediate isolation of the infected system. Dumping the memory to disk is required because the system flushes the memory every time a device is powered off. Multiple copies of the hard drive are usually made after the device is powered down, to establish master copies. These master copies are usually locked up in a safe, and investigators use working copies for both the prosecution and the defense. You can answer any charges of tampering with data by comparing working copies to the master copy that has been secured and untouched since the beginning of the investigation.

It is important to note that when making copies of hard drives, a hardware write blocker must be used to ensure that the data on the source drive has not been modified by the copy. EnCase Forensic suite from Guidance Software is a product that uses hardware write blocker.

Laws and Ethics

This section describes key laws and codes of ethics that are binding on information systems security (infosec) professionals.

For many businesses today, one of the biggest considerations for setting security policies is compliance with the law. For that reason, it is important for infosec professionals to be at least conversant in the basics of law.

In most countries, there are three types of laws:

- **Criminal:** Concerned with crimes, and its penalties usually involve the risk of fines or imprisonment, or both. If fines are paid, they are usually to the court and are used to defray court costs.

- **Civil (also called tort):** Focuses on correcting wrongs that are not crimes. An example of a civil law case is if one company sues another company for infringing on a patent. The penalty in civil law is usually monetary, although there can also be performance requirements such as ceasing to infringe on the patent. If money is awarded, it is given to the party who won the lawsuit. Imprisonment is not possible in civil law.

■ **Administrative:** Involves government agencies enforcing regulations. For example, a company may owe its employees vacation pay. An administrative court could force the company to pay and would probably also levy a fine that is payable to the agency. Therefore, in administrative law cases, monetary awards are often split between the government agency and the victim whose wrongs have been righted.

Ethics involves a standard that is higher than the law. It is a set of moral principles that adherents follow to be considered ethical. These ethics are often formalized in codes appropriately entitled "codes of ethics" by the professions formalizing the code.

The information security profession has a number of codes that have been formalized:

■ International Information Systems Security Certification Consortium, Inc. (ISC)2 Code of Ethics

■ The Computer Ethics Institute's Ten Commandments of Computer Ethics

■ RFC 1087, "Ethics and the Internet," by the Internet Activities Board (IAB)

■ Generally Accepted System Security Principles (GASSP)

Liability

Companies must take into account the legal liability for the country in which they reside. Take, for example, an Internet service provider (ISP) that has hundreds of e-businesses that rely on the ISP to run their websites with 100 percent uptime. If a hacker or a virus takes down this ISP, there is a chance for the ISP to be found liable, if it is discovered that the ISP did not take enough precautions or did not secure the network against internal or external threats.

In such cases, legal liability is likely to depend on what prevention technologies and practices are available and whether these technologies and practices are reasonably cost-effective to implement. While developing and implementing our security procedures, we must demonstrate due diligence and due care.

Showing due diligence includes everything from implementing technologies such as firewalls, intrusion-detection tools, content filters, traffic analyzers, and VPNs, to having best practices for continuous risk-assessment and vulnerability testing.

Due care is concerned with the operations and maintenance of the secure mechanisms put in place by practicing due diligence.

Lack of due care can lead to downstream liability. This is the case when a network is used by hackers as a springboard to conduct an attack against a third party. The victim of the attack could prosecute not only the hackers, but also the organization whose security was lax enough that its network was used as the launching pad for the attack.

Disaster Recovery and Business Continuity Planning

Business continuity planning and disaster recovery procedures address the continuing operations of an organization in the event of a disaster or prolonged service interruption that affects the mission of the organization. Such plans should address an emergency response phase, a recovery phase, and a return to normal operation phase. You should identify the responsibilities of personnel during an incident and the resources that are available to them.

In reality, contingency and disaster recovery plans do not address every possible scenario or assumption. Rather, they focus on the events most likely to occur and they identify an acceptable method of recovery. Periodically, you should exercise the plans and procedures to ensure that they are effective and well understood.

Business continuity planning provides a short- to medium-term framework to continue the organizational operations. The following are objectives of business continuity planning:

- Moving or relocating critical business components and people to a remote location while the original location is being repaired

- Using different channels of communication to deal with customers, shareholders, and partners until operations return to normal

Disaster recovery is the process of regaining access to the data, hardware, and software necessary to resume critical business operations after a natural or human-induced disaster. A disaster recovery plan should also include plans for coping with the unexpected or sudden loss of key personnel. A disaster recovery plan is part of a larger process known as business continuity planning.

After the events of September 11, 2001, when many companies lost irreplaceable data, the effort put into protecting such data has changed. It is believed that some companies spend up to 25 percent of their IT budget on disaster recovery planning to avoid larger losses. Research indicates that of companies that had a major loss of computerized records, 43 percent never reopened, 51 percent closed within two years, and only 6 percent survived long term (http://searchenterprisewan.techtarget.com/definition/disaster-recovery-plan and http://en.wikipedia.org/wiki/Disaster_recovery).

Not all disruptions to business operations are equal. Whether the disruption is natural or human, intentional or unintentional, the effect is the same. A good disaster recovery plan takes into account the magnitude of the disruption, recognizing that there are differences between catastrophes, disasters, and nondisasters. In each case, a disruption occurs, but the scale of that disruption can dramatically differ.

Key Topic

- **Nondisaster:** A situation where a business process is unavailable for a given period of time

- **Disaster:** A situation that makes a facility unusable for an entire day or more

- **Catastrophe:** A situation that destroys the facility

Business Continuity Concepts

Building a business continuity plan requires extensive planning, with knowledge of the business requirements, budgets, and levels of risk the organization is willing to take. Some of the building block components, however, are more easily defined. The goal, from a rather simplified point of view, is to define objectives for the recovery of host computing systems that run the applications that support the business processes. These objectives are stated as the Recovery Time Objective (RTO) and Recovery Point Objective (RPO).

RTO is the number of hours or days that management has set as the objective for resuming a business process or a system. RPO describes the age of the data you want the ability to restore to in event of a disaster. For example, if the RPO is 8 hours, systems should be restored in the state they were in no longer than 8 hours ago. The technical disaster recovery strategy depends upon meeting RTO and RPO specifications. The RTO and RPO requirements determine which option of the disaster recovery plan to implement. Recovery time and how current data is are key components in determining the level of service a business process requires in the event of a major disruption. To properly implement a disaster recovery plan, one must know the RTO and RPO that the organization is willing to accept in a disaster. The technical disaster recovery strategy of different options of recovery is based upon a combination of these requirements.

Key Concepts:

Maximum Tolerable Downtime (MTD)

The total amount of time the system owner or authorizing official is willing to accept for a mission or business process outage or disruption, and includes all impact considerations.

Recovery Time Objective (RTO)

The maximum amount of time that a system resource can remain unavailable before there is an unacceptable impact on other system resources, supported mission, or business processes.

Recovery Point Objective (RPO)

The point in time, prior to a disruption or system outage, to which mission or business process data can be recovered (given the most recent backup copy of the data) after an outage.

Summary

To have a comprehensive security solution, it is important to cover all aspects of the operation of an organization. Comprehensive security requires suitable reliance on technical, physical, and administrative controls; implementing defense in depth; and developing an all-inclusive security policy. You will also be required to demonstrate forward thinking, taking into consideration the threats of tomorrow.

In this chapter you have learned that

- The confidentiality, integrity, and availability of the data need to be protected.

- Assets, vulnerabilities, and countermeasures can be classified to assist in developing a comprehensive set of security policies.

- New trends and threats are appearing frequently in the borderless network environment where we are evolving.

- To provide a comprehensive security solution, it is essential that there be a combination of technical, physical, and administrative controls in place.

- Defense in depth is a philosophy used to provide layered security to a system by using multiple security mechanisms.

- A security policy is a set of objectives for the company, rules of behavior for users and administrators, and requirements for system and management that collectively ensures the security of network and computer systems in an organization.

References

For additional information, refer to these resources.

Publications

Harris, S. *CISSP All-in-One Exam Guide, Fifth Edition* (McGraw-Hill Professional, 2010).

McClure, S., Scambray, J., and Kurtz, G. *Hacking Exposed, Sixth Edition* (McGraw-Hill Professional, 2009).

McClure, S., Scambray, J., and Kurtz, G. *Hacking Exposed, Seventh Edition* (McGraw-Hill Professional, 2012).

NIST SP 800-27 Rev A, *Engineering Principles for Information Technology Security*.

NIST SP 800-42, *Guidelines on Network Security Testing*.

NIST SP 800-64 Rev. A, *Security Considerations in the Information System Development Life Cycle*.

Richardson, R. *2010-2011 CSI Computer Crime and Security Survey* (http://gocsi.com/survey).

Wood, C. *Information Security Policies Made Easy, Version 11* (Information Shield, 2009).

Web Resources

Insecure.org, http://www.insecure.org/nmap/

SecurityFocus, http://www.securityfocus.com/

Security-Solutions.net, http://www.security-solutions.net/download/index.html

The GNU Netcat Project (G. Giacobbi), http://netcat.sourceforge.net/

The Jargon File, http://www.catb.org/~esr/jargon/html/index.html

Review Questions

Use the questions here to review what you learned in this chapter. The correct answers are found in the appendix, "Answers to Chapter Review Questions."

1. Which are the three primary objectives of security?

   a. Integrity

   b. Confidentiality

   c. Antireplay functionality

   d. Authentication

   e. Availability

2. Which are the three categories of controls?

   a. Administrative

   b. Executive

   c. Managerial

   d. Technical

   e. Physical

3. Show that you understand the different types of controls by matching them with their related technology.

   Type of controls

   a. Preventative

   b. Deterrent

   c. Detective

   Technologies

   d. Motion sensor

   e. Video surveillance

   f. Lock

4. Match the different types of hackers and the like with their appropriate description.

Hacker types

   a. White hat
   b. Black hat
   c. Gray hat
   d. Blue hat
   e. Cracker
   f. Phreaker
   g. Script kiddy
   h. Hacktivist

Hacker descriptions

   i. Bug tester
   j. Hacker with little skill
   k. Unethical hacker
   l. Hacker of telecommunication systems
   m. Ethically questionable hacker
   n. Hacker with a political agenda
   o. Synonymous with black hat hacker
   p. Breaks security for nonmalicious reasons

5. Organize the following steps in the order in which they are used to compromise targets and applications.

   a. Escalate privilege
   b. Leverage the compromised system
   c. Perform footprint analysis
   d. Install back doors
   e. Enumerate applications and operating systems
   f. Gather additional passwords and secrets
   g. Manipulate users to gain access

6. Which of the following is (are) not part of the technical policies. (Select all that apply.)

   a. End-user policy
   b. Acceptable usage policy
   c. Email policy
   d. Governing policy
   e. Rainbow Series
   f. Network policy
   g. Common Criteria Standard
   h. Wireless policy

7. Reorder the classification levels of the private sector, from the least secure document to the most secure document.

   a. Confidential

   b. Private

   c. Public

   d. Sensitive

8. Which of the following is not a criterion used to classify data?

   a. Value

   b. Age

   c. Useful life

   d. Copyright

   e. Personal association

9. Match each of the following information classification roles with its definition.

Roles

   a. Owner

   b. Custodian

   c. User

Definitions

   d. Responsible for using the data

   e. Responsible on a day-to-day basis for the classified data

   f. Ultimately responsible for the data

10. Which of the following is a technical control?

   a. Network Admission Control system

   b. Security policies and standards

   c. Security audits

   d. Security awareness training

   e. Change and configuration management

11. Which of the following is not a characteristic of defense in depth?

   a. Security mechanisms back each other up.

   b. Security mechanisms do not depend on each other.

   c. Does not require IDS or IPS.

   d. The weakest links can be augmented so that single points of failure can be eliminated.

12. Match the definition with the appropriate attack method.

Definitions

  a. Searching a network host and open ports
  b. Capturing electrical transmission
  c. Hiding information within a transmission
  d. Intercepting traffic that passes over a physical network

Attack methods

  e. Packet sniffing
  f. Man-in-the-middle
  g. Emanation capturing
  h. Covert channel
  i. Impersonation
  j. Port scanning

13. Reorder the phases of a system development life cycle.

  a. Operations and maintenance
  b. Initiation
  c. Disposition
  d. Acquisition and development
  e. Implementation

14. Which of the following security concepts limits a user's rights to the lowest possible level needed to perform his tasks?

  a. Need to know
  b. Least privilege
  c. Universal participation
  d. Diversity of defense

Chapter 2

Security Strategy and Cisco Borderless Network

In this chapter, you learn about the Cisco vision of a security strategy for Cisco Borderless Networks. You read about the architecture, components, and underlying technologies, and see Cisco products and solutions within the architecture.

In this chapter, you learn about the following Cisco Borderless Networks topics:

- Cisco Borderless Network Architecture

- Cisco security portfolio of products solving issues of Borderless Networks

- Cisco SecureX Architecture presenting its features and benefits

- Cisco threat control and containment products and technologies

- Cisco content security products and technologies

- Cisco VPN solutions and technologies

- Security management products and technologies

Borderless Networks

Borders are dissolving in multiple dimensions in current networks.

The device border is being dissolved by the phenomenon of mobility. Expect to see billions of new network mobile devices moving into enterprises worldwide over the next few years. If you consider constant reductions and streamlining in IT budgets, organizations face serious challenges to support a growing number of mobile devices at a time when resources are being reduced.

The application border is also dissolving. This is driven by market forces in cloud computing and cloud services. Organizations of all kinds are taking advantage of offerings such as Software as a Service (SaaS) and Infrastructure as a Service (IaaS) to reduce costs and simplify the deployment of new services and applications. These cloud services add challenges in visibility (how do you identify and mitigate threats that come to and from a trusted network?), control (who controls the physical assets, encryption keys, and so on?), and trust (do you trust cloud partners to ensure that critical application data is still protected when it is off the enterprise network?).

The location border is being blurred by constant changes to the workplace experience and millions of professionals that engage in work-related activities equally from home, the office, or while traveling. Borders are blurring in the organization as well, between consumers and workers and between the various functions within the organization. The borders between the company and its partners, customers, and suppliers are also fading. As a result, the network is having an increasing demand to connect anyone, anything, anywhere, at any time.

Taken together, these trends are driving consistent innovation of network-based business processes as the Internet morphed from a network to a platform for integrating supply chains, exchanging information for business intelligence, outsourcing entire business functions, and establishing new relationships. This trend will only accelerate as cloud computing matures.

The market changes also represent a challenge to security teams within the organization. They now need to manage uncontrolled consumer devices coming into the network, and provide seamless and context-aware services to users all over the world. The location of the data and services they access is almost irrelevant. Their location could be internal to the organization, or it could be in the cloud. This makes protecting data and services a challenging proposition.

The paradigm of access anytime, anywhere, using any device changes the network management approach that has traditionally been used to design and maintain networks. Scalability, availability, performance, and other metrics become much more complex as the IT organization moves beyond the infrastructure it can directly control. These metrics are no longer linear, but multidimensional. IT organizations need to manage the same metrics, but across the device, the application, and the location border.

Cisco Borderless Network Security Architecture

The Cisco Borderless Network Architecture, shown in Figure 2-1, addresses these issues using a comprehensive set of integrated components:

- **Borderless end zone:** Implemented by security controls aimed at protecting end devices and preventing intrusion to and from those end devices. Malware, viruses, and other types of malicious code are commonplace. The borderless end zone is built to detect these threats and eradicate them, or at least mitigate them, even before users connect to the network. As users connect from multiple locations, the network reacts to suspicious behavior by controlling access based on the security posture of the connecting endpoint. This reaction mitigates the impact of endpoint-based threats and helps contain their effect in a cost-effective manner.

- **Borderless Internet:** Implemented by scanning and enforcement engines, which are deployed onsite and offsite and managed by the organization itself but also by cloud providers. These scanning and enforcement engines inspect network content from Layer 2 through Layer 7, assuming the role of firewalls, intrusion detection systems (IDS), and intrusion prevention systems (IPS), network proxies, web gateways, and so on. These engines are located throughout the corporate network, but also rely on cloud-based services for security intelligence, real-time updates, and scanning support for mobile users, remote offices, and public network-resident devices such as network sensors or supervisory control and data acquisition (SCADA) systems.

- **Borderless data center:** Data centers deserve special attention in a cloud-driven business environment. The Cisco Borderless Network Architecture leverages existing infrastructure components such as Cisco Adaptive Security Appliances (ASA), IPS sensors, and switching components such as Cisco Catalyst and Cisco Nexus switches, layering virtualized components on top to provide security solutions that are built for "in the cloud" deployment, "by the cloud" deployment, and "for the cloud" deployment.

- **Policy management layer:** Security policy is managed in central locations and then enforced throughout the network based on context-specific variables. When an employee on an untrusted network in Moscow checks email via Outlook Web Access (OWA), that employee can view messages but is precluded from downloading attachments.

- **Borderless Network Services:** Professional and technical services are provided by Cisco and its partners. Cisco and its partners help an organization achieve the full benefits of the deployment of the Cisco solutions by providing consulting services in areas such as wireless, unified communication, data center, and, of course, network security, to name a few.

Figure 2-1 *Cisco Borderless Network Security Architecture*

The type of distributed, shared security intelligence, in the form of log files, vulnerability scanning data, system configuration, and event data, is available on a "publish and subscribe" basis in industry-standard formats. Additionally, onsite security information is supplemented by security telemetry in the cloud. All of this data will be available to analysts for event detection and forensics, but the network will also consume this data itself in order to react to anomalies, enforce policies, or block attacks in real time.

Borderless End Zone

Each major component of the architecture results in specific benefits. The borderless end zone offers deployment flexibility and strong security services in multiple dimensions as users connect to the network.

PCs and mobile devices are active participants in borderless network security in several ways. In borderless security, all endpoints authenticate themselves to the organization's network and submit to a health and configuration check before gaining access. This is true for employees and third-party users. Once admitted to the network, endpoints and users are given access to specific applications and data based upon parameters such as user role, location, time of day, and so on. This does not require multiple authentications. Rather, the network understands whether a user is working from an office desk, from a home PC, or from an untrusted network around the world and enforces policies for access controls, data confidentiality, and encrypted transport accordingly. Finally, endpoints continue to have onboard security defenses, but this will evolve from current fat client software to a cloud-based model—especially for mobile devices with limited resources.

The Cisco AnyConnect client is one of the building blocks of this architectural component, providing multiple layers of defense even before users connect to the network, leveraged around Secure Sockets Layer (SSL) VPNs.

Figure 2-2 provides a summary of the advantages of the borderless end zone. Many of the concepts presented in this figure are beyond the scope of this book but are explored in greater details in other Cisco literature and courses.

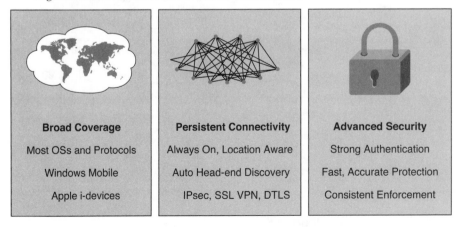

Broad Coverage	Persistent Connectivity	Advanced Security
Most OSs and Protocols	Always On, Location Aware	Strong Authentication
Windows Mobile	Auto Head-end Discovery	Fast, Accurate Protection
Apple i-devices	IPsec, SSL VPN, DTLS	Consistent Enforcement

Figure 2-2 *Borderless End Zone Advantages and Technologies*

The other side of the equation is represented by enforcement engines that make up the security array. Cisco has a strong security product line that includes firewalls, IPSs, web security, and email security. These detection and enforcement engines are evolving in two ways:

- They are built to be highly scalable and interpret and control traffic at the application level. This capability allows the network to catch up with malicious attackers, who are increasingly utilizing application layer threats to perpetrate their plans.

- They are available in multiple forms: appliance, module in a switch, or router and hybrid hosted.

Borderless Internet

The combination of intelligent endpoints and an array of scanning and enforcement engines makes the network work as a system with integrated, collaborative, and adaptive security. This is a sharp contrast with a point product approach, where function-specific products create "islands of security" constrained by independent threat, systems, and policy management. These disparate point tools are antithetical to the dynamic and integrated security that is required for borderless networks to fulfill the "any user, any content, any location, any time" nature.

The Cisco Borderless Network Architecture demands teamwork and cooperation akin to that of a symphony orchestra, where all of the individual "instruments" come together to achieve a common goal, as shown in Figure 2-3.

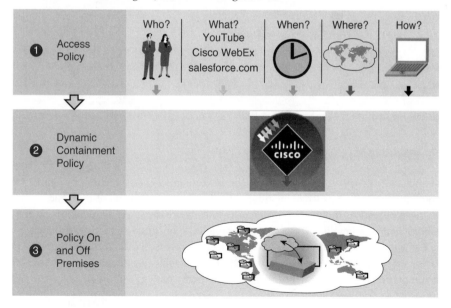

Figure 2-3 *Intelligent Access Policies Provides Context Awareness for Adaptive Securing of Endpoints*

Given the "borderless" aspect of Borderless Networks, security defenses must also extend beyond the enterprise network to mobile devices and cloud services. Using the Cisco Borderless Network Architecture, corporate LANs and WANs coordinate activities with service provider networks, distributed endpoints, and the Internet itself. No one vendor has all of the security products or resources to solve this challenge alone. Borderless network security requires industry ingenuity and collaboration. Cisco partners with leading security and networking vendors to extend the reach of the system beyond the confines of corporate networks.

Borderless Data Center

The borderless data center component of the architecture provides solutions that adjust to data center environments. Figure 2-4 illustrates the progression of service deployment in a heavily virtualized environment, such as that of data center.

Figure 2-4   *Evolution of Security in the Data Center*

Virtual appliances provide trusted access to virtualized data centers in enterprise and cloud provider environments while meeting virtualization requirements of dynamic policy-driven operation, mobility-transparent enforcement, and scale-out deployment for dense multitenancy, where one service provider might be hosting for multiple different clients. But it does not stop there. Network connectivity is also virtualized and embedded into virtual machines. Virtual switches connect virtual machines within a single physical device, integrating network switch ports into the hypervisor.

An example of this architecture is the Cisco Virtual Security Gateway (VSG), a security virtual appliance that leverages the Cisco Nexus 1000V switch to provide zone-based trust services to virtual machines. Cloud providers can leverage the Cisco VSG to significantly enhance their multitenant scaling and also generate additional revenue by offering security and monitoring services to their customers. In effect, the Cisco VSG enables a broad set of multitenant workloads having varied security profiles to share a common compute infrastructure on premises (in the enterprise virtual data center and private cloud) or off premises (in the service provider cloud). By associating one or more virtual machines (VM) into distinct trust zones, the Cisco VSG ensures that access to trust zones is controlled and monitored through established security policies.

Policy Management Layer

The policy management layer is a higher-level function that can span multiple operational devices. Cisco's vision is to make the interface between policy and enforcement systems open and built on industry standards. Therefore, if a customer chooses to use a Cisco application entitlement system and an enterprise data loss prevention (DLP) policy manager from RSA, both should work smoothly with existing network infrastructure. This significantly reduces operational complexity for Cisco customers because one set of policies can be enforced across a wide variety of infrastructure.

Borderless Network Services

Cisco Borderless Network Services covers many areas listed in Table 2-1. However, our focus for this book is restricted to the security solutions. Table 2-1 provides only a restricted list of SecureX core components. SecureX solutions and components will be presented in the next section of this chapter.

Table 2-1   *Cisco Borderless Network Services*

Category	Network Service	Solutions
Motion	Cisco Motion	Cisco CleanAir
		Cisco ClientLink
		Cisco VideoStream
Energy Management	Cisco EnergyWise	Cisco Services for Energy Management
Security	Cisco SecureX	Cisco Security Intelligence Operations
		Cisco TrustSec
		Cisco AnyConnect
Application Performance	Cisco Application Velocity	Cisco Wide Area Application Services
		Cisco UCS Express

Table 2-1   *Cisco Borderless Network Services*

Category	Network Service	Solutions
Multimedia Optimization	Cisco Enterprise Medianet	Cisco Medianet Readiness Assessment Service
Management	Management solutions	Cisco Prime for Enterprise
		Cisco Prime LAN Management Solution
		Cisco Prime Network Analysis Module
		Cisco Prime Collaboration Manager
		Cisco Prime Network Control System

Borderless Security Products

The architectural approach to security found in the Cisco Borderless Network Architecture, shown in Figure 2-5, results in distinct categories of Cisco products, technologies, and solutions. These product categories are built into the design of borderless network security and apply to multiple components of the architecture. For instance, a Cisco ASA can be found as an on-premises scanning engine in the borderless Internet component, but also as a firewall in the borderless data center.

Figure 2-5   *Policy Management Provided by Cisco Borderless Security Products*

In the following sections, we look at the pillars of security found in the Cisco Borderless Network approach.

SecureX, a Context-Aware Security Approach

Cisco SecureX is an access control strategy that allows for more effective, higher-level policy creation and enforcement for mobile users, connecting from anywhere, at any time, using any device. Because Cisco SecureX uses a broad array of parameters for policy, it allows for much more effective security and enables situational awareness, as represented in Figure 2-6. Instead of many complex firewall rules, security policy can now be based on context. For example, a salesperson accesses a global sales forecast from her laptop while in California; when she attempts to access that same sales forecast from the business center of the hotel where she is staying in China, the computer used is not detected as a corporate asset, and the request would be disallowed.

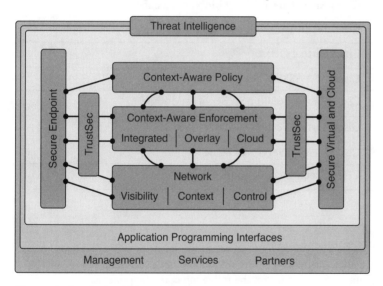

Figure 2-6 *SecureX Context Awareness*

This sort of intelligent policy enforcement uses next-generation scanning elements that are meshed into the new Cisco SecureX Architecture. Within this new architecture, the next-generation endpoint is able to automatically find the nearest scanning element somewhere in the virtual security fabric and to make a seamless connection. The behavior of a hacker halfway around the world is noted, that information is shared, and traffic from the servers of the hacker is blocked because your network now knows that it comes from someone that it cannot trust. Policy is centrally managed, but intelligence is gathered globally, with highly distributed enforcement.

Table 2-2 provides a list of Cisco security solutions that are part of the Cisco SecureX Architecture as presented in the Cisco SecureX product brochure.

Table 2-2   *Cisco SecureX Security Products*

Category	Product
Secure Network	Cisco ASA 5500 Series Adaptive Security Appliance
	Cisco Intrusion Prevention System
	Cisco Integrated Services Router Generation 2
	Cisco Security Manager
Secure Email and Web	Cisco IronPort Email Security—Cloud, Hybrid, and On Premises
	Cisco Web Security—Cloud and On Premises
	IronPort Security Management Appliance
Secure Mobility	Cisco AnyConnect Secure Mobility Client
	Cisco Adaptive Wireless IPS Software
	Cisco Virtual Office
Secure Data Center	Cisco ASA 5585-X Adaptive Security Appliance
	Cisco Catalyst 6500 ASA Services Module
	Cisco Virtual Security Gateway (VSG)
Secure Access	Cisco Identity Services Engine
	Cisco Secure Access Control System

SecureX Core Components

To enforces security policies across the entire distributed network, not just at a single point in the data stream, SecureX relies on the following core components.

Context-Aware Policies

At the core of the Cisco SecureX Architecture is context awareness, which allows enforcement elements (such as firewalls, web proxies, IPS sensors, and even network infrastructure elements such as routers and switches) to define the access policy by using information such as the identity of the user, the security posture of the connecting device, the point of access to the network, and many other components.

Cisco Security Intelligence Operations (SIO)

Many of the Cisco security products listed in Table 2-2 stay ahead of the latest threats by using real-time threat intelligence from Cisco Security Intelligence Operations (SIO). Cisco SIO is the world's largest cloud-based security ecosystem, using almost a million live data feeds from deployed Cisco email, web, firewall, and IPS solutions. Cisco SIO will be discussed further later in this chapter.

TrustSec

Cisco TrustSec relies on context awareness to enforce policy and at the same time provide access flexibility and situational access control.

Traditional access control parameters, such as the user identity, are considered. The user identity is the base component that the network gathers to initiate the determination of context. IEEE 802.1X is typically used to define the identity of those entering the network. Nonauthenticated devices, such as IP phones and printers, are also considered.

Other conditions are gathered from the Cisco AnyConnect client and the array of enforcement devices. Allowing an employee with high security clearance into the network on a weekday, using an uninfected corporate laptop from a campus office wired network, is not the same as allowing the same person (same identity) on a weekend evening to use an unknown PC, possibly infected with a virus, from a hotspot Internet café. AnyConnect and the device at the point of entry to the network determine this information.

The result is a different access policy and conditions that are based on the situational context of connectivity of individuals and devices, as illustrated by Figure 2-7.

Figure 2-7 *Context-Aware Policies Decide Access Privileges*

The same individual might be allowed into corporate resources with broad access under certain conditions, while forced into a quarantine area to update the antivirus software or unlock a user password under other conditions. The network, as a system, adapts to each circumstance.

So, as explained above, Cisco TrustSec extends context awareness through policy-based access control for any user and any device seeking access to the distributed network. Figure 2-8 illustrates the components of this function.

Figure 2-8   *Secure Resources Using TrustSec*

First, users are authenticated and authorized based on who, what, where, when, and how. Endpoint devices are also analyzed to determine if they meet corporate security policy before being granted access. Nonauthenticating devices, such as IP phones or video cameras, are also automatically identified and inventoried. Note that more and more endpoint devices, such as network printers, are 802.1x capable.

Next, traffic from any authenticated device is tagged with a unique, context-based access policy marker known a security group tag (SGT). Network devices along the data path read this tag and enforce its associated policy by restricting access to predetermined network destinations and resources. The devices do so by using security group access control lists (SGACL).

Finally, Cisco TrustSec provides data confidentiality. This is known as MAC Security (MACsec). For example, a policy may require that any employee from the finance department accessing the payroll server must have their data secured. Cisco TrustSec understands this policy and can direct the network to dynamically encrypt the data of the user.

In summary, TrustSec restricts user access using Security Group Access (SGA). Access policy is inserted as SGTs into devices. The SGA reads and enforces policy tags on TrustSec-enabled Cisco switches along data paths using SGACLs.

AnyConnect

The Cisco AnyConnect client provides a secure connectivity experience across a broad set of PC- and smartphone-based mobile devices. The enforcement devices provide posture assessment, access control services, and policy enforcement. They also start the encryption process to provide confidentiality via MACsec.

The Cisco AnyConnect Secure Mobility Solutions provide an innovative way to protect mobile employees on PC-based or smartphone platforms. These solutions use SSL or IP Security (IPsec) VPNs to deliver a more seamless, always-on, and always-protected experience to end users, while enabling IT administrators to enforce policies and block malware with cloud-based or hybrid web security. Cisco AnyConnect Secure Mobility is available to computers, tablets, and smartphones. For a complete list of Cisco AnyConnect Secure Mobility Client for Mobile Platforms, visit http://www.cisco.com/en/US/prod/collateral/vpndevc/ps5743/ps5699/ps10884/datasheet_c78-678242.html.

The Cisco AnyConnect Secure Mobility Client is a lightweight, highly modular security client that provides easily customizable capabilities. The client provides broad operating system support from traditional operating systems such as Windows and Linux, to mobile devices such as smartphones and tablets (Apple iOS, Windows Mobile, Android, and others), as illustrated in Figure 2-9.

Figure 2-9   *AnyConnect at Work*

Cisco AnyConnect provides an always-on solution that finds the nearest enforcement element and enforces multiple types of policies. This includes the use of SSL and IPsec VPNs (IKEv2 only), 802.1 X authentications and authorization, Cisco Network Admission Control (NAC), and other posture and enforcement elements. Using this consolidated client, the network implements data loss prevention, threat prevention, acceptable use policies, and access control mechanisms, all with one lightweight client that eliminates the need for multiple software elements enforcing individual security controls.

Cisco Identity Services Engine

Cisco Identity Services Engine (ISE) is the centralized policy engine for business-relevant policy definition and enforcement. Cisco ISE complements global contextual information that is offered by Cisco SIO, with localized context awareness provided by Cisco AnyConnect and the scanning and enforcement elements for effective access policy enforcement.

Cisco ISE combines the functionality of other Cisco products, such as the Cisco Secure Access Control Server for authentication, authorization, and accounting (AAA) services and Cisco NAC, into this next-generation policy server.

Threat Control and Containment

The Cisco threat control and containment solution offers comprehensive protection for your network through network-wide visibility, simplified policy control, and proactive system protection. The Cisco threat control and containment solution regulates network access, isolates infected systems, prevents intrusions, and protects critical business assets. This solution counteracts malicious traffic such as worms, viruses, and malware before it affects your business, by using centralized policy, configuration, and threat event management.

Threat prevention products have been a flagship of Cisco security for a long time. Integrated security controls found in Cisco Adaptive Security Appliance (ASA), Cisco Integrated Services Routers (ISR), and IPS sensors provide a multidimensional approach to detecting, mitigating, and responding to threats at various levels.

- **Cisco ASA:** Cisco ASAs provide proven firewall services and context- and application-aware capabilities for comprehensive, real-time threat defense. ASAs implement a truly unified threat management service, with the integration of VPN and intrusion prevention technologies in various forms.

- **Cisco ISRs:** Through software- and hardware-integrated security functions, ISRs can easily become part of the army of security controls in networks of all kinds. These functions include zone-based policy firewall, Cisco IOS IPS, and the integration of SSL and IPsec VPN technologies.

- **Cisco IPS:** Intrusion prevention is accomplished in a distributed fashion, from IPS 4200 appliances to integrated hardware modules such as the Advanced Inspection and Prevention Security Services Module (AIP-SSM) for ASA or the Intrusion Detection Services Module (IDSM) for Cisco Catalyst 6500. These IPS sensors support a variety of IPS technologies, including signature-based, anomaly-based, policy-based, and reputation-based techniques.

These threat prevention mechanisms are integrated into the fabric of the network. Flexible deployment options include standalone appliances, virtualized devices, and service modules that are embedded into routers and switches.

Note   Cisco TechWiseTV has produced excellent videos on different security products. Check them out:

"Fundamentals of Intrusion Prevention": http://youtu.be/w-z2kS9dlcI

"Fundamentals of ISE": http://youtu.be/sel1F7mKdtI

"Fundamentals of TrustSec": http://youtu.be/78-GV7Pz18I

Many other informative videos from TechWiseTV can be found at http://www.youtube.com/user/techwisetv?ob=0.

Cisco Security Intelligence Operation

Cisco SIO is the back-end security ecosystem that detects threat activity, researches and analyzes the threats, and provides real-time updates and best practices to keep organizations informed and protected. Cisco SIO, considered the largest threat analysis system providing blended threat protection, consists of three pillars:

- Threat intelligence, which is called Cisco SensorBase

- The automatic and human development process, called the IronPort Threat Operations Center

- The automated and best practices content that is pushed to network elements in the form of dynamic updates

Cisco SIO is a security intelligence center that baselines the current state of threats on a worldwide basis, and provides the network as a system with valuable information to detect, prevent, and react to threats. SIO acts as an early warning system by correlating threat information from the SensorBase, analyzed by the Threat Operations Center. SIO then feeds this information to enforcement elements, for live threat prevention based on malware outbreaks, current vulnerabilities, and zero-day attacks.

Cisco SIO weighs and processes the data, automatically categorizing threats and creating rules using more than 200 parameters. Security researchers also collect and supply information about security events that have the potential for widespread impact on networks, applications, and devices.

Rules are dynamically delivered to deploy Cisco security devices every three to five minutes. The Cisco SIO team also publishes security best practice recommendations and tactical guidance for thwarting threats.

Cisco's products participating and benefiting from Cisco SIO are IPS, ASA, IronPort Email Security Appliance (ESA), and IronPort Web Security Appliance (WSA). The

AnyConnect telemetry module can even be used to send endpoint web malware traffic information back to the web filtering infrastructure of IronPort WSA.

Some interesting statistics on Cisco SIO at the time of printing:

- It is estimated that more than 700,000 sensors participate in Cisco SIO.

- Cisco SIO analyzes more than 5 billion web requests daily coming from Cisco equipment such as IronPort WSA.

- It is estimated that 35 percent of all email traffic worldwide is checked against Cisco SIO.

Cisco SIO is a powerful way of analyzing traffic based on reputation, blocking malware and spam, and providing a granular web categorization and application classification.

Cloud Security, Content Security, and Data Loss Prevention

Cloud computing represents one of the most significant shifts in IT that many of you are likely to see in your lifetime. Reaching the point where computing functions as a utility has great potential, promising innovations that cannot yet be imagined. However, this breakthrough business model also imposes new security risks.

Not in any order of importance or severity, following is a list of the top threats to cloud computing, according to the Cloud Security Alliance (https://cloudsecurityalliance.org/):

- Abuse and nefarious use of cloud computing

- Insecure interfaces and APIs

- Malicious insiders

- Shared technology issues

- Data loss or leakage

- Account or service hijacking

- Unknown risk profile

Vendors, providers, and customers alike are concerned about the consequences if cloud computing is not properly secured, and the loss of direct control over systems for which they are nonetheless accountable.

Cloud computing is a double-edged sword: it introduces more security concerns but it provides security opportunities. Regarding security concerns about cloud computing, consider, for example, an organization that has embraced Software as a Service (SaaS) and uses cloud-based services such as Google Apps for Business and SalesForce. In a traditional cloud service, if a user leaves the organization, the administrator would need to visit both the SalesForce website and the Google Apps for Business website and proceed to nullify that user's accounts at each of those sites. However, if the organization has implemented the Cisco SaaS Access Control solution offered on Cisco IronPort WSA (discussed later), the administrator would only need to cancel the user's account from the WSA.

Content Security

Before we jump in to cloud computing, let's review some of Cisco's offerings for content security.

Content security refers to the threat prevention capabilities that provide malware protection against spyware, viruses, spam, and inappropriate content. Examples of content security products from Cisco include the following:

- Cisco IronPort Web Security Appliance (WSA), which scans the content of a web page for malware prior to passing it to the inside user who initiated the request

- Cisco IronPort Email Security Appliance (ESA), which scans incoming email against spam

- Cisco ASA 5500 Series Content Security and Control Security Services Module (CSC-SSM) running Trend Micro's antivirus and anti-spyware technologies.

Cisco IronPort WSA and ESA are discussed further later in this section.

Data Loss Prevention

Also known as data leak prevention systems or extrusion prevention systems, data loss prevention (DLP) systems monitor outbound traffic to ensure that confidential information doesn't fall into the wrong hands.

Cisco IronPort WSA and ESA both offer solutions to scan outbound traffic against preconfigured and customizable rules, thus preventing corporate or personal information from leaving the organization's premises.

Cloud-Based Security

Traditional threat prevention is now augmented to extend the system to email and web security, two key elements of the new mobile, cloud-based business environment.

Cisco offers both on-premises and cloud-based security for web and email traffic. For web security, Cisco offers the IronPort WSA as an on-premises device and IronPort ScanSafe as a cloud-based solution. For email security, Cisco offers the IronPort ESA either as an on-premises device or as a cloud-based service.

Web Security

Cisco offers both on-premises and cloud-based web security solutions, ScanSafe and the Cisco IronPort WSA, respectively. The WSA is what we commonly refer to as a web-proxy server.

Web malware is a common vehicle used to materialize threats in cloud services. Instead of creating their own malicious websites, hackers exploit the vulnerabilities of an open and dynamic web to distribute their malware. Web malware infection from reputable websites that have been compromised is not only a reality, but is now hackers' preferred route to infect victims.

This change has made traditional methods of control, such as antivirus software, less effective, and it requires an alternative approach to security.

Web security architecture from Cisco presents a flexible approach and deployment options for implementing services such as URL filtering, web content filtering, real-time scanning, web traffic and application control, malware prevention, and others. ScanSafe is a cloud-based solution that enhances security while enabling cost savings by eliminating the need to purchase, deploy, and maintain hardware required for on-premises solutions. IronPort WSA is an on-premises solution that offers data loss prevention capabilities, URL filtering, and other web security controls.

ScanSafe Web Security analyzes every web request to determine if content is malicious, inappropriate, or acceptable based on the defined security policy. This offers effective protection against threats, including zero-day threats, that would otherwise be successful.

ScanSafe Web Security is powered by Outbreak Intelligence, which is composed of numerous correlated detection technologies, automated machine-learning heuristics, and multiple "scanlets." Outbreak Intelligence builds a detailed view of each web request and the associated security risk to ensure that ScanSafe customers use the web safely.

Figure 2-10 illustrates the integration of ScanSafe with the Cisco AnyConnect client, to provide seamless deployment of context-aware policies, protected at the application layer against web malware.

Figure 2-10 *ScanSafe Integration with Cisco AnyConnect*

This is the highlighted functionality:

■ Integrated management and reporting that covers all aspects of the solution

■ Consistent policy and security for all users, regardless of location, whether they connect from their cubicle or from the boardroom in an adjacent corporate building, as an example

■ Numerous ways to integrate with existing network infrastructure and authentication services

■ Bidirectional content-based policy enforcement

■ Dynamic content classification

■ Control over HTTP and HTTPS communications

■ Accurate zero-day threat protection

■ All security extended to remote and roaming users in addition to on-premises users

Figure 2-11 also illustrates the use of IronPort Web Security Appliances on premises. In combination with ASAs, this solution implements acceptable use policies, malware prevention, and single sign-on to SaaS providers.

Figure 2-11 *Cisco IronPort WSA on Premises*

Cisco AnyConnect users use VPN technologies to connect to the corporate network via ASA, and their identity is then shared with WSAs for an integrated, context-aware web security solution.

Email Security

Cisco offers both on-premises and hosted email security solutions, using Cisco IronPort Email Security Appliance, as shown in Figure 2-12.

Figure 2-12 *Cisco IronPort Email Security Solutions*

Cisco IronPort Email Security solutions provide outstanding protection to organizations of all sizes. Sophisticated and scalable mechanisms help to do the following:

■ Minimize the downtime that is associated with email-borne malware

■ Simplify the administration of corporate mail systems

■ Reduce the burden on technical staff, while offering insight into mail system operation

Best-in-class technologies work together to prevent and respond to multilevel threats. They include the following:

- **Spam protection:** The Cisco spam protection combines best-of-breed conventional techniques with IronPort's breakthrough context-sensitive detection technology to eliminate the broadest range of known and emerging email threats.

- **Data loss prevention:** Cisco has partnered with RSA, a leader in data loss prevention technology, to provide an integrated data loss protection solution, RSA Email DLP, on Cisco IronPort ESAs. This solution ensures compliance with industry and government regulations worldwide and helps prevent confidential data from leaving customer networks.

- **Virus defense:** Cisco IronPort Virus Outbreak Filters detect new virus outbreaks in real time, then quarantine suspicious messages, offering protection before traditional antivirus solutions.

- **Email encryption tracking and reporting tools:** Cisco IronPort Preboot Execution Environment (PXE) encryption technology revolutionizes email encryption, meeting compliance requirements while delivering powerful, business-class email features.

IronPort solutions offer a choice of features and functionality available as appliance-based, cloud-based, hybrid, or managed solutions (where the solution is on premises but managed by Cisco's expert staff).

Secure Connectivity Through VPNs

Ensuring the privacy and integrity of all information is vital to your business. You can achieve privacy and integrity by using IPsec and SSL VPNs, as shown in Figure 2-13. As your company uses the flexibility and cost effectiveness of the Internet to extend its network to branch offices, telecommuters, customers, and partners, security is paramount. You must create a manageable, cost-effective communications infrastructure that will do the following:

- Improve productivity

- Enable new business applications

- Help you comply with information privacy regulations

- Enhance business efficiency

Figure 2-13 *VPN Deployment Options*

Cisco VPN solutions implement a set of products and security life-cycle services that are an essential element of the Borderless Network Architecture. By incorporating capabilities that secure the network, the endpoints, and the applications and messages, this systems-based approach delivers comprehensive security of your communications. The solution has two major elements:

- **Secure communications for remote access:** This element provides highly secure, customizable access to corporate networks and applications by establishing an encrypted tunnel across the Internet.

- **Secure communications for site-to-site connections:** This element provides an Internet-based WAN infrastructure for connecting branch offices, home offices, or the sites of business partners to all or portions of your network.

Security Management

Cisco network management systems help you automate, simplify, and integrate your network to reduce operational costs and improve productivity. The tools within the network management systems provide innovative ways to centrally and consistently manage your network to achieve critical functions such as availability, responsiveness, resilience, and security.

These network management systems also help reduce the troubleshooting and planning time that is associated with the introduction of new services such as voice, wireless, and security management. Solutions-focused tools simplify network management systems, including the management of devices, configurations, users, and services.

The tools available for security management are

- **Device managers:** Embedded into security devices in the form of HTML content. All you have to do is point your browser to an active IP address of the device, and the device manager immediately provides a comprehensive tool for one-to-one configuration and monitoring. ASDM, the Adaptive Security Device Manager, is an example of this approach for the ASA 5500 security appliances.

- **Cisco Configuration Professional:** A GUI-based device management tool for Cisco access routers. This tool simplifies routing, firewall, IPS, VPN, unified communications, WAN, and LAN configuration through GUI-based wizards. Cisco Configuration Professional is a valuable productivity enhancing tool for network administrators and channel partners for deploying routers with increased confidence and ease. This tool offers a one-click router lock-down and an innovative voice and security auditing capability to check and recommend changes to router configuration. This tool also monitors router status and troubleshoots WAN and VPN connectivity issues.

- **Cisco Security Manager:** Provides configuration and monitoring capabilities for firewalls, routers, switches, IPS sensors, and other security solutions. This tool uses multiple approaches to security management, including device-focused and policy-focused options.

Cisco Security Manager

Cisco Security Manager is a powerful but easy-to-use solution that enables you to centrally provision all aspects of device configurations and security policies for the Cisco family of security products. The solution is effective for managing even small networks consisting of fewer than ten devices, but also scales to efficiently manage large-scale networks that are composed of thousands of devices. Scalability is achieved through intelligent policy-based management techniques that can simplify administration and promote policy uniformity among devices. As a simple example, the administration might come up with a new login banner that is pushed to Cisco devices, such as routers, firewalls, and switches, using CSM. If in the future the legal department changes the wording of the login banner, CSM could deploy the new banner in a matter of minutes to all the devices.

Some of the features of Cisco Security Manager include the following:

- Supports provisioning for Cisco router platforms running a Cisco IOS Security Software image, Cisco ASA 5500 Series Adaptive Security Appliances, Cisco PIX 500 Series Security Appliances, Cisco IPS 4200 Series Sensors, and Cisco Catalyst 6500 Series Advanced Inspection and Prevention Security Services Module (AIP-SSM)

- Responds faster to threats by allowing you to define and assign new security policies to thousands of devices in a few simple steps

- Provides a rich GUI for superior ease of use

- Offers multiple views that provide flexible methods to manage devices and policies, including the ability to manage the security network visually on a topology map

- Contains extensive animated help for the new user, which reduces the learning time

- Allows you to centrally specify which policies are shared and automatically inherited by new devices to ensure that corporate policies are implemented consistently, while providing optional flexibility

- Integrates with Cisco Secure Access Control Server (ACS) to provide granular role-based access control to devices and management functions, though this functionality is removed once you upgrade to CS ACS 5.2

- Provides the ability to assign specific tasks to each administrator during the deployment of a policy, with formal change control and tracking, and allows the security and network operations staff to work together as a single team with effective coordination

Summary

In this chapter, you learned about the Cisco Borderless Network Architecture. This chapter examined the Cisco Security portfolio of products and, more specifically, reviewed the following:

- Cisco SecureX Architecture (at a high level), highlighting its features and benefits and providing examples of Cisco products that fall within this category

- Cisco threat control and containment products and technologies, such as the Cisco ASA and Cisco IPS, and illustrating their high-level features and benefits

- Cisco content security and data loss prevention technologies, such as Cisco IronPort WSA and ESA, and illustrating their high-level features and benefits

- Cisco VPN solutions and technologies, and illustrating their high-level features and benefits

- The different security management products and technologies, focusing at a high level on Cisco Security Manager

References

For additional information, refer to these Cisco.com resources:

"Borderless Networks," http://www.cisco.com/en/US/netsol/ns1015/architecture.html

Cisco AnyConnect Secure Mobility Client Administrator Guide, Release 3.0, Chapter 7, "Configuring AnyConnect Telemetry to the WSA," http://www.cisco.com/en/US/docs/security/vpn_client/anyconnect/anyconnect30/administration/guide/ac07telemetry.pdf

"Cisco AnyConnect Secure Mobility Solution," http://www.cisco.com/en/US/prod/collateral/vpndevc/ps5743/ps5699/ps10884/at_a_glance_c45-578609.pdf

"Cisco SecureX," http://www.cisco.com/en/US/netsol/ns1167/index.html

"Cisco TrustSec," http://www.cisco.com/en/US/netsol/ns1051/index.html

"Cisco Network Identity and Access Policy Solution," http://www.cisco.com/en/US/prod/collateral/vpndevc/ps5712/ps2086/network_id_vds.html

Cisco's TechWiseTV, http://www.youtube.com/ciscoCIN

Securing the Borderless Network, http://www.ciscopress.com/bookstore/product.asp?isbn=1587058863

Review Questions

Use the questions here to review what you learned in this chapter. The correct answers are found in the Appendix, "Answers to Chapter Review Questions."

1. Match each Cisco SecureX component with its definition.

   a. Context-aware enforcement

   b. Cisco TrustSec

   c. Cisco SIO

   d. Cisco AnyConnect

   _____ 1. Extends the access control functionality end to end, using security group tags.

   _____ 2. Used for real-time insight into the global threat environment.

   _____ 3. Provides a consistent user interface and consolidates traditional function-specific client software products into one.

   _____ 4. Allows enforcement elements to use identity and location information to define access policy.

2. The ASA, ISR, and IPS are all part of which product category?

   a. Threat control and containment

   b. Cisco TrustSec

   c. Cisco SecureX

   d. Cisco SIO

   e. Content security

3. Which two Cisco products provide data loss prevention in cloud services environments? (Choose two.)

   a. Cisco TrustSec

   b. Cisco ScanSafe

   c. Cisco SecureX

   d. Cisco IronPort ESA

   e. Cisco ASA

4. Using Cisco TrustSec functionality, what needs to happen before security group tags are assigned?

   a. MACsec confidentiality policy needs to be created

   b. Access policies are built in Cisco ISE

   c. Security group ACLs need to be defined

   d. User authentication mode needs to be selected

5. The Cisco ISE policy engine combines the functionality of which two Cisco products? (Choose two.)

   a. Cisco AnyConnect

   b. Cisco Secure ACS

   c. Cisco Security Manager

   d. CiscoWorks

   e. Cisco NAC

Chapter 3

Network Foundation Protection and Cisco Configuration Professional

In this chapter, you learn about Cisco IOS Network Foundation Protection (NFP) as a framework for infrastructure protection, all its components, and commonly used countermeasures as found in Cisco IOS devices. You also learn how to use Cisco Configuration Professional (CCP) to implement security controls on Cisco IOS routers.

More precisely, you learn how to do the following:

- Categorize common threats against the network infrastructure

- Describe Network Foundation Protection as a framework to develop and implement security controls to protect the network infrastructure

- List and compare security controls that protect the control plane

- List and compare security controls that protect the data plane

- List and compare security controls that protect the management plane

- Articulate the features and benefits of CCP, describing its requirements and installation options

- Demonstrate the CCP GUI, showcasing the most relevant options and features

- Describe the unique components of CCP that are used for effective security policy deployment and configuration

- Describe and implement the One-Step Lockdown and audit features found on CCP

Threats Against the Network Infrastructure

A key element in the overall security posture of an organization is the security of the network infrastructure. The network infrastructure is the foundation that is built with routers, switches, and other equipment that provides the fundamental network services to keep a network running. The infrastructure is often the target of denial of service (DoS) and other attacks that can directly or indirectly disrupt the network operation. In order to ensure the availability of the network, it is critical to implement the security tools and best practices that help protect each network element and the infrastructure as a whole.

Cisco Network Foundation Protection (NFP) provides an umbrella strategy for infrastructure protection by encompassing Cisco IOS security features.

The current network environment is complex, as networking devices offer a feature-rich set of services to cater to a variety of business needs. Business continuity requires security features and services for both network devices and infrastructure, thus ensuring the availability of the network devices under all circumstances.

Because connecting to the Internet is imperative, network devices and infrastructure are exposed to many risks and threats. Deploying security best practices helps secure the network foundation by protecting network elements and their interactions. In Internet and cloud computing environments, this means distrusting every packet and implementing policies that are aimed at categorizing traffic. Different traffic classes are then processed under different policies to ensure not only proper forwarding, but also dropping suspicious traffic, thus protecting the network devices themselves.

Table 3-1 lists some of the common threats to the network infrastructure. These threats are used not only to disrupt service via DoS attacks and routing protocol exploits, but also to create confidentiality exposure via trust exploitation attacks.

These threats exploit known vulnerabilities such as protocol weaknesses. For instance, the absence of confidentiality mechanisms in Telnet and certain versions of Simple Network Management Protocol (SNMP) can expose passwords and community names to malicious attackers. Unknown OS/software vulnerabilities can also be exploited using zero-day attacks. This exploitation can occur with software bugs and weaknesses, sometimes found in the operating systems of network devices.

The impact of these exploits and incidents is at the core of business operations. High resource utilization slows down network devices, and can even bring them down. Routing protocol operations can be disrupted, causing connectivity problems for all kinds of traffic. The problem is augmented when management sessions are slowed down in such a way that fixing the problem becomes a challenge.

Table 3-1 *Common Issues for Network Infrastructure*

Vulnerabilities	Threats	Impact
Design errors	Trust exploitation attacks	Exposed management credentials
Protocol weaknesses	Login, authentication, and password attacks	High route processor CPU utilization (near 100 percent)
Software vulnerabilities	Routing protocol exploits	Loss of protocol updates keepalives and routing
Misconfiguration	Spoofing	Route flaps and major network transitions
Multiple categories of vulnerabilities	Denial of service attacks	Slow or unresponsive management sessions
Multiple categories of vulnerabilities	Confidentiality and integrity attacks	Indiscriminate packet drops

The following are some of the symptoms and impact of network infrastructure security incidents:

- High route processor CPU utilization (near 100 percent)

- Loss of line protocol keepalives and routing protocol updates, leading to route flaps and major network transitions

- Slow or completely unresponsive interactive sessions via the CLI, due to high CPU utilization

- Route processor resource exhaustion, making resources such as memory and buffers unavailable for legitimate IP data packets

- Packet queue backup, leading to indiscriminate drops (or drops due to lack of buffer resources) of other incoming packets

It is important to apply a structured approach to network infrastructure protection. Different threats exploit different vulnerabilities in different functional areas of the network. As an example, spoofing attacks are commonly used to power DoS attacks from the external network, to exhaust edge device resources and link bandwidth. On more internal security domains, such as server farms and the campus access layer, Layer 2 attacks are typically aimed at trust exploitation and information theft using man-in-the-middle mechanisms.

Deploying the right policy and feature to the appropriate device is critical to the effective mitigation of these threats.

Cisco NFP Framework

To understand Cisco NFP architecture, it is important to understand the basics of the architecture of devices with routing capabilities. A router can be logically divided into three functional components or planes:

- Data plane
- Management plane
- Control plane

Most traffic travels through the router via the data plane. However, the route processor must manage certain packets, such as routing updates, keepalives, and network management. This traffic is often referred to as control and management plane traffic. The management plane, however, is considered separate from a functional perspective, in order to define different protection mechanisms to management traffic. In other words, the control and data planes use the central resources (CPU, memory, and so on) in Cisco network devices more intensely than does the management plane. This is depicted in Figure 3-1 by grouping them inside the same segmented lines. The data plane is typically processed in a fast-switching cache using distributed processing or in high-priority, process-independent code in the kernel.

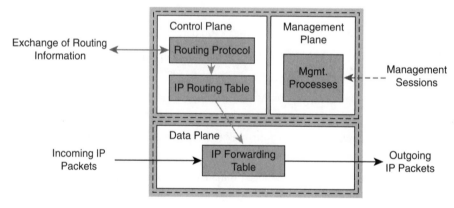

Figure 3-1   *Device Planes*

From the perspective of network traffic, a similar classification applies:

- **Data plane packets:** End-station, user-generated packets that are always forwarded by network devices to other end-station devices. From the perspective of the network device, data plane packets always have a transit destination IP address and can be managed by normal, destination IP address–based forwarding processes. Data plane packets are typically processed in a fast-switching cache.

- **Control plane packets:** Network device–generated/received packets that are used for the creation and operation of the network itself. From the perspective of the network device, control plane packets always have a receive destination IP address and are managed by the CPU in the network device route processor. Examples include protocols such as Address Resolution Protocol (ARP), Border Gateway Protocol (BGP), Open Shortest Path First (OSPF), and other protocols that hold the network together.

■ **Management plane packets:** Network device–generated/received packets, or management station–generated/received packets, that are used to manage the network. From the perspective of the network device, management plane packets always have a receive destination IP address and are managed by the CPU in the network device route processor. Examples include protocols such as Telnet, Secure Shell (SSH), TFTP, SNMP, FTP, Network Time Protocol (NTP), and other protocols that are used to manage the device or network.

Differentiating Between Control Plane, Data Plane, and Management Plane   The control path code, such as routing protocols, runs on the **control plane**.

Data packets, such as user traffic, are forwarded by the **data plane**.

Management sessions to the device, such as Secure Shell, use the **management plane**.

To deploy a protection policy to protect the different operation planes of a router, a structured approach is needed. The three distinct functions will benefit from a combined effort to protect the device, but each one affects the router operations differently. The control plane affects the ability to route packets, because it implements routing protocol functions. The management plane affects the ability to configure and monitor the device, and eventually implement the desired security controls. The data plane affects the ability to forward traffic, a critical function that must be performed efficiently.

Packet overloads on the control plane of a router can slow down routing processes and, as a result, degrade network service levels and user productivity. Packets that traverse the control plane are those destined for the CPU of that router, as opposed to network endpoints. All packets entering the control plane are redirected by the forwarding plane.

Cisco NFP is an umbrella strategy encompassing Cisco IOS security features that provides the tools, technologies, and services that enable organizations to secure their network foundations. Cisco NFP helps to establish a methodical approach to protecting router planes, forming the foundation for continuous service delivery. NFP is not a single feature or technology, nor is it a single management tool or set of commands. It is a series of Cisco IOS features designed specifically to protect the device control plane by "locking down" services and routing protocols, protect the device data plane from malicious traffic, and protect the device management plane.

Cisco NFP is not a single feature of technology but rather is the deployment of a protection strategy that is based on several mechanisms that affect all three planes. Table 3-2 summarizes some of the protection techniques available under the Cisco NFP framework. This list is only a sample of the available tools, some of which will be described and demonstrated in this chapter. More information on Cisco NFP can be found at http://www.cisco.com/go/nfp. The NFP features listed in Table 3-2 will be explained in the upcoming chapters of this book.

Table 3-2   *Some Components of Cisco NFP*

Plane	Feature	Benefit
Control plane	Control Plane Policing (CoPP)	Filter or rate limit control plane traffic with no regard to physical interface
	Control Plane Protection (CPPr)	Extend CoPP with granular traffic classification
	Routing protocol authentication	Integrity of routing and forwarding
	Cisco AutoSecure	Automate device hardening
Management plane	NTP, syslog, SNMP, SSH	Secure management and reporting
	CLI views	Obtain the benefits of role-based access control (RBAC) for command line
	Authentication, authorization, and accounting (AAA)	A comprehensive framework for RBAC
Data plane	Access control lists	Traffic filtering consistent across security device platforms
	Layer 2 controls (private VLANs, STP guards, others)	Protect the switching infrastructure
	Zone-based firewall, Cisco IOS IPS	Deployment flexibility in Cisco IOS form factor

Your network benefits from applying a structured approach to infrastructure protection using Cisco NFP. Figure 3-2 shows some of the benefits, which are explained next.

Overall, network elements benefit from a strategy that is based on role-based access control (RBAC) at the management level. Role-based access control is a strategy that associates the authority to execute certain tasks with a specific privilege level, such as certain tasks that could be executed by senior network administrators but not by junior network administrators. A simple example would be that senior administrators are allowed to perform the **show running-config** command, but junior administrators are not allowed. Network devices are organizational assets like any other, and their exploitation can cause network outages, which could be prevented using proper RBAC deployment.

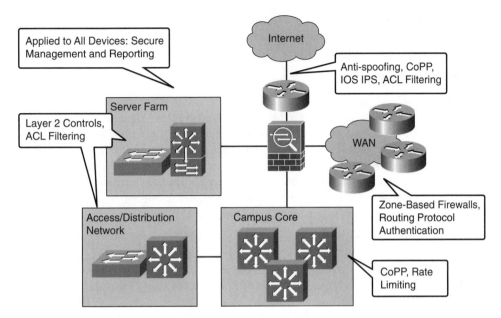

Figure 3-2   *Some of Cisco NFP in a Network*

Secure management and reporting mechanisms, such as SSH and SNMPv3, could be planned across the board for all network devices for device hardening and management plane protection.

On the other hand, traditional perimeters such as the Internet edge benefit from anti-spoofing mechanisms such as infrastructure access control list (ACL) filtering, as well as external threat protection using Cisco IOS Intrusion Prevention System (IPS). These NFP countermeasures protect not only the device itself but also the assets that those devices connect to in the organization.

Internal perimeters, such as the WAN edge, benefit from a distributed approach to security countermeasures, in the form of zone-based firewalls. These firewalls benefit from the Cisco IOS form factor to leverage existing network elements, implementing access control and data plane security in multiple edge points of the WAN in a distributed fashion.

More internal perimeters, such as server farms and the access and distribution layers, benefit from Layer 2 controls that protect the switching infrastructure.

Cisco NFP does not prevent poor network design. In that sense, building some level of redundancy into the network design is critical to the deployment of some of the NFP features. There is no substitute to designing a layered approach to security, with redundant countermeasures at different levels. Physical security and high availability are also design building blocks that need to be in place for an NFP strategy to be effective.

It is critical to apply the proper selection of Cisco NFP features to the proper device, according to a risk management plan. In that sense, Cisco NFP also assumes that a security policy is in place.

In terms of operations, the network design should follow recommended practices in change management and disaster recovery procedures.

Control Plane Security

Control Plane Policing (CoPP) is a Cisco IOS feature designed to allow users to manage the flow of traffic that is managed by the route processor of their network devices. Ideally, traffic is fast-switched from one interface to the other, as represented by the arrow in Figure 3-3. However, sometimes traffic needs to be process-switched. The CPU is shared among three main functions: routing protocols, slow data plane, and management process. Excessive traffic to any of the three main functions can overwhelm the CPU and affect the other two functions. CoPP is designed to prevent unnecessary traffic from overwhelming the route processor and the slow data path.

To protect the control plane on a router from DoS attacks, and to provide packet quality of service (QoS), the CoPP feature treats the control plane as an interface, as shown in Figure 3-3. Because the CoPP feature treats the control plane as a separate entity, a set of rules can be established and associated with the ingress and egress functions of the control plane, rules such as ACLs or rate limits.

Figure 3-3 *Goal of CoPP: Treat the CPU as an Interface*

These rules are applied only after the packet has been determined to have the control plane as its destination or when a packet exits the control plane. Thereafter, you can configure a service policy to prevent unwanted packets from progressing after a specified rate limit has been reached. For example, a system administrator can limit all TCP synchronization (SYN) packets that are destined for the control plane to a maximum rate of 1 Mbps.

Control plane security consists of implementing the following features:

- **CoPP:** CoPP lets users configure a QoS filter that manages the traffic flow of control plane packets to protect the control plane of Cisco IOS routers and switches against reconnaissance and DoS attacks.

- **CPPr:** CPPr is an extension of the policing functionality that the existing CoPP feature provides. CoPP allows QoS policing of aggregate control plane traffic that is destined to the route processor. The CPPr feature extends this policing functionality by allowing finer policing granularity by considering the CPU as three queues (subinterfaces), as shown in Figure 3-3: the host subinterface used by the routing and management processes, the Cisco Express Forwarding (CEF) subinterface, and the non-CEF subinterface.

- **Control Plane Logging:** CPPr lets you filter and rate-limit the packets that are going to the control plane of the router and discard malicious packets, or malformed packets or packets containing errors. The Control Plane Logging feature enables logging of the packets that these features drop or permit. The Control Plane Logging feature provides the logging mechanism that you need to deploy, monitor, and troubleshoot CoPP features efficiently.

CoPP

The CoPP feature provides the following benefits:

- Protection against DoS attacks that are targeted toward the network infrastructure by traffic flows and protocols that must be permitted, but where rate limiting offers substantial protection.

- Easier deployment. CoPP uses the existing Modular QoS CLI (MQC) infrastructure, which allows customers to preserve the existing interface configurations and add global control plane–specific commands to address security goals.

- A consistent implementation strategy across all Cisco hardware.

- Increased reliability, security, and availability of the network.

CPPr

Cisco CPPr extends the CoPP feature by enabling classification of the control plane traffic based on packet destination and information that is provided by the forwarding plane, allowing appropriate throttling for each category of packet. CPPr provides a finer policing. This is where you might add granularity to your policy, to accomplish tasks such as differentiating between Telnet, SSH, and HTTPS management traffic.

The functionality that is added with CPPr includes a traffic classifier, which intercepts traffic and classifies it into three control plane categories (queues, as shown in Figure 3-3). New port-filtering and queue-thresholding features have also been added. The port-filtering feature provides for policing of packets going to closed or nonlisted TCP and

UDP ports, while queue thresholding limits the number of packets for a specified protocol that will be allowed in the control plane IP input queue.

As with CoPP, CPPr is implemented using Cisco IOS MQC, a highly flexible framework that allows users to create and attach traffic policies to interfaces. The Cisco MQC mechanisms are used by CPPr to define the classification and policing descriptions for its policies. In this way, in addition to the limited permit and deny actions that are associated with simple ACLs, specific packets may be permitted but rate-limited when using the MQC structure. For example, you may wish to permit certain Internet Control Message Protocol (ICMP) packet types, but rate limit them so that the route processor is not adversely impacted. This action adds tremendously to the capabilities and flexibility of developing and deploying a useable CPPr policy.

Key Concepts:

What does Control Plane Protection provide you?

- Extends CoPP protection by providing mechanism for finer policing granularity for control plane traffic

- Allows rate limits for each traffic class individually

- Provides ease of configuration for control plane policies using modular policy CLI infrastructure

- Provides better platform reliability, security, and availability

- Provides CPU protection so it can be used for important jobs, such as routing

---

Traffic Classes

Before developing an actual CPPr policy, required traffic must be identified and separated into different classes. Multiple classification schemes can be used, but one recommended methodology involves classifying traffic into distinct groups that are based on relative importance. This approach can be illustrated with a simple classification example composed of four basic classes: critical, normal, undesirable, and default.

Table 3-3 illustrates a more complex classification scheme, along with the action to apply to each traffic class. This example uses seven different classes, which provides greater granularity and is more suitable for real-world environments. The actual number and type of classes that are needed for a given network may differ and should be selected based on local requirements, security policies, and a thorough analysis of baseline traffic.

Table 3-3   *Example of a Complex CPPr Classification Scheme*

Traffic Class Rate	Rate (pps)	Conform Action	Exceed Action
Routing Protocols (OSPF, and so on)	N/A	Transmit	Transmit
Management (HTTPS, SSH, and so on)	250	Transmit	Drop
Reporting (syslog and so on)	50	Transmit	Drop
Monitoring (SNMP and so on)	75	Transmit	Drop
Spanning Tree	25	Transmit	Drop
Undesirable	10	Drop	Drop
Default (anything else)	10	Transmit	Drop

The goal in this book is to introduce the complex topics of CoPP and CPPr. A deeper discussion of these topics can be found in the Cisco Press book *CCNP Security SECURE 642-637 Official Cert Guide*.

Routing Protocol Integrity

Other control plane security mechanisms are specific to routing protocols, such as routing protocol neighbor authentication. When configured, neighbor authentication occurs whenever neighbor routers exchange routing updates. This authentication ensures that a router receives reliable routing information from a trusted source.

Without neighbor authentication, unauthorized or deliberately malicious routing updates could compromise the security of your network traffic. A security compromise could occur if an unfriendly party diverts (rogue default gateways) or analyzes that traffic (man-in-the-middle attacks). For example, an unauthorized router could send a fictitious routing update to convince your router to send traffic to an incorrect destination.

The unfriendly party could analyze the diverted traffic to learn confidential information about your organization or merely use it to disrupt the ability of your organization to communicate effectively using the network. Neighbor authentication prevents your router from receiving any such fraudulent routing updates.

These routing protocols support neighbor authentication for IPv4: BGP, OSPF, Enhanced Interior Gateway Routing Protocol (EIGRP), Intermediate System-to-Intermediate System (ISIS), and Routing Information Protocol version 2 (RIPv2). For IPv6, the list is complete with OSPF version 3 (OSPFv3) and RIP next generation (RIPng).

The mechanism behind routing protocol integrity is hashing, which will be explained in detail in Chapter 11, "Intrusion Prevention Systems."

Cisco AutoSecure

Another example of Control Plane Protection is Cisco AutoSecure. This feature also implements protection mechanisms for the data and management planes. Cisco AutoSecure provides vital security requirements to enterprise and service provider networks by incorporating a straightforward one-touch device-lockdown process. Cisco AutoSecure enables rapid implementation of security policies and procedures to simplify the security process, without having to understand all of the Cisco IOS Software features and execute each of the many CLI commands manually. This feature uses a single command in CLI, or a single option in CCP, a one-touch device-lockdown process (discussed in the next section) that instantly configures the security posture of routers and disables nonessential system processes and services, thereby eliminating potential security threats.

Cisco AutoSecure allows two modes of operation:

- **Interactive mode:** Prompts users to select their own configuration of router services and other security-related features

- **Noninteractive mode:** Configures security-related features of the router based on a set of Cisco defaults

Interactive mode provides for greater control over the router security-related features than noninteractive mode. However, when a user needs to quickly secure a router without much human intervention, noninteractive mode is appropriate. Use AutoSecure with caution and thoroughly research its functionality prior to using it, because securing one aspect of the router might break the security of another aspect. An example of a potentially undesirable effect of using AutoSecure is that it suggests disabling Proxy ARP, which is required for the NAT process.

Table 3-4 lists some of the protection mechanisms that are activated when using Cisco AutoSecure. In general terms, Cisco AutoSecure protects the router functional planes by doing the following:

- Disabling often unnecessary and potentially insecure global services

- Enabling certain services that help further secure often necessary global services

- Disabling often unnecessary and potentially insecure interface services, which can be configured on a per-interface level

- Securing administrative access to the router

- Enabling appropriate security-related logging

Table 3-4 *Cisco AutoSecure Protection for All Three Planes*

Plane	Action
Control plane	Disables often unnecessary and potentially insecure global services (finger, HTTP, Cisco Discovery Protocol, and so on)
Management plane	Secures administrative access to the router (password existence and minimum length, AAA, SSH, and others)
Data plane	Disables often unnecessary and potentially insecure interface services, which can be configured on a per-interface level (IP redirects, IP proxy ARP, and others)

Management Plane Security

Securing the network infrastructure requires securing the management access to the infrastructure devices. If infrastructure device access is compromised, the security and management of the entire network can be compromised. Consequently, it is critical to establish the appropriate controls to prevent unauthorized access to infrastructure devices.

Network infrastructure devices often provide a range of different access mechanisms, including console and asynchronous connections, as well as remote access based on protocols such as Telnet, rlogin, HTTP, and SSH. Some mechanisms are typically enabled by default with minimal security associated with them. For example, Cisco IOS Software–based platforms are shipped with console and modem access enabled by default. For this reason, each infrastructure device should be carefully reviewed and configured to ensure that only supported access mechanisms are enabled and that they are properly secured.

The recommended practices to secure both interactive and management access to an infrastructure device are as follows:

- **Restrict device accessibility:** Limit the accessible ports and restrict the permitted communicators and the permitted methods of access by enforcing a password policy.

- **Present legal notification:** Display legal notice developed with company legal counsel for interactive sessions.

- **Authenticate access:** Ensure that access is only granted to authenticated users, groups, and services. RBAC and authentication, authorization, and accounting (AAA) services provide mechanisms to effectively authenticate access.

- **Authorize actions:** Restrict the actions and views that are permitted by any particular user, group, or service. Actions can be restricted using ACLs and views can be limited using CLI views (discussed later in this book).

■ **Ensure the confidentiality of data:** Protect sensitive data stored on management servers, such as syslog or SNMP servers, from viewing and copying. Consider the vulnerability of data in transit over a communication channel to sniffing, session hijacking, and man-in-the-middle attacks. Using management protocols with strong authentication, such as SNMPv3, mitigates confidentiality attacks that are aimed at exposing passwords, device configurations, and so on.

■ **Log and account for all access:** Record who accessed the device, what occurred, and when for auditing purposes.

■ **Integrity of logs and digital certificate:** Ensure the integrity of logs and digital certificate validation by synchronizing network time across all devices and network elements by using mechanisms such as Network Time Protocol (NTP). NTP helps the Security Information and Event Management (SIEM) server to perform more accurate correlation between multiple alarms that would have been received around the same time. NTP and its configuration will be covered in greater detail in Chapter 4, "Securing the Management Plane on Cisco IOS Devices and AAA."

Secure Management and Reporting

Figure 3-4 shows a management module with two network segments that are separated by a Cisco IOS router that acts as a firewall and a VPN termination device. The segment outside of the firewall (the production network) connects to all of the devices that require management. The segment inside of the firewall contains the management hosts themselves and the Cisco IOS routers that act as terminal servers. Remote access, such as SSH, to network devices connected on the production network is either disabled or highly restricted.

The information flow between management hosts and the managed devices can take two paths:

■ **Out-of-band (OOB):** Information flows within a network on which no production traffic resides.

■ **In-band:** Information flows across the enterprise production network, the Internet, or both.

The connection to the production network is only provided for selective Internet access, limited in-band management traffic, and IP Security (IPsec)-protected management traffic from predetermined hosts. In-band management occurs only when a management application does not function OOB, or when the Cisco device being managed does not physically have enough interfaces to support the normal management connection. This latter case employs IPsec tunnels. The Cisco IOS Firewall is configured to allow syslog information into the management segment and, in addition, Telnet, SSH, and SNMP, if these services are first initiated by the inside network. Stateful packet filtering and IPsec will be covered in detail later in this book.

Figure 3-4   *Example of Secure Management and Reporting*

Because the management network has administrative access to nearly every area of the network, it can be a very attractive target to hackers. The management module has been built with several technologies designed to mitigate such risks. The first primary threat is a hacker attempting to gain access to the management network itself. You can mitigate this threat only through the effective deployment of security features in the remaining modules in the enterprise. All of the remaining threats assume that the primary line of defense has been breached. To mitigate the threat of a compromised device, strong access control is implemented at the firewall, and at every other possible device, to prevent exploitation of the management channel. A compromised management device cannot even communicate with other hosts on the same management subnet because private VLANs (PVLAN) on the management segment switches force all traffic from the management devices directly to the Cisco IOS Firewall, where filtering takes place.

Network administrators need to securely manage all devices and hosts in the network. Management includes logging and reporting information flow, including content, configurations, and new software, from the devices to the management hosts.

From an architectural perspective, providing OOB management of network systems is the best first step in any management and reporting strategy. Devices should have a direct local connection to such a network where possible, and where this is not possible (because of geographic or system-related issues), the device should connect via a private encrypted tunnel over the production network. Such a tunnel should be preconfigured to permit only the traffic that is required for management and reporting. The tunnel should also be locked down so that only appropriate hosts can initiate and terminate tunnels.

It is important to note, however, that OOB management is not always desirable. Often, the decision depends on the type of management applications that you are running and the protocols that are required. For example, consider a management tool with the goal of determining the reachability of all the devices on the production network. If a critical link were to fail between two core switches, you would want this management console to alert an administrator.

If this management application is configured to use an OOB network, it may never determine that the link has failed, because the OOB network makes all devices appear to be attached to a single OOB management network. With management applications used to test reachability, it is therefore essential to run the management application in-band, as user traffic would do. In-band management needs to be configured in a secure manner.

SNMP management has its own set of security needs. Use SNMP version 3 (SNMPv3) where possible, because SMNPv3 supports authentication and encryption. Keeping SNMP traffic on the management segment allows the traffic to traverse an isolated segment when it pulls management information from devices. To reduce security risks, SNMP management should only pull information from devices and should not be allowed to push changes to the devices. To ensure that management information is pulled, each device is configured with a read-only SNMP community string. You can configure an SNMP read-write community string when using an OOB network. However, be aware of the increased security risk of a plaintext string that allows modification of device configurations if an older SNMP version is used. A rudimentary example of a read string would be "GET TEMPERATURE", where the network management server inquires about the internal temperature of a router. An example of a more dangerous write string would be "SET RELOAD", ordering a router to perform a reboot.

As mentioned earlier, it is important that all network devices be on the same time for proper log analysis. Time synchronization is best achieved by using NTP, which automates the process. The time distributed to the devices by NTP can be authenticated, through a process similar to routing authentication discussed earlier in this chapter. Authenticated time protects against spoofed NTP updates, which can corrupt logs and render digital certificates unusable.

Role-Based Access Control

RBAC is an access control approach that restricts user access based on the role of the user, along with their individual identity. Roles are created for job or task functions and assigned access permissions to specific assets. Users are then assigned to roles, through which assignment they acquire the permissions that are defined for the role. This means users are not assigned permissions directly, but only acquire them through role assignment, as shown in Figure 3-5. Managing the rights of an individual user becomes as simple as assigning appropriate roles to the user.

User-Based Access Control   Role-Based Access Control

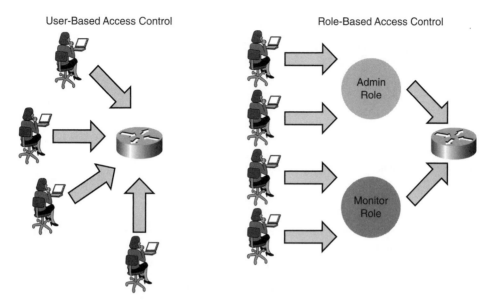

Figure 3-5 *Advantage of Role-Based Access Control*

With Cisco IOS, the role-based CLI access feature implements RBAC for router management access. This feature allows you to create different "views" of router configurations for different users. Views define which commands are accepted from different users and which configuration information is visible to them. With role-based CLI access, you can exercise better control over Cisco networking devices.

For scalability, users, permissions, and roles are usually created and maintained in a central repository, to make the access control policy available to multiple devices using it.

Deploying AAA

AAA servers are typically used as a central repository of authentication credentials (the users, answering the question "who is trying to access the device?"), authorization rules (the "what" users can accomplish), and accounting logs (the "what users did" part of the equation).

Figure 3-6 shows an example of the authentication and authorization process using an external AAA server such as Cisco Secure Access Control System (ACS) to provide AAA services to a network for management purposes.

In this chapter, we are concerned with limiting management access to our network equipment, and as such we will be discussing how to use AAA to limit the traffic to routers and switches for the purpose of owning the devices to manage them. In a later chapter, we will discuss the concept of using AAA to control traffic going through the devices.

Figure 3-6   *Authentication and Authorization Using an External AAA Server*

In step 1, the client establishes a connection with the router.

In step 2, the router prompts the user for a username and password. The user sends her credentials to the router.

In step 3, the router passes the user's credentials to the AAA server and advises the router that the user is authenticated.

In step 4, the user is authorized to access the router (administrative access) based on information found in the AAA server authorization database.

Data Plane Security

Among the laundry list of ways to protect the data plane, some that we will see in this book include

- Access control lists

- Private VLAN

- Firewalling

- Intrusion Prevention System (IPS)

Before discussing the details for data plane security, let's review the most common means of protecting it, access control list (ACL) filtering, and then discuss briefly Layer 2 protection. Both of these topics are discussed in greater detail in subsequent chapters.

Access Control List Filtering

ACLs perform packet filtering to control which packets move through the network and where. Such control provides security by helping to limit network traffic, restrict the access of users and devices to the network, and prevent traffic from leaving a network. IP access lists can reduce the chance of spoofing and DoS attacks and allow dynamic, temporary user access through a firewall.

The following are the most common reasons to use ACLs:

- **Block unwanted traffic or users:** ACLs can filter incoming or outgoing packets on an interface, thus controlling access based on source addresses, destination addresses, or user authentication. You also can use ACLs to determine which types of traffic are forwarded or blocked at the router interfaces. For example, you can permit email traffic to be routed but at the same time block all Telnet traffic.

- **Reduce the chance of DoS attacks for internal devices:** There are a number of ways to reduce the chance of DoS attacks. For example, by specifying IP source addresses, you can control whether traffic from hosts, networks, or users accesses your network. You can filter on specific Time to Live (TTL) values in packets to control how many hops a packet can take before reaching a router in your network. By configuring the TCP Intercept feature, you can prevent servers from being flooded with requests for a connection.

- **Mitigate spoofing attacks:** ACLs allow security practitioners to implement recommended practices to mitigate spoofing attacks. The guidelines that are found in several RFCs provide basic filtering, and can be easily deployed using ACLs.

- **Provide bandwidth control:** An ACL on a slow link can prevent excess traffic

- **Classify traffic to protect other planes:** You can place an ACL on inbound vty (Telnet) line access from certain nodes or networks. For the control plane, ACLs can control routing updates being sent, received, or redistributed.

Antispoofing

One efficient use of ACLs is as an antispoofing mechanism. Spoofing protection involves discarding traffic that has an invalid source address. Network security baseline includes source IP spoofing protection that is based on BCP38/RFC 2827 ingress traffic filtering.

Packets with spoofed source IP addresses represent a security risk because they are often used to conduct an attack, to evade traceability and bypass access controls. These packets may also be used to direct an attack at a spoofed source, something that is known as a reflection attack, as shown in Figure 3-7. In this figure, the hacker sends packets with a source IP address of a third party. Hosts on network 171.1.0.0 reply to what they think to be the initiator of the echo-request and send the echo-replies to 200.1.1.1, which is not the originator of the ping.

A variant of the attack shown in Figure 3-7 would be for the attacker to turn the 171.1.0.0 subnet workstations into members of a botnet, as explained in Chapter 1. The hacker could then order those zombies to launch TCP SYN packets to the victim, but spoofing as source IP address a third party. The victim would route its reply to the third-party address. This particular attack would create three casualties: the zombie site, which would have a high volume of outbound traffic; the destination victim; and the third site, whose address was invoked as the source IP address of the original request.

Figure 3-7   *Attack Involving Spoofed Address*

Spoofed traffic with an invalid source IP address may include traffic from either of the following:

■ RFC 1918, Documented Special Use Addresses (DSUA), or unallocated IP address range

■ Valid IP network address range, but not originating from the associated legitimate network

Implementing BCP38/RFC 2827 ingress traffic filtering to address source IP address spoofing renders the use of invalid source IP addresses ineffective, forcing attacks to be initiated from valid, reachable IP addresses. This implementation is beneficial because it enables greater success in tracing the originator of an attack.

ACLs are the traditional technique for filtering forged source IP addresses. However, ACLs are not dynamic in nature, requiring manual configuration changes, and may have an impact on the performance of a device. Other features, such as Unicast Reverse Path Forwarding (uRPF), can be used to complement the antispoofing strategy.

Note   Download document ID 13608, "Cisco Guide to Harden Cisco IOS Devices," from Cisco.com for an informal discussion of some Cisco IOS system device configuration settings that network administrators could consider to harden their routers, especially perimeter routers.

Layer 2 Data Plane Protection

Data plane protection mechanisms depend on feature availability for specific devices. In a switching infrastructure, these Cisco Catalyst integrated security capabilities provide data plane security on the Cisco Catalyst switches using integrated tools:

- Port security prevents MAC flooding attacks.

- DHCP snooping prevents client attacks on the DHCP server and switch.

- Dynamic ARP Inspection (DAI) adds security to ARP by using the DHCP snooping table to minimize the impact of ARP poisoning and spoofing attacks.

- IP Source Guard prevents IP spoofing addresses by using the DHCP snooping table.

Some of the above controls will be discussed later in this book.

Now that we have seen in general terms the need for protecting the network infrastructure, let's have a look at a GUI tool to help us harden our Cisco IOS routers.

Cisco Configuration Professional

CCP, shown in Figure 3-8, is a GUI-based device management tool for Cisco access routers, specifically Integrated Services Routers (ISR) and Integrated Services Routers Generation 2 (ISR G2). This tool simplifies routing, firewall, IPS, VPN, unified communications, WAN, and LAN configuration through GUI-based wizards.

Figure 3-8   *CCP GUI*

CCP is a valuable productivity-enhancing tool for network administrators, used for deploying routers with increased confidence and ease. It offers a one-click router lockdown and an innovative voice and security auditing capability to check and recommend changes to router configuration. CCP also monitors router status and troubleshoots WAN and VPN connectivity issues. The GUI includes options to configure Cisco Services-Ready Engine (SRE) modules, facilitating the integration of hardware-based functionality and centralizing their configuration in the same place where the hosting router is configured.

CCP is free, and you can download it from http://www.cisco.com/go/ciscocp. CCP can be preinstalled in the flash memory of the router, typically in its express version.

The following list summarizes the benefits of using CCP:

- Supports configuration of advanced technology deployment on ISRs and ISR - G2 through a single integrated tool

- Simplifies routing, firewall, IPS, VPN, unified communications, WAN, and LAN configuration through GUI-based easy-to-use wizards

- Monitors router status and troubleshoots WAN and VPN connectivity issues

- Provides smart wizards for routing and security configuration

- Offers license management for ISR-G2

The following are features of CCP Express:

- A lightweight version of CCP

- Router flash

- LAN and WAN interfaces

By relying on best-practice configurations that are approved by the Cisco Technical Assistance Center (TAC), network administrators can take advantage of CCP, which does the following:

- Lowers the total cost of ownership (TCO) of Cisco routers

- Reduces human errors

- Simplifies initial setup in voice deployments

- Helps ensure proper linkage between users, dialing plans, and voicemail settings

CCP offers smart wizards and advanced configuration support for the following:

- LAN and WAN interfaces

- Network Address Translation (NAT)

- Stateful and application firewall policy

- IPS, IPsec, and SSL VPNs

- Quality of service (QoS)

- Cisco Network Admission Control (NAC) policy features

CCP enables IT managers to easily organize and manage multiple routers at a single site.

CCP Initial Configuration

Devices that are shipped with CCP have a default configuration that allows you to connect a PC to an Ethernet port on the device and start configuration immediately. This initial configuration is accomplished using CCP Express. CCP Express and a factory default configuration file are installed in flash memory on routers that are shipped with CCP. You can connect a PC directly to the device, and then use CCP Express to configure LAN and WAN connections, a firewall, and NAT and make security settings before you place the device on the network in which it will operate. After you have configured the device and connected it to the network, you will be able to use CCP to connect to the device over the network and make advanced configurations.

Figure 3-9 provides a visual aid to the following configuration procedure:

Figure 3-9 *Connecting to the Default CCP Settings of an ISR*

Step 1.   The device default configuration file configures an IP address for one Ethernet interface, and that may configure the device as a DHCP server. See Table 3-5 to determine whether the device is configured as a DHCP server, and which Ethernet port to connect the PC to.

Table 3-5   Cisco Configuration Professional—Defaults According to Models

Device Model	DHCP Server	Connect PC to the Applicable Ethernet Port
Cisco 815, Cisco 86x, Cisco 88x, Cisco 180x, Cisco 1805, Cisco 1811, Cisco 1812	Yes	Depending on the model, connect to any ACT Lnk port or LAN port or SWITCH port or PWR Lnk port
Cisco 1841, Cisco 1861, Cisco 2801, Cisco 2811	No	Fast Ethernet 0/0
Cisco 28xx, Cisco 38xx	No	Gigabit Ethernet 0/0
Cisco 19xx, Cisco 29xx, Cisco 39xx	No	Gigabit Ethernet 0/0

Refer to CCP and ISR documentation on Cisco.com for an up-to-date list of defaults and detailed information on applicable Ethernet ports depending on model.

Step 2.   Connect the PC to the appropriate port listed in Table 3-5.

Step 3.   Configure the PC IP address by doing one of the following:

■ If the device is configured as a DHCP server, ensure that the PC is configured to accept an IP address from a DHCP server.

■ If the device is not configured as a DHCP server, configure the static IP address 10.10.10.2 on the PC, and use the subnet mask 255.255.255.248.

Step 4.   Open an Internet Explorer browser window, and enter the IP address **10.10.10.1** to connect to the device and start CCP Express.

Step 5.   Complete the CCP Express wizard to configure the device.

When you have completed initial setup and given the device an IP address on your LAN, you can use CCP to connect to the device and perform additional configuration.

To use CCP with an already deployed device, enter the commands shown in Table 3-6.

Table 3-6   *Command to Provision a Deployed Device with CCP Support*

Feature	Requirement	Configuration
Secure Access	SSH and HTTPS	Router(config)# ip http secure-server
		Router(config)# ip http authentication local
		Router(config)# line vty 0 4
		Router(config-line)# login local
		Router(config-line)# transport input ssh
		Router(config-line)# transport output ssh

Feature	Requirement	Configuration
Nonsecure Access (clear text)	Telnet and HTTP	Router(config)# ip http server Router(config)# ip http authentication local Router(config)# line vty 0 4 Router(config-line)# login local Router(config-line)# transport input telnet Router(config-line)# transport output telnet
User Privilege	Level 15	Router(config)# username cisco privilege 15 secret 0 cisco

Note   In the **username** command of Table 3-6, the **0** indicates that the following password is clear text, which should be avoided. If the value would have been set to **5**, it would have indicated that the following password would appear encrypted in configuration files.

Also, connecting CCP to a new device for the first time can be accomplished by choosing **Application > Setup New Device** in CCP, which you have manually installed on your PC. Connect your local PC to the console port of the router. This approach, shown in Figure 3-10, sounds counterintuitive—using a GUI through a serial port—but works, where CCP uses the console connection of your local PC to attempt to reach the router to configure it. For this to work, ensure that no other terminal monitor application is currently accessing the console port of the router.

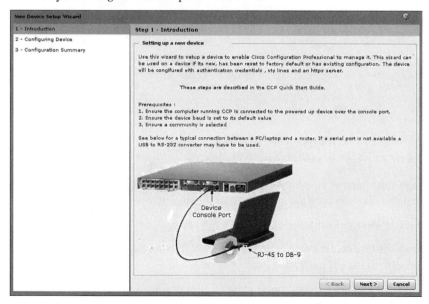

Figure 3-10   *CCP Used to Discover a Device Using the Serial Connection of a PC*

Cisco Configuration Professional User Interface and Features

Although every aspect of CCP is important and useful, due to space constraints, we will focus in the following pages only on the most relevant options and features of CCP.

Note   If you would like to follow along with these explanations of CCP, you can download the Cisco Configuration Professional Demo version from Cisco.com, using your Cisco.com user ID. This simulator is prefilled with routers and configurations so you can practice your CCP navigational and configuration skills without interfering with equipment currently in production. However, some features are not available or configurable in Demo or Offline modes.

CCP eliminates the need for multiple device managers by providing a single tool to configure and manage devices. The user interface makes it easy to manage networking features. The main parts that define the user interface are shown in Figure 3-11 and include the following:

- **Menu bar:** The row of menus across the top of the window. The menu bar offers application services, a list of open windows, and online help.

- **Toolbar:** The row of icons directly below the menu bar. These icons represent the most often used application services and most often configured networking features.

- **Left navigation pane:** This navigation pane is the scalable panel on the left side of the content pane in which you select the features to configure and monitor.

- **Content pane:** This pane is the right side of the workspace in which windows appear. You view reports here and enter information that configures networking features.

- **Status bar:** The status bar is the bar at the bottom of the window where CCP displays the status of the application. A closed lock icon refers to a secure connection and an opened lock icon refers to an unsecure connection.

Menu Bar

The row of menus across the top of the window offer application services and help. Figure 3-12 identifies the options in the Application menu, which are described here:

- **Manage Community:** Enables you to create a new community or choose an existing community. A community member would be a router that you manage with CCP.

- **Setup New Device:** Enables you to set up a new device.

- **Create User Profile:** Enables you to restrict users from using all of the features that are available in the left navigation pane.

- **Import User Profile:** Enables you to import a user profile.

Figure 3-11 *Navigating the GUI of Cisco Configuration Professional*

- **Options:** Enables you to set user preferences such as log level, show community at startup, and show CLI preview parameters.

- **Template:** Enables you to create, edit, or apply a template.

- **Work Offline:** Enables you to work with CCP in offline mode.

- **Exit:** Exits the CCP application.

Figure 3-12 *CCP Toolbar*

Toolbar

The following CCP features are available from the toolbar at the top of the window, as shown in Figure 3-12:

- **Home:** Click **Home** to display the Community View page, which summarizes the community information and allows you to add, edit, and discover devices and view the discovery and router status of each device.

- **Configure:** Click **Configure** to display the features that you can configure on a chosen device. The features are displayed in the left navigation pane, as shown in Figure 3-12. Note that if a feature (router, security, or voice) is not supported on a device, that feature is not displayed in the left navigation pane. However, if the Cisco IOS version that is installed on the device does not support a specific feature, but an upgrade does support it, then that feature is disabled (grayed out) in the left navigation pane.

- **Monitor:** Click **Monitor** to display the router and security features that you can monitor for a chosen device. The features are displayed in the left navigation pane.

- **Manage Community:** Click this icon to open the Manage Community dialog box, where you can add a new community or edit an existing community.

- **Refresh:** Click this icon to do the following:

    - Rediscover the selected device in the Select Community Member drop-down menu

    - Rediscover and reload the current feature

Note that the Refresh function is not available for offline mode, and is available in online mode only after successful discovery of one or more devices. Clicking Refresh refreshes the device that is selected in the Select Community Member drop-down menu. Choosing Home > Dashboard, selecting a device, and clicking Refresh does not refresh that device.

Navigation Pane

The following options are found in the navigation pane on the left of the screen, as shown in Figure 3-11.

Interface Management

The CCP connection wizards guide you through LAN and WAN configurations, and check the information that you enter against the existing configuration, warning you of any problems. The supported interfaces are

- LAN

- WAN

- Wireless LAN

■ Cellular WAN (3G)

■ Analog trunks

■ Digital trunks

In addition, CCP can be used to configure EnergyWise features for power management.

The Interface Management folder on the navigation pane provides configuration support for interfaces and service modules. CCP can configure the modules management, install applications, and upgrade images. The following service modules are supported:

■ Network modules

■ Enhanced network modules

■ Cisco Wide Area Application Services (WAAS) modules

■ Advanced Integration Modules (AIM)

■ Voice Network Modules (VNM)

■ Services-Ready Engine (SRE) modules

Support for Services-Ready Engine Virtualization (SRE-V) allows you to do the following:

■ Install SRE-V software on SM-SRE 700 and 900 modules

■ Edit console manager and hypervisor IP configurations

■ Launch the vSphere client user interface from CCP

■ Configure users, groups, roles and permissions, and syslog

■ View license details

Note   Cisco SRE-V is a branch-office infrastructure platform that combines computing, networking, storage, virtualization, and unified management into a cohesive system. It enables the VMware vSphere Hypervisor to be provisioned on a Cisco Services-Ready Engine (SRE) Service Module and host one or more virtual machines running Microsoft Windows Server operating system. The entire system is integrated with Generation 2 of the Cisco Integrated Services Router (ISR-G2). Further information can be found at Cisco.com.

Router

The Router folder, in the left navigation pane, displays the routing window with the configured static routes and Routing Internet Protocol (RIP), Open Shortest Path First (OSPF), and Extended Interior Gateway Routing Protocol (EIGRP) configured routes.

From this window, you can review routes, add new routes, edit existing routes, and delete routes.

Under the Router folder, the administration can also set the hostname, username, and password. Other supported routing functions include NAT, DHCP, Domain Name System (DNS), QoS, and Cisco Performance Routing (PfR).

The Router folder is also used for overall management options, related to AAA, management access, logging, and others.

Security

CCP can be used to manage functions that comprise a large portion of the topics discussed in this book. They include

- Device hardening via the One-Step Lockdown and Security Audit wizards

- VPN options for IPsec and SSL site-to-site and remote access deployments

- Zone-based firewall wizards, as well as classic Cisco IOS firewall configuration options for backwards compatibility

- Cisco IOS IPS wizards

Each is discussed in turn next.

Device Hardening   Security Audit is a feature that examines your existing router configurations and then updates your router in order to make your router and network more secure. Security Audit is based on the Cisco AutoSecure feature. It performs checks on and assists in configuration of almost all of the AutoSecure functions.

Security Audit operates in one of two modes. The first mode is the Security Audit wizard, which lets you choose which potential security-related configuration changes to implement on your router. The second mode is One-Step Lockdown, which automatically makes all recommended security-related configuration changes.

VPN   Comprehensive VPN configuration can be accomplished using CCP options. A wizard-like VPN Design Guide is available, helping you to determine which kind of VPN to configure, among site-to-site, remote access (SSL and IPsec using Easy VPN and Virtual Tunnel Interface [VTI]), Dynamic Multipoint VPN (DMVPN), and Group Encrypted Transport (GET) VPN. The input parameters include information about what type of user you are, the type of equipment that the router establishes VPN connections with, the type of traffic that the VPN will carry, and other features that you need to configure. After you provide this information, the VPN Design Guide recommends a VPN type and allows you to launch the wizard that will enable you to configure that type of VPN.

For ease of configuration, CCP offers a VPN option to create a text file that captures the VPN configuration of the local router. This file can be used to configure a remote router that enables it to establish a VPN connection to the local router.

Firewall   The firewall option simplifies access control configuration using smart wizards. Two firewall wizards are available:

- **Basic Firewall:** Creates a firewall using default rules. The use case scenario shows a typical network configuration in which this kind of firewall is used.

- **Advanced Firewall:** Leads you through the steps of configuring a firewall. You can create a demilitarized zone (DMZ) network and specify an inspection rule. The use case scenario that is shown when you choose this option shows you a typical configuration for an Internet firewall.

CCP provides preconfigured application security policies that you can use to protect the network. Using a simple slider bar, you can select the security level that you want and view a description of the security it provides. The wizard summary screen displays the policy name and the configuration statements in the policy.

Comprehensive editing tools are available to maintain the firewall ruleset, with quick edit options and a graphical view of the ruleset that allows you to understand the scope of the rule and the zones and interfaces involved.

You can also view the details of the policy by clicking the Application Security tab and choosing the name of the policy. Application inspection rules for deep packet inspection are available.

IPS   The IPS option simplifies intrusion management using a wizard-based approach to configuration. CCP allows for a simplified initialization, update, and management of IPS signatures, including intuitive options for signature tuning in order to improve the accuracy and sensitivity of the system. This allows for improved chances of managing false positives and false negatives.

The IPS option also includes a Security Dashboard, which displays threat information in the form of top threats table, and allows the administrator to visualize the events and incidents generated by the IOS IPS functionality.

Management, Monitoring, and Troubleshooting   Comprehensive monitoring and troubleshooting options are available by clicking the Monitor button in the toolbar shown in Figure 3-12. Convenient tools allow detailed troubleshooting, including connectivity testing tools that generate real traffic and provide visual cues as to potential configuration or connectivity issues.

Content Pane

The content pane, located on the right side of the workspace, is where the configuration takes place. The content pane changes depending on the selection you make on the navigation pane, located on the left of the window. In addition to configuring networking features from the content pane, you can view and monitor the equipment.

Status Bar

The status bar appears at the bottom of the window and displays the current communication status with the device. A locked padlock icon indicates that CCP has a secure connection with the chosen community member. The unlocked padlock icon indicates that CCP has a nonsecure connection with the chosen community member.

Cisco Configuration Professional Building Blocks

When using Cisco Configuration Professional, you can take advantage of the following tools to facilitate and direct the process. These building blocks simplify operations, allow RBAC, and provide bulk configuration and monitoring options for multiple devices.

- **Communities:** Groups of devices that share common components. Communities can be used to group devices based on geographic location, device function, and so on.

- **Templates:** Parameterized configuration files that can be created once with a common configuration and applied multiple times by using configuration variables that change value for each device.

- **User profiles:** GUI views that allow RBAC over CCP menus and options.

RBAC is discussed further in Chapter 4.

Communities

A community is basically a group of devices (known as community members). A single community can contain a maximum of ten devices. You can create a community and then add devices to it based on some common parameters. For example, you can create communities that are based on the location of the devices. You can create a San Jose community and add devices to it, and then you can create a Bangalore community and add devices to it, and so on.

Before you begin using CCP, you must first create a community and then add devices to that community. When you start CCP for the first time, CCP automatically creates a community for you, to which you can add devices. Devices are discovered on the network, and their configuration is uploaded to CCP.

When you add a device to a community, you must specify its IP address or hostname, credential information (username and password), and whether the communication will be secured. CCP uses this information to discover the device. After you discover the device, you can configure and monitor it. Again, up to ten devices can be added to each community.

You can create and manage communities from the Manage Community dialog box.

Creating Communities

The following list shows how to create and manage communities in CCP:

Step 1.   Use the Manage Community dialog box to create communities. The Manage Community dialog box automatically displays when you start Cisco Configuration Professional, with a community called New Community created by default.

You can also open the Manage Community dialog box in the following ways, shown in Figure 3-13:

■ From the toolbar, click the **Manage Community** icon.

■ From the menu bar, choose **Application > Manage Community**.

Figure 3-13   *Creating Communities from the Application Menu or with the Icon on the Toolbar*

Step 2. In the Manage Community dialog box, enter the IP address or hostname and the username and password information for the devices that you want to configure. If you enter the default username cisco and default password cisco, the Change Default Credentials dialog box opens. For security reasons, you must change the default credentials to new credentials.

Step 3. If you want CCP to connect securely with the device, check **Connect Securely**. To view the port information, click the down arrow next to the Connect Securely check box.

Step 4. If you want to change the default port information, click it, and then enter a new port value.

Make sure that CCP can access the device at the specified secure or nonsecure ports.

Step 5. If you want CCP to discover all the devices in a community, check **Discover All Devices**. If you want, you can choose to discover the devices later, from the Community View page.

Step 6. Click **OK**. The Community View page opens. It displays the information about the devices in the community.

Managing Communities

After you create a community and add devices to it, you can view the information for that community by clicking the only available selection in the navigation pane, a page called Community View. Clicking Community View refreshes the information appearing in the Community Information pane. From the Community Information pane, you can manage the devices (community members) in a community, such as add devices to a selected community, edit device information, delete devices, discover the devices, view information about the discovery process, and view hardware and software information about a selected device.

Figure 3-14 illustrates the Community View option in CCP. The list of devices appears in the content pane, and the selected device can be quickly chosen using the Select Community Member drop-down menu. The buttons at the bottom of the window include the Discover button, which enables you to discover or rediscover devices, the Discovery Details button, which displays a log of events and errors that may arise during the discovery process, the Manage Devices button, which enables you to manage device IP addresses and credentials, and the Router Status button, which displays the status of the devices.

Figure 3-14 *Managing Devices Within the Community*

Templates

Templates facilitate management and consistency by attributing parameters to common components of configuration files (known as parameterizing). Using the template options, you can convert specific components of the configuration files into variables, which will acquire a different value for different devices that use the template.

After the template is created, it can be applied to multiple devices in different communities. The process includes options to provide values to the variables on the template, making them specific to each device. The template remains untouched. When applying the template, you can override the existing configuration, or merge the resulting configuration into the existing configuration.

Figure 3-15 illustrates the template management options. The wizard-based process guides you through the following steps to create a template:

Step 1.   Choose **Application > Template > Create**.

Step 2.   Select the device from which you will obtain the template or select a configuration file from the local PC.

Step 3.   Check the **Include This Configuration in the Template** check box.

Step 4.   Find and select the attribute to be converted to variables, and click the **Parameterize.**

You can click Unparameterize to undo the action if the attribute is not to become a variable. The selected attribute is wrapped within a double set of curly brackets {{}}. For instance, the word demoone becomes {{demoone}} after being parameterized.

Step 5.   Click **Finish** and select the template filename and location.

Figure 3-15   *Creating Variables in CCP Templates*

After the template is created, you can apply it to multiple devices by following these steps:

Step 1.   Choose **Application > Template > Apply.**

Step 2.   Click the browse button and navigate to select the template file.

Step 3.   Click **Find Parameterized Attribute** to find and select specific text, and then change the value of the text to the value specific for the device.

Step 4.   In the Apply to Device step, shown in Figure 3-16, choose the router to apply the template from the Select Device drop-down list, and then click the respective radio button to select whether to merge with or override the running configuration. Check the **Enable Rollback** check box if rollback is desired.

Step 5.   Click the Reload Device button to apply overridden configurations, or click Rollback to return to the previous configuration and discard the changes.

Merge or Override

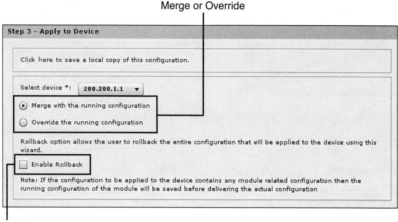

Rollback Option

Figure 3-16 *Applying a Template on a Discovered Device*

User Profiles

User profiles are a tool to define configuration views on CCP. Using profiles, administrators can define the view and configure which menus and screens are visible to the users who are acquiring the profile. This process effectively creates a different CCP option tree, where screens are available to profile users in full permission mode or in read-only mode.

Figure 3-17 illustrates the profile management options. The wizard-based process guides you through the following steps to create a profile:

Step 1.   Choose **Application > Create User Profile.**

Step 2.   Click to select the device or devices that will be part of the user profile.

Step 3.   The resulting folders represent the CCP option tree. Expand the folders to find the menus and screens.

Step 4.   Select screens to set permissions.

Step 5.   Check the check boxes to define permissions. The following permissions are available:

- **Show this screen:** Makes the screen visible to users acquiring the profile, and defines full permission over the components of the screen.

- **Restrict to read operations only:** Changes the screen permissions to view-only or read-only.

- **Disabled:** This option does not appear explicitly, but can be accomplished by clearing the two check boxes for the previously listed permissions.

Step 6.   Click **Save** to save the user profile as a file.

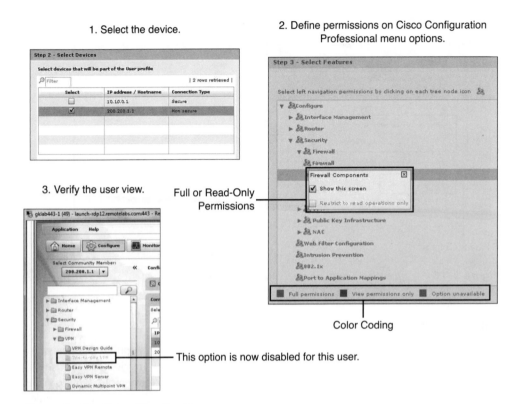

Figure 3-17   *Using User Profiles*

Following this configuration, users will see options that are grayed out when they try to access screens that have been disabled for access, and they will see buttons and check boxes that are grayed out when they try to use options on screens that have been designated as read-only.

Using CCP to Harden Cisco IOS Devices

There are two options to harden your Cisco IOS devices, as shown in Figure 3-18: the Security Audit or the One-Step Lockdown. The Security Audit approach is more granular than the One-Step Lockdown options. With the One-Step Lockdown approach, CCP evaluates and hardens your device without the option for you to review the changes about to be made.

Figure 3-18   *Security Audit Tools*

Security Audit

The Security Audit Wizard implements device hardening by testing your router configuration to determine if any potential security problems exist in the configuration. The wizard then presents you with a screen that lets you determine which security problems you want to fix. Once determined, the Security Audit Wizard makes the necessary changes to the router configuration to fix those problems using One-Step Lockdown.

Following are the steps to perform the security audit:

Step 1.   From the toolbar, choose **Configure > Security > Security Audit**.

Step 2.   Click **Perform Security Audit**. The Welcome page of the Security Audit Wizard opens.

Step 3.   Click **Next**. The Security Audit Interface Configuration page opens.

Step 4.   Input information to tell the Security Audit Wizard which of your router interfaces connect to your inside network and which connect outside of your network. For each interface listed, check either Inside or Outside to indicate where the interface connects, as shown in Figure 3-19.

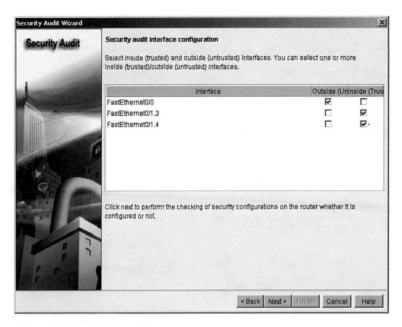

Figure 3-19 *Selecting Interfaces for a Successful Security Audit*

Step 5. Click **Next.** The Security Audit Wizard tests your router configuration to
determine if possible security problems exist. The potential problems are
determined by Cisco recommended practices. A screen showing the progress
of this action opens, listing all of the configuration options being tested for,
and whether the current router configuration passes those tests, as shown in
Figure 3-20. If you want to save this report to a file, click **Save Report.**

Figure 3-20 *Security Audit Results*

Step 6.   Click **Close**. The Security Audit Wizard displays a "report card" showing a list of possible security problems, as shown in Figure 3-21.

Figure 3-21   *Addressing Issues Reported by the CCP Security Audit*

Step 7.   Check the **Fix It** check box next to any problems that you want CCP to fix. For a description of the problem and a list of the Cisco IOS commands that will be added to your configuration, click the problem description to display a help page about that problem.

Step 8.   Click **Next**. The Security Audit Wizard may display one or more screens requiring you to enter information to fix certain problems. Enter the information as required and click **Next** for each of those screens.

Step 9.   The Summary page of the wizard shows a list of all the configuration changes that Security Audit will make. Click **Finish** to implement those changes to your router.

CCP can undo this security fix. If you want CCP to remove this security configuration, run the Security Audit Wizard. In the report card window shown in Figure 3-21, choose the option **Undo Security Configurations** from the drop-down list at the top of the window, and check the check box next to any configurations that you want to undo. Click **Next**.

One-Step Lockdown

The One-Step Lockdown option, available from the Security Audit main menu shown in Figure 3-18, tests your router configuration for potential security problems and automatically makes necessary configuration changes to correct problems that are found. The configuration is evaluated against Cisco recommended practices, similar to the Security Audit Wizard. This time, however, changes are made automatically and without prompting the user to select components to fix. Choose **Configure > Security > Security Audit > One-Step Lockdown**.

The One-Step Lockdown option streamlines device hardening by implementing the AutoSecure feature with a one-click option. To confirm the process, click the **Deliver** button in the confirmation dialog box, shown in Figure 3-22, to deliver the new settings. Notice that the confirmation dialog box also explains how to roll back the new settings using the Security Audit feature. Also, notice that the wizard lists the settings as changed before offering the option to deliver them.

Figure 3-22 *One-Step Lockdown*

Cisco IOS AutoSecure

The following list provides examples of the Cisco AutoSecure features that are implemented in CCP during the One-Step Lockdown (refer to the CCP documentation on Cisco.com for an updated list of features):

■ Disable unnecessary services and interfaces

    ■ Unused router interfaces

    ■ BOOTP server

- Cisco Discovery Protocol
- Configuration autoloading
- FTP server
- TFTP server
- NTP service
- PAD service
- TCP and UDP minor services
- DEC MOP service
- Disable commonly configured management services
  - SNMP
  - HTTP or HTTPS configuration and monitoring
  - DNS
- Ensure path integrity
  - Disable ICMP redirects
  - Disable IP source routing
  - Disable IP directed broadcast
  - Disable gratuitous and proxy ARP
  - Enable firewall on all outside interfaces
- Disable probes and scans
  - Finger
  - ICMP unreachable notifications
  - ICMP mask reply
- Ensure terminal access security
  - Enable SSH
  - Disable IP identification service
  - Enable TCP keepalives
  - Set access class on HTTP and vty
- Ensure authentication integrity
  - Enable password encryption
  - Set minimum password length
  - Set authentication failure rate

AutoSecure is a Cisco IOS feature that, like CCP, lets you more easily configure security features on your router, so that your network is better protected. CCP implements almost all of the configurations that AutoSecure provides.

The following AutoSecure features might not be implemented in CCP:

■ **Disabling Network Time Protocol (NTP):** Based on input, AutoSecure will disable NTP if it is not necessary. Otherwise, NTP will be configured with Message Digest 5 (MD5) authentication. CCP does not support disabling NTP.

■ **Configuring AAA:** If AAA is not configured, AutoSecure configures local AAA and prompts for configuration of a local username and password database on the router. CCP does not support AAA configuration.

■ **Setting Selective Packet Discard (SPD) values:** CCP does not set SPD values.

■ **Enabling TCP Intercept feature:** CCP does not enable TCP Intercept feature.

■ **Configuring antispoofing ACLs on outside interfaces:** AutoSecure creates three named ACLs used to prevent antispoofing source addresses. CCP does not configure these ACLs.

CCP implements the following Cisco AutoSecure features differently:

■ **Disable Simple Network Management Protocol (SNMP):** CCP will disable SNMP, but unlike AutoSecure, it does not provide an option for configuring SNMP version 3.

■ **Enable SSH for access to the router:** CCP will enable and configure SSH on crypto Cisco IOS images, but unlike AutoSecure, it will not enable Service Control Point (SCP) or disable other access and file transfer services, such as FTP.

For the details on what is included with CCP, and its detailed functioning (such as whether admin rights are required), read the release notes for the specific version you are working with.

Summary

This chapter had two distinct parts. In the first part, we explored Cisco Network Foundation Protection and discussed, among other things:

■ Threats that exploit network availability drive infrastructure protection.

■ Cisco Network Foundation Protection implements a divide-and-conquer approach to infrastructure protection.

■ Control plane security tools include CoPP and Cisco AutoSecure.

■ Management plane security tools include RBAC and AAA services.

■ Data plane security tools include ACLs, DHCP snooping, and Dynamic ARP spoofing.

In the second part of this chapter, we saw how Cisco Configuration Professional can be used to implement Cisco Network Foundation Protection, and how CCP provides a comprehensive and easy-to-use GUI tool for router configuration and service integration. Among other things, you learned:

■ Features include security, unified communication, license management, application management, and others.

■ Communities, templates, and user profiles provide role-based access control and streamline the process of configuring several devices.

■ The Security Audit Wizard and the One-Step Lockdown tool are device hardening options.

References

For additional information, refer to these Cisco.com resources:

Cisco Configuration Professional User Guide (Version 2.5), http://www.cisco.com/en/US/docs/net_mgmt/cisco_configuration_professional/v2_5/olh/ccp.pdf

"Cisco Network Foundation Protection (NFP)," http://www.cisco.com/en/US/products/ps6642/index.html

Review Questions

Use the questions here to review what you learned in this chapter. The correct answers are found in the Appendix, "Answers to Chapter Review Questions."

1. Which device plane processes traffic generated or received by the network device itself, used for the creation and operation of the network, and managed by the CPU in the device route processor?

   a. Control plane
   b. Data plane
   c. Forwarding plane
   d. Management plane

2. What is the main difference between Control Plane Policing (CoPP) and Control Plane Protection (CPPr)?

   a. No difference exists; both terms define the same functionality.
   b. CoPP is an extension of CPPr.
   c. CPPr is an extension of CoPP.
   d. CoPP relates to rate limiting, while CPPr defines QoS-like filters.
   e. CoPP allows more granularity on CPPr rules.

3. Which of the following are components of Control Plane Protection? (Choose two.)

    a. Routing protocol authentication

    b. SNMP

    c. Cisco SecureX

    d. Cisco AutoSecure

    e. Zone-based firewall

4. Which options are examples of data plane security controls? (Choose two.)

    a. RBAC

    b. CoPP

    c. Port security

    d. Spanning Tree Control

    e. Access control lists

    f. AAA

5. Match the plane with the right traffic type.

Planes

    a. Management

    b. Data

    c. Control

Traffic

    d. User-generated packets

    e. Packets used for the creation and operation of the network itself

    f. Packets used to manage the network

6. Which techniques could be used to mitigate a spoofing attack? (Choose two.)

    a. TTL filtering

    b. Access class

    c. Private VLANs

    d. Access list

    e. Management plane

    f. Unicast Reverse Path Forwarding

7. Which management tool is available on the router's flash and can be used to configure some LAN and WAN interfaces of the router, as well as minimal Cisco IOS Software security features?

    a. Cisco AnyConnect

    b. Cisco Configuration Professional Express

    c. Cisco Secure Desktop

    d. CiscoWorks

    e. Cisco Security Manager

    f. Cisco Configuration Professional

8. Match the Cisco Configuration Professional component with its definition.

    CCP components

    a. Communities

    b. Templates

    c. Profiles

    d. Wizards

    Component definitions

    e. Parameterized configuration files

    f. GUI views that allow role-based access control over Cisco Configuration Professional menus and options

    g. Groups of devices that share common components

    h. GUI tools to hide the complexity of commands

9. What does the Parameterize button do when creating Cisco Configuration Professional templates?

    a. Creates variables that acquire different values for different devices

    b. Designates a parameter for use across several communities

    c. Applies the same parameter to the configurations of all devices where the parameter is applied

    d. Removes the special value of a given parameter

10. Which of the following is implemented by Cisco Configuration Professional when the One-Step Lockdown option is used?

    a. Control Plane Protection

    b. Security Wizard

    c. AutoSecure

    d. Packet Tracer

Chapter 4

Securing the Management Plane on Cisco IOS Devices and AAA

This chapter describes how to securely implement the management and reporting features of Cisco IOS devices. More precisely, it discusses the following:

- Technologies used in secure management and reporting, such as syslog, Network Time Protocol (NTP), Secure Shell (SSH), and Simple Network Management Protocol version 3 (SNMPv3).

- Proper password configuration, management, and password recovery procedures and how to safeguard a copy of the operating system and configuration file with the use of authentication, authorization, and accounting (AAA) both locally and on an external database.

- The use and configuration of Cisco Secure Access Control Server (ACS) as an external AAA database

- Secure management and reporting, as well as AAA, from both the command-line interface (CLI) and from Cisco Configuration Professional (CCP).

We all know that secure management of our equipment starts with physical security. Physical controls were discussed in Chapter 1, "Network Security Concepts and Policies." In this chapter, therefore, we will focus on the secure remote access of our equipment, and proper reporting of events. We will also discuss methods to manage an administrator's credentials locally or on a centralized server.

Configuring Secure Administration Access

As discussed in Chapter 3, "Network Foundation Protection and Cisco Configuration Professional," local access to a router usually involves a direct connection to a console port on the Cisco router.

Remote access typically involves allowing Telnet, Secure Shell (SSH), HTTP, HTTPS, or Simple Network Management Protocol (SNMP) connections to the Cisco IOS device from a computer on the same subnet or a different subnet. As an example, in Chapter 3, we saw how to remotely access our Cisco IOS router using CCP.

Note Though SNMP is discussed sparsely in this section, it will be presented in greater detail later in this chapter in the section "Implementing Secure Management and Reporting."

It is preferable to allow only local access to the Cisco IOS device because some remote-access protocols, such as Telnet, send the data, including usernames and passwords, to the network device in plaintext.

If remote access is required, it is recommended that you apply one of the following options:

- Establish a dedicated management network as shown in Figure 4-1. The management network should include only identified administration hosts and connections to a dedicated interface on the router.

- Encrypt all the traffic between the administrator computer and the router.

Figure 4-1 *Dedicated Management Network*

In either case, you can configure a packet filter to allow only the identified administration hosts and preferred protocols to access the router. For example, you can configure the packet filter to permit only SSH requests from the IP address of the administration host to initiate a connection to the routers in the network.

Configuring an SSH Daemon for Secure Management Access

SSH was discussed in Chapter 3, but it's a topic worth revisiting briefly because it's part of providing secure management access to the Cisco router. The SSH daemon is a feature that enables an SSH client to make a secure, encrypted connection to a Cisco router. This connection provides functionality similar to that of an inbound Telnet connection, but it also provides strong encryption to be used with local authentication, thus ensuring secure access and communication to network devices such as routers, switches, firewalls, intrusion prevention system (IPS) sensors, and so forth. While Telnet authentication can be as simple as presenting the right password, SSH always requires presenting a username and a password. The SSH daemon in Cisco IOS Software works with publicly and commercially available SSH clients, such as PuTTY, OpenSSH, or Tera Term. To refresh your knowledge of SSH configuration, here are the steps to configure your Cisco router to support an SSH daemon using the CLI:

Step 1. Configure the IP domain name of your network using the **ip domain-name** *domain-name* command in global configuration mode:

```
Router(config)# ip domain-name cisco.com
```

Note The domain name and the hostname are used for the generation of the RSA key pairs. If there are any existing key pairs, it is recommended that you overwrite them using the command **crypto key zeroize rsa**

Step 2. Generate keys to be used with SSH by generating the Rivest, Shamir, and Adleman (RSA) keys using the **crypto key generate rsa general-keys modulus** *modulus-size* command in global configuration mode. The modulus determines the size of the RSA key. The larger the modulus, the more secure the RSA key. However, keys with large modulus values take longer to generate, and encryption and decryption operations take longer with larger keys:

```
Router(config)# crypto key generate rsa general-keys modulus 1024
```

Note The minimum recommended key length is modulus 1024. However, as per NIST SP800-313A, a modulus smaller than 2048 bits will be disallowed for federal use after 2013; see http://csrc.nist.gov/publications/nistpubs/800-131A/sp800-131A.pdf.

Step 3. Optionally, to display the generated keys, use the **show crypto key mypub-key rsa** command in privileged EXEC mode.

Step 4.   Configure the time that the router waits for the SSH client to respond using the **ip ssh time-out** *seconds* command in global configuration mode:

```
Router(config)# ip ssh time-out 120
```

Step 5.   Configure the SSH retries (the number of attempts after which the interface will reset) using the **ip ssh authentication-retries** *integer* command in global configuration mode:

```
Router(config)# ip ssh authentication-retries 4
```

Step 6.   Enable vty inbound SSH sessions:

```
Router(config)# line vty 0 4
Router(config-line)# transport input ssh
```

The SSH protocol is automatically enabled when you generate the SSH (RSA) keys. Once the keys are created, you can access the router SSH daemon using your SSH client software.

Tip   If you are using a version of Cisco IOS Software that supports both SSHv1 and SSHv2, by default SSH runs in compatibility mode; that is, both SSHv1and SSHv2 connections are honored. If you are running Cisco IOS Release 12.3(4)T or later, you can use the **ip ssh version** {1 | 2} command to configure support for only one version of SSH.

The procedure for connecting to a Cisco router SSH daemon varies depending on the SSH client application that you use. Generally, the SSH client passes your username to the router SSH daemon. The router SSH daemon prompts you for the correct password. After the password has been verified, you can configure and manage the router as if you were a standard vty user.

Tip   Cisco routers with Cisco IOS Software Releases 12.1(3)T and later can act as both SSH clients and SSH daemons. This means that you could initiate an SSH client-to-server session from your router to a central SSH daemon system using the **ssh** command. SSH employs strong encryption to protect the SSH client-to-server session. Unlike Telnet, where anyone with a sniffer can see exactly what you are sending to and receiving from your routers, SSH encrypts the entire session.

Many vulnerabilities have been reported for SSH Version 1, such as the following root exploit: http://www.doecirc.energy.gov/techbull/archive/CIRCTech02-001.shtml. It is therefore recommended to use SSH Version 2.

Configuring Passwords on Cisco IOS Devices

Strong passwords and similar secrets, such as SNMP community strings, are the primary defense against unauthorized access to your Cisco IOS devices. The first step to secure a device's administrative access is to configure secure system passwords. The best scalable way to handle most passwords is to maintain them on a TACACS+ or RADIUS authentication server, such as the Cisco Secure Access Control Server (ACS) and Cisco Identity Services Engine (ISE). (TACACS+, RADIUS, and Cisco Secure ACS will be covered later in this chapter.) However, routers can have locally configured passwords for privileged access and can have other password information in their configuration files. This section focuses only on configuring local passwords.

The first step to secure Cisco router administrative access is to configure secure system passwords.

A password can be established on individual lines, such as the console and vty, and for the privileged EXEC mode. Passwords are case sensitive.

By default, the console port does not require a password for console administrative access; however, you should always configure a console port line-level password. As shown in Example 4-1, you can use the **line console 0** command followed by the **login** and **password** subcommands to require login and establish a login password on the console line.

By default, Cisco routers support up to five simultaneous vty (Telnet) sessions. On the router, the vty ports are numbered from 0 through 4. Example 4-1 shows how you can use the **line vty 0 4** command followed by the **login** and **password** subcommands to log in to Telnet sessions. However, in Chapter 3 you were introduced to a better practice using the **login local** command, where an administrator was authenticated against a local database with the global **username** command.

Example 4-1 *Configuring the Console and Virtual Terminal Passwords*

```
R1(config)# line console 0
R1(config-line)# login
R1(config-line)# password M3rcury$12
R1(config-line)# exit
R1(config)# line vty 0 4
R1(config-line)# login
R1(config-line)# password V3nus$2012
```

The **enable secret** *password* global command restricts access to the privileged EXEC mode. You can use the **enable secret** global configuration command to configure the enable secret password. The enable secret password is always hashed inside the router configuration using a Message Digest 5 (MD5) hashing algorithm; it never appears in cleartext. Hashing will be covered in detail in Chapter 12, "Fundamentals of Cryptography and VPN."

The enable password is also used to enter enable mode, but this weak password configuration is from earlier versions of Cisco IOS Software. By default, the enable password is not encrypted in the router configuration. The **enable password** global configuration command was kept for backward compatibility in case you downgrade the router to a version of Cisco IOS Software that does not support the **enable secret** command. If both **enable password** and **enable secret** are configured, the **enable password** *password* is ignored and only the **enable secret** *password* is used.

If you forget the enable password, regardless of whether it was created using the **enable secret** command or the **enable password** command, you have no alternative but to replace it using the Cisco router password recovery procedure specific to your Cisco equipment, which you can find in Cisco Document ID 6130 at http://www.cisco.com/en/US/products/sw/iosswrel/ps1831/products_tech_note09186a00801746e6.shtml.

With the exception of the enable secret password, all Cisco router passwords are stored in plaintext by default within the router configuration. You can view these passwords with the **show running-config** command. Sniffers can also see these passwords if your TFTP server configuration files traverse an unsecured intranet or Internet connection. If an intruder gains access to the TFTP server where the router configuration files are stored, the intruder is able to obtain these passwords.

As a safeguard against this possible exploit, the **service password-encryption** command encrypts all the passwords (except the previously hashed enable secret password) in the device configuration file, and will encrypt any passwords you set after entering this command until you turn the command off with the **no** form of the command. This method, which uses the Vigenère method (also explained in Chapter 12), is not as safe as MD5, which is used with the **enable secret** command, but prevents casual discovery of the device line-level passwords. To configure password encryption, use the **service password-encryption** global command. To remove the **service password-encryption** command, use **no service password-encryption.**

Also by default, Cisco router auxiliary ports do not require a password for remote administrative access. Administrators sometimes use this port to remotely configure and monitor the router using a dialup modem connection. To combat this vulnerability, you can use the **line aux 0** command followed by the **login** and **password** subcommands to require login and establish a login password on an incoming auxiliary line.

Note   If you want to turn off the EXEC process for a specific line, such as on the auxiliary port, use the **no exec** command within the line configuration mode.

Setting Timeouts for Router Lines

Another topic important to the security of the management of the device is the line timeouts. As you learned during your CCNA studies, by default, an administrative interface stays active (and logged in) for 10 minutes after the last session activity, and you should adjust timers using the **exec-timeout** command in line configuration mode for each of the line types used. You can also use Cisco Configuration Professional, introduced in Chapter 3, to configure the exec-timeout for the vty lines.

Configuring the Minimum Length for Router Passwords

Cisco IOS Software Release 12.3(1) and later allow you to set the minimum character length for all router passwords by using the **security passwords** global configuration command. This command provides enhanced security access to the router by allowing you to specify a minimum password length (0 to 16 characters); this eliminates common passwords that are short and prevalent on most networks, such as lab and cisco. Example 4-2 demonstrates the **security passwords** command set for a minimum of ten characters.

Example 4-2   security passwords *Command*

```
R1(config)# security passwords min-length 10
```

This command affects username passwords, enable passwords and enable secret passwords, and line passwords that are created after the command is executed. Existing router passwords remain unaffected.

When creating passwords for Cisco routers, always keep the following rules in mind:

- Establish a minimum of ten characters for a password.
- Passwords can include the following:
  - Any alphanumeric character, but is case sensitive
  - A mix of uppercase and lowercase characters
  - Symbols and spaces
- Passwords should not use dictionary words.
- Password-leading spaces are ignored, but no spaces after the first character are ignored.
- Decide when and how often the passwords should be changed.

After the **security passwords** command has been enabled, any attempt to create a new password that is less than the specified length fails and results in an error message similar to this message:

```
Password too short - must be at least 10 characters. Password
configuration failed.
```

Enhanced Username Password Security

As discussed briefly in Chapter 3, Cisco routers can maintain a list of usernames and passwords for performing local login authentication. System administrators can choose to use an MD5 hashing mechanism to encrypt a user password. MD5 hashing of passwords is a much better algorithm than the standard type 7 found in the **service password-encryption** command.

MD5 hashing of a Cisco IOS user password is accomplished with the **username secret** command in global configuration mode. Administrators can choose to enter a plain-text password for MD5 hashing by the router (option **0**), or they can enter a previously encrypted MD5 secret (option **5**). The syntax for the **username secret** command is as follows:

```
username name secret { [0] password | 5 encrypted-secret}
```

Table 4-1 shows the parameters of the **username secret** command.

Table 4-1   username secret *Parameters*

Parameter	Description
name	This parameter specifies the username.
0	(Optional) This option indicates that the plaintext password is to be hashed by the router using MD5.
password	This parameter is the plaintext password to be hashed using MD5.
5	This parameter indicates that the encrypted-secret password was hashed using MD5.
encrypted-secret	This parameter is the MD5 encrypted-secret password that is stored as the encrypted user password.

Example 4-3 shows an example of the **username secret** command.

Example 4-3   username secret *Command*

```
R1(config)# username SecAdmin secret 0 Curium2012
R1(config)# username SecAdmin secret 5 $1$uypB$vAWRWP.qFQqb65.KxVxKg1
```

Dissecting the Hashed Password Format

In Example 4-3, **secret 5** means that the password is not in cleartext. The password was hashed with MD5. The hashed password, 1uypB$vAWRWP.qFQqb65.KxVxKg1, breaks down as follows:

- 1 appearing between the first dollar sign and second dollar sign indicates that the password was hashed with MD5.

- uypB appearing between the second and third dollar signs represents the randomized salt phrase added to the enable secret password prior to hashing.

- A salt value, typically 48 to 128 bits long and randomly generated, helps to produce a hash result that will not match against a lookup table of hashed dictionary words, because dictionary words have fewer bits.

- The salt phrase is stored in your configuration file, and the Cisco IOS router can use it along with the enable password you type to generate an MD5 hash value. If the value calculated from using the salt and the password you just typed in the MD5 algorithm matches the hash result stored in the configuration, such as vAWRWP.qFQqb65.KxVxKg1 in Example 4-3, the router knows that the password that was typed is legitimate.

Securing ROM Monitor

By default, Cisco IOS routers allow a break sequence during startup that forces the router into ROM monitor mode, which can be used for a password recovery procedure. This procedure, if performed correctly, leaves the router configuration intact. Anyone who gains physical access to the router console port can enter ROM monitor mode, reset the enable secret password, and discover the router configuration. You can mitigate this potential security breach by using the **no service password-recovery** global configuration command, as shown in Example 4-4. This command is a hidden Cisco IOS command and has no arguments or keywords.

Example 4-4 no service password-recovery *Command*

```
R1(config)# no service password-recovery
WARNING:
Executing this command will disable password recovery mechanism. Do not execute this
  command without another plan for password recovery.
Are you sure you want to continue? [yes/no]: yes
R1(config)#
```

Note   To recover a device after the **no service password-recovery** command has been entered, press the **Break** key within 5 seconds after the image decompresses during the boot. You are prompted to confirm the Break key action. When you confirm the action, the startup configuration is erased, the password recovery procedure is enabled, and the router boots with the factory default configuration. If you do not confirm the Break key action, the router boots normally with the No Service Password-Recovery feature enabled.

Securing the Cisco IOS Image and Configuration Files

Router files are critical to the operations of the router. Operating system images and configuration files are stored in the file system in the router's flash and nonvolatile memory. The Cisco IOS Resilient Configuration feature enables a router to secure and maintain a working copy of the running image and configuration so that those files can withstand malicious attempts to erase the contents of persistent storage (NVRAM and flash storage).

A great challenge for network operators is the total downtime that is experienced after a router has been compromised and its operating software and configuration data are erased from its persistent storage. The operator must retrieve an archived copy (hopefully one is available) of the configuration and a working Cisco IOS image to restore the router. Recovery must then be performed for each affected router, adding to the total network downtime.

The Cisco IOS Resilient Configuration feature is intended to speed up the recovery process. This feature maintains a secure working copy of the router image and the startup configuration at all times. The user cannot remove these secure files. This set of Cisco IOS image and router running configuration files is referred to as the *bootset*.

Table 4-2 describes the key commands that are required to secure the Cisco IOS image and running configuration using the **secure boot-image** command:

```
R1(config)# secure boot-image
R1(config)# secure boot-config
```

Table 4-2   secure *Commands*

Command	Description
secure boot-image	This command enables Cisco IOS image resilience. When turned on for the first time, the running image (as displayed in the **show version** command output) is secured, and a syslog entry is generated. This command functions properly only when the system is configured to run an image from a disk with an Advanced Technology Attachment (ATA) interface. Images that are booted from a TFTP server cannot be secured. Because this command has the effect of "hiding" the running image, the image file is not included in any directory listing of the disk. If the router is configured to boot with Cisco IOS resilience and an image with a different version of Cisco IOS is detected, a message similar to this is displayed at boot: "ios resilience :Archived image and configuration version 12.2 differs from running version 12.3."
secure boot-config	This command takes a snapshot of the router running configuration and securely archives it in persistent storage.

Secured files do not appear in the output of a **dir** command that is issued from an executive shell because the Cisco IOS file system prevents the secure files in a directory from being listed. ROM monitor mode does not have any such restriction and can list and boot secured files. Because the running image and running configuration archives are not visible in the output from the Cisco IOS command **dir**, use the **show secure bootset** command to verify the archive existence.

Example 4-5 shows an example of the **show secure bootset** command output. This command is important to verify that the Cisco IOS image and configuration files have been properly backed up and secured.

Example 4-5   show secure bootset *Command Output*

```
R1# show secure bootset
IOS resilience router id FHK085031MD

IOS image resilience version 12.3 activated at 05:00:59 UTC Fri Feb 10 2006
Secure archive flash:c1841-advsecurityk9-mz.123-14.T1.bin type is image (elf) []
 file size is 17533860 bytes, run size is 17699528 bytes
 Runnable image, entry point 0x8000F000, run from ram

IOS configuration resilience version 12.3 activated at 05:01:02 UTC Fri Feb 10 2
  006
Secure archive flash:.runcfg-20060210-050102.ar type is config
configuration archive size 4014 bytes
```

Configuring Multiple Privilege Levels

Cisco routers enable you to configure various privilege levels for your administrators. You can configure different passwords to control which administrators have access to the various privilege levels. Configuring various privilege levels is especially useful in a help desk environment where you want certain administrators to be able to configure and monitor every part of the router (level 15), while you want other administrators to only monitor, and not configure, the router (customized levels 2 to 14). There are 16 privilege levels, 0 to 15; level 0 is reserved for the user-level access privileges, levels 1 to 14 are levels you can customize, and level 15 is reserved for enable mode privileges.

To assign privileges to levels 2 to 14, use the **privilege** command from global configuration mode:

```
privilege mode {level level command | reset command}
```

Table 4-3 describes the parameters for this command and Example 4-6 demonstrates its use.

Table 4-3   privilege *Command Parameters*

Parameter	Description
mode	This command argument specifies the configuration mode. Use the Router(config)# **privilege ?** command to see a complete list of router configuration modes available on your router.
level	(Optional) This keyword enables setting a privilege level with a specified command.
level command	(Optional) This parameter is the privilege level that is associated with a command. You can specify up to 16 privilege levels, using numbers 0 to 15.
reset	(Optional) This keyword resets the privilege level of a command.
command	(Optional) Use this argument when you want to reset the privilege level.

Example 4-6   *Configuring Multiple Privilege Levels*

```
R1(config)# privilege exec level 2 ping
R1(config)# enable secret level 2 Cariboo2012
```

To assign a password to the custom privilege level, use the command **enable secret level** *level password* in global configuration mode.

To enter a custom privilege level, use the command **enable** *level* and enter the password that was assigned to the custom privilege level.

Example 4-6 sets the **ping** command to require privilege level 2 or above access and establishes Cariboo2012 as the secret password for privilege level 2. When you enter the **enable 2** command, as shown in Example 4-7, the router prompts you for the enable secret password for privilege level 2.

Use the **show privilege** command to display the current privilege level, as shown in Example 4-7.

Example 4-7   *Using the* **enable** *level and* **show privilege** *Commands*

```
R1> enable 2
Password: Cariboo2012
R1# show privilege
Current privilege level is 2
```

Configuring Role-Based Command-Line Interface Access

The Role-Based CLI Access feature allows you to create different "views" of router configurations for different users. Views define which commands are accepted from different users and what configuration information is visible to them. With Role-Based CLI Access, you can exercise better control over Cisco networking devices.

Note   Before you create a view, you must enable authentication, authorization, and accounting (AAA) using the **aaa new-model** command or CCP. AAA configurations are covered in the "Configuring AAA on a Cisco Router Using the Local Database" section of this chapter.

The steps used to configure and confirm a view are as follows:

Step 1.   Router> **enable view**

Step 2.   Router# **configure terminal**

Step 3.   Router(config)# **parser view** *view-name*

Step 4.   Router(config-view)# **secret 5** *encrypted-password*

Step 5.   Router(config-view)# **commands** *parser-mode* {include | include-exclusive | exclude} [all] [interface *interface-name* | *command*]

Step 6.   Router(config-view)# **exit**

Step 7.   Router(config)# **exit**

Step 8.   Router# **enable** [*view-name*]

Step 9.   Router# **show parser view** [all]

The last two steps allow you to preview the views that you have configured. The next few pages discuss these commands in detail.

The key commands specific to configuring views for Role-Based CLI Access are shown next and are presented again in Example 4-8. When a system is in "root view," it has all the access privileges of a user who has level 15 privileges. To configure any view for the system, you must be in the root view.

The difference between a user who has level 15 privileges and a root view user is that a root view user can configure a new view and add or remove commands from the view.

To access the root view, use first the **enable view** command and then the **parser view** command:

```
R1> enable view
R1# configure terminal
R1(config)# parser view view-name
R1(config-view)# secret 0 | 5 view-password
```

Table 4-4 shows the commands and parameters used to access and modify the root view.

Table 4-4   enable view *and* parser view *Command Parameters*

Parameter	Description
enable view	This command puts you in root view, from where you create views and establish view attributes.
config terminal	This command puts you in global configuration mode.
parser view *view name*	This command creates a view and enters view configuration mode.
secret 0 | 5 *view-password*	This command configures a password for this view: **secret 0** specifies that an unencrypted password follows. **secret 5** specifies that an encrypted secret follows.

Next, you must assign the allowed commands to the selected view. Use the **commands** command in view configuration mode to assign the allowed commands. The syntax for this command is as follows:

```
R1(config-view)# commands parser-mode {include | include-exclusive | exclude} [all]
[interface interface-name | command]
```

Table 4-5 shows the parameters used with the **commands** command.

Table 4-5   commands *Command Parameters*

Parameter	Description
parser-mode	The mode in which the specified command exists (for example, EXEC mode)
include	Adds a command or an interface to the view and allows the same command or interface to be added to an additional view
include-exclusive	Adds a command or an interface to the view and excludes the same command or interface from being added to all other views
exclude	Excludes a command or an interface from the view
all	A "wildcard" that allows every command in a specified configuration mode that begins with the same keyword or every subinterface for a specified interface to be part of the view
interface *interface-name*	An interface that is added to the view
command	A command that is added to the view

Example 4-8 displays a complete configuration of a new view, called NetOps.

Example 4-8   *Commands to Enable Root View and to Create New Views*

```
R1> enable view
Password:
R1# configure terminal
Enter configuration commands, one per line. End with CNTL/Z.
R1(config)# parser view NetOps
R1(config-view)# secret 0 hardtocrackpw
R1(config-view)# commands exec include ping
R1(config-view)# commands exec include all show
R1(config-view)# commands exec include telnet
R1(config-view)# commands exec include traceroute
R1(config-view)# commands exec include write
R1(config-view)# commands exec include configure
R1(config-view)# commands configure include access-list
R1(config-view)# commands configure include all interface
R1(config-view)# commands configure include all ip
```

To verify a view, use the **enable view** command. Enter the name of the view that you want to verify and provide the password to log in to the view. After you are in the view, use the question mark (**?**) command to verify that the commands available in the view are correct. Example 4-9 shows the commands only accessible from the NetOps view at the privilege mode and at the configuration mode.

Example 4-9   *Verifying Commands Available to the NetOps View*

```
R1# enable view NetOps
Password: hardtocrackpw
R1#
Jan 3 13:45:03.887: %PARSER-6-VIEW_SWITCH: successfully set to view 'NetOps'.
R1#?
Exec commands:
 configure Enter configuration mode
 enable  Turn on privileged commands
 exit  Exit from the EXEC
 ping  Send echo messages
 show  Show running system information
 telnet  Open a telnet connection
 traceroute Trace route to destination
 write  Write running configuration to memory, network, or terminal
R1# configure terminal
R1(config)#?
Configure commands:
 access-list Add an access list entry
 do   To run exec commands in config mode
 exit   Exit from configure mode
 interface Select an interface to configure
 ip   Global IP configuration subcommands
```

Implementing Secure Management and Reporting

The previous section of this chapter dealt with securing access to Cisco IOS devices. Before we look at AAA configuration and how it assists with secure access, let's have a look at secure management and reporting, because these features can be useful while troubleshooting AAA configuration.

In this section, we examine the skills necessary to implement secure management and reporting of Cisco IOS devices. The technologies will discuss in this section are as follows:

- Syslog

- Network Time Protocol (NTP)

- Simple Network Management Protocol Version 3 (SNMPv3)

In addition, we will examine some design aspects of a management infrastructure.

Planning Considerations for Secure Management and Reporting

Configuring logging for your Cisco routers is a straightforward operation when your network contains only a few Cisco routers. However, logging and reading information from hundreds of devices can prove to be a challenging proposition and can raise the following issues and considerations:

- What are the most important logs?

- How are important messages separated from routine notifications?

- How do you prevent tampering with logs?

- How do you ensure that time stamps match?

- What log data is needed in criminal investigations?

- How do you deal with the volume of log messages?

- How do you manage all the devices?

- How can you track changes when attacks or network failures occur?

Securing administrative access and device configurations is also a straightforward operation for smaller Cisco router networks. However, managing administrative access and device configurations for many devices can raise questions such as those listed.

Each of these issues is specific to your needs. To identify the priorities of reporting and monitoring, you must get input from management and from the network and security teams. The security policy that you implement should also play a large role in answering these questions.

From a reporting standpoint, most networking devices can send syslog data that can be invaluable when you are troubleshooting network problems or security threats. You can send this data to your syslog analysis host from any device whose logs you want to view. This data can be viewed in real time, on demand, and in scheduled reports. Depending on the device involved, you can choose various logging levels to ensure that the correct amount of data is sent to the logging device. You must also flag device log data within the analysis software to permit granular viewing and reporting. For example, during an attack, the log data that is provided by Layer 2 switches might not be as interesting as the data that is provided by the IPS.

Configuration change management is another issue related to secure management. When a network is under attack, it is important to know the state of critical network devices and when the last known modifications occurred. Creating a plan for change management should be a part of your comprehensive security policy; however, at a minimum, you should record changes using authentication systems on the devices and archive configurations using FTP or TFTP.

Secure Management and Reporting Architecture

In the previous chapter, Figure 3-4 showed a management module with two network segments that are separated by a Cisco IOS router that acts as a firewall and a VPN termination device. In Chapter 3, we introduced the general concept of secure management and reporting, such as the difference between out-of-band (OOB) management and in-band management. Now we will look at some specific guidelines.

Secure Management and Reporting Guidelines

The guidelines for OOB management and in-band management of the architecture are as follows:

- Management guidelines

  - Keep clocks on hosts and network devices synchronized.

  - Record changes and archive configurations.

- OOB management guidelines

  - Provide the highest level of security and mitigate the risk of passing unsecure management protocols over the production network.

- In-band management guidelines to manage or monitor devices:

  - Use VPN, SSH, or SSL (HTTPS with CCP) when possible.

  - Decide whether the management channel needs to be open at all times.

To ensure that log messages are synchronized with one another, clocks on hosts and network devices must be synchronized. For devices that support it, NTP provides a way to ensure that accurate time is kept on all devices. When you are dealing with an attack, seconds matter, because it is important to identify the order in which a specified attack occurred.

NTP is used to synchronize the clocks of various devices across a network. Synchronization of the clocks within a network is critical for digital certificates and for correct interpretation of events within the syslog data.

Enabling Time Features

Because many things that are involved in the security of your network depend on an accurate date and time stamp, such as security certificates, it is important that the router maintains the correct time.

You can use Cisco Configuration Professional to configure the date and time settings of the router in three ways:

■ Synchronize with the local PC clock

■ Manually edit the date and time

■ Configure NTP

Network Time Protocol

Time synchronization is of essence in secure management and reporting. For management, using time synchronization ensures that digital certificates are used consistently with regard to their expiration and validity. For reporting, time synchronization results in consistent correlation of events across the management infrastructure, and a more effective event and incident detection and analysis.

NTP is a method to synchronize date and time settings for devices on the network. NTP uses User Datagram Protocol (UDP) port 123 and is documented in RFC 1305. Simple Network Time Protocol (SNTP) is a simpler, less secure version of NTP.

When you implement NTP in your network, you can set up your own master clock, or you can use a publicly available NTP server on the Internet. If you implement your own master clock, you should synchronize the private network to Coordinated Universal Time (UTC) via satellite or radio.

You need to be careful when you implement NTP. An attacker can launch a denial of service (DoS) attack by sending bogus NTP data across the Internet to your network in an attempt to change the clocks on network devices, possibly causing digital certificates to become invalid. Further, an attacker could attempt to confuse a network administrator during an attack by disrupting the clocks on network devices. This scenario would make it difficult for the network administrator to determine the order of syslog events on multiple devices.

NTP version 3 (NTPv3) and later support a cryptographic authentication mechanism between NTP peers. You can use this authentication mechanism in addition to access control lists (ACL) that specify which network devices are allowed to synchronize with other network devices, to help mitigate such an attack.

Note   You should weigh the benefits of using clock time from the Internet against the possible risk of doing so and allowing unsecured packets through the firewall. Many NTP servers on the Internet don't require any authentication of peers and don't have a requirement of being accurate. Trustworthy sources of time are Symmetricom (http://www.symmetricom.com), Meingerb (http://www.meinberg-usa.com), and National Research Council Canada (http://www.nrc-cnrc.gc.ca/eng/services/time/index.html).

More information on NTP, such as the level of clock hierarchy known as stratum, can be found online at http://en.wikipedia.org/wiki/Network_Time_Protocol.

Using a Cisco IOS Router as an NTP Server

It is possible to configure your Cisco IOS router as an NTP master, which other appliances will contact to synchronize on. The following commands are used to set the router as an NTP master:

```
router# conf t
router(config)# ntp authenticate
router(config)# ntp trusted-key 99
router(config)# ntp master
router(config)# key chain NTP
router(config-keychain)# key 99
router(config-keychain-key)# key-string PR0PERT1ME
router(config-keychain-key)# end
```

Using Syslog Logging for Network Security

Syslog is the standard for logging system events. As shown in Figure 4-2, syslog implementations contain two types of systems:

- **Syslog servers:** These systems are also known as log hosts. These systems accept and process log messages from syslog clients.

- **Syslog clients:** Syslog clients are routers or other types of Cisco equipment that generate and forward log messages to syslog servers.

Figure 4-2 *Syslog Systems*

Note   Performing forensics on router logs can become very difficult if your router clocks are not running the proper time. It is recommended that you use an NTP facility to ensure that all of your routers are operating at the correct time.

If you are not running your own NTP service, you should at least consider synchronizing on an authenticated public NTP service such as the one offered by the National Research Council Canada at http://www.nrc-cnrc.gc.ca/eng/solutions/advisory/calibration/time_frequency.html#authenticated.

Also note that it is recommended to have redundant syslog servers on a network. Many approaches exist on how to use the two systems, such as

- Have the network device send its syslog messages at both servers.

- Have the network device send its syslog messages to only one server but have that server, keeping a copy of the message, forward it immediately to the second server.

Implementing Log Messaging for Security

Implementing a router logging facility is an important part of any network security policy. Cisco routers can log information regarding configuration changes, ACL violations, interface status changes, and many other types of events. Cisco routers can send log messages to several different facilities. You should configure the router to send log messages to one or more of the following items:

- **Console:** Console logging is used when modifying or testing the router while it is connected to the console. Messages sent to the console are not stored by the router and, therefore, are not very valuable as security events.

- **Terminal monitor:** The console port works at 9600 bauds and thus can't simultaneously handle a large quantity of log messages. It is therefore recommended that you remotely connect to the device, using SSH preferably, and that you issue the **terminal monitor** command to receive the log message on this current vty session. This is the subject of the next bullet.

- **Terminal lines:** You can configure enabled EXEC sessions to receive log messages on any terminal lines. Similar to console logging, this type of logging is not stored by the router and, therefore, is valuable only to the user on that line.

- **Buffered logging:** You can direct a router to store log messages in router memory. Buffered logging is a little more useful as a security tool but has the drawback of having events cleared whenever the router is rebooted. Note also that buffers can be written to flash.

- **SNMP traps:** Certain router events can be processed by the router SNMP agent and forwarded as SNMP traps to an external SNMP server. SNMP traps, addressed to destination port UDP 162, are a viable security logging facility but require the configuration and maintenance of an SNMP system.

■ **Syslog:** You can configure Cisco routers to forward log messages to an external syslog service, destination port UDP 514. This service can reside on any number of servers, including Microsoft Windows and UNIX-based systems, or since the Cisco Security MARS appliance is at end-of-life status, consider using Cisco Security Manager (CSM) or a Cisco ecosystem partner for Security Information and Event Management System (SIEM), such as Splunk, as a syslog destination. Syslog is the most popular message logging facility because it provides long-term log storage capabilities and a central location for all router messages.

Cisco router log messages fall into one of eight levels, as shown in Table 4-6. The lower the level number, the higher the severity level, as the log messages in the table denote.

Table 4-6   *Cisco Router Log Severity Messages*

Syslog Level	Definition	Example
0: LOG_EMERG	A panic condition normally broadcast to all users	Cisco IOS Software could not load.
1: LOG_ALERT	A condition that should be corrected immediately, such as a corrupted system database	Temperature too high.
2: LOG_CRIT	Critical conditions; for example, hard device errors	Unable to allocate memory.
3: LOG_ERR	Errors	Invalid memory size.
4: LOG_WARNING	Warning messages	Crypto operation failed.
5: LOG_NOTICE	Conditions that are not error conditions, but should possibly be handled specially	Interface changed state, up or down.
6: LOG_INFO	Informational messages	Packet denied by ACL.
7: LOG_DEBUG	Messages that contain information normally of use only when debugging a program	Packet type invalid.

Note   When entering logging levels in commands, you must specify the level name or the level number.

Cisco router log messages contain three main parts:

■ Time stamp

■ Log message name and severity level

■ Message text

Figure 4-3 shows a syslog entry example for a level 5 syslog message, indicating that someone has configured the router using the vty 0 port.

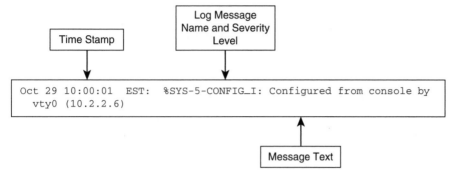

Figure 4-3 *Log Message Format*

Figure 4-4 illustrates the configuration of syslog settings using Cisco Configuration Professional. Navigate to **Configure > Router > Logging** to enable logging of system messages, and to specify logging hosts where logs can be kept.

By clicking **Edit**, you can change the syslog settings and specify the level of logging messages that you want to send and to collect, and enter the hostname or IP address of multiple logging hosts.

Figure 4-4 *Enabling Syslog Logging on CCP*

The logging settings are shown in Figure 4-4. The top of the window allows the configuration of syslog server parameters. The bottom half allows the configuration of the router buffers as receivers of router syslog messages.

When defining the logging level for a syslog server, the log collects all messages from the level you choose plus all messages from lower levels, or the router sends all messages of the level you choose plus all messages of lower levels to the logging hosts. For example, if you choose notifications (5), the log collects or sends messages of levels 0 through 5. Firewall logging messages require a logging level of debugging (7), and application security logging messages require a level of informational (6).

Using SNMP to Manage Network Devices

SNMP is another management option, not only for messaging and notifications via SNMP traps and informs, but also as a general management framework. SNMP was developed to manage nodes, such as servers, workstations, routers, switches, hubs, and security appliances, on an IP network. All versions of SNMP are application layer protocols that facilitate the exchange of management information between network devices. SNMP is part of the TCP/IP protocol suite. SNMP enables network administrators to manage network performance, find and solve network problems, and plan for network growth.

SNMP Version 1 (SNMPv1) and SNMP Version 2 (SNMPv2) are based on three concepts:

- Managers (network management systems [NMS] installed on servers)

- Agents (installed on managed nodes)

- Management Information Bases (MIB)

In any configuration, at least one manager node runs SNMP management software. Network devices that need to be managed, such as switches, routers, servers, and workstations, are equipped with an SMNP agent software module. The agent is responsible for providing access to a local MIB of objects that reflects the resources and activity at its node.

MIBs

A Management Information Base is a database of the objects that can be managed on a device. The managed objects, or variables, can be set or read to provide information on the network devices and interfaces.

The SNMP manager can retrieve, or "get," information from the agent, and change, or "set," information in the agent, as shown in Figure 4-5. Sets can change variables (settings, configuration) in the agent device or initiate actions in devices. A reply to a set indicates the new setting in the device. For example, a set can cause a router to reboot, send a configuration file, or receive a configuration file. SNMP traps enable an agent to notify the management station of significant events by sending an unsolicited SNMP message.

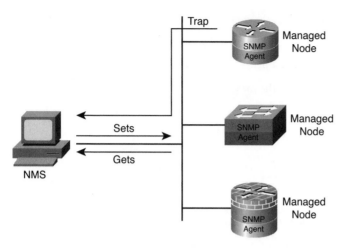

Figure 4-5 *SNMPv1/v2 Architecture*

The actions of gets and sets are the vulnerabilities that open SNMP to attack.

SNMPv1 and SNMPv2 use a community string to access router SNMP agents. SNMP community strings act like passwords. An SNMP community string is a text string that can authenticate messages between a management station and an SNMP engine:

■ If the manager sends one of the correct read-only community strings, it can get information but not set information in an agent.

■ If the manager uses one of the correct read-write community strings, it can get or set information in the agent.

In effect, having set access to a router is equivalent to having the enable password of the router.

SNMP agents accept commands and requests only from SNMP systems using the correct community string. By default, most SNMP systems use "public" as a community string. If you configure your router SNMP agent to use this commonly known community string, anyone with an SNMP system is able to read the router MIB. Because router MIB variables can point to things such as routing tables and other security-critical parts of the router configuration, it is extremely important that you create your own custom SNMP community strings.

SNMPv3 Architecture

In its natural evolution, the current version of SNMPv3 addresses the vulnerabilities of earlier versions by including three important services: authentication, privacy, and access control.

SNMPv3 is an interoperable, standards-based protocol for network management. SNMPv3 uses a combination of authenticating and encrypting packets over the network to provide secure access to devices, as shown in Figure 4-6. SNMPv3 provides the following security features:

■ **Message integrity:** Ensures that a packet has not been tampered with in transit

■ **Authentication:** Determines that the message is from a valid source

■ **Encryption:** Scrambles the contents of a packet to prevent it from being seen by an unauthorized source

Figure 4-6 *SNMPv3 Architecture*

SNMPv3 provides for a combination of both security model and security level, which determines the security mechanism that will be used when handling an SNMP packet.

A *security model* is an authentication strategy that is set up for a user and the group in which the user resides. Currently, Cisco IOS Software supports three security models: SNMPv1, SNMPv2c, and SNMPv3. A *security level* is the permitted level of security within a security model. The security level is a type of security algorithm that is performed on each SNMP packet. There are three security levels:

■ **noAuth:** This security level authenticates a packet by a string match of the username or community string.

■ **auth:** This level authenticates a packet by using either the Hashed Message Authentication Code (HMAC) with Message Digest 5 (MD5) method or the HMAC with Secure Hash Algorithms (SHA) method. Both methods are described in RFC 2104, *HMAC: Keyed-Hashing for Message Authentication*.

■ **Priv:** This level authenticates a packet by using either the HMAC MD5 or HMAC SHA algorithm and encrypts the packet using the Data Encryption Standard (DES), Triple DES (3DES), or Advanced Encryption Standard (AES) algorithm.

Note   Only SNMPv3 supports the auth and priv security levels.

Table 4-7 identifies what the combinations of security models and levels mean. As mentioned earlier, hashing and encryption will be explained in Chapter 12.

Table 4-7   *AAA Accounting Using Named Method Lists Procedure*

	Level	Authentication	Encryption	What Happens
SNMPv1	noAuthNoPriv	Community string	No	Authenticates with a community string match
SNMPv2c	noAuthNoPriv	Community string	No	Authenticates with a community string match
SNMPv3	noAuthNoPriv	Username	No	Authenticates with a username
SNMPv3	authNoPriv	MD5 or SHA	No	Provides HMAC MD5 or HMAC SHA algorithm for authentication
SNMPv3	authPriv	MD5 or SHA	Yes	Provides HMAC MD5 or HMAC SHA algorithm for authentication; provides DES, 3DES, or AES encryption in addition to authentication

Enabling SNMP Options Using Cisco CCP

Figure 4-7 illustrates the configuration of SNMP settings using Cisco Configuration Professional. Navigate to **Configure > Router > SNMP** to enable SNMP, set SNMP community strings, and enter SNMP trap receiver information.

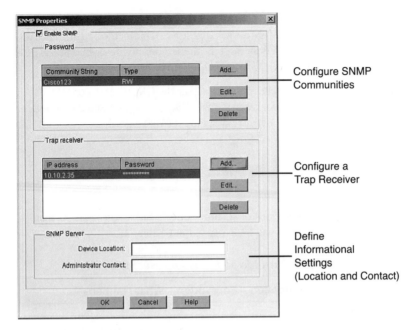

Figure 4-7   *Enabling SNMP with CCP*

Configuring AAA on a Cisco Router

Previously in this chapter, we discussed how to create a more secure management and reporting environment. A significant part of that environment is AAA. In Chapter 3, we briefly discussed the use of AAA with regard to management plane security. In this section, we will see how AAA can be implemented locally or centrally.

As mentioned, one of the options you have when configuring your network to work with AAA is to use a local username and password database to provide security greater than a simple password. It is likely that smaller organizations will configure AAA to operate locally.

Authentication, Authorization, and Accounting

Access control is the way you control who is allowed access to the access server or router and which services they are allowed to use once they have access. AAA network security services provide the primary framework through which you set up access control on your router. AAA services provide a higher degree of scalability than the line-level and privileged EXEC authentication commands alone.

Network and administrative access security in the Cisco environment, whether it involves campus access or VPN access, is based on a modular architecture that has three functional components:

- **Authentication:** Authentication requires users and administrators to prove that they really are who they say they are. Authentication is established using a username and password, challenge and response, token cards, and other methods, such as "I am user *student* and my password *validateme* proves it."

- **Authorization:** After authenticating the user and administrator, authorization services decide which resources the user and administrator are allowed to access and which operations the user and administrator are allowed to perform, such as "User *student* can access host serverXYZ using Telnet."

- **Accounting and auditing:** Accounting records what the users and administrators actually did, what they accessed, and for how long they accessed it. Accounting keeps track of how network resources are used, such as "User *student* accessed host serverXYZ using Telnet for 15 minutes."

Two examples of AAA implementation include authenticating remote users that are accessing the corporate LAN through VPN connections (as shown in Figure 4-8) and authenticating administrator access to the router console port, auxiliary port, and vty ports.

Cisco networking products support AAA access control using a local usernames and passwords database or remote security server databases. A local security database was introduced in Chapter 3 with the **username** command, and covered in detail earlier in this chapter with Table 4-1. A remote security server database is a separate server that provides AAA services for multiple network devices and a large number of network users by running RADIUS or TACACS+ protocols.

Figure 4-8 *Implementing Cisco AAA*

Note   Omitted from Figure 4-8 is "NAS services." If your Cisco router accepts dialup connections, the router is described as a network access server (NAS). With the popularity of VPN access, we don't hear as much nowadays about remote-access dialup services, but they are still around, which explains why Table 4-8 briefly discusses NAS ports.

Cisco provides many ways to implement AAA services for Cisco routers, all of which are covered in greater detail later in this chapter:

- **Self-contained AAA:** AAA services can be self-contained in the router itself. This form of authentication is also known as local authentication, with the **username** command.

- **Cisco Secure Access Control Server (ACS) for Windows:** AAA services on the router or NAS contact an external Cisco Secure ACS for Microsoft Windows system for user and administrator authentication.

Note   In 2011, Cisco announced the end of life of Cisco Secure ACS for Windows. It is still vastly used and it is still supported, and therefore we are briefly covering it in this book. However, if you are planning a new implementation for external authentication, the next two options are your current Cisco choices.

- **Cisco Secure ACS:** A policy-driven access control system and an integration point for network access control and identity management. The ACS 5.2 software runs either on a dedicated Cisco 1121 Secure Access Control System appliance or on a VMware server.

- **Cisco Identity Services Engine (ISE):** Cisco ISE is the new-generation centralized policy engine for business-relevant policy definition and enforcement. Cisco ISE consolidates features and functions that are found in Cisco Secure ACS and Network Admission Control (NAC) products, to deliver all the necessary services that are required by an enterprise network (AAA, profiling, posture, and guest management) in a single appliance platform. To learn more about ISE, check out TechWiseTV on YouTube for "Fundamentals of ISE."

Authenticating Router Access

You can use AAA to secure two different types of router access mode. The mode refers to the format of the packets that are requesting AAA services:

- **Character mode:** A user is sending a request to establish an EXEC mode process with the router, for administrative purposes. The user wishes to get the router prompt to start managing the router as the administrator.

- **Packet mode:** A user is sending a request to establish a dialup connection through the router with a device on the network. The user does not wish to get the router prompt. The sole purpose of connecting to the router is to get access to network resources. This is no longer a frequent scenario because remote users typically connect to organization resources with a VPN connection instead of a dialup connection.

With the exception of accounting commands, all the AAA commands apply to both character mode and packet mode.

For a truly secure network, you must configure the router to secure administrative access and remote LAN network access using AAA services.

Table 4-8 compares the router access modes, port types, and AAA command elements.

Table 4-8   *Router Access*

Access Type	Mode	NAS Ports	Specifications
Remote administrative access	Character (line or EXEC mode)	tty, vty, auxiliary, and console	login, exec, enable
Remote network access	Packet (interface mode)	async, group-async BRI and PRI	ppp, network

The **aaa authentication** command can be used for different authentication settings. Table 4-9 describes common options of the **aaa authentication** command. Many more options are available than those presented here.

Table 4-9   aaa authentication *Command Parameters*

Parameter	Description
enable default	Used to enable AAA authentication to determine if a user can access the privileged command level, referred to in Table 4-8 as remote administrative access, enable and exec modes.
login	Used to set AAA authentication at login, referred to in Table 4-8 as remote administrative access, login. The **aaa authentication login** command will be covered later in this chapter
ppp	Used to specify one or more AAA authentication methods for use on serial interfaces that are running Point-to-Point Protocol (PPP), referred to in Table 4-8 as remote network access mode.

Configuring AAA Authentication and Method Lists

AAA authentication is based on method lists as its building blocks. A method list is a sequential list describing the authentication methods to be queried in order to authenticate a user. Method lists enable you to designate one or more security protocols to be used for authentication, thus ensuring a backup system for authentication in case the initial method fails.

Cisco IOS Software uses the first listed method to authenticate users. If that method fails to respond, the Cisco IOS Software selects the next authentication method that is listed in the method list. This process continues until there is successful communication with a listed authentication method, or all methods that are defined in the method list are exhausted. In Figure 4-9, the default method list showcases two fallback methods. A typical configuration usually includes an AAA server database as the first method and the local database as a fallback method.

It is important to note that the Cisco IOS Software attempts authentication with the next listed authentication method only when there is no response from the previous method. If authentication fails at any point in this cycle—meaning that the security server or local username database responds by denying the user access—the authentication process stops and no other authentication methods are attempted.

Each method list is an individual configuration object. They can be assigned to multiple router components or function to provide authentication services. In Figure 4-9, the authentication methods in List 1 are assigned to both console and enable logins. List 2 methods apply to 802.1X logins, and List 3 methods apply to vty logins. Any other component not assigned a method list will use the methods on the default list.

At the bottom of Figure 4-9, we have an example where a method list called RemoteMngt is created and assigned to vty logins. When an administrator connects to the device with an SSH session, the administrator's credentials will first be checked against a TACACS+ server. If there is no communication with the TACACS+ server, the administrator's credentials will be presented to the RADIUS server, and if that communication fails as well, the administrator's credentials will be checked against the local database. The difference between the TACACS+ and RADIUS protocols will be discussed later in this chapter.

Although it is not common to see this level of complexity and granularity for different access methods on the same router, the modular configuration that is based on method lists allows for this level of granularity and flexibility.

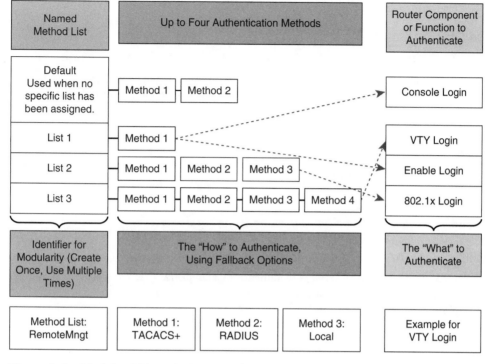

Figure 4-9 *Modular Objects in AAA Configuration*

Configuring AAA on a Cisco Router Using the Local Database

If you have only a few devices that provide remote access to your network for a limited number of users, you can store username and password security information locally on the Cisco devices. This is referred to as local authentication on a local security database. The following are local authentication characteristics:

■ Used for small networks

■ Stores usernames and passwords in the Cisco router

■ Users authenticate against the local security database in the Cisco router

■ Does not require an external database

The system administrator must populate the local security database by specifying username and password profiles for each user that might log in. This local authentication is difficult to scale because

■ There is limited persistent storage on network devices (running and startup configs).

■ If the same credentials are used to access multiple network devices, those credentials require manual replication on concerned devices.

Local authentication typically works as follows, as shown in Figure 4-10:

1. The client establishes a connection with the router.

2. The router prompts the user for a username and password.

3. The router authenticates the username and password in the local database. The user is authorized to access the network based on information in the local database.

Figure 4-10 *Implementing Authentication Using Local Services*

Configuring AAA Local Authentication

To configure AAA local services to authenticate administrator access (character mode access) or network access (packet mode) that includes VPN access, follow these general steps:

■ Add usernames and passwords to the local router database for users who need administrative access to the router.

■ Enable AAA globally on the router, or confirm that it is already enabled.

■ Configure AAA parameters on the router. These parameters include authentication policies at a minimum, using method lists for the desired access type. Authorization and accounting policies can optionally be configured.

■ Confirm and troubleshoot the AAA configuration.

The first step to configure AAA services for local authentication is to create users. Local user accounts can be configured by navigating to **Configure > Router > Router Access > User Accounts/View** and clicking Add, as shown in Figure 4-11. This window enables you to define accounts and passwords that will enable users to authenticate when logging in to the router using HTTP, Telnet, PPP, or some other means. Privilege levels and CLI views can also be configured using this option by adding a new user or editing existing users.

Figure 4-11 *Configuring Local User Accounts Using CCP*

The following are the detailed steps for adding a local user account:

Step 1.   Choose **Configure > Router > Router Access > User Accounts/View**.

Step 2.   Click **Add** to add a new user.

Step 3.   In the Add an Account dialog box, enter the username and password in the appropriate fields to define the user account.

Step 4.   From the Privilege Level drop-down list, choose **15** unless you have defined lesser privilege levels, as shown in Figure 4-11.

Step 5.   If you have defined views, you can check the **Associate a View with the User** check box and choose from the View Name drop-down list a view that you want to associate with this user.

Step 6.   Click **OK**.

Enabling AAA Authentication Policy

Authentication policies for local access can be configured by navigating to **Configure > Router > AAA > AAA Summary**. From this window, shown in Figure 4-12, you can enable AAA globally by clicking the **Enable AAA** button and then clicking **Yes** in the Enable AAA dialog box that appears. As a precaution and a first level of protection, Cisco Configuration Professional will enable authentication and authorization for the vty lines and authentication for the console line using the local database of the router. A warning message lets the administrator know about this default policy, which is also displayed in the summary window when the commands are delivered to the router. Other authentication policies can be created using authentication method lists.

Enable AAA on the Router

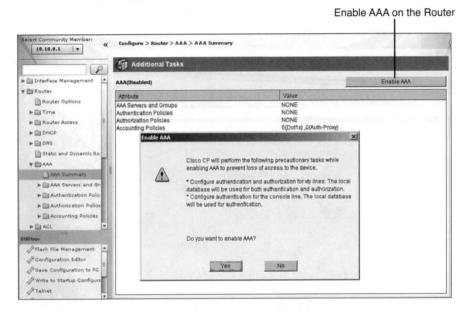

Figure 4-12 *Enabling and Disabling AAA Using CCP*

Figure 4-13 shows the resulting CCP configuration following the enabling of AAA.

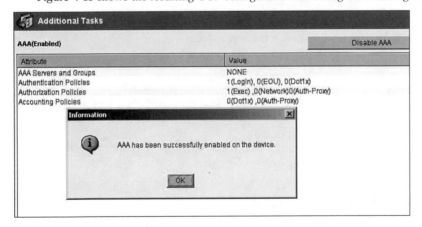

Figure 4-13 *AAA Summary After AAA Is Enabled*

Configuring Method Lists

Authentication method lists can be created or edited by navigating to **Configure > Router > AAA > Authentication Policies > Login**. The default method list is shown in the background window of Figure 4-14, as well as how to add a new list or edit an existing list.

Figure 4-14 *Configuring AAA Authentication Method Lists*

The method list requires a name so that you can later assign the list to the router function requiring authentication (management access, in our example). This name is specified in the Add a Method List for Authentication Login dialog box, shown on the left in Figure 4-14.

The authentication methods comprise a list, which you can modify by clicking Add to add a new method to the list. The resulting Select Method List(s) for Authentication Login dialog box, shown on the right in Figure 4-14, displays the available authentication methods and allows you to select among these methods. You can specify up to four methods and place them in the list in the order in which you want the router to use them. As explained earlier in conjunction with Figure 4-9, the router will attempt the first method in the list. If the authentication request receives a PASS or a FAIL response, the router does not query further. If the router does not receive a response by using the first method, it uses the next method in the list, and continues to the end of the list until it receives a PASS or a FAIL response. Each method in the list represents, then, a backup or fallback option to the previous method.

You can change the order of processing of the method list in the Add a Method List for Authentication Login dialog box. Click Move Up to move a method up the list. Click Move Down to move a method further down the list. The method "none" will always be last in the list. No other method in the list can be moved below it. This is a Cisco IOS restriction. Cisco IOS will not accept any method name after the method name "none" has been added to a method list. Method name "none" should be used with care, because it removes the requirement of having to provide authentication.

AAA Authentication CLI Configuration

Table 4-10 describes common options of the **aaa authentication login** command. More options are available than those presented here.

Table 4-10   aaa authentication login *Command Parameters*

Parameter	Description
enable	Uses the enable password for authentication.
line	Uses the line password for authentication.
local	Uses the local username database for authentication.
exec	Creates a method list that provides accounting records about user EXEC terminal sessions on the NAS, including username, date, and start and stop times.
none	Uses no authentication
group-radius	Uses the list of all RADIUS servers for authentication.
group tacacs+	Uses the list of all TACACS+ servers for authentication.
group *group-name*	Uses a subset of RADIUS or TACACS+ servers for authentication as defined by the **aaa group server radius** command or **aaa group server tacacs+** command.

Example 4-10 shows a CLI configuration for local authentication, using the following commands:

■ **aaa new-model:** Enables AAA.

■ **aaa authentication login default local:** Defines the default method list for login authentication using the local database.

■ **aaa authentication login** *list name*: Defines a custom method list for login authentication using the local database, using the enable password as a fallback option. In Example 4-10, the list name is MGT-ACCESS.

- **username:** Adds usernames and passwords to the local security database.

- **login authentication:** Assigns a method list to an access line; applied to the console line in Example 4-10.

Maximum Number of Login Attempts and Login Delay

To further secure administrative access to the router, you can specify the maximum number of failed AAA login attempts that can occur before an account is locked out, using the **aaa local authentication attempts max-fail** command in global configuration mode, as shown in Example 4-10.

Not used in Example 4-10 is the **login delay** command. The **aaa local authentication attempts max-fail** command differs from the **login delay** command in how it handles failed attempts. The **aaa local authentication attempts max-fail** command locks the user account if the authentication fails. This account stays locked until it is cleared by an administrator. The **login delay** command introduces a delay between failed login attempts without locking the account.

Example 4-10   *AAA CLI Configuration Example with Local Authentication*

```
R1(config)# aaa new-model
R1(config)# aaa local authentication attempts max-fail 10
R1(config)# aaa authentication login default local
R(config)# aaa authentication login MGT-ACCESS local enable
R1(config)# enable secret SnowyDay2012
R1(config)# username admin privilege 15 view root secret sanfran2012
R1(config)# username FWadmin privilege 10 view CCP_Firewall secret 1StopUn0w
R1(config)# line con 0
R1(config-line)# login authentication MGT-ACCESS
R1(config-line)# end
R1# debug aaa authentication
```

To display information on AAA authentication, use the **debug aaa authentication** command in privileged EXEC command mode. Example 4-11 contains debug output for an unsuccessful AAA authentication followed by a successful authentication on the router console, using the local user database defined in Example 4-10.

Example 4-11   *Troubleshooting Using the* **debug aaa authentication** *Command*

```
User Access Verification


Username: wrongusername
Password:


Feb 11 11:06:47.971: AAA/BIND(0000001B): Bind i/f
Feb 11 11:06:47.971: AAA/AUTHEN/LOGIN (0000001B): Pick method list 'MGT-ACCESS'
Feb 11 11:06:48.223: AAA/AUTHEN/ENABLE(0000001B): Processing request action LOGIN
Feb 11 11:06:48.223: AAA/AUTHEN/ENABLE(0000001B): Done status GET_PASSWORD
Feb 11 11:06:49.231: AAA/AUTHEN/ENABLE(0000001B): Processing request action LOGIN
Feb 11 11:06:49.235: AAA/AUTHEN/ENABLE(0000001B): Done status FAIL - bad password
% Authentication failed


Username: admin
Feb 11 11:06:51.239: AAA/AUTHEN/LOGIN (0000001B): Pick method list 'MGT-ACCESS'
Password:


R1>
```

AAA on a Cisco Router Using Cisco Secure ACS

Cisco Secure Access Control Server (ACS) provides a centralized identity networking solution and simplified user management experience across all Cisco devices and security management applications. This section describes Cisco Secure ACS and its uses, the requirements for installing Cisco Secure ACS for Windows, the Cisco Secure ACS installation procedure, and its configuration for router AAA services.

Cisco Secure ACS Overview

Local implementations of AAA, as previously explained, do not scale well. Most corporate environments have multiple Cisco routers and NASs with multiple router administrators and hundreds or thousands of users needing access to the corporate LAN. Maintaining local databases for each Cisco router and NAS for this size of network is not feasible.

To solve this challenge, you can use one or more Cisco Secure ACS systems (servers or engines) to manage the entire user and administrative access needs for an entire corporate network using one or more databases. External AAA systems, such as the Cisco Secure ACS for Windows, Cisco Secure ACS appliance, or Cisco Identity Services Engine (ISE), communicate with Cisco routers and NASs using the TACACS+ or RADIUS protocols to implement AAA functions. This allows you to make changes to user accounts and passwords in a centralized place (the ACS server) and have all the Cisco routers and NASs in your network access this information.

Figure 4-15 shows the following steps of the authentication and authorization process using an external Cisco Secure ACS system to provide AAA services to a network:

Step 1.   The client establishes a connection with the router.

Step 2.   The router prompts the user for a username and password.

Step 3.   The router passes the username and password to the Cisco Secure ACS (server or engine).

Step 4.   The Cisco Secure ACS authenticates the user. The user is authorized to access the router (administrative access) or the network based on information found in the Cisco Secure ACS database.

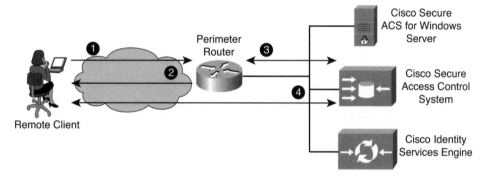

Figure 4-15   *Implementing Authentication Using External Servers*

Cisco Secure ACS, in its appliance and software form factors, is a highly scalable, high-performance ACS that operates as a centralized RADIUS and TACACS+ server that provides the following features:

■ Extends access security by combining authentication, user access, and administrator access with policy control within a centralized identity networking solution

■ Allows greater flexibility and mobility, increased security, and user-productivity gains

■ Enforces a uniform security policy for all users regardless of how they access the network

■ Reduces the administrative and management burden involved in scaling user and network administrator access to the network

Cisco Secure ACS uses a central database, which allows it to centralize the control of all user privileges and enables hundreds or thousands of access points throughout the network to reference those privileges. Cisco Secure ACS provides detailed reporting and monitoring capabilities of user behavior, access connections, and device configuration changes. This feature has become extremely important for organizations trying to comply with Sarbanes-Oxley Act regulations. Cisco Secure ACS supports a broad variety of access connections, including wired and wireless LAN, dialup, broadband, content, storage, VoIP, firewalls, switches, and VPNs.

You can leverage the Cisco Secure ACS framework to control administrator access and configuration for all the network devices in your network that support RADIUS and TACACS+. The following are some of the advanced features of Cisco Secure ACS:

■ Automatic service monitoring

■ Database synchronization and importing of tools for large-scale deployments

■ Lightweight Directory Access Protocol (LDAP) user authentication support

■ User and administrative access reporting

■ Restrictions to network access based on criteria such as the time of day and the day of week

■ User and device group profiles

■ Token-based authentication

Cisco Secure ACS is an important component of the Cisco Identity Based Networking Services (IBNS) architecture. Cisco IBNS is based on port-security standards such as IEEE 802.1x and Extensible Authentication Protocol (EAP), and extends security from the perimeter of the network to every connection point inside the LAN. You can deploy new policy control, such as per-user quotas, VLAN assignments, and ACLs, within this new architecture because of the extended capabilities of Cisco switches and wireless access points to query Cisco Secure ACS over the RADIUS protocol. Please note that IBNS is being superseded by TrustSec. Have a look at TechWiseTV's "Fundamentals of TrustSec" on YouTube to learn more.

Cisco Secure ACS is also an important component of Cisco Network Admission Control (NAC). Cisco NAC is an industry initiative sponsored by Cisco that uses the network infrastructure to enforce security-policy compliance on all devices seeking to access network computing resources, thereby limiting damage from viruses and worms. With NAC, customers can choose to allow network access only to compliant and trusted endpoint devices (for instance, PCs, servers, and personal digital assistants [PDA]) and can restrict the access of noncompliant devices. Cisco NAC is part of the Cisco Self-Defending Network initiative and is the foundation for enabling NAC on Layer 2 and Layer 3 networks. Future phases extend endpoint and network security interoperation to include dynamic incident-containment capabilities. This innovation enables compliant system elements to report misuse emanating from rogue or infected systems during an attack. Thus, infected systems can be dynamically quarantined from the rest of the network to significantly reduce virus, worm, and blended-threat propagation.

Cisco Secure ACS is a powerful access control server with many high-performance and scalability features for any organization growing its WAN or LAN. The following lists the main benefits of Cisco Secure ACS:

- **Ease of use:** A web-based user interface simplifies and distributes the configuration for user profiles, group profiles, and Cisco Secure ACS configuration.

- **Scalability:** Cisco Secure ACS is built to support large networked environments with support for redundant servers, remote databases, and database replication and backup services.

- **Extensibility:** LDAP authentication forwarding supports the authentication of user profiles that are stored in directories from leading directory vendors, including Sun, Novell, and Microsoft.

- **Management:** Microsoft Windows Active Directory support consolidates Windows username and password management and uses the Windows Performance Monitor for real-time statistics viewing.

- **Administration:** Different access levels for each Cisco Secure ACS administrator and the ability to group network devices together make it easier and more flexible to control the enforcement and changes of security policy administration over all of the devices in a network.

- **Product flexibility:** Because Cisco IOS Software has embedded support for AAA, Cisco Secure ACS can be used across virtually any NAS that Cisco sells (the Cisco IOS Software release must support RADIUS or TACACS+). Cisco Secure ACS is now available in an appliance format or in a virtual machine format. Until version 4.x, in additional to being offered as an appliance, it was also available as software call Cisco Secure ACS for Windows and as a small appliance called Cisco Secure ACS Express, mentioned later in this chapter.

- **Integration:** Tight coupling with Cisco IOS routers and VPN solutions provides features such as Multichassis Multilink PPP and Cisco IOS Software command authorization.

- **Third-party support:** Cisco Secure ACS offers token server support for any one-time password (OTP) vendor that provides an RFC-compliant RADIUS interface, such as RSA, PassGo, Secure Computing, Vasco, or CryptoCard.

- **Control:** Cisco Secure ACS provides dynamic quotas to restrict access based on the time of day, network use, number of logged sessions, and the day of the week.

Cisco Secure ACS for Windows

The last available version of Cisco Secure ACS running on Windows Server was version 4.2. This 4.2 version was also available in two additional form factors: VMware ESX Server, and as a dedicated appliance. In 2011, Cisco announced the end of life of Cisco Secure ACS 4.2 and thus the end of ACS for Windows Server. The new 5.2 version, covered later in the chapter, does not support ACS for Windows Server. Version 5.2 is only available as a VM or as a dedicated appliance. Because Cisco Secure ACS for Windows is still vastly used, we are briefly covering this option even though it has reached end-of-life status.

Cisco Secure ACS 4.2 for Windows must meet certain minimum hardware and operating system requirements, covered briefly in the next section. For third-party software requirements, such as web browsers and Java, consult the release notes.

The server that will be running Cisco Secure ACS must meet the following minimum hardware requirements:

■ Pentium IV processor that is 1.8 GHz or faster

■ 1 GB of RAM

■ At least 1 GB of free disk space; if you are running the database on the same computer, more disk space is required

■ Minimum graphics resolution of 256 colors at 800×600 pixels

Cisco Secure ACS 4.2 for Windows supports the English-language versions of the following Microsoft Windows operating systems:

■ Windows 2000 Server, with Service Pack 4 installed

■ Windows 2000 Advanced Server, with the following conditions:

    ■ Service Pack 4 installed

    ■ Without Microsoft Clustering Service installed

    ■ No other features specific to Windows 2000 Advanced Server enabled, such as Terminal Services

■ Windows Server 2003 Service Pack 1, Enterprise Edition or Standard Edition

■ Windows Server 2003, R2, Standard Edition

■ Windows Server 2003, Service Pack 2

■ Windows Server 2003, R2, Service Pack 2

Note ACS for Windows supports the multiprocessor feature on dual-processor computers. Cisco Secure ACS 4.2 supports the Japanese Windows Server 2003.

You can apply the Windows service packs before or after installing Cisco Secure ACS. If you do not install a required service pack before installing Cisco Secure ACS, the Cisco Secure ACS installation program might warn you that the required service pack is not present. If you receive a service pack message, continue the installation, and then install the required service pack before starting user authentication with Cisco Secure ACS.

Cisco Secure ACS Express

Now at end-of-life status, Cisco Secure ACS Express was an entry-level RADIUS and TACACS+ AAA server for retail branch locations, enterprise branch offices, and small businesses that have fewer than 350 users and 50 devices. It also ran on a Windows platform.

Cisco Secure ACS: Appliance and Virtual Machine

The Cisco Secure Access Control System (the non-Windows version) showcases a physical or virtual appliance form factor. It is a policy-based security server that also provides standards-compliant AAA services to your network. Cisco Secure ACS requires version 5.x of the Cisco Secure ACS software, and facilitates the administrative management of devices and applications manufactured by Cisco and other vendors.

As a dominant enterprise network access control platform, Cisco Secure ACS serves as an integration point for network access control and identity management. Two footprints are available—a Linux-based hardware appliance running the Cisco Secure ACS software, as shown in Figure 4-16, or a virtual server image for VMware ESX environments.

Figure 4-16 *Cisco 1121 Secure Access Control System*

Cisco Secure ACS provides a rule-based policy model that allows you to control network access based on dynamic conditions and attributes. The rule-based policy is designed to meet complex access policy needs.

Within the greater context of two major AAA protocols—RADIUS and TACACS+— Cisco Secure ACS provides the following basic areas of functionality:

- Under the framework of the RADIUS protocol, Cisco Secure ACS controls the wired and wireless access by users and host machines to the network and manages the accounting of the network resources used.

- Cisco Secure ACS supports multiple RADIUS-based authentication methods, including the following:

  - Password Authentication Protocol (PAP)

  - Challenge Handshake Authentication Protocol (CHAP)

  - Microsoft CHAP version 1 (MS-CHAPv1)

  - Microsoft CHAP version 2 (MS-CHAPv2)

- Cisco Secure ACS also supports many members of the Extensible Authentication Protocol (EAP) family of protocols:

  - EAP-MD5

  - Lightweight EAP (LEAP)

  - Protected EAP (PEAP)

  - EAP-Flexible Authentication via Secure Tunneling (EAP-FAST)

  - EAP-Transport Layer Security (EAP-TLS)

- In association with PEAP or EAP-FAST, Cisco Secure ACS also supports EAP-MSCHAPv2 and EAP-Generic Token Card (EAP-GTC).

- Under the framework of the TACACS+ protocol, Cisco Secure ACS helps to manage Cisco and other vendor network devices such as switches, wireless access points, routers, and gateways. It also helps to manage services and entities such as dialup, VPN, and firewall.

Cisco Secure ACS is the point in your network that identifies users and devices that try to connect to your network. This identity establishment can occur directly by using the Cisco Secure ACS internal identity repository for local user authentication or indirectly by using external identity repositories. For example, Cisco Secure ACS can use Active Directory as an external identity repository to authenticate a user and grant the user access to the network.

Cisco Secure ACS provides advanced monitoring, reporting, and troubleshooting tools that help you administer and manage your Cisco Secure ACS deployments.

Cisco Secure ACS does the following:

- Enforces access policies for VPN and wireless users

- Provides simplified device administration

Cisco Identity Services Engine

Cisco Identity Services Engine (ISE) is a next-generation identity and access control policy platform that enables enterprises to enforce compliance, enhance infrastructure security, and simplify service operations. Its unique architecture allows enterprises to gather real-time contextual information from networks, users, and devices to make proactive governance decisions by enforcing policy across the network infrastructure. Cisco ISE is an integral component of the Cisco TrustSec solution that helps secure and govern borderless networks. This rack-mounted server runs its own software, which is different from the traditional Cisco Secure ACS software.

Cisco ISE, which uses the same platform as Cisco 1121 (shown previously in Figure 4-16), provides a highly powerful and flexible attribute-based access control solution that combines AAA, posture, profiling, and guest management services on a single platform. Administrators can centrally create and manage access control policies for users and endpoints in a consistent fashion, and gain end-to-end visibility into everything that is connected to the network. Cisco ISE automatically discovers and classifies endpoints, provides the right level of access based on identity, and enforces endpoint compliance by checking the posture of a device. Cisco ISE also provides advanced enforcement capabilities, including Security Group Access (SGA) by using security group tags (SGT) and security group ACLs (SGACL).

Cisco ISE is supported in hardware and software footprints, meaning that there are three hardware appliances for small, midsize, and large scenarios, and the ESX-based virtual server footprint.

ISE

At the time of writing, ISE does not yet support TACACS+; it supports only RADIUS.

Refer to TechWiseTV on YouTube for a great video introducing ISE fundamentals: http://www.youtube.com/watch?v=sel1F7mKdtI.

TACACS+ and RADIUS Protocols

The Cisco Secure ACS family of products supports both RADIUS and TACACS+ protocols, which are the two predominant AAA protocols that are used by Cisco security appliances, routers, and switches for implementing AAA.

Cisco Secure ACS 5.2 supports RADIUS for network access control and TACACS+ for network device access control. There are several differences between TACACS+ and RADIUS, leading to their deployment in different scenarios. TACACS+ is the more secure option because it encrypts the complete transaction between the AAA client and the AAA server. It also separates authentication from authorization, making it suitable for device administration, where users are authenticated once, and device administration is then authorized granularly without the need for constant authentication. RADIUS showcases a robust application programming interface (API) for custom accounting, but it combines authentication and authorization requests. This makes it suitable for network access control, but not for device administration.

TACACS+

TACACS+ is a Cisco enhancement to the original TACACS protocol. Despite its name, TACACS+ was designed from the ground up and is therefore incompatible with any earlier version of TACACS. TACACS+ has been submitted to the Internet Engineering Task Force (IETF) as a draft proposal.

TACACS+ provides separate message types for AAA services. Because TACACS+ separates authentication and authorization, it is possible to use TACACS+ authorization and accounting while using another method of authentication.

The extensions to the TACACS+ protocol provide more types of authentication requests and response codes than were in the original specification. TACACS+ offers multiprotocol support, such as IP and AppleTalk. Normal TACACS+ operation encrypts the entire body of the packet for more secure communications and uses TCP port 49.

RADIUS

RADIUS is an open IETF standard AAA protocol for applications such as network access or IP mobility that was developed by Livingston Enterprises. RADIUS works in both local and roaming situations and is commonly used for accounting purposes. RADIUS is currently defined by RFCs 2865, 2866, 2867, and 2868.

The RADIUS protocol hides the passwords during transmission between the NAS and RADIUS server, even with the PAP protocol, using a rather complex operation that involves MD5 hashing and a shared secret. However, the rest of the packet is sent in plaintext.

RADIUS combines authentication and authorization as one process. Once users are authenticated, they are authorized as well. RADIUS uses UDP port 1645 or 1812 for authentication and UDP port 1646 or 1813 for accounting.

In addition, RADIUS is widely used by VoIP service providers. It is used to pass login credentials of a Session Initiation Protocol (SIP) endpoint (such as a broadband phone) to a SIP registrar using digest authentication, and then to a RADIUS server using RADIUS. RADIUS is also a common authentication protocol that is used by the 802.1x security standard.

The Diameter protocol is the planned replacement for RADIUS. Diameter is more secure than RADIUS because it uses the Stream Control Transmission Protocol (SCTP) or TCP rather than UDP. It also provides for failover procedures, and offers a transition path for current RADIUS implementations.

Comparing TACACS+ and RADIUS

There are several differences between TACACS+ and RADIUS, as described in the following list and summarized in Table 4-11.

Table 4-11   *TACACS+/RADIUS Comparison*

	TACACS+	RADIUS
Functionality	Separates AAA	Combines authentication and authorization
Standard	Mostly Cisco supported	Open/RFC
Transport protocol	TCP	UDP
CHAP	Bidirectional	Unidirectional

	TACACS+	RADIUS
Protocol support	Multiprotocol support	No ARA, no NetBEUI
Confidentiality	Entire packet encrypted	Password encrypted
Customization	Provides authorization of router commands on a per-user or per-group basis	Has no options to authorize router commands on a per-user or per-group basis
Accounting	Limited	Extensive

- **Functionality:** TACACS+ separates AAA functions according to the AAA architecture, allowing modularity of the security server implementation. RADIUS combines authentication and authorization, but separates accounting, thus allowing less flexibility in implementation than TACACS+.

- **Standard:** TACACS+ is a standard that is used mostly by Cisco customers. RADIUS is an open industry standard.

- **Transport protocol:** TACACS+ uses TCP. RADIUS uses UDP, which was chosen for the simplification of client and server implementations; however, it makes the RADIUS protocol less robust and requires the server to implement reliability measures such as packet retransmission and timeouts.

- **Challenge and response:** TACACS+ supports bidirectional challenge and response as used in CHAP between two routers. RADIUS supports unidirectional challenge and response from the RADIUS security server to the RADIUS client.

- **Protocol support:** TACACS+ provides more complete dialup and WAN protocol support. RADIUS does not support AppleTalk Remote Access (ARA), NetBIOS Extended User Interface (NetBEUI), NetWare Access Server Interface (NASI), and X.25 packet assembler/disassembler (PAD) connections.

- **Confidentiality:** TACACS+ encrypts the entire packet body of every packet. RADIUS encrypts only the password attribute portion of the Access-Request packet, which makes TACACS+ more secure.

- **Customization:** The flexibility that is provided in the TACACS+ protocol allows many things to be customized on a per-user basis or per-group basis, including which commands a user can execute on a router. RADIUS lacks this flexibility, and therefore many features that are possible with TACACS+ are not possible with RADIUS.

- **Accounting:** TACACS+ accounting includes a limited number of information fields. RADIUS accounting can contain more information than TACAS+ accounting records, which is the key strength of RADIUS over TACACS+.

AAA on a Cisco Router Using an External Database

Previously in this chapter, you learned how to configure a Cisco router to perform local AAA authentication and authorization. Now let's see how to configure the Cisco router to perform external AAA authentication, authorization, and accounting. By the way, AAA accounting can be performed only using an external database.

Configuration Steps for AAA Using an External Database

Follow the steps presented in this section to configure a Cisco IOS router for AAA using Cisco Secure ACS as an external AAA server. Notice that the configuration is modular and object oriented, where AAA servers are tied together into AAA server groups for ease of management. This allows you to configure multiple servers that will act as backups of each other in a high-availability fashion.

The following steps follow the same configuration approach as the previous example where the local router database was used. AAA needs to be enabled globally on the router, and method lists are configured for authentication and, optionally, for authorization and accounting. When configuring Cisco Secure ACS as an external server, the primary method is TACACS+ or RADIUS, instead of the local database.

Step 1.   Globally enable AAA.

Step 2.   Configure AAA servers and groups.

Step 3.   Enable AAA globally on the router.

Step 4.   Configure authentication policies using method lists.

Step 5.   (Optional) Configure authorization policies using method lists.

Step 6.   (Optional) Configure accounting policies using method lists.

Step 7.   Verify the AAA configuration.

Earlier, we learned how to turn on AAA globally with CCP or using the **aaa new-model** configuration command.

AAA Servers and Groups

The next step in our external AAA configuration, shown in Figure 4-17, is to configure AAA server objects. Navigate to **Configure > Router > AAA > AAA Servers and Groups > Servers** to view a snapshot of the information about the AAA servers that the router is configured to use. The IP address, server type, and other parameters are displayed for each server.

Click **Add** to add a TACACS+ or RADIUS server type, configuring the IP address for each server, as shown in Figure 4-17. You can configure timeouts and keys for TACACS+ servers, and define custom authorization and accounting ports for RADIUS servers.

Figure 4-17   *Configuring AAA Server in CCP*

The command equivalent to Figure 4-17 is as follows:

```
R1(config)# radius-server host 10.0.1.10 auth-port 1645 acct-port 1646 key 0 cisco
```

In the preceding command, **cisco** is the RADIUS key.

After you create the servers, you can group them into a server group. Server groups provide the opportunity to modularly combine AAA servers, just defined, in high-availability scenarios. You can add server groups, as shown in Figure 4-18, by navigating to **Configure > Router > AAA > AAA Server and Groups > Groups**. If you click Add to add a new group, you can choose the servers from the list and add them to the group for redundancy.

Figure 4-18 *Configuring AAA Server Group in CCP*

The command equivalent to Figure 4-18 is as follows:

```
R1(config)# aaa group server radius MYRADIUS
R1(config-sg-radius)# server 10.0.1.10 auth-port 1645 acct-port 1646
```

Note In Figure 4-18, in the Add AAA Server Group dialog box, the Server Type field is grayed out. With the current version of CCP, version 2.6, only the RADIUS server group can be created. However, you can create a TACACS+ server group at the CLI with the following configuration commands:

```
R1(config)# aaa server group tacacs+ MYTACACS
R1(config-sg-tacacs+)# server 10.0.1.67
```

AAA Authentication Method Lists

The rest of the configuration follows the familiar approach of defining named method lists, or selecting the default method list, to include the AAA servers as an option for authentication, authorization, and accounting.

AAA must be enabled globally in order to define AAA method lists. To start AAA, click the button titled **Enable AAA** found by navigating to **Configure > Router > AAA > AAA Summary**. This was demonstrated earlier in Figure 4-12.

Once AAA is enabled globally, you can navigate to **Configure > Router > AAA > Authentication Policies > Login** and click **Add** to add new authentication method lists, as shown in Figure 4-19.

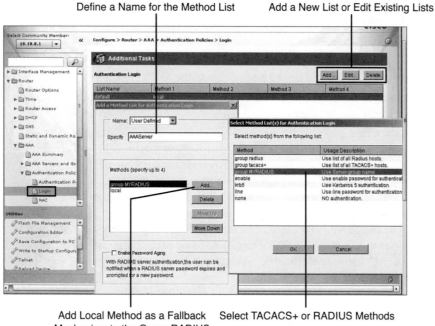

Figure 4-19 *Configuring Authentication Method Lists*

The command equivalent to Figure 4-19 is as follows:

```
R1(config)# aaa authentication login AAAServer group MYRADIUS local
```

Earlier in the chapter, Figure 4-14 showed the Cisco Configuration Professional window that is used to define AAA method lists and authentication methods. When using external AAA servers such as Cisco Secure ACS, you simply select TACACS+ or RADIUS server groups as your main method. It is recommended to add fallback methods, most typically the local router database, in case communication to the AAA servers fails, also shown in Figure 4-14.

AAA Authorization Policies

Authorization and accounting rules follow a similar approach using method lists to define the location of the authorization permissions and the accounting logs.

Because the TACACS+ protocol allows you to separate authentication from authorization, you can configure a router to restrict the user to be able to perform only certain functions after successful authentication. You can configure authorization for both character mode (EXEC authorization) and packet mode (network authorization).

To configure the router to use the Cisco Secure ACS server for authorization, you must create a user-defined authorization method list or edit the default authorization method list. The default authorization method list is automatically applied to all interfaces except those that have a user-defined authorization method list explicitly applied. A user-defined authorization method list overrides the default authorization method list.

Tip   To avoid locking yourself out of the router, make sure you configure authorization on the Cisco Secure ACS server *before* you configure the router for authorization.

Also as a precaution, consider logging on to the router console in privilege mode before starting the authorization configuration.

It is also recommended that you do *not* enable authorization on the backdoor port (for example, the console port) until you have appropriately confirmed the alternative authentication method, such as login via the AAA server, is working. In absence of console access, you may also simply open a second, concurrent Telnet/SSH session to confirm that you have appropriate access to the device, while still keeping the original session, used to log in, active. Once you have access to the device through the second vty session, you should save the configuration. A final resort, albeit not often desired, is to do a "reload in 5" and answer NO when asked to save the configuration. If the authentication/authorization mechanism fails, it will reload the router without saving in 5 minutes (adjustable time).

Figure 4-20 illustrates using an authorization method list for authorizing the use of the CLI with TACACS+. Notice that the local database is again used as a fallback option.

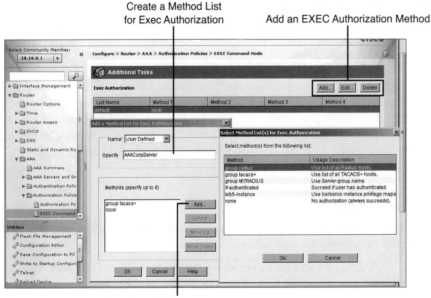

Figure 4-20   *Configuring Authorization Method Lists*

AAA Accounting Policies

Cisco Secure ACS serves as a central repository for accounting information, essentially tracking events that occur on the network. Each session that is established through Cisco Secure ACS can be fully accounted for and stored on the server. This stored information can be very helpful for management, security audits, capacity planning, and network-usage billing.

Like authentication and authorization method lists, method lists for accounting define the way accounting will be performed and the sequence in which these methods are performed. The default accounting method list is automatically applied to all interfaces except those that have a named accounting method list explicitly defined. A defined accounting method list overrides the default accounting method list.

AAA supports six different types of accounting: network, connection, exec, system, command, and resource.

Currently, AAA accounting can be configured only via the CLI. Interestingly, CCP v2.6 has an AAA Accounting Policies window. However, it does not have Add, Edit, and Delete buttons, so we can't add accounting policies using the GUI. It must be done at the CLI, and even then, it still doesn't appear in the AAA Accounting Policies window in CCP v2.6.

To configure AAA accounting using named method lists, use the commands shown in Table 4-12 while in global configuration mode.

Table 4-12   *AAA Accounting Using Named Method Lists Procedure*

Step	Command	Notes
1	`Router(config)# aaa accounting {system | network | exec | connection | commands level} {default | list-name} {start-stop | stop-only | none} [method1 [method2...]]`	This command creates an accounting method list and enables accounting. The argument *list-name* is a character string used to name the list you are creating as an account methods. To edit the default method list, use the **default** parameter. *level* refers to a specific privilege level, such as level 15. *method* refers to **local**, **group tacacs+**, **group**, and so on.
2	`Router(config)# line [aux | console | tty | vty] line-number [ending-line-number]` —or— `Router(config)# interface interface-type interface-number`	This command enters the line configuration mode or interface configuration mode for the lines or interface to which you want to apply the accounting method list.
3	`Router(config-line)# accounting {arap | commands level | connection | exec} {default | list-name}` —or— `Router(config-if)# ppp accounting {default | list-name}`	This command applies the accounting method list to a line or set of lines, or to an interface or set of interfaces.

Named accounting method lists are specific to the indicated type of accounting. The AAA accounting parameters shown in Table 4-13 describe the types of accounting that can use named accounting method lists. The **aaa accounting** command enables you to specify how much information to record for accounting. Table 4-13 also describes the AAA accounting record types.

Table 4-13 *AAA Accounting Command Parameters*

Parameter	Description
system	Performs accounting for all system-level events not associated with users, such as reloads. Note that when system accounting is used and the accounting server is unreachable at system startup time, the system will not be accessible for approximately 2 minutes.
network	This parameter creates a method list to enable accounting for all network-related service requests, including SLIP, PPP, PPP NCP, and ARAP protocols.
exec	This parameter creates a method list that provides accounting records about user EXEC terminal sessions on the NAS, including username, date, and start and stop times.
connection	This parameter creates a method list that provides accounting information about all outbound connections made from the NAS.
commands	This parameter creates a method list that provides accounting information about specific, individual EXEC commands associated with a specific privilege level.
default	This parameter uses the listed accounting methods that follow this keyword as the default list of methods for accounting services.
start-stop	This parameter instructs the TACACS+ server to send a start accounting notice at the beginning of the requested event and a stop accounting notice at the end of the event.
stop-only	This parameter instructs the TACACS+ server to send a stop record accounting notice at the end of the requested user process.
none	This parameter instructs the TACACS+ server to stop all accounting activities on this line or interface.

Note System accounting provides information about all system-level events, such as when the system reboots or when accounting is turned on or off. System accounting does not use named method lists. For system accounting, you can define only the default method list.

AAA Configuration for TACACS+ Example

Example 4-12 shows the resulting running configuration of a router that has been configured for TACACS+ services using Cisco Configuration Professional and CLI commands. This example is unrelated to the RADIUS configuration we have been doing in the preceding sections.

Example 4-12 *Example of AAA Configuration for TACACS+*

```
aaa new-model
!
aaa authentication login TACACS_SERVER group tacacs+ local
aaa authorization exec default group tacacs+
aaa authorization network default group tacacs+
aaa accounting exec default start-stop tacacs+
aaa accounting network default start-stop tacacs+
aaa accounting commands 15 default stop-only group tacacs+
!
!
tacacs-server host 10.0.1.11
tacacs-server key ciscosecure
!
line vty 0 4
 login authentication TACACS_SERVER
```

The following is an explanation of the commands displayed in Example 4-12:

- **aaa new-model:** Enables AAA.

- **aaa authentication login TACACS_SERVER group tacacs+ local:** Defines an AAA login policy entitled TACACS_SERVER that uses TACACS+ as the first authentication method and the local database as a second method if TACACS+ is unavailable. Note that the command could have been entered as **aaa authentication login TACACS_SERVER tacacs+ local,** but it would have appeared in the config as **aaa authentication login TACACS_SERVER group tacacs+ local.**

- **aaa authorization exec default group tacacs+:** Defines an AAA authorization policy that uses TACACS+ for access to an EXEC prompt. Note that the command could have been entered as **aaa authorization exec default tacacs+,** but it would have appeared in the config as **aaa authorization exec default group tacacs+.**

- **aaa authorization network default group tacacs+:** Defines an AAA authorization policy that uses TACACS+ for network access. Note that the command could have been entered as **aaa authorization network default tacacs+,** but it would have appeared in the config as **aaa authorization network default group tacacs+.**

■ **aaa accounting exec default start-stop group tacacs+:** Defines an AAA accounting policy that uses TACACS+ for logging both start and stop records for user EXEC terminal sessions. Note that the command could have been entered as **aaa accounting exec default start-stop tacacs+,** but it would have appeared in the config as **aaa accounting exec default start-stop group tacacs+.**

■ **aaa accounting network default start-stop tacacs+:** Defines an AAA accounting policy that uses TACACS+ for logging both start and stop records for all network-related service requests. Note that the command could have been entered as **aaa accounting network default start-stop tacacs+,** but it would have appeared in the config as **aaa accounting network default start-stop group tacacs+.**

■ **aaa accounting commands 15 default stop-only group tacacs+:** Defines a default commands accounting method list, where accounting services are provided by a TACACS+ security server, set for privilege level 15 commands with a stop-only restriction. Note that the command could have been entered as **aaa accounting commands 15 default stop-only tacacs+,** but it would have appeared in the config as **aaa accounting commands 15 default stop-only group tacacs+.**

■ **tacacs-server host 10.0.1.11:** Configures the IP address of the TACACS+ server.

■ **tacacs-server key ciscosecure:** Configures an encryption key of ciscosecure to be used when communicating with the TACACS+ server.

■ **line vty 0 4:** Enters line configuration mode for vty 0 through vty 4.

■ **login authentication TACACS_SERVER:** Applies the AAA authentication policy named TACACS_SERVER to all five vty lines.

Troubleshooting TACACS+

Because we are still dealing with how to configure the router, let's review the debug commands available to us. Later in this chapter, you learn the configuration that must be done on the Cisco Secure ACS server itself.

In Example 4-11, we saw the use of the **debug aaa authentication** command to get a high-level view of login activity. When the TACACS+ protocol is used on the router, you can also use the **debug tacacs** command for more detailed debugging information.

Example 4-13 shows sample output from the **debug tacacs** command for a TACACS+ login attempt that was unsuccessful, as indicated by the status FAIL.

Example 4-13   debug tacacs *Command for an Unsuccessful TACACS+ Login Attempt*

```
Router# debug tacacs

13:53:35: TAC+: Opening TCP/IP connection to 192.168.60.15 using source 192.48.0.79
13:53:35: TAC+: Sending TCP/IP packet number 416942312-1 to 192.168.60.15 (AUTHEN/
  START)
13:53:35: TAC+: Receiving TCP/IP packet number 416942312-2 from 192.168.60.15
```

```
13:53:35: TAC+ (416942312): received authen response status = GETUSER
13:53:37: TAC+: send AUTHEN/CONT packet
13:53:37: TAC+: Sending TCP/IP packet number 416942312-3 to 192.168.60.15 (AUTHEN/
  CONT)
13:53:37: TAC+: Receiving TCP/IP packet number 416942312-4 from 192.168.60.15
13:53:37: TAC+ (416942312): received authen response status = GETPASS
13:53:38: TAC+: send AUTHEN/CONT packet
13:53:38: TAC+: Sending TCP/IP packet number 416942312-5 to 192.168.60.15 (AUTHEN/
  CONT)
13:53:38: TAC+: Receiving TCP/IP packet number 416942312-6 from 192.168.60.15
13:53:38: TAC+ (416942312): received authen response status = FAIL
13:53:40: TAC+: Closing TCP/IP connection to 192.168.60.15
```

To display information from the TACACS+ helper process, use the **debug tacacs events** command in privileged EXEC mode. To disable debugging output, use the **no** form of this command.

Note   Use the **debug tacacs events** command with caution, because it can generate a substantial amount of output.

Also, because console ports communicate at 9600 bauds, it is recommended to send debug output to the syslog server and enter **no logging console** on the router.

Example 4-14 shows sample output from the **debug tacacs events** command. The example shows the opening and closing of a TCP connection to a TACACS+ server, the bytes read and written over the connection, and the TCP status of the connection.

Example 4-14   debug tacacs events *Command Output*

```
Router# debug tacacs events

%LINK-3-UPDOWN: Interface Async2, changed state to up
00:03:16: TAC+: Opening TCP/IP to 192.168.58.104/1049 timeout=15
00:03:16: TAC+: Opened TCP/IP handle 0x48A87C to 192.168.58.104/1049
00:03:16: TAC+: periodic timer started
00:03:16: TAC+: 192.168.58.104 req=3BD868 id=-1242409656 ver=193 handle=0x48A87C
  (ESTAB)
expire=14 AUTHEN/START/SENDAUTH/CHAP queued
00:03:17: TAC+: 192.168.58.104 ESTAB 3BD868 wrote 46 of 46 bytes
00:03:22: TAC+: 192.168.58.104 CLOSEWAIT read=12 wanted=12 alloc=12 got=12
00:03:22: TAC+: 192.168.58.104 CLOSEWAIT read=61 wanted=61 alloc=61 got=49
00:03:22: TAC+: 192.168.58.104 received 61 byte reply for 3BD868
```

```
00:03:22: TAC+: req=3BD868 id=-1242409656 ver=193 handle=0x48A87C (CLOSEWAIT)
  expire=9
AUTHEN/START/SENDAUTH/CHAP processed
00:03:22: TAC+: periodic timer stopped (queue empty)
00:03:22: TAC+: Closing TCP/IP 0x48A87C connection to 192.168.58.104/1049
00:03:22: TAC+: Opening TCP/IP to 192.168.58.104/1049 timeout=15
00:03:22: TAC+: Opened TCP/IP handle 0x489F08 to 192.168.58.104/1049
00:03:22: TAC+: periodic timer started
00:03:22: TAC+: 192.168.58.104 req=3BD868 id=299214410 ver=192 handle=0x489F08
  (ESTAB)
expire=14 AUTHEN/START/SENDPASS/CHAP queued
00:03:23: TAC+: 192.168.58.104 ESTAB 3BD868 wrote 41 of 41 bytes
00:03:23: TAC+: 192.168.58.104 CLOSEWAIT read=12 wanted=12 alloc=12 got=12
00:03:23: TAC+: 192.168.58.104 CLOSEWAIT read=21 wanted=21 alloc=21 got=9
00:03:23: TAC+: 192.168.58.104 received 21 byte reply for 3BD868
00:03:23: TAC+: req=3BD868 id=299214410 ver=192 handle=0x489F08 (CLOSEWAIT)
  expire=13
AUTHEN/START/SENDPASS/CHAP processed
00:03:23: TAC+: periodic timer stopped (queue empty)
```

Note   The TACACS messages are intended to be self-explanatory to IT service personnel only.

Deploying and Configuring Cisco Secure ACS

Cisco Secure ACS uses a modular approach to define AAA policies. Cisco Secure ACS 5.2 offers a new paradigm. In previous versions of ACS, the policy is group based. A user inherits network privileges and restrictions based on the group to which the user belongs. As an example, Mary from Marketing is limited to a single remote-access session, while Indy from IT is provided with up to three concurrent remote-access sessions. ACS 5.2 provides much more granular policies with its rule-based approach (not to be confused with Role-Based CLI Access). With rules-based policies, the ACS 5.2 looks at the environment used by the user: for example, the user is Indy, connecting at 2:45 p.m., from network device Switch B, port 19, and so forth. So, ACS 5.2 looks at not only who the user is, but also from which network device the user's session is initiating, what time of day the user is connecting, and so forth. In the next two sections, we will examine how prior versions of Cisco Secure ACS operate, and then we will see how the new ACS 5.2 works.

Evolution of Authorization

Cisco made a significant change in authorization when it introduced Cisco ACS 5.2

Before: Group-Based Policies

As mentioned, earlier versions of Cisco Secure ACS base policy on membership in user groups. The user groups define the access restrictions and permissions for the users who are members of the group.

Using the group-based approach, as shown in Figure 4-21, when a user requests access, the credentials of the user are authenticated with an identity store. Once authenticated, the user is associated with the appropriate user group. The authorization rules in this environment are part of the group itself, including restrictions such as time of day or point of access into the network.

Figure 4-21   *Previous Version of Cisco Secure ACS Using Group-Based Policies*

Using group-based policies, permissions are set based primarily on the identity-based association of a user with a single group. Because authorization is tied to the user group, all members of the user group have the same access restrictions and permissions all the time.

This type of authorization is suitable for simple policies, in which identity is the dominant or only condition, but it results in lack of flexibility in the presence of other requirements or conditions that define the permissions of the user.

The trends in network connectivity today call for universal access from multiple locations, at multiple times, using multiple devices, as exemplified in Figure 4-22. For example, you might want to grant an employee full access when they are on campus, but restricted access when they are working remotely over the weekend. The group-based policy approach results in complex access policies and rules because you must consider the user's choice of device (laptop versus PDA), the security posture of the device at the time of connection, and many other conditions.

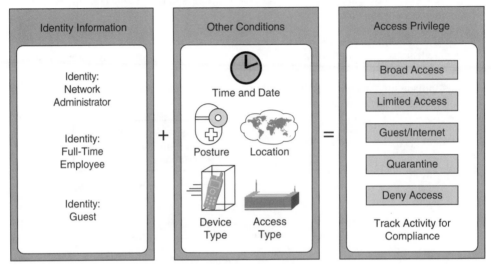

Figure 4-22   *Complexity of a Mobile Workforce and Borderless Networks*

Now: More Than Just Identities

To manage situations such as those shown in Figure 4-22, a different approach is needed—one that grants permissions on conditions other than identity alone. Using Cisco Secure ACS, starting with version 5.x, group-based policies are replaced by rule-based policies, which provide a more flexible approach that can match the variety of access conditions that are found in current networks.

Using the rule-based approach, instead of relying on the group to contain all the information, identity classification is separated from other conditions or restrictions, as shown in Figure 4-23. Permissions are also decoupled from the group, resulting in the group acting as an identity classification only and no longer containing access permissions and restrictions.

In addition to an expanded concept of identity, which is defined by the users and group membership, the idea of restrictions was also expanded to consider other session and environment attributes, such as access location, access type, time, date, end-station health, and so forth.

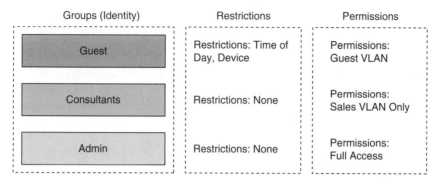

Figure 4-23 *New in Cisco Secure ACS 5.2: Rule-Based Policies*

These attributes become a contextual set of conditions that determines which permissions to apply to the network access request. In other words, the previous approach of associating permissions directly at the user and group level is replaced by a new approach in which the permissions are a separate object called an *authorization profile*. In addition, contextual conditions can be evaluated separately, eventually resulting in different sets of permissions for the same user, based on the different access conditions presented in Figure 4-24.

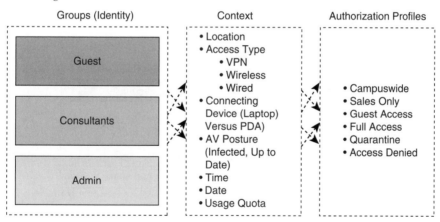

Figure 4-24 *Context-Aware Authorization Profiles*

Dynamic Access Policies on Cisco ASA

For those readers familiar with Cisco ASA, you will relate Figure 4-24 to the dynamic access policies (DAP) used in VPN settings, where the ASA assigns a policy to an incoming connection based on many criteria, including not only the user's identity, but also how the computer is used to connect, whether the computer is a corporate asset, whether the computer has antivirus protection, and so forth.

Rule-Based Policies

Authorization is now determined using a set of logical rules, which resemble the structure of if-then-else conditions, that better match the variety of network access conditions and resulting permissions. Figure 4-25 illustrates this logic. If access conditions match a certain set of attributes for the user or group, then apply a set of permissions. Using rule-based policies, the conditions can be any combination of available session attributes, including, but certainly not limited to, identity.

RULES: If <condition> then <apply profile>

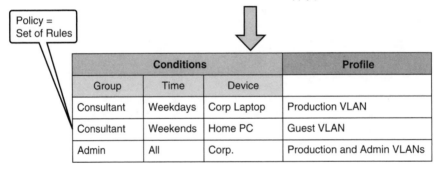

Conditions			Profile
Group	Time	Device	
Consultant	Weekdays	Corp Laptop	Production VLAN
Consultant	Weekends	Home PC	Guest VLAN
Admin	All	Corp.	Production and Admin VLANs

Figure 4-25 *Rule-Based Policies with Cisco Secure ACS 5.2*

As previously mentioned, the permissions in Cisco Secure ACS v5.x are defined in another modular object known as an authorization profile. Several profiles can be created, and multiple sets of conditions can arrive at the same profile. For instance, a user can acquire the Guest role if the user does not exist in the identity database, but a user can also acquire this role if the user is valid but tries to access the network from an unknown location, using a smartphone, over the weekend.

Authorization profiles can contain permissions in multiple dimensions; for instance, VLANs, downloadable ACLs (dACL), quality of service (QoS) settings, RADIUS attributes, and others.

The example in Figure 4-25 highlights the flexibility of the rule-based policies. Notice that a single classification of users can get different authorizations based on more than just the identity attribute. The benefits of this are that the rule conditions can be any combination of the access session attributes, and that the assignment of permissions does not have to be based on a specific identity at all. It is a set of conditions, including identity, that defines access control.

Configuring Cisco Secure ACS 5.2

Configuration of Cisco Secure ACS 5.2 will be explained using the following scenario, illustrated in Figure 4-26, which focuses on authorization policies for device administration. In our scenario, Cisco Secure ACS will be used as the policy server to grant the admin user full access to the router CLI, at privilege level 15. Similarly, the monitor user will obtain privilege level 1 for read-only access to the router's CLI. The system uses TACACS+ between the router and the policy server. Obviously, this scenario does not present the full potential of Cisco Secure ACS 5.x, which is beyond the scope of this book. The goal in this book, which focuses on Cisco IOS security, is to show you a basic configuration of Cisco Secure ACS 5.2 when it is configured for basic interaction with your network devices.

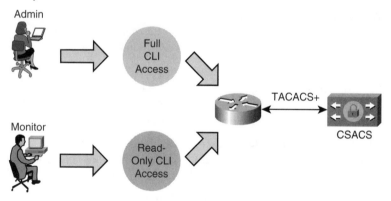

- Grant administrator user full access to router CLI at privilege level 15.
- Grant monitor user read-only access to router CLI at privilege level 1.

Figure 4-26 *Rule-Based Policies Scenario*

Configuring Authorization Policies for Device Administration

The rules-based approach is easily configured using the Cisco Secure ACS GUI. The following steps are required to build a device administration access policy using Cisco Secure ACS 5.2. This policy will define the type of CLI access that different user roles have to a router or group of routers.

The general steps used to configure Cisco Secure ACS for device administration are as follow:

Step 1.   Add network devices to Cisco Secure ACS so the router appears as an AAA client.

Step 2.   Define identity groups and identity the store.

Step 3.   Configure access services to process requests.

Step 4.   Create the identity policy.

Step 5.   Create the authorization policy.

Adding Network Devices to Cisco Secure ACS

The first step in adding a network device to Cisco Secure ACS is to define network device groups and add routers and network devices to the groups. This step allows Cisco Secure ACS to know which devices will send AAA requests.

In Cisco Secure ACS, you can define network device groups (NDG), which are sets of devices. These NDGs provide logical grouping of devices—for example, by device location or type—which you can use in policy conditions, as shown in Figure 4-27.

When Cisco Secure ACS receives a request for a device, the NDGs that are associated with that device are retrieved and compared against those in the policy table. With this method, you can group multiple devices and assign them the same policies. For example, you can group all devices in a specific location and assign to them the same policy.

The device group hierarchy is the hierarchical structure that contains the NDGs. The hierarchy provides further flexibility to create groups of devices that follow a functional classification, in addition to a geographic or location-based classification.

The access the configuration options for this step, navigate to **Network Resources > Network Device Groups** in the menu on the left side of the screen. As you can see in Figure 4-27, there are two types of NDG: one based on location and one based on device type. In this example, we are creating device type groups.

Figure 4-28 illustrates the task of adding a network device to a group under **Network Resources > Network Devices and AAA Clients.** The network device definition can be associated with a specific IP address or a subnet mask, where all IP addresses within the subnet can access the network. The device definition includes the association of the device to NDGs. You also configure here whether the device uses TACACS+ or RADIUS.

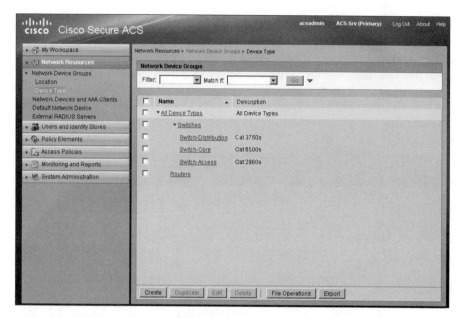

Figure 4-27   *Cisco Secure ACS and the Logical Grouping of Devices*

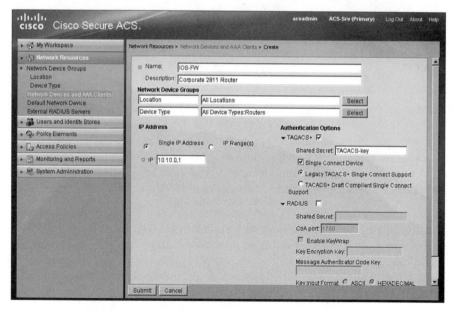

Figure 4-28   *Adding Network Devices to Cisco Secure ACS*

Defining Users, Identity Groups, and Internal Identity Stores

The second step is to define the user and identity stores. In our scenario, the internal Cisco Secure ACS store is used to validate users and credentials. The next step, then, is to define users and groups in the local Cisco Secure ACS database. This can be accomplished by navigating to **Users and Identity Stores > Internal Identity Stores > Users** and clicking **Create** to add a new user, as illustrated in Figure 4-29. This figure shows the creation of a new user in the internal identity store. The user is assigned to an existing group.

Figure 4-29 *Creating Users in Identity Store*

Configuring Access Services

The third step is to configure the access services that will define the CLI access policy. In Cisco Secure ACS 5.x, a policy is a set of rules that the server uses to evaluate an access request and return a decision. Cisco Secure ACS 5.x organizes the sequence of independent policies (a policy workflow) into an access service, which it uses to process an access request. You can create multiple access services to process different kinds of access requests, such as for device administration or network access.

When you create an access service, you define the type of policies and policy structures that it contains; for example, policies for device administration or network access, as shown in Figure 4-30. The default access services use and match RADIUS for network access policies, while using and matching TACACS+ for device administration policies. This means that, in this example, there is no need to change the default settings; we are using TACACS+ as the AAA protocol between the router and the Cisco Secure ACS server.

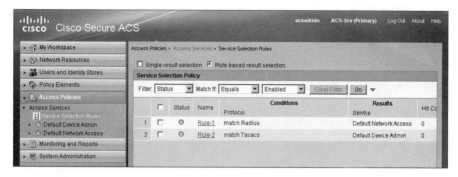

Figure 4-30 *Configuring Access Services*

Configuring the Identity Policy

The fourth step is to configure the identity policy, which defines how requests are authenticated. The navigation path for this option is **Access Policies > Access Services > Default Device Admin > Identity.** In our scenario, the access service uses the local Cisco Secure ACS store for router device administration. This means that the Default Device Admin Access Service is to be configured with the Internal Users store as an identity source, as shown in Figure 4-31. This is also the default setting. Other options include external databases, such as LDAP and Active Directory.

Figure 4-31 *Configuring Identity Policy*

Configuring the Authorization Policy

The fifth step configures the authorization policy, which defines the actual rules for Role-Based CLI Access and device administration, in our scenario shown in Figure 4-32. The navigation path is **Access Policies > Access Services > Default Device Admin > Authorization**. You then click **Create** to add a new authorization policy.

Notice the familiar framework of policies that are based on a set of conditions and a profile to apply if those conditions match an access request.

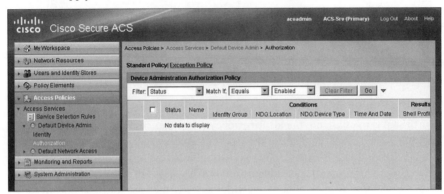

Figure 4-32 *Configuring Authorization Policy*

When you create an access service and select a service policy structure for Device Administration, ACS automatically creates a shell/command authorization policy. You can then create and modify policy rules.

The web interface supports the creation of multiple command sets for device administration. With this capability, you can maintain a smaller number of basic command sets. You can then choose the command sets in combination as rule results, rather than maintaining all the combinations themselves in individual command sets.

Figure 4-33 illustrates the creation of an authorization rule for the admin user. Notice the Conditions section, where you can define the matching conditions that would trigger the policy (in this example, membership to the Admin group and an NDG of Routers). Also notice the Results section, with its corresponding Select button. This option allows you to create customized tasks or attributes to be granted to user admin. In this example, we configure a privilege level 15 for this user.

Figure 4-34 shows the final configuration of authorization policies for both users: Admin, obtaining the shell profile FullAccess, which grants privilege level 15, and Monitor, obtaining the shell profile ReadOnly, which grants privilege level 1.

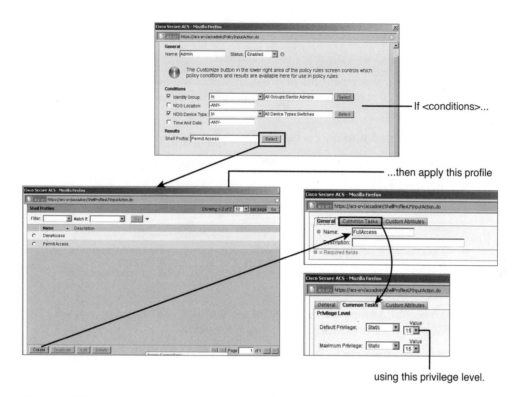

Figure 4-33 *Configuring an Authorization Rule for Admin User*

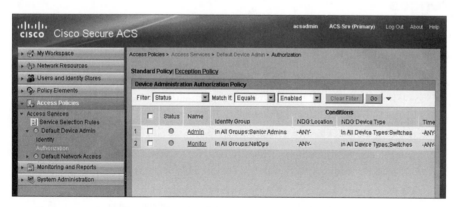

Figure 4-34 *Final Configuration of Authorization Policies for Users*

Summary

The following topics were discussed in this chapter:

- Role-based access control, use of strong authentication and cryptography, and deployment of NTP are among the recommended practices in secure management and reporting.

- Role-based access control can be accomplished on the router CLI using views.

- Syslog and SNMP provide management notification options for Cisco routers.

- AAA services can use the local router database or a remote AAA server database.

- Method lists provide redundancy and fallback options for AAA configuration using Cisco Configuration Professional.

- CLI commands can be used to verify the correct configuration of the router.

- Cisco Secure ACS can be used as an external AAA database for authentication, authorization, and accounting.

- Two popular AAA protocols, TACACS+ and RADIUS, can be used by network devices to communicate with an external AAA server.

- AAA deployment can be completed by configuring network elements to use AAA authentication and authorization.

References

For additional information, refer to these resources:

Cisco.com Resources

"Cisco Configuration Professional," http://www.cisco.com/go/ccp

"Cisco ISE Fundamentals," http://www.cisco.com/en/US/prod/collateral/vpndevc/ps5712/ps11637/ps11195/ise_fundamentals.html

"Cisco Secure Access Control System," http://www.cisco.com/go/acs

"Password Recovery Procedures," http://www.cisco.com/en/US/products/sw/iosswrel/ps1831/products_tech_note09186a00801746e6.shtml

User Guide for the Cisco Secure Access Control System 5.2, http://www.cisco.com/en/US/docs/net_mgmt/cisco_secure_access_control_system/5.2/user/guide/acsuserguide.html

RFCs

RFC 1305, "Network Time Protocol (Version 3) Specification, Implementation and Analysis," http://www.faqs.org/rfcs/rfc1305.html

RFC 2571, "An Architecture for Describing SNMP Management Frameworks," http://www.ietf.org/rfc/rfc2571.txt

Secure Shell

Wikipedia. "Secure Shell," http://en.wikipedia.org/wiki/Secure_Shell

Review Questions

Use the questions here to review what you learned in this chapter. The correct answers are found in the Appendix, "Answers to Chapter Review Questions."

1. Which port is used by NTP?

   a. UDP 49

   b. TCP 69

   c. UDP 123

   d. TCP 1211

2. Which two statements are true about passwords?

   a. The console port does not require a password for initial console administrative access.

   b. Passwords cannot include symbols and spaces.

   c. You can use either the enable password or the enable secret password to enter the enable mode when both are configured on a router.

   d. The enable secret password is always hashed inside the router configuration using a MD5 hashing algorithm.

3. What is the purpose of the 5 in the following command: **username Admin secret 5 1feb0$a104Qd9UZ./Ak00KTggPD0?**

   a. The encrypted password will be converted to cleartext in the running configuration using MD5.

   b. The user Admin has privilege level 5 in this router.

   c. The user Admin has five attempts to log in to this router.

   d. The encrypted-secret password was hashed with MD5.

4. What is the purpose of the command **parser view?**

   a. It creates different views of router configuration for different users.

   b. It provides a root view of all commands.

   c. It configures a password for a view.

   d. It is used to enter commands accessible for that view.

5. Which command would you use to enable Cisco IOS resilience?

   a. secure boot-ios

   b. secure boot-config

   c. secure boot-image

   d. secure boot-flash

6. Which command is used to enable AAA on a router?

   a. aaa enable
   b. aaa authentication new-model
   c. aaa tacacs+
   d. aaa new-model

7. Which of the following is not supported by Cisco Secure ACS?

   a. StreetTalk Directory Services
   b. Directory Services
   c. One-time passwords
   d. ODBC databases

8. Which portion of a RADIUS packet is sent in plaintext?

   a. All portions
   b. All portions except for the password
   c. All portions except for the CHAP password
   d. All portions except for the username

9. Which of the following protocols is automatically enabled once RSA keys have been generated?

   a. Telnet
   b. SDM
   c. SSH
   d. HTTPS

10. What is significantly different with Cisco Secure ACS 5.x compared to an older version of Cisco Secure ACS?

   a. Users are authenticated locally but authorized on a remote AAA server.
   b. Permissions are granted on conditions other than identity alone.
   c. The desktop is first checked against a set of policies prior to presenting the user with a login prompt.
   d. Different users can share one single AAA policies.

Chapter 5

Securing the Data Plane on Cisco Catalyst Switches

In this chapter, you learn that, like routers, both Layer 2 and Layer 3 switches have their own set of network security requirements. Access to switches is a convenient entry point for attackers who are intent on illegally gaining access to a corporate network. With access to a switch, an attacker can set up rogue access points and protocol analyzers and launch all types of attacks from within the network. Attackers can even spoof the MAC and IP addresses of critical servers to do much damage. In this chapter, you will examine various Layer 2 attacks and strategies to mitigate them. Topics covered in this chapter include the following:

- An introduction to fundamental switching concepts, starting with the building blocks of VLANs and trunking

- An introduction to other building blocks of switching technology, including Spanning Tree Protocol for high availability

- A revisit and further explanation of security threats that exploit vulnerabilities in the switching infrastructure

- A description of how to plan and develop a strategy for protecting the data plane

- A description of the Spanning Tree Protocol Toolkit found on Cisco IOS routers that prevents STP operations from having an impact on the security posture

- A review of port security and how to configure it, to illustrate security controls that are aimed at mitigating MAC spoofing and other threats

Note   Prior to covering Layer 2 data plane security, this chapter includes an overview of related technologies such as VLANs, trunking, and spanning tree. For greater details on these topics, refer to the third edition of *Cisco Press CCNA ICND2 640-816 Official Cert Guide*.

Overview of VLANs and Trunking

A virtual LAN (VLAN) is a logical broadcast domain that can span multiple physical LAN segments. Within the switched internetwork, VLANs provide segmentation and organizational flexibility. You can design a VLAN structure that lets you group stations that are segmented logically by functions, project teams, and applications without regard to the physical location of the users, as shown in Figure 5-1. You can assign each port of a switch to only one VLAN, adding a layer of security. Ports in a single VLAN share broadcasts, while ports in different VLANs do not share broadcasts. Containing broadcasts within a VLAN improves the overall performance of the network.

Within the switched internetwork, VLANs provide segmentation and organizational flexibility. Using VLAN technology, you can group switch ports and their connected users into logically defined communities, such as coworkers in the same department, a cross-functional product team, or diverse user groups sharing the same network application.

Figure 5-1   *A Building LAN Segmented with VLANs*

A VLAN can exist on a single switch or span multiple switches. VLANs can include stations in a single building or in a multiple-building infrastructure. VLANs can also connect across WANs.

A Cisco Catalyst switch operates in a network similar to a traditional bridge. Each VLAN that you configure on the switch implements address learning, forwarding and filtering decisions, and loop avoidance mechanisms as if the VLAN were a separate physical bridge.

A Cisco Catalyst switch implements VLANs by restricting traffic forwarding to destination ports that are in the same VLAN as the originating ports. So when a frame arrives on a switch port, the switch must retransmit the frame to only the ports that belong to the same VLAN. In essence, a VLAN that is operating on a switch limits transmission of unicast, multicast, and broadcast traffic. Traffic originating from a particular VLAN floods to only the other ports in that VLAN, creating a broadcast domain.

What is a VLAN? It is a single broadcast domain. It is a logical network, thus it is a subnet.

Trunking and 802.1Q

By default, a switch port carries the traffic for only a single VLAN. This is called an access port. If two interconnected switches need to exchange frames from more than one VLAN, their interconnecting ports are configured as trunks, instead of access ports. Therefore, a trunk port can carry traffic for multiple VLANs, as shown at the top of Figure 5-2.

Figure 5-2 *Trunk Ports Carry Traffic for Multiple VLANs*

A trunk is a point-to-point link between one or more Ethernet switch interfaces and another networking device such as a router or a switch. A trunk is meant to carry the traffic of multiple VLANs over that single link and allow you to extend the VLANs across an entire network.

Trunk Versus Multi-VLAN Access Port

As just mentioned, a port that carries traffic for a single VLAN is called an access port, and a port that carries traffic for multiple VLANs s is called a trunk port. However, a clarification is needed: a trunk is a port that carries traffic for multiple *data VLANs*. If a port carries traffic for both a data VLAN and a voice VLAN, it is not called a trunk: it is called a *multi-VLAN access port*. Voice VLANs are not considered data VLANs per se. Therefore, a port carrying voice VLAN traffic and data VLAN traffic is not technically carrying traffic for two data VLANs, and thus is not a trunk.

Looking at Figure 5-2, notice that connected in port Fa0/2 of Switch A is an IP Phone, from which is hanging a PC. This IP Phone has a built-in *mini* switch. The IP Phone's built-in switch, connected to port Fa0/2, passes to Switch A traffic from the PC (VLAN 20 traffic) and traffic generating by the IP Phone itself when the user places a call (VLAN 99 traffic). Port Fa0/2 on Switch A is said to be a multi-VLAN access port, and not a trunk. By comparison, port Gi1/2 on the same switch is a trunk because it is carrying traffic for more than one data VLAN: it carries traffic for data VLAN 10 and data VLAN 20, in addition to traffic for voice VLAN 99.

A trunk can be made of one or multiple interfaces combined. Interfaces belonging to a trunk require special encapsulation, which indicates the origin VLAN number of the traffic sent across the trunk. This encapsulation process will be discussed later in this section.

Cisco supports IEEE 802.1Q encapsulation. Ethernet interfaces support different trunking modes: you can configure an interface as trunking or nontrunking, or have it negotiate trunking with the neighboring interface; you can also configure which mode it will operate in and if it will be a trunk or an access port.

Besides the widely popular 802.1Q trunk encapsulation standard, Cisco has its own trunking protocol called Inter-Switch Link (ISL). However, it's not supported by all Cisco switch models.

Interfaces configured as 802.1Q ports are assigned to a trunk. All ports on a trunk are in a native VLAN, which will be covered in more detail later in this section. Every 802.1Q port is assigned an identifier value that is based on the native VLAN ID (VID) of the port (the default is VLAN 1). All untagged frames are assigned to the VLAN specified in this VID parameter.

802.1Q Tagging

IEEE 802.1Q uses an internal tagging mechanism that inserts a 4-byte Tag field into the original Ethernet frame between the source address and type or length fields, as shown in Figure 5-3. Because 802.1Q alters the frame, the trunking device recomputes the frame check sequence (FCS) on the modified frame.

Figure 5-3   *802.1Q Frame Format*

It is the responsibility of the Ethernet switch to look at the 4-byte Tag field and deter-mine where to deliver the frame. A tiny part of the 4-byte Tag field (3 bits, to be exact) is used to specify the priority of the frame. The details of this are specified in the IEEE 802.1p standard. The 802.1Q header contains the 802.1p field, so you must have 802.1Q to have 802.1p.

Native VLANs

An 802.1Q trunk and its associated trunk ports have a native VLAN value. 802.1Q does not tag frames for the native VLAN. Therefore, ordinary stations can read the native untagged frames but cannot read any other frame because the frames are tagged.

If a switch receives an untagged frame on a trunk port, the switch will associate the frame to the native VLAN. Similarly, outgoing frames that belong to the native VLAN will not be tagged using 802.1Q.

Configuring VLANs and Trunks

There are four general tasks required to configure VLANs and trunking and provide inter-VLAN routing. You will notice in the following steps that trunk ports are configured in a single step, while access ports require the configuration of a VLAN first, and then the assignment of the VLAN to the port.

Step 1.   Configure and verify 802.1Q trunks.

Step 2.   Create or modify a VLAN.

Step 3.   Assign switch ports to a VLAN and verify.

Step 4.   Configure inter-VLAN routing

Step 1: Configuring and Verifying 802.1Q Trunks

The interface configuration command to set a Fast Ethernet or Gigabit Ethernet port to trunk mode is

```
Switch(config-if)# switchport mode {access | dynamic {auto | desirable} | trunk}
```

Many Cisco Catalyst switches support the Dynamic Trunking Protocol (DTP), which manages automatic trunk negotiation.

Table 5-1 describes the four options for the **switchport mode** command.

Table 5-1   switchport mode *Command Parameters*

	Description
trunk	Configures the port into permanent 802.1Q trunk mode and negotiates with the connected device to convert the link to trunk mode.
access	Disables port trunk mode and negotiates with the connected device to convert the link to nontrunk.
dynamic desirable	Triggers the port to negotiate the link from nontrunk to trunk mode. The port negotiates to a trunk port if the connected device is in either trunk state, desirable state, or auto state. Otherwise, the port becomes a nontrunk port.
dynamic auto	Enables a port to become a trunk only if the connected device has the state set to trunk or desirable. Otherwise, the port becomes a nontrunk port.

Example 5-1 shows how to configure a port as a trunk.

Example 5-1   switchport mode *Command*

```
Switch(config)# interface fa0/1
Switch(config-if)# switchport mode trunk
```

You have the following options to control trunking for ports:

- For links that you do not intend to trunk across, use the **switchport mode access** interface configuration command to disable trunking.

- For links that you do intend to trunk across, take the following actions:

  - Use the **switchport mode trunk** interface configuration command to cause the interface to become a trunk link.

  - Use the **switchport nonegotiate** interface configuration command to prevent the generation of Dynamic Trunking Protocol frames. This command is valid only when the interface switchport mode is access or trunk (configured by using the

switchport mode access or the **switchport mode trunk** interface configuration command). This command returns an error if you attempt to execute it in dynamic (auto or desirable) mode. Use the **no** form of this command to return to the default setting. When you configure a port with the **switchport nonegotiate** command, the port trunks only if the other end of the link is specifically set to trunk. The **switchport nonegotiate** command does not form a trunk link with ports in either dynamic desirable or dynamic auto mode.

■ Use the **switchport trunk native vlan** *vlan_number* interface configuration command to set the native VLAN on the trunk to an unused VLAN. The default native VLAN is VLAN 1.

■ Use the **switchport trunk allowed vlan** *vlan_number* interface configuration command to set the list of allowed VLANs that transmit traffic from this interface in tagged format when trunking mode is on.

Verifying a Trunk

To verify a trunk configuration on many Cisco Catalyst switches, use the **show interfaces** *interface* **switchport** command or the **show interfaces** *interface* **trunk** command to display the trunk parameters and VLAN information of the port:

```
Switch# show interfaces interface [switchport | trunk]
```

In the output of the **show interfaces** *interface* **switchport** command in Example 5-2, notice the distinction between the operational mode and administrative mode for each port. This is extremely helpful in troubleshooting trunks. The administrative mode is the configured mode, while the operational mode will depend on the results of trunk negotiations. If trunk negotiations fail, the port will be administratively configured as a trunk (as shown in Example 5-2), but the operational mode will be different. It could be down, as in Example 5-2, or even fall back to an active port on the default VLAN 1.

Example 5-2   show interfaces *interface* switchport *Command*

```
SwitchX# show interfaces fa0/11 switchport
Name: Fa0/11
Switchport: Enabled
Administrative Mode: trunk
Operational Mode: down
Administrative Trunking Encapsulation: dot1q
Negotiation of Trunking: On
Access Mode VLAN: 1 (default)
Trunking Native Mode VLAN: 1 (default)
```

In the output of the **show interfaces** *interface* **trunk** command in Example 5-3, you will notice in the allowed VLANs section that traffic for a particular VLAN will not traverse the trunk if the VLAN does not show in this section.

Example 5-3   show interfaces fa0/11 trunk *Command*

```
SwitchX# show interfaces fa0/11 trunk
Port         Mode          Encapsulation Status      Native vlan
Fa0/11       desirable     802.1Q        trunking    1
Port         Vlans allowed on trunk
Fa0/11       1-4094
Port         Vlans allowed and active in management domain
Fa0/11       1-13Trunking Native Mode VLAN: 1 (default)
```

Step 2: Creating a VLAN

The maximum number of VLANs that can be created is switch-dependent. However, most Cisco Catalyst desktop switches support 128 separate spanning-tree instances, one per VLAN. VLAN 1 is the factory default Ethernet VLAN. The Cisco Discovery Protocol (CDP) advertisements and other protocols are sent on VLAN 1. The Cisco Catalyst switch IP address is in the management VLAN (VLAN 1 by default) that is the IP address used to telnet, or SSH, in the switch. This management IP address is also used by the switch if it has been configured for Simple Network Management Protocol (SNMP) or syslog.

The configuration commands to create a VLAN are as follows:

```
Switch(config)# vlan vlan-id
Switch(config-vlan)# name vlan-name
```

Table 5-2 lists the commands for creating VLANs.

Table 5-2   *Adding a VLAN Command*

Parameter	Description
vlan *vlan-id*	ID of the VLAN to be added and configured. For *vlan-id*, the range is 1 to 4094 when the enhanced software image is installed and 1 to 1005 when the standard software image is installed. Do not enter leading zeros. You can enter a single VID, a series of VIDs separated by commas, or a range of VIDs separated by hyphens.
name *vlan-name*	(Optional) Specify the VLAN name, an ASCII string from 1 to 32 characters that must be unique within the administrative domain.

Example 5-4 shows how to create a VLAN.

Example 5-4   *Example of VLAN Creation*

```
Switch(config)# vlan 2
Switch(config-vlan)# name Marketing
```

Before you create VLANs, consider these guidelines:

■ Most Cisco Catalyst desktop switches support a maximum of 128 spanning-tree instances. If the number of VLANs on the switch exceeds the number of supported spanning-tree instances, it is recommended that you configure Multiple Spanning Tree Protocol (MSTP) on your switch to map multiple VLANs to a single spanning-tree instance.

■ The maximum number of VLANs is switch-dependent. Many access layer Cisco Catalyst switches can support up to 250 user-defined VLANs.

■ Cisco Catalyst switches have a factory default configuration in which various default VLANs are preconfigured to support various media and protocol types. The default Ethernet VLAN is VLAN 1. Cisco Discovery Protocol advertisements and other protocols are sent on VLAN 1.

■ For you to be able to communicate with the Cisco Catalyst switch remotely for management purposes, the switch must have an IP address. This IP address must be in a management VLAN; the default management VLAN is VLAN 1.

After you configure the VLAN, you should validate the parameters for that VLAN. Use the **show vlan** command to display information about a particular VLAN:

```
Switch# show vlan [brief | id vlan-id | name vlan-name]
```

Example 5-5 shows the output of the **show vlan id** command.

Example 5-5 *Output of the* **show vlan id** *Command*

```
SwitchX# show vlan id 2
VLAN Name                        Status    Ports
---- --------------------        ------ ------- -------------
2    switchlab99                 active    Fa0/2, Fa0/12


VLAN Type SAID    MTU   Parent RingNo BridgeNo Stp BrdgMode Trans1 Trans2
---- ---- ------  ----  ------ ------ -------- --- -------- ------ ------
2    enet 100002 1500 -        -      -        -   -        0      0


 .    .    .
SwitchX#
```

Use the **show vlan brief** command to display one line for each VLAN that displays the VLAN name, the status, and the switch ports.

Use the **show vlan** command to display information on all configured VLANs. The **show vlan** command displays the switch ports that are assigned to each VLAN. Other VLAN parameters that are displayed include the type (the default is Ethernet); the security association ID (SAID), used for the FDDI trunk; the maximum transmission unit (MTU) (the default is 1500 for Ethernet VLAN); the STP; and other parameters that are used for Token Ring or FDDI VLANs. (Chances are you have never heard of Token Ring or FDDI network. These were competing technologies prior to the obvious emergence of Ethernet as leader.)

Step 3: Assigning Switch Ports to a VLAN

After creating a VLAN, you can manually assign a port or a number of ports to that VLAN with the following command:

```
Switch(config-if)# switchport access [vlan vlan-id | dynamic]
```

A port can belong to only one VLAN at a time. When you assign a switch port to a VLAN using this method, as shown in Example 5-6, it is known as a static-access port.

Example 5-6 *Assigning a VLAN to a Port with the* **switchport access** *Command*

```
SwitchX(config)# interface range fastethernet 0/2 - 4
SwitchX(config-if)# switchport access vlan 2


SwitchX# show vlan


VLAN  Name              Status    Ports
----  ----------------  --------  ----------------------
1     default           active    Fa0/1
2     switchlab99       active    Fa0/2, Fa0/3, Fa0/4
```

On most Cisco Catalyst switches, you configure the VLAN port assignment from interface configuration mode using the **switchport access** command. Use the **vlan** *vlan_ number* option to set static-access membership. The **dynamic** option uses the VLAN Membership Policy Server (VMPS) method and is outside of the scope of this book.

Use the **show vlan brief** privileged EXEC command to display the VLAN assignment and membership type for all switch ports, as shown in Example 5-7. It is worth mentioning that if a given port does not show under the Ports column of the table, it could be a trunk port carrying multiple VLANs.

Example 5-7   *Verifying a VLAN Assignment with the* **show vlan** *Command*

```
SwitchX# show vlan brief
VLAN Name                 Status       Ports
---- ------------------   -----------  --------- ------------------
1    default              active       Fa0/1
2    switchlab99          active       Fa0/2, Fa0/3, Fa0/4
3    vlan3                active
4    vlan4                active
1002 fddi-default         act/unsup
1003 token-ring-default   act/unsup

VLAN Name                 Status       Ports
---- ------------------   -----------  ------------------------------
1004 fddinet-default      act/unsup
1005 trnet-default        act/unsup/4
```

Step 4: Configuring Inter-VLAN Routing

Inter-VLAN communication occurs between broadcast domains via a Layer 3 device. In a VLAN environment, frames are switched only between ports within the same broadcast domain. VLANs perform network partitioning and traffic separation at Layer 2. Inter-VLAN communication cannot occur without a Layer 3 device, such as a router.

One way to accomplish inter-VLAN routing is illustrated in Figure 5-4. You can use IEEE 802.1Q to enable trunking on a router interface, and enable the router to route between VLANs. This is sometimes known as a "router on a stick" scenario, where a router is attached to a core switch. The router can receive packets on one VLAN and forward them to another VLAN. To perform inter-VLAN routing functions, the router must know how to reach all VLANs being interconnected. There must be a separate connection on the router for each VLAN, and you must enable 802.1Q trunking on those connections. The router already knows about directly connected networks. The router must learn routes to networks to which it is not directly connected.

To support 802.1Q trunking, you must subdivide the physical Fast Ethernet interface of the router into multiple, logical, addressable interfaces, one per VLAN. The resulting logical interfaces are called subinterfaces. Without this subdivision, you would have to dedicate a separate physical interface to each VLAN.

In Figure 5-4, the FastEthernet 0/0 interface is divided into two subinterfaces: FastEthernet 0/0.1 and FastEthernet0/0.2. Each subinterface represents the router in each of the VLANs for which it routes. The sample configuration in Figure 5-4 uses the **encapsulation dotlq** *vlan-id* command on each subinterface to enable 802.1Q encapsulation trunking. The subinterface number does not have to be the same as the dot1q VLAN number; however, management is easier when both numbers are the same.

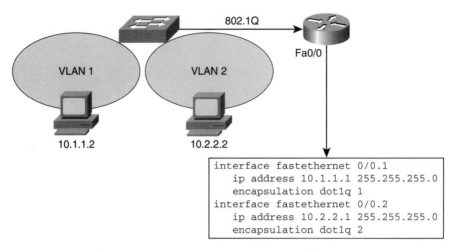

Figure 5-4 *Routing Between VLANs with 802.1Q Trunks*

Note Layer 3 switches, multilayer switches, are meant to replace the router on a stick shown in Figure 5-4 by incorporating the Layer 3 routing functionality and VLAN interfaces within the switch itself

It is also worth noting that the resulting configuration of FastEthernet0/0.1 on the router in Figure 5-4, from issuing the command **encapsulation dot1q 1,** would be **encapsulation dot1q 1 native.** The topic of native VLANs was covered earlier in the chapter.

Spanning Tree Overview

Redundant designs, such as the one shown in Figure 5-5, can mitigate the possibility of a *single point of failure*, which can cause a loss of function for the entire switched or bridged network.

Figure 5-5 *Redundant Topology*

However, you must consider problems that redundant designs can cause. Some of the problems that can occur with redundant links and devices in switched or bridged networks are as follows:

- **Broadcast storms:** Without some loop-avoidance process in operation, each switch or bridge floods broadcasts endlessly. This situation is commonly called a broadcast storm.

- **Multiple frame transmission:** Multiple copies of unicast frames may be delivered to destination stations. Many protocols expect to receive only a single copy of each transmission. Multiple copies of the same frame can cause unrecoverable errors.

- **MAC database instability:** Instability in the content of the MAC address table results from copies of the same frame being received on different ports of the switch. Data forwarding can be impaired when the switch consumes the resources that are coping with instability in the MAC address table.

Layer 2 LAN protocols, such as Ethernet, lack a mechanism to recognize and eliminate endlessly looping frames. Some Layer 3 protocols implement a Time to Live (TTL) mechanism that limits the number of times a Layer 3 networking device can retransmit a packet. Lacking such a mechanism, Layer 2 devices continue to retransmit looping traffic indefinitely.

A loop-avoidance mechanism is required to solve each of these problems. This mechanism is the Spanning Tree Protocol (STP).

STP Fundamentals

Spanning Tree Protocol (STP) provides loop resolution by managing the physical paths to given network segments. STP allows physical path redundancy while preventing the undesirable effects of active loops in the network. STP is an IEEE committee standard defined as 802.1D.

STP behaves as follows:

- STP forces certain ports into a standby state so that they do not listen to, forward, or flood data frames, as seen in Figure 5-6, where one switch has a port in blocking mode. The overall effect is that only one active path exists to the other network segment at any time.

- If there is a problem with connectivity to any of the segments within the network, STP reestablishes connectivity by automatically activating a previously inactive path, if one exists.

Figure 5-6 *Loop Resolution with STP*

RSTP, the Rapid Spanning Tree Protocol, is a version of STP enhanced for fast convergence. RSTP is defined as the IEEE standard 802.1w.

PVST+ is a Cisco implementation of RSTP that provides enhancements that are aimed at scalability of the protocol, as well as provisions for traffic load sharing across STP-enabled paths.

STP performs three steps to provide a loop-free logical network topology, as shown in Figure 5-7:

Step 1.   Selects one root bridge.

STP has a process to elect a root bridge, which will be discussed later. Only one bridge can act as the root bridge in a given network. On the root bridge, all ports are designated ports. Designated ports are normally in the forwarding state. When in the forwarding state, a port can send and receive traffic. In Figure 5-7, Switch X is the root bridge.

Figure 5-7 *STP Operation and Resulting Topology*

Step 2.   Selects the root port on the nonroot bridge.

STP establishes one root port on each nonroot bridge. The root port is the lowest-cost path from the nonroot bridge to the root bridge. Root ports are normally in the forwarding state. Spanning-tree path cost is an accumulated cost that is calculated on the bandwidth. In Figure 5-7, the lowest-cost path to the root bridge from Switch Y is through the 100BASE-T Fast Ethernet link.

Step 3.   Selects the designated port on each segment.

On each segment, STP establishes one designated port. The designated port is selected on the bridge that has the lowest-cost path to the root bridge. Designated ports are normally in the forwarding state, forwarding traffic for the segment. In Figure 5-7, the designated port for both segments is on the root bridge because the root bridge is directly connected to both segments. The 10BASE-T Ethernet port on Switch Y is a nondesignated port because there is only one designated port per segment. Nondesignated ports are normally in the blocking state to logically break the loop topology. When a port is in the blocking state, it is not forwarding traffic but can still receive traffic.

Switches and bridges running the spanning-tree algorithm exchange configuration messages with other switches and bridges at regular intervals (every 2 seconds by default). Switches and bridges exchange these messages using a multicast frame called the bridge protocol data unit (BPDU). One of the pieces of information included in the BPDU is the *bridge ID* (BID).

STP calls for each switch or bridge to be assigned a unique BID. Typically, the BID is composed of a priority value (2 bytes) and the bridge MAC address (6 bytes). The default priority, in accordance with IEEE 802.1D, is 32,768 (1000 0000 0000 0000 in binary, or 0x8000 in hex format), which is the midrange value. The root bridge is the bridge with the lowest BID.

> **Note**   A Cisco Catalyst switch uses one of its MAC addresses from a pool of MAC addresses that are assigned either to the backplane or to the supervisor module, depending on the switch model.

The bridge ID (BID) is made of the bridge priority plus the bridge MAC address.

In Figure 5-8, both switches are using the same default priority. The switch with the lowest MAC address is the root bridge. In Figure 5-8, Switch X is the root bridge with the default priority of 0x8000 (hex), or 32,768 in decimal, and a MAC address of 0c00.1111.1111.

Figure 5-8 *STP: Root Bridge Selection*

Verifying RSTP and PVRST+

PVST is enabled by default in some Cisco Catalyst switch models. You can change the mode to Rapid PVST with the **spanning-tree mode rapid-pvst** command:

```
Switch(config)# spanning-tree mode rapid-pvst
```

This spanning-tree mode is the same as PVST+ except that it uses a rapid convergence that is based on the IEEE 802.1w standard.

For verification, you can use the **show spanning-tree vlan** *vlan-range* command. Example 5-8 shows the result of this command.

Example 5-8 *Verifying Spanning-Tree Configuration for vlan 21*

```
Switch# show spanning-tree vlan 21
VLAN0021
Spanning tree enabled protocol rstp
Root ID     Priority    32789
            Address     88f0.77c5.0f80
            Cost        19
            Port        1 (FastEthernet0/1)
            Hello Time  2 sec   Max Age 20 sec   Forward Delay
15 sec


Bridge ID   Priority    32789   (priority 32768   sys-id-ext 21)
            Address
            Hello Time  d0c2.82c5.6b00
                        2 sec   Max Age 20 sec   Forward Delay
15 sec


            Aging Time  300 sec


Interface         Role Sts Cost      Prio.Nbr Type
---------------- ---- --- --------- --------- --------------
Fa0/1             Root FWD 19        128.1     P2p
Fa0/2             Desg FWD 19        128.2     P2p
Fa0/8             Desg FWD 19        128.8     P2p
```

Mitigating Layer 2 Attacks

As stated at the beginning of the chapter, like routers, both Layer 2 and Layer 3 switches have their own set of network security requirements. Access to switches is a convenient entry point for attackers who are intent on illegally gaining access to a corporate network. With access to a switch, an attacker can set up rogue access points and protocol analyzers, and launch all types of attacks from within the network. Attackers can even spoof the MAC and IP addresses of critical servers to do a great deal of damage.

Basic Switch Operation

Unlike hubs, switches can regulate the flow of data between their ports by creating "instant" networks that contain only the two end devices communicating with each other at that moment in time. When end systems send data frames, their source and destination addresses are not changed throughout the switched domain. Switches maintain content-addressable memory (CAM) lookup tables to track the source MAC addresses located on the switch ports. These lookup tables are populated by an address-learning process on the switch. If the destination MAC address of a frame is not known, or if the frame received by the switch is destined for a broadcast or multicast MAC address, the switch forwards the frame to all ports. Because of their capability to isolate traffic and create instant networks, you can use switches to divide a physical network into multiple logical segments, or VLANs, using Layer 2 traffic segmenting.

Layer 2 is the data link layer in the OSI model and is one of seven layers designed to work together but with autonomy. Layer 2 operates above the physical layer, but below the network and transport layers, as shown in Figure 5-9.

Figure 5-9 *Domino Effect If Layer 2 Is Compromised*

Layer 2 independence enables interoperability and interconnectivity. However, from a security perspective, Layer 2 independence creates a challenge because a compromise at one layer is not always known by the other layers. If the initial attack comes in at Layer 2, the rest of the network can be compromised in an instant. Network security is only as strong as the weakest link, and that link might be the data link layer.

Layer 2 Best Practices

The following list suggests Layer 2 security best practices. All of these suggestions are dependent upon your security policy.

- Manage switches in as secure a manner as possible (SSH, OOB, permit lists, and so on).
- Whenever practical, declare the VLAN ID used on trunk ports with the **switchport trunk allowed vlan** command
- Do not use VLAN 1 for anything.
- Set all user ports to nontrunking (unless you are using Cisco VoIP).
- Use port security where possible for access ports.
- Selectively use SNMP and treat community strings like root passwords.
- Enable STP attack mitigation (BPDU guard, root guard).
- Use Cisco Discovery Protocol only where necessary (with phones it is useful).
- Disable all unused ports and put them in an unused VLAN.

It is important to manage switches like routers, using secure protocols or out-of-band methods if policy permits it. Because VLAN 1 is a known management VLAN, it is recommended that you avoid using it. Turn off services that are not necessary and ports that are not being used. Implement the various security services that have been covered in this chapter as necessary and as supported by your hardware. Turn CDP off on ports that do not connect to network devices, with the exception of ports that connect to Cisco IP phones.

Layer 2 Protection Toolkit

Multiple security features and technologies are available to implement recommended practices, in a manner that streamlines configuration and management while strengthening the overall security posture. Figure 5-10 lists some of them, categorized based on type of attack (spoofing and denial of service [DoS]), type of security control (identity services and device hardening), and protocol (STP, DHCP, and Address Resolution Protocol [ARP]).

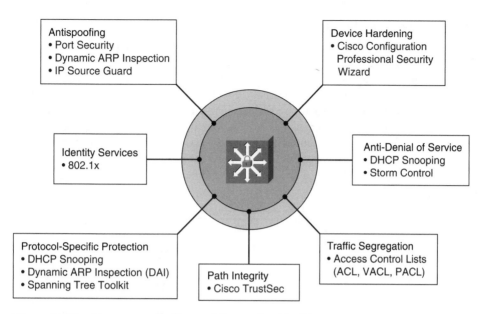

Figure 5-10   *Components of Layer 2 Protection Toolkit*

Some of these controls will be covered in more detail in this chapter, while some others, such as DHCP snooping and IP Source Guard, are covered in other Cisco Press books, such as *CCNP Security SECURE 642-637 Official Cert Guide.*

Mitigating VLAN Attacks

As mentioned at the beginning of this chapter, a VLAN is a logical broadcast domain that can span multiple physical LAN segments. Ports in a VLAN share broadcasts; ports in different VLANs do not share broadcasts. Containing broadcasts within a VLAN improves the overall performance of the network.

VLAN Hopping

The VLAN architecture simplifies network maintenance and improves performance. However, VLAN operation opens the door to abuse. VLAN hopping allows traffic from one VLAN to be seen by another VLAN without first crossing a router. Under certain circumstances, attackers can sniff data and extract passwords and other sensitive information at will. The attack works by taking advantage of an incorrectly configured trunk port. By default, trunk ports have access to all VLANs and pass traffic for multiple VLANs across the same physical link, generally between switches. The data moving across these links may be encapsulated with IEEE 802.1Q or ISL.

VLAN Hopping by Rogue Trunk

In a basic VLAN hopping attack, the attacker takes advantage of the default automatic trunking configuration on most switches. The network attacker configures a system to spoof itself as a switch. This spoofing requires that the network attacker be capable of emulating either ISL or 802.1Q signaling along with Dynamic Trunking Protocol (DTP) signaling, as shown in Figure 5-11. By tricking a switch into thinking it is another switch that needs to trunk, an attacker can gain access to all the VLANs allowed on the trunk port. To succeed, this attack requires a configuration on the port that supports trunking, such as auto. As a result, the attacker is a member of all the VLANS that are trunked on the switch and can "hop" (that is, send and receive traffic) on all of those VLANs.

Figure 5-11 *VLAN Hopping by Rogue Trunk*

A VLAN hopping attack can be launched in one of two ways:

- **Spoofing DTP messages from the attacking host to cause the switch to enter trunking mode:** From here, the attacker can send traffic tagged with the target VLAN, and the switch then delivers the packets to the destination.

- **Introducing a rogue switch and turning trunking on:** The attacker can then access all the VLANs on the victim switch from the rogue switch.

The best way to prevent a basic VLAN hopping attack is to turn off trunking on all ports except the ones that specifically require trunking. On the required trunking ports, disable DTP (auto-trunking) negotiations and manually enable trunking.

VLAN Hopping by Double Tagging

The double-tagging (or double-encapsulated) VLAN hopping attack takes advantage of the way that hardware on most switches operates. Most switches perform only one level of 802.1Q decapsulation and allow an attacker, in specific situations, to embed a hidden 802.1Q tag inside the frame. This tag allows the frame to go to a VLAN that the outer 802.1Q tag did not specify. An important characteristic of the double-encapsulated VLAN hopping attack is that it works even if trunk ports are set to off.

A double-tagging VLAN hopping attack follows four steps, as shown in Figure 5-12:

Step 1.   The attacker sends a double-tagged 802.1Q frame to the switch. The outer header has the VLAN tag of the attacker, which is the same as the native VLAN of the trunk port. For the purposes of this example, assume that this is VLAN 10. The inner tag is the victim VLAN, VLAN 20.

Step 2.   The frame arrives on the switch, which looks at the first 4-byte 802.1Q tag. The switch sees that the frame is destined for VLAN 10 and sends it out all VLAN 10 ports (including the trunk), because there is no CAM table entry. The switch does not add a VLAN 10 tag to the frames because VLAN 10 is the native VLAN, and as specified by the 802.1Q specification, native VLAN traffic is not tagged. At this point, the second VLAN tag is still intact and has not been inspected by the first switch.

Step 3.   The frame arrives at the second switch but has no knowledge that it was supposed to be for VLAN 10.

Step 4.   The second switch looks only at the 802.1Q tag (the former inner tag that the attacker sent) and sees that the frame is destined for VLAN 20 (the victim VLAN). The second switch sends the packet on to the victim port, or floods it, depending on whether there is an existing CAM table entry for the victim host.

Figure 5-12   *VLAN Hopping by Double Tagging*

It is important to note that this attack, as shown in Figure 5-12, is unidirectional and works only when the attacker and trunk port have the same native VLAN. Thwarting this type of attack is not as easy as stopping basic VLAN hopping attacks. The best approach is to ensure that the native VLAN of the trunk ports is different from the native VLAN of the user ports.

To prevent a VLAN hopping attack that uses double 802.1Q encapsulation, the switch must look further into the packet to determine whether more than one VLAN tag is attached to a given frame. Unfortunately, the application-specific integrated circuits

(ASIC) that most switches use are only hardware optimized to look for one tag and then switch the frame. The issue of performance versus security requires administrators to balance their requirements carefully.

Mitigating VLAN hopping attacks that use double 802.1Q encapsulation requires several modifications to the VLAN configuration. One of the more important elements is to use a dedicated native VLAN for all trunk ports. This attack is easy to stop if you follow the best practice that native VLANs for trunk ports should never be used anywhere else on the switch. Also, disable all unused switch ports and place them in an unused VLAN.

Mitigating Spanning Tree Attacks

Figure 5-13 shows how a network attacker can use STP to change the topology of a network so that it appears that the network attacker host is a root bridge with a higher priority. The attacker sends out BPDUs with a better bridge ID and, as a result, becomes the root bridge. Now all the traffic for this switch domain passes through the new root bridge, which is actually the attacker system.

Root Bridge Priority = 8192
MAC Address = 0000.00C0.1234

Figure 5-13   *STP Manipulation*

By manipulating the STP root bridge parameters, network attackers hope to spoof their system, or a rogue switch that they add to the network, as the root bridge in the topology. To do this, the network attacker broadcasts STP configuration and topology change BPDUs in an attempt to force spanning-tree recalculations. The BPDUs sent out by the system or switch of the network attacker announce that the attacking system has a lower bridge priority. If successful, the network attacker becomes the root bridge and sees a variety of frames that otherwise would not be seen.

Note   This attack can be used against all three security objectives of confidentiality, integrity, and availability.

PortFast

The spanning-tree PortFast feature causes an interface configured as a Layer 2 access port to transition from the blocking state to the forwarding state immediately, bypassing the listening and learning states. You can use PortFast on Layer 2 access ports that connect to a single workstation or server, as shown in Figure 5-14, to allow those devices to connect to the network immediately, instead of waiting for spanning tree to converge.

Configure PortFast

Figure 5-14   *Using PortFast*

If a port that is configured with PortFast receives a BPDU, STP can put the port into the blocking state by using a feature called BPDU guard.

Caution   Because the purpose of PortFast is to minimize the time that access ports must wait for spanning tree to converge, it should be used only on access ports. If you enable PortFast on a port connecting to another switch, you risk creating a spanning-tree loop.

Table 5-3 lists and describes the commands that you use to implement and verify PortFast on an interface.

Table 5-3   *PortFast Commands*

Command	Description
Switch(config-if)# **spanning-tree portfast [trunk]**	Enables PortFast on a Layer 2 access port and forces it to enter the forwarding state immediately. Use the **trunk** keyword for trunk interfaces not connected to switches (e.g., routers or servers with trunks).
Switch(config-if)# **no spanning-tree portfast**	Disables PortFast on a Layer 2 access port. PortFast is disabled by default.
Switch(config)# **spanning-tree portfast default**	Globally enables the PortFast feature on all nontrunking ports.
Switch# **show running-config interface** *type slot/port*	Indicates whether PortFast has been configured on a port.

BPDU Guard

To mitigate STP manipulation, use the BPDU guard and root guard enhancement commands available on Cisco switches to enforce the placement of the root bridge in the network and enforce the STP domain borders.

The STP BPDU guard feature is designed to enable network designers to keep the active network topology predictable. BPDU guard is used to protect the switched network from the problems that may be caused by the receipt of BPDUs on ports that should not be receiving them. The receipt of unexpected BPDUs might be accidental or might be part of an unauthorized attempt to add a switch to the network.

BPDU guard is best deployed toward user-facing ports to prevent rogue switch network extensions by an attacker.

The global command to activate BPDU guard on all ports with PortFast enabled is as follows:

```
Switch(config)# spanning-tree portfast bpduguard default
```

In Figure 5-15, the attacker starts sending out spoofed BPDUs in an effort to become the root bridge. Upon receipt of a BPDU, the BPDU guard feature disables the port.

Figure 5-15 *BPDU Guard*

BPDU Filters

Another command used to prevent BPDU filtering, which prevents a port from sending and receiving BPDUs, is the following the interface command:

```
Switch(config-if)# spanning-tree bpdufilter enable
```

Be careful when you enter this command because it overrides the PortFast configuration, explained previously.

This command has three states:

```
Switch(config-if)# spanning-tree bpdufilter enable
```

This command state unconditionally enables BPDU filtering on the interface.

```
Switch(config-if)# spanning-tree bpdufilter disable
```

This command state unconditionally disables BPDU filtering on the interface.

```
Switch(config-if)# no spanning-tree bpdufilter
```

This command state enables BPDU filtering on the interface if the interface is in operational PortFast state and if you configure the **spanning-tree portfast bpdufilter default** command.

Applying BPDU Guard Globally Versus Per Port

At the global level, you can enable BPDU guard on PortFast-enabled ports by using the **spanning-tree portfast bpduguard default** global configuration command. In a valid configuration, PortFast-enabled ports do not receive BPDUs. Receiving a BPDU on a PortFast-enabled port signals an invalid configuration, such as the connection of an unauthorized device, and the BPDU guard feature puts the port into the error-disabled state.

At the interface level, you can enable BPDU guard on any port by using the **spanning-tree bpduguard enable** interface configuration command without also enabling the PortFast feature. When the port receives a BPDU, it is put into the error-disabled state.

Root Guard

The root guard feature of Cisco switches is designed to provide a way to enforce the placement of root bridges in the network. Root guard limits the switch ports out of which the root bridge can be negotiated. Root guard is configured on a per-port basis. If a root guard–enabled port receives BPDUs that are superior to those that the current root bridge is sending, that port is moved to a root-inconsistent state, which is effectively equal to an STP listening state, and no data traffic is forwarded across that port. When the port stops receiving superior BPDUs, it will be unblocked again and will transition through STP states like any other port.

Because an administrator can manually set the bridge priority of a switch to zero, root guard might seem unnecessary. However, setting the priority of a switch to zero does not guarantee that switch will be elected as the root bridge, because another switch could have a priority of zero and a lower MAC address, and therefore a lower BID.

Root guard is best deployed toward ports that connect to switches that should not be the root bridge.

Recovery requires no intervention. A root guard port is in an STP-designated port state. When root guard is enabled on a port, the switch does not allow that port to become an STP root port. The port remains an STP-designated port.

The command to enable root guard on a per-interface basis is as follows:

```
Switch(config-if)# spanning-tree guard root
```

In Figure 5-16, the attacker starts sending out spoofed BPDUs in an effort to become the root bridge. Upon receipt of a BPDU, the switch with the root guard feature configured on that port ignores the BPDU and puts the port in a root-inconsistent state. The port will recover as soon as the offending BPDUs cease.

Figure 5-16   *Root Guard*

Confirming Spanning-Tree State and BPDU Guard

To display information about the state of spanning tree and BPDU guard, use the **show spanning-tree summary** command, as shown in Example 5-9.

Example 5-9   *Status of BPDU Guard with the* **show spanning-tree summary** *Command*

```
Switch# show spanning-tree summary
Root bridge for: Bridge group 1, VLAN0001, VLAN0004-VLAN1005
 VLAN1013-VLAN1499, VLAN2001-VLAN4094
EtherChannel misconfiguration guard is enabled
Extended system ID is enabled
Portfast is enabled by default
PortFast BPDU Guard is enabled
Portfast BPDU Filter is disabled by default
Loopguard is disabled by default
UplinkFast is disabled
BackboneFast is disabled
Pathcost method used is long
<output omitted>
Switch#
```

Mitigating CAM Table Overflow Attacks

The CAM table in a switch contains the MAC addresses that can be reached off a given physical port of a switch and the associated VLAN parameters for each. When a Layer 2 switch receives a frame, the switch first populates its CAM table by creating an entry listing the source MAC address of the frame it just received and the port it was received on. This entry has an idle timeout of 5 minutes; that is, if after 5 minutes no frames have been received from that MAC address on that port, the entry will be flushed out of the CAM table.

Once the switch has populated the CAM table with the source address information, it looks in the CAM table for the destination MAC address. If an entry exists for the MAC address in the CAM table, the switch forwards the frame to the MAC address port designated in the CAM table. If the MAC address does not exist in the CAM table, the switch acts like a hub and forwards the frame out every port on the switch.

The key to understanding how CAM table overflow attacks work is to know that CAM tables are limited in size. MAC flooding takes advantage of this limitation by bombarding the switch with fake source MAC addresses until the switch CAM table is full. If enough entries are entered into the CAM table before other entries are expired, the CAM table fills up to the point that no new entries can be accepted.

In a CAM table overflow attack, a network intruder floods the switch with a large number of invalid source MAC addresses until the CAM table fills up. When that occurs, the switch begins to flood all incoming traffic to all ports because there is no room in the CAM table to learn any legitimate MAC addresses. The switch, in essence, acts like a hub. As a result, the attacker can see all the frames sent from a victim host to another host without a CAM table entry. CAM table overflow floods traffic only within the local VLAN so that the intruder will see only traffic within the local VLAN to which the intruder is connected. If the intruder does not maintain the flood of invalid source MAC addresses, the switch eventually ages out older MAC address entries from the CAM table and begins to act like a switch again.

In Figure 5-17, the **macof** program is running on Host C. This tool floods a switch with packets that contain randomly generated source and destination MAC and IP addresses. Over a short period, the CAM table in the switch fills up until it cannot accept new entries. When the CAM table fills up, the switch begins to flood all frames that it receives.

Figure 5-17   *CAM Table Overflow Attack*

As long as **macof** is left running, the CAM table on the switch remains full. When this happens, the switch begins to flood all received frames out every port so that frames sent from any host are also flooded out of port 3/25 on the switch.

The CAM table overflow attack can be mitigated by configuring port security on the switch. With port security (discussed later in this chapter), you can either statically specify the MAC addresses on a particular switch port or allow the switch to dynamically learn a fixed number of MAC addresses for a switch port. Statically specifying the MAC addresses on switch ports is far too unmanageable a solution for a production environment; allowing the switch to dynamically learn a fixed number of MAC addresses for a port is a more administratively scalable solution.

Mitigating MAC Address Spoofing Attacks

MAC spoofing attacks involve the use of a known MAC address of another host to attempt to make the target switch forward frames destined for the remote host to the network attacker. By sending a single frame with the source Ethernet address of the other host, the network attacker overwrites the CAM table entry so that the switch forwards packets destined for the host to the network attacker instead. Until the host sends traffic, it does not receive any traffic. When the host sends out traffic, the CAM table entry is rewritten once more so that it moves back to the original port.

Figure 5-18 shows how MAC spoofing works. In the beginning, the switch has learned that Host A is on port 1, Host B is on port 2, and Host C is on port 3. Host B (attacker) sends out a packet identifying itself with the source MAC address of Host A. This traffic causes the switch to move the location of Host A in its CAM table from Port 1 to Port 2. Traffic from Host C destined to Host A is now visible to Host B and not to Host A.

Figure 5-18 *MAC Address Spoofing Attack*

This attack can also be mitigated by using port security.

Using Port Security

You can use the port security feature to restrict input to an interface by limiting and identifying the MAC addresses of the stations that are allowed to access the port. When you assign MAC addresses to a secure port, the port does not forward packets with source addresses outside the group of defined addresses.

Port security allows you to statically specify MAC addresses for a port or permit the switch to dynamically learn a limited number of MAC addresses. By limiting the number of permitted MAC addresses on a port to one, you can use port security to control unauthorized expansion of the network.

When a secure port receives a packet, the source MAC address of the packet is compared to the list of secure source addresses that were manually configured or autoconfigured (learned) on the port. If a MAC address of a device attached to the port differs from the list of secure addresses, either the port shuts down until it is administratively enabled (default mode) or the port drops incoming packets from the unsecure host. The behavior of the port depends on how you configure it to respond to a security violation. In Figure 5-19, traffic from Attacker 1 and Attacker 2 will be dropped at the switch because the source MAC addresses of these frames do not match MAC addresses in the list of secured (allowed) addresses.

Figure 5-19 *Port Security*

It is recommended that you configure the port security feature to shut down a port instead of just dropping packets from insecure hosts. If port security does not shut down a port, it is possible that there will be too much load from an attack, and the port will be disabled anyway.

Table 5-4 summarizes the effect of each violation mode. The parameters used to configure these violation modes will be presented later in this chapter.

Table 5-4 *Configurable Port Security Violation Modes*

Violation Mode	Traffic Is Forwarded	Sends SNMP Trap	Sends Syslog Message	Displays Error Message	Violation Counter Increment	Shuts Down Port
Protect	No	No	No	No	No	No
Restrict	No	Yes	Yes	No	Yes	No
Shutdown	No	Yes	Yes	No	Yes	Yes
Shutdown VLAN	No	Yes	Yes	No	Yes	No

Tip Port security protects against too many MAC addresses per port and can dictate which MAC address is allowed to connect against which port. However, if the hacker spoofs the MAC address permitted on that port, he will gain access to the network. If you are concerned by spoofed MAC addresses, then consider implementing an 802.1X authentication solution.

Errdisable Recovery

The errdisable recovery feature also allows you to monitor spanning tree violations. If enabled with the **errdisable recovery** command, this feature monitors ports in configurable intervals to determine their stance in terms of these violations. The feature actually tries to recover the operational status of the ports when it finds them to be in violation of the policy, making the process automatic and the recovery automated. If you do not enable the recovery for the cause, the port stays in the error-disabled state until you enter the **shutdown** and **no shutdown** interface configuration commands. If you enable the recovery for a cause, the port is brought out of the error-disabled state and allowed to retry the operation when all the causes have timed out.

Example 5-10 illustrates the syslog message that is generated upon a security violation. In this example, port Gi4/1 has been disabled due to a violation of the BPDU guard feature. The **show interfaces status** command displays the err-disabled status for the port.

Example 5-10   *Verifying the Port Status with the* **show interfaces** *interface* **status** *Command*

```
switch# show interfaces gigabitethernet 4/1 status
Port    Name          Status   Vlan  Duplex   Speed      Type
Gi4/1   err-disabled  100      full  1000     1000BaseSX
```

If errdisable recovery monitoring is enabled, you can see more detailed information as to the monitored features using the **show errdisable recovery** command, as shown in Example 5-11. There, the BPDU guard feature is being monitored every 300 seconds, and one port, Gi4/1, is error-disabled for another 290 seconds (unless you use the **shutdown/no shutdown** commands to enable it and no further violations occur). The 300 seconds is a configurable option.

Example 5-11   show errdisable recovery *Command Output*

```
switch# show errdisable recovery
ErrDisable Reason     Timer Status
-----------------     -------------
Udld                  Disabled
Bpduguard             Enabled
security-violatio     Disabled
channel-misconfig     Disabled
<output omitted>
Timer interval: 300 seconds
Interfaces that will be enabled at the next timeout:
Interface     Errdisable reason     Time left(sec)
---------     --------------------  --------------
Gi4/1         bpduguard             290
```

To configure port security on an access port, follow these steps (see Table 5-5 for command details).

Table 5-5 switchport port-security *Command Parameters*

Parameter	Description
mac-address *mac-address*	(Optional) Specify a secure MAC address for the port by entering a 48-bit MAC address. You can add additional secure MAC addresses up to the maximum value configured.
mac-address sticky [*mac-address*]	(Optional) Enable the interface for sticky learning by entering only the **mac-address sticky** keywords. When sticky learning is enabled, the interface adds all secure MAC addresses that are dynamically learned to the running configuration and converts these addresses to sticky secure MAC addresses. Specify a sticky secure MAC address by entering the **mac-address sticky** *mac-address* keywords. Note: Although you can specify a sticky secure MAC address by entering the **mac-address sticky** *mac-address* keywords, it is recommended that you use the **mac-address** *mac-address* interface configuration command to enter static secure MAC addresses.
maximum *value*	(Optional) Set the maximum number of secure MAC addresses for the interface. The maximum number of secure MAC addresses that you can configure on a switch is set by the maximum number of available MAC addresses allowed in the system. The active Switch Database Management (SDM) template determines this number. This number represents the total available MAC addresses, including those used for other Layer 2 functions and any other secure MAC addresses configured on interfaces. The default setting is 1.
vlan [*vlan-list*]	(Optional) For trunk ports, you can set the maximum number of secure MAC addresses on a specific VLAN. If the **vlan** keyword is not entered, the default value is used. **vlan:** set a per-VLAN maximum value. **vlan** *vlan-list*: set a per-VLAN maximum value on a range of VLANs separated by a hyphen or a series of VLANs separated by commas. For nonspecified VLANs, the per-VLAN maximum value is used.

Step 1.   Enter interface configuration mode:

```
Switch(config)# interface FastEthernet 0/8
```

Step 2.   Configure the interface as an access interface:

```
Switch(config-if)# switchport mode access
```

Note   An interface in the default mode (dynamic desirable) cannot be configured as a secure port.

Step 3.   Enable port security on the interface:

```
Switch(config-if)# switchport port-security [mac-address mac-address
[vlan {vlan-id | {access | voice} } ] ] | [mac-address sticky
[mac-address| vlan {vlan-id | {access | voice} } ]] [maximum value
[vlan {vlan-list | {access | voice} } ]]
```

Step 4.   (Optional) Set the maximum number of secure MAC addresses for the interface:

```
Switch(config-if)# switchport port-security maximum value
```

Note   The range is 1 to 132; the default is 1.

Step 5.   (Optional) Set the violation mode. This is the action to be taken when a security violation is detected:

```
Switch(config-if)# switchport port-security violation {protect |
restrict | shutdown | shutdown vlan}
```

Table 5-6 provides the details of the **switchport port-security violation** command parameters.

Table 5-6   switchport port-security violation *Parameters*

Parameter	Description
protect	(Optional) Set the security violation protect mode. When the number of secure MAC addresses reaches the limit allowed on the port, packets with unknown source addresses are dropped until you remove a sufficient number of secure MAC addresses or increase the number of maximum allowable addresses. You are not notified that a security violation has occurred.
restrict	(Optional) Set the security violation restrict mode. When the number of secure MAC addresses reaches the limit allowed on the port, packets with unknown source addresses are dropped until you remove a sufficient number of secure MAC addresses or increase the number of maximum allowable addresses. In this mode, you are notified that a security violation has occurred. Specifically, an SNMP trap is sent, a syslog message is logged, and the violation counter increments.

Table 5-6 switchport port-security violation *Parameters*

Parameter	Description
shutdown	(Optional) Set the security violation shutdown mode. In this mode, a port security violation causes the interface to immediately become error-disabled and turns off the port LED. It also sends an SNMP trap, logs a syslog message, and increments the violation counter. When a secure port is in the error-disabled state, you can bring it out of this state by entering the **errdisable recovery cause psecure-violation** global configuration command, or you can manually reenable it by entering the **shutdown** and **no shutdown** interface configuration commands.
shutdown vlan	Set the security violation mode to per-VLAN shutdown. In this mode, only the VLAN on which the violation occurred is error-disabled.

Tip When a secure port is in the error-disabled state, you can bring it out of this state by entering the **errdisable recovery cause secure-violation** global configuration command, or you can manually reenable it by entering the **shutdown** and **no shutdown** interface configuration commands.

Step 6. (Optional) Enter a static secure MAC address for the interface with this command:

```
Switch(config-if)# switchport port-security mac-address mac-address
```

Note Repeat this command as many times as necessary for each secure MAC address.

Step 7. (Optional) Enable sticky learning on the interface with this command:

```
Switch(config-if)# switchport port-security mac-address sticky
```

In addition to port security, consider the commands shown in Table 5-7 for making the port more secure.

Table 5-7 switchport *Command Parameters*

Parameter	Description
vlan *vlan-id*	(Optional) On a trunk port only, specify the VLAN ID and the MAC address. If no VLAN ID is specified, the native VLAN is used.
vlan access	(Optional) On an access port only, specify the VLAN as an access VLAN.
vlan voice	(Optional) On an access port only, specify the VLAN as a voice VLAN. **Note:** The **voice** keyword is available only if voice VLAN is configured on a port and if that port is not the access VLAN.

Use the **no switchport port-security** interface configuration command to return the interface to the default condition of not being a secure port. The sticky secure addresses remain part of the running configuration. To remove the sticky secure addresses from the running configuration, use the **no mac-address** *mac-address* command.

Use the **no switchport port-security maximum** *value* interface configuration command to return the interface to the default number of secure MAC addresses.

Use the **no switchport port-security violation** {**protect | restrict**} interface configuration command to return the violation mode to the default condition (shutdown mode).

You can use port security aging to set the aging time for static and dynamic secure addresses on a port. Each port supports two types of aging:

- **Absolute:** The secure addresses on the port are deleted after the specified aging time.

- **Inactivity:** The secure addresses on the port are deleted only if the secure addresses are inactive for the specified aging time.

You can use this feature to remove and add secure MAC addresses on a secure port without manually deleting the existing secure MAC addresses and still limit the number of secure addresses on a port. Also, you can enable or disable the aging of statically configured secure addresses on a per-port basis.

Use the **switchport port-security aging** {**static | time** *time* **| type** {**absolute | inactivity**}} command to enable or disable static aging for the secure port, or set the aging time or type. Table 5-8 provides the details of the **switchport port-security aging** parameters.

Table 5-8   switchport port-security aging *Parameters*

Parameter	Description
static	This command option enables aging for statically configured secure addresses on this port.
time *time*	This command option specifies the aging time for this port. The range is 0 to 1440 minutes. If the time is 0, aging is disabled for this port.
type absolute	This command option sets the aging type to absolute. All the secure addresses on this port age out exactly after the time (minutes) specified and are removed from the secure address list.
type inactivity	This command option sets the aging type to inactivity. The secure addresses on this port age out only if there is no data traffic from the secure source address for the specified time period.

Example 5-12 shows a typical port security configuration for a voice port. Two MAC addresses are allowed, and they are to be learned dynamically. One MAC address is for the IP phone, and the other IP address is for the PC connected to the IP phone.

Violations of this policy result in the port being shut down, and the aging timeout for the learned MAC addresses is set to two hours.

Example 5-12   *Port Security Configuration*

```
Switch(config-if)# switchport mode access
Switch(config-if)# switchport port-security
Switch(config-if)# switchport port-security maximum 2
Switch(config-if)# switchport port-security violation shutdown
Switch(config-if)# switchport port-security mac-address sticky
Switch(config-if)# switchport port-security aging time 120
```

Use the **show port-security** command to view port security settings for the switch, including violation count, configured interfaces, and security violation actions.

Use the **show port-security** [**interface** *interface-id*] command to view port security settings for the specified interface, including the maximum allowed number of secure MAC addresses for each interface, the number of secure MAC addresses on the interface, the number of security violations that have occurred, and the violation mode.

Example 5-13 shows that port security is enabled on port Fa0/12 with a maximum MAC address count of 2. Currently, there are no MAC addresses learned on that port, and the violation action has been set to shut down the port.

Example 5-13   show port-security *Command Output*

```
sw-class# show port-security
Secure Port   MaxSecureAddr   CurrentAddr   SecurityViolation   Security Action
              (Count)         (Count)       (Count)
-----------------------------------------------------------------------------
   Fa0/12           2              0                0               Shutdown
-----------------------------------------------------------------------------
Total Addresses in System (excluding one mac per port)   : 0
Max Addresses limit in System (excluding one mac per port) : 1024
```

Example 5-14 demonstrates output from the **show port-security interface fa0/12** command, revealing that a violation has occurred, which means that more than one MAC address has been seen on the port. The port has been shut down because of this policy violation, as confirmed by the secure-down port status.

Example 5-14   show port-security interface fa0/12 *Command Output*

```
sw-class# show port-security interface fa0/12
Port Security       : Enabled
Port status         : Secure-down
Violation mode        : Shutdown
Maximum MAC Addresses   : 1
Total MAC Addresses   : 2
Configured MAC Addresses : 0
Aging time          : 120 mins
Aging type          : Absolute
SecureStatic address aging : Disabled
Security Violation Count : 1
```

Use the **show port-security** [**interface** *interface-id*] **address** command to view all the secure MAC addresses that are configured on all switch interfaces, or on a specified interface, with aging information for each address.

Example 5-15 shows that port Fa0/12 is in VLAN 1 and has a secured MAC address of 0000.ffff.aaaa, which means that the host with the 0000.ffff aaaa MAC address can connect to port Fa0/12.

Example 5-15   show port-security address *Command Output*

```
sw-class# show port-security address
Secure Mac Address Table
------------------------------------------------------
Vlan  Mac Address    Type        Ports Remaining Age
                                (mins)
----  -----------    ----        ----- ------------
 1  0000. ffff. aaaa  SecureConfigured  Fa0/12    -
------------------------------------------------------
Total Addresses in System (excluding one mac per port)   : 0
Max Addresses limit in System (excluding one mac per port) : 1024
```

Using SNMP to Monitor Access to Switch Port

Network managers need a way to monitor who is using the network and where they are. In Figure 5-20, if port Fa2/1 is secure, an SNMP trap will be generated when MAC D disappears from the CAM table of the switch.

Figure 5-20   *Notification of Intrusions*

The MAC address notification feature sends SNMP traps to the network management station (NMS) whenever a new MAC address is added to, or an old address is deleted from, the forwarding tables. MAC notifications are generated only for dynamic and secure MAC addresses.

MAC address notification allows the network administrator to monitor MAC addresses that are learned and MAC addresses that age out and are removed from the switch.

Use the **mac address-table notification change** global configuration command to enable the MAC address notification feature on the switch.

Summary

Layer 2 security is often an overlooked aspect of network security. Buffer overflows can be the worst of these problems. The goals of endpoint security include protection from viruses, worms, and Trojan horses. SAN and voice security are also increasingly important because these technologies are growing in popularity in the modern enterprise.

The major points that were covered in this chapter are as follows:

- VLAN and trunks are susceptible to attacks such as VLAN hopping.

- A switched network can be attacked by propagating erroneous spanning tree information between participants.

- Through proper planning and implementation, a network security strategy can effectively protect the switched data plane.

- VLAN hopping and MAC spoofing attacks can be defeated by adopting effective protection of the switch data plane, such as

  - Using a dedicated VLAN ID for trunk ports while not using VLAN 1 for anything

  - Setting user ports to nontrunking (unless you are using Cisco VoIP)

  - Using port security whenever possible for access ports and enabling STP attack mitigation (BPDU guard, root guard)

- VLAN hopping and MAC spoofing attacks, which are possible on switched networks and measures that should be put in place to protect against those attacks

References

For additional information, refer to these Cisco.com resources:

Private VLAN Catalyst Switch Support Matrix (Cisco Catalyst 6500 Series Switches), http://tinyurl.com/2w22d6

"Identity Based Networking Services," http://www.cisco.com/en/US/products/ps6638/products_ios_protocol_group_home.html

"LAN Security: Introduction," http://tinyurl.com/594lpb

Securing Networks with Private VLANs and VLAN Access Control Lists (Cisco Catalyst 6000 Series Switches), http://www.cisco.com/en/US/products/hw/switches/ps700/products_tech_note09186a008013565f.shtml

Review Questions

Use the questions here to review what you learned in this chapter. The correct answers are found in the Appendix, "Answers to Chapter Review Questions."

1. Which of the following is a valid statement regarding assigning voice traffic to specific VLANs?

   a. Separation of voice from data traffic increases total throughput.
   b. Separation of voice from data traffic ensures communication privacy and nonrepudiation.
   c. Separation of voice from data traffic is seldom used in the industry.
   d. Separation of voice from data traffic makes it easier to apply VLAN access list.

2. Which of the following commands should be used on a trunk port when attempting to protect against VLAN hopping? (Choose all that apply.)

   a. switchport mode access
   b. switchport mode trunk
   c. switchport nonegotiate
   d. switchport trunk native vlan

3. Which two commands best protect a switched network from a hacker who is trying to preempt an election of the Spanning Tree Protocol?

   a. spanning-tree portfast bpduguard

   b. spanning-tree portfast default

   c. spanning-tree guard root

   d. switchport port-security violation

4. Which command limits the number of MAC addresses communicating through the same switch port?

   a. switchport mode access

   b. switchport port-security maximum

   c. switchport-security mac-address sticky

   d. switchport-security violation

5. Why should you worry about Layer 2 security?

   a. Switches cannot regulate the flow of data between their ports.

   b. You don't have to worry about Layer 2 security because it is lower than the IP layer and most attacks happen at the network layer.

   c. With the domino effect, compromising Layer 2 means compromising the higher layers.

   d. VLANs are a Layer 3 function in a switch, and therefore, as with any other Layer 3 processes, it can be easily hacked.

6. Put the following steps of a VLAN hopping attack in the proper order.

   a. The frame arrives at the second switch but has no knowledge that it was supposed to be for VLAN 10.

   b. The second switch looks only at the 802.1Q tag (the former inner tag that the attacker sent) and sees that the frame is destined for VLAN 20 (the victim VLAN). The second switch sends the packet on to the victim port, or floods it, depending on whether there is an existing CAM table entry for the victim host.

   c. The attacker sends a double-tagged 802.1Q frame to the switch. The outer header has the VLAN tag of the attacker, which is the same as the native VLAN of the trunk port. For the purposes of this example, assume that this is VLAN 10. The inner tag is the victim VLAN, VLAN 20.

   d. The frame arrives on the first switch, which looks at the first 4-byte 802.1Q tag. The switch sees that the frame is destined for VLAN 10 and sends it out all VLAN 10 ports (including the trunk), because there is no CAM table entry. The switch does not add a VLAN 10 tag to the frames because VLAN 10 is the native VLAN, and as specified by the 802.1Q specification, native VLAN traffic is not tagged. At this point, the second VLAN tag is still intact and has not been inspected by the first switch.

7. The VLAN hopping attack is the result of which condition?

   a. Layer 2 loops with STP disabled
   b. CAM table overflow
   c. Poor VLAN planning
   d. Trunking protocol vulnerabilities

8. What is one of the exceptions to the recommended practice to disable trunking on all user ports on a switch?

   a. IP phone ports
   b. Trusted VLANs
   c. Unreliable ports
   d. 802.1X ports

9. Which spanning tree protection feature disables ports when a violation occurs?

   a. Source guard
   b. BPDU guard
   c. PortFast
   d. Root guard

10. Which port security mode has as its only action to drop frames arriving on that port when a violation occurs?

   a. Shutdown
   b. Protect
   c. Dynamic
   d. Restrict

Chapter 6

Securing the Data Plane in IPv6 Environments

IPv6 shares some of the same security concerns and considerations as IPv4. Some IPv6-specific vulnerabilities and threats make it unique as it relates to your considerations and strategy to protect IPv6 infrastructures and services. In this chapter, you learn how to do the following:

- Explain the need for IPv6 from the general perspective of the transition to IPv6 from IPv4

- List and describe the fundamental features of IPv6, as well as enhancements when compared to IPv4

- Analyze the IPv6 addressing scheme, components, and design principles and configure IPv6 addressing

- Describe the IPv6 routing function

- Evaluate how common and specific threats affect IPv6

- Develop and implement a strategy for IPv6 security

The Need for IPv6

The IPv4 address space provides approximately 4.3 billion addresses. Of that address space, approximately 3.7 billion addresses are actually assignable. The other addresses are reserved for special purposes such as multicasting, private address space, loopback testing, and research.

An IPv6 address is a 128-bit binary value, which can be displayed as 32 hexadecimal digits, as shown in Figure 6-1. It provides 3.4 × 1038 IP addresses. This version of IP addressing should provide sufficient addresses for future Internet growth needs—enough to allocate the equivalent of the entire IPv4 address space to every person on the planet. Another analogy to show the enormity of the IPv6 address pool is to think that there are 667,712,614,478,140,039 addresses available per square meter of the Earth's surface, including ocean surface.

IPv4
32 Bits
= 4,294,967,296 Possible Addressable Nodes

IPv6
128 Bits: Four Times Larger in Bits
= ~3.4 x 10^{38} Possible Addressable Nodes
= 340,282,366,920,938,463,463,374,607,431,768,211,456
= 51,557,934,381,960,373,252,026,455,671 Addresses
  per Person on the Planet !!!

Figure 6-1   *Comparing IPv4 and IPv6 Addresses*

So, What Ever Happened to IPv5?

Well, IPv5 never existed. In the late 1970s, a set of protocols were defined to create the Internet Stream Protocol (ST), which was to be used, instead of IP, for streaming. The protocol was never introduced. However, the second iteration of ST (ST-II) used Internet Protocol version 5 to distinguish itself from regular IP. Though ST was never known as IPv5, IETF decided to stay away from this nomenclature to avoid confusion.

IPv6 Penetration

According to an unofficial Cisco TAC statistic, in fall 2011, about 5 percent of networks running on Cisco equipment had IPv6 in production. More formal statistics can be found at Réseaux IP Européens Network Coordination Centre, or RIPE NCC (http://www.ripe.net/). As one of four regional Internet registries that supply and administer IP addresses, it has some interesting statistics. According to RIPE NCC, in 2012 about 7.5 percent of networks worldwide were running IPv6. The largest penetration was in the Asia-Pacific region with close to 11 percent. The lowest percentage of networks running IPv6 was in North America at 5 percent. Interestingly, it's in North America that the highest number of IPv4 Class A addresses can be found. (Source: RIPE NCC, https://labs.ripe.net/Members/emileaben/interesting-graph-networks-with-ipv6-over-time.)

Google is also tracking the IPv6 adoption rate on the Internet. As of July 2012, Google was reporting that 0.78 percent of all traffic it was seeing was IPv6. (Source: http://www.google.com/intl/en/ipv6/statistics/.)

If you are interested in finding the IPv6 penetration rate in your country, visit http://v6asns.ripe.net/v/6 or http://www.google.com/ipv6/statistics.html#tab=per-country-ipv6-adoption.

In 2012, there were approximately 2.3 billion Internet users around the world. Between 2000 and 2011, there was a 480 percent growth of the Internet. In February 2011, IANA announced the allocation of the last few blocks of /8 address spaces.

The Internet will be transformed after IPv6 fully replaces IPv4. IPv4 address exhaustion is an imminent fact. Nevertheless, IPv4 will not disappear overnight. Rather, it will coexist with and then gradually be replaced by IPv6.

These facts are augmented by the tremendous increase of mobile and consumer devices connecting to the public Internet. The *consumerization* of IT services is an ongoing trend, where business workers use their consumer and mobility devices to access corporate networks. It is expected that by 2013, there will be 1 billion internet-connected devices. These trends, along with application trends, have driven peer-to-peer communications and more demand for a larger IP address space. The next wave is machine-to-machine (M2M) communications, smart grids, networked security cameras and motion sensors, connected home appliance, and so on.

The change from IPv4 to IPv6 has already begun, particularly in Europe and the Asia-Pacific region. These areas are exhausting their allotted IPv4 addresses, which makes IPv6 all the more attractive and necessary. Some countries, such as Japan, are aggressively adopting IPv6. The European Union is moving toward IPv6, and China is considering building new networks that are dedicated for IPv6. In 2008, the U.S. government mandated all federal agencies to demonstrate IPv6 connectivity over their backbone networks and that their public-facing web sites be IPv6 ready by Sept. 30, 2012.

Other IPv4 weaknesses affect the need for IPv6. IPv4 was designed without a number of modern-day network requirements for security, device roaming, quality of service, address depletion, and others. Incorporating additional features in IPv4 has been costly in terms of complexity and flexibility.

The supporting cast of IPv4 protocols and solutions that manage address scarcity (Network Address Translation [NAT], Dynamic Host Configuration Protocol [DHCP], variable-length subnet mask [VLSM], and classless interdomain routing [CIDR]) are good examples of added complexity and lower performance due to an unplanned event such as IP address space depletion.

Security is one of those requirements. The push for peer-to-peer communications, where each peer has a public address, demands security controls that work end to end and are initiated by the IP hosts themselves. IP Security (IPsec) was introduced to solve the problem of the inherent lack of security in IPv4 transmission.

Quality of service (QoS) was also an area neglected by IPv4. Resource Reservation Protocol (RSVP) and other protocols were introduced to provide QoS.

Mobility is not built in to IPv4. Mobile IP is required to deploy a roaming approach to IP addressing and service continuity.

IPv6 Features and Enhancements

IPv6 is a powerful enhancement to IPv4. Several features in IPv6 offer functional improvements. What IP developers learned from using IPv4 suggested changes to better suit current and probable network demands:

- **Larger address space:** A larger address space includes several enhancements:
  - Improved global reachability and flexibility
  - Aggregation of prefixes that are announced in routing tables
  - Multihoming to several ISPs
  - Autoconfiguration that can include data link layer addresses in the address space
  - Plug-and-play options
  - Public-to-private readdressing end to end without address translation
  - Simplified mechanisms for address renumbering and modification

- **Simpler header:** A simpler header offers several advantages over IPv4:
  - Better routing efficiency for performance and forwarding-rate scalability
  - No broadcasts and thus no potential threat of broadcast storms
  - No requirement for processing checksums
  - Simpler and more efficient extension header mechanisms
  - Flow labels or per-flow processing with no need to open the transport inner packet to identify the various traffic flows

- **Mobility and security:** Mobility and security help ensure compliance with Mobile IP and IPsec standards functionality. Mobility enables people with mobile network devices—many with wireless connectivity—to move around in networks. Mobile IP is an Internet Engineering Task Force (IETF) standard that is available for both IPv4 and IPv6, enabling mobile devices to move without breaks in established network connections. Because IPv4 does not automatically provide this kind of mobility, you must add it with additional configurations.
  - In IPv6, mobility is built in, which means that any IPv6 node can use mobility when necessary. The routing headers of IPv6 make mobile IPv6 much more efficient than Mobile IPv4 for end nodes.
  - IPsec is the IETF standard for IP network security, available for both IPv4 and IPv6. Although the functionalities are essentially identical in both environments, IPsec is mandatory in IPv6. IPsec can be used transparently on every IPv6 host without additional software, making the IPv6 Internet potentially more secure. IPsec also requires keys for each party, which implies a global key deployment and distribution.

- **Transition richness:** There are several ways to incorporate existing IPv4 capabilities with the added features of lPv6:

    - One approach is to implement a dual-stack method, with both IPv4 and IPv6 configured on the interface of a network device.

    - Tunneling is another technique that will become more prominent as the adoption of IPv6 grows. There are various IPv6-over-IPv4 tunneling methods. Some methods require manual configuration, while others are more automatic.

Cisco IOS Release 12.3(2)T and later also include Network Address Translation Protocol Translation (NAT-PT) between IPv6 and IPv4. This translation allows direct communication between hosts that use different versions of the IP protocol.

IPv6 Headers

The new IPv6 header is simpler than the IPv4 header, in the following ways:

- Half of the previous IPv4 header fields are removed. This enables simpler processing of the packets, enhancing the performance and routing efficiency.

- All fields are aligned to 64 bits, which enables direct storage and access in memory by fast lookups.

- No checksum occurs at the IP layer, and no recalculation is performed by the routers. Error detection is done by the link layer and transport layer.

IPv6 header enhancements improve hardware-based processing, which provides scalability of the forwarding rate for the next generation of high-speed networks.

IPv6 uses a different approach from IPv4 to manage optional information in the header. It defines extension headers that form a chain of headers linked by the Next Header field that is contained in each extension header. This approach provides efficiency gains over IPv4 in the way that options and special functions are packaged. It enables a faster forwarding rate and leaves the router with less work to do for each packet.

Key Topic

IPv4 Versus IPv6 Header Fields   With IPv4, the Fragmentation field is always present in the header regardless of whether the packet is fragmented or not. With IPv6, such field would appear only if the functionality is needed.

All extension headers are daisy-chained, each header pointing to the next header until they reach the transport layer data, as shown in Figure 6-2. This arrangement allows an IPv6 packet to be customized with features and functionality.

Figure 6-2   *Daisy-chaining IPv6 Extension Headers*

A good example of extension headers is the routing header (RH) in IPv6. It can be used to implement the source routing function that is widely known in IPv4, where the packet lists the intermediary hosts that it will visit before arriving at its final destination. If the Next Header field is equal to 0, the next header is a Hop-by-Hop field. This header contains information that must be examined by each node on the path.

A second routing header, with a value of 2, has been defined for use with IPv6 Mobility. It is formatted similarly to the type 0 routing header, except that it only carries one intermediate hop.

All IPv6 hosts, including end stations, process the RH.

Stateless Address Autoconfiguration

Stateless address autoconfiguration is an important feature of IPv6. It allows serverless basic configuration of the nodes and easy renumbering. It uses the Neighbor Discovery Protocol (NDP), which is based on ICMP version 6 (ICMPv6) protocol messaging, a topic we will discuss next. NDP replaces Address Resolution Protocol (ARP), and multicast replaces broadcast.

Stateless address autoconfiguration uses the information in the router advertisement messages to configure the node. The prefix included in the router advertisement is used as the /64 prefix for the node address. The other 64 bits are obtained by the dynamically created interface identifier, which, in the case of Ethernet, is the modified extended universal identifier 64-bit (EUI-64) format.

Router advertisements are sent periodically. When a host boots, it needs to have its address in the early stage of the boot process, as illustrated in Figure 6-3. Instead of waiting for the next router advertisement to get the information to configure its interfaces, a node sends a router solicitation message asking the routers on the network to reply immediately with a router advertisement so that the node can immediately autoconfigure. All the routers respond with a normal router advertisement message with the all-nodes multicast address as the destination address.

1. Router Solicitation
   (RS) Requests Prefix

ARP replaced by NDP,
broadcasts replaced by
link-local multicast.

3. Host Autoconfigured Address:
   Prefix Received + Link-Layer
   Address

2. Router Advertisement (RA)
   Sends Network-Type Information
   (Prefix, Default Route, and So On)

Figure 6-3   *IPv6 - Stateless Autoconfiguration*

Autoconfiguration enables plug-and-play configuration of an IPv6 device, which allows devices to connect themselves to the network without any configuration from an administrator and without any servers, such as DHCP servers. This key feature enables deployment of new devices on the Internet, such as smartphones, wireless devices, home appliances, and other consumer devices.

The NDP functions therefore include:

■ Router, prefix, and parameter discovery

■ Address autoconfiguration and resolution

■ Duplicate address detection

IPv6 Network Discovery Protocol (NDP) replaces IPv4 Address Resolution Protocol (ARP). NDP is a messaging protocol that relies on ICMPv6 and facilitates the discovery of neighboring devices over a network.

Internet Control Message Protocol Version 6

ICMPv6 is similar to ICMP version 4 (ICMPv4) in that it enables nodes to make diagnostic tests and report problems. Table 6-1 lists the differences between ICMPv4 and ICMPv6.

Table 6-1   *ICMPv4 and ICMPv6 Message Types*

ICMP Message Type	ICMPv4	ICMPv6
Connectivity Checks	X	X
Informational/Error Messaging	X	X
Fragmentation Needed Notification	X	X
Address Assignment		X

Table 6-1   *ICMPv4 and ICMPv6 Message Types*

ICMP Message Type	ICMPv4	ICMPv6
Address Resolution		X
Router Discovery		X
Multicast Group Management		X
Mobile IPv6 Support		X

Like ICMPv4, ICMPv6 implements two kinds of messages: error messages, such as "destination unreachable," "packet too big," or "time exceeded," and informational messages, such as "echo request" and "echo reply."

ICMPv4 is often blocked by security policies in corporate firewalls because of known attacks that are based on ICMP. ICMPv6 can be subject to similar attacks; however, there are substantial changes to its scope. The responsibilities of IMCPv6 go beyond mere messaging, and into address resolution and assignment, router discovery, and Mobile IP.

IPv6 General Features

IPv6 has many advantages over IPv4, such as

- A large address space makes global reachability possible from every IPv6 node.

- Autoconfiguration is essential for deploying many appliances. It would not be possible, practically, to manually configure IP addresses. You need some autoconfiguration mechanism that scales. DHCP may not be the right way to manage millions of clients.

- IPsec is mandated in the architecture.

- NAT includes end-to-end security in networks by requiring that you trust the end devices.

- Mobile IPv6 improves routing efficiency over IPv4.

- IPv6 is the same as IPv4 in QoS and header compression features. Both areas benefited from the work on IPv6. The IPv6 header compresses better than the IPv4 header because there are fewer fields.

- Other features are equivalent, except for a few details, such as scoped addresses (defined below) in multicast, or the concept of stateless DHCP where only static parameters are provided by the DHCP server.

RFC 4007 defines scoped addresses as follows: "Internet Protocol version 6 includes support for addresses of different 'scope'; that is, both global and non-global (e.g., link-local) addresses."

Table 6-2 summarizes the general features and benefits of IPv6 and compares them to IPv4.

Table 6-2   *IPv4 and IPv6 Compared*

IP Service	IPv4	IPv6
Addressing range	32-bit, NAT	128-bit, multiple scopes
Autoconfiguration	DHCP	Stateless, stateful (DHCPv6)
Security	IPsec	IPsec mandated, works end to end
Mobility	Mobile IP	Mobile IP with optimized routing
Quality of service	Differentiated service, integrated service	Differentiated service, integrated service
IP Multicast	Heavy application use	Heavy application and protocol stack use
ICMP	Messaging mostly	Messaging and protocol functions

Transition to IPv6

The transition from IPv4 does not require upgrades on all nodes at the same time. Many transition mechanisms enable smooth integration of IPv4 and IPv6. Other mechanisms that allow IPv4 nodes to communicate with IPv6 nodes are available. All of these mechanisms are applied to different situations. Tunnels are established manually, semiautomatically, or automatically:

- Manually
  - IPv6-in-IPv4
  - GRE (not discussed)
  - VPN (not discussed)
- Semiautomatically
  - Tunnel broker (proxying)
- Automatically
  - 6to4
  - ISATAP
  - Teredo

The three most common techniques to transition from IPv4 to IPv6 are as follows:

- **Dual stack:** Dual stack is an integration method in which a node has implementation and connectivity to both an IPv4 network and an IPv6 network. As a result, the node and its corresponding routers have two protocol stacks, as shown in Figure 6-4.

- **Tunneling:** There are several tunneling techniques available:

  - **Manual IPv6-over-IPv4 tunneling:** An integration method in which an IPv6 packet is encapsulated within the IPv4 protocol. This method requires dual-stack routers.

  - **Dynamic 6to4 tunneling:** A method that automatically establishes the connection of IPv6 islands through an IPv4 network, typically the Internet. The 6to4 tunneling method dynamically applies a valid, unique IPv6 prefix to each IPv6 island, which enables the fast deployment of IPv6 in a corporate network without address retrieval from the ISPs or registries.

  - **Intra-Site Automatic Tunnel Addressing Protocol (ISATAP) tunneling:** An automatic overlay tunneling mechanism that uses the underlying IPv4 network as a data link layer for IPv6. ISATAP tunnels allow individual IPv4 or IPv6 dual-stack hosts within a site to communicate with other such hosts on a virtual link, creating an IPv6 network using the IPv4 infrastructure.

  - **Teredo tunneling:** An IPv6 transition technology that provides host-to-host automatic tunneling instead of gateway tunneling. It is used to pass unicast IPv6 traffic when dual-stacked hosts (hosts that are miming both IPv6 and IPv4) are located behind one or multiple IPv4 NATs.

- **Proxying and translation (NAT-PT):** A translation mechanism that sits between an IPv6 network and an IPv4 network. The job of the translator is to translate IPv6 packets into IPv4 packets and vice versa.

Figure 6-4 *IPv6-in-IPv4 Tunnel*

IPv6 Addressing

IPv6 addresses are, at first, the most noticeable change compared to IPv4. Not only are IP addresses going from 32 bits to 128 bits, but how addresses are represented and how they are classified are also new. There are different types of IPv6 addresses and different representations.

IPv6 Address Representation

IPv6 addresses are 128 bits long. Addresses are represented as a series of eight 16-bit hexadecimal fields that are separated by colons. The A, B, C, D, E, and F in hexadecimal fields are not case sensitive. A typical IPv6 address would therefore look like 2001:cb7:46 d1:0:0:8a2e:370:7334.

Here are some ways to shorten the writing of IPv6 addresses:

- The leading zeros in a field are optional, so 010F = 10F and 0000 = 0.

- Successive fields of zeros can be represented as a double colon (::), but only once in an address. An address parser is able to identify the number of missing zeros by separating the two parts and filling in zeros until the 128 bits are completed. But if two double colons are placed in the address, there is no way to identify the size of each block of zeros. Therefore, only one double colon is possible in a valid IPv6 address.

The use of the double-colon technique makes many addresses very small. For example, FF01:0:0:0:0:0:0:1 becomes FF01::1, as shown in Figure 6-5. The "unspecified" address is written as a double colon (::), because it contains only zeros. The loopback address, 0:0:0:0:0:0:0:1, is represented by ::1.

Figure 6-5 shows the use of the double colon to represent multiple contiguous 16-bit chunks of zeros in an IPv6 address. The second representation that is shown in Figure 6-5 is incorrect—the double colon (::) notation can appear only once in an address, because multiple uses may make the address ambiguous. In the example, the parser cannot tell whether the missing bits (four 16-bit sections) are apportioned with 16 at the first double colon and 48 at the last double colon or some other combination.

Successive Zeros: FF01:0:0:0:0:0:0:1 → FF01::1

Loopback Address: 0:0:0:0:0:0:0:1 → ::1

Unspecified Address: 0:0:0:0:0:0:0:0 → ::

Example:
2031:0000:130F:0000:0000:09C0:876A:130B
- Can be represented as 2031:0:130f::9c0:876a:130b.
- Cannot be represented as 2031::130f::9c0:876a:130b.

Figure 6-5 *Examples of IPv6 Address Representation in Their Long Form and Shortened Form*

IPv6 addresses are presented with a prefix. The high-order bits of an IPv6 address represent the network. All the host addresses of one network would have the same first few bits. These first few network bits, *n* bits, are called the "prefix." We use /n to denote a prefix *n* bits long. If an address is presented with 2001:cb7::/32, it means that the first 32 bits belong to the network and that the other 96 bits belong to subnet and host addresses.

IPv6 Address Types

IPv6 supports three types of addresses:

- Unicast
  - Address is for a single interface
  - IPv6 has several types (for example, global, reserved, link-local, and site-local)
- Multicast
  - One-to-many
  - Enables more efficient use of the network
  - Uses a larger address range
- Anycast
  - One-to-nearest (allocated from unicast address space)
  - Multiple devices share the same address
  - All anycast nodes should provide uniform service
  - Source devices send packets to anycast address
  - Routers decide on closest device to reach that destination
  - Suitable for load balancing and content delivery services

Unicast and multicast work the same as with IPv4. As for anycast, think of it as *a shared secondary address*. As an example, think of a network topology with two routers as potential default gateways deserving the same subnet. In IPv4, a host would be configured to point to one of the two gateways. If the selected gateway is no longer available, a reconfiguration of the host would be necessary for it to start using the other gateway on the network. In IPv6, however, the two routers would be configured with the same anycast address, in addition to their own unicast address. A host would send its packets to the anycast address, and either router could provide the service.

Because there are no broadcasts with IPv6, there is no need for a broadcast address.

Each address type has specific rules regarding its construction and use, as discussed next.

IPv6 Unicast Addressing

IPv6 unicast addresses can be aggregated with prefixes of arbitrary bit length, similar to IPv4 addresses under classless interdomain routing (CIDR).

There are several types of unicast addresses in IPv6, including global addresses, site-local addresses (deprecated), unique local addresses, and link-local addresses. There are also some special-purpose subtypes of global unicast, such as the unspecified address, loopback address, and IPv6 addresses with embedded IPv4 addresses. Additional address types or subtypes could be defined in the future.

IPv6 address types have the following patterns:

- **Global:** Starts with 2000::/3 and assigned by the Internet Assigned Numbers Authority (IANA)

- **Reserved:** Used by the IETF

- **Private:** Link local (starts with FE80::/10)

- **Loopback:** (::1)

- **Unspecified:** (::)

A single interface may be assigned multiple IPv6 addresses of any type: unicast, anycast, or multicast. IPv6 addressing rules are covered by multiple RFCs, including RFC 4291.

IPv6 Global Unicast and Anycast Addresses

Global unicast addresses correspond to the principal use of IPv6 addresses for generic global IPv6 traffic and consume the most important part of the address space.

The structure of a global unicast address, shown in Figure 6-6, is as follows:

- A global routing prefix, typically a /48 assigned to a site, is a structure that enables aggregation upward, eventually to the ISP

- A subnet ID used to identify links within a site, typically 16 bits

- A 64-bit interface ID to identify the interface of the node

IPv6 has the same address format for global unicast and for anycast addresses. Every IPv6-enabled interface contains at least one loopback address (::1/128) and one link-local address. Optionally, every interface can have multiple unique local and global addresses.

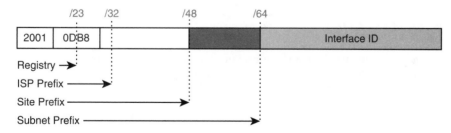

Figure 6-6 *IPv6-in-IPv4 Tunnel*

Examples of global addresses can be found in RFC 3587, "IPv6 Global Unicast Address Format." The structure that is proposed in that document provides for aggregation of routing prefixes to limit the number of entries in the global routing table. An example of aggregation is shown in Figure 6-7.

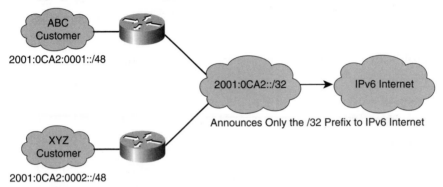

Figure 6-7 *Example of IPv6 Address Aggregation*

Link-Local Addresses

All IPv6-enabled interfaces must have a link-local address.

Link-local addresses are used for addressing on a single link, so they have a scope that is limited to the link. Link-local addresses are dynamically created on all IPv6 interfaces by using a specific link-local prefix, FE80::/10, and a 64-bit interface identifier, as shown in Figure 6-8.

Figure 6-8 *Link-Local Address*

Link-local addresses are used for automatic address configuration, neighbor discovery, and router discovery. They are also used by many routing protocols.

Link-local addresses can serve as a way to connect devices on the same local network without requiring global or unique local addresses. When communicating with a link-local address, you must specify the outgoing interface because every interface is connected to FE80::/10.

IPv6 has a 128-bit address space, but 64 bits are used for the host number on the subnet. A better way to look at the address space is to say that IPv6 supports 2^{64} subnets, and each subnet can have a practically unlimited number of hosts. In any case, there are more than enough networks and hosts for the future.

Multicast Addresses

A multicast scope is new in IPv6. Multicast is used in the context of one-to-many. A multicast address identifies a group of interfaces. Traffic that is sent to a multicast address is sent to multiple destinations at the same time. An interface may belong to any number of multicast groups. Multicast is used in the core of many functions in IPv6.

Multicast addresses are defined by the prefix FF00::/8, as shown in Figure 6-9.

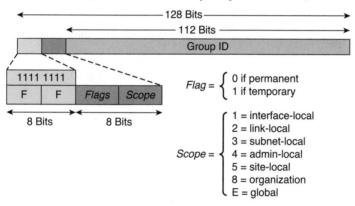

Figure 6-9 *Multicast Address*

The second octet defines the flags and the scope of the multicast address. Flags are defined as "0RPT," and these conditions apply:

- 0 is reserved and must equal 0.

- R stands for "rendezvous point" and is almost always set to 0.

- P indicates "prefix dependency" and is almost always set to 0.

- T is the "temporary" bit. For a temporary multicast address, T equals 1. For a permanent multicast address, T equals 0.

Note If R equals 1, P and T must also equal 1.

The scope parameters are used to specify in which part of the network address is valid and unique. Some addresses are unique only on the local network, while others are globally unique. Table 6-3 provides definitions of scope.

Table 6-3   *IPv6 Scope Parameters and Definitions*

Scope	Definition
1	Interface-local scope (loopback transmission)
2	Link-local scope (similar to unicast link-local scope)
3	Subnet-local scope, where subnets may span multiple links
4	Administrative-local scope (administratively configured)
5	Site-local scope
8	Organizational scope (multiple sites)
E	Global scope

For example, a multicast address starting with FF02::/16 is a permanent multicast address with a link-local scope.

The lower 112 bits of the multicast address constitute the multicast group ID.

Multicast is frequently used in IPv6 and replaces broadcast. There is no broadcast in IPv6. There is no Time to Live (TTL) in IPv6 multicast. The scoping is defined inside the address.

The multicast addresses FF00:: to FF0F:: are reserved. Inside that range, the following addresses are assigned:

- **FF02::1:** All nodes on the link-local scope
- **FF02::2:** All routers on the link-local scope
- **FF02::9:** All Routing Information Protocol (RIP) routers on the link
- **FF02::1: FFXX:XXXX:** solicited-node
- **FF05::101:** All Network Time Protocol (NTP) servers on the site-local scope
- **FF0X::103:** Rwhod (rwho plus ruptime daemon)
- **FF0X::102:** Silicon Graphics Dogfight (Internet game)
- **FF0X::127:** Cisco RP announce (multicast rendezvous point)
- **FF0X::128:** Cisco RP discovery
- **FF05::1:3:** All DHCP servers in site

Assigning IPv6 Global Unicast Addresses

Interface identifiers in IPv6 addresses are used to identify interfaces on a link. They can also be thought of as the "host portion" of an IPv6 address. Interface identifiers are required to be unique on a specific link. Interface identifiers are always 64 bits and can be dynamically derived from a Layer 2 media and encapsulation.

There are several ways to assign an IPv6 address to a device:

- Static assignment using a manual interface ID

- Static assignment using an EUI-64 interface ID

- Stateless autoconfiguration

- DHCP for IPv6 (DHCPv6)

Manual Interface Assignment

One way to statically assign an IPv6 address to a device is to manually assign both the prefix (network) and interface ID (host) portion of the IPv6 address. To configure an IPv6 address on a Cisco router interface and enable IPv6 processing on that interface, use the **ipv6 address** *ipv6-address prefix-length* command in interface configuration mode.

Example 6-1 shows how to enable IPv6 processing on the interface and configure an address based on the directly specified bits.

Example 6-1   *Manually Assigning an IPv6 Address to a Router Interface*

```
R1(config)# interface fa 0/0
R1(config-if)# ipv6 address 2001:0DB8:2222:7272::72/64
```

Note   In Example 6-1, the IPv6 address could have been configured without the leading 0 in the second most significant hexadecimal field, as shown here:
```
R1(config-if)# ipv6 address 2001:DB8:2222:7272::72/64
```

EUI-64 Interface ID Assignment

Another way to statically assign an IPv6 address is to configure the prefix (network) portion of the IPv6 address and derive the interface ID (host) portion from the Layer 2 MAC address of the device, which is known as the EUI-64 interface ID. You will see later in this chapter how the 48-bit MAC address is expanded to provide a 64-bit interface ID.

To configure an IPv6 address for an interface and enable IPv6 processing on the interface using an EUI-64 interface ID in the low-order 64 bits of the address (host), use the **ipv6 address** *ipv6-prefix/prefix-length* **eui-64** command in interface configuration mode.

Example 6-2 assigns the IPv6 address 2001:ODB8:0:1::/64 to Ethernet interface 0 and uses an EUI-64 interface ID in the low-order 64 bits of the address.

Example 6-2 *Configuring the Prefix Portion for an EUI-64 Interface ID Assignment*

```
R1(config)# interface fa 0/0
R1(config-if)# ipv6 address 2001:0DB8:0:1::/64 eui-64
```

Stateless Autoconfiguration

Autoconfiguration, as the name implies, is a mechanism that automatically configures the IPv6 address of a node. In IPv6, it is assumed that non-PC devices, as well as computer terminals, will be connected to the network. The autoconfiguration mechanism was introduced to enable plug-and-play networking of these devices, to help reduce administration overhead.

DHCPv6 (Stateful)

DHCP for IPv6 enables DHCP servers to pass configuration parameters such as IPv6 network addresses to IPv6 nodes. It offers the capability of automatic allocation of reusable network addresses and additional configuration flexibility. This protocol is a stateful counterpart to IPv6 stateless address autoconfiguration, and can be used separately or concurrently with IPv6 stateless address autoconfiguration to obtain configuration parameters.

IPv6 EUI-64 Interface Identifier

The 64-bit interface identifier in an IPv6 address identifies a unique interface on a link. A link is a network medium over which network nodes communicate using the data link layer. The interface identifier can also be unique over a broader scope. In many cases, an interface identifier is the same as, or is based on, the data link layer (MAC) address of an interface. As in IPv4, a subnet prefix in IPv6 is associated with one link.

Interface identifiers in global unicast and other IPv6 address types must be 64 bits long and can be constructed in the 64-bit EUI-64 format. As shown in Figure 6-10, this format expands the 48-bit MAC address to 64 bits by inserting "FFFE" into the middle 16 bits. The EUI-64 format interface ID is derived from the 48-bit link layer (MAC) address by inserting the hexadecimal number FFFE between the upper 3 bytes (Organizationally Unique Identifier [OUI] field) and the lower 3 bytes (serial number) of the link layer address. To ensure that the chosen address is from a unique Ethernet MAC address, the seventh bit in the high-order byte is inverted (equivalent to the IEEE G/L bit) to indicate the uniqueness of the 48-bit address. To make sure that the chosen address is from a unique Ethernet MAC address, the U/L bit is set to 0 for global scope (1 for local scope).

Figure 6-10   *Creating an EUI-64 Format Interface ID*

IPv6 and Cisco Routers

Cisco IOS Software Release 12.2(2)T and later are IPv6-ready. As soon as you configure basic IPv4 and IPv6 on the interface, the interface is dual-stacked and the router forwards IPv4 and IPv6 traffic on that interface.

There are two basic steps to activate IPv6 on a router. First, you must activate IPv6 traffic forwarding on the router, and then you must configure each interface that requires IPv6. By default, IPv6 traffic forwarding is disabled on a Cisco router.

To activate IPv6 traffic forwarding between interfaces, you must configure the global command **ipv6 unicast-routing**:

```
R1(config)# ipv6 unicast-routing
```

This command enables the forwarding of IPv6 datagrams.

The **ipv6 address** command can configure a global IPv6 address:

```
R1(config-if)# ipv6 address ipv6prefix/prefix-length eui-64
```

The link-local address is automatically configured when an address is assigned to the interface. You must specify the entire 128-bit IPv6 address or specify to use the 64-bit prefix by using the EUI-64 option, as shown in Example 6-2.

IPv6 Address Configuration Example

You can completely specify the IPv6 address or compute the host identifier (rightmost 64 bits) from the EUI-64 identifier of the interface. In Example 6-3, the IPv6 address of the interface is configured using the EUI-64 format, based on the topology shown in Figure 6-11.

Example 6-3 *Configuring and Verifying a Router for EUI-64 Interface ID Assignment*

```
R1(config)# ipv6 unicast-routing
R1(config)# interface fa0/0
R1(config-if)# ipv6 address 2001:db8:c18:1::/64 eui-64
R1# show ipv6 interface fa0/0
FastEthernet0/0 is up, line protocol is up
 IPv6 is enabled, link-local address is FE80::218:B9FF:FE21:9278
 Global unicast address(es):
 2001:DB8:c18:1:218:B9FF:FE21:9278, subnet is 2000:1:2:3::/64
 Joined group address(es):
 FF02::1:FF21:9278
 FF02::1
 FF02::2
 MTU is 1500 bytes
<output omitted>
```

LAN: 2001:DB8:C18:1::/64

Fa0/0   MAC Address:
           0260.3e47.1530

Figure 6-11 *Topology of IPv6 Networks for Example 6-3*

Alternatively, you can completely specify the entire IPv6 address to assign a router interface an address using the **ipv6 address** *ipv6-address/prefix-length* command in interface configuration mode.

Routing Considerations for IPv6

IPv6 uses longest-prefix match routing just like CIDR does for IPv4. CIDR will be covered in Chapter 8, "Access Control Lists for Threat Mitigation."

Many of the common routing protocols have been modified to manage longer IPv6 addresses and different header structures. The following updated routing protocols are currently available:

- Static

- RIPng (RFC 2080)

- OSPFv3 (RFC 2740)

- IS-IS for IPv6

- MP-BGP4 (RFC 2545/2858)

- EIGRP for IPv6

This book discusses static routing and RIPng. IPv6 routing is discussed in greater detail in *Implementing Cisco IP Routing (ROUTE) Foundation Learning Guide: Foundation Learning for the ROUTE 642-902 Exam* by Diane Teare.

You can use and configure IPv6 static routing in the same way you would with IPv4. There is an IPv6-specific requirement per RFC 2461 that a router must be able to determine the link- local address of each of its neighboring routers to ensure that the target address of a redirect message identifies the neighbor router by its link-local address. This requirement means that using a global unicast address as a next-hop address with IPv6 routing is not recommended.

Routing protocols use the link-local address as a source for exchanging routing updates, and this link-local address is actually used as next-hop address.

The Cisco IOS global command to enable IPv6 is **ipv6 unicast-routing**. You must enable IPv6 unicast routing before an IPv6-capable routing protocol or an IPv6 static route will work.

Routing Information Protocol next generation (RIPng) (RFC 2080) is a distance-vector routing protocol with a limit of 15 hops that uses split horizon and poison reverse to prevent routing loops. RIPng includes the following features:

- Based on IPv4 RIP version 2 (RIPv2) and is similar to RIPv2

- Uses IPv6 for transport

- Includes the IPv6 prefix and next-hop IPv6 address

- Uses the multicast group FF02::9, the all-RIP-routers multicast group, as the destination address for RIP updates

- Sends updates on UDP port 521

- Supported by Cisco IOS Release 12.2(2)T and later

Revisiting Threats: Considerations for IPv6

The good news, if this can be considered good, is that when considering the TCP/IP protocol stack, the Internet layer (Open Systems Interconnection [OSI] network layer) is the only difference between IPv4 and IPv6. Therefore, when the transition to IPv6 occurs, the layers above and below IPv6 will remain the same. If your web application is vulnerable to attacks in an IPv4 environment, it will also be vulnerable to attacks when IPv6 is used. This means that the threat and vulnerability landscape is similar between the two protocol stacks.

IPv4 and IPv6 are both datagram protocols, and there are many similarities between the two headers. Both headers still have a version, a quality of service (QoS) marking field, a payload length field, a counter to detect how far the packet has traveled, the value of the next upper-layer protocol, and of course a pair of addresses. Therefore, in general, many types of attacks are similar between IPv4 and IPv6, as listed below. For some attack types, additional information is provided.

- Reconnaissance
  - Not so easy in IPv6 due to large address space
  - Scanners will make router trigger NDP, wasting CPU and resources
  - Attack tools exist today (Parasit6, Fakerouter6, Scapy6, others)
- Viruses and worms
  - Scanning will probably use alternative techniques
- Application layer attacks
  - Same implications
  - Peer-to-peer nature of IPv6 augments the problem
- Unauthorized access
- Man-in-the-middle attacks
  - Still a possibility
  - Myth: mandatory IPsec resolves the issue
  - Reality: IPsec is a mandatory part of the stack, but you still have to configure it
- Sniffing or eavesdropping
- Denial of service (DoS) attacks
- Spoofed packets: forged addresses and other fields
  - Still a possibility
  - Bogons (bogus IP addresses) a reality today
- Attacks against routers and other networking devices
- Attacks against the physical or data link layers

However, there is also some bad news. IPv6 is a bit different and, as such, there are threats that have been slightly changed by the fact that IPv6 does things slightly differently than IPv4. The following is a list of threats that are only slightly modified by IPv6:

- LAN-based attacks (NDP)
- Attacks against DHCP or DHCPv6
- DoS against routers (hop-by-hop extension headers rather than router alerts)

- Fragmentation (IPv4 routers performing fragmentation versus IPv6 hosts using a fragment extension header)

- Packet amplification attacks (IPv4 uses broadcast; IPv6 uses multicast)

As far as the protocol is concerned, IPv6 is no more or less secure than IPv4, but the IPv6 protocol is unique and has its own security considerations. The fields within the IPv6 header that are unique to IPv6 include the flow label and extension headers.

Even though IPv6 does not significantly transform the IP header, there will be attacks unique to IPv6.

Following is a list of threats that are unique to IPv6 networks:

- **Reconnaissance and scanning worms:** Brute-force discovery is more difficult.

- **Attacks against ICMPv6:** ICMPv6 is a required component of IPv6.

- **Extension header (EH) attacks:** EHs need to be accurately parsed.

- **Autoconfiguration:** NDP attacks are simple to perform.

- **Attacks on transition mechanisms:** Migration techniques are required by IPv6.

- **Mobile IPv6 attacks:** Devices that roam are susceptible to multiple vulnerabilities.

- **IPv6 protocol stack attacks:** Because of the code freshness of IPv6, bugs in the protocol stack exist.

IPv6 introduces the following difficulties or vulnerabilities:

- Training and planning

  - Lack of knowledge, poor planning even for basic security controls (example: weak ingress filtering, or no filtering at all)

- End nodes are exposed to many threats:

  - **Address configuration parameters:** Rogue configuration parameters

  - **Address initialization:** Denial of address insertion

  - **Address resolution:** Address stealing

  - **Default gateway discovery:** Rogue routers

  - **Neighbor reachability tracking:** Rogue neighbor status

- Header extensions

  - Hosts process routing headers (RH)

  - Header extensions can be exploited (example: routing header for source routing and reconnaissance)

  - Amplification attacks based on routing header

The reliance of IPv6 on multicasting and ICMPv6 makes those protocols subject to multiple exploits to implement DoS, man-in-the-middle, and spoofing attacks, such as:

■ Multicasting facilitates reconnaissance (example: FF02::1 is all hosts, FF02::2 is all routers).

■ ICMPv6 is a vehicle for autoconfiguration, subject to spoofing and multiple exploits.

The built-in tunneling capabilities of IPv6 become a vulnerability when not properly controlled. Tunnels are inherently covert channels that will very likely be passed through by firewalls that do not support IPv6 or do not have a strong IPv6 filtering mechanism. Something similar happens with other network security controls such as intrusion prevention systems (IPS). Tunneling is pervasive and sometimes automatic in IPv6, so it does not take much to initiate an unwanted tunnel that could be invisible to your security controls. As an example, Teredo runs over IPv4 UDP port 41 and could also run over any UDP port. Also, most IPv4/IPv6 transition mechanisms have no authentication built in.

Dual stacking represents another issue. You might think IPv6 is not present in your network, but most operating systems support it and enable it by default. A fully protected IPv4 host can be exploited if IPv6 is a weak link. Specific dual-stacking vulnerabilities include the following:

■ IPv6 is on by default in most operating systems. You may have it on and not know that it's running.

■ Applications can be subject to attack on both IPv6 and IPv4.

■ The network is only as secure as the least secure stack.

Examples of Possible IPv6 Attacks

In Figure 6-12, the attacker manipulates the routing header to create a traffic loop. DoS attacks can be performed using this feedback loop to consume resources or amplify the packets that are sent to a victim. RH0 packets could be created with a list of embedded IPv6 addresses. The packet would be forwarded to every system in the list before finally being sent to the destination address. If the embedded IPv6 addresses in an RH0 packet were two systems on the Internet listed numerous times, it could cause a type of feedback loop.

Figure 6-12 *Traffic Loop from Exploiting Routing Header*

In Figure 6-13, the attacker abuses NDP by using a router to amplify a network scan. The router sends Neighbor Solicitation (NS) messages to all the hosts in the LAN segment, using the all-nodes multicast address.

Figure 6-13   *Network Scan from Exploiting NDP*

By combining multiple techniques, attackers can accomplish stealth attacks that result in trust exploitation and information theft. Figure 6-14 illustrates an attack that combines dual-stacked hosts, which are subject to rogue router advertisements. This type of attack could exploit the routing header (RH) to pivot using multiple hops; and by using automatic tunnels, it could stealthily go through firewalling and IPS sensors.

Figure 6-14   *Combo Attack on IPv6*

The attacker gains a foothold in the IPv4 network. The compromised host sends rogue router advertisements, triggering unwilling dual-stacked hosts to obtain an IPv6 address. These compromised hosts could trigger an automatic Teredo tunnel, which would go unnoticed by the firewall. The attacker can also use the routing header to pivot around multiple hosts in the internal network before sending traffic out.

Recommended Practices

The same best current practices for protecting IPv4 networks are still appropriate for IPv6. Standard perimeter security architecture still applies to IPv6 as it does to IPv4. Filtering at the edge and trying to protect the interior are still the order of the day. The network architecture model of core, distribution, and access will still be the way that IPv6 networks are designed. Many of the same protection mechanisms that are used in IPv4 networks will be adapted to work on IPv6. The same operational guidelines and forensic search also apply to IPv6.

The following list summarizes additional guidelines for IPv6 security. Some of these guidelines will be discussed in more detail in other chapters of this book, such as IPv6 access lists in Chapter 8 and IPv6 aware intrusion prevention in Chapter 11, "Intrusion Prevention Systems."

- Ingress filtering is key:
  - Deny Bogon addresses.
  - Filter multicast packets at your perimeter based on their scope.
  - Permit only packets that have as a destination address your allocated block of addresses or multicast group address or your link-local address for NDP.
  - Granularly filter ICMPv6 messages at the perimeter (remember, ICMPv6 is needed for protocol operations such as NDP).
  - Drop RH0 packets and unknown extension headers at the perimeter and throughout the interior of the network.
- Favor dual stack as the transition mechanism, but secure each protocol equally.
- Control the use of tunneling:
  - Configure manual tunnels if possible.
  - Do not allow tunnels through the perimeter unless required.
- Consider current and future security enhancements:
  - Secure NDS (SeND) from RFC 3971 provides a cryptographic method to Neighbor Discovery.
  - RA Guard, from RFC 6105, is an alternative and complement to SeND, filtering at Layer 2.

Summary

In this chapter, you learned about the need for IPv6. You saw that IPv6 offers more benefits than IPv4, including a larger address space, easier address aggregation, and integrated security.

A review of the IPv6 addressing scheme revealed that IPv6 address are 128 bits long, with a 48-bit global prefix, a 16-bit subnet ID, and a 64-bit interface identifier. You saw how EUI-64 addresses are derived from the MAC address. You also saw that network addresses could be assigned statically, through a stateless configuration, or through DHCPv6.

You learned that IPv6 is not automatically enabled on Cisco IOS 12.2(2)T and later; to turn it on, you have to use the **ipv6 unicast-routing** command, and to assign an IPv6 address to an interface, you have to use the **ipv6 address** interface command. You also saw that Cisco supports all major IPv6 routing protocols: RIPng, OSPFv3, and EIGRP.

The chapter also discussed the transition from IPv4 to IPv6 using dual stacks, tunneling, and possibly NAT-PT. After the overview of IPv6's general characteristics, you learned how common and specific threats could affect IPv6, and how to develop and implement a strategy for IPv6 security.

References

For additional information, refer to these resources:

Cisco Systems, Inc. *Cisco IOS IPv6 Configuration Guide, Release 12.4, Implementing IPv6 Addressing and Basic Connectivity*, http://www.cisco.com/en/US/docs/ios/ipv6/configuration/guide/ip6-addrg_bsc_con.html

Cisco Systems, Inc. *IPv6 and IPv4 Threat Comparison and Best-Practice Evaluation (v1.0)*, http://www.cisco.com/web/about/security/security_services/ciag/documents/v6-v4-threats.pdf

RFC 2464, "Transmission of IPv6 Packets over Ethernet Networks," http://www.ietf.org/rfc/rfc2464.txt

RFC 3146, "Transmission of IPv6 Packets over IEEE 1394 Networks," http://www.ietf.org/rfc/rfc3146.txt

RFC 3587, "IPv6 Global Unicast Address Format," http://www.ietf.org/rfc/rfc3587.txt

RFC 4007, "IPv6 Scoped Address Architecture," http://www.ietf.org/rfc/rfc4007.txt

RFC 4291, "IP Version 6 Addressing Architecture," http://tools.ietf.org/html/rfc4291

Review Questions

Use the questions here to review what you learned in this chapter. The correct answers are found in the Appendix, "Answers to Chapter Review Questions."

1. Which global command enables IPv6 on a Cisco router?

   a. ipv6 transition
   b. ipv6 routing
   c. ipv6 unicast-routing
   d. ipv6 anycast

2. Which are advantages of IPv6 over IPv4? (Choose two.)

   a. Larger address space
   b. Complex header
   c. Security
   d. Efficient broadcast

3. Which of the following functions is unique to ICMPv6, as compared to ICMPv4?

   a. Router discovery
   b. Connectivity checks
   c. Informational/error messaging
   d. Fragmentation requiring notification

4. Which is not a valid IPv6 address?

   a. ::
   b. FF01::1
   c. 2031::130f::9c0:876a:130b
   d. 2031::130f:9c0:876a:130b

5. Which IPv6 address types can be acquired automatically by an IPv6 host?

   a. Global unicast address
   b. Anycast address
   c. Multicast address
   d. Link-local address
   e. All of the above

6. Which IPv6 feature or component, when unprotected, is more likely to result in covert channels that go undetected by firewalls?

   a. Routing header
   b. 6to4 transition deployments
   c. ICMPv6
   d. Autoconfiguration

7. Which IPv4-to-IPv6 transition technology is implemented as a translation mechanism?

   a. Dynamic 6to4 tunnels
   b. Dual stacking
   c. ISATAP
   d. NAT-PT

8. Choose two threats that result directly from the use of the routing header alone in IPv6?

   a. Denial of service
   b. Confidentiality exploits
   c. Advanced reconnaissance
   d. Worm amplification
   e. Spoofing

9. Which of the following is a valid EUI-64 address for MAC 0021.8661.9D8B?

   a. 002186FFFF619D8B
   b. 002186FFFE619D8B
   c. 012186FFFE619D8B
   d. 022186FFFE619D8B

10. Which of the following is an IPv6 routing protocol?

   a. RIPv6
   b. OSPFv6
   c. EIGRP for IPv6
   d. MP-BGP6

Chapter 7

Planning a Threat Control Strategy

Current trends in security threat vectors require a carefully planned threat control strategy. Trends affecting security include persistent application layer exploits, using social engineering to exploit the trust architecture of the enterprise, the pervasiveness of mobility and consumerization, and the insidious motivations behind the behavior of the attackers. All of these trends result in the need for dynamic security intelligence gathering and distribution, early warning systems, and application layer inspection for mobile services where data and applications are hosted in the cloud. This chapter suggests design principles to plan a threat control and containment strategy using firewalls and intrusion prevention systems in Cisco IOS environments. (Note that in previous chapters you have started to see how to use switches and routers to provide protection; in upcoming chapters, we will further explore the protection provided by routers when used for filtering, firewalling, and encrypting traffic.) In this chapter, we will

- Evaluate the current state of enterprise security in the presence of evolving threats
- Describe design considerations for a threat protection strategy to mitigate threats as part of a risk management strategy
- Describe how Cisco strategizes threat control and containment

Threats Revisited

Previous chapters of this book discussed the evolution of threats in information security. Recent trends indicate that threats have become global in nature, increasingly sophisticated, and pervasive. New exploits are designed to have a global impact in minutes. Blended threats, which use multiple means of propagation, are more sophisticated than ever. The trends are becoming regional and global in nature. Attackers are also learning to be dynamic and reactive, changing their approach rapidly if needed. I remember a discussion I had with the director of network security for the federal reserve bank of his country; he remarked, "We have a small team of professionals working 8 hours per shift at protecting our network, but there are hundreds of hackers coming at us 24 hours per day, nonstop." This network security team had to make sure that every crease of their network was secure. The hacker had to find only one open, minuscule gap to exploit.

Threats are also becoming persistent. After the initial attack starts, subsequent attacks may come in waves as infected systems join the network. Because infections are so complex and have so many end users (employees, vendors, and contractors), multiple types of endpoints (company desktop, home, and server), and multiple types of access (wired, wireless, VPN, and dial-up), infections are difficult to eradicate.

Trends in Network Security Threats

Evolution in technology and craftiness of hackers bring in new threat vectors. Threat vectors are the methods used to get to the desired target. More recent threat vectors are increasingly sophisticated, and the motivation of the attackers is reflected in their impact. Recent threat vectors include the following:

- Cognitive threats: social networks (likejacking)

- Smartphones, tablets, and consumer electronics exploits

- Widespread website compromises

- Disruption of critical infrastructure

- Virtualization exploits

- Memory scraping

- Hardware hacking

- IPv6-based attacks

The following is a list of the specific trends that can be gathered from the evolution of threats in information security:

- **Insidious motivation, high impact:** The primary motivation of the attacker is no longer just fame and notoriety. It is mostly political and financial, aimed at economic espionage and money-making activities. Malicious attackers use a businesslike, structured process not only to write code, but also to "conduct business." It is common to see a lifecycle approach to software development and a businesslike environment where developers cooperate and make attack tools publicly available.

- **Targeted, mutating, stealth threats:** The modus operandi is increasingly stealth, using mutating malware that changes by the minute. In some instances, hundreds of variants of the same malware are created in a matter of hours.

  Cybercriminals see value in fine-tuning their efforts so that their malware reaches a single high-profile target or performs a specific function. An example of a high-profile target attack effort would include attacking critical infrastructure, government operations, and organizations with massive amounts of customer identity information.

Attackers use strength in numbers. Botnets with specific targets are the norm, whereas large-scale worms with no individual objective are less common or effective. In the past, botnets would use centralized command and control. Botnets today use peer-to-peer control, so there is no central controller to take down.

■ **Threats consistently focusing on the application layer:** Known application layer attacks such as cross-site scripting and SQL injection are still relevant, as well as other vulnerabilities such as iFrame injection, which result from programming errors in web services environments. Increasingly, attacks have demonstrated that criminals looking for financial gain can exploit vulnerabilities resulting from web programming errors as new ways of penetrating important organizations. Attacks exploiting web browser vulnerabilities are common.

■ **Social engineering front and center:** Social engineering continues to attract victims who are willing to share information with people they believe are known to them. Nowhere is this trend more visible than in social networks, a prime target of attacks. One noticeable shift in social engineering is that criminals are spending more time figuring out how to assume someone's identity, perhaps by generating emails from an individual's computer or social networking account.

■ **Threats exploiting the borderless network:** Smartphones are general-purpose computers, so worms, viruses, and other malware will increasingly target them. Open mobile platforms are a prime target, and as more workers use their consumer devices for business-critical activities, endpoint security becomes a critical security control.

Data is now stored everywhere, with the advent of cloud computing and cloud services. Cloud security is a major concern for organizations of all kinds. A technology is often the victim of its own success. As a technology becomes more popular, it appears more prominently on hackers' radar screens, thus motivating them to attack this new technology. As an example, it is expected that as IPv6 becomes more pervasive, IPv6 vulnerabilities and threats will become more commonplace.

Threat Mitigation and Containment: Design Fundamentals

The result of the recent trends in information security threats is the need for an updated, carefully planned threat control and mitigation strategy, and a revision of old design paradigms.

■ **Policies and process definition:** The nature and frequency of attacks, and the increasingly high stakes in terms of organizational and business risk, call for a more formal approach to defining threat control policies. What probably started as a reactive process, and then moved to a more socialized process, needs to become a formal process in the wake of botnets, industrial espionage, and identity theft.

- **Mitigation technologies:** The mutating and stealth nature of attacks requires more accuracy in detection and prevention technologies. It also requires a more automated process, where networks and applications react to attacks and mitigate them with little or no human intervention. This used to be a more manual process in the past; however, organizations can no longer risk the potential consequences of this manual approach.

- **End-user awareness:** Data is stored everywhere, and users access mission-critical resources from multiple locations at multiple times, using multiple types of devices. The new paradigm must get the end user more involved with security, where in the past this was a function that was fully performed by IT.

Threat Control Design Guidelines

These new paradigms result in specific design guidelines for the threat control and containment architecture:

- **Stick to the basics:** The fundamental design guidelines are still valid. Implement a layered security approach, where defense in depth defines redundant, overlapping security controls to mitigate risk and provide fault tolerance. The threat control design should consider both internal and external networks to be untrusted and apply policy for both inbound and outbound traffic.

- **Risk management:** This should be a central consideration. Logging and monitoring are still critical functions.

- **Distributed security intelligence:** Because data and access are everywhere, there should also be security "sensors" everywhere. Security needs to be embedded in network elements, operating systems, and applications. This network of sensors needs to be integrated. Actionable, relevant, highly dynamic security information should be available to security devices and controls.

- **Security intelligence analysis:** This army of sensors and security controls will produce vast amounts of information. Event management, incident management, and, in more general terms, security intelligence management require a central approach to analysis and correlation, including correlation with third parties and external sources. This analysis should result in relevant threat information that should be automatically distributed to security devices and controls in a timely manner.

- **Application layer visibility:** Application layer inspection is critical and should be implemented efficiently and effectively.

- **Incident response:** Incident response should be automated and dynamic, providing end users the means to respond and mitigate.

Application Layer Visibility

Application layer security controls provide visibility at higher layers, up to Layer 7 (as shown in Figure 7-1), necessary to match protocol and application anomalies that are purposefully crafted to exploit application and operating system vulnerabilities. This functionality is necessary in firewalls and intrusion prevention systems, and it should be implemented with effectiveness and efficiency in mind. Application layer controls are often implemented in hardware, and they require a good amount of capacity planning because they trigger deep packet inspection and are more CPU intensive than Layer 4 controls such as access control lists (ACL).

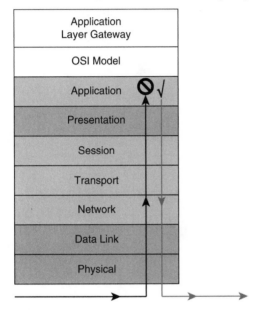

Figure 7-1 *Application Layer Visibility Analyses Traffic Up to the Application Layer*

Application layer visibility provides the intelligence to distinguish botnet command and control activity from otherwise innocuous web traffic, and can distinguish between valid encrypted data and data meant to obfuscate the application. Without application layer visibility, you cannot comprehensively detect, respond to, and investigate policy violations, exploits, and intrusions. Cisco IronPort Web Security Appliance (WSA) is a device that provides application layer visibility. The application layer visibility, which is the bread and butter of the IronPort WSA, can also be accomplished with Layer 7 filtering on the Cisco ASA firewalls and on Cisco IOS routers, though it necessitates more effort.

Distributed Security Intelligence

The distributed approach to gathering and providing relevant and actionable security intelligence follows the defense-in-depth guidelines of security architecture design. For threat management, this approach creates an army of sensors and threat controls that work collaboratively and automatically to provide a more effective threat detection and response mechanism. This results in higher threat coverage and greater accuracy, as new threats detected in one location are fed back into the system, making other locations know about the threat and update their detection and response capabilities to manage it.

This system is based on telemetry, collaboration, and proactive protection, where sensors in the field feed a central system that distributes the information to other sensors, as shown in Figure 7-2. This approach acts as an early warning system to prevent new attacks and automatically tune the response to current attacks. Cisco offers such systems with its AnyConnect telemetry module, which communicates with Cisco IronPort WSA. The web filtering infrastructure uses this data to strengthen its web security scanning algorithms, improve the accuracy of the URL categories and web reputation database, and ultimately provide better URL filtering rules for the organization.

Figure 7-2   *Distributed Security Intelligence Using Telemetry*

Security Intelligence Analysis

The proliferation of security controls could overflow the ability of the system to gather and analyze the security intelligence information. Building an effective security intelligence analysis capability becomes a crucial component of the threat control architecture design.

Event and incident management are critical components of this strategy. Monitoring and logging are fundamental guidelines that may be already in place. Local and global correlation of the monitoring and log data becomes increasingly important, for accuracy and automation, and also for forensics and post-mortem analysis.

In Figure 7-3, multiple devices send a log entry to the syslog server, on the right, regarding the single event generated by the hacker attacking the target. All these alerts are analyzed by the central event management and correlation server, and the administrator is notified once about the issue. Without proper correlation analysis, the network administrator might have been notified by the alert from the router, by the alert from the firewall, and by the alert generated by the IPS sensor. Cisco MARS, now in end-of-life status but still supported by Cisco, was an example of such central event management and correlation system. As mentioned in Chapter 4, Cisco now refers its customers to one of its Security Information and Event Management (SIEM) ecosystem partners, such as LogLogic, Splunk, and so forth. More information about SIEM partners can be found at http://www.cisco.com/en/US/solutions/ns340/ns414/ns742/ns744/ns1090/ landing_siem.html.

Figure 7-3 *Security Information and Event Management*

Integrated Threat Control Strategy

The Cisco threat control and containment solution offers comprehensive protection for your network through network-wide visibility, simplified policy control, and proactive system protection. The Cisco threat control and containment solution regulates network access, isolates infected systems, prevents intrusions, and protects critical business assets. This solution uses centralized policy, configuration, and threat event management to counteract malicious traffic, such as worms, viruses, and malware, before it affects your business.

Cisco Threat Control and Containment Categories

Threat prevention solutions have been a flagship of Cisco security for a long time. Integrated security controls found in Cisco Adaptive Security Appliance (ASA), Integrated Services Routers (ISR), and Intrusion Prevention System (IPS) sensors provide a multidimensional approach to detecting, mitigating, and responding to threats at various levels. Threat prevention mechanisms, such as application layer inspection, Modular Policy Framework (MPF), signatures, and anomaly detection and firewalling, are integrated into the fabric of the network. Flexible deployment options include standalone appliances, service modules that are embedded into routers and switches, and virtualized devices, such as Cisco ASA contexts (virtual firewalls). These mechanisms can be deployed on premises, off premises, or as part of a hybrid, managed approach using cloud services.

Table 7-1 provides an overview of the different technologies incorporated into the Cisco threat control and containment solution. These technologies are looked at more closely in the rest of this chapter.

Table 7-1 *Cisco Threat Control and Containment*

Category	Method	Recommendations
Integrated approach to threat control	Stick to the basics, formalize	Sensors everywhere
		Multiple form factors for firewall and IPS (physical and virtual appliance, hardware module, software based)
Application awareness	Distributed security intelligence	Advanced Inspection and Control (AIC)
		Modular Policy Framework (MPF)
		Flexible Packet Matching (FPM)
		Network-Based Application Recognition (NBAR)
Application-specific gateways	Application layer visibility	IronPort email and web security
		ScanSafe web security
Security management	Security intelligence analysis	Multiple options for event and log management (device managers, Cisco Configuration Professional, Cisco Security Manager)
Cisco SIO	Incident response	Global Threat Operations Centers (TOC), dynamic updates
		SensorBase and IntelliShield
		Correlation and data mining

Cisco security technologies facilitate the implementation of the design guidelines previously described by incorporating the following features and technologies:

Integrated Approach to Threat Control

The network is the system that detects and prevents threats. As such, threat control is embedded and integrated in the network using multiple deployment options: appliance-based controls, hardware modules for existing network elements, software-based controls, and virtualized security elements, are all part of this strategy to prevent intrusion and control threats.

Application Awareness

Application awareness is implemented across the board in multiple network elements and security devices, such as the Zone-Based firewall that performs application layer (Layer 7) inspection and deep packet inspection. These solutions are implemented in the form of multiple application inspection mechanisms, such as, among others, the following:

- Any alphanumeric character

- Modular Policy Framework (MPF)

- Network Based Application Recognition (NBAR)

- Flexible Packet Matching (FPM)

Application-Specific Gateways

Application awareness is also implemented in the form of application-specific gateways, geared toward the inspection and analysis of traffic related to specific applications. IronPort web and email security appliances and ScanSafe web security technologies are examples of those gateways.

Security Management

A comprehensive approach to event management is available in all security management tools, with scalable features available for different scenarios. From device managers such as Cisco IPS Device Manager (IDM), to configuration builders such as Cisco Configuration Professional, to central management applications such as Cisco Security Manager, event management and correlation are a key function in Cisco security management.

Cisco Security Intelligence Operations Site

Cisco SIO is the back-end security ecosystem that detects threat activity, researches and analyzes the threats, and provides real-time updates and best practices to keep organizations informed and protected. Cisco SIO consists of three pillars:

- Threat intelligence, which is called Cisco SensorBase, shown in Figure 7-4

- The automatic and human development process, called the Threat Operations Center

- The automated and best practices content that is pushed to network elements in the form of dynamic updates

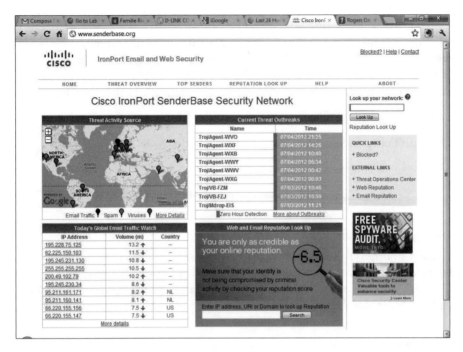

Figure 7-4 *Cisco IronPort SenderBase Web Page*

Cisco SIO is a security intelligence center that baselines the current state of threats on a worldwide basis and provides the network system with valuable information to detect, prevent, and react to threats. Cisco SIO acts as an early warning system by correlating threat information from the SensorBase, analyzed by the Threat Operations Center. Cisco SIO then feeds this information to enforcement elements for live threat prevention that is based on malware outbreaks, current vulnerabilities, and zero-day attacks.

More information on Cisco SIO can be found at http://tools.cisco.com/security/center/home.x and at http://www.senderbase.org.

Cisco Threat Control and Containment Solutions Fundamentals

Cisco offers multiple solutions in multiple different platforms to provide threat control and containment. For the purpose of the CCNA Security, we will focus on the most common technology used by small and medium businesses, which are Firewalling, including access-control lists, and Intrusion Prevention Systems. For a more exhaustive list of Cisco's offerings, visit www.cisco.com.

Cisco Security Appliances

Cisco security appliances, commonly called firewalls, are integrated devices that offer a new generation of threat control mechanisms. Solutions that include firewalling services are available in multiple footprints to implement the distributed security intelligence approach to threat prevention:

- **Cisco ASA:** These multifunction security devices include firewalls, VPNs, IPSs, and content security technologies. They are available in multiple form factors, and benefit multiple places in the network, from the small office to the data center and service provider environment.

- **Hardware modules:** Designed for data center and large enterprise networks, these security modules integrate into the Catalyst 6500 switch:

  - Cisco Catalyst 6500 ASA Services Module

  - Cisco Catalyst 6500 Firewall Services Module (FWSM)

- **Cisco IOS Firewall:** Integrated in the Cisco IOS software in Integrated Services Routers and Layer 3 switches, this Cisco IOS option implements the zone-based policy firewall and allows a distributed approach to firewall services.

- **Cisco Virtual Security Gateway (VSG):** Designed for data centers where mult-itenancy and service virtualization are common, this virtual appliance integrates with commercial server virtualization and switch virtualization environments.

Note In February 2012, Cisco announced the latest firewall OS, called Cisco ASA CX, which will bring application awareness and visibility to the traffic similarly to, but not completely the same as, how a secure web gateway would do it. Customers who wish for the full array of context awareness should still invest in a Cisco IronPort Web Security Appliance.

Cisco also announced new platforms, called the Cisco ASA 5500-X Series capable of running the Cisco ASA CX operating system. One of the many notable characteristics of the ASA 5500-X Series is its capacity to run IPS in software.

For more on Cisco ASA CX and the Cisco ASA 5500-X Series platforms, visit Cisco.com.

The different firewalls listed above implement various access control mechanisms for the new landscape of information security threats that are described in this module:

- Zone-based firewall

- ACLs

- FPM

- AIC

- MPF

- URL filtering

- User-based access control (cut-through proxy)
- Stateful failover

Cisco IPSs

Cisco IPSs are another example of integrated devices offering a new generation of threat control mechanisms. The IPS functionality is available in multiple footprints to implement the distributed security intelligence approach to threat prevention:

- **Cisco IPS 4200 Series Sensors:** These IPS appliances are available in multiple form factors, and benefit multiple places in the network, from the small office to the data center and service provider environment.

- **Hardware modules:** Integrating into ASA appliances, Catalyst 6500 switches, and ISRs, these modules embed the function of IPS sensors into the fabric of the network, and at the same time integrate with global correlation solutions such as the Cisco SIO service:

    - Cisco ASA Advanced Inspection and Prevention Security Services Module (AIP-SSM) and Cisco ASA Advanced Inspection and Prevention Security Services Card (AIP-SSC)

    - Cisco Intrusion Detection Services Module (IDSM-2) for Cisco Catalyst 6500

    - Cisco IPS Network Module Enhanced (IPS NME) and Cisco IPS Advanced Integration Module (IPS AIM) for Cisco Integrated Services Router Generation 2 (ISR G2)

- **Cisco IOS IPS:** Integrated in the Cisco IOS operating system in ISRs and Layer 3 switches, this Cisco IOS option implements IPS technologies consistent with the rest of the Cisco IPS solutions.

These IPSs implement various intrusion management solutions for the new landscape of information security threats that are described in an upcoming chapter:

- Rich set of detection mechanisms
- Signatures
    - Anomaly detection
    - Normalization
    - Correlation
- Automatic signature updates
- Multiple deployment modes
    - Inline
    - Promiscuous

Figure 7-5 illustrates the Cisco threat control and containment architecture for a small network scenario. Notice the distributed security intelligence approach, implemented through various threat control devices, including Cisco IOS zone-based and Cisco ASA firewalls, Cisco IOS IPS, and Cisco Security Manager. Application layer inspection, signature- and anomaly-based protection, and collaboration via the Cisco SIO Center are showcased in this scenario.

Figure 7-5   *Threat Control Scenario for a Small Business*

Summary

Threat vectors are stealth, targeted, aimed at the application. The motivations of attackers are increasingly based on social engineering and financial gains.

The following are the main points conveyed in this chapter:

- Threat control and containment should distribute security intelligence, improve incident analysis and correlation, and respond automatically.

- Cisco threat control and containment solutions provide multiple deployment options: appliance, hardware module, software based, and virtualized.

- Cisco threat control and containment is a solution for small, medium, and large businesses.

References

For additional information, refer to these Cisco.com resources:

"Cisco Security Intelligence Operations," http://tools.cisco.com/security/center/home.x

"Cisco 5500 Series Adaptive Security Appliances," http://www.cisco.com/en/US/products/ps6120/index.html

Review Questions

Use the questions here to review what you learned in this chapter. The correct answers are found in the Appendix, "Answers to Chapter Review Questions."

1. The term "likejacking" refers to which type of threat vector?

   a. Phishing
   b. IPv6 Teredo tunnels
   c. Social network exploits
   d. Botnets

2. Which Cisco product or service provides the global correlation service?

   a. IPS
   b. SIO
   c. Third-party SIEM systems
   d. SecureX

3. Which two security appliances best fit a data center scenario where server virtualization and multitenancy are among the main architectural components?

   a. FWSM
   b. ASA
   c. Zone-based firewall
   d. VSG

4. What is meant by end-user awareness?

   a. End users are consulted and made aware of the different applications tested by the organization.
   b. End users are aware of the potentially harmful traffic generated by other users.
   c. End users are involved in security functions that were strictly reserved to IT in the past, such as the user-acceptable policies and being conscious of potential threats.
   d. End-user awareness is a network security training program developed by IT for future dissemination to end users.

5. Which of the following is seen as the best protection against zero-day attacks?

   a. NBAR
   b. AIC
   c. SIO
   d. MPF
   e. FPM
   f. ACL

Chapter 8

Access Control Lists for Threat Mitigation

Cisco provides basic traffic filtering capabilities with access control lists (ACL). You can configure ACLs for all routed network protocols to filter packets as the packets pass through a router or security appliance. There are many reasons to configure ACLs; for example, you can use ACLs to restrict the contents of routing updates or to provide traffic flow control. One of the most important reasons to configure ACLs is to provide security for your network; this is the reason on which this chapter focuses.

This chapter outlines the types of ACLs that are available and provides guidelines that help create ACLs to provide network security in IPv4 and IPv6 environments. More precisely, this chapter

- Lists the benefits of ACLs

- Describes the building blocks and operational framework of ACLs

- Describes summarizable address blocks in the context of CIDR and VLSM environments, demonstrating how ACL wildcard masks allow for threat mitigation in those environments

- Lists design considerations when deploying ACLs

- Demonstrates the use of Cisco Configuration Professional and the CLI to deploy and verify a threat containment strategy using ACLs

- Demonstrates the use of Cisco Configuration Professional and the CLI to correlate ACL log and alarm information in order to monitor their impact and effectiveness

- Demonstrates how to configure object groups to streamline the implementation of ACLs for threat control

- Demonstrates how to configure ACLs in IPv6 environments, highlighting the operational differences with IPv4 ACLs

ACL Fundamentals

ACLs provide packet filtering for routers and firewalls to protect internal networks from the outside world. ACLs filter network traffic in both directions by controlling whether to forward or block packets at the router interfaces, based on the criteria that you specify within the ACLs. ACL criteria could be the source address of the traffic, the destination address of the traffic, the upper-layer protocol, or other information. Be aware, however, that sophisticated users (hackers) can sometimes successfully evade or fool basic ACLs not only because authentication is not required, but mainly because of the inability of an ACL to track the state of a connection.

ACLs provide a basic level of security for accessing your network. If you do not configure ACLs on your router, all packets passing through the router could get to all parts of your network. You can use ACLs on a router that is positioned between two parts of your network to control traffic entering or exiting a specific part of your internal network. An ACL on the router allows one host to access a part of your network and prevents another host from accessing the same area. The ACL shown in Figure 8-1 allows Host A to access the Human Resources network but prevents Host B from accessing the Human Resources network.

Figure 8-1 *Filtering Host B Traffic Ingress Using an ACL*

To provide the security benefits of ACLs, you should, at a minimum, configure ACLs at the perimeter of your networks. This configuration provides a basic buffer from the outside network, or from a less-controlled area of your own network into a more sensitive area of your network. On these network edge routers, you should configure ACLs for each network protocol that is configured on the router interfaces.

You can use ACLs to mitigate many threats:

- IP address spoofing (inbound)

- IP address spoofing (outbound)

- DoS TCP SYN attacks (blocking external attacks)

- DoS TCP SYN attacks (using TCP intercept)

- DoS Smurf attacks

- Filtering ICMP messages (inbound)

- Filtering ICMP messages (outbound)

- Filtering traceroute

Note   The System Administration, Networking, and Security (SANS) Institute offers a guide to protecting your Cisco IOS router, *Cisco Router Hardening Step-by-Step*, available at http://www.sans.org/reading_room/whitepapers/firewalls/cisco-router-hardening-step-by-step_794. The National Security Agency (NSA) also offers a guide on this topic, *Router Security Configuration Guide*, at http://www.nsa.gov/ia/mitigation_guidance/security_configuration_guides/cisco_router_guides.shtml.

Tip   Two terms you'll encounter in this chapter that are commonly confused are egress and ingress. *Egress* refers to traffic leaving the network or device. *Ingress* refers to traffic entering the network or device.

Cisco routers use ACLs as packet filters to decide which packets can access a router service or cross an interface. Packets that are allowed across an interface are permitted packets. Packets that are not allowed across an interface are denied packets.

An ACL enforces one or more corporate security policies. For example, a corporate security policy might allow to access the Internet only packets using source addresses from within the trusted network. Once this policy is written, you can develop an ACL that includes certain statements that, when applied to a router interface, can implement this policy.

Cisco router security depends strongly on well-written ACLs to restrict access to router network services and to filter packets as they traverse the router.

ACLs express the sets of rules that give added control over packets that enter inbound interfaces, packets that relay through the router, and packets that exit outbound interfaces of the router. ACLs do not act on packets that originate from the router itself. Instead, ACLs are statements that specify conditions of how the router handles the traffic flow through specified interfaces.

ACLs operate in two ways:

- **Inbound:** Incoming packets are processed before they are routed to an outbound interface. An inbound ACL is efficient because it saves the overhead of routing lookups if the packet will be discarded after it is denied by the filtering tests. If the packet is permitted by the tests, it is then processed for routing.

- **Outbound:** Packets arriving on the inside interface are routed to the outbound interface, and then they are processed through the outbound ACL.

Figure 8-2 shows an example of an outbound ACL. When a packet enters an interface, the router checks the routing table to see whether the packet is routable. If the packet is not routable, it is dropped.

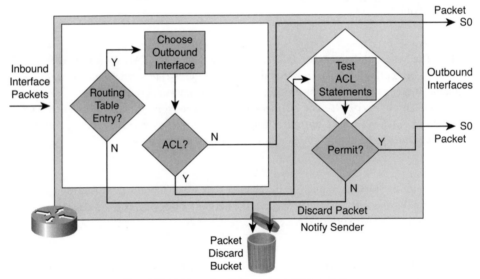

If no ACL statement matches, discard the packet.

Figure 8-2 *Outbound ACL Operation*

Next, the router checks to see whether the destination interface is grouped to an ACL. If the destination interface is not grouped to an ACL, the packet can be sent to the output buffer. Examples of outbound ACL operation are as follows:

- If the outbound interface selected by the routing process is not grouped to an outbound ACL, the packet is sent directly to that outbound interface, which is S0 in the example in Figure 8-2.

- If the outbound interface selected by the routing process is grouped to an outbound ACL, the packet is not sent out directly to that outbound interface, which is S0 in the example in Figure 8-2. The packet must first be tested by the combination of ACL statements associated with that interface. Based on the ACL tests, the packet is permitted or denied.

For outbound lists, to *permit* means to send the packet to the output buffer, and to *deny* means to discard the packet.

With an inbound ACL, when a packet enters an interface, the router checks to see whether the source interface is grouped to an ACL. If the source interface is not grouped to an ACL, the router checks the routing table to see whether the packet is routable. If the packet is not routable, the router drops the packet. Examples of inbound ACL operation are as follows:

- If the inbound interface is E0, for example, which has not been grouped to an inbound ACL, the packet is processed normally and the router checks to determine whether the packet is routable.

- If the inbound interface is E1, for example, which has been grouped to an inbound ACL, the packet is not processed and the routing table is not consulted until the packet is tested by the ACL that is associated with that interface. Based on the ACL tests, the packet is permitted or denied.

For inbound lists, *permit* means to continue to process the packet after receiving it on an inbound interface, and *deny* means to discard the packet.

ACL statements operate in a sequential, logical order, as shown in Figure 8-3. They evaluate packets from the top down, one statement at a time. If a packet header and an ACL statement match, the rest of the statements in the list are skipped, and the packet is permitted or denied as determined by the matched statement. If a packet header does not match an ACL statement, the packet is tested against the next statement in the list. This matching process continues until the end of the list is reached.

A final implied statement covers all packets for which conditions did not test true. This final test condition matches all other packets and results in a "deny" instruction. Instead of proceeding into or out of an interface, the router drops all of these remaining packets. This final statement is often referred to as the "implicit **deny any** statement." Because of this statement, an ACL should have at least one **permit** statement in it; otherwise, the ACL blocks all traffic.

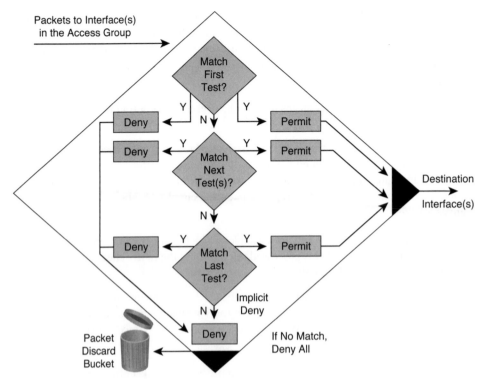

Figure 8-3   *Top-Down Process of Tests: Deny or Permit*

Types of IP ACLs

Cisco routers support two types of IP ACLs:

- **Standard ACLs:** Standard IP ACLs check the source addresses of packets that can be routed. The result either permits or denies the output for an entire protocol suite, based on the source network, subnet, or host IP address.

- **Extended ACLs:** Extended IP ACLs check both the source and destination packet addresses. They can also check for specific protocols, port numbers, and other parameters, which allows administrators more flexibility and control.

The two general methods you can use to create ACLs are as follows:

- **Numbered ACLs:** Use a number for identification.

- **Named ACLs:** Use an alphanumeric string for identification.

Using numbered ACLs is an effective method on smaller networks with more homogeneously defined traffic. Because each ACL type is limited to an assigned range of numbers, it is easy to determine the type of ACL that you are using.

Specifying an ACL number from 1 to 99 or 1300 to 1999 instructs the router to accept numbered standard IP Version 4 (IPv4) ACL statements. Specifying an ACL number from 100 to 199 or 2000 to 2699 instructs the router to accept numbered extended IPv4 ACL statements.

The named ACL feature allows you to identify IP standard and extended ACLs with an alphanumeric string (name) rather than the numeric representations. Named IP ACLs provide you more flexibility in working with the ACL entries.

Tip The number of the ACL determines which protocol it is filtering: 1 to 99 and 1300 to 1999 define standard IP ACLs. 100 to 199 and 2000 to 2699 define extended IP ACLs.

Named ACLs have been available since Cisco IOS Software Releases 11.2. Names contain alphanumeric characters. Names cannot contain spaces or punctuation and must begin with an alphabetic character. Named ACLs enable you to add or delete entries within the ACL.

There are two benefits to IP ACL entry sequence numbering:

- You can edit the order of ACL statements.

- You can remove individual statements from an ACL.

Where additions are placed in an ACL depends on whether you use sequence numbers. If you don't specify a sequence number, new ACL statements are placed at the end of the ACL.

Removing ACL statements is also streamlined with sequence numbers. If you want to remove a single entry, you can do it by referencing the entry number (or sequence number) with the **no access-list** command. It is best practice to space out the entry sequence number to leave room to add intermediate entries in the future. As an example, the first entry could be sequenced 10, the second entry 20, and so forth. Should an entry need to be inserted between 10 and 20, you could sequence it 15. Also note that Cisco lets you resequence an ACL and select the increment. A good reference on this can be found at http://www.cisco.com/en/US/docs/ios/12_2s/feature/guide/fsaclseq.html.

Note ACLs that are applied to an interface do not filter traffic that is generated by the router.

ACL Wildcard Masking and VLSM Review

Address filtering occurs when you use ACL address wildcard masking to identify how to check or ignore corresponding IP address bits. However, prior to jumping into ACL wildcard masking, let's review subnetting, including variable-length subnet masking (VLSM), which was covered amply in the CCNA material that you studied for the ICND2 exam. Please consult *CCNA Preparation Library* (Cisco Press) for thorough presentations on IP addresses, subnetting, and VLSM.

Subnetting Overview

To understand ACL filtering in classless interdomain routing (CIDR) and VLSM environments, we must start with a review of subnetting.

Remember that an IP address has 32 bits and comprises two parts—a network ID and a host ID. The length of the network ID and host ID depends on the class of the IP address. The number of hosts available also depends on the class of the IP address.

The default number of bits in the network ID is referred to as the *classful prefix length*. Therefore, a Class A address has a classful prefix length of /8, a Class B address has a classful prefix length of /16, and a Class C address has a classful prefix length of /24.

The number of hosts per subnet available depends upon the number of host ID bits not borrowed.

Subnetting Example: Class C

The subnet address is created by taking address bits from the host-number portion of Class A, Class B, and Class C addresses. Usually a network administrator assigns the subnet address locally. Like IP addresses, each subnet address must be unique.

Each time one bit is borrowed from a host field, there is one less bit remaining in the host field that can be used for host numbers, and the number of host addresses that can be assigned per subnet decreases by a power of 2. Figure 8-4 shows an example for Class C addresses.

When you borrow bits from the host field, it is important to note the number of additional subnets that are being created each time one more bit is borrowed. Borrowing two bits creates four possible subnets ($2 \times 2 = 4$). Each time another bit is borrowed from the host field, the number of possible subnets increases by a power of 2 and the number of individual host addresses decreases by a power of 2.

The following are examples of how many subnets are available, based on the number of host bits that you borrow:

- Using 3 bits for the subnet field results in 8 possible subnets ($2^3 = 8$).

- Using 4 bits for the subnet field results in 16 possible subnets ($2^4 = 16$).

- Using 5 bits for the subnet field results in 32 possible subnets ($2^5 = 32$).

- Using 6 bits for the subnet field results in 64 possible subnets ($2^6 = 64$).

Number of Bits Borrowed (s)	Number of Subnets Possible (2^s)	Number of Bits Remaining in Host ID ($8 - s = h$)	Number of Hosts Possible Per Subnet ($2^h - 2$)
1	2	7	126
2	4	6	62
3	8	5	30
4	16	4	14
5	32	3	6
6	64	2	2
7	128	1	0

Figure 8-4   *Subnetting a Class C Address*

In general, you can use the following formula to calculate the number of usable subnets, given the number of subnet bits used:

Number of subnets = 2^s (in which s is the number of subnet bits)

In general, you can use the following formula to calculate the number of hosts per subnet, given the number of host bits used:

Number of hosts per subnet = $2^h - 2$, in which h is the number of host bits not borrowed.

We subtract two host addresses from the total because one address is reserved as the network address (the address where all host bits are set to 0) and one address is reserved as the broadcast address (the address where all host bits are set to 1).

Subnetting Example

Subnet a network with a private network address of 172.16.0.0/16 so that it provides ten subnets and maximizes the number of host addresses for each subnet. Answer the following questions:

- How many bits will need to be borrowed for subnets? $2^s = 2^7 = 128$ subnets ($s = 7$ bits).

- What is the new subnet mask? Borrowing 7 host bits = 255.255.254.0 or /23.

- What are the first four subnets?

  - 172.16.0.0

  - 172.16.2.0

  - 172.16.4.0

  - 172.16.6.0

- What is the range of host addresses for the four subnets?

  - 172.16.0.1–172.16.1.254

  - 172.16.2.1–172.16.3.254

  - 172.16.4.1–172.16.5.254

  - 172.16.6.1–172.16.7.254

Variable-Length Subnet Masking

VLSM affords the options of including more than one subnet mask within a network and of subnetting an already subnetted network address. VLSM offers the following benefits:

- **More efficient use of IP addresses:** Without the use of VLSMs, companies must implement a single subnet mask within an entire Class A, B, or C network number.

  For example, consider the 172.16.0.0/16 network address divided into subnetworks using /24 masking. One of the subnetworks in this range, 172.16.14.0/24, is further divided into smaller subnetworks using /27 masking, as shown in Figure 8-5. These smaller subnetworks range from 172.16.14.0/27 to 172.16.14.224/27. In Figure 8-5, one of these smaller subnets, 172.16.14.128/27, is further divided using the /30 prefix, which creates subnets with only two hosts, to be used on the WAN links. The /30 subnets range from 172.16.14.128/30 to 172.16.14.156/30. In Figure 8-5, the WAN links used the 172.16.14.132/30, 172.16.14.136/30, and 172.16.14.140/30 subnets from the range.

- **Greater capability to use route summarization:** VLSM allows more hierarchical levels within an addressing plan and thus allows better route summarization within routing tables.

  For example, in Figure 8-5, subnet 172.16.14.0/24 summarizes all of the addresses that are further subnets of 172.16.14.0, including those from subnet 172.16.14.0/27 and from subnet 172.16.14.128/30.

- **Isolation of topology changes from other routers:** Another advantage to using route summarization in a large, complex network is that it can isolate topology changes from other routers. For example, when a specific link in the 172.16.27.0/24 domain is rapidly fluctuating between being active and inactive (called flapping), the summary route does not change. Therefore, no router that is external to the domain needs to keep modifying its routing table because of this flapping activity.

Subnet 172.16.14.0/24 is divided into smaller subnets.
• Subnet with one mask (/27).
• Then further subnet one of the unused /27 subnets into multiple /30 subnets.

Figure 8-5 *Example of Variable-Length Subnet Mask for 172.16.0.0/16*

A Working VLSM Example

The example in Figure 8-6 shows an address space defined by the subnet address 172.16.32.0/20. This address space is used for this portion of the enterprise network, and is generated from subnetting the 172.16.0.0/16 Class B network into multiple /20 subnets.

How would you define the subnets and masks to assign IP addresses to the WAN links, which require 2 host IP addresses, and the LAN segments, each one showing a requirement of 50 hosts?

By using VLSM, you can further subnet an already subnetted address. Consider again the example address space shown in Figure 8-6. Your region of the enterprise network has a subnet address of 172.16.32.0/20 and you need to assign addresses to multiple LANs, each with 50 hosts, within your region. With VLSM, you can further subnet address 172.16.32.0/20 to give you more network addresses and fewer hosts per network. For example, as shown in Figure 8-7, if you subnet 172.16.32.0/20 to 172.16.32.0/26, you gain 64 (2^6) subnets, each of which could support 62 ($2^6 - 2$) hosts.

To calculate the subnet addresses that are used on the WAN links, further subnet one of the unused /26 subnets using a similar process.

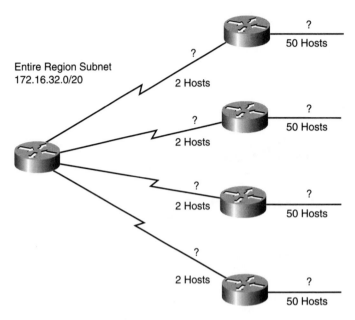

Figure 8-6   *Working VL SM Example*

Subnetted Address: 172.16.32.0/20
In Binary   10101100. 00010000.00100000.00000000

VLSM Address: 172.16.32.0/26
In Binary   10101100. 00010000.00100000.00000000

	Network		Subnet	VLSM Subnet	Host	
1st subnet:	172	16	.0010	0000.00	000000=172.16.32.0/26
2nd subnet:	172	16	.0010	0000.01	000000=172.16.32.64/26
3rd subnet:	172	16	.0010	0000.10	000000=172.16.32.128/26
4th subnet:	172	16	.0010	0000.11	000000=172.16.32.192/26
5th subnet:	172	16	.0010	0001.00	000000=172.16.33.0/26

Figure 8-7   *VLSM for 172.16.32.0/20*

The resulting address space and subnetting strategy is shown in Figure 8-8. The subnet addresses that are used on the Ethernet LANs are those generated from subdividing the 172.16.32.0/20 subnet into multiple /26 subnets.

The subnet addresses that are used on the WAN links are those generated from subdividing one of the /26 subnets, the 172.16.33.0/26 subnet, into multiple /30 subnets. This provides 16 (2^4) subnets and 2 ($2^2 - 2$) hosts for each of the WAN links.

Figure 8-8 *LANs and Point-to-Point Subnets for 172.16.32.0/20*

ACL Wildcard Bits

One of the benefits of proper summarization is the efficient use of wildcard masks in ACLs for packet filtering purposes.

In ACLs, address filtering occurs when you use ACL address wildcard masking to identify how to check or ignore corresponding IP address bits. Wildcard masking for IP address bits uses the numbers 1 and 0 to identify how to treat the corresponding IP address bits, as follows:

- **Wildcard mask bit 0:** Match the corresponding bit value in the address.

- **Wildcard mask bit 1:** Do not check (ignore) the corresponding bit value in the address.

> **Note** A wildcard mask is sometimes referred to as an inverse mask. Be aware, however, that you should use regular subnet masks if you are configuring ACLs on a Cisco ASA.

Figure 8-9 illustrates how wildcard bits are used to check the corresponding address bits.

– 0 means to match the value of the corresponding address bit
– 1 means to ignore the value of the corresponding address bit

Figure 8-9   *Wildcard Bits: How to Check the Corresponding Address Bits*

By carefully setting wildcard masks, you can permit or deny tests with one ACL statement. You can select a single IP address or any IP address.

Example: Wildcard Masking Process for IP Subnets

In Figure 8-10, an administrator wants to test a range of IP subnets that is to be permitted or denied. Assume that the IP address is a Class B address (the first two octets are the network number), with 8 bits of subnetting (the third octet is for subnets). The administrator wants to use the IP wildcard masking bits to match subnets 172.30.16.0/24 to 172.30.31.0/24.

Match for IP subnets 172.30.**16**.0/24 to 172.30.**31**.0/24.

- Address and **wildcard mask:**
  - **172.30.16.0 0.0.15.255**
  Network. Host

172.30.16.0

0	0	0	1	0	0	0	0		

Wildcard Mask:

0	0	0	0	1	1	1	1		

|<------- Match ------->|<---- Don't Care ---->| Subnet #

0	0	0	1	0	0	0	0	=	16
0	0	0	1	0	0	0	1	=	17
0	0	0	1	0	0	1	0	=	18
			:						:
0	0	0	1	1	1	1	1	=	31

Figure 8-10   *Wildcard Bits to Match IP Subnets 172.30.16.0 to 172.30.31.0*

To use one ACL statement to match this range of subnets, use the IP address 172.30.16.0 in the ACL, which is the first subnet to be matched, followed by the required wildcard mask.

First, the wildcard mask matches the first two octets (172.30) of the IP address using corresponding 0 bits in the first two octets of the wildcard mask.

Because there is no interest in an individual host, the wildcard mask ignores the final octet by using the corresponding 1 bit in the wildcard mask. For example, the final octet of the wildcard mask is 255 in decimal.

In the third octet, where the subnet address occurs, the wildcard mask of decimal 15, or binary 00001111, shown in bold, matches the high-order 4 bits of the IP address. In this case, the wildcard mask matches subnets starting with the 172.30.16.0/24 subnet. For the final (low-end) 4 bits in this octet, shown in gray, the wildcard mask indicates that the bits can be ignored. In these positions, the address value can be binary 0 or binary 1. Thus, the wildcard mask matches subnets 16, 17, 18, and so on up to subnet 31. The wildcard mask does not match any other subnets.

In Figure 8-10, the address 172.30.16.0 with the wildcard mask 0.0.15.255 matches subnets 172.30.16.0/24 to 172.30.31.0/24.

In some cases, you must use more than one ACL statement to match a range of subnets. For example, to match 10.1.4.0/24 to 10.1.8.0/24, use 10.1.4.0 0.0.3.255 and 10.1.8.0 0.0.0.255.

From your previous knowledge acquired in ICND2 (CCNA), you will remember the following command syntax, which we will review in more detail in a moment. So, suppose that you want to block all IP traffic from the range of subnets shown in Figure 8-10; the ACL could be this:

```
Router(config)# access-list 1 deny 172.30.16.0 0.0.15.255
```

The 0 and 1 bits in an ACL wildcard mask cause the ACL to either match or ignore the corresponding bit in the IP address. Working with decimal representations of binary wildcard mask bits can be tedious. For the most common uses of wildcard masking, you can use abbreviations. These abbreviations reduce how many numbers you are required to enter while configuring address test conditions.

Example: Wildcard Masking Process with a Single IP Address

In Figure 8-11, instead of entering 172.30.16.29 0.0.0.0, you can use the string **host 172.30.16.29**. Using the abbreviation **host** communicates the same test condition to the Cisco IOS ACL Software. The command syntax using the abbreviation **host** is as follows:

```
Router(config)# access-list 2 permit host 172.30.16.29
```

- 172.30.16.29 0.0.0.0 matches all of the address bits.
- Abbreviate this wildcard mask using the IP address preceded by the keyword **host** (host 172.30.16.29).

172.30.16.29

Wildcard Mask: 0.0.0.0

(Matches All Bits)

Figure 8-11   *ACL and the* host *Keyword*

And this is the same as entering the following:

```
Router(config)# access-list 2 permit 172.30.16.29 0.0.0.0
```

Should you enter the full host mask of 0.0.0.0, the router will convert the command for the **host** abbreviation automatically.

Example: Wildcard Masking Process with a Match Any IP Address

In Figure 8-12, instead of entering 0.0.0.0 255.255.255.255, you can use the word **any** by itself as the keyword. Using the abbreviation **any** communicates the same test condition to the Cisco IOS ACL Software. Both syntaxes, which accomplish the same results, are as follow, first in the long form, then using the keyword **any**:

```
Router(config)# access-list 2 permit 0.0.0.0 255.255.255.255
```

And this is the same as entering the following:

```
Router(config)# access-list 2 permit any
```

> **Tip**   As a matter of fact, you can enter any valid host IP address followed by the wildcard mask of 255.255.255.255 and the router will convert your entry to the keyword **any,** as demonstrated by the following test:
>
> ```
> YYZ(config)# access-list 3 deny 192.168.16.214 255.255.255.255
> YYZ(config)# do show access-list 3
> Standard IP access list 3
>  10 deny any
> YYZ(config)#
> ```

- 0.0.0.0 255.255.255.255 ignores all address bits.
- Abbreviate expression with the keyword any.

0. 0. 0.0

Wildcard Mask: 255.255.255.255

(Ignore All Bits)

Figure 8-12   *ACL and the* any *Keyword*

Using ACLs to Control Traffic

To configure numbered standard IPv4 ACLs on a Cisco router, you must create a standard IPv4 ACL and activate an ACL on an interface. The **access-list** command creates an entry in a standard IPv4 traffic filter list.

The following is the syntax for the **access-list** command:

```
Router(config)# access-list access-list-number {permit | deny | remark} source-
    address [mask] [log]
```

To create an ACL, use 1 to 99 for the *access-list-number* parameter. The first entry is assigned a sequence number of 10, and successive entries are incremented by 10. The default wildcard mask is 0.0.0.0 (only standard ACL). The **remark** argument lets you add a description to the ACL.

Caution   The **no access-list** *access-list-number* command removes the entire ACL.

The **log** option of the **access-list** command causes an informational logging message to be created about the packet that matches the ACE.

Tip   You control the level of messages that are logged to the console using the **logging console** command. You can also have the messages kept in buffer with the **logging buffered** command. The number of system error and debugging messages in the system logging buffer is determined by the configured size of the syslog buffer. This size of the syslog buffer is also set using the **logging buffered** command.

The logging message includes the ACL number, whether the packet was permitted or denied, the source address, and the number of packets. The message is generated for the first packet that matches, and then at five-minute intervals, including the number of packets permitted or denied in the previous five-minute interval. This five-minute interval prevents firewall resources from being consumed for repetitive packets from the same flow.

The **ip access-group** command links an existing ACL to an interface. Only one ACL per protocol, per direction, and per interface is allowed. The syntax for this command is as follows:

```
Router(config-if)# ip access-group access-list-number {in | out}
```

Note   To remove an IP ACL from an interface, first enter the **no ip access-group** command on the interface; then enter the global **no access-list** command to remove the entire ACL.

Table 8-1 provides an example of the steps required to configure and apply a numbered standard ACL on a router.

Table 8-1 *Numbered Standard ACL Configuration Procedure*

Step	Action	Notes

1	Use the **access-list** global configuration command to create an entry in a standard IPv4 ACL:
	
	`RouterX(config)# access-list 1 permit`
	`  172.16.0.0 0.0.255.255`
		Enter the global **no access-list** *access-list-number* command to remove the entire ACL. The example statement matches any address that starts with 172.16.x.x. Use the **remark** option to add a description to your ACL.

2	Use the **interface** configuration command to select an interface to which to apply the ACL: `RouterX(config)# interface ethernet 1`	After you enter the **interface** command, the CLI prompt changes from (config)# to (config-if)#.

3	Use the **ip access-group** interface configuration command to activate the existing ACL on an interface:
	
	`RouterX(config-if)# ip access-group 1`
	`  out`
		To remove an IP ACL from an interface, enter the **no ip access-group** *access-list-number* command on the interface. This example activates the standard IPv4 ACL 1 on the interface as an outbound filter.

Example: Numbered Standard IPv4 ACL—Deny a Specific Subnet

Table 8-2 describes the command syntax that is presented in Example 8-1 for the network topology shown in Figure 8-13.

Table 8-2 *Numbered Standard IPv4 ACL Example*

access-list Command Parameter	Description
1	ACL number that indicates this ACL is a standard list.
deny	Indicates that traffic that matches the selected parameters is not forwarded.
172.16.4.0	IP address of the source subnet.

access-list Command Parameter	Description
0.0.0.255	Wildcard mask; 0s indicate positions that must match, 1s indicate "don't care" positions. The mask with 0s in the first three octets indicates those positions must match; the 255 in the last octet indicates a "don't care" condition.
permit	Indicates that traffic that matches the selected parameters is forwarded.
any	Abbreviation for the IP address of the source. The abbreviation **any** indicates a source address of 0.0.0.0 and a wildcard mask of 255.255.255.255; all source addresses will match.

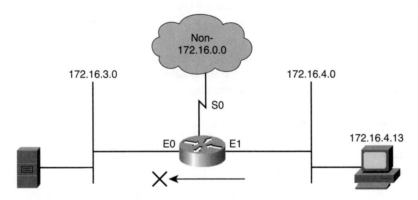

Figure 8-13 *Numbered Standard IPv4 ACL*

Example 8-1 *Numbered Standard IPv4 ACL*

```
r1(config)# access-list 1 deny 172.16.4.0 0.0.0.255
r1(config)# access-list 1 permit any
( implicit deny all = access-list 1 deny 0.0.0.0 255.255.255.255 )
r1(config)# interface ethernet 0
r1(config-if)# ip access-group 1 out
```

The ACL shown in Example 8-1 is designed to block traffic from a specific subnet, 172.16.4.0, and to allow all other traffic to be forwarded out E0. However, traffic from subnet 172.16.4.0 is not filtered when leaving by S0.

vty Access

To control traffic into and out of the router (not through the router), you protect the router virtual ports. A virtual port (or virtual terminal line) is commonly referred to as vty. By default, there are five such virtual terminal lines, numbered vty 0 through vty 4. You can configure Cisco IOS Software images to support more than five vty ports.

Restricting vty access is primarily a technique for increasing network security and defining which addresses are allowed Telnet access to the router EXEC process.

The command used to filter Telnet traffic is as follows:

```
Router(config-line)# access-class access-list-number {in | out}
```

Filtering Telnet traffic is typically considered an extended IP ACL function because it filters a higher-level protocol. However, because you are using the **access-class** command to filter incoming or outgoing Telnet sessions by source address and apply filtering to vty lines, you can use standard IP ACL statements to control vty access.

The following example applies a standard ACL to control vty access. It permits any device on network 192.168.1.0 0.0.0.255 to establish a virtual terminal session with the router. Of course, the user must know the appropriate passwords to enter user mode and privileged mode. This example assumes that the protocol used to exchange with the router is Telnet; however, other protocol can be filtered by the **access-class** command, such as Secure Shell (SSH).

```
R1(config)# access-list 12 permit 192.168.1.0 0.0.0.255
!
R1(config)# line vty 0 4
R1(config-line)# access-class 12 in
```

Notice that identical restrictions have been set on every vty line (0 to 4) because you cannot control on which vty line a user will connect. The implicit **deny any** statement still applies to the ACL when it is used as an access class entry.

Numbered Extended IPv4 ACL

To provide more precise traffic-filtering control, use extended IPv4 ACLs, which are named or numbered 100 to 199 and 2000 to 2699, because extended IPv4 ACLs check for the source and destination IPv4 addresses. In addition, with an extended ACL statement, you can specify the protocol and, optionally, TCP or UDP application to filter traffic more precisely. To specify an application, you can configure either the port number or name of a well-known application.

Table 8-3 shows some well-known port numbers of IP protocols that you can use with extended ACLs.

Table 8-3 *Well-Known Port Numbers and IP Protocols*

Well-Known Port Number (Decimal)	IP Protocol
20 (TCP)	FTP data
21 (TCP)	FTP control
22 (SSH)	Secure Shell
23 (TCP)	Telnet
25 (TCP)	SMTP
53 (TCP/UDP)	DNS
69 (UDP)	TFTP
80 (TCP)	HTTP

To configure numbered extended IPv4 ACLs on a Cisco router, create an extended IPv4 ACL and activate that ACL on an interface. Use the **access-list** command to create an entry to express a condition statement in a complex filter. Table 8-4 explains the syntax of the command for configuring a numbered extended ACL, shown here:

```
Router(config)# access-list access-list-number {permit | deny}
  protocol source source-wildcard [operator port] destination
  destination-wildcard [operator port] [established] [log]
```

Note The syntax of the **access-list** command that is presented in Table 8-4 is representative of the TCP protocol form. Not all parameters and options are given. For the complete syntax of all forms of the command, refer to the appropriate Cisco IOS Software documentation available at Cisco.com.

To link an existing extended ACL to an interface, use the following command:

```
Router(config-if)# ip access-group access-list-number (in | out)
```

Only one ACL per protocol, per direction, and per interface is allowed.

Table 8-4 *Command Parameters for a Numbered Extended ACL*

access-list Command Parameter	Description
access-list-number	This parameter identifies the list using a number in the ranges of 100 to 199 or 2000 to 2699.
permit | **deny**	This parameter indicates whether this entry allows or blocks the specified address.

access-list Command Parameter	Description
protocol	This parameter can be **ip, tcp, udp, icmp, gre,** or **igrp.**
source and *destination*	These parameters identify the source and destination IP addresses.
source-wildcard and *destination-wildcard*	In the wildcard mask, 0s indicate positions that must match, 1s indicate "don't care" positions.
operator [*port* | *app_name*]	The operator can be **lt** (less than), **gt** (greater than), **eq** (equal), or **neq** (not equal). The port number referenced can be either the source port or the destination port, depending on where in the ACL the port number is configured. As an alternative to the port number, well-known application names can be used (for example, **telnet, ftp, smtp**).
established	This option is for inbound TCP only. It allows TCP traffic to pass if the packet is a response to an outbound initiated session. This type of traffic has the acknowledgment (ACK) bits set. (See Example 8-3.)
log	This option sends a logging message to the console.

Table 8-5 describes the parameters of the **ip access-group** command.

Table 8-5 ip access-group *Command Parameters*

Parameter	Description
access-list-number	Indicates the number of the ACL that is to be linked to an interface
in | out	Selects whether the ACL is applied as an input or output filter; **out** is default

Example 8-2 shows the configuration for denying FTP access from subnet 172.16.4.0/24 to subnet 172.16.3.0/24, for the network depicted in Figure 8-14. All other traffic is allowed. By applying the ACL to the E0 interface in an outbound direction, traffic is dropped just before it would be transmitted out the E0 interface.

Example 8-2 *Numbered Extended IPv4 ACL Example*

```
r1(config)# access-list 101 deny tcp 172.16.4.0 0.0.0.255 172.16.3.0 0.0.0.255 eq 21
r1(config)# access-list 101 deny tcp 172.16.4.0 0.0.0.255 172.16.3.0 0.0.0.255 eq 20
r1(config)# access-list 101 permit ip any any
(implicit deny all)
(access-list 101 deny ip 0.0.0.0 255.255.255.255 0.0.0.0 255.255.255.255)
r1(config)# interface ethernet 0
r1(config-if)# ip access-group 101 out
```

Notice the use of wildcard masks to define how to check or ignore the corresponding IP address bits. In the example in Figure 8-14, the first access control entry (ACE) matches source addresses in the 172.16.4.0 subnet. The way to check only the first 3 bytes on this prefix is to follow the prefix with the wildcard mask 0.0.0.255. Zeroes (0) in the wildcard mask tell the ACL to check the corresponding bit of packet addresses with the prefix. Ones (1) in the wildcard mask tell the ACL not to check the corresponding bit of packet addresses with the prefix.

In Example 8-2, notice the wildcard mask. As explained earlier in the chapter, using wildcard masks is a valuable tool for creating effective and efficient ACLs, especially in CIDR environments.

Figure 8-14 *Numbered Extended IPv4 ACL Example*

In Example 8-3, the **established** parameter of the extended ACL allows responses to traffic that originate from the mail host, 200.1.1.2, to return inbound on the serial 0 interface. A match occurs if the TCP datagram has the ACK bit or reset (RST) bit set, which indicates that the packet belongs to an existing connection. Without the **established** parameter in the ACL statement, the mail host could receive SMTP traffic but not send it.

Caution   ACLs using the keyword **established** are not a substitute for a stateful firewall. The ACL only checks whether the ACK (acknowledgement) flag bit is turned on in the TCP header, without reference to other prior transmission. In other words, as long as the ACK bit is turned on and the other filtering criteria mentioned in the ACL entry are valid, the router will execute the action. It will not check to determine whether a proper TCP three-way handshake was done. It is therefore easy to fool the router using a packet-crafting tool.

Example 8-3   *Using the* established *Keyword*

```
Router(config)# access-list 102 permit tcp any host 200.1.1.2 established
Router(config)# access-list 102 permit tcp any host 200.1.1.2 eq smtp
Router(config)# interface serial 0
Router(config-if)# ip access-group 102 in
```

Displaying ACLs

When you finish the ACL configuration, use the **show** commands to verify the configuration. Use the **show access-lists** command to display the contents of all ACLs, as shown in Example 8-4. By entering the ACL name or number as an option for this command, you can display a specific ACL. To display the contents of only the IP ACLs, use the **show ip access-list** command.

Example 8-4   **show access-lists** *Command Output*

```
Router# show access-lists
Extended IP access list OUTBOUND
10 permit tcp 10.0.0.0 0.255.255.255 any eq www (67 matches)
20 permit tcp 10.0.0.0 0.255.255.255 any eq 443 (1190 matches)
30 permit udp 10.0.0.0 0.255.255.255 any eq domain
40 deny ip any any (41 matches)
```

Fast Switching and ACLs

Fast switching uses the route cache to store information about packet flows. The first packet in a flow is looked at thoroughly by the router, which performs Layer 3–to–Layer 2 mapping, selects the best route, the outbound interface, and its ACL, and decides whether the packet is allowed to leave. The decision taken on the first packet is stored in the route cache so that any subsequent packets from the same flow can be fast-switched or sent to Cisco Express Forwarding (CEF) without being looked at by the CPU, the interface ACL, and so forth.

If you enable CEF, a Layer 3 IP switching technology, and then create an ACL that uses the **log** keyword, the packets that match the ACL are not CEF switched. They are fast switched. ACL logging disables CEF.

The **show ip interfaces** command displays IP interface information and indicates whether any IP ACLs are set on the interface. In the **show ip interfaces** command output shown in Example 8-5, IP ACL OUTBOUND has been configured on the FastEthernet 0/0 interface as an inbound ACL. No outbound IP ACL has been configured on the FastEthernet interface.

Example 8-5 show ip interfaces *Command Output*

```
r1# show ip interfaces FastEthernet 0/0
FastEthernet 0/0 is up, line protocol is up
 Internet address is 10.0.2.1/24
 Broadcast address is 255.255.255.255
 Address determined by non-volatile memory
 MTU is 1500 bytes
 Helper address is not set
 Directed broadcast forwarding is disabled
 Multicast reserved groups joined: 224.0.0.5 224.0.0.6
 Outgoing access list is not set
 Inbound access list is OUTBOUND
 Proxy ARP is enabled
 <text omitted>
```

Enhancing ACLs with Object Groups

ACLs provide basic security to the network by permitting or blocking certain types of traffic. ACLs use IP addresses, protocols, and ports to filter network traffic. In some networks, the number of ACLs can become quite large and difficult to manage. The Object Groups for ACLs feature simplifies this problem. By using the Object Groups for ACLs feature, the administrator can group users, devices, or protocols into object groups and create access control entries. Each ACE can then permit or deny a group of users access to a group of servers or services.

The benefits of using Object Groups for ACL include the following:

- Increased performance when network traffic is heavy.

- Reduced storage in NVRAM compared to conventional ACLs.

- Separate ownership of the components of an ACE. For example, you can create an ACE where each department within an organization can control its group membership. You can also create an ACE to permit or deny the departments to contact each other.

- Allows you to create an object group that contains other object groups. For example, you can create an ENG-ALL address group, which contains the ENG-EAST and ENG-WEST address groups.

In Example 8-6, an access rule results in eight access control entries in an ACL.

Example 8-6   *Example of an ACL Without Object Group*

```
access-list 100 deny tcp host 10.6.252.65 host 171.8.2.12 eq www
access-list 100 deny tcp host 10.6.252.65 host 171.8.2.12 eq ftp
access-list 100 deny tcp host 10.6.252.65 host 171.8.2.13 eq www
access-list 100 deny tcp host 10.6.252.65 host 171.8.2.13 eq ftp
access-list 100 deny tcp host 10.6.252.66 host 171.8.2.12 eq www
access-list 100 deny tcp host 10.6.252.66 host 171.8.2.12 eq ftp
access-list 100 deny tcp host 10.6.252.66 host 171.8.2.13 eq www
access-list 100 deny tcp host 10.6.252.66 host 171.8.2.13 eq ftp
```

With object groups, as shown in Example 8-7, you can modularize the sources in this example using object group SOURCES, which is a network object group. Another network object group called DESTINATIONS is used to modularize the destination IP addresses, and a service object group called APPLICATIONS is used to modularize the TCP ports in the example. The resulting ACL has one line and still matches all the sources, all the destinations, and all the services. Notice how object groups extend the conventional ACL syntax to support object group–based ACLs and also add new keywords along with the source and destination addresses and ports.

Example 8-7   *Example of an ACL Using Object Groups*

```
object-group network SOURCES
 host 10.6.252.65 host 10.6.252.66
object-group network DESTINATIONS
 host 171.8.2.12 host 171.8.2.13
object-group service APPLICATIONS
 tcp www tcp ftp
access-list 100 deny object-group APPLICATIONS object-group SOURCES object-group
  DESTINATIONS
```

When configuring object group–based ACLs, all features that use or reference conventional ACLs are compatible with object group–based ACLs. Feature interactions for conventional ACLs are the same with object group–based ACLs.

These rules also apply when creating object–group based ACLs:

- You can add to, delete from, or change objects in an object group membership list dynamically (meaning without deleting and redefining the object group).

- You can add to, delete from, or change objects in an object group membership list without redefining the ACL ACE that is using the object group (meaning changing the object group without deleting the ACE and then redefining the ACE after the change).

- You can add objects to groups, delete them from groups, and then ensure that the changes are properly functioning within the object group–based ACL without reapplying the ACL to the interface.

The following components can be modularized in network object groups:

- Any IP address—includes a range from 0.0.0.0 to 255.255.255.255 (specified using the **any** command)

- Host IP addresses

- Hostnames

- Other network object groups

- Ranges of IP addresses

- Subnets

The following components can be modularized in service object groups:

- Source and destination protocol ports (such as Telnet or Simple Network Management Protocol [SNMP])

- ICMP types (such as echo, echo-reply, or host-unreachable)

- Top-level protocols (such as TCP, UDP, or Encapsulating Security Payload [ESP])

- Other service object groups

ACL Considerations

Before you start to develop any ACLs, consider the following basic rules:

- **Base your ACLs on your security policy:** Unless you anchor the ACL in a comprehensive security policy, you cannot be certain that it will effectively control access in the way that access needs to be controlled.

- **Write it out:** Never sit down at a router and start to develop an ACL without first spending some time in design. The best ACL developers suggest that you write out a list of things that you want the ACL to accomplish. Start with something as simple as "This ACL must block all SNMP access to the router except for the SNMP host at 172.19.1.15."

- **Set up a development system:** Whether you use your laptop PC or a dedicated server, you need a place to develop and store your ACLs. Word processors or text editors of any kind are suitable, as long as you can save the files in ASCII text format. Build a library of your most commonly used ACLs and use them as sources for new files. ACLs can be pasted into the router running configuration (requiring console or Telnet access) or can be stored in a router configuration file. The system that you choose should support Trivial FTP (TFTP) to make it easy to transfer any resulting configuration files to the router.

- **Access list comments:** During the configuration of the ACL, consider adding comments explaining the goal of this ACL.

> **Note** Hackers love to gain access to router configuration development systems or TFTP servers that store ACLs. A hacker can discover a lot about your network from looking at these easily read text files. For this reason, it is imperative that you choose a secure system on which to develop and store your router files.

- **Test:** If possible, test your ACLs in a secure environment before placing them into production. Testing is a commonsense approach to any router configuration changes. Most enterprises maintain their own network test beds. Although testing might appear to be an unnecessary cost, over time it can save time and money.

You should consider several caveats when working with ACLs:

- **ACLs by themselves are stateless:** ACLs are a stateless access control mechanism. As such, they may not fully support application layer behavior that requires a stateful inspection engine. Consider implementing the Cisco IOS Zone-based Policy Firewall if you need stateful inspection. Also, because ACLs check only Layer 3 and Layer 4, they can't stop packets with a malicious Layer 7 payload.

- **Only one ACL per interface, per protocol stack, per direction:** Only one ACL per protocol, per direction, and per interface is allowed. Multiple ACLs are permitted per interface, but each must be for a different protocol or different direction.

- **Implicit deny all:** All Cisco ACLs end with an implicit **deny all** statement. Although you might not actually see this statement in your ACLs, they do exist. Every ACL should have at least one **permit** statement. Otherwise, all traffic is denied. You should create the ACL before applying it to an interface. With most versions of Cisco IOS Software, an interface that has an empty ACL applied to it permits all traffic.

- **Standard ACL limitation:** Because standard ACLs are limited to packet filtering on only source addresses, you might need to create extended ACLs to implement your security policies.

- **Order of specific statements:** Certain ACL statements are more specific than others; therefore, you need to place them higher in the ACL. For example, blocking all UDP traffic at the top of the list negates the blocking of SNMP packets lower in the list. Take care that statements at the top of the ACL do not negate any statements found lower in the list.

- **Directional filtering:** Cisco ACLs have a directional filter that determines whether they examine inbound packets (ingress traffic, traffic coming toward the interface) or outbound packets (egress traffic, traffic going away from the interface). Always double-check the direction of data that your ACL is filtering.

■ **Modifying ACLs:** Cisco IOS Software Release 12.2 and earlier always appends new statements to an existing ACL to the bottom of the ACL. Because of the inherent top-down statement evaluation order of ACLs, these new entries can render the ACL unusable. When a new statement does render the ACL unusable, you must create a new ACL with the correct statement ordering, delete the old ACL, and assign the new ACL to the router interface. If you are using Cisco IOS Software Release 12.3 and later, you can use sequence numbers to ensure that you are adding a new statement into the ACL in the correct location. The ACL is processed top-down based on the sequence numbers of the statements (lowest to highest).

■ **Special packets:** Router-generated packets, such as routing table updates, are not subject to outbound ACL statements applied to interfaces on the source router. If your security policy requires filtering these types of packets, inbound ACLs on adjacent routers or other router filter mechanisms using ACLs must do the filtering task.

■ **Extended ACL placement:** If you use extended ACLs on routers too far from the source that you need to filter, packets flowing to other routers and interfaces might be adversely affected. Always consider placing extended ACLs on routers as close as possible to the source that you are filtering.

■ **Standard ACL placement:** Because standard ACLs filter packets based on the source address, placing these ACLs too close to the source can adversely affect packets destined to other destinations. Always place standard ACLs as close to the destination as possible.

Configuring ACLs for Threat Control Using Cisco Configuration Professional

Rules define how the router will respond to a particular kind of traffic. Using Cisco Configuration Professional (CCP), you can create access rules that cause the router to block certain types of traffic while permitting other types, create NAT rules that define the traffic that is to receive address translation, and create IPsec rules that specify which traffic is to be encrypted.

Rules in Cisco Configuration Professional

Cisco Configuration Professional uses the high-level concept of rules to define how the router will respond to a particular kind of traffic. ACLs are rules, but in CCP, not all rules are ACLs. Rules that can be created using CCP include the following:

■ ACLs

■ NAT rules

■ IPsec rules

- Network Admission Control (NAC) rules

- Firewall rules

- Quality of service (QoS) rules

- Unsupported rules

- Externally defined rules

Using CCP, you can create access rules that cause the router to block certain types of traffic while permitting other types, NAT rules that define the traffic that is to receive address translation, and IPsec rules that specify which traffic is to be encrypted. CCP also provides default rules that are used in guided configurations, and that you can examine and use when you create your own access rules. CCP also allows you to view rules that were not created using CCP, called external rules, and rules with syntax that CCP does not support, called unsupported rules.

On the other hand, ACLs can be used for multiple functions. An ACL is nothing more than a traffic classification mechanism that works at Layers 3 and 4. As such, it can be used to classify traffic. The action that then applies to traffic depends on where you apply the ACL. If you apply the ACL to router interfaces, the action is to permit or deny traffic traversing the interface in a particular direction. However, if you apply the ACL to a class map in Modular Policy Framework, the action might be to inspect the traffic that matches the ACL. This chapter focuses on ACLs applied to interfaces for filtering purposes.

Working with ACLs in CCP

The ACL Summary window in CCP (choose **Configure > Router > ACL > ACL Summary** to access it), shown in Figure 8-15, enables you to view a summary of the rules in the router's configuration and to navigate to other windows to create, edit, or delete rules.

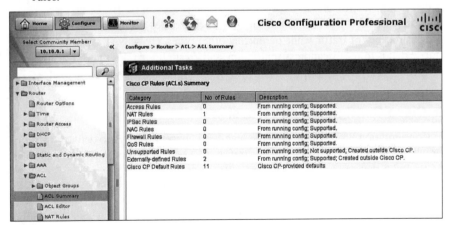

Figure 8-15 *CCP ACL Summary*

ACL Configuration Scenario Using CCP

To demonstrate the configuration of ACLs using CCP and the router CLI, we will step through the configuration scenario depicted in Figure 8-16. In this example, we will configure an outbound policy for the internal network, allowing only certain applications and protocols to originate traffic from the inside network.

The configuration steps are as follows:

Step 1.   Configure the ACL.

Step 2.   Apply the ACL to interfaces.

Step 3.   Verify and monitor the ACL.

Figure 8-16   *ACL Configuration Scenario*

ACL Editor

The ACL Editor is most commonly used to define the traffic that you want to permit or deny entry to your LAN or exit from your LAN, but ACLs can be used for other purposes as well, such as identifying traffic for NAT or for encryption.

The upper portion of the ACL Editor window, shown in Figure 8-17, lists the access rules that have been configured on this router. The lower portion of the window lists the rule entries associated with the selected rule. A rule entry consists of criteria that incoming or outgoing traffic is compared against, and the action to take on traffic matching the criteria. If traffic does not match the criteria of any of the entries in this box, it is dropped.

To add an ACL, click the **Add** button in the top-right corner of the window. This opens the Add a Rule dialog box, discussed in the following section.

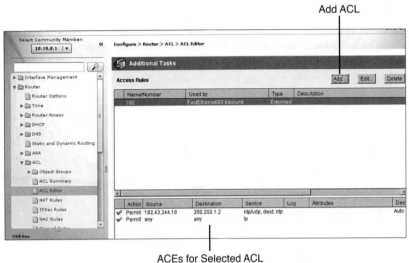

Figure 8-17 *ACL Editor*

Adding Rules

The Add a Rule dialog box, shown in Figure 8-18, lets you add a rule. (A similar dialog box, Edit a Rule, is displayed if you select a rule in the Access Rules pane and click Edit.) In the Add a Rule dialog box, you can define a name and add a description for the rule; add, change, reorder, or delete rule entries (also known as access control entries, or ACEs); and associate the rule to an interface.

The Rule Entry pane shows the entries that make up the rule. You can add, edit, and delete entries by using the buttons to the right of the pane. You can also reorder entries to change the order in which they are evaluated. Observe the following guidelines when creating rule entries:

- There must be at least one **permit** statement in the list; otherwise, all traffic will be denied.

- A **permit all** or **deny all** entry in the list must be the last entry. Remember, a default **deny all** entry is implicit and will not show in the list.

- Standard entries and extended entries cannot be mixed in the same rule.

- No duplicate entries can exist in the same rule.

Applying the log Keyword on Explicit permit or deny ip any any

The **log** keyword on the final **permit ip any any** can prove useful for testing valid configurations. After the testing period is over, you can apply the **log** keyword, changing the **permit ip any any log** to a **deny ip any any log**. This will still allow you to log the data required to characterize the threat(s) while still blocking the traffic.

ACEs can be added by clicking the Add button in the Rule Entry section of the dialog box.

Figure 8-18   *Adding a Rule with CCP*

The Add an Extended Rule Entry dialog box, shown in Figure 8-19, lets you configure the logic of the specific ACE. An extended rule entry allows you to permit or deny traffic based on its source and destination and on the protocol and service specified in the packet. In this dialog box you will complete the following sections:

- **Action:** Select the action you want the router to take when a packet matches the criteria in the rule entry. The choices are Permit and Deny.

- **Description:** Add a description for the ACE.

- **Source Host/Network:** Specify the source IP address criteria that the traffic must match. The fields in this area of the dialog box change based on the value of the Type field. They are IP Address, Wildcard Mask, Hostname, or Network Object Group.

- **Destination Host/Network:** Specify the source IP address criteria that the traffic must match. The fields and information to complete are similar to those of the Source Host/Network section, but using the components to match a destination address.

- **Protocol and Service:** Select the protocol and service, if applicable, that you want the entry to apply to. The information that you provide differs from protocol to protocol. Click the protocol to see what information you need to provide. For TCP and UDP, you can use logical operators such as these in the Service field:

- **=** : The rule entry applies to the value that you enter in the field to the right.

- **!=** : The rule entry applies to any value except the one that you enter in the field to the right.

- **<** : The rule entry applies to all port numbers lower than the number you enter.

- **>** : The rule entry applies to all port numbers higher than the number you enter.

- **Range:** The entry applies to the range of port numbers that you specify in the fields to the right

If you do not remember the name or number, click the ... button and select the value you want from the Service dialog box.

Figure 8-19 *Adding an Extended Rule*

Associating Rules with Interfaces

ACLs and other rules, by themselves, do nothing. You must apply them to interfaces and other router components. To apply an ACL to an interface, select a rule and click the **Associate** button to select the interface and direction in the Associate with an Interface dialog box, as shown in Figure 8-20. If the Associate button is not enabled, you can associate the rule with an interface by double-clicking the interface in the Interfaces and Connections window and using the Associate tab. The following are the options:

- **Select an Interface:** Select the interface to which you want this rule to apply.

- **Specify a Direction:** If you want the router to check ingress packets arriving at the interface, click **Inbound**. The router checks for a match with the rule before routing it; the router accepts or drops the packet based on whether the rule states **permit** or **deny**. If you want the router to match egress packets, click **Outbound**.

  Notice in Figure 8-20 how important it is to use the correct terminology. In the example, the ACL is called OUTBOUND, as it is aimed at filtering traffic originating on the internal network on its way to external destinations. The ACL is applied inbound to the FastEthernet0/1.4 interface because it will match ingress traffic on the interface, on its way out to the external network.

- **If another rule is already associated with the interface:** If an information box appears that states that another access rule is associated with the interface and direction you specified, you either can cancel the operation or can continue by appending the rule entries to the rule that is already applied to the interface or by disassociating the rule with the interface and associating the new rule.

Click to Associate Interface

Figure 8-20 *Associating Rules with Interfaces*

Enabling Logging with CCP

Activity on your access control rules is monitored through the creation of log entries. If logging is enabled on the router, whenever an access rule that is configured to generate log entries is invoked—for example, if a connection is attempted from a denied IP address—then a log entry is generated and can be viewed in Monitor mode.

The first step to viewing firewall activity is to enable logging on the router. To enable logging, follow these steps:

Step 1. From the toolbar, choose **Configure > Router > Logging** to open the Logging dialog box, shown in Figure 8-21.

Step 2. Click **Edit**.

Step 3. In the Syslog window that just opened, check the **Logging to Buffer** check box.

Navigate to Configure > Router > Logging > Edit

Select Logging Destination and Level

Figure 8-21 *Enabling Logging*

In addition to enabling logging, you must identify the access rules that you want to generate log entries. To configure access rules for generating log entries:

Step 1. From the toolbar, choose **Configure > Router > ACL**.

Step 2. Click **ACL Editor**. Each access rule appears in the upper table on the right side of the screen, as shown in Figure 8-17. The lower table shows the specific source and destination IP addresses and the services that are permitted or denied by the rule.

Step 3.   In the upper table, choose the rule that you want to modify and click **Edit**. The Edit a Rule dialog box appears.

Step 4.   The Rule Entry field shows each of the source IP/destination IP/service combinations that are permitted or denied by the rule. Click the rule entry that you want to configure to generate log entries, and click **Edit**.

Step 5.   In the Edit an Extended Rule Entry dialog box, check the **Log Matches Against this Entry** check box, as shown in Figure 8-22.

Step 6.   Click **OK** to close the dialog boxes that are open. The rule entry that you just modified will now generate log entries whenever a connection is attempted from the IP address range and services that define the rule entry.

Step 7.   Repeat Step 4 through Step 6 for each rule entry that you want to configure to generate log entries.

Enable Logging for This ACE

Figure 8-22   *Selecting ACEs that Will Generate Log Entries*

Monitoring ACLs with CCP

Once your logging configuration is complete, choose **Monitor > Router > Logging** and select the **Syslog** tab in the Logging dialog box, as shown in Figure 8-23. The table at the bottom shows each generated router log entry, including the time and the reason that the log entry was generated. For ACL log entries, be sure to select at least Informational from the Select a Logging Level to View drop-down menu. Notice that the table is not automatically refreshed or cleared; you need to click the Update button or the Clear button to update the view. The Search button is also important, because this table shows all syslog messages, not only those related to ACLs from the security perspective.

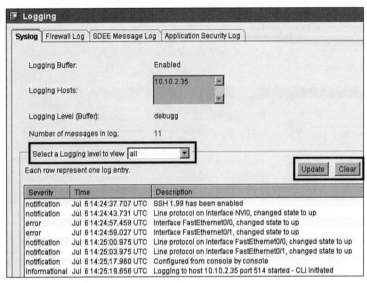

Figure 8-23 *Using CCP to View Log Entries*

The Firewall Log tab of the Logging dialog box, shown in Figure 8-24, also allows you to see logged ACEs, this time from the security perspective. The log entries shown in the top part of this tab are determined by log messages generated by the firewall. The Number of Attempts Denied by Firewall entry shows the number of connection attempts rejected by the firewall. The top-attacks table below the View drop-down menu displays the top attack entries. For ACLs, traffic matching a deny entry is considered an attack from the perspective of the firewall.

Note Logged ACLs will display events on the Firewall Log tab even if a zone-based firewall is not configured on the router.

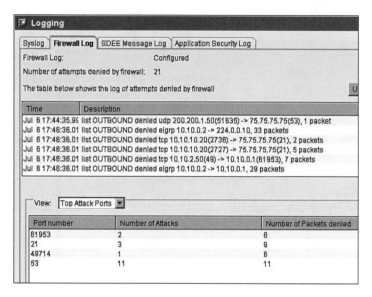

Figure 8-24 *Logged ACE Generated by the Firewall Entry*

Configuring an Object Group with CCP

You can create two types of ACL object groups:

- **Network object groups:** Can contain hostnames, host IP addresses, subnet masks, range of IP addresses, and other existing network object groups

- **Service object groups:** Can contain top-level protocols, such as TCP, UDP, and TCP-UDP; ICMP types; source and destination protocol ports; and other existing service object groups

Figure 8-25 illustrates an example of the creation of a network object group, the steps for which follow:

Step 1.   Choose **Configure > Router > ACL > Object Groups > Network Object Groups** to open the Network Object Group summary page.

Step 2.   Click **Create** to open the Create Network Object Group dialog box.

Step 3.   Enter the group name and description, specify the parameters in the Network Object Group Members area, and then click **Add**. The parameters that you entered in the left pane are added to the right pane.

Step 4.   Click **OK** to send the configured group information to the router.

Figure 8-25   *Configuring an Object Group Using CCP*

Example 8-8 shows the CLI equivalent of the configuration done in Figure 8-25.

Example 8-8   *Configuring an Object Group in the CLI*

```
Router# config t
Router(config)# object-group network INTERNAL-NETS
Router(config-network-group)# description Subnets inside the Firewall
Router(config-network-group)# 10.10.0.0 255.255.255.0
Router(config-network-group)# 10.10.1.0 255.255.255.0
Router(config-network-group)# 10.10.2.0 255.255.255.0
Router(config-network-group)# 10.10.10.0 255.255.255.0
```

After you create network object groups and/or service object groups, you can create an ACL that can permit or deny traffic to these object groups, as shown in Figure 8-26.

Use this procedure to create an ACL that can permit or deny traffic to the configured object groups.

Step 1.   Choose **Configure > Router > ACL > ACL Editor** to open the Additional Task Rules dialog box.

Step 2.   Click **Add** to open the Add a Rule dialog box.

Step 3.   Add a name and description for the rule in the appropriate fields, and then click **Add** to open the Add an Extended Rule Entry dialog box.

Step 4.   From the Action field, choose the action you want to configure. The options are Permit and Deny.

Step 5.   If you want to use object groups as an ACL source, from the Source Host/Network pane, do the following:

- Choose **Network Object Group** from the Type field.

- Click the ... (more) button—located beside the Network Object Group field—to open the Select Network Object Group dialog box.

- From the Select Network Object Group dialog box, select the network object group, and then click **OK**.

Step 6.   If you want to use an object group as an ACL destination, from the Destination Host/Network pane, do the following:

- Choose **Network Object Group** from the Type field.

- Click the ... (more) button—located beside the Network Object Group field—to open the Select Network Object Group dialog box.

- From the Select Network Object Group dialog box, select the network object group, and then click **OK**.

Step 7.   If you want to use an object group as an ACL protocol and port, from the Protocol and Service pane, do the following:

- Click the **Service Object Group** radio button.

- Click the ... (more) button—located beside the Service Object Group field—to open the Select Service Object Group dialog box.

- From the Select Service Object Group dialog box, select the service object group, and then click **OK**.

Step 8.   Click **OK** in the Add an Extended Rule Entry dialog box.

Figure 8-26   *Assigning Object Groups to ACLs*

Using ACLs in IPv6 Environments

Packet filtering in IPv6 is similar to packet filtering in IPv4. A strategy to prevent common attacks between the two protocol stacks, such as reconnaissance and spoofing attacks, typically starts with ACLs trying to match malicious traffic.

IPv6-specific attacks, such as the one depicted in Figure 8-27, require targeted filtering and IPv6-aware ACLs. IPv6 ACLs can help mitigate the following threats, among others:

- Header extension threats; for instance, amplification attacks based on Routing Header (RH 0)

- Threats based on misuse and abuse of IPv6 ICMP

- Reconnaissance based on multicast IPv6 addresses

- Threats that exploit tunneling solutions such as those used in IPv6 migration environments

Some threats require a combined approach using both protocol stacks, specifically those that exploit dual-stack environments. The scenario in Figure 8-27 depicts a Teredo tunnel launched from hosts that have been compromised via IPv6 but use IPv4 tunnels. Infrastructure filtering and firewalling for IPv4 would mitigate and contain the IPv6 threat.

Unknown IPv6 hosts autoconfigure their stack silently and initiate automatic Teredo tunnels over UDP 41.

Attacker traffic gains foothold via IPv4, sends rogue IPv6 RAs, and pivots using IPv6 hosts.

IPv4 firewall sees and allows IPv4 UDP traffic.

Figure 8-27   *Examples of IPv6 Potential Attacks*

The standard ACL functionality in IPv6 is similar to standard ACLs in IPv4. ACLs determine which traffic is blocked and which traffic is forwarded at router interfaces and allow filtering based on source and destination addresses and some Layer 4 information, inbound and outbound to a specific interface. Each ACL has an implicit **deny** statement at the end. IPv6 ACLs are defined and their deny and permit conditions are set using the **ipv6 access-list** command with the **deny** and **permit** keywords in global configuration mode. An empty ACL means that traffic is allowed. Reflexive ACLs and time-based ACLs are also available in IPv6. An IPv6 ACL can match the following IPv6 headers:

- **routing:** Matches any route header

- **mobility:** Matches any mobility header

- **dest-option-type:** Matches any destination option header

- **auth:** Matches IPsec's AH

- **undetermined-transport:** Matches any packet whose Layer 4 protocol cannot be determined (fragmented or unknown extension header) (available only with the **deny** command)

Each IPv6 ACL contains implicit **permit** rules to enable IPv6 neighbor discovery, in addition to the traditional rule that implements a default **deny** policy. The resulting implicit rules for IPv6 ACLs are shown in Example 8-9.

Example 8-9 *IPv6 ACL Implicit Entries*

```
permit icmp any any nd-na
permit icmp any any nd-na
deny ipv6 any any
```

The IPv6 neighbor discovery process makes use of the IPv6 network layer service. Therefore, by default, IPv6 ACLs implicitly allow IPv6 neighbor discovery packets to be sent and received on an interface. Neighbor discovery is similar to ARP for IPv4.

To add some context to these implicit rules, they implement what IPv4 implemented for the Address Resolution Protocol (ARP). In IPv4, ARP, which is equivalent to the IPv6 neighbor discovery process, makes use of a separate data link layer protocol. Therefore, by default, IPv4 ACLs implicitly allow ARP packets to be sent and received on an interface. The same is true for neighbor discovery in IPv6.

The user can override these rules by placing a **deny ipv6 any any** statement within an ACL.

Historically, in IPv4, administrators add the implicit **deny any** rule, along with the **log** keyword, to the end of an ACL. This is effective for monitoring and auditing ACLs, and also for logging denied packets. Doing the same in IPv6 requires adding all three implicit rules. Not doing so would result in neighbor discovery issues. In the example in Figure 8-28, a single **deny ipv6 any any** line is added to log denied packets. The two implicit rules that allow neighbor discovery in Example 8-9 are never evaluated, as all traffic is denied before it reaches the neighbor discovery rules. The solution to this problem is to explicitly add all three implicit lines, in the right order, at the end of your ACLs.

Figure 8-28 shows the topology we will use for the following named IPv6 ACL example.

Prefix: 2001:db8:2c80:1000::/64

Figure 8-28 *Example of IPv6 ACLs*

The syntax of IPv6 ACLs is similar to that of IPv4 ACLs. However, this time, the ACEs match IPv6 sources, destinations, and ports. Also notice that wildcard masks are no longer used, and the used of the /x nomenclature is pervasive across the syntax. One noticeable difference with IPv4 ACL commands is the use of the **ipv6 traffic filter** command to apply the ACL to interfaces, instead of the traditional **ip access-group** command used in IPv4 ACLs. Proper planning is required in using masks to match summarizable address blocks, given the more complex structure of IPv6 IP addresses.

The following is the syntax of IPv6 ACLs. Refer to Cisco IOS documentation for the detailed information:

```
permit protocol {source-ipv6-prefix/prefix-length | any | host
source-ipv6-address | auth} [operator [port-number]] {destination-
ipv6-prefix/prefix-length | any | host destination-ipv6- address |
auth} [operator [port-number]] [dest-option-type [doh-number | doh-
type]] [dscp value] [flow-label value] [fragments] [log] [log-
input] [mobility] [mobility-type [mh-number | mh-type]] [reflect
name [timeout value]] [routing] [routing-type routing-number]
[sequence value] [time-range name]
```

or

```
permit protocol {source-ipv6-prefix/prefix-length | any | host
source-ipv6-address | auth} [operator [port-number]] {destination-
ipv6-prefix/prefix-length | any | host destination-ipv6- address |
auth} [operator [port-number]] [dest-option-type [doh-number | doh-
type]] [dscp value] [flow-label value] [fragments] [log] [log-
input] [mobility] [mobility-type [mh-number | mh-type]] [routing]
[routing-type routing-number] [sequence value] [time-range
name] [undetermined-transport]
```

Example 8-10 illustrates an IPv6 ACL for ICMP that implements RFC 4890, which describes recommendations for filtering ICMPv6 messages in firewalls.

In networks supporting IPv6, ICMPv6 plays a fundamental role with a large number of functions, and a correspondingly large number of message types and options. ICMPv6 is essential to the functioning of IPv6, but there are a number of security risks associated with uncontrolled forwarding of ICMPv6 messages. Filtering strategies designed for the corresponding protocol, ICMP, in IPv4 networks are not directly applicable, because these strategies are intended to accommodate a useful auxiliary protocol that may not be required for correct functioning.

Example 8-10 illustrates a restrictive policy in which the required and necessary ICMPv6 message types are allowed and any unmatched types are denied. This is not a guarantee of protection against ICMPv6-based attacks, but it is a good starting point.

Example 8-10   *RFC 4890 ICMP ACL*

```
ipv6 access-list RFC4890
permit icmp any any echo-reply permit icmp any any echo-request permit icmp any any
   1 3
permit icmp any any 1 4
permit icmp any any packet-too-big permit icmp any any time-exceeded permit icmp any
   any parameter-problem permit icmp any any mld-query
permit icmp any any mld-reduction permit icmp any any mld-report permit icmp any any
   nd-na
permit icmp any any nd-ns
permit icmp any any router-solicitation
```

Summary

This chapter presented the use cases and benefits of ACLs in general. It described the building blocks and operational framework of ACLs. Prior to digging into ACLs, we reviewed how summarizable address blocks in the context of CIDR and VLSM environments work, and we then evaluated how ACL wildcard masks allow for threat mitigation in those environments.

This chapter also presented design considerations when deploying ACLs in general and demonstrated the use of Cisco Configuration Professional and the CLI to deploy and verify a threat containment strategy using ACLs and to correlate ACL log and alarm information in order to monitor their impact and effectiveness. You learned how to configure object groups to streamline the implementation of ACLs for threat control. This chapter finished by showing you how to configure ACLs in IPv6 environments, highlighting the operational differences with IPv4 ACLs.

References

For additional information, refer to these Cisco.com resources:

"Identifying Incidents Using Firewall and Cisco IOS Router Syslog Events," http://www.cisco.com/web/about/security/intelligence/identify-incidents-via-syslog.html

"IP Access List Entry Sequence Numbering," http://www.cisco.com/en/US/docs/ios/12_2s/feature/guide/fsaclseq.html

"Understanding Access Control List Logging," http://www.cisco.com/web/about/security/intelligence/acl-logging.html

Review Questions

Use the questions here to review what you learned in this chapter. The correct answers are found in the Appendix, "Answers to Chapter Review Questions."

1. Which type of threat cannot be mitigated using ACLs?

   a. Malicious payload
   b. DoS TCP SYN attack
   c. ICMP message filtering
   d. Source IP address spoofing

2. What is the range of ACL numbers for a standard access list? (Choose two.)

   a. 100–199
   b. 1–99
   c. 1300–1999
   d. 0–99

3. Which wildcard mask would match for IP subnets 172.30.16.0/24 to 172.30.31.0/24?

   a. 0.0.31.255
   b. 0.0.0.255
   c. 0.0.255.255
   d. 0.0.15.255

4. Which of the following ACLs would allow users to access their Post Office Protocol server?

   a. access-list 101 permit tcp any any eq 25
   b. access-list 101 permit tcp any eq 25 any
   c. access-list 101 permit tcp any eq 110 any
   d. access-list 101 permit tcp any any eq 110

5. Which of the following is a caveat regarding ACLs?

   a. Standard ACLs must be used to implement security policies.
   b. Beware of the explicit **deny all** at the bottom of ACLs.
   c. Place less specific statements higher in ACLs.
   d. Ensure that statements at the top of ACLs do not negate statements found lower in the list.

6. Which of the following are rules that can be configured by Cisco Configuration Professional? (Choose all that apply.)

a. NAT rules

b. Firewall rules

c. Unsupported rules

d. Sysopt rules

7. Using which keyword in the **access-list** command is a best practice method for understanding what is happening to traffic as it passes through the firewall?

a. established

b. eq

c. log

d. matches

8. Which of the following are benefits of using ACL object groups? (Choose all that apply.)

a. Optimized logging

b. Increased performance

c. Reduced storage

d. Separates ownership of the components of an ACE

9. Using which keyword in the **access-list** command designates that the packet is a response to an outbound initiated session?

a. established

b. eq

c. log

d. matches

10. Which of the following are implicit IPv6 ACLs entries? (Choose all that apply.)

a. permit icmp any any nd-na

b. deny ipv6 any any

c. permit icmp any any nd-ns

d. deny ipv6 icmp any any

Chapter 9

Firewall Fundamentals and Network Address Translation

This chapter teaches firewall concepts, technologies, and design principles. At the end of this chapter, you will be able to do the following:

■ Explain the operations of the different types of firewall technologies

■ Describe firewall technologies that historically have played, and still play, a role in network access control and security architectures

■ Introduce and describe the function and building blocks of Network Address Translation

■ List design considerations for firewall deployment

■ Describe guidelines for firewall ruleset creation

Introducing Firewall Technologies

A firewall protects network devices from intentional, hostile intrusions that could threaten information assurance (availability, confidentiality, and integrity) or lead to a denial-of-service (DoS) attack. A firewall can protect a hardware device or a software program running on a secure host computer. This chapter introduces the firewall technologies that Cisco uses in routers and security appliances.

Firewall Fundamentals

The term *firewall* is a metaphor. By segmenting a network into different physical subnetworks, firewalls can limit the damage that can spread from one subnet to another, just as the fire doors and firewalls that are used in a building limit the spread of fire, heat, and structural collapse. In network security terms, a firewall is a software or hardware barrier between an internal (trusted) network and an external (untrusted) network. In this sense, a firewall is a set of related programs that enforces an access control policy between two or more networks.

In principle, as shown in Figure 9-1, a firewall is a pair of mechanisms that perform these two separate functions, which are set by policies:

■ One mechanism blocks bad traffic.

■ The second mechanism permits good traffic.

Figure 9-1   *Firewall: Enforcing Access Control*

A firewall can be defined as follows:

> *A system or group of systems that enforces an access control policy between two networks.*

Because this definition is very generic, almost anything can be considered a firewall. Many network access technologies can be used to build a firewall:

■ Packet-filtering routers

■ LAN switches

■ Complex systems integrating many hosts into a firewall system

Note   Depending on which definition you look at regarding firewall technologies, proxy servers and gateways may or may not be included. Proxy gateways, discussed later in this chapter, are also referred to as application layer firewalls. The Cisco IronPort Web Security Appliance is an example of a proxy server.

Firewalls mean different things to different organizations, and each organization has unique requirements. Nevertheless, all firewalls usually share some common properties:

■ **Must be resistant to attacks:** Compromise of the firewall system should be very unlikely, because it would enable an attacker to disable the firewall or change its access rules.

■ **Must be the only transit point between networks:** All traffic between networks must flow through the firewall. This requirement prevents a hacker from using a backdoor connection to bypass the firewall and violate the network access policy.

■ **Enforces the access control policy of an organization:** The access control policy should define what the firewall permits or denies.

By performing network access control, you can use a firewall as a protective measure against the following:

■ **Exposure of sensitive hosts and applications to untrusted users:** A firewall hides most of the functionality of a host and permits only the minimum required connectivity to a host. Complexity is thus reduced, and many possible vulnerabilities are not exposed.

■ **Exploitation of protocol flaws:** You can program a firewall to inspect protocol messages and verify their compliance with the protocol, whether it is Layer 3, Layer 4, or a higher-layer protocol. The firewall limits what attackers can send to their target, preventing the delivery of malformed packets that are used in an attempt either to crash a system or to gain access to an application.

■ **Malicious data:** A firewall can detect and block malicious data sent to clients or servers inside the application stream, thereby stopping it from infecting the server or the client. Because firewalls are located on critical interconnection points of the network, enforcing the network access policies is simple, scalable, and robust. Sometimes a small number of firewalls can handle most of the network access control needs of an organization.

Firewalls are often misunderstood, and false assumptions are often made about their capabilities. Although it is true that firewalls would not be necessary if host and application security could be made extremely robust, many organizations use firewalls as a replacement for host or application security. Such an attitude is extremely dangerous because it can completely ignore host and application security even in extreme cases, such as connecting a sensitive server inside an Internet firewall.

Today, firewalls are such a mainstream technology that they are often considered a panacea for many security issues. While you should be aware of the benefits of the firewall model, you should also be aware of the many limitations that firewalls have and how to mitigate some of these limitations:

■ Because firewalls are used in critical points of the network, their misconfiguration can have disastrous consequences. Firewalls are often a single point of failure when it comes to security; a single mistake in a configuration rule or firewall code can compromise the network access policy.

■ Many modern applications require that the firewall handle, in addition to the primary control connection, secondary connections that are created to carry, for example, data. A typical example is an application that opens dynamic sessions from the outside to the inside after an initial client request initiated from the inside to the outside. Multimedia applications such as those for audio streaming and videoconferencing are examples where the user opens one session from the inside to the outside to request a feed. To support the streaming, however, additional sessions are opened from the outside to the inside, and by default the firewall rejects those new incoming requests. Once firewall vendors have a chance to study the new protocol, they can create a rule that forces the firewall to peek inside the payload of the original outgoing packet to gain information about the additional sessions that will be created and to prepare for those new incoming sessions.

■ End users, when faced with a restrictive firewall, might find their own methods of bypassing it. For example, inside users may use wireless broadband from the protected network to an Internet service provider (ISP) and create a backdoor connection to the protected network.

■ Because firewalls are commonly placed at chokepoints, the design of the firewall model must ensure network performance is not affected by inspecting all the traffic.

■ Tunneling unauthorized data over authorized connections (covert channels) is simple and generally impossible to detect. This activity usually requires the help of someone on the trusted side of the firewall.

Firewalls in a Layered Defense Strategy

In a layered defense scenario, firewalls provide perimeter security of the entire network and of internal network segments in the core. For example, system administrators can use a firewall to separate the human resources and financial networks of an organization from other networks or network segments within the organization.

A layered defense strategy combines different types of firewalls in layers to add depth to the information defense of an organization, as shown in Figure 9-2. For example, traffic that comes in from the untrusted network first encounters a packet filter on the outer router, located in the perimeter security. The traffic next goes to the screened host firewall or bastion host system, which applies more rules to the traffic and discards suspect packets. This bastion host system is also part of the perimeter security. The traffic then goes to an interior screening router, part of the core network security. The traffic moves to the internal destination host only after this routing. This type of demilitarized zone (DMZ) setup, located between the perimeter and the core, is called a *screened subnet configuration*. Endpoint traffic moves in the network after it has been properly authenticated by sophisticated Identity services.

Two recurring terms in this chapter are bastion host and packet filter, which are defined as the following:

■ **Bastion host:** A computer that is expected to be attacked and therefore is hardened. An example of a bastion host is firewall software installed on a workstation that is already running a commonly available operating system. Before the firewall is put into production, the workstation needs to be hardened to protect against the potential vulnerability that the operating system has.

■ **Packet filter:** Typically, a router configured with access lists used to filter out unwanted traffic.

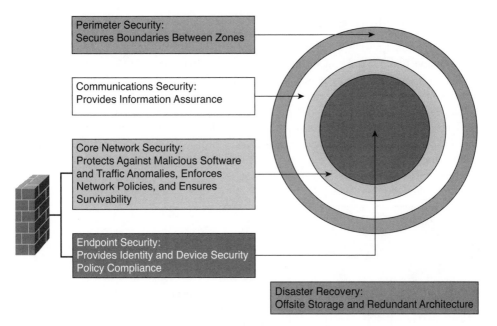

Figure 9-2   *Layered Defense Strategy*

A common misconception is that a layered firewall topology is all that you need in place to declare your internal network to be safe. This myth is probably encouraged by the booming firewall business; however, you need to consider the following factors when building a complete defense-in-depth environment:

■ A significant number of intrusions come from hosts within the network. For example, firewalls often do little to protect against viruses downloaded through email.

■ Firewalls do not protect against rogue modem or rogue wireless access point installations. In addition, and most important, a firewall is not a substitute for informed administrators and users.

■ Firewalls do not replace backup and disaster recovery mechanisms resulting from attack or hardware failure. An in-depth defense also includes offsite storage and redundant hardware topologies.

Defense in depth and diversity of defense are related topics. Defense in depth calls for multiple levels of defense; diversity of defense calls for using different types of technologies in that defense.

An example of implementing both diversity of defense and defense in depth is using a perimeter router as a packet filter and using a stateful firewall to segment the unprotected segment from the protected segment.

Static Packet-Filtering Firewalls

Packet-filtering firewalls work primarily at the network layer of the Open Systems Interconnection (OSI) model, or the IP layer of TCP/IP, as shown in Figure 9-3. Packet-filtering firewalls are generally considered Layer 3 devices, but they typically have the capability to permit or deny traffic based on Layer 4 information, such as protocol, and source and destination port numbers, in addition to the Layer 3 source and destination IP address. Packet filtering uses rules and ACLs to determine whether to permit or deny traffic based on source and destination IP addresses, protocol, source and destination port numbers, and packet type. Packet-filtering firewalls are usually part of a router firewall.

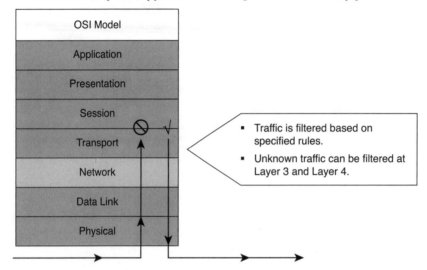

Figure 9-3   *How Static Packet Filters Map to the OSI Model*

Recall that services rely on specific ports to function; for example, Simple Mail Transfer Protocol (SMTP) servers listen to port 25 by default. Because packet-filtering firewalls filter traffic according to static packet header information, they are sometimes referred to as *static filters*. By restricting certain ports, you can restrict the services that rely on those ports. For example, blocking port 25 on a specific workstation prevents an infected workstation from broadcasting email viruses across the Internet.

Packet-filtering firewalls are similar to packet-filtering routers but with some differences in implementation. Packet filters are very scalable, application independent, and have high performance standards; however, they do not offer the complete range of security solutions required in modern networks. For example, a packet filter does not have the capability to understand dynamic protocols upon which a client request requires additional incoming connections to be initiated from the outside, toward the inside client.

Any device that uses ACLs can perform packet filtering. Cisco IOS router configurations commonly use ACLs, not only as packet-filtering firewalls but also to select specified types of traffic that is to be analyzed, forwarded, or influenced in some way. Later in this chapter, you will see examples of both ingress and egress filtering done with ACLs.

Figure 9-4 shows a simple packet-filtering example using a Cisco router.

Figure 9-4   *Static Packet Filter in Action*

In most network topologies, you need to protect the Ethernet interface connecting to the internal (inside) network, while the serial interface that connects to the Internet (outside) is unprotected. In Figure 9-4, the internal addresses that the firewall must protect are in the 10.1.1.0/24 subnet (on the Ethernet interface). The IP address of the Ethernet 0 interface is 10.1.1.1/24.

The particular network security policy shown in Figure 9-4 (ACL 101) allows all users from the inside to access Internet services on the outside. Therefore, all outgoing connections are accepted. The router checks only packets coming from the Internet (security policy ACL 102). In this case, the ACL allows Domain Name System (DNS), SMTP, and FTP services, and the return of traffic initiated from the inside. ACL 102 denies access to all other services.

Packet-filter firewalls (or packet filters) use a simple policy table lookup that permits or denies traffic based on the following possible criteria:

- Source IP address
- Destination IP address
- Source port number
- Destination port numbers
- Synchronize/start (SYN) packet receipt

The firewalls are extremely fast because they do little computation. The rules are extremely easy to implement because they require little security expertise. Router manufacturers easily embed packet-filtering logic in silicon and, consequently, packet filtering is a feature of most routers. Packet-filtering firewalls are relatively inexpensive. Even if other firewalls are used, implementing packet filtering at the router level affords an initial degree of security at the network and transport layers.

Packet filters do not represent a complete firewall solution. However, they are a key element of a secure architecture.

The following are disadvantages of packet filters:

- Packet filtering is susceptible to IP spoofing. Hackers send arbitrary packets that fit ACL criteria and pass through the filter.

- Packet filters do not filter fragmented packets well. Because fragmented IP packets carry the Layer 4 header in the first fragment and packet filters may filter based on information found in the Layer 4 header, fragments after the first fragment are passed unconditionally. A decision to use packet filters assumes that the filter of the first fragment accurately enforces the policy.

- Complex ACLs are difficult to implement and maintain correctly.

- Packet filters cannot dynamically filter certain services. For example, sessions that use dynamic port negotiations are difficult to filter without opening access to a whole range of ports.

- Packet filters are stateless. They examine each packet individually rather than in the context of the state of a connection.

Application Layer Gateways

Application layer firewalls, also called proxy firewalls or application gateways, provide a higher level of security than packet-filtering firewalls because they allow the greatest level of control. Application gateways operate on Layers 3, 4, 5, and 7 of the OSI model, as shown in Figure 9-5.

Most application layer firewalls include specialized application software and proxy servers. A *proxy* is an application that does work on behalf of something else. Proxy services are special-purpose programs that manage traffic through a firewall for a specific service, such as HTTP or FTP. Proxy services are specific to the protocol that they are designed to forward, and they can provide increased access control, perform careful detailed checks for valid data, and generate audit records about the traffic that they transfer.

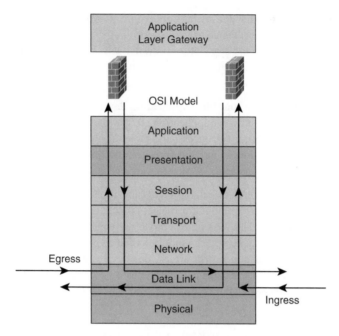

Figure 9-5 *Application Layer Gateway in Action*

Proxy firewalls act as intermediaries between networks to determine whether to allow the communication to proceed. No direct connection exists between an outside user and internal network resources, because the original connection stops in the proxy and a new connection is set between the proxy and the outside destination. For this reason, the only IP address of the network that is visible from the Internet is the IP address of the outside interface of the proxy. The client connects to the proxy server and submits an application layer request. The application layer request includes the true destination and the data request itself. The proxy server analyzes the request and can filter or change the packet contents. The server makes a copy of each incoming packet, changes the source address, and sends the packet to the destination address. The destination server replies to the proxy server, and the proxy server passes the response back to the client.

Sometimes, application layer firewalls support only a limited number of applications, or even just one application. Some of the more common applications that an application layer firewall might support include email, web services, DNS, Telnet, FTP, Usenet news, Lightweight Directory Access Protocol (LDAP), and Finger.

Application layer firewalls provide several advantages:

- **Application layer firewalls authenticate individuals, not devices:** These firewalls typically allow you to authenticate connection requests before allowing traffic to an internal or external resource. This process enables you to authenticate the user requesting the connection instead of authenticating the device.

- **Application layer firewalls make it is harder for hackers to spoof and implement DoS attacks:** An application layer firewall enables you to prevent most spoofing attacks, and DoS attacks are limited to the application firewall itself. The application firewall can detect DoS attacks, and thus reduce the burden on your internal resources.

- **Application layer firewalls can monitor and filter application data:** You can monitor all data on a connection, so you can detect application attacks such as malformed URLs, buffer-overflow attempts, unauthorized access, and more. You can even control the commands or functions you allow an individual to perform based on the authentication and authorization information.

- **Application layer firewalls can provide detailed logging:** Using application layer firewalls, you can generate detailed logs and monitor the actual data that the individual is sending across a connection. This logging can prove extremely useful if a hacker finds a new type of attack, because you can monitor what the hacker does and how the machine does it, and then address the attack. Besides using logging for security purposes, you can use it for management purposes by keeping track of who is accessing what resources, how much bandwidth is used, and how often a user accesses the resources.

The topology in Figure 9-6 represents a typical proxy server deployment. A client inside the network is requesting access to a website. The client browser uses a proxy server for all HTTP requests. Perfect examples of proxy gateways performing application layer filtering are the Cisco IronPort Web Security Appliance (WSA) and the Cisco IronPort Email Security Appliance (ESA). Network security policies force all client connections to go through the proxy server. As shown in Figure 9-6, the browser connects to the proxy server to make requests. Client-side DNS queries and client-side routing to the Internet are not needed when using a proxy server. The client has to reach only the proxy server to make the request.

When the proxy server receives the request from a client, it performs user authentication according to the rules applied to it and uses its Internet connection to access the requested website. It forwards only packets that match the firewall rules. On the return route, the proxy server analyzes the packet, including the Layer 5 and Layer 7 header and payload, to ensure that the server allows the content of the reply back in (as an example, checking whether the payload carries hidden malware) before forwarding the packet to the client.

In spite of how an application layer firewall works, with its thorough inspection of the request and response, this firewall provides only a limited number of services, such as HTTP and FTP; however, this type of firewall provides the highest level of filtering for those specific protocols.

1. A client's browser forwards its web request to the IronPort WSA.
2. After checking the policies to confirm that the client's request was acceptable, the WSA initiates a connection to the web server. In the process, its session goes through the perimeter firewall, which is most likely set up to permit outbound HTTP traffic only if the source IP address is that of the WSA.
3. The web server sends its reply addressed to the WSA.
4. The WSA performs policy checks, such as malware detection. Acceptable responses are passed to the client.

Figure 9-6   *Proxy Server Communication Process*

The main limitation of application layer firewalls is that they are process intensive because the server evaluates a significant amount of information embedded in many packets. This type of technology requires many CPU cycles and a lot of memory to process every packet that needs inspection, which sometimes creates throughput problems. In addition, the detailed logging can create disk space problems. To address these issues, you can use one of two solutions:

■ **Employ a context transfer protocol:** Using a context transfer protocol, where identity-specific information tracks users, enables you to perform only authentication and authorization; you cannot monitor data on the connection, only whether the user is authorized to go on the Internet. This solution is not a real firewall per se, because packets are checked not for their content but for the validity of their source and destination addresses. This solution would be similar to a packet filter that has the capability to learn the source and destination information dynamically and match return traffic based on that information.

■ **Monitor only key applications:** With this solution, you limit the application layer firewall to process only certain application types (such as email, Telnet, FTP, or web services) and then, perhaps, process only connections to specific internal resources. The problem with this approach is that you are not monitoring all applications and connections, and this creates a security weakness.

Application layer firewalls typically do not support all applications, such as multimedia or peer-to-peer file sharing applications (to name a few). Instead, they are generally limited to one or a few connection types, typically common applications such as email, Telnet, FTP, and web services. Therefore, an application layer firewall cannot monitor data on all applications: it monitors data only on applications it intrinsically understands.

Finally, application layer firewalls sometimes require you to install vendor-specific software on the client, which the firewall uses to handle the authentication process and any possible connection redirection. This limitation can create scalability and management problems if you must support thousands of clients.

Dynamic or Stateful Packet-Filtering Firewalls

Stateful packet filters, or stateful firewalls, are the most versatile and therefore the most common firewall technologies in use. Stateful filtering provides dynamic packet-filtering capabilities to firewalls. Stateful inspection is a firewall architecture that is classified at the network layer, although for some applications it can analyze traffic at Layer 4 and Layer 5, too, as shown in Figure 9-7. Some stateful firewalls can analyze traffic up to Layer 7 under special circumstances and additional configuration.

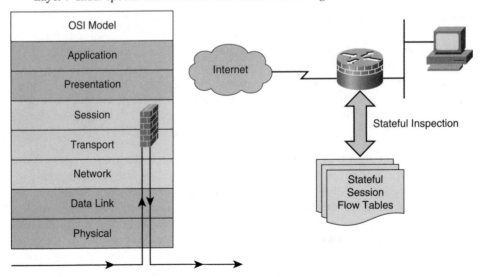

Figure 9-7   *Stateful Packet-Filtering Firewall*

Unlike static packet filtering, which examines a packet based on the information in its header, stateful inspection tracks each connection traversing all interfaces of the firewall and confirms that the session is valid. Stateful packet filtering maintains a state table and allows modification of the security rules on-the-fly. The state table is part of the internal structure of the firewall and tracks all sessions and inspects all packets passing through the firewall. If packets have the expected properties that are predicted by the state table, the firewall allows them to pass. The state table changes dynamically according to traffic flow.

Stateful firewalls use a state table to keep track of the actual communication process. From a transport layer perspective, the firewall examines information in the headers of Layer 3 packets and Layer 4 segments. For example, the firewall looks at the TCP header for SYN, reset (RST), acknowledgment (ACK), FIN, and other control codes to determine the state of the connection. In this scenario, the session layer is responsible for establishing and tearing down the connection.

When an outside service is accessed, the stateful packet filter firewall "remembers" certain details of the request by saving the state of the request in the state table. Each time a TCP or User Datagram Protocol (UDP) connection is established for inbound or outbound connections, the firewall logs the information in a stateful session flow table. When the outside system responds to the request, the firewall server compares the received packets with the saved state to allow or deny network access.

The stateful session flow table contains the source and destination addresses, port numbers, UDP connection information and TCP sequencing information, and additional flags for each TCP connection associated with a particular session. This information creates a connection object against which the firewall compares all inbound and outbound packets. The firewall permits data only if an appropriate connection exists to validate the passage of that data.

More advanced stateful firewalls include the capability to parse FTP port commands and update the state table to allow FTP to work transparently through the firewall. Advanced stateful firewalls can also provide TCP sequence number randomization, and DNS query and response matching to ensure that the firewall allows packets to return only in response to queries that originate from inside the network. These features reduce the threat of TCP RST flood attacks and DNS cache poisoning. Some stateful firewalls can also check the validity of protocol commands to ensure that intrusive and dangerous commands are not admitted on the network.

Packets inside the network must make their way to the outside network. This can possibly expose internal IP addresses to potential hackers. That is why most firewalls incorporate Network Address Translation (NAT) with stateful inspection and proxy servers for added security.

Stateful firewalls keep track of the state of a connection: they know whether the connection is in an initiation, data transfer, or termination state. This information is useful when you want to deny the initiation of connections from external devices (default behavior of a firewall) but allow your inside users to establish connections to these external devices and permit the responses to come back through the stateful firewall.

Figure 9-8 shows a successfully established HTTP TCP session that leads to a dynamic ACL rule entry on the outside interface that permits response packets from the web server to the client.

The outside ACL has three permanent entries permitting outside traffic to initiate a connection on 10.1.1.2. Our firewall also has an ACL on its inside interface, permitting traffic from inside users to anywhere outside.

1. An inside user initiates a connection.
2. The user's connection is tested against the inbound ACL on the inside interface.
3. If the traffic is permitted to progress from inside to outside, the firewall inserts a dynamic entry in the inbound ACL of the outside interface to allow the reply traffic to come in to reach the inside user.

Figure 9-8 *Stateful Packet Filtering*

Stateful packet-filtering firewalls are good to use for the following applications:

- **As a primary means of defense:** In most situations, a stateful firewall is used as a primary means of defense by filtering unwanted, unnecessary, or undesirable traffic.

- **As an intelligent first line of defense:** Networks use routing devices that support a stateful function as a first line of defense or as an additional security boost on perimeter routers.

- **As a means of strengthening packet filtering:** Stateful filtering provides more stringent control over security than packet filtering does, without adding too much cost.

- **To improve routing performance:** Stateful packet-filtering devices perform better than packet filters or proxy servers. Stateful firewalls do not require a large range of port numbers to allow returning traffic back into the network, providing that the firewall is familiar with the protocol and its behavior. The state table determines whether a packet is returning traffic. If it is not returning traffic, the filtering table filters the traffic.

■ **As a defense against spoofing and DoS attacks:** Stateful packet filtering works on packets and connections. In particular, stateful firewalls track the state of the connection in the state table listing every connection or connectionless transaction. By determining whether packets belong to an existing connection or are from an unauthorized source, stateful firewalls allow only traffic from connections that are listed in the table. As an example, during the three-way handshake of a TCP session, the firewall tracks the flag and therefore can predict what the following exchange between the client and the server will be. When the firewall removes a connection from the state table (for instance, because of the connection termination following the TCP four-way handshake as a goodbye), the firewall does not allow any more traffic from that device. In addition, the stateful firewall can log more information than a packet-filtering firewall can, including when a connection was set up, how long it was up, and when it was torn down. This logging makes connections harder to spoof.

Stateful firewalls have the following limitations:

■ **Stateful firewalls cannot prevent application layer attacks:** For example, your network might allow traffic to port 80 on a web server. Your stateful firewall examines the destination address in the Layer 3 packet and the destination port number in the segment. If there is a match, the stateful firewall allows the incoming and outgoing traffic. One problem with this approach is that the stateful firewall does not examine the actual contents of the HTTP connection.

■ **Not all protocols have a state:** UDP and Internet Control Message Protocol (ICMP) do not have a state, so a stateful firewall does not know whether the session is initiating, transmitting, or finishing, as it would with TCP. For example, UDP has no defined process for how to set up, maintain, and tear down a connection. The firewall can provide only limited support for these protocols compared to the thorough information the firewall has regarding, as an example, a TCP connection. Routers define UDP connections on an application-by-application basis.

■ **Some applications open multiple connections:** On earlier (more basic) stateful firewalls, if the client was inside the network and the server was outside the network, both stateful and packet-filtering firewalls had problems dealing with the data connection that the FTP server established to the client. You needed to open a whole range of ports to allow this second connection. Cisco IOS Firewall does not have this problem. The firewall monitors FTP control traffic and discovers information exchanged between the client and the server, which it uses to prepare the data path established from the server in the direction of the client. In this scenario, the firewall is not filtering the traffic at the application layer; it is only reading some purposeful information to prepare for the data. Here we are not talking about application inspection, discussed earlier, where the firewall reads the payload of Layer 7 to assess the FTP commands or some strings found in the FTP payload.

■ **Stateful firewalls do not authenticate users by default:** Stateful firewall technology itself does not mandate user authentication. Add-on functionality is used to provide a feature such as proxy authentication.

Other Types of Firewalls

Over the years, variations of standard stateful firewalls have emerged. Some examples of those variations, which provide additional or restrictive features, are deep packet inspection (DPI) firewalls and Layer 2 firewalls.

Application Inspection Firewalls, aka Deep Packet Inspection

Application inspection firewalls ensure the security of applications and services. Some applications require special handling by the firewall application inspection function. Applications that require special application inspection functions are those that embed IP addressing information in the user data packet or that open secondary channels on dynamically assigned ports.

The application inspection function works with NAT to help identify the location of the embedded addressing information. This arrangement allows NAT to translate embedded addresses and to update any checksum or other fields that are affected by the translation.

The application inspection function also monitors sessions to determine the port numbers for secondary channels. Many protocols open secondary TCP or UDP ports. The initial session on a well-known port negotiates dynamically assigned port numbers. The application inspection function monitors these sessions, identifies the dynamic port assignments, and permits data exchange on these ports for the duration of the specific session.

An application inspection firewall behaves in different ways according to each layer:

■ **Transport layer mechanism:** From a transport layer perspective, the application inspection firewall acts like a stateful firewall by examining information in the headers of Layer 3 packets and Layer 4 segments. For example, the application inspection firewall looks at the TCP header for SYN, RST, ACK, FIN, and other control codes to determine the state of the connection.

■ **Application layer mechanism:** The application inspection firewall checks the conformity of commands within a known protocol. For example, when the application inspection firewall checks the SMTP message type, it allows only acceptable message types on Layer 7 (such as, DATA, HELO, MAIL, NOOP, QUIT, RCPT, and RSET). In addition, the application inspection firewall checks whether the command attributes that are used (for example, length of a message type) conform to the internal rules. These rules often trust the RFC of a specific protocol. Sometimes, application layer firewalls provide protocol support for HTTP, and the application inspection firewall can determine whether the content is really an HTML website or a tunneled application, such as Instant Messaging or GoToMyPC. In the case of a tunneled application, the application inspection firewall would block the content or terminate the connection. Future development will provide application inspection support for more protocols on an application inspection firewall.

There are several advantages of an application inspection firewall:

- Application inspection firewalls are aware of the state of Layer 4 and Layer 5 connections.

- Application inspection firewalls check the conformity of application commands.

- Application inspection firewalls have the capability to check and affect Layer 7.

- Application inspection firewalls can prevent more kinds of attacks than stateful firewalls can. For example, application inspection firewalls can stop an attacker from trying to set up a virtual private network (VPN) tunnel (triggered from inside the network) through an application firewall by way of tunneled HTTP requests.

Transparent Firewalls (Layer 2 Firewalls)

Cisco IOS routers, Cisco ASA Adaptive Security Appliance Software, Cisco Firewall Services Module, and Cisco ASA Services Module offer the capability to deploy a security appliance in a secure bridging mode as a Layer 2 device to provide rich Layer 2 through 7 security services for the protected network, as illustrated in Figure 9-9. This capability enables businesses to deploy security appliances into existing network environments without the need to readdress the network. Although the security appliance can be invisible to devices on both sides of a protected network, as shown in Figure 9-9, administrators can use an exposed IP address to manage the appliance.

Note   Layer 2 firewalls, also known as transparent firewalls, are sometimes referred to as bumps in the wire or as stealth firewalls.

Figure 9-9 *Transparent Firewalling: Firewall Interfaces All in the Same Subnet*

Tip Additional information on transparent firewalls is available in *CCNP Security FIREWALL 642-618 Official Cert Guide* (Cisco Press).

NAT Fundamentals

As you read earlier in this book, IPv6 will not require NAT. However, at the time of this writing, more than 99 percent of Internet traffic is still running on IPv4. NAT enables private IPv4 internetworks that use nonregistered IPv4 addresses to connect to the Internet. NAT, defined originally in RFC 1631 and enhanced in RFC 3022, operates in routers and other devices to provide address simplification and conservation. Usually, NAT connects two networks and translates the private (inside local) addresses in the internal network into public addresses (inside global) before packets are forwarded to another network, as shown in Figure 9-10. As part of this functionality, you can configure NAT to use only one address for the entire network to the outside world. Using only one address effectively hides the internal network, thus providing additional security.

Chapter 3 mentioned RFC 1918 and the private address space. These private addresses provide a very large pool of addresses to be used inside the corporate network. These addresses, which are not routable, need to be translated for outbound traffic. A common practice is for these inside addresses to be translated by a single public IP address, often the IP address of the outside-facing interface of the firewall. This technique of translating many inside users to one single outside IP address will be discussed later in this chapter.

Multiple device types can be configured to perform NAT services. Although firewalls are most common, routers and Layer 3 switches are also capable of deploying this service.

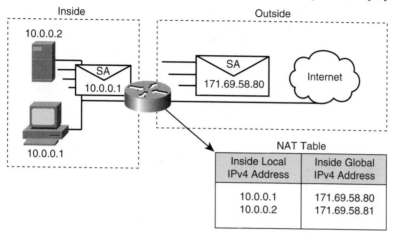

Figure 9-10 *Example of Network Address Translation*

Cisco defines the following list of NAT terms:

- **Inside local address:** The IPv4 address that is assigned to a host on the inside network. The inside local address is likely not an IPv4 address assigned by a service provider, but rather one that falls within reserved private IPv4 address spaces.

- **Inside global address:** A legitimate IPv4 address that is assigned by the network interface card (NIC) or service provider that represents one or more inside local IPv4 addresses to the outside world.

- **Outside local address:** The IPv4 address of an outside host as it appears to the inside network. Not necessarily a public address, the outside local address is allocated from a routable address space. Outside NAT (NATting the address of an outside entity when it appears on the inside network) is beyond the scope of this book.

- **Outside global address:** The IPv4 address that is assigned to a host on the outside network by the host owner. The outside global address is allocated from a globally routable address or network space.

NAT offers the following benefits:

- Eliminates the need to readdress all hosts that require external access, saving time and money.

- Conserves addresses through application port-level multiplexing. With NAT overloading, internal hosts can share a single registered IPv4 address for all external communications. In this type of configuration, relatively few external addresses are required to support many internal hosts, thus conserving IPv4 addresses. NAT overload, a term used by Cisco, is often referred to as PAT, which will be covered next.

One of the main features of NAT is dynamic Port Address Translation (PAT), which is also referred to as "NAT overload" in Cisco IOS configuration. PAT allows you to translate multiple internal addresses into a few external addresses, or even a single external address, essentially allowing the internal addresses to share one external address, as shown in Figure 9-11. With NAT overload, as shown in Figure 9-11, as long as the local host uses a unique source port, the router translates only the IP address and not the port. However, in the third entry, host 10.6.1.6 uses source port number 2031, which is already in use by host 10.6.1.2. In this situation, the router translates both source address and source port to create a unique combination that will be used to allow the return traffic to be mapped and translated back to the proper inside host.

Figure 9-11 *Example of Port Address Translation (aka NAT Overload) on Cisco IOS Router*

PAT uses unique source port numbers on the inside global IPv4 address to distinguish between translations. Because the port number is encoded in 16 bits, the total number of internal addresses that NAT can translate into one external address is, theoretically, as many as 65,536 minus the 1023 reserved ports, so about 64,000 ports. Port numbers from 0 to 1023 are used for well-known ports and thus typically aren't used for source ports.

PAT attempts to preserve the original source port. If the source port is already allocated, PAT attempts to find the first available port number. It starts from the beginning of the appropriate port group, 0 to 511, 512 to 1023, or 1024 to 65535. If PAT does not find an available port from the appropriate port group and if more than one external IPv4 address is configured, PAT moves to the next IPv4 address and tries to allocate the original source port again. PAT continues trying to allocate the original source port until it runs out of available ports and external IPv4 addresses.

Dynamic PAT is typically used when translating private addresses into routable Internet addresses, for outbound network traffic. You can configure static or dynamic inside source translation; however, dynamic PAT is typically used because there are not enough global addresses.

Example of Translating an Inside Source Address

Figure 9-12 illustrates a router that is translating a source address inside a network into a source address outside the network. The steps for translating an inside source address are as follows:

Step 1.   The user at host 1.1.1.1 opens a connection to Host B.

Step 2.   The first packet that the router receives from host 1.1.1.1 causes the router to check its NAT table.

- If a static translation entry has been configured, the router goes to Step 3.

- If no static translation entry exists, the router determines that the source address 1.1.1.1 (SA 1.1.1.1) must be translated dynamically. The router then selects a global address from the dynamic address pool and creates a translation entry (in the example, 2.2.2.2).

Step 3.   The router replaces the inside local source address of host 1.1.1.1 with the translation entry global address and forwards the packet.

Step 4.   Host B receives the packet and responds to host 1.1.1.1 by using the inside global IPv4 destination address 2.2.2.2 (DA 2.2.2.2).

Step 5.   When the router receives the packet with the inside global IPv4 address, the router performs a NAT table lookup by using the inside global address as a key. If dynamic PAT is configured, the lookup includes the destination port as well, which acts as a tiebreaker. The router finds the original host IP address and translates back to the inside local address 1.1.1.1, forwarding the packet to host 1.1.1.1.

Step 6.   Host 1.1.1.1 receives the packet and continues the conversation. The router performs Steps 2 through 5 for each packet.

Inbound access requires a different type of NAT. For servers such as host 1.1.1.1 in Figure 9-13, inbound access from the Internet requires a unique and persistent global IPv4 address. The service must have a known and unique identifier (IP address) for DNS servers to translate the service URL into the same global IPv4 address and make the service reachable.

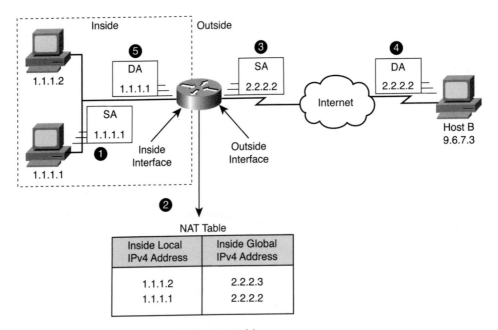

Figure 9-12 *Translating Inside Source Address*

For this reason, static NAT is used to manually configure the translation between the known inside local address, in the example 1.1.1.1, and the known global address, in the example 2.2.2.2. This is a static NAT entry that makes all packets be translated:

- A client sends a request, shown in step 1 of Figure 9-13, to 2.2.2.2 which is the public address of the server located inside our network. Upon receiving the packet, shown in Step 2, the router translates the destination address of 2.2.2.2 to 1.1.1.1.

- The router forwards the packet, with the real destination IP address, to the server, as shown in Step 3.

- The server returns its reply with source IP address of 1.1.1.1, shown in Step 4.

- The router looks at its NAT table and finds a static entry for 1.1.1.1 and translates it to its global address of 2.2.2.2 before forwarding the packet to the client, as shown in Step 5.

- Outbound packets, originated by the server 1.1.1.1, find the matching static entry as well, and all packets are translated accordingly.

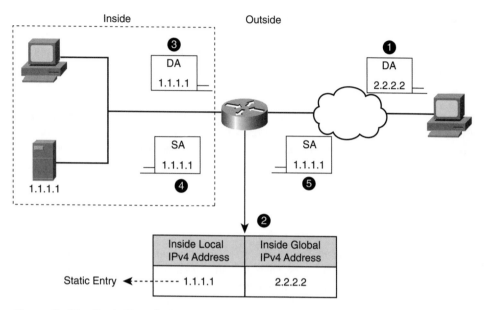

Figure 9-13 *Static Translation*

NAT Deployment Choices

The deployment modes in NAT operations are as follows:

- **Static NAT:** Maps an unregistered IPv4 address to a registered IPv4 address. One-to-one static NAT is particularly useful when a device must be accessible from outside the network.

- **Dynamic NAT:** Maps an unregistered IPv4 address to a registered IPv4 address from a group of registered IPv4 addresses. Dynamic NAT is "many-to-many" translation: in this scenario, many inside users are translated to many global addresses. These global addresses are grouped together in a NAT pool. Dynamic NAT is useful for outbound client access, when you have fewer outside global IP addresses than inside local hosts. Each inside user will have a public address that will be assigned and reserved to it for a period of time for NAT.

- **Dynamic PAT (NAT overload):** Maps multiple unregistered IPv4 addresses to a few or even a single registered IP address (many-to-one) by tracking port numbers and using different ports, if needed. NAT Overload is also known as PAT, and is a form of dynamic translation.

- **Policy NAT:** Uses ACLs to perform NAT differently based on ACL criteria (for instance source addresses, destination addresses, and ports). A group of hosts might translate to a global address pool when sending traffic to the Internet, while translating to a nonoverlapping private address when sending traffic to remote offices.

- **Static PAT:** Uses ACLs to perform translation by allowing a specific UDP or TCP port on a global address to be translated to a specific port on a local address. That is, both the address and the port numbers are translated. This is referred to as port forwarding on home routers, such as Linksys models.

> **Note**   PAT is not implemented in exactly the same way in Cisco IOS and Cisco ASA. In Cisco IOS, PAT translates the source port only if needed. With Cisco ASA, the source port of an outbound connection is *always* translated to a randomly generated port number.

Firewall Designs

Ultimately, firewalls are referred to as *firewall systems* because they implement access control using multiple technologies. These technologies might even be implemented in different physical devices. When planning your firewall system, it is important to enable and use the firewall technologies that match your security requirements.

Typically, stateful packet filtering is the building-block technology. Stateful packet filters are good central access control components. Access rules are created for Layer 3 and Layer 4 criteria to define which traffic classes can traverse the firewall. These access rules define the first level of trust relationships that are enforced through the firewall.

As you design the access rules, other firewall technologies will be necessary. Application layer inspection expands matching criteria and access control actions to upper layers, providing an additional level of security. Proxy services, including user authentication, allow for user-based rules that result in more granular and context-aware access control.

Best practices documents are a composite effort of security practitioners. This partial list of best practices is generic and serves only as a starting point for your own firewall security policy:

- Position firewalls at key security boundaries, separating security domains with different levels of trust.

- Firewalls are the primary security device, but it is unwise to rely exclusively on a firewall for security.

- Deny all traffic by default and permit only services that are needed.

- Implement various firewall technologies, matching your application mix and security policy requirements.

- Ensure that physical access to the firewall is controlled.

- Regularly monitor firewall logs. Cisco Security Manager and other Cisco management tools are available for this purpose.

- Practice change management for firewall configuration changes.

Remember that firewalls primarily protect from technical attacks originating from the outside. Inside attacks tend to be nontechnical in nature.

Firewall Policies in a Layered Defense Strategy

Firewall access rules are the building blocks for access control. An enterprise firewall could have hundreds if not thousands of rules. Access rule creation, management, and auditing are critical to implementing a sound security posture effectively and efficiently. Too many redundant rules might result in performance degradation. Ineffective or obsolete rules might result in trust exploitation and security breaches.

When defining access rules, multiple criteria can be used as a starting point:

- **Rules based on service control:** Determine the types of Internet services that can be accessed, inbound or outbound. The firewall may filter traffic based on IP address and TCP port number. It may provide proxy software that receives and interprets each service request before passing it on. It may host the server software itself, such as a web or mail service. An example of a rule based on service control would be: allow HTTP, allow HTTPS, deny everything else.

- **Rules based on direction control:** Determine the direction in which particular service requests may be initiated and allowed to flow through the firewall. An example of a rule based on direction control would be: allow HTTP outbound, but not inbound.

- **Rules based on user control:** Control access to a service according to which user is attempting to access it. This feature is typically applied to users inside the firewall perimeter (local users). It may also be applied to incoming traffic from external users. The latter requires some form of secure authentication technology, such as is provided in IP Security (IPsec). An example of a rule based on user control would be: allow campus VLANs HTTP access, deny it for wireless VLANs.

- **Rules based on behavior control:** Control how particular services are used. For example, the firewall may filter email to eliminate spam, or it may enable external access to only a portion of the information on a local web server. An example of a rule based on behavior control would be open negotiated FTP ports after learning them during connection setup.

Typically, a combination of these criteria is used to define restrictive policies that permit only the required traffic, while blocking anything else.

Access rules are typically implemented using ACLs. That is the case with Cisco IOS and Cisco ASA firewalls. For that reason, access rules are effectively ordered lists of **permit** and **deny** statements, applied to specific interfaces, as represented in Figure 9-14.

Action	Source Address	Destination Address	Service
DENY	10.1.1.0 /24	192.168.1.0 /24	Any
PERMIT	10.1.1.0 /24	172.16.0.0 /24	SSH
PERMIT	10.1.1.0 /24	ANY	HTTP
DENY	ANY	ANY	ANY

Figure 9-14 *Firewall Access Rule Structure: Top-Down Process*

The ruleset is evaluated sequentially from the top, and the rule that first matches the new connection is evaluated, permitting or denying the connection. When a rule matches a connection, all subsequent rules are ignored.

Because rules use ACLs, there is an implicit deny-all rule at the end of the list. If a connection does not match any of the rules, by default, it will be denied.

Firewall Rules Design Guidelines

When creating firewall rules, use the following guidelines:

- Use a restrictive approach, as opposed to a permissive approach, for all interfaces and all directions of traffic. This translates into simple rulesets that permit the required traffic flows and deny everything else.

- The previous guideline implies that you should take a somewhat paranoid stance and assume that malicious traffic could come from any security domain, even the most trusted ones. This stance results in outbound rules becoming as important as inbound rules, even though they apply to "trusted" internal traffic.

- A tradeoff should be made between access control, performance, and rule maintenance. Specific and granular rules provide more control over the allowed or denied traffic, but also result in longer rulesets and more change-management and maintenance challenges. Observe the use of **any** keywords matching sources, destinations, and ports, as they may allow unwanted traffic.

- For a given access requirement, more specific rules should be pushed to the top, while more generic rules should be pushed to the bottom. The top-down processing order demands this approach to prevent shadow rules when creating exceptions to a given access policy.

- Filtering impossible packets is a common practice. An example is antispoofing rules that are aimed at blocking private IPv4 address spaces in the source address of inbound Internet packets.

- Auditing and change management are crucial. Obsolete rules tend to clutter the ruleset and cause breaches to the access policy.

Lack of a formal methodology for rule creation and maintenance often results in issues that affect the security posture or the ability of the firewall to process traffic.

These issues are, among others, based on consistency, completeness, and compactness. Consistency issues result in potential security breaches.

The following is a list of potential consistency issues with firewall rules:

- **Promiscuous rules:** Allow more access than necessary to meet access requirements. An example is the use of **any** keywords in ACLs, allowing access from all IP addresses when access is only necessary from a single subnet. Another example is a rule that allows access to a system on multiple ports when only a subset of those ports is required.

- **Redundant rules:** Result when a given rule duplicates a portion of the access that is permitted or denied by another rule. An example is a rule that allows a single IP address to access a server on a particular TCP port when an existing rule already allows all IP addresses to access that port. Another example is a rule that allows access to a port on a host when other rules allow the same type of access due to the membership of the port in a service group.

- **Shadowed rules:** Result when the incorrect ordering of rules in the ruleset completely prevents the execution of one or more firewall rules. An example is configuring a rule that denies access to a particular website below a rule that allows access to all websites. Another example is placing a rule that allows access to a server on a single port from a single IP address below a rule that blocks all access to the server from all IP addresses. The existence of the first rule would shadow the second rule, rendering it useless.

- **Orphaned rules:** These are rules that exist in the firewall ruleset but never match traffic passing through the firewall. An example is a rule designed to allow access to a database server that incorrectly specifies a nonexistent destination IP address. Another example is a rule designed to allow HTTP access to a server that no longer hosts a website.

Tip   Here's a trick used by David Chapman, a technical reviewer on this book: to discover orphan rules, reset access list counters on the first of each month. At the end of the month, check which ACL entries still have their counters at zero, and flag these entries for removal.

Completeness issues might also result in security breaches:

- **Errors in rule specification:** Include errors that are made in the translation between business requirements and technical or product-specific firewall rules. Sometimes, the rules simply do not meet business requirements due to a misunderstanding about business requirements. Other times, firewall administrators fail to specify a rule necessary to meet business requirements. Specifying the incorrect port for a service is an example, such as creating a rule for port 8080 when the business requirement called for standard port 80 for the HTTP service.

■ **Data entry errors:** Include errors made when converting a technical rule definition into the firewall policy format and entering that rule into the firewall rule base. An example would be mistyping a port number, such as creating a rule for port 23 when the technical specification indicated port 53. Another example would be mistyping a source or destination address or failing to input a rule included in the technical specification.

Compactness issues typically result from obsolete rules, too much granularity, or an informal approach to defining the order of rules within the ruleset. These issues affect performance and, therefore, the ability to provide firewall services effectively. The firewall evaluates the rules inefficiently, often matching traffic flows after hundreds if not thousands of rules have been unnecessarily evaluated.

Summary

In this chapter, you have learned that a firewall is a set of rules designed to enforce an access control policy between two networks. You learned how to create firewall rules to implement your security policies. You also learned that firewall systems are a combination of packet filtering, stateful inspection, application layer inspection, and other technologies. You saw that NAT is a complementary technology to firewalling and that it allows for dynamic and static translations.

You saw that change management, ruleset auditing, and monitoring are critical firewall design considerations and that common issues found in firewall rule design include promiscuous rules, redundant rules, shadowed rules, and orphaned rules.

References

For additional information, refer to these resources:

Cisco Systems, Inc. "Configuring Network Address Translation: Getting Started," http://www.cisco.com/en/US/tech/tk648/tk361/technologies_tech_note-09186a0080094e77.shtml.

Mason, Andrew. *Cisco Firewall Technology* (Cisco Press, 2007).

Review Questions

Use the questions here to review what you learned in this chapter. The correct answers are found in the Appendix, "Answers to Chapter Review Questions."

1. Which of the following are firewalls? (Choose all that apply.)

    a. Static packet filters

    b. URL filters

    c. Application layer gateways

    d. Layer 2 switches

2. Stateful packet-filtering firewalls are good to use for all the following applications except:

   a. As a primary means of defense
   b. As an intelligent first line of defense
   c. To sanitize web traffic of malware
   d. As a means of strengthening packet filtering
   e. To improve routing performance

3. Match the following names and characteristics:

   Names

   a. Packet-filtering firewalls
   b. Application layer gateways
   c. Stateful packet filters
   d. Application inspection firewalls

   Characteristics

   1. Work primarily at the network level of the OSI model
   2. Are the most common firewalls
   3. Monitor sessions to determine the port numbers for secondary channels
   4. Were the first application layer firewalls

4. Which threats can be mitigated using ACLs? (Choose all that apply.)

   a. Malicious payloads
   b. Spam
   c. ICMP message filtering
   d. IP address spoofing

5. Cisco IronPort Web Security Appliance is an example of which of the following?

   a. Stateless packet filter
   b. Application layer gateway
   c. Stateful packet firewall
   d. Intrusion detection system

6. Match the following translation definitions and characteristics:

   Translation types

   a. Static NAT
   b. Dynamic NAT
   c. Dynamic PAT
   d. Policy NAT

   Characteristics

   1. Translation depends on both source and destination
   2. Translation is many-to-many
   3. Translation is one-to-one
   4. Translation is many-to-one

7. Match the following bases of firewall access rules with the examples:

Basis of firewall access rules:

a. Service control

b. Direction control

c. User control

d. Behavior control

Firewall access rules examples

1. Allow HTTP outbound, but not inbound

2. Allow campus VLANs HTTP access, deny it for wireless VLANs

3. Open negotiated FTP ports after learning them during connection setup

4. Allow HTTP, allow HTTPS, deny everything else

Chapter 10

Cisco Firewalling Solutions: Cisco IOS Zone-Based Firewall and Cisco ASA

Two of the Cisco Firewall solutions, Cisco IOS Zone-Based Policy Firewalls and Cisco Adaptive Security Appliance, can be configured to perform basic security operations on a network. At the end of this chapter, you will be able to do the following:

- Introduce and describe the function, operational framework, and building blocks of Cisco IOS Zone-Based Firewalls

- Describe the functions of zones and zone pairs, as well as their relationship in hierarchical policies

- Describe Cisco Common Classification Policy Language for creating zone-based firewall policies

- List the default policies for the different combinations of zone types

- Demonstrate the configuration and verification of zone-based firewalls using Cisco Configuration Professional and the CLI

- Demonstrate the configuration of NAT services for zone-based firewalls

- Describe the Cisco ASA family of products, identifying key supported features

- Describe the building blocks of Cisco ASA configuration

- Describe the navigation options, features, and requirements of Cisco ASDM

- Describe the use of access control lists on Cisco ASA

- Describe the deployment of policies using the Cisco Modular Policy Framework

- Describe the configuration procedure to deploy basic outbound access control on Cisco ASA using Cisco ASDM

The zone-based policy firewall changes the original implementation of Cisco IOS Classic Firewall stateful inspection from the older interface-based model to a more flexible, more easily understood zone-based configuration model. The first section of this chapter focuses on the features of Cisco IOS Zone-Based Policy Firewalls and how to use Cisco Configuration Professional to configure them.

Cisco Adaptive Security Appliance (ASA) implements a rich set of security technologies and can be effectively implemented as a perimeter firewall using several deployment modes. The second section of this chapter introduces Cisco ASA functionality, features, and underlying technologies and demonstrates how to configure the Cisco ASA 5505 model for basic connectivity using Cisco Adaptive Security Device Manager (ASDM).

Cisco Firewall Solutions

Cisco offers multiple different firewall solutions, each geared to a different environment. Currently, Cisco Firewall offerings include

- Cisco IOS Firewall

- Cisco ASA 5500 Adaptive Security Appliances

- Cisco ASA 1000V Cloud Firewall

- Cisco Virtual Security Gateway for Nexus 1000V Series Switch

- Cisco Catalyst 6500 Series ASA Services Module

- Cisco Catalyst 6500 Series Firewall Services Module

- Cisco Small Business SA500 Series Security Appliances

In this chapter, we cover the two first firewall technologies: Cisco IOS Firewall and Cisco ASA firewall.

Cisco IOS Zone-Based Policy Firewall

Many different types of techniques are used for firewalling. Cisco IOS routers have been using many different techniques for firewalling over the years. Recently, Cisco introduced Zone-Based Policy Firewall as an alternative to the older technology called Context-Based Access Control.

Zone-Based Policy Firewall Overview

The original implementation of Cisco IOS Classic Firewall stateful inspection used an interface-based configuration model, in which a stateful inspection policy was applied to an interface. All traffic passing through that interface received the same inspection policy. This configuration model limited the granularity of the firewall policies and caused confusion of the proper application of firewall policies, particularly in scenarios when firewall policies must be applied between multiple interfaces.

Zone-based policy firewalls (sometimes referred to as ZBF, or zone-policy firewall [ZPF]) change the firewall from the older interface-based model to a more flexible, more easily understood configuration model where interfaces are assigned to zones, and an inspection policy is applied to traffic moving between the zones. To demonstrate this model, Figure 10-1 shows three zones:

- **Untrusted:** Represents the Internet

- **DMZ:** Demilitarized zone, which contains the corporate servers accessed by the public

- **Trusted:** Represents the inside network

Note   Notably missing from Figure 10-1 is the self zone, the zone used for traffic generated by the router or destined to it, such as routing protocol traffic. The self zone is covered later in the chapter.

Interzone policies offer considerable flexibility and granularity, and thus enable you to apply different inspection policies to multiple host groups that are connected to the same router interface. The interzone policies in Figure 10-1 are as follows:

- **Public-DMZ:** DMZ policy that sets the rules for traffic originating from the untrusted zone with the DMZ as destination

- **DMZ-Private:** Private policy that sets the rules for the traffic originating from the DMZ with the trusted zone as destination

- **Private-DMZ:** DMZ policy that sets the rules for the traffic originating from the trusted zone with the DMZ as destination.

- **Private-Public:** Pubic policy that sets the rules for the traffic originating from the trusted zone with the untrusted zone as destination

Rules are bidirectional. As an example, traffic originating from the trusted zone going to the DMZ would be allowed to return due to the Private-DMZ policy, which would permit the connection and allow the return traffic to come back in the trusted zone. The DMZ-Private policy is not involved for return traffic that originated from the trusted network and for which the reply is now going from the DMZ to the trusted network. The DMZ-Private policy is only needed for traffic originating from the DMZ and destined for the trusted network. This could be the case for email: all the incoming mail could end up in the DMZ to be analyzed by the Cisco IronPort Email Security Appliance (ESA). The ESA would forward to Microsoft Exchange Server, located on the trusted network, email it considered appropriate. The connection would originate from the ESA located in the DMZ and go to MS Exchange Server located on the trusted network. In this case, the DMZ-Private policy would be invoked to permit this traffic. This is likely the only permit action on the DMZ-Private policy: let email flow from the ESA to MS Exchange Server.

The firewall will have a rule that denies email to flow directly from the Internet to MS Exchange Server located on the trusted network.

Zone-based policy firewalls are configured with the Cisco Common Classification Policy Language (C3PL), which uses a hierarchical structure to define inspection for network protocols and the groups of hosts to which the inspection will be applied.

Figure 10-1   *Cisco IOS Zone-Based Policy Firewall*

Cisco IOS Zone-Based Policy Firewalls support the following features:

- Stateful inspection

- Application inspection

- URL filtering

- Per-policy parameter

- Transparent firewall

- Virtual routing and forwarding aware firewall

First-generation firewalls, which were essentially packet filters, used only ACLs to control traffic. For this reason, it was relatively easy for attackers to breach a firewall, because no state data was examined. Second-generation firewalls, known as proxy firewalls, were concerned with the state of the connection, but they were application dependent. Third-generation firewalls, which were stateful packet filters, were developed to provide state tracking, application independence, and speed. Context-Based Access Control (CBAC), from the legacy Cisco IOS Firewall feature set, is an example of this type of third-generation firewall. CBAC performed traffic filtering using stateful filters, whereby selected outbound traffic created a temporary opening in the filter for replies to return through.

Note CBAC can still be implemented on Cisco IOS Firewalls; however, interfaces that participate in a zone-based policy firewall cannot also participate in CBAC.

The legacy stateful inspection done by CBAC was very complicated because there was a combination of ACLs and inspection rules, all of which worked together to accomplish the stateful packet filtering done by the firewall.

The Cisco IOS Zone-Based Policy Firewall completely changes the way a Cisco IOS Firewall is configured.

The first major change to the firewall configuration is the introduction of a zone-based configuration. The classic Cisco IOS Firewall stateful inspection (CBAC) used an interface-based configuration model that you configured using the **ip inspect** command. This changed with the introduction of the Cisco IOS Zone-Based Policy Firewall, which does not use the stateful inspection (CBAC) commands but rather uses C3PL. You could use the two configuration models concurrently on routers, but not on the same interfaces; you cannot configure an interface as a security zone member and for **ip inspect** simultaneously.

Zones establish the security borders of your network. A zone defines a boundary where traffic is subjected to policy restrictions as it crosses to another region of your network. The default policy of a zone-policy firewall between zones is to "deny all." If no policy is explicitly configured, all traffic moving between zones is blocked. This policy is a significant departure from the stateful inspection model, in which traffic is implicitly allowed unless it is explicitly blocked with an ACL entry.

The second major change is the introduction of the new classification policy language known as C3PL. The C3PL structure is similar to the Modular QoS CLI (MQC) structure in which class maps specify the traffic that is affected by the action that the policy map applies. C3PL will be discussed later in this chapter.

Note Interface ACLs are still relevant and are applied before zone-based policy firewalls when they are applied inbound. Interface ACLs are applied after zone-based policy firewalls when they are applied outbound.

Key benefits of zone-based policy firewall are as follows:

- It is not dependent on ACLs.

- The router security posture is restrictive (which means block unless explicitly allowed).

- C3PL makes policies easy to read and troubleshoot.

- One policy affects any given traffic instead of needing multiple ACL and inspection actions.

Zones and Zone Pairs

A zone is a collection of networks that are reachable over a specific router interface and are designated to require the same security policies. Zone-based policy firewall access control policies then control access between two or more zones that are configured on the router, using a flexible configuration language that allows you to specify simple or complex access policies in a manageable manner.

Once zones are created, default rules apply. These default rules will be presented in more detail later in this chapter. Default rules generally allow unrestricted access between interfaces that belong to the same zone, while denying all interzone traffic. Figure 10-2 shows two interfaces belonging to Zone 2. These two interfaces can pass traffic between them without any restrictions.

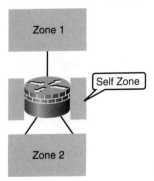

Figure 10-2   *Interfaces Belong to Zone*

Key Topic   **Note**   An interface can belong to one zone and one zone only.

A zone pair allows you to specify a unidirectional firewall policy between two security zones, thus changing the default policy. The direction of the traffic is indicated by specifying a source zone and a destination zone. The source and destination zones of a zone pair must be previously created security zones.

To permit traffic between zone-member interfaces, you must configure a policy permitting (or inspecting) traffic between that zone and another zone.

Self Zone

If desired, you can select the default or self zone as either the source zone or the destination zone. The self zone is a system-defined zone. It does not have any interfaces as members. A zone pair that includes the self zone, along with the associated policy, applies to traffic directed to the router or traffic that is generated by the router. A zone pair does not apply to traffic through the router. Traffic to or from the self zone is by default permitted.

Zone-Based Topology Examples

A zone-based firewall approach results in multiple deployment options that will represent your security domains, which is a more intuitive way to implement firewall policies than a per-interface approach.

Figure 10-3 shows a simple firewall with two security domains, suitable for remote office environments where outbound access is required only to the Internet or to a hub network. Trusted internal interfaces belong to an "inside" zone, while untrusted external interfaces belong to an "outside" zone.

Figure 10-3   *Simple Firewall Topology with Two Security Domains*

Figure 10-4 shows a medium-sized location requiring inbound access to a few public servers, in addition to outbound user access. A third zone, the DMZ, includes the interfaces and assets that are related to the servers located in DMZ interfaces, which require restricted access from the outside, and perhaps a more granular permissive policy from the inside.

If an interface doesn't belong to a zone, it can't communicate with an interface that is part of a zone.

Introduction to Cisco Common Classification Policy Language

A class is a way to identify a set of packets based on their contents. A class is a particular type of traffic; it can be thought of as a precise flow of traffic. Examples of a class of traffic would be traffic for destination port 80 or traffic with a specific subnet source IP address. Normally, you define a class to then apply to the traffic identified by that class an action that reflects a particular policy. A class is designated through class maps.

Figure 10-4   *Medium-Sized Organization with Three Zones*

An action is a specific functionality. It typically is associated with a traffic class. For example, **inspect**, **drop**, and **pass** are actions.

To create firewall policies, complete the following tasks:

Step 1.   Define a match criterion (class map).

Step 2.   Associate actions to the match criteria (policy map).

Step 3.   Attach the policy map to a zone pair (service policy).

A packet arriving at the target (such as the input interface, output interface, or zone pair) is checked against the match criterion that is configured for a class map to determine whether the packet belongs to that class. If so, the policy map defines the action that applies to the specific class. The assignment of the policy to zone pairs is configured using a service policy.

There are three major components to C3PL, as shown in Figure 10-5: class map, policy map, and service policy.

- Class maps: Identify traffic at OSI Layers 3 through 7. Use multiple matching criteria. — Classify Traffic / Class Map

- Policy maps: Define policy for traffic at Layers 3 through 7. — Define Actions / Policy Map

- Service policies: Activate policy maps for traffic flows on specific direction of zone pairs. — Activate Policy / Service Policy

Figure 10-5   *Components of Cisco Common Classification Policy Language*

Cisco Common Classification Policy Language policies are modular, object oriented, and hierarchical in nature:

- **Modular and object oriented:** These traits give the firewall administrator the flexibility to create building-block objects such as class maps and policy maps, and reuse them within a given policy and across policies.

- **Hierarchical:** This feature results in powerful policies that can be expanded to include customized inspection, application layer rules, and advanced inspection features. These advanced policies are outside the scope of this book, but are based on the hierarchical structure depicted in Figure 10-6.

Any given policy map is then applied to traffic flows that move in a given direction between zones by using service policies. The policy map processes traffic flows in that direction by matching sessions against one or more pre-created class map objects and performing access rule actions that are defined for each class.

As shown in Figure 10-6, policy maps can be thought as "if-then-else" statements, something similar to saying: "If a traffic flow matches the first class map, then the associated action is performed, and no other class map in the same policy is evaluated. Else, if the traffic flow matches the next class map in the configuration, then the associated action is performed." If traffic is not matched by any class map in a policy, a default action is performed.

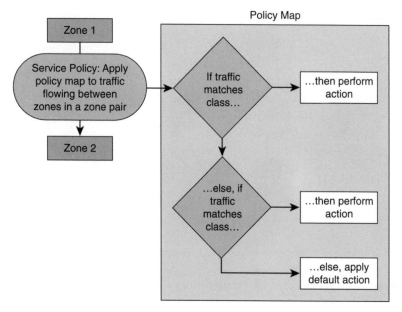

Figure 10-6 *C3PL: If-Then-Else Structure*

In Figure 10-7, two class maps—Class 1 and Class 2—are reused across policies Policy 1 and Policy 2. The class maps identity two different traffic classes that will be subject to a different policy for different interface pairs.

By the same token, the policy-level objects can also be reused. In Figure 10-7, the Policy 1 policy map is applied to two different zone pairs for the traffic source on the outside and moving toward the DMZ interfaces. However, only one of those DMZs is applied to the Policy 2 policy map, indicating a different set of policies for the same traffic in each instance.

The following are characteristics of class map objects that you should consider:

- Class maps that analyze Layer 3 and Layer 4 traffic sort the traffic based on the following criteria:

  - **Access-group:** A standard, extended, or named ACL can filter traffic based on source and destination IP addresses and source and destination ports.

■ **Protocol:** The class map can identify Layer 4 protocols such as TCP, UDP, and Internet Control Message Protocol (ICMP), and application services such as HTTP, Simple Mail Transfer Protocol (SMTP), and Domain Name System (DNS). Any well-known or user-defined service known to Port-to-Application Mapping (PAM) can be specified. PAM is used to support services that use port numbers that are different from the registered or well-known ports associated with a specific application: An example is an SMTP server listening at port 2525 instead of the standard port 25.

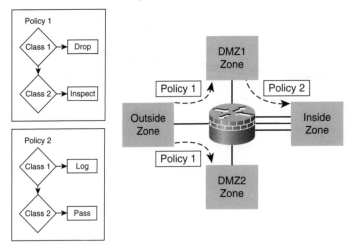

Figure 10-7 *Modular Object-Oriented Configuration Design*

■ **Class-map:** A subordinate class map that provides additional match criteria can be nested inside another class map.

■ Each class map can have multiple match statements, as shown in Figure 10-8. The match type defines how multiple match statements are processed to match the class:

■ If **match-any** is specified, traffic must meet any one of the match criteria in the class map.

■ If **match-all** is specified, traffic must match all of the class map criteria to belong to that particular class.

Figure 10-8 *Class Map with Multiple Match Statements*

Other considerations apply to policy map creation and usage:

- Class maps are evaluated in the order in which they are configured and added to the policy map. Consider pushing the more specific traffic classes to the top of the policy, while pushing the less generic traffic classes to the bottom.

- Possible actions are **inspect, pass,** and **drop** (and, optionally, **log** for dropped packets). These actions will be explained in more detail later in this section.

- In addition to user-defined classes, a system-defined class map named *class-default* represents all packets that do not match any of the user-defined classes in a policy, as shown in Figure 10-9. It is always the last class in a policy map. You can define explicit actions for this group of packets. If you do not configure any actions for class-default in an inspect policy, the default action is **drop.**

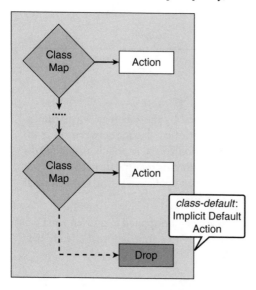

Figure 10-9   *Implicit Default Action of the class-default Map*

Zone-Based Policy Firewall Actions

The Cisco IOS Zone-Based Policy Firewall can take three possible actions when you configure it using CCP or the CLI:

- **inspect:** This action configures Cisco IOS stateful packet inspection.

- **drop:** This action is analogous to **deny** in an ACL. An additional **log** option can be added to **drop** to log dropped packets.

- **pass:** This action is analogous to **permit** in an ACL. The **pass** action does not track the state of connections or sessions within the traffic; **pass** allows the traffic only in one direction. A corresponding policy must be applied to allow return traffic to pass in the opposite direction.

Note   The **pass** action does not perform stateful inspection.

Note   Possible actions are **inspect**, **drop**, and **pass**, though some documentation might refer to **pass** as **permit**. Also remember that dropped packets can also be logged. So **log** can be considered as a fourth possible action, though only in combination with **drop**.

ZBF Terminology

When editing firewall policies, if you see:

Permit Firewall: Interpret this as "inspect according to class-map"

Permit ACL: Pass

Drop: Drop

Service Policy Zone Pair Assignments

Service policy assignments are unidirectional, as defined by the zone pair where the policy map is assigned. Remember, zone pairs define traffic behavior between zones in a unidirectional manner, based on source and destination zones. A policy map applied to a given zone pair will match traffic and perform action for that traffic in the direction defined by the zone pair. In other words, the policy map applies to traffic originating at the source zone and flowing toward the destination zone.

The final rule is that one and only one service policy can be applied to a given zone pair at any given time. If you apply a different service policy to a zone pair that already has one, you will overwrite the previous service policy.

Note   Zone pairs define traffic behavior between zones based on source and destination zones. There can be one and only one service policy per zone pair. The policy map applies to traffic originating at the source zone and flowing toward the destination zone.

Zone-Based Policy Firewall: Default Policies, Traffic Flows, and Zone Interaction

The membership of the router network interfaces in zones is subject to several rules governing interface behavior, as is the traffic moving between zone member interfaces:

- A zone must be configured before you can assign interfaces to the zone.

- You can assign an interface to only one security zone.

- Traffic is implicitly allowed to flow by default among interfaces that are members of the same zone.

- To permit traffic to and from a zone member interface, a policy allowing or inspecting traffic must be configured between that zone and any other zone.

- Traffic cannot flow between a zone member interface and any interface that is not a zone member. You can apply **pass, inspect,** and **drop** actions only between two zones.

- Interfaces that have not been assigned to a zone function as classical router ports and might still use classical stateful inspection (CBAC) configuration.

- If you do not want an interface on the router to be part of the zone-based firewall policy, it might still be necessary to put that interface in a zone and configure a "pass all" policy (sort of a dummy policy) between that zone and any other zone to which traffic flow is desired.

- From the preceding rules it follows that if traffic is to flow among all the interfaces in a router, all the interfaces must be part of the zoning model (each interface must be a member of a zone).

Table 10-1 shows a number of examples of different interface and configuration combinations.

Table 10-1   *Zone-Based Policy Firewall: Rules for Application Traffic*

Source Interface Member of Zone?	Destination Interface Member of Zone?	Zone Pair Exists?	Policy Exists?	Result
No	No	N/A	N/A	No impact of zoning/policy
Yes (zone 1)	Yes (zone 1)	N/A*	N/A	No policy lookup (pass)
Yes	No	N/A	N/A	Drop
No	Yes	N/A	N/A	Drop
Yes (zone 1)	Yes (zone 2)	No	N/A	Drop
Yes (zone 1)	Yes (zone 2)	Yes	No	Drop
Yes (zone 1)	Yes (zone 2)	Yes	Yes	Policy actions

* A zone pair must have different zones as the source and destination.

Zone-Based Policy Firewall: Rules for Router Traffic

The rules for a zone-based policy firewall are different when the router is involved in the traffic flow, whether as the source of traffic or the destination. A zone-based policy firewall is used to control router administration where the router is the destination. Table 10-2 illustrates various scenarios that involve traffic in or out of the router.

Table 10-2 *Zone-Based Policy Firewall: Rules for Router Traffic*

Source Interface Member of Zone?	Destination Interface Member of Zone?	Zone Pair Exists?	Policy Exists?	Result
Router (self)	Yes	No	N/A	Pass
Router (self)	Yes	Yes	No	Pass
Router (self)	Yes	Yes	Yes	Policy actions
Yes	Router (self)	No	N/A	Pass
Yes	Router (self)	Yes	No	Pass
Yes	Router (self)	Yes	Yes	Policy actions

When an interface is configured to be a zone member, the hosts connected to the interface are included in the zone, but traffic flowing to and from the interfaces of the router is not controlled by the zone policies. Instead, all the IP interfaces on the router are automatically made part of the self zone when a zone-based policy firewall is configured. To limit IP traffic moving to the IP addresses of the router from the various zones on a router, policies must be applied to block, allow, or inspect traffic between the zone and the self zone of the router, and vice versa. If there are no policies between a zone and the self zone, all traffic is permitted to the interfaces of the router without being inspected.

If desired, you can define a policy using the self zone as either the source or destination zone. The self zone is a system-defined zone. It does not require any interfaces to be configured as members. A zone pair that includes the self zone, along with the associated policy, applies to traffic that is directed to the router or to traffic that the router generates. It does not apply to traffic traversing the router.

The following are additional rules for zone-based policy firewalls that govern interface behavior when the router is involved in the traffic flow:

■ All traffic to and from a given interface is implicitly blocked when the interface is assigned to a zone, except traffic to or from other interfaces in the same zone, and traffic to any interface on the router.

■ All the IP interfaces on the router are automatically made part of the self zone when a zone-based policy firewall is configured. The self zone is the only exception to the default deny-all policy. All traffic to any router interface is allowed until traffic is explicitly denied.

The following considerations should be weighted when designing Cisco IOS Zone-Based Policy Firewalls:

- An interface can be assigned to one zone and one zone only.

- An interface pair can be assigned one policy and one policy only.

- Consider default traffic flows for interfaces without zones, traffic flows between zones, and traffic flows to or from the router interfaces themselves.

- Inspection actions cannot be applied to the class-default class.

- The default policy action for unclassified traffic is **drop**.

Watch for Misconfiguration

It is considered a misconfiguration to put an **inspect** action from the self zone (the router) to another zone or, vice versa, to put an **inspect** action from a zone to the self zone. The results will vary.

Configuring Basic Interzone Policies Using CCP and the CLI

The CCP Firewall Wizard helps you to implement a firewall. The wizard walks you through creating the firewall by asking you for information about the interfaces on the router, whether you want to configure a DMZ network, and what rules you want to use in the firewall.

CCP Demo Mode

Recall from Chapter 3 that a Demo Mode version of CCP is available for practice. For a helpful tutorial on CCP Demo Mode, check out Parts I and II of "Cisco Configuration Professional Demo Mode," by Doug McKillip of Global Knowledge, the URLs for which are provided in the "References" section toward the end of this chapter.

The configuration scenario shown in Figure 10-10 depicts a simple policy for a remote location that uses an untrusted network for corporate connectivity. We will configure two zones: the inside zone, which includes internal, trusted LAN interfaces, and the outside zone, which represents the untrusted network. The goal is to configure zone-based policy firewall rules that allow selected traffic to travel outbound from inside zone interfaces, while being inspected by the firewall. Inbound traffic, originating at the untrusted, outside interfaces, should be denied and logged.

Using the scenario in Figure 10-10, we will use CCP to configure and verify the firewall, and we will use the CLI to verify the configuration.

Figure 10-10 *Cisco IOS Zone-Based Firewall Configuration Scenario*

The CCP Firewall Wizard is available in two versions, Basic Firewall and Advanced Firewall. We will use the Basic Firewall wizard. These are the steps to configure a firewall using the Basic Firewall wizard:

Step 1. Start the Basic Firewall wizard.

Step 2. Select trusted and untrusted interfaces.

Step 3. Review and verify the resulting policies.

Step 4. (Optional) Enable logging.

Step 5. View firewall status and activity.

Step 6. (Optional) Modify basic policy objects.

Step 7. Verify CLI configuration.

The CCP Basic Firewall wizard will perform the specific operations related to zone-based policy firewalls. The operations include creating zones, creating zone pairs, creating C3PL components (class maps, policy maps, and service policies), and assembling the command hierarchy that implements the zone-based access control policy.

Step 1: Start the Basic Firewall Wizard

The first step is to access and run the Basic Firewall wizard, which you access by navigating to **Configure > Security > Firewall > Firewall**, clicking the **Create Firewall** tab, and then clicking the **Basic Firewall** radio button, as shown in Figure 10-11. To run the wizard, click the **Launch the Selected Task** button. The Basic Firewall wizard asks you to identify the interfaces on your router, and then it uses CCP default access rules and inspection rules to create the firewall. (The Advanced Firewall wizard, on the other hand, shows you the default inspection rules and allows you to use them in the firewall or create your own inspection rules.) CCP will use a default access rule in the firewall.

Figure 10-11   *Starting the Basic Firewall Wizard*

Note   The LAN and WAN configurations must be complete before you can configure a firewall.

Step 2: Select Trusted and Untrusted Interfaces

The first step of the Basic Firewall wizard is to identify the interfaces on the router so that the firewall will be applied to the correct interfaces, as shown in Figure 10-12. The following interface categories are available:

■ **Outside (untrusted) interface:** Select the router interface that is connected to the Internet or to your organization's WAN.

Note   Do not select the interface through which you accessed CCP as the outside (untrusted) interface. Doing so will cause you to lose your connection to CCP. Because it will be protected by a firewall, you will not be able to launch CCP from the outside (untrusted) interface after the Firewall Wizard completes.

■ **Inside (trusted) interfaces:** Check the physical and logical interfaces connecting to the LAN. You can select multiple interfaces.

The first page of the wizard also has an Allow Secure Cisco CP Access from Outside Interfaces check box. Check this box if you want users outside the firewall to be able to access the router using CCP. The wizard will display a screen that allows you to specify a host IP address or a network address. The firewall will be modified to allow access to the address you specify. If you specify a network address, all hosts on that network will be allowed through the firewall.

Click **Next** when you are finished identifying interfaces.

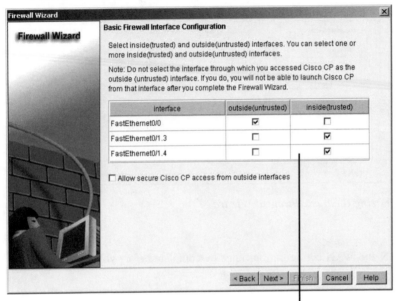

Interfaces are added to
automatically created zones.

Figure 10-12 *Selecting Trusted and Untrusted Interfaces*

The next screen of the wizard allows you to specify more lenient or strict firewall policies to match your requirements, as shown in Figure 10-13. Three levels are available, implementing the following policies:

- High Security

  - The router identifies inbound and outbound instant messaging and peer-to-peer traffic and drops it.

  - The router checks inbound and outbound HTTP traffic and email traffic for protocol compliance, and drops noncompliant traffic.

  - The router returns traffic for other TCP and UDP applications if the session was initiated inside the firewall.

- Choose this option if you want to prevent use of these applications on the network.

- Medium Security

  - The router identifies inbound and outbound instant messaging and peer-to-peer traffic, and checks inbound and outbound HTTP traffic and email traffic for protocol compliance.

  - The router returns TCP and UDP traffic on sessions initiated inside the firewall.

  - Choose this option if you want to track use of these applications on the network.

- Low Security

  - The router does not identify application-specific traffic.

  - The router returns TCP and UDP traffic on sessions initiated inside the firewall.

  - Choose this option if you do not need to track use of these applications on the network.

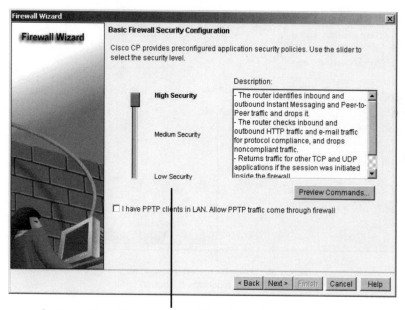

Customizable policies result from different security levels.

Figure 10-13 *Defining Security Levels for the Policy*

High Security Setting

The High Security setting enables many deep packet inspection features. Some 300 commands are then sent to the router to secure it. Use prudence with the High Security setting because it takes drastic steps to secure your firewall and the traffic going through it. Test amply in a lab environment before implementing it in a production environment. Be sure to preview the commands during your test, and to research them prior to implementing.

Step 3: Review and Verify the Resulting Policies

Click **Next**, and the wizard ends by displaying the configuration and settings, as shown in Figure 10-14. Click **Finish** to continue.

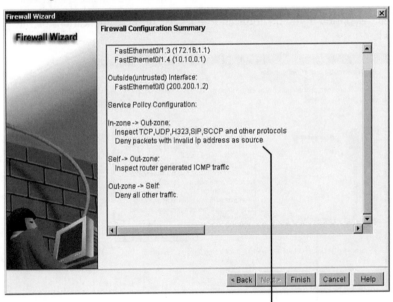

Automatic policy is created, allowing all
outbound traffic and blocking all inbound traffic.

Figure 10-14 *Reviewing the Wizard Configuration Resulting from Selecting the Low Security Setting*

Verifying and Tuning the Configuration

Firewall verification can be accomplished using several CCP tools. You can view the configured policies by navigating to **Configure > Security > Firewall > Firewall** and clicking the **Edit Firewall Policy** tab, as shown in Figure 10-15. Use this tab to view the access and inspection rules in a context that displays the interfaces that the rules are associated with. You can also use it to modify the access and inspection rules that are displayed.

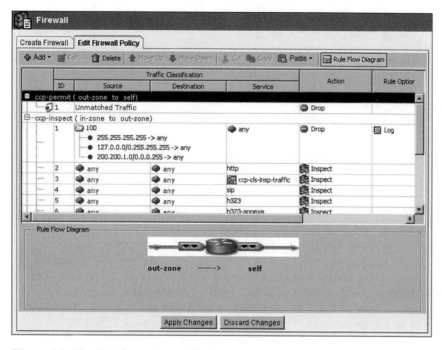

Figure 10-15 *Verifying Firewall Policies Using CCP*

Unmatched Traffic

Traffic that does not match any inspection rules which are created dynamically from allowed outbound traffic may be allowed inbound in a non-stateful manner, as long as the ACLs assigned to the interfaces permit the traffic bidirectionally.

Once the configuration is completed using CCP, you will want to turn on logging to monitor the status and activities of the firewall by viewing the logs. Depending on your findings, you might want to modify the zone-based firewall configuration.

Step 4: Enabling Logging

Activity on the firewall is monitored through the creation of log entries. If logging is enabled on the router, then whenever an access rule that is configured to generate log entries is invoked—for example, a connection is attempted from a denied IP address—a log entry is generated and can be viewed in monitor mode.

Before you attempt to view the firewall log, you must enable logging by navigating to **Configure > Router > Logging**. Then, follow these steps:

Step 1.   On the **Additional Tasks > Logging** screen, shown in the background of Figure 10-16, select **Logging to Buffer** and click **Edit** to open the Logging dialog box, shown in the foreground.

Step 2. In the Buffer Size field, enter the amount of router memory that you want to use for a logging buffer. The default value is 4096 bytes. A larger buffer will store more log entries, but you must balance your need for a larger logging buffer against potential router performance issues. Leave the other settings to their default values.

Step 3. Click **OK**.

Logging to the Console and Logging Dropped Packets

As explained in Chapter 4, it is preferable to send logging results to vty sessions rather than to the console port. The console port performs at a much lower speed than vty lines. If you decide nevertheless to send logs to the console port, use a lower level than debugging. Use at most the informational logging level.

Earlier in this chapter, we saw that it is possible to log packets that are dropped based on the policy. Though we haven't looked at the CLI for ZBF, the command would look like this: Router(config-pmap-c)# **drop log**. This log action is available for packets that are dropped because they match a policy that *explicitly* says to drop the packets. Malformed or noncompliant packets dropped by the firewall, such as those with invalid UDP Header length, incompatible TCP options, and so forth, are not logged. To see packets dropped by the firewall, use the global command **ip inspect log drop-pkt**.

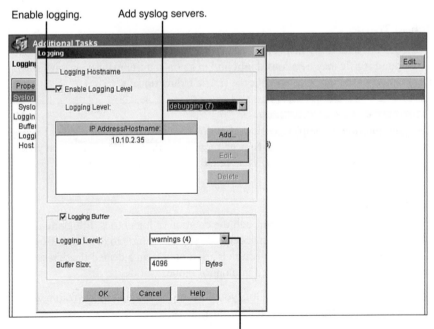

Figure 10-16 *Enabling Logging to the Buffer*

Step 5: Verifying Firewall Status and Activity

You can now view the firewall status and logs at **Monitor > Security > Firewall Status**. In the firewall statistics display, shown in Figure 10-17, you can verify that your firewall is configured and view how many connection attempts have been denied. The table shows each router log entry that is generated by the firewall, including the time and the reason that the log entry was generated.

Note   The default rule that is created by the Basic Firewall wizard enables logging for denied actions, and this log will display those messages. If logging is not enabled at the policy level, you will have to modify the policy maps to enable logging as an additional action.

Figure 10-17   *Verifying Firewall Status and Activity*

Viewing Firewall Logs

Firewall logs can also be viewed by navigating to **Monitor > Router > Logging > Firewall Log**. The log entries are determined by log messages generated by the firewall. In order for the firewall to generate log entries, you must configure the following:

- Logging for the router. To obtain firewall logging messages, you must configure a logging level of debugging (7).

- Individual access rules to generate log messages when they are invoked.

The top-attacks table below the View drop-down menu displays the top attack entries. You can use the View drop-down menu to switch from a port-based report to an attacker-based report, which displays the IP addresses of the top attackers.

Note Log entries are not refreshed automatically. You must click Update to refresh the view and display newly generated entries.

Step 6: Modifying Zone-Based Firewall Configuration Objects

The optional step of modifying zone-based policy firewall base objects uses the Configure > Security >Firewall > Firewall Components > Zones navigation option. This step allows you to add or change zones; add or modify zone pairs, as shown in the upper-right side of Figure 10-18; or add or modify C3PL objects (class maps, policy maps, and service policies), as shown in the bottom portion of Figure 10-18.

Add or Edit Zones

Figure 10-18 *Modifying ZBF Configuration Objects*

General Steps to Create ZBF

ZBF policies are built from the bottom up. You first define the class map, which specifies interesting traffic for the policy maps. You then define the policy maps, specifying which actions to take on the traffic defined in the class maps. Then, the zone pairs reference both the policy maps and the zones. The following list shows the sequence of what is created and referenced:

1. ACL to identify the traffic

2. Zones

3. Class map

4. Policy map (actions can be **inspect**, **pass**, and **drop**, and dropped traffic can also be logged)

5. Zone pair (policy map + zones)

Step 7: Verifying the Configuration Using the CLI

Example 10-1 shows an example of what the resulting CLI commands might look like after configuring a Cisco IOS Zone-Based Policy Firewall that uses two interfaces and the default inspection parameters. The breakdown is as follows:

First, the class map named OUTBOUND-PROTOCOLS is created. It identifies three protocols that are to be inspected: HTTP, SMTP, and FTP.

A policy map named ACCESS-POLICY is created. It applies stateful inspection to the protocols that are listed in the OUTBOUND-PROTOCOLS class map.

Two zones, named PRIVATE and INTERNET, are created. FastEthernet 0/0 is made a member of the PRIVATE zone and FastEthernet 0/1 is made a member of the INTERNET zone.

Finally, a zone pair named PRIV-TO-INTERNET is created with a source zone of PRIVATE, a destination zone of INTERNET, and the policy map ACCESS-POLICY applied to it.

Example 10-1   *Commands of a Basic Cisco IOS Zone-Based Policy Firewall Configuration*

```
class-map type inspect match-any OUTBOUND-PROTOCOLS
 match protocol http
 match protocol smtp
 match protocol ftp
!
policy-map type inspect ACCESS-POLICY
 class type inspect OUTBOUND-PROTOCOLS
 inspect
```

```
!
zone security PRIVATE
zone security INTERNET
!
interface fastethernet 0/0
 zone-member security PRIVATE
!
interface serial 0/0/0
 zone-member security INTERNET
!
zone-pair security PRIV-TO-INTERNET source PRIVATE destination INTERNET
 service-policy type inspect ACCESS-POLICY
!
```

Configuring NAT Services for Zone-Based Firewalls

Network Address Translation (NAT) can be added to zone-based firewall configurations by applying NAT rules at the interface level for interfaces that belong to zones. The configuration scenario that is shown in Figure 10-19 illustrates an example of outbound dynamic Port Address Translation (PAT), where trusted hosts on the inside zone are translated dynamically, using PAT, to the IP address on the router's untrusted interfaces, in this example FastEthernet 0/1.

Figure 10-19 *NAT with ZBF Configuration Scenario*

There are three main steps to configure a NAT with Cisco IOS zone-based firewall:

Step 1.   Run the Basic NAT wizard.

Step 2.   Select NAT interfaces:

- Outside interface with global IP address

- Inside interface with original IP address

Step 3.   Verify the configuration.

Step 1: Run the Basic NAT Wizard

The first step is to access and run the Basic NAT wizard by navigating to **Configure > Router > NAT** and clicking the **Create NAT Configuration** tab, as shown in Figure 10-20. The options include the following:

- **Basic NAT:** Choose the Basic NAT wizard if you want to connect your network to the Internet (or the outside), and your network has hosts but no servers. Look at the sample diagram that appears to the right when you choose Basic NAT. If your network is made up only of PCs that require access to the Internet, choose **Basic NAT** and click **Launch.**

- **Advanced NAT:** Choose the Advanced NAT wizard if you want to connect your network to the Internet (or the outside), and your network has hosts and servers, and the servers must be accessible to outside hosts (hosts on the Internet). Look at the sample diagram that appears to the right when you choose Advanced NAT.

Click the **Launch the Selected Task** button to launch the wizard.

Figure 10-20   *Starting the Basic NAT Wizard*

Step 2: Select NAT Inside and Outside Interfaces

The only configuration that is needed in the Basic NAT wizard is the definition of original versus translated interfaces:

- From the drop-down menu, shown in Figure 10-21, choose the outside interface, which connects to the Internet or untrusted network. This is the router's WAN interface.

- From the list of available networks, shown with check boxes, choose which networks will share the WAN interface in the NAT configuration. To choose a network, check its check box in the list of available networks.

Note   Do not choose a network that is connected to the WAN interface set up in this NAT configuration. Remove that network from the NAT configuration by unchecking its check box.

The list of available networks shows the following information for each network:

- IP address range allocated to the network

- Network LAN interface

- Comments entered about the network

To remove a network from the NAT configuration, uncheck its check box.

Note   If Cisco Configuration Professional detects a conflict between the NAT configuration and an existing virtual private network (VPN) configuration for the WAN interface, it will inform you with a dialog box after you click Next. The only configuration that is needed in the Basic NAT wizard is the definition of original versus translated interfaces.

Click **Next**, and the wizard ends with a summary of the configuration, as shown in Figure 10-22. Click **Finish**.

Select the Internet-facing interface from the list (outside).

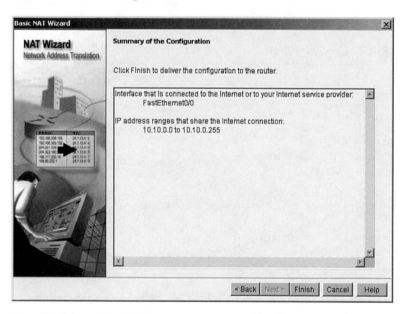

Figure 10-21 *Starting the Basic NAT Wizard*

Figure 10-22 *Finishing the Wizard*

Step 3: Verify NAT with CCP and the CLI

Verification can be accomplished by looking at the various NAT rules, found by navigating to **Configure > Router > NAT** and clicking the **Edit NAT Configuration** tab, as shown in Figure 10-23.

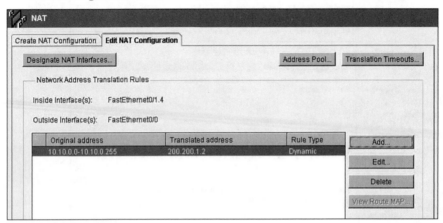

Figure 10-23   *Verifying NAT Configuration with CCP*

The resulting CLI configuration is shown in Example 10-2. Notice the commands **ip nat outside** and **ip nat inside**, which define the location of original and translated IPv4 addresses. Also notice that the original addresses are matched using an ACL, list number 1 in Example 10-2.

Example 10-2   *NAT CLI Configuration*

```
interface FastEthernet0/0
 ip address 200.200.1.2 255.255.255.0
 ip nat outside
!
interface FastEthernet0/1.4
 ip address 10.10.0.1 255.255.255.0
 ip nat inside
!
ip nat inside source list 1 interface FastEthernet0/0 overload
!
access-list 1 permit 10.10.0.0 0.0.0.255
!
```

The **show ip nat translations** command, shown in Example 10-3, displays the current translation for live traffic, including parameters such as inside local, inside global, outside local, and outside global addresses, as well as local and global ports.

Example 10-3   *Current Translation for Live Traffic*

```
Router# show ip nat translations
Pro Inside global      Inside local      Outside local    Outside global
TCP 200.200.1.51:1050  10.10.10.20:1050  75.75.75.750:23  172.16.100.10:23
TCP 200.200.1.52:1776  10.10.10.10:1776  150.150.1.40:25  150.150.1.40:25
```

ZBF: Work in Progress

Cisco keeps coming out with improvements to ZBF. One of the latest improvements, which came out with Cisco IOS Release 15, is intrazone support, which allows for zone configuration to include users both inside and outside a network. This allows for traffic inspection between users belonging to the same zone but different networks. Check Cisco.com regularly for updates to ZBF.

Cisco ASA Firewall

Cisco ASA 5505 Adaptive Security Appliance (ASA) implements a rich set of security technologies and can be effectively implemented as a perimeter firewall using several deployment modes. This section introduces Cisco ASA functionality, features, and underlying technologies. This section will demonstrate how to configure the Cisco ASA 5505 model for basic connectivity using Cisco Adaptive Security Device Manager (ASDM).

Cisco ASA 5500 Series are easy-to-deploy solutions that integrate a world-class firewall, Cisco Unified Communications (voice and video) security, Secure Sockets Layer (SSL) and IP Security (IPsec) VPNs, intrusion prevention systems (IPS), and content security services in a flexible, modular product family. The Cisco ASA 5500 Series provides intelligent threat defense and secure communications services that stop attacks before they affect business continuity. Designed to protect networks of all sizes, Cisco ASA 5500 Series security appliances enable organizations to lower their overall deployment and operations costs while delivering comprehensive multilayer security.

Cisco ASAs scale to meet a range of requirements and network sizes. At the time of publication, the Cisco ASA 5500 Series includes the Cisco ASA 5505, 5510, 5512-X, 5515-X, 5520, 5525-X, 5540, 5545-X, 5550, and 5555-X, the four different footprints of the 5585-X (each one offering a different footprint of the Security Services Processor, or SSP), and the ASA Security Services Modules.

Stateful Packet Filtering and Application Awareness

The Cisco ASA security appliance is fundamentally a stateful packet filter with application inspection and control, with a rich set of additional integrated software and hardware features that enable you to expand its functionality beyond those fundamental filtering mechanisms.

The heart of the Cisco ASA is an application-aware stateful packet inspection algorithm, which controls flows between networks that are controlled by the security appliance. The connection-oriented stateful packet inspection algorithm design creates session flows based on source and destination addresses and ports. The information is kept in a state table, as shown in Figure 10-24. The stateful packet inspection algorithm randomizes TCP sequence numbers, port numbers, and additional TCP flags before completion of the connection. This function is always in operation, monitoring return packets to ensure that they are valid, and it transparently allows any additional dynamic transport layer sessions of the same application session. This fundamental function of the security appliance allows you to minimize host and application exposure and only allow the minimal traffic on OSI network and transport layers that is required to support your applications.

Figure 10-24   *State Table Created for All Inspected Traffic*

Interface Names

You will also notice in Figure 10-24 that interfaces receive names. With the Cisco ASA, to pass traffic, an interface needs to have a name (configured with the **nameif** command), and if you wish to route IP traffic, that interface also needs an IP address, which we will cover later. The **nameif inside** command assigns automatically the security level 100. This topic will be discussed later in this section.

Network Services Offered by the Cisco ASA 5500 Series

The Cisco ASA 5500 series offers services in addition to firewalling. Some of those additional services, examined in this section, are NAT, DHCP server, and routing.

Network Address Translation

The Cisco ASA security appliance includes support for many different varieties of NAT.

Cisco ASA Pre-8.3 to 8.3 NAT

Cisco has significantly changed the way NAT is done, starting with Cisco ASA version 8.3. If you have invested time and effort learning NAT pre-8.3, read the document "ASA Pre-8.3 to 8.3 NAT Configuration Examples," found at https://supportforums.cisco.com/docs/DOC-9129. There is also a good video to help you make the transition, "Cisco ASA Version 8.3 and 8.4 NAT Configuration Example," available at https://supportforums.cisco.com/docs/DOC-12324. The terminology has changed with NAT 8.3. As an example, if you run Packet Tracer (a troubleshooting tool covered later in this chapter), you might notice the term UN-NAT, which refers to a packet using its real IP address and port (typically the private IP address). Another significant change with version 8.3 is that NAT exemption, introduced with Cisco ASA 7.0, is no longer used. For detailed information about Cisco ASA 8.3 NAT, refer to *CCNP Security FIREWALL 642-618 Official Cert Guide* (Cisco Press, 2012).

Another substantial difference with 8.3 is that when creating an ACL, you must always use the real IP address, whereas in pre-8.3, the IP address had to be either the real IP address or the NATted IP address, depending on where the ACL was applied.

Note that for the purpose of passing the IINSv2 certification exam, knowing the material presented in this section suffices.

These different varieties of NAT allow for flexible deployment of NAT services:

- **Inside and outside NAT:** These terms are typically used in reference to the physical location of the hosts that require and use NAT services. If the host resides on the inside network and its address is translated for outbound traffic flows, inside NAT is used. If the host resides on the outside network and its address is translated for inbound traffic flows, outside NAT is used. The terminology of inside and outside NAT has its origins in how the interfaces were named by the Cisco ASA predecessor, the PIX Firewall; this nomenclature is still used today: inside interface and outside interface. The inside interface, as its name implies, is the secure side of the firewall. The outside interface points to the less secure side of the firewall, usually the Internet.

- **Dynamic NAT and PAT:** Dynamic NAT translates a group of real addresses to a pool of mapped addresses that are routable on the destination network. The mapped pool may include fewer addresses than the real group, in which case source ports are used to map multiple local addresses to one or a few global addresses. When a host that you want to translate accesses the destination network, the Cisco ASA assigns to the host an IP address from the mapped pool. The translation is added only when the real host initiates the connection. The translation is in place only for the duration of the connection, and a given user does not keep the same IP address after the translation times out. Users on the destination network, therefore, cannot initiate a reliable connection to a host that uses dynamic NAT, although the connection is allowed by an ACL, and the Cisco ASA rejects any attempt to connect to a real host address directly. If all the real addresses are translated to one single IP address instead of a pool of multiple addresses, it is then referred to as Dynamic PAT. On a Cisco ASA firewall, the default dynamic NAT timeout is 3 hours. That is, after 3 hours of no activity seen for a translated address, the entry is removed from the translation table. This timer is adjustable. Note that on the Cisco IOS router, the default idle timeout for translation is 24 hours.

- **Static NAT and PAT:** Static NAT creates a fixed translation of real addresses to mapped addresses. With dynamic NAT and PAT, each host uses a different address or port for each subsequent translation. Because the mapped address is the same for each consecutive connection with static NAT, and a persistent translation rule exists, static NAT allows hosts on the destination network to initiate traffic to a translated host, if an ACL exists that allows it.

  The main difference between using dynamic NAT and using a range of addresses for static NAT is that static NAT allows a remote host to initiate a connection to a translated host (if an ACL exists that allows it), while dynamic NAT does not. You also need an equal number of mapped addresses as real addresses with static NAT.

  Static PAT is the same as static NAT, except that it lets you specify the protocol (TCP or UDP) and port for the real and mapped addresses.

- **Policy NAT:** Policy NAT lets you identify real addresses for address translation by specifying the source and destination addresses. You can also optionally specify the source and destination ports. Regular NAT can consider only the source addresses and cannot consider the destination. For example, with policy NAT, you can translate the real address to mapped address A when it accesses server A, and translate the real address to mapped address B when it accesses server B.

- **NAT exemption:** NAT exemption exempts addresses from translation and allows both real and remote hosts to originate connections. NAT exemption lets you specify the real and destination addresses when determining the real traffic to exempt (similar to policy NAT), so you have greater control using NAT exemption than dynamic identity NAT. However, unlike policy NAT, NAT exemption does not consider the ports.

Cisco ASA Connection Table

In addition to the translation table kept by the Cisco ASA, which you can look at with the **show xlate** command, the Cisco ASA maintains a connection table. You can see it with the **show conn** command. A TCP connection has a 1-hour idle timeout. A UDP connection has a 2-minutes idle timeout. These default timeouts are adjustable.

Additional Network Services

The Cisco ASA can provide a DHCP server or DHCP relay services to DHCP clients attached to Cisco ASA interfaces. The DHCP server provides network configuration parameters directly to DHCP clients. DHCP relay passes DHCP requests received on one interface to a DHCP server located behind a different interface. DHCP relay takes a DHCP broadcast and forwards it to the DHCP server located on a different network as a unicast. You can configure a DHCP server on each interface of the Cisco ASA. Each interface can have its own pool of addresses to draw from.

The Cisco ASA security appliance supports Routing Information Protocol (RIP) (versions 1 and 2), Open Shortest Path First (OSPF), and Enhanced Interior Gateway Routing Protocol (EIGRP) dynamic routing protocols to integrate into existing routing infrastructures. Where dynamic routing is not available, the Cisco ASA security appliance can use static routing instead.

Cisco ASA Security Technologies

Many other features and technologies are available in Cisco ASA. The appliances implement a rich set of firewall and security features. Some of these features are enabled by default, while others can be enabled to implement multiple levels of access and threat control and protection. In addition to the basic security features presented in this section, the following functions are available in Cisco ASAs:

- Stateful inspection and application level controls
  - ACL packet filtering
  - Object groups
  - Application Inspection and Control (AIC)
  - User-based access control (cut-through proxy)
  - Identity firewall
  - Session auditing
- Threat control and containment
  - IPS via Cisco ASA Advanced Inspection and Prevention Security Services Module (AIP-SSM) and Advanced Inspection and Prevention Security Services Card (AIP-SSC)
  - Botnet traffic filtering
  - Category-based URL filtering
  - Threat detection (basic, advanced, scanning)

- Network integration

  - Virtualization

  - Security modules

  - IPv6 and multicast support

  - NAT and DHCP services

  - Site-to-site and remote-access IPsec and SSL VPNs

  - Transparent firewall mode

  - IP routing

  - High-availability failover

The majority of these advanced functions and features are beyond the scope of this book and are covered in Cisco Press's *CCNP Security FIREWALL 642-618 Official Cert Guide*.

Cisco ASA Configuration Fundamentals

In Cisco ASA, default and custom access rules are based on interface security levels. Security levels define the level of trustworthiness of an interface, and help implement a layered, defense-in-depth approach to security. The higher the level, the more trusted the interface. The numbers themselves are not really important, but the relationship between the numbers is. In that sense, traffic flows are defined as inbound or outbound like this:

- **Inbound traffic:** Travels from a less trusted interface to a more trusted interface; that is, from a lower security level to a higher security level

- **Outbound traffic:** Travels from a more trusted interface to a less trusted interface; that is, from a higher security level to a lower security level

Each interface must have a security level from 0 (lowest) to 100 (highest). For example, as shown in Figure 10-24, you should assign your most secure network, such as the inside host network, to level 100, while the outside network connected to the Internet can be level 0. Other networks, such as DMZs, can be in between. You can assign interfaces to the same security level, but additional configuration will be needed for traffic to traverse interfaces of the same security level.

Default Security Policy

Security levels define default behavior and processing of traffic flows. Merely by assigning numbers to interfaces, this policy applies the following:

- Outbound traffic is allowed and inspected by default.

- Returning traffic is allowed because of stateful packet inspection.

- Inbound traffic is denied by default.

- When you access the Cisco ASA (for management), you have to access the nearest interface.

Remembering the Default Security Policy

Remember this rhyme: "High to low, good to go. Low to high, must die." In other words, traffic entering by an interface with security level 100 and leaving the interface with security level 0 is allowed and the returning traffic can come in. However, traffic originating from an interface with security level 50 destined for an interface with security level 100 would by default be denied.

The security level controls the following behavior:

- **Network access:** By default, there is an implicit permit from a higher security interface to a lower security interface (outbound). Hosts on the higher security interface can access any host on a lower security interface. You can limit access by applying an ACL to the interface. If you enable communication for same security level interfaces, there is an implicit permit for interfaces to access other interfaces on the same security level or lower.

- **Inspection engines:** Some application inspection engines are dependent on the security level. For same security level interfaces, inspection engines apply to traffic in either direction.

    - **NetBIOS inspection engine:** Applied only for outbound connections.

    - **SQL*Net inspection engine:** If a control connection for the SQL*Net (formerly OraServ) port exists between a pair of hosts, then only an inbound data connection is permitted through the Cisco ASA.

- **Filtering:** As an example, HTTP(S) and FTP filtering applies to outbound connections (from a higher level to a lower level). If you enable communication for same security level interfaces, you can filter traffic in either direction.

Figure 10-25 illustrates an example of security levels in action.

Figure 10-25   *Cisco ASA Security Levels and Interface Names*

The traffic flows from the inside network to the outside network are permitted by default, because they go from more trusted to less trusted interfaces. In a real network, this means that internal users on the inside interface can access resources on the DMZ freely. They can also initiate connections to the Internet with no restrictions and without the need for an additional policy or additional commands.

By the same token, traffic that is sourced on the outside network, originating from the Internet and going into either the DMZ or the inside network, is denied by default. Return traffic, however, originating on the inside network and returning via the outside interface, would be allowed.

These default traffic flows match the requirements of real-life networks. It is worth noting that firewalls should not be the only security countermeasure in your security architecture. A sound security policy, along with effective countermeasures, should be put in place. For instance, a restrictive policy for outbound traffic should be implemented to overwrite the default permissive behavior based on security levels, to prevent malicious attackers from initiating attacks from the inside network and abusing the default policies based on those security levels.

Managing the Cisco ASA Using the CLI

Cisco ASAs contain a command set that is based on Cisco IOS Software. The appliance provides five configuration modes, similar to Cisco IOS devices:

- ROM monitor mode
- User EXEC mode
- Privileged EXEC mode
- Global configuration mode
- Specific configuration modes

Upon first accessing a Cisco ASA, you are presented with a standard prompt, as shown in Figure 10-26. Multiple configuration and monitoring modes are available at this point:

- **EXEC mode:** Allows view-only capabilities on a restricted group of settings.

- **Privileged EXEC mode:** Expands the set of available commands and settings in EXEC mode to a set with full administrative privileges. It also allows for maintenance actions in addition to the read-only and monitoring capabilities.

- **Global configuration mode:** Allows changes to the system configuration.

- **Component-specific configuration modes:** Allow changes to specific components, such as interfaces.

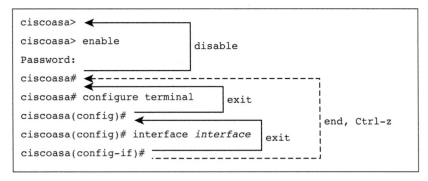

Figure 10-26 *Cisco ASA Prompts*

You can transition between modes using these commands and keystrokes:

- Use the **enable** command to access the privileged EXEC mode.

- Use **exit** or **disable** to return to the user EXEC mode.

- Use **configure terminal** to access the global configuration mode.

- Use **exit** to exit from global configuration mode, or to exit from a component-specific configuration mode into the previous level.

- Use Ctrl-Z or **end** to exit any configuration mode, any number of levels deep, and return to privileged EXEC mode.

Cisco ASA 5505

The Cisco ASA 5505 is designed for small offices, home offices, and enterprise teleworker environments. As shown in Figure 10-27, the appliance showcases an eight-port built-in Layer 2 switch that provides flexible VLAN configuration. Two of the ports are Power over Ethernet capable, and all of the ports can be assigned to specific VLANs to implement outside, inside, and DMZ subnets. Layer 2 ports are assigned to VLANs, and VLAN interfaces are created for Layer 3 connectivity. VLAN interfaces are used to assign IP addresses, security levels, and other Layer 3 components.

Figure 10-27   *Cisco ASA 5505*

There are two types of ports and interfaces to configure:

- **Physical switch ports:** The eight Fast Ethernet switch ports of the Cisco ASA forward traffic at Layer 2, using the switching function in hardware. You can configure these interfaces either in access mode or as trunk ports.

- **Logical VLAN interfaces:** Logical VLAN interfaces forward traffic between VLANs at Layer 3, using the configured security policy to apply firewall and VPN services. VLAN interfaces let you divide your Cisco ASA 5505 into separate VLANs, such as home, business, and Internet VLANs.

To segregate the switch ports into separate VLANs, you assign each switch port to a VLAN interface. Switch ports on the same VLAN can communicate with one another using hardware switching. However, when a switch port on VLAN 1 wants to communicate with a switch port on VLAN 2, for instance, the Cisco ASA applies the security policy to the traffic and routes or bridges between the two VLANs.

Other components shown Figure 10-27 include the following:

- **Power connector:** Used for attaching the power cord

- **SSC slot:** Used to install the optional Cisco AIP SSC-5 network IPS module

- **Console port:** Used to connect a computer to the Cisco ASA 5505 using an RJ-45 cable for console operations

- **Reset button:** Reserved for future use

- **USB ports:** Reserved for future use

Cisco ASDM

Cisco ASDM is to the Cisco ASA what Switch Database Management (SDM) or CCP is to Cisco IOS routers, and more. It is a configuration tool that is designed to facilitate the setup, configuration, monitoring, and troubleshooting of Cisco ASAs. The application hides the complexity of commands from administrators, and allows streamlined configurations without requiring extensive knowledge of the security appliance CLI. Cisco

ASDM can be used to monitor and configure multiple security appliances that run the same ASDM version.

Cisco ASDM features include the following:

- Runs on a variety of platforms

- Implemented in Java to provide robust, real-time monitoring

- Works with SSL, as shown in Figure 10-28, to ensure secure communication with the security appliance

- Comes preloaded in flash memory on new Cisco ASA security appliances running version 7.0 or later

- Can manage multiple security appliances from a single ASDM interface, one at a time

- Cisco ASDM sessions:

    - Five Cisco ASDM sessions per unit (single mode) or context (multimode)

    - 32 sessions per unit in multimode

- Supported on all Cisco ASAs

Figure 10-28 *Cisco ASDM*

Cisco ASDM Demo Mode

Similar to the CCP Demo Mode version mentioned earlier in the chapter, Cisco ASDM also has a Demo Mode version. For a tutorial on how to install and use the ASDM Demo Mode, check out "ASDM Demo Mode Tour," also by Doug McKillip, the URL for which is provided in the "References" section at the end of this chapter.

Preparing the Cisco ASA 5505 for ASDM

Cisco ASDM access requires some minimal configuration so that you can communicate over the network with a management interface.

With a factory default configuration, you can connect to Cisco ASDM using the following interface and network settings:

- The management interface depends on your model:

  - **Cisco ASA 5505:** The switch port to which you connect to Cisco ASDM can be any port, except for Ethernet 0/0.

  - **Cisco ASA 5510 and later:** The interface to which you connect to Cisco ASDM is Management 0/0.

- The default management address is 192.168.1.1.

- The clients that are allowed to access Cisco ASDM must be on the 192.168.1.0/24 network.

Cisco ASA 5510 and Later and Cisco ASDM

With Cisco ASA 5510 and later, the firewall looks for an interface with the name Management for the setup to be allowed to run. The **nameif management** command doesn't need to be applied to the actual Management 0/0 interface for setup to run. It's not a significant issue, but interesting to know.

If you do not have a factory default configuration, or want to change the firewall or context mode, the following steps are required.

To run Cisco ASDM on a Cisco ASA 5505, perform the following steps:

Step 1.   Assign the name "inside" to one interface.

Step 2.   Run the interactive setup dialog using the **setup** command.

Step 3.   (Optional) Specify which Cisco ASDM image file to use.

Cisco ASDM Features and Menus

Once initialized and connected, the Cisco ASDM Home page, shown in Figure 10-29, lets you view important information about your Cisco ASA. Status information in the Home page is updated every 10 seconds. This page usually has two tabs, Device Dashboard and Firewall Dashboard. If you have a hardware module such as the CSC-SSM (Content Security and Control Security Service Module) installed in your Cisco ASA, the module-specific tab also appears in the Home page. The additional tab displays status information about the software on the specific module. If you have IPS software installed in your Cisco ASA, the Intrusion Prevention tab also appears in the Home page. The additional tab displays status information about the IPS software.

Figure 10-29 *Cisco ASDM Home Pane*

The Device Dashboard tab lets you view at a glance important information about your Cisco ASA, such as the status of your interfaces, the version you are running, licensing information, and performance.

The Cisco ASDM user interface is designed to provide easy access to the many features that the Cisco ASA supports. It includes the following elements, shown in Figure 10-30:

■ A menu bar that provides quick access to files, tools, wizards, and help. Many menu items also have keyboard shortcuts.

■ A toolbar that enables you to navigate Cisco ASDM. From the toolbar, you can access the Home, Configuration, and Monitoring pages. You can also get help and navigate between pages.

■ A dockable left navigation pane to move through the Configuration and Monitoring pages. You can click one of the buttons in the header to maximize or restore this pane, make it a floating pane that you can move, hide it, or close it. To access the Configuration and Monitoring pages, you can do one of the following:

■ Click links on the left side of the application window in the left navigation pane. The content pane then displays the path in the title bar of the selected pane.

■ If you know the exact path, you can type it directly into the title bar of the content pane on the right side of the application window, without clicking any links in the left navigation pane.

■ A maximize and restore button in the right corner of the content pane that lets you hide and show the left navigation pane.

■ A dockable Device List pane with a list of devices that you can access through Cisco ASDM. You can click one of the three buttons in the header to maximize or restore this pane, make it a floating pane that you can move, hide it, or close it.

■ A status bar at the bottom of the application window that shows the time, connection status, user, memory status, running configuration status, privilege level, and SSL status.

■ The left navigation pane, as mentioned earlier, that shows various objects that you can use in the rules tables when you create access rules, NAT rules, authentication, authorization, and accounting (AAA) rules, filter rules, and service rules. The tab titles within the pane change according to the feature that you are viewing. In addition, the Cisco ASDM Assistant appears in this pane.

■ Above the left navigation pane, but not shown in Figure 10-30, is an optional Device List useful when toggling between two or more firewall configurations.

Figure 10-30   *Cisco ASDM Interface Elements*

When deploying Cisco ASAs, your access policy is made up of one or more access rules per interface or globally for all interfaces. An access rule permits or denies traffic based on the protocol, a source and destination IP address or network, and, optionally, the source and destination ports. Note that global ACLs are only available starting with Cisco ASA version 8.3.

The order of rules is important. When the Cisco ASA decides whether to forward or drop a packet, the Cisco ASA tests the packet against each rule in the order in which the rules are listed, as shown in Figure 10-31. After a match is found, no more rules are checked. For example, if you create an access rule at the beginning that explicitly permits all traffic for an interface, no further rules are ever checked.

There is an implicit deny-all rule at the end of each interface access rule list. Therefore, if a connection does not match any of the rules, by default, it will be denied.

> **Note**   Interface access rules apply to through traffic—that is, traffic entering the appliance on one interface and then leaving the appliance on the same interface or another interface. Traffic that is directed to the IP addresses or interfaces of the appliance is not subject to these rules, and requires an additional set of rules to implement access control.

Action	Source Address	Destination Address	Service
DENY	10.1.1.0 255.255.255.0	192.168.1.0 255.255.255.0	Any
PERMIT	10.1.1.0 255.255.255.0	172.16.0.0 255.255.255.0.0	SSH
PERMIT	10.1.1.0 255.255.255.0	ANY	HTTP
DENY	ANY	ANY	ANY

Figure 10-31   *Example of Stateful Packet Filtering on Cisco ASA*

Access rules apply based on the security levels described earlier in this chapter. In that sense, these defaults apply if you do not apply an interface access ruleset to an interface:

- All outbound (that is, from higher to lower security level interfaces) connections for hosts on that interface are permitted.

- All inbound (that is, from lower to higher security level interfaces) connections for hosts on that interface are denied.

You need to specifically allow connectivity between interfaces with the same security levels, as well as traffic in and out of the same interface. All such connectivity is then still controlled by the access rules of the relevant interface.

The Cisco ASA supports two types of ACLs:

- **Ingress:** Ingress ACLs apply to traffic as it enters an interface. An ingress ACL can bind an ACL to a specific interface or apply a global rule on all interfaces.

- **Egress:** Egress ACLs apply to traffic as it exits an interface. An egress ACL is useful, for example, if you want to allow only certain hosts on the inside networks to access a web server on the outside network. Rather than creating multiple ingress ACLs to restrict access, you can create a single egress ACL that allows only the specified hosts. The egress ACL prevents any other hosts from reaching the outside network.

Note   The terms *ingress* and *egress* refer to the application of an ACL on an interface, either to traffic entering the Cisco ASA on an interface or traffic exiting the Cisco ASA on an interface. These terms do not refer to the movement of traffic from a lower security interface to a higher security interface, commonly known as *inbound*, or from a higher to lower interface, commonly known as *outbound*.

Access rules can be created and maintained using the Access Rules pane in Cisco ASDM, which you can reach by navigating to **Configuration > Firewall > Access Rules**, as shown in Figure 10-32. Note that the screenshot shown in Figure 10-32 was captured on a Cisco ASA 5505 running code 8.4(2), which explains the presence of the extra column titled User.

Using the options that are shown Figure 10-32, you can add, delete, or edit rules either by using the options in the top menu or by right-clicking a particular rule and choosing from the context menu. You can also temporarily disable and enable rules.

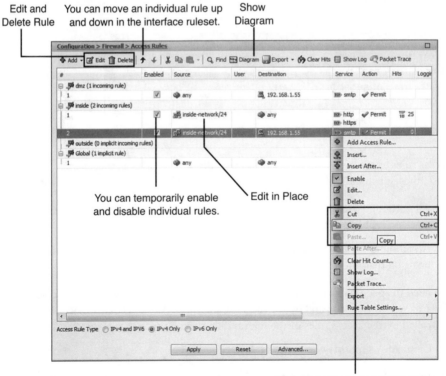

Figure 10-32   *Cisco ASA Interface Access Rules Configured with Cisco ASDM*

Cisco Modular Policy Framework

For application layer inspection, as well as other advanced options, the Cisco Modular Policy Framework (MPF) is also available on Cisco ASAs. Cisco MPF on ASAs is similar to C3PL on Cisco IOS routers. Cisco MPF uses these three configuration objects to define modular, object-oriented, hierarchical policies:

■ **Class maps:** Define a match criterion to identify qualifying traffic

■ **Policy maps:** Associate actions to the match criteria

■ **Service policies:** Attach the policy map to an interface, or globally to all interfaces of the appliance

Cisco MPF, illustrated in Figure 10-33, allows granular classification of traffic flows, in order to apply different advanced policies to different flows. These features, among others, use Cisco MPF:

■ **Hardware modules:** Traffic is redirected granularly from the Cisco ASA to the modules using Cisco MPF.

■ **Advanced Inspection and Control:** Traffic can be classified at Layers 5 through 7 for application layer inspection.

■ Rate limiting and quality of service (QoS) features.

Class maps: Identify traffic at OSI Layers 3 through 7. Use multiple matching criteria.

Policy maps: Define policy for traffic at Layers 3 through 7.

Service policies: Activate policy maps for traffic flows on specific direction of zone pairs.

Classify Traffic
Class Map

Define Actions
Policy Map

Activate Policy
Service Policy

Figure 10-33 *Cisco ASA and Modular Policy Framework*

Class Map: Identifying Traffic on Which a Policy Will Be Enforced

Cisco ASA class maps allow a richer set of match criteria, as compared to their counterparts in Cisco IOS Zone-Based Policy Firewalls. The list includes these criteria for matching information at Layers 3 and 4:

■ Access list

■ Any packet

- Default inspection traffic

- IP differentiated services code point (DSCP)

- IP flow

- TCP and UDP ports

- IP precedence

- Real-Time Transport Protocol (RTP) port numbers

- VPN tunnel group

Layers 5 through 7 class maps are also available, and provide an even richer set of criteria for application-specific parameters. For instance, you can match HTTP URLs and request methods.

Policy Map: Configuring the Action That Will Be Applied to the Traffic

Cisco ASA policy maps also allow a more rich set of actions, as compared to their router counterparts for Cisco IOS Zone-Based Policy Firewalls. The actions include not only firewall-related functions, such as application inspection and advanced connection settings, but also QoS actions, such as traffic prioritization, and traffic rerouting to hardware modules integrated into the security appliance. The list of possible actions includes

- Sending traffic to the Advanced Inspection and Prevention Security Services Module (AIP-SSM) or the Trend Micro InterScan for Cisco CSC-SSM

- Sending NetFlow information

- Prioritizing, policing, or shaping traffic (QoS)

- Configuring advanced connection settings (such as maximum number of simultaneous embryonic connections per client)

- Application inspection (such as preparing for dynamic port for FTP sessions)

When creating a policy map, you need to provide it with a name. You also need to refer to class maps, where traffic is identified.

Service Policy: Activating the Policy

The service policy, defined in the policy map configuration, will be applied to an interface or globally. You can apply only one service policy per interface. However, a service policy might contain multiple policy maps, and thus different actions to be applied on different flows of traffic.

Note   Interface service policies take precedence over the global service policy for a given feature. For example, if you have a global policy with FTP inspection and an interface policy with FTP inspection, then only the interface policy FTP inspection is applied to that interface.

Cisco ASA Modular Policy Framework: Simple Example

Figure 10-34 provides an example of MPF at work. Three map classes have been created:

- **Internet:** Traffic that has port 80 listed in its TCP header will be classified as **Internet** traffic.

- **Engineers:** Traffic with IP subnet 10.66.0.0 will be classified as **Engineers** traffic.

- **Voice:** Traffic with Layer 3 DSCP bits set to decimal value 46 will be recognized as VoIP traffic and will be classified as **Voice** traffic.

The traffic identified as **Internet** will be passed to the IPS module inserted in the Cisco ASA firewall. This module is the Advanced Inspection and Prevention Security Services Module (AIP-SSM). Traffic identified as **Engineers** will be throttled using rate limitation. Traffic identified as **Voice** will be prioritized on the way out.

With the example in Figure 10-34, the outside interface is made aware with the **service-policy** command that it is responsible for enforcing the three **policy-map** commands, which themselves list the actions to be applied on the different flows of traffic created by the **class-map** commands.

Figure 10-34   *Example of How Modular Policy Framework Can Be Used on Cisco ASA*

First Packet Dictates the Policy Used

The policy is assigned upon receipt of the first packet. As an example, in a TCP communication, the policy is "chosen" upon the SYN packet transmission. All subsequent packets from the same session will use the action that was stipulated when the policy was selected at the beginning of the connection. Any changes made to that policy during the session lifetime do not affect that specific connection. Only new connections will be affected. Therefore, if you make a change to a policy, it is best to clear all current connections that could be affected by the policy, to ensure that the new policy will be used.

Basic Outbound Access Control on Cisco ASA Using Cisco ASDM

Cisco ASDM can be used to initialize Cisco ASAs for basic operations. The Cisco ASDM Startup Wizard is available to configure interface settings, basic access control, NAT, DHCP, basic management features, and others.

Figure 10-35 describes a configuration scenario for the use of the Cisco ASDM Startup Wizard. This network, using a Cisco ASA 5505 security appliance, requires outbound access for clients on the 10.0.2.0/24 subnet. No public servers are required, and inbound access that is originated at the untrusted network should be blocked. The Cisco ASA will act as DHCP server for the 10.0.2.0/24 subnet, and will perform dynamic PAT (NAT overload) on outbound traffic using the outside interface IP address of the appliance.

Figure 10-35 *Configuration Scenario for Outbound Traffic Control on Cisco ASA*

Scenario Configuration Steps Using Cisco ASDM

The configuration steps are as follows:

Step 1.   Prepare Cisco ASA for Cisco ASDM access via the CLI.

Step 2.   Run the interactive setup dialog in Cisco ASDM.

Step 3.   Verify the configuration.

Step 4.   Verify firewall activity using the Packet Tracer tool.

The preparation steps are configured using the CLI. Once the appliance is ready, Cisco ASDM is used to invoke the Startup Wizard and continue the basic configuration. Verification is shown for both the CLI and ASDM, and the Packet Tracer tool is used for verification and troubleshooting.

Step 1: Prepare Cisco ASA for Cisco ASDM Access Using the CLI

In preparing a Cisco ASA 5505 security appliance for Cisco ASDM access, the first step is to enable an interface and configure it with a logical name. The **nameif** command, mentioned earlier in a sidebar in this chapter, assigns a name to an interface when in interface configuration mode. Security levels are automatically assigned when you issue the **nameif** command. The inside interface acquires security level 100, while other interfaces acquire level 0 by default. This default security level can be changed with the **security-level** command.

Notice that in the case of the Cisco ASA 5505 model, security levels and IP addresses are assigned to VLAN interfaces, as shown in Example 10-4. Physical interfaces in this model are Layer 2 ports, and VLAN interfaces are needed to provide Layer 3 connectivity and configure the appliance with IP addresses, security levels, ACLs, and other components.

Note   These guidelines and configuration examples apply to the Cisco ASA 5505 model. Other models, such as 5510, 5520, 5540, and 5580, are subject to different rules and requirements. As examples, with the Cisco ASA 5510, an interface would be referred to as Ethernet 0/0; with the Cisco ASA 5520, it would be referred as GigabitEthernet 0/0.

Example 10-4   *Configuring an Interface on Cisco ASA 5505*

```
asa5505(config)# interface vlan21
asa5505(config-if)# nameif inside
```

The next task is to enter the **setup** command to run the setup initialization dialog, as shown in Example 10-5. The **setup** command configures the following:

- Device settings, such as the firewall mode, clock settings, enable password, and DNS information.

- Interface settings, such as IP addresses and subnet masks.

- Cisco ASDM settings, specifically access restrictions in the form of IP addresses and subnets that are allowed to access the appliance via Cisco ASDM. In Example 10-5, this address is 10.0.2.11.

Example 10-5 *Running the Cisco ASA Setup*

```
!
asa5505(config)# interface vlan21
asa5505(config-if)# nameif inside
INFO: Security level for "inside" set to 100 by default. ciscoasa(config)# setup
Pre-configure Firewall now through interactive prompts [yes]? <Enter> Firewall Mode
[Routed]: <Enter>
Enable password [<use current password>]: cisco123
Allow password recovery [yes]? <Enter>
Clock (UTC):
 Year [2012]: <Enter>
 Month [Aug]: <Enter>
 Day [26]: <Enter>
 Time [10:21:49]: 15:34:00
Inside IP address [0.0.0.0]: 10.0.2.1
Inside network mask [255.255.255.255]: 255.255.255.0
Host name [ciscoasa]: ASA Domain name: cisco.com
IP address of host running Device Manager: 10.0.2.11
Use this configuration and write to flash? Y
!
```

Routed Versus Transparent

In the setup dialog of Example 10-5, you might have noticed **Firewall Mode [Routed]**. The Cisco IOS Firewall, like the Cisco ASA firewall, can operate in routed mode or transparent mode. The default mode is routed mode, where the firewall is a routed hop and acts as a default gateway. In transparent mode, the firewall can perform its duties at Layer 2. Transparent firewalls are beyond the scope of this book.

Optionally, you should define the location of Cisco ASDM files in the flash memory of the appliance, as shown in Example 10-6. This is especially important when using multiple versions of Cisco ASDM.

Example 10-6 *Specifying the Cisco ASDM File to Use*

```
!
asa5505(config)# asdm image disk0:/asdm-641.bin
!
```

Note Cisco ASA's internal flash is referred to as **disk0**, while its external flash (compact flash) is referred to as **disk1**. We refer to Cisco PIX Firewall flash, even when running code 8.x, as **flash0**.

Figure 10-36 illustrates and explains the CLI commands that result from the Setup Wizard. Notice how the Cisco ASA 5505 security appliance uses a VLAN interfaces to define the inside interface. The VLAN for VLAN interface 21, in this example, is assigned to the physical interface Ethernet 0/1, which is physically connected to the inside network.

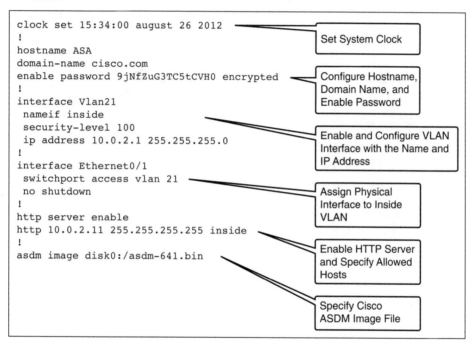

Figure 10-36 *Verifying and Understanding the Setup Configuration of a Cisco ASA*

Step 2: Run the Startup Wizard from Cisco ASDM

You can start Cisco ASDM using either of two methods, shown in Figure 10-37:

- **ASDM-IDM Launcher (Windows only):** The Launcher is an application (downloaded from the Cisco ASA using a web browser) that you can use to connect to any Cisco ASA IP address. You do not need to re-download the Launcher if you want to connect to other Cisco ASAs. The Launcher also lets you run a virtual Cisco ASDM in Demo Mode using files that are downloaded locally.

■ **Java Web Start:** For each Cisco ASA that you manage, you need to connect with a web browser and then save or launch the Java Web Start application. You can optionally save the application to your PC. However, you need separate applications for each Cisco ASA IP address.

Once started, the security appliance will prompt you for credentials for administrative access.

Note ASDM uses SSL for communications between the management station and the security appliance. By default, a self-signed certificate is generated for use by Cisco ASA. Your browser will prompt you for confirmation that you want to accept and use this digital certificate.

Figure 10-37 *Launching Cisco ASDM*

The next task is to run the Startup Wizard. To access this feature in the main Cisco ASDM application window, choose one of the following:

■ Navigate to **Wizards > Startup Wizard.**

■ Navigate to **Configuration > Device Setup > Startup Wizard,** and then click **Launch Startup Wizard.**

Step 1 of the Startup Wizard is to define the starting point in terms of configuration, as shown in Figure 10-38. The options are as follows:

■ To change the existing configuration, click the Modify Existing Configuration radio button.

■ To set the configuration to the factory default values, click the Reset Configuration to Factory Defaults radio button.

  ■ To configure the IP address and subnet mask of the Management 0/0 (Cisco ASA 5510 and later) or VLAN 1 (Cisco ASA 5505) interface to be different from the default value (192.168.1.1), check the **Configure the IP Address of the Management Interface** check box.

■ Choose the first option and click **Next** if, like in our case, you wish to modify the current configuration.

Note   If you reset the configuration to factory defaults, you cannot undo these changes by clicking Cancel or by closing this screen.

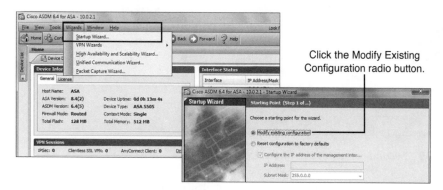

Figure 10-38   *Starting the Cisco ASDM Startup Wizard and the First Screen*

Step 2 of the Startup Wizard defines the basic configuration of the appliance, as shown in Figure 10-39. The following components can be configured:

■ **Configure the Device for Teleworker Usage:** Check this check box to specify a group of configuration settings for a remote worker. This is available only for Cisco ASA 5505 security appliances.

■ **Cisco ASA Host Name:** The hostname appears in the command-line prompt, and if you establish sessions to multiple devices, the hostname helps you keep track of where you enter commands. The hostname is also used in system messages.

■ **Domain Name:** The Cisco ASA appends the domain name as a suffix to unqualified names. For example, if you set the domain name to "example.com," and specify a syslog server by the unqualified name of "jupiter," then the security appliance qualifies the name to "jupiter.example.com."

■ **Change Privileged Mode (Enable) Password:** Checking this check box enables you to change the configured enable (privilege 15) password. The enable password lets you access privileged EXEC mode after you log in. Also, this password is used to access Cisco ASDM as the default user, which is blank. The default user shows as "enable_15" in the User Accounts pane. (If you configure user authentication for enable access, then each user has their own password, and this enable password is not used. In addition, you can configure authentication for HTTP/ASDM access.)

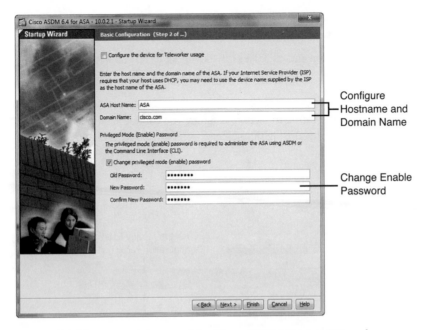

Figure 10-39   *Second Screen of the Cisco ASDM Startup Wizard*

Multiple screens allow the configuration of the appliance interfaces. In Step 3 of the wizard, (running the Plus code instead of the Base code), you group the eight Fast Ethernet switch ports on the Cisco ASA 5505 into three VLANs. These VLANs function as separate Layer 3 networks. You can then choose or create the VLANs that define your network—one for each interface: Outside, Inside, or DMZ. You have the option to not define a DMZ by not creating a DMZ VLAN.

Security levels are configured automatically when you use the wizard, but you can change them later using Cisco ASDM options. The outside interface acquires a security level of 0, the DMZ interface acquires a security level of 50, and the inside interface acquires a security level of 100.

In Figure 10-40, VLAN 21 is allocated to the inside interface, while VLAN 22 is allocated to the outside interface. No DMZ VLAN is created.

Step 4 of the wizard is switch port allocation, which lets you allocate switch ports to outside, inside, or DMZ interfaces. By default, all switch ports are assigned to VLAN 1 (inside).

Figure 10-41 shows the example for a Cisco ASA 5505 security appliance, which includes an eight-port switch. In this example, the Ethernet 0/1 interface is allocated to the inside VLAN, while the Ethernet 0/0 interface is allocated to the outside VLAN.

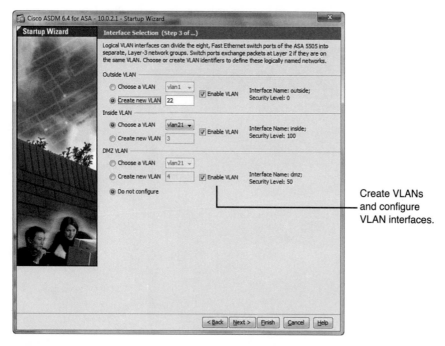

Figure 10-40   *Interface Selection from Cisco ASDM Startup Wizard*

Figure 10-41   *Switch Port Selection from Cisco ASDM Startup Wizard (Cisco ASA 5505 Only)*

Step 5 of the wizard lets you configure the IP address for each VLAN interface, as shown in Figure 10-42. Notice the options to configure Cisco ASA interfaces to obtain their IP address, as well as a default route, automatically from the network via DHCP.

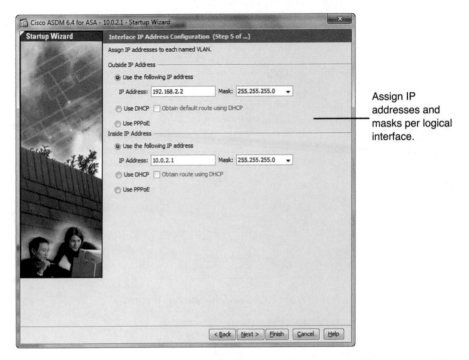

Figure 10-42   *Interface IP Address Configuration from Cisco ASDM Startup Wizard*

Step 6 of the wizard enables you to configure network services, either DHCP or PPPoE, depending on what selections you made in Step 5. Figure 10-43 illustrates the options to configure the Cisco ASA as a DHCP server. The options allow the inside interface to deliver DHCP services to DHCP clients reachable through that interface.

In our scenario, the inside interface provides DHCP servers using the range of addresses 10.0.2.100 to 10.0.2.130.

Step 7 of the wizard is to define NAT and PAT settings, if required. You can enable dynamic NAT or dynamic PAT. You have the option to define additional Cisco ASA objects such as IP addresses and IP subnets, in order to define the PAT IP addresses or the ranges of source IP addresses to match. You configure these objects in additional windows that open from the main wizard window when you choose the different options.

As shown in Figure 10-44, you can configure PAT and define the IP address on the outside interface to overload for all traffic heading outbound when originated on the inside interface.

Enable DHCP services if required.

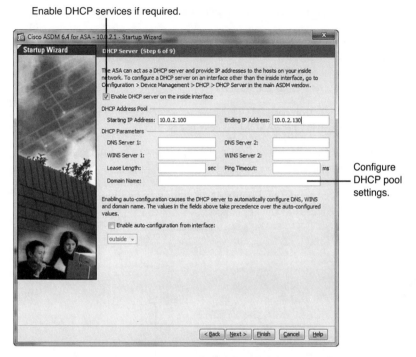

Figure 10-43 *DHCP Server Configuration from Cisco ASDM Startup Wizard*

Enable PAT.

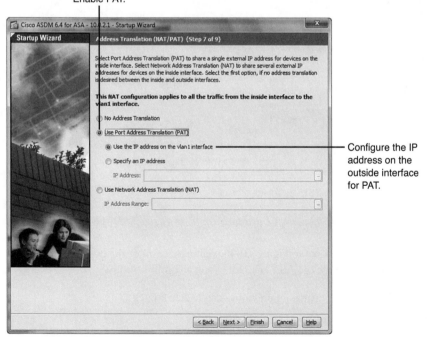

Figure 10-44 *NAT and PAT Configuration from Cisco ASDM Startup Wizard*

Step 8 of the wizard enables you to configure administrative access. The following options are available:

- Configure ASDM, Telnet, or SSH access. Clicking the Add button enables you to configure the IP address or range of addresses that are allowed to use the protocol to manage the Cisco ASA, as well as the interface where they are allowed.

- To enable a secure connection to an HTTP server to access Cisco ASDM, check the **Enable HTTP Server for HTTPS/ASDM Access** check box.

- To allow Cisco ASDM to collect and display statistics, check the **Enable ASDM History Metrics** check box.

In Figure 10-45, SSH services are defined on the inside interface to allow the whole subnet 10.0.2.0/24 to have SSH access to the appliance.

Configure access control for HTTP, SSH, or Telnet access.

Figure 10-45 *Administrative Access Configuration from Cisco ASDM Startup Wizard*

The final wizard screen, shown in Figure 10-46, summarizes all of the configuration settings that you have made for the ASA. The following are your options:

- To change any of the settings in previous screens, click Back.

- Choose one of the following:

- If you ran the Startup Wizard directly from a browser, when you click Finish, the configuration settings that you created through the wizard are sent to the Cisco ASA and saved in flash memory automatically.

- If you ran the Startup Wizard from within Cisco ASDM, you must explicitly save the configuration in flash memory by choosing **File > Save Running Configuration to Flash**.

Review and click Finish.

Figure 10-46 *Cisco ASDM Startup Wizard Summary*

Step 3: Verify the Configuration Created by the Cisco ASDM Startup Wizard

Verification can be accomplished using the Cisco ASDM Device Dashboard tab from the Home page. This screen displays interface status and statistics, as well as overall information about device health.

The access rules and NAT rules that result from the Startup Wizard can be verified by navigating to the Cisco ASDM options shown in Figure 10-47 and Figure 10-48. Note that the screenshots shown in these figures were captured on a Cisco ASA 5505 running code 8.4(2). This explains the extra column titled User, in Figure 10-47, that you might not be seeing on your Cisco ASA.

Figure 10-47 *Verifying Access Rules Created by Cisco ASDM Startup Wizard*

Figure 10-48 *Verifying NAT Rules Created by Cisco ASDM Startup Wizard*

The last required step to enable connectivity through the appliance is to define a default route for outbound traffic. This task can be accomplished by navigating to **Configuration > Device Setup > Routing > Static Routes** and clicking **Add** to create a static route. The options include the outgoing interface, the destination prefix for the route, and the next hop.

In Figure 10-49, a default route is created using the **any** keyword on the Network field. The Network field indicates the destination prefix of the route, and using **any** is similar to using 0.0.0.0 as a destination. The outgoing interface for traffic following this route is the outside interface.

Notice that this is a change made outside of the wizard, so it must be synchronized from Cisco ASDM to the appliance by clicking **Apply** at the bottom of the Static Routes window.

Configure static route specifying outgoing interface and next hop.

Apply changes when done.

Figure 10-49 *Adding a Static Route Using Cisco ASDM*

Step 4: Verify Firewall Activity Using the Packet Tracer Tool

The Packet Tracer tool provides packet tracing for packet sniffing and network fault isolation, as well as detailed information about the packets and how they are processed by the Cisco ASA. If a configuration command did not cause the packet to drop, Packet Tracer provides information about the cause in an easily readable manner.

In addition, you can use the Packet Tracer tool to trace the lifespan of a packet through the Cisco ASA to see whether the packet is operating correctly. This tool lets you do the following:

- Debug all packet drops in a production network

- Verify that the configuration is working as intended

- Show all rules applicable to a packet, along with the CLI commands that caused the rule addition

- Show a timeline of packet changes in a data path

- Inject tracer packets into the data path

To open the Packet Tracer, perform the following steps, shown in Figure 10-50:

Step 1.   In the main Cisco ASDM application window, navigate to **Tools > Packet Tracer.**

Step 2.   The Cisco ASDM Packet Tracer dialog box opens.

Step 3.   Choose the source interface for the packet trace from the Interface drop-down list.

Step 4.   Specify the protocol type for the packet trace. Available protocol types include TCP, UDP, ICMP, and IP.

Step 5.   Enter the source address for the packet trace in the Source IP Address field.

Step 6.   Choose the source port for the packet trace from the drop-down list.

Step 7.   Enter the destination IP address for the packet trace in the Destination IP Address field.

Step 8.   Choose the destination port for the packet trace from the drop-down list.

Step 9.   Click Start to trace the packet.

The information display area shows detailed messages about the packet trace.

Note   To display a graphical representation of the packet trace, check the Show Animation check box.

Figure 10-50   *Packet Tracer Tool Using Cisco ASDM*

Summary

In this chapter, you learned that a firewall is a set of rules designed to enforce an access control policy between two networks. You learned how to create firewall rules to implement your security policies. Cisco provides a range of firewall products that help you implement your security policies in a cost-effective way. ACLs provide packet-filtering capabilities for routers and firewalls to protect internal networks from the outside.

Cisco offers many different types of firewalls. In this chapter, we looked at two types: Cisco IOS Zone-Based Firewall and Cisco ASA firewall.

A zone-based policy firewall changes the firewall from the older interface-based model to a more flexible, more easily understood zone-based configuration model. Cisco IOS Zone-Based Policy Firewalls provide a more flexible way to implement your security policy on Cisco Router and Cisco Configuration Professional (CCP) makes it easier for you to configure and maintain the firewall capabilities of your routers.

The Cisco ASA family of products includes solutions for teleworkers, branch offices, Internet edge environments, and data centers. Cisco ASA uses security levels and access rules to control traffic. You also saw briefly how Modular Policy Framework rules provide a richer set of options than what is offered with a Cisco IOS Zone-Based Firewall. You learned, though, that the Cisco ASA ACLs have similar structure and operational framework than how ACLs are implemented on Cisco IOS routers. You also saw that Cisco ASDM provides protected, authenticated, GUI management for Cisco ASAs and that the Startup Wizard can be used to quickly and effectively deploy basic Cisco ASA configurations.

References

For additional information, refer to these resources

Cisco.com Resources

Cisco ASA 5500 Series Configuration Guide Using ASDM, 6.4 and 6.6, http://www.cisco.com/en/US/docs/security/asa/asa84/asdm64/configuration_guide/asdm_64_config.html

Getting Started with Cisco Configuration Professional, http://www.cisco.com/en/US/docs/net_mgmt/cisco_configuration_professional/v2_5/guides/getting_start/ccp_gsg.html

Zone-Based Policy Firewall Design and Application Guide, http://www.cisco.com/en/US/products/sw/secursw/ps1018/products_tech_note09186a00808bc994.shtml

Other Resources

Beaver, K. "Firewall Best Practices" (2009), http://www.principlelogic.com/docs/Firewall_Best_Practices.pdf

Hucaby, D., Garneau, D., and Sequeira, A. *CCNP Security FIREWALL 642-618 Official Cert Guide* (Cisco Press, 2012)

CCP and ASDM Demo Mode Tutorials

McKillip, Doug. "Cisco Configuration Professional Demo Mode – Part I," http://globalknowledgeblog.com/technology/cisco/cisco-configuration-professional-demo-mode-%E2%80%93-part-i/

McKillip, Doug. "Cisco Configuration Professional Demo Mode – Part II," http://globalknowledgeblog.com/technology/cisco/cisco-configuration-professional-demo-mode-%E2%80%93-part-ii/

McKillip, Doug. "ASDM Demo Mode Tour," http://globalknowledgeblog.com/technology/cisco/asdm-demo-mode-tour/

Review Questions

Use the questions here to review what you learned in this chapter. The correct answers are found in the Appendix, "Answers to Chapter Review Questions."

1. Which of the following is not an action of zone-based policy firewalls?

   a. drop
   b. reset
   c. pass
   d. inspect

2. When using zone-based policy, for traffic to flow among all the interfaces in a router, all of the interfaces must be which of the following?

   a. Configured with the CCP Wizard
   b. A member of a security zone
   c. Placed in a virtual template
   d. A member of a dialer interface

3. What is the role of class maps?

   a. They group interfaces to which security policies will be applied.
   b. They allow you to specify a unidirectional firewall policy between two security zones.
   c. They specify the actions to be taken when traffic matches the criteria.
   d. They identify traffic and traffic parameters that a Cisco IOS Zone-Based Policy Firewall selects for policy application.

4. What programming mechanism is used to provide zone-base firewall services in a Cisco IOS router?

   a. Adaptive Security Algorithm
   b. Access Control Lists
   c. Cisco Common Classification Policy Language
   d. Modular Policy Framework

5. In CLI, the **zone-pair** command is used to associate together which of the following? (Choose two.)

   a. zones
   b. class-map
   c. access-list
   d. service-policy
   e. interface
   f. class-type

6. An interface belongs to a zone for which a zone pair with the self zone was created. No policies have yet been created. Which action will be applied when traffic originating on the interface that belongs to the zone is destined to the router itself?

   a. inspect
   b. pass
   c. drop
   d. log
   e. drop and log

7. Multiple service policies can be applied to the same zone pair.

   a. True
   b. False

8. You want to apply a restrictive policy to traffic between interfaces that belong to the same zone in a zone-based policy firewall. Which of the following options can be used?

   a. Define the zone as the source and destination of a zone pair and create a policy for the zone pair
   b. Create a new zone and change interface zone membership
   c. Create a zone-based policy that applies ACLs to interfaces of the zone
   d. Use ACLs on the interfaces on the zone

9. Which Cisco Configuration Professional feature can be used to create zone-based firewalls?

   a. Advanced Firewall wizard only
   b. Basic Firewall wizard only
   c. Zone-based Firewall wizard
   d. Both Advanced Firewall and Basic Firewall wizards

10. Your Cisco ASA has multiple interfaces configured. There are two DMZ interfaces—DMZ1 with security level 51 and DMZ2 with security level 52. Which of the following is to be expected from this environment?

    a. All traffic between the two DMZs requires an explicit policy.
    b. Traffic originating at DMZ2 and destined to DMZ1 is allowed.
    c. Traffic originating at DMZ1 and destined to DMZ2 is allowed.
    d. None of the above.

11. Which condition would require a special configuration on Cisco ASA 8.3?

    a. Connectivity for through traffic
    b. ARP traffic for devices on the same interfaces
    c. Outbound connectivity
    d. Connectivity between interfaces of the same security level

12. What action is not available on Cisco ASA when using Modular Policy Framework?

  a. Sending SNMP traps
  b. Connection settings
  c. NetFlow-related actions
  d. QoS policies

13. Which function is not available using the Packet Tracer tool?

  a. Traffic simulation
  b. Testing ICMP traffic
  c. Capturing packets for further analysis
  d. Showing the rules applied to a packet flow

14. What is the significance of the **nameif** command with Cisco ASAs?

  a. An interface needs to have a name to pass traffic.
  b. Naming interfaces is useful for troubleshooting.
  c. The interface name appears in CDP packets.
  d. IP name resolution is based on name of interfaces.

15. Which statement is true regarding the default behavior of the Cisco ASA?

  a. Traffic is allowed to flow from a lower security level interface to a higher security level interface.
  b. Traffic is allowed to flow from a higher security level interface to a lower security level interface.
  c. Traffic is allowed to flow between interfaces of the same security level.
  d. Traffic is allowed to flow in and then out of the same interface.

Chapter 11

Intrusion Prevention Systems

This chapter describes the functions and operations of intrusion detection systems (IDS) and intrusion prevention systems (IPS). This chapter will introduce you to

- The fundamentals of intrusion prevention, comparing IDS and IPS

- The building blocks of IPS, introducing the underlying technologies and deployment options

- The use of signatures in intrusion prevention, highlighting the benefits and drawbacks

- The need for IPS alarm monitoring, evaluating the options for event managers

- Analyzing the design considerations in deploying IPS

IPS Fundamentals

Intrusion detection system (IDS) and intrusion prevention system (IPS) solutions form an integral part of a robust network defense solution. Maintaining secure network services is a key requirement of a profitable IP-based business. To show how these systems work, this chapter uses Cisco products and technologies as examples.

Introducing IDS and IPS

The evolution of threats and business models requires a new approach to intrusion prevention:

- **Targeted, mutating, stealth threats are increasingly difficult to detect.** Intrusion prevention needs to be distributed and embedded end to end along the "path of intrusion." Shared threat and security intelligence is a key feature.

■ **Attackers have insidious motivations and exploit high-impact targets, often for financial benefit or economic and political reasons.** The impact on business continuity is immense. More than ever, intrusion prevention needs to be accurate, providing a timely and precise response only to threats relevant to the infrastructure, application, and business environments of the organization.

■ **Attackers are taking advantage of new ways of communication.** Borderless networks provide a launching pad for high-impact intrusion from mobile users to consumer devices (smartphones, PDAs, tablet devices, entertainment devices, book readers, and so on), exploiting data wherever it may be stored (user's personal device, enterprise data centers, cloud service providers, and so on). The "army of intrusion sensors" requires flexible deployment options, from appliances to hardware modules on existing network elements to software-based and virtualized form factors.

Traditionally, an IDS and an IPS work together to provide a network security solution. An IDS captures packets in real time, processes them, and can respond to threats, but it works on *copies* of data traffic to detect suspicious activity by using signatures. This is called *promiscuous mode*. In the process of detecting malicious traffic, an IDS allows some malicious traffic to pass before the IDS can respond to protect the network. An IDS analyzes a copy of the monitored traffic rather than the actual forwarded packet. The advantage of operating on a copy of the traffic is that the IDS does not affect the packet flow of the forwarded traffic. The disadvantage of operating on a copy of the traffic is that the IDS cannot stop malicious traffic from single-packet attacks from reaching the target system before the IDS can apply a response to stop the attack. An IDS often requires assistance from other networking devices, such as routers and firewalls, to respond to an attack.

An IPS works inline in the data stream to provide protection from malicious attacks in real time. This is called *inline mode*. Unlike an IDS, an IPS does not allow packets to enter the trusted side of the network. An IPS monitors traffic at Layer 3 and Layer 4 to ensure that the traffic's headers, states, and so on are those specified in the protocol suite. However, the IPS sensor analyzes the payload of the packets at Layer 2 to Layer 7 for more sophisticated embedded attacks that might include malicious data. This deeper analysis lets the IPS identify, stop, and block attacks that would normally pass through a traditional firewall device. When a packet comes in through an interface on an IPS, that packet is not sent to the outbound or trusted interface until the packet has been determined to be clean. An IPS builds upon previous IDS technology; Cisco IPS platforms use a blend of detection technologies, including profile-based intrusion detection, signature-based intrusion detection, and protocol analysis intrusion detection.

The key to differentiating an IDS from an IPS is that an IPS responds immediately and does not allow any malicious traffic to pass, whereas an IDS allows malicious traffic to pass before it can respond. IDSs typically are IPSs that are configured to work on a copy of the traffic (promiscuous mode) instead of working on traffic going through it (inline mode). Because IDS devices are usually IPS devices configured differently, in this chapter we often use the term IPS, which, in our generic conversation on the topic, will also encompass IDS, unless indicated otherwise.

IDS:

- Analyzes copies of the traffic stream

- Does not slow network traffic

- Allows some malicious traffic into the network

IPS:

- Works inline in real time to monitor Layer 2 through Layer 7 traffic and content

- Needs to be able to handle network traffic

- Prevents malicious traffic from entering the network

IDS and IPS technologies share several characteristics:

- IDS and IPS technologies are deployed as sensors. An IDS or an IPS sensor can be any of the following devices:

  - A router configured with Cisco IOS IPS Software

  - An appliance specifically designed to provide dedicated IDS or IPS services

  - A network module installed in a Cisco adaptive security appliance, switch, or router

- IDS and IPS technologies typically monitor for malicious activities in two spots:

  - **Network:** To detect attacks against the network, including attacks against hosts and devices, using network IDS and network IPS.

  - **Hosts:** To detect attacks launched from or against target machines, using host IPS (HIPS). Host-based attacks are detected by reading security event logs, checking for changes to critical system files, and checking system registries for malicious entries.

- IDS and IPS technologies use signatures to detect patterns of misuse in network traffic. A signature is a set of rules that an IDS or IPS uses to detect typical intrusive activity. Signatures are usually chosen from a broad cross section of intrusion detection signatures, and can detect severe breaches of security, common network attacks, and information gathering.

- IDS and IPS technologies look for the following general patterns of misuse:

  - **Atomic pattern:** In an atomic pattern, an attempt is made to access a specific port on a specific host, and malicious content is contained in a single packet. An IDS is particularly vulnerable to an atomic attack because until the IDS finds the attack, malicious single packets are being allowed into the network. An IPS prevents these packets from entering at all.

■ **Composite pattern:** A composite pattern, also referred to as *compound*, is a sequence of operations distributed across multiple hosts over an arbitrary period of time.

Inline Sensors

Sensors, even inline, might not be completely successful at dropping packets of an attack. An attack might be underway, if only partially, before an inline sensor even starts to drop packets matching a composite pattern signature. The drop action is much more effective for atomic signatures because the sensor makes a single-packet match.

Figure 11-1 shows a sensor deployed in IDS mode and a sensor deployed in IPS mode.

Figure 11-1 *IDS and IPS Operational Differences*

The following are the steps that occur when an attack is launched in an environment monitored by an IDS:

Step 1. An attack is launched on a network that has a sensor deployed in IDS mode.

Step 2. The switch sends copies of all packets to the IDS sensor (configured in promiscuous mode, which is explained later in this section) to analyze the packets. At the same time, the target machine experiences the malicious attack.

Step 3. The IDS sensor, using a signature, matches the malicious traffic to the signature.

Step 4.   The IDS sensor sends to the switch a command to deny access to the malicious traffic.

Step 5.   The IDS sends an alarm to a management console for logging and other management purposes.

The following are the steps that occur when an attack is launched in an environment monitored by an IPS:

Step 1.   An attack is launched on a network that has a sensor deployed in IPS mode (configured in inline mode, which is explained later in this section).

Step 2.   The IPS sensor analyzes the packets as soon as they come into the IPS sensor interface. The IPS sensor, using signatures, matches the malicious traffic to the signature and the attack is stopped immediately. Traffic in violation of policy can be dropped by an IPS sensor.

Step 3.   The IPS sensor can send an alarm to a management console for logging and other management purposes.

Promiscuous Versus Inline Mode

A sensor can be deployed either in promiscuous mode or inline mode. In promiscuous mode, the sensor receives a copy of the data for analysis, while the original traffic still makes its way to its ultimate destination. By contrast, a sensor working inline analyzes the traffic live and therefore can actively block the packets before they reach their destination.

It is worth mentioning that Cisco appliances such as the Cisco ASA AIP-SSM (discussed later in this chapter), although advertised as IPS devices, can work either in promiscuous mode or in inline mode.

Management Console

The term *management console*, used in this chapter and seen in Figure 11-1, refers to a separate workstation equipped with software to configure, monitor, and report on events. The section "Monitoring Cisco IOS IPS Alarms and Event Managers" introduces some of the Cisco IPS management solutions.

Table 11-1 lists some of the advantages and limitations of deploying platform sensors in promiscuous mode; in other words, as an IDS.

Table 11-1 *Advantages and Limitations of Deploying a Sensor in Promiscuous Mode: IDS*

Advantage	Limitation
Deploying the IDS sensor does not have any impact on the network (latency, jitter, and so on).	IDS sensor response actions cannot stop the trigger packet and are not guaranteed to stop a connection. IDS sensor response actions are typically better at stopping an attacker than at stopping a specific attack itself.
The IDS sensor is not inline and, therefore, a sensor failure cannot affect network functionality.	IDS sensor response actions are less helpful in stopping email viruses and automated attackers such as worms, and IDS sensors are more vulnerable to network evasion techniques.
Overrunning the IDS sensor with data does not affect network traffic; however, it does affect the capability of the IDS sensor to analyze the data.	Users deploying IDS sensor response actions must have a well-thought-out security policy combined with a good operational understanding of their IDS deployments. Users must spend time to correctly tune IDS sensors to achieve expected levels of intrusion detection.
	Being out of band (OOB), IDS sensors are more vulnerable to network evasion techniques, which are designed to totally conceal an attack.

Table 11-2 lists some of the advantages and limitations of deploying a platform sensor in inline mode; in other words, as an IPS.

Table 11-2 *Advantages and Limitations of Deploying a Sensor in Inline Mode: IPS*

Advantage	Limitation
You can configure an IPS sensor to perform a packet drop that can stop the trigger packet, the packets in a connection, or packets from a source IP address.	Because an IPS sensor must be inline, IPS sensor errors or failure can have a negative effect on network traffic.
Being inline, an IPS sensor can use stream normalization techniques, such as fragmentation reassembly, to check the validity of the transmission, thus reducing or eliminating many of the network evasion capabilities that exist.	Overrunning IPS sensor capabilities with too much traffic negatively affects the performance of the network.
	Users deploying IPS sensor response actions must have a well-thought-out security policy combined with a good operational understanding of their IPS deployments.

Advantage	Limitation
	An IPS sensor will affect network timing because of latency, jitter, and so on. An IPS sensor must be appropriately sized and implemented so that time-sensitive applications, such as VoIP, are not negatively affected.

So, IDS or IPS? Why Not Both?

When designing a distributed IPS architecture, both IDS and IPS deployment modes can be used to improve the accuracy, intelligence, response, and performance of the architecture. When combined, IDSs in promiscuous mode and IPSs in inline mode complement each other to accomplish this objective. Figure 11-2 illustrates an example, described next.

Figure 11-2 *Using Both IDS and IPS Devices*

The IDS sensor in front of the firewall is deployed in promiscuous mode to monitor traffic in the untrusted network. It is likely that this IDS sensor will have more visibility over a wide variety of events and malicious traffic that have the potential to become security incidents. The internal network is protected initially by the firewall, and the role of the IDS sensor is to gather security intelligence in order to define a baseline of current and relevant threats. This information is then correlated and fed into the detection capabilities of the internal IPS sensor.

The IPS sensor behind the firewall can therefore focus on monitoring the internal network and detect incidents originated inside. It can also implement a more restrictive policy for external traffic, while remaining accurate, using the information gathered and baselined by the IDS sensor.

Alarm Types

As shown in the previous figures, IDS and IPS sensors produce alarms. The capability of IDS and IPS sensors to accurately detect an attack or a policy violation and generate an alarm is critical to the functionality of the sensors. Attacks can generate the following types of alarms:

- **False positive:** A false positive is an alarm triggered by normal traffic or a benign action. Consider this scenario: A signature exists that generates alarms if the enable password of any network devices is entered incorrectly. A network administrator attempts to log in to a Cisco router but enters the wrong password. The IDS cannot distinguish between a rogue user and the network administrator, and it generates an alarm.

- **False negative:** A false negative occurs when a signature is not fired when offending traffic is detected. Offending traffic could range from a corporate user pinging too aggressively a target on the Internet, to attacks against corporate web servers. A false negative should be considered a software bug if the IDS and IPS have a signature that has been designed to detect the offending traffic but failed to do so. In this situation, the failure to trigger on the offending traffic should be reported to the vendor of the IPS product.

- **True positive:** A true positive occurs when an IDS and IPS signature is correctly fired and an alarm is generated when offending traffic is detected. For example, consider a Unicode attack. Cisco IPS sensors have signatures that detect Unicode attacks against Microsoft Internet Information Services (IIS) web servers. If a Unicode attack is launched against Microsoft IIS web servers, the sensors detect the attack and generate an alarm.

- **True negative:** A true negative occurs when a signature is not fired when non-offending traffic is captured and analyzed. In other words, the sensor does not fire an alarm when it captures and analyzes "normal" network traffic.

Figure 11-3 provides a summary of the alarm types. To understand the terminology, think in terms of the question, "Was the alarm triggered?" A positive means that the alarm was triggered and a negative means that the alarm was not triggered. Thus the expression *false alarm*, which is the same as *false positive* (positive because the alarm was triggered, but false because the intrusion did not happen or the intrusion was not detected by the sensor).

		Actual Offending Traffic?	
		NO	YES
Alarm Triggered?	NO	True Negative	False Negative
	YES	False Positive	True Positive

Figure 11-3   *Making Sense of Alarm Types Terminology*

Note   Positive or negative refers to whether the alarm was triggered. Positive designates an alarm has been triggered, and negative designates an alarm has not been triggered. *True* or *false* is more complex; this answers the question, "Was the result to trigger (or not trigger) the alarm the right decision?" If the action taken by the sensor was right, then the result is true, and if the sensor took the wrong decision, the result is false. As an example, if malicious traffic travels through your network and the IPS sensor fails to detect it, it is a false negative. The *negative* refers to the alarm not triggering. The *false* means not triggering was the wrong decision for the IPS sensor to take.

Intrusion Prevention Technologies

Multiple detection technologies are typically used to provide an effective intrusion detection architecture. Table 11-3 summarizes the advantages and limitations of the various types of IDS and IPS sensors available. These will be discussed in greater detail in this section.

Table 11-3   *Types of IDS and IPS Sensors*

Sensor Type	Advantages	Limitations
Signature based	Easy configuration	No detection of unknown signatures
	Fewer false positives	Initially a lot of false positives
	Good signature design	Signatures must be created, updated, and tuned
Policy based	Simple and reliable	Generic output
	Customized policies	Policy must be created
	Can detect unknown attacks	
Anomaly based	Easy configuration	Difficult to profile typical activity in large networks
	Can detect unknown attacks	Traffic profile must be constant

Table 11-3 *Types of IDS and IPS Sensors*

Sensor Type	Advantages	Limitations
Reputation based	Leverages local, enterprise, and global correlation	More prone to false positives and false negatives
	Improved accuracy and relevancy	Requires timely updates

Signature-Based IDS/IPS

A signature-based approach is usually the starting point of an effective intrusion detection architecture. A *signature* is a set of rules that an IDS and an IPS use to detect typical intrusive activity, such as denial of service (DoS) attacks. You can easily install signatures using IDS and IPS management software such as Cisco IPS Device Manager (IDM) and Cisco IPS Express Manager (IME). Sensors allow you to modify existing signatures and define new ones.

A signature-based IDS or IPS sensor looks for specific, predefined patterns (signatures) in network traffic. It compares the network traffic to a database of known attacks, and triggers an alarm or prevents communication if a match is found. The signature can be based on a single packet or a sequence of packets. New attacks that do not match a signature do not result in detection. For this reason, the signature database needs to be constantly updated.

As sensors scan network packets, they use signatures to detect known attacks and respond with predefined actions. A malicious packet flow has a specific type of activity and signature, and an IDS or IPS sensor examines the data flow using many different signatures. When an IDS or IPS sensor matches a signature with a data flow, the sensor takes action, such as logging the event or sending an alarm to IDS or IPS management software, such as Cisco Configuration Professional (CCP).

Signature-based intrusion detection can produce false positives because certain normal network activity can be misinterpreted as malicious activity. For example, some network applications or operating systems may send out numerous Internet Control Message Protocol (ICMP) messages, which a signature-based detection system might interpret as an attempt by an attacker to map out a network segment. You can minimize false positives by tuning your sensors. You can tune built-in signatures (tuned signatures) by adjusting the many signature parameters.

Note   Protocol analysis–based intrusion detection relies on signature-based intrusion detection, where the signature performs a check to ensure that the data unit header, flags, payload, and so on respect the protocol.

Signature-based pattern matching is an approach that is rigid but simple to employ. In most cases, the pattern is matched against only if the suspect packet is associated with a particular service or, more precisely, destined to and from a particular port. This matching technique helps to lessen the amount of inspection done on every packet. However, it makes it more difficult for systems to deal with protocols that do not reside on well-defined ports, such as Trojan horses and their associated traffic, which can move at will.

At the initial stage of incorporating signature-based IDS or IPS, before the signatures are tuned, there can be many false positives (traffic generating an alert even though it is no threat to the network). After the system is tuned and adjusted to the specific network parameters, there will be fewer false positives than with the policy-based approach.

Policy-Based IDS/IPS

In policy-based systems, the IDS or IPS sensor is configured based on the network security policy. You must create the policies used in a policy-based IDS or IPS. Any traffic detected outside the policy will generate an alarm or will be dropped. Creating a security policy requires detailed knowledge of the network traffic and is a time-consuming task.

Policy-based signatures use an algorithm to determine whether an alarm should be fired. Often, policy-based signature algorithms are statistical evaluations of the traffic flow. For example, in a policy-based signature used to detect a port sweep, the algorithm issues an alarm when the threshold number of unique ports is scanned on a particular machine. Policy-based signature algorithms can be designed to analyze only specific types of packets (for example, SYN packets, where the SYN bit is turned on during the handshaking process at the beginning of the session).

The policy itself might require tuning. For example, you might have to adjust the threshold level of certain types of traffic so that the policy conforms to the utilization patterns on the network that it is monitoring. Policies can be used to look for very complex relationships.

Anomaly-Based IDS/IPS

Anomaly-based (or *profile-based*) signatures typically look for network traffic that deviates from what is seen "normally." The biggest issue with this methodology is that you first must define what *normal is*. If during the learning phase your network is the victim of an attack and you fail to identify it, the anomaly-based IPS will interpret that malicious traffic as normal, and no alarm will be triggered the next time this same attack takes place. Some systems have hard-coded definitions of normal traffic patterns and, in this case, could be considered heuristic-based systems.

Normal behavior is typically defined based on traffic patterns, traffic and protocol mix, traffic volumes, and other criteria. This is called statistical baselining. A second approach focuses on traffic that deviates from protocol standards. This is called protocol anomaly baselining.

The technique used by anomaly-based IDS/IPS systems is also referred as *network behavior analysis* or *heuristics analysis*.

Reputation-Based IPS

A more recent approach to intrusion detection is the reputation-based IPS. This technique uses reputation analysis for various traffic descriptors, such as IP addresses, URLs, Domain Name System (DNS) domains, and others. This typically translates into reputation filters, sometimes known as white lists or black lists, that round up a signature-based system by filtering known malicious sources, destinations, or application components.

A reputation-based approach typically requires communication between the sensor and the source of the reputation information. Sources can be local to the device, which builds reputation based on the history of incidents known to the local device. However, the true power of reputation-based systems lies in the correlation of reputation information with enterprise knowledge and even global knowledge, usually provided by early warning systems, honeypots, and managed security intelligence services. Cisco Security Intelligence Operations, introduced later in this chapter, is a reputation-based IPS.

Honeypots

Honeypots can also be considered to be a form of IDS. Honeypot systems use a dummy server to attract attacks. The purpose of the honeypot approach is to distract attacks away from real network devices. By staging different types of vulnerabilities in the honeypot server, you can analyze incoming types of attacks and malicious traffic patterns. You can use this analysis to tune your sensor signatures to detect new types of malicious network traffic.

Honeypot systems are used in production environments, typically by large organizations that are considered interesting targets for hackers, such as financial enterprises, governmental agencies, and so on. Also, antivirus and other security vendors tend to use them for research.

Many security experts preach the use of honeypots as an early warning system to be deployed with your IDS/IPS system, not in lieu of. Honeyd is an example of popular open source honeypot software. Although honeypots are often found as dedicated servers, it is possible to set up virtual honeypots using VMware or Windows Virtual PC. Keep in mind that should the honeypot be successfully hacked and used as a launching platform for an attack on a third party, the honeypot's owner could incur downstream liability.

IPS Attack Responses

Detection is only part of the role of an IPS. You should define and plan the reaction capabilities of sensors by defining the response that is triggered upon detection, no matter what detection techniques (or combination of techniques) you use.

When an IPS sensor detects malicious activity, it can choose from any or all of the following actions:

■ **Deny Attacker Inline:** This action terminates the current packet and future packets from this attacker address for a specified period of time. The sensor maintains a list of the attackers currently being denied by the system. You can remove entries from the list or wait for the timer to expire. The timer is a sliding timer for each entry. Therefore, if attacker A is currently being denied but issues another attack, the timer for attacker A is reset, and attacker A remains on the denied attacker list until the timer expires. If the denied attacker list is at capacity and cannot add a new entry, the packet is still denied.

■ **Deny Connection Inline:** This action terminates the current packet and future packets on this TCP flow. The packet for this flow was dropped. This is also referred to as *deny flow*.

■ **Deny Packet Inline:** This action terminates the packet. The packets are dropped.

■ **Log Attacker Packets:** This action starts IP logging on packets that contain the attacker address and sends an alert. This action causes an alert to be written to the event store, which is local to the Cisco IOS router, even if the produce-alert action is not selected. Produce alert is discussed later in a bullet.

■ **Log Pair Packets:** This action starts IP logging on packets that contain the attacker and victim address pair. This action causes an alert to be written to the event store, even if the produce-alert action is not selected.

■ **Log Victim Packets:** This action starts IP logging on packets that contain the victim address and sends an alert. This action causes an alert to be written to the event store, even if the produce-alert action is not selected.

■ **Produce Alert:** This action writes the event to the event store as an alert.

■ **Produce Verbose Alert:** This action includes an encoded dump of the offending packet in the alert. This action causes an alert to be written to the event store, even if the produce-alert action is not selected.

■ **Request Block Connection:** This action sends a request to a blocking device to block this connection.

■ **Request Block Host:** This action sends a request to a blocking device to block this attacker host.

■ **Request SNMP Trap:** This action sends a request to the notification application component of the sensor to perform Simple Network Management Protocol (SNMP) notification. This action causes an alert to be written to the event store, even if the produce-alert action is not selected.

■ **Reset TCP Connection:** This action sends TCP resets to hijack and terminate the TCP flow.

Caution Responses to deny inline actions (packet, connection, or attacker) are not available on sensors in IDS mode.

Note Packets that are dropped (denied) based on false alarms can result in network disruption if the dropped packets are required for mission-critical applications downstream of the IPS sensor. Therefore, do not be overly aggressive when assigning the deny-action to signature.

Also, "deny" discards the packet without sending a reset. Cisco recommends using "deny and reset" with alarm.

Also note that IP logging and verbose alert traces use a common capture file writing code called libpcap. This is the same format used by the famous packet-capture tool Wireshark (formerly Ethereal); by Snort, a famous freeware IDS; by NMAP, a well-known fingerprinting tool; and by Kismet, a famous wireless sniffing tool.

You can use the reset TCP connection action in conjunction with deny-packet and deny-flow actions. However, deny-packet and deny-connection actions do not automatically cause reset TCP connection actions to occur.

IPS Anti-Evasion Techniques

Attackers will do their best to get around your intrusion prevention architecture. Multiple IPS evasion techniques allow them to deploy exploits using a stealth approach, one that often renders IPS sensors unable to detect and prevent intrusion. These techniques include the following:

- **Traffic fragmentation:** Any evasion attempt where the attacker splits malicious traffic, hoping to avoid detection or filtering by confusing the network IPS sensor reassembly methods, bypassing the network IPS sensor if it does not perform any reassembly at all, or reordering split data if the network IPS sensor does not correctly order it in the reassembly process.

- **Traffic substitution:** The attacker attempts to evade detection by substituting payload data with other data in a different format but with the same meaning. If the IPS sensor does not recognize the true meaning of data, and only looks for data in a particular format, it may miss such malicious payloads. Examples include the use of Unicode strings, exploiting case sensitivity, substitution of spaces with tabs, and others.

- **Protocol-level misinterpretation:** The attacker attempts to evade detection by causing the network IPS sensor to misinterpret the end-to-end meaning of network protocols and see traffic differently from what will actually be seen and processed by the target. Consequently, the sensor will either ignore traffic that should not be ignored or vice versa.

- **Timing attacks:** The attacker attempts to evade detection of correlating signatures by performing their actions more slowly, not exceeding the thresholds inside the time windows that these signatures use to correlate different packets together.

- **Encryption and tunneling:** The attacker attempts to evade detection by encrypting packets. Sensors monitor the network and capture the packets as they traverse the network. Network-based sensors rely on the data that is being transmitted in plaintext. When packets are encrypted, the sensor captures the data but is unable to decrypt it and cannot perform meaningful analysis. This type of evasive technique assumes that the attacker has already established a secure session with the target network or host.

- **Resource exhaustion:** In this less subtle method of evading detection, the attacker relies on extreme resource consumption. It does not matter if such a denial is against the device or the personnel who are managing the device. Specialized tools can be used to create a tremendous number of alarms that consume the resources of the IPS device and prevent attacks from being logged.

The following anti-evasion features are available on Cisco IPS sensors:

- Complete session reassembly that supports the string and service engines that must examine a reliable byte stream between two network endpoints

- Data normalization (deobfuscation) inside service engines, where all signatures convert network traffic data into a normalized, canonical form before comparing it to the signature-matching rules

- IP Time to Live (TTL) analysis and TCP checksum validation to guard against end-to-end protocol-level traffic interpretation

- Configurable intervals for correlating signatures, or the use of an external correlation that does not require real-time resources

- Inspection of traffic inside Generic Routing Encapsulation (GRE) tunnels to prevent evasion through tunneling

- Smart and dynamic summarization of events to guard against too many alarms for high event rates

Table 11-4 summarizes the evasion methods and the corresponding Cisco IPS anti-evasion features that just described.

Table 11-4 *Anti-Evasion Techniques Used by Cisco IPS*

Evasion Method	Cisco IPS Anti-Evasion Features
Traffic fragmentation	Complete session reassembly in string and service engines
Traffic substitution and insertion	Data normalization (deobfuscation) in service engines

Table 11-4 *Anti-Evasion Techniques Used by Cisco IPS*

Evasion Method	Cisco IPS Anti-Evasion Features
Protocol-level misinterpretation	IP TTL analysis
	TCP checksum validation
Timing attacks	Configurable intervals
	Use of third-party SIEM system for correlation
Encryption and tunneling	GRE tunnel inspection
Resource exhaustion	Smart dynamic event summarization

Note Security Information and Event Management (SIEM) solutions include SIM (security information management) and SEM (security event management). A SIEM product provides real-time analysis of security alerts generated by network devices such as firewalls, IPS sensors, routers, and so forth. The network devices send their syslog, SNMP, or other format security logs to the SIEM for analysis, correlation, and reporting. SIEM solutions can be in the form of software installed on your server or appliance or event management services. Cisco's own SIEM solution used to be the Cisco Security Monitoring, Analysis, and Response System (MARS), which is now end-of-life status. Some of the Cisco third-party partners for SIEM solutions, at the time of writing, are Splunk, ArcSoft, LogLogic, and netForensics.

Risk-Based Intrusion Prevention

Intrusion management is all about risk. Threat vectors evolve so rapidly that it becomes impossible to possess all knowledge of all threats and all threat mutations, especially when new mutations occur within hours and even minutes of the seed malware.

A common technique that is used to improve the accuracy and context awareness of the intrusion prevention architecture is illustrated in Figure 11-4. This technique aims to build a risk rating into the detection capabilities, the goal of which is to detect and respond to relevant incidents only. In turn, this should reduce noise and allow IPS administrators to focus on mitigation and not on navigating the vast amounts of information.

For example, an IPS sensor should detect patterns of global virus outbreaks. Using risk ratings, however, it would trigger a high-severity alert if the virus exploits the operating systems that are used in the specific network being protected, but perhaps a medium severity alert if the operating system is not in use in the organization. The response would be different for unpatched or more vulnerable servers running the relevant operating system, as opposed to fully patched servers with endpoint protection. Within these subsets, the response would be different for unpatched servers have a high asset value versus unpatched servers that store public or nonvaluable information and have a lower asset value.

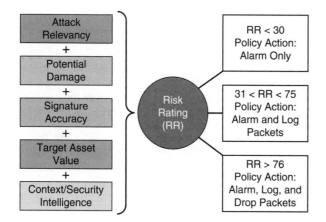

Figure 11-4   *Building a Risk Rating into the Detection Capabilities*

Using these considerations, risk ratings typically include several components:

- **Potential damage that could be caused by the activity described by the signature:** Attacks that are potentially more devastating should result in higher risk ratings, and vice versa.

- **Asset value of the target of the attack:** Attacks against higher-valued assets should result in higher risk ratings, and vice versa.

- **Accuracy of the triggering signature:** Inaccurate signatures lower confidence in correct sensor decisions. Therefore, the triggering of an inaccurate signature should result in lower risk ratings, and vice versa. Additionally, sensors running in inline mode are often more accurate than sensors running in promiscuous mode, due to their traffic normalization functions. Signatures triggering in inline mode should have a correspondingly higher risk rating.

- **Relevancy of the attack to the target:** Attacks that cannot cause damage against their target (for example, a Windows-specific attack targeting a Linux host) should be deprioritized and assigned a lower risk rating value, because they cause no or little damage.

- **Other security countermeasures (controls) in the environment:** Often, these may have some additional clues that can increase the situational awareness of the sensor, and allow it to react to the current context of network events and threats. External sources of information such as honeypots and early warning systems also fit into this category. This security intelligence may also influence risk rating by raising the risk rating for events that are caused by known threats that may be experiencing global or at least significant outbreaks outside of the protected network.

Threat Rating

Cisco IPS provides a threat rating (TR) when it detects an event. The TR is the risk rating (RR) minus values associated with protective responses, called TR adjustments. TR adjustments are actions such as denying an attacker or denying the connection. So, TR = RR − TR adjustments. For example, if a risk is rated at 80 and the protection measure (such as blocking the attacker) is rated at 45, the TR is 35.

Further discussion on threat ratings is beyond the scope of this book; however, you will find plenty of information on this topic in *CCNP Security IPS 642-627 Official Cert Guide* (Cisco Press, 2011).

IPv6-Aware IPS

IPv6 awareness is another important consideration for IPS architectures. Sensors should be IPv6 aware; they should showcase detection techniques that consider the various threats that are found both in IPv6-only environments and in dual-stack environments where IPv4 and IPv6 coexist. As an example, IPS signatures can detect Teredo tunnels and other IPv4-to-IPv6 transition techniques, often used to exploit networks implementing dual stacks.

Alarms

Alarms fire when specific parameters are met. You must balance the number of incorrect alarms that you can tolerate with the capability of the signature to detect actual intrusions. If you have too few alarms, you might be letting in more suspect packets, but network traffic will flow more quickly. If IPSs use untuned signatures, they produce many false positive alarms, which could result in masking important alarms because they would get lost among the massive number of alarms received. You should consider the following factors when implementing alarms that a signature uses:

- The level assigned to the signature determines the alarm severity level.

- A Cisco IPS signature is assigned one of four severity levels:

  - **Informational:** Activity that triggers the signature is not considered an immediate threat, but the information provided is useful information.

  - **Low:** Abnormal network activity is detected that could be perceived as malicious, but an immediate threat is not likely.

  - **Medium:** Abnormal network activity is detected that could be perceived as malicious, and an immediate threat is likely.

  - **High:** Attacks used to gain access or cause a DoS attack are detected, and an immediate threat is extremely likely.

- You can manually adjust the severity level that an alarm produces.

- To minimize false positives, study your existing network traffic patterns and then tune your signatures to recognize intrusion patterns that are atypical (out of character) for your network traffic patterns. Do not base your signature tuning on traffic patterns that are based only on industry examples. Use industry examples as a starting point, determine what your own network traffic patterns are, and then use the results in your signature alarm tuning efforts.

- As an additional source of information, consider implementing NetFlow on network access devices such as routers and firewalls. NetFlow will collect IP traffic statistics and samples, which you can later export as NetFlow records to a NetFlow collector, such as SolarWinds or one of many others. These NetFlow statistics would assist you in characterizing the type of traffic going through your network.

IPS Alarms: Event Monitoring and Management

Event monitoring and management can be divided into the following two needs:

- Real-time event monitoring and management

- Analysis based on archived information (reporting)

These functions can be handled by a single server, or they can be placed on separate servers to scale the deployment. The number of sensors that should forward alarms to a single IPS management console is a function of the aggregate number of alarms per second generated by those sensors.

There is an important difference between reporting and monitoring. Note that archives are often a significant source of data when producing reports.

- **Reporting:** Analysis based on archived information

- **Event monitoring:** Real-time monitoring

Archiving is an important aspect for proper forensics and compliance. Ensure that your archives are properly safeguarded from potential tampering and accidental loss. Your organization should have an archiving policy, often dictated by governance of the longevity of the archive (how far back you must keep your archives). Your policies also should stipulate whether archives can be kept on site or, as usually recommended, off site.

Experience with customer networks has shown that the number of sensors reporting to a single IPS management console should be limited to 25 or fewer. These customers use a mixture of default signature profiles and tuned signatures. The number of alarms generated by each sensor is determined by how sensitively the sensor is tuned; the more sensitive the tuning, the fewer the alarms that are generated and the larger the number of sensors that can report to a single IPS management console.

Note   With the evolution of technology, the limit of 25 sensors reporting to a single IPS management console is constantly being pushed. Check with your vendor for the latest information.

Multiple protocols are available for alarm generation. Common protocols are SNMP, syslog, and Security Device Event Exchange (SDEE), the latter of which is more customized for security monitoring. SDEE is a standard developed to communicate an event generated by security devices.

When implementing multiple IPS management consoles, implement either separate monitoring domains or a hierarchical monitoring structure.

It is essential to tune out false positives to maximize the scalability of the network IPS deployment. Sensors that are expected to generate a large number of alarms, such as those sitting outside the corporate firewall, should log in to a separate IPS management console, because the number of false alarms raised dramatically increases the noise-to-signal ratio and makes it difficult to identify otherwise valid events.

Recall the following:

- False positives happen when the IDS/IPS mistakes legitimate traffic for an attack.
- False negatives happen when the IDS/IPS sensor misses an attack.

Global Correlation

Figure 11-5 illustrates a distributed approach to gathering and analyzing security intelligence and threat information. By combining local, enterprise, and global intelligence, and correlating the information at all levels, you can reduce noise and focus on relevant incidents only.

- Device intelligence is gathered on a per-device basis, and when viewed locally it will be useful for pinpointing the problem to the place in the network where the sensor is located. For instance, a port-scanning reconnaissance attack on the demilitarized zone (DMZ) could be an indication of a full-blown incident, but it could also be a minor event.

- Enterprise intelligence is gathered by all sensors of the organization and typically is centralized in a SIEM system. It provides additional information to categorize events, based on the scale and scope of the event. For instance, a port-scanning attack on the DMZ network acquires more relevance when it is followed within minutes by a firewall policy violation and a password-guessing incident on a mission-critical server.

- Global intelligence is usually gathered by early warning systems, honeypots, and managed threat services outside the organization. They give incidents a global scope. For instance, if the attack pattern detected by the enterprise SIEM is known to come from the same IP sources at a global scale, this information should trigger a more timely response. The port scanning suddenly becomes a critical incident when local, enterprise, and global information is correlated.

Figure 11-5 *Device, Enterprise, and Global Correlation*

In Figure 11-5, you will also notice the event management options using Cisco IPS architectures at local, enterprise, and global levels:

- **Device event correlation:** Device-level correlation is typically accomplished with products such as Cisco Configuration Professional, IPS Device Manager, or IPS Manager Express.

- **Enterprise event correlation:** Enterprise correlation can be gathered using Cisco Security Manager or third-party, ecosystem partner SIEM systems for more specialized event management and forensics capabilities, thus providing enterprise wide intelligence. Ecosystem partner products include ArcSight, netForensics, Splunk, and others. Refer to Cisco.com for more information; specifically, look for *Cisco Security Information Event Management Deployment Guide*.

- **Global event correlation:** Global security intelligence correlation is the responsibility of the Cisco Security Intelligence Operations (SIO) cloud-based service that connects global threat information, reputation-based services, and sophisticated analysis to Cisco network security devices to provide stronger protection with faster response times.

Why Did Cisco Pay $830M for IronPort?

Why did Cisco pay $830M to acquire IronPort in 2007? IronPort was selling great email and web security appliances, but these devices would not have justified the high price tag. Cisco bought IronPort for its crown jewel, SenderBase, since renamed Cisco IronPort SensorBase. SensorBase enables your security network devices, such as firewalls, sensors, and so forth, to not only build a risk profile on IP addresses, therefore allowing risk profiles to be dynamically created on HTTP sites and Simple Mail Transfer Protocol (SMTP) email sources, but also keep a list of IP addresses known for generating malicious activities. The information is collected and analyzed globally by Cisco SIO, which is then responsible for disseminating that information to all devices subscribing to SensorBase. You can check out Cisco SenderBase for yourself at http://www.senderbase.org. Under Reputation Lookup, plug in your domain name or www.ciscopress.com. The score is neutral and you want some excitement? Type ihaveabadreputation.com. This domain belongs to IronPort and is artificially maintained with a score of Poor to be used as a target by organizations that need to test the efficacy of their Web-Based Reputation Score filtering systems. By the way, at that website you will also find the EICAR test file, used to monitor the efficacy of virus protection.

Would you like to check the score of real domains that have been known to host malware? Visit http://www.malwaredomainlist.com for a list of malware domains. Pick an offending IP address from the list, go back to www.senderbase.org, and check the reputation of that offending domain and its history. Fascinating, isn't it?

More information can be found on the power of SensorBase and Cisco Global Correlation, considered the best protection against zero-day attacks, at www.cisco.com/go/sio.

IPS Deployment

Different networks require different design and deployment options. Even within the same administrative domain, different network blocks will benefit from different IPS technologies, deployment options, and form factors. You should plan the IPS architecture carefully, using a "places in the network" approach and considering the different levels of risk for the different assets you are trying to protect.

Figure 11-7 illustrates two examples:

- A remote-access SSL VPN architecture, where the potential exists that users will connect to the SSL VPN gateway router using an infected device (PC, laptop, tablet, etc.). The focus of the signature database policy is on application layer inspection, and the objective is to mitigate threats coming from unmanaged and potentially exploited endpoints.

- A private WAN scenario, where a combination of Cisco IOS IPS and integrated hardware modules on ISR G2 routers provides a smaller footprint and cost-effective architecture. The focus on the signature database policy is on DoS, combined with a reputation-based approach on some branches.

Many other places in the network can leverage the available options to deploy an effective IPS architecture.

In this example, Cisco IPS with Global Correlation detects threats propagating in various countries and creates a new ruleset within 5 minutes to protect against the emerging threat.

Figure 11-6 *Global Correlation and Cisco SIO at Work, Preventing Zero-Day Attack*

Figure 11-7 *Examples of IPS Deployments*

Cisco IPS Offerings

When deploying an IPS architecture using Cisco technologies, various form factors are available to deploy intrusion prevention sensors using a distributed security intelligence approach, as shown in Figure 11-8.

Cisco IPS Form Factors		Small	Medium		High
	Appliances	IPS4240	IPS4255	IPS4260	IPS4270
	HW Modules – Catalyst 6500			IDSM2	IDSM2 Bundle
	HW Modules – ASA	AIP-SSC-5	AIP-SSM-10	AIP-SSM-20	AIP-SSM-40
	ISR-Integrated	IOS IPS	AIM-IPS	NME-IPS	

Throughput

Figure 11-8 *IPS Platforms from Cisco*

The following is a brief description of the available options and footprints:

- **Cisco ASA Advanced Inspection and Prevention Security Services Module (ASA AIP-SSM):** The Cisco ASA AIP-SSM uses advanced inspection and prevention technology to provide high-performance security services, such as intrusion prevention services and advanced content security services. The Cisco ASA AIP-SSM products include a Cisco ASA AIP-SSM-10 module with 1 GB of memory, a Cisco ASA AIP-SSM-20 module with 2 GB of memory, and a Cisco ASA AIP-SSM-40 module with 4 GB of memory.

- **Cisco IOS IPS:** Cisco IOS IPS is an inline, deep-packet inspection feature, available in Cisco Integrated Services Routers Generation 2 (ISR G2), which effectively mitigates a wide range of network attacks. A component of the Cisco IOS Integrated Threat Control framework and complemented by the Cisco IOS Flexible Packet Matching feature, Cisco IOS IPS provides your network with the intelligence to accurately identify, classify, and stop or block malicious traffic in real time.

- **Cisco IPS 4200 Series Sensors:** Cisco IPS 4200 Series Sensors offer significant protection to your network by helping to detect, classify, and stop threats, including worms, spyware and adware, network viruses, and application abuse. Using Cisco IPS Sensor Software Version 7.x, the Cisco IPS solution combines inline intrusion prevention services with innovative technologies that improve accuracy. As a result, more threats can be stopped without the risk of dropping legitimate network traffic.

Cisco IPS Sensor Software Version 7.x includes virtualization, enhanced detection capabilities, and improved scalability, resiliency, and performance features.

- **Cisco Catalyst 6500 Series Intrusion Detection System Services Module 2 (IDSM-2):** The Catalyst 6500 Series IDSM-2 is part of the Cisco IPS solution. It works in combination with the other components to efficiently protect your data infrastructure. With the increased complexity of security threats, achieving efficient network intrusion security solutions is critical to maintaining a high level of protection. Vigilant protection ensures business continuity and minimizes the effect of costly intrusions.

- **Cisco IPS Advanced Integration Module (IPS AIM):** Cisco offers various IPS solutions using Cisco ISR G2 platforms. Cisco IPS Sensor Software running on the Cisco IPS AIM provides advanced, enterprise-class IPS functions and meets the ever-increasing security needs of branch offices. The Cisco IPS AIM can scale in performance to match branch office WAN bandwidth requirements today and in the future. At the same time, the integration of IPS onto a Cisco ISR keeps the solution cost low and effective for businesses of all sizes.

Note Cisco IOS IPS and the Cisco IPS AIM cannot be used together. Cisco IOS IPS must be disabled when the IPS AIM is installed. Cisco IOS IPS is an IPS application that provides inspection capabilities for traffic flowing through the router. Although it is included in the Cisco IOS Advanced Security feature set, it uses the router CPU and shared memory pool to perform the inspection. Cisco IOS IPS also runs a subset of IPS signatures. The Cisco IPS AIM runs with a dedicated CPU and memory, offloading all processing of IPS signatures from the router CPU. It can load a full signature set and provide enhanced IPS features not available on Cisco IOS IPS.

New Cisco IPS Technologies and Sensors

Cisco introduced two additional IPS technologies in 2012:

- Cisco IPS 4300 Series Sensors, capable of 1-Gbps throughput.

- Cisco ASA 5500-X Series firewalls with IPS technology, including zero-day attack protection with anomaly detection, all built into the OS. These new firewalls are based on the SecureX technology and run Cisco ASA 8.6(1) code and Cisco IPS 7.1 code.

For more information on these new technologies and on all current Cisco IPS technologies, visit http://www.cisco.com/go/ips and http://www.cisco.com/go/asa.

IPS Best Practices

The following are the recommended practices for designing and deploying IPS architecture:

- Use a combination of detection technologies.

- Take advantage of multiple form factors to deploy a distributed and cost-effective IPS architecture.

- Use a "places in the network" approach, which, for Cisco, refers to the building blocks of a corporate network, such as a data center, a campus, and a branch office.

- Enable anti-evasion techniques.

- Take advantage of local, enterprise, and global correlation.

- Use a risk-based approach to improve accuracy and simplify management.

- When deploying a large number of sensors, automatically update signature packages instead of manually upgrading every sensor.

- Place the signature packages on a dedicated FTP server within the management network.

- Tune the IPS architecture constantly.

Note A Great Debate: Fail-Close or Fail-Open?

This is another topic of discussion you could add to the list of IPS best practices. Fail-close or fail-open is a philosophical debate your organization needs to engage in: "If the IPS sensor stops working, do we let the traffic go through or do we stop the traffic?" The two opposing philosophies are represented in Figure 11-9, where the network administrator needs to decide whether the traffic will be allowed to flow into the DMZ if the Cisco ASA AIP SSM fails.

It seems that the balance is tilting in favor of the fail-open approach with security experts, especially when dealing with for-profit organizations, but each organization has to define and enforce its own policy.

The default with Cisco IOS IPS is fail-open. You can verify this with the command **show** *ip ips configuration*, which should display "IPS fail closed is disabled." The output of this command is shown later in Example 11-2.

Note Readers interested in learning more about generic topics regarding IDS/IPS should consider visiting http://www.searchsecurity.com, more precisely, "Security Topics" and "Tutorials."

Figure 11-9   *Fail-Open or Fail-Close Approach*

Recommended practices are based on a series of key factors in current IPS architectures, required to manage evolving threats and business requirements:

- Intelligent, distributed detection
    - Vulnerability- and exploit-specific signatures
    - Protocol anomaly detection
    - Knowledge base anomaly detection
    - Reputation filters
- Accurate, precise response to relevant attacks
    - Risk management–based policy
    - Global correlation adding reputation
    - On-box correlation
    - "Trustworthiness" linkages with the endpoint

- Flexible deployment options

  - Passive and/or inline with flexible response (IDS/IPS)

  - Sensor virtualization

  - Physical and logical (VLAN) interface support

  - Software and hardware bypass

Cisco IPS Architecture

Cisco IPS architectures provide an effective approach to threat control and containment by implementing IPS technologies that address the key factors mentioned in the previous section. Figure 11-10 illustrates the various IPS functions that are applied to traffic as it is processed by a Cisco IPS sensor, starting with the virtual sensors. The traffic can then be analyzed by reputation filters, anti-evasion techniques, modular signature engines with automatic signature and engine updates, local and global device correlation, and risk ratings. Depending on the findings, alarm management and/or logging and forensics capabilities will be activated.

Note   Not all IPS form factors support all IPS capabilities that are shown in Figure 11-10. Please refer to the proper documentation for each IPS sensor product for specific platform details. As an example, virtual sensors are used with Cisco IPS 4x00 sensor and can be thought of as a collection of data that is defined by a set of configuration policies. A discussion on virtual sensors is beyond the scope of this book.

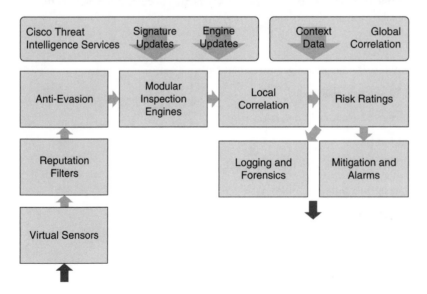

Figure 11-10   *Cisco IPS Architecture*

Cisco IOS IPS

Configuring Cisco IOS Intrusion Prevention System (IPS) is a core competency for a network security administrator. This section describes how to configure Cisco IOS IPS on routers using Cisco Configuration Professional, and includes a description of the building blocks of Cisco IOS IPS, its deployment options, and guidelines for signature tuning.

Cisco IOS IPS Features

Cisco has implemented IPS functions into its Cisco IOS Software. Cisco IOS IPS uses technology from Cisco Intrusion Detection System (IDS) and IPS Sensor product lines, including Cisco IPS 4200 Series Sensors and Cisco Catalyst 6500 Series Intrusion Detection System Services Module 2 (IDSM-2). Cisco IOS IPS combines existing Cisco IDS and IPS product features with the following three intrusion detection techniques:

- **Profile-based intrusion detection:** Profile-based intrusion detection generates an alarm when activity on the network goes outside a defined profile. With anomaly detection, profiles are created for each user or user group on your system. These profiles are then used as a baseline to define normal user and network activity. A profile could be created to monitor web traffic.

- **Signature-based intrusion detection:** Signature-based intrusion detection is less prone to triggering a false alarm when detecting unauthorized activity. A signature is a set of rules pertaining to typical intrusion activity. Signature-based intrusion detection uses signatures that are based on values in IP, TCP, UDP, and ICMP headers. Network engineers research known attacks and vulnerabilities and then develop signatures to detect these attacks and vulnerabilities on the network. These attack signatures encompass specific traffic or activity that is based on known intrusive activity.

  Cisco IOS IPS implements signatures that can look at every packet going through the network and generate alarms when necessary. Cisco IOS IPS generates alarms when a specific pattern of traffic is matched or a signature is triggered. You can configure Cisco IOS IPS to exclude signatures and modify signature parameters to work optimally in your network environment.

  A pattern-matching approach searches for a fixed sequence of bytes in a single packet. Pattern matching is a rigid approach but is simple to employ. In most cases, the pattern is matched against a packet only if the suspect packet is associated with a particular service or, more precisely, destined to or from a particular port. For example, a signature might be based on a simple pattern-matching approach such as the following: If <the packet is IPv4 and TCP> and <the destination port is 2222> and <the payload contains the string "foo"> then <fire an alarm>.

- **Protocol analysis–based intrusion detection:** Protocol analysis–based intrusion detection is similar to signature-based intrusion detection but performs a more in-depth analysis of the protocols specified in the packets. A deeper analysis examines the payloads within TCP and UDP packets, which contain other protocols. For example, a protocol such as DNS is contained within TCP or UDP, which itself is contained within IP.

The first step of protocol analysis is to decode the packet IP header information and determine whether the payload contains TCP, UDP, or another protocol. For example, if the payload is TCP, some of the TCP header information within the IP payload is processed before the TCP payload is accessed

Protocol analysis requires the IPS sensor to know how various protocols work so that it can more closely analyze the traffic of those protocols to look for suspicious or abnormal activity. For each protocol, the analysis is based not only on protocol standards, particularly the RFCs, but also on how things are implemented in the real world. Many implementations violate protocol standards. It is important that signatures reflect common and accepted practice rather than the RFC-specified ideal; otherwise, false results can be reported.

Key Topic

The following are key points of Cisco IOS IPS:

■ Software-based inline intrusion prevention sensor

■ Supports same software and signature format as other Cisco IPS products starting with 12.4(11)T

■ Supports signature-based scanning, but uses a blend of detection technologies:

  ■ Profile based

  ■ Signature based

  ■ Protocol analysis based

The following attributes describe the primary benefits of the Cisco IOS IPS solution:

■ Cisco IOS IPS uses the underlying routing infrastructure to provide an additional layer of security with investment protection.

■ Because Cisco IOS IPS is inline and is supported on a broad range of routing platforms, attacks can be effectively mitigated to deny malicious traffic from both inside and outside the network.

■ When used in combination with Cisco IDS, Cisco IOS Firewall, virtual private network (VPN), and Network Admission Control (NAC) solutions, Cisco IOS IPS provides superior threat protection at all entry points to the network.

■ Cisco IOS IPS is supported by easy and effective management tools, such as Cisco CCP, IDM, IME, and Cisco Security Manager.

- Whether threats are targeted at endpoints, servers, or the network infrastructure, Cisco IPS offers pervasive intrusion prevention solutions that are designed to integrate smoothly into the network infrastructure and to proactively protect vital resources.

- Cisco IOS IPS supports attack signatures from the same signature database that is available for Cisco IPS appliances.

Scenario: Protecting the Branch Office Against Inside Attack

The Cisco IOS IPS solution enables a distributed approach to threat mitigation by allowing intrusion prevention to be enabled on a software footprint on existing routers. Figure 11-11 depicts a typical branch protection scenario, where VPN routers connect to corporate assets across a public network. Cisco IOS IPS can be used to implement a focused intrusion prevention strategy, mitigating malware outbreaks that could originate in less protected remote locations, or partner locations that fall outside of the administration domain of corporate security teams. The smaller footprint takes full advantage of the hardware and architectural resources of ISR G2 routers and allows for inbound IPS functionality to protect the branch itself from targeted external attacks.

Figure 11-11   *Cisco IOS IPS Protecting Against an Inside Attack*

Signatures

Many of the features that make the Cisco IPS architecture effective are inherited by Cisco IOS IPS. Table 11-5 describes the features of Cisco IOS IPS–based signatures.

Table 11-5 *Cisco IOS IPS Signature Features*

Cisco IOS IPS Signature Feature	Description
Regular expression string pattern matching	Enables the creation of string patterns using regular expressions.
Response actions	Enables the sensor to take an action when the signature is triggered.
Alarm summarization	Enables the sensor to aggregate alarms. It does this to limit the number of times an alarm is sent when the signature is triggered.
Threshold configuration	Enables a signature to be tuned to perform optimally in a network.
Anti-evasive techniques	Enables a signature to defeat evasive techniques used by an attacker.
Risk ratings	Enables risk-based tuning using Event Risk Rating (ERR), which is based on attack severity, signature fidelity, and asset value.

Signature Files

As explained earlier in this chapter, a signature is a set of rules that an IDS and an IPS use to detect typical intrusive activity, such as DoS attacks.

IPS signatures are dynamically updated and posted to Cisco.com on a regular basis so that customers can access signatures that help protect their network from the latest known network attacks. The updates take the form of signature files, also known as signature packages or simply signature updates. Manual updates are also possible.

Cisco IPS devices use signature engines to load the signature files and scan signatures. Signatures that are contained within the signature packages are managed by various signature engines. The packages typically contain signature definitions for multiple engines.

Signature engines typically correspond to the protocol in which the signature occurs and look for malicious activity in that protocol. Each signature engine provides a common set of signature parameters that can be used to tune the sensitivity, scope, and actions of that particular signature engine, instead of making changes to individual signatures.

Signature Engines = Types of Interrogation

One way to think of signature engines is as types of interrogation. Each engine is an individual process that specializes in a particular type of interrogation. For example, one engine might specialize in IP headers, while another engine specializes in TCP headers, another in UDP headers, and yet another in ICMP traffic. Other engines look at application layer traffic such as SMTP or DNS. Data is processed in parallel by all the appropriate engines. Each engine specifies a set of available parameters to match malware traffic patterns.

A signature package has definitions for each signature it contains. After signatures are loaded and compiled onto a router running Cisco IOS IPS, IPS can begin detecting the new signatures immediately. Routers access signature definition information through a directory in flash that contains three configuration files—the default configuration, the delta configuration, and the Signature Event Action Processor (SEAP) configuration. SEAP is the control unit responsible for coordinating the data flow of a signature event.

Within a signatures package, signatures are categorized using signature engines and top-level categories. The first criterion to categorize signatures uses the basic and advanced signature categories. The basic signature category is appropriate for routers with less than 128 MB of available flash memory. The advanced signature category is appropriate for routers with more than 128 MB of available flash memory. Signatures are organized into signature microengines, explained further later in this section.

IOS IPS Default Category

Starting with Cisco IOS Release 15.0(1)M, in addition to the basic and advanced signature categories, there is a new category called IOS IPS default. This default category of signatures (including some lightweight signatures) is updated frequently by the Cisco signature team.

Signature files also come in different formats for the different methods to load them into the router's flash. The file naming convention indicates which method to use. The following file naming conventions are available:

- Cisco Configuration Professional signature updates use the sigv$X$-SDM-S###.zip name format, where X is the IPS architecture version, and ### is the update ID, a number that increases with every new signature package.

- You can copy files from the CLI, in which case the naming conventions change: IOS-S###-CLI.pkg applies to CLI updates, where ### is the update ID.

Unified Signatures

The signatures became unified across all Cisco platforms with version 5.x of Cisco IOS IPS. Also, you will notice in the bullets regarding the signature updates the SDM reference in the naming convention. This is a legacy from the days of Cisco Security Device Manager, the predecessor to CCP.

Signature Management

Multiple enhanced features are available in Cisco IOS IPS to simplify the signature management process. The features include the following:

- **Encrypted signature support:** Digitally signed signatures allow for trusted authentication and nonrepudiation of the source.

- **Lightweight signatures:** Lightweight signatures allow loading of larger signatures sets, without consuming significant additional memory or reducing the memory that is consumed by an existing signature set.

- **Direct download from Cisco.com capability:** This feature allows an administrator to use the CLI to specify, download, and upgrade to new signatures posted for Cisco IOS routers directly from Cisco.com. An administrator can also configure the router through the CLI to receive future periodic signature downloads automatically to eliminate the manual maintenance efforts and costs of changing or tuning IPS signatures whenever a new update is posted.

- **Tuning per top-level categories:** Top-level signature categories classify signatures for easy grouping and tuning. Group-wide parameters, such as signature event actions, can be applied to a group instead of per signature.

- **Signature tuning inheritance:** This feature allows a network administrator to preserve the customization done on a signature when a signature package is updated. A local file includes locally tuned signature parameters, taking precedence over globally administered signature updates that may reset those parameters. Network administrators can either preserve the current configuration of signature actions or override the configuration with the default settings in future signature updates.

Examining Signature Microengines

A signature microengine (SME) is a component of an IDS and IPS sensor that supports a group of signatures that are in a common category. Each SME is customized for the protocol and fields that it is designed to inspect and defines a set of legal parameters that have allowable ranges or sets of values. The SMEs look for malicious activity in a specific protocol. Signatures can be defined for any of the supported SMEs by using the parameters offered by the supporting SME. Packets are scanned by the SMEs that understand the protocols contained in the packet.

Cisco SMEs implement parallel scanning. All the signatures in a given SME are scanned in parallel fashion, rather than serially. Each SME extracts values from the packet and passes portions of the packet to the regular expression engine. The regular expression engine can search for multiple patterns at the same time (in parallel). Parallel scanning increases efficiency and results in higher throughput.

When IDS (promiscuous mode) or IPS (inline mode) is enabled, an SME is loaded (or built) on to the router. When an SME is built, the router may need to compile the regular expression found in a signature. Compiling a regular expression requires more memory than the final storage of the regular expression. Be sure to determine the final memory requirements of the finished signature before loading and merging signatures.

Note   A regular expression is a systematic way to specify a search for a pattern in a series of bytes. As an example, a regular expression to be used to prevent data containing .exe or .com or .bat from crossing the firewall could look like this:

```
.*\.[Ee][Xx][Ee]|.*\.[Cc][Oo][Mm]|.*\.[Bb][Aa][Tt]
```

Note   For the list of currently supported SMEs, refer to Cisco.com. Specifically, see "Signature Microengines Overview and Lists of Supported Engines" at http://www.cisco.com/en/US/docs/ios-xml/ios/sec_data_ios_ips/configuration/15-0m/sec-cfg-ips.html#GUID-E402D400-0222-4206-8B2D-3B2368C7EABB

Table 11-6 summarizes the types of signature engines available in Cisco IOS IPS.

Table 11-6   *Summary of Types of Supported Signature Engines*

Signature Engine	Description
Atomic	Signatures that examine single packets, for ICMP, TCP, and UDP. The atomic engine does not store persistent data across packets. Each packet is evaluated independently of preceding or following packets.
Service	Signatures that examine the many services that are attacked, such as the service HTTP engine.
String	Signatures that use regular expression–based patterns to detect intrusions. Used with TCP, UDP, and ICMP. As an example, it could be looking for destination port 23 in the TCP header.
Multi-string	Supports flexible pattern matching and supports Trend Labs signatures. Multi-string signatures inspect Layer 4 transport protocol (ICMP, TCP, and UDP) payloads using multiple string matches for one signature.
Other	Internal engine to handle miscellaneous signatures.

Table 11-7 provides more details on signature engines.

Table 11-7   *Details on Signature Microengines*

Signature Microengine	Description
ATOMIC.IP	Provides simple Layer 3 IP alarms
ATOMIC.ICMP	Provides simple ICMP alarms based on these parameters: type, code, sequence, and ID
ATOMIC.IPOPTIONS	Provides simple alarms based on the decoding of Layer 3 options
ATOMIC.UDP	Provides simple UDP packet alarms based on these parameters: port, direction, and data length
ATOMIC.TCP	Provides simple TCP packet alarms based on these parameters: port, destination, and flags
SERVICE.DNS	Analyzes the DNS service
SERVICE.RPC	Analyzes the remote procedure call (RPC) service
SERVICE.SMTP	Inspects SMTP
SERVICE.HTTP	Provides HTTP protocol decode-based string engine; includes anti-evasive URL deobfuscation
SERVICE.FTP	Provides FTP service special decode alarms
STRING.TCP	Offers TCP regular expression–based pattern inspection engine services
STRING.UDP	Offers UDP regular expression–based pattern inspection engine services
STRING.ICMP	Provides ICMP regular expression–based pattern inspection engine services
MULTI-STRING	Supports flexible pattern matching and supports Trend Labs signatures
Other	Provides internal engine to handle miscellaneous signatures

Signature Tuning

Router memory and resource constraints prevent a router from staging all Cisco IOS IPS signatures in such a way that they start utilizing router resources. When signature packages are copied into flash, the signatures are not yet staged in RAM. When Cisco IOS IPS is initialized, the signatures are loaded into the signature database. *Loading* refers to the process where Cisco IOS IPS parses the signature files and populates the signature database. However, it is the process of compiling, as shown in Figure 11-12, that stages the signatures and makes them utilize router resources. *Compiling* refers to the process where the parameter values from signatures are compiled into a regular expression table.

Figure 11-12   *Signatures Interactions with Cisco IOS*

When signatures are compiled, they are not scanned on a serial basis. A parallel signature scanning engine is used to scan for multiple patterns within a signature engine at any given time, and match intrusion activity for traffic flows that are processed by the router's interfaces. If traffic matches those patterns, an action is performed.

You can alter this process to preserve router resources and tune your intrusion prevention system. Cisco IOS IPS allows administrators to retire signatures, which prevents them from being compiled and using router resources. Similarly, unretiring signatures would compile them again. Retiring preserves the router's resources.

The system also allows administrators to enable and disable signatures. An enabled signature performs the actions that are associated with the signature, while a disabled signature does not.

Table 11-8 provides a description of the different states of signatures.

Table 11-8   *Signature States*

Signature State	Description
Retired	Cisco IOS IPS will not compile that signature into memory for scanning.
Unretired	Cisco IOS IPS will compile the signature into memory and use the signature to scan traffic.
Enabled	When triggered by a matching packet (or packet flow), the signature takes the action associated with it.
Disabled	When triggered by a matching packet (or packet flow), the signature does not take the action associated with it.

Optimal Signature Set

By default, most signatures are retired to preserve router resources. The first level of tuning in Cisco IOS IPS environments is aimed at striking a balance between performance and IPS effectiveness. Relevant signatures should be unretired and enabled to increase the effectiveness of the system. When doing this, memory and computing resources should be closely monitored. There is no magic number or rule to design the appropriate configuration for your environment. Careful planning is required. You should start with the predefined basic and advanced signature definitions that are based on the hardware resources on the router, and build from there.

It is worth noting that disabling signatures does not preserve computing resources if the signature is not retired. An unretired disabled signature, similar to an unretired enabled signature, is still processed against inspected traffic by the scanning engine. The only difference is that the associated action will not be performed in the case of the disabled signature.

It is also worth noting that only unretired *and* successfully compiled signatures will take the action when they are enabled. When a signature is retired, even though it may be enabled, it will not be compiled and will not take the action that is associated with it. Also, when a signature is disabled, even though it may be unretired and successfully compiled, it will not take the action that is associated with it.

The combinations of signature compilations and states are outlined in Table 11-9.

Table 11-9 *Combinations of Signature Compilations and States*

	Enabled	**Disabled**
Retired	No memory consumption	No memory consumption
	No action	No action
Unretired	Consumes memory	Consumes memory
	IPS action performed	No action

The predefined Cisco IOS IPS basic and advanced signature categories contain an optimum combination of signatures for all standard memory configurations, providing a good starting point.

The following list summarizes the guidelines for planning an efficient and effective Cisco IOS IPS signature definition:

- The number of signatures that can be compiled depends on the free memory available on the router.

- For routers with 128 MB of flash, start with the basic signature category.

- For routers with 256 MB+ of flash, start with the advanced signature category.

- Retire risk-irrelevant signatures according to your needs.

- Monitor free memory when retiring or unretiring signatures.

- In restrictive policies, define a fail-closed action if signatures fail to compile. This setting instructs the router to drop all packets until the signature engine is built and ready to scan traffic. If this command is issued, one of the following scenarios occurs:

  - If IPS fails to load the signature package, all packets are dropped—unless the user specifies an access control list (ACL) for packets to send to IPS.

  - If IPS successfully loads the signature package, but fails to build a signature engine, all packets that are destined for that engine are dropped.

  - If this command is not issued, all packets are passed without scanning if the signature engine fails to build.

- Disabled signatures are still scanned and processed, and will consume resources.

- Never unretire the "All" signature category.

Other signature tuning opportunities are outside the scope of this book. However, some guidelines and recommended practices are listed here. It is recommended that you tune signature parameters to customize the sensitivity, scope, response, and overall accuracy of your intrusion prevention system.

- Apply Cisco IOS IPS policies on interfaces for ingress traffic.

- Tune signature parameters to define the sensitivity, scope, response, and accuracy of signatures.

  - Matching criteria (patterns, protocol parameters, and so on)

  - Signature action

  - Thresholds and counters

- Add or remove actions based on risk rating.

  - Example: For an alarm-only signature, add a deny packet inline action if the risk rating is above a certain threshold.

- Create custom signatures for vulnerabilities and threats unique to your environment.

- Configure the router not to override tuned parameters in the next signature package update.

Monitoring IPS Alarms and Event Management

An important part of network security is the alarms generated by IPS. These alarms need to be collected and analyzed. In this section, we discuss the alarms and where they are sent.

Cisco IOS IPS Alarms Monitoring

Figure 11-13 shows how to use the Security Device Event Exchange (SDEE) protocol and a syslog-based approach to send Cisco IPS alerts. The sensor generates an alarm when an enabled signature is triggered. Alarms are stored on the sensor. A host can pull the alarms from the sensor using SDEE. Pulling alarms from a sensor allows multiple hosts to subscribe to the event "feed" to allow a host or hosts to subscribe on an as-needed basis.

Figure 11-13 *Support for SDEE and Syslog*

The support for SDEE and syslog in the Cisco IOS IPS solution is as follows:

■ Cisco IOS Software supports the SDEE protocol. When Cisco SDEE notification is enabled (by using the **ip ips notify sdee** command), by default 200 events can be stored in the event buffer, whose size can be increased to hold a maximum of 1000 events. When you disable Cisco SDEE notification, all stored events are lost. A new buffer is allocated when the notifications are reenabled.

■ SDEE uses a pull mechanism. That is, requests come from the network management application, and the IDS and IPS router responds.

■ SDEE becomes the standard format for all vendors to communicate events to a network management application.

■ You must also enable HTTP or HTTPS on the router, using the **ip http server** command, when you enable SDEE. The use of HTTPS ensures that data is secured as it traverses the network.

■ The Cisco IOS IPS router still sends IPS alerts via syslog.

When you use CCP, you can keep track of alarms that are common in SDEE system messages, including IPS signature alarms. The following is an example of an SDEE system alarm message:

```
%IPS-4-SIGNATURE:Sig:1107 Subsig:0 Sev:2 RFC1918 address
[192.168.121.1:137 ->192.168.121.255:137]
```

The preceding alarm was triggered by the fact that a packet with a private address, as listed in RFC 1918, traversed the IPS sensor.

Note   For a complete list of the Cisco IOS IPS system messages, refer to the "Interpreting Cisco IOS IPS System Messages" section in the *Cisco IOS Security Configuration Guide, Release 12.4.*

Event Management

Using SDEE and syslog, event monitoring can be accomplished at various levels, depending on the availability of local, enterprise, or global correlation and event management systems. In addition to the router's buffers, the following management applications can be used to store a single router's alarms, as also previously shown in Figure 11-5:

- Local event management and correlation
  - Cisco Configuration Professional
  - IPS Device Manager
  - IPS Manager Express
- Enterprise event management and correlation
  - Cisco Security Manager
  - Third-party ecosystem partner SIEM systems
- Global event management and correlation
  - Cisco Security Intelligence Operations (SIO)

IPS Manager Express

IPS Manager Express (IME) is a free application from Cisco that can manage alarms from up to 10 SDEE sources—either Cisco IPS Sensors or Cisco IOS IPS routers. Many of the features in IME work only with the IPS Sensors, and not with the Cisco IOS IPS routers.

Configuring Cisco IOS IPS Using Cisco Configuration Professional

Cisco IOS IPS allows you to manage intrusion prevention on routers that use Cisco IOS Software Release 12.3(8)T4 or later. Cisco Configuration Professional lets you control the application of Cisco IOS IPS on interfaces, import and edit signature files from Cisco.com, and configure the action that Cisco IOS IPS should take if a threat is detected.

Following are the configuration steps to deploy Cisco IOS IPS using CCP:

Step 1.   Download the latest Cisco IOS IPS signature package to a local PC using Cisco Configuration Professional Auto Update.

Step 2.   Launch the IPS Policies Wizard to configure Cisco IOS IPS.

Step 3.   Verify that Cisco IOS IPS configuration and signatures are properly loaded.

Step 4.   Perform signature tuning.

Step 5.   Verify alarms.

The configuration scenario is shown Figure 11-14. Configure this branch router to enable Cisco IOS IPS on both inside and outside interfaces, enabling the advanced signature category. Then, you can perform basic tuning, unretiring signatures and changing the default action.

Figure 11-14   *Cisco IOS IPS Configuration Scenario*

Step 1: Download Cisco IOS IPS Signature Package

In the first step, you navigate to the Auto Update screen. From the Cisco Configuration Professional Home page, click **Configure**, choose **Security > Intrusion Prevention** in the left navigation pane, click the **Edit IPS** tab on the right, and then click **Download** in the left column. If SDEE notification is not enabled on the router, an Information dialog box appears, as shown in Figure 11-15. Click **OK** to enable SDEE notification.

Download the latest Cisco IOS IPS signature package to a local TFTP or FTP server. On the Download panel, click the **Get the Latest Cisco CP File and CLI pkg** radio button, as shown in Figure 11-15. Next, click the **Browse** button and select a directory on your local PC in which to save the downloaded files. You can choose the TFTP or FTP server root directory, which will be used later when deploying the signature package to the router. Next click **Download**, as shown in Figure 11-15.

When prompted to provide Cisco.com login credentials, enter your Cisco.com registered username and password.

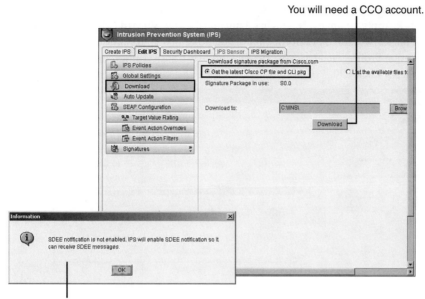

You will need a CCO account.

Message appears if SDEE
not enabled for auto-update.

Figure 11-15 *Downloading Signature Package Using CCP*

CCP connects to Cisco.com, as shown in Figure 11-16, and starts to download both the
CCP signature file (for example, sigv5-SDM-S353.zip) and the CLI signature pkg file (for
example, IOS-S353-CLI.pkg) to the directory you selected in the previous step. After
both files are downloaded, CCP prompts you to push the downloaded signature package
to the router. Choose **No** if, as with our scenario, Cisco IOS IPS has not yet been initialized on the router.

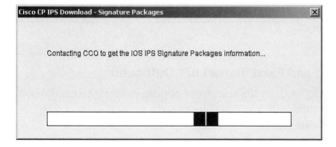

Figure 11-16 *Updating the Cisco IOS IPS Signature Package*

Step 2: Launch IPS Policies Wizard

After CCP downloads the latest Cisco IOS CLI signature package, go to the Create IPS
tab to create the initial Cisco IOS IPS configuration, as shown in Figure 11-17 (**Configure**

> Security > Intrusion Prevention > Create IPS). If prompted to apply changes to the router, click **Apply Changes.** Next, click **Launch IPS Rule Wizard** (which in fact launches the IPS Policies Wizard). An Information dialog box pops up to inform you that Cisco Configuration Professional needs to establish an SDEE subscription to the router to retrieve alerts. Click **OK.**

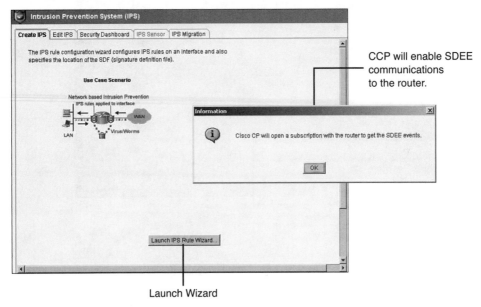

Figure 11-17 *Creating an IPS Policy by Launching the IPS Policies Wizard in CCP*

On the Select Interfaces screen of the IPS Policies Wizard, choose the interfaces on which you want to apply the Cisco IOS IPS rule by specifying whether the rule is to be applied to inbound traffic or outbound traffic, as shown in Figure 11-18. If you check both the inbound and the outbound boxes, the rule applies to traffic flowing in both directions. Click **Next** to continue.

FastEthernet 0/0 Inbound and FastEthernet 0/1 Outbound

What would happen if you configured the IPS rules to be applied to FastEthernet 0/0 inbound and FastEthernet 0/1 outbound? You could get two alarms, one generated by the ingress rule and one by the egress rule.

On the Signature File and Public Key screen of the IPS Policies Wizard, you make the signature file available to the router. This is demonstrated in Figure 11-19. In the Signature File section, click the first radio button, **Specify the Signature File You Want to Use with IOS IPS.** Then click the ... button to open the Specify Signature File dialog box, in which you specify the location of the signature package file.

Select interfaces to enable intrusion prevention.

Figure 11-18   *IPS Policies Wizard: Selecting the Interfaces*

Click to select the signature file.

Figure 11-19   *IPS Policies Wizard: Selecting the Signature File*

You will need to make the previously downloaded signature file available via TFTP, FTP, and other options, such as having it resident on the local PC. In the Specify Signature File dialog box, choose the protocol and location URL. In this example, we are uploading the signature file from the local PC. When you are finished, click **OK** to return to the Signature File and Public Key screen.

Each change to the signature configuration is saved in the delta file. This file must be digitally signed with a public key. You can obtain a key from Cisco.com and copy and paste the information in the Name and Key fields. Public keys will be discussed in Chapter 12, "Fundamentals of Cryptography and VPN Technologies."

Figure 11-20 shows **realm-cisco.pub.key.txt** entered in the Name field of the Configure Public Key section, with the appropriate public key string copied and pasted in the Key field. This public key can be downloaded from Cisco.com at http://download-sj.cisco.com/cisco/ciscosecure/ids/sigup/5.0/ios/realm-cisco.pub.key.txt.

Click **Next** to continue.

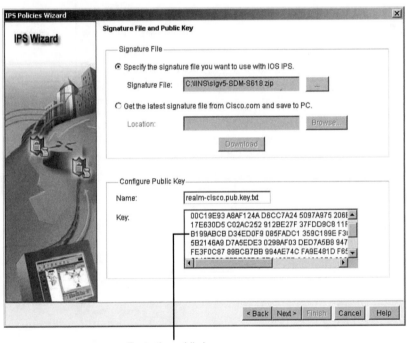

Paste the public key.

Figure 11-20 *IPS Policies Wizard: Downloading and Installing Cisco's Public Key*

In the next wizard screen, Config Location and Category, you specify a location in the router flash for storing the signature information that Cisco IOS IPS will use. This information consists of the signature file and the delta file that is created when changes are made to the signature information. Follow these steps, shown in Figure 11-21:

Step 1.   In the Config Location and Category screen, select a location where the signature definition and configuration files will be stored by clicking the ... button to the right of the Config Location field.

Step 2.   In the Add Config Location dialog box, choose the first option, **Specify the Config Location on This Router**, and then click the ... button to the right of the Directory Name field.

Step 3.   In the Choose Folder dialog box, choose the router flash folder where the IPS files will be stored. If you want IPS files to be in their own folder, click on the **New Folder** button and give an intuitive name to the new folder. In our example, we called it **IPS**.

Figure 11-21   *IPS Policies Wizard: Storing Signature Information*

After you click OK in the various dialog boxes to return to the Config Location and Category screen of the IPS Policies Wizard, choose a signature category from the Choose Category drop-down list, shown in Figure 11-22, according to the amount of flash memory that is installed on the router. Because router memory and resource constraints may prevent the use of all the available signatures, there are two categories of signatures—basic and advanced. The basic category is appropriate for routers with less than

128 MB of available flash memory. The advanced category is appropriate for routers with more than 128 MB of available flash memory. The advanced category requires additional licenses to be obtained.

Note   If you have not activated the Cisco IOS IPS License, then installation of advanced signature packages will fail. Other signature packages can be installed without the license.

In this example, select **advanced**, since we have enough memory, and click **Next**.

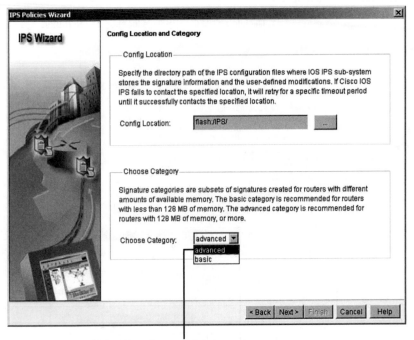

Select the advanced signature category.

Figure 11-22   *IPS Policies Wizard: Configuring Location and Signature Category*

The Summary screen, shown in Figure 11-23, provides a brief description of the tasks for the Cisco IOS IPS initial configuration. Click **Finish** on the Summary screen to deliver the configurations and signature package to the router.

Review settings and click Finish.

Figure 11-23   *IPS Policies Wizard: Summary Configuration*

Step 3: Verify Configuration and Signature Files

When the signatures are loaded, Cisco Configuration Professional then displays the Edit IPS tab (**Configure > Security > Intrusion Prevention > Edit IPS**) with the current configuration. Verify the configuration by checking which interface and in what direction Cisco IOS IPS is enabled.

On the Edit IPS tab, you can also enable or disable Cisco IOS IPS on an interface and view information about how Cisco IOS IPS is applied, by clicking IPS Policies as shown in Figure 11-24. If you enable Cisco IOS IPS on an interface, you can specify which traffic to examine for intrusion.

On the Edit IPS tab, you can click **Signatures** to verify the signature numbers and start planning your resource preservation strategy based on the router model, as shown in Figure 11-25.

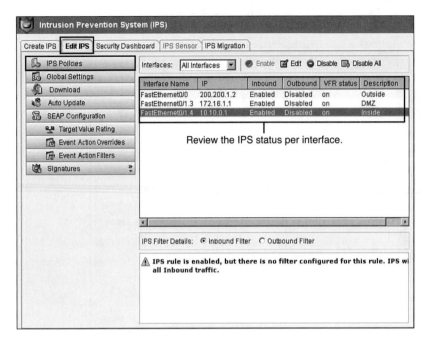

Figure 11-24   *Reviewing IPS Configuration and Interface Status*

Figure 11-25   *Reviewing IPS Signatures*

Compiled Signatures

In Figure 11-25, notice the Sub-Sig ID column. When there are multiple ways for Cisco IPS to recognize the same kind of attack, all those signatures will have the same Signature ID number (Sig ID), but each will have a different Sub-Signature ID number (Sub-Sig ID).

Also notice the Compiled count in the upper-right corner of Figure 11-25. This represents the number of unretired signatures. "Compiled" and "unretired" are synonyms in this context.

Step 4: Perform Signature Tuning

The most basic level of Cisco IOS IPS tuning manages resource preservation. Navigate to **Configure > Security > Intrusion Prevention > Edit IPS > Signatures** to tune the signatures, as shown in Figure 11-26. To find specific signatures or groups of signatures, you can use these filtering mechanisms:

- The signature tree enables you to filter the signature list on the right according to the type of signature that you want to view. First choose the branch for the general type of signature that you want to display. The signature list displays the configured signatures for the type that you chose. If a plus (+) sign appears to the left of the branch, there are subcategories that you can use to refine the filter. Click the + sign to expand the branch and then choose the signature subcategory that you want to display. If the signature list is empty, there are no configured signatures available for that type. For example:

  - To display all attack signatures, click the Attack branch folder.

  - To see the subcategories that you can use to filter the display of attack signatures, click the + sign next to the Attack folder.

  - To see denial of service signatures, click the DoS folder.

- The View By and Criteria drop-down lists enable you to filter the display according to the types of signatures that you want to view. First choose the criteria in the View By drop-down list, and then choose the value for that criteria in the Criteria drop-down list. For example, if you choose Engine in View By, Criteria changes to Engine, and you can choose among the available engines, such as ATOMIC.ICMP and SERVICE.DNS. If you choose Sig ID or Sig Name in the View By drop-down list, you must enter a value in the Criteria field.

Find signatures using these criteria.

Use signature tree to filter by category.

Figure 11-26   *Looking at the Signatures*

To retire or unretire and enable or disable signatures, select the signatures and then click Enable, Disable, Retire, or Unretire, based on your needs and the resources available on the router.

Notice how the status changes in the Enabled or the Retired column. A yellow icon appears for the signature in the column next to Enabled, as shown in Figure 11-27. The yellow icon means that changes have been made to the signature but have not been applied. Click **Apply Changes** to make the changes take effect.

Figure 11-27   *Enable, Disable, Retire, or Unretire Signatures*

To change the action that is associated with a signature, select the signature, right-click and choose **Actions,** and then check or uncheck the check boxes next to the actions to choose the actions to be associated with this signature, as shown in Figure 11-28.

Following is a summary of the options available in the context menu when you right-click a signature:

- **Actions:** Click to choose the actions to be taken when the signature is matched.

- **Set Severity To:** Click to set the severity level of a signature to high, medium, low, or informational.

- **Restore Defaults:** Click to restore the default values of the signature.

- **Remove Filter:** Click to remove a filter applied to the signature.

- **NSDB Help:** Click to display help on the Network Security Database (NSDB) (requires a Cisco.com account).

Figure 11-28   *Changing Action of Signatures*

Signature Actions

With Cisco IOS IPS, protection can be done in two ways. You can enable explicit protection on specific signatures, as shown in Figure 11-28, or it can be enabled implicitly using Event Action Overrides to protect whenever the risk rating is at or above a specified threshold. Determining which signatures should have blocking actions can be a daunting task, so the simpler alternative is to use Event Action Overrides, which uses Event Risk Rating (ERR) to make the decision on your behalf.

Cisco IOS IPS Configuration = XML

When you apply changes to the Cisco IOS IPS configuration, you will not see a command preview in CCP. This is due to the fact that Cisco IOS IPS configuration is stored in XML documents in flash, and not in the running config. The files are in flash:/ IPS, as you specified from the Config Location and Category screen of the IPS Policies Wizard.

Step 5: Verify Alarms

Cisco Configuration Professional can be used as an event viewer for Cisco IOS IPS alarms. You can view the log by navigating to **Monitor > Security > IPS Status** and clicking the **IPS Signature Statistics** tab. (The IPS Status pane also includes an IPS Alert Statistics tab, which is discussed a bit later in this section.)

Figure 11-29 illustrates the contents of the IPS Signature Statistics tab. Statistics are displayed for each enabled signature in the Cisco IOS IPS configuration. The top of the tab displays signature totals to provide a snapshot of the signature configuration. The following totals are provided:

- Total Signatures
- Total Enabled Signatures
- Total Retired Signatures
- Total Compiled Signatures

Figure 11-29 *Monitoring IPS Signature Statistics from CCP*

The statistics table displays alarm counters per signature. The table includes the signature ID, signature description, number of hits or times the signature has been matched, and a drop count that represents the number of times the packet has been dropped due to this event. If a packet that matches a signature arrives, the source and destination IP addresses are listed as well.

The table is not updated automatically. You can click **Update** to check for and include the latest signature statistics. You can also click **Clear** to set all signature statistic counters to 0.

More alarm detail can be observed by displaying the SDEE log. Click the **SDEE Log** link, shown in Figure 11-30, of the IPS Signature Statistics tab to display the log. CCP automatically navigates to **Monitor > Router > Logging** and displays the SDEE Message Log tab, shown in Figure 11-30. Some of the alarms relate to the status of the Cisco IOS IPS service, while some others relate to Cisco IOS IPS service error conditions. Click the SDEE Messages drop-down menu to filter and display Alerts only.

Figure 11-30   *Monitoring IPS Alarms from CCP*

The list includes all alarms in the router buffer, including the following components:

- **Time:** Timestamp for the individual alert

- **Type:** Alerts, Error, or Status entry

- **Description:** Includes event ID, signature IDs, risk rating, and other pieces of alarm-related information

The list is searchable. Clicking Search opens a search window, where you can choose a search type from the Search menu, enter the appropriate text in the Search field, and then click Find to display matching log entries.

The search types include the following:

■ Source IP Address

■ Destination IP Address

■ Text

Searches are not case sensitive.

The IPS Alert Statistics tab, on the other hand, displays a view from the alerts and risk rating perspective. The panel displays alert statistics in a color-coded format for easy recognition. The top part of the screen shown in Figure 11-31 displays a legend that explains the use of colors in the display.

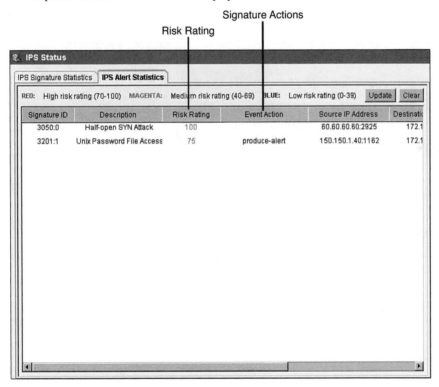

Figure 11-31   *IPS Signature Statistics*

The alert color coding is presented in Table 11-10.

Table 11-10   *Alert Color Coding*

Color	Description
Red	The event that generated the alert has a high risk rating in the range of 70 to 100.
Magenta	The event that generated the alert has a medium risk rating in the range of 40 to 69.
Blue	The event that generated the alert has a low risk rating in the range of 0 to 39.

By clicking a column heading, you sort the display based on the values of that parameter. For example, click the Signature ID heading to sort the display in ascending or descending numerical order of signature IDs. Each column is described in the following list:

- **Signature ID:** Numerical signature identifier.

- **Description:** Description of the signature.

- **Risk Rating:** Value between 0 and 100 that represents a numerical quantification of the risk associated with a particular event on the network.

- **Event Action:** Action that Cisco IOS IPS takes when an event matching the signature occurs.

- **Source IP Address:** The IP address from which the packet originated.

- **Destination IP Address:** The IP address to which the packet was addressed. If the packet is malicious, the destination IP address can be considered the target.

- **Hits:** Number of matching packets.

- **Drop Count:** The number of matching packets dropped.

- **Engine:** The signature engine associated with the signature.

Configuring Cisco IOS IPS Using the CLI

To use the command-line interface (CLI) to specify an IPS rule, use the **ip ips name** *name* command in global configuration mode as follows:

```
router(config)# ip ips name sdm_ips_rule
```

In the preceding command, the IPS rule had been created using CCP. Commands created by CCP appear in the CLI with the notation "sdm," for Security Device Manager, which was the predecessor to CCP.

To specify the location of the IPS configuration, use the **ip ips config location** *location* global configuration command, as demonstrated here:

```
router(config)# ip ips config location flash:/ips/retries 1
```

To specify the method of event notification, use the **ip ips notify** global configuration command. The following is an example of event notification sent using SDEE:

```
router(config)# ip ips notify SDEE
```

> **Note**   Examples in this section that deal with Cisco IOS IPS CLI configuration assume that the signature files are already on the router.

To configure the router to support the default basic signature set, use the **ip ips signature-category** global configuration command as follows:

```
Router(config)# ip ips signature-category
Router(config-ips-category)# category all
Router(config-ips-category-action)# retired true
Router(config-ips-category-action)# exit
Router(config-ips-category)# category ios_ips basic
Router(config-ips-category-action)# retired false
```

To apply an IPS rule to an interface, use the **ip ips** *ips_rule_name* command in interface configuration mode as demonstrated here:

```
router(config)# interface FastEthernet0/0
router(config-if)# ip ips sdm_ips_rule in
```

You should also consider turning on packets virtual reassembly on the sensing interface. Virtual Fragment Reassembly (VFR) enables the Cisco IOS Firewall to examine out-of-sequence fragments and reorder the packets into the correct order. It examines the number of fragments from a same single IP address. When VFR is enabled on the Cisco IOS Firewall, it creates the appropriate dynamic ACLs, thereby protecting the network from various fragmentation attacks. To enable VFR on an interface, use the **ip virtual-reassembly** command in interface configuration mode, as demonstrated here:

```
Router(config)# interface FastEthernet0/0
Router(config-if)# ip virtual-reassembly
```

Example 11-1 provides a combined view of the commands shown in the preceding paragraphs.

Example 11-1   *Cisco IOS IPS CLI Configuration*

```
Router(config)# ip ips name sdm_ips_rule
Router(config)# ip ips config location flash:/ips/ retries 1
Router(config)# ip ips notify SDEE
!
Router(config)# ip ips signature-category
Router(config-ips-category)# category all
Router(config-ips-category-action)# retired true
Router(config-ips-category-action)# exit
Router(config-ips-category)# category ios_ips basic
```

```
Router(config-ips-category-action)# retired false
!
Router(config)# interface Ethernet0/0
Router(config-if)# ip ips sdm_ips_rule in
Router(config-if)# ip virtual-reassembly
```

Use the **show ip ips configuration** command to display additional configuration data that is not displayed with the **show running-config** command. Example 11-2 shows some sample output from the **show ip ips configuration** command.

Example 11-2   show ip ips configuration *Command Output*

```
Router# show ip ips configuration
IPS Signature File Configuration Status
 Configured Config Locations: flash:/ips/
 Last signature default load time: 04:39:33 UTC Oct 19 2011
 Last signature delta load time: 04:41:43 UTC Oct 19 2011
 Last event action (SEAP) load time: -none-

 General SEAP Config:
 Global Deny Timeout: 3600 seconds
 Global Overrides Status: Enabled
 Global Filters Status: Enabled

IPS Auto Update is not currently configured

IPS Syslog and SDEE Notification Status
 Event notification through syslog is enabled
 Event notification through SDEE is enabled

IPS Signature Status
 Total Active Signatures: 295
 Total Inactive Signatures: 4008

IPS Packet Scanning and Interface Status
 IPS Rule Configuration
 IPS name sdm_ips_rule
 IPS fail closed is disabled
 IPS deny-action ips-interface is false
 Obsolete tuning is disabled
```

```
    Regex compile threshold (MB) 14
    Interface Configuration
    Interface FastEthernet0/0
    Inbound IPS rule is sdm_ips_rule
    Outgoing IPS rule is not set
    Interface FastEthernet0/1
    Inbound IPS rule is sdm_ips_rule
    Outgoing IPS rule is not set

IPS Category CLI Configuration:
 Category all:
  Retire: True
 Category ios_ips basic:
  Retire: False
```

You could use the **show ip ips all** command (not shown here) to display additional configuration data that is not displayed with the **show ip ips configuration** command.

Use the **show ip ips interface** command to display interface configuration data. Example 11-3 displays output from the **show ip ips interface** command, revealing that the inbound IPS audit rule **sdm_ips_rule** is applied to FastEthernet 0/0 and FastEthernet 0/1. There is no rule applied for outgoing traffic on either interface.

Example 11-3   show ip ips interfaces *Command Output*

```
Router# show ip ips interfaces
Interface Configuration
 Interface FastEthernet0/0
 Inbound IPS rule is sdm_ips_rule
 Outgoing IPS rule is not set
 Interface FastEthernet0/1
 Inbound IPS rule is sdm_ips_rule
 Outgoing IPS rule is not set
```

In Example 11-4, the output from the **show ip ips signature count** command displays summary signature information. The output shows the signature update ID, as well as the number of total, enabled, retired, compiled, and obsolete signatures. Remember that "compiled" means unretired.

Example 11-4   show ip ips signature count *Command Output*

```
Router# show ip ips signature count
Cisco SDF release version S594.0
Trend SDF release version V0.0
...
<output omitted>
...
Total Signatures: 4303
Total Enabled Signatures: 1218
Total Retired Signatures: 4008
Total Compiled Signatures: 295
Total Obsoleted Signatures: 13
Total Disallowed Signatures: 3
.
.
```

The router will also generate system log messages, providing an additional tool to monitor the health of the IPS feature. The following message is displayed when an IPS signature engine has been built and is ready to scan packets:

```
%%IPS-6-ENGINE_READY:SERVICE.HTTP - 183136 ms - packets for this engine will be
   scanned
```

The following message is displayed when packets are being dropped due to a failed IPS module, when the **ip ips fail closed** command is configured. The **ip ips fail closed** command implements a restrictive fail-closed policy when the Cisco IOS IPS feature fails.

```
%IPS-5-PACKET_DROP:SERVICE.DNS - packets dropped while engine is building
```

The following message, discussed previously in this chapter, is displayed when an IPS signature has been triggered. The signature and subsignature IDs are shown. In this particular example, the alarm is related to a potential spoofing attack, as explained earlier.

```
%IPS-4-SIGNATURE:Sig:1107 Subsig:0 Sev:2 RFC1918 address [192.168.121.1:137
   ->192.168.121.255:137]
```

Use the **show ip ips statistics** command to show a global view of signatures that have triggered, along with valuable information such as the number of packets checked per signature, the number of alarms triggered per signature, and the number of packet drops per signature. The output of Example 11-5 also shows the number of interfaces enabled for Cisco IOS IPS.

Example 11-5   show ip ips statistics *Command Output*

```
Router# show ip ips statistics
Signature statistics [process switch:fast switch]
signature 3041:0: packets checked [0:4] alarmed [0:4] dropped [0:0]
signature 3040:0: packets checked [0:1] alarmed [0:1] dropped [0:0]
signature 6062:1: packets checked [0:1] alarmed [0:1] dropped [0:0]
signature 6054:0: packets checked [0:3] alarmed [0:3] dropped [0:0]
Interfaces configured for ips 1
Session creations since subsystem startup or last reset 10101
Current session counts (estab/half-open/terminating) [15:764:0]
Maxever session counts (estab/half-open/terminating) [22:1182:0]
Last session created 00:00:08
Last statistic reset never
TCP reassembly statistics
received 2 packets out-of-order; dropped 0
peak memory usage 1 KB; current usage: 0 KB
```

Use the **show ip sdee alerts** command to see a detailed view of the alarm log, as shown in Example 11-6.

Example 11-6   show ip sdee alerts *Command Output*

```
router# show ip sdee alerts
Alert storage: 200 alerts using 96000 bytes of memory
SDEE Alerts
SigID      Sig Name            SrcIP:SrcPort       DstIP:DstPort     VRF
                               or Summary Info
1: 3040:0  TCP NULL Packet     172.17.44.101:36044 10.5.5.5:25       NONE
2: 3041:0  TCP SYN/FIN Packet  172.17.44.101:52623 10.5.5.5:25       NONE
3: 6054:0  DNS Version Request 172.17.44.101:4745  172.17.22.103:53  NONE
4: 6062:1  DNS Authors Request 172.17.44.101:4756  172.17.22.103:53  NONE
```

Summary

This chapter described how intrusion detection system (IDS) and intrusion prevention system (IPS) technology embedded in Cisco host- and network-based IDS and IPS solutions fights malware in real time. More precisely, you have learned how

- Cisco IOS IPS prevents intrusion by comparing traffic against the signatures of known attacks. A signature is a set of rules that an IDS and an IPS use to detect typical intrusive activity and how these files can be updated manually or automatically. A public key is required to use digitally signed signature files.

- Signatures can be retired or unretired, enabled or disabled.

- Cisco IOS IPS alarms are communicated using SDEE and syslog.

- The easiest way to configure Cisco IOS IPS on the router or security device is to click the Launch IPS Rule Wizard button in Cisco Configuration Professional to launch the IPS Policies Wizard.

- Cisco Configuration Professional, which includes comprehensive options for configuring IPS and for signature tuning, can also be used to manage Cisco IOS IPS events.

- CCP tools can be used to monitor IPS operations.

References

For additional information, refer to these resources.

Cisco.com Resources

"Cisco IOS IPS Q&A," http://www.cisco.com/en/US/prod/collateral/iosswrel/ps6537/ps6586/ps6634/prod_qas0900aecd806fc530.html

Cisco IOS Security Configuration Guide, Release 12.4, "Configuring Cisco IOS Intrusion Prevention System (IPS)," http://www.cisco.com/en/US/docs/ios/security/configuration/guide/12_4/sec_12_4_book.html

Cisco Security Information Event Management Deployment Guide, http://www.cisco.com/en/US/solutions/collateral/ns340/ns414/ns742/ns982/sbaSIEM_deployG.pdf

"Getting Started with IOS IPS Ð A Step-by-Step Guide," http://www.cisco.com/en/US/prod/collateral/iosswrel/ps6537/ps6586/ps6634/prod_white_paper0900aecd805c4ea8.html

"Intrusion Prevention System," http://www.cisco.com/go/ips

General IDS/IPS Resource

SearchSecurity.com, http://searchsecurity.techtarget.com/

Review Questions

Use the questions here to review what you learned in this chapter. The correct answers are found in the Appendix, "Answers to Chapter Review Questions."

1. Which two modes of IPS operation are currently available with Cisco IDS and IPS solutions?
   a. Out-of-band
   b. Promiscuous
   c. Multicasting
   d. Inline

2. IDS solutions are typically related to inline deployment of sensors. True or false?
   a. True
   b. False

3. Which general patterns of misuse do IDS and IPS technologies look for? (Choose all that apply.)

   a. Atomic pattern
   b. Molecular pattern
   c. Instrusive nonces
   d. Composite (compound) pattern
   e. Composition pattern

4. You need to customize signatures on Cisco IPS devices to detect ICMP ping exploits packet by packet. Which signature microengine should you use?

   a. Service
   b. Multi-string
   c. Atomic
   d. Sub-atomic

5. Which of the following are a type of IDS or IPS sensor? (Choose all that apply.)

   a. Signature based
   b. Policy based
   c. Transgression based
   d. Anomaly based

6. Match the technology with its definition?

   a. Signature-based IPS
   b. Policy-based IPS
   c. Reputation-based IPS
   d. Anomaly-based IPS

   1. Normal behavior typically defined based on traffic patterns, traffic and protocol mix, traffic volumes, and other criteria
   2. Typically implemented in the form of white lists or black lists
   3. Can produce false positives because certain normal network activity can be misinterpreted as malicious activity
   4. Similar to implementing a restrictive firewall policy

7. What is a signature engine?

   a. A set of rules that an IDS and an IPS use to detect typical intrusive activity
   b. A full-feature intrusion prevention tool located in the core network fabric device
   c. An internal security service module that provides dedicated CPU and memory to offload intrusion prevention processing.
   d. A component of an IDS and IPS sensor that supports a group of signatures in a common category

8. Which IPS card could integrate into an ISR router?

   a. Cisco IDSM-2
   b. Cisco ASA AIP SSM
   c. Cisco IPS AIM
   d. Cisco IPS 4200 Series Sensor

9. What is an IPS signature?

   a. A message digest encrypted with the sender's private key

   b. A set of rules used to detect typical intrusive activity

   c. A binary pattern specific to a virus

   d. An appliance that provides anti-x services

10. Compiling a regular expression found in a signature requires more memory than the final storage of the regular expression. True or false?

   a. True

   b. False

11. Which two choices are examples of techniques used to mitigate an evasion attack?

   a. Data normalization

   b. Botnet detection

   c. TCP intercept

   d. Session reassembly

   e. False positive mitigation

12. Cisco IOS IPS supports risk-based signature tuning using Cisco Event Risk Rating. True or false?

   a. True

   b. False

13. The signature package named sigv5-SDM-S592.zip is an example of what type of signature package in Cisco IOS IPS?

   a. Cisco Configuration Professional signature package

   b. CLI signature package

   c. Basic signature package

   d. Advanced signature package

   e. Default signature package

14. You are tuning IPS signatures using Cisco Configuration Professional and see a yellow icon next to the signature ID. What is the reason for this icon?

   a. The signature is a candidate for false positives.

   b. The signature is categorized with the wrong microengine.

   c. You need to click Apply.

   d. You need to enable the signature.

   e. The signature is disabled and you need to unretire it.

15. Which statement is true about this Cisco IOS IPS syslog message?

```
%IPS-5-PACKET_DROP:SERVICE.DNS - packets dropped while engine is building
```

   a. A fail-closed strategy is configured.

   b. The service.dns microengine is disabled.

   c. Packets are blocked by the action of a signature matching the traffic pattern.

   d. An inline deployment option is being used.

Chapter 12

Fundamentals of Cryptography and VPN Technologies

This chapter introduces the concepts of cryptography and VPN technologies. It covers the following topics:

- Need for VPN and VPN deployment models

- Encryption, hashing, and digital signatures and how they provide confidentiality, integrity, and nonrepudiation

- Methods, algorithms, and purposes of symmetric encryption

- Use and purpose of hashes and digital signatures in providing integrity and nonrepudiation

- Use and purpose of asymmetric encryption and Public Key Infrastructure (PKI)

An IP Security (IPsec) virtual private network (VPN) is an integral part of the security architecture of most organizations. It is used to connect branch offices, remote employees, and business partners to the resources of the organization. Providing confidentiality, integrity, and endpoint authentication, VPNs are ubiquitous and provide data loss prevention mechanisms for data in transit at multiple levels. From Secure Sockets Layer (SSL) VPNs to IPsec VPNs, site-to-site VPNs or remote access options, this security control is now embedded in networks and applications and should be made available in a transparent and manageable fashion. This chapter introduces the cryptographic elements used by VPNs, including symmetric and asymmetric algorithms, and describes the components, deployment options, and operational framework of VPN technologies.

VPN Overview

Historically, a VPN was an IP tunnel. Therefore, a generic routing encapsulation (GRE) tunnel is technically a VPN, even though GRE does not encrypt. Today, the use of a VPN implies the use of encryption. With a VPN, the information from a private network is transported over a public network, such as the Internet, to form a virtual network instead of using a dedicated Layer 2 connection, as shown in Figure 12-1. To remain private, the traffic is encrypted to keep the data confidential. VPNs are *virtual* because they are not deployed over a physical private network end to end. At some point, they will traverse a public network of some sort.

Figure 12-1 *Where VPNs Are Found*

VPNs are *private* because they use different methods of traffic segregation to keep the transferred traffic private. For instance, legacy Frame Relay networks could be considered VPNs in that they use a public network (the Frame Relay provider network), and they segregate traffic that shares the public network by encapsulating traffic within Frame Relay frames and tagging traffic that belongs to different customers with different virtual circuit identifiers. More recently, Multiprotocol Label Switching (MPLS) networks can also implement VPN-type connectivity because the customers share the provider's network (hence considered public) and their traffic is segregated using MPLS labels. It is worth mentioning that MPLS VPN does not provide confidentiality because the payload is not encrypted.

The term *private* can optionally refer to confidentiality. Even if traffic is segregated along the path of the VPN, malicious and nonmalicious attackers could technically intercept it at some point on the path and see its contents. To mitigate this risk, and to ensure traffic remains private, traffic is often encrypted to keep the data confidential. Encryption also provides other benefits, such as data integrity and authentication of the entities involved in the VPN. Encryption mechanisms are key in IPsec and SSL VPNs, the main subjects in this chapter, and will be explained in more detail throughout the rest of this book.

VPNs have many benefits:

- **Cost savings:** VPNs enable organizations to use cost-effective third-party Internet transport to connect remote offices and remote users to the main corporate site, thus eliminating expensive dedicated WAN links and modem banks. Furthermore, with the advent of cost-effective high-bandwidth technologies, such as digital subscriber line (DSL), organizations can use VPNs to reduce their connectivity costs while simultaneously increasing remote connection bandwidth.

- **Scalability:** VPNs enable corporations to use the Internet infrastructure within ISPs and devices, which makes it easy to add new users. Therefore, corporations are able to add large amounts of capacity without adding significant infrastructure.

- **Compatibility with broadband technology:** VPNs allow mobile workers, telecommuters, and people who want to extend their workday to take advantage of high-speed, broadband connectivity, such as DSL and cable, to gain access to their corporate networks, providing workers significant flexibility and efficiency. Furthermore, high-speed broadband connections provide a cost-effective solution for connecting remote offices.

- **Security:** Optionally, VPNs provide the highest level of security by using advanced encryption and authentication protocols that protect data from unauthorized access.

VPN Types

There are different types of commercially deployed VPNs. VPN are classified according to the following criteria:

- **Based on deployment mode:** Site-to-site VPN and remote-access VPN

- **Based on Open Systems Interconnection (OSI) layer:** Layer 2 VPN (legacy protocols such as Frame Relay or ATM, and Layer 2 MPLS VPN), Layer 3 VPN (IPsec and MPLS Layer 3 VPN), and Layer 7 VPN (SSL VPN)

- **Based on underlying technology:** IPsec VPN, SSL VPN, MPLS VPN, other Layer 2 technologies such as Frame Relay or ATM, and hybrid VPNs combining multiple technologies

The two basic VPN deployment models typically use either IPsec or SSL technologies to keep the communications secured. The Cisco VPN solutions, illustrated in Figure 12-2, and their associated technologies will be discussed throughout the rest of this book. Other VPN technologies, such as MPLS, are beyond the scope of this book.

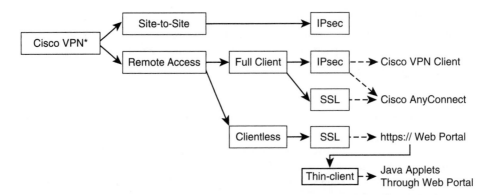

*This figure shows the most commonly used Cisco VPN technologies and those covered in this book.
Other technologies exist but they are beyond the mandate of this book.

Figure 12-2 *Cisco VPN Solutions*

Site-to-Site VPNs

A site-to-site VPN, shown in Figure 12-3, is an extension of a classic WAN network.
Site-to-site VPNs connect entire networks to each other; for example, they can connect
a branch office network to a company headquarters network. In the past, a leased line or
Frame Relay connection was required to connect sites, but because most corporations
now have Internet access, these connections can be replaced with site-to-site VPNs.

Figure 12-3 *Site-to-Site VPNs*

In a site-to-site VPN, hosts do not have Cisco VPN Client software; they send and
receive normal TCP/IP traffic through a VPN "gateway," which could be a router, firewall,
Cisco VPN Concentrator, or Cisco ASA 5500 Series Adaptive Security Appliance. The
VPN gateway is responsible for encapsulating and encrypting outbound traffic for all the

traffic from a particular site and sending it through a VPN tunnel over the Internet to a peer VPN gateway at the target site. Upon receipt, the peer VPN gateway strips the headers, decrypts the content, and relays the packet toward the target host inside its private network.

Remote-Access VPNs

In the past, corporations supported remote users by using dial-in networks and ISDN. With the advent of VPNs, a mobile user simply needs access to the Internet to communicate with the central office. In the case of telecommuters, their Internet connectivity is typically a broadband connection such as DSL or cable. Remote-access VPNs, shown in Figure 12-4, can support the needs of telecommuters, mobile users, and extranet consumer-to-business traffic. Remote-access VPNs connect individual hosts who must access their company network securely over the Internet.

Figure 12-4 *Remote-Access VPN*

Hosts in a remote-access VPN commonly have a VPN client installed. As shown in Figure 12-2, this is called "Full Client." Cisco produces two clients: Cisco AnyConnect and Cisco VPN Client. These clients use a virtual network adapter (virtual network interface card) in the host computer to send traffic back to the head office. The VPN client software encapsulates and encrypts the traffic received on the virtual NIC before sending it over the Internet to the VPN gateway at the edge of the target network. Upon receipt, the VPN gateway behaves as it does for site-to-site VPNs.

Examining Cryptographic Services

Cryptographic services are the foundation for many security implementations. The key services provided by cryptography are as follows:

- **Confidentiality:** The assurance that no one can read a particular piece of data except the receivers explicitly intended.

- **Integrity or data authentication:** The assurance that data has not been altered in transit, intentionally or unintentionally.

- **Peer authentication:** The assurance that the other entity is who he, she, or it claims to be.

- **Nonrepudiation:** A proof of the integrity and origin of data. The sender can't repudiate that he or she is the person who sent the data.

- **Key management:** The generation, exchange, storage, safeguarding, use, vetting, and replacement of keys.

VPN services use a combination of cryptographic technologies and algorithms to accomplish their goals. In the router-to-router VPN, also known as site-to-site VPN, IP packets use symmetric encryption algorithms to encrypt the payload, with keys negotiated by key management protocols. They also use asymmetric encryption algorithms to create digital signatures and authenticate the VPN peers, and use hashing functions to provide checksum-type integrity checks.

This combination of algorithms and cryptographic methods, when used as a unit to negotiate the security settings to accomplish confidentiality, integrity, and authentication, is known as a cipher suite.

Data Authentication Versus User Authentication

Data authentication, also known as message authentication, is not the same as user authentication. With user authentication, as an example, an administrator is requested to provide his username and password to gain administrative access to a network device. Simply put, data authentication is a means for senders and receivers to validate the origin of each segment of a message that is exchanged. Data authentication also ensures data integrity, a way to prove that the payload wasn't tampered with during transmission. Data authentication is covered in greater detail in this chapter when we discuss cryptographic hashes.

Cryptology Overview

Cryptology is the science of making and breaking secret codes. Cryptology is broken into two separate disciplines: *Cryptography* is the development and use of codes, and *cryptanalysis* is the breaking of those codes. A symbiotic relationship exists between the two disciplines because each makes the other one better. National security organizations employ members of both disciplines and put them to work against each other.

In the past, there have been times when each discipline has been ahead of the other. For example, during the Hundred Years' War between France and England, the cryptanalysts were ahead of the cryptographers. France believed that its cipher was unbreakable; however, the Englishmen were able to break it. Some historians believe that World War II largely turned on the fact that the winning side on both fronts was much more successful than the losing side at cracking the encryption of its adversary.

It is an ironic fact of cryptography that it is impossible to prove that an algorithm is secure. You can prove only that it is not vulnerable to known cryptanalytic attacks. If there are methods that have been developed but are unknown to the cryptographer, an algorithm might be able to be cracked. You can prove only invulnerability to known attacks, except for a brute-force attack.

All algorithms are vulnerable to brute force. If every possible key is tried, one of the keys has to work. Therefore, no algorithm is unbreakable. The best you can hope for are algorithms that are vulnerable only to brute-force attacks.

Note   Two separate techniques can be used to try to achieve secure communication. The first one is discussed in this chapter: cryptography, which is the science of encrypting a message.

The second technique is called steganography, which pertains to the method used to hide a message. The message is hidden either within another message or by other means. For example, the German Embassy in Washington, D.C., used steganography by hiding a message within a message. The first letter of each word of a telegram would make up a secret message. This method is referred to as using a null cipher. Another example of steganography was by Histiaeus, a Greek tyrant, who had the head of his most trusted slave shaved, tattooed a message on the scalp, waited for the hair to grow back, and then dispatched the slave to deliver the secret message. Obviously, the element of urgency wasn't there! Another example of steganography is encoding a message in a JPG or BMP image. The "noise" that is induced in the picture by encoding the message is not noticeable to the naked eye.

By comparison, when using cryptography, others are aware that a secret message is being transmitted, but hopefully they can't decipher the message. With steganography, third parties don't know that a message is being transmitted.

If the topic of cryptography and steganography interests you, you must read this fascinating book: *The Code Book: The Science of Secrecy from Ancient Egypt to Quantum Cryptography*, by Simon Singh (First Anchor Books Edition, 2000).

The History of Cryptography

The history of cryptography starts in diplomatic circles thousands of years ago. Messengers from a king's court would take encrypted messages to other courts. Occasionally, other courts not involved in the communication would attempt to steal any message sent to a kingdom they considered an adversary. Encryption was first used to prevent this information theft.

Not long after, military commanders started using encryption to secure messages. The messengers had far greater challenges than those of the diplomatic messengers because killing the messenger to get the message was common. With the stakes so high, military commanders resorted to encryption to secure their military communications.

The cipher attributed to Julius Caesar was a simple substitution cipher that he used on the battlefield to quickly encrypt a message that could easily be decrypted by his commanders. Thomas Jefferson, the third president of the United States, was also an inventor, and one of his inventions was an encryption system that he was believed to have used when serving as Secretary of State from 1790 to 1793.

Arthur Scherbius invented a machine in 1918 that served as a template for the machines that all the major participants in World War II used. He called the machine Enigma and sold it to Germany, estimating that if 1000 cryptanalysts tested four keys per minute, all day, every day, it would take 1.8 billion years to try them all.

During World War II, both the Germans and Allies had machines modeled after the Scherbius machine. These were the most sophisticated encryption devices ever developed, and in response, the British invented arguably the world's first computer, the Colossus, to break the encryption that was used by the Germans' Enigma machine.

Ciphers

A cipher is an algorithm for performing encryption and decryption. It is a series of well-defined steps that you can follow as a procedure. Substitution ciphers simply substitute one letter for another. In their simplest form, substitution ciphers retain the letter frequency of the original message. Table 12-1 provides a summary of popular cipher categories.

Table 12-1 *Cipher Categories*

Cipher	Description
Substitution	Substitute one character for another, such as a = e, b = f, c = g, and so on.
Polyalphabetic	Based on substitution, using multiple substitution alphabets.
Transposition	Also known as permutation. Rather than replacing characters, characters are permuted or rearranged.
One-time pad	Also known as Vernam ciphers. Use keys to apply logical operations to plaintext.

Substitution Cipher

The cipher attributed to Julius Caesar is a simple substitution cipher. Every day has a different key, and that key is used to adjust the alphabet accordingly. For example, if today's key is five, an A is moved five spaces, resulting in an encoded message using F instead; a B is a G, a C is an H, and so forth. The next day the key might be eight, and the process begins again, so A is now I, B is J, and so on.

For example, if a message has 25 occurrences of the letter S, and S is replaced by the letter Q, there will 25 occurrences of the letter Q. If the message is long enough, it will be vulnerable to frequency analysis because it retains the frequency patterns found in the language. Because of this weakness, polyalphabetic ciphers were invented.

Polyalphabetic Cipher

The Vigenère cipher, shown in Figure 12-5, is a polyalphabetic cipher that encrypts text by using a series of different Caesar ciphers based on the letters of a keyword. It is a simple form of polyalphabetic substitution and therefore invulnerable to frequency analysis.

	P L A I N T E X T L E T T E R																									
	A	B	C	D	E	F	G	H	I	J	K	L	M	N	O	P	Q	R	S	T	U	V	W	X	Y	Z
A	A	B	C	D	E	F	G	H	I	J	K	L	M	N	O	P	Q	R	S	T	U	V	W	X	Y	Z
B	B	C	D	E	F	G	H	I	J	K	L	M	N	O	P	Q	R	S	T	U	V	W	X	Y	Z	A
C	C	D	E	F	G	H	I	J	K	L	M	N	O	P	Q	R	S	T	U	V	W	X	Y	Z	A	B
D	D	E	F	G	H	I	J	K	L	M	N	O	P	Q	R	S	T	U	V	W	X	Y	Z	A	B	C
E	E	F	G	H	I	J	K	L	M	N	O	P	Q	R	S	T	U	V	W	X	Y	Z	A	B	C	D
F	F	G	H	I	J	K	L	M	N	O	P	Q	R	S	T	U	V	W	X	Y	Z	A	B	C	D	E
G	G	H	I	J	K	L	M	N	O	P	Q	R	S	T	U	V	W	X	Y	Z	A	B	C	D	E	F
H	H	I	J	K	L	M	N	O	P	Q	R	S	T	U	V	W	X	Y	Z	A	B	C	D	E	F	G
I	I	J	K	L	M	N	O	P	Q	R	S	T	U	V	W	X	Y	Z	A	B	C	D	E	F	G	H
J	J	K	L	M	N	O	P	Q	R	S	T	U	V	W	X	Y	Z	A	B	C	D	E	F	G	H	I
K	K	L	M	N	O	P	Q	R	S	T	U	V	W	X	Y	Z	A	B	C	D	E	F	G	H	I	J
L	L	M	N	O	P	Q	R	S	T	U	V	W	X	Y	Z	A	B	C	D	E	F	G	H	I	J	K
M	M	N	O	P	Q	R	S	T	U	V	W	X	Y	Z	A	B	C	D	E	F	G	H	I	J	K	L
N	N	O	P	Q	R	S	T	U	V	W	X	Y	Z	A	B	C	D	E	F	G	H	I	J	K	L	M
O	O	P	Q	R	S	T	U	V	W	X	Y	Z	A	B	C	D	E	F	G	H	I	J	K	L	M	N
P	P	Q	R	S	T	U	V	W	X	Y	Z	A	B	C	D	E	F	G	H	I	J	K	L	M	N	O
Q	Q	R	S	T	U	V	W	X	Y	Z	A	B	C	D	E	F	G	H	I	J	K	L	M	N	O	P
R	R	S	T	U	V	W	X	Y	Z	A	B	C	D	E	F	G	H	I	J	K	L	M	N	O	P	Q
S	S	T	U	V	W	X	Y	Z	A	B	C	D	E	F	G	H	I	J	K	L	M	N	O	P	Q	R
T	T	U	V	W	X	Y	Z	A	B	C	D	E	F	G	H	I	J	K	L	M	N	O	P	Q	R	S
U	U	V	W	X	Y	Z	A	B	C	D	E	F	G	H	I	J	K	L	M	N	O	P	Q	R	S	T
V	V	W	X	Y	Z	A	B	C	D	E	F	G	H	I	J	K	L	M	N	O	P	Q	R	S	T	U
W	W	X	Y	Z	A	B	C	D	E	F	G	H	I	J	K	L	M	N	O	P	Q	R	S	T	U	V
X	X	Y	Z	A	B	C	D	E	F	G	H	I	J	K	L	M	N	O	P	Q	R	S	T	U	V	W
Y	Y	Z	A	B	C	D	E	F	G	H	I	J	K	L	M	N	O	P	Q	R	S	T	U	V	W	X
Z	Z	A	B	C	D	E	F	G	H	I	J	K	L	M	N	O	P	Q	R	S	T	U	V	W	X	Y

(Row labels, top to bottom on the left margin: **K E Y W O R D   L E T T E R**)

Figure 12-5   *The Vigenère Cipher*

The method was originally described in 1553 in a book by Giovan Batista Belaso. Mistakenly, Blaise de Vigenère, a French cryptographer, has been attributed with its invention, hence its name.

To illustrate how it works, suppose that a key of SECRETKEY is used to encode ATTACK AT DAWN. The A (the first letter of ATTACK) is encoded by looking at the row starting with S (the first letter of the key SECRETKEY) for the letter in the A column. In this case, the A is replaced with S. Then you look for the row that begins with E for the letter T. This results in X as your second character. If you continue this encoding method, the message ATTACK AT DAWN is encrypted as SXVRGDKXBSAP.

> **Note** When using the Vigenère cipher and the message is longer than the key, just repeat the key.

Transposition Ciphers

In transposition ciphers, letters are simply rearranged rather than replaced. An example of this type of cipher is taking the message THE PACKAGE IS DELIVERED and transposing it to read DEREVILEDSIEGAKCAPEHT. In this example, the key is to reverse the letters.

Another example of a transposition cipher is the rail fence cipher, shown in Figure 12-6. In this transposition, the words are spelled out as if they were a rail fence. The example in Figure 12-6 uses a key of three to illustrate how this could be done.

Cipher Text:

```
T...O...I...O...L...T...E.H.C.V.R.S.L.W.F.E.A.O.C...E...E...B...N...E...N..
```

Rail Fence Cipher with a Key of Three:

```
T...O...I...O...L...T...E
.H.C.V.R.S.L.W.F.E.A.O.C.
..E...E...B...N...E...N..
```

In order to read the message, simply look diagonally, following the rail fence.

Clear Text = THE COVER IS BLOWN FLEE AT ONCE

Figure 12-6 *Transposition Cipher: Rail Fence Cipher*

The message THE COVER IS BLOWN FLEE AT ONCE would be encoded as TOIOLTEHCVRSLWFEAOCEEBNEN using this method of transposition. Once again, no letters were changed; they were just rearranged.

One-Time Pad Cipher

The one-time pad was invented and patented by Gilbert Vernam in 1917 while working at AT&T. The primary design of the one-time pad was meant to overcome the weaknesses of using the Vigenère cipher. Vernam's idea was a stream cipher that would apply the exclusive OR (XOR) operation to plaintext with a key, but still using the Vigenère cipher. Joseph Maubourgne, a captain in the U.S. Army Signal Corps, contributed the idea of using random data as a key. This combined idea is so significant that the U.S. National Security Agency (NSA) has called this patent "perhaps the most important in the history of cryptography."

Figure 12-7 shows three one-time pads used in conjunction with the Vigenère cipher.

E	M	Z	F	O
Y	P	G	A	Q
R	N	C	V	X
T	L	B	I	H
J	S	U	D	K

Sheet 1

N	S	D	F	Z
V	T	A	M	P
G	L	Y	E	X
B	R	W	U	I
Q	H	O	K	C

Sheet 2

T	E	K	C	W
N	X	P	R	Z
I	B	Y	U	L
V	O	S	H	Q
G	M	F	J	A

Sheet 3

Figure 12-7 *One-Time Pads*

There are several difficulties inherent in using one-time pads in the real world. The first of these is the challenge of creating random data. Computers, because they have a mathematical foundation, are incapable of creating random data. In addition, if the key is used more than once, it is trivial to break. Key distribution is also challenging (for example, how do you distribute the pads?).

Note   Rivest Cipher 4 (RC4) is an example of a Vernam cipher that is widely used on the Internet. It is not a one-time-pad because the key used is not random. If you have used Wired Equivalent Privacy (WEP) with a wireless network, you have used RC4.

In Figure 12-8, the plaintext "at dawn attack the high plains" is encrypted with Sheet 2 of the one-time pads, using the Vigenère cipher.

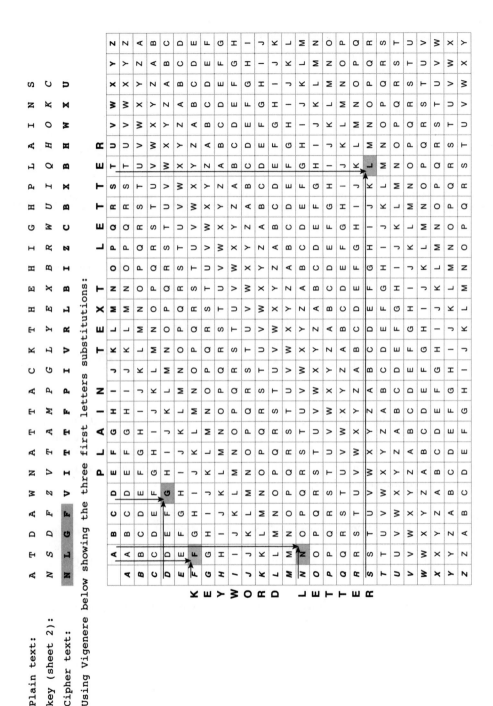

Figure 12-8 *Encryption Using One-Time Pad*

In Figure 12-9, the ciphertext is decrypted using Sheet 2 of the one-time pads.

Figure 12-9 *Decryption Using One-Time Pad*

Key Topic

Classical ciphers are either transposition ciphers or substitution ciphers.

Recall that a transposition cipher exchanges the position of letters, whereas a substitution cipher replaces one letter with another letter based on a secret key.

Figure 12-10 illustrates an example of a simple computer version of a substitution cipher, where the word WOLFE is translated in ASCII. The key MAJOR is also translated in ASCII. The key is applied to the cleartext using in this example the logical operation XOR. The result is ciphertext. The result of applying the key, using again the XOR operation, is the deciphering of the ciphertext to its original cleartext.

Clear Text = WOLFE
Key = MAJOR
Substitution Algorithm: XOR

Exclusive or = Logical Operation of **Exclusive Disjunction**
(When the elements are the same, the result is 0, and when the elements are different, the result is 1.)

WOLFE in ASCII: 01010111 01001111 01001100 01000110 01000101
MAJOR in ASCII: 01001101 01000001 01001010 01001111 01010010
Cipher Text: 00011010 00001110 00000110 00001001 00010111

Re-applying the Key On the Cipher Text to Find the Clear Text:
Cipher Text: 00011010 00001110 00000110 00001001 00010111
MAJOR in ASCII: 01001101 01000001 01001010 01001111 01010010
Clear Text ASCII: 01010111 01001111 01001100 01000110 01000101

The clear text ASCII found in the last operation corresponds to WOLFE in ASCII.

Figure 12-10 *Computer Version of a Substitution Cipher*

XOR is a type of logical disjunction on two operands that results in a value of true if only one of the operands has a value of true. In other words, for the result to be true (result of 1), the two operands must be different (one operand must be 0 and the other operand must be 1). In mathematics, operands are the input values used on the operation. With the formula 4 * 5, 4 and 5 are operands, and * (multiplication) is the operation.

Figure 12-10 is an example of both a substitution cipher and symmetric encryption. Symmetric encryption is discussed later in this chapter.

Block and Stream Ciphers

Algorithms can operate in two modes:

- **Block mode:** The algorithm can work on only fixed chunks of data.

- **Stream mode:** The algorithm can process data bit by bit.

Block Ciphers

Block ciphers transform a fixed-length block of plaintext into a block of ciphertext. Applying the reverse transformation to the ciphertext block and using the same secret key results in decryption. Currently, the fixed length (also known as the block size) for many block ciphers is typically 128 bits. DES has a block size of 64 bits.

> **Note** *Block size* refers to how much data is encrypted at any one time, whereas *key length* refers to the size of the encryption key. For example, DES encrypts blocks in 64-bit chunks, including an 8-bit parity check, thus yielding a 56-bit effective key strength.

Block ciphers usually result in output data that is larger than the input data because the ciphertext must be a multiple of the block size. To accomplish this, block algorithms take data one chunk at a time (for example, 8 bytes) and use padding to add artificial data (blanks) if there is less input data than one full block.

The following are common block ciphers:

- DES and 3DES, running in either Electronic Code Book (ECB) mode or Cipher Block Chaining (CBC) mode

- Advanced Encryption Standard (AES)

- International Data Encryption Algorithm (IDEA)

- Secure and Fast Encryption Routine (SAFER)

- Skipjack

- Blowfish

- Rivest-Shamir-Alderman (RSA)

Figure 12-11 illustrates the differences between ECB mode and CBC mode.

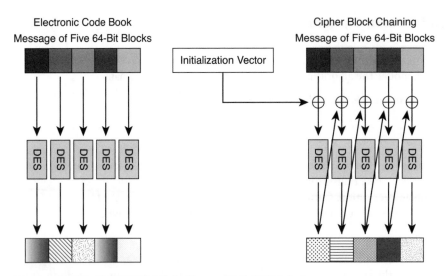

Figure 12-11   *DES ECB Mode Versus DES CBC Mode*

ECB mode serially encrypts each 64-bit plaintext block using the same 56-bit key. If two identical plaintext blocks are encrypted using the same key, their ciphertext blocks are the same. Therefore, an attacker could identify similar or identical traffic flowing through a communications channel and use that information to build a catalog of messages, which have a certain meaning, and replay them later without knowing their real meaning. For example, an attacker might capture a login sequence of someone with administrative privilege whose traffic is protected by ECB mode and then replay that sequence. That risk is undesirable, so CBC mode was invented to mitigate this risk.

In CBC mode, each 64-bit plaintext block is exclusive ORed (XORed) bitwise with the previous ciphertext block and then is encrypted using the DES key. Because of this process, the encryption of each block depends on previous blocks.

Encryption of the same 64-bit plaintext block can result in different ciphertext blocks. CBC mode can help guard against certain attacks, but it cannot help against sophisticated cryptanalysis or an extended brute-force attack.

Stream Ciphers

Unlike block ciphers, stream ciphers operate on smaller units of plaintext, typically bits. With a stream cipher, the transformation of these smaller plaintext units varies, depending on when they are encountered during the encryption process. Stream ciphers can be much faster than block ciphers, and generally do not increase the message size, because they can encrypt an arbitrary number of bits.

In stream cipher mode, the cipher uses previous ciphertext and the secret key to generate a pseudorandom stream of bits, which only the secret key can generate. To encrypt data, the data is XORed with the pseudorandom stream bit by bit, or sometimes byte by byte, to obtain the ciphertext. The decryption procedure is the same: The receiver generates the same random stream using the secret key, and XORs the ciphertext with the pseudo-random stream to obtain the plaintext.

Common stream ciphers include the following:

- DES and 3DES, running in output feedback (OFB) or cipher feedback (CFB) mode

- Rivest Cipher 4 (RC4)

- Software-optimized Encryption Algorithm (SEAL)

The Process of Encryption

Encryption is the process of disguising a message in such a way as to hide its original contents, as shown in Figure 12-12. With encryption, the plaintext readable message is converted to ciphertext, which is the unreadable, "disguised" message. Decryption reverses the process. The purpose of encryption is to guarantee confidentiality so that only authorized entities can read the original message.

Figure 12-12   *Transforming Plaintext into Ciphertext*

Old encryption algorithms, such as the Caesar cipher or the Enigma machine, were based on the secrecy of the algorithm to achieve confidentiality. With modern technology, where reverse engineering is often simple, public-domain algorithms are often used. With most modern algorithms, successful decryption requires knowledge of the appropriate cryptographic keys; that is, the security of encryption lies in the secrecy of the keys, not the algorithm.

Encryption can provide confidentiality at an OSI layer, such as the following:

- Encrypt application layer data, such as secure email, secure database sessions (Oracle SQL*Net), and secure messaging (Lotus Notes sessions)

- Encrypt session layer data, using a protocol such as SSL or Transport Layer Security (TLS)

- Encrypt network layer data, using protocols such as those provided in the IPsec protocol suite

- Encrypt link layer data, using proprietary link-encrypting devices

Nowadays, encryption algorithms such as Triple Data Encryption Standard (3DES) and Advanced Encryption Standard (AES) are readily distributed. So, because we all share the same algorithms, they have no need for protection (except for the fact that Western countries define cryptography as munitions, and therefore encryption algorithms are subject to the same export regulations as weapons).

Because we all share algorithms, what we protect are the cryptographic keys used with the algorithms. Cryptographic keys are sequences of bits that are input into an encryption algorithm together with the data to be encrypted.

Encryption Application Examples

The IPsec protocols can provide the encryption functionality for all the packets routed over an untrusted network. The encrypting IPsec peer takes a packet with the plaintext payload, encrypts the payload into ciphertext, and forwards the packet to the untrusted network (for example, the Internet). Its IPsec partner receives the ciphertext payload packet and decrypts the payload into the original plaintext. The two IPsec peers share the same encryption and decryption algorithm and proper keys.

The SSL protocol provides an encrypted channel on top of an existing TCP session. For example, HTTPS, which is HTTP encapsulated inside SSL, also known as HTTP over SSL or HTTP Secure, provides, among other services, confidentiality of the session between a web browser and a web server, using symmetric cryptography.

Both IPsec and SSL are used to set up a VPN. An IPsec VPN is application independent and requires a specialized IP stack on the end system or in the packet path that includes IPsec. Originally, SSL-based VPN supported only web-based applications with the SSL software included with all Internet browsers. Nowadays, SSL-based VPN also provides full tunnel support. Both SSL and IPsec are explained in more detail later in this book.

In contrast to IPsec and SSL, Layer 2 encryption, also known as data link layer encryption and depicted in Figure 12-13, encrypts the whole frame, including the physical address fields located in the header of the frame, and therefore can be used only on point-to-point links where no network switching or routing equipment is required for path decision.

Figure 12-13 *Cisco ASA Configured as a Layer 2 Firewall*

Note   IPsec implementation is a mandatory part of IPv6.

Cryptanalysis

Cryptanalysis is the practice of breaking codes to obtain the meaning of encrypted data. An attacker who tries to break an algorithm or encrypted ciphertext might use one of the following attacks:

- Brute-force attack

- Ciphertext-only attack

- Known-plaintext (the usual brute-force) attack

- Chosen-plaintext attack

- Chosen-ciphertext attack

- Birthday attack

- Meet-in-the-middle attack

The sections that follow describe these attacks in greater detail.

Brute-Force Attack

In a brute-force attack, an attacker tries every possible key with the decryption algorithm, knowing that eventually one of them will work. All encryption algorithms are vulnerable to this attack. On average, a brute-force attack will succeed about 50 percent of the way through the keyspace (see "Keyspaces," later in this chapter, for more information). The objective of modern cryptographers is to have a sufficiently large keyspace so that it takes too much money and too much time to accomplish a brute-force attack.

Note   As reported by Distributed.net in 1999, a DES cracking machine was used to recover a 56-bit DES key in 22 hours using brute force. It is estimated that it would take 149 trillion years to crack AES using the same method.

Ciphertext-Only Attack

In a ciphertext-only attack, the attacker has the ciphertext of several messages, all of which have been encrypted using the same encryption algorithm, but the attacker has no knowledge of the underlying plaintext. The job of the attacker is to recover the ciphertext of as many messages as possible or, better yet, to deduce the key or keys used to encrypt the messages so as to decrypt other messages encrypted with the same keys. The attacker could use statistical analysis to achieve the result. Those attacks are no longer practical today because modern algorithms produce pseudorandom output that is resistant to statistical analysis.

Known-Plaintext Attack

In a known-plaintext attack, the attacker has access to the ciphertext of several messages, but also knows something about the plaintext underlying that ciphertext. With knowledge of the underlying protocol (HTTP, FTP, SMTP), file type (web page, file transferred, email message), and some characteristic strings that might appear in the plaintext, the attacker uses a brute-force attack to try keys until decryption with the correct key produces a meaningful result. This attack may be the most practical attack, because attackers can usually assume the type and some features of the underlying plaintext, if they can only capture ciphertext. However, modern algorithms with enormous keyspaces make it unlikely for this attack to succeed, because on average an attacker would have to search through at least half of the keyspace to be successful.

> **Note**   A known-plaintext attack was used in the cracking of the Enigma machine. During World War II, Alan Turing, a famous British crypto-mathematician, discovered that at around 6 a.m. each day the Germans were sending an encrypted weather report. Turing was sure that within the ciphertext captured around that time of day the word WETTER (weather in German) could be found. With the ciphertext equivalent to the plaintext WEATHER, Turing had a good start to continue reverse engineering the rest of the message.
>
> In cryptanalysis, a sample of ciphertext suspected to be a resulting plaintext is called a *crib*.

Chosen-Plaintext Attack

In a chosen-plaintext attack, the attacker chooses what data the encryption device encrypts and observes the ciphertext output. A chosen-plaintext attack is more powerful than a known-plaintext attack because the attacker gets to choose the plaintext blocks to encrypt, allowing the attacker to choose plaintext that might yield more information about the key. This attack might not be very practical, because it is often difficult or impossible to capture both the ciphertext and plaintext, unless the trusted network has been broken into and the attacker already has access to confidential information.

Chosen-Ciphertext Attack

In a chosen-ciphertext attack, the attacker can choose different ciphertexts to be decrypted and has access to the decrypted plaintext. With the pair, the attacker can search through the keyspace and determine which key decrypts the chosen ciphertext in the captured plaintext. For example, the attacker has access to a tamperproof encryption device with an embedded key. His job is to deduce the embedded key by sending data through the box. This attack is analogous to the chosen-plaintext attack. This attack might not be very practical, because it is often difficult or impossible to capture both the ciphertext and plaintext, unless the trusted network has been broken into and the attacker already has access to confidential information.

Birthday Attack

The birthday attack gets its name from the amazing statistical probability involved in two individuals having the same birthday. According to statisticians, the probability that 2 people in a group of 23 people share the same birthday is greater than 50 percent.

This particular attack is a form of brute-force attack against hash functions. If some function, when supplied with a random input, returns one of k equally likely values, then by repeating the function with different inputs, the same output is expected after $1.2k^{1/2}$ number of times.

Tip To test the birthday theory, input 365 in the place of *k*.

Meet-in-the-Middle

The meet-in-the-middle attack is a known-plaintext attack. Do not confuse this with the *man-in-the-middle attack*, which is discussed later. In a meet-in-the-middle attack, the attacker knows a portion of the plaintext and the corresponding ciphertext. The plaintext is encrypted with every possible key, and the results are stored. The ciphertext is then decrypted using every key until one of the results matches one of the stored values.

Desirable Encryption Algorithm Features

The following are features that a good encryption algorithm provides:

- Resists cryptographic attacks
- Supports variable and long key lengths and scalability
- Creates an avalanche effect

Note When deciding on a algorithm for your organization, keep in mind the export regulations of cryptographic equipment, which might limit your choice.

A good cryptographic algorithm is designed in such a way that it resists common cryptographic attacks. The best way to break data protected by the algorithm is to try to decrypt the data using all the possible keys. The length of time that such an attack requires to succeed depends on the number of possible keys, but is generally very, very long. With appropriately long keys, such attacks are usually considered infeasible.

Variable key lengths and scalability are also desirable attributes of a good encryption algorithm. The longer the encryption key, the longer it takes an attacker to break it. For example, a 16-bit key would mean that there are 65,536 possible keys, but a 56-bit key would mean there are $7.2 * 10^{16}$ possible keys. Scalability provides flexible key lengths and allows you to select the strength and speed of encryption that you need.

When changing only a few bits of the plaintext message causes its ciphertext to change completely, this is known as an *avalanche effect*. The avalanche effect is a desired feature of an encryption algorithm because it allows very similar messages to be sent over an untrusted medium, with the encrypted (ciphertext) messages being completely different.

You must carefully consider export and import restrictions when you use encryption internationally. Some countries do not allow the export of encryption algorithms, or allow only the export of these algorithms with shorter keys, and some countries impose import restrictions on cryptographic algorithms.

In January 2000, and again in 2010, the restrictions that the U.S. Department of Commerce placed on export regulations were dramatically relaxed. As an example of the loosening of the rules, cryptographic products were made exportable under a license exception unless the end users were governments outside the United States or under embargo. For more information on the current U.S. Department of Commerce export regulations, see http://www.commerce.gov.

Key Management

Key management is often considered the most difficult part of designing a cryptosystem. Many cryptosystems have failed because of mistakes in their key management, and all modern cryptographic algorithms require the services of key management procedures. In practice, most attacks on cryptographic systems will be aimed at the key management level rather than at the cryptographic algorithm itself.

Key Management Components

Key management consists of the following components:

- **Key generation:** In a modern cryptographic system, key generation is usually auto-mated and not left to the end user. The use of good random number generators is needed to ensure that all keys are likely to be equally generated so that the attacker cannot predict which keys are more likely to be used.

- **Key verification:** Almost all cryptographic algorithms have some weak keys that should not be used, and with the help of key verification procedures, you can regen-erate these keys if they occur.

- **Key storage:** On a modern multiuser operating system that uses cryptography, a key can be stored in memory. This presents a possible problem when that memory is swapped to the disk, because a Trojan horse program, installed on the PC of a user, could then have access to the private keys of that user. A possible solution is to store the key on a USB stick and require a password to unlock that key.

- **Key exchange:** The key management procedures should also provide a secure key exchange mechanism, which allows secure agreement on the keying material with the other party, probably over an untrusted medium.

- **Key revocation and destruction:** Key revocation notifies all the interested parties that a certain key has been compromised and should no longer be used. Key destruc-tion erases old keys in such a manner that malicious attackers cannot recover them.

Key Topic

Key management deals with the secure generation, verification, exchange, storage, revo-cation, and destruction of keys.

Keyspaces

The keyspace of an algorithm is the set of all possible key values. A key that has n bits produces a keyspace that has 2^n possible key values. By adding 1 bit to the key, you effectively double the keyspace. For example, DES with its 56-bit keys has a keyspace of more than 72,000,000,000,000,000 (2^{56}) possible keys, but by adding 1 bit to the key length, the keyspace doubles, and an attacker needs twice the amount of time to search the keyspace.

As previously mentioned, almost every algorithm has some weak keys in its keyspace that enable an attacker to break the encryption via a shortcut. Weak keys show regularities in encryption or poor encryption. For instance, DES has four keys for which encryption is the same as decryption. This means that if one of these weak keys is encrypted twice, the original plaintext is recovered.

The weak keys of DES are those that produce 16 identical subkeys. This occurs when the key bits are

- Alternating 1s + 0s (0101010101010101)

- Alternating F + E (FEFEFEFEFEFEFEFE)

- E0E0E0E0F1F1F1F1

- 1F1F1F1F0E0E0E0E

It is unlikely that such keys would be chosen, but implementations should still verify all keys and prevent weak keys from being used. With manual key generation, you must take special care to avoid defining weak keys.

Key Length Issues

If the cryptographic system is trustworthy, the only way to break it is with a brute-force attack. A brute-force attack is a search through the entire keyspace, trying all the possible keys, to find a key that decrypts the data. If the keyspace is large enough, the search should require an enormous amount of time, making such an exhaustive effort infeasible. On average, an attacker has to search through half of the keyspace before the correct key is found. The time that is needed to accomplish this search depends on the computer power available to the attacker. However, current key lengths can easily make any attempt insignificant, because it would take many millions or billions of years to complete the search when a sufficiently long key is used.

With modern algorithms that are trusted, the strength of protection depends solely on the length of the key. Choose the key length so that it protects data confidentiality or integrity for an adequate period of time. Data that is more sensitive and needs to be kept secret longer must use longer keys.

The funding of the attacker should also affect your choice of key length. When you assess the risk of someone breaking the encryption algorithm, you must estimate the resources of the attacker and how long you must protect the data. For example, if the attacker has $1 million of funding, and the data must be protected for one year, classic DES is not a good choice because it can be broken by a $1 million machine in a couple of minutes. However, it would take an attacker some million years or more to crack 168-bit 3DES or 128-bit RC4, which makes either of these key length choices more than adequate.

Performance is another issue that can influence the choice of key length. You must find a good balance between the speed and protection strength of an algorithm, because some algorithms, such as RSA, run slower with larger key sizes. Strive for adequate protection while also enabling unhindered communication over untrusted networks.

Because of the rapid advances in technology and cryptanalytic methods, the key size needed for a particular application is constantly increasing. Go to the BlueKrypt website at http://www.keylength.com/en/4/ to see updated NIST key length recommendations.

Example of the Impact of Key Length

Part of the strength of the RSA algorithm is the difficulty of factoring large numbers. If a 1024-bit number is hard to factor, then a 2048-bit number is going to be even harder to factor. Even with the fastest computers available today, it would take many lifetimes to factor a 1024-bit number that is a factor of two 512-bit prime numbers. Of course, this advantage is lost if an easy way to factor large numbers is found. However, cryptographers consider this possibility unlikely, and the rule "the longer the key, the better" is valid, except for possible performance reasons.

As of 2005, the best known attack on 3DES required around 2^{32} known plaintexts, 2^{113} steps, 2^{90} single DES encryptions, and 2^{88} memory operations. This is not currently practical. If the attacker seeks to discover any one of many cryptographic keys, there is a memory-efficient attack that will discover one of 2^{28} keys, given a handful of chosen plaintexts per key and around 2^{84} encryption operations. This attack is highly parallelizable and verges on the practical, given billion-dollar budgets and years to mount the attack, although the circumstances in which it would be useful are limited.

Symmetric and Asymmetric Encryption Overview

An encryption algorithm, which is also called a cipher, is a mathematical function that is used to encrypt and decrypt data. Generally, there are two functions, one to encrypt and one to decrypt. If the security of an encryption system is based on the secrecy of the algorithm itself, the algorithm code must be heavily guarded. If the algorithm is revealed, every party that is involved must change the algorithm.

Modern cryptography takes a different approach: all algorithms are public, and cryptographic keys are used to ensure the secrecy of data. There are two classes of encryption algorithms, which differ in their use of keys:

- **Symmetric encryption algorithms:** Use the same key to encrypt and decrypt data

- **Asymmetric encryption algorithms:** Use different keys to encrypt and decrypt data

Key Topic

A *key* is a required parameter for encryption algorithms. There are two concepts regarding keys:

- **Symmetric encryption:** The same key encrypts and decrypts.

- **Asymmetric encryption:** One key encrypts, and a different key decrypts.

Symmetric Encryption Algorithms

Symmetric encryption algorithms are algorithms in which the encryption and decryption keys are the same, as shown in Figure 12-14. Therefore, the sender and the receiver must share the same secret key before communicating securely. The security of a symmetric algorithm rests in the secrecy of the symmetric key; by obtaining the key, anyone can encrypt and decrypt messages. Symmetric encryption is often called secret-key encryption. Symmetric, or secret-key, encryption is the more traditional form of cryptography. The typical key length range of symmetric encryption algorithms is 40 to 256 bits. Best practice considers that anything less than 128-bit key material is not considered strong enough for business use.

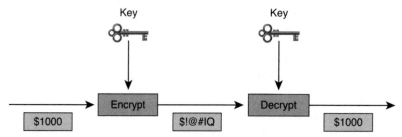

Figure 12-14 *Symmetric Encryption at Work*

The following are well-known encryption algorithms that use symmetric keys:

- **DES:** 56-bit keys

- **Triple DES (3DES):** 112- and 168-bit keys

- **AES:** 128-, 192-, and 256-bit keys

- **IDEA:** 128-bit keys

- **The RC series (RC2, RC4, RC5, and RC6):**

  - **RC2:** 40- and 64-bit keys

  - **RC4:** 1- to 256-bit keys

  - **RC5:** 0- to 2040-bit keys

  - **RC6:** 128-, 192-, and 256-bit keys

- **Blowfish:** 32- to 448-bit keys

The most commonly used techniques in symmetric encryption cryptography are block ciphers, stream ciphers, and message authentication codes (MAC).

Because symmetric algorithms are usually quite fast, they are often used for wire-speed encryption in data networks. Symmetric algorithms are based on simple mathematical operations and can easily be accelerated by hardware. Because of their speed, you can use symmetric algorithms for bulk encryption when data privacy is required (for example, to protect a VPN).

On the other hand, key management can be a challenge. The communicating parties must exchange the symmetric, secret key using a secure channel before any encryption can occur. Therefore, the security of any cryptographic system depends greatly on the security of the key exchange method.

Because of their speed, symmetric algorithms are frequently used for encryption services, with additional key management algorithms providing secure key exchange.

Some of the characteristics of symmetric algorithms are as follows:

- Faster than asymmetric algorithms.

- Much stronger than asymmetric algorithms.

- Much shorter key lengths than asymmetric algorithms.

- Simpler mathematics than asymmetric algorithms.

- One key is used for both encryption and decryption.

- Sometimes referred to as private-key encryption.

Modern symmetric algorithms use key lengths that range from 40 to 256 bits. This range gives symmetric algorithms keyspaces that range from 240 (1,099,511,627,776 possible keys) to 2^{256} ($1.5 * 10^{77}$) possible keys. (Keyspaces are described in depth later in this chapter.) This large range is the difference between whether or not the algorithm is vulnerable to a brute-force attack. If you use a key length of 40 bits, your encryption is likely to be broken easily using a brute-force attack. In contrast, if your key length is 256 bits, it is unlikely that a brute-force attack will be successful, because the keyspace is too large.

On average, a brute-force attack will succeed halfway through the keyspace. Key lengths that are too short can have the entire possible keyspace stored in RAM on a server cluster of a cracker, which makes it possible for the algorithm to be cracked in real time.

Table 12-2 illustrates ongoing expectations for valid key lengths, assuming that the algorithms are mathematically and cryptographically sound. What is also assumed in such calculations is that computing power will continue to grow at its present rate and the ability to perform brute-force attacks will grow at the same rate.

Table 12-2 *Acceptable Key Lengths in Bits*

	Symmetric Key	Asymmetric Key	Digital Signature	Hash
Protection up to 3 years	80	1248	160	160
Protection up to 10 years	96	1776	192	192
Protection up to 20 years	112	2432	224	224
Protection up to 30 years	128	3248	256	256

Caution If a method other than brute-force is discovered against a particular algorithm, the key lengths in Table 12-2 become obsolete.

Note Note the comparatively short symmetric key lengths, illustrating that symmetric algorithms are the strongest type of algorithm.

Comparing Symmetric Encryption Algorithms

Symmetric encryption algorithms operate under the same framework, but they present considerable differences. Table 12-3 provides a summary analysis of their respective characteristics.

Table 12-3 *Characteristics of Symmetric Encryption Algorithms*

Algorithm	Description
DES	Block cipher, encrypts 64-bit data blocks.
	Fixed-length 64-bit key (only 56 bits used for encryption).
3DES	Applies DES three times in a row using three different keys. Key sizes of 168 and 112 bits.
AES	Iterated block cipher with variable block and key lengths. 128- or 192- or 256-bit keys.
Rivest ciphers	Widely deployed family of algorithms.
	Variable block and key sizes.

DES

Data Encryption Standard (DES) is a symmetric encryption algorithm, as shown in Figure 12-14. It usually operates in block mode, in which it encrypts data in 64-bit blocks.

The DES algorithm is essentially a sequence of permutations and substitutions of data bits, combined with the encryption key. The same algorithm and key are used for both encryption and decryption. Cryptography researchers have scrutinized DES for nearly 35 years and have found no significant flaws.

Because DES is based on simple mathematical functions, it can easily be implemented and accelerated in hardware.

DES has a fixed key length. The key is actually 64 bits long, but only 56 bits are used for encryption, with the remaining 8 bits used for parity; the least significant bit of each key byte is used to indicate odd parity.

A DES key is always 56 bits long. When you use DES with a weaker encryption of a 40-bit key, it actually means that the encryption key is 40 secret bits and 16 known bits, which makes the key length 56 bits. In this case, DES actually has a key strength of 40 bits.

DES Modes of Operation

To encrypt or decrypt more than 64 bits of data, DES uses two different types of ciphers:

- **Block ciphers:** Operate on fixed-length groups of bits, termed blocks, with an unvarying transformation

- **Stream ciphers:** Operate on individual digits one at a time with the transformation varying during the encryption

DES Security Guidelines

You should consider doing several things to protect the security of DES-encrypted data:

- Change keys frequently to help prevent brute-force attacks.

- Use a secure channel to communicate the DES key from the sender to the receiver.

- Consider using DES in CBC mode. With CBC, the encryption of each 64-bit block depends on previous blocks. CBC is the most widely used mode of DES.

- Verify that a key is not part of the weak or semi-weak key list before using it. DES has 4 weak keys and 12 semi-weak keys. Because there are 2^{56} possible DES keys, the chance of picking one of these keys is small. However, because testing the key has no significant impact on the encryption time, it is recommended that you test the key. The keys that should be avoided are listed in Section 3.6 of Publication 74 of the Federal Information Processing Standards, found at http://www.itl.nist.gov/fipspubs/fip74.htm.

> **Note**   If possible, use 3DES rather than DES. You should use DES only for very short-term confidentiality.

3DES

With advances in computer processing power, the original 56-bit DES key became too short to withstand even medium-budget attackers. One way to increase the DES effective key length, without changing the well-analyzed algorithm itself, is to use the same algorithm with different keys several times in a row.

The technique of applying DES three times in a row to a plaintext block is called 3DES. Brute-force attacks on 3DES are considered infeasible today, and because the basic algorithm has been well tested in the field for more than 35 years, it is considered very trustworthy.

3DES uses a method called 3DES-Encrypt-Decrypt-Encrypt (3DES-EDE) to encrypt plaintext, as shown in Figure 12-15. 3DES-EDE includes the following steps:

Step 1.   The message is encrypted using the first 56-bit key, known as K1.

Step 2.   The data is decrypted using the second 56-bit key, known as K2.

Step 3.   The data is encrypted again, now using the third 56-bit key, known as K3.

The 3DES-EDE procedure provides encryption with an effective key length of 168 bits. If keys K1 and K3 are equal, as in some implementations, a less-secure encryption of 112 bits is achieved.

- EDE (Encrypt-Decrypt-Encrypt) Method – 3DES-EDE Method:
  - Data is encrypted using K1.
  - Data is decrypted using K2.
  - Data is encrypted using K3.
- If K1 = K3, Key Yields 112-Bit Key Length
- If K1 ≠ K3, Key Yields 168-Bit Key Length

Figure 12-15   *3DES Encryption Process*

The following procedure is used to decrypt a 3DES-EDE block:

Step 1.   Decrypt the ciphertext using key K3.

Step 2.   Encrypt the data using key K2.

Step 3.   Decrypt the data using key K1.

> **Note**   Encrypting the data three times with three different keys does not significantly increase security. The 3DES-EDE method must be used. For example, it can be shown that encrypting data three times in a row using different 56-bit keys equals an effective 58-bit key strength and not the full 168-bit key strength, as you would expect.
>
> Also, here's why 3DES can be either 56-, 112-, or 168-bit strong: 3DES keying option 1, which provides 168-bit strength, uses three independent 56-bit values for K1, K2, and K3 (3 × 56 bits). With keying option 2, K1 and K3 use the same value and K2 is a different value, so two different 56-bit keys produce a 112-bit strength (2 × 56). Keying option 1 uses only one 56-bit value for K1, K2, and K3, offering only 56-bit strength.

AES

For a number of years, it was recognized that DES would eventually reach the end of its usefulness. In 1997, the AES initiative was announced, and the public was invited to propose candidate encryption schemes, one of which could be chosen as the encryption standard to replace DES. There were rigorous reviews of 15 original candidates. Rijndael, Twofish, and RC6 were among the finalists. Rijndael was ultimately selected.

The Rijndael Cipher

On October 2, 2000, the U.S. National Institute of Standards and Technology (NIST) announced the selection of the Rijndael cipher as the AES algorithm. The Rijndael cipher, developed by Joan Daemen and Vincent Rijmen, has a variable block length and key length. The algorithm currently specifies how to use keys with a length of 128, 192, or 256 bits to encrypt blocks with a length of 128, 192, or 256 bits, which provides nine different combinations of key length and block length. Both block length and key length can be extended very easily in multiples of 32 bits.

The U.S. Secretary of Commerce approved the adoption of AES as an official U.S. government standard, effective May 26, 2002. AES is listed in Annex A of FIPS Publication 140-2 as an approved security function.

> **Note**   Go to http://csrc.nist.gov/publications/fips/fips197/fips-197.pdf for more information about AES.

Rijndael is an iterated block cipher, which means that the initial input block and cipher key undergo multiple transformation cycles before producing output. The algorithm can operate over a variable-length block using variable-length keys; a 128-, 192-, or 256-bit key can be used to encrypt data blocks that are 128, 192, or 256 bits long, and all nine combinations of key and block length are possible. The accepted AES implementation of Rijndael contains only some of the capabilities of the Rijndael algorithm. The algorithm is written so that the block length or the key length or both can easily be extended in multiples of 32 bits, and the system is specifically designed for efficient implementation in hardware or software on a range of processors.

AES Versus 3DES

AES was chosen to replace DES and 3DES because the key length of AES makes it stronger than DES and AES runs faster than 3DES on comparable hardware. AES is more efficient than DES and 3DES on comparable hardware, usually by a factor of five when it is compared with DES. Also, AES is more suitable for high-throughput, low-latency environments, especially if pure software encryption is used. However, AES is a relatively young algorithm, and, as the golden rule of cryptography states, a more mature algorithm is always more trusted. 3DES is therefore a more conservative and more trusted choice in terms of strength, because it has been analyzed for around 35 years.

Rivest Ciphers

The RC family of algorithms is widely deployed in many networking applications because of their favorable speed and variable key length capabilities.

The RC algorithms were designed all or in part by Ronald Rivest. Some of the most widely used RC algorithms are as follows:

- **RC2:** A variable-key-size block cipher that was designed as a "drop-in" replacement for DES.

- **RC4:** A variable-key-size Vernam stream cipher often used in file encryption products and for secure communications, such as within SSL. It is not considered a one-time pad because its key is not random. The cipher can be expected to run very quickly in software and is considered secure, although it can be implemented insecurely, as in WEP.

- **RC5:** A fast block cipher that has variable block size and variable key size. With a 64-bit block size, RC5 can be used as a drop-in replacement for DES.

- **RC6:** A block cipher that was designed by Rivest, Sidney, and Yin and is based on RC5. Its main design goal was to meet the requirement of AES.

SEAL

Although it is beyond the scope of this book, it is good to know that Cisco also provides support for SEAL encryption. The Software-optimized Encryption Algorithm is an alternative algorithm to software-based DES, 3DES, and AES. SEAL encryption uses a 160-bit encryption key and has a lower impact on the CPU compared to other software-based algorithms. The SEAL encryption feature provides support for the SEAL algorithm in Cisco IOS IPsec implementations. SEAL support was added to Cisco IOS Software Release 12.3(7)T.

Asymmetric Encryption Algorithms

Asymmetric algorithms, also sometimes called *public-key algorithms*, are designed in such a way that the key used for encryption differs from the key used for decryption, as shown in Figure 12-16.

Figure 12-16 *Asymmetric Encryption at Work*

The decryption key cannot, in any reasonable amount of time, be calculated from the encryption key, and vice versa. The typical key length range for asymmetric algorithms is 512 to 4096 bits. You cannot directly compare the key length of asymmetric and symmetric algorithms because the underlying design of the two algorithm families differs greatly.

Note   For further reference, consult the book *Applied Cryptography*, by Bruce Schneier. Mr. Schneier also maintains an informative and entertaining blog/newsletter, which you can subscribe to at http://www.schneier.com/crypto-gram.html.

The best-known asymmetric cryptographic algorithms are RSA, ElGamal, Digital Signature Algorithm (DSA), and elliptic curve algorithms.

> **Note** Rivest, Shamir, and Aldeman, who met while at the Massachusetts Institute of Technology (MIT), released the RSA algorithm in 1977.

Asymmetric algorithms are substantially slower than symmetric algorithms. Their design is based on computational problems, such as factoring extremely large numbers or computing discrete logarithms of extremely large numbers. Because they lack speed, asymmetric algorithms are typically used in low-volume cryptographic mechanisms, such as digital signatures and key exchange. However, the key management of asymmetric algorithms tends to be simpler than that of symmetric algorithms, because usually one of the two encryption or decryption keys can be made public.

Because symmetric ciphers are faster than asymmetric algorithms, they are used for bulk data encryption.

Asymmetric algorithms are explained in greater detail later in this book.

Public Key Confidentiality

The confidentiality objective of asymmetric algorithms is achieved when the encryption process is started with the public key. When the public key is used to encrypt the data, the private key must be used to decrypt the data. Because only one host has the private key, confidentiality is achieved.

Public key (encrypt) + Private key (decrypt) = Confidentiality

In Figure 12-17, Alice and Bob exchange data with the goal of confidentiality. They follow these steps:

Step 1. Alice acquires Bob's public key (how the public key is acquired will be discussed later in this chapter when we discuss certificate authorities).

Step 2. Alice uses Bob's public key to encrypt a message, which is often a symmetric key, using an agreed upon algorithm.

Step 3. Alice transmits the encrypted message.

Step 4. Bob uses his private key to decrypt, and reveal, the message.

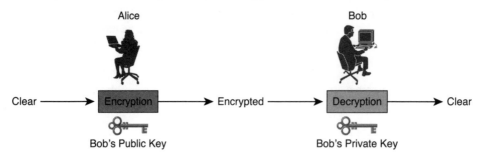

Figure 12-17 *Asymmetric Confidentiality Process*

We just saw how asymmetric encryption can be used to provide confidentiality. In an upcoming section, we will see how asymmetrical encryption is used to provide proof of authenticity and integrity by using digital signatures.

Encryption Algorithm Selection

Choosing an encryption algorithm is one of the most important steps of building a cryptography-based solution. You should consider two main criteria when selecting an encryption algorithm for your organization:

- **Trust in the algorithm by the cryptographic community:** Most new algorithms are broken quickly, so algorithms that have been resisting attacks for a number of years are preferred. Inventors and promoters often oversell the benefits of new algorithms. The truth is that there are few or no revolutions in cryptography.

- **Protection against brute-force attacks:** If the algorithm is considered trusted, there is no shortcut to break it, and the attacker must search through the keyspace to guess the correct key. The algorithm must allow key lengths that satisfy the confidentiality requirements of an organization. For example, DES no longer provides enough protection for most modern needs because of its short key length.

The following symmetric encryption algorithms are considered trustworthy:

- 3DES

- IDEA

- AES

The following asymmetric encryption algorithms, all covered in more detail later in this book, are considered trustworthy:

- RSA

- Elliptic Curve Digital Signature Algorithm (ECDSA)

- Diffie-Hellman (DH)

For symmetric algorithms, each bit in a key doubles the difficulty of finding the key. But with asymmetric algorithms, such as RSA, each additional bit only nominally increases the difficulty of factoring the composite number that is used by the algorithm. Therefore, comparatively shorter key lengths for symmetric algorithms are similar to larger key lengths using asymmetric algorithms, when both types of algorithm are used for similar objectives (for instance, when comparing the two types of algorithm in terms of confidentiality and payload encryption). Symmetric and asymmetric keys compare as follow:

- An 80-bit symmetric key is considered equal to a 1024-bit key using the RSA algorithm.

- A 112-bit symmetric key is considered equal to a 2048-bit key using the RSA algorithm.

- A 128-bit symmetric key is considered equal to a 3072-bit key using the RSA algorithm.

For more information about the comparison of the key strengths of symmetric algorithms to RSA, refer to http://www.rsasecurity.com/rsalabs/node.asp?id=2004.

Cryptographic Hashes and Digital Signatures

Cryptographic hashes and digital signatures play an important part in modern cryptosystems. They provide verification and authentication and play an important role in nonrepudiation. It is important to understand the basic mechanisms of these algorithms and some of the issues involved in choosing a particular hashing algorithm or digital signature method.

Hashing is a mechanism used for data integrity assurance. The hashing process uses a hash function, which is a one-way function of input data that produces a fixed-length digest of output data, also known as a fingerprint. The digest is cryptographically very strong. Hashes are functions that are relatively easy to compute, but *significantly* harder to reverse. Grinding coffee is a good example of a one-way function: it is easy to grind coffee beans, but it is impractical (not to say impossible) to put all the tiny pieces back together to rebuild the original beans.

If the input data changes just a little bit, the digest changes substantially. This is known as the *avalanche effect*. Essentially, the fingerprint that results from hashing data uniquely identifies that data. If you are given only a fingerprint, it is computationally infeasible to generate data that would result in that fingerprint.

Figure 12-18 illustrates how hashing is performed. Data of arbitrary length is input into the hash function. Hashing is similar to the calculation of cyclic redundancy check (CRC) checksums, but it is much stronger cryptographically. That is, given a CRC value, it is easy to generate data with the same CRC. However, with hash functions, it is computationally infeasible for an attacker to have two different sets of data that would come up with the same fingerprint.

Note Extrapolating from the explanation above, it is easy to understand the possibility that two different pieces of data could produce the same hash result. This is called a collision. As an example, a few years ago I transferred my Microsoft Outlook PST file to a new computer. Upon launching MS Outlook from my new computer, I was asked for the password of the PST file. I couldn't remember it because it had been cached in the settings of my previous laptop for years and, therefore, I never had to type it in. Knowing that MS Outlook PST passwords are kept as a CRC32 hash in the PST file itself, I used freeware designed for this purpose and was able to get the hash result of my password. I then proceeded to find a CRC32 hash-guessing freeware tool and get the hash result found in the

PST file. The hash-guessing tool provided me with a long alphanumeric code which, when hashed, produced the same result as the hashed password for my PST file. This code was obviously not my real password, but at least it provided the same hash result, so I proceeded to use that code as the password to open my PST file. This is how I cracked my own MS Outlook file. And, by the way, I immediately proceeded to change the Outlook password to a string I could remember.

This is an example of having two separate seed values producing the same hash results is an example of collision.

Figure 12-18   *Cryptographic Hashes*

The hashing process is not reversible; it is a *one-way function* with a fixed-length output. If you hash the word "Hello" with MD5 (covered later), the output, called the *message digest*, will be 128 bits long. If you process the *Oxford English Dictionary* through MD5, the message digest will be 128 bits long. It is impossible to take a message digest of 128 bits long and try to reverse-engineer it into a 1200-page dictionary; thus the expression that hashing is a one-way function.

Hashing is often applied in the following situations:

- To generate one-time and one-way responses to challenges in authentication protocols such as PPP Challenge Handshake Authentication Protocol (PPP CHAP), Microsoft NT Domain, and Extensible Authentication Protocol-Message Digest 5 (EAP-MD5)

- To provide proof of the integrity of data, such as that provided with file integrity checkers, digitally signed contracts, and PKI certificates

- To provide proof of authenticity when it is used with a symmetric secret authentication key, such as IPsec or routing protocol authentication

Key Topic

Hashing algorithms are one-way processes.

A hash function, H, is a transformation that takes an input, (x), and returns a fixed-size string, which is called the hash value, b. The formula for the calculation is $b = H(x)$.

A cryptographic hash function should have the following general properties:

- The input can be any length.

- The output has a fixed length.

- $H(x)$ is relatively easy to compute for any given x.

- $H(x)$ is one way and not reversible.

- $H(x)$ is collision free.

If a hash function is hard to invert, it is considered a one-way hash. "Hard to invert" means that given a hash value b, it is computationally infeasible to find some input, (x), such that $H(x) = b$. H is said to be a weakly collision-free hash function if, given a message x, it is computationally infeasible to find a message y not equal to x such that $H(x) = H(y)$. A strongly collision-free hash function, H, is one for which it is computationally infeasible to find any two messages x and y such that $H(x) = H(y)$.

Figure 12-18 illustrates the hashing process. Data of arbitrary length is input into the hash function, and the result of the hash function is the fixed-length digest, or fingerprint. Hashing is similar to the calculation of CRC checksums, but is cryptographically stronger. That is, given a CRC value, it is easy to generate data with the same CRC. However, as mentioned before, with hash functions, it is computationally infeasible for an attacker, given a hash value b, to find some input, (x), such that $H(x) = b$.

Figure 12-19 illustrates hashing in action. The sender wants to ensure that the message is not altered on its way to the receiver. The sending device inputs the message into a hashing algorithm and computes its fixed-length digest. This fingerprint is then attached to the message, where the message and the hash are in plaintext. The message, and its fingerprint attached, is sent to the receiver. The receiving device removes the fingerprint from the message and inputs the message into the same hashing algorithm. If the hash that is computed by the receiving device is equal to the one that is attached to the message, the message has not been altered during transit.

Hashing does not add security to the message. When the message traverses the network, a potential attacker could intercept the message, change it, recalculate the hash, and append it to the message. Hashing only prevents the message from being changed accidentally, such as by a communication error. There is nothing unique to the sender in the hashing procedure; therefore, anyone can compute a hash for any data, as long as they have the correct hash function.

Thus, hash functions are helpful to ensure that data did not change accidentally, but it cannot ensure that data was not deliberately changed.

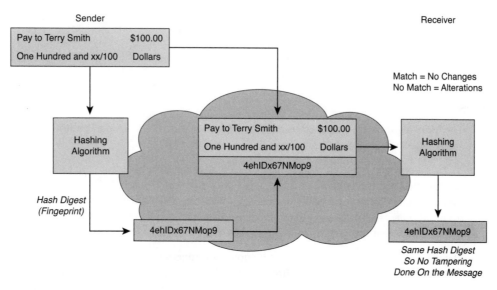

Figure 12-19 *Data Integrity: Hashing in Action*

These are two well-known hash functions:

- Message Digest 5 (MD5) with 128-bit digests
- Secure Hash Algorithm 1 (SHA-1) with 160-bit digests

Hashing Algorithms

The two most commonly used cryptographic hash functions are MD5 and SHA-1. SHA-2 is an additional and newer option. Table 12-4 compares the three algorithms in terms of strength, key size, and vulnerability to cryptanalytic attacks.

Table 12-4 *Comparing Hashing Algorithms*

Algorithm	Description
MD5	Ubiquitous hashing algorithm
	128-bit message digest
	Not recommended for new applications
SHA-1	160-bit message digest
	Preferred to MD5 because, although slower, is the stronger algorithm
SHA-2	Similar to SHA-1, with message digest of 224, 256, 384, or 512 bits
	Adopted by U.S. federal government as secure hash standard in 2008

> **Note**   Although originally thought to be collision resistant, both MD5 and SHA were later found to be vulnerable to such forms of attack.

MD5

The MD5 algorithm is a ubiquitous hashing algorithm that was developed by Ron Rivest and is used in a variety of Internet applications today.

MD5 is a one-way function, which makes it easy to compute a hash from the given input data but makes it infeasible to compute input data given only a hash. MD5 is also collision resistant, which means that two messages with the same hash are very unlikely to occur. MD5 is essentially a complex sequence of simple binary operations, such as XORs and rotations, that are performed on input data and produce a 128-bit digest.

The main algorithm itself is based on a compression function, which operates on blocks. The input is a data block plus a feedback of previous blocks. Each 512-bit block is divided into sixteen 32-bit subblocks. These blocks are then rearranged with simple operations in a main loop, which consists of four rounds. The output of the algorithm is a set of four 32-bit blocks, which concatenate to form a single 128-bit hash value. The message length is also encoded into the digest.

MD5 is based on MD4, an earlier algorithm. MD4 has been broken, and currently MD5 is considered less secure than SHA-1 by many authorities on cryptography, such as ICSA Labs (http://www.icsalabs.com). These authorities consider MD5 less secure than SHA-1 because some noncritical weaknesses have been found in one of the MD5 building blocks, causing uneasy feelings inside the cryptographic community. The availability of the SHA-1 and RACE Integrity Primitives Evaluation Message Digest (RIPEMD)-160 HMAC functions, which do not show such weaknesses and use a stronger (160-bit) digest, makes MD5 a second choice as far as hash methods are concerned.

SHA-1

The U.S. National Institute of Standards and Technology (NIST) developed the Secure Hash Algorithm (SHA), the algorithm that is specified in the Secure Hash Standard (SHS). SHA-1 is a revision to the SHA that was published in 1994; the revision corrected an unpublished flaw in SHA. Its design is similar to the MD4 family of hash functions that Ron Rivest developed.

The SHA-1 algorithm takes a message of less than 2^{64} bits in length and produces a 160-bit message digest. The algorithm is slightly slower than MD5, but the larger message digest makes it more secure against brute-force collision and inversion attacks. More details on SHA-1 collision attacks can be found at http://www.rsa.com/rsalabs/node.asp?id=2927.

You can find the official text for the standard at http://www.itl.nist.gov/fipspubs/fip180-1.htm.

> **Note** SHA also has 224-, 256-, 384-, and 512-bit versions.

SHA-2

Secure Hash Algorithm 2 (SHA-2) specifies five SHAs—SHA-1, SHA-224, SHA-256, SHA-384, and SHA-512—for computing a condensed representation of electronic data. When a message of any length less than 264 bits (for SHA-224 and SHA-256) or less than 2128 bits (for SHA-384 and SHA-512) is input to a hash algorithm, the result is a message digest that ranges in length from 224 to 512 bits, depending on the algorithm.

The SHA-2 family of hash functions was approved by NIST for use by federal agencies in 2006, for all applications using SHAs. The publication encouraged all federal agencies to stop using SHA-1 for digital signatures, digital time stamping, and other applications that require collision resistance as soon as practical, and it mandated the use of the SHA-2 family of hash functions for these applications after 2010. After 2010, federal agencies used SHA-1 only for the following applications: HMACs, key derivation functions (KDF), and random number generators (RNG). This change was triggered in 2005 when security flaws were identified for SHA-1 in theoretical exploits that exposed weaknesses to collision attacks.

Hashed Message Authentication Codes

Hash functions are the basis of the protection mechanism of Hashed Message Authentication Codes (HMAC). HMACs use existing hash functions, but with a significant difference; HMACs add a secret key as input to the hash function. Only the sender and the receiver know the secret key, and the output of the hash function now depends on the input data and the secret key. Therefore, only parties who have access to that secret key can compute the digest of an HMAC function. This behavior defeats man-in-the-middle attacks and provides authentication of the data origin. If two parties share a secret key and use HMAC functions for authentication, a properly constructed HMAC digest of a message that a party has received indicates that the other party was the originator of the message, because it is the only other entity possessing the secret key.

Cisco technologies use two well-known HMAC functions:

- Keyed MD5, based on the MD5 hashing algorithm
- Keyed SHA-1, based on the SHA-1 hashing algorithm

Figure 12-20 illustrates how an HMAC digest is created. Data of an arbitrary length is input into the hash function, together with a secret key. The result is the fixed-length hash that depends on the data and the secret key.

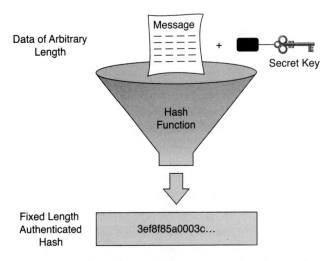

- Same procedure is used for generation and verification of secure fingerprints.

Figure 12-20 *HMAC Digest Creation*

Figure 12-21 illustrates an HMAC in action. The sender wants to ensure that the message is not altered in transit and wants to provide a way for the receiver to authenticate the origin of the message.

Figure 12-21 *HMAC in Action*

The sending device inputs data and the secret key into the hashing algorithm and calculates the fixed-length HMAC digest. This authenticated fingerprint is then attached to the message and sent to the receiver. The receiving device removes the fingerprint from the message and uses the plaintext message with the secret key as input to the same hashing function. If the fingerprint calculated by the receiving device is equal to the fingerprint that was sent, the message has not been altered. In addition, the origin of the message is authenticated, because only the sender possesses a copy of the shared secret key. The HMAC function has ensured the authenticity of the message.

Note IPsec VPNs rely on HMAC functions to authenticate the origin and provide data integrity checking of every packet.

Cisco products use hashing for entity-authentication, data-integrity, and data-authenticity purposes:

- IPsec gateways and clients use hashing algorithms, such as MD5 and SHA-1 in HMAC mode, to provide packet integrity and authenticity.

- Cisco IOS routers use hashing with secret keys in an HMAC-like manner, to add authentication information to routing protocol updates.

- Cisco software images that you can download from Cisco.com have an MD5-based checksum available so that customers can check the integrity of downloaded images.

- Hashing can also be used in a feedback-like mode to encrypt data; for example, TACACS+ uses MD5 to encrypt its session.

Overview of Digital Signatures

When data is exchanged over untrusted networks, several major security issues must be determined:

- **Whether data has changed in transit:** Hashing and HMAC functions rely on a cumbersome exchange of secret keys between parties to provide the guarantee of integrity.

- **Whether a document is authentic:** Hashing and HMAC can provide some guarantee of authenticity, but only by using secret keys between two parties. Hashing and HMAC cannot guarantee authenticity of a transaction or a document to a third party.

Digital signatures are often used in the following situations:

- To provide a unique proof of data source, which can be generated only by a single party, such as with contract signing in e-commerce environments

- To authenticate a user by using the private key of that user and the signature it generates

- To prove the authenticity and integrity of PKI certificates

- To provide a secure time stamp, such as with a central trusted time source

Suppose a customer sends transaction instructions via an email to a stockbroker, and the transaction turns out badly for the customer. It is conceivable that the customer could claim never to have sent the transaction order, or that someone forged the email. The brokerage could protect itself by requiring the use of digital signatures before accepting instructions via email.

Handwritten signatures have long been used as a proof of authorship of, or at least agreement with, the contents of a document. Digital signatures can provide the same functionality as handwritten signatures, and much more.

Digital signatures provide three basic security services in secure communications:

- **Authenticity of digitally signed data:** Digital signatures authenticate a source, proving that a certain party has seen and has signed the data in question.

- **Integrity of digitally signed data:** Digital signatures guarantee that the data has not changed from the time it was signed.

- **Nonrepudiation of the transaction:** The recipient can take the data to a third party, which accepts the digital signature as a proof that this data exchange did take place. The signing party cannot repudiate that it has signed the data.

Note   To better understand nonrepudiation, consider the use of HMAC functions, which also provide authenticity and integrity guarantees. With HMAC functions, two or more parties share the same authentication key and can compute the HMAC fingerprint. Therefore, taking received data and its HMAC fingerprint to a third party does not prove that the other party sent this data; you could have generated the same HMAC fingerprint yourself, because you have a copy of the HMAC authentication key. With digital signatures, each party has a unique, secret signature key, which is not shared with any other party, making nonrepudiation possible.

To achieve the preceding goals, digital signatures have the following properties:

- **The signature is authentic:** The signature convinces the recipient of the document that the signer signed the document.

- **The signature is not forgeable:** The signature is proof that the signer, and no one else, signed the document.

- **The signature is not reusable:** The signature is a part of the document and cannot be moved to a different document.

- **The signature is unalterable:** After a document is signed, the document cannot be altered without detection.

- **The signature cannot be repudiated:** The signature and the document are physical things. The signer cannot claim later that they did not sign it.

Well-known asymmetric algorithms, such as RSA or DSA, are typically used to perform digital signing.

In some countries, including the United States, digital signatures are considered equivalent to handwritten signatures, if they meet certain provisions. Some of these provisions include the proper protection of the certificate authority, the trusted signer of all other public keys, and the proper protection of the private keys of the users. In such a scenario, users are responsible for keeping their private keys private, because a stolen private key can be used to "steal" their identity.

Later in this chapter you will have the opportunity to delve deeper into the mechanics of digital signatures, but for now Figure 12-22 illustrates the basic functioning of digital signatures:

Step 1. When someone wants to sign some data, they use a signature algorithm with their signature key. Only the signer knows this signature key. Therefore, the signer must keep the signature key secret.

Step 2. Based on the input data and a signature key, the signature algorithm generates its output, which is called a digital signature.

Step 3. The sending device attaches the digital signature to the message and sends the message to the receiver.

Step 4. The receiving device verifies the signature with the verification key, which is usually public.

Step 5. The receiving device inputs the message, the digital signature, and the verification key into the verification algorithm, which checks the validity of the digital signature.

Step 6. If the check is successful, the document has not been changed after signing and the document was originated by the signer of the document.

Figure 12-22 *Digital Signatures in Action*

Digital Signatures = Encrypted Message Digest

A digital signature is the result of encrypting, with the user's private key, the digest and appending that encrypted digest to the plaintext or encrypted message to verify the identity of the sender. The digest will be decrypted with the corresponding public key.

A digital signature provides authentication and integrity. If the recipient is successful at decrypting the digest using the public key of the sender, the recipient has proof of the origin of the message. Also, if both hashes have the same value—the hash calculated by the recipient upon receiving the message and the decrypted hash that was appended to the message in the first place—the recipient has proof that the message wasn't tampered with during transmission, and thus proof of its integrity.

Digital signatures are commonly used to provide assurance of the code authenticity and integrity of both mobile and classic software. As an example, you might have noticed that some executable files (or possibly the whole installation package of a program) are wrapped with a digitally signed envelope, which allows the end user to verify the signature before installing the software.

Digitally signing code provides several assurances about the code:

■ The code has not been modified since it left the software publisher.

■ The code is authentic and is actually sourced by the publisher.

■ The publisher undeniably publishes the code. This provides nonrepudiation of the act of publishing.

The digital signature could be forged only if someone obtained the private key of the publisher. The assurance level of digital signatures is extremely high if the private key is protected properly.

The user of the software must also obtain the public key, which is used to verify the signature. The user can obtain the key in a secure fashion; for example, the key could be included with the installation of the operating system, or transferred securely over the network (for example, using the PKI and certificate authorities).

Diffie-Hellman

Earlier, we discussed how symmetric encryption is faster than asymmetric encryption. However, a significant drawback of symmetric encryption is key generation and distribution. The Diffie-Hellman algorithm is one answer to this problem. The topic of key management, such as key generation and distribution, is covered in more detail in the next section. For now, let's only focus on the mathematical function that could be used to solve these problems.

The goal of DH is that each peer deduces the same secret number following the exchange of some values, in cleartext. That secret number that both peers deduce could then be used as the symmetric encryption key.

The DH algorithm is the basis of most modern automatic key exchange methods. The Internet Key Exchange (IKE) protocol in IPsec VPNs uses DH algorithms extensively to provide a reliable and trusted method for key exchange over untrusted channels.

Whitfield Diffie and Martin Hellman invented the DH algorithm in 1976. Its security stems from the difficulty of calculating the discrete logarithms of very large numbers. The DH algorithm, depicted in Figure 12-23, provides secure key exchange over unsecure channels and is frequently used in modern key management to provide keying material for other symmetric algorithms, such as DES, 3DES, and AES. Don't be too intimidated by Figure 12-23 and the explanation that follows. Later we will demonstrate an example of DH and you'll see it's not too complicated.

To start a DH exchange, the two parties must agree on two nonsecret numbers. The first number is g, the generator, and the second number is p, the modulus. These numbers can be made public and are usually chosen from a table of known values. g is usually a very small number, such as 2, 3, or 4, and p is a very large prime number.

Next, every party generates its own secret value. Then, based on g, p, and the secret value of each party, each party calculates its public value. The public value is computed according to the following formula:

$$Y = g^x \bmod p$$

In this formula, x is the secret value of the entity, and Y is the public value of the entity.

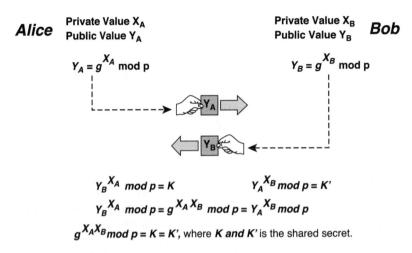

First, Alice and Bob need to agree on
g (generator) and p (modulus ~ prime).

Figure 12-23 *Diffie-Hellman Key Exchange Algorithm*

After computing the public values, the two parties exchange their public values. Each party then exponentiates the received public value with its secret value to compute a common shared-secret value, represented by K and K' in Figure 12-23. When the algorithm completes, both parties have the same shared secret, which they have computed from their secret value and the public value of the other party.

No one listening on the channel can compute the secret value, because only g, p, Y_A, and Y_B are known; at least one secret value is needed to calculate the shared secret. Unless attackers can compute the discrete algorithm of the preceding equation to recover X_A or X_B, they cannot obtain the shared secret.

The following steps describe a DH exchange:

Step 1. Alice and Bob agree on generator g and modulus p.

Step 2. Alice chooses a random large integer, X_A, and sends Bob its public value, Y_A, where $Y_A = g^{x_A} \bmod p$.

Step 3. Bob chooses a random large integer, X_B, and sends Alice his public value, Y_B, where $Y_B = g^{x_B} \bmod p$.

Step 4. Alice computes $K = Y_B^{x_A} \bmod p$.

Step 5. Bob computes $K' = Y_A^{x_B} \bmod p$.

Step 6. Both K and K' are the equal to $g^{x_A x_B} \bmod p$.

Alice and Bob now have a shared secret ($K = K'$), and even if someone has listened on the untrusted channel, there is no way the listener could compute the secret from the captured information, assuming that computing a discrete logarithm of Y_A or Y_B is practically infeasible.

Note RFC 2409 (http://www.ietf.org/rfc/rfc2409) and RFC 3526 (http://www.ietf.org/rfc/rfc3526) provide more details about the values of *g* and *p*.

Diffie-Hellman Example

As you just read, a modulus operation is at the heart of DH. In simple terms, a modulus gives you the remainder of a division when the result of that division is an integer; you don't want a fraction here. Figure 12-24 shows a simple modulus operation.

27 mod 6 = ?

Remember the goal of the modulus: to find the remainder when a division produces an integer.

How many times does 6 go into 27? Four times.

$$\begin{array}{r|l} 27 & 6 \\ -24 & 4 \\ \hline 3 & \end{array}$$

What is the remainder? 3

So, 27 mod 6 = 3

Figure 12-24 *Simple Modulus Calculation*

So, let's try a Diffie-Hellman together. Follow along with Figure 12-25.

Step 1 In the clear, Alice and Bob agree on: generator = 7
Prime number for modulus = 13

Alice

Private Value, $X_A = 3$ Step 2   Private Value, $X_B = 2$ **Bob**

$Y_A = g^{X_A}$ mod p $Y_B = g^{X_B}$ mod p

$Y_A = 7^3$ mod 13   Step 3 $Y_B = 7^2$ mod 13

$Y_A = 343$ mod 13 $Y_B = 49$ mod 13

$Y_A = 5$ Public $Y_B = 10$ Public
         Value   Value Bob
         Alice

Step 4

$Y_B{}^{X_A}$ mod p = $Y_A{}^{X_B}$ mod p

10^3 mod 13 =   Step 5 5^{10} mod 13

1000 mod 13 = <u>12</u>   25 mod 13 = <u>12</u>

Shared Key = 12   12 will be the symmetrical encryption key used for their secure communication.

Figure 12-25 *Diffie-Hellman Example*

Step 1. In cleartext, Alice and Bob agree on a generator and on a modulus. The generator is usually a small number. In our example, shown in Figure 12-25, the peers, Alice and Bob, agree that the generator will be 7. Typically, the modulus is a very large prime number. To keep our calculations simple, we are using a very small modulus number, 13.

Step 2. Alice and Bob independently come up with a random private value that they will keep secret. Alice randomly generates as Alice's private value 3. Bob randomly generates as Bob's private value 2.

Step 3. Alice and Bob proceed to derive their public value, using the generator and primer they agreed on in Step 1 and their own private value they generated in Step 2. Review Figure 12-24 to confirm the procedures of modulus calculations of Step 3. Through the modulus operation, Alice derives that her public value is 5 and Bob derives that his public value is 10.

Step 4. They proceed at sharing their public value with each other, in the clear. Thus, Alice hears that Bob's public value is 10 and Bob hears that Alice's public value is 5.

Step 5. They use their peer's public value, their own private value, and the generator and the prime number of Step 1 to finally calculate a key of 12. The result in Step 5, though independently calculated, will be the same. This will be the shared key that will be used for symmetric encryption. In our example, the key is decimal 12, which is very small. It's only 4 bits long. In real life, with AES as an example, the symmetric keys are 128, 192, or 256 bits long.

If you had sniffed the communication, what would you have learned? The generator (7), the prime number (13), Alice's public value (3), and Bob's public value (2). But you would not know the private values used by Alice and Bob, so it would be impossible for you to proceed with Step 5. DH hasn't been broken yet.

Key Topic

The result of a DH calculation, which will be the same result on both peers, could be used as the encryption key for symmetric algorithms, such as when encrypting with DES, 3DES, or AES.

Additional information can be found at http://www.rsa.com/rsalabs/node.asp?id=2248. There is also a great and colorful explanation of Diffie-Hellman at http://en.wikipedia.org/wiki/Diffie%E2%80%93Hellman_key_exchange.

Cryptographic Processes in VPNs

In the previous pages, you learned about encryption algorithms such as AES, hashing algorithms such as SHA, and key management algorithms such as DH. The combination of symmetric algorithms, hashing functions, and key management algorithms is what comprises IPsec. In Chapter 14, you will see how all these pieces fit together.

Similarly, the SSL and TLS protocols support the use of a variety of different cryptographic algorithms, or ciphers, for use in operations. In Chapter 15, you will see in more detail how SSL and TLS work.

Different protocols support different cryptographic algorithms to accomplish these goals. The selection of the protocol is part of the design phase of VPN implementations, and is directly tied to the strength of the protocol itself, as well as the strength of the keys. The strength of the keys, as you know, is directly related to the key size.

The prevalent algorithms today are 160-bit hashes, provided by SHA-1, and 1024-bit DH keys, among others.

Federal Information Processing Standard (FIPS) 140-2 is the current version of the FIPS 140 publication that specifies requirements for cryptography modules in the United States. NIST issued the FIPS 140 series to uphold the standards that describe the U.S. federal government requirements that IT products should meet. The 2011 specification calls for the following cryptographic algorithms: encryption with AES-128, key generation with Diffie-Hellman 2048 bit, digital signature with RSA 2048 bit, and hashing with SHA 256-bit. These stricter requirements are an indication of the ever-evolving and dynamic nature of threats and acceptable levels of risk in information security. Note that FIPS 140-3 is currently available in its draft format.

Asymmetric Encryption: Digital Signatures

Asymmetric encryption algorithms accomplish two primary objectives: confidentiality and authentication. Asymmetric algorithms are slower than symmetric algorithms because they use more complex mathematics. Because asymmetric algorithms are slower, they are usually used as key exchange protocols and are rarely used for bulk encryption. The sections that follow cover the principles behind asymmetric encryption for digital signatures. Later in the chapter, we will also see how asymmetric encryption is used for PKI environments.

Asymmetric Encryption Overview

To provide the two main objectives of confidentiality and authentication, asymmetric algorithms are based on mathematical formulas that are considerably more complex than the formulas symmetric algorithms are based on. As a result, computation takes more time for asymmetric algorithms. Despite this slower computation trait, asymmetric algorithms are often used as key exchange protocols for symmetric algorithms, which have no inherent key exchange technology.

Also known as *public-key encryption*, asymmetric algorithms have two keys: a public key and a private key. Both keys are capable of the encryption process. However, the complementary matched key is required for decryption. For example, if a public key encrypts the data, the matching private key decrypts the data. The opposite is also true. If a private key encrypts the data, the corresponding public key decrypts the data.

Examples of public-key encryption algorithms are RSA, DSA, DH, ElGamal, and elliptic curve cryptography (ECC). The mathematical operations differ with each algorithm, but the algorithms all share one trait: the mathematics are complicated.

Asymmetric algorithms are designed in such a way that the key that is used for encryption is different from the key that is used for decryption (Figure 12-16, shown earlier, illustrates the mechanics of asymmetric encryption). The decryption key cannot, in any reasonable amount of time, be calculated from the encryption key, and vice versa. The usual key length for asymmetric algorithms ranges from 512 to 4096 bits. Asymmetric algorithm key lengths cannot be directly compared to symmetric algorithm key lengths because the two algorithm families differ greatly in their underlying design.

To illustrate this point, it is generally thought that an encryption key of RSA that is 2048 bits is roughly equivalent to a 128-bit key of RC4 in terms of resistance against brute-force attacks.

Public Key Authentication

The authentication objective of asymmetric algorithms is achieved when the encryption process is started with the private key. When the private key is used to encrypt the data, the public key must be used to decrypt the data. Because only one host has the private key, only that host could have encrypted the message, therefore providing authentication of the sender.

Private key (encrypt) + Public key (decrypt) = Authentication.

Typically, no attempt is made to preserve the secrecy of the public key, so any number of hosts can decrypt the message. When a host successfully decrypts a message using a public key, it is trusted that the private key encrypted the message, which verifies who the sender is; this is a form of authentication.

In Figure 12-26, Alice and Bob exchange data with the goal of authentication. They follow these steps:

Step 1.   Alice, using her private key, creates a digital signature and appends it to the message.

Step 2.   Alice transmits the signed message to Bob.

Step 3.   Bob acquires Alice's public key.

Step 4.   Bob uses Alice's public key to verify the signature.

Figure 12-26 *Asymmetric Authentication Process = Digital Signature*

If Bob wishes to also sign a document, he will need to go through Steps 1 and 2 using his private key, and Alice will need to acquire Bob's public key to check his signature. Therefore, the authentication is unidirectional. Each party is responsible for creating his or her own signature.

Safekeeping the Private Key

As you can imagine, the private key must be kept secret. As an example, in some organizations, the private key is kept on a USB thumb drive. When the owner of the private key wishes to use it, he inserts it into the USB port and is typically asked for the PIN to unlock the private key. Using a private key provides strong authentication. Strong authentication requires using two separate authentication methods. To unlock the private key, we are therefore using strong authentication: something you have (the USB thumb drive) and something you know (the PIN).

Caution If the private key is compromised, another key pair must be generated to replace the compromised key.

RSA and Digital Signatures

RSA is one of the most common asymmetric algorithms. Ron Rivest (discussed earlier in this chapter), Adi Shamir, and Len Adleman invented the patented public-key RSA algorithm in 1977. The patent expired in September 2000, and the algorithm is now in the public domain. Of all the public-key algorithms that were proposed over the years, RSA is by far the easiest to understand and implement.

The RSA algorithm is very flexible because it has a variable key length that allows speed to be traded for the security of the algorithm if necessary.

The RSA keys are usually 512 to 2048 bits long. RSA has withstood years of extensive cryptanalysis, and although the security of RSA has been neither proved nor disproved, it does suggest a confidence level in the algorithm. The security of RSA is based on the difficulty of *factoring* very large numbers, which means breaking large numbers into multiplicative factors. If an easy method of factoring these large numbers were discovered, the effectiveness of RSA would be destroyed.

The RSA algorithm is based on the fact that each entity has two keys: a public key and a private key. The public key can be published and given away, but the private key must be kept very secret. It is not possible to determine, using any computationally feasible algorithm, the private key from the public key, and vice versa. What one of the keys encrypts, the other key decrypts, and vice versa.

RSA keys are long term and are usually changed or renewed after some months or even years.

The current procedures for signing digital signatures are not simply implemented by public-key operations. In fact, a modern digital signature is based on a hash function and a public-key algorithm. Figure 12-27 illustrates this procedure.

Figure 12-27 *RSA Digital Signatures*

The signature process shown in Figure 12-27 is as follows:

Step 1. The signer (Alice) makes a hash, or fingerprint, of the document, which uniquely identifies the document and all of its contents.

Step 2. Alice encrypts the hash only with her private key.

Step 3. The encrypted hash, known as the signature, is appended to the document.

The verification process works as follows:

Step 1.   The verifier (Bob) obtains Alice's public key.

Step 2.   Bob decrypts the signature using Alice's public key. This step unveils the assumed hash value of the signer.

Step 3.   Bob makes a hash of the received document, without its signature, and compares this hash to the decrypted signature hash. If the hashes match, the document is authentic; that is, it has been signed by Alice, and has not changed since it was signed.

This example illustrates how the authenticity and integrity of the message are ensured even though the actual text is public. Both encryption and digital signatures are required to ensure that the message is private and has not changed.

Note   The RSA algorithm is currently the most common method for signature generation and is used widely in e-commerce systems and Internet protocols in that role.

RSA is substantially slower than DES in both hardware and software implementations. This performance problem is the main reason that RSA is typically used only to protect small amounts of data. RSA is mainly used for two services:

■ To ensure confidentiality of data by performing encryption

■ To perform authentication of data, nonrepudiation of data, or both by generating digital signatures

Note   RSA encryption is faster than decryption, and verification is faster than signing.

Public Key Infrastructure

The example in the previous section of authentication using asymmetric encryption and digital signatures suffers from one critical drawback: scalability. If applied to two parties, such as the Bob and Alice example, you need two sets of private/public keys to authenticate the two parties. As the number of parties increases, and if you want to maintain authentication separate for each pair of entities, the number of private/public keys increases exponentially, and the number of validations to verify the signatures does as well.

For instance, if 10 individuals need to validate each other, 95 validations would need to be performed before everyone would have validated everyone else. Adding a single individual to the group would require an additional 20 validations because each of the original 10 individuals would need to authenticate the new individual, and the new individual would need to authenticate the original 10. This method does not scale well.

The impact is more tangible in real-life environments involving large organizations. In those scenarios, it is impractical for all parties to continually exchange identification documents. For example, Cisco goes to reasonable measures to identify employees and contractors, and then issues ID badges. The badge is relatively difficult to forge. Measures are in place to protect the integrity of the badge and the badge issuance. Because of these measures, all Cisco personnel accept this badge as authoritative as to the identity of any individual.

The badge scenario is an example of a trusted third-party protocol. This concept involves the use of a trusted introducer to all the parties trying to communicate. All individuals agree to accept the word of this neutral third party. In this way, parties that need to validate each other rely on the in-depth authentication of an agreed-upon third party instead of performing their own authentication. Presumably, the third party does an in-depth investigation before the issuance of credentials. After this in-depth investigation, the third-party issues credentials that are difficult to forge. From that point forward, all individuals who trust the third party simply accept the credentials that the third party issues.

Passports and driver's licenses are real-life examples of a trusted third-party environment that uses the concept of a trusted introducer. Certificate authority (CA) servers are an example of this concept in PKI environments.

Note   Certificate servers are an example of a trusted third party.

In Figure 12-28, Alice applies to the license bureau for a driver's license. In this process, she submits evidence of her identity and her qualifications to drive. Her application is approved and a license is issued.

Alice applies for a driver's license.

She receives her driver's license after her identity is proven.

Alice attempts to cash a check.

Her identity is accepted after her driver's license is checked.

Figure 12-28   *Trusted Third Party Example*

Later, Alice needs to cash a check at the bank. Upon presenting the check to the bank teller, the bank teller asks her for ID. Alice presents her driver's license. The bank, because it trusts the government agency that issued the driver's license, verifies her identity, and cashes her check.

> **Note**   Certificate servers function like the license bureau in this example. The driver's license is analogous to a certificate in a PKI or a technology that supports certificates.

A PKI provides a framework upon which you can base security services, such as encryption, authentication, and nonrepudiation. A PKI allows for very scalable solutions, and is becoming an extremely important authentication solution for VPNs. A PKI uses specific terminology to name its components.

PKI Terminology and Components

When these concepts are applied in practice, it is important to understand the supporting framework. A PKI is the service framework that is needed to support large-scale, public-key-based technologies. PKI is a set of technical, organizational, and legal components that are needed to establish a system that enables large-scale use of public-key cryptography to provide authenticity, confidentiality, integrity, and nonrepudiation services.

Three very important terms must be defined when talking about a PKI:

- **PKI:** A service framework needed to support large-scale PK-based technologies

- **Certificate authority (CA):** The trusted third party that signs the public keys of entities in a PKI-based system

- **Certificate:** A document that in essence binds together the name of the entity and its public key and that has been signed by the CA

> **Note**   The certificate of a user is always signed by a CA. Moreover, every CA has its own certificate, containing its public key, signed by itself. This is called a *CA certificate*, or more properly, a *self-signed CA certificate*, or more commonly, a *root certificate*.

A PKI is more than just a CA and its users. And implementing the enabling technology and building a large PKI involves a huge amount of organizational and legal work. There are five main areas of a PKI:

- CAs for key management

- PKI users, such as people, devices, servers, and so on

- Storage and protocols

- Supporting organizational framework, known as practices and user authentication using local registration authorities (LRA)

- Supporting legal framework

Many vendors offer CA servers as a managed service or as an end-user product:

- VeriSign

- Entrust Technologies

- RSA

- Cybertrust

- Microsoft

- Novell

Certificate Classes

CAs, especially outsourced ones, can issue certificates of a number of classes, which determine how trusted a certificate is. A single outsourcing vendor (for example, VeriSign) might run a single CA, issuing certificates of different classes, and its customers will use the CA they need depending on the desired level of trust.

A certificate class is usually a number; the higher the number, the more trusted the certificate is considered. The trust in the certificate is usually determined by how rigorous the procedure was that verified the identity of the holder when the certificate was issued. For example, a class 0 certificate might be issued without any checks, such as for testing purposes. A class 1 certificate might require an email reply from the future certificate holder to confirm his wish to enroll. This confirmation is a weak authentication of the holder. For a class 3 or 4 certificate, the future holder must prove his identity and authenticate his public key by showing up in person with at least two official ID documents.

Certificate Authorities

PKIs form different topologies of trust. In the simple model shown in Figure 12-29, a single CA, which is also known as the root CA, issues all the certificates to the end users. The benefit in such a setup is simplicity, but there are several pitfalls:

- It is difficult to scale this topology to a large environment.

- This topology needs a strictly centralized administration.

- There is a critical vulnerability in using a single-signing private key; if this key is stolen, the whole PKI falls apart because the CA can no longer be trusted as a unique signer.

Figure 12-29 *PKI Topology Using a Single-Root CA*

Because of its simplicity, VPNs that are managed by a single organization often use this topology.

Going beyond the single-root CA, topologies that are more complex can be devised that involve multiple CAs within the same organization. One such topology is the hierarchical CA system, shown in Figure 12-30. With the hierarchical topology, CAs can issue certificates to end users and to subordinate CAs, which in turn issue their certificates to end users, other CAs, or both. Therefore, a tree of CAs and end users is built in which every CA can issue certificates to lower-level CAs and end users.

Figure 12-30 *PKI Topology Using Hierarchical CAs*

The main benefits of a hierarchical PKI topology are increased scalability and manageability; trust decisions can now be hierarchically distributed to smaller branches. This distribution works well in most large organizations. For example, a large company may have a root CA that issues certificates to level-2 CAs. These level-2 CAs issue the certificates to the end users. Because the root-signing key is seldom used after the subordinate CA certificates are issued, it is less exposed and therefore much more trusted. Also, if a sub-ordinate CA has its private key stolen, only a branch of the PKI is rendered untrusted. All other users can consider this by no longer trusting that particular CA.

One issue with hierarchical PKI topologies lies in finding the certification path for a certificate (in other words, determining the chain of the signing process). The more CAs involved in establishing the trust between the root CA and the end user, the more difficult the task.

Another approach to hierarchical PKIs is called cross-certifying, as shown in Figure 12-31. In this scenario, multiple flat single-root CAs establish trust relationships horizontally, by cross-certifying their own CA certificates.

Figure 12-31 *PKI Topology Using Cross-Certifying CAs*

Some PKIs might offer the possibility or even require the use of two key pairs per entity:

- One public and private key pair is intended only for encryption operations. The public key encrypts, and the private key decrypts.

- The other public and private key pair is intended only for signing operations. The private key signs, and the public key verifies the signature.

These keys are sometimes called "usage" or "special" keys. They may differ in key length and even in the choice of the public-key algorithm. If the PKI requires two key pairs per entity, a user has two certificates:

- An encryption certificate containing the public key of the user who encrypts the data

- A signature certificate containing the public key of the user who verifies the digital signature of the user

The following scenarios typically use usage keys:

- When encryption is used much more frequently than signing, a certain public and private key pair is more exposed due to its frequent usage. In this case, it might be a good idea to shorten its lifetime and change it more often, while having a separate signing private and public key pair with a longer lifetime.

- When different levels of encryption and digital signing are required, because of legal, export, or performance issues, usage keys allow you to assign different key lengths to the two pairs.

- When key recovery is desired (for example, a copy of a user's private key is kept in a central repository for various backup reasons), usage keys allow you to back up only the private key of the encrypting pair; the signing private key remains with the user, enabling true nonrepudiation.

The CA, with its private key, is the security-critical component in a PKI system. To make the operation of a CA simpler, and therefore more secure, many key management tasks are often offloaded to registration authorities (RA). RAs are PKI servers that perform management tasks on behalf of the CA, so that the CA can focus on the signing process.

Usually, the following tasks are offloaded to the RA:

- Authentication of users when they enroll with the PKI

- Key generation for users who cannot generate their own keys

- Distribution of certificates after enrollment

PKI Standards

Standardization and interoperability of different PKI vendors are still issues when interconnecting PKIs. The X.509 standards and the Internet Engineering Task Force (IETF) Public-Key Infrastructure X.509 (PKIX) workgroup have made progress toward publishing a common set of standards for PKI protocols and data formats.

A PKI also uses a number of supporting services, such as Lightweight Directory Access Protocol (LDAP)-accessible X.500 directories.

Interoperability between a PKI and its supporting services is a concern because many vendors have proposed and implemented proprietary solutions instead of waiting for standards to develop. The state of interoperability can still be described as basic, even after 10 years of PKI software development.

Note   The IETF has formed a working group that is dedicated to promoting and standardizing PKI in the Internet. The working group has published a draft set of standards detailing common data formats and PKI-related protocols in a network. The goals and milestones of the PKI working group can be tracked at http://www.ietf.org/html.charters/pkix-charter.html.

The X.509 standard describes an identity and how to store an authentication key, more precisely defining basic PKI formats, such as certificate and certificate revocation list (CRL) formats, to enable basic interoperability. Abstract Syntax Notation One (ASN.1) provides information about the format of the X.509 certificate and the syntax of the fields in the certificate. The X.509 standard has been widely used for years with many Internet applications, such as SSL and IPsec.

The X.509 Version 3 (X.509v3) standard defines the format of a digital certificate. This format is already extensively used in the infrastructure of the Internet, in the following ways:

- Secure web servers use X.509v3 for website authentication in the SSL and TLS protocols.

- Web browsers use X.509v3 for services that implement client certificates in the SSL protocol.

- User mail agents that support mail protection using the Secure/Multipurpose Internet Mail Extensions (S/MIME) protocol use X.509.

- IPsec VPNs where certificates can be used as a public-key distribution mechanism for IKE RSA-based authentication use X.509.

Certificates are public information. They contain the binding between an entity's names and public keys and are usually published in a centralized directory so that other PKI users can easily access them.

In the CA authentication procedure, the first step of the user, when contacting the PKI, is to securely obtain a copy of the public key of the CA. The public key of the CA verifies all the certificates issued by the CA and is vital for the proper operation of the PKI.

The public key of the CA is also distributed in the form of a certificate issued by the CA itself. This certificate is also called a *self-signed certificate*, because the signer and the holder are the same entity. Only a root CA issues self-signed certificates to itself.

Public-Key Cryptography Standards (PKCS) provide basic interoperability of applications, which use public-key cryptography. The PKCS define the low-level standardized formats for the secure exchange of arbitrary data, such as a standard format for an encrypted piece of data, a signed piece of data, and so on. The origin and purpose of PKCS are described on the RSA Laboratories website: "The Public-Key Cryptography Standards are specifications produced by RSA Laboratories in cooperation with secure systems developers worldwide for the purpose of accelerating the deployment of public-key cryptography."

There are many defined PKCS standards:

- **PKCS #1:** RSA Cryptography Standard

- **PKCS #3:** Diffie-Hellman Key Agreement Standard

- **PKCS #5:** Password-Based Cryptography Standard

- **PKCS #6:** Extended-Certificate Syntax Standard

- **PKCS #7:** Cryptographic Message Syntax Standard

- **PKCS #8:** Private-Key Information Syntax Standard

- **PKCS #9:** Selected Attribute Types

- **PKCS #10:** Certification Request Syntax Standard

- **PKCS #11:** Cryptographic Token Interface Standard

- **PKCS #12:** Personal Information Exchange Syntax Standard

- **PKCS #13:** Elliptic Curve Cryptography Standard

- **PKCS #15:** Cryptographic Token Information Format Standard

Note   For more information about these standards, visit http://www.rsa.com/rsalabs/node.asp?id=2124.

Public-key technology is becoming more widely deployed and is becoming the basis for standards-based security, such as the IPsec and IKE protocols. With the use of public-key certificates in network security protocols comes the need for a certificate management protocol that PKI clients and CA servers can use to support certificate lifecycle operations, such as certificate enrollment and revocation, and certificate and CRL access. The goal of the Simple Certificate Enrollment Protocol (SCEP) is to support the secure issuance of certificates to network devices in a scalable manner, using existing technology wherever possible.

As shown in Figure 12-32, an end entity starts an enrollment transaction by creating a certificate signing request using PKCS#10. The PKCS#10 signing request is encapsulated in a PKCS#7 and sent to the CA or RA. PKCS#7 is a syntax standard for cryptographic messages. After the CA or RA receives the request, it either automatically approves the request and sends the certificate back, or it compels the end entity to wait until the operator can manually authenticate the identity of the requesting end entity.

Figure 12-32 *Certificate Signing Request*

Distinguished names (DN) provide a way to identify an entity by using multiple fields to provide hierarchical identification. DNs are used on a certificate in the Subject field.

Note An example of a distinguished name used as the Subject Name field in an X.509 user certificate would appear as

CN=Harry Wales,OU=Sales,O=My Computer,L=My Company,L=Chicago,S=Ohio,C=US

where

- CN= commonName

- OU= organizationalUnitName

- O= Organization

- L= Locality (City)

- S= State

- C= US

The merging of the X.509 standard with public-key encryption allows the introduction of a trusted third party: the CA. The CA has a pair of asymmetric keys, a private key, and a public key. An X.509 certificate is created to identify the CA. The certificate of the CA contains the following information:

- The identity of the CA (for example, a subject containing the identity in the DN format)

- Other parameters (such as serial number, algorithms used, and validity period)

- The public key of the CA (for example, an RSA public key)

- The signature using the private key of the CA (for example, self-signing using the private key of the CA with RSA encryption and the SHA-1 hash algorithm)

Caution   The certificate is freely distributed. The receiver of the certificate should verify the authenticity of the certificate of the CA out-of-band.

Also, browsers such as Microsoft Internet Explorer come with certificates of large CAs, such as VeriSign, GoDaddy, and so on, already provisioned in the installation. That's how our personal computers are able to established HTTPS sessions with banks and Internet retailers without having to install additional software.

In Figure 12-33, the following steps occur to retrieve the CA certificate:

Step 1.   Alice and Bob request the CA certificate that contains the CA public key.

Step 2.   Upon receipt of the CA certificate, Alice's and Bob's systems verify the validity of the certificate using public-key cryptography.

Step 3.   Alice and Bob follow up the technical verification done by their systems by telephoning the CA administrator and verifying the public key and serial number of the certificate.

Figure 12-33   *Retrieving a CA Certificate*

After retrieving the CA certificate, Alice and Bob perform the following steps to submit certificate requests to the CA, as shown in Figure 12-34:

Step 1.   Alice's and Bob's systems forward a certificate request that includes their public keys along with some identifying information. All of this information is encrypted using the public key of the CA.

Step 2.   Upon receipt of the certificate requests, the CA administrator telephones Alice and Bob to confirm their submittals and the public keys.

Step 3.   The CA administrator issues the certificate by adding some additional data to the certificate request, and digitally signing it all.

Step 4.   Either the end user manually retrieves the certificate or SCEP automatically retrieves the certificate, and the certificate is installed onto the system.

Figure 12-34   *Certificate Enrollment*

Having installed certificates signed by the same CA, Bob and Alice are now ready to authenticate each other, as shown in Figure 12-35:

Step 1.   Bob and Alice exchange certificates. The CA is no longer involved.

Step 2.   Each party verifies the digital signature on the certificate by hashing the plaintext portion of the certificate, decrypting the digital signature using the CA public key, and comparing the results. If the results match, the certificate is verified as being signed by a trusted third party, and the verification by the CA that Bob is Bob and Alice is Alice is accepted.

Figure 12-35   *Authentication Using Certificates*

Certificate Revocation

Digital certificates can be revoked if keys are thought to be compromised, or if the business use of the certificate calls for revocation (for example, VPN access, network logon, and so on). If keys are thought to be compromised, generating new keys will force the creation of a new digital certificate, rendering the old certificate invalid and a candidate for revocation. On the other hand, a consultant could obtain a digital certificate for VPN access into the corporate network only for the duration of the contract.

Certificate revocation is also a centralized function, providing "push" and "pull" methods to obtain a list of revoked certificates frequently or on demand from a centralized entity. In some instances, the CA server often acts as the issuer of certificate revocation information, as shown in Figure 12-36.

Figure 12-36 *Certificate Revocation Process*

Several methods can be used for certificate revocation. The most prevalent today is the use of CRLs, but other methods such as Online Certificate Status Protocol (OCSP) overcome some of the limitations of CRLs and are often used. An alternative method is Cisco-proprietary and involves querying the AAA server to see if the user exists. If the user exists, the entity checking the validity of the certificate presumes that the certificate is good because the user is valid in the AAA server. Table 12-5 lists benefits and limitations of each method.

Table 12-5 *Certificate Revocation Methods*

Certificate Revocation List	Online Certificate Status Protocol	AAA Server Certificate Authorization
A list of revoked certificate serial numbers is distributed as a time-stamped, CA-signed file.	Revocation information is immediately pushed to an online database.	Cisco-proprietary alternative to OCSP.

Table 12-5   *Certificate Revocation Methods*

Certificate Revocation List	Online Certificate Status Protocol	AAA Server Certificate Authorization
PKI entities regularly poll the CRL repository to pull the current CRL. Clients cache a local copy of CRLs. The client downloads a newer CRL once the current one expires.	Entities can query the OCSP server at any time to check for validity of the received certificate.	Entities can query the AAA server at any time to check for validity of the received certificate.
There is a window of opportunity for attackers while the new CRL is not yet propagated. This is why it is recommended to have an overlapping period between the two CRLs.	This protocol is not widely deployed.	It is not integrated with the PKI, so it requires a separate authorization database.

Certificates were traditionally used at the application layer to provide strong authentication for applications. Each application may have a different implementation of the actual authentication process, but they all use a similar type of certificate in the X.509 format.

Certificate Use

SSL is probably the most widely used certificate-based authentication. SSL includes the negotiation of keys that are used to encrypt the SSL session. Many applications use SSL to provide authentication and encryption. The most widely used application is HTTPS. Other well-known applications that were using poor authentication and no encryption were modified to use SSL, such as Simple Mail Transfer Protocol (SMTP), LDAP, and Post Office Protocol version 3 (POP3).

Email has experienced many extensions. One of the important extensions was the introduction of Multipurpose Internet Mail Extensions (MIME), which allowed arbitrary data to be included in an email. Another extension was to provide security to entire mail messages or parts of mail messages. S/MIME authenticates and encrypts email messages.

Pretty Good Privacy (PGP) is an application that was originally developed by Phil Zimmerman, a privacy advocate, so that end users could engage in confidential communications using encryption. The most frequent use of PGP has been to secure email.

Certificates are also used at the network layer, or at the application layer, by network devices. Cisco routers, Cisco VPN concentrators, and Cisco ASA firewalls can use certificates to authenticate IPsec peers.

Cisco switches can use certificates to authenticate end devices connecting to LAN ports. Authentication uses IEEE 802.1X between the adjacent devices. The authentication can be proxied to a central access control server (ACS) via EAP-TLS.

Cisco routers can also provide Telnet 3270 support that does not include encryption or strong authentication. Cisco routers can now use SSL to establish Secure Telnet 3270 sessions.

Figure 12-37 illustrates a network where certificates are used for various purposes. A single CA server can facilitate many applications that require digital certificates for authentication purposes. Using CA servers is therefore a solution that simplifies the management of authentication and provides strong security due to the strength of cryptographic mechanisms that are used in combination with digital certificates.

Figure 12-37 *Where We Find Certificates Being Used*

Digital Certificates and CAs

Compared to other authentication mechanisms, a PKI has the following characteristics:

■ To authenticate each other, users have to obtain the certificate of the CA and their own certificate. These steps require the out-of-band verification of the processes. After this verification is complete, the presence of the CA is no longer required until one of the certificates that is involved expires.

■ Public-key systems use asymmetric keys where one is public and the other one is private. One of the features of these algorithms is that whatever is encrypted using one key can only be decrypted using the other key. This provides nonrepudiation.

■ Key management is simplified because two users can freely exchange the certificates. The validity of the received certificates is verified using the public key of the CA, which the users have in their possession.

■ Because of the strength of the algorithms involved, you can set a very long lifetime for the certificates, typically a lifetime measured in years.

The disadvantages of using trusted third parties relate to key management:

- **A user certificate is compromised (stolen private key):** Other users should not accept compromised certificates. The only way to prevent the compromised certificates from being used is to keep a list of all revoked certificates. A server, not necessarily the CA server, must be accessible to users so that they can periodically download the latest CRL and use the list when authenticating other users. If the CRL lists the received certificate of the user, the authentication fails.

- **The certificate of the CA is compromised (stolen private key):** This invalidates all certificates signed by the CA. A single CA environment requires the creation of a new CA certificate and the creation of new user certificates. A hierarchical CA environment requires the use of an authority revocation list (ARL), where all child certificates of the compromised CA become invalid if the ARL lists the CA.

- **The CA administrator:** The human factor is an additional limitation of the CA-based solution. To lessen the impact, the CA administrator should follow strict rules when issuing certificates to users. A security policy should define the steps required to create certificates (for example, mandatory out-of-band verification of all initial enrollment procedures or verification steps for CA administrators before approving certificate requests).

When you use certificates in IP networks, you might need to combine public-key authentication with another authentication mechanism to increase the level of security and provide more authorization options. For example, IPsec using certificates for authentication and Extended Authentication (XAUTH) with one-time password hardware tokens would be a superior authentication scheme when compared to certificates alone. XAUTH is used for user authentication during IPsec remote access VPN, while the digital certificate is used typically for asset authentication (machine authentication).

Summary

The key points covered in this chapter are as follows:

- A cryptosystem is made up of a combination of hashing, symmetric, and asymmetric algorithms.

- Symmetric algorithms use a single key for encrypting and decrypting. Generally speaking, symmetric algorithms are the strongest and fastest algorithms and therefore are used for most encryption.

- Hashing algorithms use a one-way process designed to provide integrity. Usually, successful decryption of a digest provides proof of integrity and authenticity.

- Asymmetric algorithms use a key pair for the encrypting/decrypting process. One key encrypts, and the other key decrypts.

- RSA is a widely used algorithm for public-key cryptography.

- A PKI uses asymmetric encryption to provide confidentiality, integrity, and authentication services.

- PKI solutions are based on digital certificates and a trusted third party trust model.

- X.509v3, PKCS, and others provide standards for certificate formats and interoperability.

- CRL, OCSP, and AAA server certificate authorization are means to validate a certificate.

- The hierarchical trust model of PKI solutions includes CAs and RAs.

References

For additional information, refer to these resources.

Books and Articles

Giry, D. "Cryptographic Key Length Recommendation," http://www.keylength.com/en/3/

Kahn, D. *The Codebreakers: The Comprehensive History of Secret Communication from Ancient Times to the Internet* (Scribner, 1996).

Kaliski, B. "TWIRL and RSA Key Size," http://www.rsasecurity.com/rsalabs/node.asp?id=2004.

Singh, S. *The Code Book: The Science of Secrecy from Ancient Egypt to Quantum Cryptography* (Knopf Publishing Group, 1999).

Standards

IETF. *Public-Key Infrastructure (X.509) (pkix)*, http://tools.ietf.org/html/rfc5280

NIST. "Advanced Encryption Standard (AES)" (FIPS PUB 197), http://csrc.nist.gov/publications/fips/fips197/fips-197.pdf.

NIST. "Secure Hash Standard" (FIPS PUB 180-1), http://www.itl.nist.gov/fipspubs/fip180-1.htm.

RSA Laboratories. *Public-Key Cryptography Standards (PKCS)*, http://www.rsa.com/rsalabs/node.asp?id=2124.

Wikipedia. "Diffie-Hellman," http://en.wikipedia.org/wiki/Diffie%E2%80%93Hellman_key_exchange.

Encryption Regulations

U.S. Department of Commerce, http://www.commerce.gov.

"EAR Controls for Items That Use Encryption," http://www.bis.doc.gov/encryption/default.htm.

Review Questions

Use the questions here to review what you learned in this chapter. The correct answers are found in the Appendix, "Answers to Chapter Review Questions."

1. Which three business benefits are directly associated with VPNs?

   a. Cost savings
   b. Traffic segregation
   c. Telemetry
   d. Scalability
   e. Productivity

2. Asymmetric encryption utilizes which of the following?

   a. A complex solution to leverage certificates
   b. Key pairs to accomplish encryption
   c. All types of authentication as long as they support PKI procedures
   d. A certificate authority that signs public keys in a network

3. Select all the desirable features of an encryption algorithm.

   a. Resistance to known cryptanalytic attack
   b. Short lengths and scalability of the key for easy storage
   c. No export or import restrictions
   d. Susceptible to the avalanche effect; a small change in plaintext causes substantial changes in ciphertext

4. A cipher suite is _____.

   a. The place of storage of cipher keys
   b. A combination of cryptographic methods that work together
   c. A chain of crypto keys
   d. The prevalent set of algorithms at a given point in time

5. The selection of asymmetric encryption algorithms is based on a tradeoff between security and _____.

   a. Operational efficiency
   b. Reliability
   c. Performance
   d. Key length

6. RC4 is a(n) _____ encryption algorithm.

   a. Asymmetric
   b. Polyalphabetic
   c. Elliptic curve
   d. Symmetric

7. Which two options determine the strength of protection of modern cryptography algorithms?

    a. Length of key
    b. Mathematical complexity
    c. Number of permutations
    d. Level of trust toward the algorithm itself
    e. Resistance to brute force attacks

8. Which combination does asymmetric encryption use in confidentiality scenarios?

    a. The private key is used to encrypt and the public key is used to decrypt.
    b. The public key is used to encrypt and the private key is used to decrypt.
    c. A digital certificate is used to encrypt and the private key is used to decrypt.
    d. The public key is used to encrypt and the corresponding digital certificate is used to decrypt.

9. Which of the following is not involved in RSA user authentication?

    a. A hashing function
    b. A public key
    c. Digital signatures
    d. A shared secret

10. Which of the following cipher categories transforms plaintext into ciphertext by operating bit by bit?

    a. Transposition
    b. Stream
    c. Polyalphabetic
    d. Block

11. DES operates in which two block cipher modes?

    a. ECB
    b. CFB
    c. CBC
    d. OFB

12. Which algorithm is used in AES?

    a. Twofish
    b. RC6
    c. RC4
    d. Rijndael

13. Which statement best describes MD5?

    a. MD5 is a one-way function that makes it difficult to compute a hash from the given input data, but makes it feasible to compute input data given only a hash.

    b. MD5 is a one-way function that makes it easy to compute a hash from the given output data, but makes it infeasible to compute input data given only a hash.

    c. MD5 is a one-way function that makes it difficult to compute a hash from the given output data, but makes it feasible to compute input data given only a hash.

    d. MD5 is a one-way function that makes it easy to compute a hash from the given input data, but makes it infeasible to compute the exact input data given only a hash.

14. Which of the following statements regarding public-key authentication is true?

    a. When the private key is used to encrypt, the corresponding public key is used to decrypt.

    b. Because the public key is present on only one system, authentication is assured when its private key decrypts the message.

    c. Great effort is made to maintain the secrecy of the public keys.

    d. Public-key scenario is used for producing fingerprint.

15. Which set of algorithms provides the most secure communication?

    a. AES, SHA-1

    b. 3DES, SHA-1

    c. 3DES, MD5

    d. AES, MD5

16. Which of the following statements best describes a digital signature?

    a. A digital signature is a message digest encrypted with the sender's public key.

    b. A digital signature is a message digest encrypted with the receiver's public key.

    c. A digital signature is a message digest encrypted with the sender's private key.

    d. A digital signature is a message digest encrypted with the receiver's public key.

17. Complete the sentence with the best statement: The Vigenère cipher is a(n) _____ .

    a. Polyalphabetic cipher

    b. Polymorphic cipher

    c. Polybius square cipher

    d. Alphabetum cipher

18. Which of the following is not a term that is related to hierarchical CA topologies?

    a. Certificate chain

    b. Subordinate CAs

    c. PKI

    d. Single point of failure

19. Which protocol encrypts at the session layer of the OSI model?

    a. IPsec

    b. Enigma

    c. SSL

    d. MD5

20. Which statement is most accurate when describing aspects of a birthday attack?

    a. An attacker tries every possible key with the decryption algorithm.

    b. The attacker has the ciphertext of several messages, all of which have been encrypted using the same encryption algorithm.

    c. If some function, when supplied with a random input, returns one of k equally likely values, then by repeating the function with different inputs, the same output would be expected after $1.2k^{\frac{1}{2}}$ number of times.

    d. The attacker knows a portion of the plaintext and the corresponding ciphertext.

21. Which of the following terms identifies a standard that describes the structure of digital certificates?

    a. PKCS#10

    b. SCEP

    c. X.509v3

    d. RSA

22. Out-of-band authentication, in the context of certificate authorities, typically involves which of the following? (Choose two.)

    a. Certificate request

    b. Separate network

    c. Digital signature

    d. Public key

    e. Serial number

Chapter 13

IPsec Fundamentals

This chapter addresses the protocols and algorithms that IPsec uses and the different security services that IPsec provides. More precisely, this chapter

- Analyzes the architecture of the IPsec protocol

- Details the role and operational impact of IPsec's main components

- Describes IPsec modes of operation in various scenarios

- Describes the phases of IPsec connectivity

- Describes the role and component of IKE

- Provides an overview of the operations of IPv6 VPNs

An IP Security (IPsec) virtual private network (VPN) is an essential tool for providing a secure network for business communication. This chapter addresses the different protocols and algorithms that IPsec uses and the different security services that IPsec provides. This chapter also introduces the different VPN technologies and some of the best practices that you should use with them.

IPsec Framework

IPsec is an Internet Engineering Task Force (IETF) standard that defines how a VPN can be set up using the IP addressing protocol; it was originally defined in RFCs 2401 to 2412. IPsec works at the network layer, protecting and authenticating IP packets between participating IPsec devices (peers). IPsec is not bound to any specific encryption, authentication, or security algorithms or keying technology. IPsec is a framework of open standards.

Because IPsec is not bound to specific algorithms, IPsec allows newer and better algorithms to be implemented without patching the existing IPsec standards. IPsec provides data confidentiality, data integrity, origin authentication, and antireplay protection between participating peers at the IP layer. IPsec secures a path between a pair of gateways or between a gateway and a host, as shown in Figure 12-2 in Chapter 12, "Fundamentals of Cryptography and VPN Technologies." IPsec could also secure a path between two hosts.

IPsec provides the following essential security functions:

- **Confidentiality:** IPsec ensures confidentiality by using encryption. Data encryption prevents third parties from reading the data, especially data transmitted over public networks or over wireless networks.

- **Integrity:** IPsec ensures that data arrives unchanged at the destination; that is, that the data has not been manipulated at any point along the communication path. IPsec ensures data integrity by using checksums, which are a simple redundancy check. The IPsec protocol adds up the basic components of a message, typically the number of bytes, and stores the total value. IPsec performs a checksum operation on received data and compares the result to the authentic checksum. If the sums match, the assumption is that the data has not been manipulated.

- **Authentication:** Authentication ensures that the connection is made with the desired communication partner. IPsec uses Internet Key Exchange (IKE) to authenticate users and devices that can carry out communication independently. IKE uses several types of authentication:

  - Username and password

  - One-time password

  - Biometric

  - Preshared keys (PSK)

  - Digital certificates

> **Note** IKE is discussed in more detail in the section, "IKE Protocol," later in the chapter.

- **Antireplay protection:** Antireplay protection verifies that each packet is unique and is not duplicated. IPsec packets are protected by comparing the sequence number of the received packets with a sliding window on the destination host or security gateway. A packet that has a sequence number that comes before the sliding window is considered either late or a duplicate packet. Late and duplicate packets are dropped.

Essential services provided by IPsec are as follows:

- Confidentiality

- Integrity

- Authentication

- Antireplay

The main reason we use IPsec is typically to provide confidentiality to our transmission. Confidentiality is reached by encrypting sensitive payload. The following explains the recent improvement to encryption.

Suite B Cryptographic Standard

In most cryptographic functions, the key length is an important security parameter. Both academic and private organizations provide recommendations and mathematical formulas to approximate the minimum key size requirement for security. Despite the availability of these publications, choosing an appropriate key size to protect systems and networks from attacks remains a challenge.

As computing power increases, the feasibility of deploying complex encryption algorithms commercially also increases. The main principle is that the degree of security depends on the length of the key of the encryption algorithm. The time that it takes to process all of the possibilities is a function of the computing power of the computer. Therefore, the shorter the key, the easier it is to break the key.

In 2005, the U.S. National Security Agency (NSA) identified a set of cryptographic algorithms that, when used together, provides the preferred method for ensuring the security and integrity of information that is passed over public networks such as the Internet. The NSA called the set of algorithms "Suite B." Today, Suite B is globally recognized as an advanced, publicly available standard for cryptography. Suite B provides a security level of 128 bits or higher, significantly higher than many commonly used standards.

Integrated into IETF standards, Suite B algorithms make it easier to collaborate in environments where costs or logistics traditionally hindered information sharing. Secure sharing of information over the Internet and other nontrusted networks supports various missions at all levels of government. Examples include intelligence agencies and the military in a government context, or private sector companies that are required to increase the security of transmitting sensitive content such as intellectual property or private customer and employee information.

Another advantage of Suite B is that it helps public and private sector organizations meet compliance requirements. These requirements include compliance with Payment Card Industry Data Security Standard (PCI DSS), Health Insurance Portability and Accountability Act (HIPAA), Federal Information Processing Standards (FIPS), and others.

As described in RFC 4869, "Suite B Cryptographic Suites for IPsec," Suite B cryptography secures information traveling over networks using four well-established, public-domain cryptographic algorithms:

- Encryption that is based on AES using 128- or 256-bit keys

- Digital signatures with the Elliptic Curve Digital Signature Algorithm (ECDSA) using curves with 256- and 384-bit prime moduli

- Key exchange, either preshared or dynamic, using the Elliptic Curve Diffie-Hellman (ECDH) method.

- Hashing (digital fingerprinting) based on Secure Hash Algorithm 2 (SHA-2)

The NSA has stated that these four algorithms in combination provide adequate information assurance for classified information. RFC 4869 has gained acceptance in the industry.

> **Note** In December 2006, NSA submitted an Internet Draft on implementing Suite B for IPsec, which was accepted for publication by the IETF as RFC 4869. However, RFC 4869 was later obsoleted by RFC 6379 in October 2011. The curriculum of IINSv2 exam 640-554 was developed with RFC 4869 in mind.
>
> Also note that with the use of 384-bit elliptic curve, SHA-384 and AES with 256-bit keys are necessary for the protection of top secret information.

Commercial Suite B devices do not require the special handling requirements that are traditionally associated with government-specific cryptographic devices. The less stringent requirements simplify adoption, strengthen the overall architecture security, and minimize operational costs.

Essential services provided by the Suite B cryptographic standard include the following:

- Confidentiality = AES

- Integrity = SHA-2

- Authentication = ECDSA

- Key management = ECDH

Encryption Algorithms

Chapter 12 provided an in-depth analysis of the different encryption technologies. You saw that the degree of security depends on the length of the key and on the encryption algorithm. The time that it takes to process all the possibilities is a function of the computing power of the computer. Therefore, the shorter the key, the easier it is to break the key.

The following are some of the encryption algorithms and key lengths that VPNs use:

- **Date Encryption Standard (DES):** DES was developed by IBM. DES uses a 56-bit key, ensuring high-performance encryption. DES is a symmetric key cryptosystem.

- **3DES:** The 3DES algorithm is a variant of the 56-bit DES. 3DES operates in a way that is similar to how DES operates, in that data is broken into 64-bit blocks. 3DES then processes each block three times, each time with an independent 56-bit key.

3DES provides significant encryption strength over 56-bit DES. 3DES is a symmetric key cryptosystem.

- **Advanced Encryption Standard (AES):** The National Institute of Standards and Technology (NIST) has recently adopted AES to replace the existing DES encryption in cryptographic devices. AES provides stronger security than DES and is computationally more efficient than 3DES. AES offers three different key lengths: 128-, 192-, and 256-bit keys. AES is the standard prescribed in RFC 4869, "Suite B Cryptographic Suites for IPsec."

- **Rivest, Shamir, and Adleman (RSA):** RSA is an asymmetrical key cryptosystem. It uses a key length of 512, 768, 1024, or larger. IPsec does not use RSA for data encryption. IKE uses RSA encryption only during the peer-authentication phase.

- **Software-Optimized Encryption Algorithm (SEAL) algorithm:** SEAL is a stream cipher, developed in 1993 by Phillip Rogaway and Don Coppersmith, and uses a 160-bit key for encryption.

Key Exchange: Diffie-Hellman

Encryption algorithms, such as DES and 3DES, explained in Chapter 12, require a symmetric shared-secret key to perform encryption and decryption. You can use email, courier, or overnight express to send the shared-secret keys to the administrators of the devices. But the easiest key-exchange method is a public-key exchange method between the encrypting and decrypting devices. The method has two variants:

- The Diffie-Hellman (DH) key agreement, explained in great detail in Chapter 12, is a cryptographic protocol that provides a way for two peers to establish a shared-secret key, which only they know, even though they are communicating over an unsecure channel.

- ECDH is a variant of the DH protocol using elliptic curve cryptography (ECC). It is part of the Suite B standards.

That shared-secret key, created by the Diffie-Hellman key exchange method, is then used as the encryption key to exchange data.

These algorithms are used within IKE to establish session keys. They support different key sizes that are identified by different DH or ECDH groups. DH groups determine the strength of the key that is used in the key exchange process. Higher group numbers are more secure, but they require additional time to compute the key. The DH groups are referred to as DHx; for example, Diffie-Hellman Group 1 is referred to as DH1. The following is a quick listing of the different DH groups (which are covered in more detail later in this chapter, in the "IKE Protocol" section):

- DH1: 768-bit key
- DH2: 1024-bit key

- DH5: 1536-bit key

- DH7: 163-bit ECDH key

- DH14: 2048-bit key

- DH15: 3072-bit key

- DH16: 4096-bit key

- DH19: 256-bit ECDH key

- DH20: 384-bit ECDH key

- DH24: 2048-bit ECDH key

Data Integrity

VPN data is typically transported over the public Internet. Potentially, this data could be intercepted and modified. To guard against this problem, you can use a data-integrity algorithm, explained in Chapter 12. A data-integrity algorithm adds a hash to the message, which guarantees the integrity of the original message. If the transmitted hash matches the received hash, the message has not been tampered with. However, if there is no match, the message was altered.

A Hashed Message Authentication Code (HMAC) is a data-integrity algorithm that guarantees the integrity of the message. At the local end, the message and a shared-secret key are sent through a hash algorithm, which produces a hash value. The message and hash are sent over the network. Refer to Figure 12-18 in Chapter 12 for a detailed presentation on HMAC.

General HMAC concepts were explained in Chapter 12. Now, let's look at three common HMAC algorithms:

- **HMAC-Message Digest 5 (HMAC-MD5):** HMAC-MD5 uses a 128-bit shared-secret key of any size. The variable-length message and shared-secret key are combined and run through the HMAC-MD5 hash algorithm. The output is a 128-bit hash. The hash is appended to the original message and is forwarded to the remote end.

- **HMAC-Secure Hash Algorithm 1 (HMAC-SHA-1):** HMAC-SHA-1 uses a secret key of any size. The variable-length message and the shared-secret key are combined and run through the HMAC-SHA-1 hash algorithm. The output is a 160-bit hash. The hash is appended to the original message and is forwarded to the remote end.

- **HMAC-Secure Hash Algorithm 2 (HMAC-SHA-2):** The SHA-2 family of HMACs is based on the same base algorithm as SHA-1. The SHA-2 family (the second generation of SHA algorithms) includes the algorithms of 256 and 384 bit, referred to as SHA-256 bit hash algorithm and SHA-384 bit hash algorithm. This functionality is part of the Suite B standard.

Authentication

When you are conducting business long distance, it is necessary to know who is at the other end of the phone, email, or fax. The same is true of VPN networks. The device on the other end of the VPN tunnel must be authenticated before the communication path is considered secure. Four peer-authentication methods exist:

■ **Preshared keys:** A secret key value is entered into each peer manually and is used to authenticate the peer. This is a shared secret that both parties must exchange ahead of time. Think of it as a secret password that they offer to each other to confirm the identity of the other party. At each end, the PSK is combined with other information to form the authentication key.

■ **RSA signatures:** In addition to sending its digital certificate to the remote end, the sender also includes the hash value of a message encrypted with its private key. This acts like a signature. At the remote end, once the receiver has validated the sender's digital certificate, the encrypted hash is decrypted using the public key of the sender, found in the sender's digital certificate. If the decrypted hash matches the recomputed hash, the signature is genuine.

■ **RSA encrypted nonces:** A *nonce* is a random number generated by the peer. It is similar to a nonce word, used only once. RSA encrypted nonces use RSA to encrypt the nonce value and other values. This method requires that the public key of the two peers be present on the other peer before the third and fourth messages of an IKE exchange can be accomplished. For this reason, public keys must be manually copied to each peer as part of the configuration process, and therefore this method is limited by the available memory of the receiver. This method is the least used of the four authentication methods.

■ **Elliptic Curve Digital Signature Algorithm (ECDSA):** The ECDSA is the elliptic curve analog of the DSA, which is part of the Digital Signature Standard (DSS) method. ECDSA signatures are smaller than RSA signatures of similar cryptographic strength. ECDSA public keys (and certificates) are smaller than similar-strength DSA keys, resulting in improved communications efficiency. Furthermore, on many platforms, ECDSA operations can be computed more quickly than similar-strength RSA operations. These advantages of signature size, bandwidth, and computational efficiency may make ECDSA an attractive choice for many IKE and IKE version 2 (IKEv2) implementations.

IPsec is a framework of open standards. IPsec spells out the messaging to secure the communications but relies on existing algorithms to implement the encryption, authentication, and key exchange. Figure 13-1 illustrates some of the standard algorithms that IPsec uses.

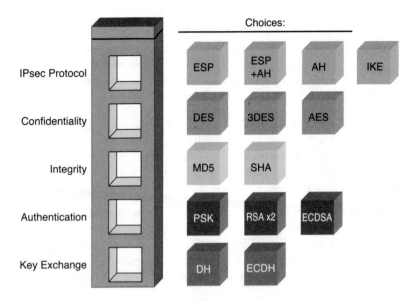

Figure 13-1   *IPsec Framework Components*

When you configure an IPsec gateway to provide security services, you will call from the components that make the IPsec framework. This framework includes IPsec protocols and many other categories of components, as shown in Figure 13-1. You must first choose an IPsec protocol. The choices are Encapsulating Security Payload (ESP) or ESP with Authentication Header (AH). AH can also be used alone. The second element is an encryption algorithm. Choose the encryption algorithm that is appropriate for the desired level of security: DES, 3DES, or AES. The third element is authentication. Choose an authentication algorithm to provide data integrity: MD5 or SHA. The last element is the DH algorithm group. Choose which group to use, DH Group 1 (DH1), DH Group 2 (DH2), or DH Group 5 (DH5). IPsec provides the framework, and the administrator chooses the algorithms that are used to implement the security services within that framework.

IPsec Protocol

IPsec is a framework of open standards. There are two distinct stages to building IPsec tunnels: IKE and the IPsec protocol itself. IKE is responsible for establishing the rules of engagement and confirming the identity of the peers with whom communication is about to start. IPsec tunnels are responsible for passing data in a secure communication. To make an analogy, consider the FTP protocol, which uses two ports. Port 21 is used as the control port and port 20 is used as the data port. Port 21 is responsible for validating the identity of the parties and negotiating the requests. The actual data (file) exchange is done through the data port, port 20. The process is similar with the IPsec framework. IKE has a similar role as port 21, with responsibility for negotiating the type of connection, the identity of the entities, and so forth. IPsec tunnels are similar to port 20, because they are the secured carrier of the data exchanged between the two peers (the procedure for which will be covered in detail later in this chapter). Think of IKE as the control plane and IPsec as the data plane. For now, let's focus on the actual tunnels that provide secure data exchanges between peers, the actual IPsec tunnels.

IPsec spells out the messaging to secure the communications but relies on existing algorithms, listed in Figure 13-1. There are two main IPsec framework protocols, as depicted in Figure 13-2:

- **Authentication Header (AH):** AH, which is IP protocol 51, is the appropriate protocol to use when confidentiality is not required or permitted. It provides data authentication and integrity for IP packets passed between two systems. It is a means of verifying that any message that is passed from Router A to Router B has not been modified during transit. It verifies that the origin of the data was either Router A or Router B. AH does not provide data confidentiality (encryption) of packets. All text is transported in the clear. If the AH protocol is used alone, it provides weak protection. Consequently, Encapsulating Security Payload uses the AH protocol to provide data encryption and tamper-aware security features.

- **Encapsulating Security Payload (ESP):** ESP is a security protocol that can provide confidentiality and authentication. ESP, which is IP protocol 50, provides confidentiality by performing encryption on the IP packet. IP packet encryption conceals the data payload and the identities of the ultimate source and destination. ESP provides authentication for the inner IP packet and ESP header. Authentication provides data-origin authentication and data integrity. Although both encryption and authentication are optional in ESP, at a minimum, one of them must be selected.

Authentication Header (AH) – Protocol 51

Router A

All Data In Plaintext

Router B

AH provides the following:

- Authentication
- Integrity
- Anti-replay

Encapsulating Security Payload (ESP) – Protocol 50

Router A

Data Payload Is Encrypted

Router B

ESP provides the following:

- Encryption
- Authentication
- Integrity
- Antireplay

Figure 13-2 *IPsec Security Protocols*

Authentication Header

AH achieves authenticity by applying a keyed one-way hash function to the packet to create a hash, or message digest. The hash is combined with the text and is transmitted. The receiver detects changes in any part of the packet that occur during transit by performing the same one-way hash function on the received packet and comparing the result to the value of the message digest that the sender has supplied. The fact that the one-way hash also involves the use of a shared-secret key between the two systems means that authenticity is assured.

The AH function is applied to the entire datagram except for any mutable IP header fields that change in transit; for example, Time to Live (TTL) fields that are modified by the routers along the transmission path. Figure 13-3 illustrates the AH process, which is as follows.

Figure 13-3   *AH Authentication and Integrity*

Step 1.   The IP header and data payload are hashed.

Step 2.   The hash builds a new AH header, which is prepended to the original packet.

Step 3.   The new packet is transmitted to the IPsec peer router.

Step 4.   The peer router hashes the IP header and data payload, extracts the transmitted hash from the AH header, and compares the two hashes. The hashes must match exactly. Even if 1 bit is changed in the transmitted packet, the hash output on the received packet changes and the AH header will not match.

AH supports the HMAC-MD5 and HMAC-SHA-1 algorithms.

Note AH protects the entire IP packet, which includes the IP header, against tampering during transmission. Because NAT modifies the IP header, it is incompatible with AH. Fixes, such as tunnel mode, discussed later, remedy this problem.

Also, note that the Cisco firewalls, starting at code 7, do not offer the AH option. Only ESP can be performed.

Essential services provided by AH are

■ Data integrity through hashing

■ Data origin authentication through hashing

■ Antireplay protection

AH in Production

AH has its place for secure communication. When most of us hear the term "secure communication," we think encrypted payload. However, there are situations where confidentiality is not necessary but authenticity and integrity are. Take the example of a car manufacturer that places an order to its brake pads supplier every morning at 8 a.m. for just-in-time delivery the next day. There is nothing secret about today's order of 8000 brake pads. So, payload encryption is not necessary. However, the brake pads supplier, upon receiving the order, wants to confirm that the order really came from the car manufacturer and not from Johnny the Joker, and that the order of 8000 brake pads wasn't tampered with. The order for 8000 brake pads would be released with the payload in cleartext; however, an encrypted hash of the packet is included in the transmission, thus providing a proof of origin and integrity.

Encapsulating Security Payload

ESP provides confidentiality by encrypting the payload. It supports a variety of symmetric encryption algorithms. The lowest common algorithm for IPsec is 56-bit DES. Cisco products also support the use of 3DES and especially AES for stronger encryption.

ESP can also provide integrity and authentication of the datagrams. First, the payload is encrypted. Next, the encrypted payload is sent through a hash algorithm, HMAC-MD5 or HMAC-SHA-1. The hash provides authentication and data integrity for the data payload.

Optionally, ESP can also enforce antireplay protection by requiring that a receiving host set the replay bit in the header to indicate that the packet has been seen.

The original data is well protected by ESP because the entire original IP datagram is encrypted, as shown in Figure 13-4. An ESP header and trailer are added to the encrypted payload. With ESP authentication, the encrypted IP datagram and the ESP header and trailer are included in the hashing process. Lastly, a new IP header is prepended to the authenticated payload. The new IP address is used to route the packet through the Internet.

Figure 13-4 *ESP Protocol*

When both authentication (AH) and encryption (ESP) are selected, encryption occurs first. One reason for this order of processing is that it facilitates rapid detection and rejection of replayed or bogus packets by the receiving device. Before decrypting the packet, the receiver can authenticate inbound packets. By doing this, it can quickly detect problems and potentially reduce the impact of denial-of-service (DoS) attacks.

Essential services provided by ESP are

■ Data confidentiality through encryption

■ Data integrity through hashing

■ Data origin authentication through hashing

■ Antireplay protection

IPsec Modes of Operations

ESP and AH can be used in two different ways, or *modes*. The encapsulation can be done in tunnel mode or in transport mode. The encapsulation performed on an ESP packet with each mode is illustrated in Figure 13-5.

Figure 13-5 *Encapsulation with Tunnel Mode and Transport Mode*

Transport Mode

In transport mode, security is provided only for the transport layer and above. Transport mode protects the payload of the packet but leaves the original IP address in the clear. The original IP address is used to route the packet through the Internet. ESP transport mode is used between hosts and is therefore not compatible with Network Address Translation (NAT).

Note Transport mode works well with generic routing encapsulation (GRE) because GRE hides the addresses of the end stations by adding its own IP header.

Tunnel Mode

ESP tunnel mode provides security for the complete original IP packet. The original IP packet is encrypted, and then it is encapsulated in another IP packet. The outside IP address is used to route the packet through the Internet.

ESP tunnel mode is used between a host and a security gateway or between two security gateways, as shown in Figure 13-6. For gateway-to-gateway applications, rather than load IPsec on all the computers at the remote and corporate offices, it is easier to have the security gateways perform the IP-in-IP encryption and encapsulation.

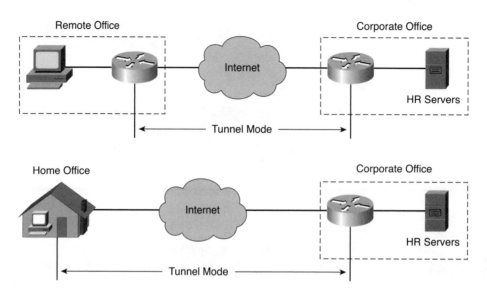

Figure 13-6   *IPsec Tunnel Mode*

ESP tunnel mode is used in the IPsec remote-access application. At a home office, there might be no router to perform the IPsec encapsulation and encryption. In this case, an IPsec client running on the PC performs the IPsec IP-in-IP encapsulation and encryption. At the corporate office, the router de-encapsulates and decrypts the packet.

IKE Protocol

IPsec implements a VPN solution using an encryption process that involves the periodic changing of encryption keys. IPsec uses the IKE protocol to authenticate a peer computer and to generate encryption keys. IKE negotiates a security association (SA), which is an agreement between two peers engaging in an IPsec exchange and consists of all the required parameters necessary to establish successful communication. An IPsec peer accepting incoming IKE requests listens on UDP port 500.

IPsec uses the IKE protocol to provide these functions:

■ Negotiation of SA characteristics

■ Automatic key generation

■ Automatic key refresh

■ Manageable manual configuration

There are two versions of the IKE protocol: IKEv1 and IKEv2. IKEv2 was created to overcome some of the limitations of IKEv1. IKEv2 provides the following enhancements:

■ Simplicity, by requiring fewer transactions to establish security associations. A simplified initial exchange of messages reduces latency and increases connection establishment speed.

- Stronger security, through DoS protection and other functions.

- Reliability, by using sequence numbers, acknowledgements, and error correction.

- Flexibility, through support for Extensible Authentication Protocol (EAP) as a method for authenticating VPN endpoints.

- Mobility, by using the IKEv2 Mobility and Multihoming Protocol (MOBIKE) extension. This enhancement allows mobile users to roam and change IP addresses without disconnecting their IPsec session.

Because the IKEv2 base specification includes all the functionality of IKEv1, we'll look at the IKEv1 modes and phases first, followed by a brief overview of the enhancements in IKEv2, and then summarize the differences between these two versions.

Note   Because a picture is worth a thousand words, Figure 13-7 is the visual representation of IPsec sequence of events when tunnels are being built with IKEv1. The process starts at the bottom of the figure with IKE Phase 1, followed by IKE Phase 2, and finally with the two unidirectional IPsec tunnels coming up to exchange the encrypted data.

Figure 13-7   *Visual Representation of IKEv1 and IPsec Tunnels Being Built from the Ground Up*

IKEv1 Modes

To establish a secure communication channel between two peers, the IKE protocol uses the following three modes of operation:

- **Main mode:** In main mode, which takes place in IKEv1 Phase 1, an IKE session begins with one computer (the initiator) sending a proposal or proposals to another computer (the responder). The proposal sent by the initiator defines what encryption and authentication protocols are acceptable, how long keys should remain active, and whether Perfect Forward Secrecy (PFS) should be enforced. (PFS is covered later in this chapter.) There are three exchanges typical of main mode, for a total of six packets:

  - The first exchange between the initiator and the responder establishes the basic security policy. The initiator sends all its Internet Security Association and Key Management Protocol (ISAKMP) policies. The responder chooses a proposal best suited to the security situation and then sends that proposal to the initiator. This exchange totals two packets.

  - The next exchange passes DH public keys between the two users. DH key exchange is a cryptographic protocol that allows two parties that have no prior knowledge of each other to establish a shared-secret key over an unsecure communications channel. All further negotiation is encrypted within the IKE SA.

  - The third exchange authenticates an ISAKMP session. The fifth and sixth packets are the first packets exchanged encrypted, as depicted earlier in Figure 13-7, which shows authentication being conducted inside the ISAKMP tunnel. Once the IKE SA is established, IPsec quick mode negotiation begins.

- **Aggressive mode:** Aggressive mode compresses into three packets the IKE SA negotiation phases just described. In aggressive mode, which takes place in IKEv1 Phase 1, the initiator passes all data that is required for the SA. The responder sends the proposal, key material, and ID and authenticates the session in the next packet. The initiator replies by authenticating the session. Negotiation is quicker, and the initiator and responder IDs pass in plaintext.

- **Quick mode:** Quick mode IPsec negotiation, which happens in IKEv1 Phase 2, takes place after successful IKE SA negotiation. Quick mode is similar to aggressive mode IKE negotiation, except that negotiation is protected within an IKE SA. Quick mode negotiates the SA for the data encryption and manages the key exchange for that IPsec SA, as shown in Figure 13-7. This means that it negotiates a shared IPsec transform, derives shared-secret keying material that the IPsec security algorithms will use, and establishes IPsec SAs. During quick mode, the peers exchange the list of protected networks: the subnets at each end that must use the encrypted tunnel when communicating amongst themselves.

IKEv1 Phases

To establish a secure communication channel between two peers, the IKE protocol executes the following phases:

- **IKE Phase 1:** Two IPsec peers perform the initial negotiation of SAs. In this phase, the SA negotiations are bidirectional; data may be sent and received using the same encryption key. In IKE Phase 1, the transform sets, hash methods, and other parameters are determined. Optionally, IKE Phase 1 can include authentication, in which each peer in the SA negotiation is able to verify the identity of the other. Even if the SA negotiation data stream between the two IPsec peers is compromised, there is little chance that the encryption keys could be guessed and thus the traffic decrypted.

- **IKE Phase 2:** SAs are negotiated by the IKE process ISAKMP on behalf of other services, such as IPsec, that need encryption key material for operation. Quick mode negotiates the IKE Phase 2 SAs. In this phase, the SAs that IPsec uses are unidirectional; therefore, a separate key exchange is required for each data flow.

Note Other, optional parameters are sometimes negotiated between IKE Phase 1 and IKE Phase 2, such as level of DH, encryption algorithms, and methods of authentication.

IKEv1 Phase 1

The basic purpose of IKE Phase 1, shown in Figure 13-8, is to negotiate IKE policy sets, authenticate the peers, and set up a secure channel between the peers. IKE Phase 1 occurs in two modes: main mode and aggressive mode.

Figure 13-8 *IKE Phase 1*

Main Mode

Main mode has three two-way exchanges between the initiator and receiver:

- **First exchange:** Peers negotiate and agree on the algorithms and hashes that will be used to secure the IKE communications.

- **Second exchange:** DH generates public and private values. The peers exchange their public values, and the result is a shared secret. The shared-secret key is used to generate all the other encryption and authentication keys.

- **Third exchange:** The identity of the other side is verified. The main outcome of main mode is a secure communications path for subsequent exchanges between the peers.

Note   In aggressive mode, fewer exchanges are done, and the exchanges have fewer packets. As an example, with aggressive mode, the peers will exchange their identity and a hash of the PSK even though the DH calculations have not been performed yet, and therefore there is no shared secret to send data in an encrypted format.

Aggressive Mode

Aggressive mode, as explained earlier, compresses the IKE SA negotiation phases into a total of three messages. Negotiation is quicker, and the initiator and responder IDs pass in plaintext.

Main Mode Versus Aggressive Mode

The use of main mode or aggressive mode is a tradeoff between performance and security. Main mode requires more messages but does not expose the identity of the peers. This identity is protected by the policies and keys that are negotiated in the first two exchanges. Aggressive mode requires fewer messages and therefore is more efficient. However, peer identities are exposed before negotiating a secure channel, so it assumes a trusted transport and a more protected environment outside of IPsec. The choice of mode is a configurable option in most IPsec implementations.

IKEv1 Phase 1 Example

When you are trying to make a secure connection between Host A and Host B through the Internet, a secure path (a tunnel) is established between Router A and Router B. Through the tunnel, the IPsec encryption, authentication, and other protocols are negotiated.

IKEv1 First Exchange: IKE Policy Is Negotiated

The ultimate goal of IPsec is to have a secure tunnel through which we can transmit encrypted data. Before we start exchanging encrypted data with a peer, though, we need to confirm who we are dealing with and how we will be sending encrypted data to it. You would never send your credentials in cleartext to your peer for authentication, so IPsec needs to start with transmission of other information in cleartext. This is the beginning of IKEv1 Phase 1.

In the cleartext, the two peers agree on the following:

- **Encryption algorithm they will use for their IKE tunnel:** DES, 3DES, or EAS

- **Hashing algorithm they will use for integrity check:** MD5 or SHA

- **Authentication method they will use:** PSK, RSA Signatures, RSA encrypted nonces, or ECDSA

- **DH group:** The DH group used to generate the symmetrical key used to encrypt IKE traffic between the two peers, such as authentication credentials, which shouldn't be sent in cleartext. An IKE tunnel is made of different protocols, one of which is called Internet Security Associate Key Management Protocol (ISAKMP). ISAKMP is an encrypted tunnel through which peers will be exchanging, among other things, their credentials. To have an encrypted tunnel, both peers must have the same symmetrical key. The DH group designates the length of the symmetrical key that will be generated during the upcoming Diffie-Hellman operation.

- **Duration of ISAKMP tunnel:** This is referred to as the *lifetime*.

IKE HAGLE

Use the acronym HAGLE to assist you in remembering the five elements that peers agree upon during IKEv1 Phase 1:

H = Hash

A = Authentication

G = Group (DH group)

L = Lifetime

E = Encryption

Rather than negotiate each protocol individually, the protocols are grouped into sets, called *IKE policy sets*. IKE policy sets are exchanged during the IKE main mode, first exchange phase. If a policy match is found between peers, main mode continues. If no match is found, the tunnel is torn down.

Of the five values that both peers must agree on, only lifetime can be adjusted dynamically. It will be adjusted to the smallest values exchanged between the two peers. All the other elements of IKEv1 Phase 1 negotiations (hash, authentication, DH group, encryption) must have a perfect match between the two peers.

In Figure 13-9, Router A sends IKE policy sets 10, 20, and 30 to Router B. Router B compares its sets with those received from Router A. In this instance, there is a policy match. Policy set 10 of Router A matches policy set 20 of Router B and is selected over policy set 30 on both sides, because the lowest policy priority number wins.

Figure 13-9   *IKEv1 Phase 1, First Exchange: Policy Is Negotiated*

Note   Policy set numbers are only locally significant to a VPN device. The policy set numbers do not have to match between two VPN peers.

In a point-to-point application, each end may need only a single IKE policy set to be defined. However, in a hub-and-spoke environment, the central site may require multiple IKE policy sets to satisfy all the remote peers.

IKEv1 Second Exchange: DH Key Exchange

When the IKE policy is agreed on, including the size of the prime number to be used for DH, the two peers run the DH key exchange protocol. You will remember from Chapter 12 that, as shown in Figure 13-10, the result of DH will be the creation of a shared secret, where $K = K'$, that is needed by the various symmetric encryption and hashing algorithms upon which IKE and IPsec will ultimately agree.

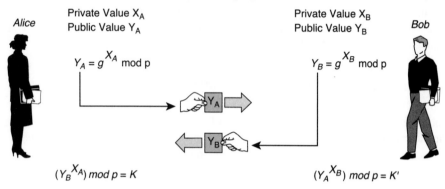

Figure 13-10 *IKEv1 Phase 1, Second Exchange: DH Key Exchange*

Several levels of DH key exchanges are available in Cisco IOS Software:

- **DH Group 1:** A key exchange that uses a 768-bit prime number. This group is the usual choice when the encryption algorithm is DES.

- **DH Group 2:** A key exchange that uses a 1024-bit prime number. This group is the usual choice when using 3DES for encryption.

- **DH Group 5:** A key exchange that uses a 1536-bit prime number. DH 5 should be used with AES.

- **DH Group 7 (ECC):** A key exchange that generates IPsec keys when the elliptic curve field is 163 bits. This group was designed to be used with low-powered hosts such as PDAs.

- **DH Group 14:** A key exchange that results in 2048 bits of keying material.

- **DH Group 15:** A key exchange that results in 3072 bits of keying material.

- **DH Group 16:** A key exchange that results in 4096 bits of keying material.

- **DH Group 19:** A key exchange that results in 256 bits of keying material.

- **DH Group 20:** A key exchange that results in 384 bits of keying material.

- **DH Group 24:** A key exchange that results in 2048 bits of keying material.

> **Note**   Groups 5, 14, 15, and 16 should be used with AES. Groups 19, 20, and 24 should be used with ECDH.

The group that is chosen must be strong enough (have enough bits) to protect the IPsec keys during negotiation. A generally accepted guideline recommends the use of a 2048-bit group after the year 2013 (until the year 2030). Either DH14 or DH24 can be selected to meet this guideline. Even if a longer-lived security method is needed, the use of ECC is recommended, but G15 and DH16 can also be considered.

IKEv1 Third Exchange: Authenticate Peer Identity

When you are conducting business over the Internet, it is necessary to know who is at the other end of the tunnel. The device on the other end of the VPN tunnel must be authenticated before the communications path is considered secure. The last exchange of IKE Phase 1 authenticates the remote peer, as illustrated in Figure 13-11.

Figure 13-11   *IKEv1 Phase 1, Third Exchange: Authenticate Peer Identity*

As mentioned earlier, there are four data origin authentication methods with IKEv1:

- **PSKs:** Pre-shared keys are a secret key value that is entered into each peer manually and is used to authenticate the peer.

- **RSA signatures:** RSA signatures are the exchange of digital certificates that is used to authenticate the peers in addition to sending a hash value of a message encrypted with its private key as proof of its identity.

- **RSA encrypted nonces:** Nonces are random numbers that are generated by each peer and then encrypted and exchanged between peers. The two nonces are used during the peer-authentication process.

- **ECDSA signatures:** Exchange of certificates. ECDSA certificates are smaller than RSA signatures of similar cryptographic strength, resulting in improved communications efficiency. ECDSA is available with Suite B.

IKEv1 Phase 2

The purpose of IKEv1 Phase 2 is to negotiate the IPsec security parameters, as shown in Figure 13-12, that will be used to secure the IPsec tunnel. IKEv2 Phase 2 performs the following functions.

Figure 13-12   *IKE Phase 2*

- Negotiates IPsec security parameters, known as IPsec transform sets.

- Establishes IPsec SAs.

- Periodically renegotiates IPsec SAs to ensure security.

- Optionally, performs an additional DH exchange to generate IPsec SA keys that have no relation to the IKE keys. Generating IPsec keys from scratch for the purpose of IPsec SAs is referred to as Perfect Forward Secrecy (PFS), which is described after IKEv2 quick mode.

IKEv2 Quick Mode

IKE Phase 2 has one mode, called quick mode. Quick mode occurs after IKE has established the secure tunnel in Phase 1. It negotiates a shared IPsec transform, derives shared-secret keying material that the IPsec security algorithms will use, and establishes IPsec SAs. Quick mode also exchanges nonces that are used to generate new shared-secret key material and to prevent replay attacks from generating false SAs.

Quick mode also renegotiates a new IPsec SA when the IPsec SA lifetime expires. Basically, quick mode refreshes the keying material that creates the shared-secret key, which is based on the keying material derived from the DH exchange in Phase 1.

Perfect Forward Secrecy

The basic principle of PFS is that new keys (shared secrets) cannot be derived from older keys. The idea is that if keys are compromised, previous and subsequent keys are secured because they were generated from scratch and not derived. Therefore, PFS exists when a DH exchange is done at each rekeying interval, which is preferable, but might not be necessary, instead of deriving the new keys from the previous keys.

IKE Version 2

In IKEv2, there is a simplified initial exchange of messages that, compared to IKEv1, reduces latency and increases the connection establishment speed. The IKEv2 base specification includes all the functionality of IKEv1 as well as additional functionality. It preserves most of the features of version 1, including the two negotiation phases. However, the specific operations of the two phases differ:

- **Phase 1:** In IKEv2, there is only one mode or set of network flows defined for Phase 1 negotiation. The set requires four messages, two from the initiator and two from the responder. The first two of these four messages flow in the clear on the network. The other two messages are encrypted. Still, this mode is equivalent to main mode in IKEv1, and not to aggressive mode.

  The negotiation of the first Phase 2 SA is accomplished within these four flows, still in Phase 2. When the fourth message flows, both Phase 1 and Phase 2 SAs are activated. Either the initiator or the responder can later activate additional Phase 2 SAs using this Phase 1 SA.

- **Phase 2:** The purpose of Phase 2 negotiation is to establish a set of parameters, known as an SA, which is used to protect specific types of IP traffic. The Phase 2 SA contains the keys that are used to encrypt and decrypt IPsec packets on the host, authenticate IPsec packets on the host, or both. Because the first Phase 2 SA is created during Phase 1, all subsequent Phase 2 SAs are called child SAs. The identity of the remote peer is implicitly authenticated when the Phase 2 SA is used.

IKEv2, illustrated in Figure 13-13, uses fewer messages to accomplish the same (and more) objectives as IKEv1. In addition, the parent-child relationship of Phase 2 SAs streamlines the process. The first Phase 2 SA is created during phase 1, and negotiated parameters are added here for child Phase 2 SAs.

For instance, rekeying in IKEv2 negotiates new keys, but it does not reauthenticate the identity of the peer. When an IKEv1 Phase 1 SA is refreshed, new keys are negotiated, and identity of the IKE peer is reauthenticated.

Figure 13-13 *IKEv2: A Simplified Approach*

IKEv1 Versus IKEv2

A full lecture on IKEv2 is beyond the scope of this book; however, Table 13-1 provides you with a summary of the differences between IKEv1 and IKEv2.

Table 13-1 *Differences Between IKE Version 1 and Version 2*

Benefit	Enhancement	IKEv1	IKEv2
Simplicity	RFC documents	RFC 2407, 2408, 2409, 4109, 4995	RFC 5996
	Negotiation		
	Phase 1	6 messages (main mode) or 3 messages (aggressive mode)	4 messages
	Phase 2	3 messages	2 messages
Security	Identity hiding	Optional, only in main mode	Always
	DoS protection	No	Yes, optional

Table 13-1 *Differences Between IKE Version 1 and Version 2*

Benefit	Enhancement	IKEv1	IKEv2
Reliability	Message ACK	None	Reliable; all messages are acknowledged and sequenced
Flexibility	Backward compatibility	No	Yes
	Authentication	None	Extensible Authentication Protocol
	Rekeying	Requires reauthentication	No reauthentication required
	Mobility	None	MOBIKE for Layer 3 roaming

The notable differences with IKE version 2 are

- **Fewer RFCs:** The specifications for IKEv1 were covered in at least three RFCs and even more. IKEv2 combines the specifications into one RFC.

- **Simplified message exchange:** IKEv2 has one four-message initial exchange mechanism while IKEv1 provides eight distinctly different initial exchange mechanisms, each one of which has slight advantages and disadvantages.

- **Security:** Identities are always hidden during Phase 1 in IKEv2. DoS attacks are mitigated because IKEv2 does not process a request until it determines the requester. IKEv1 can be tricked to perform much cryptographic (and expensive) processing from false locations (spoofing).

- **NAT traversal (NAT-T):** ESP as is couldn't be used with PAT because there are no ports that could be translated by the Internet-facing router configured for PATting outbound connections. To mitigate this problem, NAT-T was created. VPN clients, sitting behind a PAT device, encapsulate IKE and ESP in UDP port 4500, which enables these protocols to pass through a device performing NAT. NAT-T is used by both IKEv1 and IKEv2.

- **Reliability:** IKEv2 uses sequence numbers and acknowledgments to provide reliability and mandates some error processing logistics and shared state management.

- **Support for EAP:** By using EAP, IKEv2 can leverage existing authentication infrastructure and credential databases. EAP allows users to choose a method suitable for existing credentials, and also makes separation of the IKEv2 responder (VPN gateway) from the EAP authentication endpoint (backend authentication, authorization, and accounting [AAA] server) easier.

■ **Mobility:** Through MOBIKE, IKEv2 allows for Layer 3 roaming that changes the peer's IP address. The main scenario for MOBIKE is enabling a remote-access VPN user to move from one address to another without reestablishing all SAs with the VPN gateway. For instance, a user could start from fixed Ethernet in the office and then disconnect the laptop and move to the office wireless LAN. When the user leaves the office, the laptop could start using General Packet Radio Service (GPRS). When the user arrives home, the laptop could switch to the home wireless LAN.

IPv6 VPNs

IPsec is the baseline protocol that was established for enabling packet security during transmission of packets in IPv6. Even though the IPv6 standards mandate that IPsec be implemented, they do not mandate that IPsec be used for all IPv6 communications. Such a mandate might not be realistic, given the limited computing resources of a personal digital assistant (PDA), telephone, printer, sensor, toaster, or refrigerator. These small embedded devices can lack the computing resources to perform encryption functions.

IPsec is also native to IPv6. It defines new protocol headers that add authentication and confidentiality to IPv6 packets. The original IPsec RFCs defined the use of an AH to secure the header information and the content of the packet and the use of an ESP to secure the contents of the packet. The IPsec architecture for IPv4 and the IPsec architecture for IPv6 are similar as far as the standards are concerned. In IPv4, AH and ESP were IP protocol headers. The difference is that IPv6 uses the extension header approach, as learned in the CCNA and as shown in Figure 13-14. In IPv6, ESP uses the next-header value of 50 and AH uses the next-header value of 51.

Next Header = 51 (AH) or 50 (ESP)

Figure 13-14 *IPv6 Extension Header Approach*

Because of the ubiquitous nature of the IPv6 Internet (at least in the future), some of the more recent features and functionalities that are found in IPsec become crucial when the protocol is used in IPv6 networks. The latest cryptography suites (Suite B and beyond) and the mobility enhancements that are found in IKEv2 are key.

Here is a summary of IPsec for IPv6 characteristics:

■ IPsec is mandatory for IPv6.

■ IPsec is native to IPv6.

- Includes built-in confidentiality, integrity, authentication, and antireplay.

- Offers flexibility and low overhead through extension headers.

- The IPsec framework and behavior are the same as IPsec for IPv4.

- Strong encryption (Suite B) and mobility enhancements (IKEv2) are key in IPv6.

- Only site-to-site tunnel mode VPNs are supported in Cisco IOS as of version 15.1.

IPsec Services for Transitioning to IPv6

In the early stages of the transition to IPv6, much of the world's networks and the Internet will continue to use IPv4. Several options are available for transitioning to IPv6. Some of them involve tunneling IPv6 in IPv4 (such as manual IPv6 tunnels, automatic IPv4-compatible tunnels, GRE, automatic 6to4 tunnels, and Intra-Site Automatic Tunnel Addressing Protocol [ISATAP] tunnels).

Using these methods, you can transport IPsec-protected IPv6 traffic over an IPv4 WAN. If you only have IPv4 connectivity between your remote locations and your central site, you can use a tunnel. The tunnel interface can carry the IPv6 packets within an IPv4 tunnel.

Figure 13-15 shows the resulting packet structure. The IPv4 packet is encapsulated by IPsec with a header and a trailer. The result is encapsulated with an IPv4 header that allows forwarding across the IPv4 Internet. The recommended IPsec mode (per RFC 4891) is transport mode.

Figure 13-15 *IPv6 Transition Using IPv6-over-IPv4 Tunnel*

ESP uses the next-header value of 50 and AH uses the next-header value of 51.

Solutions for transitioning IPsec services to IPv6 are

```
Key
Topic
```

- **Tunneling IPv6 over IPv4:** A common transition strategy

- **IPv4 IPsec:** Can be used to provide VPN services to IPv6

- **IPsec transport mode:** Typically used

Summary

The key points covered in this chapter are as follows:

- IPsec is a ubiquitous VPN technology that provides confidentiality, data-integrity, authentication, and antireplay services.

- ESP, AH, and IKE perform major functions within IPsec.

- IKEv1 phases 1 and 2 are enhanced by IKEv2.

- IPsec is mandatory and native to IPv6.

References

For additional information, refer to these resources.

Books

Carmouche, J. H. *IPSec Virtual Private Network Fundamentals* (Cisco Press, 2007).

Naganand, D., and Harkins, D. *IPSec: The New Security Standard for the Internet, Intranets, and Virtual Private Networks, Second Edition* (Prentice Hall, 2003).

Cisco.com Resources

"Cisco IOS IPsec," http://www.cisco.com/en/US/products/ps6635/products_ios_protocol_group_home.html

"Export Compliance & Regulatory Affairs: Encryption Control Guidance," http://www.cisco.com/wwl/export/faq.html

Review Questions

Use the questions here to review what you learned in this chapter. The correct answers are found in the Appendix, "Answers to Chapter Review Questions."

1. Which of the following is not a security function provided by IPsec?
   - **a.** Confidentiality
   - **b.** Key management
   - **c.** Antireplay
   - **d.** Authentication
   - **e.** Integrity

2. Which of the following are peer-authentication methods with IPsec? (Choose all that apply.)

   a. PSK
   b. RSA signatures
   c. RSA encrypted nonces
   d. HMAC-SHA1
   e. HMAC-MD5

3. Which three modes are used by IKE to secure communications?

   a. Main mode
   b. Basic mode
   c. Advanced mode
   d. Quick mode
   e. Aggressive mode
   f. Simple mode

4. Match the Diffie-Hellman group with the size of its keying material.

   Groups

   a. Group 5
   b. Group 2
   c. Group 7
   d. Group 1
   e. Group 16
   f. Group 19

   Bits

   g. 4096
   h. 163
   i. 1024
   j. 1536
   k. 256
   l. 768

5. Which statement is true regarding how ESP segments are encapsulated in IP packets?

   a. In transport mode, security is provided only for the transport layer and below.
   b. In tunnel mode, security is provided for the complete original IP packet.
   c. In tunnel mode, security is provided only for the transport layer and above.
   d. In transport mode, security is provided for the entire IP packet.

6. Match the IPsec component with its category.

   a. ESP

   b. IKE

   c. EDCH

   d. EDCSA

   1. Key Exchange

   2. Authentication

   3. Negotiation

   4. Confidentiality

7. In IPsec tunnel mode, the original IP address is used to route the packet through the untrusted network. True or false?

   a. True

   b. False

8. You require DoS protection and mobility for your IPsec phase 1 negotiation. Which protocol would you select?

   a. Diffie-Hellman.

   b. IKEv2

   c. IKEv1

   d. AH

9. In IPv6 environments, IPsec is mandatory for all IPv6 communications. True or false?

   a. True

   b. False

10. You want to prevent filtering IPsec traffic across the path of a VPN. Which three protocols should be allowed in the firewall policy?

   a. IP protocol 50

   b. TCP 50

   c. UDP 51

   d. TCP 51

   e. UDP 500

   f. UDP 4500

Chapter 14

Site-to-Site IPsec VPNs with Cisco IOS Routers

Building a site-to-site IPsec VPN is an essential part of many plans to meet the security requirements of customers. In this chapter, you will learn how to use the command-line interface (CLI) to configure a site-to-site IPsec VPN to securely connect two or more subnets over the Internet or an intranet.

This chapter teaches you how to configure a site-to-site IPsec VPN with preshared keys, using Cisco Configuration Professional. This ability includes being able to meet these objectives:

- Evaluate the requirements and configuration of site-to-site IPsec VPNs

- Use Cisco Configuration Professional to configure site-to-site IPsec VPNs

- Use CLI commands and Cisco Configuration Professional monitoring options to validate the VPN configuration

- Use CLI commands and Cisco Configuration Professional monitoring options to monitor and troubleshoot the VPN configuration

Site-to-Site IPsec: Planning and Preparation

Site-to-site VPNs are the option of choice for organizations of all kinds in implementing a corporate network across public and private networks. Internet-based VPN environments and Multiprotocol Label Switching (MPLS) VPN environments benefit from the flexibility of deployment and standards-based implementation of cryptographic mechanisms.

The choice of device-terminating VPNs, such as a firewall or a router, becomes a key factor in implementing site-to-site VPNs. Organizations benefit from leveraging their existing network elements and using an integrated approach to VPN deployments. This chapter highlights the use of Cisco IOS routers as site-to-site VPN termination points in IP Security (IPsec) environments.

Site-to-Site IPsec VPN Operations

IPsec VPN negotiation can be broken down into five steps, as shown in Figure 14-1, including Phase 1 and Phase 2 of Internet Key Exchange (IKE):

Step 1.   An IPsec tunnel is initiated when Host A sends "interesting" traffic to Host B. Traffic is considered interesting when it travels between the IPsec peers and meets the criteria that is defined in the crypto access control list (ACL).

Step 2.   In IKE Phase 1, the IPsec peers (routers A and B) negotiate the established IKE SA policy. Once the peers are authenticated, a secure tunnel is created using ISAKMP.

Step 3.   In IKE Phase 2, the IPsec peers use the authenticated and secure tunnel to negotiate IPsec SA transforms. The negotiation of the shared policy determines how the IPsec tunnel is established.

Step 4.   The IPsec tunnel is created and data is transferred between the IPsec peers based on the IPsec parameters configured in the IPsec transform sets.

Step 5.   The IPsec tunnel terminates when the IPsec SAs are deleted or when their lifetime expires.

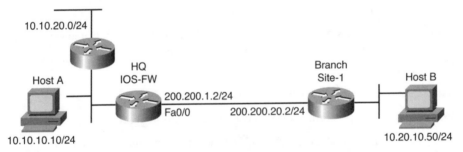

1. Host A sends interesting traffic to Host B.
2. Router IOS-FW and Router Site-1 negotiate an IKE Phase 1 session.

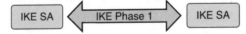

3. Router IOS-FW and Router Site-1 negotiate an IKE Phase 2 session.

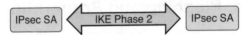

4. Hosts A and B communicate via IPsec tunnel.

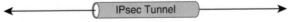

5. IPsec tunnel is terminated.

Figure 14-1   *Site-to-Site IPsec VPN*

Planning and Preparation Checklist

The following items should be considered in planning and preparing for a site-to-site VPN deployment:

- **Verify connectivity between peers:** IPsec uses distinct protocols and ports for its operations. Ensure that protocol 50 (Encapsulating Security Payload [ESP]), protocol 51 (Authentication Header [AH]), and UDP port 500 (ISAKMP) traffic is not blocked at interfaces that are used by IPsec.

- **Define interesting traffic:** It is common in site-to-site VPNs to find deployments where some traffic will use the VPN and some traffic will bypass it. This concept is known as *split tunneling*. It is important to define which traffic will trigger the establishment of the VPN (interesting traffic) and which traffic will travel outside the tunnel (noninteresting traffic).

- **Determine the cipher suite requirements:** The choice of encryption algorithms for Phase 1 and Phase 2 of IPsec, as well as for the different services (confidentiality, integrity, and authentication), define the strength of protection and capacity planning considerations. The cipher suite is defined by the assets the organization is trying to protect and the level of risk it is willing to take. However, other considerations apply, such as compliance regulations. It is important to know that the cipher suite can be different for different peers. Multiple policies can be built on a given device, and they are negotiated differently with different peers. The resulting tunnels will provide varying levels of risk.

- **Manage monitoring, troubleshooting, and change:** It is important to build all three areas in the planning process. This chapter illustrates some of the tools that are available to accomplish these tasks.

Building Blocks of Site-to-Site IPsec

IPsec has specific procedures that require configuration on the security appliance for the successful establishment of a VPN tunnel.

Interesting Traffic and Crypto ACLs

Interesting traffic is defined by crypto ACLs in site-to-site IPsec VPN configurations. Crypto ACLs perform these functions, illustrated in Figure 14-2:

- **Outbound:** For outbound traffic, the crypto ACL defines the flows that IPsec should protect. Traffic that is not selected is sent in plaintext.

- **Inbound:** The same ACL is processed for inbound traffic. The ACL defines traffic that should have been protected by IPsec, and discards packets if they are selected but arrive unprotected (unencrypted).

Figure 14-2   *Outbound and Inbound Access Control Lists*

Ultimately, traffic will be processed against ACL statements. Traffic matching a **permit** action in the ACL will be protected and sent through the VPN. Traffic matching a **deny** action in the ACL will be sent outside the VPN in cleartext.

These recommendations apply when defining interesting traffic:

■ Try to be as restrictive as possible when defining which packets to protect in a crypto ACL. If you must use the **any** keyword in a **permit** statement, you must preface that statement with a series of **deny** statements to filter out any traffic (that would otherwise fall within that **permit** statement) that you do not want to be protected.

■ Because crypto ACLs are processed for both outbound and inbound traffic, it is important to create mirrored crypto ACLs in each VPN endpoint.

Mirrored Crypto ACLs

When crypto ACLs are incorrectly configured or missing, traffic might only flow in one direction across the VPN tunnel, or it might not be sent across the tunnel at all. When a router receives encrypted packets from an IPsec peer, it uses the same ACL to determine which inbound packets to decrypt by viewing the source and destination addresses in the ACL in reverse order. Any unprotected inbound traffic that matches a **permit** entry in the crypto ACL for a **crypto map** entry that is highlighted as IPsec is dropped. This drop occurs because this traffic was expected to be protected by IPsec.

In Figure 14-3, the VPN protects traffic from both LANs behind each router acting as VPN peer. The crypto ACL created on router Site-1 is the exact mirror of the crypto ACL created on router IOS-FW. The definition of source traffic on router IOS-FW becomes the definition of destination traffic on router Site-1. Similarly, the definition of destination traffic on router IOS-FW becomes the definition of source traffic on router Site-1.

You will notice in Figure 14-3 that we have included all the HQ subnets in our crypto ACLs, thus the wildcard mask of 16 bits for 10.10.0.0. The branch office has only one subnet, 10.20.10.0, thus the wildcard mask of 24 bits.

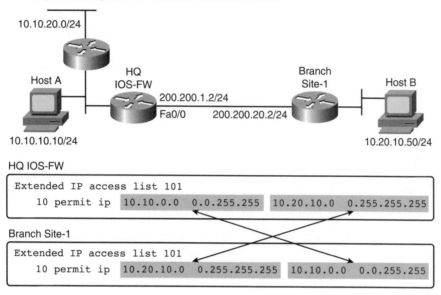

Figure 14-3 *Mirrored Crypto ACLs*

Cipher Suite

The cipher suite selection should follow guidelines in terms of encryption algorithms, key sizes, and key lifetimes. Table 14-1 illustrates an example. Advanced Encryption Standard (AES), for instance, is considered a stronger encryption algorithm than Triple Data Encryption Standard (3DES). Similarly, Secure Hash Algorithm 2 (SHA-2) is considered a stronger hashing function than SHA-1 and Message Digest 5 (MD5). In fact, some of these algorithms might have been broken already, in real networks or in a lab.

Table 14-1 *Example of Cipher Suite Selection Decision*

Parameter	Weaker	Stronger
Encryption algorithm	3DES	AES
Hash algorithm	MD5	SHA-1/SHA-2
Authentication method	Preshare	RSA signature
Diffie-Hellman key exchange	DH Group 1	DH Group 5
IKE SA lifetime	86,400 seconds	< 86,400 seconds

Similar considerations apply to authentication methods, where digital certificates are considered a stronger method to uniquely identify VPN peers, and they are a more scalable solution in the presence of a high volume of peers. Diffie-Hellman (DH) groups define the size of encryption keys, and will have an effect on device performance.

Key lifetimes also define the level of risk and the strength of the cryptography solution. The shorter the lifetimes, the more frequently peers will perform rekeying and refresh the cryptography materials, mitigating the effect of man-in-the-middle attacks and other exploits that expose keys and other components.

Crypto Map

Crypto map entries that you create for IPsec combine the needed configuration parameters of IPsec SAs, including the following parameters:

- Which traffic should be protected by IPsec using a crypto ACL

- The granularity of the flow to be protected by a set of SAs

- Who the remote IPsec peer is, which determines where the IPsec-protected traffic is sent

- The local address that is to be used for the IPsec traffic (optional)

- Which IPsec security should be applied to this traffic, choosing from a list of one or more transform sets

Crypto maps, illustrated in Figure 14-4, are applied to router interfaces in order for the IPsec VPN to start working. You can apply only one crypto map set to a single interface. Crypto maps can negotiate different policies for different peers on the same interface. In that case, the same crypto map will have multiple entries. These multiple entries are known as a *crypto map set*.

You must create multiple crypto map entries for a given interface if any of these conditions exist:

- Different data flows are to be managed by separate IPsec peers.

- You want to apply different IPsec security to different types of traffic (to the same or separate IPsec peers). An example would be if you want traffic between one set of subnets to be authenticated and traffic between another set of subnets to be both authenticated and encrypted. In this case, you should define the different types of traffic in two separate ACLs, and you must create a separate crypto map entry for each crypto ACL.

- If you are not using IKE to establish a particular set of SAs, and you want to specify multiple ACL entries, you must create separate ACLs (one per permit entry) and specify a separate crypto map entry for each ACL.

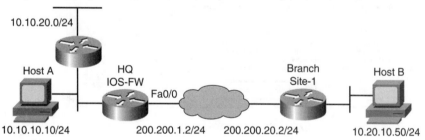

Figure 14-4   *Crypto Map and Its Role*

Configuring a Site-to-Site IPsec VPN Using CCP

The following pages show you how to configure a site-to-site IPsec VPN with preshared keys by using Cisco Configuration Professional wizards. All screen shots and configuration examples that follow use the same scenario that is depicted in Figure 14-5. The goal is to establish a site-to-site VPN between router IOS-FW and router Site-1, protecting traffic that travels between the two LAN segments behind each router.

To ensure secure communications, a strong cipher suite is required, which involves using preshared keys, AES, SHA-1, and DH5, as an example.

Figure 14-5   *Scenario for Configuring a Site-to-Site IPsec VPN with Preshared Keys Using CCP VPN Wizard*

Initiating the VPN Wizard

The Cisco Configuration Professional VPN wizard can be used to simplify the process of configuring the site-to-site VPN. The wizard is located by following this option path: **Configure > Security > VPN > Site-to-Site VPN**.

The Create Site to Site VPN tab includes two types of wizard:

- **Create a Site to Site VPN:** This option allows you to create a VPN network connecting two routers.

- **Create a Secure GRE Tunnel (GRE over IPsec):** This option allows you to configure a Generic Routing Encapsulation (GRE) protocol tunnel between your router and a peer system.

As shown in Figure 14-6, click **Create a Site-to-Site VPN** and click **Launch the Selected Task.**

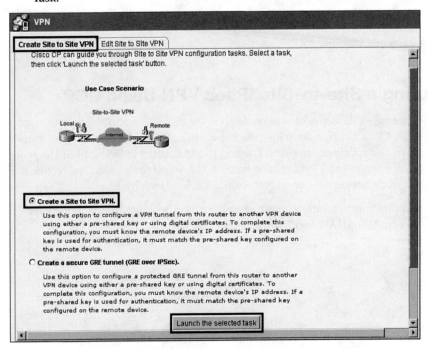

Figure 14-6   *Launching CCP Site-to-Site VPN Wizard*

As shown in Figure 14-7, the Site-to-Site VPN Wizard starts with a choice of quick setup or a step-by-step wizard:

- Using quick setup, CCP will automatically provide a default IKE policy to govern authentication, a default transform set to control the encryption of data, and a default IPsec rule that will encrypt all traffic between the router and the remote device. Quick setup is best used when both the local router and the remote system are Cisco routers using CCP. Quick setup will configure 3DES encryption if it is supported by the Cisco IOS image. Otherwise, it will configure DES encryption. If you need AES or Software-Optimized Encryption Algorithm (SEAL) encryption, you must use the step-by-step wizard. Using quick setup, you can view the default IKE policy, transform set, and IPsec rule that will be used to configure the one-step VPN.

■ Using the step-by-step wizard, you can configure a site-to-site VPN using parameters that you specify. The result is a custom configuration for the VPN, allowing the use of any of the CCP defaults that you need. The step-by-step wizard, selected in Figure 14-7, allows you to specify stronger encryption than the quick setup wizard allows.

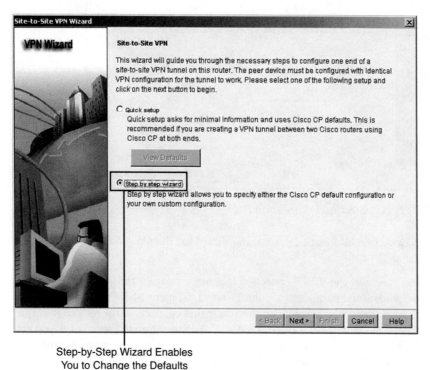

Step-by-Step Wizard Enables
You to Change the Defaults

Figure 14-7 *Wizard Gives a Choice Between Quick Setup or Step-by-Step Approach*

VPN Connection Information

You can use the VPN Connection Information page of the Site-to-Site VPN Wizard, shown in Figure 14-8, to identify the IP address or hostname of the remote site that will terminate the VPN tunnel that you are configuring, to specify the router interface to use, and to enter the preshared key that both routers will use to authenticate each other.

Figure 14-8   *VPN Connection Information Page*

The VPN Connection Information page of the wizard has three distinct sections, as shown in Figure 14-8.

The first component of the VPN Connection Information page is the local router interface that will initiate and terminate the tunnel, shown in Figure 14-9. From the interface drop-down menu, select the interface on this router that connects to the remote site. The router presented in Figure 14-9 is the HQ IOS-FW. As also shown in Figure 14-9, you can click Details to view the details of the interface, in terms of other configured features, such as Network Address Translation (NAT), existing ACLs, quality of service (QoS) rules, or Cisco IOS Intrusion Prevention System (IPS) rules. This is important to determine the compatibility of those features with IPsec configurations on the same interface.

The second component of the VPN Connection Information page is the Peer Identity section, shown in Figure 14-10. Enter the IP address of the remote IPsec peer that will terminate the VPN tunnel that you are configuring. The remote IPsec peer might be another router, a VPN concentrator, or any other gateway device that supports IPsec. Three options are available in the Peer Identity section, the first two of which are located in the drop-down menu:

- **Peer(s) with dynamic IP addresses:** Choose this option if the peers that the router connects to use a dynamically assigned IP address.

- **Peer with static IP address:** Choose this option if the peer that the router connects to uses a fixed IP address.

■ **Enter the IP address of the remote peer:** This is enabled when Peer With Static IP Address is chosen. Enter the IP address of the remote peer.

Figure 14-9   *First Component of VPN Connection Information Page: Interface Selection*

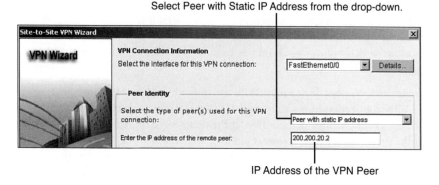

Figure 14-10   *Second Component of VPN Connection Information Page: Peer Identity*

The third component of the VPN Connection Information page, the Authentication section, is where you specify the preshared key used for IPsec authentication, as shown in Figure 14-11.

In the Authentication section of this page, you can click the Pre-shared Keys button if the VPN peers use a preshared key to authenticate connections from each other. This key must be the same on each side of the VPN. Question marks (?) and spaces must not be used in the preshared key. The preshared key can contain a maximum of 128 characters. Optionally, you can configure digital certificates as the authentication option. Click Next to move to the next page.

Figure 14-11   *Third Component of VPN Connection Information Page: Authentication*

IKE Proposals

The next wizard page, IKE Proposals, shown in Figure 14-12, lists all of the IKE policies that have been configured on the router. If no user-defined policies have been configured, the page lists the Cisco Configuration Professional default IKE policy. IKE policies govern the way in which devices in a VPN authenticate themselves during Phase 1. The local router uses the IKE policies listed on this page to negotiate authentication with the remote router.

The local router and the peer device must both use the same policy. The router that initiates the VPN connection offers all its policies to the receiver, which analyzes them starting with the lowest priority number first. If the remote system rejects that policy, it considers the policy with the next lowest number, and continues in this fashion until it finds a match, as shown previously in Figure 13-8. You must coordinate closely with the administrator of the peer system so that you can configure identical policies on both routers.

If you want to add an IKE policy that is not included in this list, you can click Add and create the policy in the Add IKE Policy dialog box that is displayed. You can edit an existing policy by selecting it and clicking Edit. CCP default policies are read-only and cannot be edited. In Figure 14-12, the Add IKE Policy dialog box displays the desired policy for the requirements, which are encryption using AES, authentication using preshared keys, hashing using SHA-1, and key exchange using DH 5.

> **Note**   Adding a new policy creates a new line with a higher priority in the IKE policy list. In the Add IKE Policy dialog box, you can control the priority number and define the cipher suite of your choice. Be sure to select the new policy from the list of IKE policies before you click **Next** to continue.

Select this proposal from the list.

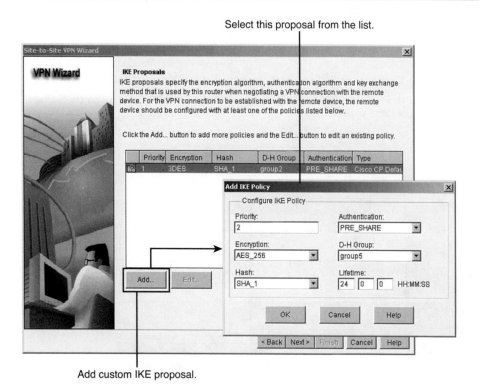

Add custom IKE proposal.

Figure 14-12   *IKE Proposals Configured Through the VPN Wizard*

Transform Set

The next step of the VPN Wizard is to define the transform sets, which define the cipher suite for IPsec Phase 2. The Transform Set page, shown in Figure 14-13, lists the CCP default transform sets and the additional transform sets that have been configured on this router. These transform sets will be available for use by the VPN. A *transform set* represents a certain combination of security protocols and algorithms. During the IPsec security association negotiation, the peers agree to use a particular transform set for protecting a particular data flow. A *transform* describes a particular security protocol with its corresponding algorithms.

A list of all configured transform sets is available in the Select Transform Set drop-down menu. Selecting one allows you to view the settings and add entries to the transform set.

Click **Add** to create the transform set in the Add Transform Set dialog box. You may choose to perform this action if the router is to negotiate different Phase 2 policies for

different peers. This is common in hub-and-spoke VPN topologies. For nondefault transform sets, you can also click Edit to modify the settings.

In Figure 14-13, the Add Transform Set dialog box is configured with the desired policy.
ESP is the IPsec protocol that will define authentication, integrity, and payload encryption to create Phase 2 tunnels, using SHA-1 as the integrity algorithm, and AES as the
encryption algorithm. The default is tunnel mode.

Click **Next** to continue the wizard and the VPN configuration.

Note   Adding a new policy will add options to the Select Transform Set drop-down
menu. Be sure to select the newly created policy from this drop-down menu before you
click **Next** to continue with the wizard.

Figure 14-13   *Transform Set Configured Through the VPN Wizard*

Traffic to Protect

The next step of the wizard is to define interesting traffic. The Traffic to Protect page,
shown in Figure 14-14, lets you define the traffic that this VPN protects. The VPN can

protect traffic between specified subnets, or protect the traffic that is specified in an IPsec rule that you select. There are two options available:

- **Protect all traffic between the following subnets:** Use this option to specify a single source subnet (a subnet on the LAN) whose outgoing traffic you want to encrypt, and one destination subnet that is supported by the peer that you specified on the VPN Connection Information page. All traffic flowing between other source and destination pairs will be sent unencrypted.

- **Create/Select an access-list for IPSec traffic:** Use this option if you need to specify multiple sources and destinations, or if you need to encrypt specific types of traffic. An IPsec rule can consist of multiple entries, each specifying different traffic types and different sources and destinations. Click the ... button next to the field and specify an existing IPsec rule that defines the traffic you want to encrypt, or create an IPsec rule to use for this VPN.

In Figure 14-14, the protected networks from the perspective of router IOS-FW are 10.10.0.0/16 as the source (the LAN behind IOS-FW) and 10.20.10.0/24 as the destination (the LAN behind router Site-1).

Click **Next** to continue the wizard and the VPN configuration.

Figure 14-14 *Protecting Traffic Through the VPN Wizard*

Configuration Summary

The last step of the wizard is to review and accept the configuration, as shown in Figure 14-15. This page shows you the VPN configuration that you created. After you review the configuration on this page, you can either click the Back button to make changes if you want, or click Finish to complete the wizard. Note that a testing option is available. You can check the Test VPN Connectivity After Configuring check box to test the VPN connection you have just configured. The results of the test will be shown in another window. This option is demonstrated later in this chapter.

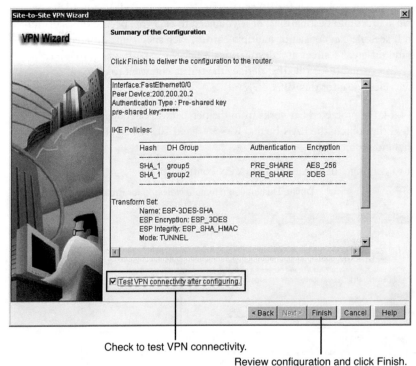

Check to test VPN connectivity.

Review configuration and click Finish.

Figure 14-15   *Summary of the Site-to-Site VPN Wizard Configuration*

Note   If NAT is configured on this router, a CCP warning box, shown in Figure 14-16, will appear after you click **Finish**; this warning will offer to convert your NAT rules with route maps in order for the VPN to work properly. CCP assumes, rightly so, that you would like to skip the NAT process for traffic going through the IPsec tunnel. Therefore, traffic from 10.10.0.0/16 will appear with its original (real) IP address when transiting on the 10.20.10.0/24 network and vice versa. In other words, sessions between 10.10.0.0/16 and 10.20.10.0/24 will not have their source address translated.

Figure 14-16   *VPN Wizard Warning About NAT Rules*

Creating a Mirror Configuration for the Peer Site

Site-to-site VPNs require both sides to be configured with matching policies. You also need to create mirrored crypto ACLs in each VPN endpoint and ensure that the peers know each other's IP addresses. Typically, the same process that is configured by the wizard has to be replicated on the other peer. In Cisco Configuration Professional, you can navigate to **Configure > Security > VPN > Site-to-Site VPN**, click the **Edit Site-to-Site VPN** tab, and then click **Generate Mirror** to automatically create a mirror configuration for the peer.

Clicking this button, as shown in Figure 14-17, creates a text file that captures the VPN configuration of the local router so that a remote router can be given a VPN configuration that enables it to establish a VPN connection to the local router. This button is disabled if you have selected a dynamic site-to-site VPN tunnel.

Note   The text file that you generate must not be copied into the configuration file of the remote system, but it must be edited and used only to show what has been configured on the local router so that the remote device can be configured in a way that is compatible. Identical names for IPsec policies, IKE policies, and transform sets may be used on the remote router, but the policies and transform sets may be different. If the text file is simply copied into the remote configuration file, configuration errors are likely to result.

Note   Any previously configured VPN connections that are detected by Cisco Configuration Professional that do not use ISAKMP crypto maps will appear as read-only entries in the VPN connection table and cannot be edited.

Figure 14-17   *Creating a Mirror Configuration for the Peer Router*

Verifying the IPsec Configuration Using CCP and CLI

You can verify the VPN configuration on the Edit Site to Site VPN tab, as shown in Figure 14-18. Use this tab to manage the VPN connections to remote systems.

The Status column shows the status of the connection, which is indicated by the intuitive icons. You can also create, edit, and delete VPN connections, and reset existing connections.

The Clear Connection, Generate Mirror, and Test Tunnel buttons are also available from this tab.

Verifying IPsec Configuration Using CLI

The Cisco IOS CLI can also be used to verify the site-to-site VPN configuration. Table 14-2 shows some of the available commands.

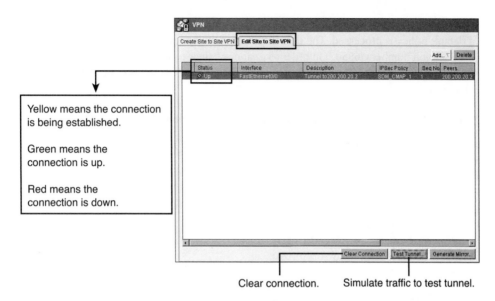

Yellow means the connection is being established.

Green means the connection is up.

Red means the connection is down.

Clear connection.   Simulate traffic to test tunnel.

Figure 14-18   *Editing VPN Configuration Using CCP*

Table 14-2   *Commands to Verify IPsec Configuration*

Parameters	Description
show crypto isakmp policy	Displays configured IKE policies
show crypto ipsec transform-set	Displays configured IPsec transform sets
show crypto map	Displays configured crypto maps
show crypto ipsec sa	Displays established IPsec tunnels

Verifying IKE Policy Using the CLI

Use the **show crypto isakmp policy** command to display configured IKE policies and the default IKE policy settings. This command is useful because it reveals your ISAKMP (IKE) configuration with one command.

The command output, shown in Example 14-1, displays all sections of the IKE policy for router Site-1 according to the topology originally presented in Figure 14-5. The numbers that identify each section (in this example, section numbers 1 and 2) are used to process different sections for peers with different IKE policies. Sections are processed in order, from lower to higher numbers.

If you do not configure IKE policies, or if traffic does not match any configured policy, a default policy is processed. The default policy includes several sections that start with high section numbers (65507) in order to guarantee their processing as an option of last resort. This default policy can be displayed with the **show crypto isakmp default policy** command.

Example 14-1 *Output of* **show crypto isakmp policy** *Command*

```
IOS-FW# show crypto isakmp policy
Global IKE policy
Protection suite of priority 1
    encryption algorithm: Three key triple DES
    hash algorithm: Secure Hash Standard
    authentication method: Pre-Shared Key
    Diffie-Hellman group: #2 (1024 bit)
lifetime: 86400 seconds, no volume limit
```

Verifying IKE Phase 2 Policy Using the CLI

You can use the **show crypto ipsec transform-set** command to show all of the configured transform sets. Because transform sets determine the level of protection that your data will have as it is tunneled, it is important to verify the strength of your IPsec protection policy.

In Example 14-2, the first transform set was created by Cisco Configuration Professional for our example. The remaining transform sets are preconfigured as part of the default policy.

Example 14-2 *Output of* **show crypto ipsec transform-set** *Command*

```
IOS-FW# show crypto ipsec transform-set
Transform set ESP-3DES-SHA: { esp-3des esp-sha-hmac }
   will negotiate = { Tunnel, },
Transform set #$!default_transform_set_1: { esp-aes esp-sha-hmac }
   will negotiate = { Transport, },
Transform set #$!default_transform_set_0: { esp-3des esp-sha-hmac }
   will negotiate = { Transport, },
```

Verifying Crypto Maps Using the CLI

To see all of the configured crypto maps, use the **show crypto map** command, as shown in Example 14-3. This command verifies configurations and shows the configured and current peers, as well as the crypto ACL that defines traffic flows to be protected. The output also shows the interface where the crypto map is assigned.

The information provided by the crypto ACL is most important, as it allows you to monitor and troubleshoot the accuracy and validity of interesting traffic.

The **show running-config** command also reveals many of these same settings.

> **Note** In production, you could reduce the length of the **show run** command by using the **show run brief** command or the **show run | section crypto** command. The equivalent command on a Cisco ASA firewall would be **show run crypto**.

Example 14-3   *Output of* **show crypto map** *Command*

```
IOS-FW# show crypto map
Crypto Map "SDM_CMAP_1" 1 ipsec-isakmp
     Description: Tunnel to200.200.20.2
     Peer = 200.200.20.2
     Extended IP access list 101
      access-list 101 permit ip 10.10.0.0 0.0.255.255 10.20.10.0 0.0.0.255
     Current peer: 200.200.20.2
     Security association lifetime: 4608000 kilobytes/3600 seconds
     Responder-Only (Y/N): N
     PFS (Y/N): N
     Transform sets={
             ESP-3DES-SHA:  { esp-3des esp-sha-hmac } ,
     }
     Interfaces using crypto map SDM_CMAP_1:
          FastEthernet0/0
```

Monitoring Established IPsec VPN Connections

Cisco Configuration Professional monitoring is streamlined by using the VPN Status window, which displays a tree of VPN connections that are possible on the router, including all types of VPNs (remote access, site-to-site, and others).

Site-to-site tunnels are displayed as IPsec tunnels. This group displays statistics about each IPsec VPN that is configured on the router. Each row in the table represents one IPsec VPN. You will need to click Update to refresh the IPsec tunnel table and display the most current data from the router.

Figure 14-19 showcases the Monitor Tunnel and Test Tunnel options, which are essential to the troubleshooting process.

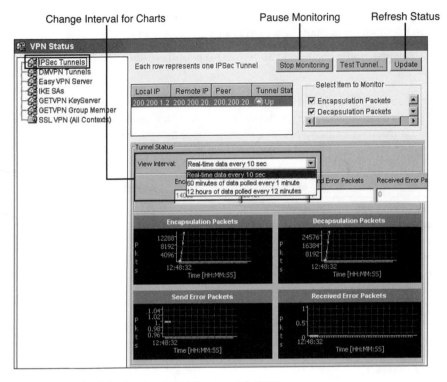

Figure 14-19   *Monitoring VPN Status with CCP*

IKE Policy Negotiation

The Test Tunnel option allows you to send simulated data through the VPN tunnel. You can click the Start button to start the test. The results are shown on the left side of Figure 14-20.

If the test fails, a popup window prompts you to confirm the initiation of a troubleshooting phase, used by CCP to generate simulated traffic and enable IPsec debugging, in order to automate the troubleshooting process. Clicking Yes to accept this debugging phase presents additional options to either allow CCP to simulate VPN traffic or let you define the profile of the simulated traffic by specifying a destination IP address.

VPN Troubleshooting

Figure 14-21 illustrates the report window of a failed VPN test. The icons shown in Figure 14-20 provide visual cues to determine the severity of the test and to define which of the multiple tests performed by CCP passed or failed. The panel at the bottom suggests the failure reason and spells out recommended actions to resolve the problem.

Figure 14-20   *Testing Site-to-Site IPsec Tunnel*

Figure 14-21   *VPN Troubleshooting Status Window*

Monitoring IKE Security Association

Monitoring and troubleshooting can also be accomplished by using the Cisco IOS CLI. The **show crypto isakmp sa** command shows the status and settings of IKE Phase 1 SAs.

Notice the status of the tunnel under the Status column. Also notice the difference between the Status column and the State column. *State* refers to the progress of the negotiation within Phase 1, while *status* refers to VPN high availability (HA), showing a state of ACTIVE for SAs on the HA active router, and STANDBY for the SAs on the standby router. This means that a status of ACTIVE is not related to active tunnels; in fact, the Status column is not an indication of health of each Phase 1 SA. A state of QM_IDLE is considered normal for an established Phase 1 tunnel.

Table 14-3 and 14-4 list and describe the possible values for state and status.

Table 14-3   *Values for IKE Security Association State*

State	Description
MM_NO_STATE	The Phase 1 SA has been created, but nothing else has happened yet.
MM_SA_SETUP	The peers have agreed on parameters for the Phase 1 SA.
MM_KEY_EXCH	DH negotiation was successful, but the Phase 1 SA remains unauthenticated.
MM_KEY_AUTH	The Phase 1 SA has been authenticated.
QM_IDLE	The Phase 1 SA is idle, in quiescent state.

Table 14-4   *Values for IKE Security Association Status*

Status	Description
ACTIVE	The Phase 1 SA is terminated on the active device of an HA cluster.
STANDBY	The Phase 1 SA is terminated on the standby device of an HA cluster.

Monitoring IPsec Security Association

IPsec Phase 2 can also be monitored by using the **show crypto ipsec sa** command, as shown in Example 14-4. Increasing encrypt and decrypt counters are a general indication of an operational IPsec Phase 2 tunnel.

Example 14-4 *Output of the* **show crypto ipsec sa** *Command*

```
RouterA# show crypto ipsec sa
interface: FastEthernet0/0
   Crypto map tag: SDM_CMAP_1, local addr 200.200.1.2


   protected vrf: (none)
   local ident (addr/mask/prot/port): (10.10.0.0/255.255.0.0/0/0)
   remote ident (addr/mask/prot/port): (10.20.10.0/255.255.255.0/0/0)
   current_peer 200.200.20.2 port 500
     PERMIT, flags={origin_is_acl,}
   #pkts encaps: 4030, #pkts encrypt: 4030, #pkts digest: 4030
   #pkts decaps: 4033, #pkts decrypt: 4033, #pkts verify: 4033
   #pkts compressed: 0, #pkts decompressed: 0
   #pkts not compressed: 0, #pkts compr. failed: 0
   #pkts not decompressed: 0, #pkts decompress failed: 0
   #send errors 0, #recv errors 0
```

Note   The **show crypto ipsec sa** command shows different information depending on whether it is issued from a Cisco IOS router or an ASA firewall:

- **Cisco IOS router:** IPsec SAs show the local and remote identities even if the tunnel is not up. The key item to look for is the presence of inbound and outbound Security Profile Indexes (SPI). Increasing encapsulation/decapsulation counters are also a way to confirm that actual traffic is going through the tunnel.

- **ASA devices:** IPsec SAs do not show identities unless the tunnel is up. Also, the presence of encapsulated packets but no decapsulated packets (or vice versa) is usually a sign of bad routes on one end of the tunnel and/or an ACL in the middle of the flow that is blocking ESP or UDP 4500 (NAT-T) traffic.

Summary

The key points covered in this chapter are as follows:

- Planning an IPsec site-to-site VPN includes selecting the cipher suite and building monitoring and contingency planning into the IPsec site-to site VPN configuration checklist.

- Cisco Configuration Professional provides a step-by-step wizard to guide configuration.

- Use the Monitor Tunnel options to verify configuration.

- Use the Test VPN option and CLI commands to test and troubleshoot.

References

For additional information, refer to these resources:

Carmouche, J. H. *IPsec Virtual Private Network Fundamentals* (Cisco Press, 2007).

Cisco Systems, Inc. "Cisco IOS IPsec," http://www.cisco.com/en/US/products/ps6635/products_ios_protocol_group_home.html.

Deal, R. *The Complete Cisco VPN Configuration Guide* (Cisco Press, 2005).

Review Questions

Use the questions here to review what you learned in this chapter. The correct answers are found in the Appendix, "Answers to Chapter Review Questions."

1. Which command is best suited to show that traffic is flowing through the VPN tunnel?

    a. show crypto map
    b. show crypto ipsec transform-set
    c. show crypto isakmp policy
    d. show crypto ipsec sa

2. Which command would help troubleshoot a Phase I issue?

    a. debug crypto sa
    b. debug crypto phase 1
    c. debug crypto isakmp
    d. show crypto sa

3. Which command would be the most helpful to compare the configuration of peer, ACL, SA lifetime, and transform sets?

    a. debug crypto sa
    b. show crypto isakmp sa
    c. show crypto map sa
    d. show crypto map

4. You are deploying IPsec VPNs with the Cisco Configuration Professional wizard. Which of the following is true about traffic that is denied by the crypto ACL?

    a. The traffic will be denied access to the VPN.
    b. The traffic will be dropped if it does not match the crypto policy.
    c. The traffic is permitted if it matches the crypto policy.
    d. The traffic is permitted in cleartext.

5. Which of the following options is available in the VPN Status window of Cisco Configuration Professional?

    a. Create Mirror
    b. Monitor Tunnel
    c. Clear Connection
    d. Add Policy

6. Which of the following is considered a stable state for a Phase 1 security association in IPsec VPNs, using the **show crypto isakmp sa** command?

   a. QM_IDLE
   b. QM_NO_STATE
   c. QM_ACTIVE
   d. QM_ESTABLISHED

7. You issue the command **show crypto isakmp sa**. You discover that the IKE tunnel is down. Issuing the **show crypto ipsec sa** command will be helpful at troubleshooting the connectivity problem. True or false?

   a. True
   b. False

8. You use the Test Tunnel option of CCP. The test fails. What, if any, happens next?

   a. CCP returns a fail message and the Test Tunnel option closes.
   b. CCP pings automatically the IP address of the peer to ensure that it is live.
   c. CCP presents a popup window prompting you to confirm the initiation of a troubleshooting phase.
   d. CCP opens a CLI window and issues **show crypto** commands to the router.

Chapter 15

SSL VPNs with Cisco ASA

Upon completing this chapter, you will be able to describe the Secure Sockets Layer (SSL) VPN operational framework. You will be able to demonstrate the deployment of basic SSL VPNs on Cisco Adaptive Security Appliances (ASA) using Cisco Adaptive Security Device Manager (ASDM) and the Cisco AnyConnect VPN Client. This chapter prepares you to meet these objectives:

- Describe the use cases and operational requirements of Cisco SSL VPNs

- Describe the protocol framework for SSL and TLS

- Describe a configuration that is based on SSL VPN deployment options and other design considerations

- Describe the steps to configure Cisco VPN clientless mode on Cisco ASA and demonstrate the configuration on Cisco ASDM

- Describe the steps to configure Cisco full-tunnel mode on Cisco ASA and demonstrate the configuration on Cisco ASDM using the Cisco AnyConnect VPN Client

Mobility and IT consumer market trends influence the need for comprehensive remote-access security policies. SSL VPNs are commonly used as a remote-access service. As such, SSL VPNs must integrate strong cryptography and standards-based components with deployment and operational efficiencies and endpoint security. This chapter describes the SSL protocol framework and describes the benefits of the Cisco SSL VPN solution. The chapter also demonstrates the configuration of clientless and full-tunnel SSL VPNs using Cisco ASDM and the Cisco AnyConnect VPN Client.

SSL VPNs in Borderless Networks

Remote-access and mobility services have gone through drastic changes in the past few years. There are three market transitions driving the network architectures of the future:

- **Mobility:** Over the next three years, there will be more than 1.3 billion new networked mobile devices. These devices will include mobile Internet devices, notebooks, smartphones, notebooks, tablets, and other devices.

- **Video:** Video has truly become pervasive in both consumer and business environments. No longer simply a means of communication, it has become a key factor in reducing training and travel costs. It is also beginning to reshape business models, especially in retail.

- **IT consumerization:** This is essentially what can be called the new workplace experience, in which consumer demand and new consumer devices influence technology decisions made by IT departments. Globalization has created a need for partners, customers, and employees to connect to each other and to the Internet over traditional boundaries from a variety of environments and devices.

These three market transitions are changing the IT environment and the strategic role that the network plays in delivery of new services. These market factors will influence the features that are found in remote-access products and technologies.

These transitions are also placing significant demands on the typical functions of the IT organization. Functional needs have remained similar: scalability, availability, performance, security, manageability, and cost of ownership. But as new (and potentially untrusted) devices connect to the network from multiple (and potentially untrusted) places, and as the IT organization moves beyond the infrastructure it can directly control, these parameters have become much more complex. In fact, the parameters are no longer linear; they are multidimensional, and the IT organizations, therefore, are struggling to meet their requirements in terms of the underlying network infrastructure.

The main challenges to IT organizations in providing remote and mobile access to corporate resources include the following:

- They need to provide an improved access experience, providing everywhere connectivity and management whether through wired, wireless, or remote access.

- To support the increasing number of mobile workers, corporate security administrators must provide context-aware security and policy enforcement. They must extend the application experience, regardless of the locations of the end users, what devices they are using, what network they are on, and where the information they are accessing is located. Administrators must also be able to support a heterogeneous set of laptops and mobile devices to encourage choice for their clients—the end users. Finally, they must provide this security unobtrusively and agnostic of the access network to minimize end-user concerns.

- The days of the standard corporate device are over. Businesses must meet the first two challenges in a way that will allow them to embrace the wave of new devices—smartphones and tablets, in addition to the traditional laptops—that workers are using.

Cisco SSL VPN

The Cisco SSL VPN technology provides remote-access connectivity from almost any Internet-enabled location with a web browser and its native SSL encryption. Cisco SSL VPN provides the flexibility to support secure access for all users, regardless of the end-point host from which they establish a connection. If application access requirements are modest, SSL VPN does not require a software client to be preinstalled on the endpoint host. This ability enables companies to extend their secure enterprise networks to any authorized user by providing remote-access connectivity to corporate resources from any Internet-enabled location.

Cisco SSL VPN currently delivers three modes of Cisco SSL VPN access: clientless, thin client, and full client, as shown in Figure 12-2, earlier in this book. Cisco SSL VPNs allow users to access web pages and services, including the ability to access files, send and receive email, and run TCP-based applications without IPsec VPN client software. Cisco SSL VPNs are appropriate for user populations that require per-application or per-server access control, or access from desktops not owned by the enterprise.

In many cases, IPsec and Cisco SSL VPNs are complementary because they solve different problems. This complementary approach allows a single device to address all remote-access user requirements.

The primary benefit of Cisco SSL VPN is its ubiquity and versatility. SSL is available on computers, tablets, and smartphones. You use it when you shop or bank online.

An additional benefit of Cisco SSL VPN is that it is compatible with Dynamic Multipoint VPNs (DMVPN), Cisco IOS Firewalls, IPsec, intrusion prevention systems (IPS), Cisco Easy VPN, and Network Address Translation (NAT).

SSL VPNs and IPsec VPNs are complementary technologies that you can deploy together to better address the unique access requirements of diverse user communities. Both offer access to virtually any network application or resource. Cisco SSL VPNs offer additional features such as easy connectivity from desktops outside your company's management, little or no desktop software maintenance, and user-customized web portals upon login.

Table 15-1 shows the most significant differences between IPsec VPNs and Clientless SSL VPNs. IPsec excels in the number of applications that are supported, the strength of its encryption, the strength of its authentication, and its overall security. The areas in which Clientless SSL VPN excels are its ease of use and ease of deployment.

Table 15-1   *Clientless SSL VPN Versus IPsec VPN*

	Clientless SSL VPN	IPsec VPN
Applications	Web-enabled applications, file sharing applications, email.	All IP-based applications.
Encryption	Moderate. Key lengths range from 40 bits to 128 bits. (Note: If your browser supports AES 256, then the encryption strength is the same as IPsec.)	Stronger. Key lengths range from 56 bits to 256 bits.
Authentication	Moderate. One-way or two-way authentication.	Strong. Two-way authentication using shared secrets or digital certificates.
Ease of use	Very high.	Moderate. Can be challenging to nontechnical users.
Overall security	Moderate. Any device can connect.	Strong. Only specific devices with specific configurations can connect.
Summary	Anywhere access	Any application

When used for VPN connectivity, SSL does not require any special-purpose client software to be preinstalled on the system. Cisco SSL VPNs are also known as "clientless VPNs" because they rely on the existence of web browsers on the connecting host, a preinstalled client that already supports the protocol. This feature makes SSL VPNs capable of "anywhere" connectivity from company-managed desktops and non-company-managed desktops, such as employee-owned PCs, contractor or business partner desktops, and Internet kiosks. Any software that is required for application access across the SSL VPN connection is dynamically downloaded on an as-needed basis, minimizing desktop software maintenance.

Traditionally, when security was a primary issue, IPsec was the preferred choice. If support and ease of deployment were the primary issues, then SSL was considered. Nowadays, SSL VPN is usually considered the preferred choice, especially because it provides security comparable to IPsec. Cisco VPN products support both technologies in order to satisfy the largest number of customer requirements.

SSL and TLS Protocol Framework

Transport Layer Security (TLS) and its predecessor, SSL, are cryptographic protocols that provide secure communications on the Internet for such things as web browsing, email, Internet faxing, instant messaging, and other data transfers. Originally developed by Netscape, SSL has been universally accepted on the World Wide Web to transfer information privately over the Internet. Virtually all online transactions and browser-based monetary interactions that occur on the Internet are secured by SSL.

As mentioned earlier, SSL has evolved from Netscape's original implementation. TLS is a standards-based alternative to SSL.

SSL and TLS provide confidentiality, integrity, and authentication services to the applications that use them. In that sense, these protocols encrypt and authenticate from the session layer up, including the presentation and application layers.

SSL is used to encrypt and authenticate the session layer and above. As such, it encrypts more than just HTTP (called HTTPS); it can also encrypt FTP (thus FTPS), POP (for POPS), LDAP (for LDAPS), wireless security (EAP-TLS), and others.

Cryptographically, SSL and TLS rely on public key infrastructure (PKI) and digital certificates for authenticating the VPN endpoints. In e-commerce environments, typically only the server side is authenticated and requires a digital certificate. Other applications are increasingly using mutual authentication, where both the client and the server use digital certificates to identify themselves.

Figure 15-1 shows the encapsulation of SSL/TLS.

SSL ex: HTTPS

Figure 15-1 *SSL/TLS Encapsulation*

SSL and TLS

There are slight differences between SSL and TLS, but the protocols remain largely similar. The terms are sometimes used interchangeably, but interestingly, the protocols are not interoperable. Some implementations include provisions to switch to the other protocol if necessary for a given session, especially in the case of TLS, which incorporates mechanisms to switch to SSL if the client connection requires it.

TLS 1.0 originated from SSL 3.0, and later versions of both protocols show a similar development path. Table 15-2 lists some of the differences.

Table 15-2   *SSL and TLS*

SSL	TLS
Developed by Netscape in the 1990s	Standard developed by IETF
Starts with security and proceeds directly to secured communications	Can start with an insecure "hello" and switch to secured communications only after the handshake is successful
Wider and more prevalent support on client-side applications	Granular and more pervasive support on server-side applications
More weaknesses identified in older SSL versions	Stronger implementation due to standards process and universal support

---

DTLS

TLS has a sister protocol called DTLS, for Datagram Transport Layer Security. The main difference between TLS and DTLS is that DTLS gets encapsulated in UDP at Layer 4, while TLS gets encapsulated in TCP, as shown in Figure 15-1.

SSL Cryptography

The SSL and TLS protocols support the use of a variety of different cryptographic algorithms, or ciphers, for use in operations such as authenticating the server and client to each other, transmitting certificates, and establishing session keys. Symmetric algorithms are used for bulk encryption, asymmetric algorithms are used for authentication and the exchange of keys, and hashing is used as part of the authentication process. Figure 15-2 illustrates some of the supported algorithms (in the figure, EC stands for Elliptic Curve).

Note   The listed encryption algorithms are just examples for SSL and TLS support. Multiple other cipher suites are supported but not listed.

Figure 15-2   *Supported SSL Cryptographic Cipher Suites*

SSL Tunnel Establishment

Figure 15-3 gives a simplified explanation of the key steps in establishing an SSL session:

Step 1.   The user makes an outbound connection to TCP port 443.

Step 2.   The security appliance responds with a digital certificate, which contains a public key that is digitally signed by a trusted certificate authority (CA). The ASA can also present a self-signed certificate. The client will have to accept the security warning mentioning that the validity of the signature cannot be confirmed, but the self-signed certificate is useable.

Step 3.   The user computer generates a shared-secret, symmetric key that both parties will use.

Step 4.   The shared secret is encrypted with the public key of the security appliance and transmitted to the router. The security appliance software is able to easily decrypt the packet using its private key. Now both participants in the session know the shared-secret key.

SSL utilizes encryption algorithms with key lengths that range from 40 to 256 bits.

Figure 15-3   *Major Steps of SSL VPN Tunnel Establishment*

SSL Tunnel Establishment Example

SSL and PKI, as explained in Chapter 12, are complex topics. Figure 15-4 and the following steps explain the essence of how an HTTPS session is established. This example is not meant to provide you with a detailed and accurate account of how an HTTPS session is set up, but rather to provide an understandable example without all the technicalities.

Figure 15-4   *Example of an HTTPS Session*

Steps A to I illustrate steps between the Blue Bank server and VeriSign.

Steps 1 to 11 illustrate steps between the HTTPS client and the Blue Bank server.

Step A.   As a root CA, the VeriSign server has created a key pair. It used its own private key to sign its own public key—this is called a self-signed certificate. (Signing of certificates will be covered in Step E.) By the way, serious organizations such as VeriSign do not use their top root certificate to sign client certificates. (The hierarchy of CAs is beyond the scope of this book.)

Step B.   Blue Bank wants to start offering an online banking service. It selects VeriSign as the public CA server (CA theory was covered in Chapter 12). The Blue Bank server acquires the digital certificate of VeriSign. (The creation of digital certificates will be covered in Step D.) It is highly probably that the Blue Bank server would already have installed on it the VeriSign digital certificate. Popular desktops and server OSs, such as those from Microsoft, already have this CA certificate installed in the certificate store. One of the easiest ways to see the content of the certificate store, and thus to see the trusted root certificates installed on a server or a workstation, is to start Internet Explorer and navigate to **Tools > Internet Options**, click the **Content** tab, click the **Certificates** button, and then click the **Trusted Root Certification Authorities** tab.

Step C.   Blue Bank generates a private and public key pair.

Step D.   Blue Bank petitions VeriSign to validate its public key in order to generate a digital certificate.

Step E.   VeriSign proceeds to turn the Blue Bank public key into a digital certificate by adding information to the public key. Some of the fields added to the public key, as shown in Figure 15-4, are Subject Name (it could be Blue Bank URL), Validity (dates), and so forth.

Step F.   VeriSign hashes some of the fields included with the information of the Blue Bank digital certificate and produces a digest.

Step G.   VeriSign encrypts the digest and encrypts it with its private key. We now have a digital signature; so the definition of a digital signature is: *a hash encrypted with a private key*.

Step H.   The Blue Bank digital certificate has been created. What is the Blue Bank digital certificate? It's a validated public key signed by the CA.

What is a validated public key? It's the public key, with fields added to it.

What is a signature? It's the hash result encrypted with the CA private key.

Step I.   Blue Bank installs its digital certificate, which is Blue Bank's public key, signed by the CA.

Now, as a Blue Bank customer, you wish to open an online banking session, using your laptop.

Step 1.   Your laptop is equipped with the root certificate of the CA used by Blue Bank, VeriSign. If the server on which you want to open an SSL session had its digital certificate issued by a CA that you are unfamiliar with, you would need to download the root certificate onto your computer. In our scenario, the laptop is running a popular OS and already has a copy of the VeriSign digital certificate in its certificate store.

Step 2.   Your laptop browser queries the Blue Bank server to see if it accepts HTTPS sessions.

Step 3.   Because Blue Bank accepts SSL sessions, the server sends a copy of its digital certificate to the laptop. Actually, sending a copy of the Blue Bank digital certificate happens only the first time that the particular laptop connects to the Blue Bank server. After that, the server and the client will only check whether they are using the right Digital Certificate Serial number (it's one of the fields in Step E). When Blue Bank puts a new certificate in production, either because the previous one has expired or because the key has been compromised, it will ask the laptop for a certificate number that the laptop hasn't heard about yet. In that case, the Blue Bank server will then push the new certificate to the laptop.

Step 4.   The client proceeds to validate the certificate. It checks for the validity date and the name of the issuer. Because the client already knows about the issuer of the certificate, in this case VeriSign, it proceeds to validate the signature. To do so, it first hashes the pre-agreed fields from the digital certificate to get a digest.

Step 5.   Continuing with the validation of the Blue Bank digital certificate, the client decrypts the signature originally created by VeriSign's private key (Step G). To decrypt that signature, the client uses the VeriSign public key acquired in Step 1. If the hash digest calculated by the client in Step 4 matches the result found by decrypting the digital signature in Step 5, then the client knows two things for sure: the issuer (signing authority) was indeed VeriSign, and no one tampered with the content of the certificate. The authenticity of the certificate is proven by the fact that the client was successful at decrypting the signature using VeriSign's public key, which means that the signature was created in the first place by VeriSign's private key. And who has VeriSign's private key? Only VeriSign—and it's guarded ferociously.

Step 6.   The ultimate goal of the client is to have an HTTPS session with the server, as shown in Step 12. This HTTPS session will use symmetric cryptography because it is much faster than asymmetric cryptography. The client and the server must at this stage agree on the encryption that they will use for the symmetric encrypted session in Step 12. Let's say for our scenario that the client and the server agree that the encryption algorithm will be RC4-128 (Rivest Cipher, 128-bit) and exchange other essential information.

Step 7.   As part of the process of coming up with a symmetric encryption key that will be used in Step 12, the client generates a value (called the pre-master value, also referred as a session key in Figure 15-4) that will be used to finalize the symmetric key used by the server and client.

Step 8.   The pre-master value (session value) needs to be shared confidentially with the server, so the client encrypts it with the server's public key, found with the Blue Bank digital certificate received in Step 3.

Step 9.   The encrypted pre-master value (session value) is sent to the server.

Step 10.   Using its private key, the Blue Bank server can decrypt the data it just received from the client and discover the pre-master value (session value) that is to be used in the fabrication of a symmetric encryption key.

Step 11.   Both the client and the server now have a copy of the pre-master value (session value) and all the other values necessary to generate the same session key. They independently arrive at the same result, and that result is the symmetric key they will use for their SSL session.

Step 12.   The SSL tunnel comes up. Only then will some browsers show you a padlock near the URL bar, and only then will Blue Bank present you with the login page where you will be required to provide your banking card number and password.

When the client gracefully logs out of the session or when the session times out, the client and the server both forget the session key that was generated in Step 11.

Cisco SSL VPN Deployment Options and Considerations

As shown in Chapter 12 (in Figure 12-2), Cisco SSL VPNs offer different types of access options: SSL Clientless and SSL full client mode, referred to as Cisco AnyConnect SSL VPN. A third option exists as SSL Clientless thin-client, which provides some more functionality with the SSL Clientless. Figure 15-5 shows the use case for the different ways to access the corporate network remotely.

Figure 15-5 shows the usage scenario for the following three types of SSL access:

■ **Clientless:** This option enables a user to connect to the network with few requirements beyond a basic web browser. The access provides the ability to reach web servers or webified resources such as file shares.

■ **Thin client:** A small applet or application (generally under 100 KB) is downloaded that provides access to a subset of application resources, generally TCP, and often an outbound and static port. This thin-client is part of the Clientless option.

■ **SSL VPN client:** A larger client is delivered to the end user and is required when users need full application access. The applications that can be accessed are very similar to those available via IPsec VPN. This client is delivered via a web page (the device that the user is connecting to) and never needs to be manually distributed or installed. This client is referred to as Cisco AnyConnect.

Figure 15-5 *SSL VPN Access Scenarios*

The architecture includes VPN termination points (Cisco IOS routers or ASA) and the Cisco AnyConnect VPN Client.

Figure 15-6 illustrates the differences between the two main deployment modes that are found in Cisco SSL VPN solutions:

■ Clientless mode is easier to deploy but presents additional challenges in terms of endpoint security and application access.

■ Full network access supports a wider variety of applications but presents additional operational challenges in downloading and maintaining the client software on remote hosts.

SSL VPNs provide a flexible way of extending network resources and applications to remote users. When using a clientless SSL VPN deployment model, corporations have the additional flexibility of providing access to corporate resources even when the remote device is not corporately managed. In this deployment model, the Cisco ASA is used as a proxy device to network resources and provides a web portal interface for remote devices to navigate the network. Additionally, to access the SSL VPN network, the remote device system only requires a supported web browser with built-in SSL functionality. Although more flexible than client-based SSL VPNs, clientless SSL VPNs provide only limited network application or resource access and include additional security risks when using non-corporate-managed clients.

Figure 15-6 *Two Main SSL Deployment Modes*

Full network access SSL VPNs operate much like standard IPsec VPN clients in the way that they provide network access. In comparison to the clientless SSL VPN deployment model, there are no network access restrictions for resources or applications. Full network access SSL VPNs require more planning for network deployment because they require a client to be installed on the remote systems. This requirement makes it difficult to deploy on non-corporate-managed systems because most SSL VPN clients require administrator privileges to install. The use of corporate-managed systems provides tighter control over endpoint security.

Cisco SSL VPN Client: Full Network Access

With an SSL VPN client (Layer 3), an SSL-VPN tunneling client is needed because users need full application access. Users need to use applications such as Microsoft Outlook, Cisco IP Communicator, Lotus Notes, Lotus Sametime, PeopleCube Meeting Maker, Telnet, Secure Shell (SSH), X Window System, and so on, but without having to install and administer an IPsec VPN software package. Cisco SSL VPN clientless and port-forwarding modes are not capable of this level of functionality.

The Cisco AnyConnect VPN client, using secure SSL connections to the security appliance, provides remote users with full VPN tunneling to corporate resources. This client is delivered via a web page (hosted on the Cisco ASA to which the user is connecting) and never needs to be manually distributed or installed.

The following are among the many features of the Cisco AnyConnect VPN client:

- **Optimal gateway selection:** Determines and establishes connectivity to the most optimal network access point, eliminating the need for end users to determine the nearest location.

- **Mobility-friendly:** Designed for mobile users, it can be configured so that the VPN connection remains established during IP address changes, loss of connectivity, hibernation, or standby.

- **Broad operating system support:**

  - Windows 7 32-bit (x86) and 64-bit (x64)

  - Windows Vista 32-bit (x86) and 64-bit (x64), including Service Packs 1 and 2 (SP1/SP2)

  - Windows XP SP2+ 32-bit (x86) and 64-bit (x64)

  - Mac OS X 10.5 and 10.6.x

  - Linux Intel (2.6.x kernel)

  - Apple iOS 4 (requires an optional AnyConnect Mobile license)

  - Windows Mobile 5.0, 6.0, and 6.1 (Professional and Classic) (requires an optional AnyConnect Mobile license)

  - Android 2.1 and up

- **Wide range of deployment and connection options:**

  - Predeployment, including Microsoft Installer, or automatic headend deployment (administrative rights are required for initial installation) via ActiveX (Windows only) and Java

  - Connection modes:

    - Standalone via system icon

    - Browser initiated (web launch)

    - Clientless portal initiated

    - CLI initiated

    - Application programming interface (API) initiated

- **Ease of client administration:** Allows an administrator to automatically distribute software and policy updates from the headend security appliance, eliminating administration that is associated with client software updates.

- **Preconnection posture assessment (Premium license required):** In conjunction with Cisco Secure Desktop, Host Scan verification checking seeks to detect the presence of antivirus software, personal firewall software, and Windows service packs on the endpoint system before granting network access.

- **Client firewall policy:** Added protection for split tunneling configurations, used in conjunction with Cisco Secure Mobility to allow for local access exceptions (for example, printing, tethered device support, and so on).

The Many Faces of AnyConnect

When we hear references to AnyConnect, most of us think of the SSL VPN full tunnel client mode. However, AnyConnect is now much more than that. AnyConnect Release 3.0 integrates many modules that offer functionality on wired, wireless, and remote-access networks; many of those modules were standalone clients in the past. As an example, in the past, looking under your Start menu, you might see a Cisco SSL VPN client, a Cisco 802.1x client, a Cisco ScanSafe client, a Cisco NAC client, a Cisco VPN IPsec client, and so forth. Those independent Cisco clients have been migrated to modules that now are integrated under the Cisco AnyConnect umbrella. So, Cisco AnyConnect now is your "network access unified client." In this chapter, however, we will strictly see the SSL VPN full tunnel client mode aspect of AnyConnect.

SSL VPN on Cisco ASA in Clientless Mode

The following is the procedure for configuring a clientless SSL VPN using Cisco ASDM. The configuration process is demonstrated in this section following the presentation of the configuration scenario.

Task 1.   Launch the Clientless SSL VPN Wizard from ASDM.

Task 2.   Configure the SSL VPN interface.

Task 3.   Configure user authentication.

Task 4.   Configure user group policy.

Task 5.   Configure a bookmark list.

Task 6.   Verify the Clientless SSL VPN Wizard configuration.

Clientless Configuration Scenario

Figure 15-7 shows a sample configuration topology that we will use for our scenario. All screen shots that follow are based on this scenario. We will use ASDM to configure the ASA firewall.

Figure 15-7 *Clientless SSL VPN Configuration Topology*

In this scenario, a clientless SSL VPN session is established from a remote client and terminates on the ASA. The user will land on the ASA default portal page, customized to include bookmarks to provide access to internal resources such as file servers.

Task 1: Launch the Clientless SSL VPN Wizard from ASDM

In Cisco ASDM, choose **Wizards > VPN Wizards > Clientless SSL VPN Wizard**, as shown in Figure 15-8. When the wizard launches, the first page provides an introduction to the Cisco AnyConnect VPN client product. Although it's not labeled as such, the introduction page is the first step of the wizard.

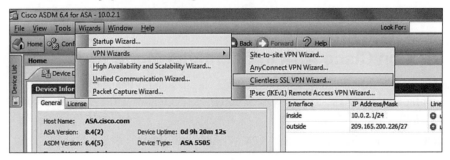

Figure 15-8 *Launching the Clientless SSL VPN Wizard from ASDM on Cisco ASA*

Task 2: Configure the SSL VPN Interface

Step 2 of the SSL VPN Wizard is the SSL VPN Interface page. By default, the ASA will use a self-signed certificate to send to the client for authentication. If required, the ASA may be configured to use a certificate that is purchased from a well-known certificate authority, such as VeriSign, to connect clients. In the event that a certificate is purchased, you may select it in the Certificate drop-down menu of the Digital Certificate section, as described in the following steps.

To configure the SSL VPN interface, complete the following steps, demonstrated in Figure 15-9:

Step 1. Enter a name for the clientless SSL VPN connection in the Connection Profile Name field.

Step 2. In the SSL VPN Interface drop-down menu, choose the interface to be used with the clientless SSL VPN connection.

Step 3. (Optional) Select a third-party certificate that has been installed on the ASA for use in connecting SSL VPN clients. If no certificates were installed, as in our scenario, the ASA will use a self-signed certificate.

Step 4. Click Next.

Note The SSL VPN Interface screen in the SSL VPN Wizard provides several links in the Information section. These links identify the URLs that need to be used for the SSL VPN service access (login) and for Cisco ASDM access (to access the Cisco ASDM software download).

Figure 15-9   *Configuring the SSL VPN Interface on Cisco ASA*

Task 3: Configure User Authentication

User authentication may be managed by external authentication servers (such as RADIUS) or it may be managed locally by using the ASA local user database.

To configure user authentication using the local user database, complete the following steps, illustrated in Figure 15-10:

Step 1.   Click the **Authenticate Using the Local User Database** radio button.

Step 2.   Enter a username and password for the desired user.

Step 3.   Click **Add** to add the user to the local user database.

Step 4.   Click **Next**.

Figure 15-10   *Configuring User Authentication for Cisco SSL VPN on Cisco ASA*

Task 4: Configure User Group Policy

On the Group Policy wizard page, you may select an existing user group policy to modify or you may add a new user group policy for the clientless SSL VPN connection.

To create a new user group policy, complete the following steps, as shown in Figure 15-11:

Step 1. Click the **Create New Group Policy** radio button.

Step 2. Enter a name for the new user group policy.

Step 3. Click **Next**.

Note By default, the created user group policy inherits its settings from the default group policy, DfltGrpPolicy. You may modify these settings after you have completed the SSL VPN Wizard by navigating to the **Configuration > Remote Access VPN > Clientless SSL VPN Access > Group Policies** submenu.

Configure New Group Policy

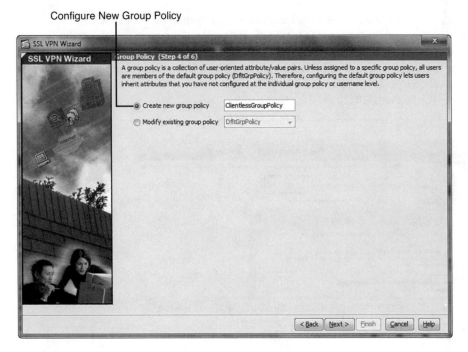

Figure 15-11 *Configuring User Group Policy for Cisco SSL VPN on Cisco ASA*

Task 5: Configure a Bookmark List

A bookmark list is a set of URLs that is configured to be used in the clientless SSL VPN web portal. By default, there are no configured bookmark lists and they must be configured by the network administrator.

To create a bookmark list and add bookmark entries to it, complete the following steps, as shown in Figures 15-12 and 15-13:

Step 1.   Click **Manage** to create a new bookmark list.

Step 2.   In the Configure GUI Customization Objects dialog box, click **Add** to add a bookmark list that is based on the included template.

Step 3.   In the Add Bookmark List dialog box, enter the bookmark list name in the corresponding field and click **Add** to create bookmarks for this list.

Step 4.   The Add Bookmark dialog box opens, shown in Figure 15-13. Enter a name for the bookmark in the Bookmark Title field.

Bookmark List

Think of the bookmark list as a bookmark container. Within that container, you will have listed multiple URLs for HTTP, HTTPS, FTP, and CIFS servers, which will be demonstrated next. Also, you could have destinations to SSL thin-client services listed in this bookmark list, such as RDP, Telnet, and SSH. For more details on thin clients, refer to *CCNP Security VPN 642-648 Official Cert Guide*, Second Edition, by Howard Hooper (Cisco Press, 2012).

Figure 15-12   *Configuring a Bookmark List for Cisco SSL VPN on Cisco ASA*

Step 5.   Enter the URL value for the bookmark as cifs. The following list of URL values is displayed in the drop-down menu:

- http

- https

- cifs

- ftp

Step 6.   Enter the server destination IP address or hostname to be used with the bookmark entry.

Step 7.   (Optional) Enter the URL endpoint browser that can fetch certain information that is sent along to the webserver or web application.

Step 7.   (Optional) Enter the name in the Subtitle field. The subtitle will appear under the bookmark entry on the web portal.

Step 8.   (Optional) Select the thumbnail image to be used with this bookmark entry in the Thumbnail field.

When you're finished creating a bookmark and click OK, you are brought back to the Add Bookmark List page. Click OK on the Add Bookmark List page to return to the wizard bookmark list page, where you click Next to return to the Summary page.

Choose the appropriate protocol.

Define the URL.

Figure 15-13   *Creating a Bookmark List*

Note To use thumbnails with bookmarks, the images must first be uploaded to the ASA.

Task 6: Verify the Clientless SSL VPN Wizard Configuration

Verify that the information that was entered in the SSL VPN Wizard is correct. As shown in Figure 15-14, click **Finish** to finish the wizard and send the configuration to the ASA.

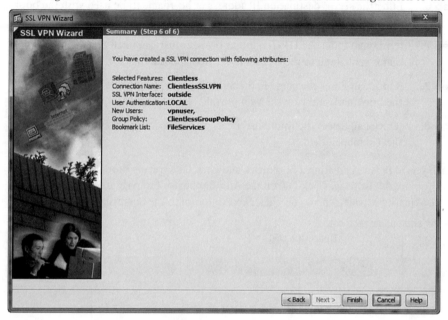

Figure 15-14 *Verifying the SSL VPN Configuration Created by the ASDM SSL VPN Wizard*

Log In to the VPN Portal: Clientless SSL VPN

For verification, open a compliant web browser and enter the login URL for the SSL VPN into the address field, as shown in the upper-left portion of Figure 15-15. The address that you enter should be the configured address URL.

Enter the previously configured username and password and click **Login**.

Note The prefix to the path changes depending on whether you require authentication. The security appliance uses /+CSCOE+/ for objects that require authentication, and uses /+CSCOU+/ for objects that do not. The security appliance displays /+CSCOE+/ objects on the portal page only, while /+CSCOU+/ objects are visible and usable in either the login page or the portal page.

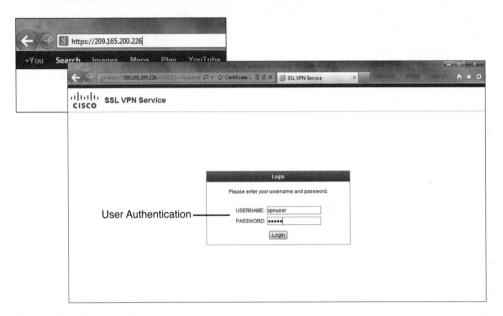

Figure 15-15 *Logging In to the VPN Portal Using Clientless SSL VPN*

Once the user is logged in, the main portal page will be displayed to the user, as shown in Figure 15-16. The default homepage displays configured web application bookmarks and Common Internet File System (CIFS) bookmarks. In the event that many bookmarks are available, one or the other type of bookmarks may be selected for display by using the buttons in the left navigation pane.

To the left of each configured bookmark is the imported thumbnail image file that is used by the bookmark. If there are other sites that must be accessed but that are not configured as bookmarks, they may be accessed using the Address bar at the top of the portal page.

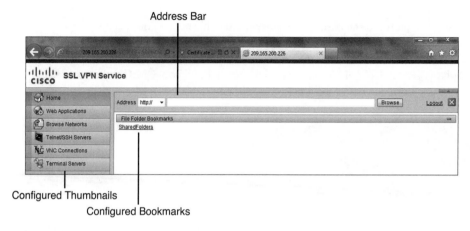

Figure 15-16 *Resources Accessible in the Portal*

Portal Customization

The login page shown in Figure 15-15, the portal page shown in Figure 15-16, and the logout page (not shown) can all be customized with colors, corporate logos, and so forth. More information on this topic can be found in the Cisco Press book *CCNP Security VPN 642-648 Official Cert Guide, 2nd Edition.*

SSL VPN on ASA Using the Cisco AnyConnect VPN Client

Suppose that you need more functionality than what Clientless SSL VPN, via the portal, can give you. For example, let's say you are an engineer and need to run customized software that reaches the computer-aided design (CAD) server and prints on a plotter.

Because Clientless SSL VPN doesn't provide you with the adequate functionality, you wish to use the Full client. You will need to configure both the ASA and the client. Though the Remote Access client, Cisco AnyConnect VPN Client gives you a choice of IPsec (IKEv2 only) or SSL full client remote access; in our scenario, we will focus only on the SSL VPN full client mode.

There are three major phases to configuring SSL VPN full-tunnel mode using Cisco ASDM so that remote clients will connect using Cisco AnyConnect:

Phase 1.   Configure Cisco ASA for Cisco AnyConnect.

Phase 2.   Configure the Cisco AnyConnect VPN Client.

Phase 3.   Verify VPN Connectivity with Cisco AnyConnect.

These phases are discussed in turn following the presentation of the configuration scenario.

Cisco AnyConnect Configuration Scenario

For this scenario, we will use the same topology as for the portal, as shown earlier in Figure 15-7. We will add one element to this topology: an address pool for the VPN AnyConnect client. The VPN gateway, which in our example is the Cisco ASA, will provide IP addresses to connecting clients using the address pool 10.33.33.100 to 10.33.33.200.

In our scenario, we will first initiate a clientless session. After working from the web clientless portal, we will discover that a full VPN tunnel is required to progress in our work. From the clientless portal, we will click the AnyConnect option to proceed with the Cisco AnyConnect VPN Client download and installation. We will then start an SSL VPN full-tunnel session using the newly installed AnyConnect client. All screen shots that follow are based on this scenario. We will use ASDM to configure the Cisco ASA firewall.

Phase 1: Configure Cisco ASA for Cisco AnyConnect

Eight tasks are required for configuring the Cisco ASA for AnyConnect, which will be further outlined in this section:

1. Configure the connection profile.

2. Configure VPN protocols and the device certificate.

3. Configure the client image.

4. Configure the authentication methods.

5. Configure the client address management.

6. Configure the network name resolution servers.

7. Configure the network address translation exemption.

8. Configure the AnyConnect client deployment summary.

To configure the Cisco ASA, we will use the AnyConnect VPN Connection Setup Wizard. From Cisco ASDM, choose **Wizards > VPN Wizards > AnyConnect VPN Wizard** to open the Introduction page of the wizard, shown in Figure 15-17.

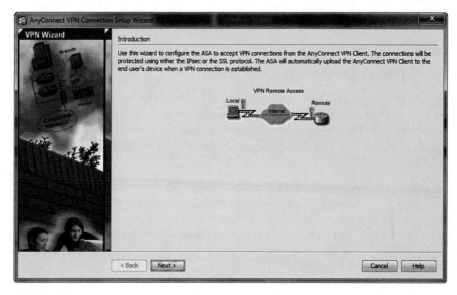

Figure 15-17   *Launching the AnyConnect VPN Connection Setup Wizard from Cisco ASDM*

Task 1: Connection Profile Identification

After you click **Next** on the Introduction page of the wizard, the first task is to configure the connection profile identification, used to identify the ASA to the remote-access users, as shown in Figure 15-18.

Figure 15-18   *Setting the Connection Profile Identification*

Complete the following steps:

Step 1.   In the Connection Profile Name field, enter a name that remote-access users will access for VPN connections. Connection profiles appear as **tunnel-group** in the CLI. This connection profile name will be displayed in a drop-down list on the initial clientless session, allowing the user to log in using the profile and download the Cisco AnyConnect VPN Client. The drop-down list appears whenever you have created connection profiles in addition to the default connection profile named DefaultRAGroup—it is called group because what is called a connection profile within ASDM is called a Tunnel-Group at the CLI. So, connection profiles (found in ASDM) are also called Tunnel-Group (at the CLI).

Step 2.   In the VPN Access Interface drop-down menu, choose an interface that remote-access users will access for VPN connections.

Step 3.   Click **Next** to continue to the next page of the AnyConnect VPN Connection Setup Wizard.

Task 2: VPN Protocols and Device Certificate

The next task is to specify the VPN protocol allowed for this connection profile, as shown in Figure 15-19. The Cisco AnyConnect VPN Client defaults to SSL. If you enable IPsec as a VPN tunnel protocol for the connection profile, you must also create and deploy a client profile with IPsec enabled using the profile editor from Cisco ASDM. AnyConnect IPsec supports only IKEv2.

Select protocols. Selecting both is an option.

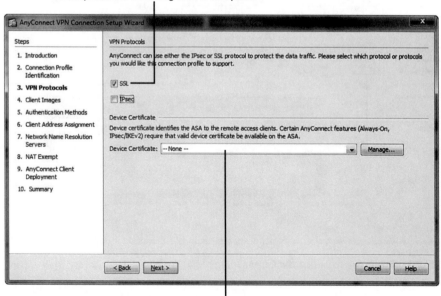

No certificate selection results in use of ASA self-signed certificate.

Figure 15-19   *Selecting the VPN Protocol and the Certificate*

Complete the following steps to define protocols and certificates:

Step 1. Check the check box for each of the desired protocols. In this example, only SSL is chosen.

Step 2. Choose an identity certificate from the Device Certificate drop-down list. This certificate identifies the ASA to remote-access clients. Clicking the Manage button opens the Manage Identity Certificates dialog box, which allows you to create new certificates and manipulate existing certificates.

Step 3. Click **Next** to continue to the next page of the AnyConnect VPN Connection Setup Wizard.

Task 3: Client Image

ASA can automatically upload the latest Cisco AnyConnect VPN Client package to the client device when it accesses the enterprise network. You can use a regular expression to match the user agent of a browser to an image. You can also minimize connection setup time by moving the most commonly encountered operating system for your organization, for example Windows, to the top of the list.

To configure the location of the Cisco AnyConnect SSL VPN Client, complete the following steps:

Step 1. Click **Add** to add a new image definition, as shown in Figure 15-20.

Figure 15-20 *Browsing to Select the Client Image*

Step 2.   Click **Browse Flash** if the image file is already located on the Cisco ASA, or click **Upload** if you have a copy on the local machine to upload to the security appliance.

Step 3.   The Browse Flash dialog box opens, as shown in Figure 15-21, allowing you to navigate through files and folders in flash memory. Select the image of the Cisco AnyConnect VPN Client, and click OK to continue.

Figure 15-21   *Selecting the Client Image*

Step 4.   Click **Next** to continue to the next page of the AnyConnect VPN Connection Setup Wizard.

Task 4: Authentication Methods

User authentication may be managed by external authentication servers (such as RADIUS) or it may be managed locally using the ASA local user database.

In Figure 15-22, the requirements call for configuring user authentication using the local user database.

Use local user database.

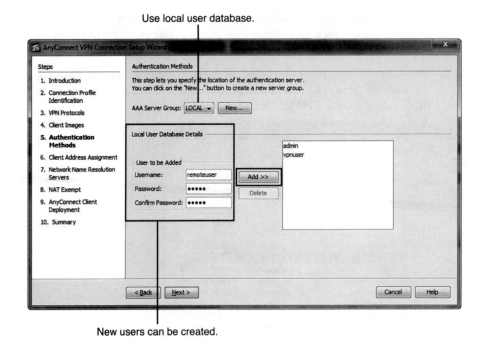

New users can be created.

Figure 15-22   *Selecting the Authentication Method*

Complete the following steps:

Step 1.   Choose the LOCAL value from the AAA Server Group drop-down menu.

Step 2.   Configure a username and password for the desired user. Notice that existing users appear in the pane on the right.

Step 3.   Click **Add** to add the user to the local user database. The username will move to the pane on the right.

Step 4.   Click **Next** to continue to the next page of the SSL VPN Connection Setup Wizard.

Task 5: Client Address Assignment

SSL VPN clients receive new IP addresses when they connect to the ASA. Clientless connections do not require new IP addresses. Address pools define a range of addresses that remote clients can receive. The IP address pool configuration is required for successful client-based SSL VPN connectivity. Without an available IP address pool, the full-tunnel Cisco AnyConnect SSL VPN to the security appliance will fail.

Full Client Virtual Adapter

Later in this chapter, we will see that a remote-access user wishing to use a Full client—usually to have more functionality than what the clientless portal can offer—sees a virtual adapter added to the list of network adapters in his computer. We are used to seeing wireless and wired adapters listed under network properties. These network adapters, to fully join a network, usually use DHCP to receive an IP address, a DNS, and so forth. AnyConnect installs a virtual adapter on your workstation, which enables your workstation to look and feel as if it's connected on the corporate network, though you are physically a distance away. This virtual adapter, similar to your wired and wireless adapters, requires and receives from the ASA an IP address, and a DNS server, so it becomes a client of your corporate LAN. So, for the next few tasks, we will configure for AnyConnect connectivity similar attributes that we would need to configure for our DHCP clients.

Using the options on the Client Address Assignment wizard page, you can select an existing IP address pool or click New to create a new pool, as shown in Figure 15-23. For our particular scenario, complete these steps as follow:

Step 1. Click **New** to define the desired address pool.

Step 2. In the Add IP Pool dialog box, create the pool by configuring the following items:

- **Name:** A name to be associated with the IP address pool.

- **Starting IP Address:** Starting IP address of the range to be assigned to the client SSL VPN connections.

- **Ending IP Address:** Ending IP address of the range to be assigned to the client SSL VPN connections.

- **Subnet Mask:** Choose the desired subnet mask of the IP address pool from the drop-down menu.

Step 3. Click **OK** to accept the newly configured IP address pool.

Step 4. Click **Next** to continue to the next page of the SSL VPN Connection Setup Wizard.

Figure 15-23   *Selecting the Address Pool That Will Be Assigned to AnyConnect Clients*

Task 6: Network Name Resolution Servers

The next step, shown in Figure 15-24, lets you specify which domain names are resolved for the remote user when accessing the internal network. Simply complete these fields, if necessary:

- **DNS Servers:** Enter the IP address of the DNS server.

- **WINS Servers:** Enter the IP address of the WINS server.

- **Domain Name:** Type the default domain name.

Click **Next** to continue to the next page of the SSL VPN Connection Setup Wizard.

Task 7: Network Address Translation Exemption

If NAT is enabled on the ASA, the VPN traffic must be exempt from this translation. Complete the following steps, shown in Figure 15-25, to configure NAT exemption, which is necessary in our scenario:

Step 1.   Check the **Exempt VPN Traffic from Network Address Translation** check box.

Step 2.   Choose the interface connected to the internal network that needs to be exempted from NAT. In this example, the inside interface contains the hosts that the VPN clients will access.

Step 3.   Type the host or subnet IP addresses that are to bypass NAT in the Local Network field. You can also click the ... button and select the addresses from the Browse Local Network dialog box. The traffic between Cisco AnyConnect VPN Clients and the internal networks defined here will be exempt from NAT.

Step 4.   Click **Next** to move to the next page of the SSL VPN Connection Setup Wizard.

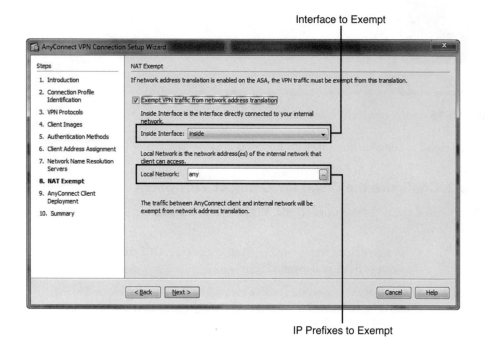

Figure 15-24   *Selecting Network Name Resolution Servers*

Figure 15-25   *Configuring NAT Exemption*

Task 8: AnyConnect Client Deployment Summary

The final two wizard pages are informational:

- **AnyConnect Client Deployment:** The message explains how you can install the Cisco AnyConnect VPN Client program to a client device using either of two methods. The first method is web launch, which installs automatically when accessing the ASA using a web browser. The second method is predeployment, which manually installs the Cisco AnyConnect VPN Client package.

- **Summary:** Provides a summary, shown in Figure 15-26, of your selections from the previous wizard pages.

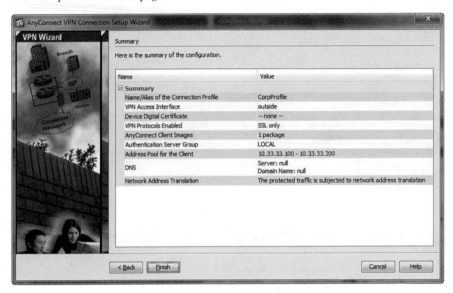

Figure 15-26 *AnyConnect Wizard Summary*

Click **Finish** to complete the SSL VPN Connection Setup Wizard.

Phase 2: Configure the Cisco AnyConnect VPN Client

To download the Cisco AnyConnect SSL VPN Client to the host system, you must complete the following steps:

Step 1.   Open a compliant web browser and enter the login URL for the SSL VPN into the address field, as shown in Figure 15-27.

Step 2.   Ensure that the connection profile created for the client is selected in the Group drop-down menu, enter the previously configured username and password, and click **Login**.

Figure 15-27   *Connecting to the Portal to Eventually Request an AnyConnect Installation Download*

Installing AnyConnect

AnyConnect can be preinstalled on the remote client using the standalone installation program that Cisco offers. Another option is to have the AnyConnect installation downloaded to the remote-access computer from the ASA using the AnyConnect version available in flash, as shown earlier in Figure 15-21. This is the approach we will take in our scenario. Other variants of this option exist, such as having the AnyConnect installation pushed to your remote client as soon as the ASA receives an authenticated HTTPS session. Those variants are explained in detail in the Cisco Press book *CCNP Security VPN 642-648 Official Cert Guide*, Second Edition.

In our scenario, start with a clientless session but then choose to upgrade to a full client session by clicking the AnyConnect option on the left side of the portal page. A process will begin a series of compliance checks for the target system. The following items are checked on the host system:

- **Platform Detection:** The ASA first queries the client system in an attempt to identify the type of client connecting to the security appliance. Based on the platform that is identified, the proper software package may be auto-downloaded.

- **ActiveX:** Detects whether ActiveX is available on the host system for client download. For ActiveX to operate properly with the Cisco ASA, it is important that the security appliance is added as a trusted network site. ActiveX will be used for client download in the event that a web portal is not in use.

- **Java Detection:** Detects whether a supported version of Java is available on the host system for client download. Java will be used for client download in the event that a web portal page has been configured.

If all the preceding checks succeed, Cisco AnyConnect will be downloaded and installed automatically on your remote system. All along, the progress is shown, under the title WebLaunch, for the system inspection and the status of the download. Once the client completes the auto-download of the Cisco AnyConnect SSL VPN Client, the web session automatically launches the Cisco AnyConnect SSL VPN Client and attempts to log the user into the network using the same credentials that are supplied when logging into the web portal.

If the ActiveX or Java checks are not successful, the ASA will nevertheless offer you the chance to download manually the Cisco AnyConnect VPN Client located in its flash, as shown in Figure 15-28.

Figure 15-28 *Cisco AnyConnect Installed from a VPN Clientless Session*

After the download, the Cisco AnyConnect VPN Client is installed. You can then proceed to launch AnyConnect, as shown in Figure 15-29, which will initiate the SSL full client VPN connection to your ASA. You will have concurrently both a clientless session and a full SSL session on the ASA.

Figure 15-29   *Starting Cisco AnyConnect Client*

When the AnyConnect connection is established, an icon with a sphere and a lock will appear in the system tray, identifying that the client has successfully connected to the SSL VPN network, as shown in Action 1 of Figure 15-30.

Figure 15-30   *AnyConnect Icon in Computer System Tray and Details on the Connection*

Phase 3: Verify VPN Connectivity with Cisco AnyConnect VPN Client

Additional connection statistics and information may be shown by clicking the icon in the system tray shown in Figure 15-30, Action 1, and then selecting Advanced, as shown in Figure 15-30, Action 2. This client interface may also be used to log the user out.

The Statistics tab on the Client interface presents more information, and allows you to review packet and byte counters, shown in Action 3, as well as the overall settings of the VPN (crypto suite, IP address obtained, split tunneling policy, and others).

In our scenario, future SSL VPN sessions may be launched through the web portal or through the installed Cisco AnyConnect SSL VPN Client.

Verifying VPN Connectivity from Cisco ASA

In Cisco ASDM, you can monitor established VPN sessions by navigating to **Monitoring > VPN > VPN Statistics > Sessions**. From the window, shown in Figure 15-31, you can view session statistics for the ASA.

Filter by VPN Type (AnyConnect Client)

Possibility for Bulk Logouts

Figure 15-31 *Monitoring the VPN Sessions Status from ASDM*

The top pane shows a summary of active, cumulative, peak concurrent, and inactive VPN sessions. This pane includes VPN sessions of all types, including IPsec, clientless SSL, and site-to-site sessions.

The bottom pane displays individual VPN sessions. You can filter the type of session to display by using the Filter By drop-down menu above the pane. This menu allows you to specify the type of sessions that the statistics in the bottom pane represent. You will need to click Filter to refresh the output according to the filter.

This bottom pane includes the username and IP addresses used in each session, as well as the connection profiles that were matched, the cipher suite in use for the session, and other session statistics such as duration and packet/byte counters.

Clicking Details to the right of the bottom pane provides additional details for each VPN session, as shown in Figure 15-32.

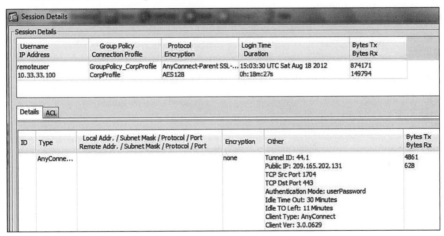

Figure 15-32 *Detailed Information on Current VPN Session*

Summary

The key points covered in this chapter are as follows:

- Market trends drive the need for effective remote-access security and present challenges to the IT organization.

- The SSL protocol uses the cryptology concepts presented in this chapter.

- Cisco SSL VPN solutions include clientless and full client tunnel modes of operation.

- Cisco SSL VPN clientless mode can be configured on Cisco ASA using Cisco ASDM.

- Cisco SSL VPN full client tunnel mode can be configured on Cisco ASA using Cisco ASDM and the Cisco AnyConnect VPN Client.

References

For additional information, refer to this resource:

CCNP Security VPN 642-648 Official Cert Guide, Second Edition (Cisco Press)

Review Questions

Use the questions here to review what you learned in this chapter. The correct answers are found in the Appendix, "Answers to Chapter Review Questions."

1. Which two current market trends create challenges to remote connectivity and Cisco SSL VPN services?

   a. Consumerization
   b. Bandwidth availability
   c. Ubiquitous access to corporate resources
   d. Increase in malware
   e. Cost of VPN infrastructures

2. Which option is the main difference between TLS and SSL?

   a. SSL operates at the transport layer.
   b. TLS is standards-based.
   c. SSL uses digital certificates.
   d. TLS supports Suite B algorithms.

3. When deploying Cisco SSL VPNs, which of the following options provides the most depth in application support?

   a. EasyVPN
   b. Thin Client
   c. Full Client
   d. Clientless

4. Which solution would you recommend for a user who requires access strictly to web-based applications?

   a. EasyVPN
   b. Thin Client
   c. Full Client
   d. Clientless

5. You wish to use the SSL VPN to access your network. However, the administrator has not installed a third-party certificate for Cisco SSL VPN sessions. What will happen to your SSL VPN session?

   a. The SSL VPN session will fail because it requires a server-side certificate.
   b. The ASA will present a self-signed certificate.
   c. A root certificate will need to be imported into ASA.
   d. The SSL VPN will fail because the client automatically rejects untrusted certificates.

6. Clientless SSL VPN is best suited for?

   a. Complex applications
   b. Users who needs to print on a LAN printer
   c. Web-enabled applications, file sharing, email
   d. All IP-based applications

7. Match the cryptographic algorithms with their function within SSL. Multiple algorithms can be matched to one single function.

   Function

   a. Confidentiality
   b. Integrity
   c. Authentication
   d. Key management

   Algorithm

   1. RC4
   2. DSA
   3. SHA-2
   4. 3DES
   5. MD5
   6. DSS
   7. AES
   8. DH

Answers to Chapter Review Questions

Chapter 1

1. a, b, and e
2. a, d, and e
3. a. Preventative = f. Lock
   b. Deterrent = e. Video surveillance
   c. Detective = d. Motion sensor
4. a. White hat = p. Breaks security for nonmalicious reasons
   b. Black hat = k. Unethical hacker
   c. Gray hat = m. Ethically questionable hacker
   d. Blue hat = i. Bug tester
   e. Cracker = o. Synonymous with black hat hacker
   f. Phreaker = l. Hacker of telecommunication systems
   g. Script kiddy = j. Hacker with little skill
   h. Hacktivist = n. Hacker with a political agenda
5. a. Escalate privilege = Step 4
   b. Leverage the compromised system = Step 7
   c. Perform footprint analysis = Step 1
   d. Install back doors = Step 6
   e. Enumerate applications and operating systems = Step 2
   f. Gather additional passwords and secrets = Step 5
   g. Manipulate users to gain access = Step 3
6. d, e, and g

7. a. Confidential = 4

b. Private = 3

c. Public = 1

d. Sensitive = 2

8. d

9. a. Owner = f. Ultimately responsible for the data

b. Custodian = e. Responsible on a day-to-day basis for the classified data

c. User = d. Responsible for using the data

10. b

11. b

12. a. Searching a network host and open ports = j. Port scanning

b. Capturing electrical transmission = g. Emanation capturing

c. Hiding information within a transmission = h. Covert channel

d. Intercepting traffic that passes over a physical network = e. Packet sniffing

13. a. Operations and maintenance = Step 4

b. Initiation = Step 1

c. Disposition = Step 5

d. Acquisition and development = Step 2

e. Implementation = Step 3

14. b

Chapter 2

1. a. Context-aware enforcement = 4

b. Cisco TrustSec = 1

c. Cisco SIO = 2

d. Cisco AnyConnect = 3

2. a

3. b and d

4. c

5. b and e

Chapter 3

1. a

2. c

3. a and d

4. c and e

5.   a.   Management = f. Packets used to manage the network

      b.   Data = d. User-generated packets

      c.   Control = e. Packets used for the creation and operation of the network itself

6.   d and f

7.   b

8.   a.   Communities = g. Groups of devices that share common components

      b.   Templates = e. Parameterized configuration files

      c.   Profiles = f. GUI views that allow role-based access control over Cisco Configuration Professional menus and options

      d.   Wizards = h. GUI tools to hide the complexity of commands

9.   a

10. c

Chapter 4

1.   c

2.   a and d

3.   d

4.   a

5.   c

6.   d

7.   a

8.   b

9.   c

10. b

Chapter 5

1.   d

2.   b, c, and d

3.   a and c

4.   b

5.   c

6.   a.   = Step 3

      b.   = Step 4

      c.   = Step 1

      d.   = Step 2

7.   c

8. a

9. b

10. b

Chapter 6

1. c

2. a and c

3. a

4. c

5. e

6. b

7. d

8. a and c

9. d

10. c

Chapter 7

1. c

2. b

3. a and d

4. c

5. c

Chapter 8

1. a

2. b and c

3. d

4. d

5. d

6. a, b, and c

7. c

8. b, c, and d

9. a

10. a, b, and c

Chapter 9

1. a and c
2. c
3. a. Packet-filtering firewalls = 1 Work primarily at the network level of the OSI model
   b. Application layer gateways = 4 Were the first application layer firewalls
   c. Stateful packet filters = 2 Are the most common firewalls
   d. Application inspection firewalls = 3 Monitor sessions to determine the port numbers for secondary channels
4. c and d
5. b
6. a. Static NAT = 3 Translation is one-to-one
   b. Dynamic NAT = 2 Translation is many-to-many
   c. Dynamic PAT = 4 Translation is many-to-one
   d. Policy NAT = 1 Translation depends on both source and destination
7. a. Service control = 4 Allow HTTP, allow HTTPS, deny everything else
   b. Direction control = 1 Allow HTTP outbound, but not inbound
   c. User control = 2 Allow campus VLANs HTTP access, deny it for wireless VLANs
   d. Behavior control = 3 Open negotiated FTP ports after learning them during connection setup

Chapter 10

1. b
2. b
3. d
4. c
5. a and d
6. b
7. b
8. b
9. d
10. b
11. d
12. a
13. c
14. a
15. b

Chapter 11

1. b and d
2. b
3. a and d
4. c
5. a, b, and d
6. a. Signature-based IPS = 3. Can produce false positives because certain normal network activity can be misinterpreted as malicious activity

   b. Policy-based IPS = 4. Similar to implementing a restrictive firewall policy

   c. Reputation-based IPS = 2. Typically implemented in the form of white lists or black lists

   d. Anomaly-based IPS = 1. Normal behavior typically defined based on traffic patterns, traffic and protocol mix, traffic volumes, and other criteria
7. d
8. c
9. b
10. a
11. a and d
12. a
13. a
14. c
15. a

Chapter 12

1. a, d, and e
2. b
3. a, c, and d
4. b
5. c
6. d
7. a and e
8. b
9. d
10. b
11. a and c
12. d
13. d

14. a

15. b

16. c

17. a

18. d

19. c

20. c

21. c

22. d and e

Chapter 13

1. b

2. a, b, and c

3. a, d, and e

4. a. Group 5 = g. 4096

    b. Group 2 = h. 163

    c. Group 7 = i. 1024

    d. Group 1 = j. 1536

    e. Group 16 = k. 256

    f. Group 19= l. 768

5. b

6. a. ESP = 4. Confidentiality

    b. IKE = 3. Negotiation

    c. EDCH = 1. Key Exchange

    d. EDCSA = 2. Authentication

7. b

8. b

9. b

10. a, e, and f

Chapter 14

1. d

2. c

3. d

4. d

5. b

6. a

7. b

8. c

Chapter 15

1. a and c

2. b

3. c

4. d

5. b

6. c

7.   a. Confidentiality = 1, 4, 7

b. Integrity = 3, 5

c. Authentication = 2

d. Key management = 6, 8

Index

Numerics

A

B

H

I

N

NAC (Network Admission Control), 200

named ACLs, 324

NAT (network address translation), 384-390

  for Cisco ASA 5500 series, 428-431

  deployment modes, 389-390

  inside source address translation, 387

  PAT, 386-387

NAT overload, 389

native VLANs, 237

NAT-TP, 284

navigation pane, CCP

  Device Hardening folder, 140

  Firewall option, 141

  Interface Management option, 138-139

  IPS option, 141

  Router folder, 139-140

  Security folder, 140

NDP (Neighbor Discovery Protocol), 280-281

need for network security, 12

  business goals, 12

  risk management, 12-13

negative alarms, 475

NetCat, 22

network borders

  application border, 86

  device border, 85

  location border, 86

network infrastructure, threats against, 112-113

network security

  assumptions made regarding networks, 2

  compliance regulations, 50-53

  need for, 12

    business goals, 12

    risk management, 12-13

  podcasts regarding, 17

  posture assessment, 69-70

  requirements, 2-3

  testing, 70-72

    techniques, 71

    tools, 71-72

  trends affecting, 16-19

    changes in workplace experience, 16

    cloud computing, 16

    exploitation of trust, 17-18

    malware, 18

    regulatory compliance, 18-19

NFP (Cisco Network Foundation Protection), 112-118

  control plane, 118-122

    CoPP, 118-119

    CPPr, 119

  data plane, 128-131

    ACL filtering, 128-129

    antispoofing, 129-130

    Layer 2 protection, 131

  management plane, 123-128

    AAA, deploying, 127-128

    RBAC, 126-127

    secure management and reporting, 124-126

S